Physics Galaxy

15 Papers

2002-2016 (Offline & Online)

JEE MAIN

Chapter-Wise Solutions

Physics

Ashish Arora

First edition : Dec, 2000

Second edition : May, 2016

Revised Edition : April, 2022

Title : Physics Galaxy 2022 : JEE Main Physics - Chapter-Wise Solutions (2002-2016)

Language : English

Author's Name : Ashish Arora

Typeset & Published by :

Career Launcher Infrastructure (P) Ltd.

A-45, Mohan Cooperative Industrial Area, Near Mohan Estate Metro Station, New Delhi - 110044

Marketed by :

G.K. Publications (P) Ltd.

Plot No. 9A, Sector-27A, Mathura Road, Faridabad, Haryana-121003

ISBN : 978-93-92837-71-5

Printer's Details : Printed in India, New Delhi.

For product information :
Visit ***www.gkpublications.com*** or email to ***gkp@gkpublications.com***

Dedicated

to

My Parents, Son, Daughter

and

My beloved wife

In his teaching career since 1992 Ashish Arora personally mentored more than 10000 IITians and students who reached global heights in various career and profession chosen. It is his helping attitude toward students with which all his students remember him in life for his contribution in their success and keep connections with him live. Below is the list of some of the successful students in IITJEE, NEET & International Olympiad personally mentored by him.

NAVNEET LOIWAL	*International GOLD Medal in IPhO-2000 at LONDON*, Also secured **AIR-4** in **IIT JEE 2000**
	PROUD FOR INDIA : Navneet Loiwal was the first Indian Student who won first International GOLD Medal for our country in International Physics Olympiad.
DUNGRA RAM CHOUDHARY	**AIR-1** in **IIT JEE 2002**
HARSHIT CHOPRA	*National Gold Medal in INPhO-2002* and got **AIR-2** in **IIT JEE-2002**
KUNTAL LOYA	A Girl Student got position **AIR-8** in **IIT JEE 2002**
LUV KUMAR	*National Gold Medal in INPhO-2003* and got **AIR-3** in **IIT JEE-2003**
RAJHANS SAMDANI	*National Gold Medal in INPhO-2003* and got **AIR-5** in **IIT JEE-2003**
SHANTANU BHARDWAJ	*International SILVER Medal in IPhO-2002 at INDONESIA*
SHALEEN HARLALKA	*International GOLD Medal in IPhO-2003 at CHINA* and got **AIR-46** in **IIT JEE-2003**
TARUN GUPTA	*National GOLD Medal in INPhO-2005*
APEKSHA KHANDELWAL	*National GOLD Medal in INPhO-2005*
ABHINAV SINHA	*Hon'ble Mension Award in APhO-2006* at *KAZAKHSTAN*
RAMAN SHARMA	*International GOLD Medal in IPhO-2007* at *IRAN* and got **AIR-20** in **IIT JEE-2007**
PRATYUSH PANDEY	*International SILVER Medal in IPhO-2007* at *IRAN* and got **AIR-85 in IIT JEE-2007**
GARVIT JUNIWAL	*International GOLD Medal in IPhO-2008* at *VIETNAM* and got **AIR-10** in **IIT JEE-2008**
ANKIT PARASHAR	*National GOLD Medal in INPhO-2008*
HEMANT NOVAL	*National GOLD Medal in INPhO-2008* and got **AIR-25** in **IIT JEE-2008**
ABHISHEK MITRUKA	*National GOLD Medal in INPhO-2009*
SARTHAK KALANI	*National GOLD Medal in INPhO-2009*
ASTHA AGARWAL	*International SILVER Medal in IJSO-2009* at *AZERBAIJAN*
RAHUL GURNANI	*International SILVER Medal in IJSO-2009* at *AZERBAIJAN*
AYUSH SINGHAL	*International SILVER Medal in IJSO-2009* at *AZERBAIJAN*
MEHUL KUMAR	*International SILVER Medal in IPhO-2010* at *CROATIA* and got **AIR-19** in **IIT JEE-2010**
ABHIROOP BHATNAGAR	*National GOLD Medal in INPhO-2010*
AYUSH SHARMA	*International Double GOLD Medal in IJSO-2010* at *NIGERIA*
AASTHA AGRAWAL	*Hon'ble Mension Award in APhO-2011* at *ISRAEL* and got **AIR-93** in **IIT JEE 2011**
ABHISHEK BANSAL	*National GOLD Medal in INPhO-2011*
SAMYAK DAGA	*National GOLD Medal in INPhO-2011*
SHREY GOYAL	*National GOLD Medal in INPhO-2012* and secured **AIR-24** in **IIT JEE 2012**
RAHUL GURNANI	*National GOLD Medal in INPhO-2012*
JASPREET SINGH JHEETA	*National GOLD Medal in INPhO-2012*
DIVYANSHU MUND	*National GOLD Medal in INPhO-2012*
SHESHANSH AGARWAL	*International SILVER Medal in IAO-2012 at KOREA*
SWATI GUPTA	*International SILVER Medal in IJSO-2012 at IRAN*
PRATYUSH RAJPUT	*International SILVER Medal in IJSO-2012 at IRAN*
SHESHANSH AGARWAL	*International BRONZE Medal in IOAA-2013 at GREECE*
SHESHANSH AGARWAL	*International GOLD Medal in IOAA-2014 at ROMANIA*
SHESHANSH AGARWAL	*International SILVER Medal in IPhO-2015 at INDIA* and secured **AIR-58** in **JEE(Advanced)-2015**
VIDUSHI VARSHNEY	*International SILVER Medal in IJSO-2015 at SOUTH KOREA*
AMAN BANSAL	AIR-1 in JEE Advanced 2016
KUNAL GOYAL	AIR-3 in JEE Advanced 2016
GOURAV DIDWANIA	AIR-9 in JEE Advanced 2016
DIVYANSH GARG	*International SILVER Medal in IPhO-2016 at SWITZERLAND*
NALIN KHANDELWAL	AIR-1 in NEET 2019
MRIDUL AGARWAL	AIR-1 in JEE Advanced 2021

ABOUT THE AUTHOR

The complexities of Physics have given nightmares to many, but the homegrown genius of Jaipur-Ashish Arora has helped several students to live their dreams by decoding it.

Newton Law of Gravitation and Faraday's Magnetic force of attraction apply perfectly well with this unassuming genius. A Pied Piper of students, his webportal https://www.physicsgalaxy.com, The world's largest encyclopedia of video lectures on high school Physics possesses strong gravitational pull and magnetic attraction for students who want to make it big in life.

Ashish Arora, gifted with rare ability to train masterminds, has mentored over 10,000 IITians in his past 24 years of teaching sojourn including lots of students made it to Top 100 in IIT-JEE/JEE(Advance) including AIR-1 and many in Top-10. Apart from that, he has also groomed hundreds of students for cracking International Physics Olympiad. No wonder his student Navneet Loiwal brought laurel to the country by becoming the first Indian to win a Gold medal at the 2000 - International Physics Olympiad in London (UK).

His special ability to simplify the toughest of the Physics theorems and applications rates him as one among the best Physics teachers in the world. With this, Arora simply defies the logic that perfection comes with age. Even at 18 when he started teaching Physics while pursuing engineering, he was as engaging as he is now. Experience, besides graying his hair, has just widened his horizon.

Now after encountering all tribes of students - some brilliant and some not-so-intelligent - this celebrated teacher has embarked upon a noble mission to make the entire galaxy of Physics inform of his webportal PHYSICSGALAXY.COM to serve and help global students in the subject. Today students from 183 countries are connected with this webportal. On any topic of physics students can post their queries in comment section in Physics Galaxy Youtube channel on which many Physics experts with Ashish Arora reply to several queries posted online by students.

Dedicated to global students of middle and high school level, his website *www.physicsgalaxy.com* also has teaching sessions dubbed in American accent and subtitles in 87 languages. For students in India preparing for JEE & NEET, his online courses will be available soon on PHYSICSGALAXY.COM.

In 2007 he started authoring Physics Galaxy Youtube Channel which has now become World's Largest Youtube Channel for online physics lectures on high school physics and preparation of JEE & NEET. Daily about 1.5 lakh+ video lectures are being watched on the channel by students preparing for JEE, NEET & High school Physics.

FOREWORD

I am extremely happy to share my views about this book written by Er. Ashish Arora. He has contributed immensely to the teaching-learning of Physics though many innovative ways. His approach has always been student centric and this contribution is yet another example of the same.

As the title states "Physics Galaxy JEE Main Solutions" the book provides valuable information and covers the necessary components by offering solution to all questions asked in old JEE Main (all Online & Offline 2002-2016) with detailed explanations. All questions are categorized into 30 topics based on weightage of questions asked in the past 15 years (2002-2016) however in this book total 15 papers of all online and offline shifts of JEE Main are included with detailed comprehensive solutions and upto 2016 all solutions to questions are linked with video solutions available on YouTube channel of Physics Galaxy. This is to indicate and promote understanding of the methods or reasons for specific/particular solutions. Aspirants can also scan the respective QR code given in the book to see its video explanation as and when required. All solutions of the questions are based on the conceptual analysis covered in the popular Physics Galaxy book series (5 volumes) so that aspirants following the book series will be able to relate and recall all the explanations already done.

I am sure the book promotes the concept of deeper learning in the domain of Physics. My best wishes to the many aspirants who will certainly find this book a very valuable tool to enhance thorough understanding of the subject.

Prof. Sandeep Sancheti

April, 2022

Ph. D. (U.K.), B.Tech. FIETE, MIEEE
VC, SRMIST, Chennai &
President, AIU, New Delhi

PREFACE

For a science student, preparing for JEE Main or NEET, Physics is the most important subject, unlike to other subjects it requires logical reasoning and high imagination of brain. Without improving the level of physics it is very difficult to achieve a goal in the present age of competitions. To score better, one does not require hard working at least in physics. It just requires a simple understanding and approach to think a physical situation. Actually physics is the surrounding of our everyday life. If you wish to make the concepts of physics strong, you should try to understand core concepts of physics in practical approach rather than theoretical.

This book "*PHYSICS GALAXY JEE Main Solutions*" is designed in a totally different and friendly approach to develop the physics concepts psychologically. The book covers detailed solutions to all the questions previously asked in JEE Main all online and offline papers from 2002 to 2016. From the analysis of 2021 all four attempts papers it is clearly seen that all these papers held were designed on the basis of past 15 year papers. More than 60% questions are based on concepts asked in previous years which were matching in style with the questions of these old papers, called derived PYQs.

All the questions of these online and offline papers are divided in 30 topics for topic level understanding of questions asked in JEE Main. In my classroom teaching also I found that topic level understanding of previous year papers of exam helps students a lot in concept visualization from the point of view of preparation of final exam as well as for the purpose of last moment revision of all topics.

For every question asked in these old JEE Main papers, video solutions are recorded and made available for students on YouTube channel of Physics Galaxy as well as these video solutions can be accessed through Physics Galaxy mobile app available on iOS and Android play store. While following the book if students face any doubt in understanding the solution of the specific question then they can scan the QR codes given at the end of the book for all the questions to directly start the video solution of that question.

I don't have words for my best friend my wife Anuja for always being together with me to complete this book in the unique style and format along with the whole series of Physics Galaxy book series and lecture notes series.

I would like to pay my gratitude to Sh. Dayashankar Prajapati in assisting me to complete the task in Design Labs of PHYSICSGALAXY.COM and presenting the book in totally new format of second edition.

At last but the most important person, my father who has devoted his valuable time to finally present the book in such a format and a simple language, thanks is a very small word for his dedication in this book.

In this first edition of book I have tried my best to make this book error free but owing to the nature of work, inadvertently, there is possibility of errors left untouched. I shall be grateful to the readers, if they point out me regarding errors and oblige me by giving their valuable and constructive suggestions via emails for further improvement of the book.

Date : April, 2022

Ashish Arora

PHYSICSGALAXY.COM
B-80, Model Town, Malviya Nagar, Jaipur-302017
e-mails: ashisharora@physicsgalaxy.com

CONTENTS

* * * * *

CHAPTER 1

UNITS AND DIMENSIONS

1.1 MEASUREMENTS AND DIMENSIONAL ANALYSIS

1. Identify the pair whose dimensions are equal : **[2002]**
(A) Torque and work (B) Stress and energy
(C) Force and stress (D) Force and work

2. The physical quantities not having same dimensions are : **[2003]**
(A) torque and work
(B) momentum and planck's constant
(C) stress and young's modulus
(D) speed and $(\mu_0\varepsilon_0)^{-1/2}$

3. Dimensions of $\frac{1}{\mu_0\varepsilon_0}$, where symbols have their usual meaning, are : **[2003]**
(A) $[L^{-1}T]$ (B) $[L^{-2}T^2]$
(C) $[L^2T^{-2}]$ (D) $[LT^{-1}]$

4. Which one of the following represents the correct dimensions of the coefficient of viscosity ? **[2004]**
(A) $[ML^{-1}T^{-1}]$ (B) $[MLT^{-1}]$
(C) $[ML^{-1}T^{-2}]$ (D) $[ML^{-2}T^{-2}]$

5. Out of the following pair, which one does NOT have identical dimensions : **[2005]**
(A) Impulse and momentum
(B) Angular momentum and planck's constant
(C) Work and torque
(D) Moment of inertia and moment of a force

6. Which of the following units denotes the dimensions $\frac{ML^2}{Q^2}$, where Q denotes the electric charge ? **[2006]**
(A) Wb/m^2 (B) Henry (H)
(C) H/m^2 (D) Weber (Wb)

7. The dimensions of magnetic field in M, L, T and C (coulomb) is given as : **[2008]**
(A) $[MLT^{-1}C^{-1}]$ (B) $[MT^2C^{-2}]$
(C) $[MT^{-1}C^{-1}]$ (D) $[MT^{-2}C^{-1}]$

8. Given that K = energy, V = velocity, T = time. If they are chosen as the fundamental units, then what is dimensional formula for surface tension ? **[2012 (Online)]**
(A) $[KV^{-2}T^{-2}]$ (B) $[K^2V^2T^{-2}]$
(C) $[K^2V^{-2}T^{-2}]$ (D) $[KV^2T^2]$

9. Let $[\epsilon_0]$ denote the dimensional formula of the permittivity of vacuum. If M = mass, L = length, T = time and A = electric current, then : **[2013]**
(A) $\epsilon_0 = [M^{-1}L^{-3}T^2A]$ (B) $\epsilon_0 = [M^{-1}L^{-3}T^4A^2]$
(C) $\epsilon_0 = [M^1L^2T^1A^2]$ (D) $\epsilon_0 = [M^1L^2T^1A]$

10. The dimensions of angular momentum, latent heat and capacitance are, respectively : **[2013 (Online)]**
(A) $ML^2T^1A^2, L^2T^{-2}, M^{-1}L^{-2}T^2$
(B) $ML^2T^{-2}, L^2T^2, M^{-1}L^{-2}T^4A^2$
(C) $ML^2T^{-1}, L^2T^{-2}, ML^2TA^2$
(D) $ML^2T^{-1}, L^2T^{-2}, M^{-1}L^{-2}T^4A^2$

11. If the time period t of the oscillation of a drop of liquid of density d, radius r, vibrating under surface tension s is given by the formula $t = \sqrt{r^{2b}s^c d^{a/2}}$. It is observed that the time period is directly proportional to $\sqrt{\frac{d}{s}}$. The value of b should therefore be : **[2013 (Online)]**
(A) $\frac{3}{4}$ (B) $\sqrt{3}$
(C) $\frac{3}{2}$ (D) $\frac{2}{3}$

12. In terms of resistance R and time T, the dimensions of ratio $\frac{\mu}{\varepsilon}$ of the permeability μ and permittivity ε is : **[2014 (Online)]**
(A) $[RT^{-2}]$ (B) $[R^2T^{-1}]$
(C) $[R^2]$ (D) $[R^2T^2]$

13. From the following combinations of physical constants (expressed through their usual symbols) the only combination, that would have the same value in different systems of units, is : **[2014 (Online)]**
(A) $\frac{ch}{2\pi\epsilon_e^2}$
(B) $\frac{e^2}{2\pi\epsilon_0 Gm_e^2}$ (m_e = mass of electron)
(C) $\frac{\mu_0\epsilon_0}{c^2}\frac{G}{he^2}$
(D) $\frac{2\pi\sqrt{\mu_0\epsilon_0}}{ce^2}\frac{h}{G}$

14. If the capacitance of a nanocapacitor is measured in terms of a unit 'u' made by combining the electric charge 'e', Bohr radius 'a_0', Planck's constant 'h' and speed of light 'c' then : **[2015 (Online)]**

(A) $u = \dfrac{e^2 h}{a_0}$ (B) $u = \dfrac{hc}{e^2 a_0}$

(C) $u = \dfrac{e^2 c}{h a_0}$ (D) $u = \dfrac{e^2 a_0}{hc}$

15. If electronic charge e, electron mass m, speed of light in vacuum c and Planck's constant h are taken as fundamental quantities, the permeability of vacuum μ_0 can be expressed in units of : **[2015 (Online)]**

(A) $\left(\dfrac{h}{me^2}\right)$ (B) $\left(\dfrac{hc}{me^2}\right)$

(C) $\left(\dfrac{h}{ce^2}\right)$ (D) $\left(\dfrac{mc^2}{he^2}\right)$

16. In the following 'I' refers to current and other symbols have their usual meaning, Choose the option that corresponds to the dimensions of electrical conductivity : **[2016 (Online)]**

(A) $M^{-1} L^{-3} T^3 I$ (B) $M^{-1} L^{-3} T^3 I^2$

(C) $M^{-1} L^3 T^3 I$ (D) $M L^{-3} T^3 I^2$

17. A, B, C and D are four different physical quantities having different dimensions. None of them is dimensionless. But we know that the equation $AD = C \ln (BD)$ holds true. Then which of the combination is not a meaningful quantity ? **[2016 (Online)]**

(A) $\dfrac{C}{BD} - \dfrac{AD^2}{C}$ (B) $A^2 - B^2C^2$

(C) $\dfrac{A}{B} - C$ (D) $\dfrac{(A - C)}{D}$

* * * * *

CHAPTER

2 MOTION IN A STRAIGHT LINE

2.1 MOTION IN ONE DIMENSION

1. If a body loses half of its velocity on penetrating 3 cm in a wooden block, then how much will it penetrate more before coming to rest? **[2002]**

(A) 1 cm (B) 2 cm

(C) 3 cm (D) 4 cm

2. From a building two balls A and B are thrown with equal speeds such that A is thrown upwards and B downwards (both vertically). If v_A and v_B are their respective velocities on reaching the ground, then : **[2002]**

(A) $v_B > v_A$

(B) $v_A = v_B$

(C) $v_A > v_B$

(D) their velocities depends on their masses

3. Speeds of two identical cars are u and $4u$ at a specific instant. At constant retardation the ratio of the respective distances at which the two cars are stopped from that instant is : **[2002]**

(A) 1 : 1 (B) 1 : 4

(C) 1 : 8 (D) 1 : 16

4. A car moving with a speed of 50 km/hr, can be stopped by brakes after at least 6 m. If the same car is moving at a speed of 100 km/hr, the minimum stopping distance is : **[2003]**

(A) 12 m (B) 18 m

(C) 24 m (D) 6 m

5. A ball is released from the top of a tower of height h metres. It takes T seconds to reach the ground. What is the position of the ball after $T/3$ seconds? **[2004]**

(A) $h/9$ metre from the ground

(B) $7h/9$ metre from the ground

(C) $8h/9$ metre from the ground

(D) $17h/9$ metre from the ground

6. An automobile travelling with a speed of 60 km/h, can brake to stop within a distance of 20 m. If the car is going twice as fast, i.e. 120 km/h, the stopping distance will be : **[2004]**

(A) 20 m (B) 40 m

(C) 60 m (D) 80 m

7. The relation between time t and distance x is $t = ax^2 + bx$, where a and b are constants. The acceleration is : **[2005]**

(A) $-2abv^2$ (B) $2bv^2$

(C) $-2av^3$ (D) $2av^3$

8. A car, starting from rest, accelerates at the rate f through a distance S, then continues at constant speed for time t and then decelerates at the rate $f/2$ to come to rest. If the total distance travelled is 15S, then : **[2005]**

(A) $S = ft$ (B) $S = \frac{1}{6}ft^2$

(C) $S = \frac{1}{72}ft^2$ (D) $S = \frac{1}{4}ft^2$

9. A particle is moving eastwards with a velocity of 5 ms^{-1}. In 10 second the velocity changes to 5 ms^{-1} northwards. The average acceleration in this time is : **[2005]**

(A) $\frac{1}{\sqrt{2}}$ ms^{-1} towards north-west

(B) $\frac{1}{2}$ ms^{-2} towards north

(C) Zero

(D) $\frac{1}{2}$ ms^{-2} towards north-west

10. A parachutist after bailing out falls 50 m without friction. When parachute opens, it decelerates at 2 m/s^2. He reaches the ground with a speed of 3 m/s. At what height, did he bail out? **[2005]**

(A) 91 m (B) 182 m

(C) 293 m (D) 111 m

11. A particle located at $x = 0$ at time $t = 0$, starts moving along the positive x-direction with a velocity v that varies as $v = \alpha\sqrt{x}$. The displacement of the particle varies with time as : **[2006]**

(A) $t^{1/2}$ (B) t^3

(C) t^2 (D) t

12. The velocity of a particle is $v = v_0 + gt + ft^2$. If its position is $x = 0$ at $t = 0$, then its displacement after unit time ($t = 1$) is : **[2007]**

(A) $v_0 + 2g + 3f$ (B) $v_0 + \frac{g}{2} + \frac{f}{3}$

(C) $v_0 + g + f$ (D) $v_0 + \frac{g}{2} + f$

13. An object, moving with a speed of 6.25 m/s, is decelerated at a rate given by $\frac{dv}{dt} = -2.5\sqrt{v}$ where v is the instantaneous speed. The time taken by the object, to come to rest, would be: **[2011]**

(A) 1s (B) 2s
(C) 4s (D) 8s

14. A good train accelerating uniformly on a straight railway track, approaches an electric pole standing on the side of track. Its engine passes the pole with velocity u and the guard's room passes with velocity v. The middle wagon of the train passes the pole with a velocity : **[2012 (Online)]**

(A) $\frac{u+v}{2}$ (B) $\frac{1}{2}\sqrt{u^2+v^2}$
(C) $\sqrt{uv}$ (D) $\sqrt{\left(\frac{u^2+v^2}{2}\right)}$

15. The graph of an object's motion (along the x-axis) is shown in the figure. The instantaneous velocity of the object at point A and B are v_A and v_B respectively. Then : **[2012 (Online)]**

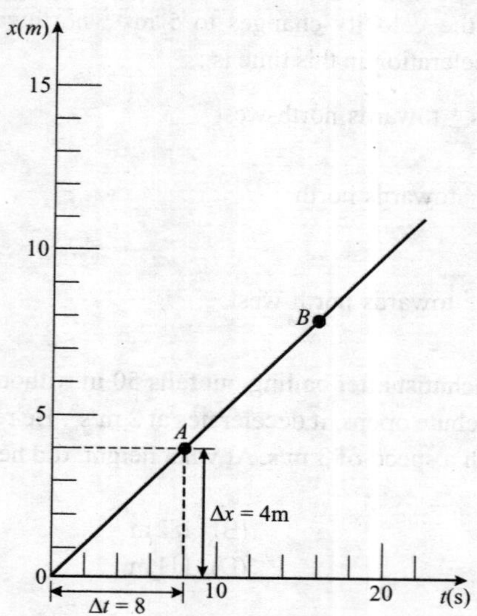

(A) $v_A = v_B = 0.5$ m/s (B) $v_A = 0.5$ m/s $< v_B$
(C) $v_A = 0.5$ m/s $> v_B$ (D) $v_A = v_B = 2$ m/s

16. The distance travelled by a body moving along a line in time t is proportional to t^3. The acceleration-time (a, t) graph for the motion of the body will be : **[2012 (Online)]**

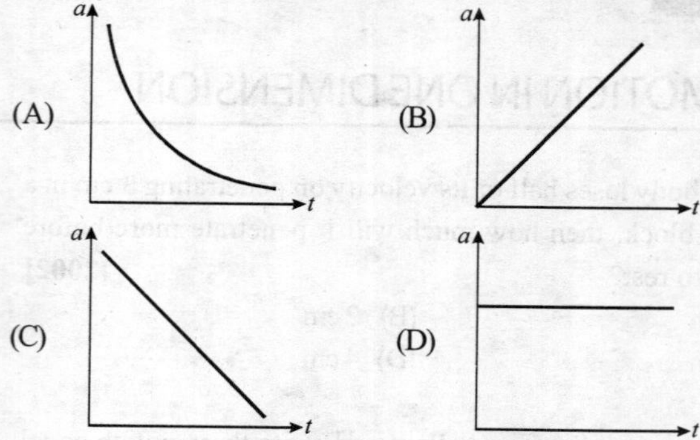

17. A car covers the first half of the distance between two places at 40 km/h and other half at 60 km/h. The average speed of the car is : **[2012 (Online)]**

(A) 40 km/h (B) 45 km/h
(C) 48 km/h (D) 60 km/h

18. From a tower of height H, a particle is thrown vertically upwards with a speed u. The time taken by the particle, to hit the ground, is n times that taken by it to reach the highest point of its path. The relation between H, u and n is : **[2014]**

(A) $2gH = n^2u^2$ (B) $gH = (n-2)^2 u^2$
(C) $2gH = nu^2(n-2)$ (D) $gH = (n-2)u^2$

19. A person climbs up a stalled escalator in 60 s. If standing on the same but escalator running with constant velocity he takes 40 s. How much time is taken by the person to walk up the moving escalator ? **[2014 (Online)]**

(A) 37 s (B) 27 s
(C) 24 s (D) 45 s

* * * * *

CHAPTER

3 MOTION IN A PLANE

3.1 MOTION IN TWO DIMENSIONS

1. A ball whose kinetic energy is E, is projected at an angle of 45° to the horizontal. The kinetic energy of the ball at the highest point of its flight will be : **[2002]**

(A) E (B) $E/\sqrt{2}$
(C) $E/2$ (D) Zero

2. A boy playing on the roof of a 10 m high building throws a ball with a speed of 10 m/s at an angle of 30° with the horizontal. How far from the throwing point will the ball be at the height of 10 m from the ground? **[2002]**

[$g = 10$ m/s^2, $\sin 30° = 1/2$, $\cos 30° = \frac{\sqrt{3}}{2}$]

(A) 5.20 m (B) 4.33 m
(C) 2.60 m (D) 8.66 m

3. The coordinates of a moving particle at any time t are given by $x = \alpha t^3$ and $y = \beta t^3$. The speed of the particle at time t is given by : **[2003]**

(A) $\sqrt{\alpha^2+\beta^2}$ (B) $3t^2\sqrt{\alpha^2+\beta^2}$
(C) $t^2\sqrt{\alpha^2+\beta^2}$ (D) $\sqrt{\alpha^2+\beta^2}$

4. A ball is thrown from a point with a speed v_0 at angle of projection θ. From the same point and at the same instant, a person starts running with a constant speed $v_0/2$ to catch the ball? If yes, what should be the angle of projection? **[2004]**

(A) Yes, 60° (B) Yes, 30°
(C) No (D) Yes, 45°

5. If $\vec{A}\times\vec{B} = \vec{B}\times\vec{A}$, then the angle between A and B is : **[2004]**

(A) $\frac{\pi}{2}$ (B) $\frac{\pi}{3}$
(C) π (D) $\frac{\pi}{4}$

6. A projectile can have the same range 'R' for two angles of projection. If 'T_1' and 'T_2' to be time of flights in the two cases, then the product of the two time of flights is directly proportional to : **[2004]**

(A) R (B) $\frac{1}{R}$
(C) $\frac{1}{R^2}$ (D) R^2

7. A particle is projected at 60° to the horizontal with a kinetic energy K. The kinetic energy at the highest point is : **[2007]**

(A) K (B) Zero
(C) $K/4$ (D) $K/2$

8. A particle has an initial velocity of $3\hat{i}+4\hat{j}$ and an acceleration of $0.4\hat{i}+0.3\hat{j}$. Its speed after 10 s is : **[2009]**

(A) $7\sqrt{2}$ units (B) 7 units
(C) 8.5 units (D) 10 units

9. A particle is moving with velocity $\vec{v} = K(y\hat{i}+x\hat{j})$, where K is a constant. The general equation for its path is : **[2010]**

(A) $y = x^2$ + constant (B) $y^2 = x$ + constant
(C) xy = constant (D) $y^2 = x^2$ + constant

10. A water fountain on the ground sprinkles water all around it. If the speed of water coming out of the fountain is v, the total area around the fountain that gets wet is : **[2011]**

(A) $\pi\frac{v^4}{g^2}$ (B) $\frac{\pi}{2}\frac{v^4}{g^2}$
(C) $\pi\frac{v^2}{g^2}$ (D) $\pi\frac{v^4}{g}$

11. A boy can throw a stone up to a maximum height of 10 m. The maximum horizontal distance that the boy can throw the same stone up to, will be : **[2012]**

(A) $20\sqrt{2}$ m (B) 10 m
(C) $10\sqrt{2}$ m (D) 20 m

12. A projectile is given an initial velocity of $(\hat{i}+2\hat{j})$ m/s, where $\hat{i}$ is along the ground and $\hat{j}$ is along the vertical. If $g = 10$ m/s^2, the equation of its trajectory is : **[2013]**

(A) $y = 2x - 5x^2$ (B) $4y = 2x - 5x^2$
(C) $4y = 2x - 25x^2$ (D) $y = x - 5x^2$

13. The maximum range of a bullet fired from a toy pistol mounted on a car at rest is $R_0 = 40$ m. What will be the acute angle of inclination of the pistol for maximum range when the car is moving in the direction of firing with uniform velocity $v = 20$ m/s, on a horizontal surface ? ($g = 10$ m/s^2) : **[2013 (Online)]**

(A) 30° (B) 60°
(C) 75° (D) 45°

14. A ball projected from ground at an angle of 45° just clears a wall in front. If point of projection is 4m from the foot of wall and ball strikes the ground at a distance of 6 m on the other side of the wall, the height of the wall is : **[2013 (Online)]**

(A) 4.4 m (B) 2.4 m
(C) 3.6 m (D) 1.6 m

15. The initial speed of a bullet fired from a rifle is 630 m/s. The rifle is fired at the centre of a target 700 m away at the same level as the target. How far above the centre of the target ? **[2014 (Online)]**

(A) 1.0 m (B) 4.2 m
(C) 6.1 m (D) 9.8 m

16. The position of a projectile launched from the origin at $t = 0$ is given by $\vec{r} = (40\hat{i} + 50\hat{j})$ m at $t = 2$ s. If the projectile was launched at an angle θ from the horizontal, then θ is : (take $g = 10\ ms^{-2}$) : **[2014 (Online)]**

(A) $\tan^{-1}\frac{2}{3}$ (B) $\tan^{-1}\frac{3}{2}$
(C) $\tan^{-1}\frac{7}{4}$ (D) $\tan^{-1}\frac{4}{5}$

17. A vector $\vec{A}$ is rotated by a small angle $\Delta\theta$ radian ($\Delta\theta << 1$) to get a new vector $\vec{B}$. In that case $|\vec{B} - \vec{A}|$ is : **[2015 (Online)]**

(A) $|\vec{A}|\Delta\theta$ (B) $|\vec{B}|\Delta\theta - |\vec{A}|$
(C) $|\vec{A}|\left(1 - \frac{\Delta\theta^2}{2}\right)$ (D) 0

* * * * *

CHAPTER

3 MOTION IN A PLANE

3.2 RELATIVE MOTION

1. A body is at rest at $x = 0$. At $t = 0$, it starts moving in the positive x-direction with a constant acceleration. At the same instant another body passes through $x = 0$ moving in the positive x-direction with a constant speed. The position of the first body is given by $x_1(t)$ after time 't' and that of second body by $x_2(t)$ after the same time interval. Which of the following graphs correctly describes $(x_1 - x_2)$ as a function of time 't' ? **[2008]**

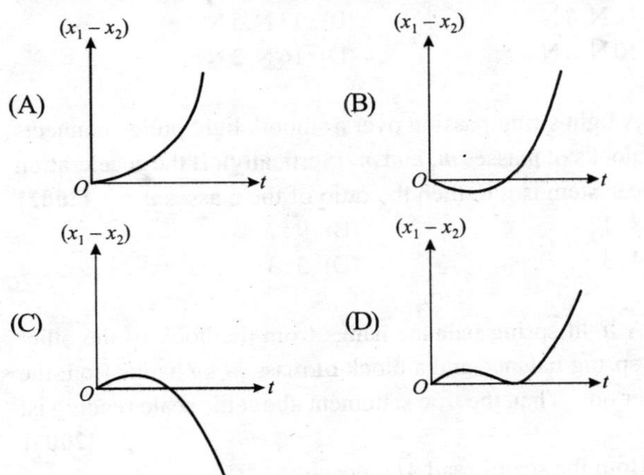

2. Two fixed frictionless inclined planes making an angle 30° and 60° with the vertical are shown in the figure. Two blocks A and B are placed on the two planes. What is the relative vertical acceleration of A with respect to B? **[2010]**

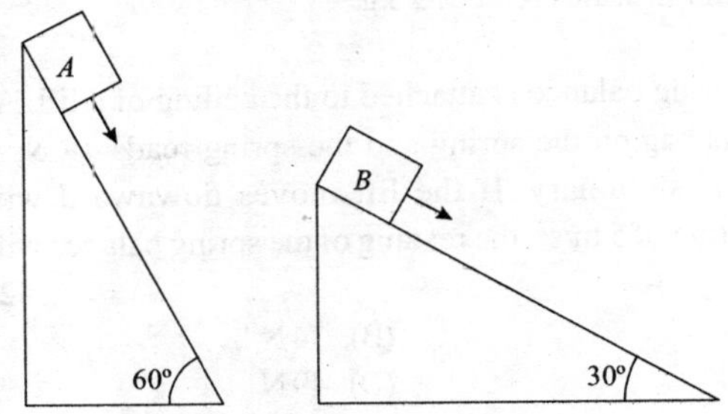

(A) 4.9 ms^{-2} in horizontal direction
(B) 9.8 ms^{-2} in vertical direction
(C) Zero
(D) 4.9 ms^{-2} in vertical direction

3. Two stones are thrown up simultaneously from the edge of a cliff 240 m high with initial speed of 10 m/s and 40 m/s respectively. Which of the following graph best represents the time variation of relative position of the second stone with respect of the first ?

(Assume stones do not rebound after hitting the ground and neglect air resistance, take $g = 10$ m/s^2)

(The figure are schematic and not drawn to scale) **[2015]**

(A)

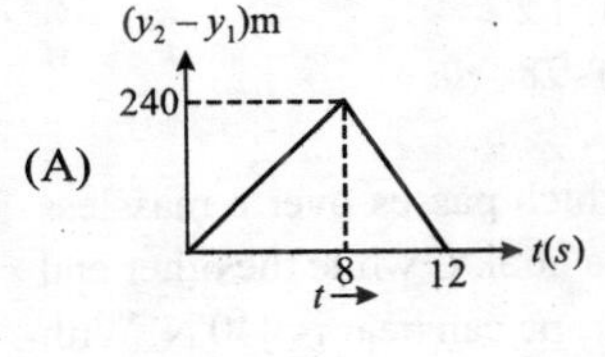

(B)

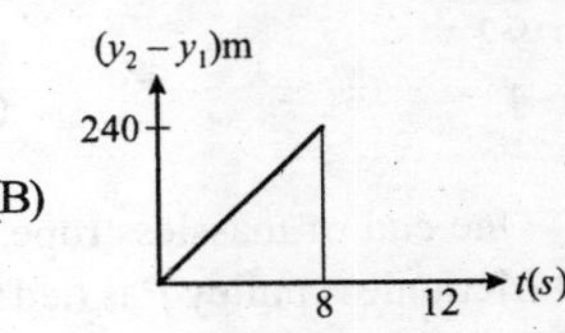

(C)

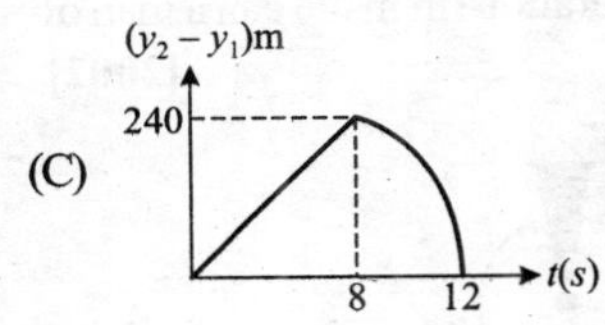

(D)

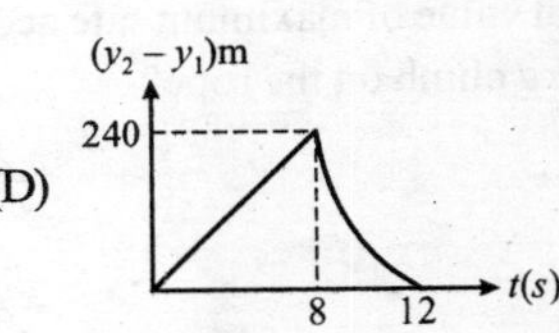

* * * * *

CHAPTER

4 LAWS OF MOTION

4.1 NEWTON'S LAWS OF MOTION

1. When forces F_1, F_2, F_3 are acting on a particle of mass m such that F_2 and F_3 are mutually perpendicular, then the particle remains stationary. If the force F_1 is now removed then the acceleration of the particle is : **[2002]**

(A) F_1/m (B) F_2F_3/mF_1

(C) $(F_2 - F_3)/m$ (D) F_2/m

2. Three identical blocks of masses $m = 2$ kg are drawn by a force F with an acceleration of 0.6 ms^{-2} on a frictionless surface, then what is the tension (in N) in the string between the blocks B and C : **[2002]**

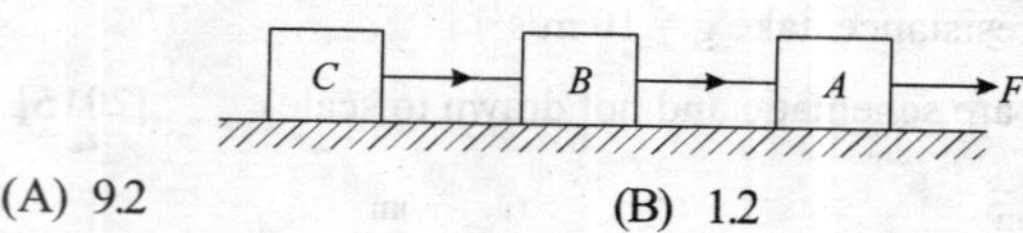

(A) 9.2 (B) 1.2

(C) 4 (D) 9.8

3. One end of massless rope, which passes over a massless and frictionless pulley P is tied to a hook C while the other end is free. Maximum tension that the rope can bear is 840 N. With what value of maximum safe acceleration (in ms^{-2}) can a man of 60 kg climb on the rope? **[2002]**

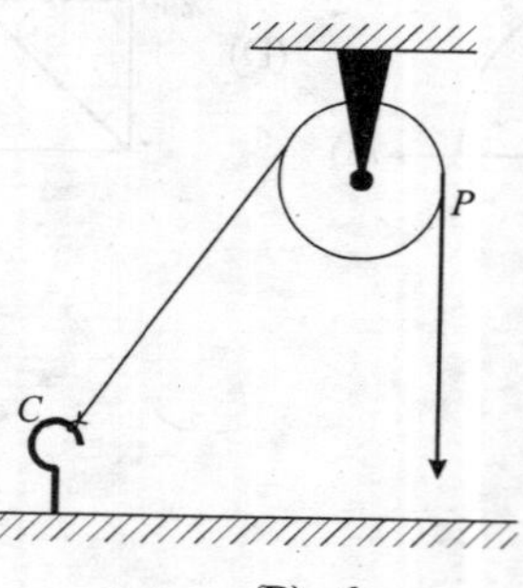

(A) 16 (B) 6

(C) 4 (D) 8

4. A solid sphere, a hollow sphere and a ring are released from top of an inclined plane (frictionless) so that they slide down the plane. Then maximum acceleration down the plane is for (no rolling) : **[2002]**

(A) Solid sphere (B) Hollows sphere

(C) Ring (D) All same

5. A lift is moving down with acceleration a. A man in the lift drops a ball inside the lift. The acceleration of the ball as observed by the man in the lift and a man standing stationary on the ground are respectively : **[2002]**

(A) g, g (B) $g - a, g - a$

(C) $g - a, g$ (D) a, g

6. Two forces are such that the sum of their magnitudes is 18 N and their resultant is 12 N which is perpendicular to the smaller force. Then the magnitudes of the forces are : **[2002]**

(A) 12 N, 6 N (B) 13 N, 5 N

(C) 10 N, 8 N (D) 16 N, 2 N

7. A light string passing over a smooth light pulley connects two blocks of masses m_1 and m_2 (vertically). If the acceleration of the system is $g/8$, then the ratio of the masses is : **[2002]**

(A) 8 : 1 (B) 9 : 7

(C) 4 : 3 (D) 5 : 3

8. A light spring balance hangs from the hook of the other light spring balance and a block of mass M kg hangs from the former one. Then the true statement about the scale reading is: **[2003]**

(A) Both the scales read M kg each

(B) The scale of the lower one reads M kg and of the upper one zero

(C) The reading of the two scales can be anything but the sum of the readings will be M kg

(D) Both the scales read $M/2$ kg

9. A spring balance is attached to the ceiling of a lift. A man hangs his bag on the spring and the spring reads 49 N, when the lift is stationary. If the lift moves downward with an acceleration of 5 m/s^2, the reading of the spring balance will be : **[2003]**

(A) 24 N (B) 74 N

(C) 15 N (D) 49 N

10. A rocket which has a mass of 3.5×10^4 kg is blasted upwards with an initial acceleration of 10 m/s^2. Then the initial thrust of the blast is : **[2003]**

(A) 3.5×10^5 N (B) 7.0×10^5 N

(C) 14.0×10^5 N (D) 1.75×10^5 N

11. Three forces start acting simultaneously on a particle moving with velocity $\vec{v}$. These forces are represented in magnitude and direction by the three sides of a triangle ABC (as shown). The particle will now move with velocity : **[2003]**

(A) Less than $\vec{v}$

(B) Greater than $\vec{v}$

(C) $|v|$ in the direction of largest force BC

(D) $\vec{v}$, remaining unchanged

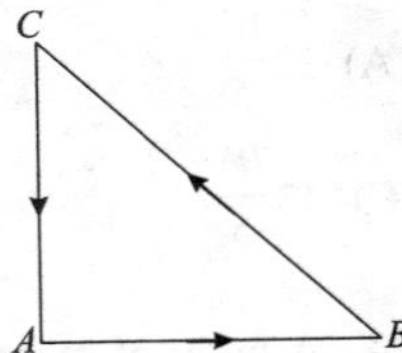

12. A block of mass M is pulled along a horizontal frictionless surface by a rope of mass m. If a force P is applied at the free end of the rope, the force exerted by the rope on the block is : **[2003]**

(A) $\dfrac{Pm}{M+m}$ (B) $\dfrac{Pm}{M-m}$

(C) P (D) $\dfrac{PM}{M+m}$

13. Two masses $m_1 = 5$ kg and $m_2 = 4.8$ kg tied to a string are hanging over a light frictionless pulley. What is the acceleration of the masses when they are free to move ? ($g = 9.8$ m/s^2) : **[2004]**

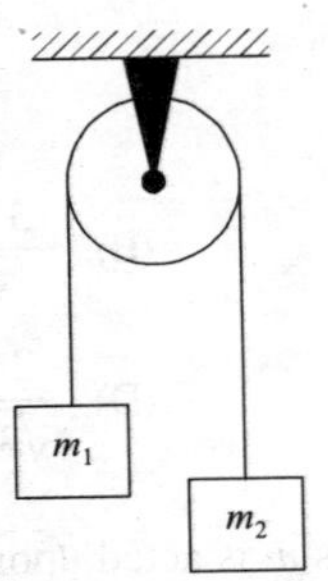

(A) 0.2 m/s^2 (B) 9.8 m/s^2

(C) 5 m/s^2 (D) 4.8 m/s^2

14. A machine gun fires a bullet of mass 40 g with a velocity 1200 ms^{-1}. The man holding it, can exert maximum force of 144 N on the gun. How many bullets can he fire per second at the most? **[2004]**

(A) One (B) Four

(C) Two (D) Three

15. A block is kept on a frictionless inclined surface with angle of inclination α. The incline is given an acceleration a to keep the block stationary. Then a is equal to : **[2005]**

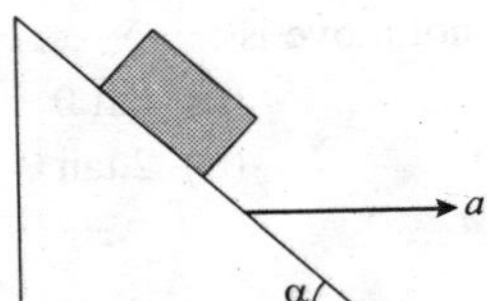

(A) $g/\tan\alpha$ (B) g cosec α

(C) g (D) $g\tan\alpha$

16. A player caught a cricket ball of mass 150 g moving at a rate of 20 m/s. If the catching process is completed in 0.1 s, the force of the blow exerted by the ball on the hand of the player is equal to : **[2006]**

(A) 150 N (B) 3 N

(C) 30 N (D) 300 N

17. A ball of mass 0.2 kg is thrown vertically upwards by applying a force by hand. If the hand moves 0.2 m while applying the force and the ball goes upto 2 m height further, find the magnitude of the force. (Consider $g = 10$ m/s^2) : **[2006]**

(A) 4 N (B) 16 N

(C) 20 N (D) 22 N

18. A block of mass m is connected to another block of mass M by a spring (massless) of spring constant k. The blocks are kept on a smooth horizontal plane. Initially the blocks are at rest and the spring is unstretched. Then a constant force F starts acting on the block of mass M to pull it. Find the force on the block of mass m : **[2007]**

(A) $\dfrac{mF}{M}$ (B) $\dfrac{(M+m)F}{m}$

(C) $\dfrac{mF}{(m+M)}$ (D) $\dfrac{MF}{(m+M)}$

19. If a spring of stiffness 'k' is cut into two parts 'A' and 'B' of length $l_A : l_B = 2 : 3$, then the stiffness of spring 'A' is given by : **[2011]**

(A) $\dfrac{5}{2}k$ (B) $\dfrac{3k}{5}$

(C) $\dfrac{2k}{5}$ (D) k

20. A particle of mass m is at rest at the origin at time $t = 0$. It is subjected to a force $F(t) = F_0 e^{-bt}$ in the x-direction. Its speed $v(t)$ is depicted by which of the following curves ? **[2012]**

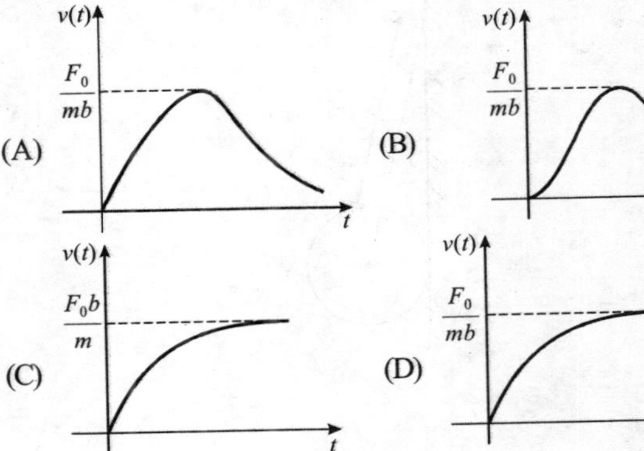

21. This question has Statement-1 and Statement-2. Of the four choices given after the Statements, choose the one that best describes the two Statements. **[2012 (Online)]**

Statement-1 : If you push on a cart being pulled by a horse so that it does not move, the cart pushes you back with an equal and opposite force :

Statement-2 : The cart does not move because the force described in Statement-1 cancel each other.

(A) Statement-1 is true, Statement-2 is true, Statement-2 is the correct explanation of Statement-1

(B) Statement-1 is false, Statement-2 is true

(C) Statement-1 is true, Statement-2 is false

(D) Statement-1 is true, Statement-2 is true, Statement-2 is not the correct explanation of Statement-1.

22. Two blocks of mass $M_1 = 20$ kg and $M_2 = 12$ kg are connected by a metal rod of mass 8 kg. The system is pulled vertically up by applying a force of 480 N as shown. The tension at the mid-point of the rod is : **[2013 (Online)]**

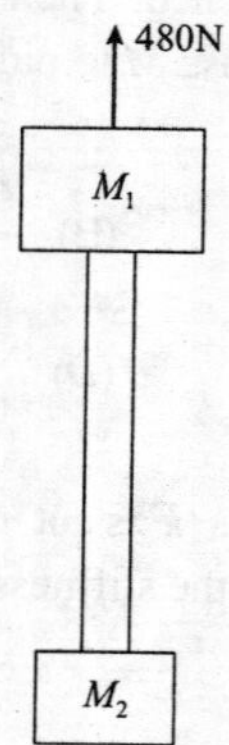

(A) 144 N (B) 96 N
(C) 240 N (D) 192 N

23. A uniform sphere of weight W and radius 5 cm is being held by a string as shown in the figure. The tension in the string will be : **[2013 (Online)]**

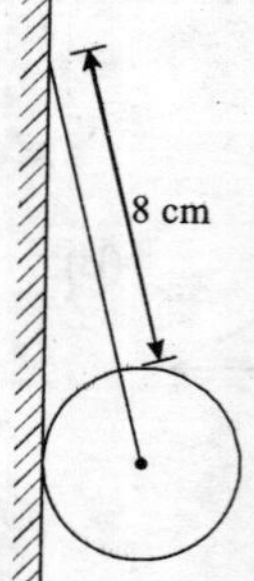

(A) $12\dfrac{W}{5}$ (B) $5\dfrac{W}{12}$

(C) $13\dfrac{W}{5}$ (D) $13\dfrac{W}{12}$

24. A body of mass 5 kg under the action of constant force $\vec{F} = F_x\hat{i} + F_y\hat{j}$ has velocity at $t = 0$ s as $\vec{v} = (6\hat{i} - 2\hat{j})$ m/s and at $t = 10$ s as $\vec{v} = +6\hat{j}$ m/s. The force $\vec{F}$ is : **[2014 (Online)]**

(A) $(-3\hat{j} + 4\hat{j})$ N (B) $\left(-\dfrac{3}{5}\hat{i} + \dfrac{4}{5}\hat{j}\right)$N

(C) $(3\hat{i} - 4\hat{j})$N (D) $\left(\dfrac{3}{5}\hat{i} - \dfrac{4}{5}\hat{j}\right)$N

25. A heavy box is to dragged along a rough horizontal floor. To do so, person A pushes it at an angle 30º from the horizontal and requires a minimum force F_A, while person B pulls the box at an angle 60º from the horizontal and needs minimum force F_B. If the coefficient of friction between the box and the floor is $\dfrac{\sqrt{3}}{5}$, the ratio $\dfrac{F_A}{F_B}$ is : **[2014 (Online)]**

(A) $\sqrt{3}$ (B) $\dfrac{5}{\sqrt{3}}$

(C) $\sqrt{\dfrac{3}{2}}$ (D) $\dfrac{2}{\sqrt{3}}$

26. A particle of mass m is acted upon by a force F given by the empirical law $F = \dfrac{R}{t^2} v(t)$. If this law is to be tested experimentally by observing the motion starting from rest, the best way is to plot : **[2016 (Online)]**

(A) log $v(t)$ against $\dfrac{1}{t}$ (B) $v(t)$ against t^2

(C) log $v(t)$ against $\dfrac{1}{t^2}$ (D) log $v(t)$ against t

27. A rocket is fired vertically from the earth with an acceleration of 2 g, where g is the gravitational acceleration. On an inclined plane inside the rocket, making an angle θ with the horizontal, a point object of mass m is kept. The minimum coefficient of friction μ_{min} between the mass and the inclined surface such that the mass does not move is : **[2016 (Online)]**

(A) tan 2θ (B) tan θ
(C) 3 tan θ (D) 2 tan θ

* * * * *

CHAPTER

4 LAWS OF MOTION

4.2 FRICTION

1. A horizontal force of 10 N is necessary to just hold a block stationary against a wall. The coefficient of friction between the block and the wall is 0.2. The weight of the block is : **[2003]**

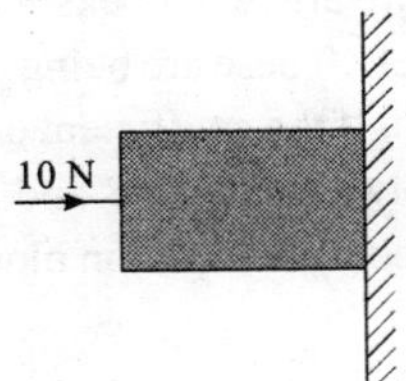

(A) 20 N (B) 50 N
(C) 100 N (D) 2 N

2. A marble block of mass 2 kg lying on ice when given a velocity of 6 m/s is stopped by friction in 10 s. Then the coefficient of friction is : **[2003]**
(A) 0.02 (B) 0.03
(C) 0.06 (D) 0.01

3. A block rests on a rough inclined plane making an angle of 30° with the horizontal. The coefficient of static friction between the block and the plane is 0.8. If the frictional force on the block is 10 N, the mass of the block (in kg) is : (taken $g = 10$ m/s^2) : **[2004]**

(A) 2.0 (B) 4.0
(C) 1.6 (D) 2.5

4. A smooth block is released at rest on a 45° incline and then slides a distance d. The time taken to slide is n times as much to slide on rough incline than on a smooth incline. The coefficient of friction is : **[2005]**

(A) $\mu_k = 1 - \frac{1}{n^2}$ (B) $\mu_k = \sqrt{1 - \frac{1}{n^2}}$

(C) $\mu_s = 1 - \frac{1}{n^2}$ (D) $\mu_s = \sqrt{1 - \frac{1}{n^2}}$

5. The upper half of an inclined plane with inclination ϕ is perfectly smooth, while the lower half is rough. A body starting from rest at the top will again come to rest at the bottom, if the coefficient of friction for the lower half is given by : **[2005]**
(A) $2 \sin \phi$ (B) $2 \cos \phi$
(C) $2 \tan \phi$ (D) $\tan \phi$

6. Consider a car moving on a straight road with a speed of 100 m/s. The distance at which car can be stopped, is : [$\mu_k = 0.5$] **[2005]**
(A) 800 m (B) 1000 m
(C) 100 m (D) 400 m

7. The minimum force required to start pushing a body up a rough (frictional coefficient μ) inclined plane is F_1 while the minimum force needed to prevent it from sliding down is F_2. If the inclined plane makes an angle θ from the horizontal such that $\tan \theta = 2\mu$ then the ratio $\frac{F_1}{F_2}$ is : **[2011]**

(A) 4 (B) 1
(C) 2 (D) 3

8. An insect crawls up a hemispherical surface very slowly. The coefficient of friction between the insect and the surface is 1/3. If the line joining the centre of the hemispherical surface to the insect makes an angle α with the vertical, the maximum possible value of α so that the insect does not slip is given by: **[2012 (Online)]**

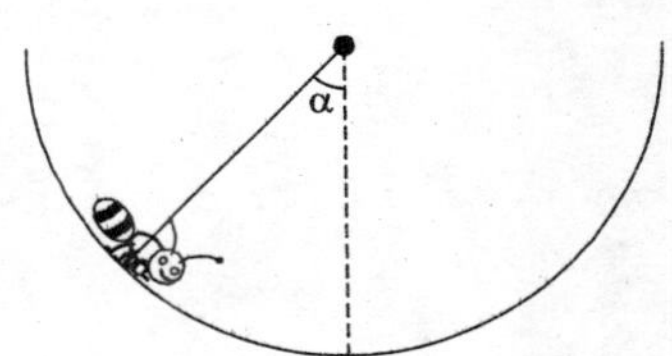

(A) $\cot \alpha = 3$ (B) $\sec \alpha = 3$
(C) $\operatorname{cosec} \alpha = 3$ (D) $\cos \alpha = 3$

9. A block of weight W rest on a horizontal floor with coefficient of static friction μ. It is desired to make the block move by applying minimum amount of force. The angle θ from the horizontal at which the force should be applied and magnitude of the force F are respectively : **[2012 (Online)]**

(A) $\theta = \tan^{-1}(\mu), F = \frac{\mu W}{\sqrt{1+\mu^2}}$

(B) $\theta = \tan^{-1}\left(\frac{1}{\mu}\right), F = \frac{\mu W}{\sqrt{1+\mu^2}}$

(C) $\theta = 0, F = \mu W$

(D) $\theta = \tan^{-1}\left(\frac{\mu}{1+\mu}\right), F = \frac{\mu W}{1+\mu}$

10. A body starts from rest on a long inclined plane of slope 45°. The coefficient of friction between the body and the plane varies as $\mu = 0.3\,x$, where x is distance travelled down the plane. The body will have maximum speed : **[2013 (Online)]**

(A) 9.8 m (B) 27 m

(C) 12 m (D) 3.33 m

11. A block is placed on a rough horizontal plane. A time dependent horizontal force $F = kt$ acts on the block, where k is a positive constant. The acceleration-time graph of the block is: **[2013 (Online)]**

(A) 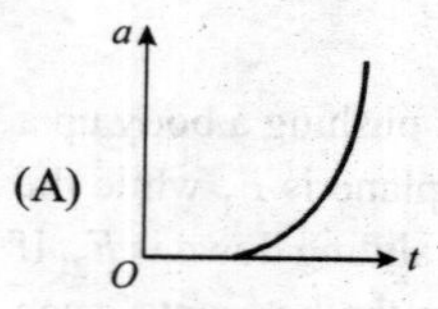

(B) 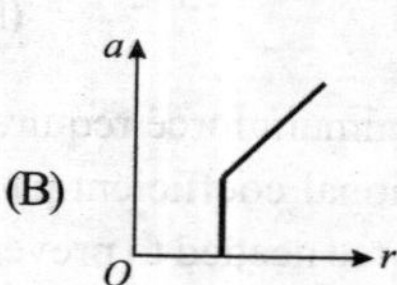

(C) 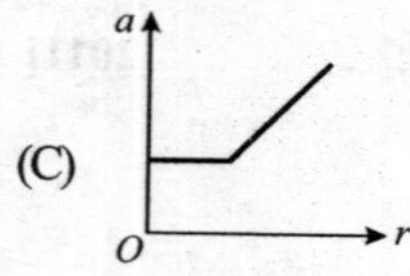

(D) 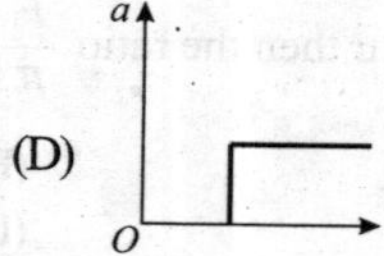

12. A block of mass m is placed on a surface with a vertical cross section given by $y = \frac{x^3}{6}$. If the coefficient of friction is 0.5, the maximum height above the ground at which the block can be placed without slipping is : **[2014]**

(A) $\frac{1}{6}m$ (B) $\frac{2}{3}m$

(C) $\frac{1}{3}m$ (D) $\frac{1}{2}m$

13. Given in the figure are two blocks A and B of weight 20 N and 100 N, respectively. These are being pressed against a wall by a force F as shown. If the coefficient of friction between the blocks is 0.1 and between block B and the wall is 0.15, the frictional force applied by the wall on block B is : **[2015]**

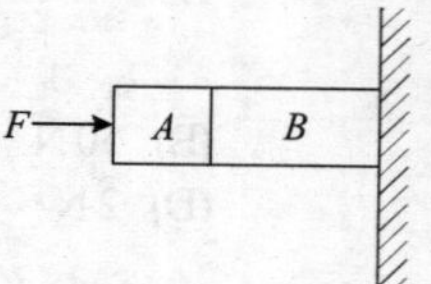

(A) 100 N (B) 80 N

(C) 120 N (D) 150 N

* * * * *

CHAPTER 5

WORK ENERGY POWER & APPLICATIONS

5.1 WORK ENERGY POWER

1. A spring of force constant 800 N/m has an extension of 5 cm. The work done in extending it from 5 cm to 15 cm is : **[2002]**

(A) 16 J (B) 8 J
(C) 32 J (D) 24 J

2. A spring of spring constant 5×10^3 N/m is stretched initially by 5 cm from the unstretched position. Then the work required to stretch it further by another 5 cm is : **[2003]**

(A) 12.50 N-m (B) 18.75 N-m
(C) 25.00 N-m (D) 6.25 N-m

3. A body is moved along a straight line by a machine delivering a constant power. The distance moved by the body in time t is proportional to : **[2003]**

(A) $t^{3/4}$ (B) $t^{3/2}$
(C) $t^{1/4}$ (D) $t^{1/2}$

4. A particle moves in a straight line with retardation proportional to its displacement. Its loss of kinetic energy for any displacement x is proportional to : **[2004]**

(A) x^2 (B) e^x
(C) x (D) $\log_e x$

5. A body of mass m accelerates uniformly from rest to v_1 in time t_1. The instantaneous power delivered to the body as a function of time t is : **[2004]**

(A) $\dfrac{mv_1 t}{t_1}$ (B) $\dfrac{mv_1^2 t}{t_1^2}$

(C) $\dfrac{mv_1 t^2}{t_1}$ (D) $\dfrac{mv_1^2 t}{t_1}$

6. A uniform chain of length 2 m is kept on a table such that a length of 60 cm hangs freely from the edge of the table. The total mass of the chain is 4 kg. What is the work done in pulling the entire chain on the table : **[2004]**

(A) 7.2 J (B) 3.6 J
(C) 120 J (D) 1200 J

7. A force $\vec{F} = (5\vec{i} + 3\vec{j} + 2\vec{k})N$ is applied over a particle which displaces it from its origin to the point $\vec{r} = (2\vec{i} - \vec{j})m$. The work done on the particle in joule is : **[2004]**

(A) +10 (B) +7
(C) −7 (D) +13

8. A bullet fired into a fixed target loses half of its velocity after penetrating 3 cm. How much further it will penetrate before coming to rest, assuming that it faces constant resistance to motion ? **[2005]**

(A) 3.0 m (B) 2.0 m
(C) 1.5 cm (D) 1.0 cm

9. The block of mass M moving on the frictionless horizontal surface collides with the spring of spring constant k and compresses it by length L. The maximum momentum of the block after collision is : **[2005]**

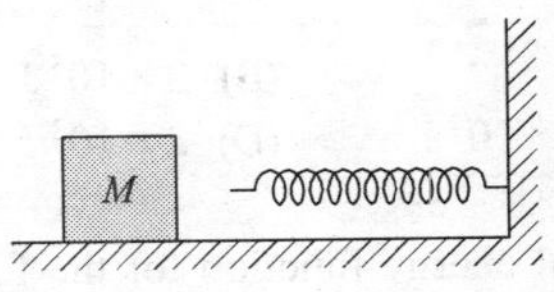

(A) $\sqrt{Mk}\,L$ (B) $\dfrac{kL^2}{2M}$

(C) Zero (D) $\dfrac{ML^2}{k}$

10. A spherical ball of mass 20 kg is stationary at the top of a hill of height 100 m. It rolls down a smooth surface to the ground, then climbs up another hill of height 30 m and finally rolls down to a horizontal base at a height of 20 m above the ground. The velocity attained by the ball is : **[2005]**

(A) 20 m/s (B) 40 m/s
(C) $10\sqrt{30}$ m/s (D) 10 m/s

11. A particle of mass 100 g is thrown vertically upwards with a speed of 5 m/s. The work done by the force of gravity during the time the particle goes up is : **[2006]**

(A) −0.5 J (B) −1.25 J
(C) 1.25 J (D) 0.5 J

12. The potential energy of a 1 kg particle free to move along the x-axis is given by $V(x) = \left(\dfrac{x^4}{4} - \dfrac{x^2}{2}\right)$ J. The total mechanical energy of the particle is 2 J. Then, the maximum speed (in m/s) is: **[2006]**

(A) $3/\sqrt{2}$ (B) $\sqrt{2}$
(C) $1/\sqrt{2}$ (D) 2

13. A mass of M kg is suspended by a weightless string. The horizontal force that is required to displace it until the string makes an angle of 45° with the initial vertical direction is : **[2006]**

(A) $Mg(\sqrt{2}+1)$ (B) $Mg\sqrt{2}$

(C) $\frac{Mg}{\sqrt{2}}$ (D) $Mg(\sqrt{2}-1)$

14. A 2 kg block slides on a horizontal floor with a speed of 4 m/s. It strikes an uncompressed spring, and compresses it till the block is motionless. The kinetic friction force is 15 N and spring constant is 10,000 N/m. The spring compresses by : **[2007]**

(A) 5.5 cm (B) 2.5 cm

(C) 11.0 cm (D) 8.5 cm

15. An athlete in the Olympic games covers distance of 100 m in 10 s. His kinetic energy can be estimated to be in the range : **[2008]**

(A) 200 J – 500 J (B) 2×10^5 J – 3×10^5 J

(C) 2×10^4 J – 3×10^4 J (D) 2×10^3 J – 5×10^3 J

16. The potential energy function for the force between two atoms in a diatomic molecule is approximately given by $U(x)=\frac{a}{x^{12}}-\frac{b}{x^6}$, where a and b are constant and x is the distance between the atoms. If the dissociation energy of the molecule is $D=[U(x=\infty)-U_{\text{at equilibrium}}]$, D is : **[2010]**

(A) $\frac{b^2}{6a}$ (B) $\frac{b^2}{2a}$

(C) $\frac{b^2}{12a}$ (D) $\frac{b^2}{4a}$

17. At time $t = 0$s particle starts moving along the x-axis. If its kinetic energy increases uniformly with time 't', the net force acting on it must be proportional to : **[2011]**

(A) $\sqrt{t}$ (B) Constant

(C) t (D) $\frac{1}{\sqrt{t}}$

18. This question has Statement-1 and Statement-2. Of the four choices given after the statements, choose the one that best describes the two statements.

If two springs S_1 and S_2 of force constants k_1 and k_2, respectively, are stretched by the same force, it is found that more work is done on spring S_1 than on spring S_2.

Statement-1 : If stretched by the same amount, work done on S_1, will be more than that on S_2

Statement-2 : $k_1 < k_2$. **[2012]**

(A) Statement-1 is true, Statement-2 is true and Statement-2 is not the correct explanation of Statement-1.

(B) Statement-1 is false, Statement-2 is true

(C) Statement-1 is true, Statement-2 is false

(D) Statement-1 is true, Statement-2 is true and Statement-2 is the correct explanation of Statement-1.

19. The force $\vec{F} = F\hat{i}$ on a particle of mass 2 kg, moving along the x-axis is given in the figure as a function of its position x. The particle is moving with a velocity of 5 m/s along the x-axis at $x = 0$. What is the kinetic energy of the particle at $x = 8$ m? **[2012 (Online)]**

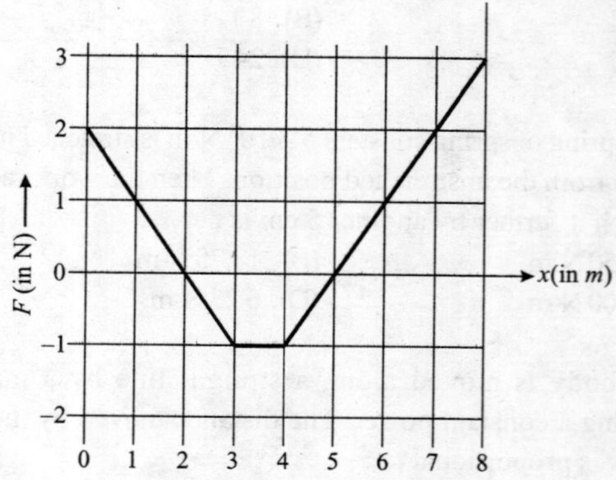

(A) 34 J (B) 34.5 J

(C) 4.5 J (D) 29.4 J

20. A particle gets displaced by $\Delta\vec{r} = (2\hat{i}+3\hat{j}+4\hat{k})$ m under the action of a force $\vec{F}\ (7\hat{i}+4\hat{j}+3\hat{k})$. The change in its kinetic energy is : **[2012 (Online)]**

(A) 38 J (B) 70 J

(C) 52.5 J (D) 126 J

21. The springs of force constants 300 N/m (Spring A) and 400 N/m (Spring B) are joined together in series. The combination is compressed by 8.75 cm. The ratio of energy stored in A and B is $\frac{E_A}{E_B}$. Then $\frac{E_A}{E_B}$ is equal : **[2013 (Online)]**

(A) $\frac{4}{3}$ (B) $\frac{16}{9}$

(C) $\frac{3}{4}$ (D) $\frac{9}{16}$

22. A 70 kg man leaps vertically into the air from a crouching position. To take the leap the man pushes the ground with a constant force F to raise himself. The center of gravity rises by 0.5 m before he leaps. After the leap the c.g. rises by another 1 m. The maximum power delivered by the muscles is : [Take $g = 10$ ms^{-2}] **[2013 (Online)]**

(A) 6.26×10^3 Watts at the start

(B) 6.26×10^3 Watts at take off

(C) 6.26×10^4 Watts at the start

(D) 6.26×10^4 Watts at take off

23. When a rubber-band is stretched by a distance x, it exerts a restoring force of magnitude $F = ax + bx^2$ where a and b are constants. The work done in stretching the unstretched rubber-band by L is : **[2014]**

(A) $aL^2 + bL^3$ (B) $\frac{1}{2}(aL^2 + bL^3)$

(C) $\frac{aL^2}{2} + \frac{bL^3}{3}$ (D) $\frac{1}{2}\left(\frac{aL^2}{2} + \frac{bL^3}{3}\right)$

24. A spring of unstretched length 1 has a mass m with one end fixed to a rigid support. Assuming spring to be made of a uniform wire, the kinetic energy possessed by it if its free end is pulled with uniform velocity v is : **[2014 (Online)]**

(A) $\frac{1}{2}mv^2$ (B) mv^2

(C) $\frac{1}{3}mv^2$ (D) $\frac{1}{6}mv^2$

25. A wind-powered generator converts wind energy into electrical energy. Assume that the generator converts a fixed fraction of the wind energy intercepted by its blades into electrical energy. For wind speed v, the electrical power output will be most likely proportional to : **[2014 (Online)]**

(A) v^4 (B) v^2

(C) v (D) v^3

26. A bullet looses $\left(\frac{1}{n}\right)^{th}$ of its velocity passing through one plank. The number of such planks that are required to stop the bullet can be : **[2014 (Online)]**

(A) $\frac{n^2}{2n-1}$ (B) $\frac{2n^2}{n-1}$

(C) Infinite (D) n

27. A small ball of mass m starts at a point A with speed v_0 and moves along a frictionless track AB as shown. The track BC has coefficient of friction μ. The ball comes to stop at C after travelling a distance L which is : **[2014 (Online)]**

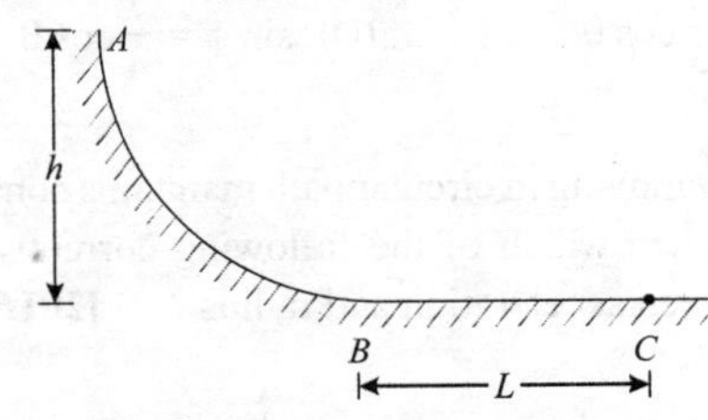

(A) $\frac{2h}{\mu} + \frac{v_0^2}{2\mu g}$ (B) $\frac{h}{\mu} + \frac{v_0^2}{2\mu g}$

(C) $\frac{h}{2\mu} + \frac{v_0^2}{\mu g}$ (D) $\frac{h}{2\mu} + \frac{v_0^2}{2\mu g}$

28. A point particle of mass m, moves along the uniformly rough track PQR as shown in the figure. The coefficient of friction, between the particle and the rough track equals m. The particle released, from rest, from the point P and it comes to rest at a point R. The energies, lost by the ball, over the parts, PQ and QR, of the track, are equal to each other, and no energy is lost when particle changes direction from PQ to QR The values of the coefficient of friction m and the distance $x(= QR)$, are, respectively close to : **[2016]**

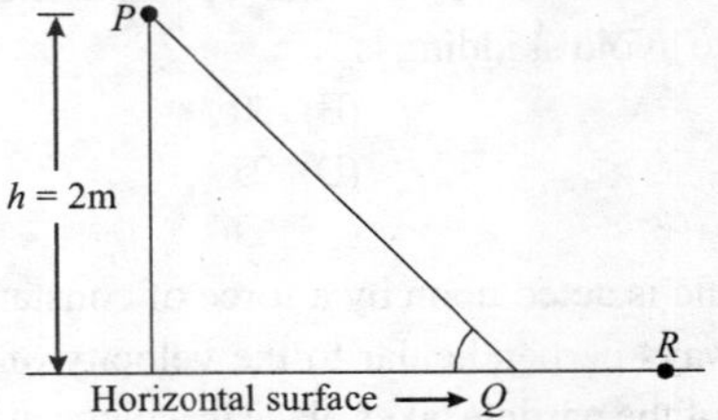

(A) 0.2 and 6.5 m (B) 0.2 and 3.5 m

(C) 0.29 and 3.5 m (D) 0.29 and 6.5 m

29. A person trying to lose weight by burning fat lifts a mass of 10 kg upto a height of 1 m 1000 times. Assume that the potential energy lost each time he lowers the mass is dissipated. How much fat will he use up considering the work done only when the weight is lifted up? Fat supplies 3.8×10^7 J of energy per kg which is converted to mechanical energy with a 20% efficiency rate. Take $g = 9.8$ ms^{-2} : **[2016]**

(A) 2.45×10^{-3} kg (B) 6.45×10^{-3} kg

(C) 9.89×10^{-3} kg (D) 12.89×10^{-3} kg

30. Velocity-time graph for a body of mass 10 kg is shown in figure. Work-done on the body in first two seconds of the motion is : **[2016 (Online)]**

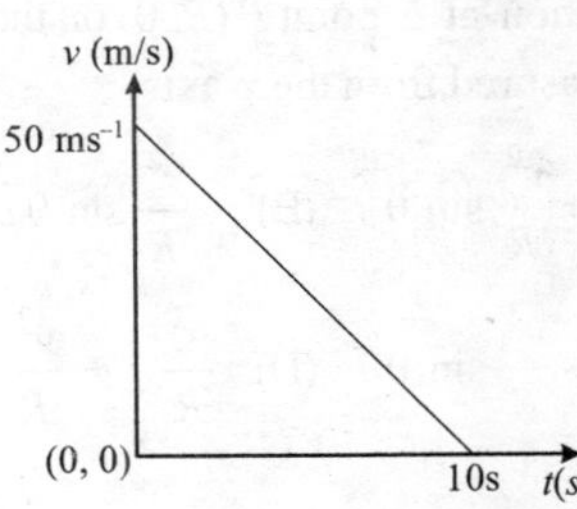

(A) –9300 J (B) 12000 J

(C) –4500 J (D) – 12000 J

31. A car of weight W is on an inclined road that rises by 100 m over a distance of 1 Km and applies a constant frictional force $\frac{W}{20}$ on the car. While moving uphill on the road at a speed of 10 ms^{-1}, the car needs power P. If it needs power $\frac{P}{2}$ while moving downhill at speed v then value of v is : **[2016 (Online)]**

(A) 20 ms^{-1} (B) 5 ms^{-1}

(C) 15 ms^{-1} (D) 10 ms^{-1}

* * * * *

CHAPTER 5

WORK ENERGY POWER & APPLICATIONS

5.2 CIRCULAR MOTION

1. The minimum velocity (in ms^{-1}) with which a car driver must traverse a flat curve of radius 150 m and coefficient of friction 0.6 to avoid skidding is : **[2002]**

(A) 60 (B) 30

(C) 15 (D) 25

2. A particle is acted upon by a force of constant magnitude which is always perpendicular to the velocity of the particle. The motion of the particle takes place in a plane, it follows that: **[2004]**

(A) Its velocity is constant

(B) Its acceleration is constant

(C) Its kinetic energy is constant

(D) It moves in a straight line

3. Which of the following statements is false for a particle moving in a circle with a constant angular speed? **[2004]**

(A) The velocity vector is tangent to the circle

(B) The acceleration vector is tangent to the circle

(C) The acceleration vector point to the center of the circle

(D) The velocity and acceleration vectors are perpendicular to each other

4. For a particle in uniform circular motion in anticlockwise sense the acceleration at $\bar{a}$ point $P(R, \theta)$ on the circle of radius R is (Here θ is measured from the x-axis) : **[2010]**

(A) $-\frac{v^2}{R}\cos\theta\,\hat{i} + \frac{v^2}{R}\sin\theta\,\hat{j}$ (B) $-\frac{v^2}{R}\sin\theta\,\hat{i} + \frac{v^2}{R}\cos\theta\,\hat{j}$

(C) $-\frac{v^2}{R}\cos\theta\,\hat{i} - \frac{v^2}{R}\sin\theta\,\hat{j}$ (D) $\frac{v^2}{R}\,\hat{i} + \frac{v^2}{R}\,\hat{j}$

5. A point P moves in counter-clockwise direction on a circular path as shown in the figure. The movement of 'P' is such that it sweeps out a length $s = t^3 + 5$, where s is in metres and t is in seconds. The radius of the path is 20 m. The acceleration of 'P' when $t = 2$ s is nearly : **[2010]**

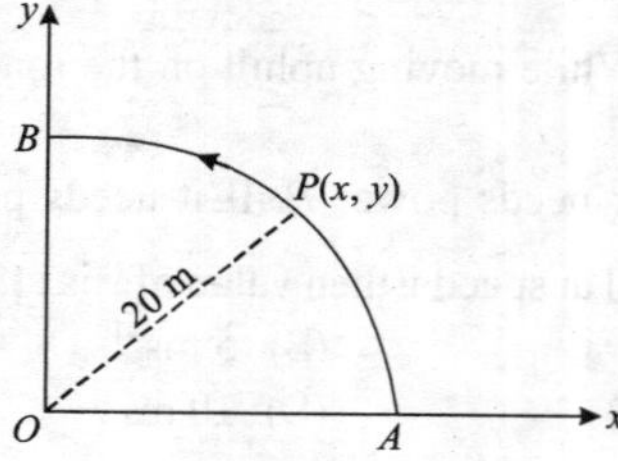

(A) 13 m/s² (B) 12 m/s²

(C) 7.2 m/s² (D) 14 m/s²

6. Two cars of masses m_1 and m_2 are moving in circles of radii r_1 and r_2, respectively. Their speeds are such that they make complete circles in the same time t. The ratio of their centripetal acceleration is : **[2012]**

(A) $m_1 r_1 : m_2 r_2$ (B) $m_1 : m_2$

(C) $r_1 : r_2$ (D) $1 : 1$

7. A body of mass 'm' is tied to one end of a spring and whirled round in a horizontal plane with a constant angular velocity. The elongation in the spring is 1 cm. If the angular velocity is doubled, the elongation in the spring is 5 cm. The original length of the spring is : **[2013 (Online)]**

(A) 15 cm (B) 12 cm

(C) 16 cm (D) 10 cm

8. A particle is released on a vertical smooth semicircular track from point X so that OX makes angle θ from the vertical (see figure). The normal reaction of the track on the particle vanishes at point Y where OY makes angle ϕ with the horizontal. Then : **[2014 (Online)]**

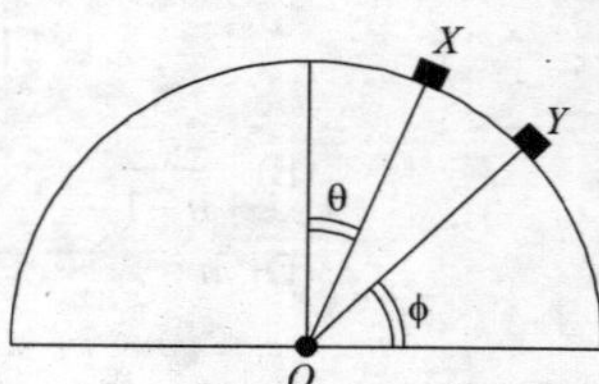

(A) $\sin\phi = \cos\phi$ (B) $\sin\phi = \frac{1}{2}\cos\theta$

(C) $\sin\phi = \frac{2}{3}\cos\theta$ (D) $\sin\phi = \frac{3}{4}\cos\theta$

9. If a body moving in circular path maintains constant speed of 10 ms^{-1}, then which of the following correctly describes relation between acceleration and radius ? **[2015 (Online)]**

(A)

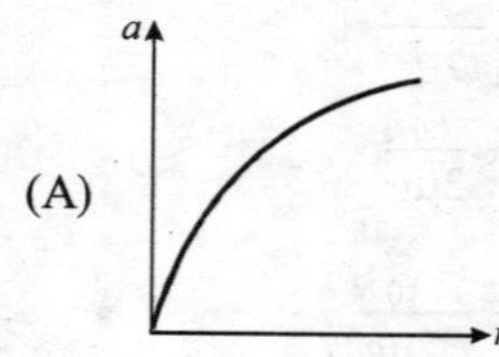

(B)
a
r

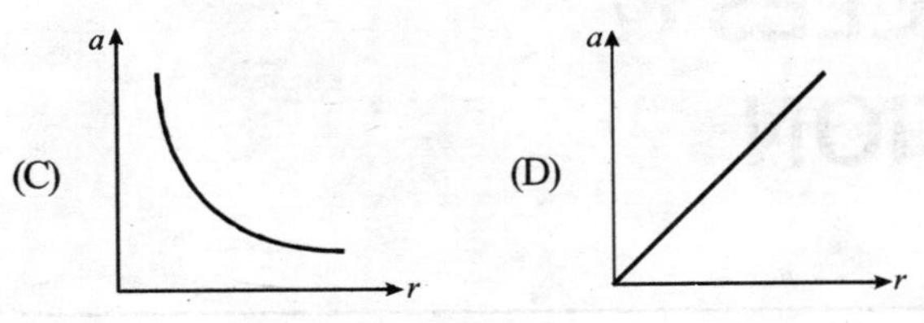

10. A particle is moving in a circle of radius r under the action of a force $F = \alpha r^2$ which is directed towards centre of the circle. Total mechanical energy (kinetic energy + potential energy) of the particle is (take potential energy = 0 for $r = 0$) : **[2015 (Online)]**

(A) $\frac{1}{2}\alpha r^3$ (B) $\frac{5}{6}\alpha r^3$

(C) $\frac{4}{3}\alpha r^3$ (D) αr^3

11. A particle of mass M is moving in a circle of fixed radius R in such a way that its centripetal acceleration at time t is given by $n^2 R t^2$ where n is a constant. The power delivered to the particle by the force acting on it, is : **[2016 (Online)]**

(A) $\frac{1}{2} M n^2 R^2 t^2$ (B) $M n^2 R^2 t$

(C) $M n R^2 t^2$ (D) $M n R^2 t$

12. Concrete mixture is made by mixing cement, stone and sand in a rotating cylinder drum. If the drum rotates too fast, the ingredients remain stuck to the wall of the drum and proper mixing of ingredients does not take place. The maximum rotational speed of the drum in revolutions per minute (rpm) to ensure proper mixing is close to : [Take the radius of the drum to be 1.25 m and its axle to be horizontal] **[2016 (Online)]**

(A) 27.0 (B) 0.4

(C) 1.3 (D) 8.0

* * * * *

CHAPTER

6 SYSTEM OF PARTICLES & ROTATIONAL MOTION

6.1 SYSTEM OF PARTICLES

1. Two identical particles move towards each other with velocity $2v$ and v respectively. The velocity of centre of mass is: **[2002]**

(A) v (B) $v/3$
(C) $v/2$ (D) Zero

2. Consider the following two statements :
A : Linear momentum of a system of particles is zero
B : Kinetic energy of a system of particles is zero
Then : **[2003]**

(A) A does not imply B and B does not imply A
(B) A implies B but B does not imply A
(C) A does not imply B but B implies A
(D) A implies B and B implies A

3. Two spherical bodies of mass M and $5M$ and radii R and $2R$ respectively are released in free space with initial separation between their centres equal to $12R$. It they attract each other due to gravitational force only, then the distance covered by the smaller body just before collision is : **[2003]**

(A) $2.5R$ (B) $4.5R$
(C) $7.5R$ (D) $1.5R$

4. A body A of mass M while falling vertically downwards under gravity breaks into two parts; a body B of mass $1/3M$ and, a body C of mass $2/3M$. The centre of mass of bodies B and C taken together shifts compared to that of body A towards : **[2005]**

(A) Depends on height of breaking
(B) Does not shift
(C) Body C
(D) Body B

5. A mass m moves with a velocity v and collides inelastically with another identical mass. After collision the I[st] mass moves with velocity $v/\sqrt{3}$ in a direction perpendicular to the initial direction of motion. Find the speed of the second mass after collision : **[2005]**

(A) v (B) $\sqrt{3}\,v$
(C) $\frac{2}{\sqrt{3}}v$ (D) $\frac{v}{\sqrt{3}}$

6. A T shaped object with dimensions shown in the figure, is lying on a smooth floor. A force $\vec{F}$ is applied at the point P parallel to AB, such that the object has only the translational motion without rotation. Find the location of P with respect to C : **[2005]**

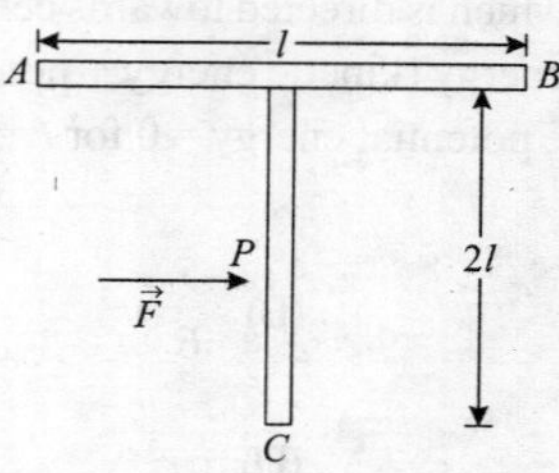

(A) $\frac{2}{3}l$ (B) $\frac{3}{2}l$
(C) $\frac{4}{3}l$ (D) l

7. A bomb of mass 16 kg at rest explodes into two pieces of masses 4 kg and 12 kg. The velocity of the 12 kg mass is 4 ms^{-1}. The kinetic energy of the other mass is : **[2006]**

(A) 144 J (B) 288 J
(C) 192 J (D) 96 J

8. Consider a two particle system with particles having masses m_1 and m_2. If the first particle is pushed towards the centre of mass through a distance d, by what distance should the second particle be moved, so as to keep the centre of mass at the same position ? **[2006]**

(A) $\frac{m_2}{m_1}d$ (B) $\frac{m_1}{m_1+m_2}d$
(C) $\frac{m_1}{m_2}d$ (D) d

9. A block of mass 0.50 kg is moving with a speed of 2.00 ms^{-1} on a smooth surface. It strikes another mass of 1.00 kg and then they move together as a single body. The energy loss during the collision is : **[2008]**

(A) 0.16 J (B) 1.00 J
(C) 0.67 J (D) 0.34 J

10. A thin rod of length 'L' is lying along the x-axis with its ends at $x = 0$ and $x = L$. It linear density (mass/length) varies with x as $k\left(\frac{x}{L}\right)^n$ where n can be zero or any positive number. If the position x_{CM} of the centre of mass of the rod is plotted against 'n', which of the following graphs best approximates the dependence of x_{CM} on n ? **[2008]**

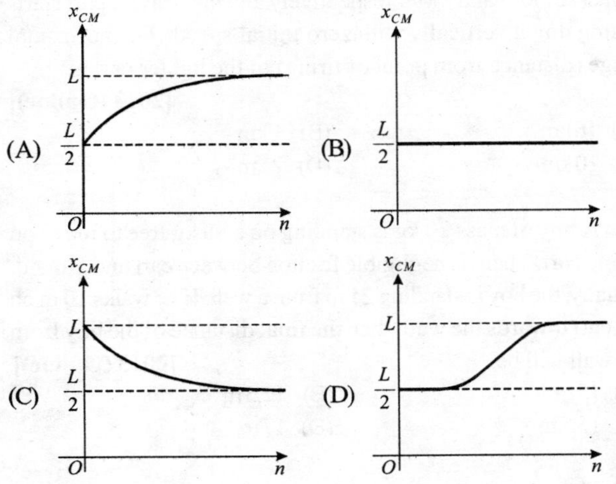

11. Consider a rubber ball freely falling from a height $h = 4.9$ m onto a horizontal elastic plate. Assume that the duration of collision is negligible and the collision with the plate is totally elastic. Then the velocity as a function of time and the height as a function of time will be : **[2009]**

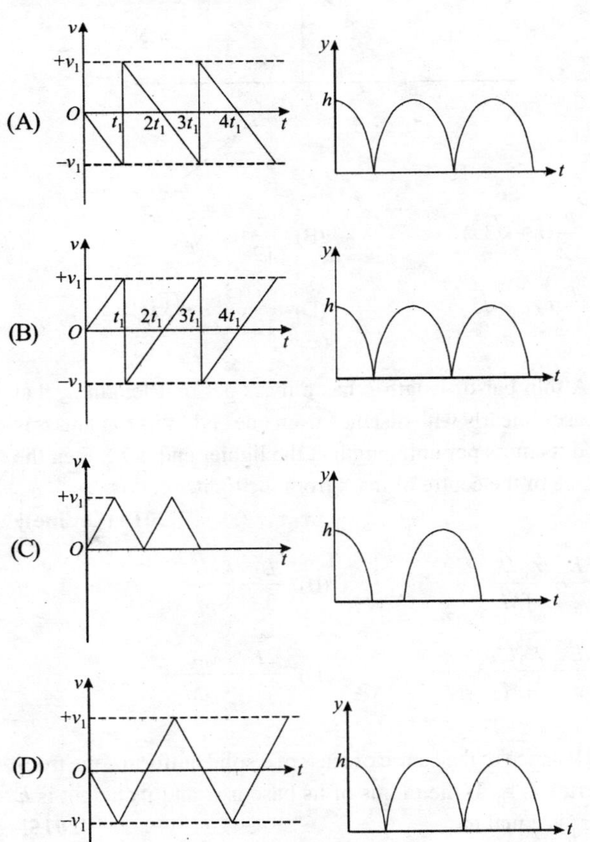

12. The figure shows the position-time (x-t) graph of one dimensional motion of a body of mass 0.4 kg. The magnitude of each impulse is : **[2010]**

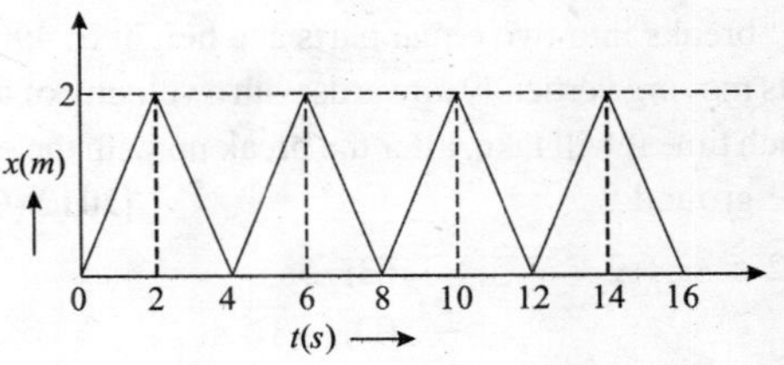

(A) 0.4 Ns (B) 0.8 Ns
(C) 1.6 Ns (D) 0.2 Ns

Directions : This Questions contain Statement-1 and Statement-2.
Of the four choices given after the statements, choose the one that best describes the two statements.

13. Statement-1 : Two particles moving in the same direction do not lose all their energy in a completely inelastic collision.
Statement-2 : Principle of conservation of momentum holds true for all kinds of collisions. **[2010]**
(A) Statement-1 is true, Statement-2 is false
(B) Statement-1 is true, Statement-2 is true; Statement-2 is the correct explanation of Statement-1
(C) Statement-1 is true, Statement-2 is true; Statement-2 is not the correct explanation of Statement-1
(D) Statement-1 is false, Statement-2 is true

14. A particle of mass 'm' is projected with a velocity v making an angle of 30° with the horizontal. The magnitude of angular momentum of the projectile about the point of projection when the particle is at its maximum height 'h' is: **[2011]**

(A) $\frac{\sqrt{3}}{2}\frac{mv^2}{g}$ (B) Zero

(C) $\frac{mv^3}{\sqrt{2}g}$ (D) $\frac{\sqrt{3}}{16}\frac{mv^3}{g}$

15. A spring is compressed between two blocks of masses m_1 and m_2 placed on a horizontal frictionless surface as shown in the figure. When the blocks are released, they have initial velocity of v_1 and v_2 as shown. The block travel distances x_1 and x_2 respectively before coming to rest. The ratio (x_1/x_2) is : **[2012 (Online)]**

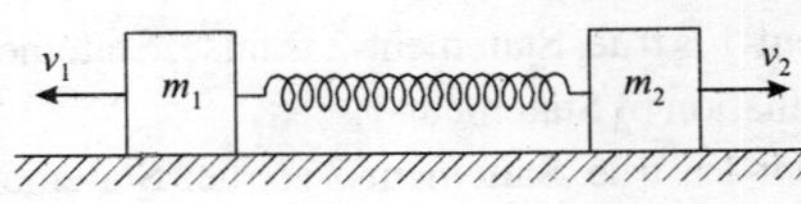

(A) $\frac{m_2}{m_1}$ (B) $\frac{m_1}{m_2}$

(C) $\sqrt{\frac{m_2}{m_1}}$ (D) $\sqrt{\frac{m_1}{m_2}}$

16. A projectile moving vertically upwards with a velocity of 200 ms^{-1} breaks into two equal parts at a height of 490 m. One part starts moving vertically upwards with a velocity of 400 ms^{-1}. How much time it will take, after the break up with the other part to hit the ground ? **[2012 (Online)]**

(A) $2\sqrt{2}$ s (B) 5s
(C) 10s (D) $\sqrt{10}$ s

17. Two bodies A and B of mass m and $2m$ respectively are placed on a smooth floor. They are connected by a spring of negligible mass. A third body C of mass m is placed on the floor. The body C moves with a velocity v_0 along the line joining A and B and collides elastically with A. At a certain time after the collision it is found that the instantaneous velocities of A and B are same and the compression of the spring is x_0. The spring constant k will be : **[2012 (Online)]**

(A) $m\dfrac{v_0^2}{x_0^2}$ (B) $m\dfrac{v_0}{2x_0}$

(C) $2m\dfrac{v_0}{x_0}$ (D) $\dfrac{2}{3}m\left(\dfrac{v_0}{x_0}\right)^2$

18. A moving particle of mass m, makes a head on elastic collision with another particle of mass $2m$, which is initially at rest. The percentage loss in energy of the colliding particle on collision, is close to : **[2012 (Online)]**

(A) 33% (B) 67%
(C) 90% (D) 10%

Directions : This Questions contain Statement-1 and Statement-2.

Of the four choices given after the statements, choose the one that best describes the two statements.

19. This question has statement-1 and statement-2. Of the four choices given after the statements, choose the one that best describes the two statements.

Statement-1 : A point particle of mass m moving with speed v collides with stationary point particle of mass M. If the maximum energy loss possible is given as $f\left(\frac{1}{2}mv^2\right)$ then $f=\left(\frac{m}{M+m}\right)$.

Statement-2 : Maximum energy loss occurs when the particles get stuck together as a result of the collision. **[2013]**

(A) Statement-1 is true, Statement-2 is false; Statement-2 is the correct explanation of Statement-1.
(B) Statement-1 is true, Statement-2 is true; Statement-2 is not the correct explanation of Statement-2
(C) Statement-1 is true, Statement-2 is false
(D) Statement-1 is false, Statement-2 is true

20. A projectile of mass M is fired so that the horizontal range is 4 km. At the highest point the projectile explodes in two parts of masses $M/4$ and $3M/4$ respectively and the heavier part starts falling down vertically with zero initial speed. The horizontal range (distance from point of firing) of the lighter part is : **[2013 (Online)]**

(A) 16 km (B) 1 km
(C) 10 km (D) 2 km

21. A boy of mass 20 kg is standing on a 80 kg free to move on a long cart. There is negligible friction between cart and ground. Initially, the boy is standing 25 m from a wall. If he walks 10 m on the cart towards the wall, then the final distance of the boy from the wall will be : **[2013 (Online)]**

(A) 15 m (B) 12.5 m
(C) 15.5 m (D) 17 m

22. Three masses m, $2m$ and $3m$ are moving in x-y plane with speed $3u$, $2u$ and u respectively as shown in figure. The three masses collide at the same point at P and stick together. The velocity of resulting mass will be : **[2014 (Online)]**

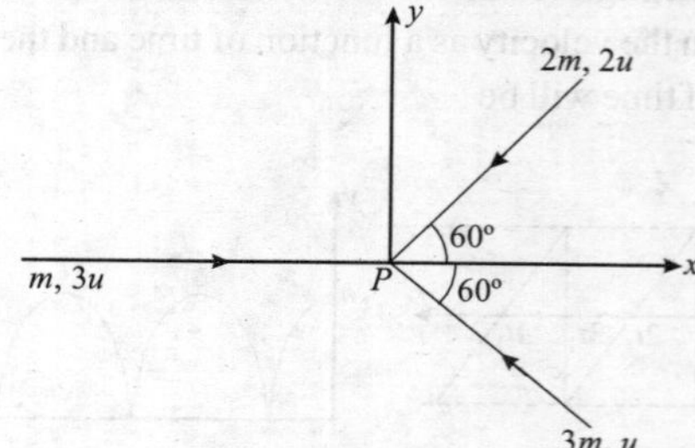

(A) $\dfrac{u}{12}(\hat{i}+\sqrt{3}\hat{j})$ (B) $\dfrac{u}{12}(\hat{i}-\sqrt{3}\hat{j})$

(C) $\dfrac{u}{12}(-\hat{i}+\sqrt{3}\hat{j})$ (D) $\dfrac{u}{12}(-\hat{i}-\sqrt{3}\hat{j})$

23. A thin bar of length L has a mass per unit length λ, that increases linearly with distance from one end. If its total mass is M and its mass per unit length at the lighter end is λ_0, then the distance of the centre of mass from the lighter end is : **[2014 (Online)]**

(A) $\dfrac{L}{2}-\dfrac{\lambda_0 L^2}{4M}$ (B) $\dfrac{L}{3}+\dfrac{\lambda_0 L^2}{8M}$

(C) $\dfrac{L}{3}+\dfrac{\lambda_0 L^2}{4M}$ (D) $\dfrac{2L}{3}-\dfrac{\lambda_0 L^2}{6M}$

24. Distance of the centre of mass of a solid uniform cone from its vertex is z_0. If the radius of its base is R and its height is h then z_0 is equal to : **[2015]**

(A) $\dfrac{h^2}{4R}$ (B) $\dfrac{3h}{4}$

(C) $\dfrac{5h}{8}$ (D) $\dfrac{3h^2}{8R}$

25. A particle of mass m moving in the x direction with speed $2v$ is hit by another particle of mass $2m$ moving in the y direction with speed v. If the collision is perfectly inelastic, the percentage loss in the energy during the collision is close to : **[2015]**

(A) 44% (B) 50%
(C) 56% (D) 62%

26. A bullet of mass 4 g is fired horizontally with a speed of 300 m/s into 0.8 kg block of wood at rest on a table. If the coefficient of friction between the block and the table is 0.3, how far will the block slide approximately ? **[2015 (Online)]**

(A) 0.19 m (B) 0.379 m
(C) 0.569 m (D) 0.758 m

27. A block of mass $m = 0.1$ kg is connected to a spring of unknown spring constant k. It is compressed to a distance x from its equilibrium position and released from rest. After approaching half the distance $\left(\frac{x}{2}\right)$ from equilibrium position, it hits another block and comes to rest momentarily, while the other block moves with a velocity 3 ms^{-1}. The total initial energy of the spring is : **[2015 (Online)]**

(A) 0.3 J (B) 0.6 J
(C) 0.8 J (D) 1.5 J

28. A block of mass $m = 10$ kg rest on a horizontal table. The coefficient of friction between the block and the table is 0.05. When hit by a bullet of mass 50 g moving with speed v, that gets embedded in it, the block moves and comes to stop after moving a distance of 2 m on the table. If a freely falling object were to acquire speed $\frac{v}{10}$ after being dropped from height H, then neglecting energy losses and taking $g = 10$ ms^{-2}, the value of H is close to : **[2015 (Online)]**

(A) 0.05 km (B) 0.02 km
(C) 0.03 km (D) 0.04 km

29. A large number (n) of identical beads, each of mass m and radius r are strung on a thin smooth rigid horizontal rod of length L ($L >> r$) and are at rest at random positions. The rod is mounted between two rigid supports (see figure). If one of the beads is now given a speed v, the average force experienced by each support after a long time is (assume all collisions are elastic): **[2015 (Online)]**

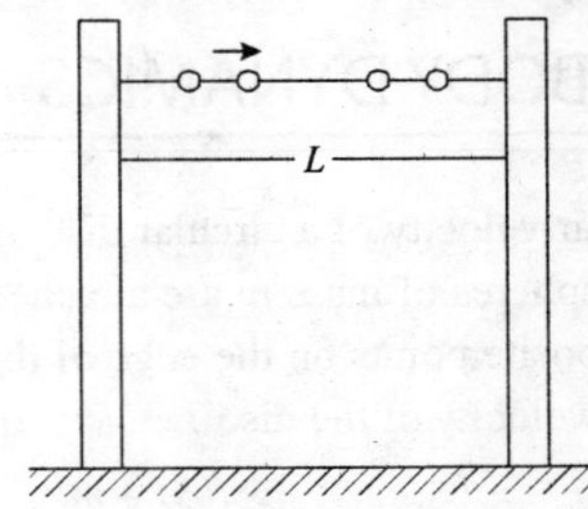

(A) $\frac{mv^2}{2(L-nr)}$ (B) $\frac{mv^2}{L-2nr}$

(C) $\frac{mv^2}{L-nr}$ (D) Zero

30. A uniform thin rod AB of length L has linear mass density $\mu(x) = a + \frac{bx}{L}$, where x is measured from A. If the CM of the rod lies at a distance of $\left(\frac{7}{12}\right)L$ from A, then a and b are related as: **[2015 (Online)]**

(A) $a = 2b$ (B) $2a = b$
(C) $a = b$ (D) $3a = 2b$

31. In the figure shown ABC is a uniform wire. If centre of mass of wire lies vertically below point A, then $\frac{BC}{AB}$ is close to : **[2016 (Online)]**

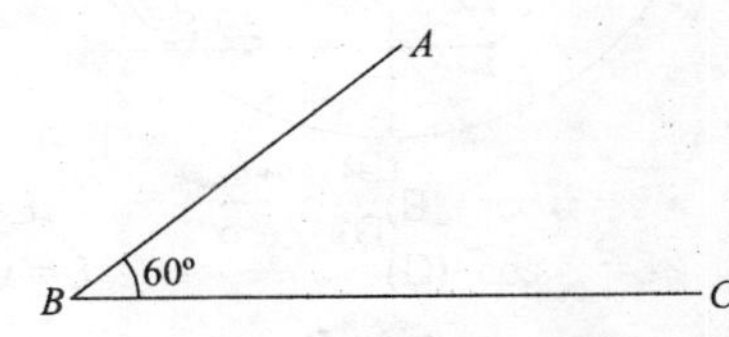

(A) 1.85 (B) 1.5
(C) 1.37 (D) 3

* * * * *

CHAPTER 6

SYSTEM OF PARTICLES & ROTATIONAL MOTION

6.2 RIGID BODY DYNAMICS

1. Initial angular velocity of a circular disc of mass M is ω_1. Then two small spheres of mass m are attached gently to two diametrically opposite points on the edge of the disc. What is the final angular velocity of the disc ? **[2002]**

(A) $\left(\frac{M+m}{M}\right)\omega_1$ (B) $\left(\frac{M+m}{m}\right)\omega_1$

(C) $\left(\frac{M}{M+4m}\right)\omega_1$ (D) $\left(\frac{M}{M+2m}\right)\omega_1$

2. Moment of inertia of a circular wire of mass M and radius R about its diameter is : **[2002]**

(A) $MR^2/2$ (B) MR^2

(C) $2MR^2$ (D) $MR^2/4$

3. A particle of mass m moves along line PC with velocity v as shown. What is the angular momentum of the particle about O ? **[2002]**

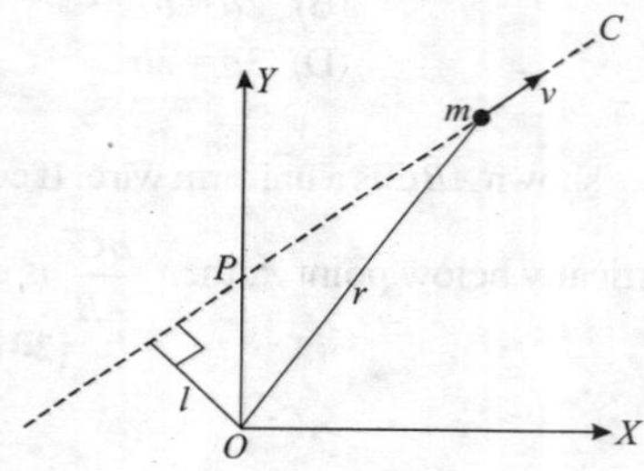

(A) mvL (B) mvl

(C) mvr (D) Zero

4. A circular disc X of radius R is made from an iron plate of thickness t and another disc Y of radius $4R$ is made from an iron plate of thickness $t/4$. Then the relation between the moment of inertia I_X and I_Y is : **[2003]**

(A) $I_Y = 32\, I_X$ (B) $I_Y = 16\, I_X$

(C) $I_Y = I_X$ (D) $I_Y = 64\, I_X$

5. A particle performing uniform circular motion has angular momentum L. If its angular frequency is doubled and its kinetic energy halved, then the new angular momentum is : **[2003]**

(A) $\frac{L}{4}$ (B) $2L$

(C) $4L$ (D) $\frac{L}{2}$

6. Let $\vec{F}$ be the force acting on particle having position vector $\vec{r}$ and $\vec{\tau}$ be the torque of this force about the origin. Then : **[2003]**

(A) $\vec{r}\cdot\vec{\tau}=0$ and $\vec{F}\cdot\vec{\tau}\neq 0$ (B) $\vec{r}\cdot\vec{\tau}\neq 0$ and $\vec{F}\cdot\vec{\tau}=0$

(C) $\vec{r}\cdot\vec{\tau}\neq 0$ and $\vec{F}\cdot\vec{\tau}\neq 0$ (D) $\vec{r}\cdot\vec{\tau}=0$ and $\vec{F}\cdot\vec{\tau}=0$

7. A solid sphere is rotating in free space. If the radius of the sphere is increased keeping mass same which one of the following will not be affected ? **[2004]**

(A) Moment of inertia (B) Angular momentum

(C) Angular velocity (D) Rotational kinetic energy

8. One solid sphere A and another hollow sphere B are of same mass and same outer radii. Their moment of inertia about their diameters are respectively I_A and I_B such that : **[2004]**

(A) $I_A = I_B$ (B) $I_A > I_B$

(C) $I_A < I_B$ (D) $\frac{I_A}{I_B}=\frac{d_A}{d_B}$

Where d_A and d_B are their densities.

9. An annular ring with inner and outer radii R_1 and R_2 is rolling without slipping with a uniform angular speed. The ratio of the forces experienced by the two particles situated on the inner and outer parts of the ring F_1/F_2 is : **[2005]**

(A) $\frac{R_2}{R_1}$ (B) $\left(\frac{R_1}{R_2}\right)^2$

(C) 1 (D) $\frac{R_1}{R_2}$

10. The moment of inertia of uniform semicircular disc of mass M and radius r about a line perpendicular to the plane of the disc through the centre is : **[2005]**

(A) $\frac{1}{4}Mr^2$ (B) $\frac{2}{5}Mr^2$

(C) Mr^2 (D) $\frac{1}{2}Mr^2$

11. Four point masses, each of value m, are placed at the corners of a square $ABCD$ of side l. The moment of inertia of this system about an axis passing through A and parallel to BD is : **[2006]**

(A) $2ml^2$ (B) $\sqrt{3}\, ml^2$

(C) $3ml^2$ (D) ml^2

12. A force of $-F\hat{k}$ acts on O, the origin of the co-ordinate system. The torque about the point (1, –1) is : **[2006]**

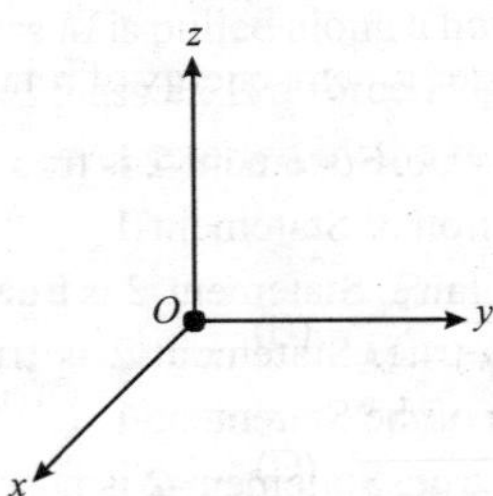

(A) $F(\hat{i}-\hat{j})$ (B) $-F(\hat{i}+\hat{j})$

(C) $F(\hat{i}+\hat{j})$ (D) $-F(\hat{i}-\hat{j})$

13. A thin circular ring of mass m and radius R is rotating about its axis with a constant angular velocity ω. Two objects each of mass M are attached gently to the opposite ends of a diameter of the ring. The ring now rotates with an angular velocity ω'= : **[2006]**

(A) $\frac{\omega(m+2m)}{M}$ (B) $\frac{\omega(m-2m)}{(m+2M)}$

(C) $\frac{\omega m}{(m+M)}$ (D) $\frac{\omega m}{(m+2M)}$

14. For the given uniform square lamina $ABCD$, whose centre is O: **[2007]**

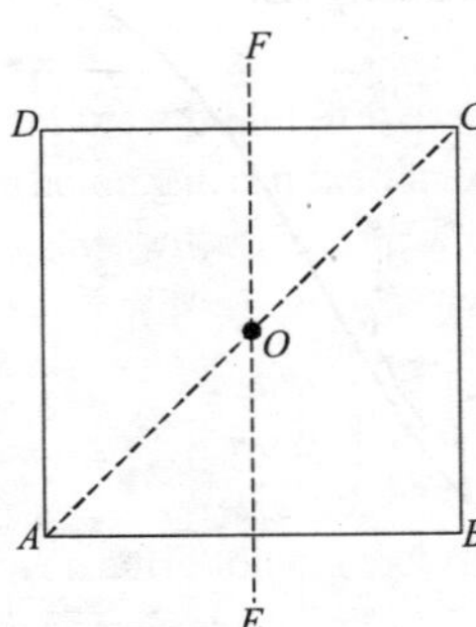

(A) $\sqrt{2}\,I_{AC}=I_{EF}$ (B) $I_{AD}=3I_{EF}$

(C) $I_{AC}=I_{EF}$ (D) $I_{AC}=\sqrt{2}\,I_{EF}$

15. A circular disc of radius R is removed from a bigger circular disc of radius 2 R such that the circumferences of the discs coincide. The centre of mass of the new disc is αR from the centre of the bigger disc. The value of α is : **[2007]**

(A) 1/3 (B) 1/2

(C) 1/6 (D) 1/4

16. A round uniform body of radius R, mass M and moment of inertia I, rolls down (without slipping) an inclined plane making an angle θ with the horizontal. Then its acceleration is : **[2007]**

(A) $\frac{g\sin\theta}{1+I/MR^2}$ (B) $\frac{g\sin\theta}{1+MR^2/I}$

(C) $\frac{g\sin\theta}{1-I/MR^2}$ (D) $\frac{g\sin\theta}{1-MR^2/I}$

17. Angular momentum of the particle rotating with a central force is constant due to : **[2007]**

(A) Constant force (B) Constant linear momentum

(C) Zero torque (D) Constant torque

18. Consider a uniform square plate of side 'a' and mass 'm' the moment of inertia of this plate about an axis perpendicular to its plane and passing through one of its corners is : **[2008]**

(A) $\frac{5}{6}ma^2$ (B) $\frac{1}{12}ma^2$

(C) $\frac{7}{12}ma^2$ (D) $\frac{2}{3}ma^2$

19. A thin uniform rod of length l and mass m is swinging freely about a horizontal axis passing through its end. Its maximum angular speed is ω. Its centre of mass rises to a maximum height of : **[2009]**

(A) $\frac{1}{6}\frac{l\omega}{g}$ (B) $\frac{1}{2}\frac{l^2\omega^2}{g}$

(C) $\frac{1}{6}\frac{l^2\omega^2}{g}$ (D) $\frac{1}{3}\frac{l^2\omega^2}{g}$

20. A small particle of mass m is projected at an angle θ with the x-axis with an initial velocity v_0 in the x-y plane as shown in the figure. At a time $t < \frac{v_0\sin\theta}{g}$, the angular momentum of the particle is : **[2010]**

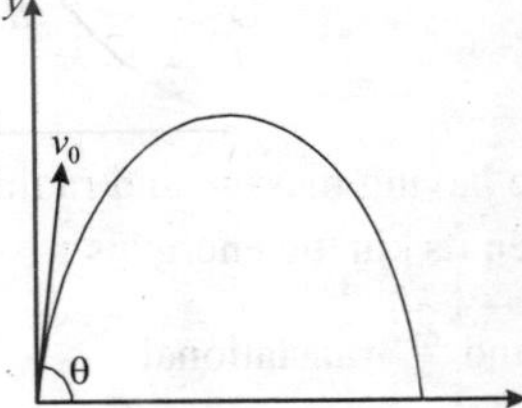

(A) $\frac{1}{2}mg\,v_0\,t^2\cos\theta\,\hat{i}$ (B) $-mg\,v_0\,t^2\cos\theta\,\hat{j}$

(C) $mg\,v_0\,t\cos\theta\,\hat{k}$ (D $-\frac{1}{2}mg\,v_0\,t^2\cos\theta\,\hat{k}$

Where $\hat{i},\hat{j}$ and $\hat{k}$ are unit vectors along x, y and z-axis respectively.

21. A mass m hangs with the help of a string wrapped around a pulley on a frictionless bearing. The pulley has mass m and radius R. Assuming pulley to be a perfect uniform circular disc, the acceleration of the mass m, if the string does not slip on the pulley, is : **[2011]**

(A) g (B) $\frac{2}{3}g$

(C) $\frac{g}{3}$ (D) $\frac{3}{2}g$

22. A thin horizontal circular disc is rotating about a vertical axis passing through its centre. An insect is at rest at a point near the rim of the disc. The insect now moves along a diameter of the disc to reach its other end. During the journey of the insect, then angular speed of the disc : **[2011]**

(A) Continuously increases
(B) First increases and then decreases
(C) Remains unchanged
(D) Continuously decreases

23. A pulley of radius $2m$ is rotated about its axis by a force $F = (20t - 5t^2)$ newton (where t is measured in seconds) applied tangentially. If the moment of inertia of the pulley about its axis of rotation is 10 kg-m^2, the number of rotations made by the pulley before its direction of motion it reversed, is : **[2011]**

(A) More than 6 but less than 9
(B) More than 9
(C) Less than 3
(D) More than 3 but less than 6

24. A diameter R is cut from a disc of mass M and radius R; the circumference of the cut passes through the centre of the disc. The moment of inertia of the remaining portion of the disc about an axis perpendicular to the disc and passing through its centre is : **[2012 (Online)]**

(A) $\left(\frac{15}{32}\right)MR^2$ (B) $\left(\frac{1}{8}\right)MR^2$

(C) $\left(\frac{3}{8}\right)MR^2$ (D) $\left(\frac{13}{32}\right)MR^2$

25. A solid sphere having mass m and radius r rolls down an inclined plane. Then its kinetic energy is : **[2012 (Online)]**

(A) $\frac{5}{7}$ rotational and $\frac{2}{7}$ translational

(B) $\frac{2}{7}$ rotational and $\frac{5}{7}$ translational

(C) $\frac{2}{5}$ rotational and $\frac{3}{5}$ translational

(D) $\frac{1}{2}$ rotational and $\frac{1}{2}$ translational

26. This question has Statement-1 and Statement-2. Of the four choices given after the Statements, choose the one the best describes the two Statements. **[2012 (Online)]**

Statement-1 : When moment of inertia I of a body rotating about an axis with angular speed ω increases, its angular momentum L is unchanged but the kinetic energy K increases if there is no torque applied on it.

Statement-2 : $L = I\omega$, kinetic energy of rotation $= \frac{1}{2}I\omega^2$:

(A) Statement-1 is true, Statement-2 is true, Statement-2 is not the correct explanation of Statement-1
(B) Statement-1 is false, Statement-2 is true
(C) Statement-1 is true, Statement-2 is true, Statement-2 is correct explanation of the Statement-1
(D) Statement-1 is true, Statement-2 is false

27. A stone of mass m, tied to the end of a string, is whirled around in a circle on a horizontal frictionless table. The length of the string is reduced gradually keeping the angular momentum of the stone about the centre of the circle constant. Then, the tension in the string is given by $T = Ar^n$, where A is a constant, r is the instantaneous radius of the circle. The value of n is equal to : **[2012 (Online)]**

(A) -1 (B) -2
(C) -4 (D) -3

28. A solid sphere is rolling on a surface as shown in figure, with a translational velocity v ms^{-1}. If it is to climb the inclined surface continuing to roll without slipping, then minimum velocity for this to happen is : **[2012 (Online)]**

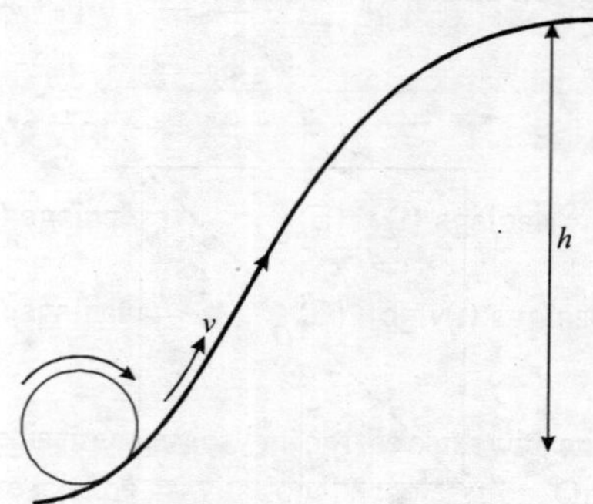

(A) $\sqrt{2gh}$ (B) $\sqrt{\frac{7}{5}gh}$

(C) $\sqrt{\frac{7}{2}gh}$ (D) $\sqrt{\frac{10}{7}gh}$

29. A thick-walled hollow sphere has outside radius R_0. It rolls down an incline without slipping and its speed at the bottom is v_0. Now the incline is waxed, so that it is practically frictionless and the sphere is observed to slide down (without any rolling). Its speed at the bottom is observed to be $5v_0/4$. The radius of gyration of the hollow sphere about an axis through its centre is : **[2012 (Online)]**

(A) $3R_0/2$ (B) $3R_0/4$
(C) $9R_0/16$ (D) $3R_0$

30. Two point masses of mass $m_1 = fM$ and $m_2 = (1-f)M$ $(f < 1)$ are in outer space (far from gravitational influence of other objects) at a distance R from each other. They move in circular orbits about their centre of mass with angular velocities ω_1 for m_1 and ω_2 for m_2. In that case : **[2012 (Online)]**

(A) $(1-f)\,\omega_1 = f\omega$
(B) $\omega_1 = \omega_2$ and independent of f
(C) $f\omega_1 = (1-f)\,\omega_2$
(D) $\omega_1 = \omega_2$ and depend on f

31. A hoop of radius r and mass m rotating with an angular velocity ω_0 is placed on a rough horizontal surface. The initial velocity of the centre of the hoop is zero. What will be the velocity of the centre of the hoop when it ceases to slip ? **[2013]**

(A) $\dfrac{r\omega_0}{4}$ (B) $\dfrac{r\omega_0}{3}$
(C) $\dfrac{r\omega_0}{2}$ (D) $r\omega_0$

32. A bullet of mass 10 g and speed 500 m/s is fired into a door and gets embedded exactly at the centre of the door. The door is 1.0 m wide and weighs 12 kg. It is hinged at one end and rotates about a vertical axis practically without friction. The angular speed of the door just after the bullet embeds into it will be : **[2013 (Online)]**

(A) 6.25 rad/sec (B) 0.625 rad/sec
(C) 3.35 rad/sec (D) 0.335 rad/sec

33. A particle of mass 2 kg is moving such that at time t, its position, in meter, is given by $\vec{r}\,(t) = 5\hat{i} - 2t^2\hat{j}$. The angular momentum of the particle at $t = 2$s about the origin in kg m^{-2} s^{-1} is : **[2013 (Online)]**

(A) $-80\,\hat{k}$ (B) $(10\hat{i} - 16\hat{j})$
(C) $-40\,\hat{k}$ (D) $40\,\hat{k}$

34. A tennis ball (treated as hollow spherical shell) starting from O rolls down a hill. At point A the ball becomes air borne leaving at an angle of 30° with the horizontal. The ball strikes the ground at B. What is the value of the distance AB ? (Moment of inertia of a spherical shell of mass m and radius R about its diameter = $2/3mR^2$) : **[2013 (Online)]**

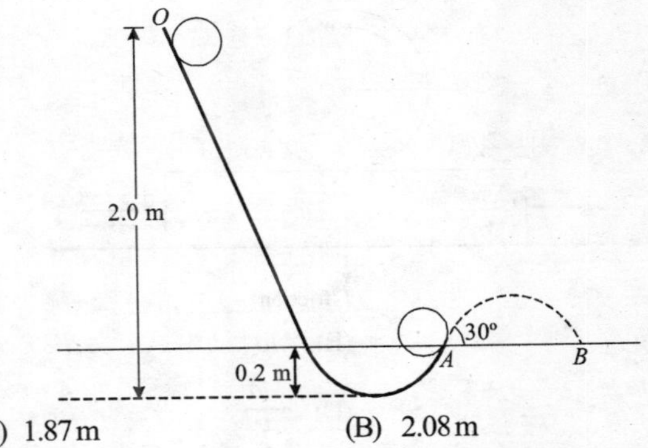

(A) 1.87 m (B) 2.08 m
(C) 1.57 m (D) 1.77 m

35. A ring of mass M and radius R is rotating about its axis with angular velocity ω. Two identical bodies each of mass m are now gently attached at the two ends of a diameter of the ring. Because of this, the kinetic energy loss will be : **[2013 (Online)]**

(A) $\dfrac{m(M+2m)}{M}\omega^2 R^2$ (B) $\dfrac{Mm}{(M+m)}\omega^2 R^2$
(C) $\dfrac{Mm}{(M+2m)}\omega^2 R^2$ (D) $\dfrac{(M+m)M}{(M+2m)}\omega^2 R^2$

36. A mass 'm' is supported by a massless string wound around a uniform hollow cylinder of mass m and radius R. If the string does not slip on the cylinder, with what acceleration will the mass fall on release ? **[2014]**

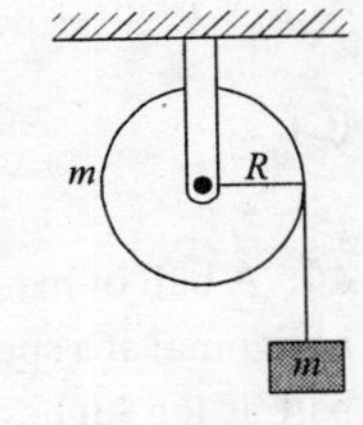

(A) $\dfrac{2g}{3}$
(B) $\dfrac{g}{2}$
(C) $\dfrac{5g}{6}$
(D) g

37. A bob of mass m attached to an inextensible string of length l is suspended from a vertical support. The bob rotates in a horizontal circle with an angular speed ω rad/s about the vertical. About, the point of suspension : **[2014]**

(A) Angular momentum is conserved
(B) Angular momentum changes in magnitude but not in direction
(C) Angular momentum changes in direction but not in magnitude
(D) Angular momentum changes both in direction and magnitude

38. Consider a cylinder of mass M resting on a rough horizontal rug that is pulled out from under it with acceleration 'a' perpendicular to the axis of the cylinder. What is $F_{friction}$ at point P ? It is assumed that the cylinder does not slip : **[2014 (Online)]**

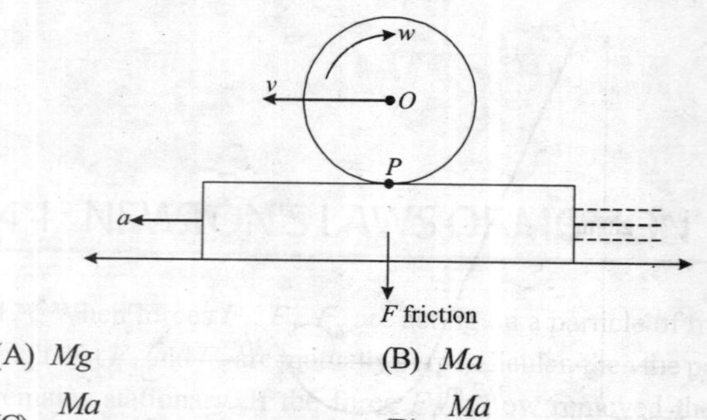

(A) Mg (B) Ma

(C) $\frac{Ma}{2}$ (D) $\frac{Ma}{3}$

39. A cylinder of mass M_C and sphere of mass M_S are placed at point A and B of two inclines, respectively (See figure). If they roll on the incline without slipping such that their acceleration are the same, then the ratio $\frac{\sin\theta_C}{\sin\theta_S}$ is : **[2014 (Online)]**

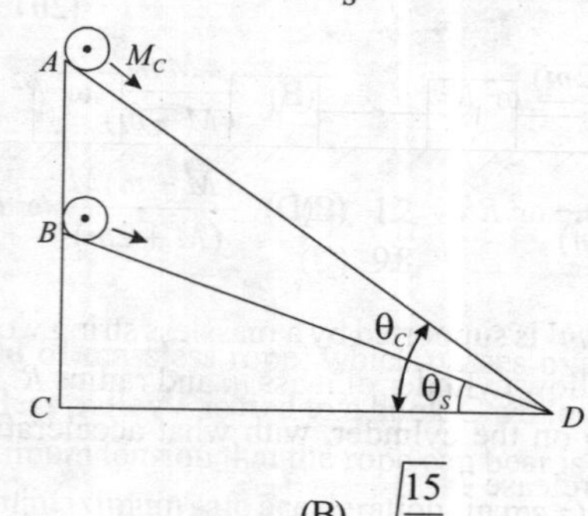

(A) $\sqrt{\frac{8}{7}}$ (B) $\sqrt{\frac{15}{14}}$

(C) $\frac{8}{7}$ (D) $\frac{15}{14}$

40. A ball of mass 160 g is thrown up at an angle of 60° to the horizontal at a speed of 10 ms^{-1}. The angular momentum of the ball at the highest point of the trajectory with respect to the point from which the ball is thrown is nearly ($g = 10\ ms^{-2}$) : **[2014 (Online)]**

(A) 1.73 kg m^2/s (B) 3.0 kg m^2/s

(C) 3.46 kg m^2/s (D) 6.9 kg m^2/s

41. A particle of mass m is moving in a circular path of radius a, with a constant velocity v as shown in the figure. The centre of circle is marked by 'C'. The angular momentum from the origin O can be written as : **[2014 (Online)]**

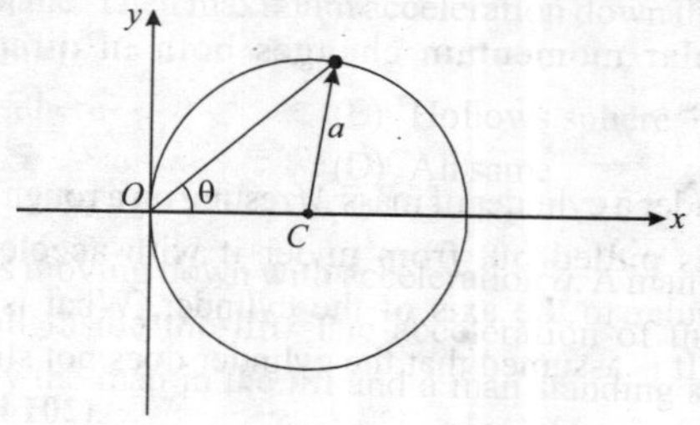

(A) $mva(1 + \cos 2\theta)$ (B) $mva(1 + \cos\theta)$

(C) $mva \cos 2\theta$ (D) mva

42. From a solid sphere of mass M and radius R a cube of maximum possible volume is cut. Moment of inertia of cube about an axis passing through its center and perpendicular to one of its faces is : **[2015]**

(A) $\frac{MR^2}{32\sqrt{2}\pi}$ (B) $\frac{MR^2}{16\sqrt{2}\pi}$

(C) $\frac{4MR^2}{9\sqrt{3}\pi}$ (D) $\frac{4MR^2}{3\sqrt{3}\pi}$

43. A uniform solid cylindrical roller of mass 'm' is being pulled on a horizontal surface with force F parallel to the surface and applied at its centre. If the acceleration of the cylinder is 'a' and it rolling without slipping then the value of 'F' is : **[2015 (Online)]**

(A) ma (B) $\frac{5}{3}ma$

(C) $\frac{3}{2}ma$ (D) $2ma$

44. A particle of mass 2 kg is on a smooth horizontal table and moves in a circular path of radius 0.6 m. The height of the table from the ground is 0.8 m. If the angular speed of the particle is 12 rad s^{-1}, the magnitude of its angular momentum about a point on the ground right under the centre of the circle is : **[2015 (Online)]**

(A) 14.4 kg m^2 s^{-1} (B) 8.64 kg m^2 s^{-1}

(C) 0.16 kg m^2 s^{-1} (D) 11.52 kg m^2 s^{-1}

45. Consider a thin uniform square sheet made of a rigid material. If its side is 'a' mass m and moment of inertia I about one of its diagonals, then : **[2015 (Online)]**

(A) $I > \frac{ma^2}{12}$ (B) $\frac{ma^2}{24} < I < \frac{ma^2}{12}$

(C) $I = \frac{ma^2}{24}$ (D) $I = \frac{ma^2}{12}$

46. A particle of mass m is moving along the side of a square of side 'a', with a uniform speed v in x-y plane as shown in the figure : **[2016]**

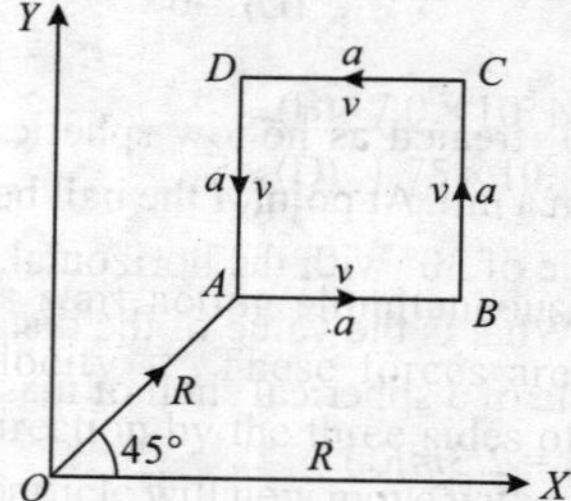

Which of the following statements is false for the angular momentum $\vec{L}$ about the origin ?

(A) $\vec{L} = mv\left[\frac{R}{\sqrt{2}} + a\right]\hat{k}$ when the particle is moving from B to C

(B) $\vec{L} = \frac{mv}{\sqrt{2}}R\hat{k}$ when the particle is moving from D to A

(C) $\vec{L} = -\frac{mv}{\sqrt{2}}R\hat{k}$ when the particle is moving from A to B

(D) $\vec{L} = mv\left[\frac{R}{\sqrt{2}} - a\right]\hat{k}$ when the particle is moving from C to D

47. A roller is made by joining together two cones at their vertices O. It is kept on two rails AB and CD, which are placed asymmetrically (see figure), with its axis perpendicular to CD and its centre O at the centre of line joining AB and CD (see figure). It is given a light push so that its starts rolling with its centre O moving parallel to CD in the direction shown. As it moves, the roller will tend to : **[2016]**

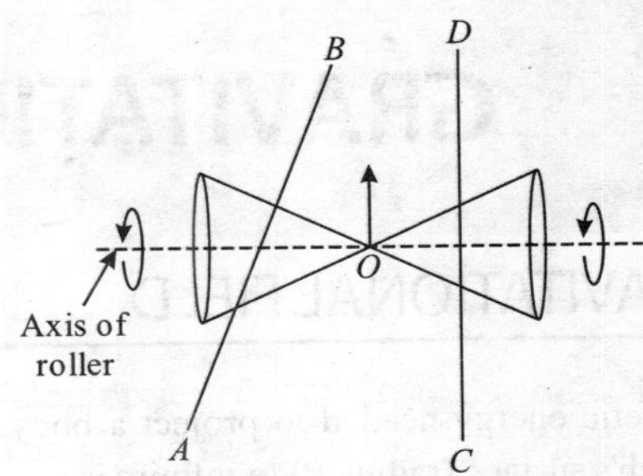

(A) Go straight
(B) Turn left and right alternately
(C) Turn left
(D) Turn right

48. A cubical block of side 30 cm is moving with velocity 2 ms^{-1} on a smooth horizontal surface. The surface has a bump at a point O as shown in figure. The angular velocities (in rad/s) of the block immediately after it hits the bump, is : **[2016 (Online)]**

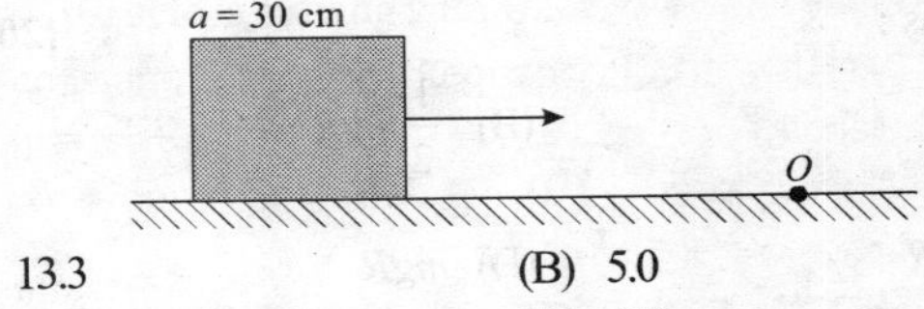

(A) 13.3
(B) 5.0
(C) 9.4
(D) 6.7

* * * * *

CHAPTER 7

GRAVITATION

7.1 GRAVITATIONAL FIELD

1. The kinetic energy needed to project a body of mass m from the earth's surface (radius R) to infinity is : **[2002]**

(A) $\frac{mgR}{2}$ (B) $2mgR$

(C) mgR (D) $\frac{mgR}{4}$

2. If g is the acceleration due to gravity on the earth's surface, the gain in the potential energy of an object of mass m raised from the surface of the earth to a height equal to the radius R of the earth, is : **[2004]**

(A) $2mgR$ (B) $\frac{1}{2}mgR$

(C) $\frac{1}{4}mgR$ (D) mgR

3. A particle of mass 10 g is kept on the surface of a uniform sphere of mass 100 kg and radius 10 cm. Find the work to be done against the gravitational force between them, to take the particle far away from the sphere : [you may take $G = 6.67 \times 10^{-11}$ Nm^2/kg^2] **[2005]**

(A) 13.34×10^{-10} J (B) 3.33×10^{-10} J

(C) 6.67×10^{-9} J (D) 6.67×10^{-10} J

4. The change in the value of g at a height h above the surface of the earth is the same as at a depth d below the surface of earth. When both d and h are much smaller than the radius of earth, then which one of the following is correct ? **[2005]**

(A) $d = \frac{h}{2}$ (B) $d = \frac{3h}{2}$

(C) $d = 2h$ (D) $d = h$

5. Average density of the earth : **[2005]**

(A) Does not depend on g

(B) Is a complex function of g

(C) Is directly proportional to g

(D) Is inversely proportional to g

6. If g_E and g_M are the accelerations due to gravity on the surfaces of the earth and the moon respectively and if Millikan's oil drop experiment could be performed on the two surfaces, one will find the ratio $\frac{\text{electronic charge on the moon}}{\text{electronic charge on the earth}}$ to be : **[2007]**

(A) 1 (B) Zero

(C) g_E / g_M (D) g_M / g_E

7. This question contains statement-1 and statement-2 of the four choices given after the statements, choose the one that best describes the two statements. **[2008]**

Statement 1 : For a mass M kept at the centre of a cube of side 'a', the flux of gravitational field passing through its sides is $4\pi GM$.

Statement 2 : If the direction of a field due to a point source is radial and its dependence on the distance 'r' from the source is given as I/r^2, its flux through a closed surface depends only on the strength of the source enclosed by the surface and not on the size or shape of the surface.

(A) Statement-1 is false, Statement-2 is true

(B) Statement-1 is true, Statement-2 is true; Statement-2 is a correct explanation for Statement-1

(C) Statement-1 is true, Statement-2 is true; Statement-2 is not a correct explanation for Statement-1

(D) Statement-1 is true, Statement-2 is false

8. The height at which the acceleration due to gravity becomes $\frac{g}{9}$ (where g = the acceleration due to gravity on the surface of the earth) in terms of R, the radius of the earth, is : **[2009]**

(A) $\frac{R}{2}$ (B) $\sqrt{2}R$

(C) $2R$ (D) $\frac{R}{\sqrt{2}}$

9. Two bodies of masses m and $4m$ are placed at a distance r. The gravitational potential at a point on the line joining them where the gravitational field is zero is : **[2011]**

(A) $-\frac{6Gm}{r}$ (B) $-\frac{9Gm}{r}$

(C) Zero (D) $-\frac{4Gm}{r}$

10. The mass of a spaceship is 1000 kg. It is to be launched from the earth's surface out into free space. The value of 'g' and

'R' (radius of earth) are 10 m/s^2 and 6400 km respectively. The required energy for this work will be : **[2012]**

(A) 6.4×10^{10} J (B) 6.4×10^{11} J
(C) 6.4×10^{8} J (D) 6.4×10^{9} J

11. Assuming the earth to be a sphere of uniform density, the acceleration due to gravity inside the earth at a distance of r from the centre is proportional to : **[2012 (Online)]**

(A) r (B) r^{-1}
(C) r^2 (D) r^{-2}

12. The variation of acceleration due to gravity g with distance d from centre of the earth is best represented by (R = Earth's radius) : **[2012 (Online)]**

(A) 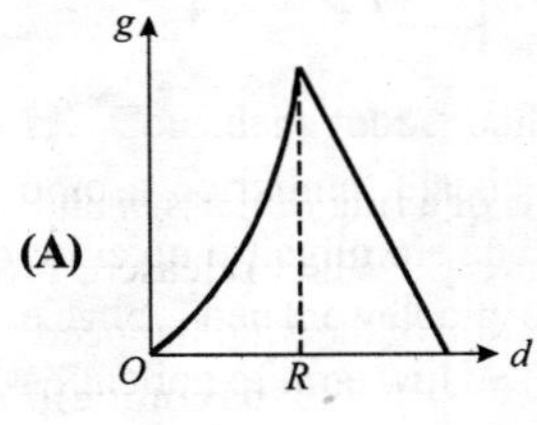

(B) 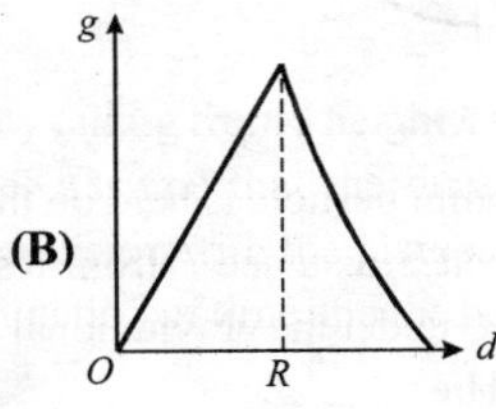

(C) 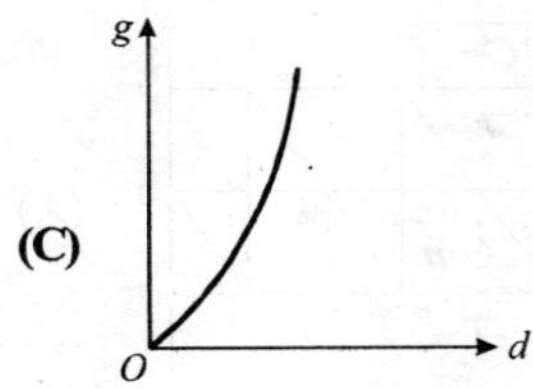

(D) 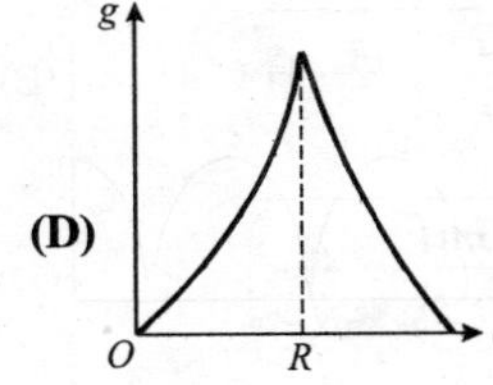

13. The gravitational field, due to the 'left over part' of a uniform sphere (from which a part as shown, has been 'removed out'), at a very far off point P, located as shown, would be (nearly) : **[2013 (Online)]**

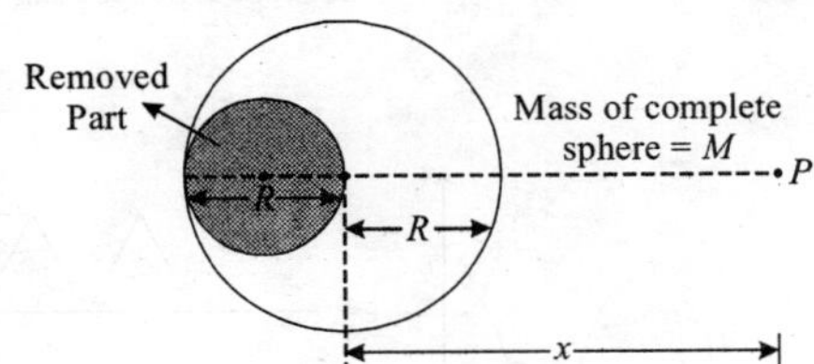

(A) $\frac{5}{6}\frac{GM}{x^2}$ (B) $\frac{8}{9}\frac{GM}{x^2}$

(C) $\frac{7}{8}\frac{GM}{x^2}$ (D) $\frac{6}{7}\frac{GM}{x^2}$

14. The change in the value of acceleration of earth towards sun, when the moon comes from the position of solar eclipse to the position on the other side of earth in line with sun is : (mass of the moon = 7.36×10^{22} kg, radius of the moon's orbit = 3.8×10^8 m) **[2013 (Online)]**

(A) 6.73×10^{-5} m/s^2 (B) 6.73×10^{-3} m/s^2
(C) 6.73×10^{-2} m/s^2 (D) 6.73×10^{-4} m/s^2

15. Four particles, each of mass M and equidistant from each other, move along a circle of radius R under the action of their mutual gravitational attraction. The speed of each particle is : **[2014]**

(A) $\sqrt{\frac{GM}{R}}$ (B) $\sqrt{2\sqrt{2}\frac{GM}{R}}$

(C) $\sqrt{\frac{GM}{R}(1+2\sqrt{2})}$ (D) $\frac{1}{2}\sqrt{\frac{GM}{R}(1+2\sqrt{2})}$

16. A capillary tube is immersed vertically in water and the height of the water column is x. When this arrangement is taken into a mine of depth d, the height of the water column is y. If R is the radius of earth, the ratio $\frac{x}{y}$ is : **[2014 (Online)]**

(A) $\left(1-\frac{d}{R}\right)$ (B) $\left(1-\frac{2d}{R}\right)$

(C) $\left(\frac{R-d}{R+d}\right)$ (D) $\left(\frac{R+d}{R-d}\right)$

17. The gravitational field in a region is given by $\vec{g}$ = 5 N/kg $\hat{i}$ + 12 N/kg $\hat{j}$. The change in the gravitational potential energy of a particle of mass 1 kg when it is taken from the origin to a point (7 m, –3 m) is : **[2014 (Online)]**

(A) 71 J (B) $13\sqrt{58}$ J
(C) –71 J (D) 1 J

18. From a sphere of mass M and radius R, a smaller sphere of radius $\frac{R}{2}$ is carved out such that the cavity made in the original sphere is between its centre and the periphery (See figure). For the configuration in the figure where the distance between the centre of the original sphere and the removed sphere is $3R$, the gravitational force between the two sphere is : **[2014 (Online)]**

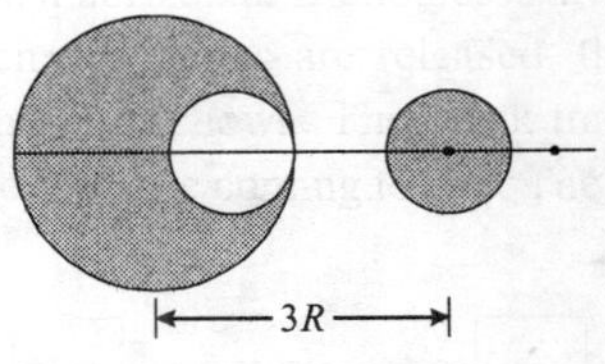

(A) $\frac{41GM^2}{3600R^2}$ (B) $\frac{41GM^2}{450R^2}$

(C) $\frac{59GM^2}{450R^2}$ (D) $\frac{GM^2}{225R^2}$

19. Two hypothetical planets of masses m_1 and m_2 are at rest when they are infinite distance apart. Because of the gravitational force they move towards each other along the line joining their centres. What is their speed when their separation is 'd' ? (Speed of m_1 is v_1 and that of m_2 is v_2) **[2014 (Online)]**

(A) $v_1 = v_2$

(B) $v_1 = m_2\sqrt{\frac{2G}{(d(m_1+m_2)}}$ $\quad v_2 = m_1\sqrt{\frac{2G}{(d(m_1+m_2)}}$

(C) $v_1 = m_1\sqrt{\frac{2G}{(d(m_1+m_2)}}$ $\quad v_2 = m_2\sqrt{\frac{2G}{(d(m_1+m_2)}}$

(D) $v_1 = m_2\sqrt{\frac{2G}{m_1}}$ $\quad v_2 = m_2\sqrt{\frac{2G}{m_2}}$

20. From a solid sphere of mass M and radius R, a spherical portion of radius $\frac{R}{2}$ is removed, as shown in figure. Taking gravitational potential $V = 0$ at $r = \infty$, the potential at the centre of the cavity thus formed is : **[2015]**
(G = gravitational constant)

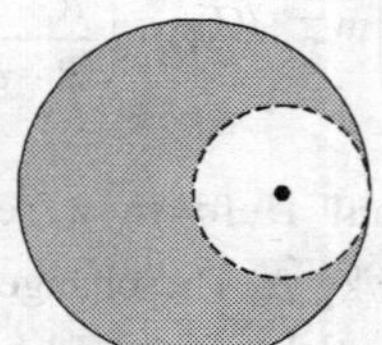

(A) $\frac{-GM}{2R}$ (B) $\frac{-GM}{R}$

(C) $\frac{-2GM}{3R}$ (D) $\frac{-2GM}{R}$

21. Which of the following most closely depicts the correct variation of the gravitational potential $V(r)$ due to a large planet of radius R and uniform mass density ? (Figures are not drawn to scale) **[2015 (Online)]**

(A) 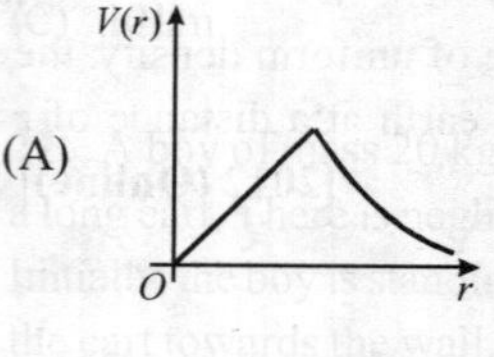

(B) 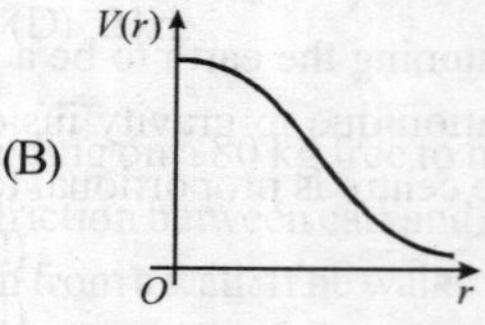

(C) 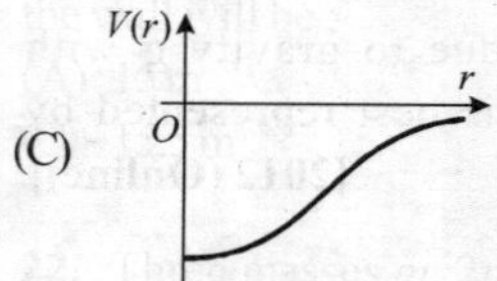

(D) 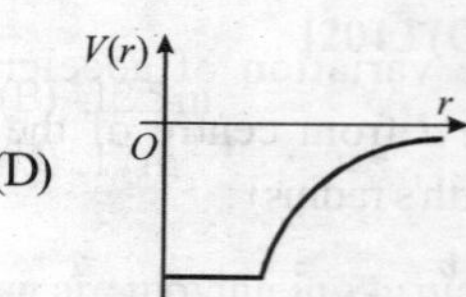

22. A point particle is held on the axis of a ring of mass m and radius r at a distance r from it's centre C. When released, it reaches C under the gravitational attraction of the ring. Its speed at C will be : **[2016 (Online)]**

(A) $\sqrt{\frac{2Gm}{r}(\sqrt{2}-1)}$ (B) $\sqrt{\frac{Gm}{r}}$

(C) $\sqrt{\frac{2Gm}{r}\left(1-\frac{1}{\sqrt{2}}\right)}$ (D) $\sqrt{\frac{2Gm}{r}}$

* * * * *

CHAPTER

7 GRAVITATION

7.2 SATELLITE MOTION

1. If suddenly the gravitational force of attraction between earth and a satellite revolving around it becomes zero, then the satellite will : **[2002]**

(A) Continue to move in its orbit with same velocity

(B) Move tangentially to the original orbit with same velocity

(C) Become stationary in its orbit

(D) Move towards the earth

2. Energy required to move a body of mass *m* from an orbit of radius 2*R* to 3*R* is : **[2002]**

(A) $GMm/12R$ (B) $GMm/3R$

(C) $GMm/8R$ (D) $GMm/6R$

3. The escape velocity of a body depends upon mass as : **[2002]**

(A) m^0 (B) m^1

(C) m^2 (D) m^3

4. The time period of a satellite of earth is 5 hours. If the separation between the centre of earth and the satellite is increased to 4 times the previous value, the new time period will become : **[2003]**

(A) 10 h (B) 80 h

(C) 40 h (D) 20 h

5. The escape velocity for a body projected vertically upwards from the surface of earth is 11 km/h. If the body is projected at an angle of 45° with the vertical, the escape velocity will be : **[2003]**

(A) $11\sqrt{2}$ km/s (B) 22 km/s

(C) 11 km/s (D) $\frac{11}{\sqrt{2}}$ km/s

6. Suppose the gravitational force varies inversely as the nth power of distance. Then the time period of a planet in circular orbit of radius *R* around the sun will be proportional to : **[2004]**

(A) $R^{\left(\frac{n+1}{2}\right)}$ (B) $R^{\left(\frac{n-1}{2}\right)}$

(C) R^n (D) $R^{\left(\frac{n-2}{2}\right)}$

7. The time period of an earth satellite in circular orbit is independent of : **[2004]**

(A) The mass of the satellite

(B) Radius of its orbit

(C) Both the mass and radius of the orbit

(D) Neither the mass of the satellite nor the radius of its orbit

8. A satellite of mass *m* revolves around the earth of radius *R* at a height *x* from its surface. If *g* is the acceleration due to gravity on the surface of the earth, the orbital speed of the satellite is : **[2004]**

(A) gx (B) $\frac{gR}{R-x}$

(C) $\frac{gR^2}{R+x}$ (D) $\left(\frac{gR^2}{R+x}\right)^{1/2}$

9. A planet in a distant solar system is 10 times more massive than the earth and its radius is 10 times smaller. Given that the escape velocity from the earth is 11 km s^{-1}, the escape velocity from the surface of the planet would be : **[2008]**

(A) 1.1 km s^{-1} (B) 11 km s^{-1}

(C) 110 km s^{-1} (D) 0.11 km s^{-1}

10. Two particles of equal mass '*m*' go around a circle of radius *R* under the action of their mutual gravitational attraction. The speed of each particle with respect to their centre of mass is : **[2011]**

(A) $\sqrt{\frac{Gm}{R}}$ (B) $\sqrt{\frac{Gm}{4R}}$

(C) $\sqrt{\frac{Gm}{3R}}$ (D) $\sqrt{\frac{Gm}{2R}}$

11. India's Mangalyan was sent to the Mars by launching it into a transfer orbit EOM around the sun. It leaves the earth at *E* and meets Mars at *M*. If the semi-major axis of Earth's orbit is $a_e = 1.5 \times 10^{11}$ m, that of Mars orbit $a_m = 2.28 \times 10^{11}$ m, taken Kepler's laws give the estimate of time for Mangalyan to reach Mars from Earth to be close to : **[2014 (Online)]**

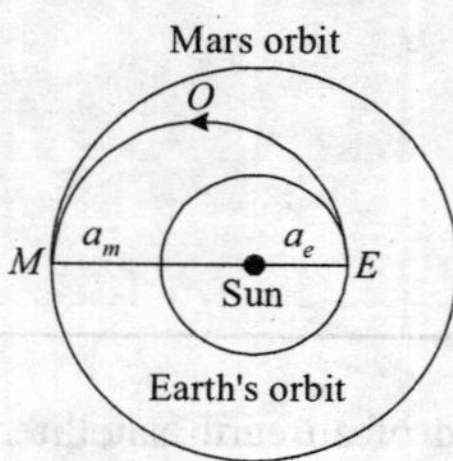

(A) 500 days (B) 320 days
(C) 260 days (D) 220 days

12. A very long (length L) cylindrical galaxy is made of uniformly distributed mass and has radius R ($R << L$). A star outside the galaxy is orbiting the galaxy in a plane perpendicular to the galaxy and passing through its centre. If the time period of star is T and its distance from the galaxy's axis is r, then : **[2015 (Online)]**

(A) $T \propto r$ (B) $T \propto \sqrt{r}$
(C) $T \propto r^2$ (D) $T^2 \propto r^3$

13. A satellite is revolving in a circular orbit at a height 'h' from the earth's surface (radius of earth R; $h << R$). The minimum increase in its orbital velocity required, so that the satellite could escape from the earth's gravitational field, is close to : (Neglect the effect of atmosphere.) **[2016]**

(A) $\sqrt{2gR}$ (B) $\sqrt{gR}$
(C) $\sqrt{gR/2}$ (D) $\sqrt{gR}(\sqrt{2}-1)$

14. Figure shows elliptical path *abcd* of a planet around the sun S such that the area of triangle *csa* is 1/4 the area of the ellipse. (See figure) With *db* as the semimajor axis and *ca* as the semiminor axis. If t_1 is the time taken for planet to go over path *abc* and t_2 for path taken over *cda* then : **[2016 (Online)]**

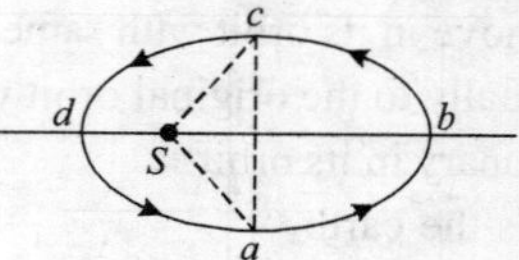

(A) $t_1 = 4t_2$ (B) $t_1 = 2t_2$
(C) $t_1 = 3t_2$ (D) $t_1 = t_2$

15. An astronaut of mass m is working on a satellite orbiting the earth at a distance h from the earth's surface. The radius of the earth is R, while its mass is M. The gravitational pull F_G on the astronaut is : **[2016 (Online)]**

(A) Zero since astronaut feels weightless

(B) $\frac{GMm}{(R+h)^2} < F_G < \frac{GMm}{R^2}$

(C) $F_G = \frac{GMm}{(R+h)^2}$ (D) $0 < F_G < \frac{GMm}{R^2}$

* * * * *

CHAPTER 8

MECHANICAL PROPERTIES OF SOLIDS

8.1 ELASTICITY

1. A wire suspended vertically from one of its ends is stretched by attaching a weight of 200 N to the lower ends. The weight stretches the wire by 1 mm. Then the elastic energy stored in the wire is : **[2003]**

(A) 0.2 J (B) 10 J
(C) 20 J (D) 0.1 J

2. A wire fixed at the upper end stretches by length l by applying a force F. The work done in stretching is : **[2004]**

(A) $\frac{F}{2l}$ (B) Fl
(C) $2Fl$ (D) $\frac{Fl}{2}$

3. If S is stress and Y is Young's modulus of material of a wire, the energy stored in the wire per unit volume is : **[2005]**

(A) $2S^2Y$ (B) $\frac{S^2}{2Y}$
(C) $\frac{2Y}{S^2}$ (D) $\frac{S}{2Y}$

4. A wire elongates by l mm when a load W is hanged from it. If the wire goes over a pulley and two weights W each are hung at the two ends, the elongation of the wire will be (in mm) : **[2006]**

(A) l (B) $2l$
(C) Zero (D) $l/2$

5. Two wires are made of the same material and have the same volume. However wire 1 has cross-sectional area A and wire 2 has cross-sectional area $3A$. If the length of wire 1 increases by Δx on applying force F, how much force is needed to stretch wire 2 by the same amount ? **[2009]**

(A) $6F$ (B) $9F$
(C) F (D) $4F$

6. The load versus elongation graphs for four wires of same length and made of the same material are shown in the figure. The thinnest wire is represented by the line : **[2012 (Online)]**

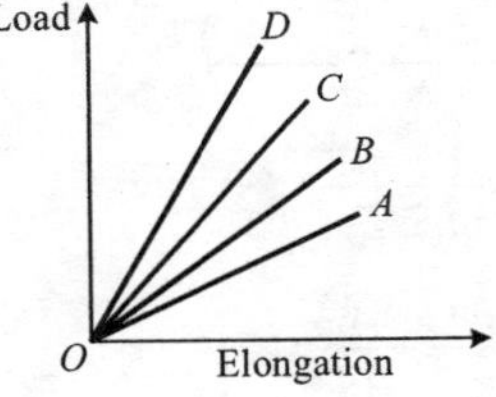

(A) OA (B) OC
(C) OD (D) OB

7. A structural steel rod has a radius of 10 mm and length of 1.0 m. A 100 kN for stretches it along its length. Young's modulus of structural steel is 2×10^{11} Nm^{-2}. The percentage strain is about : **[2012 (Online)]**

(A) 0.16% (B) 0.32%
(C) 0.08% (D) 0.24%

8. A steel wire can sustain 100 kg weight without breaking. If the wire is cut into two equal parts, each can sustain a weight of : **[2012 (Online)]**

(A) 50 kg (B) 400 kg
(C) 100 kg (D) 200 kg

9. Two blocks of masses m and M are connected by means of a metal wire of cross-sectional area A passing over a frictionless fixed pulley as shown in the figure. The system is then released. If $M = 2m$, then the stress produced in the wire is : **[2013 (Online)]**

(A) $\frac{2mg}{3A}$

(B) $\frac{4mg}{3A}$

(C) $\frac{mg}{A}$

(D) $\frac{3mg}{4A}$

10. If the ratio of lengths, radii and Young's moduli of steel and brass wires in the figure are a, b and c respectively, then the corresponding ratio of increase in their lengths is : **[2013 (Online)]**

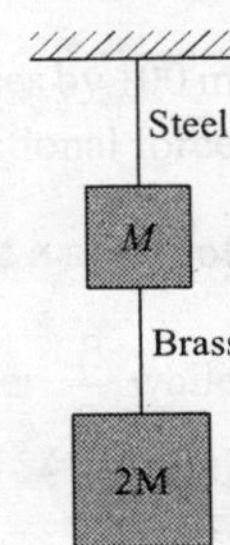

(A) $\frac{3c}{2ab^2}$

(B) $\frac{2a^2c}{b}$

(C) $\frac{3a}{2b^2c}$

(D) $\frac{2ac}{b^2}$

11. A uniform wire (Young's modulus 2×10^{11} Nm^{-2}) is subjected to longitudinal tensile stress of 5×10^7 Nm^{-2}. If the overall volume change in the wire is 0.02%, the fractional decrease in the radius of the wire is close to : **[2013 (Online)]**

(A) 1.0×10^{-4} (B) 1.5×10^{-4}
(C) 0.25×10^{-4} (D) 5×10^{-4}

12. A copper wire of length 1.0 m and a steel wire of length 0.5 m having equal cross-sectional areas are joined end to end. The composite wire is stretched by a certain load which stretches the copper wire by 1 mm. If Young's moduli of copper and steel are respectively 1.0×10^{11} Nm^{-2} and 2.0×10^{11} Nm^{-2}, the total extension of the composite wire is : **[2013 (Online)]**

(A) 1.75 mm (B) 2.0 mm
(C) 1.50 mm (D) 1.25 mm

13. In materials like aluminium and copper, the correct order of magnitude of various elastic moduli is : **[2014 (Online)]**

(A) Young's modulus < shear modulus < bulk modulus
(B) Bulk modulus < shear modulus < Young's modulus
(C) Shear modulus < Young's modulus < bulk modulus
(D) Bulk modulus < Young's modulus < shear modulus

14. The bulk moduli of ethanol, mercury and water are given as 0.9, 25 and 2.2 respectively in units of 10^9 Nm^{-2}. For a given value of pressure, the fractional compression in volume is $\frac{\Delta V}{V}$. Which of the following statements about $\frac{\Delta V}{V}$ for these three liquids is correct ? **[2014 (Online)]**

(A) Ethanol > Water > Mercury
(B) Water > Ethanol > Mercury
(C) Mercury > Ethanol > Water
(D) Ethanol > Mercury > Water

15. Steel ruptures when a shear of 3.5×10^8 Nm^{-2} is applied. The force needed to punch a 1 cm diameter hole in a steel sheet 0.3 cm thick is nearly : **[2014 (Online)]**

(A) 1.4×10^4 N (B) 2.7×10^4 N
(C) 3.3×10^4 N (D) 1.1×10^4 N

16. A uniform tapering conical wire is made from a material of Young's modulus Y and has a normal, unextended length L. The radii, at the upper and lower ends of this conical wire, have values R and $3R$, respectively. The upper end of the wire is fixed to a rigid support and a mass M is suspended from its lower end. The equilibrium extended length, of this wire, would equal: **[2016 (Online)]**

(A) $L\left(1+\frac{2}{9}\frac{Mg}{\pi YR^2}\right)$ (B) $L\left(1+\frac{1}{9}\frac{Mg}{\pi YR^2}\right)$
(C) $L\left(1+\frac{1}{3}\frac{Mg}{\pi YR^2}\right)$ (D) $L\left(1+\frac{2}{3}\frac{Mg}{\pi YR^2}\right)$

17. A bottle has an opening of radius a and length b. A cork of length b and radius $(a + \Delta a)$ where $(\Delta a << a)$ is compressed to fit into the opening completely (see figure). If the bulk modulus of cork is B and frictional coefficient between the bottle and cork is μ then the force needed to push the cork into the bottle is : **[2016 (Online)]**

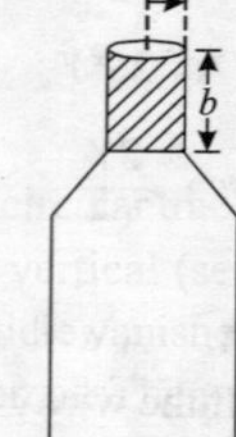

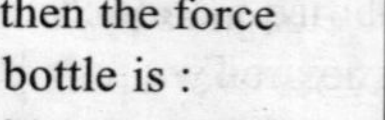

(A) $(\pi\mu Bb)\,a$ (B) $(2\pi\mu Bb)\,\Delta a$
(C) $(\mu\pi Bb)\,\Delta a$ (D) $(4\pi\mu Bb)\,\Delta a$

* * * * *

CHAPTER

9 MECHANICAL PROPERTIES OF FLUIDS

9.1 FLUID STATICS

1. A jar is filled with two non-mixing liquids 1 and 2 having densities ρ_1 and ρ_2, respectively. A solid ball, made of a material of density ρ_3, is dropped in the jar. It comes to equilibrium in the position shown in the figure. Which of the following is true for ρ_1, ρ_2 and ρ_3 : **[2008]**

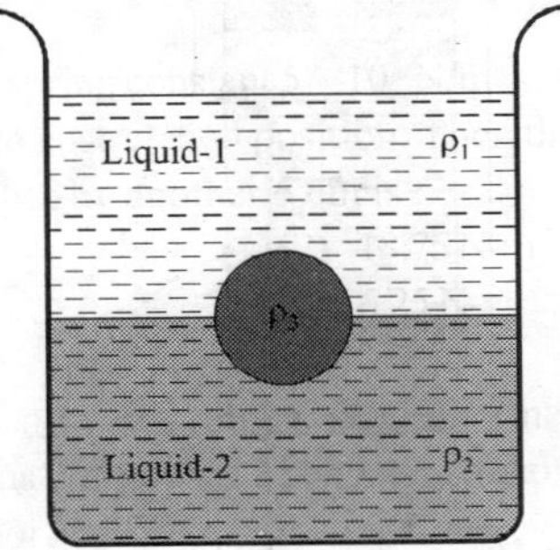

(A) $\rho_3 < \rho_1 < \rho_2$ (B) $\rho_3 < \rho_2 < \rho_1$
(C) $\rho_1 < \rho_2 < \rho_3$ (D) $\rho_1 < \rho_3 < \rho_2$

2. A ball is made of a material of density ρ where $\rho_{oil} < \rho < \rho_{water}$ with ρ_{oil} and ρ_{water} representing the densities of oil and water, respectively. The oil and water are immiscible. If the above ball is in equilibrium in a mixture of this oil and water, which of the following pictures represents its equilibrium position ? **[2010]**

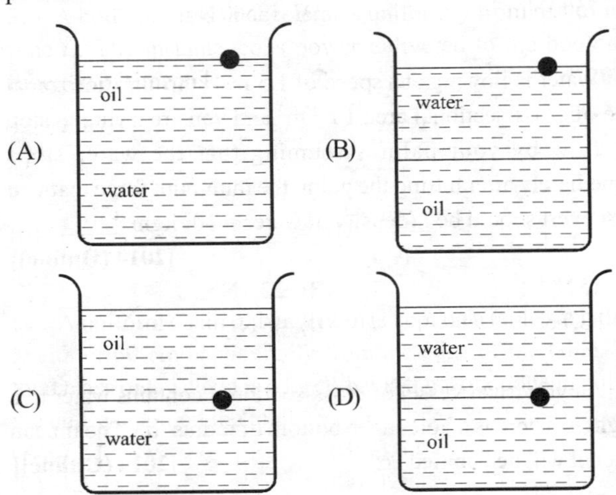

3. A uniform cylinder of length L and mass M having cross-sectional area A is suspended, with its length vertical, from a fixed point by a massless spring, such that it is half submerged in a liquid of density σ at equilibrium position. The extension x_0 of the spring when it is in equilibrium is : **[2013]**

(A) $\frac{Mg}{k}\left(1-\frac{LA\sigma}{M}\right)$ (B) $\frac{Mg}{k}\left(1-\frac{LA\sigma}{2M}\right)$

(C) $\frac{Mg}{k}\left(1+\frac{LA\sigma}{M}\right)$ (D) $\frac{Mg}{k}$

4. There is a circular tube in a vertical plane. Two liquids which do not mix and of densities d_1 and d_2 are filled in the tube. Each liquid subtends 90° angle at centre. Radius joining their interface makes an angle α with vertical. Ratio d_1/d_2 is : **[2014]**

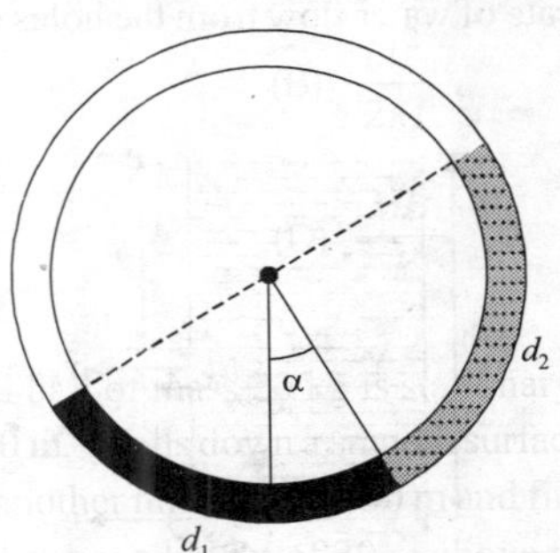

(A) $\frac{1+\sin\alpha}{1-\sin\alpha}$ (B) $\frac{1+\cos\alpha}{1-\cos\alpha}$

(C) $\frac{1+\tan\alpha}{1-\tan\alpha}$ (D) $\frac{1+\sin\alpha}{1-\cos\alpha}$

* * * * *

CHAPTER 9

MECHANICAL PROPERTIES OF FLUIDS

9.2 FLUID DYNAMICS

1. A cylinder of height 20 m is completely filled with water. The velocity of efflux of water (in ms^{-1}) through a small hole on the side wall of the cylinder near its bottom, is : **[2002]**

(A) 10
(B) 20
(C) 25.5
(D) 5

2. Water is flowing continuously from a tap having an internal diameter 8×10^{-3} m. The water velocity as it leaves the tap is 0.4 ms^{-1}. The diameter of the water stream at a distance 2×10^{-1} m below the tap is close to : **[2011]**

(A) 9.6×10^{-3} m
(B) 3.6×10^{-3} m
(C) 5.0×10^{-3} m
(D) 7.5×10^{-3} m

3. A square hole of side length l is made at a depth of h and a circular hole of radius r is made at a depth of 4h from the surface of water in a water tank kept on a horizontal surface. If $l << h$, $r << h$ and the rate of water flow from the holes is the same, then r is equal to : **[2012]**

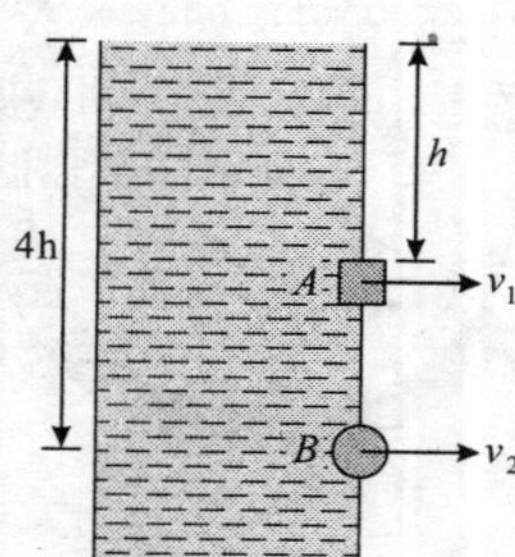

(A) $\frac{l}{\sqrt{2\pi}}$
(B) $\frac{l}{\sqrt{3\pi}}$
(C) $\frac{l}{3\pi}$
(D) $\frac{l}{2\pi}$

4. Water is flowing through a horizontal tube having cross-sectional area of its two ends being A and A' such that the ratio A/A' is 5. If the pressure difference of water between the two ends is 3×10^5 Nm^{-2}, the velocity of water with which it enters the tube will be (neglect gravity effects) : **[2012 (Online)]**

(A) 5 ms^{-1}
(B) 10 ms^{-1}
(C) 25 ms^{-1}
(D) $50\sqrt{10}$ ms^{-1}

5. In a cylindrical water tank, there are two small holes A and B on the wall at a depth of h_1, from the surface of water and at a height of h_2 from the bottom of water tank. Surface of water is at height H from the bottom of water tank. Water coming out from both holes strikes the ground at the same point S. Find the ratio of h_1 and h_2 : **[2012 (Online)]**

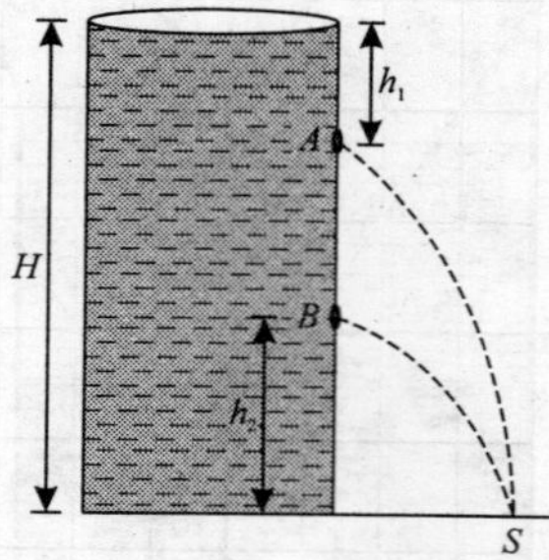

(A) Depends on H
(B) 1 : 1
(C) 2 : 2
(D) 1 : 2

6. Air of density 1.2 kg m^{-3} is blowing across the horizontal wings of an aeroplane in such a way that its speeds above and below the wings are 150 ms^{-1} and 100 ms^{-1}, respectively. The pressure difference between the upper and lower sides of the wings, is : **[2013 (Online)]**

(A) 60 Nm^{-2}
(B) 180 Nm^{-2}
(C) 7500 Nm^{-2}
(D) 12500 Nm^{-2}

7. Water is flowing at a speed of 1.5 ms^{-1} through horizontal tube of cross-sectional area 10^{-2} m^2 and you are trying to stop the flow by your palm. Assuming that the water stops immediately after hitting the palm, the minimum force that you must exert should be : (density of water = 10^3 kgm^{-3}) **[2014 (Online)]**

(A) 15 N
(B) 22.5 N
(C) 33.7 N
(D) 45 N

8. A cylindrical vessel of cross-section A contains water to a height h. There is a hole in the bottom of radius 'a'. The time in which it will be emptied is : **[2014 (Online)]**

(A) $\frac{2A}{\pi a^2}\sqrt{\frac{h}{g}}$
(B) $\frac{\sqrt{2}A}{\pi a^2}\sqrt{\frac{h}{g}}$
(C) $\frac{2\sqrt{2}A}{\pi a^2}\sqrt{\frac{h}{g}}$
(D) $\frac{A}{\sqrt{2}\pi a^2}\sqrt{\frac{h}{g}}$

9. A tank with a small hole at the bottom has been filled with water and kerosene (specific gravity 0.8). The height of water is 3 m and that of kerosene 2 m. When the hole is opened the velocity of fluid coming out from it is nearly : (take $g = 10\ \text{ms}^{-2}$ and density of water $= 10^3\ \text{kg m}^{-3}$) : **[2014 (Online)]**

(A) $10.7\ \text{ms}^{-1}$ (B) $9.6\ \text{ms}^{-1}$
(C) $8.5\ \text{ms}^{-1}$ (D) $7.6\ \text{ms}^{-1}$

10. In the diagram shown, the difference in the two tubes of the manometer is 5 cm, the cross section of the tube at A and B is $6\ \text{mm}^2$ and $10\ \text{mm}^2$ respectively. The rate at which water flows through the tube is ($g = 10\ \text{ms}^{-2}$) : **[2014 (Online)]**

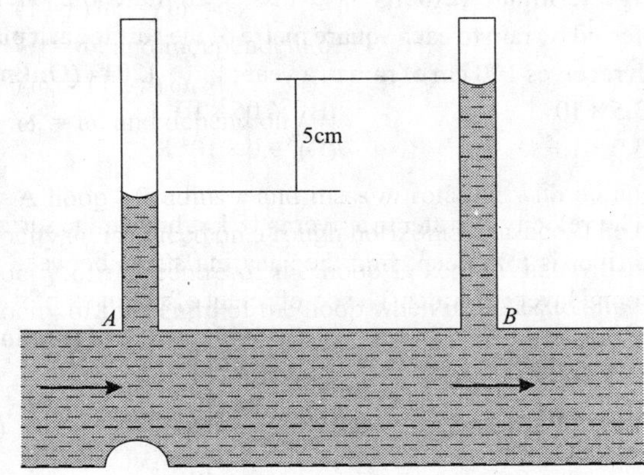

(A) 7.5 cc/s (B) 8.0 cc/s
(C) 10.0 cc/s (D) 12.5 cc/s

11. Consider a water jar of radius R that has water filled up to height H and is kept on a stand of height h (see figure). Through a hole of radius r ($r << R$) at its bottom, the water leaks out and the stream of water coming down towards the ground has a shape like a funnel as shown in the figure. If the radius of the cross-section of water stream when it hits the ground is x. Then: **[2016 (Online)]**

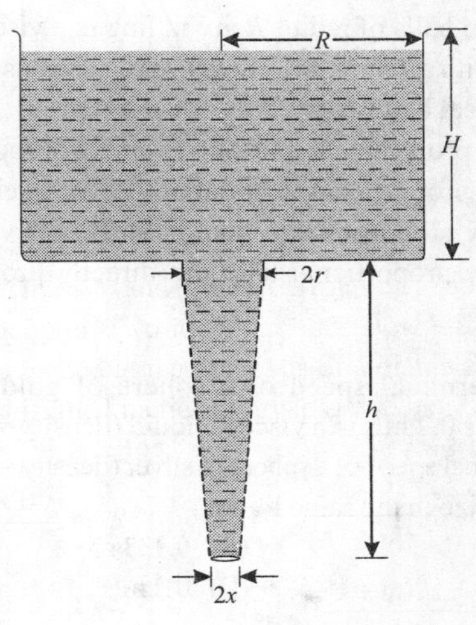

(A) $x = r\left(\dfrac{H}{H+h}\right)^{\frac{1}{4}}$ (B) $x = r\left(\dfrac{H}{H+h}\right)$

(C) $x = r\left(\dfrac{H}{H+h}\right)^{2}$ (D) $x = r\left(\dfrac{H}{H+h}\right)^{\frac{1}{2}}$

* * * * *

CHAPTER 9

MECHANICAL PROPERTIES OF FLUIDS

9.3 VISCOSITY

1. Spherical balls of radius R are falling in a viscous fluid of viscosity η with a velocity v. The retarding viscous force acting on the spherical ball is : **[2004]**

(A) Directly proportional to R but inversely proportional to v

(B) Directly proportional to both radius R and velocity v

(C) Inversely proportional to both radius R and velocity v

(D) Inversely proportional to R but directly proportional to velocity v

2. If the terminal speed of a sphere of gold (density = 19.5 kg/m^3) is 0.2 m/s in a viscous liquid (density = 1.5 kg/m^3), find the terminal speed of a sphere of silver (density = 10.5 kg/m^3) of the same size in the same liquid : **[2006]**

(A) 0.4 m/s (B) 0.133 m/s

(C) 0.1 m/s (D) 0.2 m/s

3. A spherical solid ball of volume V is made of a material of density ρ_1. It is falling through a liquid of density ρ_2 ($\rho_2 < \rho_1$). Assume that the liquid applies a viscous force on the ball that is proportional to the square of its speed v, i.e., $F_{viscous} = -kv^2$ ($k > 0$). Then terminal speed of the ball is : **[2008]**

(A) $\sqrt{\frac{Vg(\rho_1 - \rho_2)}{k}}$ (B) $\frac{Vg\rho_1}{k}$

(C) $\sqrt{\frac{Vg\rho_1}{k}}$ (D) $\frac{Vg(\rho_1 - \rho_2)}{k}$

4. If a ball of steel (density $\rho = 7.8$ g cm^{-3}) attains a terminal velocity of 10 cm s^{-1} when falling in a tank of water (coefficient of viscosity $\eta_{water} = 8.5 \times 10^{-4}$ Pa.s) then its terminal velocity in glycerine : **[2011]**

($\rho = 12$ g cm^{-3}, $\eta = 13.2$ Pa.s) would be nearly :

(A) 1.6×10^{-5} cm s^{-1} (B) 6.25×10^{-4} cm s^{-1}

(C) 6.45×10^{-4} cm s^{-1} (D) 1.5×10^{-5} cm s^{-1}

5. The terminal velocity of a small sphere of radius a in a viscous liquid is proportional to : **[2012 (Online)]**

(A) a^2 (B) a^3

(C) a (D) a^{-1}

6. In an experiment, a small steel ball falls through a liquid at a constant speed of 10 cm/s. If the steel ball is pulled upward with a force equal to twice its effective weight, how fast will it move upward ? **[2013 (Online)]**

(A) 5 cm/s (B) Zero

(C) 10 cm/s (D) 20 cm/s

7. The average mass of rain drops is 3.0×10^{-5} kg and their average terminal velocity is 9 m/s. Calculate the energy transferred by rain to each square metre of the surface at a place which receives 100 cm of rain in a year : **[2014 (Online)]**

(A) 3.5×10^5 J (B) 4.05×10^4 J

(C) 3.0×10^5 J (D) 9.0×10^4 J

8. The velocity of water in a river is 18 km/hr near the surface. If the river is 5 m deep, find the shearing stress between the horizontal layers of water. The co-efficient of viscosity of water $= 10^{-2}$ poise : **[2014 (Online)]**

(A) 10^{-1} N/m^2 (B) 10^{-2} N/m^2

(C) 10^{-3} N/m^2 (D) 10^{-4} N/m^2

9. If it takes 5 minutes to fill a 15 litre bucket from a water tap of diameter $\frac{2}{\sqrt{\pi}}$ cm then the Reynolds number for the flows is (density of water = 10^3 kg/m^3) and viscosity of water = 10^{-3} Pa.s) close to : **[2015 (Online)]**

(A) 1100 (B) 11,000

(C) 550 (D) 5500

10. Which of the following option correctly describes the variation of the speed v and acceleration 'a' of a point mass falling vertically in a viscous medium that applies a force $F = -kv$, where 'k' is a constant, on the body ? (Graphs are schematic and not drawn to scale) : **[2016 (Online)]**

(A)
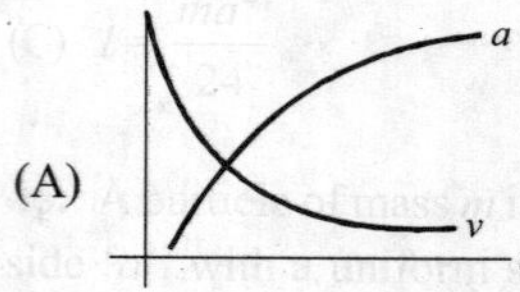

(B)
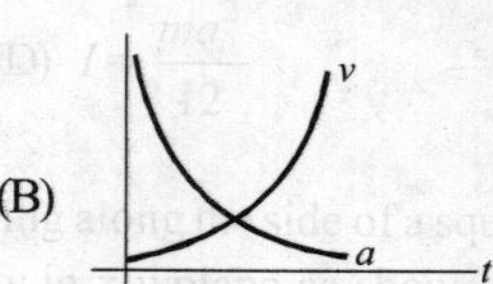

(C)
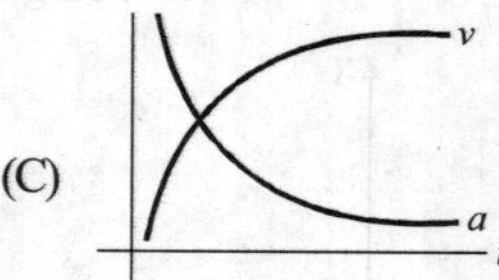

(D)
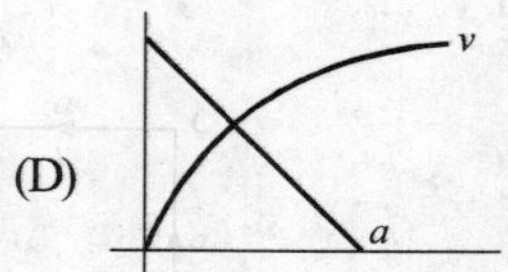

* * * * *

CHAPTER

10 THERMAL PROPERTIES OF MATTER

10.1 THERMAL EXPANSION

1. A metal rod of Young's modulus Y and coefficient of thermal expansion α is held at its two ends such that its length remains invariant. If its temperature is raised by t°C, the linear stress developed in it is : **[2011]**

(A) $\frac{\alpha t}{Y}$ (B) $\frac{Y}{\alpha t}$

(C) $Y\alpha t$ (D) $\frac{1}{(Y\alpha t)}$

2. An aluminium sphere of 20 cm diameter is heated from 0°C to 100°C. Its volume changes by (given that coefficient of linear expansion for aluminium $\alpha_{Al} = 23 \times 10^{-6}$/°C) : **[2011]**

(A) 28.9 cc (B) 2.89 cc

(C) 9.28 cc (D) 49.8 cc

3. A wooden wheel of radius R is made of two semicircular parts (see figure). The two parts are held together by a ring made of a metal strip of cross sectional area S and Length L. L is slightly less than $2\pi R$. To fit the ring on the wheel, it is heated so that its temperature rises by ΔT and it just steps over the wheel. As it cools down to surrounding temperature, it presses the semicircular parts together. If the coefficient of linear expansion of the metal is α, and its Young's modulus is Y, the force that one part of the wheel applies on the other part is : **[2012]**

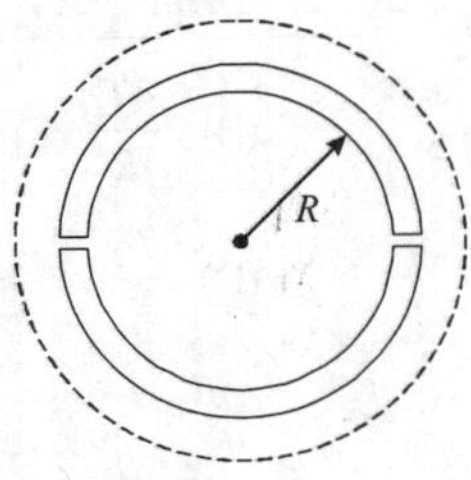

(A) $2SY\alpha\Delta T$ (B) $2\pi SY\alpha\Delta T$

(C) $SY\alpha\Delta T$ (D) $\pi SY\alpha\Delta T$

4. On a linear temperature scale Y, water freezes at – 160°Y and boils at – 50°Y. On this Y scale, a temperature of 340 K would be read as : (water freezes at 273 K and boils at 373 K) : **[2013 (Online)]**

(A) –73.7°Y (B) –233.7°Y

(C) –86.3°Y (D) –106.3°Y

5. The ratio of the coefficient of volume expansion of a glass container to that of a viscous liquid kept inside the container is 1 : 4. What fraction of the inner volume of the container should the liquid occupy so that the volume of the remaining vacant space will be same at all temperatures ? **[2013 (Online)]**

(A) 2 : 5 (B) 1 : 4

(C) 1 : 64 (D) 1 : 8

6. The pressure that has to be applied to the ends of a steel wire of length 10 cm to keep its length constant when its temperature is raised by 100°C is (For steel Young's modulus is 2×10^{11} Nm^{-2} and coefficient of thermal expansion is 1.1×10^{-5} K^{-1}) : **[2014]**

(A) 2.2×10^{8} Pa (B) 2.2×10^{9} Pa

(C) 2.2×10^{7} Pa (D) 2.2×10^{6} Pa

7. A pendulum clock loses 12 s a day if the temperature is 40°C and gains 4 s a day if the temperature is 20°C. The temperature at which the clock will show correct time, and the co-efficient of linear expansion (α) of the metal of the pendulum shaft are respectively : **[2016]**

(A) 25°C; $\alpha = 1.85 \times 10^{-5}$/°C (B) 60°C; $\alpha = 1.85 \times 10^{-4}$/°C

(C) 30°C; $\alpha = 1.85 \times 10^{-3}$/°C (D) 55°C; $\alpha = 1.85 \times 10^{-2}$/°C

* * * * *

9. This question has Statement-1 and Statement-2. Of the four choices given after the Statements, choose the one that best describes the two Statements. **[2013 (Online)]**

Statement-1 : A capillary is dipped in a liquid and liquid rises to a height h in it. As the temperature of the liquid is raised, the height h increases (if the density of the liquid and the angle of contact remain the same).

Statement-2 : Surface tension of a liquid decreases with the rise in its temperature.

(A) Statement-1 is true, Statement-2 is true; Statement-2 is not the correct explanation for Statement-1

(B) Statement-1 is false, Statement-2 is true

(C) Statement-1 is true, Statement-2 is false

(D) Statement-1 is true, Statement-2 is true; Statement-2 is the correct explanation for Statement-1

10. Wax is coated on the inner wall of a capillary tube and the tube is then dipped in water. Then, compared to the unwaxed capillary, the angle of contact θ and the height h upto which water rises change. These changes are : **[2013 (Online)]**

(A) θ increases and h also increases

(B) θ decreases h also decreases

(C) θ increases and h decreases

(D) θ decreases and h increases

11. On heating water, bubbles being formed at the bottom of the vessel detach and rise. Take the bubbles to be spheres of radius R and making a circular contact of radius r with the bottom of the vessel. If $r << R$ and the surface tension of water is T, value of r just before bubbles detach is : (density of water is ρ_w) : **[2014]**

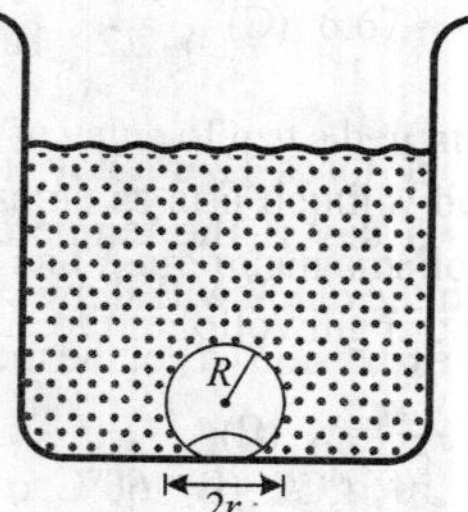

(A) $R^2\sqrt{\frac{2\rho_w g}{3T}}$ (B) $R^2\sqrt{\frac{\rho_w g}{6T}}$

(C) $R^2\sqrt{\frac{\rho_w g}{T}}$ (D) $R^2\sqrt{\frac{3\rho_w g}{T}}$

12. An air bubble of radius 0.1 cm is in a liquid having surface tension 0.06 N/m and density 10^3 kg/m^3. The pressure inside the bubble is 1100 Nm^{-2} greater than the atmospheric pressure. At what depth is the bubble below the surface of the liquid ? ($g=9.8$ ms^{-2}) : **[2014 (Online)]**

(A) 0.1 m (B) 0.15 m

(C) 0.20 m (D) 0.25 m

13. Two soap bubbles coalesce to form a single bubble. If V is the subsequent change in volume of contained air and S change in total surface are, T is the surface tension and P atmospheric pressure, then which of the following relation is correct ? **[2014 (Online)]**

(A) $4PV+3ST=0$ (B) $3PV+4ST=0$

(C) $2PV+3ST=0$ (D) $3PV+2ST=0$

14. If two glass plates have water between them and are separated by very small distance (see figure), it is very difficult to pull them apart. It is because the water in between form cylindrical surface on the side that gives rise to lower pressure in the water in comparison to atmosphere. If the radius of the cylindrical surface is R and surface tension of water is T then the pressure in water between the plates is lower by : **[2015 (Online)]**

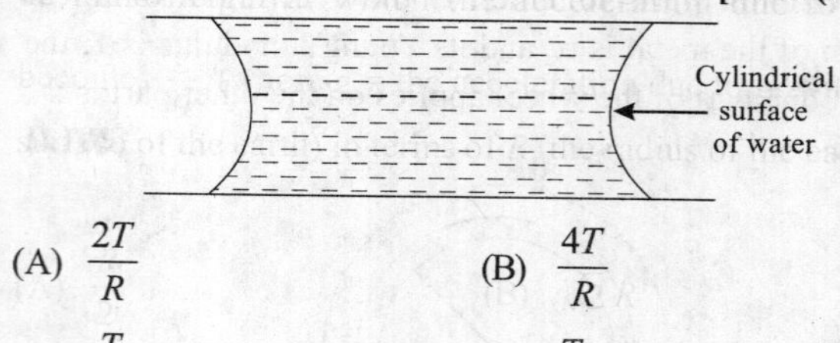

(A) $\frac{2T}{R}$ (B) $\frac{4T}{R}$

(C) $\frac{T}{4R}$ (D) $\frac{T}{R}$

* * * * *

CHAPTER 9 MECHANICAL PROPERTIES OF FLUIDS

9.4 SURFACE TENSION

1. If two soap bubbles of different radii are connected by a tube : **[2004]**

(A) Air flows from the bigger bubble to the smaller bubble till the sizes become equal

(B) Air flows from bigger bubble to the smaller bubble till the sizes are interchanged

(C) Air flows from the smaller bubble to the bigger bubble

(D) There is no flow of air

2. A 20 cm long capillary tube is dipped in water. The water rises upto 8 cm. If the entire arrangement is put in a freely falling elevator, the length of water column in the capillary tube will be: **[2005]**

(A) 8 cm (B) 10 cm

(C) 4 cm (D) 20 cm

3. A capillary tube (A) is dipped in water. Another identical tube (B) is dipped in a soap-water solution. Which of the following shows the relative nature of the liquid columns in the two tubes : **[2008]**

(A)

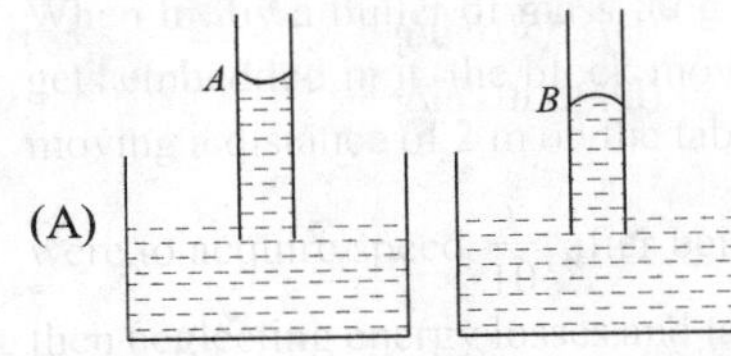

(B)

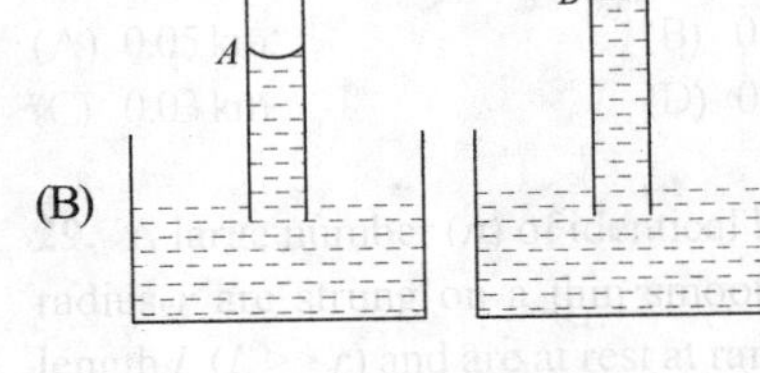

(C)

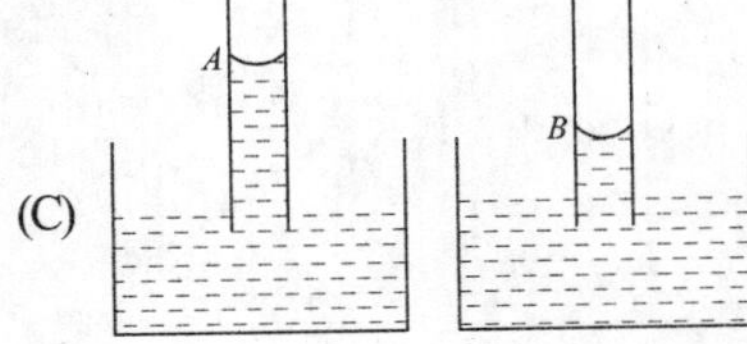

(D)

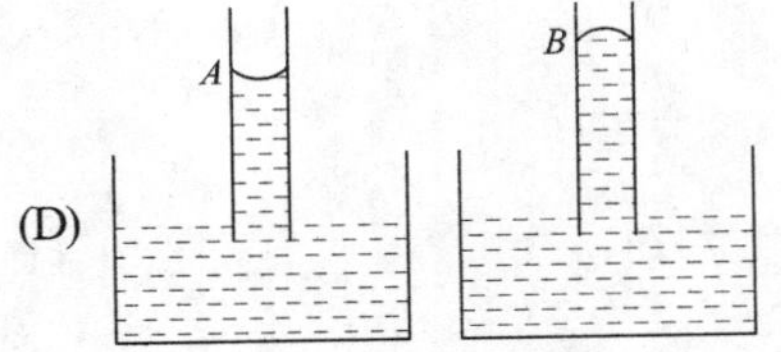

4. Two mercury drops (each of radius 'r') merge to form a bigger drop. The surface energy of the bigger drop, if T is the surface tension, is : **[2011]**

(A) $2^{5/3}\pi r^2 T$ (B) $4\pi r^2 T$

(C) $2\pi r^2 T$ (D) $2^{8/3}\pi r^2 T$

5. Work done in increasing the size of a soap bubble from a radius of 3 cm to 5 cm is nearly (Surface tension of soap solution $= 0.03\ \text{Nm}^{-1}$) : **[2011]**

(A) 2π mJ (B) 0.4π mJ

(C) 4π mJ (D) 0.2π mJ

6. A thin liquid film formed between a U-shaped wire and a light slider supports a weight of 1.5×10^{-2} N (see figure). The length of the slider is 30 cm and its weight negligible. The surface tension of the liquid film is : **[2012]**

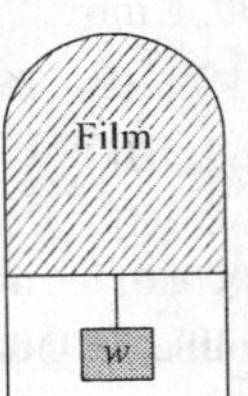

(A) $0.025\ \text{Nm}^{-1}$ (B) $0.012525\ \text{Nm}^{-1}$

(C) $0.125\ \text{Nm}^{-1}$ (D) $0.0525\ \text{Nm}^{-1}$

7. A large number of liquid drops each of radius r coalesce to from a single drop of radius R. The energy released in the process is converted into kinetic energy of the big drop so formed. The speed of the big drop is (given, surface tension of liquid T, density ρ) : **[2012 (Online)]**

(A) $\sqrt{\dfrac{T}{\rho}\left(\dfrac{1}{r}-\dfrac{1}{R}\right)}$ (B) $\sqrt{\dfrac{2T}{\rho}\left(\dfrac{1}{r}-\dfrac{1}{R}\right)}$

(C) $\sqrt{\dfrac{4T}{\rho}\left(\dfrac{1}{r}-\dfrac{1}{R}\right)}$ (D) $\sqrt{\dfrac{6T}{\rho}\left(\dfrac{1}{r}-\dfrac{1}{R}\right)}$

8. Assume that a drop of liquid evaporates by decrease in its surface energy, so that its temperature remains unchanged. What should be the minimum radius of the drop for this to be possible ? The surface tension is T, density of liquid is ρ and L is its latent heat of vaporization : **[2013]**

(A) $\sqrt{T/\rho L}$ (B) $T/\rho L$

(C) $2T/\rho L$ (D) $\rho L/T$

CHAPTER

10 THERMAL PROPERTIES OF MATTER

10.2 CALORIMETRY

1. Heat given to a body which raises its temperature by 1°C is: **[2002]**
(A) Water equivalent (B) Thermal capacity
(C) Specific heat (D) Temperature gradient

2. If mass-energy equivalence is taken into account, when water is cooled to form ice, the mass of water should : **[2002]**
(A) Increase (B) Remain unchanged
(C) Decrease (D) First increase then decrease

3. Given that 1 g of water in liquid phase has volume 1 cm^3 and in vapour phase 1671 cm^3 at atmospheric pressure and the latent heat of vaporization of water is 2256 J/g; the change in the internal energy in joules for 1 g of water at 373 K when it changes from liquid phase to vapour phase at the same temperature is : **[2013 (Online)]**
(A) 2256 (B) 167
(C) 2089 (D) 1

4. 500 g of water and 100 g of ice at 0°C are in a calorimeter whose water equivalent is 40 g. 10 g of steam at 100°C is added to it. Then water in the calorimeter is : (Latent heat of ice = 80 cal/g, Latent heat of steam = 540 cal/g) : **[2013 (Online)]**
(A) 580 g (B) 590 g
(C) 600 g (D) 610 g

5. Water of volume 2L in a closed container is heated with a coil of 1 kW. While water is heated, the container loses energy at a rate of 160 J/s. In how much time will the temperature of water rise from 27°C to 77°C ? (Specific heat of water is 4.2 kJ/kg and that of the container is negligible) : **[2014 (Online)]**
(A) 8 min 20 s (B) 6 min 2 s
(C) 7 min (D) 14 min

6. An experiment takes 10 minutes to raise the temperature of water in a container from 0°C to 100°C and another 55 minutes to convert it totally into steam by a heater supplying heat at a uniform rate. Neglecting the specific heat of the container and taking specific heat of water to be 1 cal/g °C, the heat of vapourization according to this experiment will come out to be: **[2015 (Online)]**
(A) 560 cal/g (B) 550 cal/g
(C) 540 cal/g (D) 530 cal/g

* * * * *

CHAPTER

10 THERMAL PROPERTIES OF MATTER

10.3 HEAT TRANSFER

1. Two spheres of the same material have radii 1 m and 4 m and temperatures 4000 K and 2000 K respectively. The ratio of the energy radiated per second by the first sphere to that by the second is : **[2002]**

(A) 1 : 1 (B) 16 : 1
(C) 4 : 1 (D) 1 : 9

2. Infrared radiations are detected by : **[2002]**

(A) Spectrometer (B) Pyrometer
(C) Nanometer (D) Photometer

3. Which of the following is more close to a black body : **[2002]**

(A) Black board paint (B) Green leaves
(C) Black holes (D) Red roses

4. The earth radiates in the infra-red region of the spectrum. The spectrum is correctly given by : **[2003]**

(A) Rayleigh Jeans law (B) Plank's law of radiation
(C) Stefan's law of radiation (D) Wien's law

5. According to Newton's law of cooling, the rate of cooling of a body is proportional to $(\Delta\theta)^n$, where $\Delta\theta$ is the difference of the temperature of the body and the surroundings, and n is equal to : **[2003]**

(A) Two (B) Three
(C) Four (D) One

6. If the temperature of the sun were to increase from T to $2T$ and its radius from R to $2R$, then the ratio of the radiant energy received on earth to what it was previously, will be : **[2004]**

(A) 4 (B) 16
(C) 32 (D) 64

7. The temperature of the two outer surfaces of a composite slab, consisting of two materials having coefficients of thermal conductivity K and $2K$ and thickness x and $4x$, respectively are T_2 and T_1 $(T_2 > T_1)$. The rate of heat transfer through the slab, in a steady state is $\left(\frac{A(T_2 - T_1)K}{x}\right) f$, with f equals to (A = cross sectional area) : **[2004]**

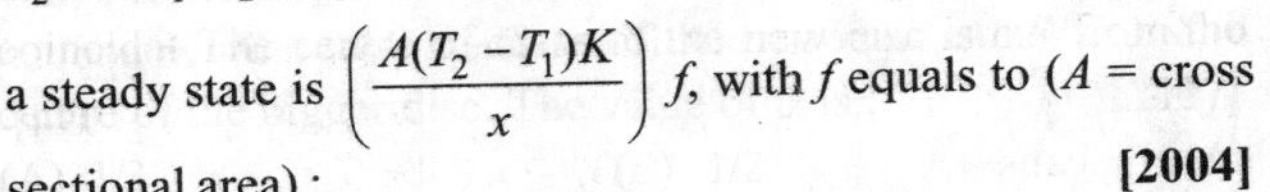

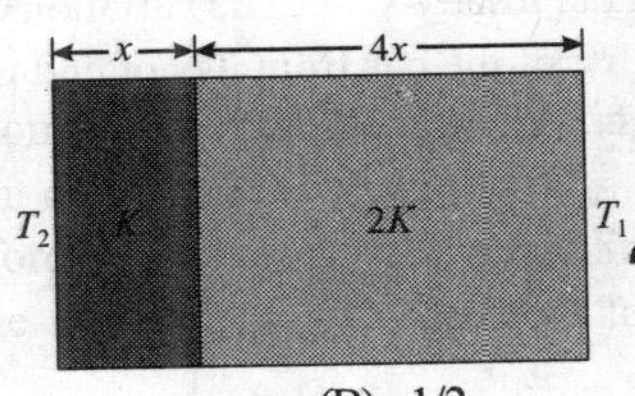

(A) 1 (B) 1/2
(C) 2/3 (D) 1/3

8. The figure shows a system of two concentric spheres of radii r_1 and r_2 and kept at temperatures T_1 and T_2, respectively. The radial rate of flow of heat in a substance between the two concentric spheres, is proportional to : **[2005]**

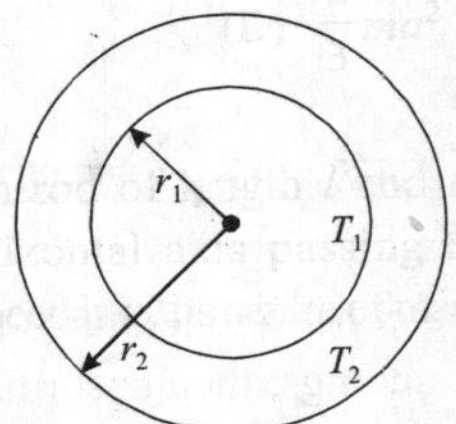

(A) $\frac{(r_2 - r_1)}{(r_1 r_2)}$ (B) $\ln\left(\frac{r_2}{r_1}\right)$

(C) $\frac{r_1 r_2}{(r_2 - r_1)}$ (D) $(r_2 - r_1)$

9. Assuming the sun to be a spherical body of radius R at a temperature of T K, evaluate the total radiant power, incident on earth, at a distance r from the sun-(when radius of earth is r_0) : **[2006]**

(A) $4\pi r_0^2 R^2 \sigma T^4/r^2$ (B) $\pi r_0^2 R^2 \sigma T^4/r^2$
(C) $r_0^2 R^2 \sigma T^4/4\pi r^2$ (D) $R^2 \sigma T^4/r^2$

10. One end of a thermally insulated rod is kept at a temperature T_1 and the other at T_2. The rod is composed of two sections of lengths l_1 and l_2 and thermal conductivities K_1 and K_2 respectively. The temperature at the interface of the two sections is : **[2007]**

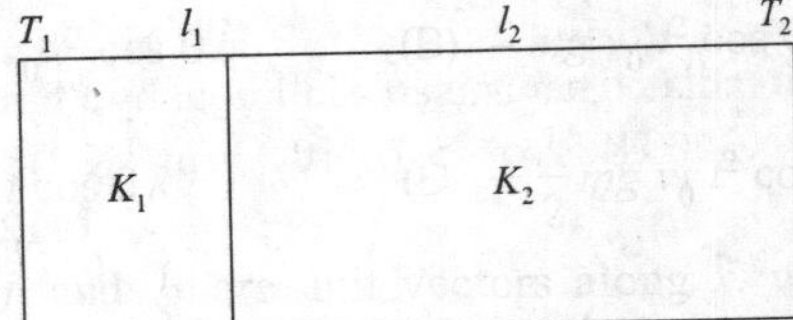

(A) $(K_2l_2T_1 + K_1l_1T_2)/(K_1l_1 + K_2l_2)$
(B) $(K_2l_1T_1 + K_1l_2T_2)/(K_2l_1 + K_1l_2)$
(C) $(K_1l_2T_1 + K_2l_1T_2)/(K_1l_2 + K_2l_1)$
(D) $(K_1l_1T_1 + K_2l_2T_2)/(K_1l_1 + K_2l_2)$

11. A long metallic bar is carrying heat from one of its ends to the other end under steady-state. The variation of temperature θ along the length x of the bar from its hot end is best described by which of the following figures? **[2009]**

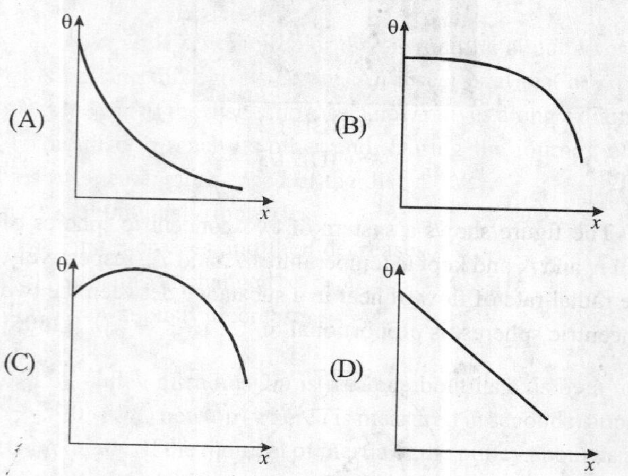

12. A liquid in a beaker has temperature $\theta(t)$ at time t and θ_0 is temperature of surroundings, then according to Newton's law of cooling the correct graph between $\log_e(\theta - \theta_0)$ and t is : **[2012]**

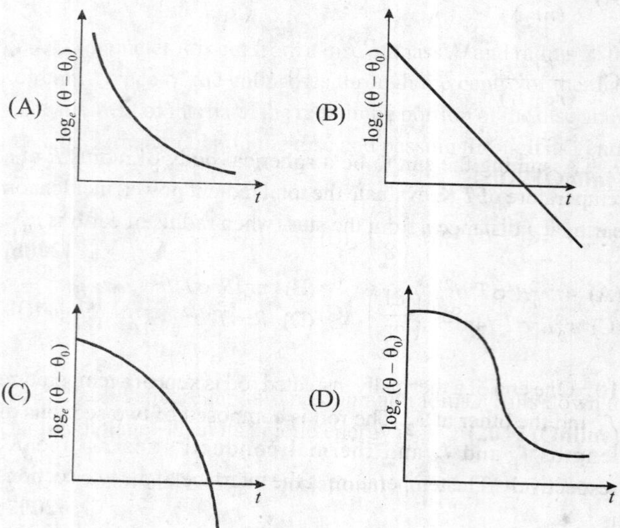

13. The heat radiated per unit area in 1 hour by a furnace whose temperature is 3000 K is ($\sigma = 5.7 \times 10^{-8}$ Wm^{-2} K^{-4}) : **[2012 (Online)]**

(A) 1.7×10^{10} J
(B) 1.1×10^{12} J
(C) 2.8×10^{8} J
(D) 4.6×10^{6} J

14. A large cylindrical rod of length L is made by joining two identical rods of copper and steel of length $\left(\frac{L}{2}\right)$ each. The rods are completely insulated from the surroundings. If the free end of copper rod is maintained at 100°C and that of steel at 0°C then the temperature of junction is (Thermal conductivity of copper is 9 times that of steel) : **[2012 (Online)]**

(A) 90°C
(B) 50°C
(C) 10°C
(D) 67°C

15. If a piece of metal is heated to temperature θ and then allowed to cool in a room which is at temperature θ_0 the graph between the temperature T of the metal and time t will be closed to : **[2013]**

(A)

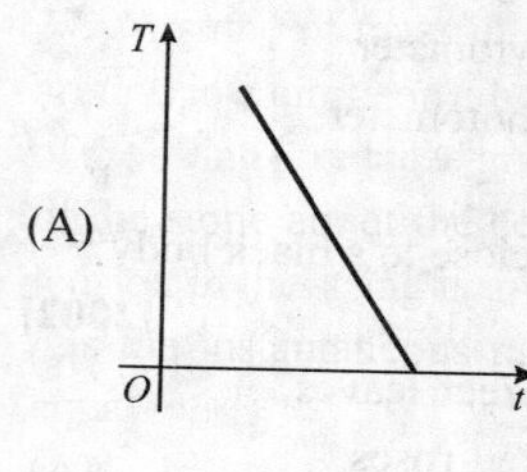

(B)

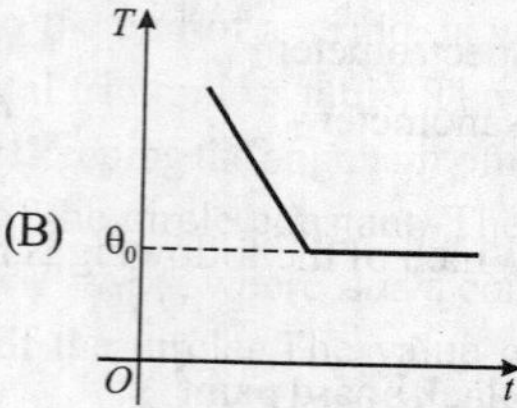

(C)

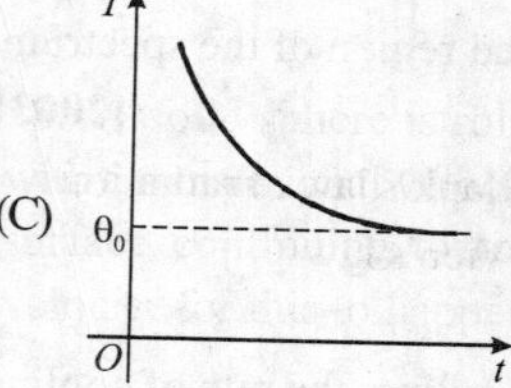

(D)

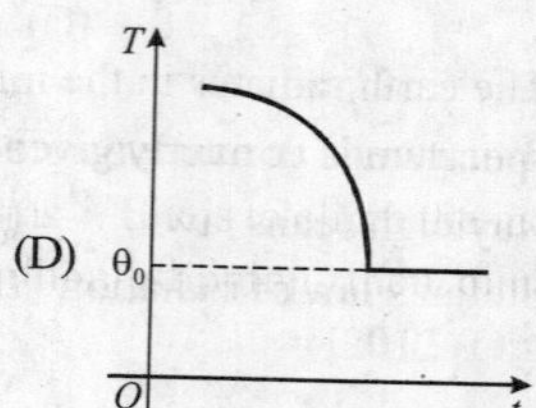

16. A mass of 50g of water in a closed vessel, with surroundings at a constant temperature takes 2 minutes to cool from 30°C to 25°C. A mass of 100 g of another liquid in an identical vessel with identical surroundings takes the same time to cool from 30° C to 25°C. The specific heat of the liquid is : (The water equivalent of the vessel is 30 g) : **[2013 (Online)]**

(A) 2.0 kcal/kg
(B) 7 kcal/kg
(C) 3 kcal/kg
(D) 0.5 kcal/kg

17. Three rods of Copper, Brass and Steel are welded together to form a Y-shaped structure. Area of cross-section of each rod = 4 cm^2. End of copper rod is maintained at 100°C where as ends of brass and steel are kept at 0°C. Lengths of the copper, brass and steel rods are 46, 13 and 12 cms respectively. The rods are thermally insulated from surroundings except at ends. Thermal conductivities of copper, brass and steel are 0.92, 0.26 and 0.12 CGS units respectively. Rate of heat flow through copper rod is : **[2014]**

(A) 1.2 cal/s
(B) 2.4 cal/s
(C) 4.8 cal/s
(D) 6.0 cal/s

18. A black coloured solid sphere of radius R and mass M is inside a cavity with vacuum inside. The walls of the cavity are maintained at temperature T_0. The initial temperature of the sphere is $3T_0$. If the specific heat of the material of the sphere varies as αT^3 per unit mass with the temperature T of the sphere, where α is a constant, then the time taken for the sphere to cool down to temperature $2T_0$ will be (σ is Stefan Boltzmann constant): **[2014 (Online)]**

(A) $\frac{M\alpha}{4\pi R^2\sigma}\ln\left(\frac{3}{2}\right)$ (B) $\frac{M\alpha}{4\pi R^2\sigma}\ln\left(\frac{16}{3}\right)$

(C) $\frac{M\alpha}{16\pi R^2\sigma}\ln\left(\frac{16}{3}\right)$ (D) $\frac{M\alpha}{16\pi R^2\sigma}\ln\left(\frac{3}{2}\right)$

19. A hot body, obeying Newton's law of cooling is cooling down from its peak value 80°C to an ambient temperature of 30°C. it takes 5 minutes in cooling down from 80°C to 40°C. How much time will it take to cool down from 62°C to 32°C? (Given In 2 = 0.693, In 5 = 1.609) : **[2014 (Online)]**

(A) 3.75 minutes (B) 8.6 minutes
(C) 9.6 minutes (D) 6.5 minutes

20. Hot water cools from 60°C to 50°C in the first 10 minutes and to 42°C in the next 10 minutes. The temperature of the surroundings is : **[2014 (Online)]**

(A) 25°C (B) 10°C
(C) 15°C (D) 20°C

* * * * *

CHAPTER

11 THERMODYNAMICS

11.1 LAWS OF THERMODYNAMICS

1. Which statement is incorrect ? **[2002]**

(A) All reversible cycles have same efficiency

(B) Reversible cycle has more efficiency than an irreversible one

(C) Carnot cycle is a reversible one

(D) Carnot cycle has the maximum efficiency in all cycles

2. Even carnot engine cannot give 100% efficiency because we cannot : **[2002]**

(A) Prevent radiation

(B) Find ideal sources

(C) Reach absolute zero temperature

(D) Eliminate friction

3. A carnot engine takes 3×10^6 cal of heat from a reservoir at 627 °C and gives it to a sink at 27 °C. The work done by the engine is : **[2003]**

(A) 4.2×10^6 J (B) 8.4×10^6 J

(C) 16.8×10^6 J (D) Zero

4. During an adiabatic process, the pressure of a gas is found to be proportional to the cube of its absolute temperature. The ratio C_P/C_V for the gas is : **[2003]**

(A) 4/3 (B) 2

(C) 5/3 (D) 3/2

5. Which of the following parameters does not characterise the thermodynamic state of matter ? **[2003]**

(A) Temperature (B) Pressure

(C) Work (D) Volume

6. "Heat cannot be itself flow from a body at lower temperature to a body at higher temperature" is a statement or consequence of : **[2003]**

(A) Second law of thermodynamics

(B) Conservation of momentum

(C) Conservation of mass

(D) First law of thermodynamics

7. Which of the following statements is correct for any thermodynamic system ? **[2004]**

(A) The internal energy changes in all processes

(B) Internal energy and entropy are state functions

(C) The change in entropy can never be zero

(D) The work done in an adiabatic process is always zero

8. A system goes from A to B via two processes I and II as shown in figure. If ΔU_1 and ΔU_2 are the changes in internal energies in the processes I and II respectively then : **[2005]**

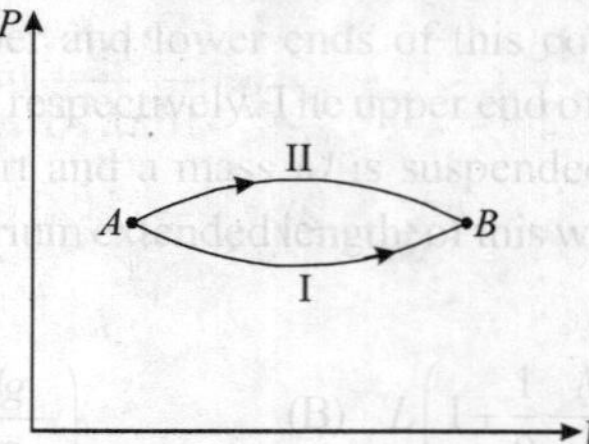

(A) $\Delta U_1 = \Delta U_2$

(B) Relation between ΔU_1 and ΔU_2 cannot be determined

(C) $\Delta U_2 > \Delta U_1$ (D) $\Delta U_2 < \Delta U_1$

9. The temperature-entropy diagram of a reversible engine cycle is given in the figure. Its efficiency is : **[2005]**

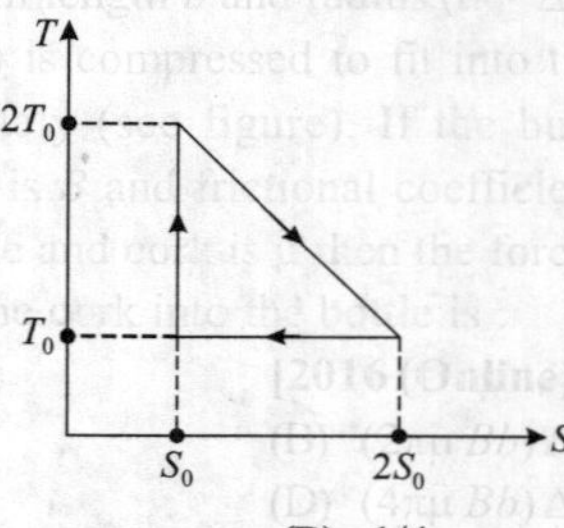

(A) 1/2 (B) 1/4

(C) 1/3 (D) 2/3

10. Which of the following is incorrect regarding the first law of thermodynamics ? **[2005]**

(A) It is applicable to any cyclic process

(B) It is a restatement of the principle of conservation of energy

(C) It introduces the concept of the internal energy

(D) It introduced the concept of the entropy

11. The work of 146 kJ is performed in order to compress one kilo mole of a gas adiabatically and in this process the temperature of the gas increases by 7°C. The gas is : $[R = 8.3 \text{ J mol}^{-1} \text{K}^{-1}]$ **[2006]**

(A) Diatomic (B) Triatomic

(C) A mixture of monoatomic and diatomic

(D) Monoatomic

12. When a system is taken from state i to state f along the path iaf, it is found that $Q = 50$ cal and $W = 20$ cal. Along the path ibf $Q = 36$ cal. W along the path ibf is : **[2007]**

(A) 6 cal (B) 16 cal
(C) 66 cal (D) 14 cal

13. A carnot engine, having an efficiency of $\eta = 1/10$ as heat engine, is used as a refrigerator. If the work done on the system is 10 J, the amount of energy absorbed from the reservoir at lower temperature is : **[2007]**
(A) 99 J (B) 90 J
(C) 1 J (D) 100 J

14. Directions : This question is based on the following paragraph. Two moles of helium gas are taken over the cycle *ABCDA*, as shown in the *P-T* diagram.

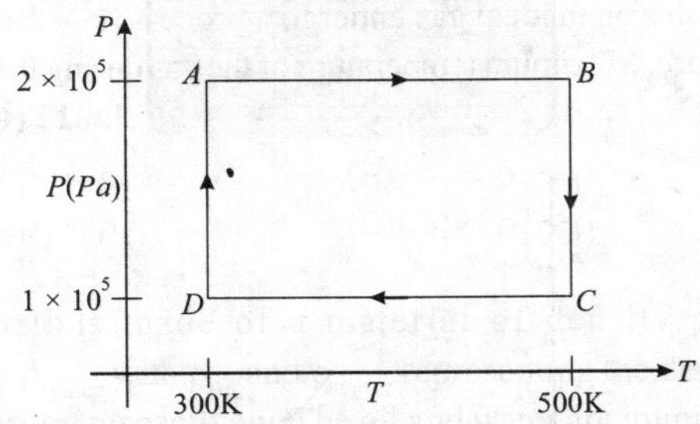

Assuming the gas to be ideal, the work done on the gas in taking it from *A* to *B* is : **[2009]**
(A) 400 R (B) 500 R
(C) 200 R (D) 300 R

15. Directions : This question is based on the following paragraph. Two moles of helium gas are taken over the cycle *ABCDA*, as shown in the *P-T* diagram. **[2009]**

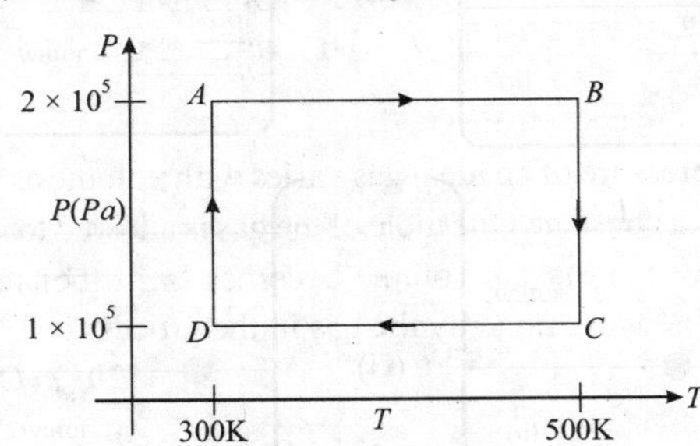

The work done on the gas in taking it from *D* to *A* is :
(A) −690 R (B) +690 R
(C) −414 R (D) +414 R

16. Directions : This question is based on the following paragraph.
Two moles of helium gas are taken over the cycle *ABCDA*, as shown in the *P-T* diagram.

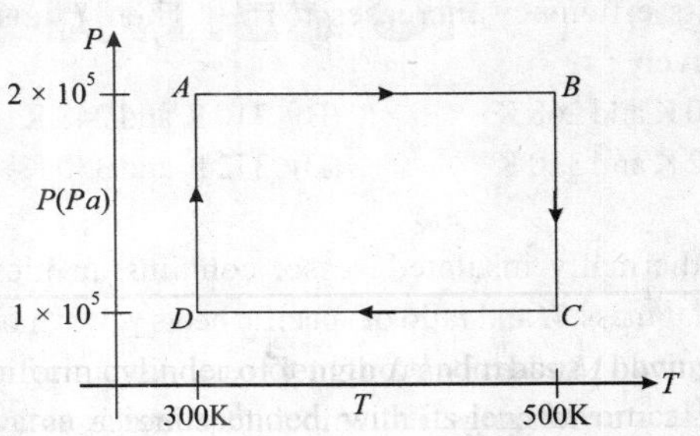

The net work done on the gas in the cycle *ABCDA* is : **[2009]**
(A) 1076 R (B) 1904 R
(C) Zero (D) 276 R

17. A diatomic ideal gas is used in a carnot engine as the working substance. If during the adiabatic expansion part of the cycle the volume of the gas increases from V to $32V$, the efficiency of the engine is : **[2010]**
(A) 0.25 (B) 0.5
(C) 0.75 (D) 0.99

18. 100 g of water is heated from 30°C to 50°C Ignoring the slight expansion of the water, the change in its internal energy is (specific heat of water is 4184 J/kg/K) : **[2011]**
(A) 84 kJ (B) 2.1 kJ
(C) 4.2 kJ (D) 8.4 kJ

19. A container with insulating walls is divided into two equal parts by a partition fitted with a valve. One part is filled with an ideal gas at a pressure P and temperature T, whereas the other part is completely evacuated. If the valve is suddenly opened, the pressure and temperature of the gas will be : **[2011]**
(A) $\frac{P}{2}, T$ (B) $\frac{P}{2}, \frac{T}{2}$
(C) P, T (D) $P, \frac{T}{2}$

20. The specific heat capacity of a metal at low temperature (T) is given as $C_p(\text{kJK}^{-1}\,\text{kg}^{-1}) = 32\left(\frac{T}{400}\right)^3$. A 100 gram vessel of this metal is to be cooled from 20 K to 4 K by a special refrigerator operating at room temperature (27°C). The amount of work required to cool the vessel is : **[2011]**
(A) Equal to 0.002 kJ
(B) Greater than 0.148 kJ
(C) Between 0.148 kJ and 0.028 kJ
(D) Less than 0.028 kJ

21. A Carnot engine operating between temperatures T_1 and T_2 has efficiency has efficiency 1/6. When T_2 is lowered by

62 K, its efficiency increases to 1/3. Then T_1 and T_2 are, respectively : **[2011]**

(A) 330 K and 268 K (B) 310 K and 248 K
(C) 372 K and 310 K (D) 372 K and 330 K

22. A thermally insulated vessel contains an ideal gas of molecular mass M and ratio of specific heats γ. It is moving with speed v and is suddenly brought to rest. Assuming no heat is lost to the surroundings, its temperature increases by : **[2011]**

(A) $\frac{\gamma M v^2}{2R}$ K (B) $\frac{(\gamma-1)}{2R} Mv^2$ K

(C) $\frac{(\gamma-1)}{2(\gamma+1)R} Mv^2$ K (D) $\frac{(\gamma-1)}{2\gamma R} Mv^2$ K

23. A Carnot engine, whose efficiency is 40% takes in heat from a source maintained at a temperature of 500 K. It is desired to have an engine of efficiency 60%. Then, the intake temperature for the same exhaust (sink) temperature must be : **[2012]**

(A) 600 K
(B) Efficiency of Carnot engine cannot be made larger than 50%
(C) 1200 K
(D) 750 K

24. Helium gas goes through a cycle $ABCDA$ (consisting of two isochoric and two isobaric lines) as shown in figure. Efficiency of this cycle is nearly (Assume the gas to be close to ideal gas) **[2012]**

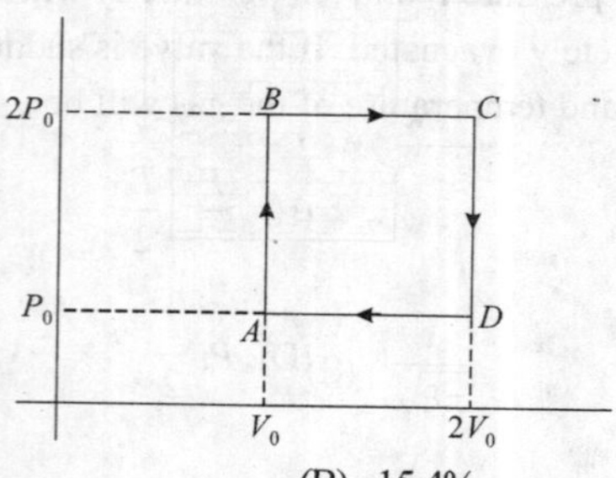

(A) 12.5% (B) 15.4%
(C) 9.1% (D) 10.5%

25. This question has Statement-1 and Statement-2. Of the four choices given after the Statements, choose the one that best describes the two Statements. **[2012 (Online)]**

Statement-1 : An inventor claims to have constructed an engine that has an efficiency of 30% when operated between the boiling and freezing points of water. This is not possible.

Statement-2 : The efficiency of a real engine is always less than the efficiency of a carnot engine operating between the same two temperatures.

(A) Statement-1 is true; Statement-2 is true, Statement-2 not the correct explanation of Statement-1
(B) Statement-1 is true, Statement-2 is false
(C) Statement-1 is false, Statement-2 is true
(D) Statement-1 is true, Statement-2 is true, Statement-2 is the correct explanation of Statement-1

26. This question has Statement-1 and Statement-2. Of the four choices given after the Statements, choose the one that best describes the two Statements. **[2012 (Online)]**

Statement-1 : In an adiabatic process, change in internal energy of a gas is equal to work done on/by the gas in the process.

Statement-2 : The temperature of a gas remains constant in an adiabatic process.

(A) Statement-1 is true; Statement-2 is true, Statement-2 is a correct explanation of Statement-1
(B) Statement-1 is true, Statement-2 is true
(C) Statement-1 is false, Statement-2 is true
(D) Statement-1 is false, Statement-2 is true, Statement-2 is not a correct explanation of Statement-1

27. n moles of an ideal gas undergo a process $A \to B$ as shown in the figure. Maximum temperature of the gas during the process is : **[2012 (Online)]**

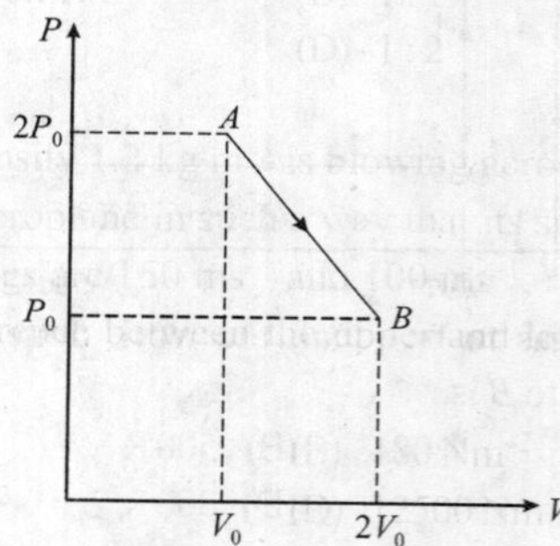

(A) $\frac{9P_0V_0}{nR}$ (B) $\frac{3P_0V_0}{2nR}$

(C) $\frac{9P_0V_0}{2nR}$ (D) $\frac{9P_0V_0}{4nR}$

28. The pressure of an ideal gas varies with volume as $P = \alpha V$, where α is a constant. One mole of the gas is allowed to undergo expansion such that its volume becomes 'm' times its initial volume. The work done by the gas in the process is : **[2012 (Online)]**

(A) $\frac{\alpha V}{2}(m^2-1)$ (B) $\frac{\alpha^2 V^2}{2}(m^2-1)$

(C) $\frac{\alpha}{2}(m^2-1)$ (D) $\frac{\alpha V^2}{2}(m^2-1)$

29. An ideal monatomic gas with pressure P, volume V and temperature T is expanded isothermally to a volume $2V$ and a final pressure P_i. If the same gas is expanded adiabatically to a volume $2V$, the final pressure is P_a. The ratio $\frac{P_a}{P_i}$ is : **[2012 (Online)]**

(A) $2^{-1/3}$ (B) $2^{1/3}$
(C) $2^{2/3}$ (D) $2^{-2/3}$

30. A given ideal gas with $\gamma = \frac{C_p}{C_v} = 1.5$ at a temperature T. If the gas is compressed adiabatically to one-fourth of its initial volume, the final temperature will be : **[2012 (Online)]**

(A) $2\sqrt{2}T$ (B) $4T$
(C) $2T$ (D) $8T$

31. The door of a working refrigerator is left open in a well insulated room. The temperature of air in the room will : **[2012 (Online)]**

(A) Decrease
(B) Increase in winters and decrease in summers
(C) Remains the same
(D) Increase

32. The above *p-v* diagram represents the thermodynamic cycle of an engine, operating with an ideal monoatomic gas. The amount of heat, extracted from the source in a single cycle is : **[2013]**

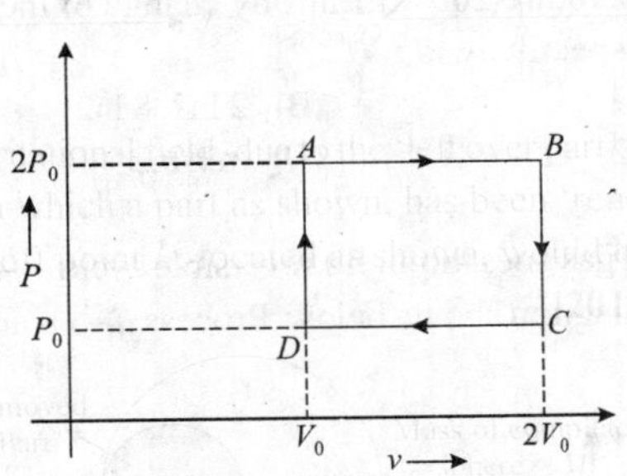

(A) p_0v_0 (B) $\left(\frac{13}{2}\right)p_0v_0$
(C) $\left(\frac{11}{2}\right)p_0v_0$ (D) $4p_0v_0$

33. An ideal gas at atmospheric pressure is adiabatically compressed so that its density becomes 32 times of its initial value. If the final pressure of gas is 128 atmospheres, the value of 'γ' of the gas is : **[2013 (Online)]**

(A) 1.5 (B) 1.4
(C) 1.3 (D) 1.6

34. A certain amount of gas is taken through a cyclic process (*A, B, C, D, A*) that has two isobars, one isochore and one isothermal. The cycle can be represented on a *P-V* indicator diagram as : **[2013 (Online)]**

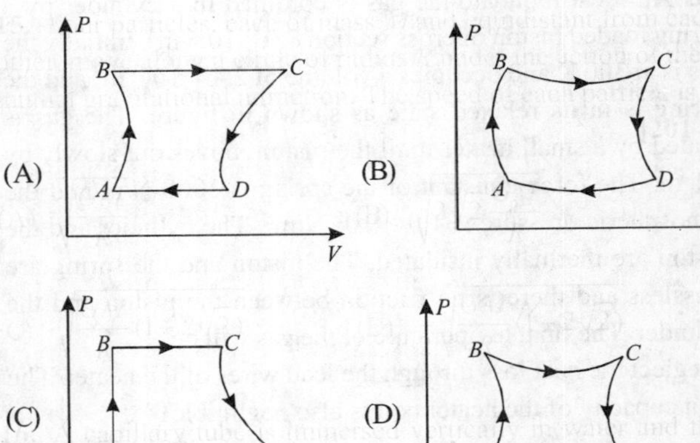

35. In the isothermal expansion of 10 g of gas from volume V to 2 V the work done by the gas is 575 J. What is the root mean square speed of the molecules of the gas at that temperature ? **[2013 (Online)]**

(A) 398 m/s (B) 520 m/s
(C) 499 m/s (D) 532 m/s

36. One mole of diatomic ideal gas undergoes a cyclic process *ABC* as shown in figure. The process *BC* is adiabatic. The temperatures at *A, B* and *C* are 400 K, 800 K and 600 K respectively. Choose the correct statement : **[2014]**

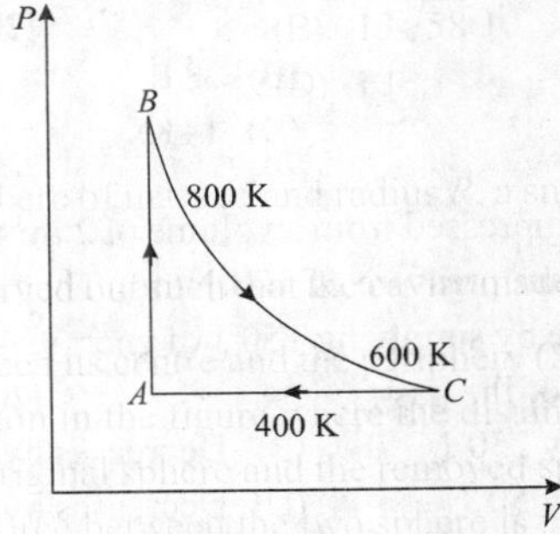

(A) The change in internal energy in whole cyclic process is 250 R
(B) The change in internal energy in the process *CA* is 700 R
(C) The change in internal energy in the process *AB* is –350 R
(D) The change in internal energy in the process *BC* is –500 R

37. The equation of state for a gas is given by $PV = nRT + \alpha V$, where n is the number of moles and α is a positive constant. The initial temperature and pressure of one mole of the gas contained in a cylinder are T_0 and P_0 respectively. The work done by the gas when its temperature doubles isobarically will be : **[2014 (Online)]**

(A) $\frac{P_0T_0R}{P_0 - \alpha}$ (B) $\frac{P_0T_0R}{P_0 + \alpha}$
(C) $P_0T_0R \ln 2$ (D) P_0T_0R

38. An ideal monoatomic gas is confined in a cylinder by a spring loaded piston of cross section 8.0×10^{-3} m^2. Initially the gas is at 300 K and occupies a volume of 2.4×10^{-3} m^3 and the spring is in its relaxed state as shown in figure. The gas is heated by a small heater until the piston moves out slowly by 0.1 m. The force constant of the spring is 8000 N/m and the atmospheric pressure is 1.0×10^5 N/m^2. The cylinder and the piston are thermally insulated. The piston and the spring are massless and there is no friction between the piston and the cylinder. The final temperature of the gas will be :
(Neglect the heat loss through the lead wires of the heater. The heat capacity of the heater coil is also negligible) : **[2014 (Online)]**

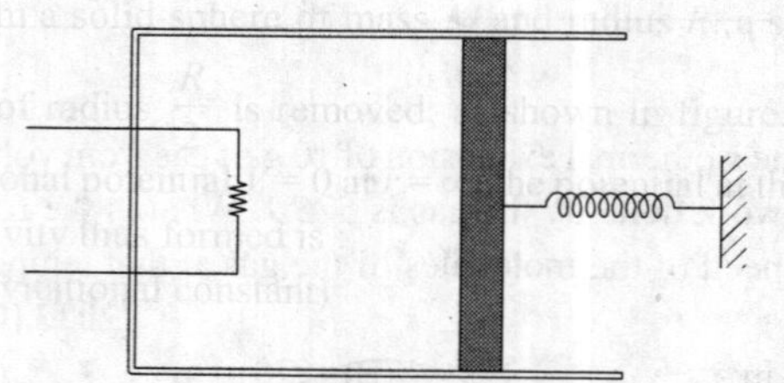

(A) 300 K (B) 800 K
(C) 500 K (D) 1000 K

39. During an adiabatic compression, 830 J of work is done on 2 moles of a diatomic ideal gas to reduce its volume by 50%. The change in its temperature is nearly : $[R = 8.3\ \text{JK}^{-1}\ \text{mol}^{-1}]$ **[2014 (Online)]**

(A) 40 K (B) 33 K
(C) 20 K (D) 14 K

40. A gas is compressed from a volume of 2 m^3 to a volume of 1 m^3 at a constant pressure of 100 N/m^2. Then it is heated at constant volume by supplying 150 J of energy. As a result, the internal energy of the gas : **[2014 (Online)]**

(A) Increases by 250 J (B) Decreases by 250 J
(C) Increases by 50 J (D) Decreases by 50 J

41. A Carnot engine absorbs 1000 J of heat energy from a reservoir at 127°C and rejects 600 J of heat energy during each cycle. The efficiency of engine and temperature of sink will be : **[2014 (Online)]**

(A) 20% and – 43°C (B) 40% and – 33°C
(C) 50% and – 20°C (D) 70% and – 10°C

42. Consider an ideal gas confined in an isolated closed chamber. As the gas undergoes an adiabatic expansion, the average time of collision between molecules increases as V^q, where V is the volume of the gas. The value of q is $\left(\gamma = \frac{C_p}{C_v}\right)$: **[2015]**

(A) $\frac{3\gamma+5}{6}$ (B) $\frac{3\gamma-5}{6}$
(C) $\frac{\gamma+1}{2}$ (D) $\frac{\gamma-1}{2}$

43. Consider a spherical shell of radius R at temperature T. The black body radiation inside it can be considered as an ideal gas of photons with internal energy per unit volume $u = \frac{U}{V} \propto T^4$ and pressure $p = \frac{1}{3}\left(\frac{U}{V}\right)$. If the shell now undergoes an adiabatic expansion the relation between T and R is : **[2015]**

(A) $T \propto \frac{1}{R}$ (B) $T \propto \frac{1}{R^3}$
(C) $T \propto e^{-R}$ (D) $T \propto e^{-3R}$

44. A solid body of constant heat capacity 1 J/°C is being heated by keeping it in contact with reservoirs in two ways : **[2015]**

(i) Sequentially keeping in contact with 2 reservoirs such that each reservoir supplied same amount of heat
(ii) Sequentially keeping in contact with 8 reservoirs such that each reservoir supplies same amount of heat

In both the cases body is brought from initial temperature 100°C to final temperature 200°C. Entropy change of the body in the two cases respectively is :

(A) ln2, 2 ln2 (B) 2 ln2, 8 ln2
(C) ln2, 4 ln2 (D) ln2, ln2

45. An ideal gas goes through a reversible cycle $a \to b \to c \to d$ has the V-T diagram shown below. Process $d \to a$ and $b \to c$ are adiabatic.

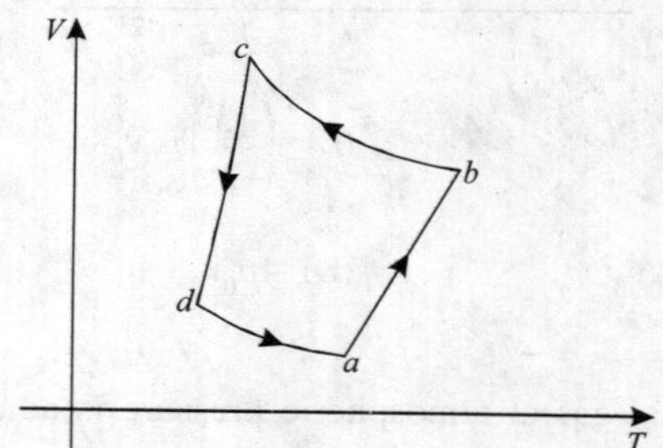

The corresponding P-V diagram for the process is (all figures are schematic and not drawn to scale) : **[2015 (Online)]**

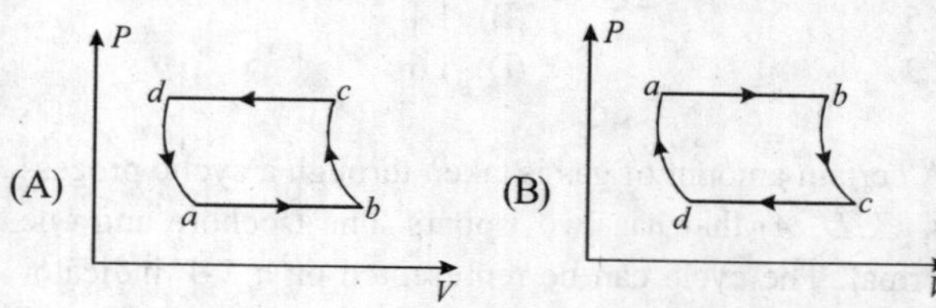

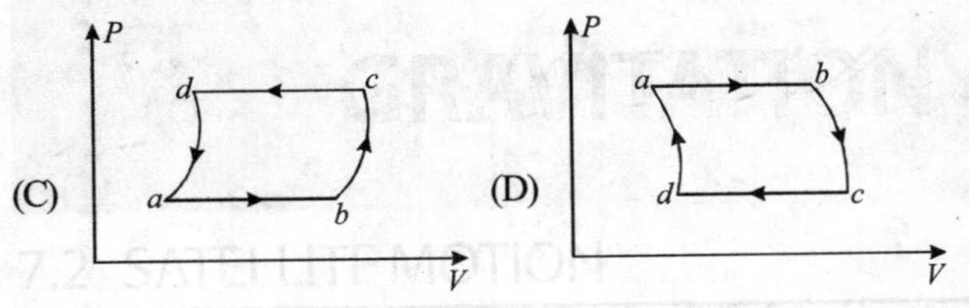

46. '*n*' moles of an ideal gas undergoes a process $A \to B$ as shown in the figure. The maximum temperature of the gas during the process will be : **[2016]**

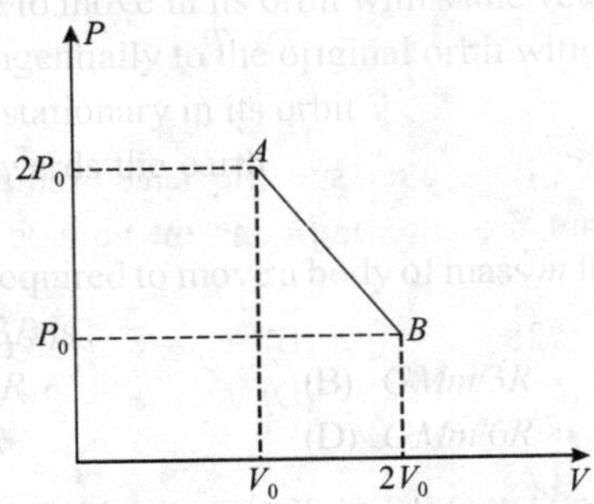

(A) $\frac{9P_0V_0}{4nR}$ (B) $\frac{3P_0V_0}{2nR}$

(C) $\frac{9P_0V_0}{2nR}$ (D) $\frac{9P_0V_0}{nR}$

47. An ideal gas undergoes a quasi static, reversible process in which its molar heat capacity C remains constant. If during this process the relation of pressure P and volume V is given by PV^n = constant, then n is given by (Here C_P and C_V are molar specific heat at constant pressure and constant volume, respectively) : **[2016]**

(A) $n = \frac{C_P}{C_V}$ (B) $n = \frac{C - C_P}{C - C_V}$

(C) $n = \frac{C_P - C}{C - C_V}$ (D) $n = \frac{C - C_V}{C - C_P}$

48. A Carnot freezer takes heat from water at 0°C inside it and rejects it to the room at a temperature of 27°C. The latent heat of ice is 336×10^3 J kg^{-1}. If 5 kg of water at 0°C is converted into ice at 0°C by the freezer, then the energy consumed by the freezer is closed to : **[2016 (Online)]**

(A) 1.51×10^5 J (B) 1.68×10^6 J

(C) 1.71×10^7 J (D) 1.67×10^5 J

49. The ratio of work done by an ideal monoatomic gas to the heat supplied to it in an isobaric process is : **[2016 (Online)]**

(A) $\frac{2}{5}$ (B) $\frac{3}{2}$

(C) $\frac{3}{5}$ (D) $\frac{2}{3}$

50. 200 g water is heated from 40°C to 60°C. Ignoring the slight expansion of water, the change in its internal energy is close to (Given specific heat of water = 4184 J/kg K) : **[2016 (Online)]**

(A) 167.4 kJ (B) 8.4 kJ

(C) 4.2 kJ (D) 16.7 kJ

* * * * *

CHAPTER

12 KINETIC THEORY

12.1 KINETIC THEORY OF GASES

1. Cooking gas containers are kept in a lorry moving with uniform speed. The temperature of the gas molecules inside will : **[2002]**

(A) Increase (B) Decrease
(C) Remains same
(D) Decrease for some, while increase for others

2. At what temperature is the rms velocity of a hydrogen molecule equal to that of an oxygen molecules at 47° C? **[2002]**

(A) 80 K (B) –73 K
(C) 3 K (D) 20 K

3. 1 mole of a gas with $\gamma = 7/5$ is mixed with 1 mole of a gas with $\gamma = 5/3$, then the value of γ for the resulting mixture is : **[2002]**

(A) 7/5 (B) 2/5
(C) 24/16 (D) 12/7

4. Two thermally insulated vessels 1 and 2 are filled with air at temperatures (T_1, T_2), volume (V_1, V_2) and pressure (P_1, P_2) respectively. If the valve joining the two vessels is opened, the temperature inside the vessel at equilibrium will be : **[2004]**

(A) $T_1 + T_2$ (B) $\frac{(T_1 + T_2)}{2}$

(C) $\frac{T_1T_2(P_1V_1 + P_2V_2)}{P_1V_1T_2 + P_2V_2T_1}$ (D) $\frac{T_1T_2(P_1V_1 + P_2V_2)}{P_1V_1T_1 + P_2V_2T_2}$

5. One mole of ideal monoatomic gas ($\gamma = 5/3$) is mixed with one mole of diatomic gas ($\gamma = 7/5$). What is γ for the mixture ? γ denotes the ratio of specific heat at constant pressure, to that at constant volume : **[2004]**

(A) 3/2 (B) 23/15
(C) 35/23 (D) 4/3

6. A gaseous mixture consists of 16 g of helium and 16 g of oxygen. The ratio C_p/C_v of the mixture is : **[2005]**

(A) 1.59 (B) 1.62
(C) 1.4 (D) 1.54

7. Two rigid boxes containing different ideal gases are placed on a table. Box A contains one mole of nitrogen at temperature T_0, while box B contains one mole of helium at temperature (7/3) T_0. The boxes are then put into thermal contact with each other, and heat flows between them until the gases reach a common final temperature (Ignore the heat capacity of boxes). Then, the final temperature of gases, T_f in terms of T_0 is : **[2006]**

(A) $T_f = \frac{3}{7}T_0$ (B) $T_f = \frac{7}{3}T_0$

(C) $T_f = \frac{3}{2}T_0$ (D) $T_f = \frac{5}{2}T_0$

8. If C_P and C_V denote the specific heats of nitrogen per unit mass at constant pressure and constant volume respectively, then : **[2007]**

(A) $C_P - C_V = R/28$ (B) $C_P - C_V = R/14$
(C) $C_P - C_V = R$ (D) $C_P - C_V = 28R$

9. An insulated container of gas has two chambers separated by an insulating partition. One of the chambers has volume V_1 and contains ideal gas at pressure P_1 and temperature T_1. The other chamber has volume V_2 and contains ideal gas at pressure P_2 and temperature T_2. If the partition is removed without doing any work on the gas, the final equilibrium temperature of the gas in the container will be : **[2008]**

(A) $\frac{T_1T_2(P_1V_1 + P_2V_2)}{P_1V_1T_2 + P_2V_2T_1}$ (B) $\frac{P_1V_1T_1 + P_2V_2T_2}{P_1V_1 + P_2V_2}$

(C) $\frac{P_1V_1T_2 + P_2V_2T_1}{P_1V_1 + P_2V_2}$ (D) $\frac{T_1T_2(P_1V_1 + P_2V_2)}{P_1V_1T_1 + P_2V_2T_2}$

10. One kg of a diatomic gas is at a pressure of 8×10^4 N/m^2. The density of the gas is 4 kg/m^3. What is the energy of the gas due to its thermal motion ? **[2009]**

(A) 6×10^4 J (B) 7×10^4 J
(C) 3×10^4 J (D) 5×10^4 J

11. Three perfect gases at absolute temperatures T_1, T_2 and T_3 are mixed. The masses of molecules are m_1, m_2, and m_3 and the number of molecules are n_1, n_2 and n_3 respectively. Assuming no loss of energy, then final temperature of the mixture is : **[2011]**

(A) $\frac{n_1T_1^2 + n_2T_2^2 + n_3T_3^2}{n_1T_1 + n_2T_2 + n_3T_3}$ (B) $\frac{n_1^2T_1^2 + n_2^2T_2^2 + n_3^2T_3^2}{n_1T_1 + n_2T_2 + n_3T_3}$

(C) $\frac{T_1 + T_2 + T_3}{3}$ (D) $\frac{n_1T_1 + n_2T_2 + n_3T_3}{n_1 + n_2 + n_3}$

12. A perfect gas at 27°C is heated at constant pressure so as to double its volume. The final temperature of the gas will be, close to : **[2012 (Online)]**

(A) 327°C (B) 200°C

(C) 54°C (D) 300°C

13. A thin tube sealed at both ends in 100 cm long. It lies horizontally, the middle 20 cm containing mercury and two equal ends containing air at standard atmospheric pressure. If the tube is now turned to a vertical position, by what amount will the mercury be displaced ? (Given : cross-section of the tube can be assumed to be uniform) **[2013 (Online)]**

(A) 2.95 cm

(B) 5.18 cm

(C) 8.65 cm

(D) 0.0 cm

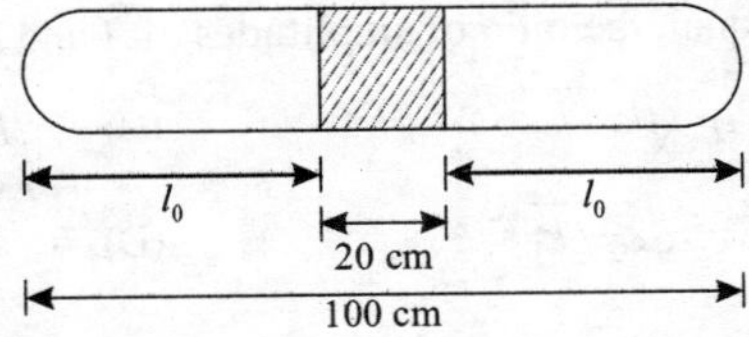

14. Figure shows the variation in temperature (ΔT) with the amount of heat supplied (Q) in an isobaric process corresponding to a monoatomic (M), diatomic (D) and a polyatomic (P) gas. The initial state of all the gases are the same and the scales for the two axes coincide. Ignoring vibrational degrees of freedom, the lines a, b and c respectively correspond to : **[2013 (Online)]**

(A) P, M and D

(B) M, D and P

(C) P, D and M

(D) D, M and P

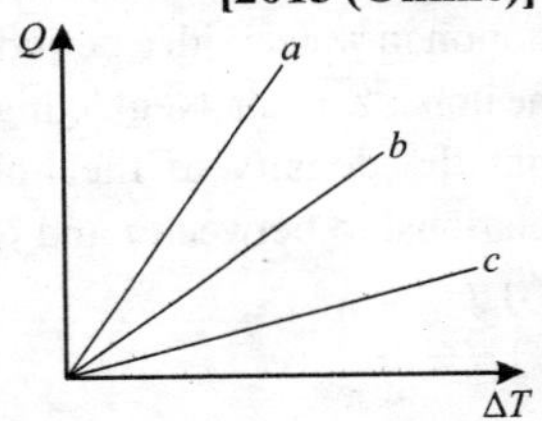

15. There are two identical chambers, completely thermally insulated from surroundings. Both chambers have a partition wall dividing the chambers in two compartments. Compartment 1 is filled with an ideal gas and Compartment 3 is filled with a real gas. Compartments 2 and 4 are vacuum. A small hole (orifice) is made in the partition walls and the gases are allowed to expand in vacuum. **[2013 (Online)]**

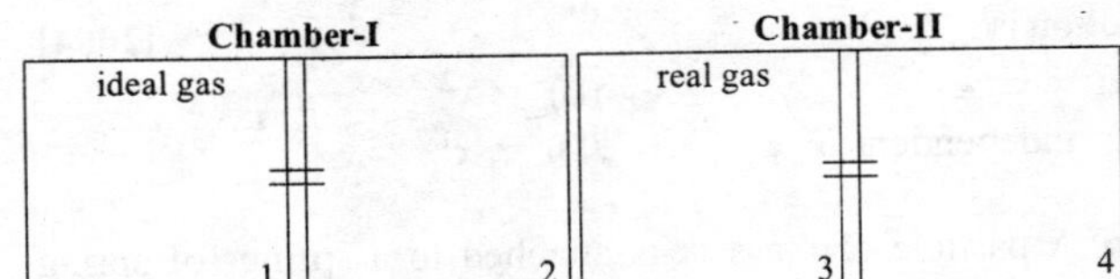

Statement-1 : No change in temperature of the gas takes place when ideal gas expands in vacuum. However, the temperature of real gas goes down (cooling) when it expands in vacuum.

Statement-2 : The internal energy of an ideal gas in only kinetic. The internal energy of a real gas is kinetic as well as potential.

(A) Statement-1 is false and Statement-2 is true

(B) Statement-1 and Statement-2 both are true. Statement-2 is the correct explanation of Statement-1

(C) Statement-1 is true and Statement-2 is false

(D) Statement-1 and Statement-2 both are true. Statement-2 is not correct explanation of Statement-1

16. An open glass tube is immersed in mercury in such a way that a length of 8 cm extends above the mercury level. The open end of the tube is then closed and sealed and the tube is raised vertically up by additional 46 cm. What will be length of the air column above mercury in the tube now ?
(Atmospheric pressure = 76 cm of Hg) **[2014]**

(A) 16 cm (B) 22 cm

(C) 38 cm (D) 6 cm

17. Modern vacuum pumps can evacuate a vessel down to a pressure of 4.0×10^{-15} atom. At room temperature (300 K). Taking $R = 8.0\ \text{JK}^{-1}\ \text{mole}^{-1}$, atom $= 10^5\ Pa$ and $N_{\text{Avogadro}} = 6 \times 10^{23}\ \text{mole}^{-1}$, the mean distance between molecules of gas in an evacuated vessel will be of the order of : **[2014 (Online)]**

(A) 0.2 μm (B) 0.2 mm

(C) 0.2 cm (D) 0.2 nm

18. At room temperature a diatomic gas is found to have an r.m.s. speed of 1930 ms^{-1}. The gas is : **[2014 (Online)]**

(A) H_2 (B) Cl_2

(C) O_2 (D) F_2

19. A gas molecule of mass M at the surface of the earth has kinetic energy equivalent to 0°C. If it were to go up straight without colliding with any other molecules, how high it would rise ? Assume that the height attained in much less than radius of the earth. (k_B is Boltzmann constant) : **[2014 (Online)]**

(A) 0 (B) $\dfrac{273k_B}{2Mg}$

(C) $\dfrac{546k_B}{3Mg}$ (D) $\dfrac{819k_B}{2Mg}$

20. Using equipartition of energy, the specific heat (in J kg^{-1} K^{-1}) of aluminium at room temperature can be estimated to be (atomic weight of aluminium = 27) : **[2015 (Online)]**

(A) 410 (B) 25

(C) 1850 (D) 925

21. In an ideal gas at temperature T, the average force that a molecule applies on the walls of a closed container depends on T as T^q. A good estimate for q is : **[2015 (Online)]**

(A) $\dfrac{1}{2}$ (B) 2

(C) 1 (D) $\dfrac{1}{4}$

* * * * *

CHAPTER

13 OSCILLATIONS

13.1 SIMPLE HARMONIC MOTION

1. If a spring has time period T, and is cut into n equal parts, then the time period of each part will be : **[2002]**

(A) $T\sqrt{n}$ (B) $\frac{T}{\sqrt{n}}$

(C) nT (D) T

2. In a simple harmonic oscillator, at the mean position : **[2002]**

(A) Kinetic energy is minimum, potential energy is maximum

(B) Both kinetic and potential energies are maximum

(C) Kinetic energy is maximum, potential energy is minimum

(D) Both kinetic and potential energies are minimum

3. A child swinging on a swing in sitting position, stands up, then the time period of the swing will : **[2002]**

(A) Increase

(B) Decrease

(C) Remain same

(D) Increase if the child is long and decrease if the child is short

4. A mass M is suspended from a spring of negligible mass. The spring is pulled a little and then released so that the mass executes SHM of time period T. If the mass is increased by m, the time period becomes $5T/3$, then the ratio of m/M is :**[2003]**

(A) $\frac{3}{5}$ (B) $\frac{25}{9}$

(C) $\frac{16}{9}$ (D) $\frac{5}{3}$

5. The displacement of a particle varies according to the relation $x = 4(\cos\pi t + \sin\pi t)$. The amplitude of the particle is : **[2003]**

(A) -4 (B) 4

(C) $4\sqrt{2}$ (D) 8

6. A body executes simple harmonic motion. The potential energy (PE), the kinetic energy (KE) and total energy (TE) are measured as function of displacement x. Which of the following statements is true ? **[2003]**

(A) KE is maximum when $x = 0$

(B) TE is zero when $x = 0$

(C) KE is maximum when x is maximum

(D) PE is maximum when $x = 0$

7. Two particles A and B of equal masses are suspended from two massless springs of spring constants k_1 and k_2, respectively. If the maximum velocities, during oscillations are equal, the ratio of amplitudes of A and B is : **[2003]**

(A) $\sqrt{k_1/k_2}$ (B) k_1/k_2

(C) $\sqrt{k_2/k_1}$ (D) k_2/k_1

8. The length of a simple pendulum executing simple harmonic motion is increased by 21%. The percentage increase in the time period of the pendulum of increased length is : **[2003]**

(A) 11% (B) 21%

(C) 42% (D) 10%

9. The bob of a simple pendulum executes simple harmonic motion in water with a period t, while the period of oscillation of the bob is t_0 in air. Neglecting frictional force of water and given that the density of the bob is $(4/3) \times 1000$ kg/m^3. What relationship between t and t_0 is true? **[2004]**

(A) $t = t_0$ (B) $t = t_0/2$

(C) $t = 2t_0$ (D) $t = 4t_0$

10. A particle at the end of a spring executes simple harmonic motion with a period t_1, while the corresponding period for another spring is t_2. If the period of oscillation with the two springs in series is T, then : **[2004]**

(A) $T = t_1 + t_2$ (B) $T^2 = t_1^2 + t_2^2$

(C) $T^{-1} = t_1^{-1} + t_2^{-1}$ (D) $T^{-2} = t_1^{-2} + t_2^{-2}$

11. The total energy of a particle, executing simple harmonic motion is : **[2004]**

(A) $\propto x$ (B) $\propto x^2$

(C) independent of x (D) $\propto x^{1/2}$

12. A particle of mass m is attached to a spring (of spring constant k) and has a natural angular frequency ω_0. An external force $F(t)$ proportional to $\cos\omega t$ ($\omega \neq \omega_0$) is applied to the oscillator. The time displacement of the oscillator will be proportional to : **[2004]**

(A) $\frac{m}{\omega_0^2 - \omega^2}$ (B) $\frac{1}{m(\omega_0^2 - \omega^2)}$

(C) $\frac{1}{m(\omega_0^2 + \omega^2)}$ (D) $\frac{m}{(\omega_0^2 + \omega^2)}$

13. In forced oscillation of a particle the amplitude is maximum for a frequency ω_1 of the force while the energy is maximum for a frequency ω_2 of the force; then : **[2004]**
(A) $\omega_1 < \omega_2$ when damping is small and $\omega_1 > \omega_2$ when damping is large
(B) $\omega_1 > \omega_2$
(C) $\omega_1 = \omega_2$
(D) $\omega_1 < \omega_2$

14. A particle of mass 0.3 kg is subjected to a force $F = -kx$ with $k = 15$ N/m. What will be its initial acceleration, if it is released from a point 20 cm away from the origin ? **[2005]**
(A) 3 m/s^2 (B) 15 m/s^2
(C) 5 m/s^2 (D) 10 m/s^2

15. The function $\sin^2(\omega t)$ represents : **[2005]**
(A) A periodic, but not simple harmonic, motion with a period $2\pi/\omega$
(B) A periodic, but not simple harmonic, motion with a period π/ω
(C) A simple harmonic motion with a period $2\pi/\omega$
(D) A simple harmonic motion with a period π/ω

16. If a simple harmonic motion is represented by $\frac{d^2x}{dt^2} + \alpha x = 0$, its time period is : **[2005]**
(A) $\frac{2\pi}{\alpha}$ (B) $\frac{2\pi}{\sqrt{\alpha}}$
(C) $2\pi\alpha$ (D) $2\pi\sqrt{\alpha}$

17. The bob of a simple pendulum is a spherical hollow ball filled with water. A plugged hole near the bottom of the oscillating bob gets suddenly unplugged. During observation, till water is coming out, the time period of oscillation would : **[2005]**
(A) First increase and then decrease to the original value
(B) First decrease and then increase to the original value
(C) Remain unchanged
(D) Increase towards a saturation value

18. Two simple harmonic motions are represented by the equations $y_1 = 0.1 \sin\left(100\pi t + \frac{\pi}{3}\right)$ and $y_2 = 0.1 \cos 100\pi t$. The phase difference of the velocity of particle 1, with respect to the velocity of particle 2 is : **[2005]**
(A) $\frac{-\pi}{6}$ (B) $\frac{\pi}{3}$
(C) $\frac{-\pi}{3}$ (D) $\frac{\pi}{6}$

19. The maximum velocity of a particle, executing simple harmonic motion with an amplitude 7 mm, is 4.4 m/s. The period of oscillation is : **[2006]**
(A) 0.01 s (B) 10 s
(C) 0.1 s (D) 100 s

20. Starting from the origin a body oscillates simple harmonically with a period of 2s. After what time will its kinetic energy be 75% of the total energy ? **[2006]**
(A) $\frac{1}{6}$ s (B) $\frac{1}{4}$ s
(C) $\frac{1}{3}$ s (D) $\frac{1}{12}$ s

21. A coin is placed on a horizontal platform which undergoes vertical simple harmonic motion of angular frequency ω. The amplitude of oscillation is gradually increased. The coin will leave contact with the platform for the first time : **[2006]**
(A) At the mean position of the platform
(B) For an amplitude of $\frac{g}{\omega^2}$
(C) For an amplitude of $\frac{g^2}{\omega^2}$
(D) At the highest position on the platform

22. The displacement of an object attached to a spring and executing simple harmonic motion is given by $x = 2 \times 10^{-2} \cos \pi t$ metre. The time at which the maximum speed first occurs is : **[2007]**
(A) 0.5 s (B) 0.75 s
(C) 0.125 s (D) 0.25 s

23. A point mass oscillates along the x-axis according to the law $x = x_0 \cos(\omega t - \pi/4)$ If the acceleration of the particle is written as- $a = A\cos(\omega t + \delta)$, then : **[2007]**
(A) $A = x_0, \delta = -\pi/4$ (B) $A = x_0\omega^2, \delta = \pi/4$
(C) $A = x_0\omega^2, \delta = -\pi/4$ (D) $A = x_0\omega^2, \delta = 3\pi/4$

24. Two springs, of force constants k_1 and k_2, are connected to a mass m as shown. The frequency of oscillation of the mass is f. If both k_1 and k_2 are made four times their original values, the frequency of oscillation becomes : **[2007]**

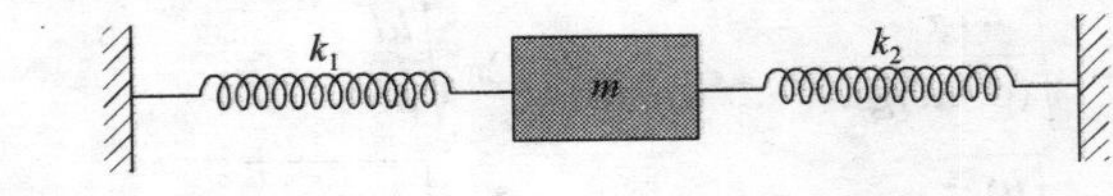

(A) $f/2$ (B) $f/4$
(C) $4f$ (D) $2f$

25. A particle of mass m executes simple harmonic motion with amplitude a and frequency ν. The average kinetic energy during its motion from the position of equilibrium to the end is : **[2007]**

(A) $\pi^2 ma^2\nu^2$ (B) $\frac{1}{4}ma^2\nu^2$
(C) $4\pi^2 ma^2\nu^2$ (D) $2\pi^2 ma^2\nu^2$

26. If x, v and a denote the displacement, the velocity and the acceleration of a particle executing simple harmonic motion of time period T, then, which of the following does not change with time ? **[2009]**

(A) $aT+2\pi v$ (B) $\frac{aT}{v}$
(C) $a^2T^2+4\pi^2v^2$ (D) $\frac{aT}{x}$

27. A mass M, attached to a horizontal spring, executes S.H.M. with amplitude A_1. When the mass M passes through its mean position then a smaller mass m is placed over it and both of them move together with amplitude A_2. The ratio of $\left(\frac{A_1}{A_2}\right)$ is : **[2011]**

(A) $\left(\frac{M}{M+m}\right)^{1/2}$ (B) $\left(\frac{M+m}{M}\right)^{1/2}$
(C) $\frac{M}{M+m}$ (D) $\frac{M+m}{M}$

28. Two particles are executing simple harmonic motion of the same amplitude A and frequency ω along the x-axis. Their mean position is separated by distance X_0 $(X_0 > A)$. If the maximum separation between them is $(X_0 + A)$, the phase difference between their motion is : **[2011]**

(A) $\frac{\pi}{4}$ (B) $\frac{\pi}{6}$
(C) $\frac{\pi}{2}$ (D) $\frac{\pi}{3}$

29. A wooden cube (density of wood 'd') of side 'l' floats in a liquid of density 'ρ' with its upper and lower surfaces horizontal. If the cube is pushed slightly down and released, it performs simple harmonic motion of period 'T'. Then, 'T' is equal to : **[2011]**

(A) $2\pi\sqrt{\frac{l\pi}{(\rho-d)g}}$ (B) $2\pi\sqrt{\frac{ld}{\rho g}}$
(C) $2\pi\sqrt{\frac{l\rho}{dg}}$ (D) $2\pi\sqrt{\frac{ld}{(\rho-d)g}}$

30. If a simple pendulum has significant amplitude (up to a factor of $1/e$ of original) only in the period between $t = 0s$ to $t = \tau s$, then τ may be called the average life of the pendulum. When the spherical bob of the pendulum suffers a retardation (due to viscous drag) proportional to its velocity, with 'b' as the constant of proportionality, the average life time of the pendulum is (assuming damping is small) in seconds : **[2012]**

(A) $\frac{2}{b}$ (B) $\frac{0.693}{b}$
(C) b (D) $\frac{1}{b}$

31. A ring is suspended from a point S on its rim as shown in the figure. When displaced from equilibrium, it oscillates with time period of 1 second. The radius of the ring is : (take $g = \pi^2$): **[2012 (Online)]**

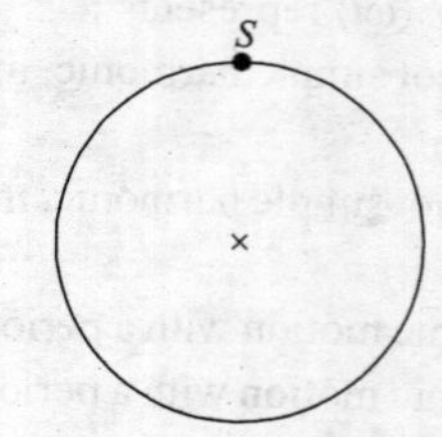

(A) 0.125 m (B) 1.5 m
(C) 1.0 m (D) 0.5 m

32. The displacement $y(t) = A\sin(\omega t + \phi)$ of a pendulum for $\phi = \frac{2\pi}{3}$ is correctly represented by : **[2012 (Online)]**

(A) 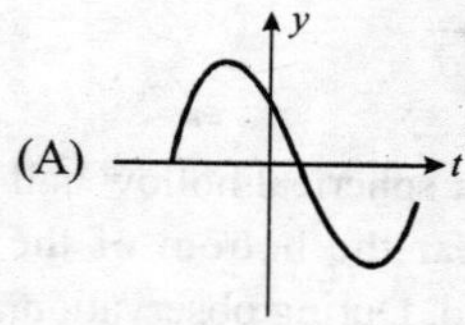

(B) 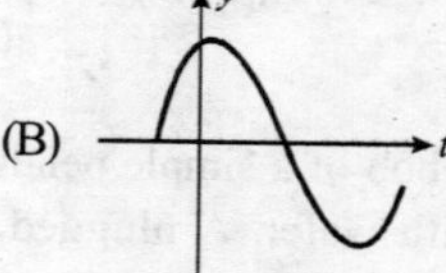

(C) 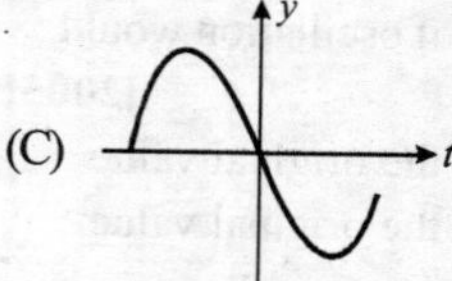

(D) 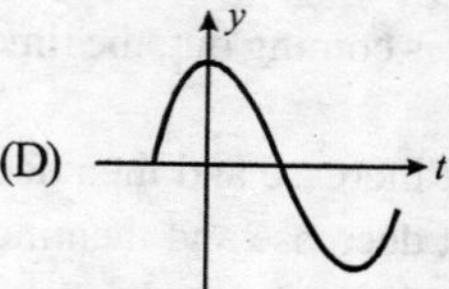

33. An ideal gas enclosed in a vertical cylindrical container supports a freely moving piston of mass M. The piston and the cylinder have equal cross sectional area A. When the piston is in equilibrium, the volume of the gas is V_0 and its pressure is P_0. The piston is slightly displaced from the equilibrium position and released. Assuming that the system is completely isolated from its surrounding, the piston executes a simple harmonic motion with frequency : **[2013]**

(A) $\frac{1}{2\pi}\frac{A\gamma P_0}{V_0 M}$ (B) $\frac{1}{2\pi}\frac{V_0 M P_0}{A^2\gamma}$
(C) $\frac{1}{2\pi}\sqrt{\frac{A^2\gamma P_0}{MV_0}}$ (D) $\frac{1}{2\pi}\sqrt{\frac{MV_0}{A\gamma P_0}}$

34. The amplitude of a damped oscillator decreases to 0.9 times its original magnitude in 5s. In another 10s it will decrease to α times its original magnitude, where α equals : **[2013]**

(A) 0.7 (B) 0.81
(C) 0.729 (D) 0.6

35. Two simple pendulums of length 1 m and 4 m respectively are both given small displacement in the same direction at the same instant. They will be again in phase after the shorter pendulum has completed number of oscillations equal to : **[2013 (Online)]**

(A) 2 (B) 7
(C) 5 (D) 3

36. A mass $m = 1.0$ kg is put on a flat pan attached to a vertical spring fixed on the ground. The mass of the spring and the pan is negligible. When pressed slightly and released, the mass executes simple harmonic motion. The spring constant is 500 N/m. What is the amplitude A of the motion, so that the mass m tends to get detached from the pan? (Take $g = 10$ m/s^2) The spring is stiff enough so that it does not get distorted during the motion : **[2013 (Online)]**

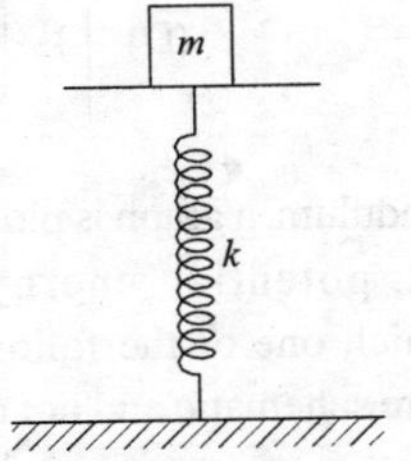

(A) $A > 2.0$ cm (B) $A = 2.0$ cm
(C) $A < 2.0$ cm (D) $A = 1.5$ cm

37. A uniform cylinder of length L and mass M having cross-sectional area A is suspended, with its length vertical, from a fixed point by a massless spring, such that it is half submerged in a liquid of density σ at equilibrium position. When the cylinder is given a downward push and released, it starts oscillating vertically with a small amplitude. The time period T of the oscillations of the cylinder will be : **[2013 (Online)]**

(A) Smaller than $2\pi\left[\dfrac{M}{(k + A\sigma g)}\right]^{1/2}$

(B) $2\pi\sqrt{\dfrac{M}{k}}$

(C) Larger than $2\pi\left[\dfrac{M}{(k + A\sigma g)}\right]^{1/2}$

(D) $2\pi\left[\dfrac{M}{(k + A\sigma g)}\right]^{1/2}$

38. Bob of a simple pendulum of length l is made of iron. The pendulum is oscillating over a horizontal coil carrying direct current. If the time period of the pendulum is T then : **[2013 (Online)]**

(A) $T < 2\pi\sqrt{\dfrac{l}{g}}$ and damping is smaller than in air alone

(B) $T = 2\pi\sqrt{\dfrac{l}{g}}$ and damping is larger than in air alone

(C) $T > 2\pi\sqrt{\dfrac{l}{g}}$ and damping is smaller than in air alone

(D) $T < 2\pi\sqrt{\dfrac{l}{g}}$ and damping is larger than in air alone

39. A particle moves with simple harmonic motion in a straight line. In first τ, s after starting from rest it travels a distance a, and in next τ s it travels $2a$, in same direction, then : **[2014]**

(A) Amplitude of motion is $3a$
(B) Time period of oscillations is 8τ
(C) Amplitude of motion is $4a$
(D) Time period of oscillations is 6τ

40. The amplitude of a simple pendulum, oscillating in air with a small spherical bob, decreases from 10 cm to 8 cm in 40 seconds. Assuming that Stokes law is valid, and ratio of the coefficient of viscosity of air to that of carbon dioxide is 1.3. The time in which amplitude of this pendulum will reduce from 10 cm to 5 cm in carbon dioxide will be close to :
(In 5 = 1.601, In 2 = 0.693) **[2014 (Online)]**

(A) 231 s (B) 208 s
(C) 161 s (D) 142 s

41. In an experiment for determining the gravitational acceleration g of a place with the help of a simple pendulum, the measured time period square is plotted against the string length of the pendulum in the figure. What is the value of g at the place ? **[2014 (Online)]**

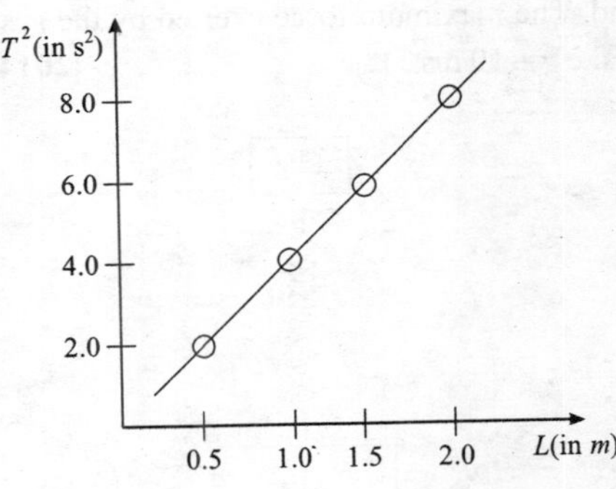

(A) 9.81 m/s^2 (B) 9.87 m/s^2
(C) 9.91 m/s^2 (D) 10.0 m/s^2

42. A particle which is simultaneously subjected to two perpendicular simple harmonic motions represented by; $x = a_1 \cos \omega t$ and $y = a_2 \cos 2\omega t$ traces a curve given by : **[2014 (Online)]**

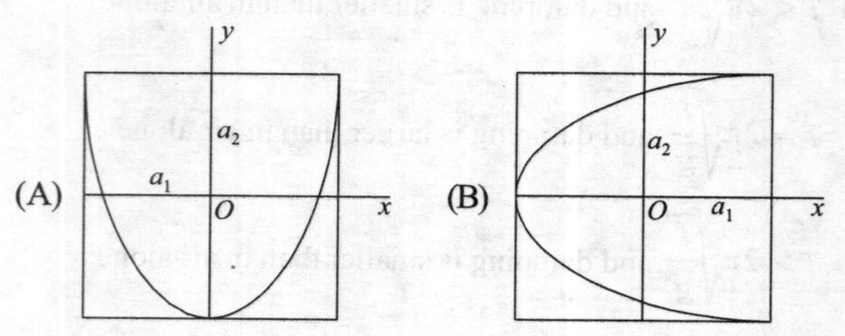

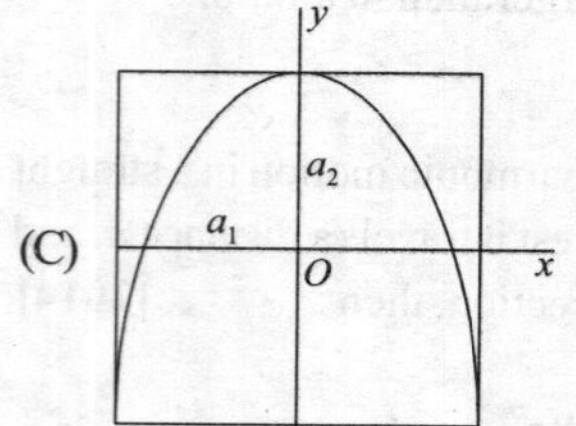

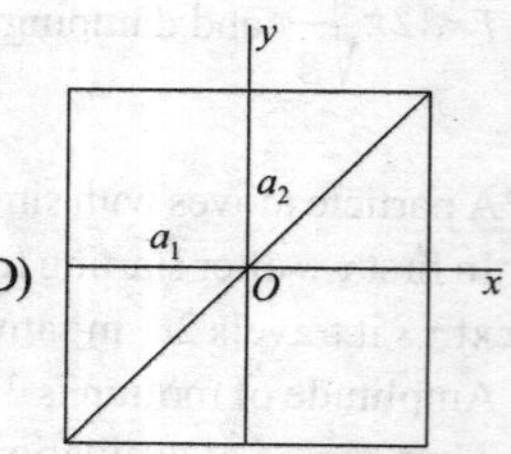

43. Which of the following expressions corresponds to simple harmonic motion along a straight line, where x is the displacement and a, b, c are positive constants ? **[2014 (Online)]**

(A) $a + bx - cx^2$ (B) bx^2
(C) $a - bx + cx^2$ (D) $- bx$

44. A body is in simple harmonic motion with time period half second ($T = 0.5$ s) and amplitude one cm ($A = 1$ cm). Find the average velocity in the interval in which it moves form equilibrium position to half of its amplitude : **[2014 (Online)]**

(A) 4 cm/s (B) 6 cm/s
(C) 12 cm/s (D) 16 cm/s

45. Two bodies of masses 1 kg and 4 kg are connected to a vertical spring, as shown in the figure. The smaller mass executes simple harmonic motion of angular frequency 25 rad/s, and amplitude 1.6 cm while the bigger mass remains stationary on the ground. The maximum force exerted by the system on the floor is (take $g = 10$ ms^{-2}) : **[2014 (Online)]**

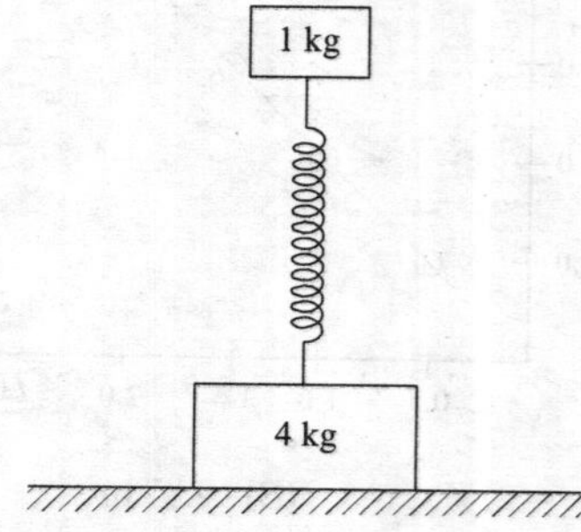

(A) 20 N (B) 10 N
(C) 60 N (D) 40 N

46. The angular frequency of the damped oscillator is given by, $\omega = \sqrt{\frac{k}{m} - \frac{r^2}{4m^2}}$ where k is the spring constant, m is the mass of the oscillator and r is the damping constant. If the ratio $\frac{r^2}{mk}$ is 8%, the change in time period compared to the undamped oscillator is approximately as follows : **[2014 (Online)]**

(A) Increases by 1% (B) Increases by 8%
(C) Decreases by 1% (D) Decreases by 8%

47. A pendulum made of a uniform wire of cross sectional area A has time period T. When an additional mass M is added to its bob, the time period changes to T_M. If the Young's modulus of the material of the wire is Y then $1/Y$ is equal to (g = gravitational acceleration) : **[2015]**

(A) $\left[\left(\frac{T_M}{T}\right)^2 - 1\right]\frac{A}{Mg}$ (B) $\left[\left(\frac{T_M}{T}\right)^2 - 1\right]\frac{Mg}{A}$
(C) $\left[1 - \left(\frac{T_M}{T}\right)^2\right]\frac{A}{Mg}$ (D) $\left[1 - \left(\frac{T}{T_M}\right)^2\right]\frac{A}{Mg}$

48. For a simple pendulum, a graph is plotted between its kinetic energy (KE) and potential energy (PE) against its displacement d. Which one of the following represents these correctly ? (Graph are schematic and not drawn to scale) **[2015]**

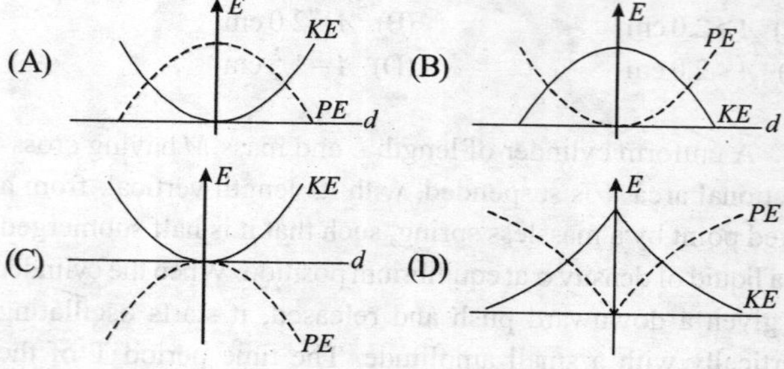

49. A pendulum with time period of 1s is losing energy. At certain time its energy is 45 J. If after completing 15 oscillations, its energy has become 15 J, its damping constant (in s^{-1}) is : **[2015 (Online)]**

(A) $\frac{1}{2}$ (B) $\frac{1}{30} \ln 3$
(C) 2 (D) $\frac{1}{15} \ln 3$

50. x and y displacements of a particle are given as $x(t) = a \sin \omega t$ and $y(t) = a \sin 2\omega t$. Its trajectory will look like : **[2015 (Online)]**

(A) 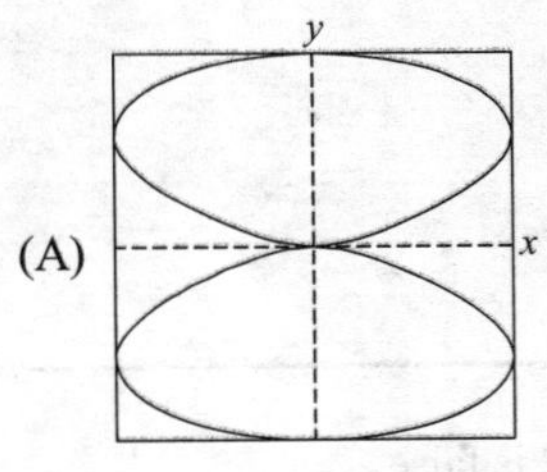

(B) 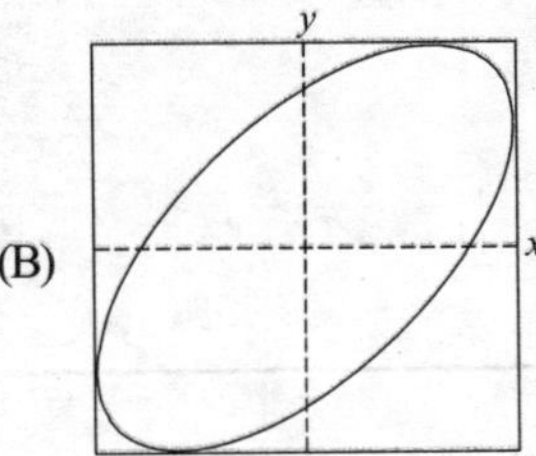

(C) 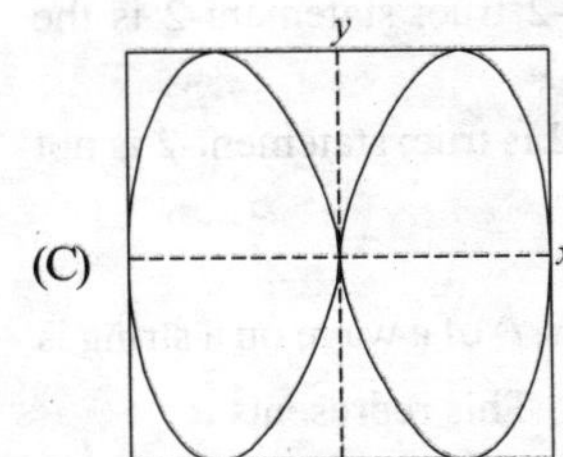

(D) 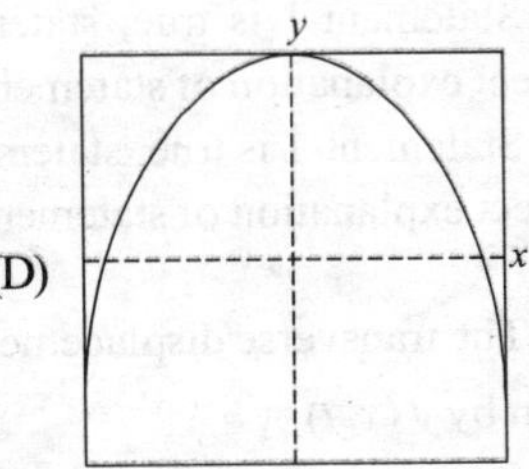

51. A simple harmonic oscillator of angular frequency 2 rad s^{-1} is acted upon by an external force $F = \sin t$ N. If the oscillator is at rest in its equilibrium position at $t = 0$, its position at later times is proportional to : **[2015 (Online)]**

(A) $\sin t + \frac{1}{2}\cos 2t$ (B) $\cot t - \frac{1}{2}\sin 2t$

(C) $\sin t - \frac{1}{2}\sin 2t$ (D) $\sin t + \frac{1}{2}\sin 2t$

52. A particle performs simple harmonic motion with amplitude A. Its speed is trebled at the instant that it is at a distance $\frac{2A}{3}$ from equilibrium position. The new amplitude of the motion is : **[2016]**

(A) $\frac{A}{3}\sqrt{41}$ (B) $3A$

(C) $A\sqrt{3}$ (D) $\frac{7A}{3}$

53. In an engine the piston undergoes vertical simple harmonic motion with amplitude 7 cm. A washer rests on top of the piston and moves with it. The motor speed is slowly increased. The frequency of the piston at which the washer no longer stays in contact with the piston, is close to : **[2016 (Online)]**

(A) 0.7 Hz (B) 1.9 Hz

(C) 1.2 Hz (D) 0.1 Hz

54. Two particles are performing simple harmonic motion in a straight line about the same equilibrium point. The amplitude and time period for both particles are same and equal to A and T, respectively. At time $t = 0$ one particle has displacement A while the other one has displacement $-A/2$ and they are moving towards each other. If they cross each other at time t, then t is : **[2016 (Online)]**

(A) $\frac{5T}{6}$ (B) $\frac{T}{3}$

(C) $\frac{T}{4}$ (D) $\frac{T}{6}$

* * * * *

CHAPTER 14

WAVES

14.1 WAVE MOTION

1. The displacement y of a wave travelling in the x-direction is given by $y = 10^{-4} \sin\left(600t - 2x + \frac{\pi}{3}\right)$ metre, where, x is expressed in metres and t in seconds. The speed of the wave-motion, in ms^{-1} is : **[2003]**

(A) 300 (B) 600
(C) 1200 (D) 200

2. A sound absorber attenuates the sound level by $20dB$. The intensity decreases by a factor of : **[2007]**

(A) 1000 (B) 10000
(C) 10 (D) 100

3. A wave travelling along the x-axis is described by the equation $y(x, t) = 0.005 \cos(\alpha x - \beta t)$. If the wavelength and the time period of the wave in 0.08 m and 2.0 s respectively then α and β in appropriate units are : **[2008]**

(A) $\alpha = 25.00\pi, \beta = \pi$ (B) $\alpha = \frac{0.08}{\pi}, \beta = \frac{2.0}{\pi}$

(C) $\alpha = \frac{0.04}{\pi}, \beta = \frac{1.0}{\pi}$ (D) $\alpha = 12.50\pi, \beta = \frac{\pi}{2.0}$

4. The speed of sound in oxygen (O_2) at a certain temperature is 460 ms^{-1}. The speed of sound in helium (He) at the same temperature will be (assume both gases to be ideal) : **[2008]**

(A) $460\sqrt{\frac{200}{21}}\ ms^{-1}$ (B) $500\sqrt{\frac{200}{21}}\ ms^{-1}$

(C) $650\sqrt{2}\ ms^{-1}$ (D) $330\sqrt{2}\ ms^{-1}$

5. The equation of a wave on a string of linear mass density 0.04 kg m^{-1} is given by $y = 0.02\ (m) \sin\left[2\pi\left(\frac{t}{0.04(s)} - \frac{x}{0.50(m)}\right)\right]$. The tension in the string is : **[2010]**

(A) 6.25 N (B) 4.0 N
(C) 12.5 N (D) 0.5 N

6. **Statement-1 :** Two longitudinal waves given by equations: $y_1(x, t) = 2a \sin(\omega t - kx)$ and $y_2(x, t) = a \sin(2\omega t - 2kx)$ will have equal intensity.

Statement-2 : Intensity of waves of given frequency in same medium is proportional to square of amplitude only. **[2011]**

(A) Statement-1 is false, statement-2 is true
(B) Statement-1 is true, statement-2 is false
(C) Statement-1 is true, statement-2 true; statement-2 is the correct explanation of statement-1
(D) Statement-1 is true, statement-2 is true; statement-2 is not correct explanation of statement-1

7. The transverse displacement $y(x, t)$ of a wave on a string is given by $y(x, t) = e^{-(ax^2 + bt^2 + 2\sqrt{ab}xt)}$. This represents a : **[2011]**

(A) Standing wave of frequency $\sqrt{b}$
(B) Standing wave of frequency $\frac{1}{\sqrt{b}}$
(C) Wave moving in $+x$ direction with speed $\sqrt{\frac{a}{b}}$
(D) Wave moving in $-x$ direction with speed $\sqrt{\frac{b}{a}}$

8. The disturbance $y(x, t)$ of a wave propagating in the positive x-direction is given by $y = \frac{1}{1+x^2}$ at time $t = 0$ and by $y = \frac{1}{[1+(x-1)^2]}$ at $t = 2$s, where x and y are in meters. The shape of the wave disturbance does not change during the propagation. The velocity of wave in m/s is : **[2012 (Online)]**

(A) 2.0 (B) 4.0
(C) 0.5 (D) 1.0

9. When two sound waves travel in the same direction in a medium, the displacements of a particle located at 'x' at time 't' is given by :

$$y_1 = 0.05 \cos(0.50\pi x - 100\pi t)$$
$$y_2 = 0.05 \cos(0.45\pi x - 92\pi t)$$

where y_1, y_2 and x are in meters and t in seconds. The speed of sound in the medium is : **[2013 (Online)]**

(A) 92 m/s (B) 200 m/s
(C) 100 m/s (D) 332 m/s

10. In a transverse wave the distance between a crest and neighbouring trough at the same instant is 0.4 cm and the distance between a crest and trough at the same place is 1.0 cm. The next crest appears at the same place after a time interval of 0.4s. The maximum speed of the vibrating particles in the medium is : **[2013 (Online)]**

(A) $\frac{3\pi}{2}$ cm/s (B) $\frac{5\pi}{2}$ cm/s

(C) $\frac{\pi}{2}$ cm/s (D) 2π cm/s

11. An engine approaches a hill with a constant speed. When it is at a distance of 0.9 km, it blows a whistle whose echo is heard by the driver after 5 seconds. If the speed of sound in air is 330 m/s, then the speed of the engine is : **[2013 (Online)]**

(A) 32 m/s (B) 27.5 m/s

(C) 60 m/s (D) 30 m/s

12. A transverse wave is represented by

$$y = \frac{10}{\pi}\sin\left(\frac{2\pi}{T}t - \frac{2\pi}{\lambda}x\right)$$

For what value of the wavelength the wave velocity is twice the maximum particle velocity ? **[2014 (Online)]**

(A) 40 cm (B) 20 cm

(C) 10 cm (D) 60 cm

13. A uniform string of length 20 m is suspended from a rigid support. A short wave pulse is introduced at its lowest end. It starts moving up the string. The time taken to reach the support is : (take $g = 10\ ms^{-2}$) : **[2016]**

(A) $2\pi\sqrt{2}$ s (B) 2s

(C) $2\sqrt{2}$ s (D) $\sqrt{2}$ s

* * * * *

CHAPTER

14 WAVES

14.2 STATIONARY WAVES AND BEATS

1. Tube A has both ends open while tube B has one end closed, otherwise they are identical. The ratio of fundamental frequency of tubes A and B is : **[2002]**

(A) 1 : 2 (B) 1 : 4
(C) 2 : 1 (D) 4 : 1

2. A tuning fork arrangement (pair) produces 4 beats/s with one fork of frequency 288 cps. A little wax is placed on the unknown fork and it then produces 2 beats/s. The frequency of the unknown fork is : **[2002]**

(A) 286 cps (B) 292 cps
(C) 294 cps (D) 288 cps

3. Length of a string tied to two rigid supports is 40 cm. Maximum length (wavelength in cm) of a stationary wave produced on it, is : **[2002]**

(A) 20 (B) 80
(C) 40 (D) 120

4. A wave $y = a \sin(\omega t - kx)$ on a string meets with another wave producing a node at $x = 0$. Then the equation of the unknown wave is : **[2002]**

(A) $y = a \sin(\omega t + kx)$ (B) $y = -a \sin(\omega t + kx)$
(C) $y = a \sin(\omega t - kx)$ (D) $y = -a \sin(\omega t - kx)$

5. A tuning fork of known frequency 256 Hz makes 5 beats per second with the vibrating string of a piano. The beat frequency decreases to 2 beats per second when the tension in the piano string is slightly increased. The frequency of the piano string before increasing the tension was : **[2003]**

(A) $(256 + 2)$ Hz (B) $(256 - 2)$ Hz
(C) $(256 - 5)$ Hz (D) $(256 + 5)$ Hz

6. When two tuning forks (fork 1 and fork 2) are sounded simultaneously, 4 beats per second are heard. Now, some tape is attached on the prong of the fork 2. When the tuning forks are sounded again, 6 beats per second are heard. If the frequency of fork 1 is 200 Hz, then what was the original frequency of fork 2? **[2005]**

(A) 200 Hz (B) 202 Hz
(C) 196 Hz (D) 204 Hz

7. A string is stretched between fixed points separated by 75.0 cm. It is observed to have resonant frequencies of 420 Hz and 315 Hz. Their are no other resonant frequencies between these two. Then, the lowest resonant frequency for this string is : **[2006]**

(A) 105 Hz (B) 1.05 Hz
(C) 1050 Hz (D) 10.5 Hz

8. While measuring the speed of sound by performing a resonance column experiment, a student gets the first resonance condition at column length of 18 cm during winter. Repeating the same experiment during summer, student measures the column length to be x cm for the second resonance. Then : **[2008]**

(A) $18 > x$ (B) $x > 54$
(C) $54 > x > 36$ (D) $36 > x > 18$

9. Three sound waves of equal amplitudes have frequencies $(\nu - 1)$, ν, $(\nu + 1)$. They superpose to give beats. The number of beats produced per second will be : **[2009]**

(A) 2 (B) 1
(C) 4 (D) 3

10. A travelling wave represented by $y = A \sin(\omega t - kx)$ is superimposed on another wave represented by $y = A \sin(\omega t + kx)$. The resultant is : **[2011]**

(A) A standing wave having nodes at $x = \left(n + \frac{1}{2}\right)\frac{\lambda}{2}, n = 0, 1, 2$
(B) A wave travelling along $+x$ direction
(C) A wave travelling along $-x$ direction
(D) A standing wave having nodes at $x = \frac{n\lambda}{2}; n = 0, 1, 2$

11. A cylindrical tube, open at both ends, has a fundamental frequency f, in air. The tube is dipped vertically in water so that half of it is in water. The fundamental frequency of the air-column is now : **[2012]**

(A) $2f$ (B) f
(C) $f/2$ (D) $3f/4$

12. Following are expressions for four plane simple harmonic waves : **[2012 (Online)]**

(i) $y_1 = A \cos 2\pi\left(n_1 t + \frac{x}{\lambda_1}\right)$

(ii) $y_2 = A \cos 2\pi\left(n_1 t + \frac{x}{\lambda_1} + \pi\right)$

(iii) $y_3 = A\cos 2\pi\left(n_2 t + \frac{x}{\lambda_2}\right)$

(iv) $y_4 = A\cos 2\pi\left(n_2 t - \frac{x}{\lambda_2}\right)$

The pair of waves which will produce destructive interference and stationary wave respectively in a medium, are :

(A) (iii, iv), (i, ii) (B) (i, iii), (ii, iv)
(C) (i, iv), (ii, iii) (D) (i, ii), (iii, iv)

13. A wave represented by the equation $y_1 = a\cos(kx - \omega t)$ is superimposed with another wave to form a stationary wave such that the point $x - 0$ is node. The equation for the other wave is : **[2012 (Online)]**

(A) $a\cos(kx - \omega t - \pi)$ (B) $a\cos(kx + \omega t + \pi)$

(C) $a\cos\left(kx + \omega t + \frac{\pi}{2}\right)$ (D) $a\cos\left(kx - \omega t + \frac{\pi}{2}\right)$

14. A uniform tube of length 60.5 cm is held vertically with its lower end dipped in water. A sound source of frequency 500 Hz sends sound waves into the tube. When the length of tube above water is 16 cm and again when it is 50 cm, the tube resonates with the source of sound. Two lowest frequencies (in Hz), to which tube will resonate when it is taken out of water, are (approximately) : **[2012 (Online)]**

(A) 281, 562 (B) 281, 843
(C) 276, 552 (D) 272, 544

15. An air column in a pipe, which is closed at one end, will be in resonance with a vibrating tuning fork of frequency 264 Hz if the length of the column in cm is (velocity of sound = 330 m/s): **[2012 (Online)]**

(A) 125.00 (B) 93.75
(C) 62.50 (D) 187.50

16. A sonometer wire of length 1.5 m is made of steel. The tension in it produces an elastic strain of 1%. What is the fundamental frequency of steel if density and elasticity of steel are 7.7×10^3 kg/m^3 and 2.2×10^{11} N/m^2 respectively? **[2013]**

(A) 188.5 Hz (B) 178.2 Hz
(C) 200.5 Hz (D) 770 Hz

17. A sonometer wire of length 114 cm is fixed at both the ends. Where should the two bridges be placed so as to divide the wire into three segments whose fundamental frequencies are in the ratio 1 : 3 : 4 ? **[2013 (Online)]**

(A) At 36 cm and 84 cm from one end
(B) At 24 cm and 72 cm from one end
(C) At 48 cm and 96 cm from one end
(D) At 72 cm and 96 cm from one end

18. A pipe of length 85 cm is closed from one end. Find the number of possible natural oscillations of air column in the pipe whose frequencies lie below 1250 Hz. The velocity of sound in air is 340 m/s : **[2014]**

(A) 12 (B) 8
(C) 6 (D) 4

19. The total length of a sonometer wire between fixed ends is 110 cm. Two bridges are placed to divide the length of wire in ratio 6 : 3 : 2. The tension in the wire is 400 N and the mass per unit length is 0.01 kg/m. What is the minimum common frequency with which three parts can vibrate ? **[2014 (Online)]**

(A) 1100 Hz (B) 1000 Hz
(C) 166 Hz (D) 100 Hz

20. A pipe open at both ends has a fundamental frequency f in air. The pipe is dipped vertically in water so that half of it is in water. The fundamental frequency of the air column is now : **[2016]**

(A) $\frac{f}{2}$ (B) $\frac{3f}{4}$
(C) $2f$ (D) f

* * * * *

CHAPTER

14 WAVES

14.3 DOPPLER'S EFFECT

1. An observer moves towards a stationary source of sound, with a velocity one-fifth of the velocity of sound. What is the percentage increase in the apparent frequency ? **[2005]**

(A) Zero (B) 0.5%
(C) 5% (D) 20%

2. A whistle producing sound waves of frequencies 9500 Hz and above is approaching a stationary person with speed v ms^{-1}. The velocity of sound in air is 300 ms^{-1}. If the person can hear frequencies upto a maximum of 10,000 Hz, the maximum value of v upto which he can hear the whistle is : **[2006]**

(A) $15\sqrt{2}$ ms^{-1} (B) $15/\sqrt{2}$ ms^{-1}
(C) 15 ms^{-1} (D) 30 ms^{-1}

3. A motor cycle starts from rest and accelerates along a straight path at 2 m/s^2. At the starting point of the motor cycle there is a stationary electric siren. How far has the motor cycle gone when the driver hears the frequency of the siren at 94% of its value when the motor cycle was at rest ? (Speed of sound = 330 ms^{-1}) : **[2009]**

(A) 147 m (B) 196 m
(C) 49 m (D) 98 m

4. This question has Statement-1 and Statement-2. Of the four choices given after the Statements, choose the one that best describes the two Statements. **[2012 (Online)]**

Statement-1 : Bats emitting ultrasonic waves can detect the location of a prey by hearing the waves reflected from it.

Statement-2 : When the source and the detector are moving, the frequency of reflected waves is changed.

(A) Statement-1 is false, Statement-2 is true
(B) Statement-1 is true, Statement-2 is false
(C) Statement-1 is true, Statement-2 is true, Statement-2 is not the correct explanation of Statement-1
(D) Statement-1 is true, Statement-2 is true, Statement-2 is the correct explanation of Statement-1

5. A and B are two sources generating sound waves. A listener is situated at C. The frequency of the source at A is 500 Hz. A, now, moves towards C with a speed 4 m/s. The number of beats heard at C is 6. When A moves away from C with speed 4 m/s, the number of beats heard at C is 18. The speed of sound is 340 m/s. The frequency of the source at B is : **[2013 (Online)]**

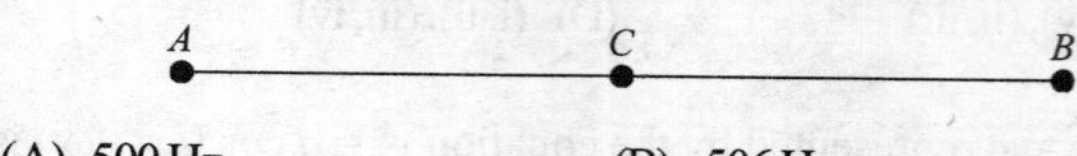

(A) 500 Hz (B) 506 Hz
(C) 512 Hz (D) 494 Hz

6. Two factories are sounding their sirens at 800 Hz. A man goes from one factory to other at a speed of 2 m/s. The velocity of sound is 320 m/s. The number of beats heard by the person in one second will be : **[2014 (Online)]**

(A) 2 (B) 4
(C) 8 (D) 10

7. A source of sound A emitting waves of frequency 1800 Hz is falling towards ground with a terminal speed v. The observer B on the ground directly beneath the source receives waves of frequency 2150 Hz. The source A receives waves, reflected from ground of frequency nearly : (Speed of sound = 343 m/s) : **[2014 (Online)]**

(A) 2150 Hz (B) 2500 Hz
(C) 1800 Hz (D) 2400 Hz

8. A train is moving on a straight track with speed 20 ms^{-1}. It is blowing its whistle at the frequency of 1000 Hz. The percentage change in the frequency heard by a person standing near the track as the train passes him is (speed of sound = 320 ms^{-1}) close to : **[2015]**

(A) 6% (B) 12%
(C) 18% (D) 24%

9. A bat moving at 10 ms^{-1} towards a wall sends a sound signal of 8000 Hz towards it. On reflection it hears a sound of frequency f. The value of f in Hz is close to (speed of sound = 320 ms^{-1}) : **[2015 (Online)]**

(A) 8516 (B) 8258
(C) 8424 (D) 800

10. A source of sound emits sound waves at frequency f_0. It is moving towards an observer with fixed speed v_s ($v_s < v$, where v is the speed of sound in air). If the observer were to move towards the source with speed v_0, one of the following two graphs (A and B) will given the correct variation of the frequency f heard by the observer as v_0 is changed : **[2015 (Online)]**

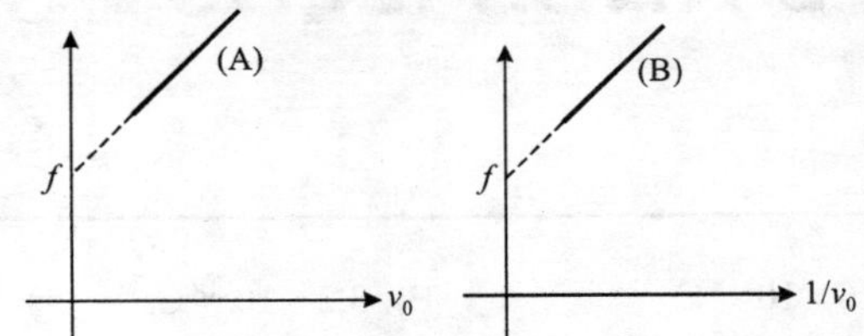

The variation of f with v_0 is given correctly by :

(A) Graph A with slope $= \dfrac{f_0}{(v+v_s)}$

(B) Graph B with slope $= \dfrac{f_0}{(v-v_s)}$

(C) Graph A with slope $= \dfrac{f_0}{(v-v_s)}$

(D) Graph B with slope $= \dfrac{f_0}{(v+v_s)}$

11. Two engines pass each other moving in opposite directions with uniform speed of 30 m/s. One of them is blowing a whistle of frequency 540 Hz. Calculate the frequency heard by driver of second engine before they pass each other. Speed of sound is 330 m/sec : **[2016 (Online)]**

(A) 450 Hz (B) 540 Hz
(C) 270 Hz (D) 648 Hz

12. A toy-car, blowing its horn, is moving with a steady speed of 5 m/s, away from a wall. An observer, towards whom the toy car is moving, is able to hear 5 beats per second. If the velocity of sound in air is 340 m/s, the frequency of the horn of the toy car is close to : **[2016 (Online)]**

(A) 680 Hz (B) 510 Hz
(C) 340 Hz (D) 170 Hz

* * * * *

CHAPTER

15 ELECTRIC CHARGES AND FIELDS

15.1 ELECTRIC FORCE AND ELECTRIC FIELD

1. If a charge q is placed at the centre of the line joining two equal charges Q such that the system is in equilibrium then the value of q is : **[2002]**

(A) $Q/2$ (B) $-Q/2$

(C) $Q/2$ (D) $-Q/4$

2. Three charges $-q_1$, $+q_2$ and $-q_3$ are place as shown in the figure. The x-component of the force on $-q_1$ is proportional to: **[2003]**

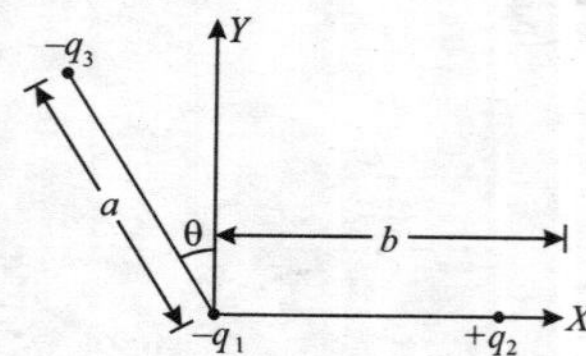

(A) $\frac{q_2}{b^2} - \frac{q_3}{a^2}\cos\theta$ (B) $\frac{q_2}{b^2} + \frac{q_3}{a^2}\sin\theta$

(C) $\frac{q_2}{b^2} + \frac{q_3}{a^2}\cos\theta$ (D) $\frac{q_2}{b^2} - \frac{q_3}{a^2}\sin\theta$

3. Four charges equal to $-Q$ are placed at the four corners of a square and a charge q is at its centre. If the system is in equilibrium, the value of q is : **[2004]**

(A) $-\frac{Q}{4}(1+2\sqrt{2})$ (B) $\frac{Q}{4}(1+2\sqrt{2})$

(C) $-\frac{Q}{2}(1+2\sqrt{2})$ (D) $\frac{Q}{2}(1+2\sqrt{2})$

4. Two spherical conductors B and C having equal radii and carrying equal charges in them, repel each other with a force F when kept apart at some distance. A third spherical conductor having same radius as that of B but uncharged, is brought in contact with B, then brought in contact with C and finally removed away from both. The new force of repulsion between B and C is : **[2004]**

(A) $\frac{F}{4}$ (B) $\frac{3F}{4}$

(C) $\frac{F}{8}$ (D) $\frac{3F}{8}$

5. A charged oil drop is suspended in a uniform field of 3×10^4 v/m so that it neither falls nor rises. The charge on the drop will be (Take the mass of the charge $= 9.9 \times 10^{-15}$ kg and $g = 10$ m/s^2) : **[2004]**

(A) 1.6×10^{-18} C (B) 3.2×10^{-18} C

(C) 3.3×10^{-18} C (D) 4.8×10^{-18} C

6. Two point charges $+8q$ and $-2q$ are located at $x = 0$ and $x = L$ respectively. The location of a point on the x-axis at which the net electric field due to these two point charges is zero is : **[2005]**

(A) $2L$ (B) $L/4$

(C) $8L$ (D) $4L$

7. A charged ball B hangs from a silk thread S, which makes an angle θ with a large charged conducting sheet P, as shown in the figure. The surface charge density σ of the sheet is proportional to : **[2005]**

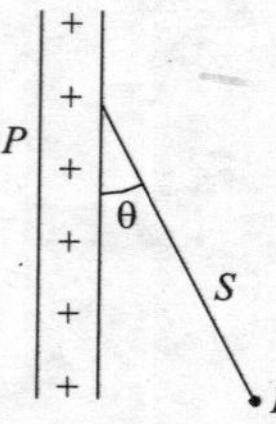

(A) $\cos\theta$ (B) $\cot\theta$

(C) $\sin\theta$ (D) $\tan\theta$

8. A thin spherical shell of radius R has a charge Q spread uniformly over its surface. Which of the following graphs most closely represents the electric field $E(r)$ produced by the shell in the range $0 \le r < \infty$, where r is the distance from the centre of the shell : **[2008]**

(A)

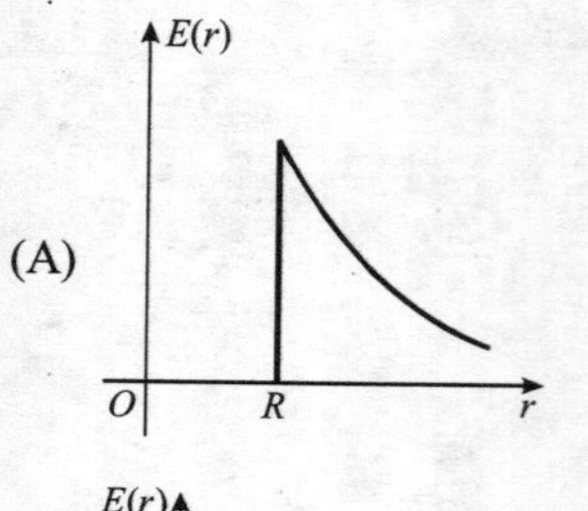

(B)

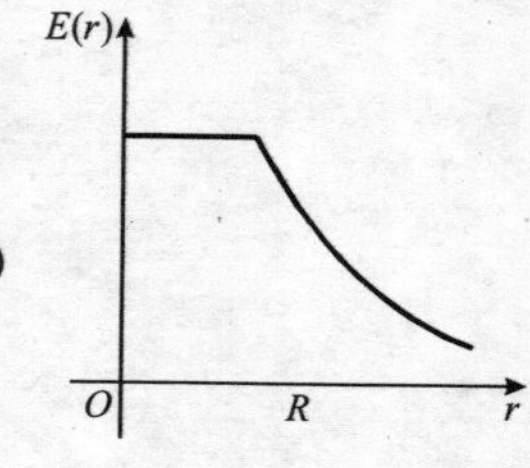

(C)

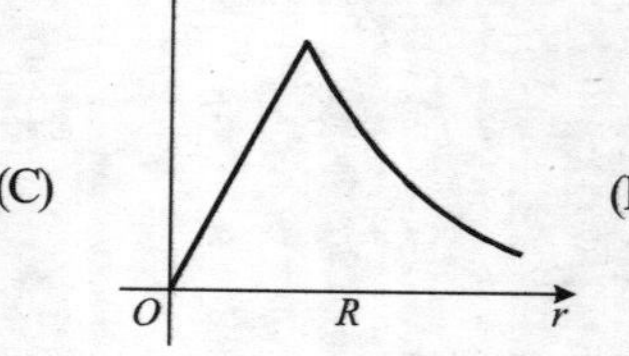

(D)

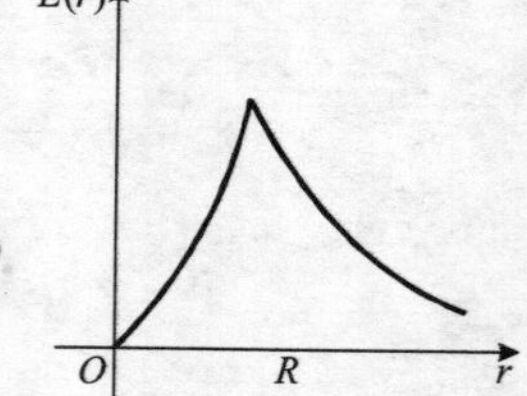

9. A charge Q is placed at each of the opposite corners of a square. A charge q is placed at each of the other two corners. If the net electrical force on Q is zero, then $\frac{Q}{q}$ equals : **[2009]**

(A) 1 (B) $-\frac{1}{\sqrt{2}}$

(C) $-2\sqrt{2}$ (D) -1

10. Let $\rho(r) = \frac{Q}{\pi R^4} r$ be the charge density distribution for a solid sphere of radius R and total charge Q. For a point 'p' inside the sphere at distance r_1 from the centre of the sphere, the magnitude of electric field is : **[2009]**

(A) $\frac{Qr_1^2}{4\pi \epsilon_0 R^4}$ (B) $\frac{Qr_1^2}{3\pi \epsilon_0 R^4}$

(C) 0 (D) $\frac{Q}{4\pi \epsilon_0 r_1^2}$

11. Two identical charged spheres are suspended by strings of equal lengths. The strings make an angle of 30° with each other. When suspended in a liquid of density 0.8 g cm^{-3}, the angle remains the same. If density of the material of the sphere is 1.6 g cm^{-3}, the dielectric constant of the liquid is : **[2010]**

(A) 1 (B) 4

(C) 3 (D) 2

12. Let there be a spherically symmetric charge distribution with charge density varying as $\rho(r) = \rho_0\left(\frac{5}{4} - \frac{r}{R}\right)$ upto $r = R$, and $\rho(r) = 0$ for $r > R$, where r is the distance from the origin. The electric field at a distance r $(r < R)$ from the origin is given by : **[2010]**

(A) $\frac{\rho_0 r}{3 \epsilon_0}\left(\frac{5}{4} - \frac{r}{R}\right)$ (B) $\frac{4\pi\rho_0 r}{3 \epsilon_0}\left(\frac{5}{3} - \frac{r}{R}\right)$

(C) $\frac{\rho_0 r}{4 \epsilon_0}\left(\frac{5}{3} - \frac{r}{R}\right)$ (D) $\frac{4\rho_0 r}{3 \epsilon_0}\left(\frac{5}{4} - \frac{r}{R}\right)$

13. A thin semi-circular ring of radius r has a positive charge q distributed uniformly over it. The net field $\vec{E}$ at the centre O is: **[2010]**

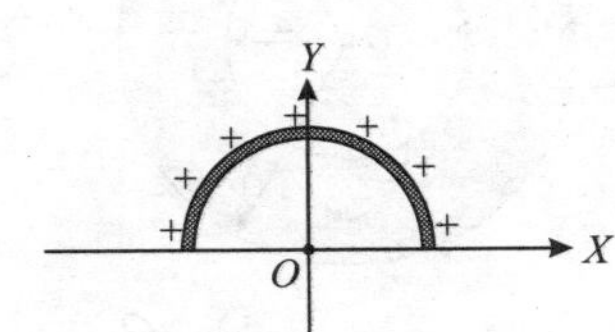

(A) $\frac{q}{2\pi^2 \epsilon_0 r^2}\hat{j}$ (B) $\frac{q}{4\pi^2 \epsilon_0 r^2}\hat{j}$

(C) $-\frac{q}{4\pi^2 \epsilon_0 r^2}\hat{j}$ (D) $-\frac{q}{2\pi^2 \epsilon_0 r^2}\hat{j}$

14. Two identical charged spheres suspended from a common point by two massless string of length l are initially a distance $d(d << l)$ apart because of their mutual repulsion. The charge begins to leak from both the spheres at a constant rate. As a result the charges approach each other with a velocity v. Then as a function of distance x between them : **[2011]**

(A) $v \propto x^{1/x}$ (B) $v \propto x$

(C) $v \propto x^{-1/2}$ (D) $v \propto x^{-1}$

15. In a uniformly charged sphere of total charge Q and radius R, the electric field E is plotted as a function of distance from the centre. The graph which would correspond to the above will be : **[2012]**

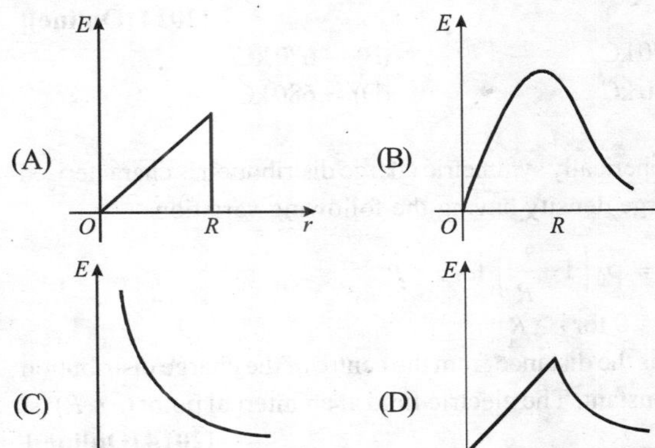

16. Two charges, each equal to q, are kept at $x = -a$ and $x = a$ on the x-axis. A particle of mass m and charge $q_0 = \frac{q}{2}$ is placed at the origin. If charge q_0 is given a small displacement $(y << a)$ along the y-axis, the net force acting on the particle is proportional to : **[2013]**

(A) y (B) $-y$

(C) $\frac{1}{y}$ (D) $-\frac{1}{y}$

17. A liquid drop having 6 excess electrons is kept stationary under a uniform electric field of 25.5 kVm^{-1}. The density of liquid is 1.26×10^3 kg m^{-3}. The radius of the drop is (neglect buoyancy) : **[2013 (Online)]**

(A) 4.3×10^{-7} m (B) 7.8×10^{-7} m

(C) 0.078×10^{-7} m (D) 3.4×10^{-7} m

18. The surface charge density of a thin charged disc of radius R is σ. The value of the electric field at the centre of the disc is $\frac{\sigma}{2\epsilon_0}$. With respect to the field at the centre, the electric field along the axis at a distance R from the centre of the disc : **[2013 (Online)]**

(A) Reduces by 70.7% (B) Reduces by 29.3%

(C) Reduces by 9.7% (D) Reduces by 14.6%

19. Two balls of same mass and carrying equal charge are hung from a fixed support of length l. At electrostatic equilibrium, assuming that angles made by each thread is small, the separation, x between the balls is proportional to : **[2013 (Online)]**

(A) l
(B) l^2
(C) $l^{2/3}$
(D) $l^{1/3}$

20. The magnitude of the average electric field normally present in the atmosphere just above the surface of the Earth is about 150 N/C, directed inward towards the center of the Earth. This gives the total net surface charge carried by the Earth to be : [Given $\varepsilon_0 = 8.85 \times 10^{-12}$ C^2/N-m^2, $R_E = 6.37 \times 10^6$ m] **[2014 (Online)]**

(A) +670 kC
(B) −670 kC
(C) −680 kC
(D) +680 kC

21. A spherically symmetric charge distribution is characterised by a charge density having the following variations :

$$\rho(r) = \rho_0\left(1 - \frac{r}{R}\right) \text{ for } r < R$$

$$\rho(r) = 0 \text{ for } r \geq R$$

Where r is the distance from the centre of the charge distribution ρ_0 is a constant. The electric field at an internal point $(r < R)$ is: **[2014 (Online)]**

(A) $\frac{\rho_0}{4\varepsilon_0}\left(\frac{r}{3} - \frac{r^2}{4R}\right)$
(B) $\frac{\rho_0}{\varepsilon_0}\left(\frac{r}{3} - \frac{r^2}{4R}\right)$
(C) $\frac{\rho_0}{3\varepsilon_0}\left(\frac{r}{3} - \frac{r^2}{4R}\right)$
(D) $\frac{\rho_0}{12\varepsilon_0}\left(\frac{r}{3} - \frac{r^2}{4R}\right)$

22. A thin disc of radius $b = 2a$ has a concentric hole of radius 'a' in it (see figure). It carries uniform surface charge 'σ' on it. If the electric field on its axis at height 'h' ($h << a$) from its centre is given as 'Ch' then value of 'C' is : **[2015 (Online)]**

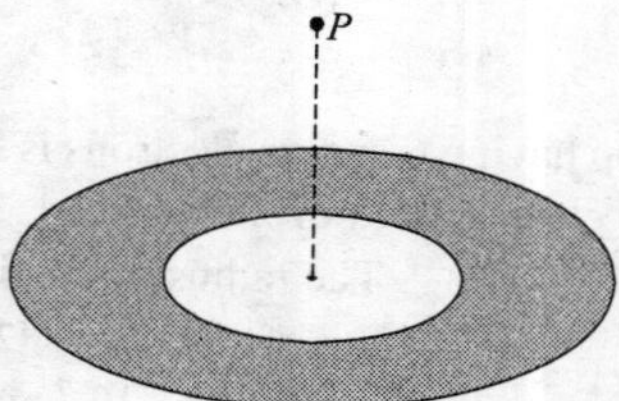

(A) $\frac{\sigma}{4a\,\epsilon_0}$
(B) $\frac{\sigma}{8a\,\epsilon_0}$
(C) $\frac{\sigma}{a\,\epsilon_0}$
(D) $\frac{\sigma}{2a\,\epsilon_0}$

23. A wire of length L (= 20 cm), is bent into a semicircular arc. If the two equal halves of the arc were each to be uniformly charged with charges $\pm Q$, [$|Q| = 10^3\varepsilon_0$ Coulomb where ε_0 is the permittivity (in SI units) of free space] the net electric field at the centre O of the semicircular arc would be : **[2015 (Online)]**

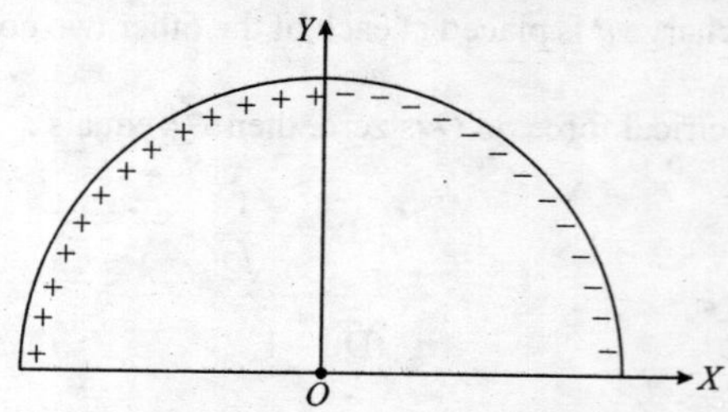

(A) $(50 \times 10^3\text{ N/C})\,\hat{j}$
(B) $(50 \times 10^3\text{ N/C})\,\hat{i}$
(C) $(25 \times 10^3\text{ N/C})\,\hat{j}$
(D) $(25 \times 10^3\text{ N/C})\,\hat{i}$

24. Shown in the figure are two point charges $+Q$ and $-Q$ inside the cavity of a spherical shell. The charges are kept near the surface of the cavity on opposite sides of the centre of the shell. If σ_1 is the surface charge on the inner surface and Q_1 net charge on it and σ_2 the surface charge on the outer surface and Q_2 net charge on it then : **[2015 (Online)]**

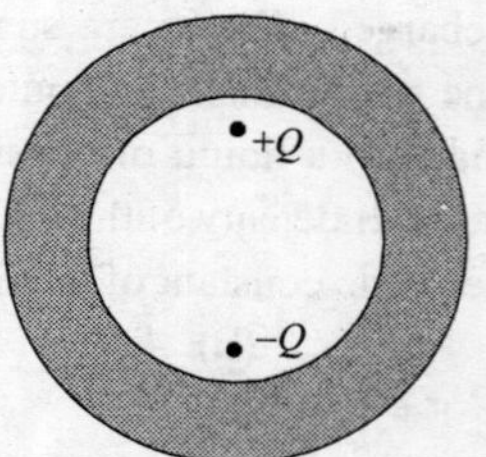

(A) $\sigma_1 \neq 0, Q_1 = 0$; $\sigma_2 \neq 0, Q_2 = 0$
(B) $\sigma_1 \neq 0, Q_1 = 0$; $\sigma_2 = 0, Q_2 = 0$
(C) $\sigma_1 = 0, Q_1 = 0$; $\sigma_2 = 0, Q_2 = 0$
(D) $\sigma_1 \neq 0, Q_1 \neq 0$; $\sigma_2 \neq 0, Q_2 \neq 0$

25. The region between two concentric spheres of radii 'a' and 'b' respectively (see figure), has volume charge density $\rho = \frac{A}{r}$, where A is a constant and r is the distance from the centre. At the centre of the spheres is a point charge Q. The value of A such that the electric field in the region between the spheres will be constant, is : **[2016]**

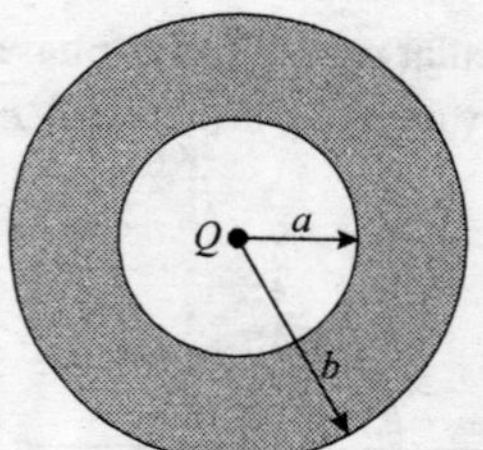

(A) $\frac{Q}{2\pi a^2}$
(B) $\frac{Q}{2\pi(b^2 - a^2)}$
(C) $\frac{2Q}{\pi(a^2 - b^2)}$
(D) $\frac{2Q}{\pi a^2}$

* * * * *

CHAPTER

15 ELECTRIC CHARGES AND FIELDS

15.2 ELECTRIC FLUX AND GAUSS'S LAW

1. A charged particle q is placed at the centre O of cube of length L ($ABCDEFGH$). Another same charge q is placed at a distance L from O. Then the electric flux through $ABCD$ is : **[2002]**

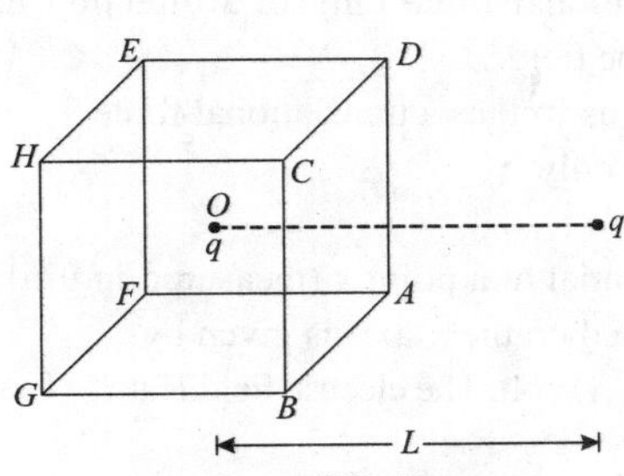

(A) $q/4\pi\epsilon_0 L$ (B) Zero
(C) $q/2\pi\epsilon_0 L$ (D) $q/3\pi\epsilon_0 L$

2. If the electric flux entering and leaving an enclosed surface respectively is ϕ_1 and ϕ_2, the electric charge inside the surface will be : **[2003]**

(A) $(\phi_2 - \phi_1)\varepsilon_0$ (B) $(\phi_1 - \phi_2)/\varepsilon_0$
(C) $(\phi_2 - \phi_1)/\varepsilon_0$ (D) $(\phi_1 - \phi_2)\varepsilon_0$

3. The electrostatic potential inside a charged spherical ball is given by $\phi = ar^2 + b$ where r is the distance from the centre; a, b are constant. Then the charge density inside the ball is : **[2011]**

(A) $-24\pi a \epsilon_0$ (B) $-6 a \epsilon_0$
(C) $-24\pi a \epsilon_0 r$ (D) $-6 a \epsilon_0 r$

4. The flat base of a hemisphere of radius a with no charge inside it lies in a horizontal plane. A uniform electric field $\vec{E}$ is applied at an angle $\pi/4$ with the vertical direction. The electric flux through the curved surface of the hemisphere is : **[2012 (Online)]**

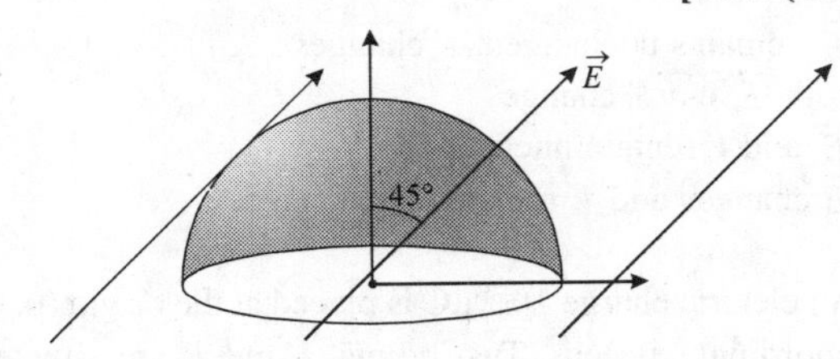

(A) $\pi a^2 E$ (B) $\dfrac{\pi a^2 E}{\sqrt{2}}$

(C) $\dfrac{\pi a^2 E}{2\sqrt{2}}$ (D) $\dfrac{(\pi + 2a\pi)^2 E}{(2\sqrt{2}^2)}$

5. Three positive charges of equal value q are placed at vertices of an equilateral triangle. The resulting lines of force should be sketched as in : **[2012 (Online)]**

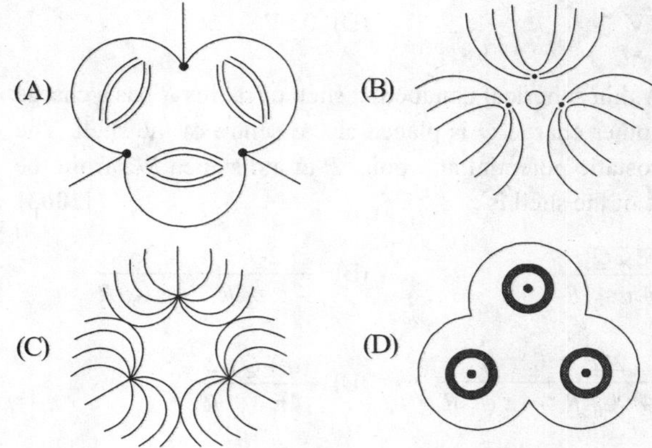

6. The electric potential $V(x)$ in a region around the origin is given by $V(x) = 4x^2$ volts. The electric charge enclosed in a cube of 1m side with its centre at the origin is (in coulomb) : **[2012 (Online)]**

(A) $8\varepsilon_0$ (B) $-4\varepsilon_0$
(C) 0 (D) $-8\varepsilon_0$

7. The electric field in a region of space is given by, $\vec{E} = E_0\hat{i} + 2E_0\hat{j}$ where $E_0 = 100$ N/C. The flux of the field through a circular surface of radius 0.02 m parallel to the Y-Z plane is nearly : **[2014 (Online)]**

(A) 0.125 Nm²/C (B) 0.02 Nm²/C
(C) 0.005 Nm²/C (D) 3.14 Nm²/C

8. A long cylindrical shell carries positive surface charge ρ in the upper half and negative surface charge $-\sigma$ in the lower half. The electric field lines around the cylinder will look like figure given in (figures are schematic and not drawn to scale) : **[2015]**

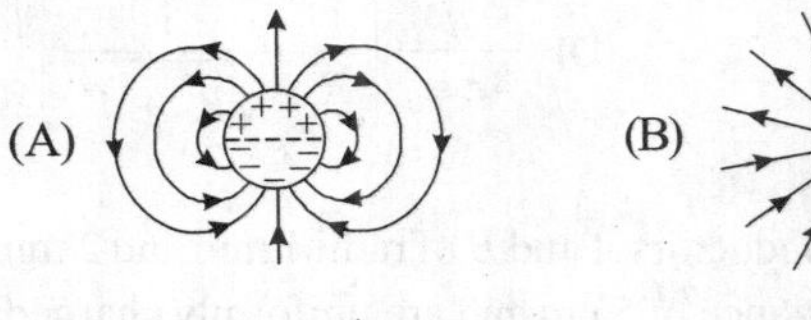

(C)
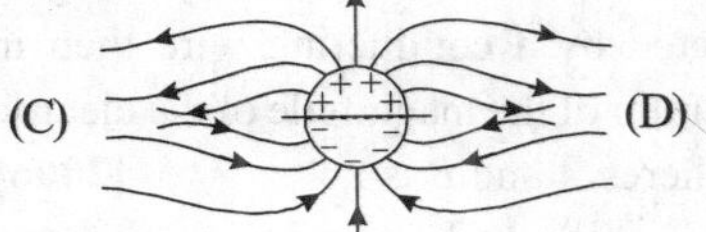

(D)
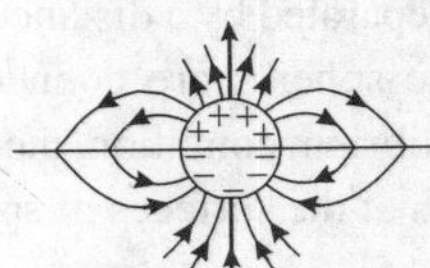

* * * * *

CHAPTER

16 ELECTRIC POTENTIAL AND CAPACITANCE

16.1 ELECTRIC POTENTIAL AND DIPOLE

1. On moving a charge of 20 C by 2 cm, 2 J of work is done, then the potential difference between the points is : **[2002]**

(A) 0.1 V (B) 8 V

(C) 2 V (D) 0.5 V

2. A thin spherical conducting shell of radius R has a charge q. Another charge Q is placed at the centre of the shell. The electrostatic potential at a point P at a distance $R/2$ from the centre of the shell is : **[2003]**

(A) $\frac{2Q}{4\pi \epsilon_0 R}$ (B) $\frac{2Q}{4\pi \epsilon_0 R} - \frac{2q}{4\pi \epsilon_0 R}$

(C) $\frac{2Q}{4\pi \epsilon_0 R} + \frac{q}{4\pi \epsilon_0 R}$ (D) $\frac{(q+Q)\,2}{4\pi \epsilon_0 R}$

3. A charged particle q is shot towards another charged particle Q which is fixed, with a speed v. It approaches Q upto a closest distance r and then returns. If q was given a speed $2v$, the closest distance of approach would be : **[2004]**

(A) r (B) $2r$

(C) $r/2$ (D) $r/4$

4. Two thin wire rings each having a radius R are placed at a distance d apart with their axes coinciding. The charges on the two rings are $+q$ and $-q$. The potential difference between the centres of the two rings is : **[2005]**

(A) $\frac{qR}{4\pi \epsilon_0 d^2}$ (B) $\frac{q}{2\pi \epsilon_0}\left[\frac{1}{R} - \frac{1}{\sqrt{R^2+d^2}}\right]$

(C) Zero (D) $\frac{q}{4\pi \epsilon_0}\left[\frac{1}{R} - \frac{1}{\sqrt{R^2+d^2}}\right]$

5. Two spherical conductors A and B of radii 1 mm and 2 mm are separated by a distance of 5 cm and are uniformly charged. If the spheres are connected by a conducting wire then in equilibrium condition, the ratio of the magnitude of the electric fields at the surfaces of spheres A and B is : **[2006]**

(A) 4 : 1 (B) 1 : 2

(C) 2 : 1 (D) 1 : 4

6. An electric dipole is placed at an angle of 30° to a non-uniform electric field. The dipole will experience : **[2006]**

(A) A translational force only in the direction of the field

(B) A translational force only in a direction normal to the direction of the field

(C) A torque as well as a translational force

(D) A torque only

7. The potential at a point x (measured in μm) due to some charges situated on the x-axis is given by :
$V(x) = 20/(x^2 - 4)$ volt. The electric field E at $x = 4$ μm is given by: **[2007]**

(A) $\frac{5}{3}$ V/μm and in the $-ve$ x direction

(B) $\frac{5}{3}$ V/μm and in the $+ve$ x direction

(C) $\frac{10}{9}$ V/μm and in the $-ve$ x direction

(D) $\frac{10}{9}$ V/μm and in the $+ve$ x direction

8. Charges are placed on the vertices of a square as shown. Let $\vec{E}$ be the electric field and V the potential at the centre. If the charges on A and B are interchanged with those on D and C respectively, then : **[2007]**

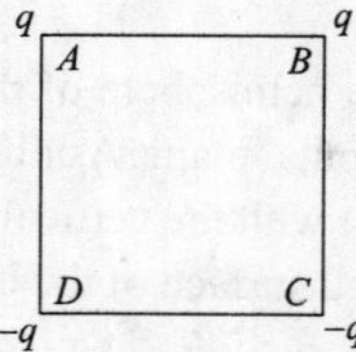

(A) $\vec{E}$ remains unchanged, V changes

(B) both $\vec{E}$ and V change

(C) $\vec{E}$ and V remain unchanged

(D) $\vec{E}$ changes and V remains unchanged

9. An electric charge 10^{-3} μC is placed at the origin (0, 0) of X-Y coordinate system. Two points A and B are situated at $(\sqrt{2}, \sqrt{2})$ and (2, 0) respectively. The potential difference between the points A and B will be : **[2007]**

(A) 9V (B) Zero

(C) 2V (D) 4.5 V

10. Statement-1 : For a charged particle moving from point P to point Q the net work done by an electrostatic field on the particle is independent of the path connecting point P to point Q.
Statement-2 : The net work done by a conservative force on an object moving along closed loop is zero. **[2009]**
(A) Statement-1 is true, Statement-2 is true; Statement-2 is not the correct explanation of Statement-1
(B) Statement-1 is false, Statement-2 is true
(C) Statement-1 is true, Statement-2 is false
(D) Statement-1 is true, Statement-2 is true; Statement-2 is the correct explanation of Statement-1

11. Two points P and Q are maintained at the potential of 10V and –4V, respectively. The work done in moving 100 electrons from P to Q is : **[2009]**
(A) -2.24×10^{-16} J (B) 2.24×10^{-16} J
(C) -9.60×10^{-17} J (D) 9.60×10^{-17} J

12. Two positive charges of magnitude 'q' are placed at the ends of a side (side-1) of a square of side '$2a$'. Two negative charges of the same magnitude are kept at the other corners. Starting from rest, if a charge Q moves from the middle of side-1 to the centre of square, its kinetic energy at the centre of square is : **[2011]**
(A) $\frac{1}{4\pi \epsilon_0}\frac{2qQ}{a}\left(1-\frac{1}{\sqrt{5}}\right)$ (B) Zero
(C) $\frac{1}{4\pi \epsilon_0}\frac{2qQ}{a}\left(1+\frac{1}{\sqrt{5}}\right)$ (D) $\frac{1}{4\pi \epsilon_0}\frac{2qQ}{a}\left(1-\frac{2}{\sqrt{5}}\right)$

13. An insulating solid sphere of radius R has a uniformly positive charge density ρ. As a result of this uniform charge distribution there is a finite value of electric potential at the centre of the sphere, at the surface of the sphere and also at a point out side the sphere. The electric potential at infinity is zero.
Statement-1 : When a charge 'q' is taken from the centre to the surface of the sphere, its potential energy changes by $\frac{q\rho}{3\epsilon_0}$.
Statement-2 : The electric field at a distance $r(r < R)$ from the centre of the sphere is $\frac{\rho r}{3\epsilon_0}$. **[2012]**
(A) Statement-1 is true, Statement-2 is true and Statement-2 is the correct explanation of Statement-1
(B) Statement-1 is true, Statement-2 is true and Statement-2 is not the correct explanation of Statement-1
(C) Statement-1 is true, Statement-2 is false
(D) Statement-1 is false, Statement-2 is true

14. A charge of total amount Q is distributed over two concentric hollow spheres of radii r and $R(R > r)$ such that the surface charge densities on the two spheres are equal. The electric potential at the common centre is : **[2012 (Online)]**
(A) $\frac{1}{4\pi\varepsilon_0}\frac{(R-r)Q}{(R^2+r^2)}$ (B) $\frac{1}{4\pi\varepsilon_0}\frac{(R+r)Q}{2(R^2+r^2)}$
(C) $\frac{1}{4\pi\varepsilon_0}\frac{(R+r)Q}{(R^2+r^2)}$ (D) $\frac{1}{4\pi\varepsilon_0}\frac{(R-r)Q}{(R^2+r^2)}$

15. A charge Q is uniformly distributed over a long rod AB of length L as shown in the figure. The electric potential at the point O lying at a distance L from the end A is : **[2013]**
(A) $\frac{Q}{8\pi \epsilon_0 L}$ (B) $\frac{3Q}{4\pi \epsilon_0 L}$
(C) $\frac{Q}{4\pi \epsilon_0 L \ln 2}$ (D) $\frac{Q \ln 2}{4\pi \epsilon_0 L}$

16. Two point dipoles of dipole moment $\vec{P}_1$ and $\vec{P}_2$ are at a distance x from each other and $\vec{P}_1 \parallel \vec{P}_2$. The force between the dipoles is : **[2013 (Online)]**
(A) $\frac{1}{4\pi\varepsilon_0}\frac{4p_1p_2}{x^4}$ (B) $\frac{1}{4\pi\varepsilon_0}\frac{3p_1p_2}{x^3}$
(C) $\frac{1}{4\pi\varepsilon_0}\frac{6p_1p_2}{x^4}$ (D) $\frac{1}{4\pi\varepsilon_0}\frac{8p_1p_2}{x^4}$

17. This question has Statement-1 and Statement-2. Of the four choices given after the Statements, choose the one that best describes the two Statements. **[2013 (Online)]**
Statement-1 : No work is required to be done to move a test charge between any two points on an equipotential surface.
Statement-2 : Electric lines of force at the equipotential surfaces are mutually perpendicular to each other.
(A) Statement-1 is true, Statement-2 is true, Statement-2 is the correct explanation of Statement-1
(B) Statement-1 is true, Statement-2 is true, Statement-2 is not the correct explanation of Statement-1
(C) Statement-1 is true, Statement-2 is false
(D) Statement-1 is false, Statement-2 is true

18. A point charge of magnitude + 1 μC is fixed at (0, 0, 0). An isolated uncharged spherical conductor, is fixed with its center at (4, 0, 0). The potential and the induced electric field at the centre of the sphere is : **[2013 (Online)]**
(A) 1.8×10^5 V and -5.625×10^6 V/m
(B) 0 V and 0 V/m
(C) 2.25×10^5 V and -5.625×10^6 V/m
(D) 2.25×10^5 V and 0 V/m

19. Consider a finite insulated, uncharged conductor placed near a finite positively charged conductor. The uncharged body must have a potential : **[2013 (Online)]**

(A) Less than the charged conductor and more than at infinity
(B) More than the charged conductor and less than at infinity
(C) More than the charged conductor and more than at infinity
(D) Less than the charged conductor and less than at infinity

20. Two small equal point charges of magnitude q are suspended from a common point on the ceiling by insulating mass less strings of equal lengths. They come to equilibrium with each string making angle θ from the vertical. If the mass of each charge is m, then the electrostatic potential at the centre of line joining them will be $\left(\frac{1}{4\pi\epsilon_0} = k\right)$: **[2013 (Online)]**

(A) $2\sqrt{kmg \tan\theta}$ (B) $\sqrt{kmg \tan\theta}$
(C) $4\sqrt{kmg / \tan\theta}$ (D) $4\sqrt{kmg \tan\theta}$

21. Assume that an electric field $\vec{E} = 30x^2\hat{i}$ exists in space. Then the potential difference $V_A - V_O$, where V_O is the potential at the origin and V_A the potential at $x = 2$ m is : **[2014]**

(A) 120 V (B) -120 V
(C) -80 V (D) 80 V

22. A uniformly charged solid sphere of radius R has potential V_0 (measured with respect to ∞) on its surface. For this sphere the equipotential surfaces with potentials $\frac{3V_0}{2}$, $\frac{5V_0}{4}$, $\frac{3V_0}{4}$ and $\frac{V_0}{4}$ have radius R_1, R_2, R_3, and R_4 respectively. Then : **[2015]**

(A) $R_1 = 0$ and $R_2 > (R_4 - R_3)$
(B) $R_1 \neq 0$ and $(R_2 - R_1) > (R_4 - R_3)$
(C) $R_1 = 0$ and $R_2 < (R_4 - R_3)$
(D) $2R < R_4$

23. An electric field $\vec{E} = (25\hat{i} + 30\hat{j})NC^{-1}$ exists in a region of space. If the potential at the origin is taken to be zero then the potential at $x = 2$m, $y = 2$m is : **[2015 (Online)]**

(A) -110 J/C (B) -140 J/C
(C) -120 J/C (D) -130 J/C

24. The potential (in volts) of a charge distribution is given by

$V(z) = 30 - 5z^2$ for $|z| \leq 1$m

$V(z) = 35 - 10|z|$ for $|z| \geq 1$m

$V(z)$ does not depend on x and y. If this potential is generated by a constant charge per unit volume ρ_0 (in units of ε_0) which is spread over a certain region, then choose the correct statement: **[2016 (Online)]**

(A) $\rho_0 = 20\,\varepsilon_0$ in the entire region
(B) $\rho_0 = 10\,\varepsilon_0$ for $|z| \leq 1$ m and $p_0 = 0$ elsewhere
(C) $\rho_0 = 20\,\varepsilon_0$ for $|z| \leq 1$ m and $p_0 = 0$ elsewhere
(D) $\rho_0 = 40\,\varepsilon_0$ in the entire region

25. Within a spherical charge distribution of charge density $\rho(r)$, N equipotential surfaces of potential V_0, $V_0 + \Delta V$, $V_0 + 2\Delta V$, ... $V_0 + N\Delta V (\Delta V > 0)$, are drawn and have increasing radii r_0, r_1, r_2, ... r_N, respectively. If the difference in the radii of the surfaces is constant for all values of V_0 and ΔV then : **[2016 (Online)]**

(A) $\rho(r) =$ constant (B) $\rho(r) \propto \frac{1}{r^2}$
(C) $\rho(r) \propto \frac{1}{r}$ (D) $\rho(r) \propto r$

* * * * *

CHAPTER

16 ELECTRIC POTENTIAL AND CAPACITANCE

16.2 CAPACITANCE

1. Capacitance (in F) of a spherical conductor having radius 1 m, is : **[2002]**

(A) 1.1×10^{-10} (B) 10^{-6}

(C) 9×10^{-9} (D) 10^{-3}

2. If there are n capacitors in parallel connected to V volt source, then the energy stored is equal to : **[2002]**

(A) CV (B) $\frac{1}{2}nCV^2$

(C) CV^2 (D) $\frac{1}{2n}CV^2$

3. The work done in placing a charge of 8×10^{-18} C on a condenser of capacity 100 micro-farad is : **[2003]**

(A) 16×10^{-32} J (B) 3.1×10^{-26} J

(C) 4×10^{-10} J (D) 32×10^{-32} J

4. A sheet of aluminium foil of negligible thickness is introduced between the plates of a capacitor. The capacitance of the capacitor : **[2003]**

(A) Decreases (B) Remains unchanged

(C) Becomes infinite (D) Increases

5. A parallel plate capacitor is made by stacking n equally spaced plates connected alternatively. If the capacitance between any two adjacent plates is C, then the resultant capacitance is : **[2005]**

(A) $(n-1)C$ (B) $(n+1)C$

(C) C (D) nC

6. A fully charged capacitor has a capacitance C. It is discharged through a small coil of resistance wire embedded in a thermally insulated block of specific heat capacity s and mass m. If the temperature of the block is raised by ΔT, the potential difference V across the capacitance is : **[2005]**

(A) $\sqrt{\frac{2mC\Delta T}{s}}$ (B) $\frac{mC\Delta T}{s}$

(C) $\frac{ms\Delta T}{C}$ (D) $\sqrt{\frac{2ms\Delta T}{C}}$

7. Two insulating plates are both uniformly charged in such a way that the potential difference between them is $V_2 - V_1 = 20$ V. (i.e., plate 2 is at a higher potential). The plates are separated by $d = 0.1$ m and can be treated as infinitely large. An electron is released from rest on the inner surface of plate 1. What is its speed when it hits plate 2? **[2006]**

($e = 1.6 \times 10^{-19}$ C, $m_0 = 9.11 \times 10^{-31}$ kg)

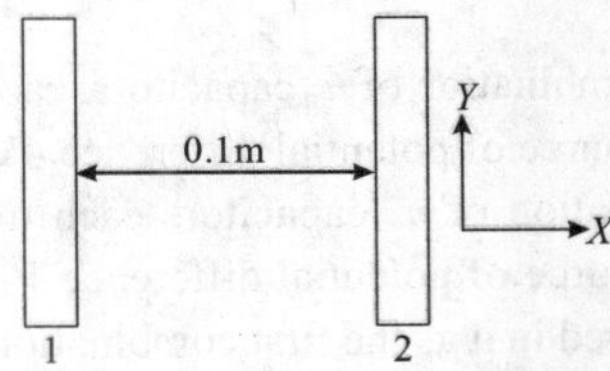

(A) 2.65×10^{6} m/s (B) 7.02×10^{12} m/s

(C) 1.87×10^{6} m/s (D) 32×10^{-19} m/s

8. A parallel plate condenser with a dielectric of dielectric constant K between the plates has a capacity C and is charged to a potential V volts. The dielectric slab is slowly removed from between the plates and then re-inserted. The net work done by the system in this process is : **[2007]**

(A) $\frac{1}{2}(K-1)CV^2$ (B) $CV^2(K-1)/K$

(C) $(K-1)CV^2$ (D) Zero

9. A battery is used to charge a parallel plate capacitor till the potential difference between the plates becomes equal to the electromotive force of the battery. The ratio of the energy stored in the capacitor and the work done by the battery will be : **[2007]**

(A) 1 (B) 2

(C) 1/4 (D) 1/2

10. A parallel plate capacitor with air between the plates has a capacitance of 9 pF. The separation between its plates is 'd'. The space between the plates is now filled with two dielectrics. One of the dielectric has dielectric constant $K_1 = 3$ and thickness $\frac{d}{3}$ while the other one has dielectric constant $K_2 = 6$ and thickness $\frac{2d}{3}$. Capacitance of the capacitor is now : **[2008]**

(A) 1.8 pF (B) 45 pF

(C) 40.5 pF (D) 20.25 pF

11. Two circuits (a) and (b) have charged capacitors of capacitance C, 2C and 3C with open switches. Charges on each of the capacitor are as shown in the figures. On closing the switches : **[2012 (Online)]**

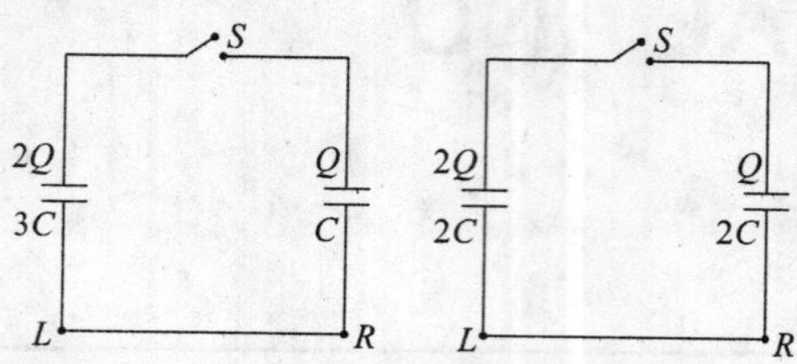

(A) No charge flows in (a) but charge flows from R to L in (b)
(B) Charges flow from L to R in both (a) and (b)
(C) Charges flows from R to L in (a) and from L to R in (b)
(D) No charge flows in (a) but charge flows from L to R in (b)

12. A series combination of n_1 capacitors, each of capacity C_1 is charged by source of potential difference 4V. When another parallel combination of n_2 capacitors each of capacity C_2 is charged by a source of potential difference V, it has the same total energy stored in it as the first combination has. The value of C_2 in terms of C_1 is then : **[2012 (Online)]**

(A) $16\frac{n_2}{n_1}C_1$ (B) $\frac{2C_1}{n_1 n_2}$
(C) $2\frac{n_2}{n_1}C_1$ (D) $\frac{16C_1}{n_1 n_2}$

13. This question has Statement-1 and Statement-2. Of the four choices given after the Statements, choose the one that best describes the two Statements. **[2012 (Online)]**
Statement-1 : It is not possible to make a sphere of capacity 1 farad using a conducting material.
Statement-2 : It is possible for earth as its radius is 6.4×10^6 m.
(A) Statement-1 is true, Statement-2 is true, Statement-2 is the correct explanation of Statement-1
(B) Statement-1 is false, Statement-2 is true
(C) Statement-1 is true, Statement-2 is true, Statement-2 is not the correct explanation of Statement-1
(D) Statement-1 is true, Statement-2 is false

14. Two capacitors C_1 and C_2 are charged to 120V and 200V respectively. It is found that by connecting them together the potential on each one can be made zero. Then : **[2013]**
(A) $5C_1 = 3C_2$ (B) $3C_1 = 5C_2$
(C) $3C_1 + 5C_2 = 0$ (D) $9C_1 = 4C_2$

15. A uniform electric field $\vec{E}$ exists between the plates of a charged condenser. A charged particle enters the space between the plates and perpendicular to $\vec{E}$. The path of the particle between the plates is a : **[2013 (Online)]**
(A) Straight line (B) Hyperbola
(C) Parabola (D) Circle

16. To establish an instantaneous current of 2 A through a 1 μF capacitor; the potential difference across the capacitor plates should be changed at the rate of : **[2013 (Online)]**
(A) 2×10^4 V/s (B) 4×10^6 V/s
(C) 2×10^6 V/s (D) 4×10^4 V/s

17. A parallel plate capacitor having a separation between the plates d, plate are A and material with dielectric constant K has capacitance C_0. Now one-third of the material is replaced by another material with dielectric constant 2 K, so that effectively there are two capacitors one with area $\frac{1}{3}A$, dielectric constant 2K and another with area $\frac{2}{3}A$ and dielectric constant K. If the capacitance of this new capacitor is C then C/C_0 is : **[2013 (Online)]**
(A) 1 (B) 4/3
(C) 2/3 (D) 1/3

18. A parallel plate capacitor is made of two circular plates separated by a distance of 5 mm and with a dielectric of dielectric constant 2.2 between them. When the electric field in the dielectric is 3×10^4 V/m, the charge density of the positive plate will be closed to : **[2014]**
(A) 6×10^{-7} C/m² (B) 3×10^{-7} C/m²
(C) 3×10^4 C/m² (D) 6×10^4 C/m²

19. The gap between the plates of a parallel plate capacitor of area A and distance between plates d, is filled with a dielectric whose permittivity varies linearly from ϵ_1 at one plate to ϵ_2 at the other. The capacitance of capacitor is: **[2014 (Online)]**
(A) $\epsilon_0(\epsilon_1 + \epsilon_2)A/d$ (B) $\epsilon_0(\epsilon_2 + \epsilon_1)A/2d$
(C) $\epsilon_0 A/[d\ln(\epsilon_2/\epsilon_1)]$ (D) $\epsilon_0(\epsilon_2 - \epsilon_1)A/[d\ln(\epsilon_2/\epsilon_1)]$

20. Three capacitors, each of $3\mu F$, are provided these cannot be combined to provide the resultant capacitance of : **[2014 (Online)]**
(A) 1 μF (B) 2 μF
(C) 4.5 μF (D) 6 μF

21. A parallel plate capacitor is made of two plates of length l, width w and separated by distance d. A dielectric slab (dielectric constant K) that fits exactly between the plates is held near the edge of the plates. It is pulled into the capacitor by a force $F = -\frac{\partial U}{\partial x}$ where U is the energy of the capacitor when dielectric is inside the capacitor up to distance x (See figure). If the charge on the capacitor is Q then the force on the dielectric when it is near the edge is : **[2014 (Online)]**

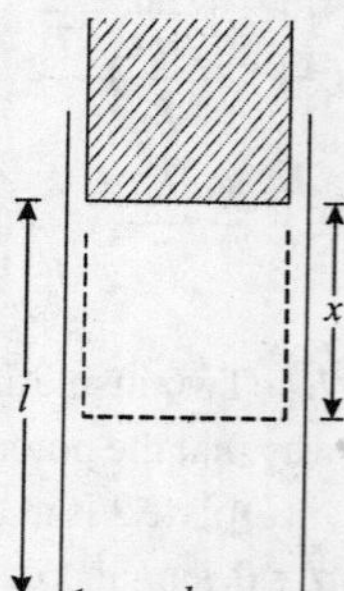

(A) $\frac{Q^2 d}{2\omega l^2 \varepsilon_0}K$
(B) $\frac{Q^2 w}{2\omega l^2 \varepsilon_0}(K-1)$
(C) $\frac{Q^2 d}{2wl^2 \varepsilon_0}(K-1)$
(D) $\frac{Q^2 w}{2dl^2 \varepsilon_0}K$

22. The space between the plates of a parallel plate capacitor is filled with a 'dielectric' whose 'dielectric constant' varies with distance as per the relation :

$K(x) = K_0 + \lambda x (\lambda = a \text{ constant})$

The capacitance C, of the capacitor, would be related to its vacuum capacitance C_0 for the relation : **[2014 (Online)]**

(A) $C = \frac{\lambda d}{\ln(1+K_0\lambda d)} C_0$ (B) $C = \frac{\lambda}{d \cdot \ln(1+K_0\lambda d)} C_0$

(C) $C = \frac{\lambda d}{\ln(1+\lambda d / K_0)} C_0$ (D) $C = \frac{\lambda}{d \cdot \ln(1+K_0/\lambda d)} C_0$

23. In the given circuit, charge Q_2 on the 2 μF capacitor changes as C is varied from 1 μF to 3 μF. Q_2 as a function of 'C' is given properly by : (figures are drawn schematically and are not to scale) : **[2015]**

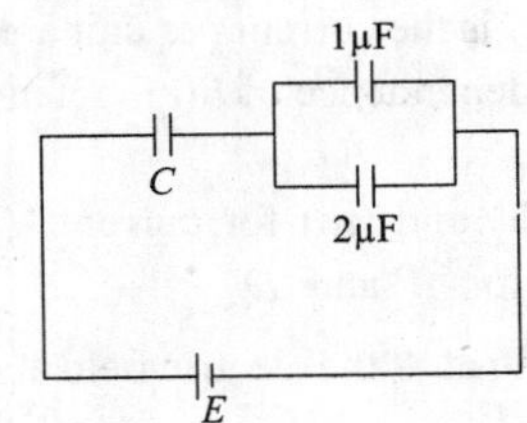

(A) 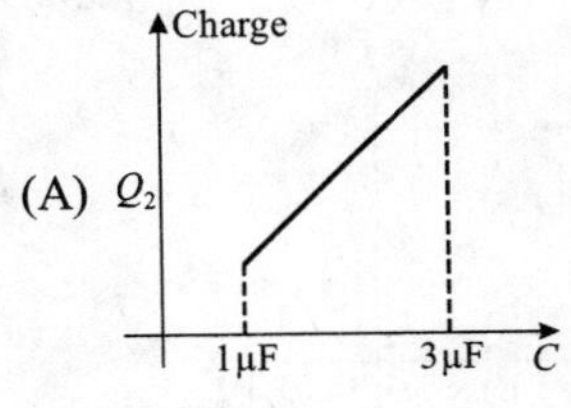

(B) 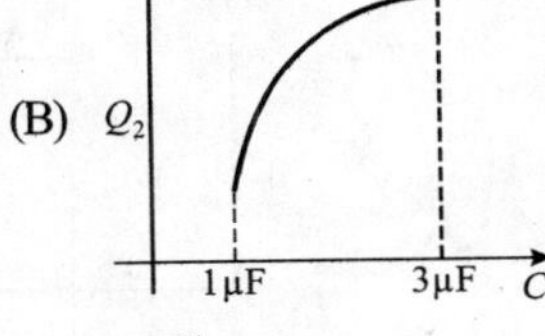

(C) 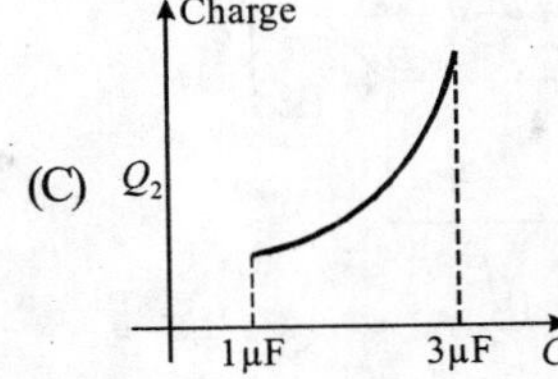

(D) 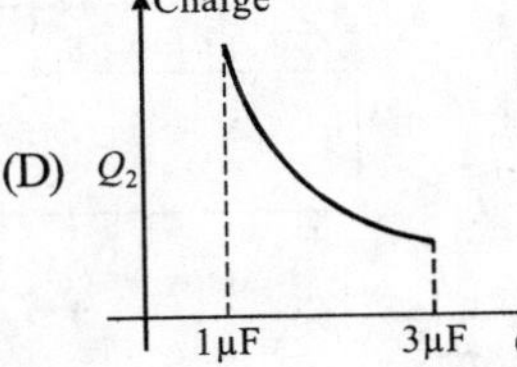

24. In figure a system of four capacitors connected across a 10 V battery is shown. Charge that will flow from switch S when it is closed is : **[2015 (Online)]**

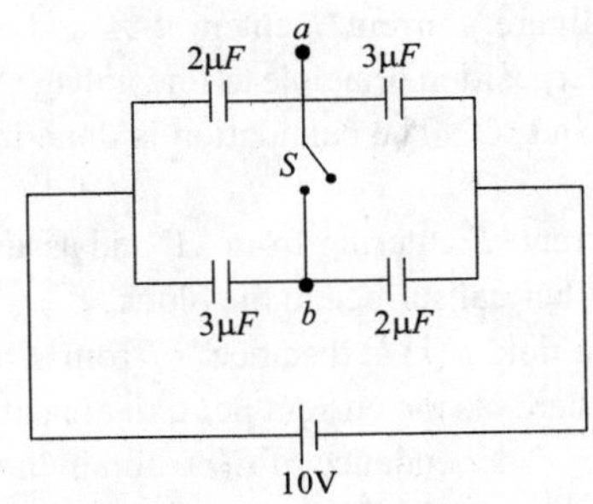

(A) 5 μC from b to a (B) 20 μC from a to b

(C) Zero (D) 5 μC from a to b

25. A combination of capacitors is set up as shown in the figure. The magnitude of the electric field, due to a point charge Q (having a charge equal to the sum of the charges on the 4 μF and 9 μF capacitors), at a point distant 30 m from it, would equal : **[2016]**

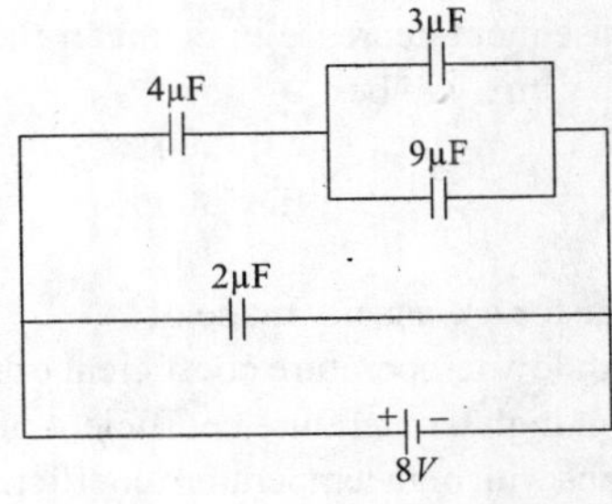

(A) 240 N/C (B) 360 N/C

(C) 420 N/C (D) 480 N/C

26. Three capacitors each of 4 μF are to be connected in such a way that the effective capacitance is 6 μF. This can be done by connecting them : **[2016 (Online)]**

(A) All in series

(B) All in parallel

(C) Two in parallel and one in series

(D) Two in series and one in parallel

27. Figure shows a network of capacitors where the numbers indicates capacitances in micro Farad. The value of capacitance C if the equivalent capacitance between point A and B is to be 1 μF is : **[2016 (Online)]**

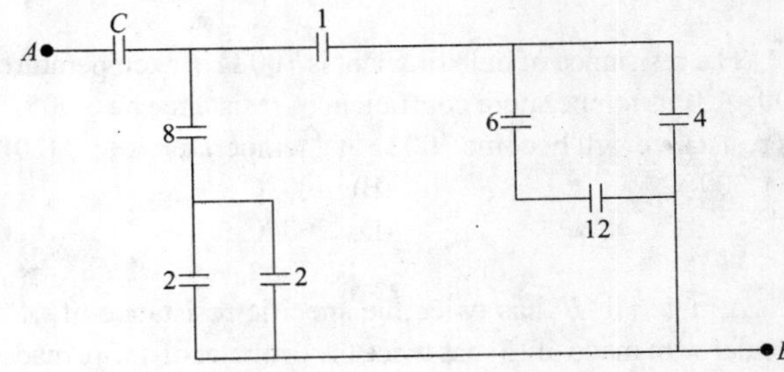

(A) $\frac{32}{23} \mu F$ (B) $\frac{31}{23} \mu F$

(C) $\frac{33}{23} \mu F$ (D) $\frac{34}{23} \mu F$

* * * * *

CHAPTER

17 CURRENT ELECTRICITY

17.1 CURRENT ELECTRICITY

1. The length of a given cylindrical wire is increased by 100%. Due to the consequent decrease in diameter the change in the resistance of the wire will be : **[2003]**

(A) 200 % (B) 100 %

(C) 50 % (D) 300 %

2. The thermistor are usually made of : **[2004]**

(A) metals with low temperature coefficient of resistivity

(B) metals with high temperature coefficient of resistivity

(C) metal oxides with high temperature coefficient of resistivity

(D) semiconducting materials having low temperature coefficient of resistivity

3. An electric current is passed through a circuit containing two wires of the same material, connected in parallel. If the lengths and radii of the wires are in the ratio of 4/3 and 2/3, then the ratio of the currents passing through the wire will be : **[2004]**

(A) 3 (B) 1/3

(C) 8/9 (D) 2

4. The resistance of the series combination of two resistance is S. When they are joined in parallel, the total resistance is P. If $S = nP$, then the minimum possible value of n is : **[2004]**

(A) 4 (B) 3

(C) 2 (D) 1

5. The resistance of bulb filament is 100 Ω at a temperature of 100°C. If its temperature coefficient of resistance be 0.005 /°C, its resistance will become 200 Ω at a temperature of : **[2006]**

(A) 300 °C (B) 400 °C

(C) 500 °C (D) 200 °C

6. A material 'B' has twice the specific resistance of 'A'. A circular wire made of 'B' has twice the diameter of a wire made of 'A'. Then for the two wires to have the same resistance, the ratio l_B/l_A of their respective lengths must be: **[2006]**

(A) 1 (B) $\frac{1}{2}$

(C) $\frac{1}{4}$ (D) 2

7. The resistance of a wire is 5 ohm at 50°C and 6 ohm at 100°C. The resistance of the wire at 0°C will be : **[2007]**

(A) 3 ohm (B) 2 ohm

(C) 1 ohm (D) 4 ohm

8. Consider a block of conducting material of resistivity 'ρ' shown in the figure. Current 'I' enters at 'A' and leaves from 'D'. We apply superposition principle to find voltage 'ΔV' developed between 'B' and 'C'. The calculation is done in the following steps :

(i) Take current 'I' entering from 'A' and assume it to spread over a hemispherical surface in the block.

(ii) Calculate field $E(r)$ at distance 'r' from A by using Ohm's law $E = \rho j$, where j is the current per unit area at 'r'

(iii) From the 'r' dependence of $E(r)$, obtain the potential $V(r)$ at r.

(iv) Repeat (i), (ii) and (iii) for current 'I' leaving 'D' and superpose results for 'A' and 'D'

For current entering at A, the electric field at a distance 'r' from A is : **[2008]**

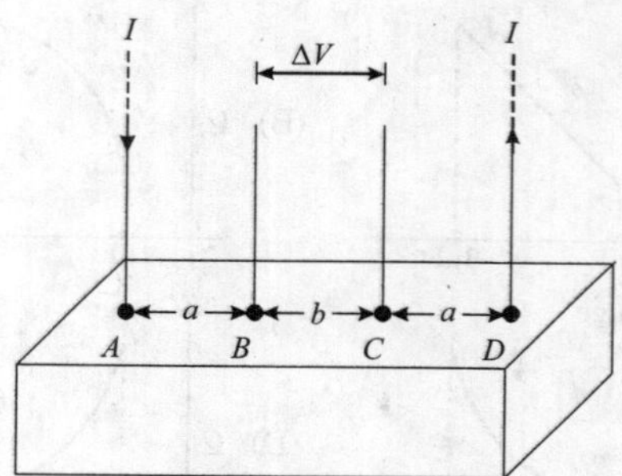

(A) $\frac{\rho I}{8\pi r^2}$ (B) $\frac{\rho I}{r^2}$

(C) $\frac{\rho I}{2\pi r^2}$ (D) $\frac{\rho I}{4\pi r^2}$

9. Consider a block of conducting material of resistivity 'ρ' shown in the figure. Current 'I' enters at 'A' and leaves from 'D'. We apply superposition principle to find voltage 'ΔV' developed between 'B' and 'C'. The calculation is done in the following steps :

(i) Take current 'I' entering from 'A' and assume it to spread over a hemispherical surface in the block.

(ii) Calculate field $E(r)$ at distance 'r' from A by using Ohm's law $E = \rho j$, where j is the current per unit area at 'r'

(iii) From the 'r' dependence of $E(r)$, obtain the potential $V(r)$ at r.

(iv) Repeat (i), (ii) and (iii) for current 'I' leaving 'D' and superpose results for 'A' and 'D'

ΔV measured between B and C is : **[2008]**

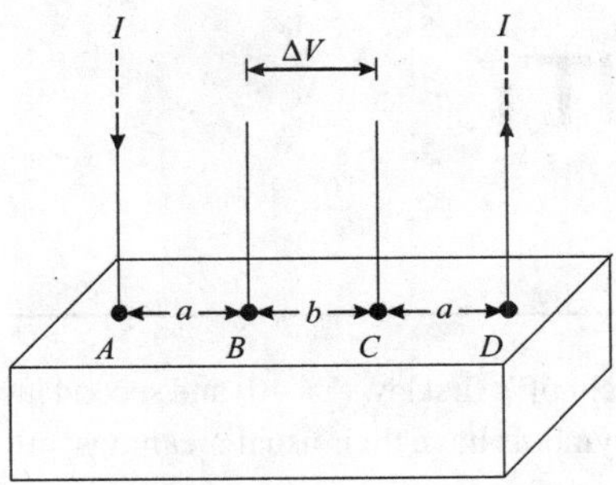

(A) $\frac{\rho I}{\pi a}-\frac{\rho I}{\pi(a+b)}$ (B) $\frac{\rho I}{a}-\frac{\rho I}{(a+b)}$

(C) $\frac{\rho I}{2\pi a}-\frac{\rho I}{2\pi(a+b)}$ (D) $\frac{\rho I}{2\pi(a+b)}$

10. Statement-1 : The temperature dependence of resistance is usually given as $R = R_0(1 + \alpha\Delta t)$. The resistance of a wire changes from 100 Ω to 150 Ω when its temperature is increased from 27°C to 227°C. This implies that $\alpha = 2.5 \times 10^{-3}$ /°C.

Statement-2 : $R = R_0(1 + \alpha\Delta t)$ is valid only when the change in the temperature ΔT is small and $\Delta R = (R - R_0) << R_0$. **[2009]**

(A) Statement-1 is true, Statement-2 is true; Statement-2 is not the correct explanation of Statement-1

(B) Statement-1 is false, Statement-2 is true

(C) Statement-1 is true, Statement-2 is false

(D) Statement-1 is true, Statement-2 is true; Statement-2 is the correct explanation of Statement-1

11. Two conductors have the same resistance at 0°C but their temperature coefficients of resistance are α_1 and α_2. The respective temperature coefficients of their series and parallel combinations are nearly : **[2010]**

(A) $\frac{\alpha_1+\alpha_2}{2}, \frac{\alpha_1+\alpha_2}{2}$ (B) $\frac{\alpha_1+\alpha_2}{2}, \alpha_1+\alpha_2$

(C) $\alpha_1+\alpha_2, \frac{\alpha_1+\alpha_2}{2}$ (D) $\alpha_1+\alpha_2, \frac{\alpha_1\alpha_2}{\alpha_1+\alpha_2}$

12. If 400 Ω of resistance is made by adding four 100 Ω resistance of tolerance 5%, then the tolerance of the combination is : **[2011]**

(A) 20% (B) 5%

(C) 10% (D) 15%

13. If a wire is stretched to make it 0.1 % longer, its resistance will : **[2011]**

(A) Decrease by 0.2% (B) Decrease by 0.05%

(C) Increase by 0.05% (D) Increase by 0.2%

14. The resistance of a wire is R. It is bent at the middle by 180° and both the ends are twisted together to make a shorter wire. The resistance of the new wire is : **[2012 (Online)]**

(A) $2R$ (B) $R/2$

(C) $R/4$ (D) $R/8$

15. When 5 V potential difference is applied across a wire of length 0.1 m, the drift speed of electrons is 2.5×10^{-4} ms^{1}. If the electron density in the wire is 8×10^{28} m^{-3}, the resistivity of the material is close to : **[2015]**

(A) 1.6×10^{-8} Ωm (B) 1.6×10^{-7} Ωm

(C) 1.6×10^{-6} Ωm (D) 1.6×10^{-5} Ωm

16. Suppose the drift velocity v_d in a material varied with the applied electric field E as $v_d \propto \sqrt{E}$. The $V - I$ graph for a wire made of such a material is best given by : **[2015 (Online)]**

(A)
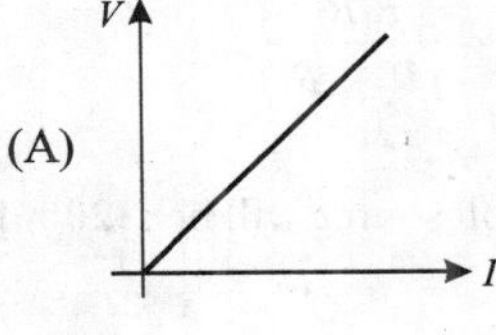

(B)
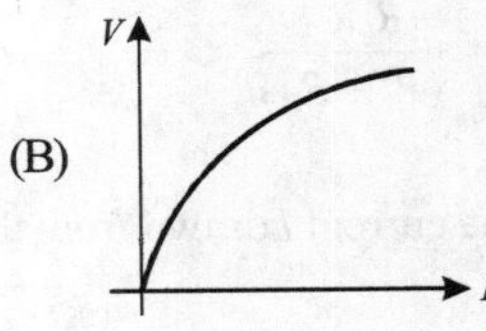

(C)
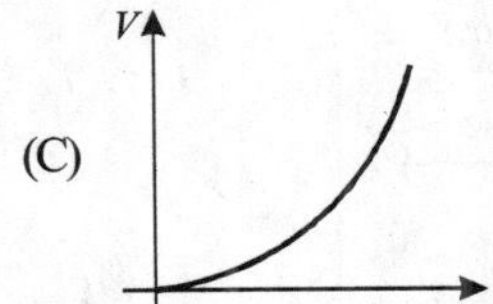

(D)
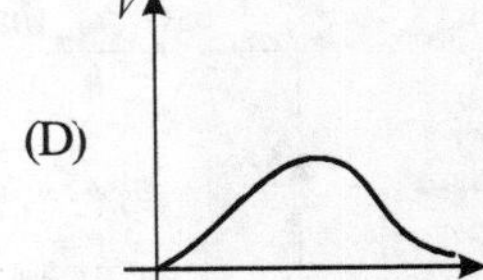

* * * * *

CHAPTER

17 CURRENT ELECTRICITY

17.2 CIRCUIT ANALYSIS

1. A 3 volt battery with negligible internal resistance is connected in a circuit as shown in the figure. The current I, in the circuit will be : **[2003]**

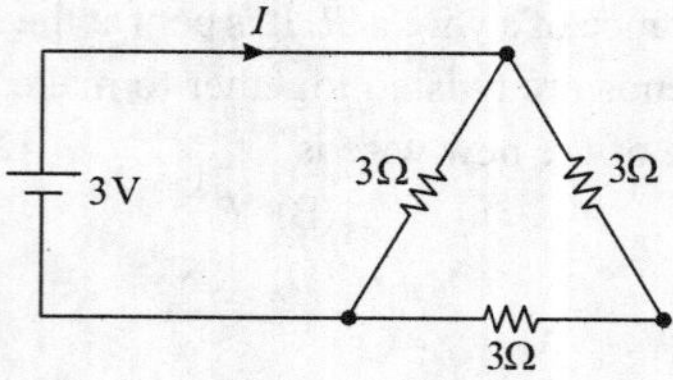

(A) 1 A (B) 1.5 A
(C) 2 A (D) 1/3 A

2. Two sources of equal emf are connected to an external resistance R. The internal resistances of the two sources are R_1 and R_2 ($R_2 > R_1$). If the potential difference across the source having internal resistance R_2, is zero, then : **[2005]**

(A) $R = \dfrac{R_2 \times (R_1 + R_2)}{(R_2 - R_1)}$ (B) $R = R_2 - R_1$

(C) $R = \dfrac{R_1 R_2}{(R_1 + R_2)}$ (D) $R = \dfrac{R_1 R_2}{(R_2 - R_1)}$

3. The current I drawn from the 5 volt source will be : **[2006]**

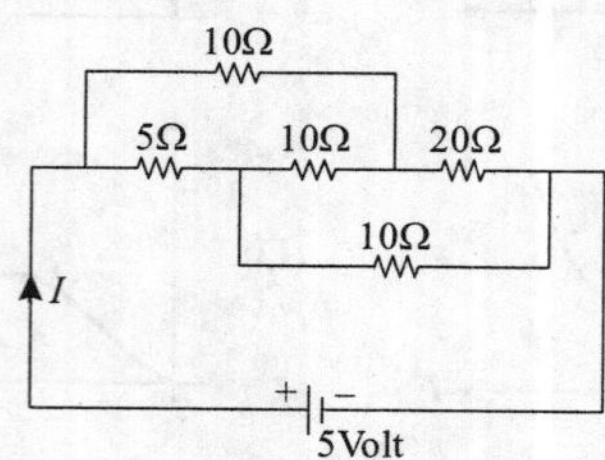

(A) 0.33 A (B) 0.5 A
(C) 0.67 A (D) 0.17 A

4. In a Wheatstone's bridge, three resistances P, Q and R are connected in the three arms and the fourth arm is formed by two resistances S_1 and S_2 connected in parallel. The condition for the bridge to be balanced will be : **[2006]**

(A) $\dfrac{P}{Q} = \dfrac{2R}{S_1 + S_2}$ (B) $\dfrac{P}{Q} = \dfrac{R(S_1 + S_2)}{S_1 S_2}$

(C) $\dfrac{P}{Q} = \dfrac{R(S_1 + S_2)}{2 S_1 S_2}$ (D) $\dfrac{P}{Q} = \dfrac{R}{S_1 + S_2}$

5. The kirchhoff's first law ($\Sigma i = 0$) and second law ($\Sigma iR = \Sigma E$), Where the symbols have their usual meanings, are respectively based on : **[2006]**

(A) conservation of charge, conservation of momentum
(B) conservation of energy, conservation of charge
(C) conservation of momentum, conservation of charge
(D) conservation of charge, conservation of energy

6. A 5 V battery with internal resistance 2 Ω and a 2 V battery with internal resistance 1 Ω are connected to a 10 Ω resistor as shown in the figure. The current in the 10 Ω resistor is : **[2008]**

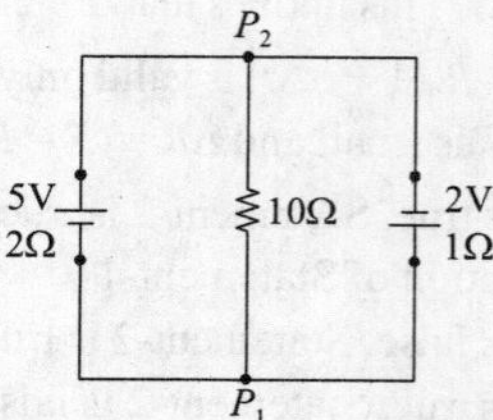

(A) 0.27 A P_2 to P_1 (B) 0.03 A P_1 to P_2
(C) 0.03 A P_2 to P_1 (D) 0.27 A P_1 to P_2

7. A d.c. source of emf E_1 = 100 V and internal resistance r = 0.5 Ω, a storage battery of emf E_2 = 90 V and an external resistance R are connected as shown in figure. For what value of R no current will pass through the battery ? **[2013 (Online)]**

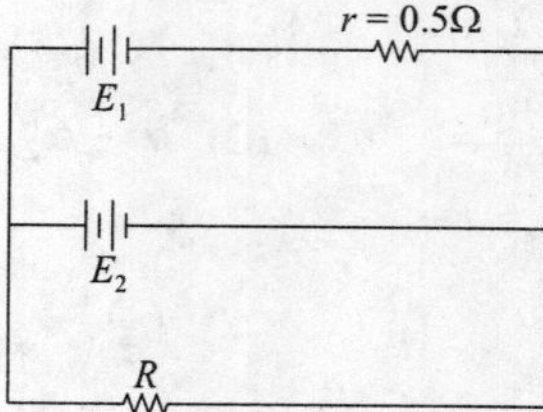

(A) 5.5 Ω (B) 3.5 Ω
(C) 4.5 Ω (D) 2.5 Ω

8. A letter 'A' is constructed of a uniform wire with resistance 1.0 Ω per cm. The sides of the letter are 20 cm and the cross piece in the middle is 10 cm long. The apex angle is 60°. The resistance between the ends of the legs is closed to : **[2013 (Online)]**

(A) 50.0 Ω (B) 10 Ω
(C) 36.7 Ω (D) 26.7 Ω

9. Six equal resistances are connected between points P, Q and R as shown in figure. Then net resistance will be maximum between : **[2013 (Online)]**

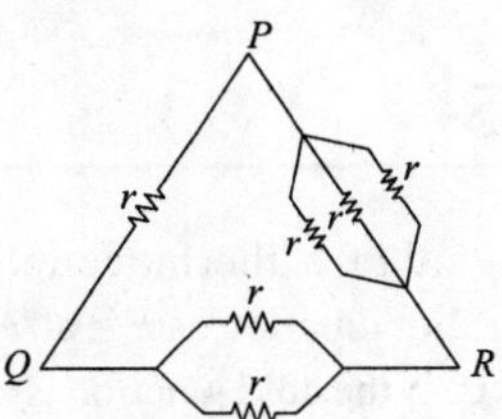

(A) P and R (B) P and Q
(C) Q and R (D) Any two points

10. A d.c. main supply of e.m.f. 220 V is connected across a storage battery of e.m.f. 200 V through a resistance of 1 Ω. The battery terminals are connected to an external resistance 'R'. The minimum value of 'R', so that a current passes through the battery to charge it is : **[2014 (Online)]**

(A) 7 Ω (B) 9 Ω
(C) 11 Ω (D) Zero

11. In the circuit shown, current (in A) through 50 V and 30 V batteries are, respectively : **[2014 (Online)]**

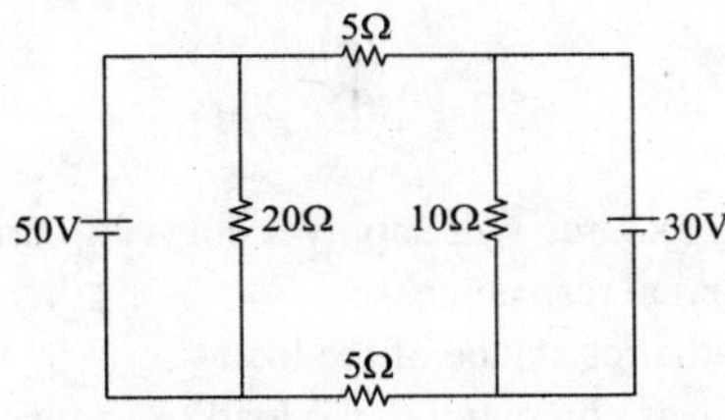

(A) 2.5 and 3 (B) 3.5 and 2
(C) 4.5 and 1 (D) 3 and 2.5

12. In the circuit shown, the current in the 1 Ω resistor is : **[2015]**

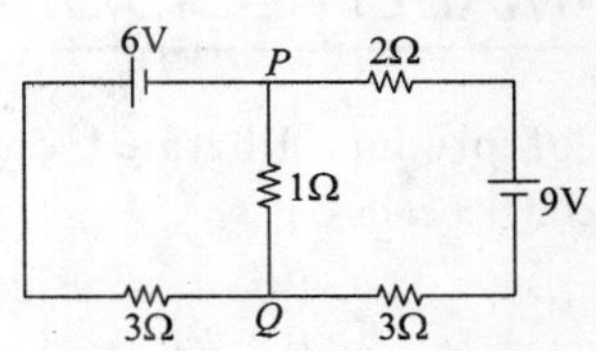

(A) 1.3 A, from P to Q (B) 0 A
(C) 0.13 A, from Q to P (D) 0.13 A, from P to Q

13. In the electric network shown, when no current flows through the 4 Ω resistor in the arm EB, the potential difference between the points A and D will be : **[2015 (Online)]**

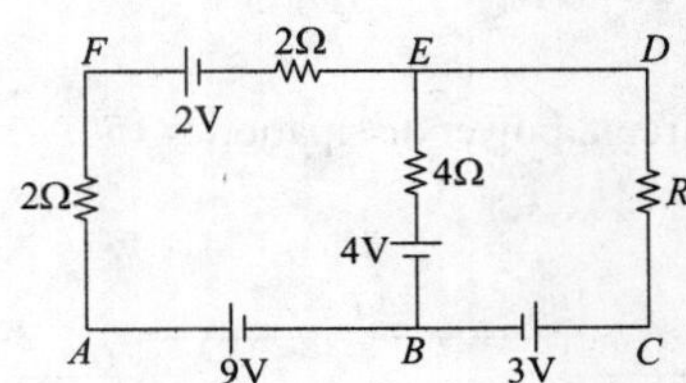

(A) 6V (B) 3V
(C) 5V (D) 4V

* * * * *

CHAPTER

17 CURRENT ELECTRICITY

17.3 THERMAL EFFECTS OF CURRENT & RC CIRCUITS

1. The mass of product liberated on anode in an electrochemical cell depends on : **[2002]**

(A) $(It)^{1/2}$ (B) It

(C) I/t (D) I^2t

2. A wire when connected to 220 V mains supply has power dissipation P_1. Now the wire is cut into two equal pieces which are connected in parallel to the same supply. Power dissipation in this case is P_2. Then $P_2 : P_1$ is: **[2002]**

(A) 1 (B) 4

(C) 2 (D) 3

3. If in the circuit, power dissipation is 150 W, then R is : **[2002]**

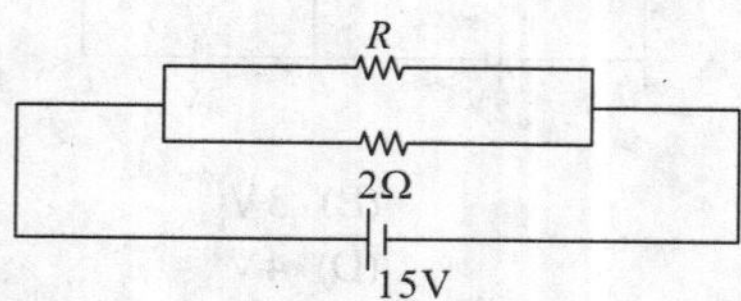

(A) 2 Ω (B) 6 Ω

(C) 5 Ω (D) 4 Ω

4. The thermo e.m.f. of a thermo-couple is 25μ V/°C at room temperature. A galvanometer of 40 ohm resistance, capable of detecting current as low as 10^{-5} A, is connected with the thermo couple. The smallest temperature difference that can be detected by this system is : **[2003]**

(A) 16°C (B) 12°C

(C) 8°C (D) 20°C

5. The negative *Zn* pole of a Daniell cell, sending a constant current through a circuit, decreases in mass by 0.13 g in 30 minutes. If the electrochemical equivalent of *Zn* and *Cu* are 32.5 and 31.5 respectively, the increase in the mass of the positive *Cu* pole in this time is : **[2003]**

(A) 0.180 g (B) 0.141 g

(C) 0.126 g (D) 0.242 g

6. A 220 volt, 1000 watt bulb is connected across a 110 volt mains supply. The power consumed will be : **[2003]**

(A) 750 watt (B) 500 watt

(C) 250 watt (D) 1000 watt

7. The thermo emf of a thermocouple varies with the temperature θ of the hot junction as $E = a\theta + b\theta^2$ in volts where the ratio a/b is 700°C. If the cold junction is kept at 0°C, then the neutral temperature is : **[2004]**

(A) 1400 °C

(B) 350 °C

(C) 700 °C

(D) No neutral temperature is possible for this thermocouple

8. The electrochemical equivalent of a metal is 3.35×10^{-7} kg per Coulomb. The mass of the metal liberated at the cathode when a 3A current is passed for 2 seconds will be : **[2004]**

(A) 6.6×10^{57} kg (B) 9.9×10^{-7} kg

(C) 19.8×10^{-7} kg (D) 1.1×10^{-7} kg

9. Time taken by a 836 W heater to heat one litre of water from 10°C to 40°C is : **[2004]**

(A) 150 s (B) 100 s

(C) 50 s (D) 200 s

10. An energy source will supply a constant current into the load, if its internal resistance is : **[2005]**

(A) Equal to the resistance of the load

(B) Very large as compared to the load resistance

(C) Zero

(D) Non-zero but less than the resistance of the load

11. Two voltameters, one of copper and another of silver, are joined in parallel. When a total charge q flows through the voltameters, equal amount of metals are deposited. If the electrochemical equivalents of copper and silver are Z_1 and Z_2 respectively the charge which flows through the silver voltameter is : **[2005]**

(A) $\dfrac{q}{1+\dfrac{Z_2}{Z_1}}$ (B) $\dfrac{q}{1+\dfrac{Z_1}{Z_2}}$

(C) $q\dfrac{Z_2}{Z_1}$ (D) $q\dfrac{Z_1}{Z_2}$

12. A heater coil is cut into two equal parts and only one part is now used in the heater. The heat generated will now be : **[2005]**

(A) Four times (B) Doubled

(C) Halved (D) One fourth

13. The resistance of hot tungsten filament is about 10 times the cold resistance. What will be the resistance of 100 W and 200 V lamp when not in use ? **[2005]**

(A) 20 Ω (B) 40 Ω
(C) 200 Ω (D) 400 Ω

14. A thermocouple is made from two metals, Antimony and Bismuth. If one junction of the couple is kept hot and the other is kept cold, then, an electric current will : **[2006]**

(A) Flow from Antimony to Bismuth at the hot junction
(B) Flow from Bismuth to Antimony at the cold junction
(C) Now flow through the thermocouple
(D) Flow from Antimony to Bismuth at the cold junction

15. An electric bulb is rated 220 V-100 W. The power consumed by it when operated on 110 V will be : **[2006]**

(A) 75 W (B) 40 W
(C) 25 W (D) 50 W

16. Let C be the capacitance of a capacitor discharging through a resistor R. Suppose t_1 is the time taken for the energy stored in the capacitor to reduce to half its initial value and t_2 is the time taken for the charge to reduce to one-fourth its initial value. Then the ratio t_1/t_2 will be : **[2010]**

(A) 2 (B) 1
(C) 1/2 (D) 1/4

17. Combination of two identical capacitors, a resistor R and a *dc* voltage source of voltage 6 V is used in an experiment on $(C-R)$ circuit. It is found that for a parallel combination of the capacitor the time in which the voltage of the fully charged combination reduces to half its original voltage is 10 second. For series combination the time needed for reducing the voltage of the fully charged series combination by half is : **[2011]**

(A) 20 second (B) 10 second
(C) 5 second (D) 2.5 second

18. A resistor 'R' and $2\mu F$ capacitor in series is connected through a switch to 200 V direct supply. Across the capacitor is a neon bulb that lights up at 120 V. Calculate the value of R to make the bulb light up 5s after the switch has been closed. $(\log_{10} 2.5 = 0.4)$: **[2011]**

(A) $2.7 \times 10^6\ \Omega$ (B) $3.3 \times 10^7\ \Omega$
(C) $1.3 \times 10^4\ \Omega$ (D) $1.7 \times 10^5\ \Omega$

19. Two electric bulbs marked 25W-220 V and 100 W-220 V are connected in series to a 440 V supply. Which of the bulbs will fuse ? **[2012]**

(A) Neither (B) Both
(C) 100 W (D) 25 W

20. The figure shows an experimental plot for discharging of a capacitor in an R–C circuit. The time constant τ of this circuit lies between : **[2012]**

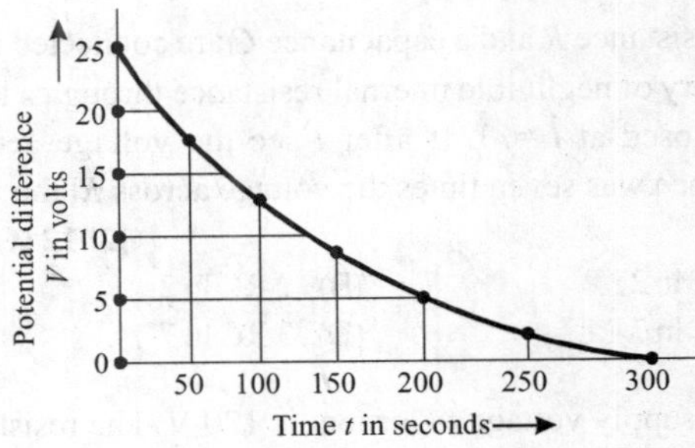

(A) 100 sec and 150 sec (B) 150 sec and 200 sec
(C) 0 and 50 sec (D) 50 sec and 100 sec

21. This question has Statement-1 and Statement-2. Of the four choice given after the Statements, choose the one that best describes the two Statements.

Statement-1 : The possibility of an electric bulb fusing is higher at the time of switching ON.

Statement-2 : Resistance of an electric bulb when it is not lit up is much smaller than when it is lit up. **[2012 (Online)]**

(A) Statement-1 is true, Statement-2 is false
(B) Statement-1 is false, Statement-2 is true, Statement-2 is not a correct explanation of Statement-1
(C) Statement-1 is true, Statement-2 is true, Statement-2 is a correct explanation of Statement-1
(D) Statement-1 is false, Statement-2 is true

22. Three resistors of 4 Ω, 6 Ω and 12 Ω are connected in parallel and the combination is connected in series with a 1.5 V battery of 1 Ω internal resistance. The rate of Joule heating in the 4 Ω resistor is : **[2012 (Online)]**

(A) 0.55 W (B) 0.33 W
(C) 0.25 W (D) 0.86 W

23. A 6.0 volt battery is connected to two light bulbs as shown in figure. Light bulb-1 has resistance 3 ohm while light bulb-2 has resistance 6 ohm. Battery has negligible internal resistance. Which bulb will glow brighter ? **[2012 (Online)]**

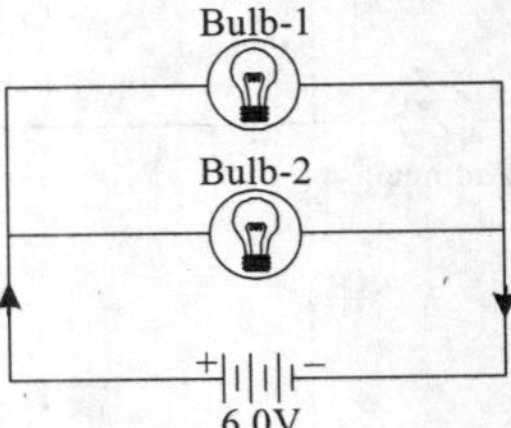

(A) Bulb-1 will glow more first and then its brightness will become less than bulb-2

(B) Bulb-1
(C) Bulb-2
(D) Both glow equally

24. A resistance R and a capacitance C are connected in series to a battery of negligible internal resistance through a key. The key is closed at $t = 0$. If after t sec the voltage across the capacitance was seven times the voltage across R, the value of t is : **[2012 (Online)]**

(A) 3 RC ln 2 (B) 2 RC ln 2
(C) 2 RC ln 7 (D) 3 RC ln 7

25. The supply voltage to a room is 120 V. The resistance of the lead wires is 6 Ω. A 60 W bulb is already switched on. What is the decrease of voltage across the bulb, when a 240 W heater is switched on in parallel to the bulb? **[2013]**

(A) Zero Volt (B) 2.9 Volt
(C) 13.3 Volt (D) 10.04 Volt

26. Which of the four resistances P, Q, R and S generate the greatest amount of heat when a current flows from A to B? **[2013 (Online)]**

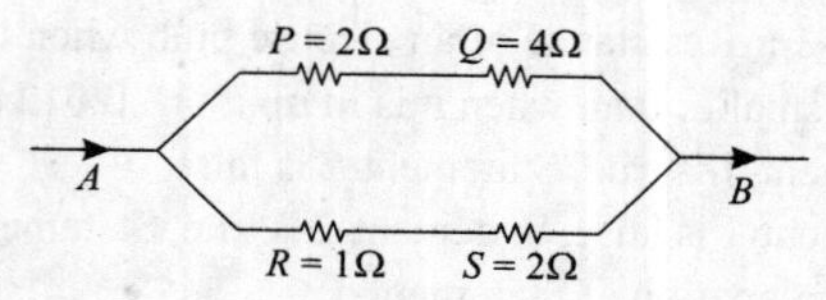

(A) Q (B) S
(C) P (D) R

27. In a large building, there are 15 bulbs of 40 W, 5 bulbs of 100 W, 5 fans of 80 W and 1 heater of 1 kW. The voltage of the electric mains is 220 V. The minimum capacity of the main fuse of the building will be : **[2014]**

(A) 8 A (B) 10 A
(C) 12 A (D) 14 A

28. Four bulbs B_1, B_2, B_3 and B_4 of 100 W each are connected to 220 V main as shown in the figure. The reading in an ideal ammeter will be : **[2014 (Online)]**

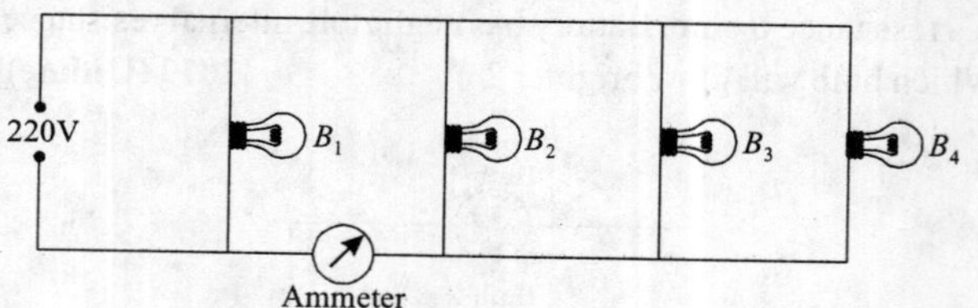

(A) 0.45 A (B) 0.90 A
(C) 1.35 A (D) 1.80 A

29. The circuit shown here has two batteries of 8.0 V and 16.0 V and three resistors 3 Ω, 9 Ω and 9 Ω and a capacitor of 5.0 μF. How much is the current I in the circuit in steady state ? **[2014 (Online)]**

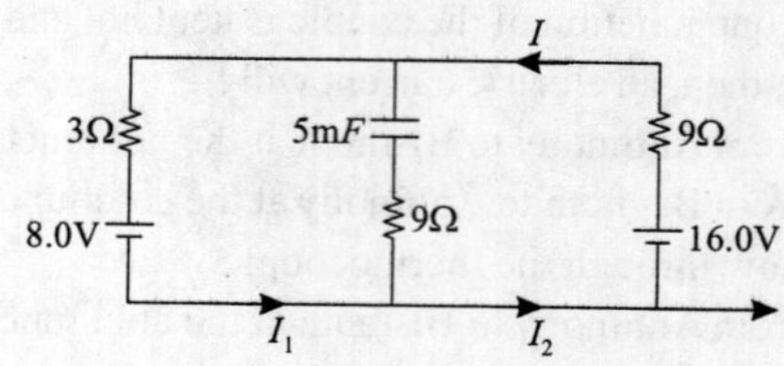

(A) 1.6 A (B) 0.67 A
(C) 2.5 A (D) 0.25 A

30. In the circuit shown, the resistance r is a variable resistance. If for $r = fR$, the heat generation in r is maximum then the value of f is : **[2016 (Online)]**

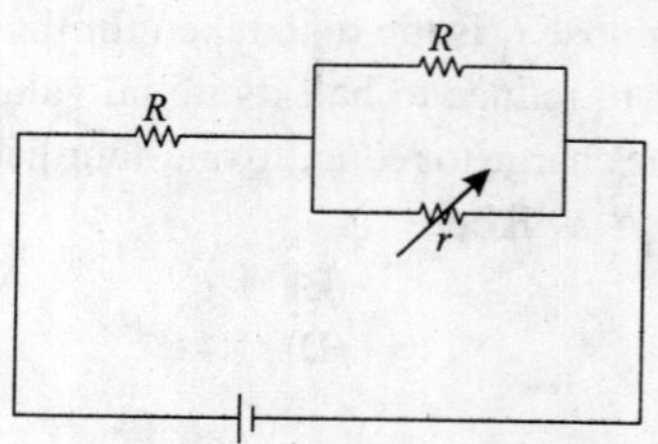

(A) $\frac{1}{2}$ (B) 1
(C) $\frac{1}{4}$ (D) $\frac{3}{4}$

31. The resistance of an electrical toaster has a temperature dependence given by $R(T) = R_0[1 + \alpha(T - T_0)]$ in its range of operation. At $T_0 = 300$ K, $R = 100\ \Omega$ and at $T = 500$ K, $R = 120\ \Omega$. The toaster is connected to a voltage source at 200 V and its temperature is raised at a constant rate from 300 to 500 K in 30 s. The total work done in raising the temperature is : **[2016 (Online)]**

(A) $400 \ln \frac{5}{6}$ J (B) $200 \ln \frac{2}{3}$ J
(C) 300 J (D) $400 \ln \frac{1.5}{1.3}$ J

* * * * *

CHAPTER

17 CURRENT ELECTRICITY

17.4 ELECTRICAL MEASURING INSTRUMENTS

1. If an ammeter is to be used in place of a voltmeter, then we must connect with the ammeter *a* : **[2002]**

(A) low resistance in parallel
(B) high resistance in parallel
(C) high resistance in series
(D) low resistance in series

2. An ammeter reads upto 1 A. Its internal resistance is 0.81 Ω. To increase the range to 10 A, the value of the required shunt is : **[2003]**

(A) 0.03 Ω (B) 0.3 Ω
(C) 0.9 Ω (D) 0.09 Ω

3. The length of a wire of a potentiometer is 100 cm, and the emf of its stand and cell is *E* volt. It is employed to measure the emf of a battery whose internal resistance is 0.5 Ω. If the balance point is obtained at $l = 30$ cm from the positive end, the emf of the battery is : **[2003]**

(A) $\frac{30E}{100.5}$ (B) $\frac{30E}{100-0.5}$

(C) $\frac{30(E-0.5i)}{100}$, where *i* is the current in the potentiometer wire

(D) $\frac{30E}{100}$

4. In a metre bridge experiment, null point is obtained at 20 cm from one end of the wire when resistance *X* is balanced against another resistance *Y*. If $X < Y$, then where will be the new position of the null point from the same end, if one decides to balance a resistance of 4*X* against *Y* ? **[2004]**

(A) 50 cm (B) 80 cm
(C) 40 cm (D) 70 cm

5. In a potentiometer experiment the balancing with a cell is at length 240 cm. On shunting the cell with a resistance of 2 Ω, the balancing length becomes 120 cm. The internal resistance of the cell is : **[2005]**

(A) 1 Ω (B) 0.5 Ω
(C) 4 Ω (D) 2 Ω

6. In the circuit, the galvanometer *G* shows zero deflection. If the batteries *A* and *B* have negligible internal resistance, the value of the resistor *R* will be : **[2005]**

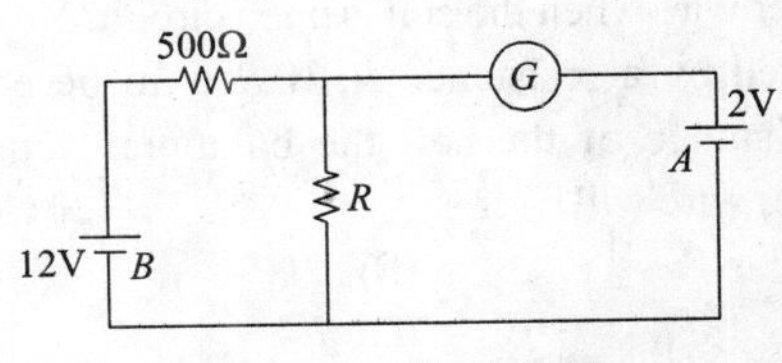

(A) 200 Ω (B) 100 Ω
(C) 500 Ω (D) 1000 Ω

7. A moving coil galvanometer has 150 equal divisions. Its current sensitivity is 10 divisions per milli ampere and voltage sensitivity is 2 divisions per millivolt. In order that each division reads 1 V, the resistance in Ohm's needed to be connected in series with the coil will be : **[2005]**

(A) 10^3 (B) 10^5
(C) 99995 (D) 9995

8. Shown in the figure below is a meter-bridge set up with null deflection in the galvanometer. The value of the unknown resistor *R* is : **[2008]**

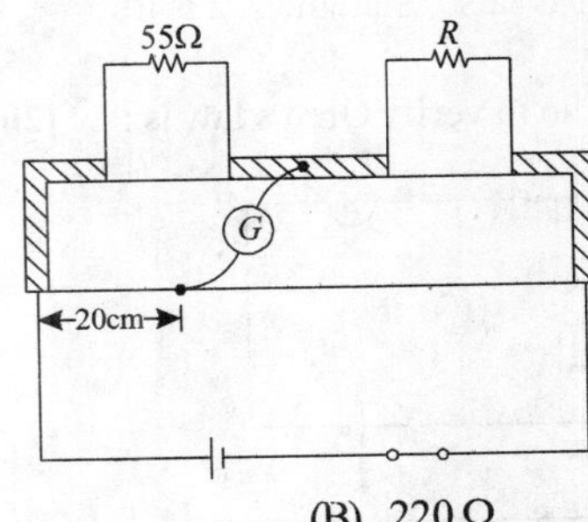

(A) 13.75 Ω (B) 220 Ω
(C) 110 Ω (D) 55 Ω

9. The current in the primary circuit of a potentiometer is 0.2 A. The specific resistance and cross-section of the potentiometer wire are 4×10^{-7} ohm metre and 8×10^{-7} m^2 respectively. The potential gradient will be equal to : **[2011]**

(A) 0.2 V/m (B) 1 V/m
(C) 0.5 V/m (D) 0.1 V/m

10. It is preferable to measure the e.m.f. of a cell by potentiometer than by a voltmeter because of the following possible reasons : **[2012 (Online)]**

(i) In case of potentiometer, no current flows through the cell
(ii) The length of the potentiometer allows greater precision
(iii) Measurement by the potentiometer is quicker

(iv) The sensitivity of the galvanometer, when using a potentiometer is not relevant

(A) (i), (iii), (iv) (B) (i), (iii), (iv)
(C) (i), (ii) (D) (i), (ii), (iii), (iv)

11. In an experiment of potentiometer for measuring the internal resistance of primary cell a balancing length l is obtained on the potentiometer wire when the cell is open circuit. Now the cell is short circuited by a resistance R. If R is to be equal to the internal resistance of the cell the balancing length on the potentiometer wire will be : **[2012 (Online)]**

(A) l (B) $2l$
(C) $l/2$ (D) $l/4$

12. This question has Statement-1 and Statement-2. Of the four choice given after the Statements, choose the one that best describes the two Statements.

Statement-1 : Higher the range, greater is the resistance of ammeter.

Statement-2 : To increase the range of ammeter, additional shunt needs to be used across it **[2013]**

(A) Statement-1 is true, Statement-2 is true, Statement-2 is the correct explanation of Statement-1
(B) Statement-1 is true, Statement-2 is true, Statement-2 is not the correct explanation of Statement-1
(C) Statement-1 is true, Statement-2 is false
(D) Statement-1 is false, Statement-2 is true

13. Correct set up to verify Ohm's law is : **[2013 (Online)]**

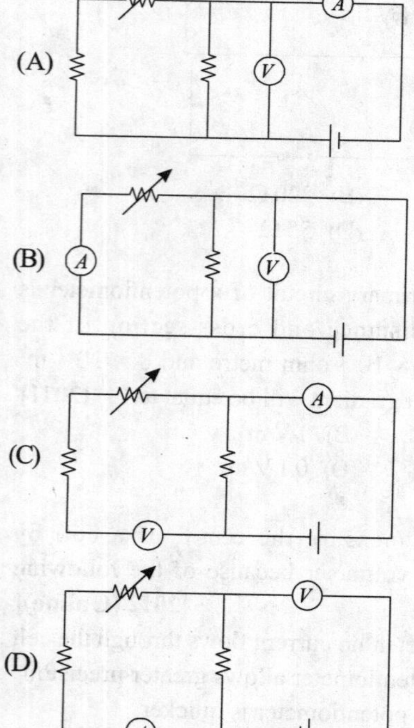

14. In a metre bridge experiment null point is obtained at 40 cm from one end of the wire when resistance X is balanced against another resistance Y. If $X < Y$, then the new position of the null point from the same end, if one decides to balance a resistance of $3X$ against Y, will be close to : **[2013 (Online)]**

(A) 80 cm (B) 75 cm
(C) 67 cm (D) 50 cm

15. A shunt of resistance 1 Ω is connected across a galvanometer of 120 Ω resistance. A current of 5.5 ampere gives full scale deflection in the galvanometer. The current that will give full scale deflection in the absence of the shunt is nearly : **[2013 (Online)]**

(A) 5.5 ampere (B) 0.5 ampere
(C) 0.004 ampere (D) 0.045 ampere

16. To find the resistance of a galvanometer by the half deflection method the following circuit is used with resistances $R_1 = 9970\ \Omega$, $R_2 = 30\ \Omega$ and $R_3 = 0$. The deflection in the galvanometer is d. With $R_3 = 107\ \Omega$ the deflection changed to $\frac{d}{2}$. The galvanometer resistance is approximately : **[2013 (Online)]**

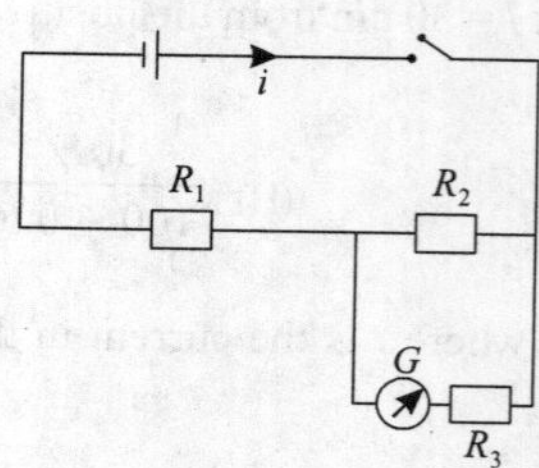

(A) 107 Ω (B) 137 Ω
(C) 107/2 Ω (D) 77 Ω

17. In the circuit diagrams (A, B, C and D) shown below, R is a high resistance and S is a resistance of the order of galvanometer resistance G. The correct circuit, corresponding to the half deflection method for finding the resistance and figure of merit of the galvanometer, is the circuit labelled as : **[2014 (Online)]**

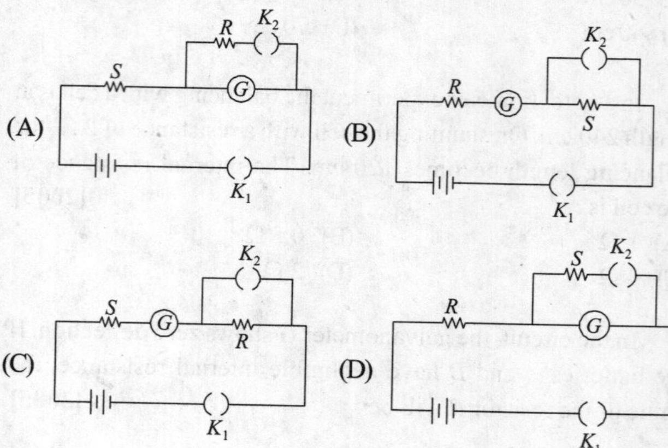

(A) Circuit A with $G=\dfrac{RS}{(R-S)}$

(B) Circuit B with $G=S$

(C) Circuit C with $G=S$

(D) Circuit D with $G=\dfrac{RS}{(R-S)}$

18. A 10 V battery with internal resistance 1 Ω and a 15 V battery with internal resistance 0.6 Ω are connected in parallel to a voltmeter (see figure). The reading in the voltmeter will be close to : **[2015 (Online)]**

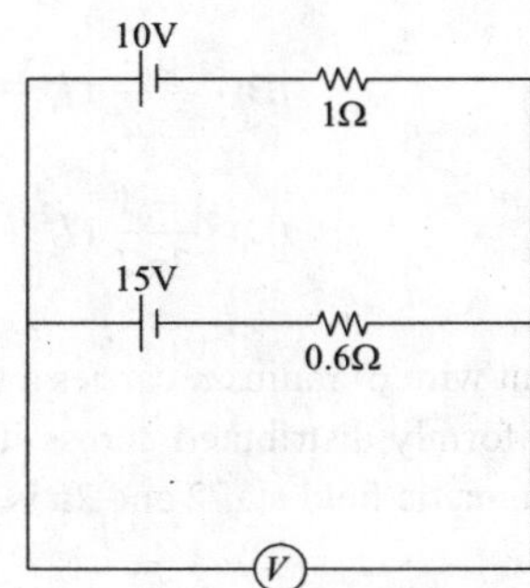

(A) 12.5 V (B) 24.5 V
(C) 13.1 V (D) 11.9 V

19. A galvanometer having a coil resistance of 100 Ω gives a full scale deflection, when a current of 1 mA is passed through it. The value of the resistance, which can convert this galvanometer into ammeter giving a full scale deflection for a current of 10 A, is : **[2016]**

(A) 0.01 Ω (B) 2 Ω
(C) 0.1 Ω (D) 3 Ω

20. To know the resistance G of a galvanometer by half deflection method, a battery of emf V_E and resistance R is used to deflect the galvanometer by angle θ. If a shunt of resistance S is needed to get half deflection then G, R and S related by the equation : **[2016 (Online)]**

(A) $S(R+G)=RG$ (B) $2S(R+G)=RG$
(C) $2G=S$ (D) $2S=G$

21. A 50 Ω resistance is connected to a battery of 5 V. A galvanometer of resistance 100 Ω is to be used as an ammeter to measure current through the resistance, for this a resistance r_s is connected to the galvanometer. Which of the following connections should be employed if the measured current is within 1% of the current without the ammeter in the circuit ? **[2016 (Online)]**

(A) $r_s=0.5\,\Omega$ in series with the galvanometer
(B) $r_s=1\,\Omega$ in series with galvanometer
(C) $r_s=1\,\Omega$ in parallel with galvanometer
(D) $r_s=0.5\,\Omega$ in parallel with the galvanometer

22. A galvanometer has a 50 division scale. Battery has no internal resistance. It is found that there is deflection of 40 divisions when $R = 2400\,\Omega$. Deflection becomes 20 divisions when resistance taken from resistance box is 4900 Ω. Then we can conclude : **[2016 (Online)]**

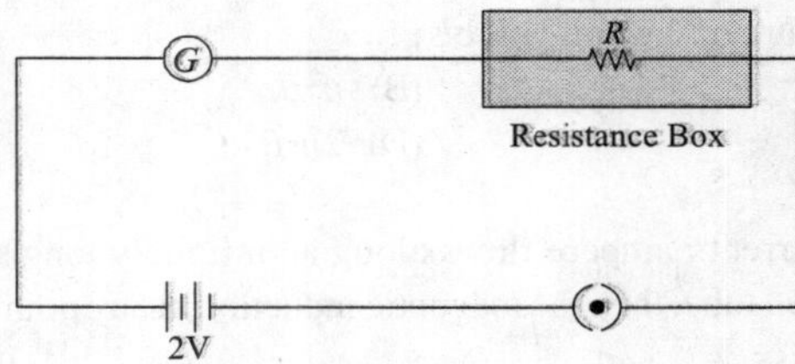

(A) Current sensitivity of galvanometer is 20 μA/division
(B) Resistance of galvanometer is 200 Ω
(C) Resistance required on $R.B.$ for a deflection of 10 divisions is 9800 Ω
(D) Full scale deflection current is 2 mA

* * * * *

CHAPTER

18 MOVING CHARGES & MAGNETISM

18.1 MAGNETIC EFFECTS OF CURRENT

1. If in a circular coil A of radius R, current i is flowing and in another coil B of radius $2R$ a current $2i$ is flowing, then the ratio of the magnetic fields, B_A and B_B produced by them will be : **[2002]**

(A) 1 (B) 2
(C) 1/2 (D) 4

2. The magnetic field due to a current carrying circular loop of radius 3 cm at a point on the axis at a distance of 4 cm from the centre is 54 μT. What will be its value at the centre of the loop ? **[2004]**

(A) 250 μT (B) 150 μT
(C) 125 μT (D) 75 μT

3. A long wire carries a steady current. It is bent into a circle of one turn and the magnetic field at the centre of the coil is B. It is then bent into a circular loop of n turns. The magnetic field at the centre of the coil will be : **[2004]**

(A) nB (B) n^2B
(C) $2nB$ (D) $2n^2B$

4. A current i ampere flows along an infinitely long straight thin walled tube, then the magnetic induction at any point inside the tube is : **[2004]**

(A) $\frac{\mu_0}{4\pi}\cdot\frac{2i}{r}$ tesla (B) Zero
(C) Infinite (D) $\frac{2i}{r}$ tesla

5. Two concentric coils each of radius equal to 2π cm are placed at right angles to each other. 3 A and 4 A are the currents flowing in each coil respectively. The magnetic induction in Wb/m^2 at the centre of the coils will be : [$\mu_0 = 4\pi \times 10^{-7}$ Wb/Am] **[2005]**

(A) 12×10^{-5} (B) 10^{-5}
(C) 5×10^{-5} (D) 7×10^{-5}

6. A long solenoid has 200 turns per cm and carries a current i. The magnetic field at its centre is 6.28×10^{-2} weber/m^2. Another long solenoid has 100 turns per cm and it carries a current $i/3$. The value of the magnetic field at its centre is : **[2006]**

(A) 1.05×10^{-2} weber/m^2 (B) 1.05×10^{-5} weber/m^2
(C) 1.05×10^{-3} weber/m^2 (D) 1.05×10^{-4} weber/m^2

7. Two identical conducting wires AOB and COD are placed at right angles to each other. The wire AOB carries an electric current I_1 and COD carries a current I_2. The magnetic field on a point lying at a distance d from O, in a direction perpendicular to the plane of the wires AOB and COD, will be given by : **[2007]**

(A) $\frac{\mu_0}{2\pi}\left(\frac{I_1+I_2}{d}\right)^{1/2}$ (B) $\frac{\mu_0}{2\pi d}(I_1^2+I_2^2)^{1/2}$
(C) $\frac{\mu_0}{2\pi d}(I_1+I_2)$ (D) $\frac{\mu_0}{2\pi d}(I_1^2+I_2^2)$

8. A long straight wire of radius a carries a steady current i. The current is uniformly distributed across its cross section. The ratio of the magnetic field at $a/2$ and $2a$ is : **[2007]**

(A) 1/2 (B) 1/4
(C) 4 (D) 1

9. A current I flows along the length of an infinitely long, straight, thin walled pipe. Then : **[2007]**

(A) The magnetic field at all points inside the pipe is the same, but not zero
(B) The magnetic field is zero only on the axis of the pipe
(C) The magnetic field is different at different points inside the pipe
(D) The magnetic field at any point inside the pipe is zero

10. A horizontal overhead powerline is at a height of 4 m from the ground and carries a current of 100 A from east to west. The magnetic field directly below it on the ground is : [$\mu_0 = 4\pi \times 10^{-7}$ TmA^{-1}] : **[2008]**

(A) 2.5×10^{-7} T southward (B) 5×10^{-6} T northward
(C) 5×10^{-6} T southward (D) 2.5×10^{-7} T northward

11. The magnitude of the magnetic field (B) due to the loop $ABCD$ at the origin (O) is : **[2009]**

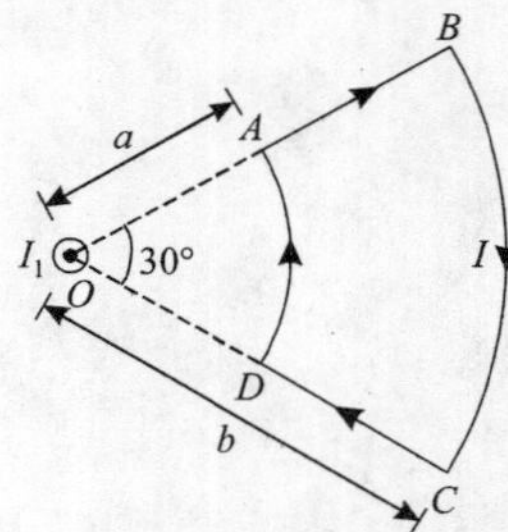

(A) $\frac{\mu_0 I}{4\pi}\left[\frac{b-a}{ab}\right]$ (B) $\frac{\mu_0 I}{4\pi}\left[2(b-a)+\frac{\pi}{3}(a+b)\right]$

(C) Zero (D) $\frac{\mu_0 I(b-a)}{24ab}$

12. Due to the presence of the current I_1 at the origin : **[2009]**

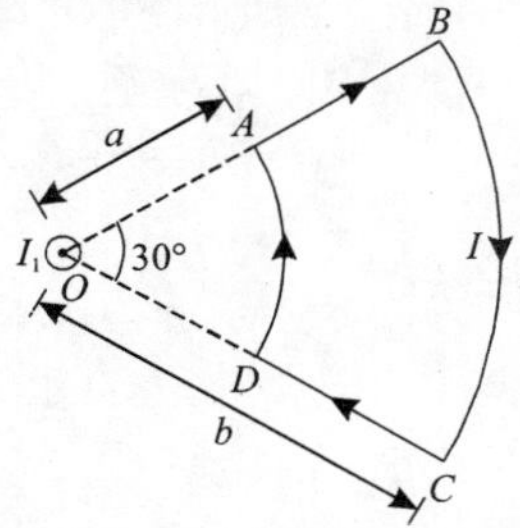

(A) The magnitude of the net force on the loop is given by $\frac{I_1 I}{4\pi}\mu_0\left[2(b-a)+\frac{\pi}{3}(a+b)\right]$

(B) The magnitude of the net force on the loop is given by $\frac{\mu_0 I I_1}{24ab}(b-a)$

(C) The forces on AB and DC are zero

(D) The forces on AD and BC are zero

13. Two long parallel wire are at a distance 2d apart. They carry steady equal currents flowing out of the plane of the paper as shown. The variation of the magnetic field B along the line XX' is given by : **[2010]**

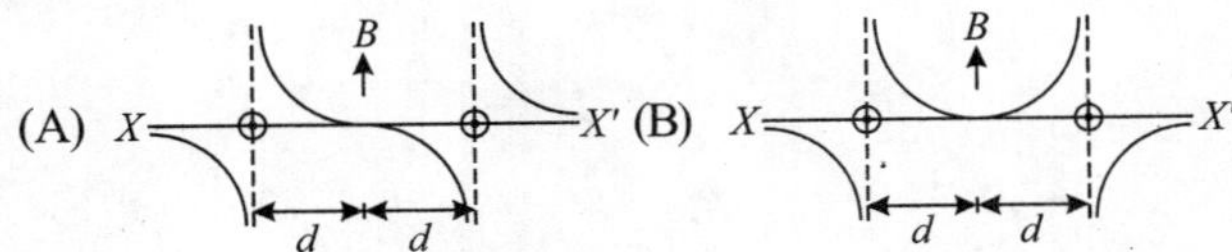

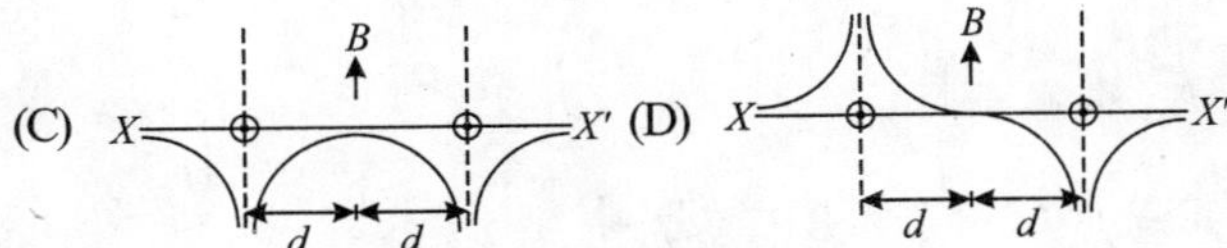

14. A current I flows in an infinity long wire with cross section in the from of a semicircular ring of radius R. The magnitude of the magnetic induction along its axis is : **[2011]**

(A) $\frac{\mu_0 I}{2\pi R}$ (B) $\frac{\mu_0 I}{4\pi R}$

(C) $\frac{\mu_0 I}{\pi^2 R}$ (D) $\frac{\mu_0 I}{2\pi^2 R}$

15. A charge Q is uniformly distributed over the surface of non-conducting disc of radius R. The disc rotates about an axis perpendicular to its plane and passing through its centre with an angular velocity ω. As a result of this rotation a magnetic field of induction B is obtained at the centre of the disc. If we keep both the amount of charge placed on the disc and its angular velocity to be constant and vary the radius of the disc then the variation of the magnetic induction at the centre of the disc will be represented by the figure : **[2012]**

(A)

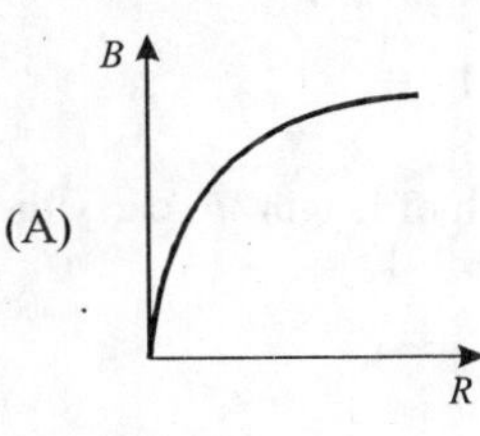

(B)

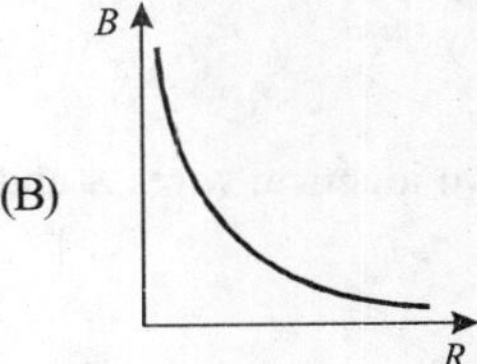

(C)

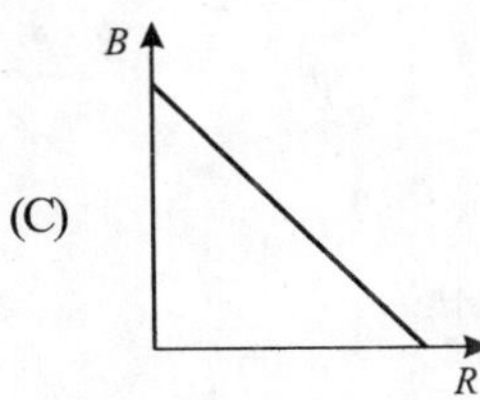

(D)

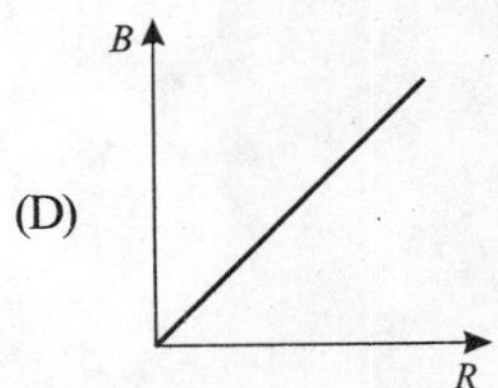

16. An electric current is flowing through a circular coil of radius R. The ratio of the magnetic field at the centre of the coil and that at a distance $2\sqrt{2}R$ from the centre of the coil and on its axis is : **[2013 (Online)]**

(A) $2\sqrt{2}$ (B) 27

(C) 36 (D) 8

17. A current i is flowing in a straight conductor of length L. The magnetic induction at a point on its axis at a distance $L/4$ from its centre will be : **[2013 (Online)]**

(A) Zero (B) $\frac{\mu_0 i}{2\pi L}$

(C) $\frac{\mu_0 i}{\sqrt{2}L}$ (D) $\frac{4\mu_0 i}{\sqrt{5}\mu L}$

18. Choose the correct sketch of the magnetic field lines of a circular current loop shown by the dot ⊙ and the cross ⊗ : **[2013 (Online)]**

(A)

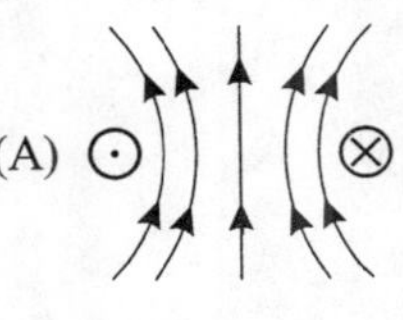

(B)

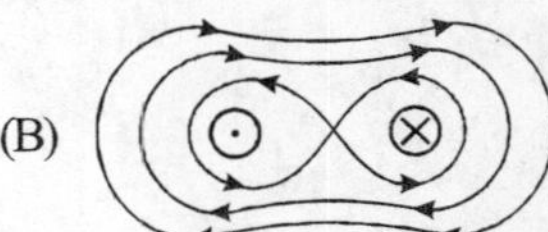

(C)

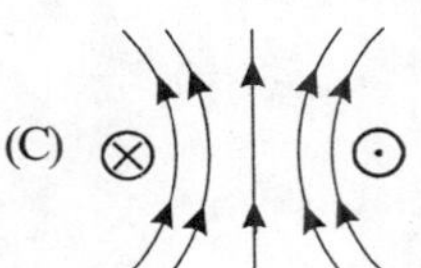

(D)

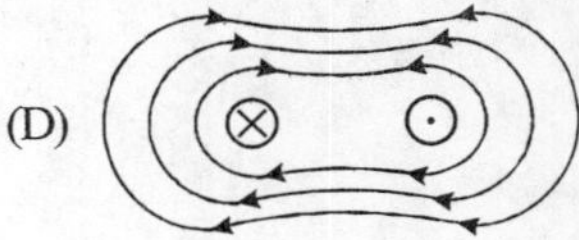

19. Consider two thin identical conducting wires covered with very thin insulating material. One of the wires is bent into a loop and produces magnetic field B_1, at its centre when a current I passes through it. The second wire is bent into a coil with three identical loops adjacent to each other and produces magnetic field B_2 at the centre of the loops when a current $I/3$ passes through it. Then ratio $B_1 : B_2$ is : **[2014 (Online)]**

(A) 1 : 1 (B) 1 : 3
(C) 1 : 9 (D) 9 : 1

20. Two identical wires A and B, each of length 'l', carry the same current I. Wire A is bent into a circle of radius R and wire B is bent to form a square of side 'a'. If B_A and B_B are the values of magnetic field at the centres of the circle and square respectively, then the ratio $\frac{B_A}{B_B}$ is : **[2016]**

(A) $\frac{\pi^2}{8}$ (B) $\frac{\pi^2}{16\sqrt{2}}$
(C) $\frac{\pi^2}{16}$ (D) $\frac{\pi^2}{8\sqrt{2}}$

* * * * *

CHAPTER

18 MOVING CHARGES & MAGNETISM

18.2 MAGNETIC FORCE ON MOVING CHARGES

1. Wires 1 and 2 carrying currents i_1 and i_2 respectively are inclined at an angle θ to each other. What is the force on a small element dl of wire 2 at a distance r from wire 1 (as shown in figure) due to the magnetic field of wire 1 ? **[2002]**

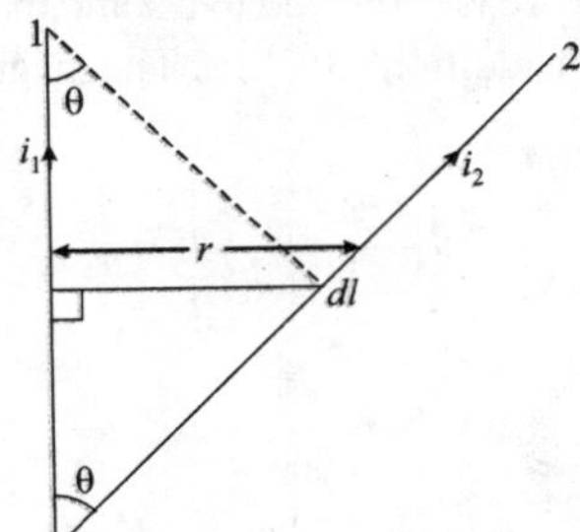

(A) $\frac{\mu_0}{2\pi r} i_1 i_2 \, dl \tan\theta$ (B) $\frac{\mu_0}{2\pi r} i_1 i_2 \, dl \sin\theta$

(C) $\frac{\mu_0}{2\pi r} i_1 i_2 \, dl \cos\theta$ (D) $\frac{\mu_0}{4\pi r} i_1 i_2 \, dl \sin\theta$

2. The time period of a charged particle undergoing a circular motion in a uniform magnetic field is independent of its : **[2002]**

(A) Speed (B) Mass
(C) Charge (D) Magnetic induction

3. If a current is passed through a spring then the spring will : **[2002]**
(A) Expand (B) Compress
(C) Remain same (D) None of these

4. If an electron and a proton having same momentum enter perpendicularly to a magnetic field, then : **[2002]**
(A) Curved path of electron and proton will be same (ignoring the sense of revolution)
(B) They will move undeflected
(C) Curved path of electron is more curved than that of proton
(D) Path of proton is more curved

5. A particle of charge -16×10^{-18} C moving with velocity 10 ms^{-1} along the x-axis enters a region where a magnetic field of induction B is along the y-axis and an electric field of magnitude 10^4 V/m is along the negative z-axis If the charged particle continues moving along the x-axis, the magnitude of B is : **[2003]**
(A) 10^3 Wb/m^2 (B) 10^5 Wb/m^2
(C) 10^{16} Wb/m^2 (D) 10^{-3} Wb/m^2

6. A magnetic needle laying parallel to a magnetic field requires W unit of work to turn it through 60°. The torque needed to maintain the needle in this position will be : **[2003]**
(A) $\sqrt{3}\,W$ (B) W
(C) $(\sqrt{3}/2)\,W$ (D) $2\,W$

7. A particle of mass M and charge Q moving with velocity $\vec{v}$ describes a circular path of radius R when subjected to a uniform transverse magnetic field of induction B. The work done by the field when the particle completes one full circle is : **[2003]**

(A) $\left(\frac{Mv^2}{R}\right) 2\pi R$ (B) Zero
(C) $BQ\,2\pi R$ (D) $BQv\,2\pi R$

8. Two long conductors, separated by a distance d carry currents I_1 and I_2 in the same direction. They exert a force F on each other. Now the current in one of them is increased to two times and its direction is reversed. The distance is also increased to $3d$. The new value of the force between them is : **[2004]**
(A) $-2F$ (B) $F/3$
(C) $-2F/3$ (D) $-F/3$

9. A charged particle of mass m and charge q travels on a circular path of radius r that is perpendicular to a magnetic field B. The time taken by the particle to complete one revolution is : **[2005]**

(A) $\frac{2\pi mq}{B}$ (B) $\frac{2\pi q^2 B}{m}$

(C) $\frac{2\pi qB}{m}$ (D) $\frac{2\pi m}{qB}$

10. Two thin, long, parallel wires, separated by a distance d carry a current of 'i' in the same direction. They will : **[2005]**

(A) attract each other with a force of $\frac{\mu_0 i^2}{(2\pi d)}$

(B) repel each other with a force of $\frac{\mu_0 i^2}{(2\pi d)}$

(C) attract each other with a force of $\frac{\mu_0 i^2}{(2\pi d^2)}$

(D) repel each other with a force of $\frac{\mu_0 i^2}{(2\pi d^2)}$

11. A uniform electric field and a uniform magnetic field are acting along the same direction in a certain region. If an electron is projected along the direction of the fields with a certain velocity then : **[2005]**

(A) Its velocity will increase
(B) Its velocity will decrease
(C) It will turn towards left of direction of motion
(D) It will turn towards right of direction of motion

12. In a region, steady and uniform electric and magnetic fields are present. These two fields are parallel to each other. A charged particle is released from rest in this region. The path of the particle will be a : **[2006]**

(A) helix (B) straight line
(C) ellipse (D) circle

13. A charged particle moves through a magnetic field perpendicular to its direction. Then : **[2007]**

(A) the momentum changes but the kinetic energy is constant
(B) both momentum and kinetic energy of the particle are not constant
(C) both momentum and kinetic energy of the particle are constant
(D) kinetic energy changes but the momentum is constant

14. A charged particle with charge q enters a region of constant, uniform and mutually orthogonal fields $\vec{E}$ and $\vec{B}$ with a velocity $\vec{V}$ perpendicular to both $\vec{E}$ and $\vec{B}$, and comes out without any change in magnitude or direction of $\vec{V}$. Then : **[2007]**

(A) $\vec{V}=\dfrac{\vec{E}\times\vec{B}}{B^2}$ (B) $\vec{V}=\dfrac{\vec{B}\times\vec{E}}{B^2}$
(C) $\vec{V}=\dfrac{\vec{E}\times\vec{B}}{E^2}$ (D) $\vec{V}=\dfrac{\vec{B}\times\vec{E}}{E^2}$

15. A thin circular disk of radius R is uniformly charged with density $\sigma > 0$ per unit area. The disk rotates about its axis with a uniform angular speed ω. The magnetic moment of the disk is : **[2011]**

(A) $2\pi R^4\sigma\omega$ (B) $\pi R^4\sigma\omega$
(C) $\dfrac{\pi R^4}{2}\sigma\omega$ (D) $\dfrac{\pi R^4}{4}\sigma\omega$

16. An electric charge $+q$ moves with velocity $\vec{V}=3\hat{i}+4\hat{j}+\hat{k}$, in an electromagnetic field given by : $\vec{E}=3\hat{i}+\hat{j}+2\hat{k}$. $\vec{B}=\hat{i}+\hat{j}-3\hat{k}$. The y-component of the force experienced by $+q$ is : **[2011]**

(A) $2q$ (B) $11q$
(C) $5q$ (D) $3q$

17. Proton, Deuteron and alpha particle of the same kinetic energy are moving in circular trajectories in a constant magnetic field. The radii of proton, deuteron and alpha particle are respectively r_p, r_d and r_α. Which one of the following relations is correct ? **[2012]**

(A) $r_\alpha = r_d > r_p$ (B) $r_\alpha = r_d = r_p$
(C) $r_\alpha = r_p < r_d$ (D) $r_\alpha > r_d > r_p$

18. The circuit in figure consists of wires at the top and bottom and identical springs as the left and right sides. The wire at the bottom has a mass of 10 g and is 5 cm long. The wire is hanging as shown in the figure. The springs stretch 0.5 cm under the weight of the wire and the circuit has a total resistance of 12 Ω. When the lower wire is subjected to a static magnetic field, the springs, stretch an additional 0.3 cm. The magnetic field is : **[2012 (Online)]**

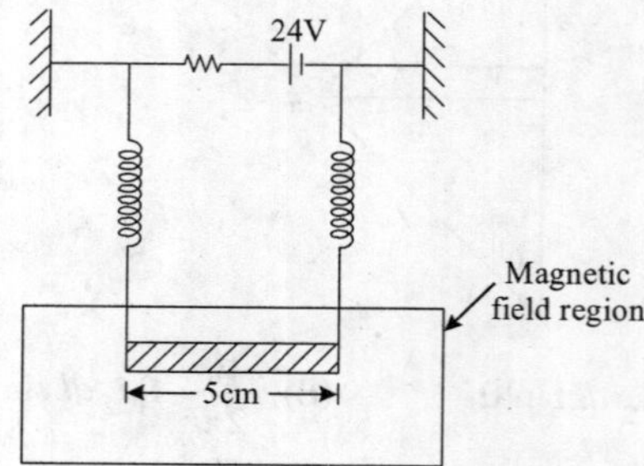

(A) 0.6 T and directed out of page
(B) 1.2 T and directed into the plane of page
(C) 0.6 T and directed into the plane of page
(D) 1.2 T and directed out of page

19. Currents of a 10 ampere and 2 ampere are passed through two parallel thin wires A and B respectively in opposite directions. Wire A is infinitely long and the length of the wire B is 2 m. The force acting on the conductor B, which is situated at 10 cm distance from A will be : **[2012 (Online)]**

(A) 8×10^{-5} N (B) 5×10^{-5} N
(C) $8\pi\times10^{-7}$ N (D) $4\pi\times10^{-7}$ N

20. The velocity of certain ions that pass undeflected through crossed electric field $E = 7.7$ k V/m and magnetic field $B = 0.14$ T is : **[2012 (Online)]**

(A) 18 km/s (B) 77 km/s
(C) 55 km/s (D) 1078 km/s.

21. The magnetic force acting on charged particle of charge 2 μC in magnetic field of 2T acting in y-direction, when the particle velocity is $(2\hat{i}+3\hat{j})\times10^6$ ms^{-1} is : **[2012 (Online)]**

(A) 8 N in z-direction (B) 8 N in y-direction
(C) 4 N in y-direction (D) 4 N in z-direction

22. A proton and a deuteron are both accelerated through the same potential difference and enter in a magnetic field perpendicular to the direction of the field. If the deuteron follows a path of radius R, assuming the neutron and proton masses are nearly equal, the radius of the proton's path will be : **[2012 (Online)]**

(A) $\sqrt{2}R$ (B) $\frac{R}{\sqrt{2}}$

(C) $\frac{R}{2}$ (D) R

23. This question has Statement-1 and Statement-2. Of the four choices given after the Statements, choose the one that best describes the two Statements.

Statement-1 : A charged particle is moving at right angle to a static magnetic field. During the motion the kinetic energy of the charge remains unchanged.

Statement-2 : Static magnetic field exert force on a moving charge in the direction perpendicular to the magnetic field : **[2012 (Online)]**

(A) Statement-1 is false, Statement-2 is true

(B) Statement-1 is true, Statement-2 is true, Statement-2 is not the correct explanation of Statement-1

(C) Statement-1 is true, Statement-2 is false

(D) Statement-1 is true, Statement-2 is true, Statement-2 is the correct explanation of Statement-1

24. A rectangular loop of wire, supporting a mass m, hangs with one end in a uniform magnetic field $\vec{B}$ pointing out of the plane of the paper. A clockwise current is set up such that $i > mg/Ba$, where a is the width of the loop. Then : **[2013 (Online)]**

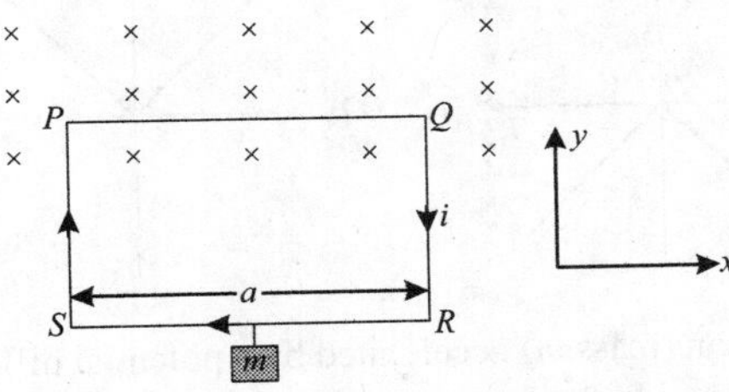

(A) The weight rises due to a vertical force caused by the magnetic field and work is done on the system

(B) The weight do not rise due to vertical for caused by the magnetic field and work is done on the system

(C) The weight rises due to a vertical force caused by the magnetic field but no work is done on the system

(D) The weight rises due to a vertical force caused by the magnetic field and work is extracted from the magnetic field

25. A particle of charge 16×10^{-16} C moving with velocity 10 ms^{-1} along x-axis enters a region where magnetic field of induction $\vec{B}$ is along the y-axis and an electric field of magnitude 10^4 Vm^{-1} is along the negative z-axis. If the charged particle continues moving along x-axis, the magnitude of $\vec{B}$ is : **[2013 (Online)]**

(A) 16×10^3 Wb m^{-2} (B) 2×10^3 Wb m^{-2}

(C) 1×10^3 Wb m^{-2} (D) 4×10^3 Wb m^{-2}

26. A metal sample carrying a current along X-axis with density J_X is subjected to magnetic field B_Z (along Z-axis). The electric field E_Y developed along Y-axis is directly proportional to J_X as well as B_Z. The constant of proportionality has SI unit : **[2013 (Online)]**

(A) $\frac{\text{m}^2}{\text{A}}$ (B) $\frac{\text{m}^3}{\text{As}}$

(C) $\frac{\text{m}^2}{\text{As}}$ (D) $\frac{\text{As}}{\text{m}^3}$

27. A conductor lies along the z-axis at $-1.5 \le z < 1.5$ m and carries a fixed current of 10.0 A in $-\hat{a}_Z$ direction (see figure). For a field $\vec{B} = 3.0 \times 10^{-4} e^{-0.2x} \hat{a}_y$ T, find the power required to move the conductor at constant speed to $x = 2.0$ m, $y = 0$ m in 5×10^{-3} s. Assume parallel motion along the x-axis: **[2014]**

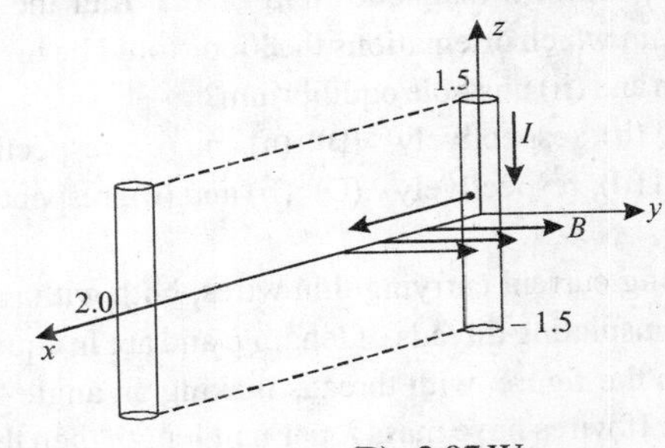

(A) 1.57 W (B) 2.97 W

(C) 14.85 W (D) 29.7 W

28. Three straight parallel current carrying conductors are shown in the figure. The force experienced by the middle conductor of length 25 cm is : **[2014 (Online)]**

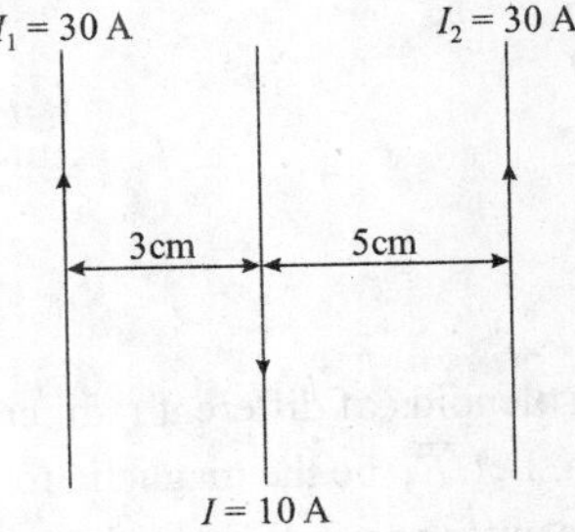

(A) 3×10^{-4} N toward right (B) 6×10^{-4} N toward right

(C) 9×10^{-4} N toward right (D) Zero

29. A positive charge 'q' of mass 'm' is moving along the $+x$ axis. We wish to apply a uniform magnetic field B for time Δt so that the charge reverses its direction crossing the y-axis at a distance d. Then : **[2014 (Online)]**

(A) $B = \frac{mv}{qd}$ and $\Delta t = \frac{\pi d}{v}$ (B) $B = \frac{mv}{2qd}$ and $\Delta t = \frac{\pi d}{2v}$

(C) $B = \frac{2mv}{qd}$ and $\Delta t = \frac{\pi d}{2v}$ (D) $B = \frac{2mv}{qd}$ and $\Delta t = \frac{\pi d}{v}$

30. A rectangular loop of sides 10 cm and 5 cm carrying a current I of 12 A is placed in different orientations as shown in the figures below :

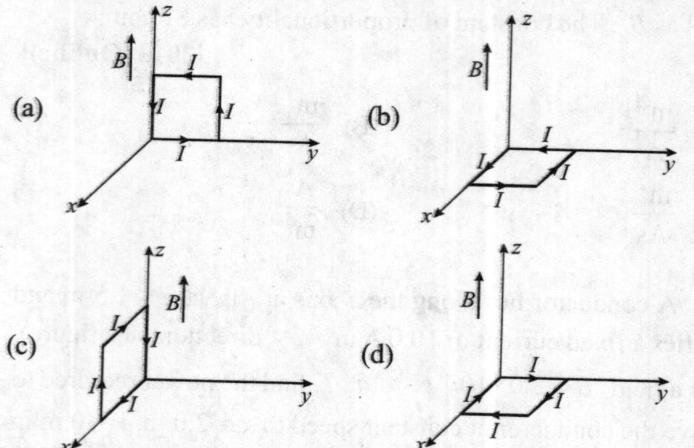

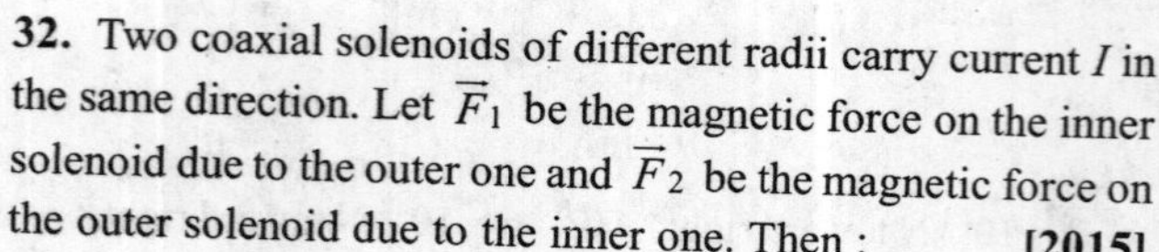

If there is a uniform magnetic field of 0.3 T in the positive z direction, in which orientations the loop would be in (i) stable equilibrium and (ii) unstable equilibrium? **[2015]**

(A) (a) and (b), respectively (B) (a) and (c), respectively

(C) (b) and (d), respectively (D) (b) and (c), respectively

31. Two long current carrying thin wires, both with current I, are held by insulating threads of length L and are in equilibrium as shown in the figure, with threads making an angle 'θ' with the vertical. If wires have mass λ per unit length then the value of I is : (g = gravitational acceleration) : **[2015]**

(A) $\sin\theta\sqrt{\dfrac{\pi\lambda gL}{\mu_0\cos\theta}}$

(B) $2\sin\theta\sqrt{\dfrac{\pi\lambda gL}{\mu_0\cos\theta}}$

(C) $2\sqrt{\dfrac{\pi gL}{\mu_0}\tan\theta}$

(D) $\sqrt{\dfrac{\pi\lambda gL}{\mu_0}\tan\theta}$

32. Two coaxial solenoids of different radii carry current I in the same direction. Let $\vec{F}_1$ be the magnetic force on the inner solenoid due to the outer one and $\vec{F}_2$ be the magnetic force on the outer solenoid due to the inner one. Then : **[2015]**

(A) $\vec{F}_1 = \vec{F}_2 = 0$

(B) $\vec{F}_1$ is radially inwards and $\vec{F}_2$ is radially outwards

(C) $\vec{F}_1$ is radially inwards and $\vec{F}_2 = 0$

(D) $\vec{F}_1$ is radially outwards and $\vec{F}_2 = 0$

33. A wire carrying current I is tied between points P and Q and is in the shape of a circular arc of radius R due to a uniform magnetic field B (perpendicular to the plane of the paper, shown by ×××) in the vicinity of the wire. If the wire subtends an angle $2\theta_0$ at the centre of the circle (of which it forms an arc) then the tension in the wire is : **[2015 (Online)]**

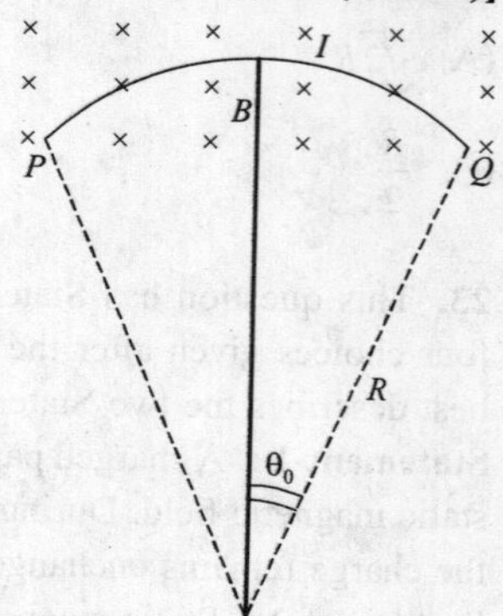

(A) $\dfrac{IBR}{2\sin\theta_0}$

(B) $\dfrac{IBR\theta_0}{\sin\theta_0}$

(C) IBR

(D) $\dfrac{IBR}{\sin\theta_0}$

34. Two long straight parallel wires, carrying (adjustable) current I_1 and I_2, are kept at a distance d apart. If the force 'F' between the two wires is taken as 'positive' when the wires repel each other and 'negative' when the wires attract each other, the graph showing the dependence of 'F', on the product $I_1 I_2$, would be : **[2015 (Online)]**

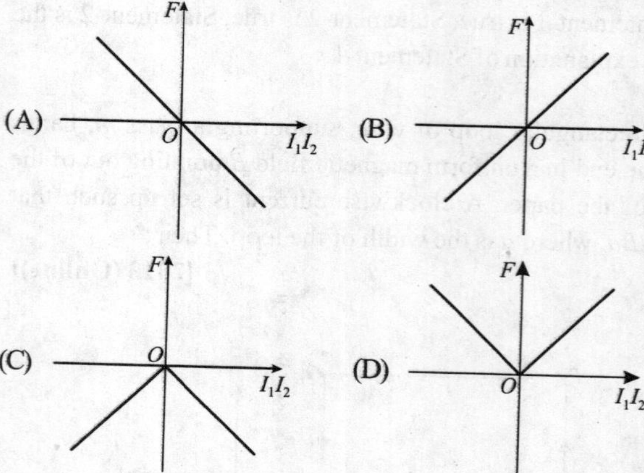

35. A proton (mass m) accelerated by a potential difference V flies through a uniform transverse magnetic field B. The field occupies a region of space by width 'd'. If α be the angle of deviation of proton from initial direction of motion (see figure), the value of sin α will be : **[2015 (Online)]**

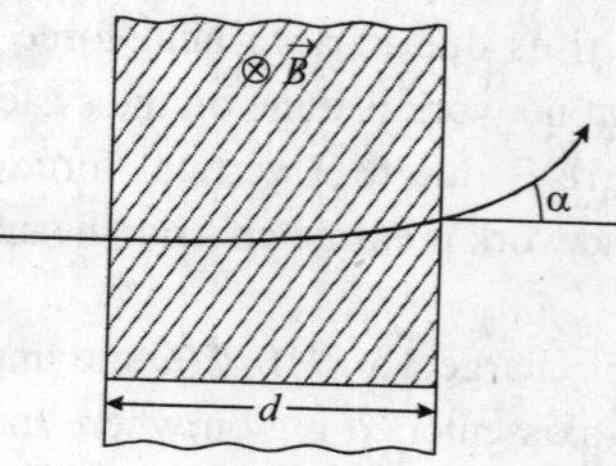

(A) $qV\sqrt{\dfrac{Bd}{2m}}$ (B) $\dfrac{B}{2}\sqrt{\dfrac{qd}{mV}}$

(C) $\dfrac{B}{d}\sqrt{\dfrac{q}{2mV}}$ (D) $Bd\sqrt{\dfrac{q}{2mV}}$

* * * * *

CHAPTER

19 MAGNETISM AND MATTER

19.1 CLASSICAL AND TERRESTRIAL MAGNETISM

1. The magnetic lines of force inside a bar magnet : **[2003]**

(A) are from north-pole to south-pole of the magnet

(B) do not exist

(C) depend upon the area of cross-section of the bar magnet

(D) are from south-pole to north-pole of the magnet

2. A thin rectangular magnet suspended freely has a period of oscillation equal to T. Now it is broken into two equal halves (each having half of the original length) and one piece is made to oscillate freely in the same field. If its period of oscillation is T', the ratio $\frac{T'}{T}$ is : **[2003]**

(A) $\frac{1}{2\sqrt{2}}$ (B) $\frac{1}{2}$

(C) 2 (D) $\frac{1}{4}$

3. The length of a magnet is large compared to its width and breadth. The time period of its oscillation in a vibration magnetometer is 2 s. The magnet is cut along its length into three equal parts and these parts are then placed on each other with their like poles together. The time period of this combination will be : **[2004]**

(A) $2\sqrt{3}$ s (B) $\frac{2}{3}$ s

(C) 2 s (D) $\frac{2}{\sqrt{3}}$ s

4. A magnetic needle is kept in a non-uniform magnetic field. It experiences : **[2005]**

(A) a torque but not a force (B) neither a force nor a torque

(C) a force and a torque (D) a force but not a torque

5. A bar magnet of length 6 cm has a magnetic moment of 4 JT^{-1}. Find the strength of magnetic field at a distance of 200 cm from the centre of the magnet along its equatorial line : **[2012 (Online)]**

(A) 4×10^{-8} tesla (B) 3.5×10^{-8} tesla

(C) 5×10^{-8} tesla (D) 3×10^{-8} tesla

6. Two short bar magnets of length 1 cm each have magnetic moments 1.20 Am^2 and 1.00 Am^2 respectively. They are placed on a horizontal table parallel to each other with their N poles pointing towards the South. They have a common magnetic equator and are separated by a distance of 20.0 cm. The value of the resultant horizontal magnetic induction at the mid-point O of the line joining their centres is close to : (Horizontal component of earth's magnetic induction is 3.6×10^{-5} Wb/m^2) : **[2013]**

(A) 3.6×10^{-5} Wb/m^2 (B) 2.56×10^{-4} Wb/m^2

(C) 3.50×10^{-4} Wb/m^2 (D) 5.80×10^{-4} Wb/m^2

7. The earth's magnetic field lines resemble that of a dipole at the centre of the earth. If the magnetic moment of this dipole at the centre of the earth. If the magnetic moment of this dipole is close to 8×10^{22} Am^2, the value of earth's magnetic field near the equator is close to (radius of the earth = 6.4×10^6 m) : **[2013 (Online)]**

(A) 0.6 Gauss (B) 1.2 Gauss

(C) 1.8 Gauss (D) 0.32 Gauss

8. The mid points of two small magnetic dipoles of length d in end-on positions, are separated by a distance x, ($x >> d$). The force between them is proportional to x^{-n} where n is : **[2014 (Online)]**

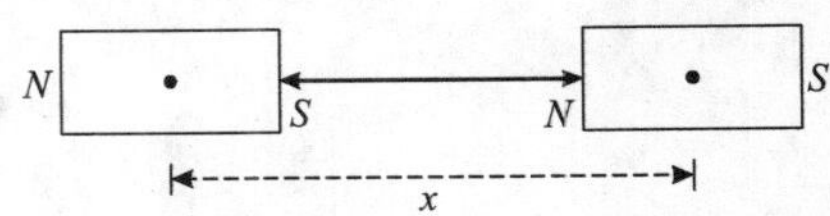

(A) 1 (B) 2

(C) 3 (D) 4

9. The magnetic field of earth at the equator is approximately 4×10^{-5} T. The radius of earth is 6.4×10^6 m. Then the dipole moment of the earth will be nearly of the order of : **[2014 (Online)]**

(A) 10^{23} A m^2 (B) 10^{20} A m^2

(C) 10^{16} A m^2 (D) 10^{10} A m^2

10. A short bar magnet is placed in the magnetic meridian of the earth with north pole pointing north. Neutral points are found at a distance of 30 cm from the magnet on the East-West line, drawn through the middle point of the magnet. The magnetic moment of the magnet in Am^2 is close to : (Given $\frac{\mu_0}{4\pi} = 10^{-7}$ in SI units and B_H = Horizontal component of earth's magnetic field = 3.6×10^{-5} tesla) : **[2015 (Online)]**

(A) 14.6 (B) 19.4
(C) 9.7 (D) 4.9

11. A 25 cm long solenoid has radius 2 cm and 500 total number of turns. It carries a current of 15 A. If it is equivalent to a magnet of the same size and magnetization $\overrightarrow{M}$ (magnetic moment/volume), then $|\overrightarrow{M}|$ is : **[2015 (Online)]**

(A) $30000\,\pi\,\text{Am}^{-1}$ (B) $3\,\pi\,\text{Am}^{-1}$
(C) $30000\,\text{Am}^{-1}$ (D) $300\,\text{Am}^{-1}$

12. A magnetic dipole is acted upon by two magnetic fields which are inclined to each other at an angle of 75°. One of the fields has a magnitude of 15 mT. The dipole attains stable equilibrium at an angle of 30° with this field. The magnitude of the other field (in *mT*) is close to : **[2016 (Online)]**

(A) 1 (B) 11
(C) 36 (D) 1060

* * * * *

CHAPTER

19 MAGNETISM AND MATTER

19.2 MAGNETIC PROPERTIES OF MATERIALS

1. Curie temperature is the temperature above which : **[2003]**
(A) A ferromagnetic material becomes paramagnetic
(B) A paramagnetic material becomes diamagnetic
(C) A ferromagnetic material becomes diamagnetic
(D) A paramagnetic material becomes ferromagnetic

2. The materials suitable for making electromagnets should have : **[2004]**
(A) High retentivity and low coercivity
(B) Low retentivity and low coercivity
(C) High retentivity and high coercivity
(D) Low retentivity and high coercivity

3. Needles N_1, N_2 and N_3 are made of a ferromagnetic, a paramagnetic and a diamagnetic substance respectively. A magnet when brought close to them will : **[2006]**
(A) Attract N_1 and N_2 strongly but repel N_3
(B) Attract N_1 strongly, N_2 weakly and repel N_3 weakly
(C) Attract N_1 strongly, but repel N_2 and N_3 weakly
(D) Attract all three of them

4. Relative permittivity and permeability of a material ε_r and μ_r, respectively. Which of the following values of these quantities are allowed for a diamagnetic material ? **[2008]**
(A) $\varepsilon_r = 0.5, \mu_r = 1.5$ (B) $\varepsilon_r = 1.5, \mu_r = 0.5$
(C) $\varepsilon_r = 0.5, \mu_r = 0.5$ (D) $\varepsilon_r = 1.5, \mu_r = 1.5$

5. The coercivity of a small magnet where the ferromagnet gets demagnetized is 3×10^3 A m^{-1}. The current required to be passed in a solenoid of length 10 cm and number of turns 100, so that the magnet gets demagnetized when inside the solenoid, is : **[2014]**
(A) 30 mA (B) 60 mA
(C) 3 A (D) 6 A

6. Three identical bars A, B and C are made of different magnetic materials. When kept in a uniform magnetic field, the field lines around them look as follows :

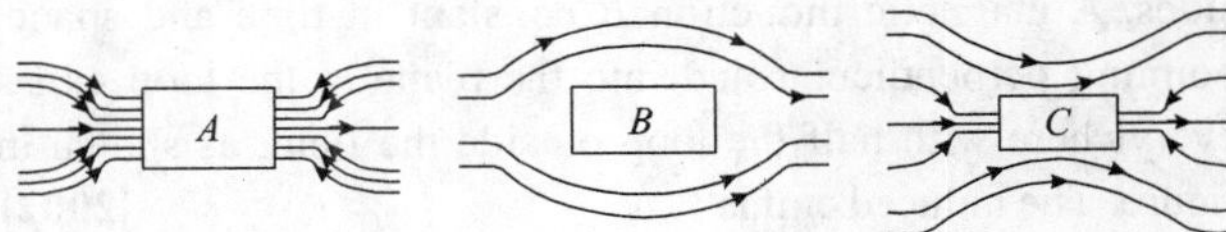

Make the correspondence of these bars with their material being diamagnetic (D), ferromagnetic (F) and paramagnetic (P) : **[2014 (Online)]**
(A) $A \leftrightarrow D, B \leftrightarrow P, C \leftrightarrow F$ (B) $A \leftrightarrow F, B \leftrightarrow D, C \leftrightarrow P$
(C) $A \leftrightarrow P, B \leftrightarrow F, C \leftrightarrow D$ (D) $A \leftrightarrow F, B \leftrightarrow P, C \leftrightarrow D$

7. An example of a perfect diamagnet is a superconductor. This implies that when a superconductor is put in a magnetic field of intensity B, the magnetic field B_s inside the superconductor will be such that : **[2014 (Online)]**
(A) $B_s = -B$ (B) $B_s = 0$
(C) $B_s = B$ (D) $B_s < B$ but $Bs \neq 0$

8. Hysteresis loops for two magnetic materials A and B are given below :

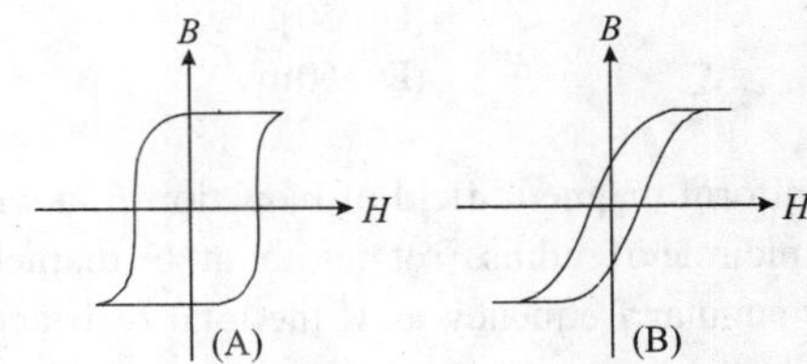

These materials are used to make magnets for electric generators, transformer core and electromagnet core. Then it is proper to use : **[2016]**
(A) A for electric generators and transformers
(B) A for electromagnets and B for electric generators
(C) A for transformers and B for electric generators
(D) B for electromagnets and transformers

* * * * *

CHAPTER 20 ELECTROMAGNETIC INDUCTION

20.1 ELECTROMAGNETIC INDUCTION

1. A conducting square loop of side L and resistance R moves in its plane with a uniform velocity v perpendicular to one of its sides. A magnetic induction B constant in time and space, pointing perpendicular and into the plane at the loop exists everywhere with half the loop outside the field, as shown in figure. The induced emf is : **[2002]**

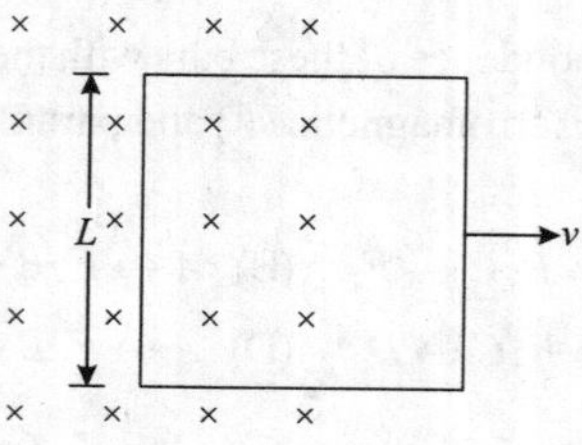

(A) Zero (B) RvB

(C) $\frac{vBL}{R}$ (D) vBL

2. A metal conductor of length 1 m rotates vertically about one of its ends at angular velocity 5 radians per second. If the horizontal component of earth's magnetic field is 0.2×10^{-4} T, then the emf developed between the two ends of the conductor is : **[2004]**

(A) $5\mu V$ (B) $50\mu V$

(C) 5mV (D) 50mV

3. In a uniform magnetic field of induction B, a wire in the form of semicircle of radius r rotates about the diameter of the circle with angular frequency ω. If the total resistance of the circuit is R, the mean power generated per period of rotation is: **[2004]**

(A) 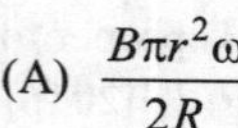 $\frac{B\pi r^2\omega}{2R}$ (B) $\frac{(B\pi r^2\omega)^2}{8R}$

(C) $\frac{(B\pi r\omega)^2}{2R}$ (D) $\frac{(B\pi r\omega^2)^2}{8R}$

4. A coil having n turns and resistance $R\,\Omega$ is connected with a galvanometer of resistance $4\,R\Omega$. This combination is moved in time t seconds from a magnetic field W_1 weber to W_2 weber. The induced current in the circuit is : **[2004]**

(A) $\frac{W_2 - W_1}{5\,Rnt}$ (B) $-\frac{n(W_2 - W_1)}{5\,Rt}$

(C) $-\frac{(W_2 - W_1)}{Rnt}$ (D) $-\frac{n(W_2 - W_1)}{Rt}$

5. One conducting U-tube can slide inside another as shown in figure, maintaining electrical contacts between the tubes. The magnetic field B is perpendicular to the plane of the figure. If each tube moves towards the other at a constant speed v, then the emf induced in the circuit in terms of B, l and v, where l is the width of each tube, will be : **[2005]**

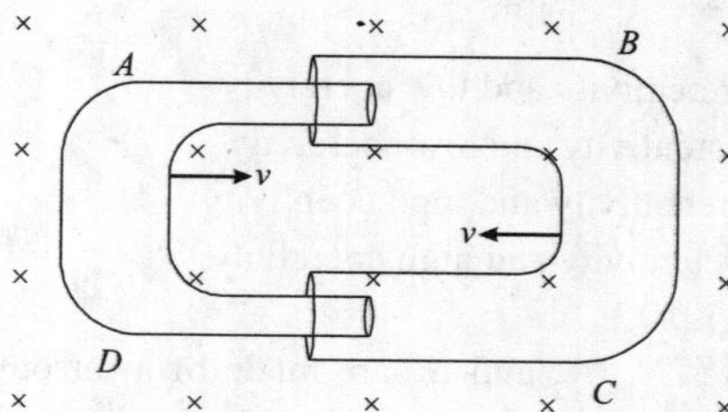

(A) Blv (B) $-Blv$

(C) zero (D) $2Blv$

6. A rectangular loop has a sliding connector PQ of length l and resistance $R\Omega$ and it is moving with a speed v as shown. The set-up is placed in a uniform magnetic field going into the plane of the paper. The three currents I_1, I_2 and I are : **[2010]**

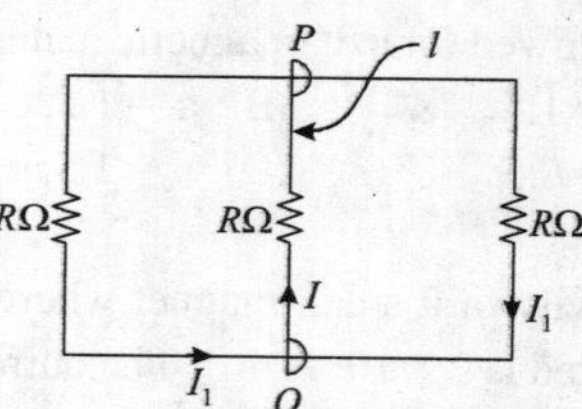

(A) $I_1 = I_2 = \frac{Blv}{6R}, I = \frac{Blv}{3R}$ (B) $I_1 = -I_2 = \frac{Blv}{R}, I = \frac{2Blv}{R}$

(C) $I_1 = I_2 = \frac{Blv}{3R}, I = \frac{2Blv}{3R}$ (D) $I_1 = I_2 = , I = \frac{Blv}{R}$

7. A horizontal straight wire 20 m long extending from east to west is falling with a speed of 5.0 m/s, at right angles to the horizontal component of the earth's magnetic field 0.30×10^{-4} Wb/m^2. The instantaneous value of the e.m.f. induced in the wire will be : **[2011]**

(A) 6.0mV (B) 3mV

(C) 4.5mV (D) 1.5mV

8. A boat is moving due east in a region where the earth's magnetic field is 5.0×10^{-5} NA^{-1} m^{-1} due north and horizontal. The boat carries a vertical aerial 2 m long. If the speed of the boat is 1.50 ms^{-1}, the magnitude of the induced emf in the wire of aerial is : **[2011]**

(A) 0.50 mV (B) 0.15 mV
(C) 1 mV (D) 0.75 mV

9. A coil is suspended in a uniform magnetic field, with the plane of the coil parallel to the magnetic lines of force. When a current is passed through the coil it starts oscillating; it is very difficult to stop. But if an aluminium plate is placed near to the coil, it stops. This is due to : **[2012]**

(A) Electromagnetic induction in the aluminium plate giving rise to electromagnetic damping
(B) Development of air current when the plate is placed
(C) Induction of electrical charge on the plate
(D) Shielding of magnetic lines of force as aluminium is a paramagnetic material

10. Magnetic flux through a coil of resistance 10 Ω is changed by $\Delta\phi$ in 0.1 s. The resulting current in the coil varies with time as shown in the figure. Then $|\Delta\phi|$ is equal to (in weber) : **[2012 (Online)]**

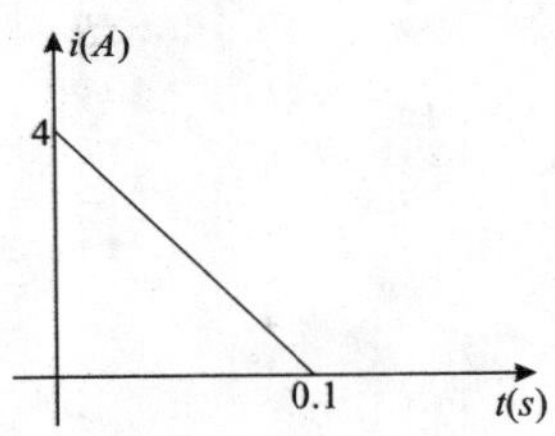

(A) 6 (B) 4
(C) 2 (D) 8

11. A circular loop of radius 0.3 cm lies parallel to a much bigger circular loop of radius 20 cm. The centre of the small loop is on the axis of the bigger loop. The distance between their centres is 15 cm. If a current of 2.0 A flows through the smaller loop, then the flux linked with bigger loop is : **[2013]**

(A) 9.1×10^{-11} weber (B) 6×10^{-11} weber
(C) 3.3×10^{-11} weber (D) 6.6×10^{-9} weber

12. A metallic rod of length 'l' is tied to a string of length $2l$ and made to rotate with angular speed ω on a horizontal table with one end of the string fixed. If there is a vertical magnetic field 'B' in the region, the e.m.f. induced across the ends of the rod is : **[2013]**

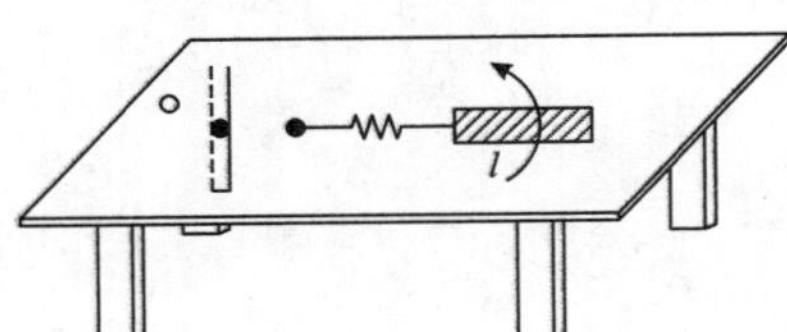

(A) $\frac{2B\omega l^2}{2}$ (B) $\frac{3B\omega l^2}{2}$
(C) $\frac{4B\omega l^2}{2}$ (D) $\frac{5B\omega l^2}{2}$

13. A square frame of side 10 cm and a long straight wire carrying current 1 A are in the plate of the paper. Starting from close to the wire, the frame moves towards the right with a constant speed of 10 ms^{-1} (see figure).
The e.m.f. induced at the time the left arm of the frame is at x = 10 cm from the wire is: **[2014 (Online)]**

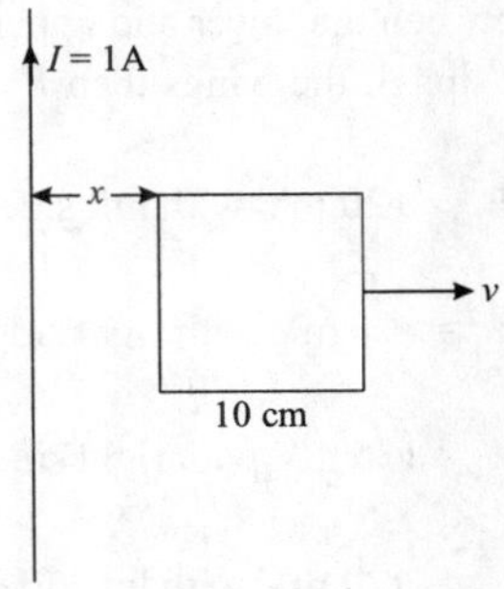

(A) 2 μV (B) 1 μV
(C) 0.75 μV (D) 0.5 μV

14. A coil of circular cross-section having 1000 turns and 4 cm^2 face area is placed with its axis parallel to a magnetic field which decreases by 10^{-2} Wb m^{-2} in 0.01 s. The e.m.f. induced in the coil is : **[2014 (Online)]**

(A) 400 mV (B) 200 mV
(C) 4 mV (D) 0.4 mV

15. Figure shows a circular area of radius R where a uniform magnetic field $\vec{B}$ is going into the plane of paper and increasing in magnitude at a constant rate.
In that case, which of the following graphs, drawn schematically, correctly shows the variation of the induced electric field $E(r)$? **[2014 (Online)]**

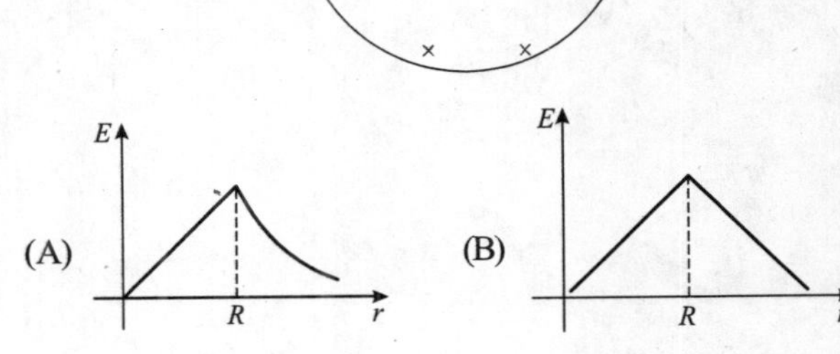

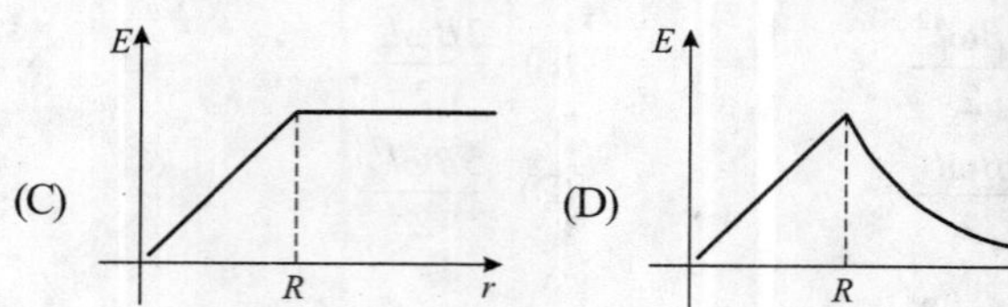

16. A fighter plane of length 20 m, wing span (distance from tip of one wing to the tip of the other wing) of 15 m and height 5 m is lying towards east over Delhi. Its speed is 240 ms^{-1}. The earth's magnetic field over Delhi is 5×10^{-5} T with the declination angle ~ 0° and dip of θ such that $\sin\theta = 2/3$. If the voltage developed is V_B between the lower and upper side of the plane of V_W between the tips of the wings then V_B and V_W are close to: **[2016 (Online)]**

(A) $V_B = 40$ mV; $V_w = 120$ mV with left side of pilot at higher voltage

(B) $V_B = 45$ mV; $V_W = 120$ mV with right side of pilot at higher voltage

(C) $V_B = 40$ mV; $V_W = 135$ mV with right side of pilot at higher voltage

(D) $V_B = 45$ mV; $V_W = 120$ mV with left side of pilot at higher voltage

17. Consider a thin metallic sheet perpendicular to the plane of the paper moving with speed 'v' in a uniform magnetic field B going into the plane of the paper (See figure). If charge densities σ_1 and σ_2 are induced on the left and right surfaces, respectively, of the sheet then (ignore fringe effects) : **[2016 (Online)]**

(A) $\sigma_1 = \dfrac{-\epsilon_0 vB}{2}, \sigma_2 = \dfrac{\epsilon_0 vB}{2}$

(B) $\sigma_1 = \epsilon_0 vB, \sigma_2 = -\epsilon_0 vB$

(C) $\sigma_1 = \dfrac{\epsilon_0 vB}{2}, \sigma_2 = \dfrac{-\epsilon_0 vB}{2}$

(D) $\sigma_1 = \sigma_2 = \epsilon_0 vB$

18. A conducting metal circular-wire-loop of radius r is placed perpendicular to a magnetic field which varies with time as $B = B_0 e^{-t/\tau}$, where B_0 and τ are constants, at time $t = 0$. If the resistance of the loop is R then the heat generated in the loop after a long time $(t \to \infty)$ is : **[2016 (Online)]**

(A) $\dfrac{\pi^2 r^2 B_0^4}{2\tau R}$ (B) $\dfrac{\pi^2 r^4 B_0^2}{2\tau R}$

(C) $\dfrac{\pi^2 r^4 B_0^2 R}{\tau}$ (D) $\dfrac{\pi^2 r^4 B_0^2}{\tau R}$

* * * * *

CHAPTER

20 ELECTROMAGNETIC INDUCTION

20.2 SELF AND MUTUAL INDUCTION

1. The inductance between A and D is : **[2002]**

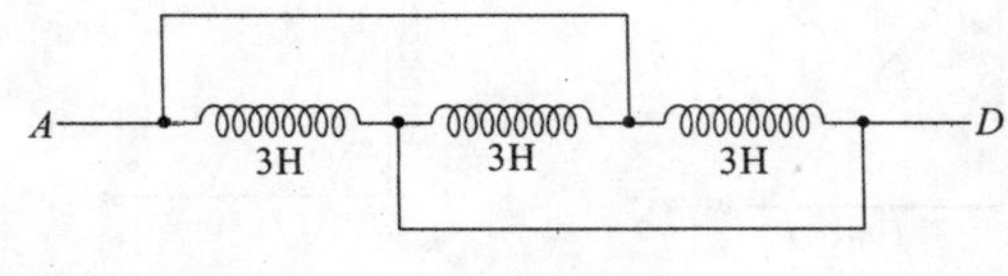

(A) 3.66 H (B) 9 H
(C) 0.66 H (D) 1 H

2. When the current changes from +2 A to – 2 A in 0.05 s, an emf of 8 V is induced in a coil. The coefficient of self-induction of the coil is : **[2003]**

(A) 0.2 H (B) 0.4 H
(C) 0.8 H (D) 0.1 H

3. Two coils are placed close to each other. The mutual inductance of the pair of coils depends upon : **[2003]**

(A) the rates at which currents are changing in the two coils
(B) relative position and orientation of the two coils
(C) the materials of the wires of the coils
(D) the currents in the two coils

4. A coil of inductance 300 mH and resistance 2 Ω is connected to a source of voltage 2 V. The current reaches half of its steady state value in : **[2005]**

(A) 0.05 s (B) 0.1 s
(C) 0.15 s (D) 0.3 s

5. The flux linked with a coil at any instant 't' is given by : $\phi = 10t^2 - 50t + 250$. The induced emf at $t = 3$ s is : **[2006]**

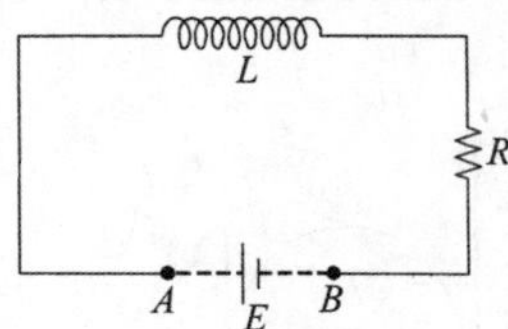

(A) –190 V (B) –10 V
(C) 10V (D) 190V

6. An inductor (L = 100 mH), a resistor (R = 100 Ω) and a battery (E = 100 V) are initially connected in series as shown in the figure. After a long time the battery is disconnected after short circuiting the points A and B. The current in the circuit 1 ms after the short circuit is : **[2006]**

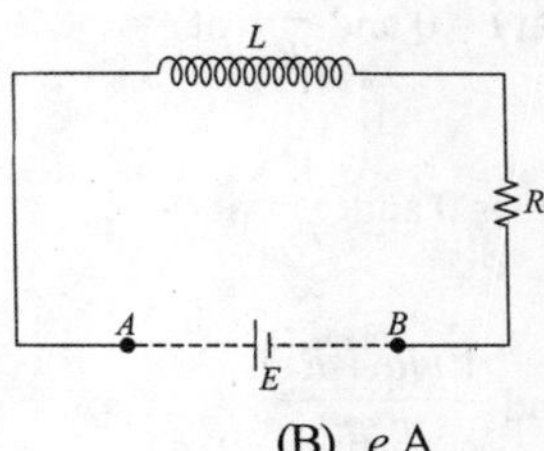

(A) $1/e$ A (B) e A
(C) 0.1 A (D) 1 A

7. An ideal coil of 10 H is connected in series with a resistance of 5 Ω and a battery of 5 V. 2 s after the connection is made, the current flowing (in ampere) in the circuit is : **[2007]**

(A) $(1 - e)$ (B) e
(C) e^{-1} (D) $(1 - e^{-1})$

8. Two coaxial solenoids are made by winding thin insulated wire over a pipe of cross-sectional area A = 10 cm^2 and length = 20 cm. If one of the solenoids has 300 turns and the other 400 turns, their mutual inductance is : $[\mu_0 = 4\pi \times 10^{-7}\ \text{TmA}^{-1}]$: **[2008]**

(A) $2.4\ \pi \times 10^{-5}$ H (B) $4.8\ \pi \times 10^{-4}$ H
(C) $4.8\ \pi \times 10^{-5}$ H (D) $2.4\ \pi \times 10^{-4}$ H

9. An inductor of inductance L = 400 mH and resistors of resistances $R_1 = 2\ \Omega$ and $R_2 = 2\ \Omega$ are connected to a battery of emf 12 V as shown in the figure. The internal resistance of the battery is negligible. The switch S is closed at $t = 0$. The potential drop across L as a function of time is : **[2009]**

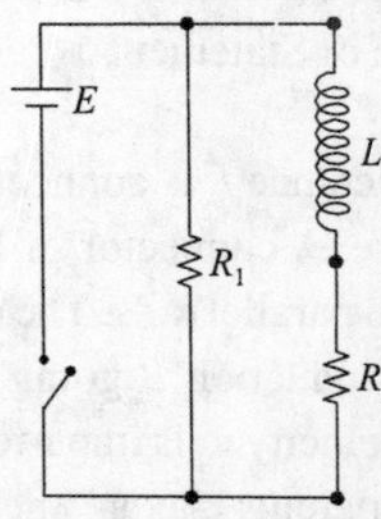

(A) $6(1 - e^{-t/0.2})$ V (B) $12e^{-5t}$ V
(C) $6e^{-5t}$ V (D) $\frac{12}{t}e^{-3t}$ V

10. In the circuit show below, the key K is closed at $t = 0$. Th current through the battery is : **[201**

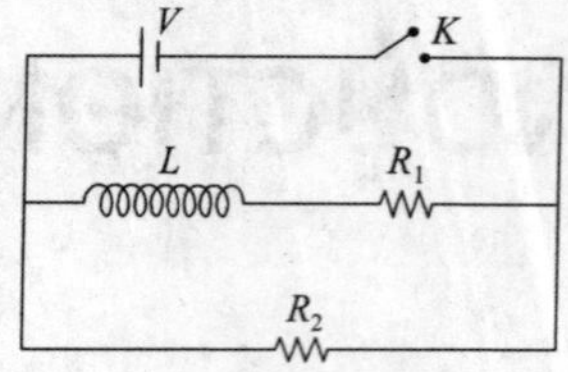

(A) $\dfrac{V(R_1+R_2)}{R_1R_2}$ at $t=0$ and $\dfrac{V}{R_2}$ at $t=\infty$

(B) $\dfrac{VR_1R_2}{\sqrt{R_1^2+R_2^2}}$ at $t=0$ and $\dfrac{V}{R_2}$ at $t=\infty$

(C) $\dfrac{V}{R_2}$ at $t=0$ and $\dfrac{V(R_1+R_2)}{R_1R_2}$ at $t=\infty$

(D) $\dfrac{V}{R_2}$ at $t=0$ and $\dfrac{VR_1R_2}{\sqrt{R_1^2+R_2^2}}$ at $t=\infty$

11. This question has Statement-1 and Statement-2. Of the four choices given after the Statements, choose the one that best describes the two Statements.

Statement-1 : Self inductance of a long solenoid of length L, total number of turns N and radius r is less than $\dfrac{\pi\mu_0 N^2 r^2}{L}$.

Statement-2 : The magnetic induction in the solenoid in Statement-1 carrying current I is $\dfrac{\mu_0 NI}{L}$ in the middle of the solenoid but becomes less as we move towards its ends : **[2012 (Online)]**

A) Statement-1 is true, Statement-2 is false
) Statement-1 is true, Statement-2 is true, Statement-2 is the rect explanation of Statement-1
Statement-1 is false, Statement-2 is true
Statement-1 is true, Statement-2 is true, Statement-2 is not rrect explanation of Statement-1

oil of self inductance L is connected at one end of two hown in figure. A connector of length l, mass m can over the two parallel rails. The entire set up is placed tic field of induction B going into the page. At an an initial velocity v_0 is imparted to it and as a result 's moving along x-axis. The displacement of the presented by the figure : **[2012 (Online)]**

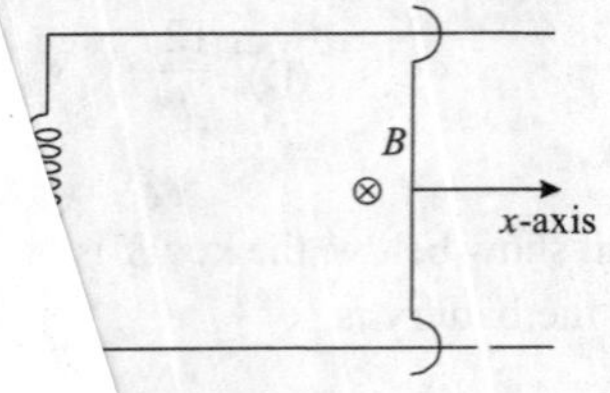

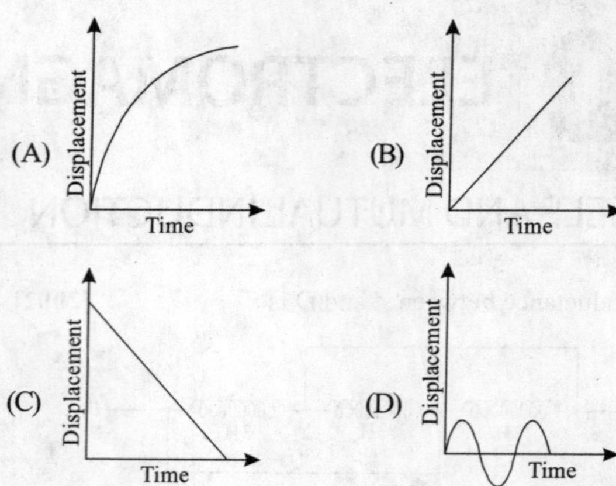

13. In an LCR circuit as shown below both switches are open initially. Now switch S_1 is closed, S_2 kept open. (q is charge on the capacitor and $\tau = RC$ is Capacitive time constant). Which of the following statement is correct? **[2013]**

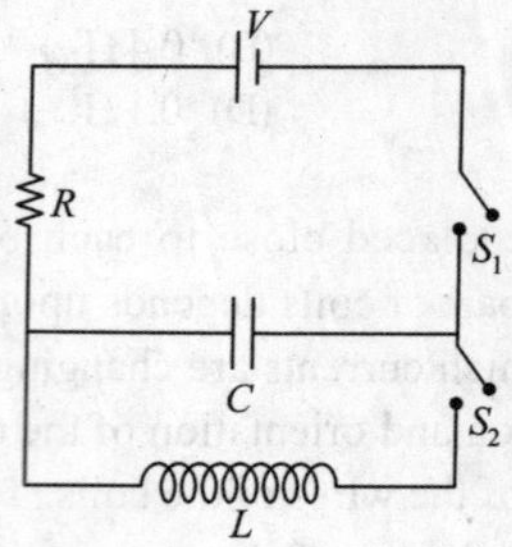

(A) Work done by the battery is half of the energy dissipated in the resistor

(B) At, $t=\tau$, $q = CV/2$

(C) At, $t = 2\tau$, $q = CV(1-e^{-2})$

(D) At, $t = 2\tau$, $q = CV(1-e^{-1})$

14. Two coils, X and Y, are kept in close vicinity of each other. When a varying current, $I(t)$, flows through coil X, the induced e.m.f ($V(t)$) in coil Y, varies in the manner shown here. The variation of $I(t)$, with time, can then be represented by the graph labelled as graph : **[2013 (Online)]**

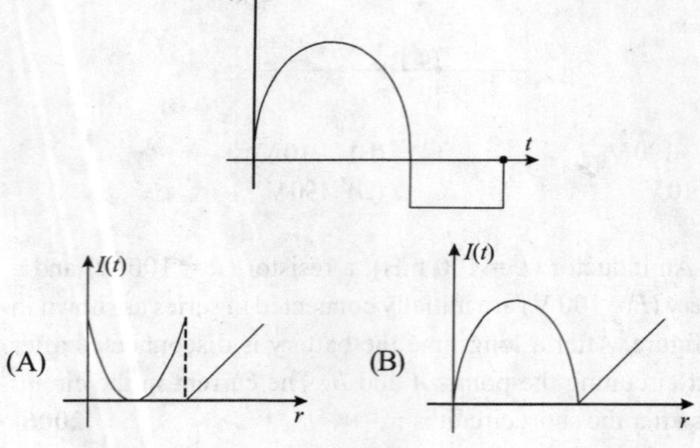

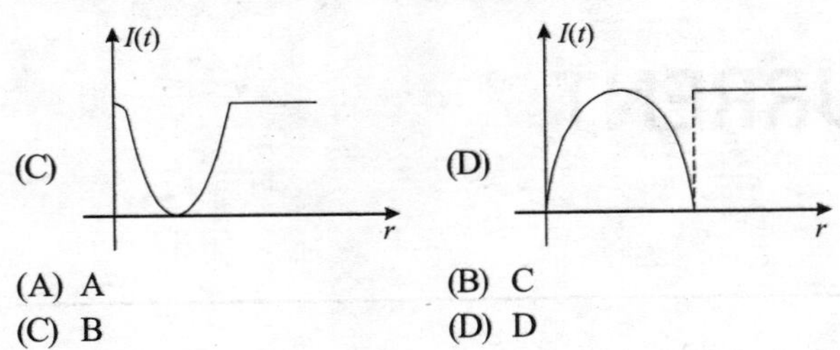

(A) A (B) C
(C) B (D) D

15. In the circuit shown here, the point 'C' is kept connected to point 'A' till the current flowing through the circuit becomes constant. Afterward, suddenly, point 'C' is disconnected from point 'A' and connected to point 'B' at time $t = 0$. Ratio of the voltage across resistance and the inductor at $t = L/R$ will be equal to : **[2014]**

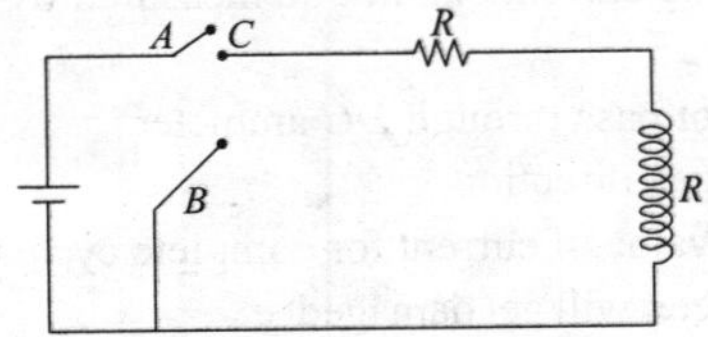

(A) $\frac{e}{1-e}$ (B) 1

(C) -1 (D) $\frac{1-e}{e}$

16. An LCR circuit is equivalent to a damped pendulum. In an LCR circuit the capacitor is charged to Q_0 and then connected to the L and R as shown below :

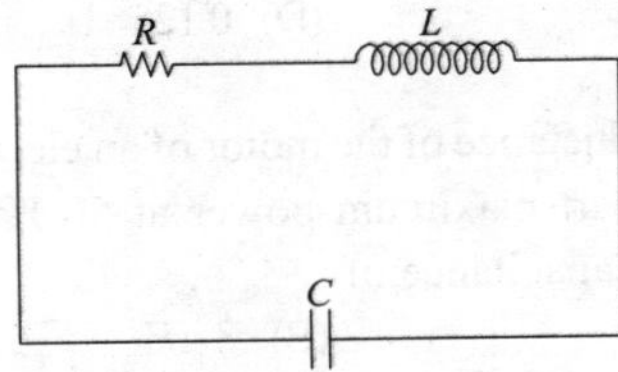

If a student plots graphs of the square of maximum charge (Q^2_{Max}) on the capacitor with time (t) for two different values L_1 and $L_2(L_1 > L_2)$ of L then which of the following represents this graph correctly? (plots are schematic and not drawn to scale) : **[2015]**

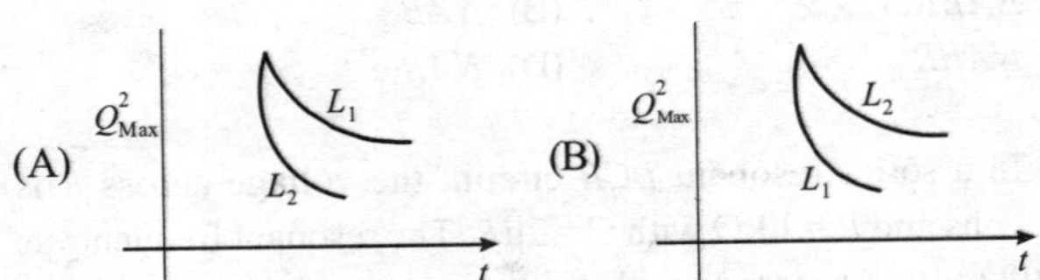

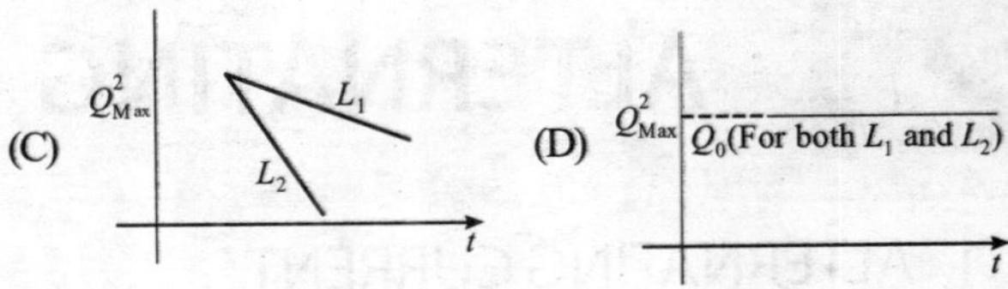

17. An inductor ($L = 0.03$ H) and a resistor ($R = 0.15$ kΩ) are connected in series to a battery of 15V EMF in a circuit shown below. The key K_1 has been kept closed for a long time. Then at $t = 0$, K_1 is opened and key K_2 is closed simultaneously. At $t = 1$ ms, the current in the circuit will be: ($e^5 \cong 150$) : **[2015]**

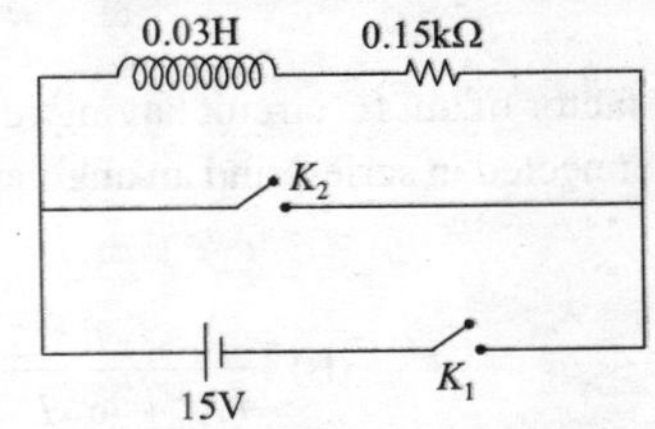

(A) 100 mA (B) 67 mA
(C) 6.7 mA (D) 0.67 mA

18. When current in a coil changes from 5 A to 2A in 0.1 s, average voltage of 50 V is produced. The self-inductance of the coil is : **[2015 (Online)]**

(A) 6 H (B) 0.67 H
(C) 3 H (D) 1.67 H

19. In the circuits (a) and (b) switches S_1 and S_2 are closed at $t = 0$ and are kept closed for a long time. The variation of current in the two circuits for $t \geq 0$ are roughly shown by figure (figures are schematic and not drawn to scale) : **[2015 (Online)]**

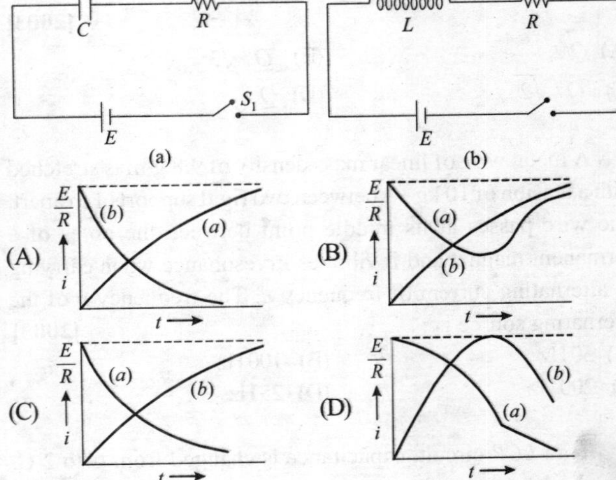

* * * * *

CHAPTER

21 ALTERNATING CURRENT

21.1 ALTERNATING CURRENT

1. In a transformer, number of turns in the primary are 140 and that in the secondary are 280. If current in primary is 4 A, then that in the secondary is : **[2002]**

(A) 4 A (B) 2 A
(C) 6 A (D) 10 A

2. The power factor of an *AC* circuit having resistance *R* and inductance *L* (connected in series) and an angular velocity ω is: **[2002]**

(A) $\frac{R}{\omega L}$ (B) $\frac{R}{(R^2+\omega^2 L^2)^{1/2}}$

(C) $\frac{\omega L}{R}$ (D) $\frac{R}{(R^2-\omega^2 L^2)^{1/2}}$

3. The core of any transformer is laminated so as to : **[2003]**

(A) reduce the energy loss due to eddy currents
(B) make it light weight
(C) make it robust and strong
(D) increase the secondary voltage

4. In an oscillating *LC* circuit the maximum charge on the capacitor is *Q*. The charge on the capacitor when the energy is stored equally between the electric and magnetic fields is : **[2003]**

(A) $Q/2$ (B) $Q/\sqrt{3}$
(C) $Q/\sqrt{2}$ (D) Q

5. A metal wire of linear mass density of 9.8 g/m is stretched with a tension of 10 kg-wt between two rigid supports 1 m apart. The wire passes at its middle point between the poles of a permanent magnet and it vibrates in resonance when carrying an alternating current of frequency *n*. The frequency *n* of the alternating source is : **[2003]**

(A) 50 Hz (B) 100 Hz
(C) 200 Hz (D) 25 Hz

6. In an *LCR* circuit, capacitance is changed from *C* to 2 C. For the resonant frequency to remain unchanged, the inductance should be changed from *L* to : **[2004]**

(A) 4*L* (B) 2*L*
(C) *L*/2 (D) *L*/4

7. In an *LCR* series ac circuit, the voltage across each of the components. *L*, *C* and *R* is 50 V. The voltage across the *LC* combination will be : **[2004]**

(A) 50 *V* (B) $50\sqrt{2}V$
(C) 100 *V* (D) 0

8. Alternating current can not be measured by *DC* ammeter because : **[2004]**

(A) *AC* cannot pass through *DC* ammeter
(B) *AC* changes direction
(C) Average value of current for complete cycle is zero
(D) *DC* ammeter will get damaged

9. The phase difference between the alternating current and emf is π/2. which of the following cannot be the constituent of the circuit ? **[2005]**

(A) *C* alone (B) *R*, *L*
(C) *L*, *C* (D) *L* alone

10. A circuit has a resistance of 12 Ω and an impedance of 15 Ω. The power factor of circuit will be : **[2005]**

(A) 0.8 (B) 0.4
(C) 1.25 (D) 0.125

11. The self-inductance of the motor of an electric fan is 10 H. In order to impart maximum power at 50 Hz, it should be connected to a capacitance of : **[2005]**

(A) 4 μ*F* (B) 8 μ*F*
(C) 1 μ*F* (D) 2 μ*F*

12. In an *AC* generator, a coil with *N* turns, all of the same area *A* and total resistance *R*, rotates with frequency ω in a magnetic field *B*. The maximum value of emf generated in the coil is : **[2006]**

(A) *NABR*ω (B) *NAB*
(C) *NABR* (D) *NAB*ω

13. In a series resonant *LCR* circuit, the voltage across *R* is 100 volts and *R* = 1 kΩ with *C* = 2μ*F*. The resonant frequency ω is 200 rad/s. At resonance the voltage across *L* is : **[2006]**

(A) 2.5×10^{-2} V (B) 40 V
(C) 250 V (D) 4×10^{-3} V

14. In an AC circuit the voltage applied is $E = E_0 \sin\omega t$. The resulting current in the circuit is $I = I_0 \sin\left(\omega t - \frac{\pi}{2}\right)$. The power consumption in the circuit is given by : **[2007]**

(A) $P = \frac{E_0 I_0}{\sqrt{2}}$ (B) $P = \text{zero}$

(C) $P = \frac{E_0 I_0}{2}$ (D) $P = \sqrt{2} E_0 I_0$

15. In a series LCR circuit $R = 200\ \Omega$ and the voltage and the frequency of the main supply is 220 V and 50 Hz respectively. On taking out the capacitance from the circuit the current lags behind the voltage by 30°. On taking out the inductor from the circuit the current leads the voltage by 30°. The power dissipated in the LCR circuit is : **[2010]**

(A) 242 W (B) 305 W
(C) 210 W (D) Zero

16. A fully charged capacitor C with initial charge q_0 is connected to a coil of self inductance L at $t = 0$. The time at which the energy is stored equally between the electric and the magnetic fields is : **[2011]**

(A) $2\pi\sqrt{LC}$ (B) $\sqrt{LC}$

(C) $\pi\sqrt{LC}$ (D) $\frac{\pi}{4}\sqrt{LC}$

17. The capacitor of an oscillatory circuit is enclosed in a container. When the container is evacuated, the resonance frequency of the circuit is 10 kHz. When the container is filled with a gas, the resonance frequency changes by 50 Hz. The dielectric constant of the gas is : **[2012 (Online)]**

(A) 1.001 (B) 2.001
(C) 1.01 (D) 3.01

18. In an LCR circuit shown in the following figure, what will be the readings of the voltmeter across the resistor and ammeter if an a.c. source of 220 V and 100 Hz is connected to it as shown ? **[2012 (Online)]**

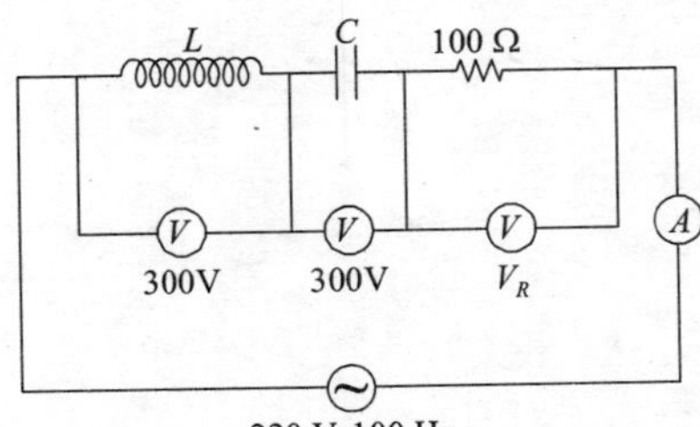

(A) 800 V, 8 A (B) 110 V, 1.1 A
(C) 300 V, 3 A (D) 220 V, 2.2 A

19. An LCR circuit as shown in the figure is connected to a voltage source V_{ac} whose frequency can be varied. The frequency, at which the voltage across the resistor is maximum, is : **[2013 (Online)]**

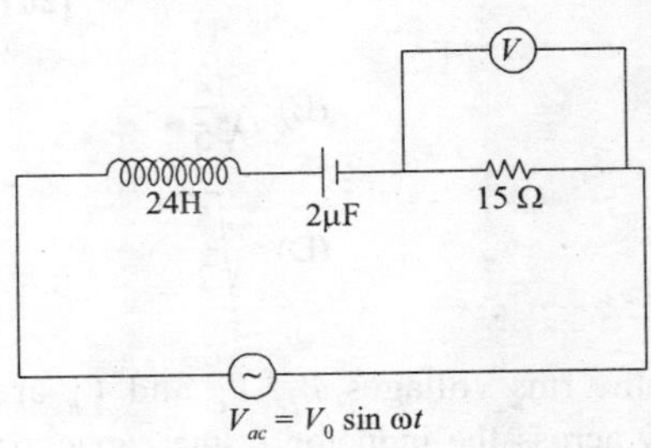

(A) 902 Hz (B) 143 Hz
(C) 23 Hz (D) 345 Hz

20. In a series L-C-R circuit, $C = 10^{-11}$ Farad, $L = 10^{-5}$ Henry and $R = 100$ Ohm, when a constant D.C. voltage E is applied to the circuit, the capacitor acquires a charge 10^{-9} C. The D.C. source is replaced by a sinusoidal voltage source in which the peak voltage E_0 is equal to the constant D.C. voltage E. At resonance the peak value of the charge acquired by the capacitor will be : **[2013 (Online)]**

(A) 10^{-15} C (B) 10^{-6} C
(C) 10^{-10} C (D) 10^{-8} C

21. The plot given below is of the average power delivered to and LRC circuit versus frequency. The quality factor of the circuit is : **[2013 (Online)]**

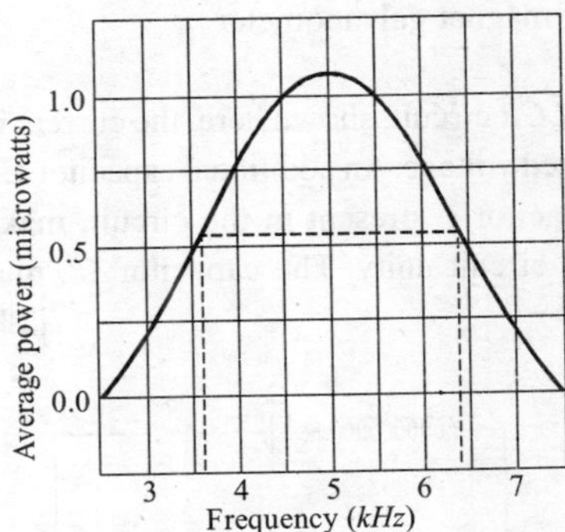

(A) 5.0 (B) 2.0
(C) 2.5 (D) 0.4

22. When resonance is produced in a series LCR circuit, then which of the following is not correct ? **[2013 (Online)]**

(A) Current in the circuit is in phase with the applied voltage
(B) Inductive and capacitive reactances are equal
(C) If R is reduced, the voltage across capacitor will increase
(D) Impedance of the circuit is maximum

23. A series LR circuit is connected to an ac source of frequency ω and the inductive reactance is equal to 2 R. A capacitance of capacitive reactance equal to R is added in series with L and R. The ratio of the new power factor to the old one is : **[2013 (Online)]**

(A) $\sqrt{\frac{2}{3}}$ (B) $\sqrt{\frac{2}{5}}$

(C) $\sqrt{\frac{3}{2}}$ (D) $\sqrt{\frac{5}{2}}$

24. When the rms voltages V_L, V_C and V_R are measured respectively across the inductor L, the capacitor C and the resistor R in a series LCR circuit connected to an AC source, it is found that the ratio $V_L : V_C : V_R = 1 : 2 : 3$. If the rms voltage of the AC sources is 100 V, the V_R is close to : **[2014 (Online)]**

(A) 50 V (B) 70 V

(C) 90 V (D) 100 V

25. A sinusoidal voltage $V(t) = 100 \sin (500t)$ is applied across a pure inductance of $L = 0.02$ H. The current through the coil is: **[2014 (Online)]**

(A) $10 \cos (500\,t)$ (B) $-10 \cos (500t)$

(C) $10 \sin (500t)$ (D) $-10 \sin (500t)$

26. The AC voltage across a resistance can be measured using a : **[2015 (Online)]**

(A) Hot wire voltmeter

(B) Moving coil galvanometer

(C) Potential coil galvanometer

(D) Moving magnet galvanometer

27. For the LCR circuit, shown here, the current is observed to lead the applied voltage. An additional capacitor C', when joined with the capacitor C present in the circuit, makes the power factor of the circuit unity. The capacitor C', must have been connected in : **[2015 (Online)]**

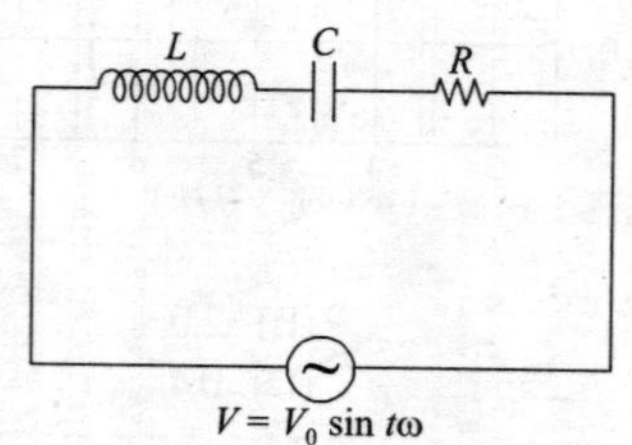

(A) Series with C and has a magnitude $\frac{C}{(\omega^2 LC - 1)}$

(B) Series with C and has a magnitude $\frac{1 - \omega^2 LC}{\omega^2 L}$

(C) Parallel with C and has a magnitude $\frac{1 - \omega^2 LC}{\omega^2 L}$

(D) Parallel with C and has a magnitude $\frac{C}{(\omega^2 LC - 1)}$

28. An arc lamp requires a direct current of 10 A at 80 V to function. If it is connected to a 220 V (rms), 50 Hz AC supply, the series inductor needed for it to work is close to : **[2016]**

(A) 80 H (B) 0.08 H

(C) 0.044 H (D) 0.065 H

29. A series LR circuit is connected to a voltage source with $V(t) = V_0 \sin \omega t$. After very large time, current (t) behaves as $\left(t_0 >> \frac{L}{R}\right)$: **[2016 (Online)]**

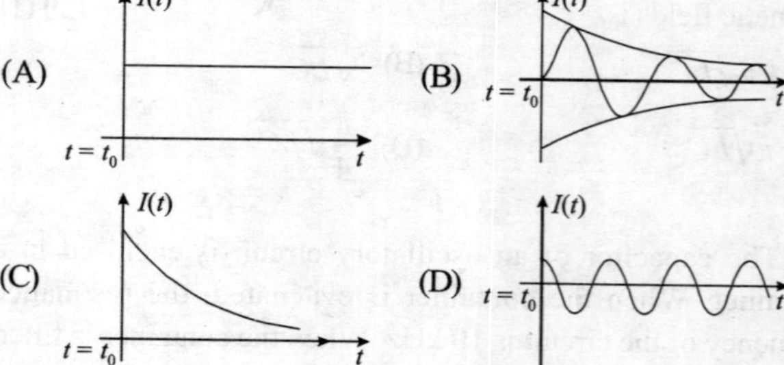

* * * * *

CHAPTER

22 ELECTROMAGNETIC WAVES

22.1 ELECTROMAGNETIC WAVE

1. An electromagnetic wave of frequency $\nu = 3.0$ MHz passes from vacuum into a dielectric medium with permittivity $\in = 4.0$. Then : **[2004]**

(A) Wave length is halved and frequency remains unchanged
(B) Wave length is doubled and frequency becomes half
(C) Wave length is doubled and the frequency remains unchanged
(D) Wave length and frequency both remain unchanged

2. If a source of power 4 kW produces 10^{20} photons/second, the radiation belongs to apart of the spectrum called : **[2010]**

(A) γ-rays (B) X-rays
(C) ultraviolet rays (D) microwaves

3. An electromagnetic wave in vacuum has the electric and magnetic field $\vec{E}$ and $\vec{B}$, which are always perpendicular to each other. The direction of polarization is given by $\vec{X}$ and that of wave propagation by $\vec{k}$. Then : **[2012]**

(A) $\vec{X} \parallel \vec{B}$ and $\vec{k} \parallel \vec{B} \times \vec{E}$ (B) $\vec{X} \parallel \vec{E}$ and $\vec{k} \parallel \vec{E} \times \vec{B}$
(C) $\vec{X} \parallel \vec{B}$ and $\vec{k} \parallel \vec{E} \times \vec{B}$ (D) $\vec{X} \parallel \vec{E}$ and $\vec{k} \parallel \vec{B} \times \vec{E}$

4. The frequency of *X*-rays; γ-rays and ultraviolet rays are respectively *a*, *b* and *c* then : **[2012 (Online)]**

(A) $a < b;\ b > c$ (B) $a > b;\ b > c$
(C) $a < b < c$ (D) $a = b = c$

5. An electromagnetic wave with frequency ω and wavelength λ travels in the $+y$ direction. Its magnetic field is along $+x$-axis. The vector equation for the associated electric field (of amplitude E_0) is : **[2012 (Online)]**

(A) $\vec{E} = -E_0 \cos\left(\omega t + \frac{2\pi}{\lambda} y\right)\hat{x}$

(B) $\vec{E} = E_0 \cos\left(\omega t - \frac{2\pi}{\lambda} y\right)\hat{x}$

(C) $\vec{E} = E_0 \cos\left(\omega t - \frac{2\pi}{\lambda} y\right)\hat{z}$

(D) $\vec{E} = -E_0 \cos\left(\omega t + \frac{2\pi}{\lambda} y\right)\hat{z}$

6. The magnetic field in a travelling electromagnetic wave has a peak value of 20 nT. The peak value of electric field strength is : **[2013]**

(A) 3 V/m (B) 6 V/m
(C) 9 V/m (D) 12 V/m

7. Photons of an electromagnetic radiation has an energy 11 keV each. To which region of electromagnetic spectrum does it belong ? **[2013 (Online)]**

(A) X-rays region (B) Ultra violet region
(C) Infrared region (D) Visible region

8. Select the correct statement from the following : **[2013 (Online)]**

(A) Electromagnetic waves cannot travel in vacuum
(B) Electromagnetic waves are longitudinal waves
(C) Electromagnetic waves are produced by charges moving with uniform velocity
(D) Electromagnetic waves carry both energy and momentum as they propagate through space

9. A plane electromagnetic wave in a non-magnetic dielectric medium is given by $\vec{E} = \vec{E}_0(4 \times 10^{-7} x - 50t)$ with distance being in meter and time in seconds. The dielectric constant of the medium is : **[2013 (Online)]**

(A) 2.4 (B) 5.8
(C) 8.2 (D) 4.8

10. During the propagation of electromagnetic waves in a medium: **[2014]**

(A) Electric energy density is double of the magnetic energy density
(B) Electric energy density is half of the magnetic energy density
(C) Electric energy density is equal to the magnetic energy density
(D) Both electric and magnetic energy densities are zero

11. If microwaves, X-rays, infrared, gamma rays, ultra-violet, radio waves and visible parts of the electromagnetic spectrum are denoted by *M, X, I, G, U, R* and *V* then which of the following is the arrangement in ascending order of wavelength ? **[2014 (Online)]**

(A) *R, M, I, V, U, X* and *G* (B) *M, R, V, X, U, G* and *I*
(C) *G, X, U, V, I, M* and *R* (D) *I, M, R, U, V, X* and *G*

12. An electromagnetic wave of frequency 1×10^{14} hertz is

propagating along z-axis. The amplitude of electric field is 4 V/m. If $\varepsilon_0 = 8.8 \times 10^{-12}$ C^2/N-m^2, then average energy density of electric field will be : **[2014 (Online)]**

(A) 35.2×10^{-10} J/m^3 (B) 35.2×10^{-11} J/m^3
(C) 35.2×10^{-12} J/m^3 (D) 35.2×10^{-13} J/m^3

13. A lamp emits monochromatic green light uniformly in all directions. The lamp is 3% efficient in converting electrical power to electromagnetic waves and consumes 100 W of power. The amplitude of the electric field associated with the electromagnetic radiation at a distance of 5 m from the lamp will be nearly : **[2014 (Online)]**

(A) 1.34 V/m (B) 2.68 V/m
(C) 4.02 V/m (D) 5.36 V/m

14. An electromagnetic wave travelling in the x-direction has frequency of 2×10^{14} Hz and electric field amplitude of 27 Vm^{-1}. From the options given below, which one describes the magnetic field for this wave ? **[2015 (Online)]**

(A) $\vec{B}(x,t) = (3\times10^{-8}\text{T})\hat{j}\,;\sin[2\pi(1.5\times10^{-8}x - 2\times10^{14}t)]$
(B) $\vec{B}(x,t) = (9\times10^{-8}\text{T})\hat{i}\,;\sin[2\pi(1.5\times10^{-8}x - 2\times10^{14}t)]$
(C) $\vec{B}(x,t) = (9\times10^{-8}\text{T})\hat{j}\,;\sin[1.5\times10^{-6}x - 2\times10^{14}t]$
(D) $\vec{B}(x,t) = (9\times10^{-8}\text{T})\hat{k}\,;\sin[2\pi(1.5\times10^{-6}x - 2\times10^{14}t)]$

15. For plane electromagnetic waves propagating in the z-direction, which one of the following combination gives the correct possible direction for $\vec{E}$ and $\vec{B}$ field respectively ? **[2015 (Online)]**

(A) $(2\hat{i}+3\hat{j})$ and $(\hat{i}+2\hat{j})$ (B) $(-2\hat{i}-3\hat{j})$ and $(3\hat{i}-2\hat{j})$
(C) $(3\hat{i}+4\hat{j})$ and $(4\hat{i}-3\hat{j})$ (D) $(\hat{i}+2\hat{j})$ and $(2\hat{i}-\hat{j})$

16. Arrange the following electromagnetic radiations per quantum in the order of increasing energy : **[2016]**

A : Blue B : Yellow light
C : X-ray D : Radiowave

(A) C, A, B, D (B) B, A, D, C
(C) D, B, A, C (D) A, B, D, C

17. Microwave oven acts on the principle of : **[2016 (Online)]**

(A) Giving rotational energy to water molecules
(B) Giving translational energy to water molecules
(C) Giving vibrational energy to water molecules
(D) Transferring electrons from lower to higher energy levels in water molecule

18. Consider an electromagnetic wave propagating in vacuum. Choose the correct statement : **[2016 (Online)]**

(A) For an electromagnetic wave propagating in $+y$ direction the electric field is $\vec{E} = \frac{1}{\sqrt{2}}E_{yz}(x,t)\hat{z}$ and the magnetic field is $\vec{B} = \frac{1}{\sqrt{2}}B_z(x,t)\hat{y}$

(B) For an electromagnetic wave propagating in $+y$ direction the electric field is $\vec{E} = \frac{1}{\sqrt{2}}E_{yz}(x,t)\hat{y}$ and the magnetic field is $\vec{B} = \frac{1}{\sqrt{2}}B_{yz}(x,t)\hat{z}$

(C) For an electromagnetic wave propagating in $+x$ direction the electric field is $\vec{E} = \frac{1}{\sqrt{2}}E_{yz}(y,z,t)\,(\hat{y}+\hat{z})$ and the magnetic field is $\vec{B} = \frac{1}{\sqrt{2}}B_{yz}(y,z,t)(\hat{y}+\hat{z})$

(D) For an electromagnetic wave propagating in $+x$ direction the electric field is $\vec{E} = \frac{1}{\sqrt{2}}E_{yz}(x,t)(\hat{y}-\hat{z})$ and the magnetic field is $\vec{B} = \frac{1}{\sqrt{2}}B_{yz}(x,t)(\hat{y}+\hat{z})$

* * * * *

CHAPTER 23

RAY OPTICS AND OPTICAL INSTRUMENTS

23.1 GEOMETRICAL OPTICS I - REFLECTION OF LIGHT

1. If two mirrors are kept at 60° to each other, then the number of images formed by them is : **[2002]**

(A) 5 (B) 6
(C) 7 (D) 8

2. To get three images of a single object, one should have two plane mirrors at an angle of : **[2003]**

(A) 60° (B) 90°
(C) 120° (D) 30°

3. A car is fitted with a convex side-view mirror of focal length 20 cm. A second car 2.8 m behind the first car is overtaking the first car at a relative speed of 15 m/s. The speed of the image of the second car as seen in the mirror of the first one is : **[2011]**

(A) 10 m/s (B) 15 m/s
(C) $\frac{1}{10}$ m/s (D) $\frac{1}{15}$ m/s

4. You are asked to design a shaving mirror assuming that a person keeps it 10 cm from his face and views the magnified image of the face at the closest comfortable distance of 25 cm. The radius of curvature of the mirror would then be : **[2015 (Online)]**

(A) 60 cm (B) –24 cm
(C) –60 cm (D) 24 cm

* * * * *

CHAPTER 23

RAY OPTICS AND OPTICAL INSTRUMENTS

23.2 GEOMETRICAL OPTICS II - REFRACTION OF LIGHT

1. Which of the following is used in optical fibres ? **[2002]**

(A) Total internal reflection (B) Scattering

(C) Diffraction (D) Refraction

2. A light ray is incident perpendicular to one face of a 90° prism and is totally internally reflected at the glass-air interface. If the angle of reflection is 45°, we conclude that the refractive index n : **[2004]**

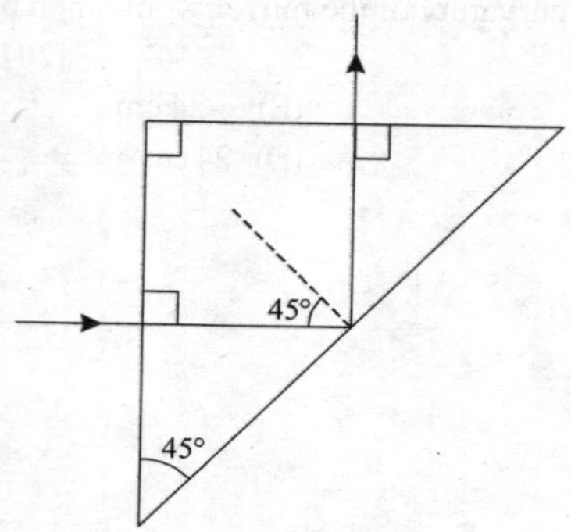

(A) $n < \frac{1}{\sqrt{2}}$ (B) $n > \sqrt{2}$

(C) $n > \frac{1}{\sqrt{2}}$ (D) $n < \sqrt{2}$

3. A fish looking up through the water sees the outside world, contained in a circular horizon. If the refractive index of water is 4/3 and the fish is 12 cm below the water surface, the radius of this circle in cm is : **[2005]**

(A) $36\sqrt{7}$ (B) $\frac{36}{\sqrt{7}}$

(C) $36\sqrt{5}$ (D) $4\sqrt{5}$

4. A transparent solid cylindrical rod has a refractive index of $\frac{2}{\sqrt{3}}$. It is surrounded by air. A light ray is incident at the mid-point of one end of the rod as shown in the figure :

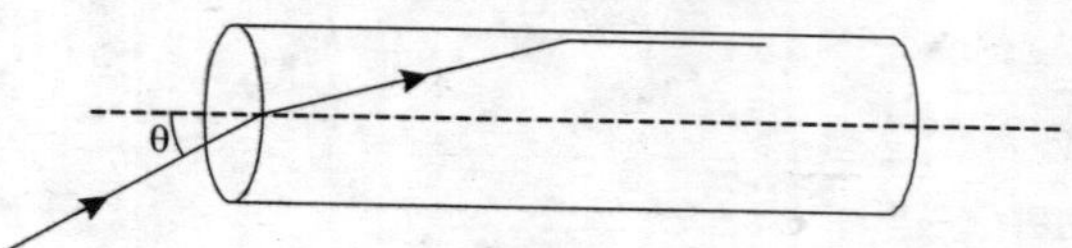

The incident angle θ for which the light ray grazes along the wall of the rod is : **[2009]**

(A) $\sin^{-1}\left(\frac{2}{\sqrt{3}}\right)$ (B) $\sin^{-1}\left(\frac{1}{\sqrt{3}}\right)$

(C) $\sin^{-1}\left(\frac{1}{2}\right)$ (D) $\sin^{-1}\left(\frac{\sqrt{3}}{2}\right)$

5. Let the x-y plane be the boundary between two transparent media. Medium 1 in $z \geq 0$ has a refractive index of $\sqrt{2}$ and medium 2 with $z < 0$ has a refractive index of $\sqrt{3}$. A ray of light in medium 1 given by the vector $\vec{A} = 6\sqrt{3}\hat{i} + 8\sqrt{3}\hat{j} - 10\hat{k}$ is incident on the plane of separation. The angle of refraction in medium 2 is : **[2011]**

(A) 60° (B) 75°

(C) 30° (D) 45°

6. A beaker contains water up to a height h_1 and kerosene of height h_2 above water so that the total height of (water + kerosene) is $(h_1 + h_2)$. Refractive index of water is μ_1 and that of kerosene is μ_2. The apparent shift in the position of the bottom of the beaker when viewed from above is : **[2011]**

(A) $\left(1-\frac{1}{\mu_1}\right)h_2 + \left(1-\frac{1}{\mu_2}\right)h_1$ (B) $\left(1+\frac{1}{\mu_1}\right)h_1 - \left(1+\frac{1}{\mu_2}\right)h_2$

(C) $\left(1-\frac{1}{\mu_1}\right)h_1 + \left(1-\frac{1}{\mu_2}\right)h_2$ (D) $\left(1+\frac{1}{\mu_1}\right)h_2 - \left(1+\frac{1}{\mu_2}\right)h_1$

7. A glass prism of refractive index 1.5 is immersed in water (refractive index 4/3) as shown in figure. A light beam incident normally on the face AB is totally reflected to reach the face BC, if: **[2012 (Online)]**

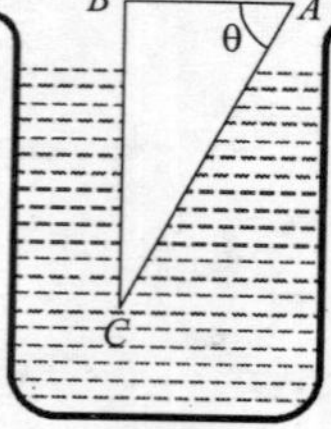

(A) $\sin\theta > \frac{5}{9}$ (B) $\sin\theta > \frac{2}{3}$

(C) $\sin\theta > \frac{8}{9}$ (D) $\sin\theta > \frac{1}{3}$

8. The graph between angle of deviation (δ) and angle of incidence (i) for a triangular prism is represented by : **[2013]**

(A) 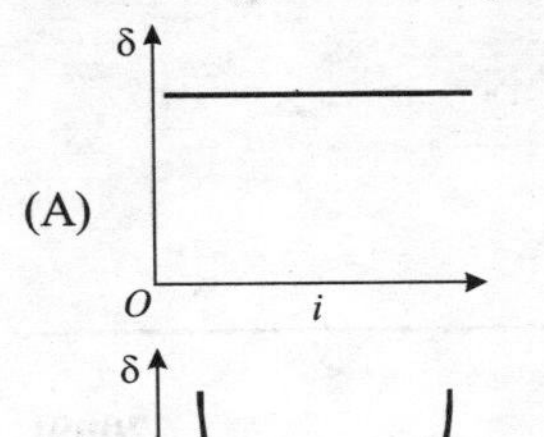

(B) 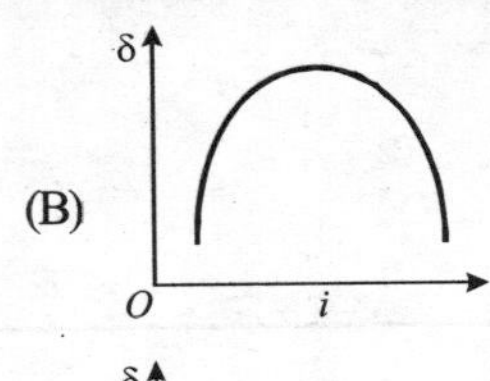

(C) 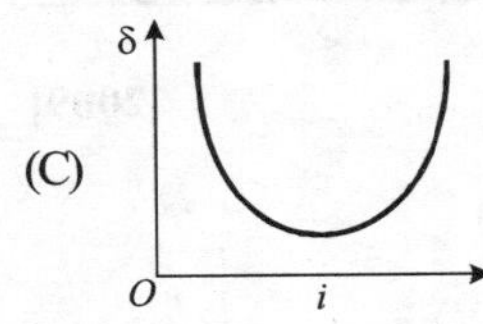

(D) 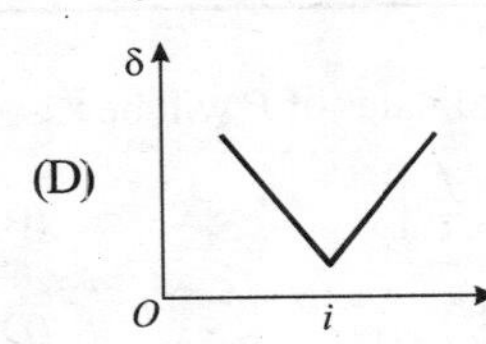

9. Light is incident from a medium into air at two possible angles of incidence (A) 20° and (B) 40°. In the medium light travels 3.0 cm in 0.2 ns. The ray will : **[2013 (Online)]**

(A) Suffer total internal reflection in both cases (A) and (B)

(B) Suffer total internal reflection in case (B) only

(C) Have partial reflection and partial transmission in case (B)

(D) Have 100% transmission in case (A)

10. A light ray falls on a square glass slab as shown in the diagram. The index of refraction of the glass, if total internal reflection is to occur at the vertical face, is equal to : **[2013 (Online)]**

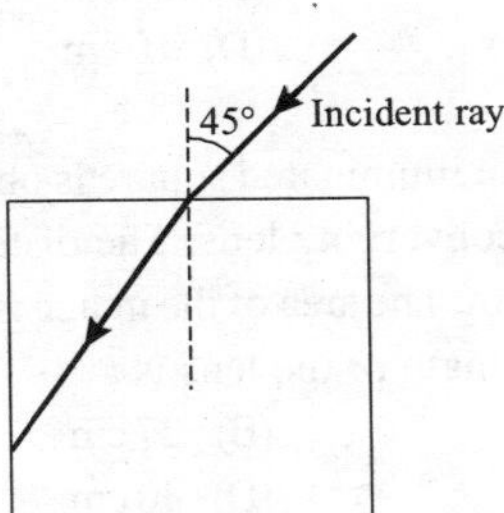

(A) $\frac{(\sqrt{2}+1)}{2}$ (B) $\sqrt{\frac{5}{2}}$

(C) $\frac{3}{2}$ (D) $\sqrt{\frac{3}{2}}$

11. A printed page is pressed by a glass of water. The refractive index of the glass and water is 1.5 and 1.33, respectively. If the thickness of the bottom of glass is 1 cm and depth of water is 5 cm, how much the page will appear to be shifted if viewed from the top ? **[2013 (Online)]**

(A) 1.033 cm (B) 3.581 cm

(C) 1.3533 cm (D) 1.90 cm

12. A diver looking up through the water sees the outside world contained in a circular horizontal. The refractive index of water is 4/3, and the diver's eyes are 15 cm below the surface of water. Then the radius of the circle is : **[2014 (Online)]**

(A) $15\times3\times\sqrt{5}$ cm (B) $15\times3\sqrt{5}$ cm

(C) $\frac{15\times\sqrt{7}}{3}$ cm (D) $\frac{15\times3}{\sqrt{7}}$ cm

13. Monochromatic light is incident of a glass prism of angle A. If the refractive index of the material of the prism is μ, a ray, incident at an angle θ, on the face AB would get transmitted through the face AC of the prism provided : **[2015]**

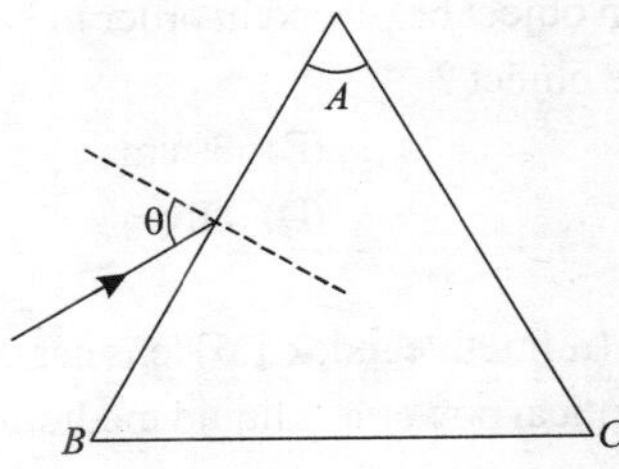

(A) $\theta > \sin^{-1}\left[\mu\sin\left(A-\sin^{-1}\left(\frac{1}{\mu}\right)\right)\right]$

(B) $\theta < \sin^{-1}\left[\mu\sin\left(A-\sin^{-1}\left(\frac{1}{\mu}\right)\right)\right]$

(C) $\theta > \cos^{-1}\left[\mu\sin\left(A+\sin^{-1}\left(\frac{1}{\mu}\right)\right)\right]$

(D) $\theta < \cos^{-1}\left[\mu\sin\left(A+\sin^{-1}\left(\frac{1}{\mu}\right)\right)\right]$

14. In an experiment for determination of refractive index of glass of a prism by $i-\delta$, plot, it was found that a ray incident at angle 35°, suffers a deviation of 40° and that it emerges at angle 79°. In that case which of the following is closest to the maximum possible value of the refractive index ? **[2016]**

(A) 1.5 (B) 1.6

(C) 1.7 (D) 1.8

15. A hemispherical glass body of radius 10 cm and refractive index 1.5 is silvered on its curved surface. A small air bubble is 6 cm below the flat surface inside it along the axis. The position of the image of the air bubble made by the mirror is seen : **[2016 (Online)]**

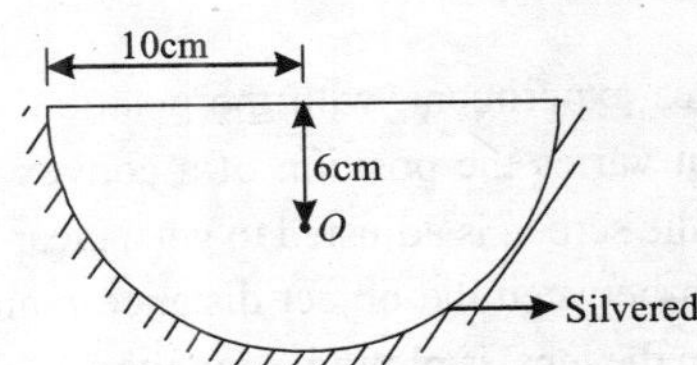

(A) 14 cm below flat surface (B) 20 cm below flat surface

(C) 16 cm below flat surface (D) 30 cm below flat surface

* * * * *

CHAPTER 23

RAY OPTICS AND OPTICAL INSTRUMENTS

23.3 GEOMETRICAL OPTICS III - THIN LENSES

1. A plano-convex lens of refractive index 1.5 and radius of curvature 30 cm is silvered at the curved surface. Now, this lens has been used to form the image of an object. At what distance from this lens, an object be placed in order to have a real image of the size of the object ? **[2004]**

(A) 20 cm (B) 30 cm

(C) 60 cm (D) 80 cm

2. A thin glass (refractive index 1.5) lens has optical power of – 5 D in air. Its optical power in a liquid medium with refractive index 1.6 will be : **[2005]**

(A) 1 D (B) – 1 D

(C) 25 D (D) – 25 D

3. Two lenses of power – 15 D and + 5 D are in contact with each other. The focal length of the combination is : **[2007]**

(A) – 20 cm (B) – 10 cm

(C) + 20 cm (D) + 10 cm

4. A student measures the focal length of a convex lens by putting an object pin at a distance 'u' from the lens and measuring the distance 'v' of the image pin. The graph between 'u' and 'v' plotted by the student should look like : **[2008]**

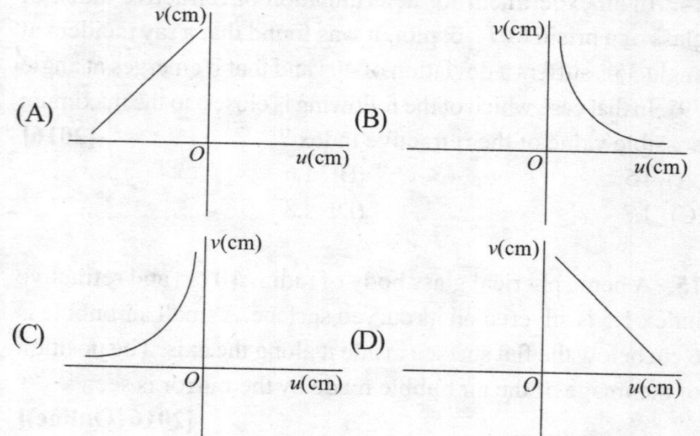

5. In an optics experiment, with the position of the object fixed, a student varies the position of a convex lens and for each position, the screen is adjusted to get a clear image of the object. A graph between the object distance u and the image distance v, from the lens, is plotted using the same scale for the two axes. A straight line passing through the origin and making an angle of 45° with the x-axis meets the experimental curve at P. The coordinates of P will be : **[2009]**

(A) $\left(\frac{f}{2}, \frac{f}{2}\right)$ (B) (f, f)

(C) $(4f, 4f)$ (D) $(2f, 2f)$

6. An object 2.4 m in front of a lens forms a sharp image on a film 12 cm behind the lens. A glass plate 1 cm thick, of refractive index 1.50 is interposed between lens and film with its plane faces parallel to film. At what distance (from lens) should object be shifted to be in sharp focus on film ? **[2012]**

(A) 5.6 m (B) 7.2 m

(C) 2.4 m (D) 3.2 m

7. Diameter of a plano-convex lens is 6 cm and thickness at the centre is 3 mm. If speed of light in material of lens is 2×10^8 m/s, the focal length of the lens is : **[2013]**

(A) 15 cm (B) 20 cm

(C) 30 cm (D) 10 cm

8. The image of an illuminated square is obtained on a screen with the help of a converging lens. The distance of the square from the lens is 40 cm. The area of the image is 9 times that of the square. The focal length of the lens is : **[2013 (Online)]**

(A) 36 cm (B) 27 cm

(C) 60 cm (D) 30 cm

9. A thin convex lens made from crown glass $\left(\mu = \frac{3}{2}\right)$ has focal length f. When it is measured in two different liquids having refractive indices 4/3 and 5/3, it has the focal lengths f_1 and f_2 respectively. The correct relation between the focal length is : **[2014]**

(A) $f_1 = f_2 < f$

(B) $f_1 > f$ and f_2 becomes negative

(C) $f_2 > f$ and f_1 becomes negative

(D) f_1 and f_2 both becomes negative

10. An object is located in a fixed position in front of a screen. Sharp image is obtained on the screen for two positions of a thin lens separated by 10 cm. The size of the images in two situations are in the ratio 3 : 2. What is the distance between the screen and the object ? **[2014 (Online)]**

(A) 124.5 cm (B) 144.5 cm

(C) 65.0 cm (D) 99.0 cm

11. The refractive index of the material of a concave lens is μ. It is immersed in a medium of refractive index μ_1. A parallel beam of light is incident on the lens. The path of the emergent rays when $\mu_1 > \mu$ is : **[2014 (Online)]**

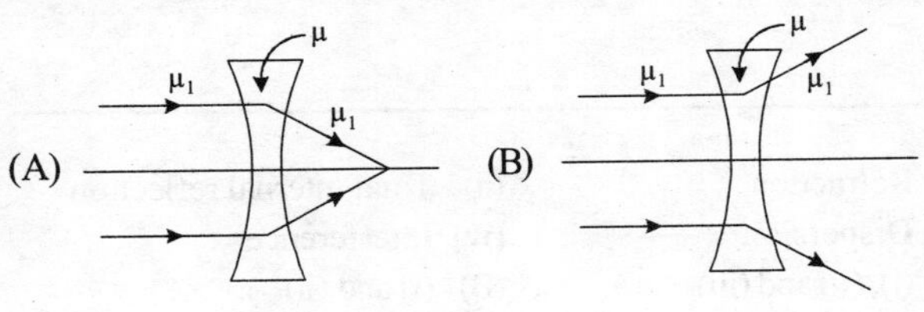

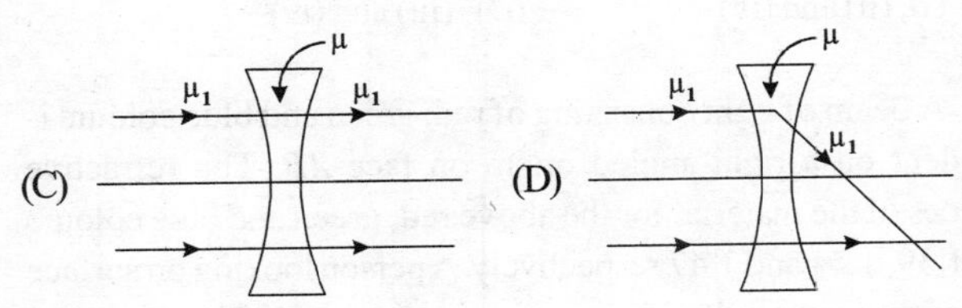

12. A thin convex lens of focal length 'f' is put on a plane mirror as shown in the figure. When an object is kept at a distance 'a' from the lens-mirror combination, its image is formed at a distance $a/3$ in front of the combination. The value of 'a' is : **[2015 (Online)]**

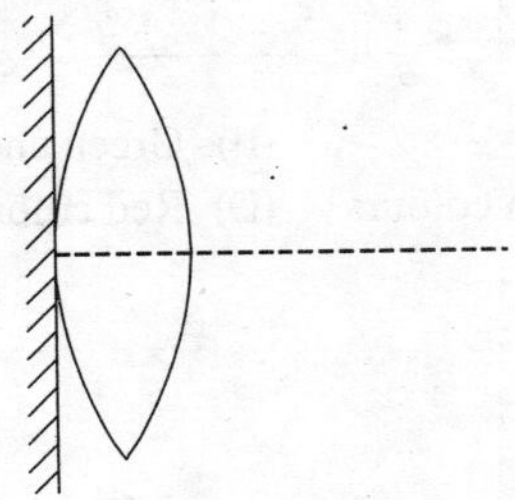

(A) $3f$ (B) $\frac{3}{2}f$

(C) f (D) $2f$

13. To find the focal length of a convex mirror, a student records the following data :

Object Pin	Convex Lens	Convex Mirror	Image Pin
22.2 cm	32.2 cm	45.8 cm	71.2 cm

The focal length of the convex lens is f_1 and that of mirror is f_2. Then taking index correction to be negligibly small, f_1 and f_2 are close to : **[2016 (Online)]**

(A) $f_1 = 7.8$ cm $f_2 = 12.7$ cm

(B) $f_1 = 12.7$ cm $f_2 = 7.8$ cm

(C) $f_1 = 15.6$ cm $f_2 = 25.4$ cm

(D) $f_1 = 7.8$ cm $f_2 = 25.4$ cm

14. A convex lens, of focal length 30 cm, a concave lens of focal length 120 cm, and a plane mirror are arranged as shown. For an object kept at a distance of 60 cm from the convex lens, the final image, formed by the combination, is a real image, at a distance of : **[2016 (Online)]**

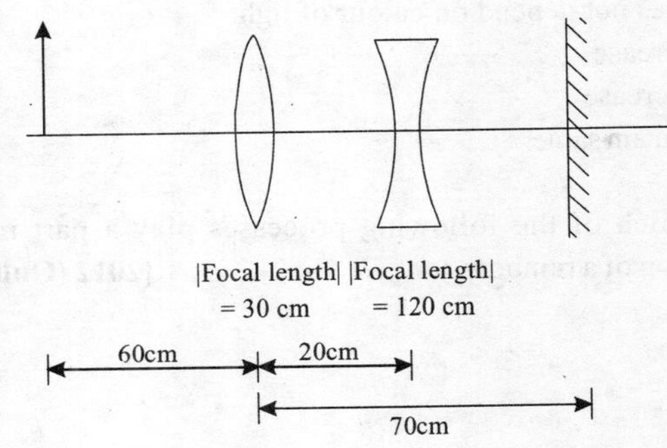

(A) 60 cm from the convex lens

(B) 60 cm from the concave lens

(C) 70 cm from the convex lens

(D) 70 cm from the concave lens

* * * * *

CHAPTER 23

RAY OPTICS AND OPTICAL INSTRUMENTS

23.4 DISPERSION OF LIGHT

1. The refractive index of glass is 1.520 for red light and 1.525 for blue light. Let D_1 and D_2 be angles of minimum deviation for red and blue light respectively in a prism of this glass. Then : **[2006]**

(A) $D_1 < D_2$

(B) $D_1 = D_2$

(C) D_1 can be less than or greater than D_2 depending upon the angle of prism

(D) $D_1 > D_2$

2. When monochromatic red light is used instead of blue light in a convex lens, its focal length will : **[2011]**

(A) Does not depend on colour of light

(B) Increase

(C) Decrease

(D) Remain same

3. Which of the following processes play a part in the formation of a rainbow ? **[2012 (Online)]**

(i) Refraction (ii) Total internal reflection

(iii) Dispersion (iv) Interference

(A) (i), (ii) and (iii) (B) (i) and (ii)

(C) (i), (ii) and (iv) (D) (iii) and (iv)

4. A beam of light consisting of red, green and blue colours is incident on a right-angled prism on face *AB*. The refractive indices of the material for the above red, green and blue colours are 1.39, 1.44 and 1.47 respectively. A person looking on surface *AC* of the prism will see : **[2012 (Online)]**

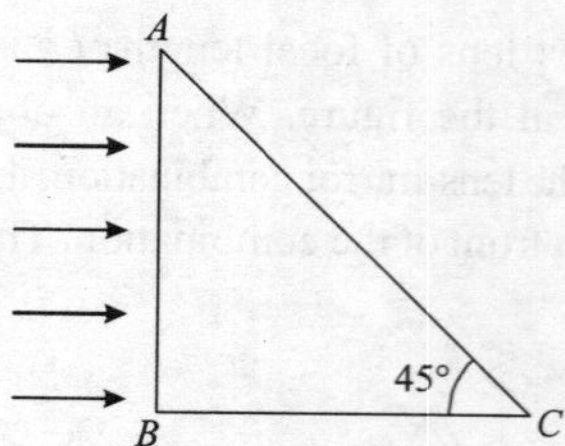

(A) No light (B) Green and blue colours

(C) Red and green colours (D) Red colour only

* * * * *

CHAPTER

23 RAY OPTICS AND OPTICAL INSTRUMENTS

23.5 OPTICAL INSTRUMENTS

1. An astronomical telescope has a large aperture to : **[2002]**
(A) Reduced spherical aberration
(B) Have high resolution
(C) Increase span of observation
(D) Have low dispersion

2. Wavelength of light used in a optical instrument are $\lambda_1 = 4000$ Å and $\lambda_2 = 5000$ Å, then ratio of their respective resolving powers (corresponding to λ_1 and λ_2) is : **[2002]**
(A) 16:25 (B) 9:1
(C) 4:5 (D) 5:4

3. The image formed by an objective of a compound microscope is : **[2003]**
(A) Virtual and diminished (B) Real and diminished
(C) Real and enlarged (D) Virtual and enlarged

4. Two point white dots are 1 mm apart on a black paper. They are viewed by eye of pupil diameter 3 mm. Approximately, what is the maximum distance at which these dots can be resolved by the eye ? [Take $\lambda = 500$ nm] : **[2005]**
(A) 5 m (B) 1 m
(C) 6 m (D) 3 m

5. An experiment is performed to find the refractive index of glass using a travelling microscope. In this experiment distances are measured by : **[2008]**
(A) A vernier scale provided on the microscope
(B) A standard laboratory scale
(C) A meter scale provided on the microscope
(D) A screws gauge provided on the microscope

6. We wish to make a microscope with the help of two positive lenses both with a focal length of 20 mm each and the object is positioned 25 mm from the objective lens. How far apart the lenses should be so that the final image is formed at infinity ? **[2012 (Online)]**
(A) 20 mm (B) 100 mm
(C) 120 mm (D) 80 mm

7. A telescope of aperture 3×10^{-2} m diameter is focused on a window at 80 m distance fitted with a wire mesh of spacing 2×10^{-3} m. Given : $\lambda = 5.5 \times 10^{-7}$ m, which of the following is true for observing the mesh through the telescope? **[2012 (Online)]**
(A) Yes, it is possible with the same aperture size
(B) Possible also with an aperture half the present diameter
(C) No, it is not possible
(D) Given data is not sufficient

8. The focal length of the objective and the eyepiece of a telescope are 50 cm and 5 cm respectively. If the telescope is focussed for distinct vision on a scale distant 2 m from its objective, then its magnifying power will be : **[2013 (Online)]**
(A) –4 (B) –8
(C) +8 (D) –2

9. This question has Statement-1 and Statement-2. Of the four choices given after the Statements, choose the one that best describes the two Statements. **[2013 (Online)]**

Statement-1 : Very large size telescopes are reflecting telescopes instead of refracting telescopes :

Statement-2 : It is easier to provide mechanical support to large size mirrors than large size lenses :
(A) Statement-1 is true and Statement-2 is false
(B) Statement-1 is false and Statement-2 is true
(C) Statement-1 and Statement-2 are true and Statement-2 is correct explanation for Statement-1
(D) Statement-1 and Statement-2 are true and Statement-2 is not the correct explanation for Statement-1

10. The focal lengths of objective lens and eye lens of a Galilean telescope are respectively 30 cm and 3.0 cm. Telescope produces virtual, erect image of an object situated far away from it at least distance of distinct vision from the eye lens. In this condition, the magnifying power of the Galilean telescope should be : **[2014 (Online)]**
(A) +11.2 (B) –11.2
(C) –8.8 (D) +8.8

11. In a compound microscope, the focal length of objective lens is 1.2 cm and focal length of eye piece is 3.0 cm. When object is kept at 1.25 cm in front of objective, final image is formed at infinity. Magnifying power of the compound microscope should be : **[2014 (Online)]**
(A) 200 (B) 100
(C) 400 (D) 150

12. Assuming human pupil to have a radius of 0.25 cm and a comfortable viewing distance of 25 cm, the minimum separation between two objects that human eye can resolve at 500 nm wavelength is : **[2015]**

(A) 1 μm (B) 30 μm
(C) 100 μm (D) 300 μm

13. A telescope has an objective lens of focal length 150 cm and an eyepiece of focal length 5 cm. If a 50 m tall tower at a distance of 1 km is observed through this telescope in normal setting, the angle formed by the image of the tower is θ, then θ is close to : **[2015 (Online)]**

(A) 30° (B) 15°
(C) 60° (D) 1°

14. An observer looks at a distant tree of height 10 m with a telescope of magnifying power of 20. To the observer the tree appears : **[2016]**

(A) 10 times taller (B) 10 times nearer
(C) 20 times taller (D) 20 times nearer

15. To determine refractive index of glass slab using a travelling microscope, minimum number of readings required are : **[2016 (Online)]**

(A) Two (B) Four
(C) Three (D) Five

* * * * *

CHAPTER

24 WAVE OPTICS

24.1 INTERFERENCE OF LIGHT

1. To demonstrate the phenomenon of interference we require two sources which emit radiations of : **[2003]**

(A) nearly the same frequency
(B) the same frequency
(C) different wavelength
(D) the same frequency and having a definite phase relationship

2. The maximum number of possible interference maxima for slit-separation equal to twice the wavelength in Young's double-slit experiment, is : **[2004]**

(A) infinite (B) five
(C) three (D) zero

3. A Young's double slit experiment uses a monochromatic source. The shape of the interference fringes formed on a screen is : **[2005]**

(A) hyperbola (B) circle
(C) straight line (D) parabola

4. In a Young's double slit experiment the intensity at a point where the path difference is $\lambda/6$ (λ being the wavelength of the light used) is I. If I_0 denotes the maximum intensity, I/I_0 is equal to : **[2007]**

(A) $\dfrac{1}{\sqrt{2}}$ (B) $\dfrac{\sqrt{3}}{2}$

(C) $\dfrac{1}{2}$ (D) $\dfrac{3}{4}$

5. A mixture of light, consisting of wavelength 590 nm and an unknown wavelength, illuminates Young's double slit and gives rise to two overlapping interference patterns on the screen. The central maximum of both lights coincide. Further, it is observed that the third bright fringe of known light coincides with the 4th bright fringe of the unknown light. From this data, the wavelength of the unknown light is : **[2009]**

(A) 442.5 nm (B) 776.8 nm
(C) 393.4 nm (D) 885.0 nm

Direction : Below questions from 6 to 8 are based on the following paragraph.

An initially parallel cylindrical beam travels in a medium of refractive index $\mu(I) = \mu_0 + \mu_2 I$, where μ_0 and μ_2 are positive constants and I is the intensity of the light beam. The intensity of the beam is decreasing with increasing radius :

6. The initial shape of the wavefront of the beam is : **[2010]**

(A) planar
(B) convex
(C) concave
(D) convex near the axis and concave near the periphery

7. The speed of the light in the medium is : **[2010]**

(A) maximum on the axis of the beam
(B) minimum on the axis of the beam
(C) the same everywhere in the beam
(D) directly proportional to the intensity I

8. As the beam enters the medium, it will : **[2010]**

(A) travel as a cylindrical beam
(B) diverge
(C) converge
(D) diverge near the axis and converge near the periphery

9. Direction : The question has a paragraph followed by two statement, Statement-1 and statement-2. Of the given four alternatives after the statements, choose the one that describes the statements.

A thin air film is formed by putting the convex surface of a plane-convex lens over a plane glass plate. With monochromatic light, this film gives an interference pattern due to light reflected from the top (convex) surface and the bottom (glass plate) surface of the film

Statement-1 : When light reflects from the air-glass plate interface, the reflected wave suffers a phase change of π.

Statement-2 : The centre of the interference pattern is dark. **[2011]**

(A) Statement-1 is true, Statement-2 is true and Statement-2 is not the correct explanation of Statement-1
(B) Statement-1 is false, Statement-2 is true
(C) Statement-1 is true, Statement-2 is false
(D) Statement-1 is true, Statement-2 is true and Statement-2 is the correct explanation of statement-1

10. In a Young's double slit experiment, the two slits act as coherent sources of waves of equal amplitude A and wavelength λ. In another experiment with the same arrangement the two slits are made to act as incoherent sources of waves of same amplitude and wavelength. If the intensity at the middle point of the screen in the first case is I_1 and in the second case I_2, then the ratio I_1/I_2 is : **[2011]**

(A) 4 (B) 2

(C) 1 (D) 0.5

11. At two points P and Q on screen in Young's double slit experiment, waves from slits S_1 and S_2 have a path difference of 0 and $\lambda/4$ respectively. The ratio of intensities at P and Q will be : **[2011]**

(A) 3 : 2 (B) 2 : 1

(C) $\sqrt{2}:1$ (D) 4 : 1

12. In Young's double slit experiment, one of the slit is wider than other, so that the amplitude of the light from one slit is double of that from other slit. If I_m be the maximum intensity, the resultant intensity I when they interfere at phase difference ϕ is given by : **[2012]**

(A) $\frac{I_m}{9}\left(1+8\cos^2\frac{\phi}{2}\right)$ (B) $\frac{I_m}{9}(4+5\cos\phi)$

(C) $\frac{I_m}{9}\left(1+2\cos^2\frac{\phi}{2}\right)$ (D) $\frac{I_m}{5}\left(1+4\cos^2\frac{\phi}{2}\right)$

13. In a Young's double slit experiment with light of wavelength λ, fringe pattern on the screen has fringe width β. When two thin transparent glass (refractive index μ) plates of thickness t_1 and t_2 ($t_1 > t_2$) are placed in the path of the two beams respectively, the fringe pattern will shift by a distance : **[2012 (Online)]**

(A) $\frac{\beta(\mu-1)}{\lambda}\left(\frac{t_1}{t_2}\right)$ (B) $\frac{\mu\beta}{\lambda}\frac{t_1}{t_2}$

(C) $\frac{\beta(\mu-1)}{\lambda}(t_1-t_2)$ (D) $(\mu-1)\frac{\lambda}{\beta}(t_1+t_2)$

14. The maximum number of possible interference maxima for slit separation equal to 1.8 λ, where λ is the wavelength of light used, in a Young's double slit experiment is : **[2012 (Online)]**

(A) Zero (B) 3

(C) Infinite (D) 5

15. In Young's double slit interference experiment, the slit widths are in the ratio 1 : 25. Then the ratio of intensity at the maxima and minima in the interference pattern is : **[2012 (Online)]**

(A) 3 : 2 (B) 1 : 25

(C) 9 : 4 (D) 1 : 5

16. Two coherent plane light waves of equal amplitude makes a small angle $\alpha(<< 1)$ with each other. The fall almost normally on a screen. If λ is the wavelength of light waves, the fringe width Δx of interference patterns of the two sets of waves on the screen is : **[2012 (Online)]**

(A) $\frac{2\lambda}{\alpha}$ (B) $\frac{\lambda}{\alpha}$

(C) $\frac{\lambda}{(2\alpha)}$ (D) $\frac{\lambda}{\sqrt{\alpha}}$

17. Two coherent point sources S_1 and S_2 are separated by a small distance 'd' as shown. The fringes obtained on the screen will be : **[2013]**

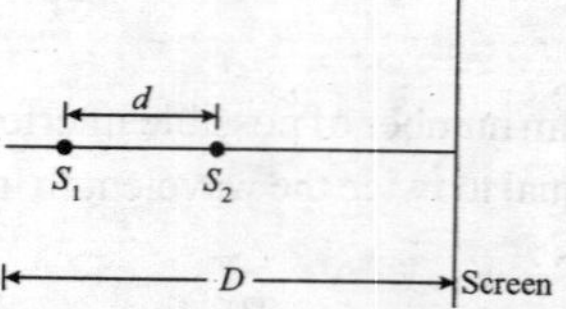

(A) points (B) straight lines

(C) semi-circles (D) concentric circles

18. This question has Statement-1 and Statement-2. Of the four choices given after the Statements, choose the one that best describes the two Statements.

Statement-1 : In young's double slit experiment, the number of fringes observed in the field of view is small with longer wavelength of light and is large with shorter wavelength of light.

Statement-2 : In the double slit experiment the fringe width depends directly on the wavelength of light. **[2013 (Online)]**

(A) Statement-1 is true, Statement-2 is true and the Statement-2 is correct explanation of the Statement-1

(B) Statement-1 is false and the Statement-2 is true

(C) Statement-1 is true Statement-2 is true and the Statement-2 is not correct explanation of the Statement-1

(D) Statement-1 is true and the Statement-2 is false

19. The source that illuminates the double-slit in 'double-slit interference experiment' emits two distinct monochromatic waves of wavelength 500 nm and 600 nm, each of them producing its own pattern on the screen. At the central point of the pattern when path difference is zero, maxima of both the patterns coincide and the resulting interference pattern is most distinct at the region of zero path difference. But as one moves out of this central region, the two fringe systems are gradually out of step such that maximum due to on wavelength coincides with the minimum due to the other and the combined fringe system becomes completely indistinct. This may happen when path difference in nm is : **[2013 (Online)]**

(A) 2000 (B) 3000

(C) 1000 (D) 1500

20. A ray of light of intensity I is incident on a parallel glass slab at point A as shown in diagram. It undergoes partial reflection and refraction. At each reflection, 25% of incident energy is reflected. The rays AB and $A'B'$ undergo interference. The ratio of I_{max} and I_{min} is : **[2013 (Online)]**

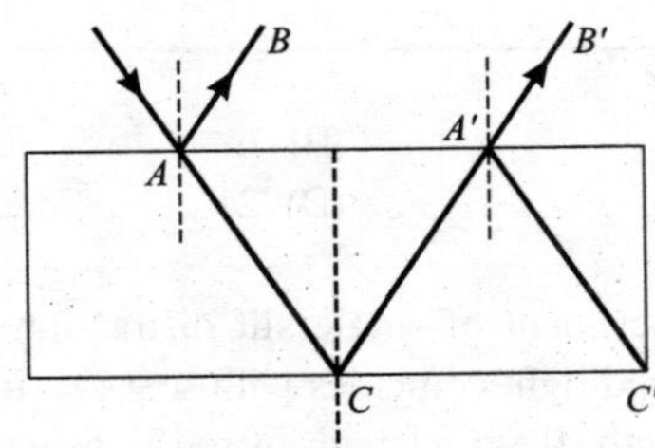

(A) 49 : 1 (B) 7 : 1

(C) 4 : 1 (D) 8 : 1

21. n identical waves each of intensity I_0 interfere with each other. The ratio of maximum intensities if the interference is (i) coherent and (ii) incoherent is : **[2013 (Online)]**

(A) n^2 (B) $\frac{1}{n}$

(C) $\frac{1}{n^2}$ (D) n

22. Two monochromatic light beams of intensity 16 and 9 units are interfering. The ratio of intensities of bright and dark parts of the resultant pattern is : **[2014 (Online)]**

(A) $\frac{16}{9}$ (B) $\frac{4}{3}$

(C) $\frac{7}{1}$ (D) $\frac{49}{1}$

23. On a hot summer night, the refractive index of air is smallest near the ground and increase with height from the ground. When a light beam is directed horizontally, the Huygen's principle leads us to conclude that as it travels, the light beam : **[2015]**

(A) becomes narrower

(B) goes horizontally without any deflection

(C) bends downwards

(D) bends upwards

24. In a Young's double slit experiment with light of wavelength λ the separation of slits is d and distance of screen is D such that $D >> d >> \lambda$. If the fringe width is β, the distance from point of maximum intensity to the point where intensity falls to half of maximum intensity on either side is : **[2015 (Online)]**

(A) $\frac{\beta}{6}$ (B) $\frac{\beta}{3}$

(C) $\frac{\beta}{4}$ (D) $\frac{\beta}{2}$

* * * * *

CHAPTER

24 WAVE OPTICS

24.2 DIFFRACTION OF LIGHT

1. If I_0 is the intensity of the principle maximum in the single slit diffraction pattern, then what will be its intensity when the slit width is doubled : **[2005]**

(A) $2I_0$ (B) $4I_0$
(C) I_0 (D) $I_0/2$

2. The first diffraction minimum due to the single slit diffraction is seen at $\theta = 30°$ for a light of wavelength 5000 Å falling perpendicularly on the slit. The width of the slit is : **[2012 (Online)]**

(A) 2.5×10^{-5} cm (B) 1.25×10^{-5} cm
(C) 10×10^{-5} cm (D) 5×10^{-5} cm

3. This question has Statement-1 and Statement-2. Of the four choices given after the Statements, choose the one that best describes the two Statements. **[2013 (Online)]**

Statement-1 : Out of radio waves and microwaves, the radio waves undergo more diffraction.

Statement-2 : Radio waves have greater frequency compared to microwaves.

(A) Statement-1 is true, Statement-2 is true and Statement-2 is the correct explanation of Statement-1
(B) Statement-1 is false, Statement-2 is true
(C) Statement-1 is true, Statement-2 is false
(D) Statement-1 is true, Statement-2 is true but Statement-2 is not the correct explanation of Statement-1

4. The diameter of the objective lens of microscope makes an angle β at the focus of the microscope. Further, the medium between the object and the lens is an oil of refractive index n. Then the resolving power of the microscope: **[2014 (Online)]**

(A) Increases with decreasing value of n
(B) Increases with decreasing value of β
(C) Increases with increasing value of $n \sin 2\beta$
(D) Increases with increasing value of $\frac{1}{n \sin 2\beta}$

5. In a Young's double slit experiment, the distance between the two identical slits is 6.1 times larger than the slit width. Then the number of intensity maxima observed within the central maximum of the single slit diffraction pattern is : **[2014 (Online)]**

(A) 3 (B) 6
(C) 12 (D) 24

6. In an experiment of single slit diffraction pattern, first minimum for red light coincides with first maximum of some other wavelength. If wavelength of red light is 6600 Å, then wavelength of first maximum will be : **[2014 (Online)]**

(A) 3300 Å (B) 4400 Å
(C) 5500 Å (D) 6600 Å

7. The box of a pin hole camera, of length L, has a hole of radius a. It is assumed that when the hole is illuminated by a parallel beam of light of wavelength λ the spread of the spot (obtained on the opposite wall of the camera) is the sum of its geometrical spread and the spread due to diffraction. The spot would then have its minimum size (say b_{min}) when : **[2016]**

(A) $a = \frac{\lambda^2}{L}$ and $b_{min} = \left(\frac{2\lambda^2}{L}\right)$

(B) $a = \sqrt{\lambda L}$ and $b_{min} = \left(\frac{2\lambda^2}{L}\right)$

(C) $a = \sqrt{\lambda L}$ and $b_{min} = \sqrt{4\lambda L}$

(D) $a = \frac{\lambda^2}{L}$ and $b_{min} = \sqrt{4\lambda L}$

8. In Young's double slit experiment, the distance between slits and the screen is 1.0 m and monochromatic light of 600 nm is being used. A person standing near the slits is looking at the fringe pattern. When the separation between the slits is varied, the interference pattern disappears for a particular distance d_0 between the slits. If the angular resolution of the eye is 1°/60, the value of d_0 is close to : **[2016 (Online)]**

(A) 1 mm (B) 3 mm
(C) 2 mm (D) 4 mm

9. Two stars are 10 light years away from the earth. They are seen through a telescope of objective diameter 30 cm. The wavelength of light is 600 nm. To see the stars just resolved by the telescope, the minimum distance between them should be (1 light year = 9.46×10^{15} m) of the order of: **[2016 (Online)]**

(A) 10^8 km (B) 10^{10} km
(C) 10^{11} km (D) 10^6 km

* * * * *

CHAPTER

24 WAVE OPTICS

24.3 POLARIZATION OF LIGHT

1. Electromagnetic waves are transverse in nature is evident by : **[2002]**

(A) polarization (B) interference

(C) reflection (D) diffraction

2. The angle of incidence at which reflected light is totally polarized for reflection from air to glass (refractive index n), is : **[2004]**

(A) $\tan^{-1}(1/n)$ (B) $\sin^{-1}(1/n)$

(C) $\sin^{-1}(n)$ (D) $\tan^{-1}(n)$

3. When an unpolarized light of intensity I_0 is incident on a polarizing sheet, the intensity of the light which does not get transmitted is : **[2005]**

(A) $1/2I_0$ (B) $1/4I_0$

(C) Zero (D) I_0

4. Statement-1 : On viewing the clear blue portion of the sky through a Calcite Crystal, the intensity of transmitted light varies as the crystal is rotated. **[2011]**

Statement-2 : The light coming from the sky is polarized due to scattering of sun light by particles in the atmosphere. The scattering is largest for blue light.

(A) Statement-1 is false, statement-2 is true

(B) Statement-1 is true, statement-2 is false

(C) Statement-1 is true, statement-2 true; statement-2 is the correct explanation of statement-1

(D) Statement-1 is true, statement-2 is true; statement -2 is not correct explanation of statement-1

5. Two polaroids have their polarizing directions parallel so that the intensity of a transmitted light is maximum. The angle through which either polaroid must be turned if the intensity is to drop by one-half is : **[2012 (Online)]**

(A) 135° (B) 90°

(C) 120° (D) 180°

6. A beam of unpolarised light of intensity I_0 is passed through a polaroid A and then through another polaroid B which is oriented so that its principal plane makes an angle of 45° relative to that of A. The intensity of the emergent light is : **[2013]**

(A) I_0 (B) $I_0/2$

(C) $I_0/4$ (D) $I_0/8$

7. A person lives in a high-rise building on the bank of a river 50 m wide. Across the river is a well lit tower of height 40 m. When the person, who is at a height of 10 m, looks through a polarizer at an appropriate angle at light of the tower reflecting from the river surface, he notes that intensity of light coming from distance X from his building is the least and this corresponds to the light coming from light bulbs at height 'Y' on the tower. The values of X and Y are respectively close to (refractive index of water = 4/3) : **[2013 (Online)]**

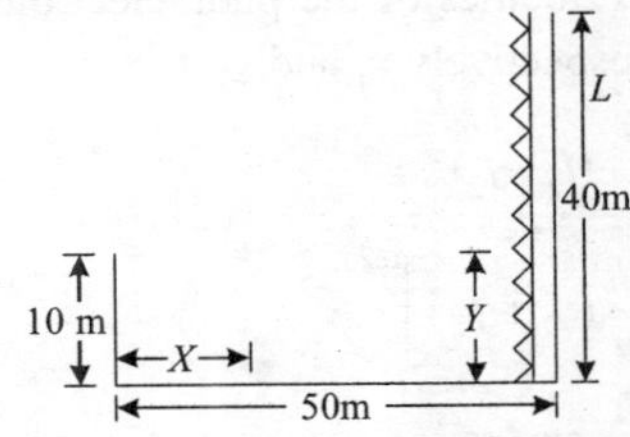

(A) 25 m, 10 m (B) 13 m, 27 m

(C) 22 m, 13 m (D) 17 m, 20 m

8. Two beams, A and B, of plane polarized light with mutually perpendicular planes of polarization are seen through a polaroid. From the position when the beam A has maximum intensity (and beam B has zero intensity), a rotation of polaroid through 30° makes the two beams appear equally bright. If the initial intensities of the two beams are I_A and I_B respectively, then I_A/I_B equals : **[2014]**

(A) 3 (B) 3/2

(C) 1 (D) 1/3

9. A ray of light is incident from a denser to a rarer medium. The critical angle for total internal reflection is θ_{iC} and Brewster's angle of incidence is θ_{iB}, such that $\sin\theta_{iC}/\sin\theta_{iB} = \eta = 1.28$. The relative refractive index of the two media is : **[2014 (Online)]**

(A) 0.2 (B) 0.4

(C) 0.8 (D) 0.9

10. Unpolarized light of intensity I_0 is incident on surface of a block of glass at Brewster's angle. In that case, which one of the following statements is true ? **[2015 (Online)]**

(A) Reflected light is completely polarized with intensity less than $I_0/2$

(B) Transmitted light is completely polarized with intensity less than $I_0/2$

(C) Transmitted light is partially polarized with intensity $I_0/2$

(D) Reflected light is partially polarized with intensity $I_0/2$

* * * * *

CHAPTER 25

DUAL NATURE OF RADIATION, MATTER & X-RAYS

25.1 PHOTOELECTRIC EFFECT

1. Sodium and copper have work functions 2.3 eV and 4.5 eV respectively. Then the ratio of their threshold wavelengths is nearest to : **[2002]**

(A) 1 : 2 (B) 4 : 1
(C) 2 : 1 (D) 1 : 4

2. Two identical, photocathodes receive light of frequencies f_1 and f_2. If the velocities of the photoelectrons (of mass m) coming out are respectively v_1 and v_2, then : **[2003]**

(A) $v_1^2 - v_2^2 = \frac{2h}{m}(f_1 - f_2)$

(B) $v_1 + v_2 = \left[\frac{2h}{m}(f_1 + f_2)\right]^{1/2}$

(C) $v_1^2 + v_2^2 = \frac{2h}{m}(f_1 + f_2)$

(D) $v_1 + v_2 = \frac{2h}{m}\left[\frac{2h}{m}(f_1 - f_2)\right]^{1/2}$

3. The work function of a substance is 4.0 eV. The longest wavelength of light that can cause photoelectron emission from this substance is approximately : **[2004]**

(A) 540 nm (B) 400 nm
(C) 310 nm (D) 220 nm

4. According to Einstein's photoelectric equation, the plot of the kinetic energy of the emitted photoelectrons from a metal *Vs* the frequency, of the incident radiation gives a straight line whose slope : **[2004]**

(A) depends on the nature of the metal used
(B) depends on the intensity of the radiation
(C) depends both on the intensity of the radiation and the metal used
(D) is the same for all metals and independent of the intensity of the radiation

5. A photocell is illuminated by a small bright source placed 1 m away. When the same source of light is place 0.5 m away, the number of electrons emitted by photocathode would : **[2005]**

(A) decrease by a factor of 4 (B) increase by a factor of 4
(C) decrease by a factor of 2 (D) increase by a factor of 2

6. The anode voltage of a photocell is kept fixed. The wavelength λ of the light falling on the cathode is gradually changed. The plate current I of the photocell varies as follows : **[2006]**

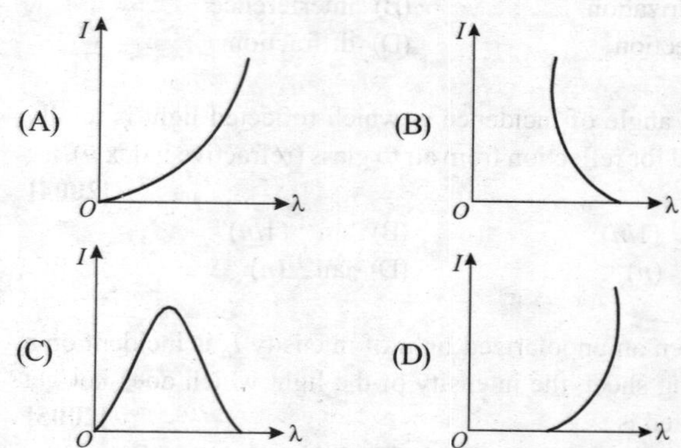

7. The threshold frequency for a metallic surface corresponds to an energy of 6.2 eV and the stopping potential for a radiation incident on this surface is 5 V. The incident radiation lies in : **[2006]**

(A) ultra-violet region (B) infra-red region
(C) visible region (D) *X*-ray region

8. The surface of a metal is illuminated with the light of 400 nm. The kinetic energy of the ejected photoelectrons was found to be 1.68 eV. The work function of the metal is : [hc = 1240 eV-nm] **[2009]**

(A) 1.51 eV (B) 1.68 eV
(C) 3.09 eV (D) 1.42 eV

9. Directions : Question contain Statement-1 and Statement-2. Of the four choices given after the statements, choose the one that best discribes the two statements. **[2010]**

Statement-1 : When ultraviolet light is incident on a photocell, its stopping potential is V_0 and the maximum kinetic energy of the photoelectrons is K_{max}. When the ultraviolet light is replaced by X-rays, both V_0 and K_{max} increase.

Statement-2 : Photoelectrons are emitted with speeds ranging from zero to a maximum value because of the range of frequencies present in the incident light.

(A) Statement-1 is true, Statement-2 is false
(B) Statement-1 is true, Statement-2 is true; Statement-2 is the correct explanation of Statement-1
(C) Statement-1 is true, Statement-2 is true; Statement-2 is not the correct explanation of Statement-1
(D) Statement-1 is false, Statement-2 is true

10. This question has Statement-1 and Statement-2. Of the four choices given after the statements, choose the one that best describes the two statements. **[2011]**

Statement-1 : A metallic surface is irradiated by a monochromatic light of frequency $\nu > \nu_0$ (the threshold frequency). The maximum kinetic energy and the stopping potential are K_{max} and V_0 respectively. If the frequency incident on the surface is doubled, both the K_{max} and V_0 are also doubled.

Statement-2 : The maximum kinetic energy and the stopping potential of photoelectrons emitted from a surface are linearly dependent on the frequency of incident light.

(A) Statement-1 is true, Statement-2 is true, Statement-2 is not the correct explanation of Statement-1

(B) Statement-1 is false, Statement-2 is true

(C) Statement-1 is true, Statement-2 is false

(C) Statement-1 is true, Statement-2 is true, Statement-2 is the correct explanation of Statement-1

11. This question has Statement-1 and Statement-2. Of the four choices given after the Statements, choose the one that best describes the two Statements. **[2012 (Online)]**

Statement-1 : A metallic surface is irradiated by a monochromatic light of frequency $\upsilon > \upsilon_0$ (the threshold frequency). If the incident frequency is now doubled, the photocurrent and the maximum kinetic energy are also doubled.

Statement-2 : The maximum kinetic energy of photoelectrons emitted from a surface is linearly dependent on the frequency of the incident light. The photocurrent depends only on the intensity of the incident light :

(A) Statement-1 is true, Statement-2 is true, Statement-2 is the correct explanation of Statement-1

(B) Statement-1 is false, Statement-2 is true

(C) Statement-1 is true, Statement-2 is false

(D) Statement-1 is true, Statement-2 is true, Statement-2 is not the correct explanation of Statement-1

12. Photoelectrons are ejected from a metal when light of frequency ν falls on it. Pick out the wrong statement from the following : **[2012 (Online)]**

(A) No electrons are emitted if ν is less than W/h, where W is the work function of the metal

(B) The ejection of the photoelectrons is instantaneous

(C) The maximum energy of the photoelectrons is $h\nu$

(D) The maximum energy of the photoelectrons is independent of the intensity of the light

13. The anode voltage of photocell is kept fixed. The wavelength λ of the light falling on the cathode is gradually changed. The plate current I of the photocell varies as follows: **[2013]**

(A)

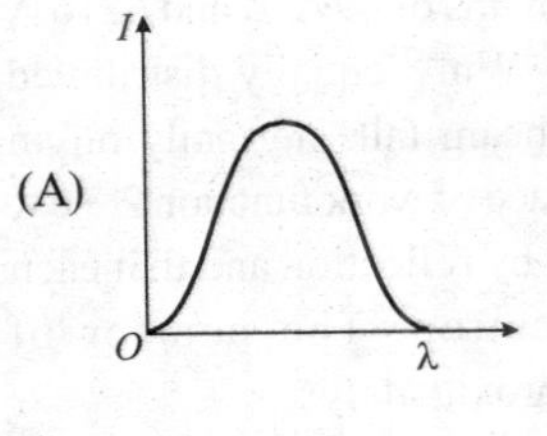

(B)

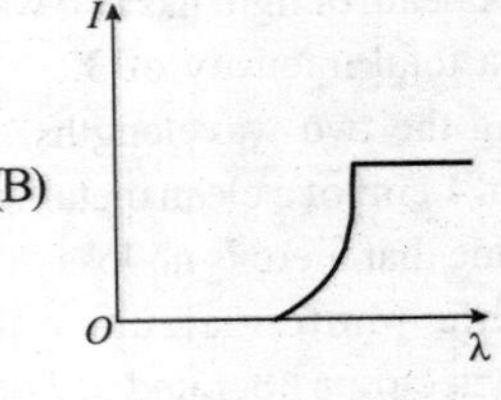

(C)

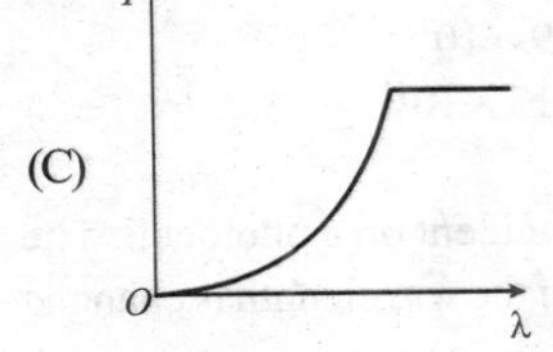

(D)

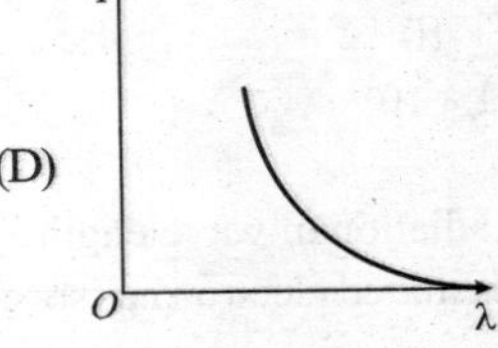

14. A copper ball of radius 1 cm and work function 4.47 eV is irradiated with ultraviolet radiation of wavelength 2500 Å. The effect of irradiation results in the emission of electrons from the ball. Further the ball will acquire charge and due to this there will be a finite value of the potential on the ball. The charge acquired by the ball is : **[2013 (Online)]**

(A) 5.5×10^{-13} C (B) 7.5×10^{-13} C

(C) 4.5×10^{-12} C (D) 2.5×10^{-11} C

15. In an experiment on photoelectric effect, a student plots stopping potential V_0 against reciprocal of the wavelength λ of the incident light for two different metals A and B. These are shown in the figure.

Looking at the graphs, you can most appropriately say that : **[2013 (Online)]**

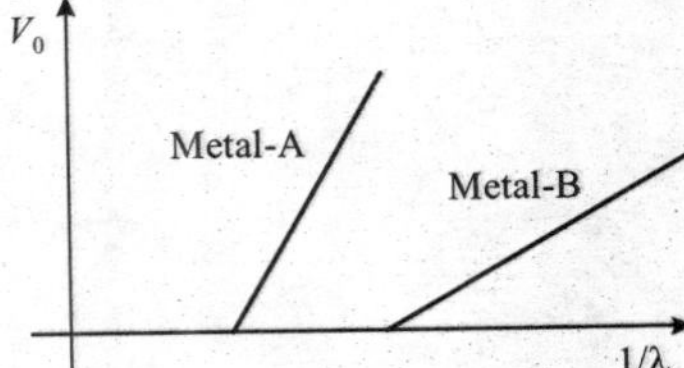

(A) Work function of metal B is greater than that of metal A

(B) For light of certain wavelength falling on both metal, maximum kinetic energy of electrons emitted from A will be greater than those emitted from B

(C) Work function of metal A is greater than that of metal B

(D) Students data is not correct

16. The radiation corresponding to $3 \rightarrow 2$ transition of hydrogen atom falls on a metal surface to produce photoelectrons. These electrons are made to enter a magnetic field of 3×10^{-4} T. If the radius of the largest circular path followed by these electrons is 10.0 mm, the work function of the metal is close to : **[2014]**

(A) 1.8 eV (B) 1.1 eV

(C) 0.8 eV (D) 1.6 eV

17. A beam of light has two wavelengths of 4972 Å and 6216 Å with a total intensity of 3.6×10^{-3} Wm^{-2} equally distributed among the two wavelengths. The beam falls normally on an area of 1 cm^2 of a clean metallic surface of work function 2.3 eV. Assume that there is no loss of light by reflection and that each capable photon ejects one electron. The number of photoelectrons liberated in 2s is approximately : **[2014 (Online)]**

(A) 6×10^{11} (B) 9×10^{11}
(C) 11×10^{11} (D) 15×10^{11}

18. Radiation of wavelength λ, is incident on a photocell. The fastest emitted electron has speed v. If the wavelength is changed to $\frac{3\lambda}{4}$, the speed of the fastest emitted electron will be : **[2016]**

(A) $> v\left(\frac{4}{3}\right)^{\frac{1}{2}}$ (B) $< v\left(\frac{4}{3}\right)^{\frac{1}{2}}$
(C) $= v\left(\frac{4}{3}\right)^{\frac{1}{2}}$ (D) $= v\left(\frac{3}{4}\right)^{\frac{1}{2}}$

19. When photons of wavelength λ_1 are incident on an isolated sphere, the corresponding stopping potential is found to be V. When photons of wavelength λ_2 are used, the corresponding stopping potential was thrice that of the above value. If light of wavelength λ_3 is used then find the stopping potential for this case : **[2016 (Online)]**

(A) $\frac{hc}{e}\left[\frac{1}{\lambda_3}+\frac{1}{\lambda_2}-\frac{1}{\lambda_1}\right]$ (B) $\frac{hc}{e}\left[\frac{1}{\lambda_3}+\frac{1}{2\lambda_2}-\frac{1}{\lambda_1}\right]$
(C) $\frac{hc}{e}\left[\frac{1}{\lambda_3}-\frac{1}{\lambda_2}-\frac{1}{\lambda_1}\right]$ (D) $\frac{hc}{e}\left[\frac{1}{\lambda_3}+\frac{1}{2\lambda_2}-\frac{3}{2\lambda_1}\right]$

20. A photoelectric surface is illuminated successively by monochromatic light of wavelengths λ and $\frac{\lambda}{2}$. If the maximum kinetic energy of the emitted photoelectrons in the second case is 3 times that in the first case, the work function of the surface is : **[2016 (Online)]**

(A) $\frac{hc}{2\lambda}$ (B) $\frac{hc}{\lambda}$
(C) $\frac{hc}{3\lambda}$ (D) $\frac{3hc}{\lambda}$

* * * * *

CHAPTER 25

DUAL NATURE OF RADIATION, MATTER & X-RAYS

25.2 MATTER WAVES & X-RAYS

1. Formation of covalent bonds in compounds exhibits : **[2002]**

(A) wave nature of electron
(B) particle nature of electron
(C) both wave and particle nature of electron
(D) none of the above

2. A radiation of energy E falls normally on a perfectly reflecting surface. The momentum transferred to the surface is: **[2004]**

(A) E/c (B) $2E/c$
(C) Ec (D) E/c^2

3. If the kinetic energy of a free electron doubles, its de-Broglie wavelength changes by the factor : **[2005]**

(A) $\frac{1}{2}$ (B) 2
(C) $\frac{1}{\sqrt{2}}$ (D) $\sqrt{2}$

4. Photon of frequency ν has a momentum associated with it. If c is the velocity of light, the momentum is : **[2007]**

(A) ν/c (B) $h\nu c$
(C) $h\nu/c^2$ (D) $h\nu/c$

5. **Directions For question 5 and 6 :** These questions are based on the following paragraph.

Wave property of electrons implies that they will show diffraction effects. Davisson and Germer demonstrated this by diffracting electrons from crystals. The law governing the diffraction from a crystal is obtained by requiring that electron waves reflected from the planes of atoms in a crystal interfere constructively (see figure).

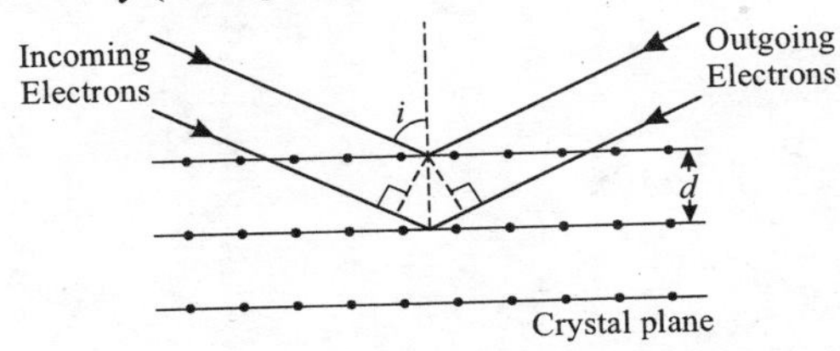

Electrons accelerated by potential V are diffracted from a crystal. If $d = 1$ Å and $i = 30°$ V should be about ($h = 6.6 \times 10^{-34}$ Js, $m_e = 9.1 \times 10^{-31}$ kg, $e = 1.6 \times 10^{-19}$ C) : **[2008]**

(A) 2000 V (B) 50 V
(C) 500 V (D) 1000 V

6. If a strong diffraction peak is observed when electrons are incident at an angle 'i' from the normal to the crystal planes with distance 'd' between them (see figure), de-Broglie wavelength λ_{dB} of electrons can be calculated by the relationship (n is an integer): **[2008]**

(A) $d \sin i = n\lambda_{dB}$ (B) $2d \cos i = n\lambda_{dB}$
(C) $2d \sin i = n\lambda_{dB}$ (D) $d \cos i = n\lambda_{dB}$

7. This question has Statement-1 and Statement-2. Of the four choices given after the statements, choose the one that best describes the two statements. **[2012]**

Statement-1 : Davisson-Germer experiment established the wave nature of electrons.

Statement-2 : If electrons have wave nature, they can interfere and show diffraction.

(A) Statement-1 is true, Statement-2 is true and Statement-2 is not the correct explanation of Statement-1
(B) Statement-1 is false, Statement-2 is true
(C) Statement-1 is true, Statement-2 is false
(D) Statement-1 is true, Statement-2 is true and Statement-2 is the correct explanation of statement-1

8. Electrons are accelerated through a potential difference V and protons are accelerated through a potential difference 4 V. The de-Broglie wavelengths are λ_e and λ_p for electrons and protons respectively. The ratio of $\frac{\lambda_e}{\lambda_p}$ is given by: (given m_e is mass of electron and m_p is mass of proton) : **[2013 (Online)]**

(A) $\frac{\lambda_e}{\lambda_p} = \sqrt{\frac{m_p}{m_e}}$ (B) $\frac{\lambda_e}{\lambda_p} = \sqrt{\frac{m_e}{m_p}}$
(C) $\frac{\lambda_e}{\lambda_p} = \frac{1}{2}\sqrt{\frac{m_e}{m_p}}$ (D) $\frac{\lambda_e}{\lambda_p} = 2\sqrt{\frac{m_p}{m_e}}$

9. Match List-I (Experiment performed) with List-II (Phenomena discovered/associated) and select the correct option from the options given below the lists : **[2014 (Online)]**

List-I	List-II
(1) Davisson and germer experiment	(i) Wave nature of electrons
(2) Millikan's oil drop experiment	(ii) Charge of an electron
(3) Rutherford experiment	(iii) Quantisation of energy levels
(4) Franck-Hertz experiment	(iv) Existence of nucleus

(A) (1)→(i); (2)→(ii); (3)→(iii); (4)→(iv)
(B) (1)→(i); (2)→(ii); (3)→(iv); (4)→(iii)
(C) (1)→(iii); (2)→(iv); (3)→(i); (4)→(ii)
(D) (1)→(iv); (2)→(iii); (3)→(ii); (4)→(i)

10. A photon of wavelength λ is scattered from an electron, which was at rest. The wavelength shift $\Delta\lambda$ is three times of λ and the angle of scattering θ is 60°. The angle at which the electron recoiled is ϕ. The value of tan ϕ is : (electron speed is much smaller than the speed of light) : **[2014 (Online)]**
(A) 0.16 (B) 0.22
(C) 0.25 (D) 0.28

11. For which of the following particles will it be most difficult to experimentally verify the de-Broglie relationship ? **[2014 (Online)]**
(A) An electron (B) A proton
(C) An α-particle (D) A dust particle

12. Match List-I (Fundamental Experiment) with List-II (its conclusion) and select the correct option from the choices given below the list : **[2015]**

List-I	List-II
(p) Franck-Hertz Experiment	(i) Particle nature of light
(q) Photo-electric experiment	(ii) Discrete energy levels of atom
(r) Davisson-Germer Experiment	(iii) Wave nature of electron
	(iv) Structure of atom

(A) (p)→(i); (q)→(iv); (r)→(iii)
(B) (p)→(ii); (q)→(iv); (r)→(iii)
(C) (p)→(ii); (q)→(i); (r)→(iii)
(D) (p)→(iv); (q)→(iii); (r)→(ii)

13. If one were to apply Bohr model to a particle of mass 'm' and charge 'q' moving in a plane under the influence of a magnetic field 'B', the energy of the charged particle in the nth level will be : **[2015 (Online)]**
(A) $n\left(\frac{hqB}{2\pi m}\right)$ (B) $n\left(\frac{hqB}{8\pi m}\right)$
(C) $n\left(\frac{hqB}{4\pi m}\right)$ (D) $n\left(\frac{hqB}{\pi m}\right)$

14. The de-Broglie wavelength associated with the electron in the $n = 4$ level is : **[2015 (Online)]**
(A) 1/4th of the de-Broglie wavelength of the electron in the ground state
(B) Four times the de-Broglie wavelength of the electron in the ground state
(C) Two times the de-Broglie wavelength of the electron in the ground state
(D) Half of the de-Broglie wavelength of the electron in the ground state

15. de-Broglie wavelength of an electron accelerated by a voltage of 50 V is close to ($|e| = 1.6 \times 10^{-19}$ C, $m_e = 9.1 \times 10^{31}$ kg, $h = 6.6 \times 10^{-34}$ Js) : **[2015 (Online)]**
(A) 2.4 Å (B) 0.5 Å
(C) 1.7 Å (D) 1.2 Å

16. A parallel beam of electrons travelling in x-direction falls on a slit of width d (see figure). If after passing the slit, an electron acquires momentum P_y in the y-direction then for a majority of electrons passing through the slit (h is Plank's constant) : **[2015 (Online)]**

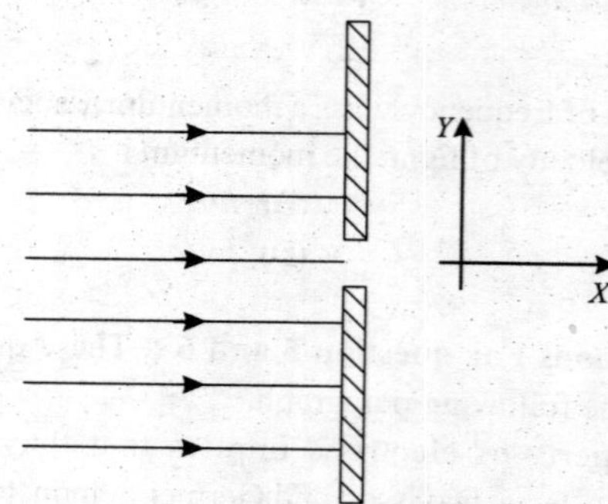

(A) $|P_y|d > h$ (B) $|P_y|d < h$
(C) $|P_y|d = h$ (D) $|P_y|d >> h$

* * * * *

CHAPTER

26 ATOMS

26.1 ATOMIC STRUCTURE

1. If the binding energy of the electron in a hydrogen atom is 13.6 eV, the energy required to remove the electron from the first excited state of Li^{2+} is : **[2002]**

(A) 30.6 eV (B) 13.6 eV
(C) 3.4 eV (D) 122.4 eV

2. The wavelengths involved in the spectrum of deuterium ($_1^2D$) are slightly different from that of hydrogen spectrum, because : **[2003]**

(A) sizes of the two nuclei are different
(B) nuclear forces are different in the two cases
(C) masses of the two nuclei are different
(D) attraction between the electron and the nucleus is different in the two cases

3. If 13.6 eV energy is required to ionize the hydrogen atom, then the energy required to remove an electron from $n = 2$ is : **[2003]**

(A) 10.2 eV (B) 0 eV
(C) 3.4 eV (D) 6.8 eV

4. The diagram shows the energy levels for an electron in a certain atom. Which transition shown represents the emission of a photon with the most energy? **[2005]**

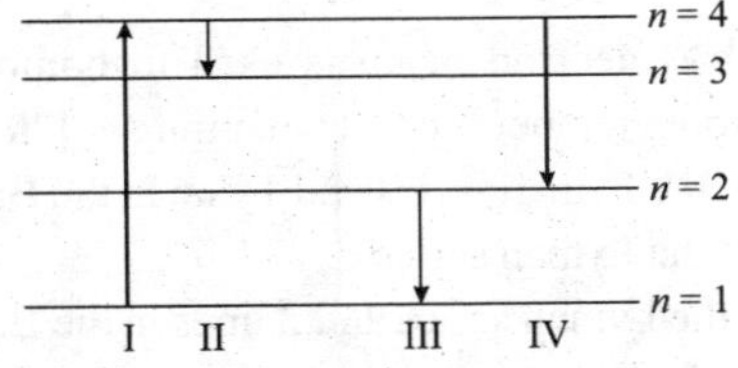

(A) III (B) IV
(C) I (D) II

5. Which of the following transitions in hydrogen atoms emit photons of highest frequency ? **[2007]**

(A) $n = 2$ to $n = 6$ (B) $n = 6$ to $n = 2$
(C) $n = 2$ to $n = 1$ (D) $n = 1$ to $n = 2$

6. Suppose an electron is attracted towards the origin by a force k/r where 'k' is a constant and 'r' is the distance of the electron from the origin. By applying Bohr model to this system, the radius of the nth orbital of the electron is found to be 'r_n' and the kinetic energy of the electron to be 'T_n'. Then which of the following is true? **[2008]**

(A) $T_n \propto \frac{1}{n^2}, r_n \propto n^2$
(B) T_n independent of n, $r_n \propto n$
(C) $T_n \propto \frac{1}{n}, r_n \propto n$
(D) $T_n \propto \frac{1}{n}, r_n \propto n^2$

7. The transition from the state $n = 4$ to $n = 3$ in a hydrogen like atom results in ultraviolet radiation. Infrared radiation will be obtained in the transition from : **[2009]**

(A) $4 \to 2$ (B) $5 \to 4$
(C) $2 \to 1$ (D) $3 \to 2$

8. Energy required for the electron excitation in Li^{++} from the first to the third Bohr orbit is : **[2011]**

(A) 108.8 eV (B) 122.4 eV
(C) 12.1 eV (D) 36.3 eV

9. A diatomic molecule is made of two masses m_1 and m_2 which are separated by a distance r. If we calculate its rotational energy by applying Bohr's rule of angular momentum quantization, its energy will be given by : (n is an integer) : **[2012]**

(A) $\frac{(m_1+m_2)n^2h^2}{2m_1m_2r^2}$ (B) $\frac{(m_1+m_2)^2n^2h^2}{2m_1^2m_2^2r^2}$

(C) $\frac{n^2h^2}{2(m_1+m_2)r^2}$ (D) $\frac{2n^2h^2}{(m_1+m_2)r^2}$

10. Hydrogen atom is excited from ground state to another state with principal quantum number equal to 4. Then the number of spectral lines in the emission spectra will be : **[2012]**

(A) 6 (B) 2
(C) 3 (D) 5

11. The electron of a hydrogen atom makes a transition from the $(n + 1)^{th}$ orbit to the nth orbit. For large n the wavelength of the emitted radiation is proportional to : **[2012 (Online)]**

(A) n (B) n^3
(C) n^4 (D) n^2

12. A hypothetical atom has only three energy levels. The ground level has energy, $E_1 = -8$ eV. The two excited states have energies, $E_2 = -6$ eV and $E_3 = -2$ eV. Then which of the following wavelengths will not be present in the emission spectrum of this atom? **[2012 (Online)]**

(A) 207 nm (B) 465 nm
(C) 310 nm (D) 620 nm

13. A doubly ionised Li atom is excited from its ground state ($n = 1$) to $n = 3$ state. The wavelengths of the spectral lines are given by λ_{32}, λ_{31} and λ_{21}. The ratio $\lambda_{32}/\lambda_{31}$ and $\lambda_{21}/\lambda_{31}$ are, respectively : **[2012 (Online)]**

(A) 8.1, 0.67 (B) 8.1, 1.2
(C) 6.4, 1.2 (D) 6.4, 0.67

14. Which of the plots shown in the figure represents speed (v_n) of the electron in a hydrogen atom as a function of the principal quantum number (n) ? **[2012 (Online)]**

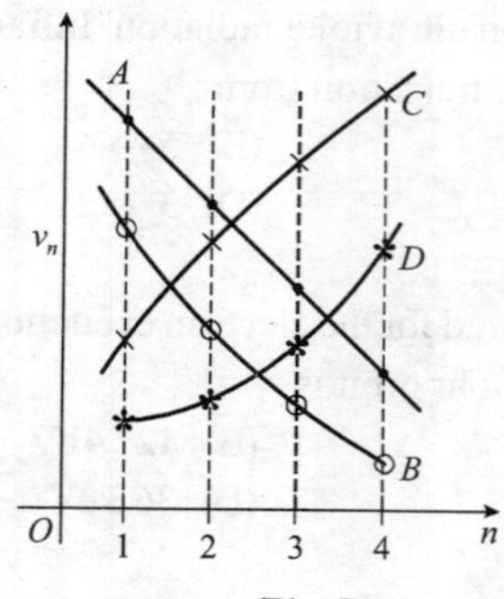

(A) B (B) D
(C) C (D) A

15. In the Rutherford experiment, α-particles are scattered from a nucleus as shown. Out of the four paths, which path is not possible ? **[2012 (Online)]**

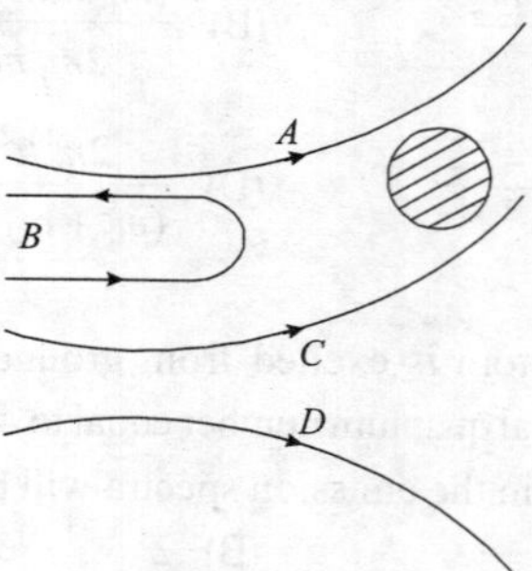

(A) D (B) B
(C) C (D) A

16. Ionisation energy of Li (Lithium) atom in ground state is 5.4 eV. Binding energy of an electron in Li^+ ion in ground state is 75.6 eV. Energy required to remove all three electrons of Lithium (Li) atom is : **[2012 (Online)]**

(A) 81.0 eV (B) 135.4 eV
(C) 203.4 eV (D) 156.6 eV

17. In a hydrogen like atom electron makes transition from an energy level with quantum number n to another with quantum number $(n - 1)$. If $n >> 1$, the frequency of radiation emitted is proportional to : **[2013]**

(A) $\frac{1}{n}$ (B) $\frac{1}{n^2}$
(C) $\frac{1}{n^{3/2}}$ (D) $\frac{1}{n^3}$

18. In the Bohr model an electron moves in a circular orbit around the proton. Considering the orbiting electron to be a circular current loop, the magnetic moment of the hydrogen atom, when the electron is in n^{th} excited state, is : **[2013 (Online)]**

(A) $\left(\frac{e}{2m}\frac{n^2 h}{2\pi}\right)$ (B) $\left(\frac{e}{m}\right)\frac{nh}{2\pi}$
(C) $\left(\frac{e}{2m}\right)\frac{nh}{2\pi}$ (D) $\left(\frac{e}{m}\right)\frac{n^2 h}{2\pi}$

19. Orbits of a particle moving in a circle are such that the perimeter of the orbit equals an integer number of de-Broglie wavelengths of the particle. For a charged particle moving in a plane perpendicular to a magnetic field, the radius of the nth orbital will therefore be proportional to : **[2013 (Online)]**

(A) n^2 (B) n
(C) $n^{1/2}$ (D) $n^{1/4}$

20. A 12.5 eV electron beam is used to bombard gaseous hydrogen at room temperature. It will emit : **[2013 (Online)]**

(A) 2 lines in the Lyman series and 1 line in the Balmer series
(B) 3 lines in the Lyman series
(C) 1 line in the Lyman series and 2 lines in the Balmer series
(D) 3 lines in the Balmer series

21. In the Bohr's model of hydrogen-like atom the force between the nucleus and the electron is modified as $F = \frac{e^2}{4\pi\varepsilon_0}\left(\frac{1}{r^2} + \frac{\beta}{r^3}\right)$, where β is a constant. For this atom, the radius of the nth orbit in terms of the Bohr radius $\left(a_0 = \frac{\varepsilon_0 h^2}{m\pi e^2}\right)$ is : **[2013 (Online)]**

(A) $r_n = a_0 n - \beta$ (B) $r_n = a_0 n^2 + \beta$
(C) $r_n = a_0 n^2 - \beta$ (D) $r_n = a_0 n + \beta$

22. Hydrogen ($_1H^1$), Deuterium ($_1H^2$), singly ionised Helium $(_2He^4)^+$ and dubly ionised lithium $(_3Li^6)^{++}$ all have one electron around the nucleus. Consider an electron transition from $n = 2$ to $n = 1$. If the wave lengths of emitted radiation are λ_1, λ_2, λ_3 and λ_4 respectively then approximately which one of the following is correct? **[2014]**

(A) $4\lambda_1 = 2\lambda_2 = 2\lambda_3 = \lambda_4$
(B) $\lambda_1 = 2\lambda_2 = 2\lambda_3 = \lambda_4$
(C) $\lambda_1 = \lambda_2 = 4\lambda_3 = 9\lambda_4$
(D) $\lambda_1 = 2\lambda_2 = 3\lambda_3 = 4\lambda_4$

23. The binding energy of the electron in a hydrogen atom is 13.6 eV, the energy required to remove the electron from the first excited state of Li^{++} is : **[2014 (Online)]**

(A) 122.4 eV
(B) 30.6 eV
(C) 13.6 eV
(D) 3.4 eV

24. As an electron makes a transition from an excited state to the ground state of a hydrogen-like atom/ion : **[2015]**

(A) its kinetic energy increases but potential energy and total energy decrease
(B) kinetic energy, potential energy and total energy decrease
(C) kinetic energy decreases, potential energy increases but total energy remains same
(D) kinetic energy and total energy decrease but potential energy increases

25. A neutron moving with a speed 'v' makes a head on collision with a stationary hydrogen atom in ground state. The minimum kinetic energy of the neutron for which inelastic collision will take place is : **[2016 (Online)]**

(A) 20.4 eV
(B) 10.2 eV
(C) 12.1 eV
(D) 16.8 eV

26. A hydrogen atom makes a transition from $n = 2$ to $n = 1$ and emits a photon. This photon strikes a doubly ionized lithium atom ($Z = 3$) in excited state and completely removes the orbiting electron. The least quantum number for the excited state of the ion for the process is : **[2016 (Online)]**

(A) 2
(B) 4
(C) 5
(D) 3

* * * * *

CHAPTER

27 NUCLEI

27.1 RADIOACTIVITY

1. At a specific instant emission of radioactive compound is deflected in a magnetic field. The compound can emit : **[2002]**

(i) electrons (ii) protons

(iii) He^{2+} (iv) neutrons

The emission at the instant can be :

(A) i, ii, iii (B) i, ii, iii, iv

(C) iv (D) ii, iii

2. If N_0 is the original mass of the substance of half-life period $t_{1/2}$ = 5 years, then the amount of substance left after 15 years is : **[2002]**

(A) $\frac{N_0}{8}$ (B) $\frac{N_0}{16}$

(C) $\frac{N_0}{2}$ (D) $\frac{N_0}{4}$

3. A radioactive sample at any instant has its disintegration rate 5000 disintegration per minute. After 5 minutes, the rate is 1250 disintegrations per minute. Then, the decay constant (per minute) is : **[2003]**

(A) 0.4 ln 2 (B) 0.2 ln 2

(C) 0.1 ln 2 (D) 0.8 ln 2

4. Which of the following radiations has the least wavelength ? **[2003]**

(A) γ-rays (B) β-rays

(C) α-rays (D) X-rays

5. A nucleus disintegrates into two nuclear parts which have their velocities in the ratio 2 : 1. The ratio of their nuclear sizes will be : **[2004]**

(A) $2^{1/3} : 1$ (B) $1 : 3^{1/2}$

(C) $3^{1/2} : 1$ (D) $1 : 2^{1/3}$

6. If radius of the ${}^{27}_{13}Al$ nucleus is estimated to be 3.6 fermi, then the radius of ${}^{125}_{52}Te$ nucleus be nearly : **[2005]**

(A) 6 fermi (B) 8 fermi

(C) 4 fermi (D) 5 fermi

7. Starting with a sample of pure ^{66}Cu, 7/8 of it decays into Zn in 15 min. The corresponding half-life is : **[2005]**

(A) 10 min (B) 15 min

(C) 5 min (D) $7\frac{1}{2}$ min

8. The half-life period of a radioactive element *X* is same as the mean life time of another radioactive element *Y*. Initially they have the same number of atoms. Then : **[2007]**

(A) *X* will decay faster than *Y*

(B) *Y* will decay faster than *X*

(C) *Y* and *X* have same decay rate initially

(D) *X* and *Y* decay at same rate always

9. The half life of a radioactive substance is 20 minutes. The approximate time interval $(t_2 - t_1)$ between the time t_2 when 2/3 of it has decayed and time t_1 when 1/3 of it had decayed is : **[2011]**

(A) 20 min (B) 28 min

(C) 7 min (D) 14 min

10. Half-lives of two radioactive elements *A* and *B* are 20 minutes and 40 minutes, respectively. Initially, the samples have equal number of nuclei. After 80 minutes, the ratio of decayed numbers of *A* and *B* nuclei will be : **[2012]**

(A) 1 : 16 (B) 4 : 1

(C) 1 : 4 (D) 5 : 4

11. The counting rate observed from a radioactive source at $t = 0$ was 1600 counts s^{-1}, and $t = 8$ s, it was 100 counts s^{-1}. The counting rate observed as counts s^{-1} at $t = 6$ s will be : **[2012 (Online)]**

(A) 250 (B) 400

(C) 300 (D) 200

12. A sample originally contained 10^{20} radioactive atoms, which emit α-particles. The ratio of α-particles emitted in the third year to that emitted during the second year is 0.3. How many α-particles were emitted in the first year ? **[2012 (Online)]**

(A) 3×10^{18} (B) 3×10^{19}

(C) 5×10^{18} (D) 7×10^{19}

13. Which of the following Statements is correct ? **[2012 (Online)]**

(A) The rate of radioactive decay cannot be controlled but that of nuclear fission can be controlled

(B) Nuclear forces are short range, attractive and charge dependent

(C) Nuclei of atoms having same number of neutrons are known as isobars

(D) Wavelength of matter waves is given by de-Broglie formula but that of photons is not given by the same formula

14. The decay constants of a radioactive substance for α and β emission are λ_α and λ_β respectively. If the substance emits α and β simultaneously, then the average half life of the material will be : **[2012 (Online)]**

(A) $\frac{2T_\alpha T_\beta}{T_\alpha + T_\beta}$ (B) $T_\alpha + T_\beta$

(C) $\frac{T_\alpha T_\beta}{T_\alpha + T_\beta}$ (D) $\frac{1}{2}(T_\alpha + T_\beta)$

15. The half-life of a radioactive element *A* is the same as the mean-life of another radioactive element *B*. Initially both substances have the same number of atoms, then : **[2013 (Online)]**

(A) *A* and *B* decay at the same rate always
(B) *A* and *B* decay at the same rate initially
(C) A will decay at a faster rate than *B*
(D) *B* will decay at a faster rate than *A*

16. A radioactive nuclei with decay constant 0.5/s is being produced at a constant rate of 100 nuclei/s. If at $t = 0$ there were no nuclei, the time when there are 50 nuclei is : **[2014 (Online)]**

(A) 1 s (B) $2\ln\left(\frac{4}{3}\right)$ s

(C) ln 2 s (D) $\ln\left(\frac{4}{3}\right)$ s

17. A piece of bone of an animal from a ruin is found to have ^{14}C activity of 12 disintegrations per minute per *gm* of its carbon content. The ^{14}C activity of a living animal is 16 disintegrations per minute per *gm*. How long ago nearly did the animal die? (Given half life of ^{14}C is $t_{1/2} = 5760$ years) : **[2014 (Online)]**

(A) 1672 years (B) 2391 years
(C) 3291 years (D) 4453 years

18. A piece of wood from a recently cut tree shows 20 decays per minute. A wooden piece of same size placed in a museum (obtained from a tree cut many years back) shows 2 decays per minute. If half life of C^{14} is 5730 years, then age of the wooden piece placed in the museum is approximately : **[2014 (Online)]**

(A) 10439 years (B) 13094 years
(C) 19039 years (D) 39049 years

19. Let N_β be the number of β particles emitted by 1 gram of Na^{24} radioactive nuclei (half life = 15 hrs) in 7.5 hours, N_β is close to (Avogadro number = 6.023×10^{23}/g. mole) : **[2015 (Online)]**

(A) 6.2×10^{21} (B) 7.5×10^{21}
(C) 1.25×10^{22} (D) 1.75×10^{22}

* * * * *

CHAPTER

27 NUCLEI

27.2 NUCLEAR PHYSICS

1. In the nuclear fusion reaction, ${}_1^2H + {}_1^3H \rightarrow {}_2^4He + n$ given that the repulsive potential energy between the two nuclei is 7.7×10^{-14} J, the temperature at which the gases must be heated to initiate the reaction is nearly [Boltzmann's constant $k = 1.38 \times 10^{-23}$ J/K] : **[2003]**
(A) 10^7 K (B) 10^5 K
(C) 10^3 K (D) 10^9 K

2. Which of the following cannot be emitted by radioactive substances during their decay ? **[2003]**
(A) Protons (B) Neutrinos
(C) Helium nuclei (D) Electrons

3. A nucleus with $Z = 92$ emits the following in a sequence : α, α, β^-, β^-, α, α, α, α, β^-, β^-, α, β^+, β^+, α. The Z of the resulting nucleus is : **[2003]**
(A) 76 (B) 78
(C) 82 (D) 74

4. When U^{238} nucleus originally at rest, decays by emitting an alpha particle having a speed u, the recoil speed of the residual nucleus is : **[2003]**
(A) $\frac{4u}{238}$ (B) $-\frac{4u}{234}$
(C) $\frac{4u}{234}$ (D) $-\frac{4u}{238}$

5. An α-particle of energy 5 MeV is scattered through 180° by a fixed uranium nucleus. The distance of the closest approach is of the order of : **[2004]**
(A) 1 Å (B) 10^{-10} cm
(C) 10^{-12} cm (D) 10^{-15} cm

6. The binding energy per nucleon of deuteron $\left({}_1^2H\right)$ and helium nucleus $\left({}_2^4He\right)$ is 1.1 MeV and 7 MeV respectively. If two deuteron nuclei react to form a single helium nucleus, then the energy released is : **[2004]**
(A) 13.9 MeV (B) 26.9 MeV
(C) 23.6 MeV (D) 19.2 MeV

7. A nuclear transformation is denoted by $X(n, \alpha) \rightarrow {}_3^7Li$. Which of the following is the nucleus of element X? **[2005]**
(A) ${}_6^{12}C$ (B) ${}_5^{10}B$
(C) ${}_5^9B$ (D) ${}_4^{11}Be$

8. The intensity of gamma radiation from a given source is I. On passing through 36 mm of lead, it is reduced to $I/8$. The thickness of lead, which will reduce the intensity to $I/2$ will be : **[2005]**
(A) 6 mm (B) 9 mm
(C) 18 mm (D) 12 mm

9. The energy spectrum of β-particles [number $N(E)$ as a function of β-energy E] emitted from a radioactive source is: **[2006]**

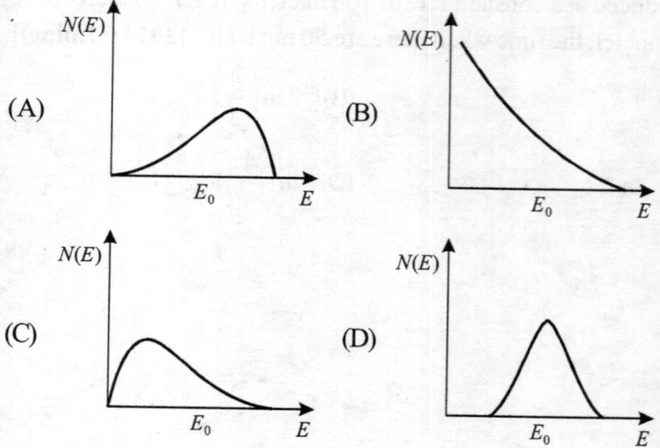

10. When $_3Li^7$ nuclei are bombarded by protons and the resultant nuclei are $_4Be^8$, the emitted particles will be : **[2006]**
(A) alpha particles (B) beta particles
(C) gamma photons (D) neutrons

11. An alpha nucleus of energy $1/2\ mv^2$ bombards a heavy nuclear target of charge Ze. Then the distance of closest approach for the alpha nucleus will be proportional to : **[2006]**
(A) v^2 (B) $1/m$
(C) $1/v^4$ (D) $1/Ze$

12. If the binding energy per nucleon in ${}_3^7Li$ and ${}_2^4He$ nuclei are 5.60 MeV and 7.06 MeV respectively, then in the reaction: $p + {}_3^7Li \rightarrow 2\,{}_2^4He$ energy of proton must be : **[2006]**
(A) 28.24 MeV (B) 17.28 MeV
(C) 1.46 MeV (D) 39.2 MeV

13. In gamma ray emission from a nucleus : **[2007]**
(A) both the neutron number and the proton number change
(B) there is no change in the proton number and the neutron number
(C) only the neutron number changes
(D) only the proton number changes

14. If M_0 is the mass of an oxygen isotope $_8O^{17}$, M_p and M_n are the masses of a proton and a neutron, respectively, the nuclear binding energy of the isotope is : **[2007]**
(A) $(M_o - 8M_p)c^2$ (B) $(M_o - 8M_p - 9M_n)c^2$
(C) $M_o c^2$ (D) $(M_o - 17M_n)c^2$

15. Which of the following are the constituents of the nucleus? **[2007]**
(A) Electrons and protons (B) Neutrons and protons
(C) Electrons and neutrons (D) Neutrons and positrons

16. This question contains Statement-1 and Statement-2. Out of the four choices given after the statements, choose the one that best describes the two statements. **[2008]**
Statement-1 : Energy is released when heavy nuclei undergo fission or light nuclei undergo fusion.
Statement-2 : For heavy nuclei, binding energy per nucleon increases with increasing Z while for light nuclei it decreases with increasing Z.
(A) Statement-1 is false, Statement-2 is true
(B) Statement-1 is true, Statement-2 is true; Statement-2 is a correct explanation for Statement-1
(C) Statement-1 is true, Statement-2 is true; Statement-2 is not a correct explanation for Statement-1
(D) Statement-1 is true, Statement-2 is false

17. The above is a plot of binding energy per nucleon E_b, against the nuclear mass M; A, B, C, D, E, F correspond to different nuclei. Consider four reactions : **[2009]**

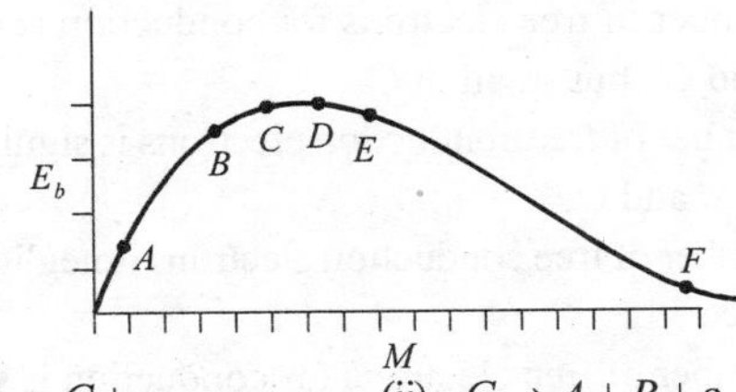

(i) $A + B \rightarrow C + \varepsilon$ (ii) $C \rightarrow A + B + \varepsilon$
(iii) $D + E \rightarrow F + \varepsilon$ (iv) $F \rightarrow D + E + \varepsilon$
where ε is the energy released ? In which reactions is ε positive ?
(A) (ii) and (iv) (B) (ii) and (iii)
(C) (i) and (iv) (D) (i) and (iii)

18. A radioactive nucleus (initial mass number A and atomic number Z) emits 3 α-particles and 2 positrons. The ratio of number of neutrons to that of protons in the final nucleus will be : **[2010]**
(A) $\dfrac{A-Z-4}{Z-2}$ (B) $\dfrac{A-Z-8}{Z-4}$
(C) $\dfrac{A-Z-4}{Z-8}$ (D) $\dfrac{A-Z-12}{Z-4}$

19. A nucleus of mass $M + \Delta m$ is at rest and decays into two daughter nuclei of equal mass $M/2$ each. Speed of light is c. The binding energy per nucleon for the parent nucleus is E_1 an that for the daughter nuclei is E_2. Then : **[2010]**
(A) $E_1 = 2E_2$ (B) $E_2 = 2E_1$
(C) $E_1 > E_2$ (D) $E_2 > E_1$

20. A nucleus of mass $M + \Delta m$ is at rest and decays into two daughter nuclei of equal mass $M/2$ each. Speed of light is c. The speed of daughter nuclei is : **[2010]**
(A) $c\sqrt{\dfrac{\Delta m}{M+\Delta m}}$ (B) $c\dfrac{\Delta m}{M+\Delta m}$
(C) $c\sqrt{\dfrac{2\Delta m}{M}}$ (D) $c\sqrt{\dfrac{\Delta m}{M}}$

21. Statement-1 : A nucleus having energy E_1 decays β^- emission to daughter nucleus having energy E_2, but the β^- rays are emitted with a continuous energy spectrum having end point energy $E_1 - E_2$. **[2011]**
Statement-2 : To conserve energy and momentum in β-decay at least three particles must take part in the transformation.
(A) Statement-1 is incorrect, statement-2 is correct
(B) Statement-1 is correct, statement-2 is incorrect
(C) Statement-1 is correct, statement-2 correct; statement-2 is the correct explanation of statement-1
(D) Statement-1 is correct, statement-2 is correct; statement-2 is not the correct explanation of statement-1

22. After absorbing a slowly moving neutron of mass m_N (momentum ~ 0) a nucleus of mass M breaks into two nuclei of masses m_1 and 5 m_1 (6 $m_1 = M + m_N$), respectively. If the de Broglie wavelength of the nucleus with mass m_1 is λ, then de Broglie wavelength of the other nucleus will be : **[2011]**
(A) 25λ (B) 5λ
(C) $\dfrac{\lambda}{5}$ (D) λ

23. When Uranium is bombarded with neutrons, it undergoes fission. The fission reaction can be written as :

$$_{92}U^{235} + {_0n^1} \rightarrow {_{56}Ba^{141}} + {_{36}Kr^{92}} + 3x + Q \text{ (energy)}$$

where three particles named x are produced and energy Q is released. What is the name of the particle x ? **[2013 (Online)]**
(A) Electron (B) α-particle
(C) Neutron (D) Neutrino

* * * * *

CHAPTER

28 SEMICONDUCTORS ELECTRONICS

28.1 SEMICONDUCTOR

1. The energy band gap is maximum in : **[2002]**
(A) Metals (B) Superconductors
(C) Insulators (D) Semiconductors

2. By increasing the temperature, the specific resistance of a conductor and a semiconductor : **[2002]**
(A) Increases for both (B) Decreases for both
(C) Increases, decreases (D) Decreases, increases

3. At absolute zero, *Si* acts as : **[2002]**
(A) Non-metal (B) Metal
(C) Insulator (D) None of these

4. A strip of copper and another of germanium are cooled from room temperature to 80 K. The resistance of: **[2003]**
(A) Each of these decreases
(B) Copper strip increases and that of germanium decreases
(C) Copper strip decreases and that of germanium increases
(D) Each of these increases

5. The difference in the variation of resistance with temperature in a metal and a semiconductor arises essentially due to the difference in the : **[2003]**
(A) Crystal structure
(B) Variation of the number of charge carriers with temperature
(C) Type of bonding
(D) Variation of scattering mechanism with temperature

6. When *p-n* junction diode is forward biased then : **[2004]**
(A) Both the depletion region and barrier height are reduced
(B) The depletion region is widened and barrier height is reduced
(C) The depletion region is reduced and barrier height is increased
(D) Both the depletion region and barrier height are increased

7. The electrical conductivity of a semiconductor increases when electromagnetic radiation of wavelength shorter than 2480 nm is incident on it. The band gap in (*eV*) for the semiconductor is : **[2005]**
(A) 2.5 eV (B) 1.1 eV
(C) 0.7 eV (D) 0.5 eV

8. If the ratio of the concentration of electrons to that of holes in a semiconductor is 7/5, and the ratio of currents is 7/4, then what is the ratio of their drift velocities ? **[2006]**
(A) $\frac{5}{8}$ (B) $\frac{4}{5}$
(C) $\frac{5}{4}$ (D) $\frac{4}{7}$

9. A solid which is not transparent to visible light and whose conductivity increases with temperature is formed by : **[2006]**
(A) Ionic bonding (B) Covalent bonding
(C) Vander Waals bonding (D) Metallic bonding

10. If the lattice constant of this semiconductor is decreased, then which of the following is correct ? **[2006]**

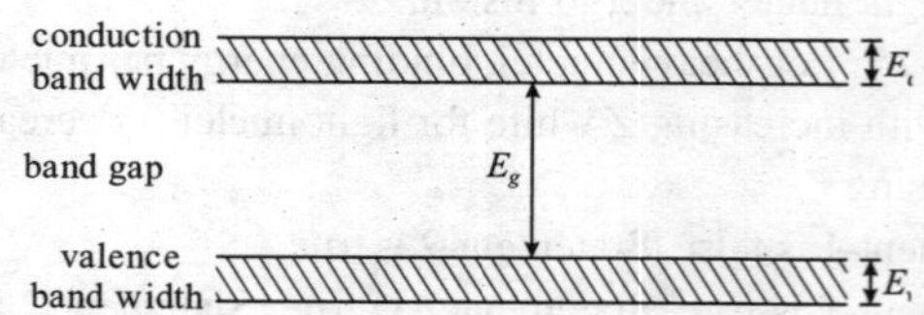

(A) All E_C, E_g, E_v increase
(B) E_c and E_v increase, but E_g decrease
(C) E_c and E_v decrease, but E_g increases
(D) All E_c, E_g, E_v decrease

11. Carbon, silicon and germanium have four valence electrons each. At room temperature which one of the following statements is most appropriate ? **[2007]**
(A) The number of free electrons for conduction is significant only in *Si* and *Ge* but small in *C*
(B) The number of free conduction electrons is significant in *C* but small in *Si* and *Ge*
(C) The number of free conduction electrons is negligibly small in all the three
(D) The number of free electrons for conduction is significant in all the three

12. This question has Statement-1 and Statement-2. Of the four choices given after the Statements, choose the one that best describes the two Statements. **[2012 (Online)]**
Statement-1 : A pure semiconductor has negative temperature coefficient of resistance.
Statement-2 : On raising the temperature, more charge carriers

are released into the conduction band

(A) Statement-1 is false, Statement-2 is true

(B) Statement-1 is true, Statement-2 is false

(C) Statement-1 is true, Statement-2 is true, Statement-2 is not a correct explanation of Statement-1

(D) Statement-1 is true, Statement-2 is true, Statement-2 is the correct explanation of Statement-1

13. The temperature dependence of resistances of Cu and undoped Si in the temperature range 300 – 400K, is best described by : **[2016]**

(A) Linear increase for Cu, exponential decrease of Si

(B) Linear decrease for Cu, linear decrease for Si

(C) Linear increase for Cu, linear increase for Si

(D) Linear increase for Cu, exponential increase for Si

* * * * *

CHAPTER

28 SEMICONDUCTORS ELECTRONICS

28.2 PN JUNCTION AND DIODES

1. In the middle of the depletion layer of a reverse-biased *p-n* junction, the : **[2003]**

(A) Electric field is zero (B) Potential is maximum

(C) Electric field is maximum (D) Potential is zero

2. A strip of copper and another of germanium are cooled from room temperature to 80 K. The resistance of : **[2004]**

(A) Each of these decreases

(B) Copper strip increases and that of germanium decreases

(C) Copper strip decreases and that of germanium increases

(D) Each of these increases

3. The circuit has two oppositely connected ideal diodes in parallel. What is the current flowing in the circuit ? **[2006]**

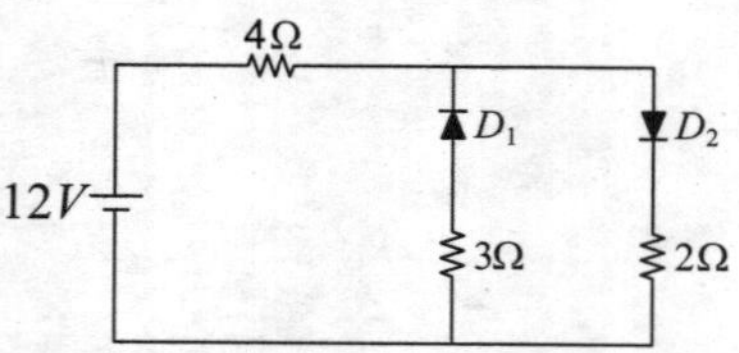

(A) 1.71 A (B) 2.00 A

(C) 2.31 A (D) 1.33 A

4. In the following, which one of the diodes reverse biased ? **[2006]**

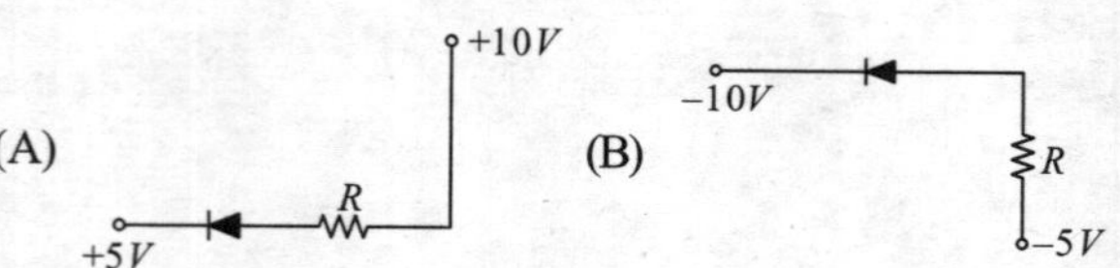

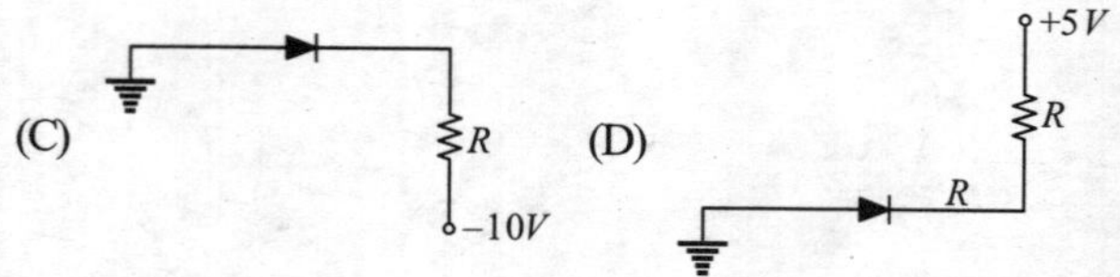

5. If in a *p-n* junction diode, a square input signal of 10 V is applied as shown **[2007]**

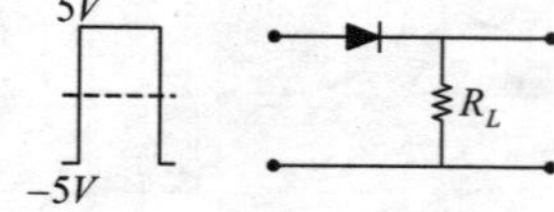

Then the output signal across R_L will be :

(A)
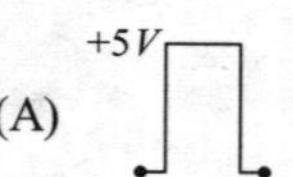

(B)
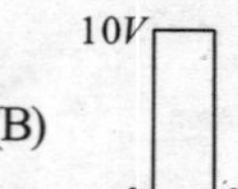

(C)
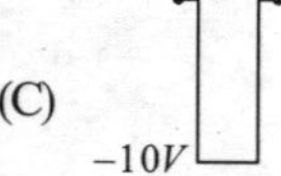

(D) −5V

6. A p-n junction (D) shown in the figure can act as a rectifier. An alternating current source (V) is connected in the circuit. **[2009]**

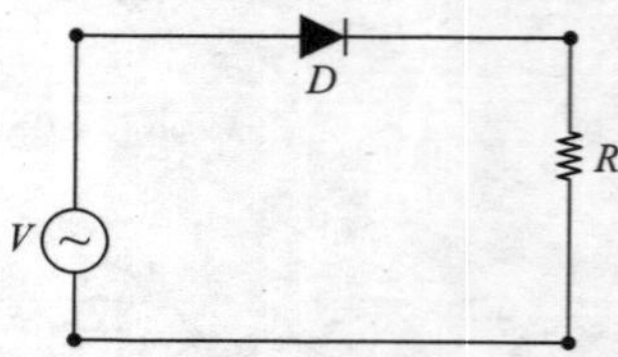

The current (*I*) in the resistor (*R*) can be shown by

(A)
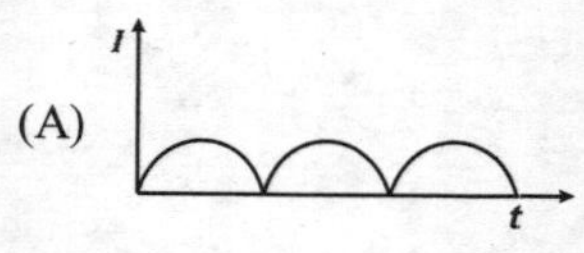

(B)
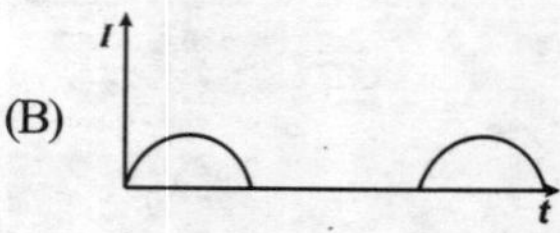

(C)
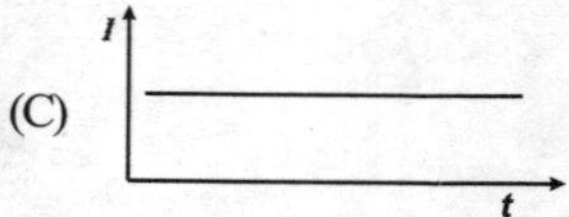

(D)
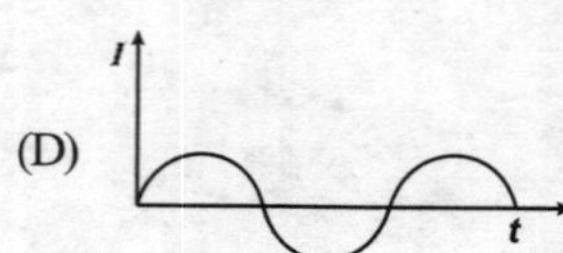

7. The I-V characteristic of an LED is : **[2013]**

(A)
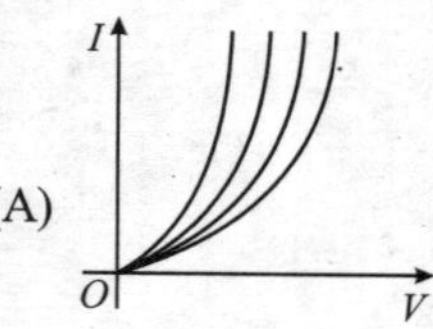

(B)
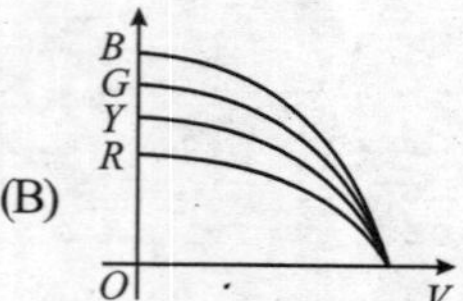

(C)
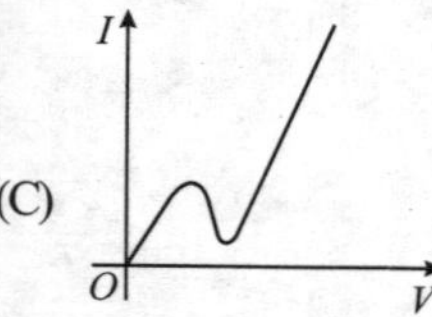

(D)
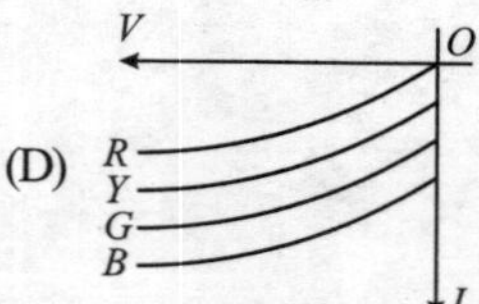

8. Figure shows a circuit in which three identical diodes are used. Each diode has forward resistance of 20 Ω and infinite backward resistance. Resistors $R_1 = R_2 = R_3 = 50\ \Omega$. Battery voltage is 6 V. The current through R_3 is : **[2013 (Online)]**

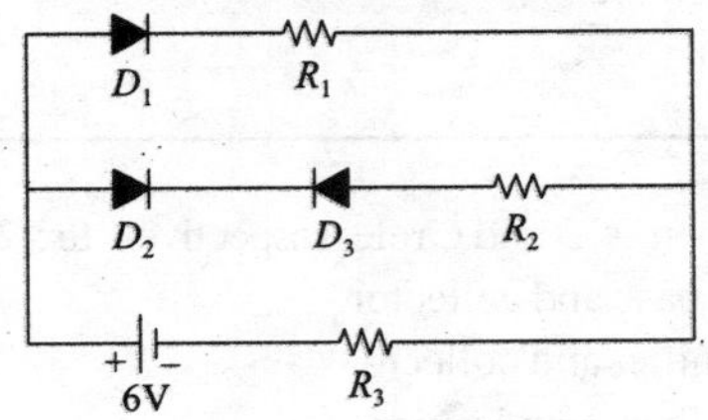

(A) 50 mA (B) 100 mA
(C) 60 mA (D) 25 mA

9. The forward biased diode connection is : **[2014]**

(A) +2V —▷|—— −2V
(B) −3V —▷|—— −3V
(C) 2V —▷|—— 4V
(D) −2V —▷|—— +2V

10. A Zener diode is connected to a battery and a load as shown below : **[2014 (Online)]**

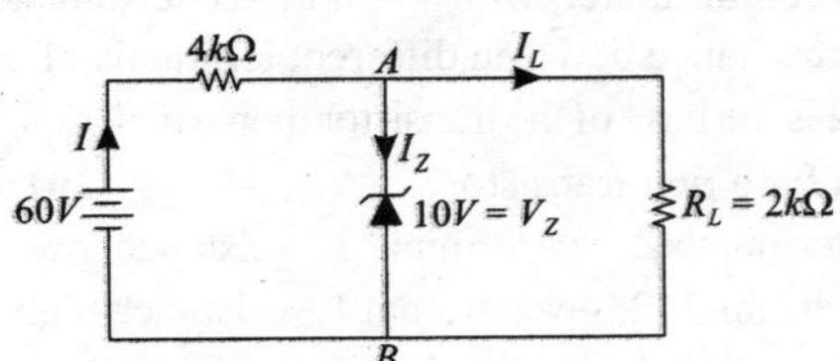

The currents, I, I_Z and I_L are respectively :
(A) 15 mA, 5 mA, 10 mA (B) 15 mA, 7.5 mA, 7.5 mA
(C) 12.5 mA, 5 mA, 7.5 mA (D) 12.5 mA, 7.5 mA, 5 mA

11. For LED's to emit light in visible region of electromagnetic light, it should have energy band gap in the range of : **[2014 (Online)]**

(A) 0.1 eV to 0.4 eV (B) 0.5 eV to 0.8 eV
(C) 0.9 eV to 1.6 eV (D) 1.7 eV to 3.0 eV

12. A red LED emits light at 0.1 watt uniformly around it. The amplitude of the electric field of the light at a distance of 1 m from the diode is : **[2015]**

(A) 5.48 V/m (B) 7.75 V/m
(C) 1.73 V/m (D) 2.45 V/m

13. In an unbiased n-p junction electrons diffuse from n-region to p-region because : **[2015 (Online)]**

(A) Hole in p-region attract them
(B) Electrons travel across the junction due to potential difference
(C) Only electrons move from n to p region and not the vice-versa
(D) Electron concentration in n-region is more compared to that in p-region

14. A 2 V battery is connected across AB as shown in the figure. The value of the current supplied by the battery when in one case battery's positive terminal is connected to A and in other case when positive terminal of battery is connected to B will respectively be : **[2015 (Online)]**

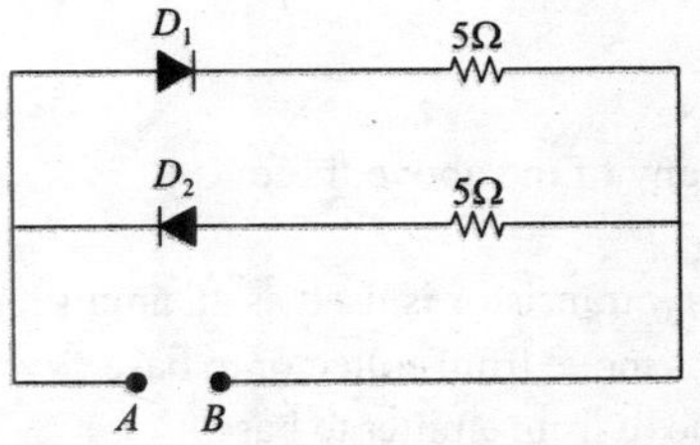

(A) 0.4 A and 0.2 A (B) 0.2 A and 0.4 A
(C) 0.1 A and 0.2 A (D) 0.2 A and 0.1 A

15. Identify the semiconductor devices whose characteristics are given below, in the order (i), (ii), (iii), (iv) : **[2016]**

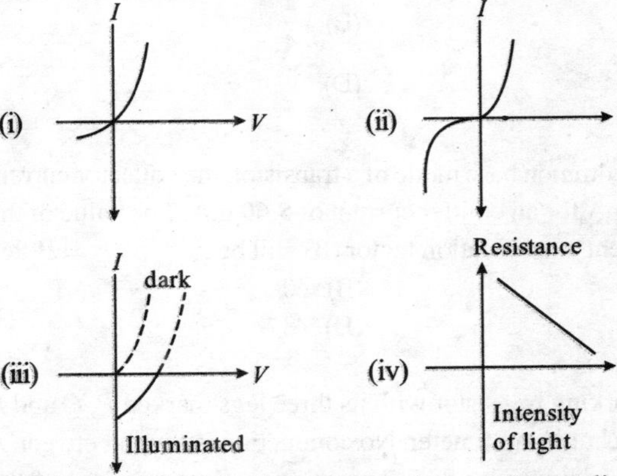

(A) Solar cell, Light dependent resistance, Zener diode, simple diode
(B) Zener diode, Solar cell, simple diode, Light dependent resistance
(C) Simple diode, Zener diode, Solar cell, Light dependent resistance
(D) Zener diode, Simple diode, Light dependent resistance, Solar cell

16. An experiment is performed to determine the 1-V characteristic of a Zener diode, which has a protective resistance of $R = 100\ \Omega$, and a maximum power of dissipation rating of 1 W. The minimum voltage range of the DC source in the circuit is : **[2016 (Online)]**

(A) 0 – 5 V (B) 0 – 24 V
(C) 0 – 12 V (D) 0 – 8 V

* * * * *

CHAPTER

28 SEMICONDUCTORS ELECTRONICS

28.3 TRANSISTORS

1. The part of a transistor which is most heavily doped to produce large number of majority carriers is : **[2002]**

(A) Emmiter

(B) Base

(C) Collector

(D) Can be any of the above three

2. When *npn* transistor is used as an amplifier : **[2004]**

(A) Electrons move from collector to base

(B) Holes move from emitter to base

(C) Electrons move from base to collector

(D) Holes move from base to emitter

3. In a common base amplifier, the phase difference between the input signal voltage and output voltage is : **[2005]**

(A) π (B) $\frac{\pi}{4}$

(C) $\frac{\pi}{2}$ (D) 0

4. In a common base mode of a transistor, the collector current is 5.488 mA for an emitter current of 5.60 mA. The value of the base current amplification factor (β) will be : **[2006]**

(A) 49 (B) 50

(C) 51 (D) 48

5. A working transistor with its three legs marked *P*, *Q* and *R* is tested using a multimeter. No conduction is found between *P* and *Q*. By connecting the common (negative) terminal of the multimeter to *R* and the other (positive) terminal to *P* or *Q*, some resistance is seen on the multimeter. Which of the following is true for the transistor ? **[2008]**

(A) It is an *npn* transistor with *R* as base

(B) It is a *pnp* transistor with *R* as base

(C) It is a *pnp* transistor with *R* as emitter

(D) It is an *npn* transistor with *R* as emitter

6. An *n-p-n* transistor has three leads *A*, *B* and *C*. Connecting *B* and *C* by moist fingers, *A* to the positive lead of an ammeter, and *C* to the negative lead of the ammeter, one finds large deflection. Then, *A*, *B* and *C* refer respectively to : **[2014 (Online)]**

(A) Emitter, base and collector

(B) Base, emitter and collector

(C) Base, collector and emitter

(D) Collector, emitter and base

7. For a common emitter configuration, if α and β have their usual meanings, the incorrect relationship between α and β is : **[2016]**

(A) $\alpha = \frac{\beta}{1+\beta}$ (B) $\alpha = \frac{\beta^2}{1+\beta^2}$

(C) $\frac{1}{\alpha} = \frac{1}{\beta} + 1$ (D) None of these

8. An unknown transistor needs to be identified as a *npn* or *pnp* type. A multimeter, with +*ve* and –*ve* terminals, is used to measure resistance between different terminals of transistor. If terminal 2 is the base of the transistor then which of the following is correct for a *pnp* transistor? **[2016 (Online)]**

(A) +*ve* terminals 2, –*ve* terminal 3, resistance low

(B) +*ve* terminals 2, –*ve* terminal 1, resistance high

(C) +*ve* terminals 1, –*ve* terminal 2, resistance high

(D) +*ve* terminals 3, –*ve* terminal 2, resistance high

9. A realistic graph depicting the variation of the reciprocal of input resistance in an input characteristics measurement in a common emitter transistor configuration is : **[2016 (Online)]**

(A) 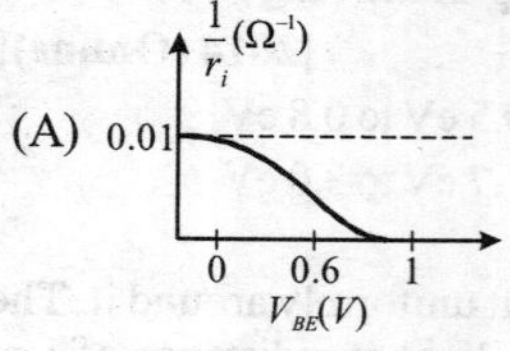

(B) 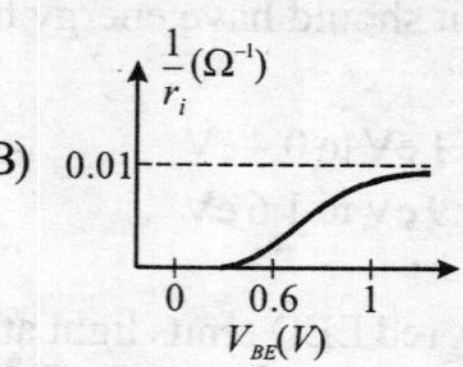

(C) 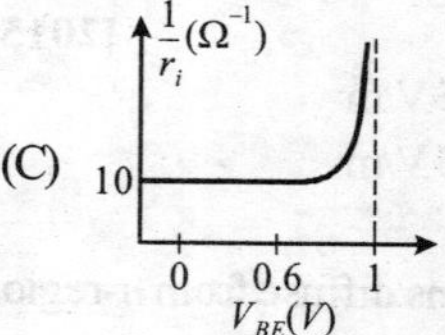

(D) 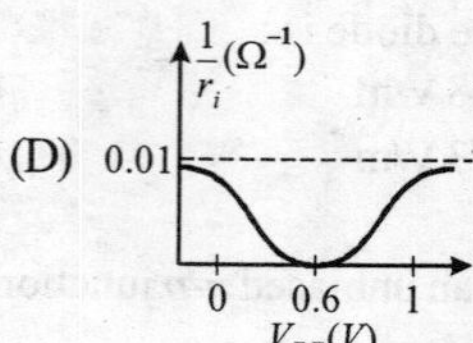

* * * * *

CHAPTER

28 SEMICONDUCTORS ELECTRONICS

28.4 LOGIC GATES

1. In the circuit below, A and B represent two inputs and C represents the output. **[2008]**

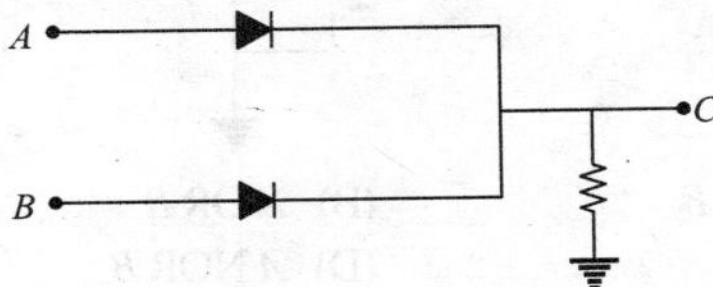

The circuit represents :

(A) NOR gate (B) AND gate
(C) NAND gate (D) OR gate

2. The logic circuit shown below has the input waveforms 'A' and 'B' as shown. Pick out the correct output waveform : **[2009]**

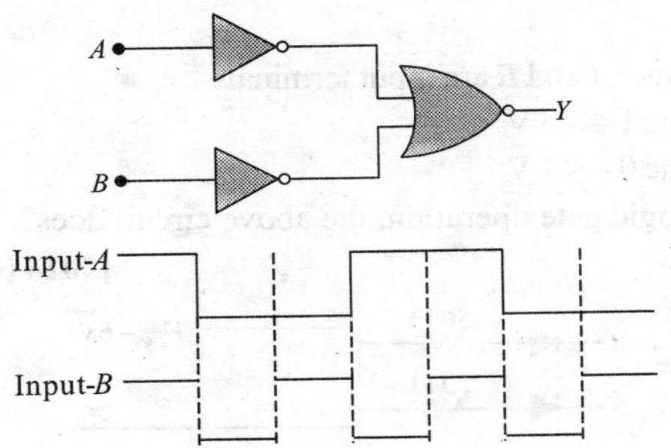

Output is :

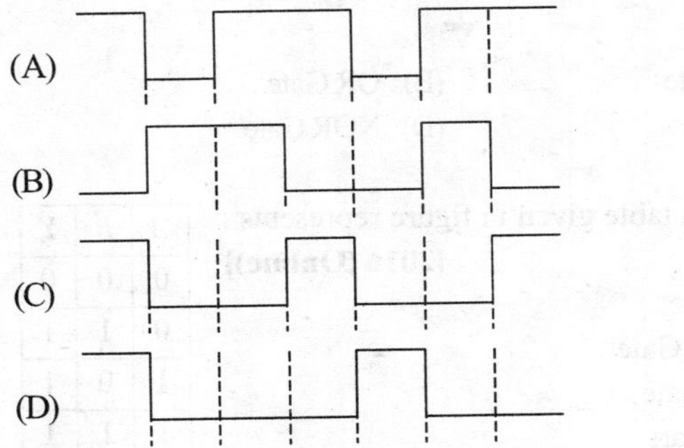

3. The combination of gates shown below yields : **[2010]**

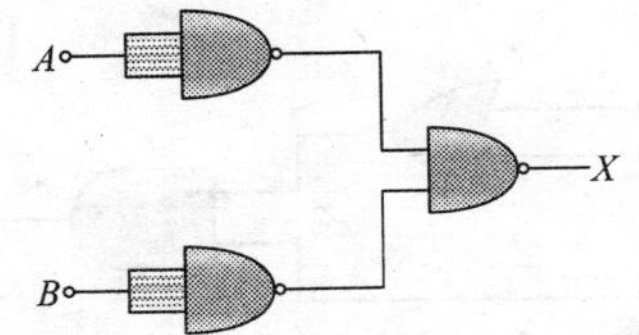

(A) OR gate (B) NOT gate
(C) XOR gate (D) NAND gate

4. The output of an OR gate is connected to both the inputs of a NAND gate. The combination will serve as : **[2011]**

(A) NOT gate (B) NOR gate
(C) AND gate (D) OR gate

5. Truth table for system of four NAND gates as shown in figure is : **[2012]**

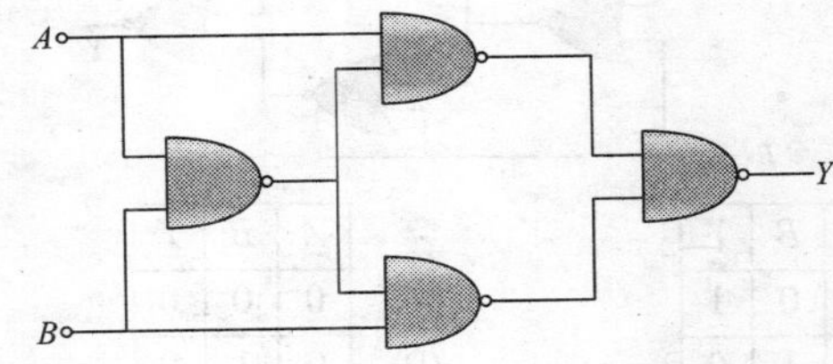

(A)

A	B	Y
0	0	0
0	1	1
1	0	1
1	1	0

(B)

A	B	Y
0	0	0
0	1	0
1	0	1
1	1	1

(C)

A	B	Y
0	0	1
0	1	1
1	0	0
1	1	0

(D)

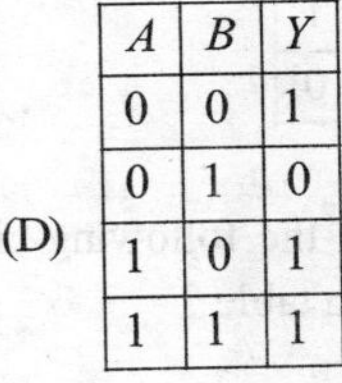

A	B	Y
0	0	1
0	1	0
1	0	1
1	1	1

6. Which logic gate with inputs A and B performs the same operation as that performed by the following circuit ? **[2012 (Online)]**

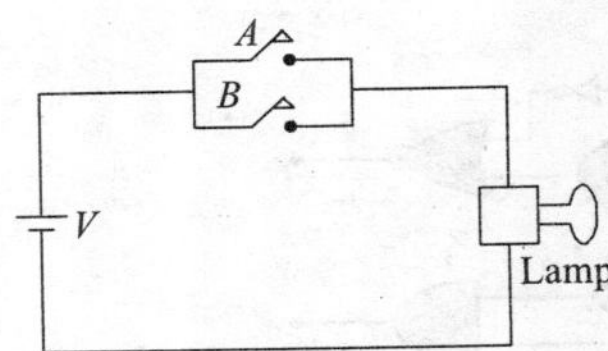

(A) NAND gate (B) OR gate
(C) NOR gate (D) AND gate

7. Which one of the following is the Boolean expression for NOR gate ? **[2012 (Online)]**

(A) $Y=\overline{A+B}$ (B) $Y=\overline{A\cdot B}$
(C) $Y=A\cdot B$ (D) $Y=\overline{A}$

8. The figure shows a combination of two NOT gates and a NOR gate. The combination is equivalent to a : **[2012 (Online)]**

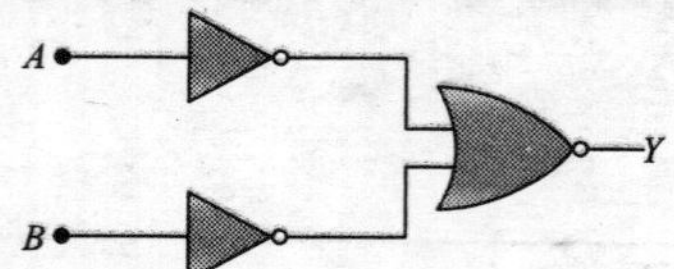

(A) NAND gate (B) NOR gate
(C) AND gate (D) OR gate

9. A system of four gates is set up as shown. The 'truth table' corresponding to this system is : **[2013 (Online)]**

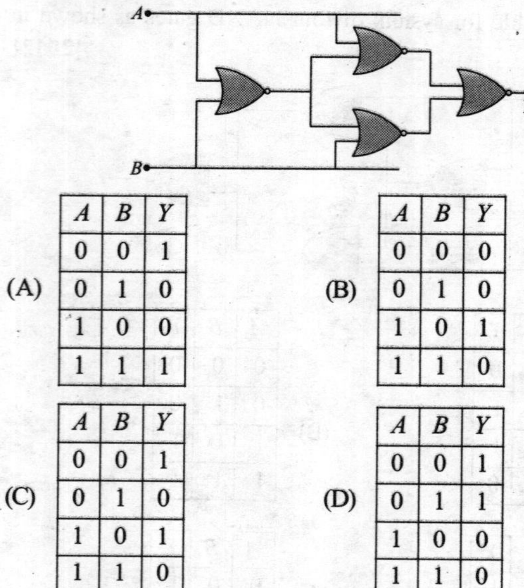

(A)

A	B	Y
0	0	1
0	1	0
1	0	0
1	1	1

(B)

A	B	Y
0	0	0
0	1	0
1	0	1
1	1	0

(C)

A	B	Y
0	0	1
0	1	0
1	0	1
1	1	0

(D)

A	B	Y
0	0	1
0	1	1
1	0	0
1	1	0

10. Which of the following circuits correctly represents the following truth table ? **[2013 (Online)]**

A	*B*	*C*
0	0	0
0	1	0
1	0	1
1	1	0

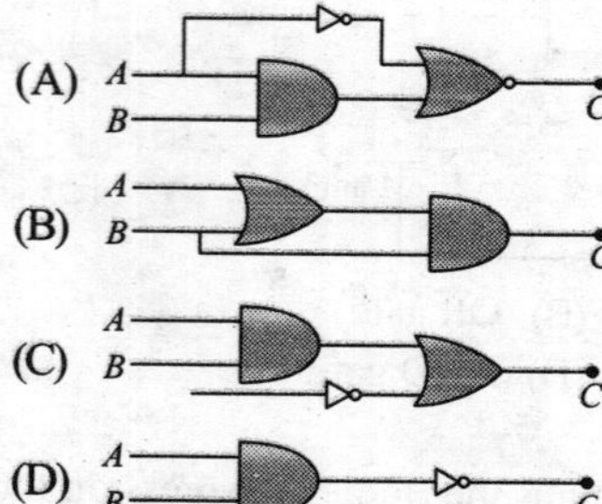

11. Consider two *npn* transistors as shown in figure. If 0 Volts corresponds to false and 5 Volts correspond to true then the output at *C* corresponds to : **[2013 (Online)]**

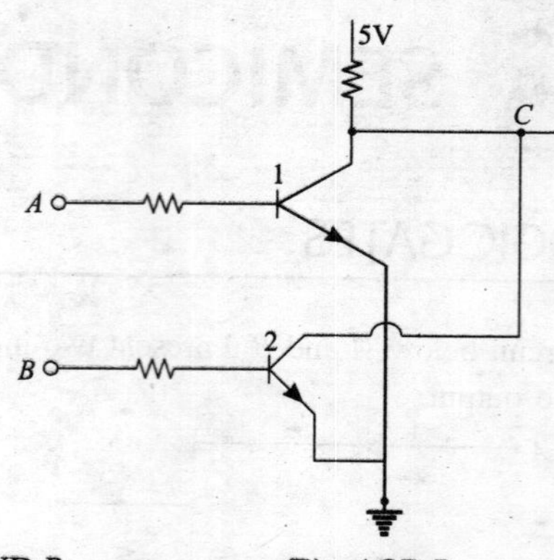

(A) *A* NAND *B* (B) *A* OR *B*
(C) *A* AND *B* (D) *A* NOR *B*

12. Identify the gate and match *A*, *B*, *Y* in bracket to check : **[2014 (Online)]**

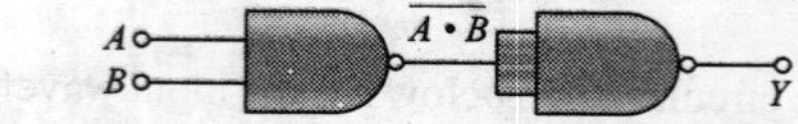

(A) AND ($A=1, B=1, Y=1$) (B) OR ($A=1, B=1, Y=0$)
(C) NOT ($A=1, B=1, Y=1$) (D) XOR ($A=0, B=0, Y=0$)

13. Given : *A* and *B* are input terminals
Logic 1 => 5 V
Logic 0 =< 1 V
Which logic gate operation, the above circuit does? **[2014 (Online)]**

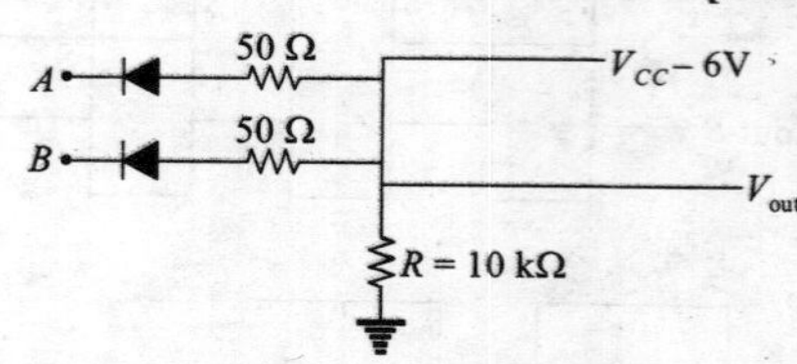

(A) AND Gate (B) OR Gate
(C) XOR Gate (D) NOR Gate

14. The truth table given in figure represents : **[2016 (Online)]**

A	B	Y
0	0	0
0	1	1
1	0	1
1	1	1

(A) OR – Gate
(B) NAND – Gate
(C) AND – Gate
(D) NOR – Gate

15. To get an output of 1 from the circuit shown in figure the input must be : **[2016 (Online)]**

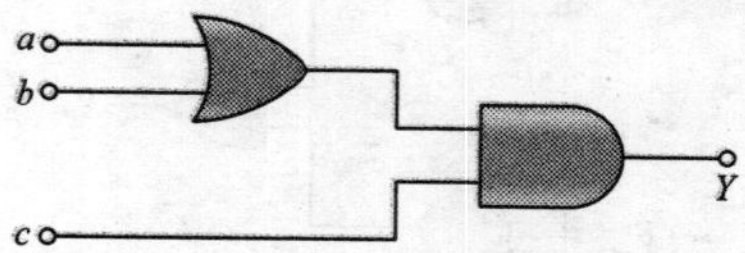

(A) $a=0, b=0, c=1$ (B) $a=1, b=0, c=0$
(C) $a=1, b=0, c=1$ (D) $a=0, b=1, c=0$

* * * * *

CHAPTER

29 COMMUNICATION SYSTEMS

29.1 COMMUNICATION SYSTEMS

1. Consider telecommunication through optical fibres. Which of the following statements is not true? **[2003]**
(A) Optical fibres can be of graded refractive index
(B) Optical fibres are subject to electromagnetic interference from outside
(C) Optical fibres have extremely low transmission loss
(D) Optical fibres may have homogeneous core with a suitable cladding

2. This question has Statement-1 and Statement-2. Of the four choices given after the statements, choose the one that best describes the two statements. **[2011]**
Statement-1 : Sky wave signals are used for long distance radio communication. These signals are in general, less stable than ground wave signals.
Statement-2 : The state of ionosphere varies from hour to hour, day to day and season to season.
(A) Statement-1 is true, Statement-2 is true, Statement-2 is the correct explanation of Statement-1
(B) Statement-1 is true, Statement-2 is true, Statement-2 is not the correct explanation of Statement-1
(C) Statement-1 is false, Statement-2 is true
(D) Statement-1 is true, Statement-2 is false

3. A radar has a power of 1 kW and is operating at a frequency of 10 GHz. It is located on a mountain top of height 500 m. The maximum distance upto which it can detect object located on the surface of the earth **[2012]**
(Radius of earth = 6.4×10^6 m) is :
(A) 80 km (B) 16 km
(C) 40 km (D) 64 km

4. A 10 kW transmitter emits radio waves of wavelength 500 m. The number of photons emitted per second by the transmitter is of the order of : **[2012 (Online)]**
(A) 10^{37} (B) 10^{31}
(C) 10^{25} (D) 10^{43}

5. A radio transmitter transmits at 830 kHz. At a certain distance from the transmitter magnetic field has amplitude 4.82×10^{-11} T. The electric field and the wavelength are respectively : **[2012 (Online)]**
(A) 0.014 N/C, 36 m (B) 0.14 N/C, 36 m
(C) 0.14 N/C, 360 m (D) 0.014 N/C, 360 m

6. This question has Statement-1 and Statement-2. Of the four choices given after the Statements, choose the one that best describes the two Statements. **[2013]**
Statement-1 : Short wave transmission is achieved due to the total internal reflection of the *e-m* wave from an appropriate height in the ionosphere.
Statement-2 : Refractive index of a plasma is independent of the frequency of *e-m* waves.
(A) Statement-1 is true, Statement-2 is false
(B) Statement-1 is false, Statement-2 is true
(C) Statement-1 is true, Statement-2 is true but Statement-2 is not the correct explanation of Statement-1
(D) Statement-1 is true, Statement-2 is true and Statement-2 is the correct explanation of Statement-1

7. Which of the following statement is NOT correct ?
(A) Ground wave signals are more stable than the sky wave signals **[2013]**
(B) The critical frequency of an ionospheric layer is the highest frequency that will be reflected back by the layer when it is vertically incident
(C) Electromagnetic waves of frequencies higher than about 30 MHz cannot penetrate the ionosphere
(D) Sky wave signals in the broadcast frequency range are stronger at night than in the day time

8. A transmitting antenna at the top of a tower has height 32 m and height of the receiving antenna is 50 m. What is the maximum distance between them for satisfactory communication in line of sight (LOS) mode ? **[2014 (Online)]**
(A) 55.4 km (B) 45.5 km
(C) 54.5 km (D) 455 km

9. For sky wave propagation, the radio waves must have a frequency range in between : **[2014 (Online)]**
(A) 1 MHz to 2 MHz (B) 5 MHz to 25 MHz
(C) 35 MHz to 40 MHz (D) 45 MHz to 50 MHz

10. Long range radio transmission is possible when the radio waves are reflected from the ionosphere. For this to happen the frequency of the radio waves must be in the range : **[2014 (Online)]**
(A) 80 - 150 MHz (B) 8 - 25 MHz
(C) 1 - 3 MHz (D) 150 - 1500 kHz

* * * * *

CHAPTER

29 COMMUNICATION SYSTEMS

29.2 MODULATION AND DEMODULATION

1. Which of the following four alternatives is not correct ? We need modulation : **[2011]**

(A) To reduce the time lag between transmission and reception of the information signal

(B) To reduce the size of antenna

(C) To reduce the fractional band width, that is the ratio of the signal band width to the centre frequency

(D) To increase the selectivity

2. Given the electric field of a complete amplitude modulated wave as

$$\vec{E} = \hat{i}E_c\left(1+\frac{E_m}{E_c}\cos\omega_m t\right)\cos\omega_c t$$

Where the subscript stands for the carrier wave and m for the modulating signal. The frequencies present in the modulated wave are : **[2012 (Online)]**

(A) ω_c and $\sqrt{\omega_c^2+\omega_m^2}$ (B) ω_c, $\omega_c+\omega_m$ and $\omega_c-\omega_m$

(C) ω_c and ω_m (D) ω_c and $\sqrt{\omega_c\omega_m}$

3. Which of the following modulated signal has the best noise-tolerance ? **[2013]**

(A) Long-wave (B) Short-wave

(C) Medium-wave (D) Amplitude-modulated

4. A diode detector is used to detect an amplitude modulated wave of 60% modulation using a condenser of capacity 250 picofarad in parallel with a load resistance 100 kilo ohm. Find the maximum modulated frequency which could be detected by it : **[2013]**

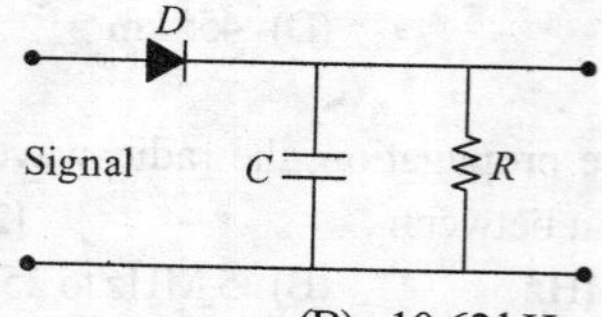

(A) 10.62 MHz (B) 10.62 kHz

(C) 5.31 MHz (D) 5.31 kHz

5. If a carrier wave $c(t) = A\sin\omega_c t$ is amplitude modulated by a modulator signal $m(t) = A\sin\omega_m t$ then the equation of modulated signal $[C_m(t)]$ and its modulation index are respectively : **[2013 (Online)]**

(A) $C_m(t) = A(1+\sin\omega_m t)\sin\omega_c t$ and 2

(B) $C_m(t) = A(1+\sin\omega_m t)\sin\omega_m t$ and 1

(C) $C_m(t) = A(1+\sin\omega_m t)\sin\omega_c t$ and 1

(D) $C_m(t) = A(1+\sin\omega_c t)\sin\omega_m t$ and 2

6. A signal of 5 kHz frequency is amplitude modulated on a carrier wave of frequency 2 MHz. The frequencies of the resultant signal is/are : **[2015]**

(A) 2005 kHz, 2000 kHz and 1995 kHz

(B) 2000 kHz and 1995 kHz

(C) 2 MHz only (D) 2005 kHz and 1995 kHz

7. Choose the correct statement : **[2016]**

(A) In frequency modulation the amplitude of the high frequency carrier wave is made to vary in proportion to the amplitude of the audio signal

(B) In frequency modulation the amplitude of the high frequency carrier wave is made to vary in proportional to the frequency of the audio signal

(C) In amplitude modulation the amplitude of the high frequency carrier wave is made to vary in proportion to the amplitude of the audio signal

(D) In amplitude modulation the frequency of the high frequency carrier wave is made to vary in proportion to the amplitude of the audio signal

8. A modulated signal $C_m(t)$ has the form $C_m(t) = 30\sin 300\pi t + 10(\cos 200\pi t - \cos 400\pi t)$. The carrier frequency f_c, the modulating frequency (message frequency) f_w and the modulation index μ are respectively given by : **[2016 (Online)]**

(A) $f_c = 200$ Hz; $f_w = 50$ Hz; $\mu = 1/2$

(B) $f_c = 150$ Hz; $f_w = 50$ Hz; $\mu = 2/3$

(C) $f_c = 150$ Hz; $f_w = 30$ Hz; $\mu = 1/3$

(D) $f_c = 200$ Hz; $f_w = 30$ Hz; $\mu = 1/2$

9. An audio signal consists of two distinct sounds : one a human speech signal in the frequency band of 200 Hz to 2700 Hz, while the other is a high frequency music signal in the frequency band of 10200 Hz to 15200 Hz. The ratio of the AM signal band width required to send both the signals together to the *AM* signal bandwidth required to send just the human speech is : **[2016 (Online)]**

(A) 2 (B) 5

(C) 6 (D) 3

* * * * *

CHAPTER

30 ERRORS AND EXPERIMENTS

30.1 ERRORS AND EXPERIMENTS

1. Two full turns of the circular scale of a screw gauge cover a distance of 1 mm on its main scale. The total number of divisions on the circular scale is 50. Further, it is found that the screw gauge has a zero error of – 0.03 mm. While measuring the diameter of a thin wire, a student notes the main scale reading of 3 mm and the number of circular scale divisions in line with the main scale as 35. The diameter of the wire is : **[2008]**

(A) 3.32 mm (B) 3.73 mm
(C) 3.67 mm (D) 3.38 mm

2. A body of mass $m = 3.513$ kg is moving along the x-axis with a speed of 5.00 ms^{-1}. The magnitude of its momentum is recorded as : **[2008]**

(A) 17.6 kg ms^{-1} (B) 17.565 kg ms^{-1}
(C) 17.56 kg ms^{-1} (D) 17.57 kg ms^{-1}

3. In an experiment the angles are required to be measured using an instrument, 29 divisions of the main scale exactly coincide with the 30 divisions of the vernier scale. If the smallest division of the main scale is half a degree (= 0.5°), then the least count of the instrument is : **[2009]**

(A) half minute (B) one degree
(C) half degree (D) one minute

4. The respective number of significant figures for the numbers 23.023, 0.0003 and 2.1×10^{-3} are : **[2009]**

(A) 5, 1, 2 (B) 5, 1, 5
(C) 5, 5, 2 (D) 4, 4, 2

5. A screw gauge gives the following reading when used to measure the diameter of a wire.

Main scale reading : 0 mm

Circular scale reading : 52 divisions **[2011]**

Given that 1 mm on main scale corresponds to 100 divisions of the circular scale. The diameter of wire from the above data is :

(A) 0.052 cm (B) 0.026 cm
(C) 0.005 cm (D) 0.52 cm

6. A spectrometer gives the following reading when used to measure the angle of a prism.

Main scale reading : 58.5 degree

Vernier scale reading : 09 divisions

Given that 1 division on main scale corresponds to 0.5 degree. Total divisions on the Vernier scale is 30 and match with 29 divisions of the main scale. The angle of the prism from the above data is : **[2012]**

(A) 58.59 degree (B) 58.77 degree
(C) 58.65 degree (D) 59 degree

7. Resistance of a given wire is obtained by measuring the current flowing in it and the voltage difference applied across it. If the percentage errors in the measurement of the current and the voltage difference are 3% each, then error in the value of resistance of the wire is : **[2012]**

(A) 6% (B) Zero
(C) 1% (D) 3%

8. A student measured the diameter of a wire using a screw gauge with the least count 0.001 cm and listed the measurements. The measured value should be recorded as : **[2012 (Online)]**

(A) 5.3200 cm (B) 5.3 cm
(C) 5.32 cm (D) 5.320 cm

9. N divisions on the main scale of a vernier calliper coincide with $(N + 1)$ divisions of the vernier scale. If each division of main scale is 'a' units, then the least count of the instrument is : **[2012 (Online)]**

(A) a (B) $\frac{a}{N}$
(C) $\frac{N}{N+1} \times a$ (D) $\frac{a}{N+1}$

10. A student measured the length of a rod and wrote it as 3.50 cm. Which instrument did he use to measure it ? **[2014]**

(A) A meter scale

(B) A vernier calliper where the 10 divisions in vernier scale matches with 9 division in main scale and main scale has 10 divisions in 1 cm

(C) A screw gauge having 100 divisions in the circular scale and pitch as 1 mm

(D) A screw gauge having 50 divisions in the circular scale and pitch as 1 mm

11. The current voltage relation of a diode is given by $I = (e^{1000\,V/T} - 1)$ mA, where the applied voltage V is in volt and the temperature T is in degree kelvin. If a student makes an error measuring ± 0.01 V while measuring the current of 5 mA at 300 K, what will be the error in the value of current in mA ? **[2014]**

(A) 0.2 mA (B) 0.02 mA
(C) 0.5 mA (D) 0.05 mA

12. An experiment is performed to obtain the value of acceleration due to gravity g by using a simple pendulum of length L. In this experiment time for 100 oscillations is measured by using a watch of 1 second least count and the value is 90.0 seconds. The length L is measured by using a meter scale of least count 1 mm and the value is 20.0 cm. The error in the determination of g would be : **[2014 (Online)]**

(A) 1.7% (B) 2.7%
(C) 4.4% (D) 2.27%

13. In the experiment of calibration of voltmeter, a standard cell of e.m.f. 1.1 volt is balanced against 440 cm of potential wire. The potential difference across the ends of resistance is found to balance against 220 cm of the wire. The corresponding reading of voltmeter is 0.5 volt. The error in the reading of voltmeter will be : **[2014 (Online)]**

(A) – 0.15 volt (B) 0.15 volt
(C) 0.5 volt (D) – 0.05 volt

14. Match List-I (Event) with List-II (Order of the time interval for happening of the event) and select the correct option from the options given below the lists : **[2014 (Online)]**

List-I	List-II
(1) Rotation period of earth	(i) 10^5s
(2) Revolution period of earth	(ii) 10^7s
(3) Period of light wave	(iii) 10^{-15}s
(4) Period of sound wave	(iv) 10^{-3}s

(A) (1)→(i), (2)→(ii), (3)→(iii), (4)→(iv)
(B) (1)→(ii), (2)→(i), (3)→(iv), (4)→(iii)
(C) (1)→(i), (2)→(ii), (3)→(iv), (4)→(iii)
(D) (1)→(ii), (2)→(i), (3)→(iii), (4)→(iv)

15. The period of oscillation of a simple pendulum is $T = 2\pi\sqrt{\frac{L}{g}}$. Measured value of L is 20.0 cm know to 1 mm accuracy and time for 100 oscillations of the pendulum is found to be 90 s using a wrist watch of 1 s resolution. The accuracy in the determination of g is : **[2015]**

(A) 1% (B) 5%
(C) 2% (D) 3%

16. Diameter of a steel ball is measured using a Vernier callipers which has divisions of 0.1 cm on its main scale (MS) and 10 divisions of its vernier scale (VS) match 9 divisions on the main scale. Three such measurements for a ball are given as : **[2015 (Online)]**

S.No.	MS(cm)	VS divisions
1.	0.5	8
2.	0.5	4
3.	0.5	6

If the zero error is – 0.03 cm, then mean corrected diameter is :

(A) 0.52 cm (B) 0.59 cm
(C) 0.56 cm (D) 0.53 cm

17. A student measures the time period of 100 oscillations of a simple pendulum four times. The data set is 90 s, 91 s, 95 s, and 92 s. If the minimum division in the measuring clock is 1 s, then the reported mean time should be : **[2016]**

(A) 92 ± 1.8 s (B) 92 ± 3 s
(C) 92 ± 1.5 s (D) 92 ± 5.0 s

18. A screw gauge with a pitch of 0.5 mm and a circular scale with 50 divisions is used to measure the thickness of a thin sheet of Aluminium. Before starting the measurement, it is found that wen the two jaws of the screw gauge are brought in contact, the 45th division coincides with the main scale line and the zero of the main scale is barely visible. What is the thickness of the sheet if the main scale reading is 0.5 mm and the 25th division coincides with the main scale line ? **[2016]**

(A) 0.70 mm (B) 0.50 mm
(C) 0.75 mm (D) 0.80 mm

* * * * *

ANSWER KEY

1.1 Measurements and Dimensional Analysis

1. (A) 2. (B) 3. (C) 4. (A) 5. (D)

6. (B) 7. (C) 8. (A) 9. (B) 10. (D)

11. (C) 12. (C) 13. (B) 14. (D) 15. (C)

16. (B) 17. (A, D)

2.1 Motion in One Dimension

1. (A) 2. (B) 3. (D) 4. (C) 5. (C)

6. (D) 7. (C) 8. (C) 9. (A) 10. (C)

11. (C) 12. (B) 13. (B) 14. (D) 15. (A)

16. (B) 17. (C) 18. (C) 19. (C)

3.1 Motion in Two Dimensions

1. (C) 2. (D) 3. (B) 4. (A) 5. (C)

6. (A) 7. (C) 8. (A) 9. (D) 10. (A)

11. (D) 12. (A) 13. (B) 14. (B) 15. (C)

16. (C) 17. (A)

3.2 Relative Motion

1. (B) 2. (D) 3. (C)

4.1 Newton's Laws of Motion

1. (A) 2. (B) 3. (C) 4. (D) 5. (C)

6. (B) 7. (B) 8. (A) 9. (A) 10. (B)

11. (D) 12. (D) 13. (A) 14. (D) 15. (D)

16. (C) 17. (D) 18. (C) 19. (A) 20. (D)

21. (A) 22. (D) 23. (D) 24. (A) 25. (D)

26. (A) 27. (B)

4.2 Friction

1. (D) 2. (C) 3. (A) 4. (A) 5. (C)

6. (B) 7. (D) 8. (A) 9. (A) 10. (D)

11. (B) 12. (A) 13. (C)

5.1 Work Energy Power

1. (B) 2. (B) 3. (B) 4. (A) 5. (B)

6. (B) 7. (B) 8. (D) 9. (A) 10. (B)

11. (B) 12. (A) 13. (D) 14. (A) 15. (D)

16. (D) 17. (D) 18. (B) 19. (D) 20. (A)

21. (A) 22. (B) 23. (C) 24. (D) 25. (D)

26. (A) 27. (B) 28. (C) 29. (D) 30. (C)

31. (C)

5.2 Circular Motion

1. (B) 2. (C) 3. (B) 4. (C) 5. (D)

6. (C) 7. (A) 8. (C) 9. (C) 10. (B)

11. (B) 12. (A)

6.1 System of Particles

1. (C) 2. (C) 3. (C) 4. (B) 5. (C)

6. (C) 7. (B) 8. (C) 9. (C) 10. (A)

11. (A) 12. (B) 13. (B) 14. (D) 15. (A)

16. (C) 17. (D) 18. (C) 19. (D) 20. (C)

21. (D) 22. (D) 23. (D) 24. (B) 25. (C)

26. (B) 27. (B) 28. (D) 29. (B) 30. (B)

31. (C)

6.2 Rigid Body Dynamics

1. (C) 2. (A) 3. (B) 4. (D) 5. (A)

6. (D) 7. (B) 8. (C) 9. (D) 10. (D)

11. (C) 12. (B) 13. (D) 14. (C) 15. (A)

16. (A) 17. (C) 18. (D) 19. (C) 20. (D)

21. (B) 22. (B) 23. (D) 24. (D) 25. (B)

26. (B) 27. (D) 28. (D) 29. (B) 30. (B)

31. (C) 32. (B) 33. (A) 34. (A) 35. (C)

36. (B) 37. (C) 38. (D) 39. (D) 40. (B)

41. (A) 42. (C) 43 (C) 44. (A) 45. (D)

46. (A, C) 47. (C) 48. (B)

7.1 Gravitational Field

1. (C) 2. (B) 3. (D) 4. (C) 5. (A)

6. (A) 7. (B) 8. (C) 9. (B) 10. (A)

11. (A) 12. (B) 13. (C) 14. (A) 15. (D)

16. (A) 17. (D) 18. (A) 19. (B) 20. (B)

21. (C) 22. (C)

7.2 Satellite Motion

1. (B) 2. (A) 3. (A) 4. (C) 5. (C)

6. (A) 7. (A) 8. (D) 9. (C) 10. (B)

11. (C) 12. (A) 13. (D) 14. (C) 15. (C)

8.1 Elasticity

1. (D) 2. (D) 3. (B) 4. (A) 5. (B)

6. (A) 7. (A) 8. (C) 9. (B) 10. (C)

11. (C) 12. (D) 13. (C) 14. (A) 15. (C)

16. (C) 17. (D)

9.1 Fluid Statics

1. (D) 2. (C) 3. (B) 4. (C)

9.2 Fluid Dynamics

1. (B) **2.** (B) **3.** (A) **4.** (A) **5.** (B)
6. (C) **7.** (B) **8.** (B) **9.** (B) **10.** (A)
11. (A)

9.3 Viscosity

1. (B) **2.** (C) **3.** (A) **4.** (B) **5.** (A)
6. (C) **7.** (B) **8.** (C) **9.** (D) **10.** (C)

9.4 Surface Tension

1. (C) **2.** (D) **3.** (C) **4.** (D) **5.** (B)
6. (A) **7.** (D) **8.** (C) **9.** (B) **10.** (C)
11. (A) **12.** (A) **13.** (B) **14.** (D)

10.1 Thermal Expansion

1. (C) **2.** (A) **3.** (A) **4.** (C) **5.** (B)
6. (A) **7.** (A)

10.2 Calorimetry

1. (B) **2.** (C) **3.** (C) **4.** (B) **5.** (A)
6. (B)

10.3 Heat Transfer

1. (A) **2.** (B) **3.** (A) **4.** (D) **5.** (D)
6. (D) **7.** (D) **8.** (C) **9.** (B) **10.** (C)
11. (D) **12.** (B) **13.** (A) **14.** (A) **15.** (C)
16. (D) **17.** (C) **18.** (C) **19.** (B) **20.** (B)

11.1 Laws of Thermodynamics

1. (A) **2.** (C) **3.** (B) **4.** (D) **5.** (C)
6. (A) **7.** (B) **8.** (A) **9.** (C) **10.** (D)
11. (A) **12.** (A) **13.** (A) **14.** (A) **15.** (D)
16. (D) **17.** (C) **18.** (D) **19.** (A) **20.** (C)
21. (C) **22.** (B) **23.** (D) **24.** (B) **25.** (D)
26. (B) **27.** (D) **28.** (D) **29.** (D) **30.** (C)
31. (D) **32.** (C) **33.** (B) **34.** (C) **35.** (C)
36. (D) **37.** (A) **38.** (B) **39.** (C) **40.** (A)
41. (B) **42.** (C) **43.** (A) **44.** (D) **45.** (B)
46. (A) **47.** (B) **48.** (D) **49.** (A) **50.** (D)

12.1 Kinetic Theory of Gases

1. (C) **2.** (D) **3.** (C) **4.** (C) **5.** (A)
6. (B) **7.** (C) **8.** (A) **9.** (A) **10.** (D)
11. (D) **12.** (A) **13.** (B) **14.** (C) **15.** (A)
16. (A) **17.** (B) **18.** (A) **19.** (D) **20.** (D)
21. (C)

13.1 Simple Harmonic Motion

1. (B) **2.** (C) **3.** (B) **4.** (C) **5.** (C)
6. (A) **7.** (C) **8.** (D) **9.** (C) **10.** (B)
11. (C) **12.** (B) **13.** (C) **14.** (D) **15.** (D)
16. (B) **17.** (A) **18.** (A) **19.** (A) **20.** (A)
21. (B) **22.** (A) **23.** (D) **24.** (D) **25.** (A)
26. (D) **27.** (B) **28.** (D) **29.** (B) **30.** (A)
31. (A) **32.** (A) **33.** (C) **34.** (C) **35.** (A)
36. (A) **37.** (D) **38.** (D) **39.** (D) **40.** (C)
41. (B) **42.** (A) **43.** (D) **44.** (C) **45.** (C)
46. (A) **47.** (A) **48.** (B) **49.** (D) **50.** (C)
51. (C) **52.** (D) **53.** (B) **54.** (D)

14.1 Wave Motion

1. (A) **2.** (D) **3.** (A) **4.** (A) **5.** (A)
6. (B) **7.** (D) **8.** (C) **9.** (B) **10.** (B)
11. (D) **12.** (A) **13.** (C)

14.2 Stationary Waves and Beats

1. (C) **2.** (B) **3.** (B) **4.** (B) **5.** (C)
6. (C) **7.** (A) **8.** (B) **9.** (B) **10.** (A)
11. (B) **12.** (D) **13.** (B) **14.** (D) **15.** (B)
16. (B) **17.** (D) **18.** (C) **19.** (B) **20.** (D)

14.3 Doppler's Effect

1. (D) **2.** (C) **3.** (D) **4.** (C) **5.** (C)
6. (D) **7.** (B) **8.** (B) **9.** (A) **10.** (C)
11. (D) **12.** (D)

15.1 Electric Force and Electric Field

1. (D) **2.** (B) **3.** (B) **4.** (D) **5.** (C)
6. (A) **7.** (D) **8.** (A) **9.** (C) **10.** (A)
11. (D) **12.** (C) **13.** (A) **14.** (C) **15.** (D)
16. (A) **17.** (B) **18.** (A) **19.** (D) **20.** (C)
21. (B) **22.** (A) **23.** (D) **24.** (B) **25.** (A)

15.2 Electric Flux and Gauss's Law

1. (B) **2.** (A) **3.** (B) **4.** (B) **5.** (C)
6. (D) **7.** (A) **8.** (A)

16.1 Electric Potential and Dipole

1. (A) **2.** (C) **3.** (D) **4.** (B) **5.** (C)
6. (C) **7.** (D) **8.** (D) **9.** (B) **10.** (D)
11. (B) **12.** (A) **13.** (D) **14.** (C) **15.** (D)
16. (C) **17.** (C) **18.** (C) **19.** (A) **20.** (D)
21. (C) **22.** (D, C) **23.** (A) **24.** (B) **25.** (C)

16.2 Capacitance

1. (A) 2. (B) 3. (D) 4. (B) 5. (A)
6. (D) 7. (A) 8. (D) 9. (D) 10. (C)
11. (C) 12. (D) 13. (D) 14. (B) 15. (C)
16. (C) 17. (B) 18. (A) 19. (D) 20. (D)
21. (C) 22. (C) 23. (B) 24. (A) 25. (C)
26. (D) 27. (A)

17.1 Current Electricity

1. (D) 2. (C) 3. (B) 4. (A) 5. (B)
6. (D) 7. (D) 8. (C) 9. (A) 10. (B)
11. (A) 12. (B) 13. (D) 14. (C) 15. (D)
16. (C)

17.2 Circuit Analysis

1. (B) 2. (B) 3. (B) 4. (B) 5. (D)
6. (C) 7. (C) 8. (D) 9. (B) 10. (C)
11. (C) 12. (C) 13. (C)

17.3 Thermal Effects of Current & RC Circuits

1. (B) 2. (B) 3. (B) 4. (A) 5. (C)
6. (C) 7. (D) 8. (C) 9. (A) 10. (B)
11. (A) 12. (B) 13. (B) 14. (D) 15. (C)
16. (D) 17. (D) 18. (A) 19. (D) 20. (A)
21. (C) 22. (C) 23. (B) 24. (A) 25. (D)
26. (B) 27. (C) 28. (C) 29. (B) 30. (A)
31. (None)

17.4 Electrical Measuring Instruments

1. (C) 2. (D) 3. (D) 4. (A) 5. (D)
6. (B) 7. (D) 8. (B) 9. (D) 10. (C)
11. (C) 12. (D) 13. (A) 14. (C) 15. (D)
16. (D) 17. (D) 18. (C) 19. (A) 20. (A)
21. (D) 22. (A)

18.1 Magnetic Effect of Current

1. (A) 2. (A) 3. (B) 4. (B) 5. (C)
6. (A) 7. (B) 8. (D) 9. (D) 10. (C)
11. (D) 12. (D) 13. (A) 14. (B) 15. (B)
16. (B) 17. (A) 18. (A) 19. (A) 20. (D)

18.2 Magnetic Force on Moving Charges

1. (C) 2. (A) 3. (B) 4. (A) 5. (A)
6. (A) 7. (B) 8. (C) 9. (D) 10. (A)
11. (B) 12. (B) 13. (A) 14. (A) 15. (D)
16. (B) 17. (C) 18. (A) 19. (A) 20. (C)
21. (A) 22. (B) 23. (D) 24. (C) 25. (C)
26. (B) 27. (B) 28. (A) 29. (C) 30. (C)
31. (B) 32. (A) 33. (C) 34. (A) 35. (D)

19.1 Classical and Terrestrial Magnetism

1. (D) 2. (B) 3. (B) 4. (C) 5. (C)
6. (B) 7. (D) 8. (D) 9. (A) 10. (C)
11. (C) 12. (B)

19.2 Magnetic Properties of Materials

1. (A) 2. (B) 3. (B) 4. (B) 5. (C)
6. (B) 7. (B) 8. (D)

20.1 Electromagnetic Induction

1. (D) 2. (B) 3. (B) 4. (B) 5. (D)
6. (C) 7. (B) 8. (B) 9. (A) 10. (C)
11. (A) 12. (D) 13. (B) 14. (A) 15. (A)
16. (D) 17. (B) 18. (B)

20.2 Self and Mutual Induction

1. (D) 2. (D) 3. (B) 4. (B) 5. (B)
6. (A) 7. (D) 8. (D) 9. (B) 10. (C)
11. (B) 12. (D) 13. (C) 14. (None) 15. (C)
16. (A) 17. (D) 18. (D) 19. (C)

21.1 Alternating Current

1. (B) 2. (B) 3. (A) 4. (C) 5. (A)
6. (C) 7. (D) 8. (C) 9. (B) 10. (A)
11. (C) 12. (D) 13. (C) 14. (B) 15. (A)
16. (D) 17. (C) 18. (D) 19. (B) 20. (D)
21. (B) 22. (D) 23. (D) 24. (C) 25. (B)
26. (A) 27. (C) 28. (D) 29. (D)

22.1 Electromagnetic Wave

1. (A) 2. (B) 3. (B) 4. (A) 5. (C)
6. (B) 7. (A) 8. (D) 9. (B) 10. (C)
11. (C) 12. (C) 13. (B) 14. (D) 15. (B)
16. (C) 17. (C) 18. (D)

23.1 Geometrical Optics I - Reflection of Light

1. (A) 2. (B) 3. (D) 4. (C)

23.2 Geometrical Optics II - Refraction of Light

1. (A) 2. (B) 3. (B) 4. (B) 5. (D)
6. (C) 7. (C) 8. (C) 9. (B) 10. (D)
11. (None) 12. (D) 13. (A) 14. (A) 15. (B)

23.3 Geometrical Optics III - Thin Lenses

1. (A) 2. (A) 3. (B) 4. (C) 5. (D)
6. (A) 7. (C) 8. (D) 9. (B) 10. (D)
11. (A) 12. (D) 13. (A) 14. (A)

23.4 Dispersion of Light

1. (A) 2. (B) 3. (A) 4. (D)

23.5 Optical Instruments

1. (B) 2. (D) 3. (C) 4. (A) 5. (A)
6. (C) 7. (A) 8. (D) 9. (C) 10. (D)
11. (A) 12. (B) 13. (C) 14. (C) 15. (C)

24.1 Interference of Light

1. (D) 2. (C) 3. (A) 4. (D) 5. (A)
6. (A) 7. (B) 8. (C) 9. (D) 10. (B)
11. (B) 12. (A) 13. (C) 14. (B) 15. (C)
16. (B) 17. (D) 18. (A) 19. (D) 20. (A)
21. (D) 22. (D) 23. (D) 24. (C)

24.2 Diffraction of Light

1. (B) 2. (C) 3. (C) 4. (C) 5. (C)
6. (B) 7. (C) 8. (C) 9. (A)

24.3 Polarization of Light

1. (A) 2. (D) 3. (A) 4. (C) 5. (A)
6. (C) 7. (B) 8. (D) 9. (C) 10. (A)

25.1 Photoelectric Effect

1. (C) 2. (A) 3. (C) 4. (D) 5. (B)
6. (B) 7. (A) 8. (D) 9. (A) 10. (B)
11. (B) 12. (C) 13. (D) 14. (A) 15. (D)
16. (B) 17. (B) 18. (A) 19. (None) 20. (A)

25.2 Matter Waves and X-Rays

1. (A) 2. (B) 3. (C) 4. (D) 5. (B)
6. (B) 7. (D) 8. (D) 9. (B) 10. (C)
11. (D) 12. (C) 13. (C) 14. (B) 15. (C)
16. (A)

26.1 Atomic Structure

1. (A) 2. (C) 3. (C) 4. (A) 5. (C)
6. (B) 7. (B) 8. (A) 9. (A) 10. (A)
11. (B) 12. (B) 13. (C) 14. (A) 15. (C)
16. (C) 17. (D) 18. (C) 19. (C) 20. (A)
21. (C) 22. (C) 23. (B) 24. (A) 25. (A)
26. (B)

27.1 Radioactivity

1. (A) 2. (A) 3. (A) 4. (A) 5. (D)
6. (A) 7. (C) 8. (B) 9. (A) 10. (D)
11. (D) 12. (D) 13. (A) 14. (C) 15. (D)
16. (B) 17. (B) 18. (C) 19. (B)

27.2 Nuclear Physics

1. (D) 2. (A) 3. (B) 4. (C) 5. (C)
6. (C) 7. (B) 8. (D) 9. (C) 10. (C)
11. (B) 12. (B) 13. (B) 14. (B) 15. (B)
16. (D) 17. (C) 18. (C) 19. (C) 20. (C)
21. (C) 22. (D) 23. (C)

28.1 Semiconductor

1. (C) 2. (C) 3. (C) 4. (C) 5. (B)
6. (A) 7. (D) 8. (C) 9. (B) 10. (C)
11. (A) 12. (D) 13. (A)

28.2 PN Junction and Diodes

1. (C) 2. (C) 3. (B) 4. (D) 5. (A)
6. (B) 7. (A) 8. (A) 9. (A) 10. (C)
11. (D) 12. (D) 13. (D) 14. (A) 15. (C)
16. (B)

28.3 Transistors

1. (A) 2. (D) 3. (D) 4. (A) 5. (B)
6. (C) 7. (B) 8. (B) 9. (C)

28.4 Logic Gates

1. (D) 2. (D) 3. (A) 4. (B) 5. (A)
6. (B) 7. (A) 8. (C) 9. (A) 10. (A)
11. (A) 12. (A) 13. (None) 14. (A) 15. (C)

29.1 Communication Systems

1. (B) 2. (A) 3. (A) 4. (B) 5. (D)
6. (A) 7. (C) 8. (B) 9. (B) 10. (B)

29.2 Modulation and Demodulation

1. (A) 2. (B) 3. (B) 4. (B) 5. (C)
6. (A) 7. (C) 8. (B) 9. (C)

30.1 Errors and Experiments

1. (D) 2. (A) 3. (D) 4. (A) 5. (A)
6. (C) 7. (A) 8. (D) 9. (D) 10. (B)
11. (A) 12. (B) 13. (D) 14. (A) 15. (D)
16. (B) 17. (C) 18. (D)

* * * * *

SOLUTIONS

1.1 Measurements and Dimensional Analysis

Sol. 1 (A) Torque $\tau = Fr \rightarrow [MLT^{-2}][L] = [ML^2T^{-2}]$
Work $W = Fs \rightarrow [MLT^{-2}][L] = [ML^2T^{-2}]$ } same

(B) Stress $= \dfrac{F}{A} \rightarrow \dfrac{[MLT^{-2}]}{[L^2]} = [ML^{-1}T^{-2}]$
Energy $\rightarrow$ [Work] $\rightarrow [ML^2T^{-2}]$ } different

(C) Force $\rightarrow [MLT^{-2}]$
Stress $\rightarrow [ML^{-1}T^{-2}]$ } different

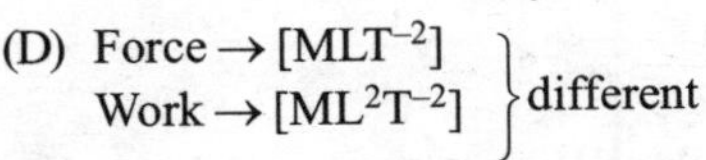

(D) Force $\rightarrow [MLT^{-2}]$
Work $\rightarrow [ML^2T^{-2}]$ } different

Ans. (A)

Sol. 2 (A) Torque $\tau = Fr \rightarrow [MLT^{-2}][L] = [ML^2T^{-2}]$
Work $W = Fs \rightarrow [ML^2T^{-2}]$ } same

(B) Momentum $P = mv \rightarrow [M][LT^{-2}] = [MLT^{-1}]$
Plank's constant $h = \dfrac{E}{\nu} \rightarrow \dfrac{[ML^2T^{-2}]}{[T^{-1}]} = [ML^2T^{-1}]$ } different

(C) Stresss $= \dfrac{F}{A} \rightarrow \dfrac{[MLT^{-2}]}{[L^2]} = [ML^{-1}T^{-2}]$
Young's modulus $Y = \dfrac{\text{Stress}}{\text{strain}} = [\text{stress}] = ML^{-1}T^{-2}]$ } same

(D) speed (m/s) and $\dfrac{1}{\sqrt{\mu_0 \in_0}}$ = speed of light (m/s) } same

Ans. (B)

Sol. 3 Speed of light in free space is given as

$$c = \frac{1}{\sqrt{\mu_0 \in_0}}$$

$$\Rightarrow \quad \frac{1}{\mu_0 \in_0} = c^2$$

$$\Rightarrow \quad D\left(\frac{1}{\mu_0 \in_0}\right) = D(c^2) = [LT^{-1}]^2 = [L^2T^{-2}]$$

Ans. (C)

Sol. 4 From stokes rule we have viscous force on a sphere of radius r moving at a speed v in a medium of coefficient of viscosity η is given as

$$F = 6\pi\eta rv$$

$$\Rightarrow \quad \eta = \frac{F}{6\pi rv}$$

$$\Rightarrow \quad D(\eta) = \frac{[F]}{[r][v]} = \frac{[MLT^{-2}]}{[L][LT^{-1}]} = [ML^{-1}T^{-1}]$$

Ans. (A)

Sol. 5 (A) Impulse $J = Ft \rightarrow [MLT^{-2}][T] = [MLT^{-1}]$
Momentum $P = mv \rightarrow [M][LT^{-1}] = [MLT^{-1}]$ } same

(B) Angular momentum $L = mvr \rightarrow [M][LT^{-1}][L] = [ML^2T^{-1}]$
Planck's constant $h = \dfrac{E}{\nu} \rightarrow \dfrac{[ML^2T^{-2}]}{[T^{-1}]} = [ML^2T^{-1}]$ } same

(C) Work $W \rightarrow [ML^2T^{-2}]$
Torque $\tau = Fr \rightarrow [MLT^{-2}][L] = [ML^2T^{-2}]$ } same

(D) Moment of inertia $I = Mr^2 \rightarrow [ML^2]$
Moment of a force $\tau = Fr \rightarrow [ML^2T^{-2}]$ } Different

Ans. (D)

Sol. 6 Dimensions of $\dfrac{ML^2}{Q^2}$ is given as

$$D\left(\frac{ML^2}{Q^2}\right) = \frac{[ML^2]}{[AT]^2} = [ML^2A^{-2}T^{-2}]$$

(A) Wb/m^2 $\rightarrow$ unit of magnetic induction (B)

$$D(B) = [MT^{-2}A^{-1}]$$

(B) Henry $\rightarrow$ unit for self Induction (L)

We use energy in inductance $E = \dfrac{1}{2}LI^2 \Rightarrow L = \dfrac{2E}{I^2}$

$$\Rightarrow \quad D(L) = \frac{[ML^{-2}T^{-2}]}{[A^2]} = [ML^2T^{-2}A^{-2}]$$

(C) H/m^2 $\rightarrow D\left(\dfrac{H}{m^2}\right) = \dfrac{[ML^2T^{-2}A^{-2}]}{[L^2]} = [MT^2A^{-2}]$

(D) Wb $\rightarrow$ unit for magnetic flux ϕ

$$\Rightarrow \quad D(\phi) = D(B.S)$$
$$= [MT^{-2}A^{-1}][L^2]$$
$$= [ML^2T^{-2}A^{-1}]$$

Ans. (B)

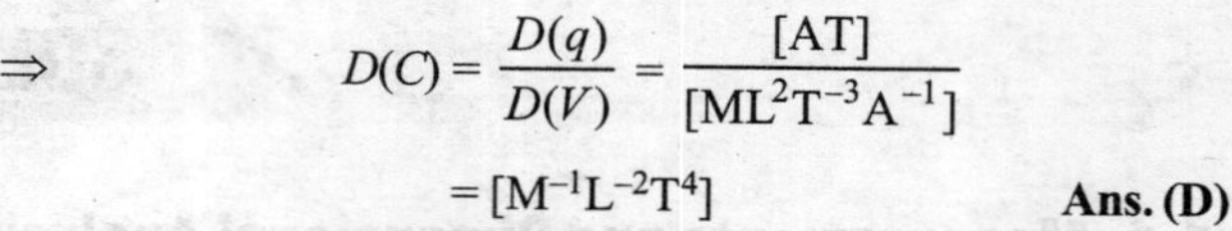

Sol. 7 The force on moving charge in magnetic field is given as $F = qvB$

$$\Rightarrow \quad B = \frac{F}{qv}$$

$$\Rightarrow \quad D[B] = \frac{[F]}{[q][v]} = \frac{[MLT^{-2}]}{[C][LT^{-1}]} = [MT^{-1}C^{-1}]$$ **Ans. (C)**

Sol. 8 If surface tension S is expressed in terms of K, V and T with dimensions a, b and c then we use

$$[S] = [K]^a [V]^b [T]^c$$

$$\Rightarrow \quad [MT^{-2}] = [ML^2T^{-2}]^a [LT^{-1}]^b [T]^c$$

Comparing dimensions on LHS & RHS we have

$$\Rightarrow \quad a = 1$$

$$2a + b = 0 \Rightarrow b = -2$$

$$-2a - b + c = -2 \Rightarrow c = 2a + b - 2 \Rightarrow c = -2$$

$$\Rightarrow \quad [S] = [K^1V^{-2}T^{-2}]$$ **Ans. (A)**

Sol. 9 By Coulomb's law we use the force between two point charges is given as

$$F = \frac{1}{4\pi \epsilon_0} \frac{q_1 q_2}{r^2}$$

$$\Rightarrow \quad \epsilon_0 = \frac{1}{4\pi} \frac{q_1 q_2}{Fr^2}$$

$$\Rightarrow \quad D(\epsilon_0) = \frac{[\text{charge}]^2}{[F][L^2]} = \frac{[IT]^2}{[MLT^{-2}][L^2]}$$

$$\Rightarrow \quad D(\epsilon_0) = [M^{-1}L^{-3}T^4I^2] = [M^{-1}L^{-3}T^4A^2]$$ **Ans. (B)**

Sol. 10 Angular momentum is expressed as

$$L = mvr$$

$$\Rightarrow \quad D[L] = [M][LT^{-1}][L] = [ML^2T^{-1}]$$

Latent heat of a substance is expressed as

$$L_f = \frac{Q}{m}$$

$$\Rightarrow \quad D(L_f) = \frac{[ML^2T^{-2}]}{[M]} = [L^2T^{-2}]$$

Capacitance is expressed as

$$C = \frac{q}{V}$$

Potential difference V is expressed as

$$V = \frac{W}{q}$$

$$\Rightarrow \quad D(V) = \frac{[ML^2T^{-2}]}{[AT]}$$

$$\Rightarrow \quad D(V) = [ML^2T^{-3}A^{-1}]$$

$$\Rightarrow \quad D(C) = \frac{D(q)}{D(V)} = \frac{[AT]}{[ML^2T^{-3}A^{-1}]}$$

$$= [M^{-1}L^{-2}T^4]$$ **Ans. (D)**

Sol. 11 Time period $t = r^b s^{c/2} d^{a/4}$ ...(1)

and it is also given that $t \propto \sqrt{\frac{d}{s}} = d^{1/2}s^{-1/2}$ ...(2)

$$t = kd^{1/2}s^{-1/2}$$ ...(3)

Here k involves the terms of r

From (1) and (3) we have

$$\frac{c}{2} = -\frac{1}{2} \Rightarrow c = -1$$

and $$\frac{a}{4} = \frac{1}{2} \Rightarrow a = 2$$

Writing dimensions of LHS & RHS in equation (1), gives

$$[T] = [L]^b[MT^{-2}]^{c/2}[ML^{-3}]^{a/4}$$

in above equation on RHS dimensions of L and M must be zero

$$\Rightarrow \quad b - \frac{3a}{4} = 0 \Rightarrow b = \frac{3a}{4} = \frac{3 \times 2}{4} = \frac{3}{2}$$ **Ans. (C)**

Sol. 12 Dimensions of R, h, $\in$ are

$$[R] = [ML^2T^{-3}I^{-2}]$$

$$[\in] = [M^{-1}L^{-3}T^4I^2]$$

$$[\mu] = [MLT^{-2}I^{-2}]$$

$$\Rightarrow \quad D\left(\frac{\mu}{\in}\right) = \frac{[MLT^{-2}I^{-2}]}{[M^{-1}L^{-3}T^4I^2]} = [M^2L^4T^{-6}I^{-4}]$$

$$= [R^2]$$ **Ans. (C)**

Sol. 13 Only a dimensionless constants (without units) have same values in different system of unit.

$$[e] = [IT]$$

$$[\epsilon_0] = [M^{-1}L^{-3}T^4I^2]$$

$$[h] = [ML^2T^{-1}]$$

$$[c] = [LT^{-1}]$$

$$[G] = [M^{-1}L^3T^{-2}]$$

We can also use $c = \dfrac{1}{\sqrt{\mu_0 \epsilon_0}}$

(A) $$D\left(\frac{ch}{2\pi \epsilon_0^2}\right) = \frac{[LT^{-1}][ML^2T^{-1}]}{[M^{-1}L^{-3}T^4I^2]}$$

→ Not dimensionless

(B) $$D\left(\frac{e^2}{2\pi \epsilon_0 \, Gm_e^2}\right) = \frac{[IT]^2}{[M^{-1}L^{-3}T^4I^2][M^{-1}L^3T^{-2}][M]^2}$$

→ Dimensionless

So this value does not change with system of units.

(C) $D\left(\frac{\mu_0 \in_0 G}{c^2 he^2}\right) = D\left(\frac{G}{c^4 he^2}\right)$

$$= \frac{[M^{-1}L^3T^{-2}]}{[LT^{-1}]^2[ML^2T^{-1}][IT]^2}$$

→ Not dimensionless

(D) $D\left(\frac{2\pi\sqrt{\mu_0 \in_0}}{ce^2}\frac{h}{G}\right) = D\left(\frac{h}{c^2e^2G}\right)$

$$= \frac{[M^1L^2T^{-1}]}{[LT^{-1}]^2[IT]^2[M^{-1}L^{-3}T^{-2}]}$$

→ Not dimensionless **Ans. (B)**

Sol. 14 By dimensional analysis we use

$$D(u) = [e]^a[a_0]^b[h]^c[c]^d$$

Comparing dimensions on LHS & RHS we have

$$\Rightarrow \quad c = -1$$

$$b + 2c + d = -2 \Rightarrow b = 1$$

$$a - c - d = 4 \Rightarrow d = -1$$

$$a = 2$$

$$\Rightarrow \quad u = e^2 a_0^{\,1} h^{-1}c^{-1}$$

$$\Rightarrow \quad u = \frac{e^2 a_0}{hc}$$ **Ans. (D)**

Sol. 15 Here we use

$$\mu_0 = ke^am^bc^ch^d$$

As speed of light $c = \frac{1}{\sqrt{\mu_0 \in_0}}$

$$\Rightarrow \quad D(\mu_0) = \frac{1}{D(c)^2.D(\in_0)}$$

Then to find dimensions of e, m, c and h we compare the dimensions on LHS & RHS

$$\Rightarrow \quad D(\mu_0) = [IT]^a[M]^b[LT^{-1}]^c[ML^2T^{-1}]^d$$

$$\Rightarrow \quad [MLT^{-2}I^{-2}] = [IT]^a[M]^b[LT^{-1}]^c[ML^2T^{-1}]^d$$

$$\Rightarrow \quad b + d = 1 \Rightarrow b = 0$$

$$c + 2d = 1 \Rightarrow d = 1$$

$$a - c - d = -2 \Rightarrow c + d = 0 \Rightarrow c = -1$$

$$a = -2$$

$$\Rightarrow \quad \mu_0 = ke^{-2}m^0c^{-1}h^1$$

$$\Rightarrow \quad \mu_0 = k\left(\frac{h}{ce^2}\right)$$ **Ans. (C)**

Sol. 16 Resistance of a conductor is given as

$$R = \rho\frac{l}{A}$$

Conductivity $\sigma = \frac{1}{\rho} = \frac{l}{RA}$

by Ohm's law $V = IR \Rightarrow R = \frac{V}{I}$

$$\Rightarrow \quad \sigma = \frac{lI}{VA} \quad \text{(for dimensions)}$$

Electric potential $V = \frac{W}{q}$

$$\Rightarrow \quad D(V) = \frac{[ML^2T^{-2}]}{[I][T]} = [ML^2T^{-3}I^{-1}]$$

and $D(\sigma) = \frac{[L][I]}{[V][L^2]} = \frac{[L][I]}{[ML^2T^{-3}I^{-1}][L^2]}$

$$= [M^{-1}L^{-3}I^2T^3]$$ **Ans. (B)**

Sol. 17 From given equation $[BD]$ → dimensionless

and $[AD] \equiv [C]$

(A) $D\left[\frac{C}{BD}\right] \equiv D[C]$ and $D\left[\frac{AD^2}{C}\right] = D[D]$

$$\Rightarrow \quad \underbrace{\frac{C}{BD}}_{[C]} - \underbrace{\frac{AD^2}{C}}_{[D]}$$

⇒ Two physical quantities having different dimensions are subtracted here so this is not a meaningful quantity.

(B) $D(A^2) \equiv D\left(\frac{C^2}{D^2}\right)$ and $D(B^2C^2] \equiv D\left(\frac{C^2}{D^2}\right)$

$$\Rightarrow \quad \underbrace{A^2}_{\left[\frac{C^2}{D^2}\right]} - \underbrace{B^2C^2}_{\left[\frac{C^2}{D^2}\right]}$$

⇒ This equation is dimensionally homogeneous, so it is meaningful

(C) $D\left(\frac{A}{B}\right) \equiv D(AD)$ and $D(C) \equiv D(AD)$

$$\Rightarrow \quad \underbrace{\frac{A}{B}}_{[AD]} - \underbrace{C}_{[AD]}$$

⇒ This equation is dimensionally homogeneous.

This is a meaningful quantity.

(D) $D(A) \neq D(C)$

⇒ A-C will not give a meaningful quantity. **Ans. (A) & (D)**

2.1 Motion in One Dimension

Sol. 1 Considering uniform retardation

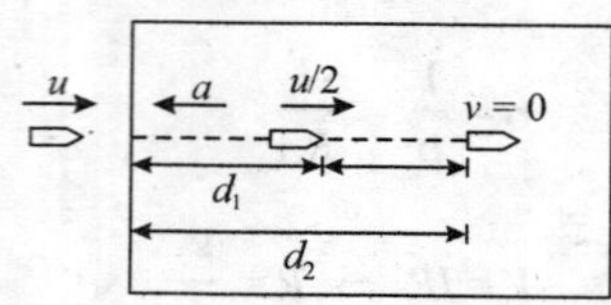

We use $v^2 = u^2 - 2ad$

Initially $\left(\frac{u}{2}\right)^2 = u^2 - 2ad_1$

$\Rightarrow \quad \frac{3}{4}u^2 = 2a(3)$

$\Rightarrow \quad a = \frac{u^2}{8}$

Finally $(0)^2 = u^2 - 2ad_2$

$\Rightarrow \quad d_2 = 4$ cm

$\Rightarrow$ more distance is $d_2 - d_1 = 4 - 3 = 1$ cm **Ans. (A)**

Sol. 2

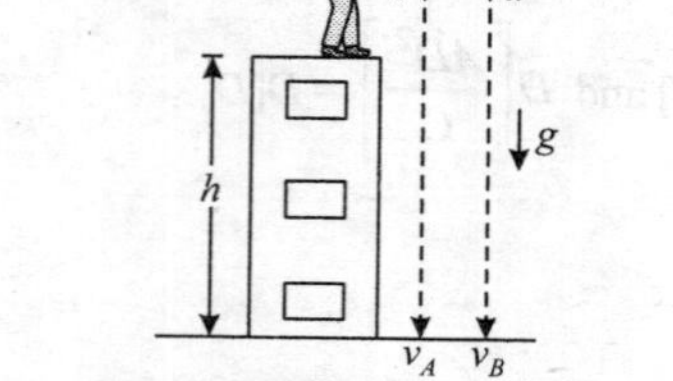

for both balls A & B, we use

$$v^2 = u^2 + 2gh$$

$\Rightarrow \quad v_A = v_B$ **Ans. (B)**

Sol. 3

u, $v_f = 0$, s, a

$$s_1 = \frac{u^2}{2a}$$

for car having initial speed $4u$

$$s_2 = \frac{(4u)^2}{2a} = \frac{8u^2}{a}$$

$$\frac{s_1}{s_2} = \frac{1}{16}$$ **Ans. (D)**

Sol. 4 We use $v^2 = u^2 - 2as$; a = constant

For stopping $v = 0$

$\Rightarrow$ stopping distance

$$s = \frac{u^2}{2a}$$

$\Rightarrow \quad s \propto u^2$

if u becomes doubled

$\Rightarrow \quad s_f = 4s_i = 4 \times 6 = 24$ m **Ans. (C)**

Sol. 5

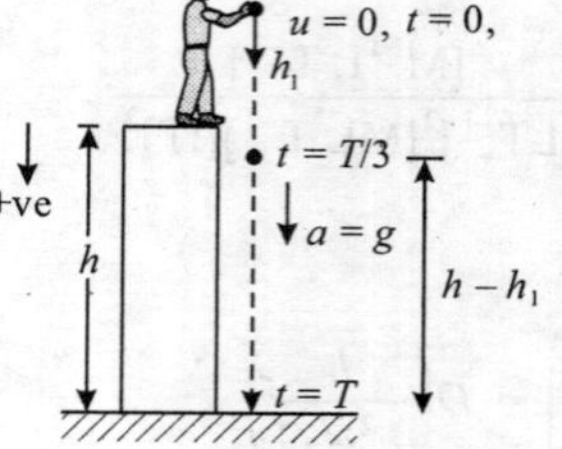

We use $h = ut + \frac{1}{2}gt^2 = \frac{1}{2}gt^2$

$$h = \frac{1}{2}gT^2$$

at $t = T/3, h = h_1$

$$\Rightarrow \quad h_1 = \frac{1}{2}g\left(\frac{T}{3}\right)^2 = \frac{1}{2}g\left(\frac{T}{9}\right)^2 = \frac{h}{9}$$

distance from ground $h - h_1 = h - \frac{h}{9} = \frac{8h}{9}$ **Ans. (C)**

Sol. 6 With reference to solution of question 4 came in 2003, we use

stopping distance $s \propto u^2$

As u is getting doubled

$\Rightarrow \quad s_f = 4s_i$

$s_f = 4 \times 20$

$= 80$ m **Ans. (D)**

Sol. 7 We are given $t = ax^2 + bx$

differentiate w.r.t. to time gives

$$1 = 2ax\left(\frac{dx}{dt}\right) + b\left(\frac{dx}{dt}\right) \quad \ldots(1)$$

$$\Rightarrow \quad x = \frac{1 - b\left(\frac{dx}{dt}\right)}{2a\left(\frac{dx}{dt}\right)}$$

again differentiating equation-(1) w.r.t. to time gives

$$0 = 2a\left[\left(\frac{dx}{dt}\right)^2 + x\left(\frac{d^2x}{dt^2}\right)\right] + b\left[\frac{d^2x}{dt^2}\right]$$

Acceleration is given as

$$\Rightarrow \quad a_c = \frac{d^2x}{dt^2} = \frac{-2a\left(\frac{dx}{dt}\right)^2}{2ax + b}$$

[considering $v = dx/dt$]

$$a_c = \frac{-2av^2}{2a\left(\frac{1 - bv}{2av}\right) + b} = -2av^3$$ **Ans. (C)**

Sol. 8 We draw *v-t* curve for motion of car as shown in figure and for first part of journey, we use

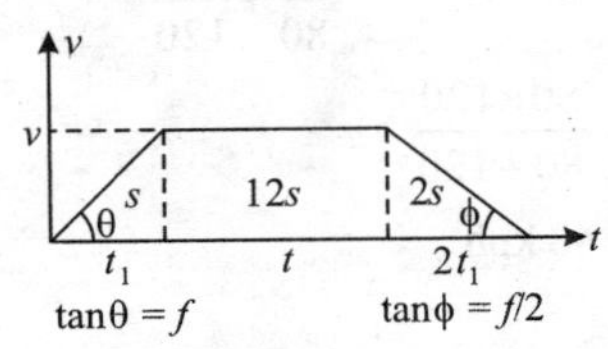

$$v = \sqrt{2fs}$$

$$\Rightarrow \quad 12s = vt$$

$$\Rightarrow \quad 12s = \sqrt{2fs}\,.\,t$$

$$\Rightarrow \quad 144s^2 = 2fs.\,t^2$$

$$\Rightarrow \quad s = \frac{1}{72}ft^2$$

Ans. (C)

Sol. 9 Average acceleration is given as

$$\bar{a} = \left|\frac{\vec{v}_f - \vec{v}_i}{\Delta t}\right| = \frac{|\Delta\vec{v}|}{\Delta t} = \frac{5\sqrt{2}}{10}\text{ m/s}^2$$

$$\bar{a} = \frac{1}{\sqrt{2}}\text{ m/s}^2$$

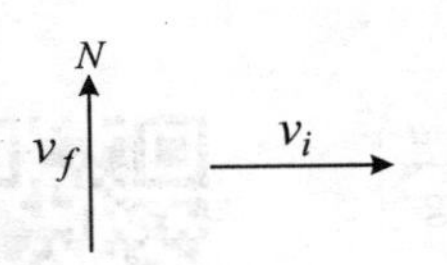

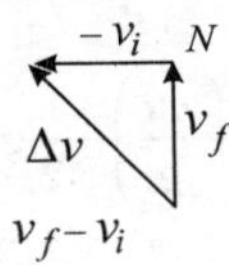

here $\quad |\overrightarrow{\Delta v}| = \sqrt{5^2 + 5^2} = 5\sqrt{2}$ m/s

along N-W direction. **Ans. (A)**

Sol. 10 We use $\quad v^2 = u^2 - 2ah$

(for motion after parachute opens)

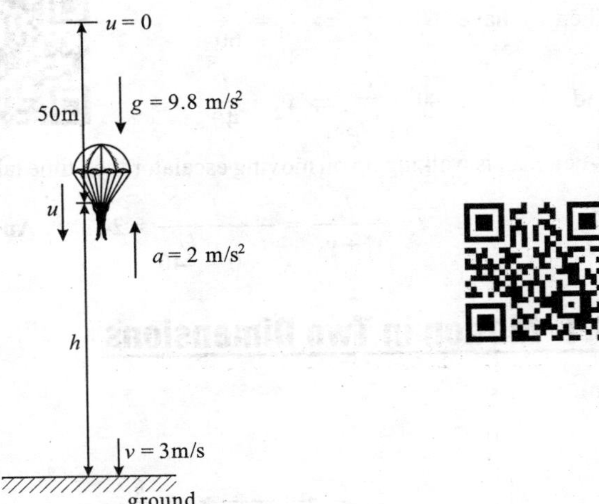

Here we use $\quad u = \sqrt{2gs} = \sqrt{2\times 9.8\times 50} = \sqrt{980}$ m/s

$$\Rightarrow \quad (3)^2 = 980 - 2\times 2\times h$$

$$\Rightarrow \quad h = \frac{971}{4} = 242.7\text{ m}$$

Total height $\quad h_T = 242.7 + 50 = 292.7$ m **Ans. (C)**

Sol. 11 We are given $v = \alpha\sqrt{x}$

$$\Rightarrow \quad \frac{dx}{dt} = \alpha\sqrt{x}$$

$$\Rightarrow \quad \frac{dx}{\sqrt{x}} = \alpha dt$$

Integrating above relation gives

$$\int_{x=0}^{x=x}\frac{dx}{\sqrt{x}} = \int_{t=0}^{t=t}\alpha dt$$

$$\Rightarrow \quad [2\sqrt{x}]_0^x = \alpha[t]_0^t$$

$$\Rightarrow \quad 2\sqrt{x} = \alpha t$$

$$\Rightarrow \quad x = \frac{1}{4}\alpha^2 t^2$$

$$\Rightarrow \quad x \propto t^2$$

Ans. (C)

Sol. 12 We are given $v = v_0 + gt + ft^2$

$$\Rightarrow \quad \frac{dx}{dt} = v_0 + gt + ft^2$$

$$\Rightarrow \quad dx = (v_0 + gt + ft^2)\,dt$$

integrating above relation gives

$$\int_{x=0}^{x=x} dx = \int_{t=0}^{t=1}(v_0 + gt + ft^2)dt$$

$$\Rightarrow \quad x = \left[v_0 t + \frac{1}{2}gt^2 + \frac{1}{3}ft^3\right]_0^1$$

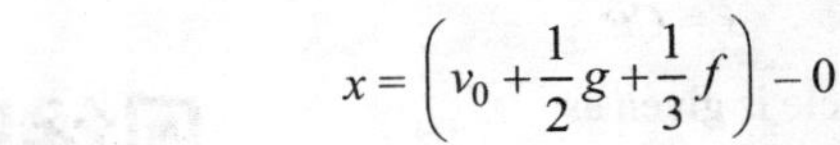

$$\Rightarrow \quad x = \left(v_0 + \frac{1}{2}g + \frac{1}{3}f\right) - 0$$

Ans. (B)

Sol. 13 Deceleration of particle is

$$a = \frac{dv}{dt} = -2.5\sqrt{v}$$

$$\Rightarrow \quad \frac{dv}{\sqrt{v}} = -2.5\,dt$$

Integrating above relation gives

$$\int_{6.25}^{0}\frac{dv}{\sqrt{v}} = \int_{t=0}^{t=t} -2.5dt$$

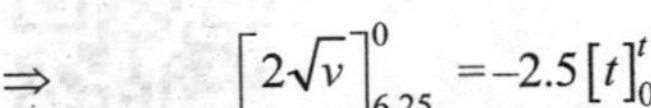

$$\Rightarrow \quad \left[2\sqrt{v}\right]_{6.25}^{0} = -2.5\left[t\right]_0^t$$

$$\Rightarrow \quad -2\times 2.5 = -2.5t \Rightarrow t = 2\text{s}$$

Ans. (B)

Sol. 14 As train is moving at constant acceleration, we use

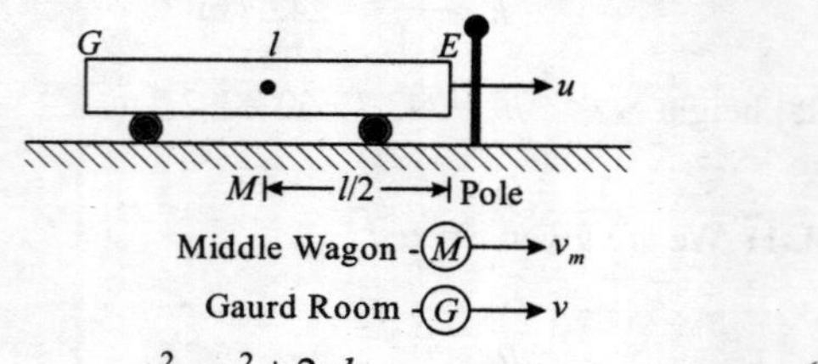

$$v^2 = u^2 + 2al \quad \dots(1)$$

and $$v_m^2 = u^2 + 2a(l/2) \quad \dots(2)$$

from (1) $$al = \frac{v^2 - u^2}{2}$$

from (2) $$v_m^2 = u^2 + \frac{v^2 - u^2}{2}$$

$\Rightarrow$ $$v_m = \sqrt{\frac{u^2 + v^2}{2}}$$ **Ans. (D)**

Sol. 15 As graph is a straight line the instantaneous velocity is equal to the average velocity.

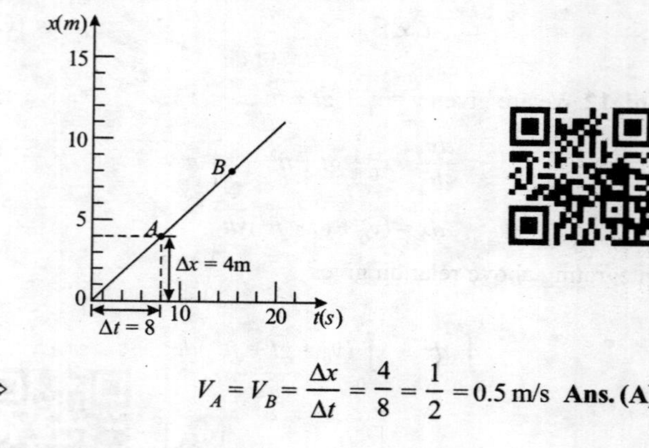

$\Rightarrow$ $$V_A = V_B = \frac{\Delta x}{\Delta t} = \frac{4}{8} = \frac{1}{2} = 0.5 \text{ m/s}$$ **Ans. (A)**

Sol. 16 We are given that

$$x = Ct^3$$

Velocity of particle is given as

$$v = \frac{dx}{dt} = 3Ct^2$$

$\Rightarrow$ Acceleration of particle

$$a = \frac{dv}{dt} = 6Ct \Rightarrow a \propto t$$ **Ans. (B)**

Sol. 17 Total time taken

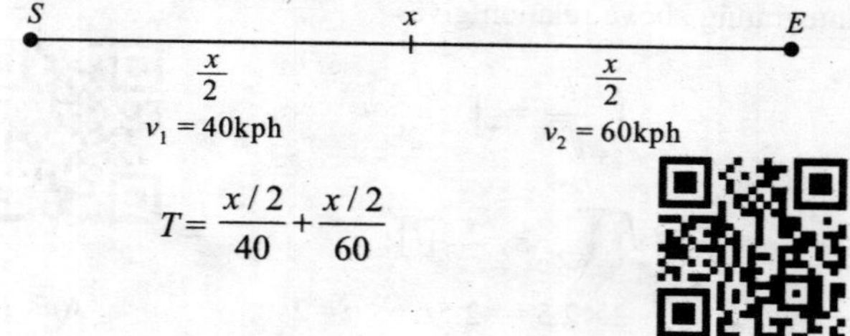

$$T = \frac{x/2}{40} + \frac{x/2}{60}$$

$$\text{Average speed} = \frac{\text{distance}}{\text{time}} = \frac{x}{\frac{x}{80} + \frac{x}{120}}$$

$$= \frac{80 \times 120}{80 + 120}$$

$$= 48 \text{ kph}$$ **Ans. (C)**

Sol. 18

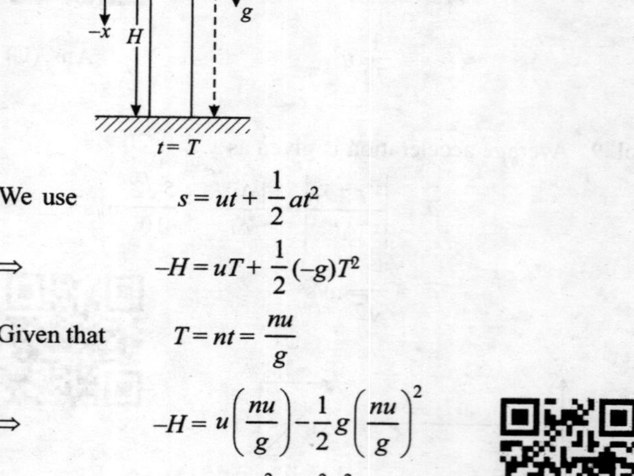

We use $$s = ut + \frac{1}{2}at^2$$

$\Rightarrow$ $$-H = uT + \frac{1}{2}(-g)T^2$$

Given that $$T = nt = \frac{nu}{g}$$

$\Rightarrow$ $$-H = u\left(\frac{nu}{g}\right) - \frac{1}{2}g\left(\frac{nu}{g}\right)^2$$

$\Rightarrow$ $$H = -\frac{nu^2}{g} + \frac{n^2u^2}{2g}$$

$\Rightarrow$ $$2gH = nu^2(n-2)$$ **Ans. (C)**

Sol. 19 If length of escalator is l and velocity of man's walks is v_1 and velocity escalator's motion is v_2.

Then we have $$60 = \frac{l}{v_1} \Rightarrow v_1 = \frac{l}{60}$$

and $$40 = \frac{l}{v_2} \Rightarrow v_2 = \frac{l}{40}$$

When man is walking up on moving escalator then time taken is

$$t = \frac{l}{v_1 + v_2} = \frac{l}{l/60 + l/40} = 24 \text{ s}$$ **Ans. (C)**

3.1 Motion in Two Dimensions

Sol. 1

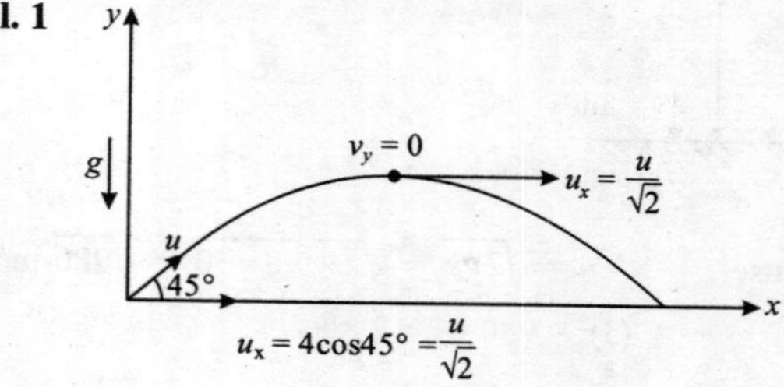

Initial KE of ball $E = \frac{1}{2}mu^2$

KE of ball at highest point of flight

$$E_H = \frac{1}{2}m\left(\frac{u}{\sqrt{2}}\right)^2 = \frac{1}{4}mu^2 = E/2 \quad \textbf{Ans. (C)}$$

Sol. 2

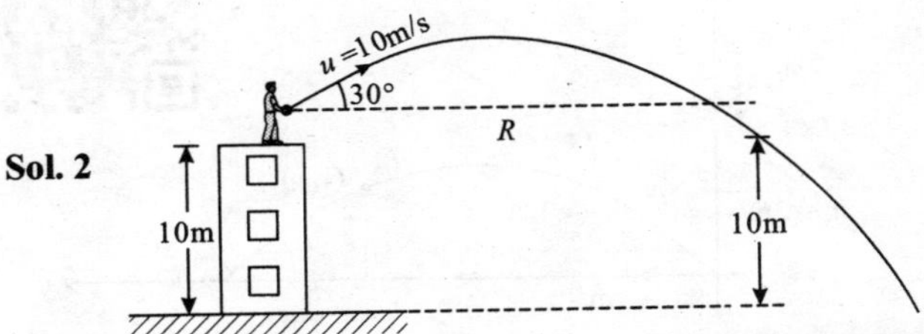

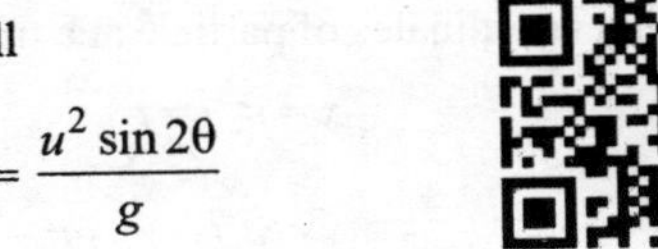

Horizontal Range of ball

$$R = \frac{u^2 \sin 2\theta}{g}$$

$$\Rightarrow \quad R = \frac{(10)^2 \sin(60°)}{10} = 10 \times \frac{\sqrt{3}}{2} = 5\sqrt{3}\text{ m}$$

$$\Rightarrow \quad R = 8.66\text{ m} \quad \textbf{Ans. (D)}$$

Sol. 3 As $\quad x = \alpha t^3;\quad y = \beta t^3$

$$v_x = \frac{dx}{dt} = 3\alpha t^2;\quad v_y = \frac{dy}{dt} = 3\beta t^2$$

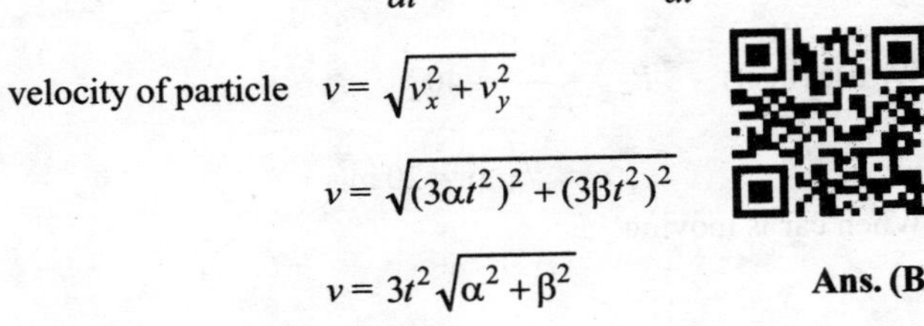

velocity of particle $\quad v = \sqrt{v_x^2 + v_y^2}$

$$v = \sqrt{(3\alpha t^2)^2 + (3\beta t^2)^2}$$

$$v = 3t^2\sqrt{\alpha^2 + \beta^2} \quad \textbf{Ans. (B)}$$

Sol. 4

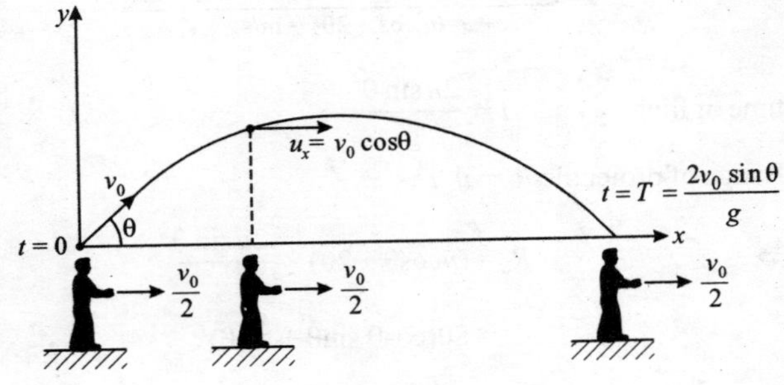

$$R = \frac{v_0}{2}T$$

$$\Rightarrow \quad \frac{v_0^2 \sin 2\theta}{g} = \frac{v_0}{2} \times \frac{2v_0 \sin\theta}{g}$$

$$2\sin\theta\cos\theta = \sin\theta \Rightarrow \cos\theta = 1/2$$

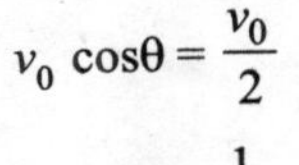

Person will be able to catch the ball if

$$v_0 \cos\theta = \frac{v_0}{2}$$

$$\Rightarrow \quad \cos\theta = \frac{1}{2}$$

$$\Rightarrow \quad \theta = 60° \quad \textbf{Ans. (A)}$$

Sol. 5 $\quad \vec{A}\times\vec{B} - \vec{B}\times\vec{A} = 0$

$$\Rightarrow \quad \vec{A}\times\vec{B} + \vec{A}\times\vec{B} = 0$$

$$\Rightarrow \quad 2(\vec{A}\times\vec{B}) = 0$$

$$\Rightarrow \quad \vec{A}\times\vec{B} = 0$$

$$\Rightarrow \quad AB\sin\theta = 0$$

$\Rightarrow$ Either $A = 0$ or $B = 0$ or $\theta = 0, \pi, 2\pi$ **Ans. (C)**

Sol. 6 Same range of projectile angles are complementary θ, $90 - \theta$ so time of flight in the two cases are

$$T_1 = \frac{2u\sin\theta}{g}$$

and $$T_2 = \frac{2u\cos\theta}{g}$$

here $$T_1T_2 = \frac{4u^2\sin\theta\cos\theta}{g^2} = \frac{2u^2\sin 2\theta}{g^2} = \frac{2R}{g}$$

$$\Rightarrow \quad T_1T_2 \propto R \quad \textbf{Ans. (A)}$$

Sol. 7

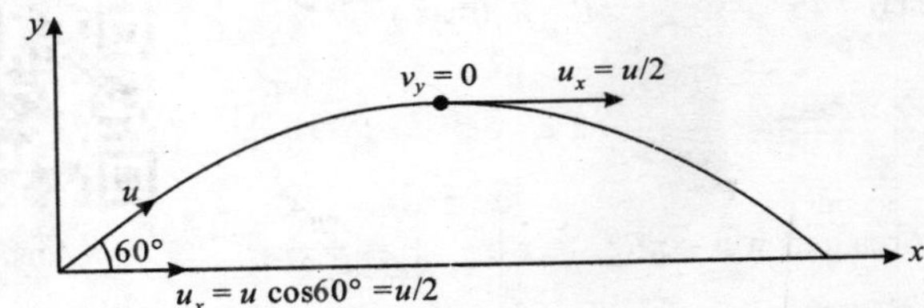

Initial kE $\quad K = \frac{1}{2}mu^2$

KE of particle at highest point

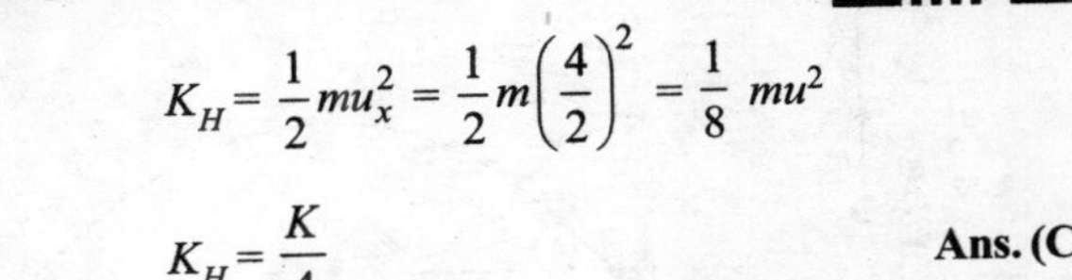

$$K_H = \frac{1}{2}mu_x^2 = \frac{1}{2}m\left(\frac{4}{2}\right)^2 = \frac{1}{8}mu^2$$

$$\Rightarrow \quad K_H = \frac{K}{4} \quad \textbf{Ans. (C)}$$

Sol. 8 We can use vector speed equation

$$\vec{v} = \vec{u} + \vec{a}\,t$$

After 10 s, find velocity is

$$\vec{v} = (3\hat{i} + 4\hat{j}) + (0.4\hat{i} + 0.3\hat{j}) \times 10$$

$$\vec{v} = 7\hat{i} + 7\hat{j}$$

$$|\vec{v}| = \sqrt{7^2 + 7^2}$$

$$= 7\sqrt{2} \text{ units}$$

Ans. (A)

Sol. 9 We are given velocity components of particle as

$$v_x = \frac{dx}{dt} = Ky \quad \ldots(1)$$

and $$v_y = \frac{dy}{dt} = Kx \quad \ldots(2)$$

By (1)/(2) $\Rightarrow$ $$\frac{dx}{dy} = \frac{y}{x}$$

$$x\,dx = y\,dy$$

integrating above relation gives

$$\int x\,dx = \int y\,dx$$

$$\Rightarrow \quad \frac{x^2}{2} = \frac{y^2}{2} + C$$

$$\Rightarrow \quad x^2 = y^2 + C$$

$$\Rightarrow \quad y^2 = x^2 + C_1$$

Ans. (D)

Sol. 10

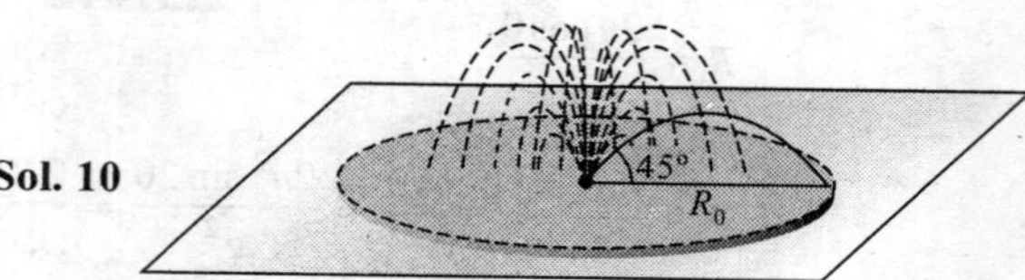

Maximum horizontal range

$$R = \frac{u^2 \sin 2\theta}{g}$$

at $\theta = 45° \rightarrow$ $$R = R_0 \text{(max.)}$$

$$\Rightarrow \quad R_0 = \frac{u^2}{g}$$

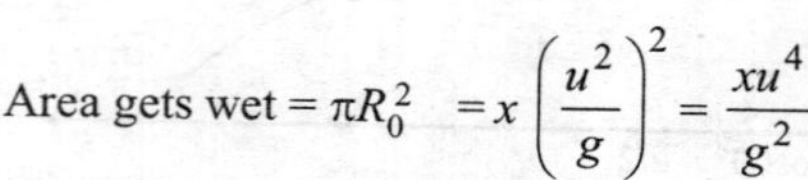

Area gets wet $= \pi R_0^2 = x\left(\frac{u^2}{g}\right)^2 = \frac{xu^4}{g^2}$

Ans. (A)

Sol. 11

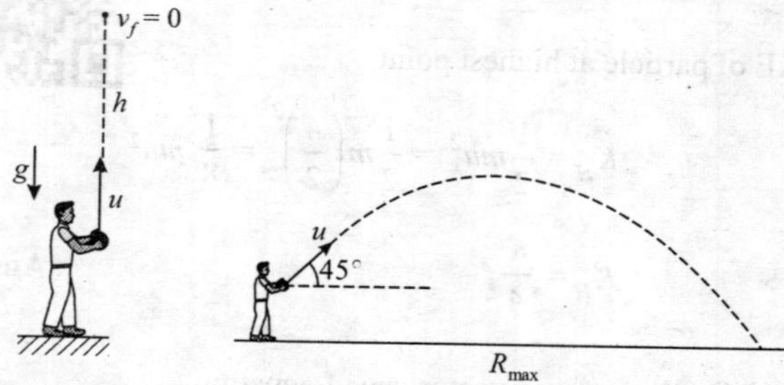

When stories thrown up, maximum height is given as

$$h = \frac{u^2}{2g} = 10 \text{ m}$$

$$\Rightarrow \quad u^2 = 200$$

For projectile maximum range is given for same projection speed, is

$$R_{max} = \frac{u^2}{g} = \frac{200}{10} = 20 \text{ m}$$

Ans. (D)

Sol. 12

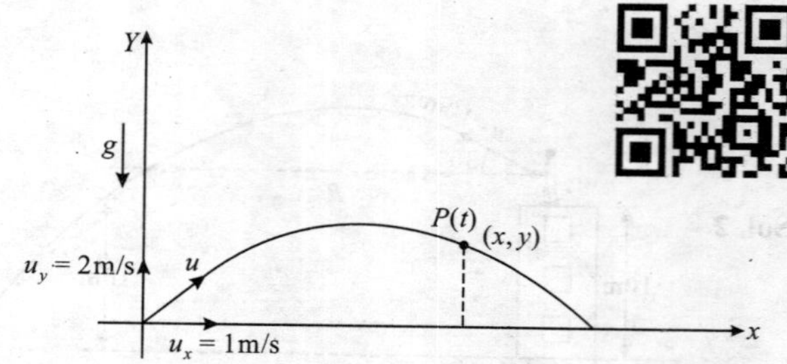

Position coordinates of particle at a time t are

$$x = u_x t = t \quad \ldots(1)$$

and $$y = u_y t - \frac{1}{2} gt^2 - 5t^2 \quad \ldots(2)$$

Eliminating t we get

$$\Rightarrow \quad y = 2x - 5x^2$$

Ans. (A)

Sol. 13 When car is at rest

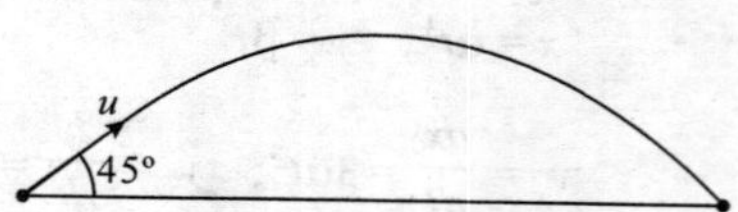

We use (max) $$R_{max} = \frac{u^2}{g} = 40$$

$$\Rightarrow \quad u = \sqrt{400} = 20 \text{ m/s}$$

When car is moving

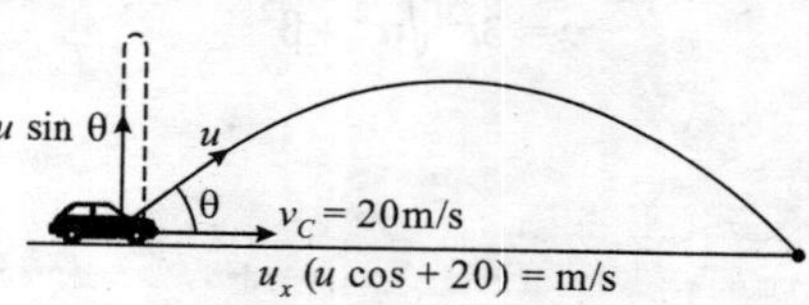

time of flight $$t = \frac{2u\sin\theta}{g}$$

Range of projectile $R_x = u_x t$

$$\Rightarrow \quad R_x = (u\cos\theta + 20) \times \frac{2u\sin\theta}{g}$$

$$= 80(\cos\theta \sin\theta + \sin\theta)$$

$$\Rightarrow \quad R_x = 80\left[\frac{1}{2}\sin 2\theta + \sin\theta\right]$$

R_x is max when $\frac{dR_x}{d\theta} = 0$

$$\frac{dR_x}{d\theta} = 80[\cos 2\theta + \cos\theta]$$

$\Rightarrow \quad \cos 2\theta = -\cos\theta$

$\Rightarrow \quad \cos 2\theta = \cos(180 - \theta) \Rightarrow 2\theta = 180 - \theta$

$\Rightarrow \quad \theta = 60°$ **Ans. (B)**

Sol. 14

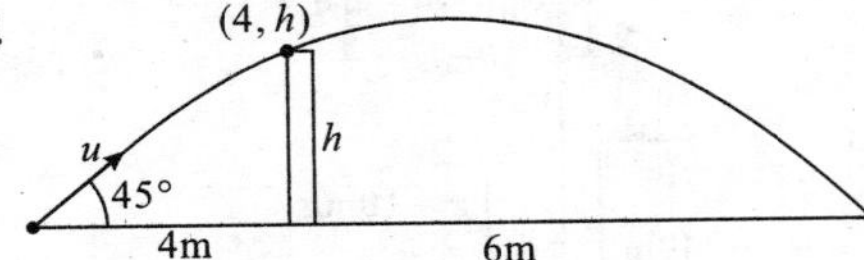

Maximum Range of projectile is

$$\frac{u^2}{g} = 10$$

$$\Rightarrow \quad u = \sqrt{100} = 10 \text{ m/s}$$

Equation of trajectory of projectile

$$y = x\tan\theta - \frac{gx^2}{2u^2\cos^2\theta}$$

$$\Rightarrow \quad y = x - \frac{10x^2}{2(10)^2\left(\frac{1}{\sqrt{2}}\right)^2}$$

$$\Rightarrow \quad y = x - \frac{x^2}{10}$$

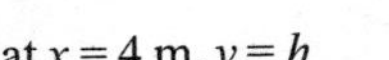

at $x = 4$ m, $y = h$

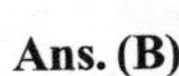

$$\Rightarrow \quad h = 4 - \frac{16}{10} = 2.4 \text{ m}$$ **Ans. (B)**

Sol. 15

As θ small the time taken by bullet to hit the target is

$$t = \frac{700}{4\cos\theta} = \frac{700}{630} = \frac{10}{9} \text{ s}$$

($\cos\theta \sim 1$ for small θ)

Distance fallen by bullet in time t is

$$h = \frac{1}{2}gt^2$$

$$= \frac{1}{2} \times 10 \times \left(\frac{10}{9}\right)^2 = 6.1 \text{ m}$$ **Ans. (C)**

Alternative :

Considering projectile motion we use

$$\frac{u^2 \sin 2\theta}{g} = 700 \text{ m}$$

$$\frac{u^2(2\sin\theta\cos\theta)}{g} = 700$$

For small θ, we take $\cos\theta \sim 1$ and $\sin\theta \sim \tan\theta$

$$\Rightarrow \quad 2\sin\theta = \frac{700 \times 10}{(630)^2}$$

here $\quad \tan\theta = \frac{h}{700}$

$$\Rightarrow \quad h = 700\tan\theta \text{ m}$$

$$\Rightarrow \quad h \simeq 700\sin\theta$$

$$\Rightarrow \quad h = 700 \times \frac{700 \times 10}{2 \times (630)^2} = 6.1 \text{ m}$$ **Ans. (C)**

Sol. 16

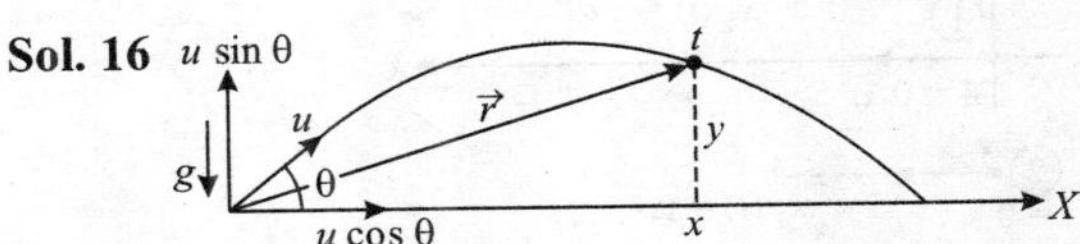

For a given projectile position vector at time t is given as

$$\vec{r} = (u\cos\theta . t)\,\hat{i} + \left(u\sin\theta \cdot t - \frac{1}{2}gt^2\right)\hat{i}$$

$$\vec{r} = 40\hat{i} + 50\hat{j} \text{ (given at } 2s)$$

By Comparing with given values

$$u\cos\theta(2) = 40$$

$$\Rightarrow \quad u\cos\theta = 20 \qquad \ldots(1)$$

$$u\sin\theta(2) - 20 = 50 \qquad \ldots(2)$$

By (2)/(1) $\Rightarrow \quad \tan\theta = \frac{35}{20} = \frac{7}{4}$ **Ans. (C)**

Sol. 17 $|\vec{A}| = |\vec{B}| = A$

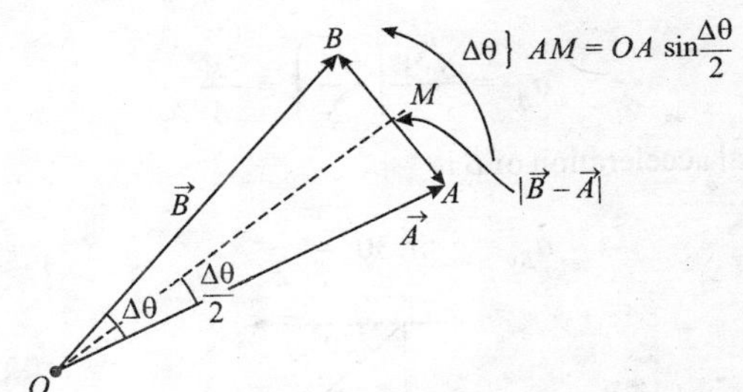

$$|\vec{A}| = |\vec{B}| = A$$

The magnitude of $\vec{B} - \vec{A}$ is given as

$$|\vec{B} - \vec{A}| = AB = 2A\sin\left(\frac{\Delta\theta}{2}\right)$$

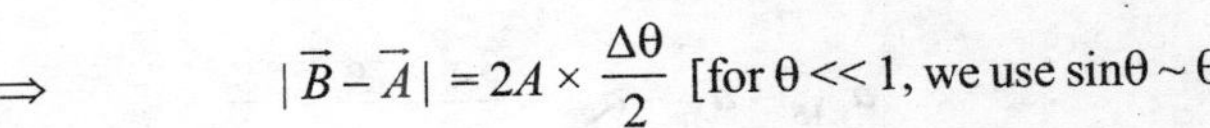

$$\Rightarrow \quad |\vec{B} - \vec{A}| = 2A \times \frac{\Delta\theta}{2} \quad [\text{for } \theta << 1, \text{ we use } \sin\theta \sim \theta]$$

$$\Rightarrow \quad |\vec{B} - \vec{A}| = A\,\Delta\theta$$ **Ans. (A)**

Alternatively : From below figure it can be directly seen the magnitude of $|\vec{B}-\vec{A}| = A\,\Delta\theta$.

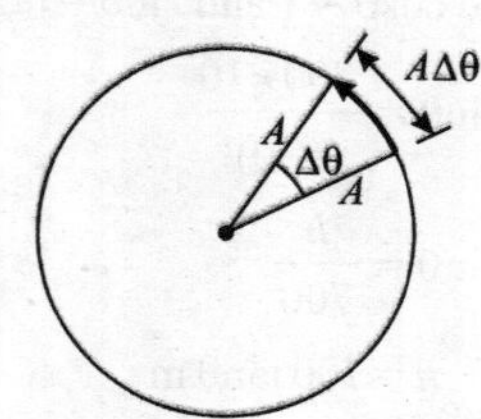

3.2 Relative Motion

Sol. 1

$x_1(t) = \frac{1}{2}at^2$

① $4 = 0, a$ $\quad t \quad X$

② $t = 0$ $\quad x_2(t) = vt$

$t=0 \qquad x_2(t) = vt$

$$\Rightarrow \quad x_1 - x_2 = \frac{1}{2}at^2 - vt$$

at $t = 0+$ we have $x_1 - x_2 \to -\text{ve}$

Initially $x_1 - x_2$ is negative in option-(B) only. **Ans. (B)**

Sol. 2 Vertical acceleration of A is

$$a_{Ay} = g\sin 60° = \frac{\sqrt{3}g}{2}$$

$$\Rightarrow \quad a_{Ay} = \frac{\sqrt{3}g}{2}\left(\frac{\sqrt{3}}{2}\right) = \frac{3g}{4}$$

Vertical acceleration of B is

$$a_{By} = g\sin 30° = \frac{g}{2}$$

$$\Rightarrow \quad a_{By} = \frac{g}{2}\left(\frac{1}{2}\right) = \frac{g}{4}$$

Acceleration of B w.r.t. A is vertical direction is

$$a_{yAB} = a_{Ay} - a_{By} = \frac{3g}{u} - \frac{g}{u} = \frac{g}{2}$$

$$= 4.9 \text{ m/s}^2$$

Ans. (D)

Sol. 3 For $u = 10$ m/s, $h_1 = \frac{u_1^2}{2g} = \frac{100}{2\times 10} = 5$ m

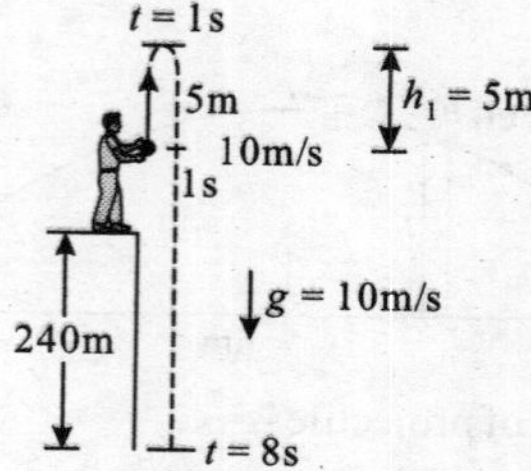

Time of downward journey

$$t_2 = \sqrt{\frac{2h}{g}}$$

$$t_2 = \sqrt{\frac{2\times 245}{10}} = 7 \text{ s}$$

For $u = 40$ m/s, $h_2 = \frac{u^2}{2g} = \frac{(40)^2}{2\times 10} = 80$ m

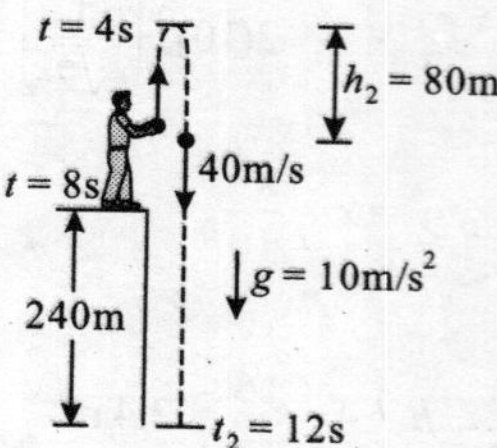

Time for downward journey of stone

$$t_2 = \sqrt{\frac{2h}{g}}$$

$$t_2 = \sqrt{\frac{2\times 320}{10}} = 8\text{s}$$

If y_1 and y_2 are height above ground for the two stones, we have

$$y_1 = 240 + (10t - 5t^2)$$
$$y_1 = 240 + 10t - 5t^2$$
$$y_2 = 240 + (40t - 5t^2)$$
$$y_2 = 240 + 40t - 5t^2$$

$\Rightarrow$ from $t = 0$ to $t = 8$ s when first stone reaches ground

$$y_2 - y_1 = 30t$$

at $\quad t = 8\text{s} \qquad y_2 - y_1 = 240\text{ m}$

after $t = 8$s, first stone is at rest $\Rightarrow y_1 = 0$

$$\Rightarrow \qquad \Delta y = y_2 - y_1 = 240 + 40t - 5t^2$$

slope of graph

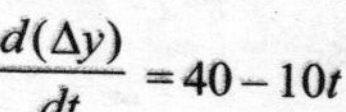

$$\frac{d(\Delta y)}{dt} = 40 - 10t$$

As for $t > 8$ s slope of graph is increasing **Ans. (C)**

4.1 Newton's Laws of Motion

Sol. 1 As particle remain stationary

$$\Rightarrow \quad \vec{F_1}+\vec{F_2}+\vec{F_3}=0$$

$$\vec{F_1}+\vec{F_R}=0$$

$$\vec{F_1}=-\vec{F_R}$$

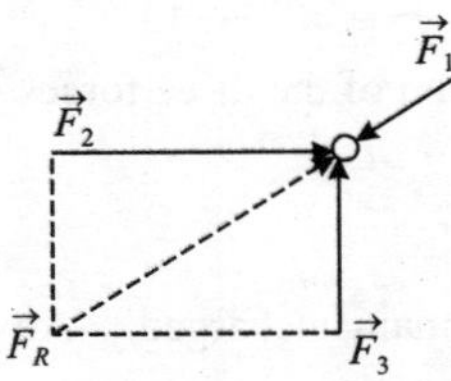

when $\vec{F_1}$ is removed, particle will move in under the influence of $\vec{F_R}$

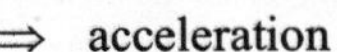

$\Rightarrow$ acceleration

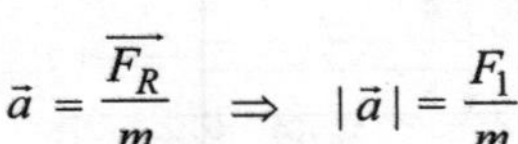

$$\vec{a}=\frac{\vec{F_R}}{m} \Rightarrow |\vec{a}|=\frac{F_1}{m}$$ **Ans. (A)**

Sol. 2

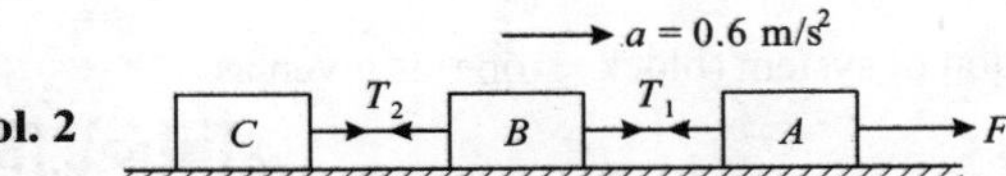

For block C, its equation of motion is

$$T_2=m_C a$$
$$=2\times 0.6$$
$$=1.2\,\text{N}$$ **Ans. (B)**

Sol. 3 When man is at rest

$$T=60\text{g}=600\,\text{N}$$

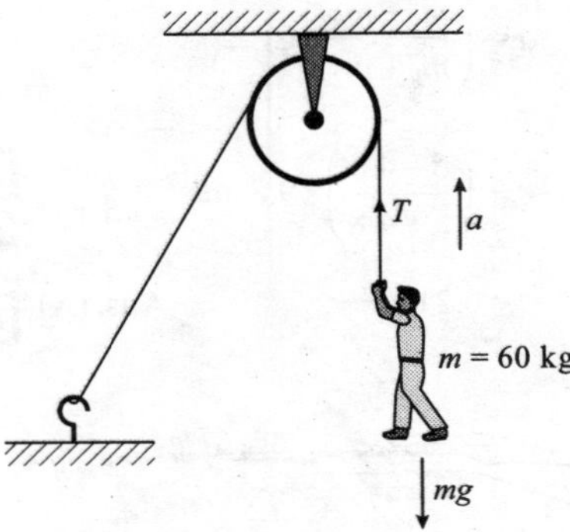

When man starts climbing up the rope at acceleration a, its equation of motion is

$$T-mg=ma$$
$$\Rightarrow \quad 840-600=60a$$
$$\Rightarrow \quad a=4\ \text{m/s}^2$$ **Ans. (C)**

Sol. 4

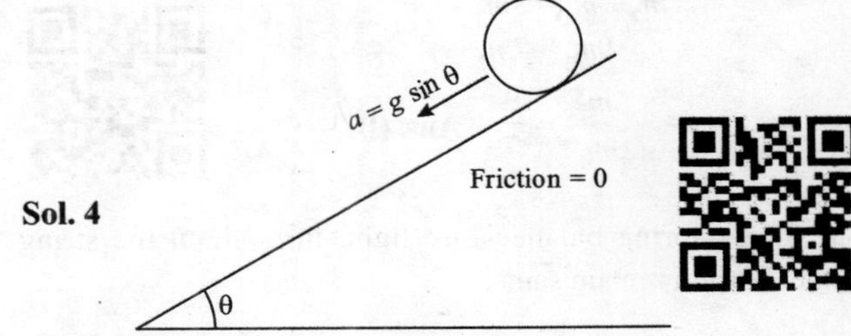

As no friction is there, all bodies slide with acceleration $g \sin\theta$.

Ans. (D)

Sol. 5 Acceleration of ball w.r.t. lift

$$\vec{a}_{BL}=\vec{a}_B-\vec{a}_L$$
$$a_{BL}=g-a$$

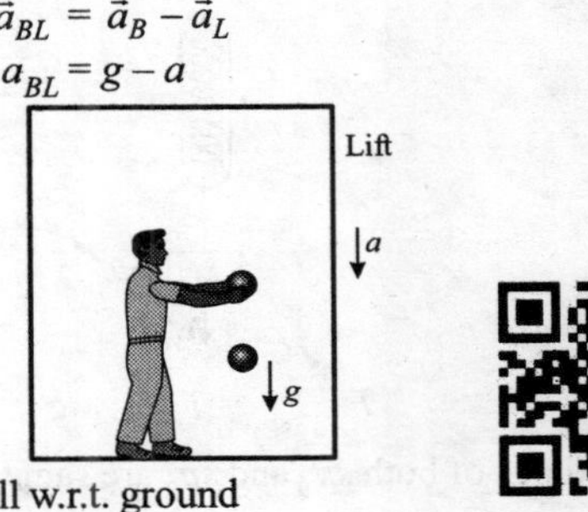

Acceleration of ball w.r.t. ground

$$a_B=g$$ **Ans. (C)**

Sol. 6 Given that

$$F_1+F_2=18\,\text{N} \qquad \ldots(1)$$

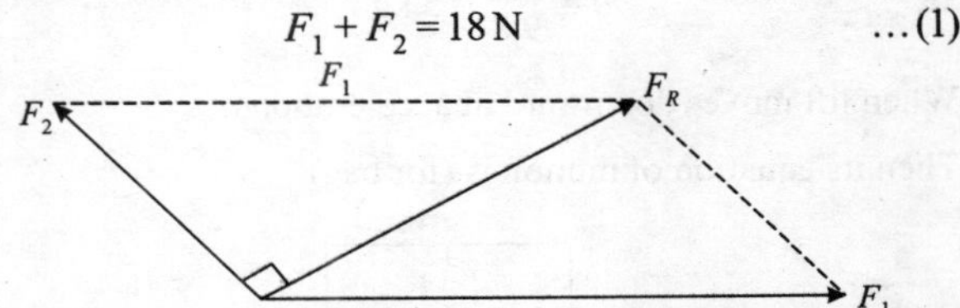

From the given vector triangle, we use

$$F_2^2+F_R^2=F_1^2$$
$$\Rightarrow \quad F_1^2-F_2^2=F_R^2=144$$
$$\Rightarrow \quad (F_1+F_2)(F_1-F_2)=144$$

from (1) $\Rightarrow$ $F_1-F_2=\frac{144}{18}=8 \qquad \ldots(2)$

from (1) and (2) $\quad 2F_1=26 \Rightarrow F_1=13\,\text{N}$

$\quad 2F_2=10 \Rightarrow F_2=5\,\text{N}$ **Ans. (B)**

Sol. 7 Acceleration of Atwood's machine is given as

$$a=\frac{m_2-m_1}{m_2+m_1}\cdot g$$

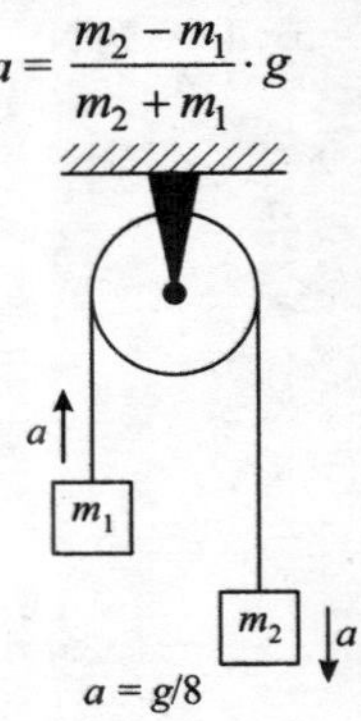

$$m_2 + m_1 = 8m_2 - 8m_1$$
$$9m_1 = 7m_2$$
$$\Rightarrow \quad \frac{m_2}{m_1} = \frac{9}{7}$$ **Ans. (B)**

Sol. 8 As spring balances are light, throughout the string length tension remain same.

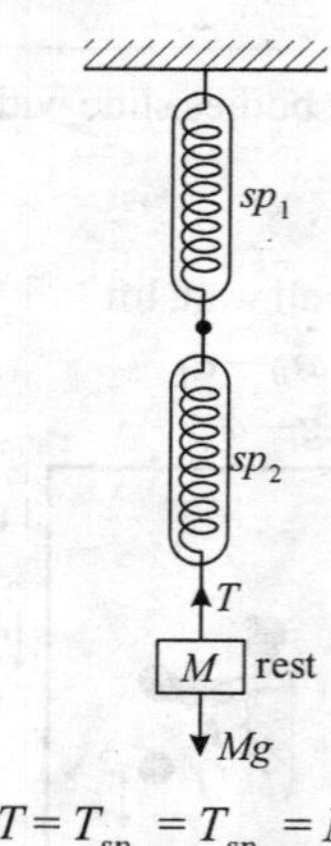

$$T = T_{sp_1} = T_{sp_2} = Mg$$

$\Rightarrow$ Readings of both sp_1 and sp_2 are same **Ans. (A)**

Sol. 9 At rest $T = 49\text{N} = mg$

$$\Rightarrow \quad m = \frac{49}{9.8} = 5\text{ kg}$$

When lift moves downward at acceleration a

Then its equation of motion is (for bag)

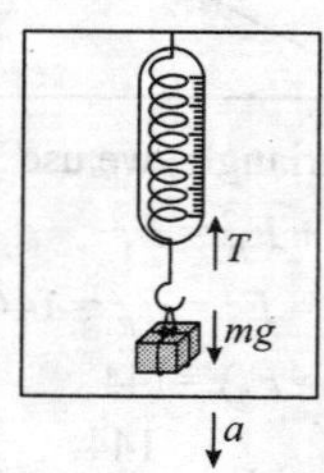

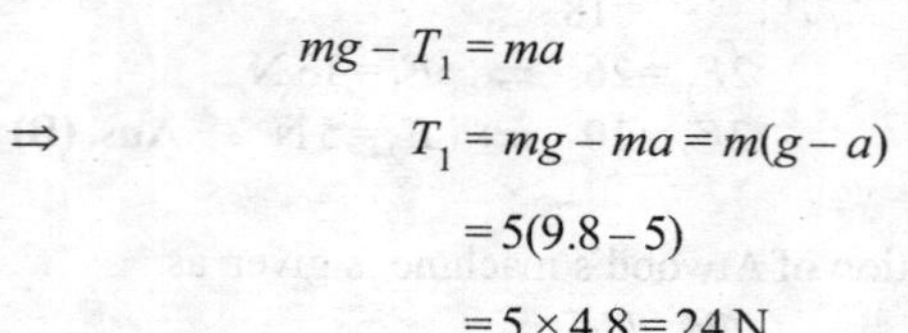

$$mg - T_1 = ma$$
$$\Rightarrow \quad T_1 = mg - ma = m(g - a)$$

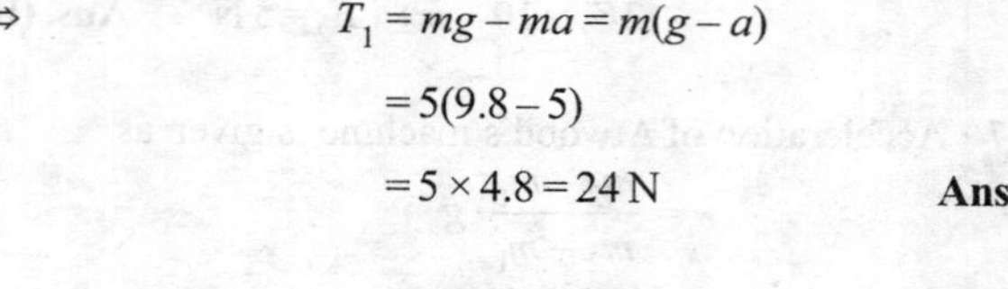

$$= 5(9.8 - 5)$$
$$= 5 \times 4.8 = 24\text{ N}$$ **Ans. (A)**

Sol. 10

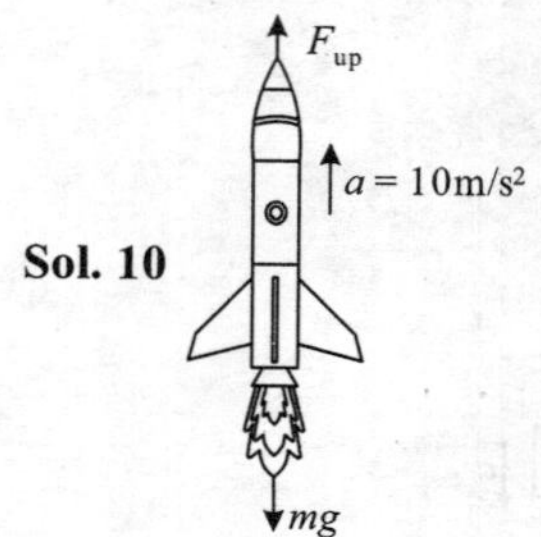

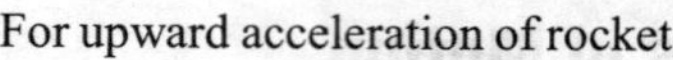

For upward acceleration of rocket

$$a = 10\text{ m/s}^2$$

We use

$$F_{up} - mg = ma$$
$$\Rightarrow \quad F_{up} = mg + ma$$
$$\Rightarrow \quad F_{up} = m(g + a) = 3.5 \times 10^4[10 + 10]$$
$$= 7 \times 10^5\text{ N}$$ **Ans. (B)**

Sol. 11 As vector sum of the three forces is equal to zero

$$\Rightarrow \quad \vec{a} = 0$$

$\Rightarrow \quad \vec{v} \rightarrow$ remain uncharged. **Ans. (D)**

Sol. 12 *FBD* of block is shown in figure

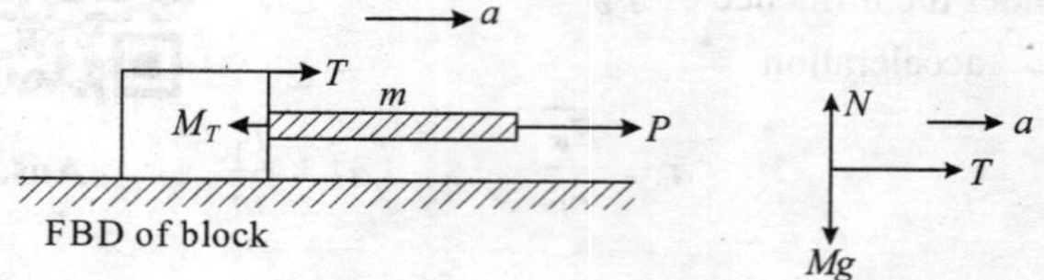

Acceleration of system (block + rope) is given as

$$a = \left(\frac{P}{M + m}\right)$$

Equation of motion of block

$$T = Ma = \frac{MP}{M + m}$$ **Ans. (D)**

Sol. 13 Acceleration of masses in Atwood's machine is given as

$$a = \left(\frac{m_1 - m_2}{m_1 + m_2}\right)g$$

$$= \left(\frac{5 - 4.8}{5 + 4.8}\right) \times 9.8\text{ m/s}^2$$

$$= 0.2\text{ m/s}^2$$ **Ans. (A)**

Sol. 14

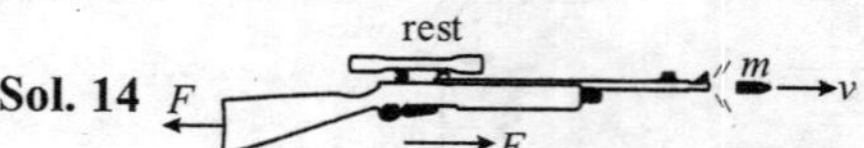

Man has to apply an equal force to keep the gun at rest

F = rate of charge of linear momentum

If N bullets are fired per second

$$\Rightarrow \quad F = N \cdot mv$$

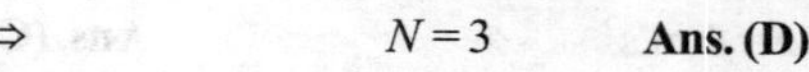

$$144 = N \times 40 \times 10^{-3} \times 1200$$

$$\Rightarrow \quad N = 3$$ **Ans. (D)**

Sol. 15

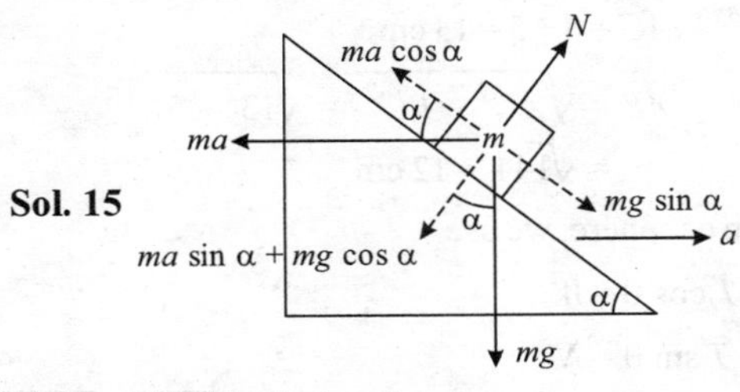

To keep the block at rest, we use

$$mg \sin \alpha = ma \cos \alpha$$

$$a = g \tan \alpha \qquad \textbf{Ans. (D)}$$

Sol. 16

In the process of catching the ball, force on hand is

$$F = \frac{\Delta P}{\Delta t} = \frac{P_i - P_f}{\Delta t} = \frac{150 \times 10^{-3} \times 20}{0.1}$$

$$\Rightarrow \quad F = 30\,\text{N} \qquad \textbf{Ans. (C)}$$

Sol. 17 In free fall motion of ball we use

$$v^2 = u^2 - 2gh$$

$$\Rightarrow \quad 0 = u^2 - 2 \times 10 \times 2$$

$$\Rightarrow \quad u = \sqrt{40}\ \text{m/s}$$

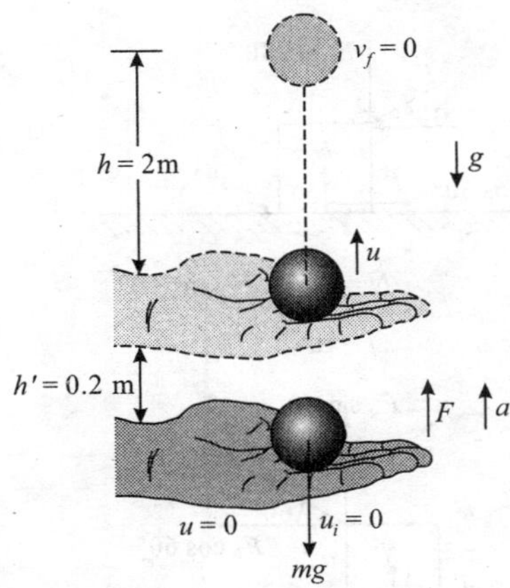

When ball was being pushed by hand, we use

$$u^2 = u_i^2 + 2ah'$$

$$40 = 0 + 2a(0.2)$$

$$\Rightarrow \quad a = 100\ \text{m/s}^2$$

equation of motion of ball is given as

$$F - mg = ma$$

$$\Rightarrow \quad F = m(g + a) = 0.2(10 + 100)$$

$$\Rightarrow \quad F = 0.2 \times 110 = 22\,\text{N} \qquad \textbf{Ans. (D)}$$

Sol. 18

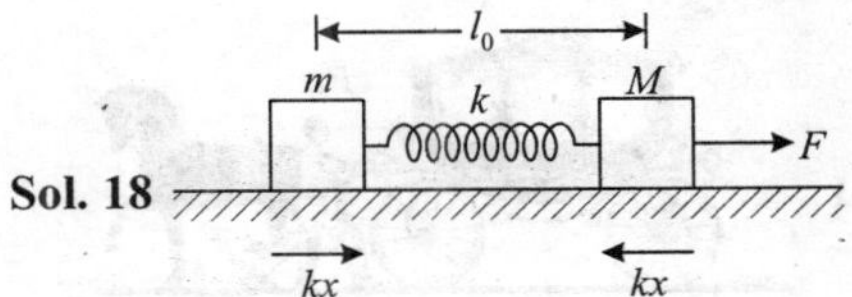

When both the blocks will start moving at same acceleration, say spring has an extension x_0

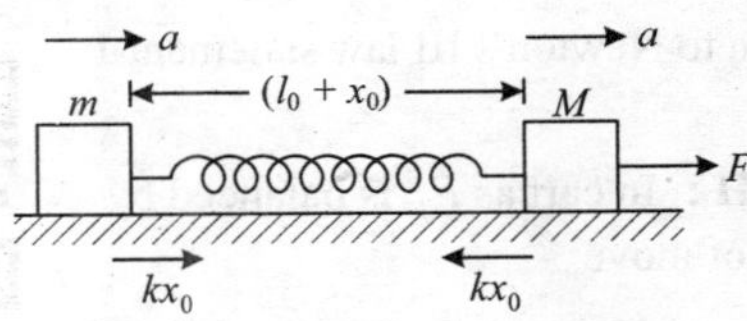

Common acceleration

$$a = \frac{F}{m + M}$$

equation of motion of blocks are

and $\quad F - kx_0 = Ma$

$$kx_0 = ma$$

$$kx_0 = \frac{mF}{m + M} \qquad \textbf{Ans. (C)}$$

Sol. 19 If a spring of length l is cut in different parts then force constant of a part of length l_1 is given as

$$k_1 = \frac{kl}{l_1} \qquad [k = \text{force constant of original spring}]$$

For spring A and B we have

$$l_A = 2l_0;\ l_B = 3l_0;\ l = l_A + l_B = 5l_0$$

Thus force constant of spring A is

$$k_A = \frac{kl}{l_A} = k\left(\frac{5l_0}{2l_0}\right) = \frac{5}{2}k \qquad \textbf{Ans. (A)}$$

Sol. 20 Acceleration of particle

$$a = \frac{F}{m} = \frac{F_0}{m}e^{-bt}$$

$$\Rightarrow \quad a = \frac{dv}{dt} = \frac{F_0}{m}e^{-bt}$$

$$\Rightarrow \quad dv = \frac{F_0}{m}e^{-bt}dt$$

Integrating above relation gives

$$\int_{v=0}^{v=v} dv = \int_{t=0}^{t=t} \frac{F_0}{m}e^{-bt}dt$$

$$\Rightarrow \quad v = \frac{F_0}{m}\left[\frac{e^{-bt}}{-b}\right]_0^t$$

$$\Rightarrow \quad v_{(t)} = \frac{F_0}{mb}[1 - e^{-bt}] \qquad \textbf{Ans. (D)}$$

Sol. 21 Statement-I :

As cart does not move

$\Rightarrow$ $F_H = F_B$ (ignoring friction on cart)

Acceleration to Newton's III law statement-I is true

Statement-II : In cart as F_H is balanced by F_B it does not move

$\Rightarrow$ Statement-II is also true and it is explaining statement-I also. **Ans. (A)**

Sol. 22

Equation of motion of system is

$$480 - 400 = 40a$$

$$\Rightarrow \quad a = \frac{80}{40} = 2\text{m/s}^2$$

for mass below point M, we use below FBD as shown

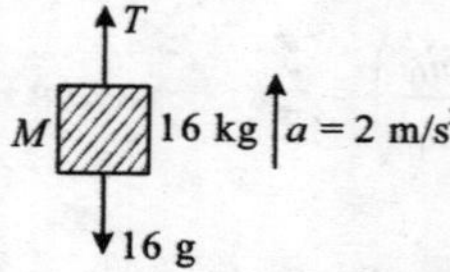

Equation of motion for above FBD is

$$T - 160 = 16 \times 2 = 32$$

$$\Rightarrow \quad T = 192\text{ N}$$

Ans. (D)

Sol. 23

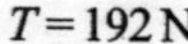
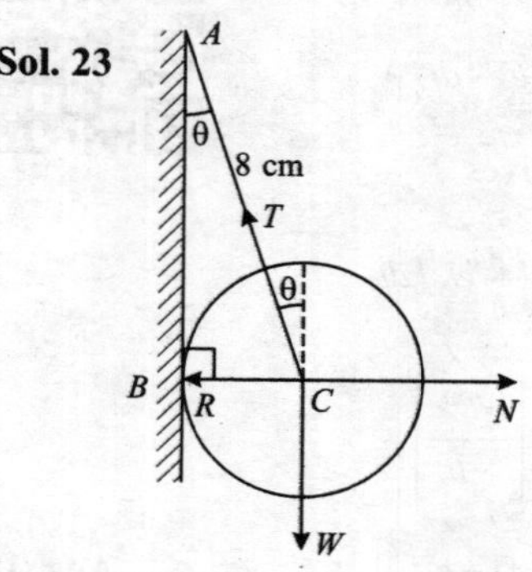

$R = 5$ cm

$$AC = 8 + 5 = 13\text{ cm}$$

and $AB = \sqrt{AC^2 - BC^2} = \sqrt{13^2 - 5^2}$

$$= \sqrt{144} = 12\text{ cm}$$

For equilibrium of sphere, we use

$$T\cos\theta = W$$

$$T\sin\theta = N$$

$$\Rightarrow \quad T = \frac{W}{\cos\theta}$$

Here $\cos\theta = \frac{AB}{AC} = \frac{12}{13}$

$$\Rightarrow \quad T = \frac{13W}{12}$$

Ans. (D)

Sol. 24 As $\vec{F}$ = constant

$\Rightarrow$ $\vec{a}$ = constant

We can use $\vec{a} = \frac{\vec{v}_2 - \vec{v}_1}{\Delta t}$

$$\Rightarrow \quad \vec{a} = \frac{6\hat{i} - (6\hat{i} - 2\hat{j})}{10} = \frac{-6\hat{i} + 8\hat{j}}{10}$$

$$\Rightarrow \quad \vec{a} = \frac{-3\hat{i} + 4\hat{j}}{5}\text{ m/s}^2$$

Force on particle is

$$\vec{F} = m\vec{a} = 5\left(\frac{-3\hat{i} + 4\hat{j}}{5}\right) = -3\hat{i} + 4\hat{j}\text{ N}$$ **Ans. (A)**

Sol. 25

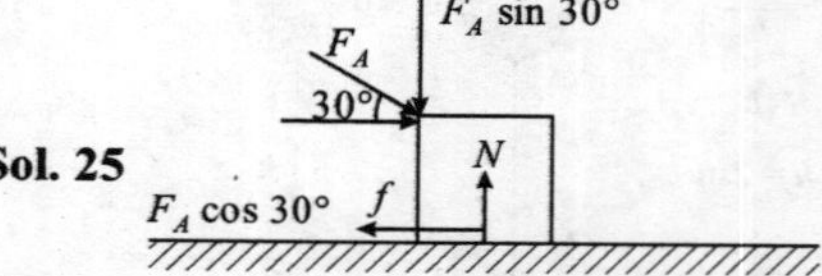

$$N = Mg + F_A\sin 30°$$

$$f = \mu N$$

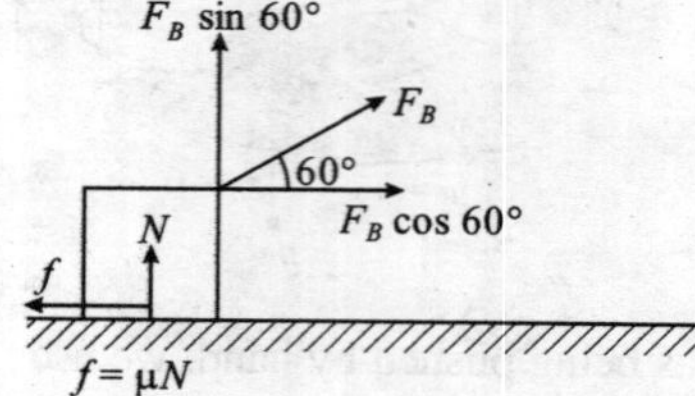

$$N = Mg - F_B\sin 60°$$

to drag the box by person A, we use

$$F_A\cos 30° \geq \mu(Mg + F_A\sin 30°)$$

$$F_A \geq \frac{2\mu Mg}{\sqrt{3} - \mu} \quad \ldots(1)$$

$$\Rightarrow \quad F_A\left(\frac{\sqrt{3}}{2} - \frac{\mu}{2}\right) \geq \mu Mg$$

to drag the box by person B, we use

$$F_B \cos 60° \geq \mu(Mg - F_B \sin 60°)$$

$$\Rightarrow \quad F_B \geq \frac{2\mu Mg}{1+\mu\sqrt{3}} \quad \ldots(2)$$

$$\Rightarrow \quad F_B\left(\frac{1}{2}+\frac{\mu\sqrt{3}}{2}\right) \geq \mu Mg$$

The ratio $\frac{F_A}{F_B}$ can be obtained by equation-(1) & (2)

$$\Rightarrow \quad \frac{F_A}{F_B} = \frac{1+\mu\sqrt{3}}{\sqrt{3}-\mu}$$

$$\Rightarrow \quad \frac{F_A}{F_B} = \frac{1+\left(\frac{\sqrt{3}}{5}\right)\sqrt{3}}{\sqrt{3}-\frac{\sqrt{3}}{5}} = \frac{1+3/5}{\sqrt{3}(4/5)} = \frac{2}{\sqrt{3}}$$

Ans. (D)

Sol. 26 Given that

$$F = ma = \frac{R}{t^2}v$$

$$\Rightarrow \quad \frac{dv}{dt} = \frac{R}{mt^2}v$$

$$\Rightarrow \quad \int \frac{dv}{v} = \int \frac{R}{mt^2}dt$$

$$\Rightarrow \quad \ln(v) = -\frac{R}{mt}+C$$

$$\Rightarrow \quad \ln(v) = -\left(\frac{R}{m}\right)\frac{1}{t}+C$$

here above expression stations that graph of ln v and $\frac{1}{t}$ is a straight line with slope $-\frac{R}{m}$

Ans. (A)

Sol. 27

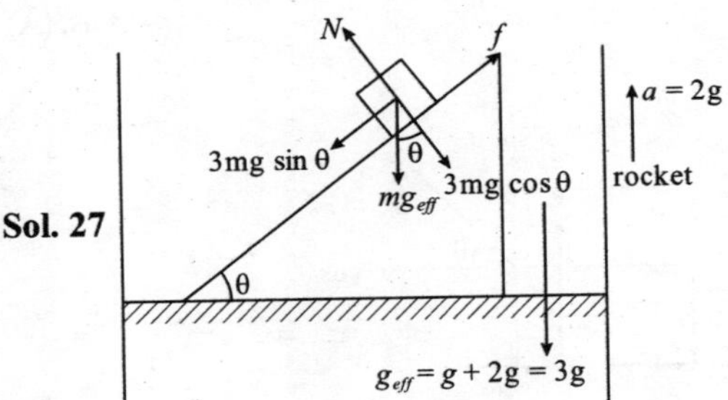

Limiting friction on the block is

$$f_L = \mu N = 3\mu\, mg \cos\theta$$

for block not to slide (f_L)

$$3\,mg \sin\theta < 3m\, mg \cos\theta$$

$$\mu > \tan\theta$$

$$\Rightarrow \quad \mu_{min} = \tan\theta$$

Ans. (B)

4.2 Friction

Sol. 1

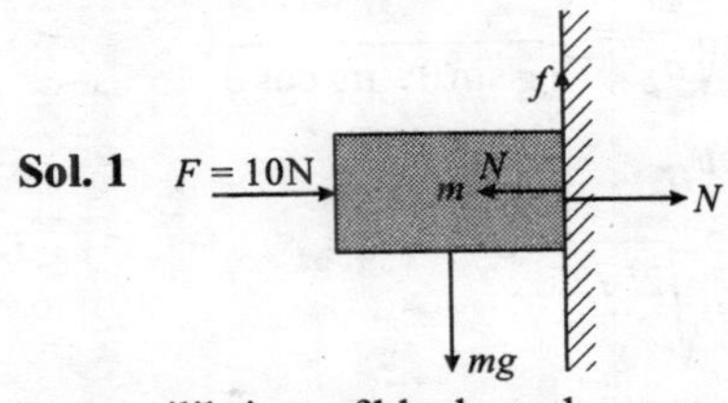

For equilibrium of block, we have

$$N = F = 10\,\text{N}$$

$$mg = f = \mu N$$

$$\Rightarrow \quad mg = 0.2 \times 10 = 2\,\text{N}$$

Ans. (D)

Sol. 2

Retardation due to friction on block is

$$a = -\mu g$$

we use

$$V = u + at$$

$$\Rightarrow \quad 0 = 6 - \mu(10)(10)$$

$$\Rightarrow \quad \mu = 0.06$$

Ans. (C)

Sol. 3

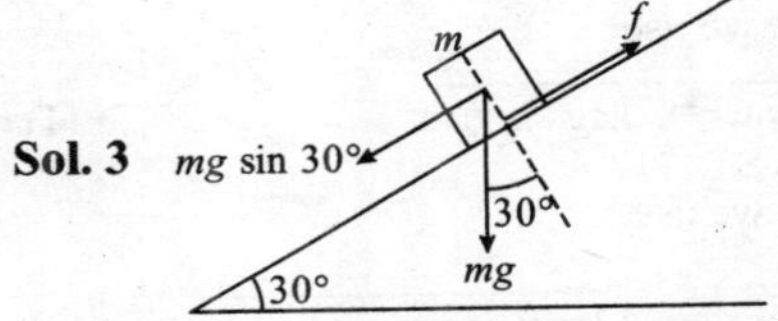

As block is rest on incline plane we use

$$f = mg \sin 30°$$

$$\Rightarrow \quad 10 = m(10)\left(\frac{1}{2}\right)$$

$$\Rightarrow \quad m = 2\,\text{kg}$$

Ans. (A)

Sol. 4

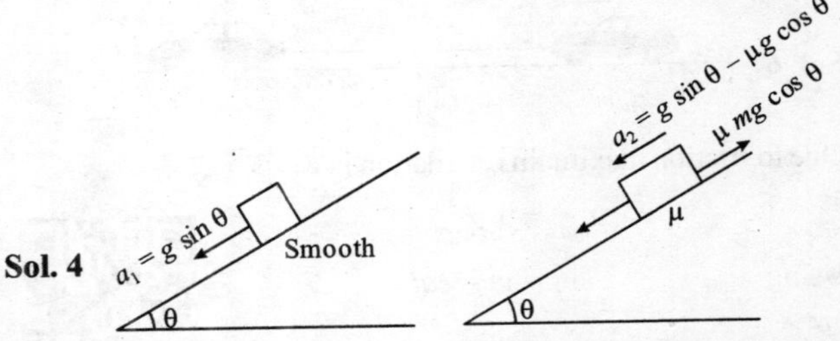

To slide a distance l along incline, time required for smooth incline

$$t_1 = \sqrt{\frac{2l}{a_1}} = \sqrt{\frac{2l}{g\sin\theta}}$$

For rough incline

$$t_2 = \sqrt{\frac{2l}{a_2}} = \sqrt{\frac{2l}{g\sin\theta - \mu g\cos\theta}}$$

Given that $\quad t_2 = nt_1$

$$\Rightarrow \quad \sqrt{\frac{2l\sqrt{2}}{g(1-\mu)}} = n\sqrt{\frac{2l\sqrt{2}}{g}}$$

$$\Rightarrow \quad \sqrt{\frac{1}{1-\mu}} = n$$

$$\Rightarrow \quad 1-\mu = \frac{1}{n^2}$$

$$\Rightarrow \quad \mu_k = 1 - \frac{1}{n^2}$$

Ans. (A)

Sol. 5

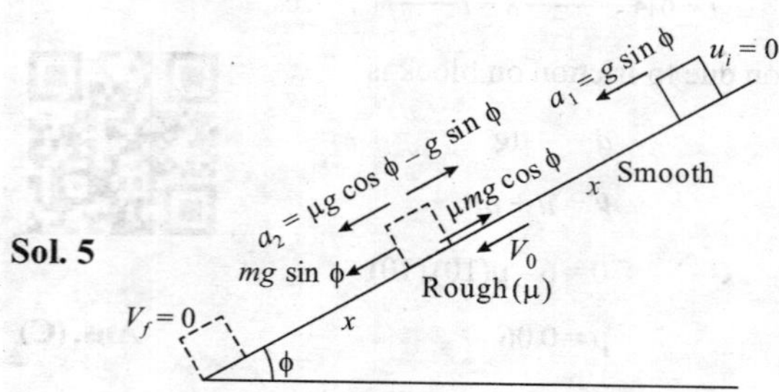

for upper half of motion, we use

$$V_0 = \sqrt{2a_1 x} = \sqrt{2g\sin\phi \cdot x} \quad \ldots(1)$$

for lower half of motion, we use

$$V_0 = \sqrt{2a_2 x} = \sqrt{2g(\mu\cos\phi - \sin\phi)x} \quad \ldots(2)$$

from (1) & (2), we have

$$2xg\sin\phi = 2xg(\mu\cos\phi - \sin\phi)$$

$$\Rightarrow \quad 2\sin\phi = \mu\cos\phi$$

$$\Rightarrow \quad \mu = 2\tan\phi$$

Ans. (C)

Sol. 6

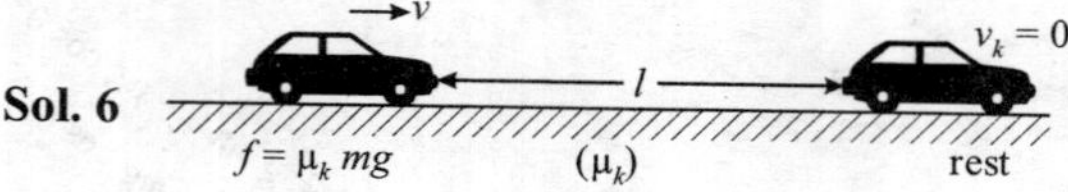

Due to friction maximum retardation in car is

$$a_{max} = \mu_k g$$

Using $\quad v_f^2 = v^2 - 2al$

$$\Rightarrow \quad l = \frac{v^2}{2a} \quad [\text{As } v_f = 0]$$

$$\Rightarrow \quad l = \frac{(100)^2}{2\times 0.5\times 10} = \frac{10000}{10}$$

$$\Rightarrow \quad l = 1000\,\text{m}$$

Ans. (B)

Sol. 7

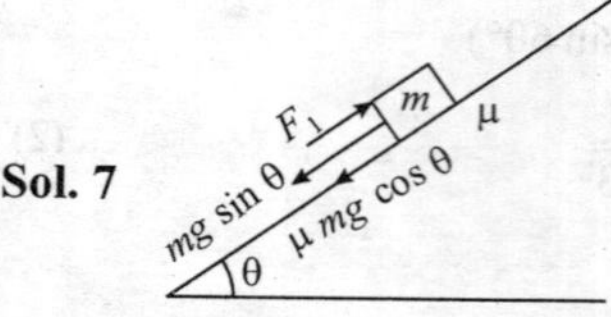

To push the block up on incline plane, minimum, force required is

$$F_1 = mg\sin\theta + \mu mg\cos\theta$$

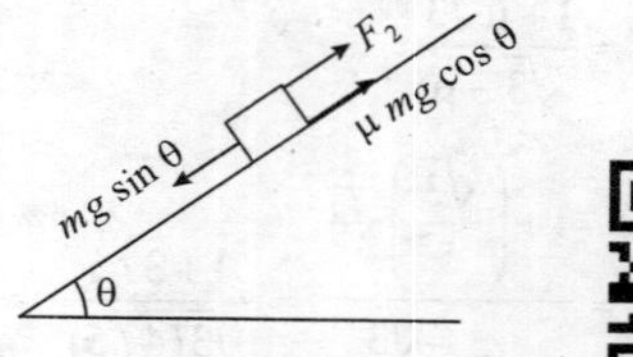

To prevent the body sliding down

$$F_2 = mg\sin\theta - \mu mg\cos\theta.$$

$$\Rightarrow \quad \frac{F_1}{F_2} = \frac{\sin\theta + \mu\cos\theta}{\sin\theta - \mu\cos\theta} = \frac{\tan\theta + \mu}{\tan\theta - \mu} = \frac{3\mu}{\mu} = 3$$

Ans. (D)

Sol. 8 For insect not to slip α is the angle of repose

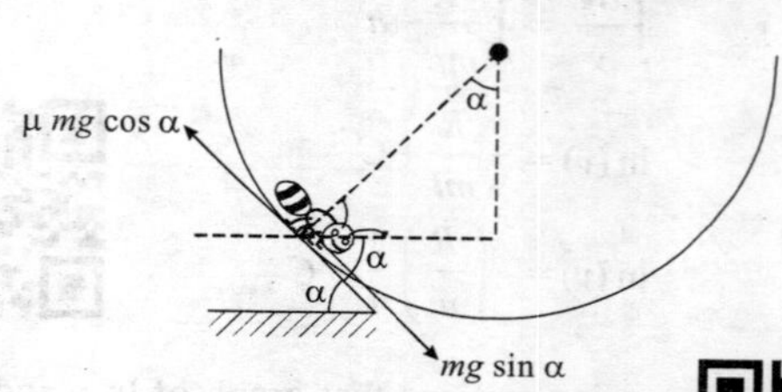

$$mg\sin\alpha \le \mu mg\cos\alpha$$

$$\Rightarrow \quad \mu \ge \tan\alpha \quad \Rightarrow \quad \tan\alpha = \frac{1}{3}$$

$$\Rightarrow \quad \cot\alpha = 3$$

Ans. (A)

Sol. 9

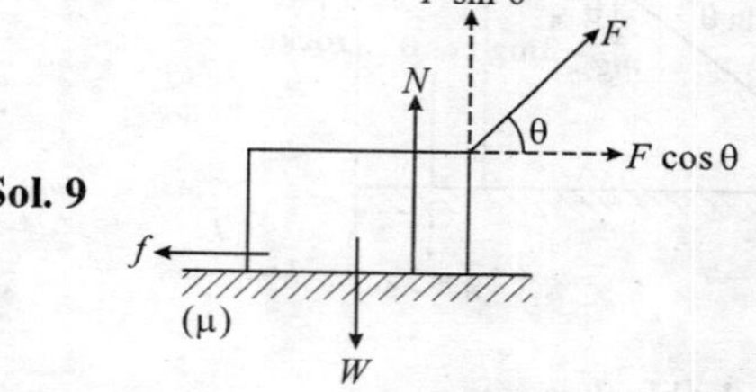

$$N = W - F\sin\theta$$

To slide the block we use

$$F\cos\theta = \mu(W - F\sin\theta)$$

$$\Rightarrow \quad F = \frac{\mu W}{\cos\theta + \mu\sin\theta} \quad \ldots(1)$$

F is minimum when

$$\frac{dF}{d\theta}=0$$

$\Rightarrow \quad -\sin\theta+\mu\cos\theta=0$

$\Rightarrow \quad \mu=\tan\theta$

$\Rightarrow \quad \theta=\tan^{-1}(\mu)$

$\Rightarrow \quad \sin\theta=\dfrac{\mu}{\sqrt{1+\mu^2}}\ ;\ \cos\theta=\dfrac{1}{\sqrt{1+\mu^2}}$

Minimum value of force can be given as

$$F_{\min}=\frac{\mu W}{\dfrac{1}{\sqrt{1+\mu^2}}+\dfrac{\mu^2}{\sqrt{1+\mu^2}}}=\frac{\mu W}{\sqrt{1+\mu^2}}$$

Ans. (A)

Sol. 10

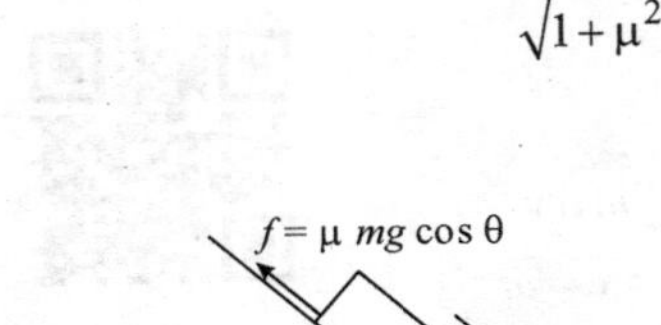

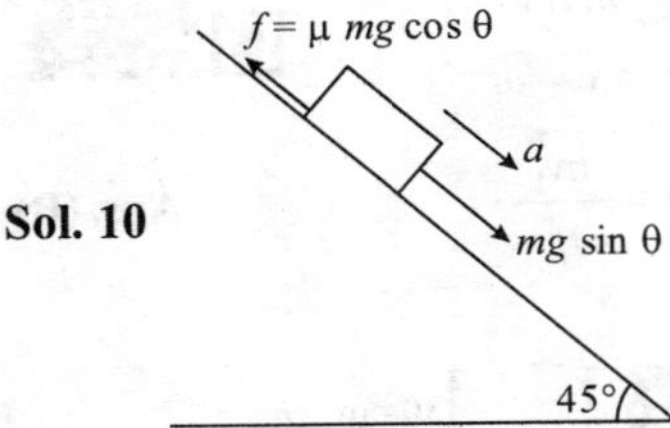

Acceleration body down the plane is

$$a=g\sin\theta-mg\cos\theta \qquad (\mu=0.3x)$$

Speed of body increases until $a=0$

After some time at a specific distance

$$a=0$$

$\Rightarrow \quad g\left(\dfrac{1}{\sqrt{2}}\right)-0.3x\,g\cos 45°=0$

$\Rightarrow \quad x=\dfrac{1}{0.3}=3.33\text{ m}$

Ans. (D)

Sol. 11

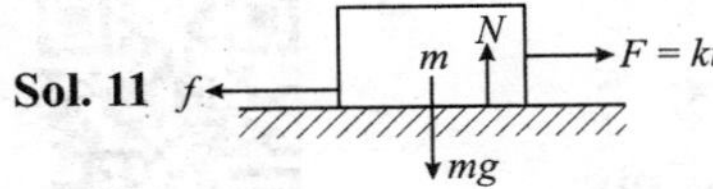

Limiting value of friction $=\mu mg$

for small values of F,

$$f=F$$

static friction and block static sliding at time $t=t_0$ when

$$kt_0=\mu mg$$

and for $t>t_0$, equation of motion, we use

$$kt-\mu mg=ma$$

$\Rightarrow \quad a=\dfrac{kt}{m}-mg$

The graph will be a line with $+ve$ slope after

$$t=t_0$$

Ans. (B)

Sol. 12

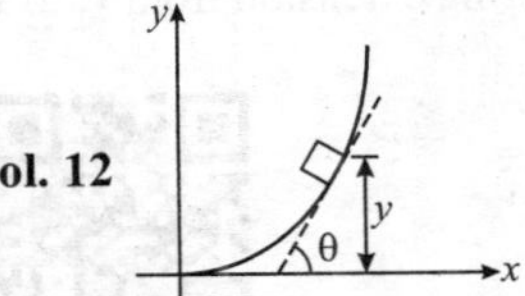

Block will remain at rest at a height y where

if $\quad \tan\theta=\mu$

$\theta\rightarrow$ Angle of Repose

here $\quad \tan\theta=\dfrac{dy}{dx}=\dfrac{d}{dx}\left(\dfrac{x^3}{6}\right)=\dfrac{x^2}{2}=0.5$

$\Rightarrow \quad x^2=0.5\times 2=1$

$\Rightarrow \quad x=\pm 1$

$\Rightarrow \quad y=\dfrac{1}{6}m \quad$ **Ans. (A)**

Sol. 13

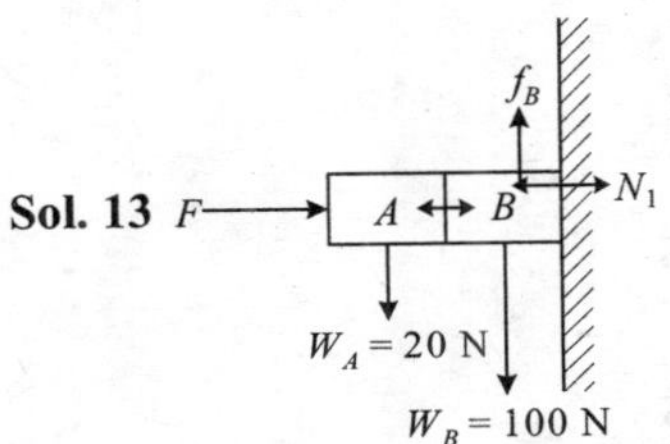

We consider blocks to be at rest and combined *FBD* of blocks with static friction is shown as

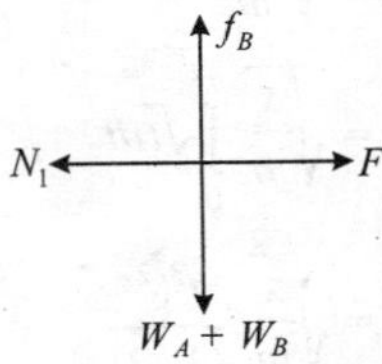

For equilibrium of blocks we have

$$f_B=W_A+W_B=120\text{ N}$$

Ans. (C)

5.1 Work Energy Power

Sol. 1 The energy stored in a spring having extension x is

$$U=\frac{1}{2}kx^2$$

Work done in extending the extension in spring from x_1 to x_2 is

$$W=U_f-U_i$$

$\Rightarrow \quad W=\dfrac{1}{2}k(x_2^2-x_1^2)$

$\Rightarrow \quad W=\dfrac{1}{2}\times 800[(0.15)^2-(0.05)^2]$

$\Rightarrow \quad W=400[0.0225-0.0025]=8\text{J}$

Ans. (B)

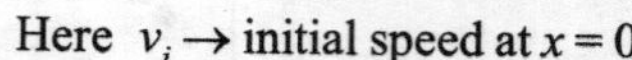

Sol. 2 Work done in extending spring extension from x_1 to x_2 is

$$W = U_f - U_i = \frac{1}{2}kx_2^2 - \frac{1}{2}kx_1^2$$

$$\Rightarrow \quad W = \frac{1}{2}(5 \times 10^3) \times [(0.1)^2 - (0.05)^2]$$

$$\Rightarrow \quad W = 18.75 \text{ J}$$

Ans. (B)

Sol. 3 Along a straight line motion, power is given as

$$P = F.v = mav$$

$$\Rightarrow \quad m\left(\frac{dv}{dt}\right)v = P \rightarrow \text{constant}$$

$$\Rightarrow \quad vdv = \frac{P}{m}dt$$

Integrating this relation gives

$$\int_0^v vdv = \frac{P}{m}\int_0^t dt$$

$$\Rightarrow \quad \frac{v^2}{2} = \frac{P}{m}t$$

$$\Rightarrow \quad v = \sqrt{\frac{2P}{m}t}$$

$$\Rightarrow \quad \frac{dx}{dt} = \sqrt{\frac{2P}{m}}\sqrt{t}$$

$$\Rightarrow \quad dx = \sqrt{\frac{2P}{m}}\sqrt{t}\,dt$$

$$\Rightarrow \quad \int_0^x dx = \sqrt{\frac{x}{m}}\int_0^t \sqrt{t}dt$$

$$\Rightarrow \quad x = \sqrt{\frac{x}{m}}\frac{t^{3/2}}{(3/2)}$$

$$\Rightarrow \quad x \propto t^{3/2}$$

Ans. (B)

Sol. 4 Given that

$$a \propto -x$$

$$\Rightarrow \quad v\frac{dv}{dx} = a = -Cx$$

$$\Rightarrow \quad \int_{v_i}^{v_f} vdv = -\int_{x=0}^{x} Cx\,dx$$

$$\Rightarrow \quad \left[\frac{v^2}{2}\right]_{v_i}^{v_f} = -\frac{Cx^2}{2}$$

$$\Rightarrow \quad \frac{v_i^2}{2} - \frac{v_f^2}{2} = -\frac{Cx^2}{2}$$

If equation is multiplied with mass of particle m

Here $v_i \rightarrow$ initial speed at $x = 0$

$v_f \rightarrow$ final speed after covering displacement x

$$\frac{1}{2}mv_i^2 - \frac{1}{2}mv_f^2 = \frac{1}{2}mCx^2$$

$$\Rightarrow \quad \Delta K = \frac{1}{2}mCx^2$$

$$\Rightarrow \quad \Delta K \propto x^2$$

Ans. (A)

Sol. 5 $t = 0$, $u = 0$ — a → — $t = t_1$, v_1 → x

Using $\quad v = u + at$

$$v_1 = at_1$$

$$\Rightarrow \quad a = \frac{v_1}{t_1}$$

Instantaneous power

$$P = F \cdot v = m\,a\,v$$

After time t_1 speed of particle is $v = at$

$$\Rightarrow \quad P = ma^2t = \frac{mv_1^2}{t_1^2} \cdot t$$

Ans. (B)

Sol. 6

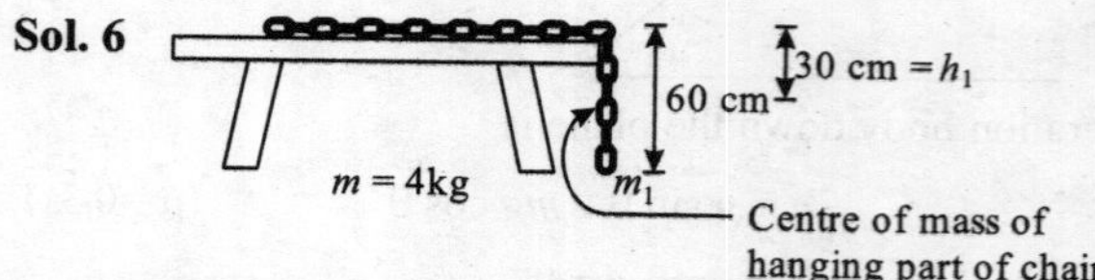

Mass of hanging part of chain is

$$m_1 = \frac{4}{2} \times 0.6 = 1.2 \text{ kg}$$

Work done in lifting hanging part of chain is

$$W = m_1 g h_1 = 1.2 \times 10 \times 0.3$$

$$= 3.6 \text{ J}$$

Ans. (B)

Sol. 7 Work done in displacing a particle is given as

$$w = \vec{F} \cdot \vec{r}$$

$$\Rightarrow \quad w = (5\hat{i} + 3\hat{j} + 2\hat{k}) \cdot (2\hat{i} - \hat{j})$$

$$\Rightarrow \quad w = 10 - 3 = 7 \text{ J}$$

Ans. (B)

Sol. 8

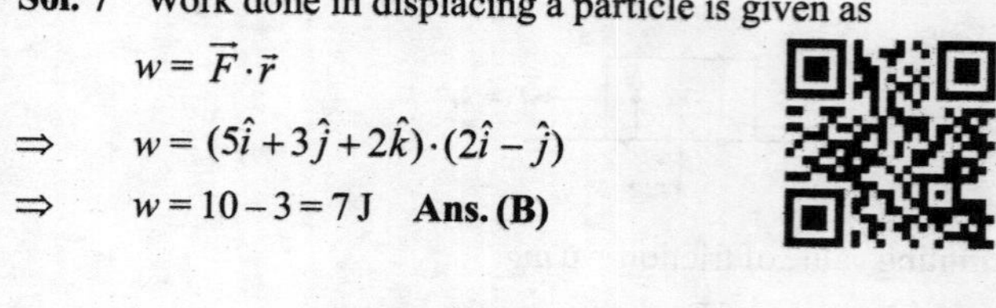

We use $\quad v^2 = u^2 + 2as$

For first part of motion

$$\left(\frac{v}{2}\right)^2 = (v)^2 - 2a(3)$$

$$\Rightarrow \quad \frac{3v^2}{4} = 6a$$

$$\Rightarrow \quad a = \frac{v^2}{8}$$

For second part of motion

$$(0)^2 = \left(\frac{v}{2}\right)^2 - 2as$$

$$\Rightarrow \quad s = \frac{v^2}{8a} = 1 \text{ cm}$$

Ans. (D)

Sol. 9 By conservation of energy

$$\frac{1}{2}Mv^2 = \frac{1}{2}kL^2$$

$$\Rightarrow \quad v = \sqrt{\frac{k}{M}}\,L$$

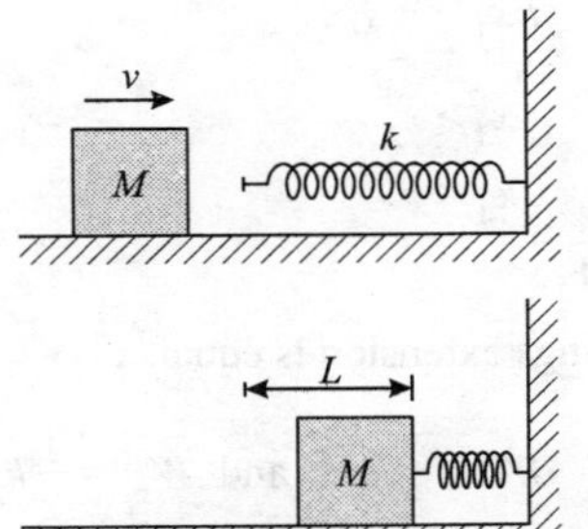

Maximum momentum of the block is

$$P_{max} = Mv = M\sqrt{\frac{k}{M}}\cdot L = \sqrt{kM}\cdot L$$

Ans. (A)

Sol. 10 All surface are smooth

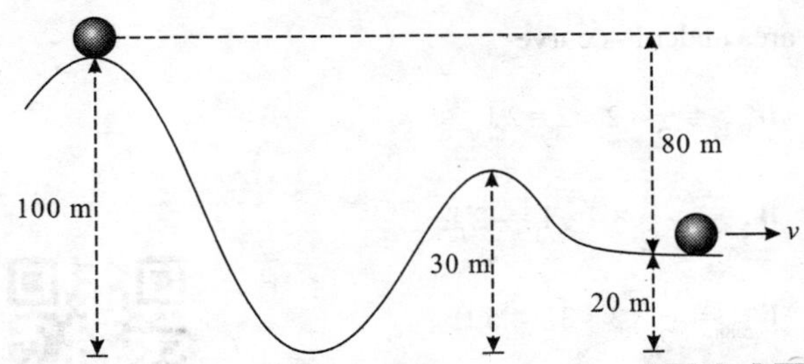

Using work energy theorem, we have

$$0 + mg(80) = \frac{1}{2}mv^2$$

$$\Rightarrow \quad v = \sqrt{1600} = 40 \text{ m/s}$$

Ans. (B)

Sol. 11

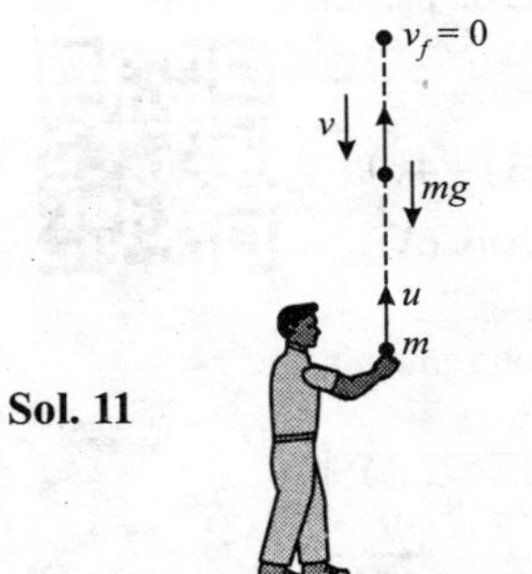

By applying work-energy theorem, we have

$$\frac{1}{2}mu^2 + W_g = 0$$

$$\Rightarrow \quad W_g = \frac{1}{2}mu^2 = -\frac{1}{2}\times 100\times 10^{-3}\times (5)^2$$

$$\Rightarrow \quad W_g = -1.25 \text{ J}$$

Ans. (B)

Sol. 12 At any instant total mechanical energy is given as

$$E = K + U$$

$$\Rightarrow \quad K = E - U = 2 - \left(\frac{x^4}{4} - \frac{x^2}{2}\right)$$

K is maximum when

$$\frac{dK}{dx} = 0 = -\frac{4x^3}{4} + \frac{2x}{2}$$

$$\Rightarrow \quad -x^3 + x = 0$$

$$\Rightarrow \quad x = 0, -1, +1$$

$$K_{x=0} = 2\text{J}$$

and

$$K_{x=\pm 1} = 2 - \frac{1}{4} + \frac{1}{2} = \frac{9}{4}\text{ J (max)}$$

$$\Rightarrow \quad \frac{1}{2}mv_{max}^2 = \frac{9}{4}$$

$$\Rightarrow \quad v_{max} = \sqrt{\frac{9}{2}} = \frac{3}{\sqrt{2}} \text{ m/s}$$

Ans. (A)

Sol. 13 As initial and final kinetic energy of mass is zero, using work-energy theorem, we have

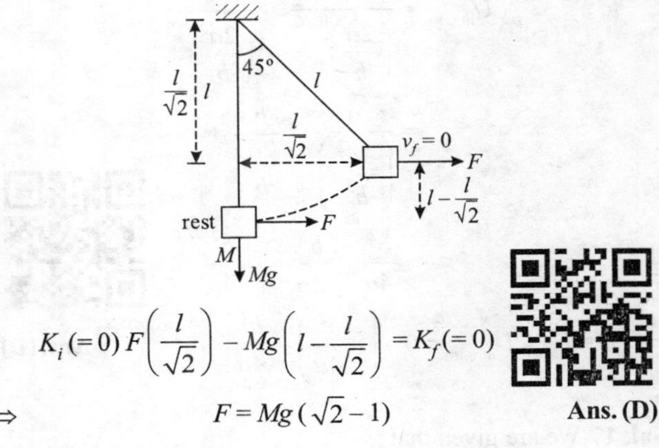

$$K_i(=0)\; F\left(\frac{l}{\sqrt{2}}\right) - Mg\left(l - \frac{l}{\sqrt{2}}\right) = K_f(=0)$$

$$\Rightarrow \quad F = Mg(\sqrt{2} - 1)$$

Ans. (D)

Sol. 14 Using work-energy theorem for the compression of spring, we have

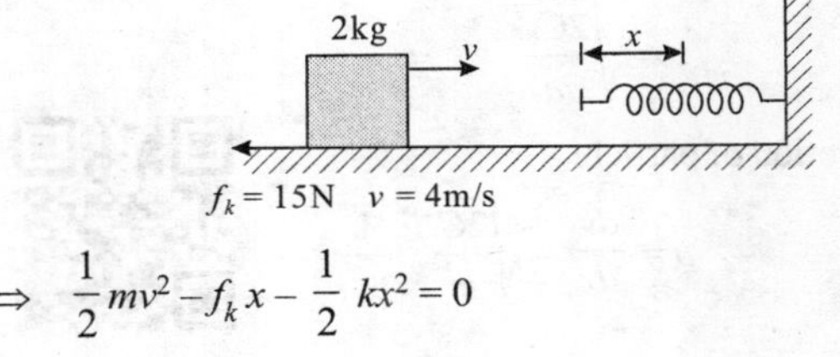

$$\Rightarrow \quad \frac{1}{2}mv^2 - f_k x - \frac{1}{2}kx^2 = 0$$

$$\Rightarrow \quad \frac{1}{2} \times 2 \times (4)^2 - 15x - \frac{1}{2} \times 10000\,x^2 = 0$$

$$\Rightarrow \quad 5000x^2 + 15x - 16 = 0$$

$$\Rightarrow \quad x = \frac{-15 \pm \sqrt{225 + 4 \times 5000 \times 16}}{10000} = 0.055\text{ m}$$

$$\Rightarrow \quad x = 5.5\text{ cm}$$

Ans. (A)

Sol. 15 Speed of athlete can be taken as

$$\bar{v} = \frac{100}{10} = 10\text{m/s}$$

KE of athlete $K = \frac{1}{2} m\bar{v}^2$

$$= \frac{1}{2} \times 60 \times (10)^2 = 3000\text{ J}$$

mass of an athlete can be estimated ~ 60 kg **Ans. (D)**

Sol. 16 At $x = \infty$, $U(x) = 0$

at equilibrium, force on atoms = 0

we use $F = -\frac{dU}{dx} = \frac{12a}{x^{13}} - \frac{6b}{x^7} = 0$

$$\Rightarrow \quad x^6 = \frac{2a}{b}$$

$$\Rightarrow \quad x = \left(\frac{2a}{b}\right)^{1/6}$$

PE at equilibrium is given as

$$U_{\text{at eqm}} = \frac{a}{\left(\frac{2a}{b}\right)^{12/6}} - \frac{b}{\left(\frac{2a}{b}\right)^{6/6}}$$

$$= \frac{a}{\left(\frac{4a^2}{b^2}\right)} - \frac{b}{\frac{2a}{b}}$$

$$= \frac{b^2}{4a} - \frac{b^2}{2a} = -\frac{b^2}{4a}$$

$$\Rightarrow D = U_\infty - U_{\text{at eqm}} = 0 - \left(-\frac{b^2}{4a}\right) = \frac{b^2}{4a}$$

Ans. (D)

Sol. 17 We are given that

$$K = \frac{1}{2} mv^2 = Ct$$

$$\Rightarrow \quad v = \sqrt{\frac{2Ct}{m}}$$

$\Rightarrow$ Acceleration of particle

$$a = \frac{dv}{dx} = \sqrt{\frac{2C}{m}} \cdot \frac{1}{2\sqrt{t}}$$

$\Rightarrow$ Force on particle is given as

$$a = \frac{dv}{dx} = \sqrt{\frac{2C}{m}} \cdot \frac{1}{2\sqrt{t}} = \sqrt{\frac{Cm}{2t}}$$

$$\Rightarrow \quad F \propto \frac{1}{\sqrt{t}}$$

Ans. (D)

Sol. 18 We are given that applied force $F = k_1x_1 = k_2x_2$

and $W_{s_1} > W_{s_2}$

$$\frac{1}{2}k_1x_1^2 > \frac{1}{2}k_1x_2^2$$

$$\Rightarrow \quad \frac{1}{2}Fx_1 > \frac{1}{2}Fx_2$$

$$\Rightarrow \quad x_1 > x_2$$

$$\Rightarrow \quad k_1 < k_2$$

$\Rightarrow$ S_{II} is correct

If in the two springs extension is equal, x

$$\Rightarrow \quad W_{s_1} = \frac{1}{2}k_1x^2 \text{ and } W_{s_2} = \frac{1}{2}k_2x^2$$

$$\Rightarrow \quad W_{s_1} < W_{s_2}$$

$\Rightarrow$ S_{I} is false **Ans. (B)**

Sol. 19 Using work-energy theorem we have

$$\frac{1}{2}mv_i^2 + W_F = \frac{1}{2}mv_f^2$$

By area under F-x curve

$$W_{0.2s} = \frac{1}{2} \times 2 \times 2 = 2\text{ J}$$

$$W_{2.5s} = -\frac{1}{2} \times 4 \times 1 = -2\text{ J}$$

$$W_{5.8s} = \frac{1}{2} \times 3 \times 3 = 4.5\text{ J}$$

$$\Rightarrow k_f = \frac{1}{2} \times 2 \times (5)^2 + [W_{0.2} + W_{2.5} + W_{5.8}]$$

$$\Rightarrow k_f = 25 + [2 - 2 + 4.5] = 29.5\text{ J}$$

Ans. (D)

Sol. 20 By work-energy theorem

Gain (change) in KE = Work done on particle

$$\Delta k = \vec{F} \cdot \overrightarrow{\Delta r}$$

$$\Rightarrow \quad \Delta k = (7\hat{i} + 4\hat{j} + 3\hat{k}) \cdot (2\hat{i} + 3\hat{j} + 4\hat{k})$$

$$\Rightarrow \quad \Delta k = 14 + 12 + 12 = 38\text{ J}$$ **Ans. (A)**

Sol. 21 For springs in series, tension remain same

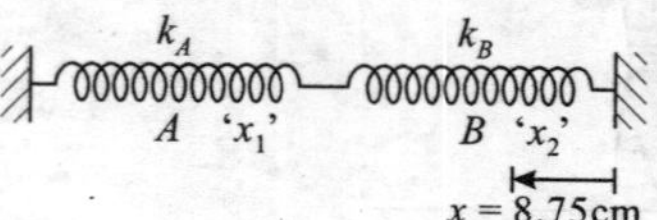

If compression in A and B are x_1 and x_2

$$\Rightarrow \quad k_A x_1 = k_B x_2$$

and
$$3x_1 = 4x_2$$

$$x_1 + x_2 = 8.75$$

$$\Rightarrow \quad x_1 + \frac{3}{4}x_1 = 8.75$$

$$\Rightarrow \quad x_1 = \frac{8.75 \times 4}{7} = 5 \text{ cm}$$

$$\Rightarrow \quad x_2 = 3.75 \text{ cm}$$

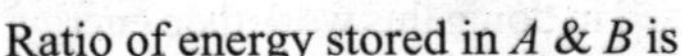
Ratio of energy stored in A & B is

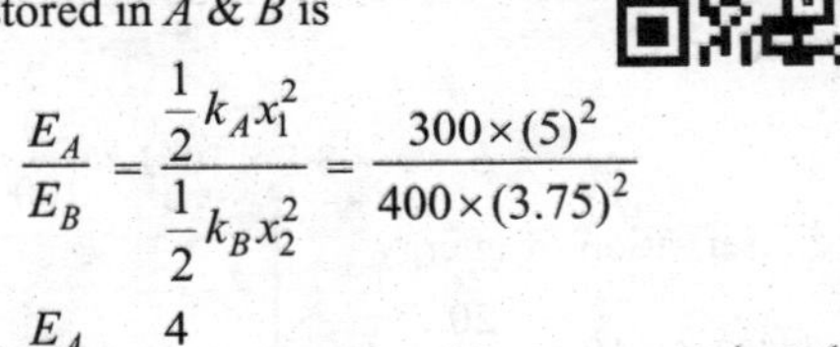
$$\frac{E_A}{E_B} = \frac{\frac{1}{2}k_A x_1^2}{\frac{1}{2}k_B x_2^2} = \frac{300 \times (5)^2}{400 \times (3.75)^2}$$

$$\Rightarrow \quad \frac{E_A}{E_B} = \frac{4}{3}$$

Ans. (A)

Sol. 22 If a is upward acceleration of man, we can use

$$v = \sqrt{2ah_1} = \sqrt{2gh_2}$$

$v_f = 0$, $h_2 = 1\text{m}$, take off point, $u = 0$, a, g, v, $h_1 = 0.5\text{m}$, F, F

$W = mg = 700$ N

$$\Rightarrow \quad a = \frac{gh_2}{h_1} = \frac{10 \times 1}{0.5} = 20 \text{ m/s}^2$$

$\Rightarrow$ Velocity at take off is

$$v = \sqrt{2 \times 10 \times 1} = \sqrt{20} \text{ m/s}$$

Power delivered by muscles is

$$P = ma.v$$

$$\Rightarrow \quad P = 70 \times 20 \times \sqrt{20}$$

$$\Rightarrow \quad P = 6.26 \times 10^3 \text{ W}$$

Ans. (B)

Sol. 23 When the rubber band is stretched by a distance x than work done in further stretching it by dx is given as

$$dW = Fdx = (ax + bx^2)\, dx$$

$$\Rightarrow \quad W = \int dW = \int_0^L (ax + bx^2)dx$$

$$\Rightarrow \quad W = \left[\frac{ax^2}{2} + \frac{bx^3}{3}\right]_0^L$$

$$\Rightarrow \quad W = \frac{aL^2}{2} + \frac{bL^3}{3}$$

Ans. (C)

Sol. 24 To find KE of spring, we consider an elemental part of spring as shown mass of element is $dm = \frac{m}{l}dx$

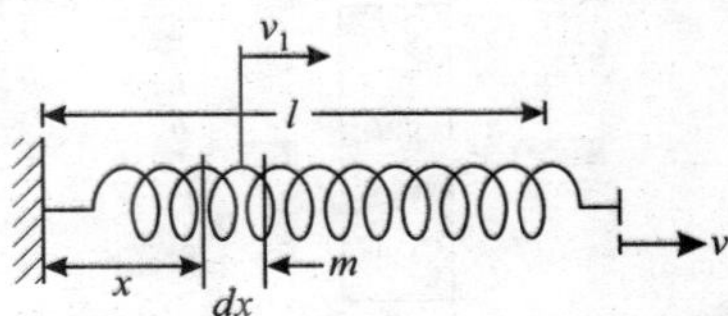

As spring is uniformly stretched, the speed of element is

$$v_1 = \frac{v}{l} \cdot x$$

KE of element is $dK = \frac{1}{2}dmv_1^2$

$$\Rightarrow \quad dK = \frac{1}{2}\left(\frac{m}{l}dx\right)\left(\frac{v}{l}x\right)^2$$

$$\Rightarrow \quad \int dK = \frac{1}{2}\frac{mv^2}{l^3}\int_0^l x^2 dx$$

Total KE of spring is given as

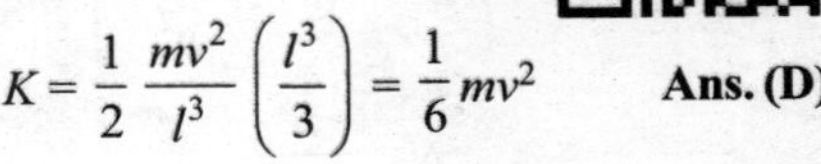
$$K = \frac{1}{2}\frac{mv^2}{l^3}\left(\frac{l^3}{3}\right) = \frac{1}{6}mv^2$$

Ans. (D)

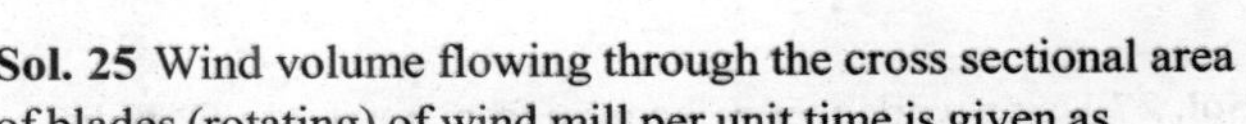
Sol. 25 Wind volume flowing through the cross sectional area of blades (rotating) of wind mill per unit time is given as

$$V = Av$$

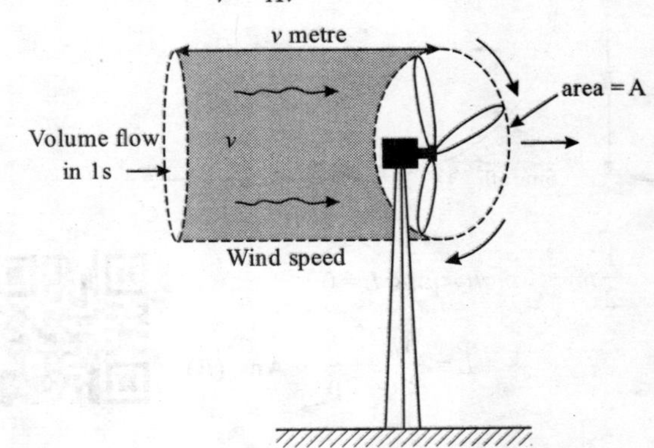

Mass of wind intercepting the blades per second is

$$m = \rho Av \quad [\rho \rightarrow \text{wind density of air}]$$

Kinetic energy of wind mass intercepting the section of blades per second is

$$\text{KE/sec} = \frac{1}{2}mv^2 = \frac{1}{2}\rho Av^3$$

$\Rightarrow$ Electrical power (J/s) $\propto v^3$ **Ans. (D)**

Sol. 26 If plank thickness is x, we have

$$u^2\left(1 - \frac{1}{n}\right)^2 = u^2 - 2ax$$

$$\Rightarrow \quad 2ax = u^2\left[1 - \left(\frac{n-1}{n}\right)^2\right]$$

$$\Rightarrow \qquad 2ax = u^2\left[\frac{2n-1}{n^2}\right] \qquad \ldots(1)$$

Plank

u a $u-\frac{u}{n}$

x

Using constant retardation, we have

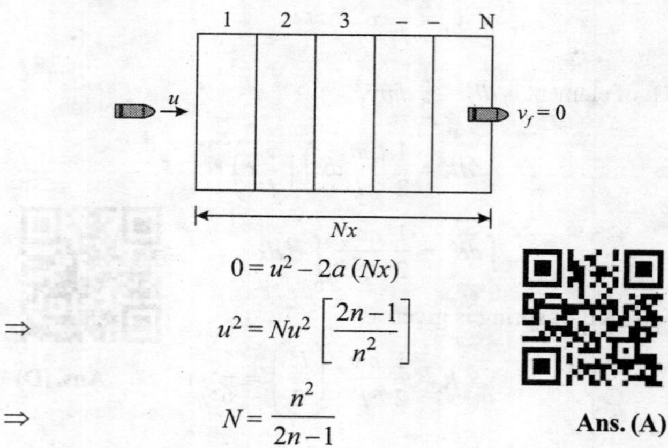

$$0 = u^2 - 2a\,(Nx)$$

$$\Rightarrow \qquad u^2 = Nu^2\left[\frac{2n-1}{n^2}\right]$$

$$\Rightarrow \qquad N = \frac{n^2}{2n-1}$$

Ans. (A)

Sol. 27 Using work energy theorem from point A to C, we have

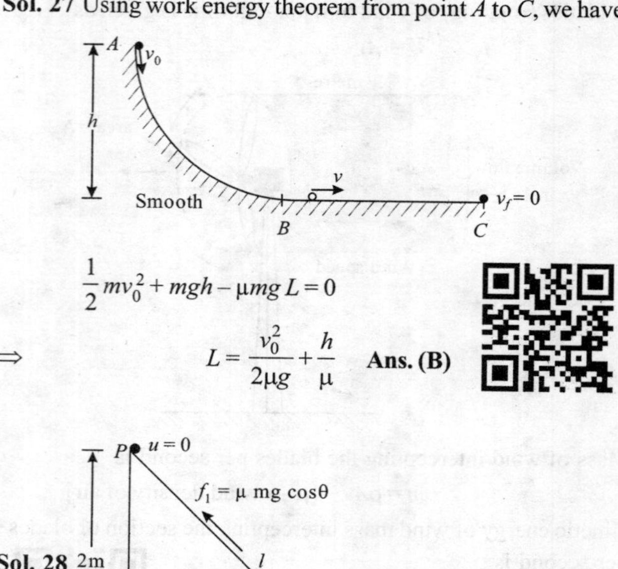

$$\frac{1}{2}mv_0^2 + mgh - \mu mg\,L = 0$$

$$\Rightarrow \qquad L = \frac{v_0^2}{2\mu g} + \frac{h}{\mu}$$

Ans. (B)

Sol. 28

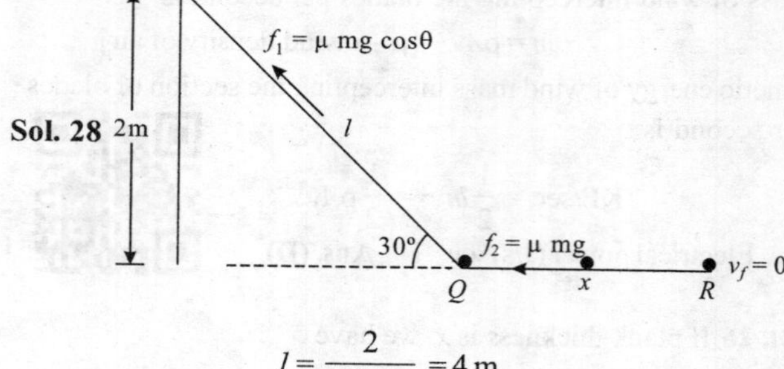

$$l = \frac{2}{\sin 30^\circ} = 4\text{ m}$$

As work done by friction is equal in part PQ & QR

$$\mu mg \cos 30^\circ\,(\mu) = \mu mg\,x$$

$$\Rightarrow \qquad x = 2\sqrt{3}\text{ m} = 3.464\text{ m} \simeq 3.5\text{ m}$$

We use work energy theorem from P to R as

$$K_i(=0) + \text{mg}\,(2) - 2\mu\, mg\,x = K_f(=0)$$

$$\Rightarrow \qquad x = 3.5 = \frac{1}{\mu}$$

$$\Rightarrow \qquad \mu = \frac{1}{3.5} = 0.29$$

Ans. (C)

Sol. 29 Work done in lifting 10 kg mass by 1 m, 1000 times is

$$W = mgh \times 1000 = 10 \times 9.8 \times 1 \times 1000\text{ J}$$

If m in kg mass of fat will be used in doing this work then energy released is

$$E = m \times 3.8 \times 10^7\text{ J} \times \frac{20}{100}$$

By conservation of energy

$$m \times 3.8 \times 10^7 \times \frac{20}{100} = 10 \times 9.8 \times 1 \times 1000$$

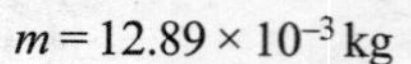

$$\Rightarrow \qquad m = 12.89 \times 10^{-3}\text{ kg}$$

Ans. (D)

Sol. 30 Time function of body's speed

$$v = -5t + 50\text{ m/s}$$

at $t = 0$; $v_1 = 50$ m/s

at $t = 2s$; $v_2 = -5 \times 2 + 50 = 40$ m/s

Work done on body is equal to gain in kinetic energy

$$\Rightarrow \quad W = \frac{1}{2}m\,(v_2^2 - v_1^2) = \frac{1}{2} \times 10 \times ((40)^2 - (50)^2) = -4500\text{ J}$$

Ans. (C)

Sol. 31 To rise up at constant speed v_0, we have driving force

$$f_D = \left(\frac{W}{20} + \frac{W}{10}\right)$$

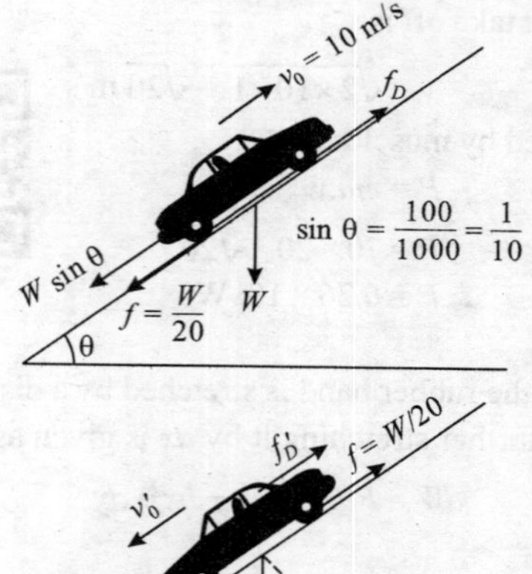

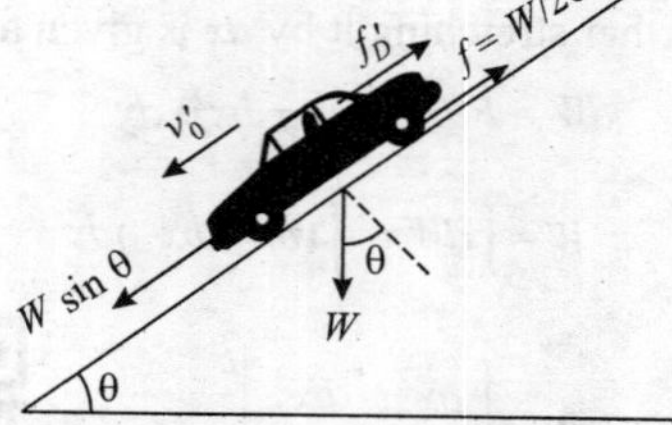

Given that power needed is

$$P = f_D\,v_0 = W\left(\frac{1}{20} + \frac{1}{10}\right) \times 10 \qquad \ldots(1)$$

To move down at constant speed v, we have

$$f'_D = \left(\frac{W}{10} - \frac{W}{20}\right) \text{ and power is } \frac{P}{2}$$

$$\Rightarrow \quad \frac{P}{2} = f'_D v'_0 = W\left(\frac{1}{10} - \frac{1}{20}\right) v'_0 \quad \ldots(2)$$

$$\text{By (1)/(2)} \Rightarrow \quad 2 = \frac{3/2}{1/20v'_0}$$

$$\Rightarrow \quad v_0' = \frac{30}{2} = 15 \text{ m/s} \quad \textbf{Ans. (C)}$$

5.2 Circular Motion

Sol. 1 Friction provides the necessary centripetal force for circular motion so we use

$$f = \frac{mv^2}{R}$$

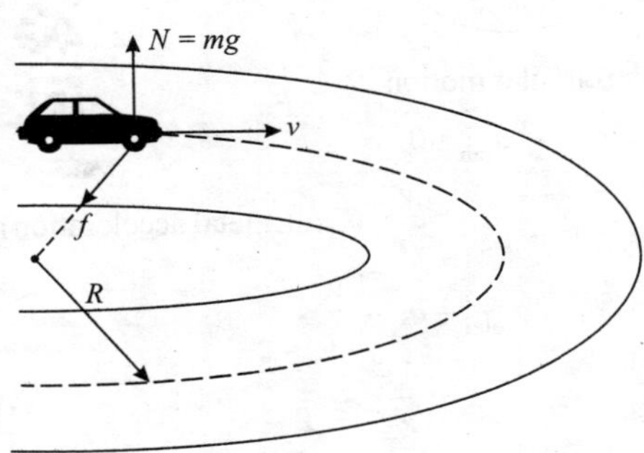

For skidding $\quad f = \dfrac{mv^2}{R} \geq \mu mg$

to avoid skidding

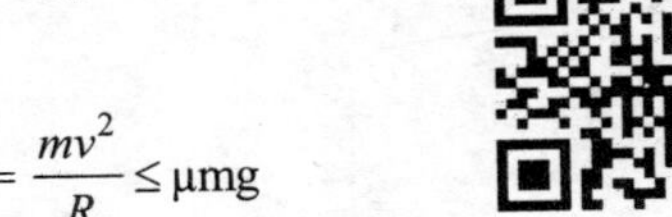

$$f = \frac{mv^2}{R} \leq \mu mg$$

$$\Rightarrow \quad v_{max} = \sqrt{\mu Rg} = \sqrt{0.6 \times 150 \times 10}$$

$$\Rightarrow \quad v_{max} = \sqrt{900} = 30 \text{ m/s} \quad \textbf{Ans. (B)}$$

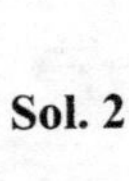

Sol. 2

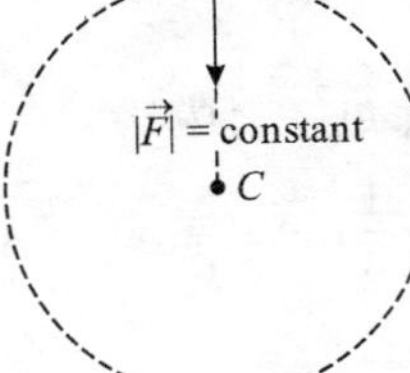

$$|\vec{F}| = \frac{mv^2}{R} \text{ (centripetal force) = constant}$$

$\Rightarrow \quad |v| \to$ constant

$\Rightarrow \quad$ KE $\to$ constant $\quad$ **Ans. (C)**

Sol. 3

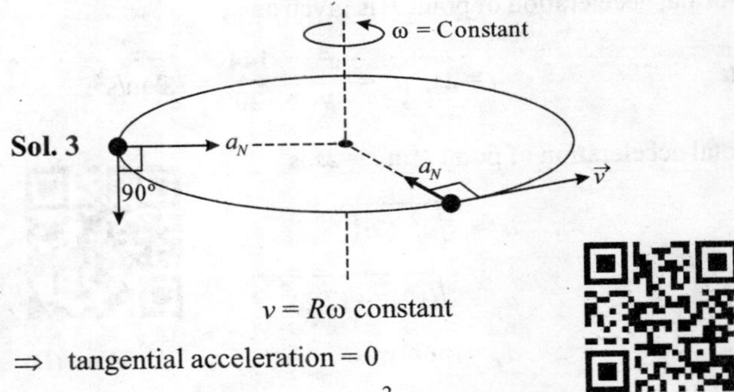

$v = R\omega$ constant

$\Rightarrow$ tangential acceleration = 0

Here normal acceleration $a_N = \dfrac{v^2}{R} = \omega^2 R$ (constant in magnitude)

Option (B) is false here. **Ans. (B)**

Sol. 4

Y, v, P (R, θ), θ, R, a_N, θ, O, X, $a_N = \dfrac{v^2}{R}$

As in uniform circular motion $a_{tangential} = 0$

and only centripetal acceleration is there so its vector is given as

$$\vec{a} = -a_N \cos\theta\,\hat{i} - a_N \sin\theta\,\hat{j}$$

$$\vec{a} = -\frac{v^2}{R}\cos\theta\,\hat{i} - \frac{v^2}{R}\sin\theta\,\hat{j} \quad \textbf{Ans. (C)}$$

Sol. 5

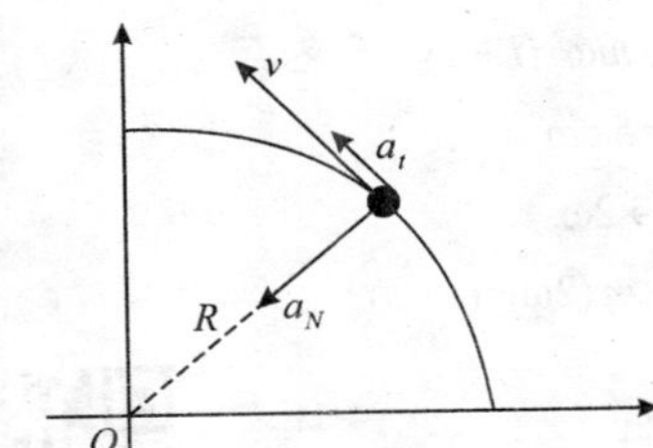

Tangential acceleration of point P is given as

$$a_t = \frac{dv}{dt} = \frac{d^2v}{dt^2} = 6t$$

at $t = 2$s, $a_t = 6 \times 2 = 12$ m/s^2

$$s = t^3 + 5$$

$$\Rightarrow \quad v = \frac{ds}{dt} = 3t^2$$

at $\quad t = 2$s

$$v = 3 \times 4$$

$$\Rightarrow \quad v = 12 \text{ m/s}$$

Normal acceleration of point P is given as

at $\quad t = 2\text{s},\ a_N = \dfrac{v^2}{R} = \dfrac{144}{20} = 7.2\ \text{m/s}^2$

Total acceleration of point P at $t = 2$s is

$$a_T = \sqrt{a_t^2 + a_N^2}$$

$$\Rightarrow \quad a_T = \sqrt{(12)^2 + (7.2)^2}$$

$$\Rightarrow \quad a_T = 13.99\ \text{m/s}^2$$

Ans. (D)

Sol. 6 As cars complete the circles in same time $\Rightarrow$ Their angular speeds are equal

Centripetal acceleration of cars

$$a_{N_1} = \omega^2 r_1$$

$$a_{N_2} = \omega^2 r_2$$

$$\Rightarrow \quad \frac{a_{N_1}}{a_{N_2}} = \frac{r_1}{r_2}$$

Ans. (C)

Sol. 7

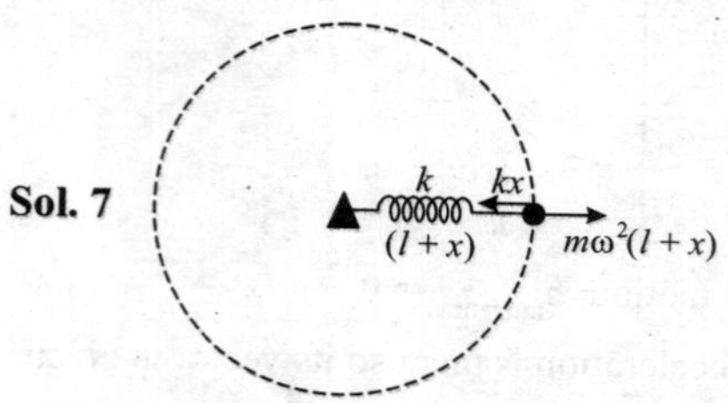

Case-I : $\quad x = 1$ cm

If original length of spring is l, we use

For circular motion of body we have along radial direction

$$x = 1\ \text{cm}$$

$$k(1) = m\omega^2 (l + 1) \quad \ldots(1)$$

Case-II : $\quad x = 5$ cm

$$\omega \to 2\omega$$

$$k(5) = m(2\omega)^2 (l + 5) \quad \ldots(2)$$

$$(2)/(1) \Rightarrow \quad \frac{4(l+5)}{l+1} = \frac{5}{1}$$

$$\Rightarrow \quad 4l + 20 = 5l + 5$$

$$\Rightarrow \quad l = 15\ \text{cm}$$ **Ans. (A)**

Sol. 8

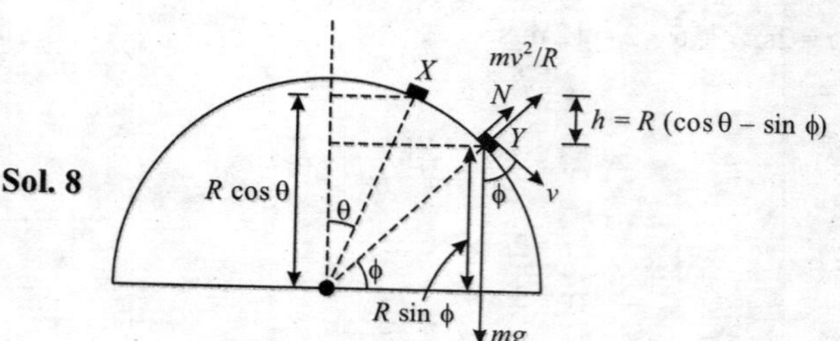

By work energy theorem, we use

$$mgh = \frac{1}{2}mv^2$$

$$\Rightarrow \quad v = \sqrt{2gR(\cos\theta - \sin\phi)}$$

At point Y we have along radial direction in circular motion (in frame of particle)

$$N + \frac{mv^2}{R} = mg\sin\phi$$

As $N = 0$

$$\Rightarrow \quad 2\,mg\,(\cos\theta - \sin\phi) = mg\sin\phi$$

$$\Rightarrow \quad 2\cos\theta = 3\sin\phi$$

Ans. (C)

Sol. 9

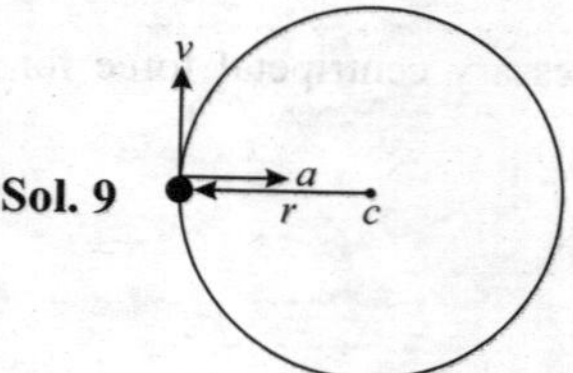

For uniform circular motion

$$a_{\tan} = 0$$

and $\quad a_N = \dfrac{v^2}{r}$ (Centripetal acceleration)

$$\Rightarrow \quad a_{\text{total}} = a_N = \frac{v^2}{r}$$

$$a \propto \frac{1}{r}$$

Ans. (C)

Sol. 10

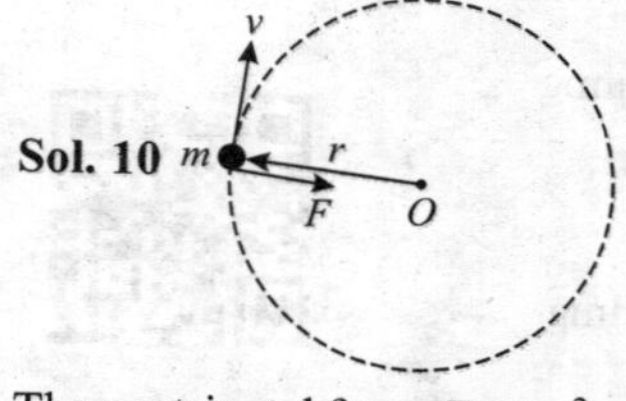

The centripetal force $F = \alpha r^2$

The PE of particle in the field of this force is given as

$$U = -\int_0^r \vec{F}\cdot\vec{dr} = \int_0^r F\,dr = \int_0^r \alpha r^2\,dr = \frac{\alpha r^3}{3} - 0$$

We also use

$$F = \frac{mv^2}{r} = \alpha r^2 \Rightarrow \text{KE} = \frac{1}{2}mv^2 = \frac{1}{2}\alpha r^3$$

Total mechanical energy $= \dfrac{1}{2}\alpha r^3 + \dfrac{1}{3}\alpha r^3 = \dfrac{5}{6}\alpha r^3$ **Ans. (B)**

Sol. 11

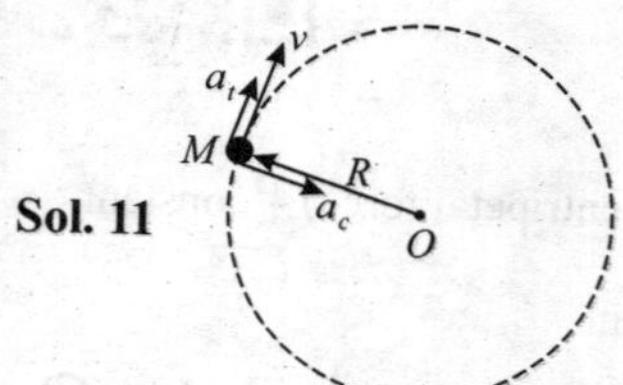

Centripetal acceleration of particle is given as

$$a_c = n^2Rt^2 = \frac{v^2}{R}$$

$$\Rightarrow \quad v^2 = n^2R^2t^2$$

$$\Rightarrow \quad v^2 = nRt \;\Rightarrow\; a_t = \frac{dv}{dt} = nR$$

As v increases, tangential acceleration is in the direction of velocity

Power delivered to the particle is given as

$$P = ma_t v = m\,(nR)\,(nRt)$$

$$\Rightarrow \quad P = mn^2R^2t$$

Ans. (B)

Sol. 12

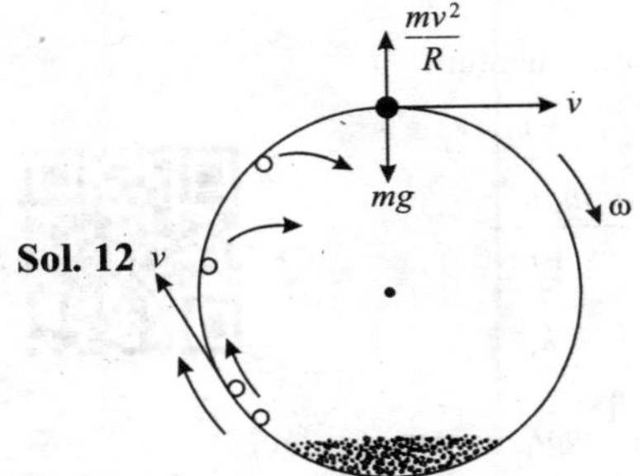

In the frame of rotating drum at the topmost point particle (mixture ingredients) will not loose contact from drum wall if

$$\frac{mv^2}{R} \geq mg \;\Rightarrow\; v \geq \sqrt{Rg}$$

If $v \geq \sqrt{Rg}$ than proper mixing will not take place

Thus for proper mixing $v < \sqrt{Rg}$

$$\Rightarrow \quad \omega = \frac{v}{R} = \sqrt{\frac{g}{R}} = \sqrt{\frac{10}{1.25}}\ \text{rad/s}$$

$$\omega \text{ in rpm is } \omega_{RPM} = \frac{60}{2\pi}\sqrt{\frac{10}{1.25}} \gtrsim 27\ \text{rpm}$$

$\Rightarrow$ If $\omega \simeq 27$ rpm then before reaching top, ingredients fall and mix properly

Ans. (A)

6.1 System of Particles

Sol. 1 $m \xrightarrow{2V}$ $\quad \xleftarrow{V} m$

$-ve \longleftrightarrow +ve$

Velocity of centre of mass is given as

$$\vec{v}_{cm} = \frac{m_1\vec{V_1} + m_2\vec{V_2}}{m_1 + m_2}$$

$$= \frac{m(2V) + m(-v)}{2m}$$

$$= \frac{v}{2}$$

Ans. (C)

Sol. 2 Linear Momentum $\rightarrow$ vector

Kinetic energy $\rightarrow$ scalar

If KE $= 0 \;\Rightarrow\;$ Speeds of all particles of system will be individually zero

$\Rightarrow$ linear momentum $= 0$

Ans. (C)

Sol. 3

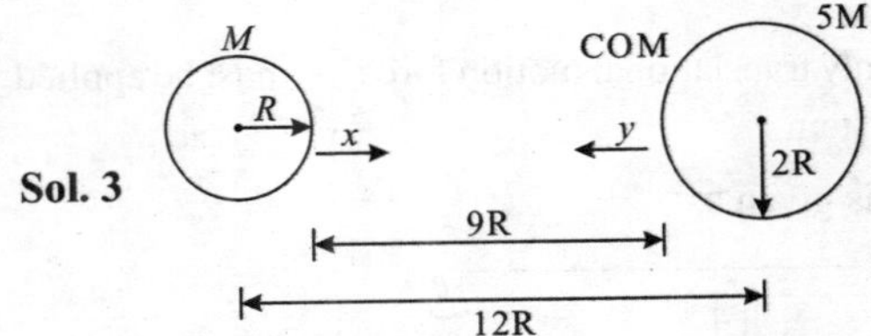

Due to internal gravitational force bodies move such that their centre of mass remain at rest

If M and $5\,M$ travels distances x and y before collision

$$\Rightarrow \quad x + y = 9\,R$$

In motion displacement of centre of mass is zero

$$\Rightarrow \quad \Delta x_{CM} = \frac{M\Delta x_1 + 5M\Delta x_2}{M + 5M} = 0$$

$$\Rightarrow \quad \Delta x_{CM} = Mx - 5\,M(9\,R - x) = 0$$

$$\Rightarrow \quad x = 7.5\,R$$ **Ans. (C)**

Sol. 4

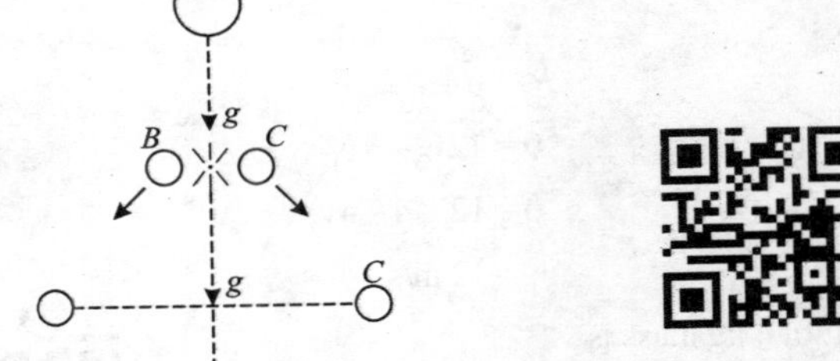

Breaking is due to internal forces which do not affect the motion of centre of mass

$\Rightarrow$ Centre of mass of bodies B & C continue to move as if body A is not broken.

Ans. (B)

Sol. 5

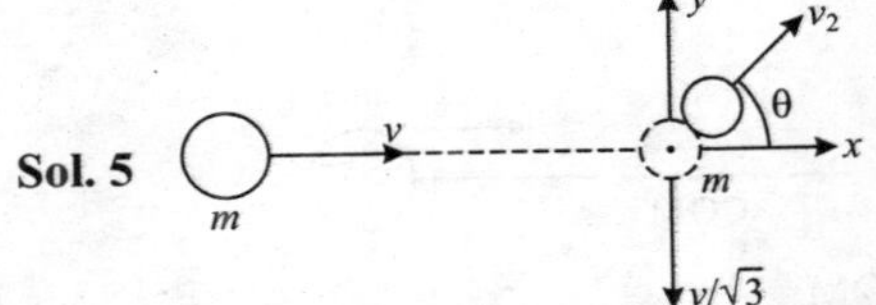

As no external force is present linear momentum of system will remain conserved so we use

in x-dir $\quad mv = mv_2 \cos\theta$

in y-dir $\quad 0 = mv_2 \sin\theta - \dfrac{mv}{\sqrt{3}}$

$\Rightarrow \qquad v_2 \cos\theta = v \qquad \ldots(1)$

and $\qquad v_2 \sin\theta = \dfrac{v}{\sqrt{3}} \qquad \ldots(2)$

Squaring and adding equation-(1) and (2) gives

$$v_2 = \sqrt{v^2 + \frac{v^2}{3}} = \sqrt{\frac{4v^2}{3}} = \frac{2v}{\sqrt{3}} \quad \textbf{Ans. (C)}$$

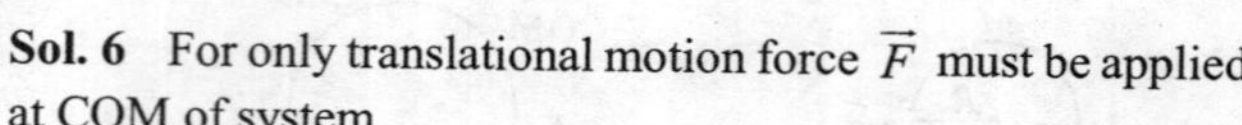

Sol. 6 For only translational motion force $\vec{F}$ must be applied at COM of system

Distance PC is given as

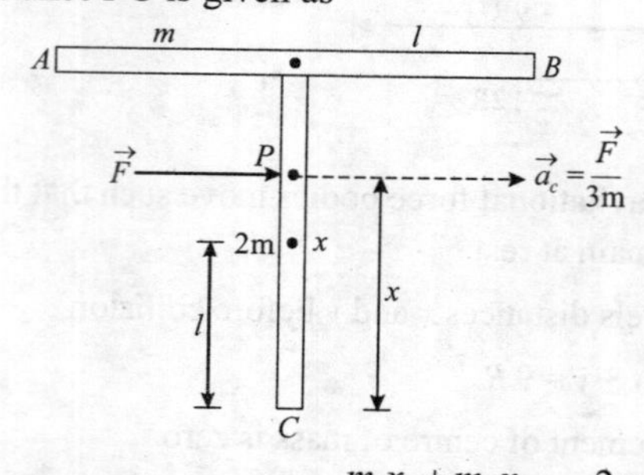

$$x = \frac{m_1x_1 + m_2x_2}{M_1 + m_2} = \frac{2m(l) + m(2l)}{2m + m} = \frac{4l}{3}$$

Ans. (C)

Sol. 7

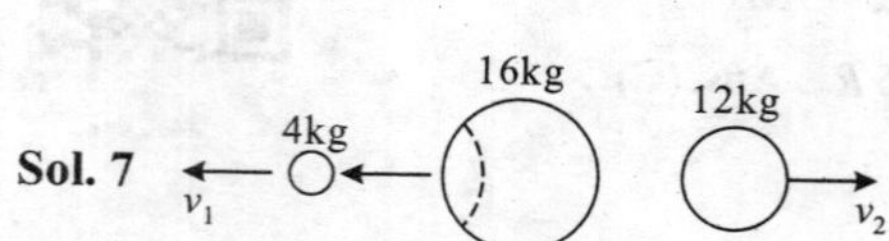

Rest

$$P_i = 0 = P_f$$

$\Rightarrow \qquad 0 = 12v_2 - 4v_1$

$\Rightarrow \qquad 0 = 12 \times 4 - 4v_1$

$\Rightarrow \qquad v_1 = 12\text{ m/s}$

KE of 4 kg mass is

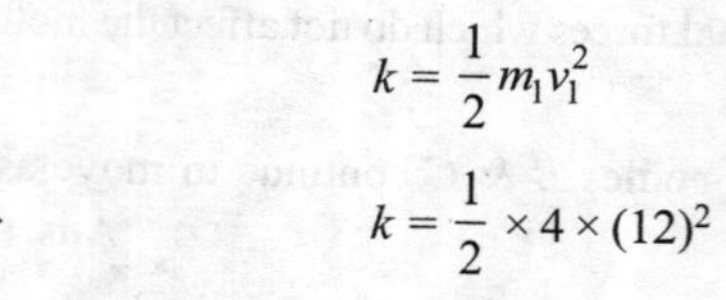

$$k = \frac{1}{2}m_1v_1^2$$

$\Rightarrow \qquad k = \dfrac{1}{2} \times 4 \times (12)^2$

$\Rightarrow \qquad k = 288\text{ J} \qquad$ **Ans. (B)**

Sol. 8

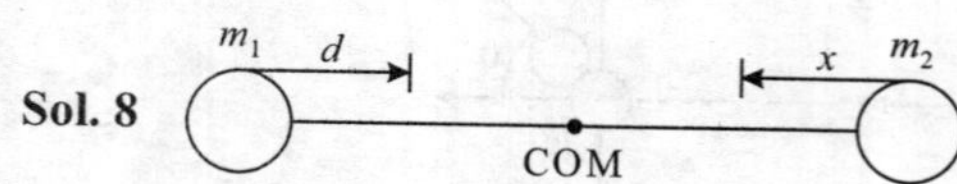

Displacement of COM

$$\Delta x_{COM} = 0$$

We use

$$\bar{\Delta}x_{COM} = \frac{m_1\overline{\Delta x_1} + m_2\overline{\Delta x_2}}{m_1 + m_2}$$

$\Rightarrow \qquad 0 = \dfrac{m_1 d + m_2 x}{m_1 + m_2}$

$\Rightarrow \qquad x = -\dfrac{m_1}{m_2}d$

[– *ve* sign indicates opposite direction]

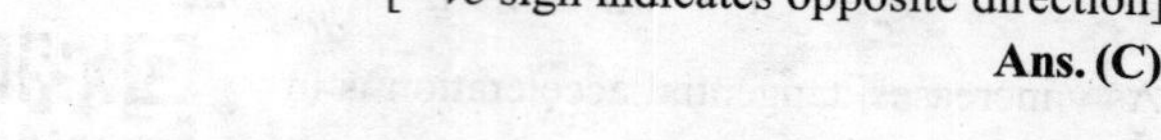

Ans. (C)

Sol. 9

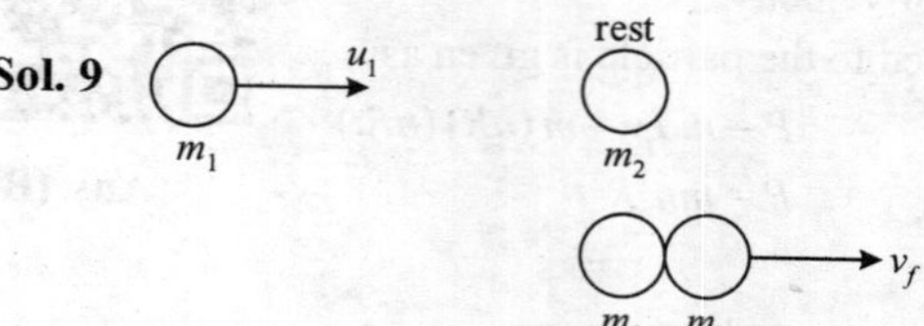

By conservation of linear momentum

$$m_1u_1 = (m_1 + m_2)V_f$$

$\Rightarrow \qquad V_f = \dfrac{m_1u_1}{m_1 + m_2}$

loss in energy $\qquad \Delta E_L = k_i - k_f$

$\Rightarrow \qquad \Delta E_L = \dfrac{1}{2}m_1u_1^2 - \dfrac{1}{2}(m_1 + m_2)v_f^2$

$\Rightarrow \qquad \Delta E_L = \dfrac{1}{2}\left(\dfrac{m_1m_2}{m_1 + m_2}\right)u_1^2$

$\Rightarrow \qquad \Delta E_L = \dfrac{1}{2} \times \dfrac{0.5 \times 1}{0.5 + 1} \times (2)^2 = \dfrac{2}{3}\text{ J} \qquad$ **Ans. (C)**

Sol. 10

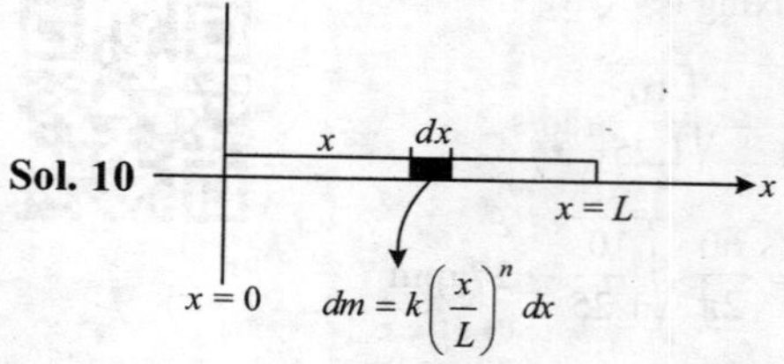

Mass of rod $\qquad M = \int dm = \int_0^L \dfrac{k}{L^n} \cdot \left[\dfrac{x^{n+1}}{n+1}\right]_0^L = \left(\dfrac{k}{n+1}\right)L$

Centre of mass position of rod

$$x_{cm} = \frac{1}{M}\int dmx$$

$\Rightarrow \qquad x_{cm} = \dfrac{1}{\left(\dfrac{k}{n+1}\right)L} \cdot \int_0^L \dfrac{k}{L^n} \cdot x^{n+1}dx$

$\Rightarrow \qquad x_{cm} = \dfrac{n+1}{L^{n+1}}\left(\dfrac{x^{n+2}}{n+2}\right)_0^L = \left(\dfrac{n+1}{n+2}\right)L$

at $n = 0 \rightarrow x_{cm} = \dfrac{L}{2}$ and at $n \rightarrow \infty$ we have $x_{cm} = L \qquad$ **Ans. (A)**

Sol. 11

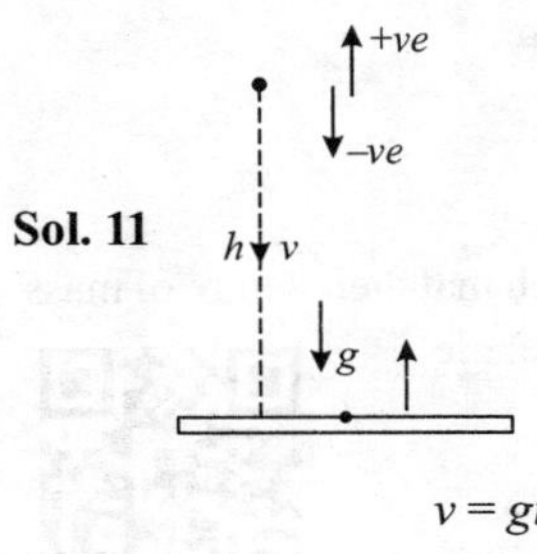

$$v = gt$$ **Ans. (A)**

Sol. 12 Slope of x-t curve from $t = 0$ to $t = 2$ s

$$v_1 = \frac{2}{2} = 1 \text{ m/s} \quad +ve$$

Slope of x-t curve from $t = 2$ s to $t = 4$ s

$$v_2 = \frac{2}{2} = -1 \text{ m/s}$$

Impulse

$$\Rightarrow \quad \vec{J} = \Delta\vec{P} = m\vec{v}_2 - m\vec{v}_1$$

$$\Rightarrow \quad |\vec{J}| = |0.4(-1-1)|$$

$$|\vec{J}| = 0.4 \times 2 = 0.8 \text{ Ns}$$ **Ans. (B)**

Sol. 13

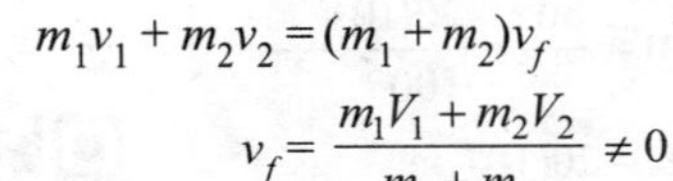

$$m_1v_1 + m_2v_2 = (m_1 + m_2)v_f$$

$$\Rightarrow \quad v_f = \frac{m_1V_1 + m_2V_2}{m_1 + m_2} \neq 0$$

$\Rightarrow \quad k_f \neq 0$ **Ans. (B)**

$\Rightarrow$ S-1 and S-2 are true and S-2 is explaining S-1

Sol. 14

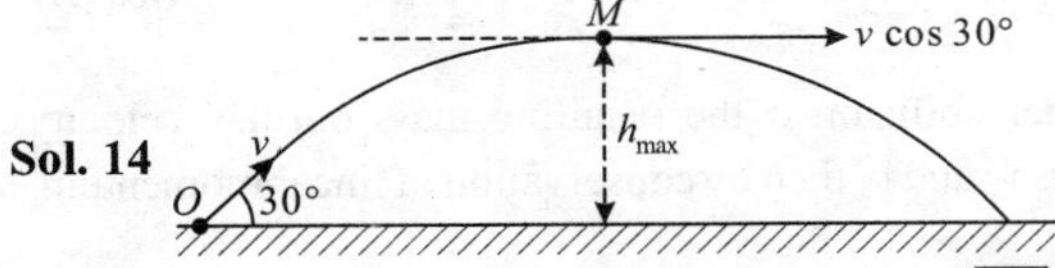

Maximum height of projectile

$$h_{max} = \frac{v^2 \sin^2(30°)}{2g}$$

Angular momentum of particle at M about O is given as

$$L_{MO} = m(V\cos 30°) \times h_{max}$$

$$\Rightarrow \quad L_{MO} = mv\left(\frac{\sqrt{3}}{2}\right) \times \frac{v^2}{2g}\left(\frac{1}{4}\right) = \frac{\sqrt{3}mv^3}{16g}$$

Ans. (D)

Sol. 15 As finally blocks come to rest

$$\Rightarrow \quad m_1V_1 = m_2V_2$$

$$\Rightarrow \quad V_{CM} = 0$$

Thus COM of system will remain at rest

$\Rightarrow$ displacement of $COM = 0$

Thus we use

$$\Delta x_{cm} = \frac{m_2x_2 - m_1x_1}{m_1 + m_2} = 0$$

$$\Rightarrow \quad m_1x_1 = m_2x_2$$

$$\Rightarrow \quad \frac{x_1}{x_2} = \frac{m_2}{m_1}$$ **Ans. (A)**

Sol. 16

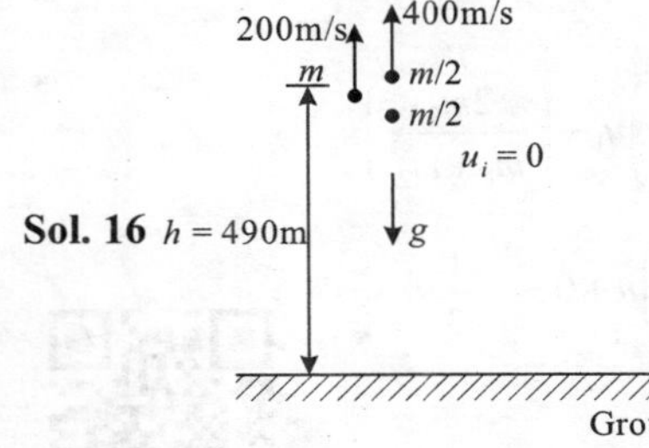

Initial upward momentum of moving body is

$$P_i = m(200)$$

Final upward momentum of $m/2$ (one part) is

$$P_f = \frac{m}{2}(400) = m(200)$$

As the moving part carries the same momentum as that of the initial body, No momentum is left in the other part

$$\Rightarrow \quad v_{\text{other part}} = 0$$

As it is in free fall, time taken to hit the ground is

$$t = \sqrt{\frac{2h}{g}} = \sqrt{\frac{2 \times 490}{9.8}} = \sqrt{100} = 10 \text{ s}$$ **Ans. (C)**

Sol. 17

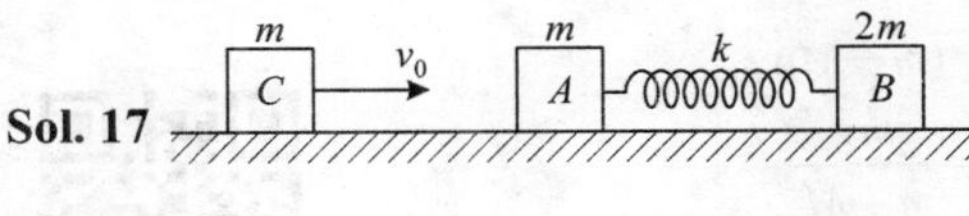

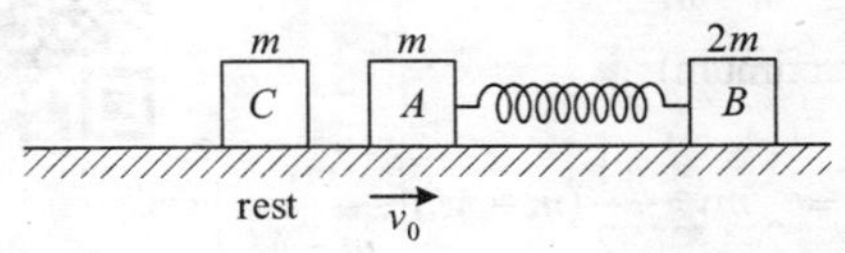

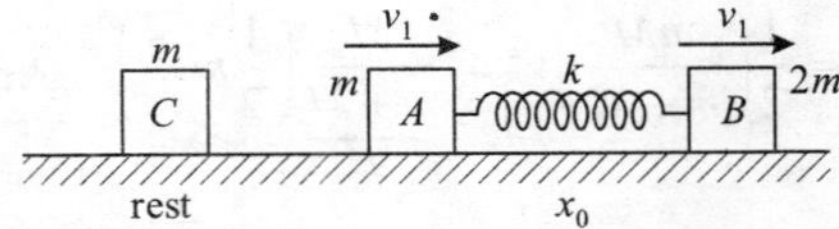

By conservation of linear momentum, we have

$$mv_0 = 3mv_1 \quad \Rightarrow \quad v_1 = \frac{v_0}{3}$$

By conservation of energy, we have

$$\frac{1}{2}mv_0^2 = \frac{1}{2}(3m)\left(\frac{v_0}{3}\right)^2 + \frac{1}{2}kx_0^2$$

$$\Rightarrow \frac{1}{2}mv_0^2\left(1-\frac{1}{3}\right) = \frac{1}{2}kx_0^2$$

$$\Rightarrow \qquad k = \frac{2}{3}mv_0^2\left(\frac{1}{x_0^2}\right) \qquad \textbf{Ans. (D)}$$

Sol. 18 m u — $2m$ rest; m v_1, $2m$ v_2; $k_i = \frac{1}{2}mu^2$

For elastic collision (Head-on), The final velocity of particle m is given as

$$v_1 = \left(\frac{m_1 - m_2}{m_1 + m_2}\right)u_1 + \left(\frac{2m_2}{m_1 + m_2}\right)u_2$$

$$\Rightarrow \qquad v_1 = \left(\frac{m - 2m}{m + 2m}\right)u + 0 = -\frac{1}{3}u$$

Final KE of particle – 1 is

$$k_f = \frac{1}{2}m\left(\frac{u}{3}\right)^2 = \frac{1}{2}mu^2\left(\frac{1}{9}\right)$$

% loss in KE of first particle is % loss

$$\Delta k_L = \frac{k_i - k_f}{k_i} \times 100 = \left(1 - \frac{1}{9}\right) \times 100\,\%$$

$$\Rightarrow \qquad \Delta k_L \simeq 89\% \qquad \textbf{Ans. (C)}$$

Sol. 19 As maximum energy loss occurs in completely inelastic collision

$\Rightarrow$ Statement-2 is true

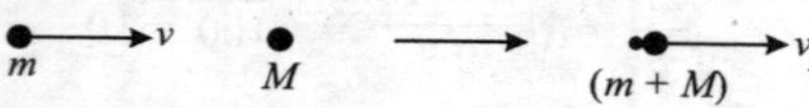

by conservation of momentum

$$mv = (m + M)v_f$$

$$\Rightarrow \qquad v_f = \frac{mv}{m + M}$$

Energy loss (maximum)

$$\Delta E_{\max} = \frac{1}{2}mv^2 - \frac{1}{2}(m + M)\left(\frac{mv}{m + M}\right)^2$$

$$\Delta E_{\max} = \frac{1}{2}\left(\frac{mM}{m + M}\right)v^2 = \underbrace{\frac{M}{m + M}}_{f}\left(\frac{1}{2}mv^2\right) \qquad \textbf{Ans. (D)}$$

Sol. 20

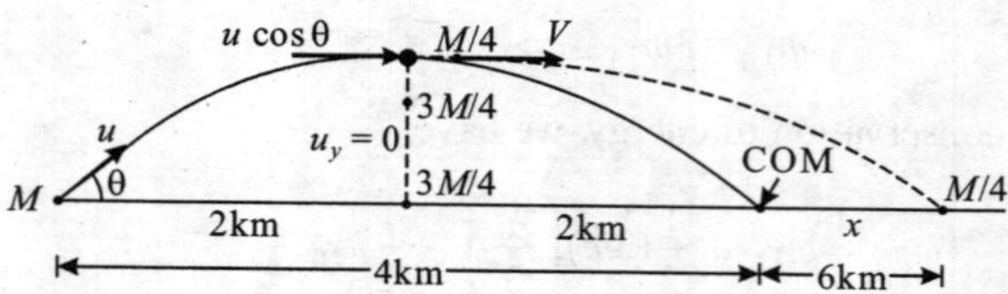

By Conservation of linear momentum

$$M(u\cos\theta) = \frac{M}{u}\cdot v$$

$$\Rightarrow \qquad v = 4u\cos\theta$$

$3M/4$ and $M/4$ will fall on ground such that their centre of mass is located at the original path of projectile

$$\Rightarrow \qquad \frac{3M}{4} \times 2 = \frac{M}{4} \times x$$

$$\Rightarrow \qquad x = 6\,\text{km}$$

$$\text{Range} = 4 + 6 = 10\,\text{km} \qquad \textbf{Ans. (C)}$$

Sol. 21

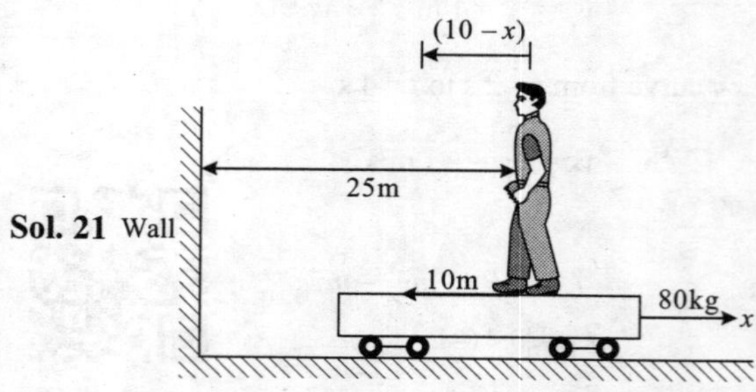

Due to motion of boy, if cart displaces toward right by x such that

$$\Delta x_{COM} = 0 = \frac{M_1x_1 + M_2x_2}{M_1 + M_2}$$

$$\Rightarrow \qquad 0 = \frac{80x - 20(10 - x)}{100}$$

$$\Rightarrow \qquad 80x = 20(10 - x)$$

$$\Rightarrow \qquad 5x = 10$$

$$\Rightarrow \qquad x = 2\,\text{m}$$

Final distance of boy from wall is

$$d = 25 - (10 - 2) = 17\,\text{m} \qquad \textbf{Ans. (D)}$$

Sol. 22 After collision if the resulting mass $6m$ has velocity components v_x and v_y then by conservation of linear momentum, we have

Along x-direction

$$+m(3u) - 2m(2u)\cos 60° - 3mu\cos 60° = 6mv_x$$

$$\Rightarrow \qquad 3u - 2u - \frac{3}{2}u = 6v_x$$

$$\Rightarrow \qquad v_x = -\frac{u}{12}$$

Along y-direction

$$-(2m)(2u)\sin 60° + 3mu\sin 60° = 6mv_y$$

$$\Rightarrow \qquad -4mu\left(\frac{\sqrt{3}}{2}\right) + 3mu\left(\frac{\sqrt{3}}{2}\right) = 6mv_y$$

$$\Rightarrow \qquad -\frac{\sqrt{3}}{2}u = 6v_y$$

$$\Rightarrow \quad v_y = -\frac{\sqrt{3}}{12}u$$

$$\Rightarrow \quad \vec{v} = v_x\hat{i} + v_y\hat{i}$$

$$\Rightarrow \quad \vec{v}_{6m} = -\frac{u}{12}\hat{i} - \frac{\sqrt{3}}{12}u\hat{j}$$

$$= \frac{u}{12}(-i - \sqrt{3}\hat{j})$$

Ans. (D)

Sol. 23

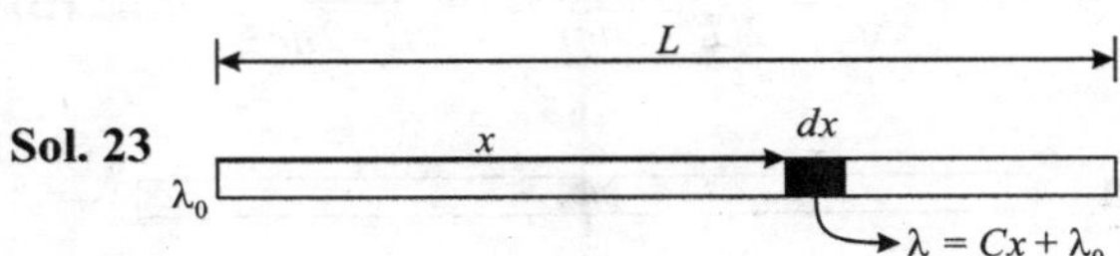

Mass of element is

$$M = \int dm = \int_0^L \lambda dx = \int_0^L (Cx + \lambda_0)dx$$

$$\Rightarrow \quad M = \int_0^L (Cx + \lambda_0)dx$$

$$\Rightarrow \quad M = \frac{CL^2}{2} + \lambda_0 L$$

$$\Rightarrow \quad C = \frac{2}{L^2}(M - \lambda_0 L)$$

Distance of COM from lighter end is

$$x_{COM} = \frac{1}{M}\int dmx = \frac{1}{M}\int_0^L (Cx^2 + \lambda_0 x)dx$$

$$\Rightarrow \quad x_{COM} = \frac{1}{M}\left(\frac{LC^3}{3} + \frac{\lambda_0 L^2}{2}\right) = \frac{L^2}{M}\left(\frac{CL}{3} + \frac{\lambda_0}{2}\right)$$

$$\Rightarrow \quad x_{COM} = \frac{L^2}{M}\left(\frac{2}{3L}(M - \lambda_0 L) + \frac{\lambda_0}{2}\right)$$

$$\Rightarrow \quad x_{COM} = \frac{2}{3}L - \frac{L^2}{M}\left(-\frac{2}{3}\lambda_0 + \frac{\lambda_0}{2}\right)$$

$$\Rightarrow \quad x_{COM} = \frac{2L}{3} - \frac{\lambda_0 L^2}{6M}$$

Ans. (D)

Sol. 24

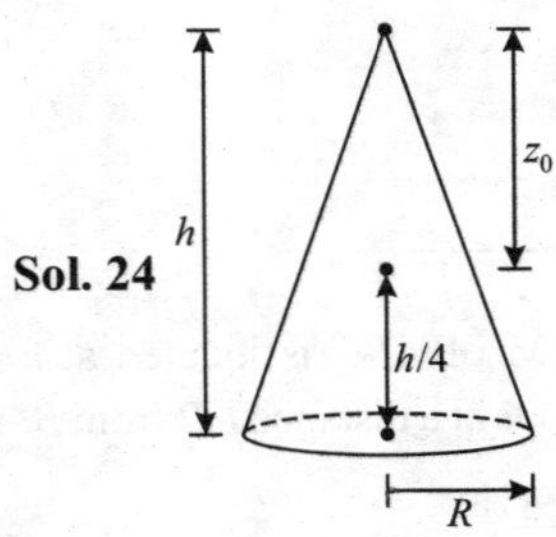

COM distance from vertex

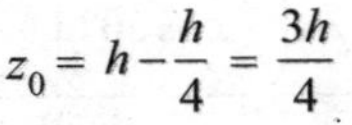

$$z_0 = h - \frac{h}{4} = \frac{3h}{4}$$

Ans. (B)

Sol. 25

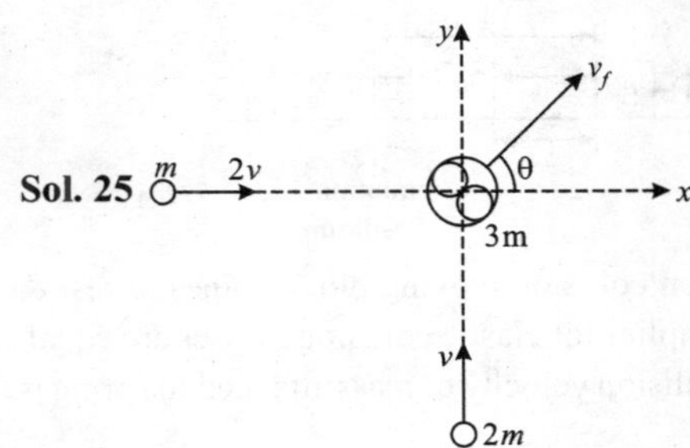

By conservation of linear momentum

in x-direction $\quad 2mv = 3mv_f\cos\theta \quad \ldots(1)$

in y-direction $\quad 2mv = 3mv_f\sin\theta \quad \ldots(2)$

Squaring and adding (1) and (2)

$$2v_f = \sqrt{8}v$$

$$\Rightarrow \quad v_f = \frac{2\sqrt{2}}{3}v$$

Initial KE of system is

$$k_i = \frac{1}{2}m(2V)^2 + \frac{1}{2}2m(V)^2 = 3mv^2$$

Final KE of system is

$$k_f = \frac{1}{2}3m\left(\frac{2\sqrt{2}}{3}v\right)^2 = \frac{4}{3}mv^2$$

Loss in energy during collision

$$\Delta E_L = k_i - k_y = \frac{5}{3}mv^2$$

$$\% \text{ loss} = \frac{k_i - k_f}{k_i} \times 100\%$$

$$\Rightarrow \quad \% \text{ loss} = \frac{500}{9} = 55.55\%$$

Ans. (C)

Sol. 26

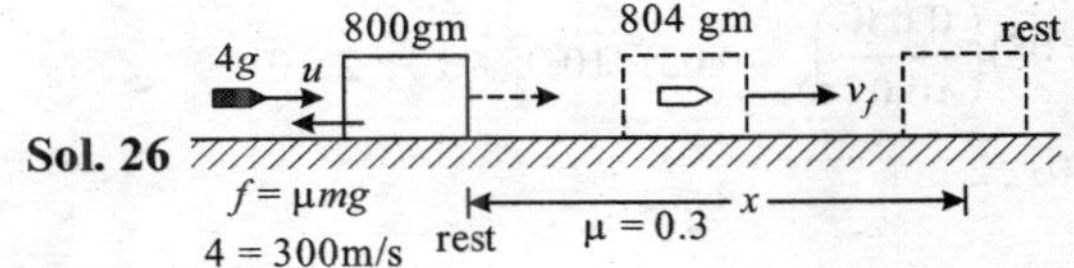

By conservation of momentum we use

$$4u + 0 = 804v_f$$

$$v_f = \frac{4 \times 300}{804} = \frac{1200}{804} = 1.49 \text{ m/s}$$

using work energy theorem for block sliding on rough surface, we have

$$\frac{1}{2}mv_f^2 - \mu mgx = 0$$

$$\Rightarrow \quad x = \frac{V_f^2}{2\mu g} = \frac{(1.49)^2}{2 \times 0.3 \times 10} = 0.379 \text{ m}$$

Ans. (B)

Sol. 27

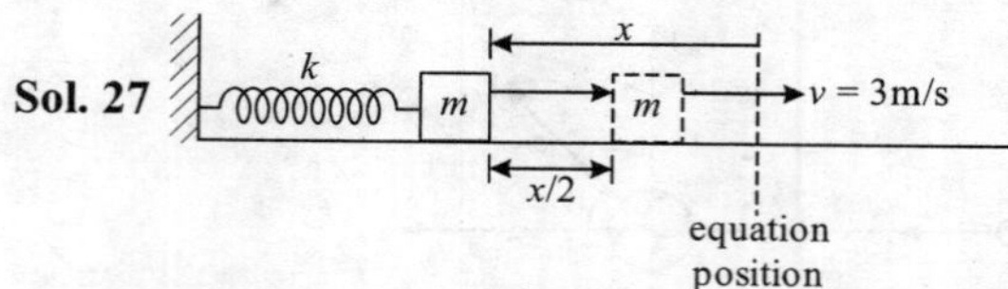

As it is given that on collision moving block comes to rest & other moves, this implies for elastic collision masses are equal. Thus just before collision velocity of mass attached to spring is 3 m/s.

By conservation of energy, we use

$$\frac{1}{2}kx^2 = \frac{1}{2}k\left(\frac{x}{2}\right)^2 + \frac{1}{2}mv^2$$

$$\Rightarrow \quad \frac{1}{2}kx^2\left(1-\frac{1}{4}\right) = \frac{1}{2}\times 0.1\times(3)^2$$

$$\Rightarrow \quad \frac{1}{2}kx^2 = \frac{0.9}{2}\times\frac{4}{3}$$

$$\Rightarrow \quad \frac{1}{2}kx^2 = 0.6\text{ J}$$

initial stored energy in spring. **Ans. (B)**

Sol. 28

If after collision block moves at speed v_1 we have by momentum conservation

$$0.05V = 10.05v_1$$

$$\Rightarrow \quad v_1 = \frac{0.05v}{10.05}$$

Using work-energy theorem after collision we have

$$\frac{1}{2}(10.05)\,v_1^2 - \mu\,(m+M)gx = 0$$

$$\Rightarrow \quad \frac{1}{2}(10.05)\left(\frac{0.05v}{10.05}\right)^2 - 0.05\times 10.05\times 10\times 2 = 0$$

$$\Rightarrow \quad v = 201\sqrt{2}\text{ m/s}$$

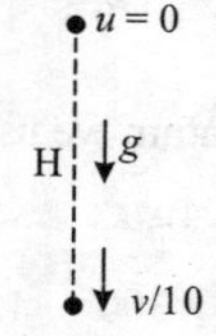

We have

$$\Rightarrow \quad \frac{v}{10} = \sqrt{2gH}$$

$$\Rightarrow \quad H = \frac{v^2}{200g} = \frac{(201\sqrt{2})^2}{2\times 10^3} \cong 40\text{ m}$$ **Ans. (D)**

Sol. 29 When a bead strikes with speed v and rebond the change in momentum is

$$\Delta P = mv - (-me) = 2mv$$

Between two supoort, the distance beads travel on rod is

$$r = L - n(2r) \text{ (diameter of each bead)}$$

Time between two successive collisions on same support is

$$\Delta t = \frac{2r}{v} = \frac{2[L-2nr]}{v}$$

Average force on each support is

$$F = \frac{\Delta P}{\Delta t} = \frac{2mv}{2(L-2nr)}\times v = \frac{mv^2}{L-2nr}$$ **Ans. (B)**

Sol. 30

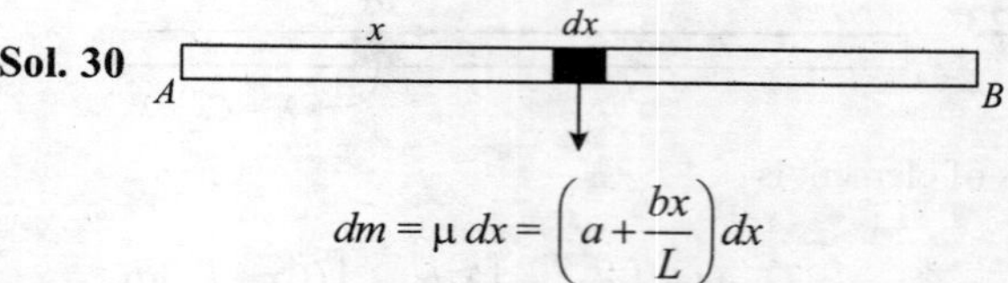

$$dm = \mu\,dx = \left(a+\frac{bx}{L}\right)dx$$

COM of rod is given as

$$x_{cm} = \frac{\int dm\,x}{\int dm} = \frac{\int_0^L\left(a+\frac{bx}{L}\right)x\,dx}{\int_0^L\left(a+\frac{bx}{L}\right)dx}$$

$$\Rightarrow \quad x_{cm} = \frac{\left(\frac{aL^2}{2}+\frac{bL^2}{3L}\right)}{\left(aL+\frac{bL^2}{2L}\right)} = \frac{7L}{12}$$

$$\Rightarrow \quad \frac{7L}{12} = \frac{\frac{a}{2}+\frac{b}{3}}{a+\frac{b}{2}}$$

$$\Rightarrow \quad 7a+\frac{7b}{2} = 6a+4b$$

$$\Rightarrow \quad a = \frac{b}{2}$$

$$\Rightarrow \quad b = 2a$$ **Ans. (B)**

Sol. 31

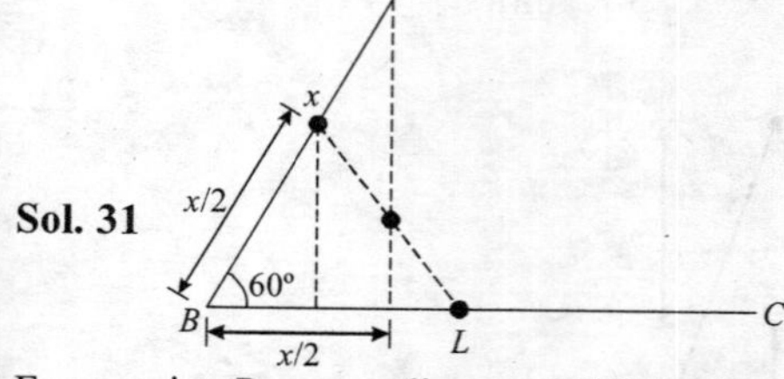

From point B, x coordinate of COM of ABC is located at a distance $x/2$ from B and for BC, COM is at a distance $L/2$ from B.

$$\Rightarrow \quad x_{cm} = \frac{m_1x_1+m_2x_2}{m_1+m_2}$$

$$\Rightarrow \quad \frac{x}{2} = \frac{\lambda x\left(\frac{x}{2}\cos 60^\circ\right)+\lambda L\left(\frac{L}{2}\right)}{\lambda x+\lambda L}$$

If λ kg/m is linear mass density of wire

$\Rightarrow \quad m_1 = \lambda x \quad \& \quad m_2 = \lambda L$
$\quad (AB) \qquad\qquad (BC)$

$$\Rightarrow \quad \frac{x}{2}(x+L) = \frac{x^2}{4} + \frac{L^2}{2}$$

$$\Rightarrow \quad \frac{x^2}{2} + \frac{xL}{2} = \frac{x^2}{4} + \frac{L^2}{2}$$

$$\Rightarrow \quad \frac{x^2}{4} + \frac{xL}{2} = \frac{L^2}{2}$$

$$\Rightarrow \quad \left(\frac{L}{x}\right)^2 - \left(\frac{L}{x}\right) - \frac{1}{2} = 0$$

$$\Rightarrow \quad \frac{L}{x} = \frac{1+\sqrt{1+4(1/2)}}{2} = \frac{1+\sqrt{3}}{2} \simeq 1.37$$

Ans. (C)

6.2 Rigid Body Dynamics

Sol. 1

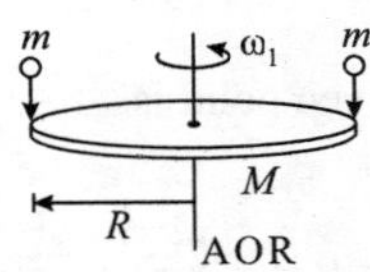

Initial MI of disc

$$I_1 = \frac{1}{2}MR^2$$

Initial MI of disc with small spheres

$$I_2 = \frac{1}{2}MR^2 + 2mR^2$$

As no external torque is applied on disc, its angular momentum remain conserved.

$$\Rightarrow \quad I_1\omega_1 = I_2\omega_2 \text{ (where } \omega_2 \text{ is final angular speed)}$$

$$\Rightarrow \quad \omega_2 = \frac{I_1\omega_1}{I_2} = \left(\frac{M}{M+4m}\right)\omega_1$$

Ans. (C)

Sol. 2

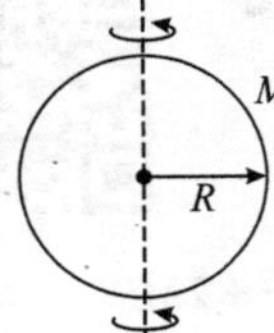

MI of a circular ring about its diametrical axis is given as

$$I = \frac{1}{2}MR^2$$

Ans. (A)

Sol. 3

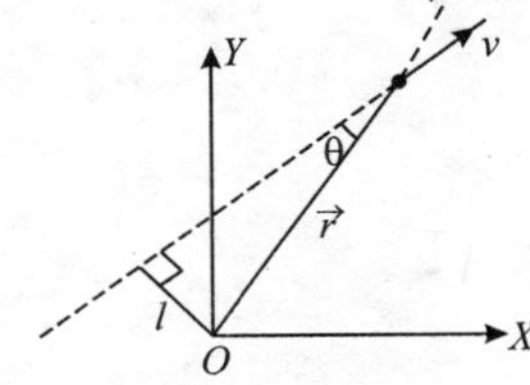

Angular momentum

$$\vec{L} = m(\vec{r} \times \vec{v}) = mvr\sin\theta = mvl$$

Ans. (B)

Sol. 4

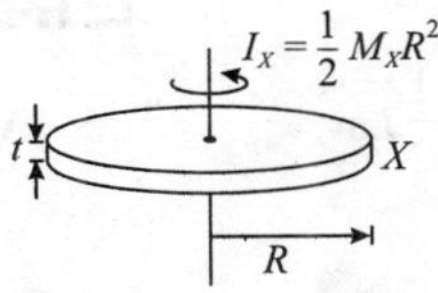

Mass of disc X is

$$M_x = \rho(\pi R^2 t)$$

$$\Rightarrow \quad I_x = \frac{1}{2}\rho\pi R^4 t$$

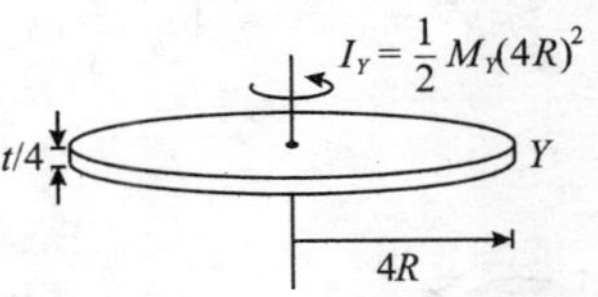

Mass of disc Y is

$$M_y = \rho(\pi(4R)^2(t/4)) = 4\rho\pi R^2 t$$

$$\Rightarrow \quad I_Y = \frac{1}{2}(64\rho\pi R^4 t)$$

$$\Rightarrow \quad I_y = 64\, I_X$$

Ans. (D)

Sol. 5 For a particle in circular motion, we have

Angular momentum $L = I\omega \Rightarrow I = \dfrac{L}{\omega}$

Kinetic Energy $\quad K = \dfrac{1}{2}I\omega^2 = \dfrac{1}{2}\left(\dfrac{L}{\omega}\right)\omega^2$

$$\Rightarrow \quad L = \frac{2K}{\omega}$$

If $\quad K \to K/2$ and $\omega \to 2\omega$

Then final angular momentum is

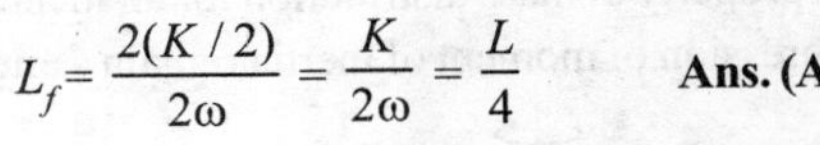

$$L_f = \frac{2(K/2)}{2\omega} = \frac{K}{2\omega} = \frac{L}{4}$$

Ans. (A)

Sol. 6 For the given particle, we know

$$\vec{\tau} = \vec{r} \times \vec{F}$$

$\Rightarrow \quad \vec{\tau}$ is $\perp$ to $\vec{r}$ and also $\vec{\tau}$ is $\perp$ to $\vec{F}$

$$\Rightarrow \quad \vec{r}\cdot\vec{\tau} = 0 \text{ and } \vec{F}\cdot\vec{\tau} = 0$$

Ans. (D)

Sol. 7

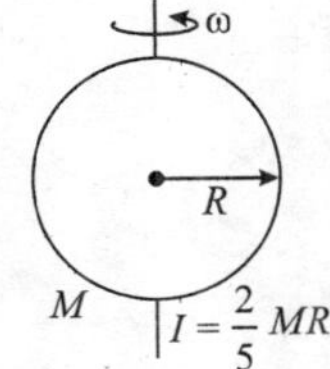

If R increases $\Rightarrow$ I increases

As no external torque is applied

$\Rightarrow$ Angular momentum remain conserved

So as I increases, ω decreases

Rotational KE $\quad K = \frac{1}{2}I\omega^2 = \frac{1}{2}L\omega$ **Ans. (B)**

Sol. 8

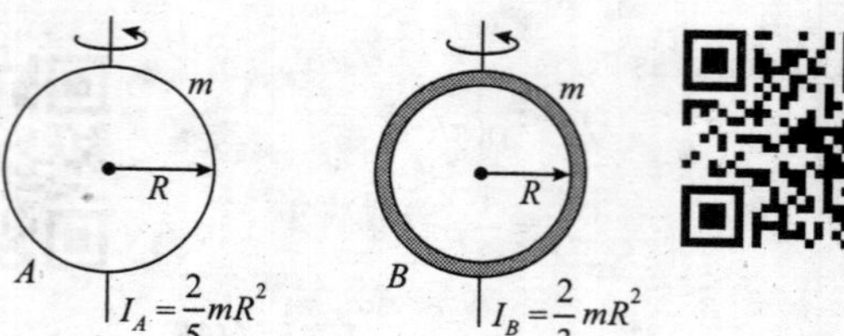

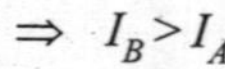

$\Rightarrow$ $I_B > I_A$

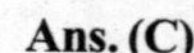

Ans. (C)

Sol. 9

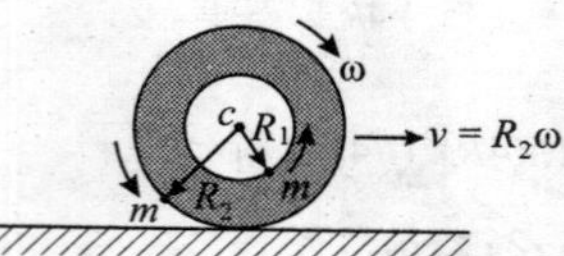

With respect to ring centre the two particles on inner and outer parts of ring are in uniform circular motion at speed ω.

$\Rightarrow$ Forces on the two particles are

$$F_1 = m\omega^2 R_1 \text{ and } F_2 = m\omega^2 R_2$$

$$\Rightarrow \quad \frac{F_1}{F_2} = \frac{R_1}{R_2}$$ **Ans. (D)**

Sol. 10

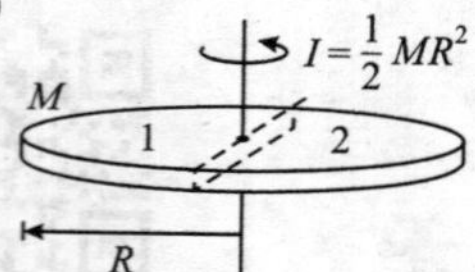

By property of mass distribution for all identical parts of a body, expression of moment of inertia remain same.

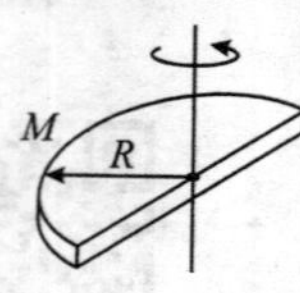

$$\Rightarrow \quad I = \frac{1}{2}MR^2$$ **Ans. (D)**

Sol. 11

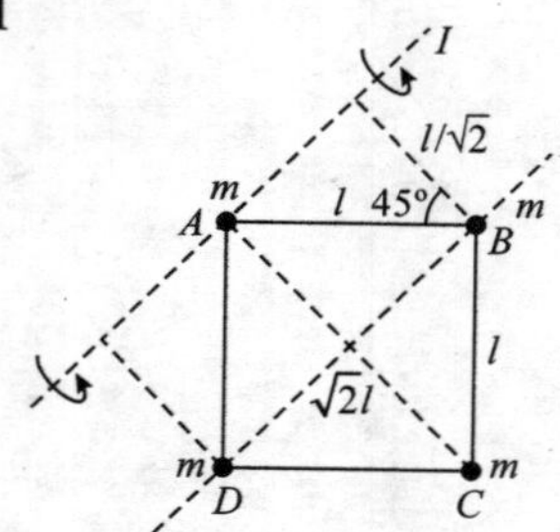

MI of all the masses about given AOR is

$$I = I_A + I_B + I_C + I_D$$

$$\Rightarrow \quad I = 0 + m\left(\frac{l}{\sqrt{2}}\right)^2 + m(\sqrt{2}l)^2 + m\left(\frac{l}{\sqrt{2}}\right)^2$$

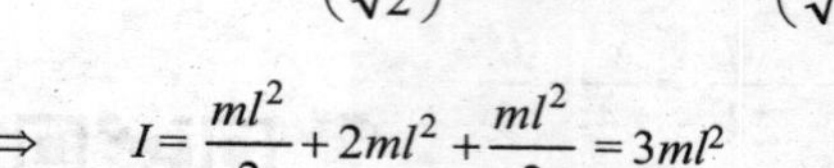

$$\Rightarrow \quad I = \frac{ml^2}{2} + 2ml^2 + \frac{ml^2}{2} = 3ml^2$$ **Ans. (C)**

Sol. 12

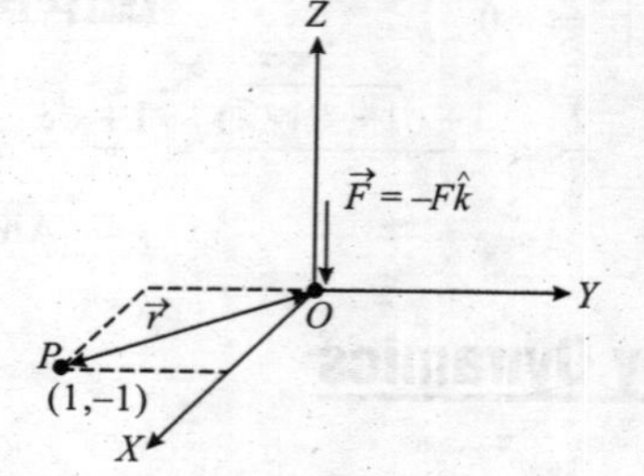

Position vector of origin about the given point is

$$\vec{r} = -\hat{i} + \hat{j}$$

Torque of the given force about point P is

$$\vec{\tau} = \vec{r} \times \vec{F} = (-\hat{i} + \hat{j}) \times (-F\hat{k})$$

$$\Rightarrow \quad \vec{\tau} = F(-\hat{j} - \hat{i}) = -F(\hat{i} + \hat{j})$$ **Ans. (B)**

Sol. 13

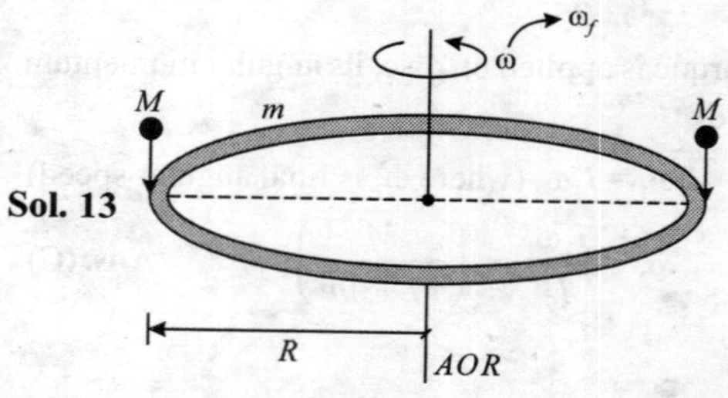

As no external torque is applied on ring, its angular momentum remain conserved

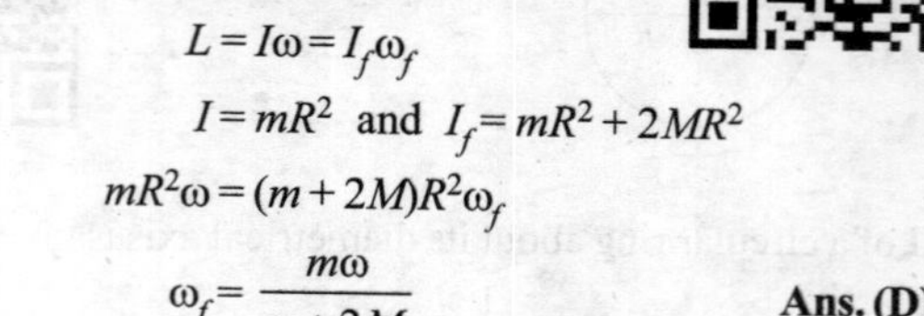

$$L = I\omega = I_f\omega_f$$

here $\quad I = mR^2$ and $I_f = mR^2 + 2MR^2$

$$\Rightarrow \quad mR^2\omega = (m + 2M)R^2\omega_f$$

$$\Rightarrow \quad \omega_f = \frac{m\omega}{m + 2M}$$ **Ans. (D)**

Sol. 14

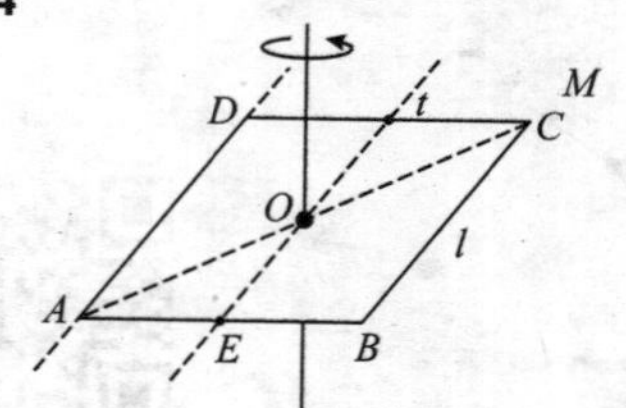

MI of a square plate about AOR passing through its center and $\perp$ to its plane is given as

$$I_0 = \frac{1}{6}Ml^2$$

For any AOR in the plane of lamina passing through its center MI can be given as

$$2I_P = \frac{1}{6}Ml^2$$

$$\Rightarrow \quad I_P = \frac{1}{12}Ml^2 = I_{EF} = I_{AC}$$

$$\Rightarrow \quad I_{AD} = I_{EF} + \frac{Ml^2}{4} = \frac{Ml^2}{3}$$

Ans. (C)

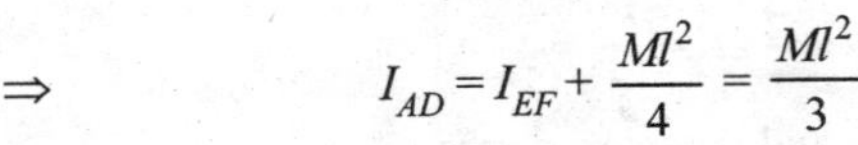

Sol. 15

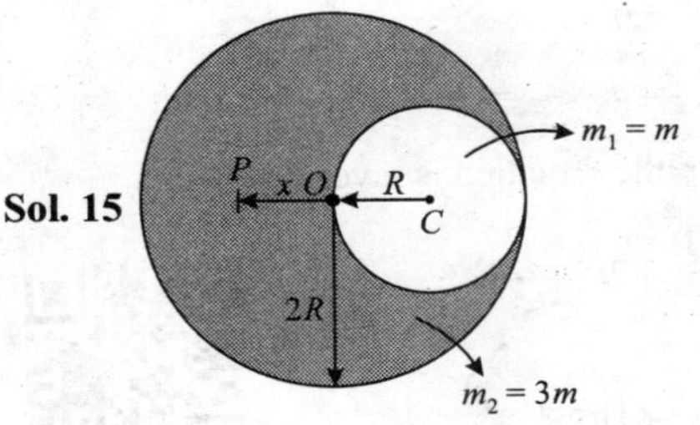

As disc is uniform, its mass is proportional to its surface area

$$\Rightarrow \quad m_1 = C\cdot\pi R^2 = m$$

and $$m_2 = C[\pi(2R)^2 - \pi R^2] = C(3\pi R^2) = 3m$$

As point O is the COM of bigger disc of radius $2R$, we use

$$3mx = mR$$

$$\Rightarrow \quad x = \frac{R}{3} = \alpha R$$

$$\Rightarrow \quad \alpha = \frac{1}{3}$$

Ans. (A)

Sol. 16

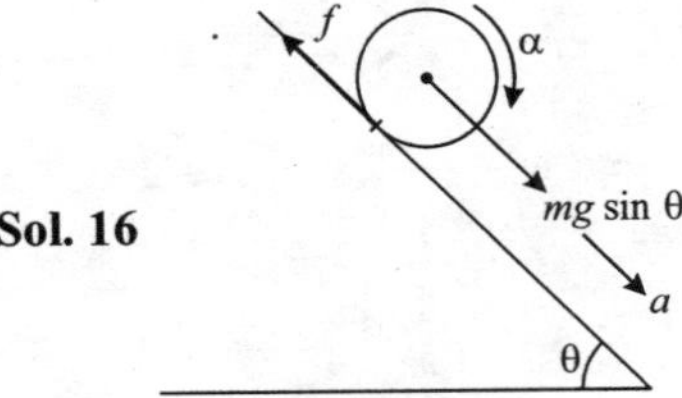

Equation of motion of body

$$mg\sin\theta - f = ma \quad \ldots(1)$$

$$\Rightarrow \quad fR = I\left(\frac{a}{R}\right) \quad \ldots(2)$$

[For pure rolling $a = R\alpha$]

$$(1)+(2) \Rightarrow \quad mg\sin\theta = a\left(M + \frac{I}{R^2}\right)$$

$$\Rightarrow \quad a = \frac{g\sin\theta}{\left(1 + \frac{I}{MR^2}\right)}$$

Ans. (A)

Sol. 17

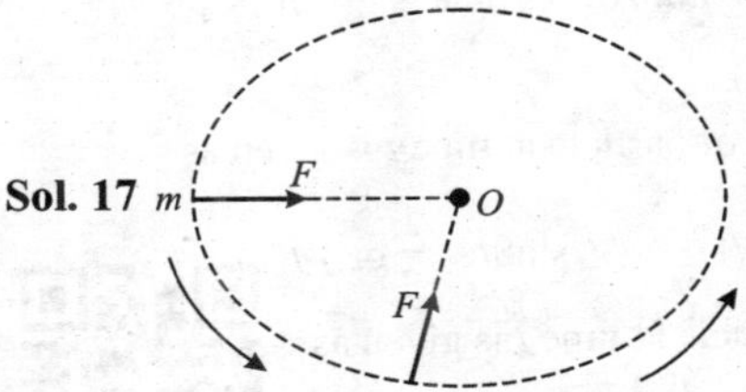

Due to central force which always passes through centre so the torque due to this force about O is always zero during motion.

As $\quad \vec{\tau}_0 = 0$

$\Rightarrow$ Angular momentum about O remain conserved. **Ans. (C)**

Sol. 18

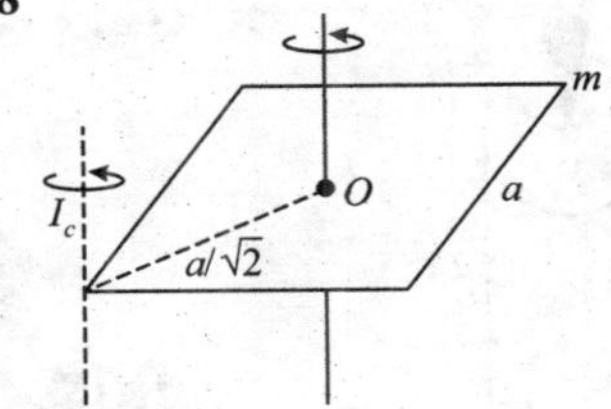

MI of square plate about its central AOR is

$$I_0 = \frac{1}{6}Ma^2$$

From parallel AOR, we have

$$I_c = I_0 + Md^2$$

$$\Rightarrow \quad I_c = \frac{1}{6}Ma^2 + \frac{1}{2}Ma^2 = \frac{2}{3}Ma^2$$

Ans. (D)

Sol. 19 By conservation of energy, we have

$$\frac{1}{2}I\omega^2 = mgh$$

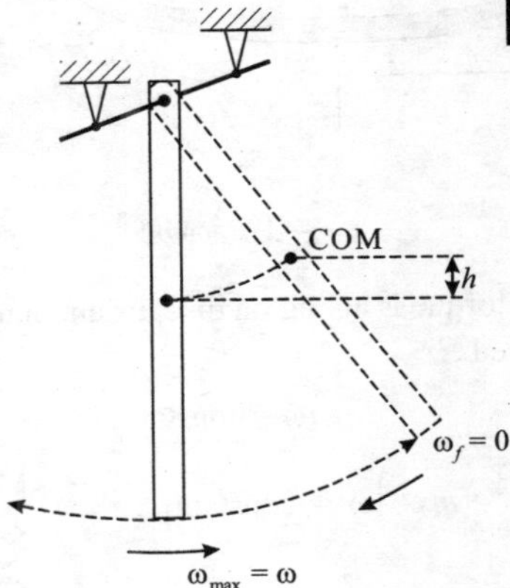

$$\Rightarrow \quad h = \frac{I\omega^2}{2mg} = \frac{\omega^2}{2mg}\left(\frac{Ml^2}{3}\right) = \frac{\omega^2 l^2}{6g}$$

Ans. (C)

Sol. 20 Angular momentum of particle is given as

$$\vec{L} = m(\vec{r} \times \vec{v})$$

where position vector of particle at time t is given as

$$\vec{r} = (v_0 \cos\theta t)\,\hat{i} + (v_0 \sin\theta t - \frac{1}{2}gt^2)\,\hat{j}$$

velocity vector of particle at time t is given as

$$\vec{v} = (v_0 \cos\theta)\,\hat{i} + (v_0 \sin\theta - gt)\,\hat{j}$$

$$\Rightarrow \quad \vec{L} = -\frac{1}{2} mgv_0 t^2 \cos\theta\,\hat{k}$$

Ans. (D)

Sol. 21 Equation of motion for mass m

$$mg - T = ma \qquad \ldots(1)$$

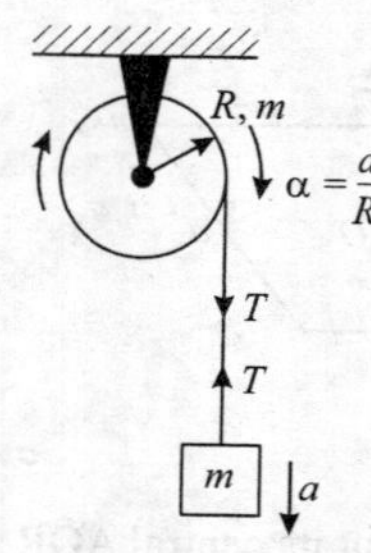

For pulley

$$T.R = \left(\frac{1}{2}mR^2\right)\left(\frac{a}{R}\right) \qquad \ldots(2)$$

$$(1)+(2) \quad \Rightarrow \quad mg = \frac{3}{2}ma$$

$$\Rightarrow \quad a = \frac{2g}{3}$$

Ans. (B)

Sol. 22

$$I = \frac{1}{2}MR^2 + mx^2$$

An no external torque is acting on disc, its angular momentum remain conserved

$$\Rightarrow \quad L = I\omega = \text{constant}$$

$$\Rightarrow \quad \left(\frac{1}{2}MR^2 + mx^2\right)\omega = \text{constant}$$

$$\Rightarrow \quad \omega = \frac{\text{constant}}{\frac{1}{2}MR^2 + mx^2}$$

As $x \downarrow \Rightarrow \omega\uparrow$ and after passing centre O $x \uparrow \Rightarrow \omega\downarrow$ **Ans (B)**

Sol. 23 Torque on pulley

$$\tau = rF = 40t - 10t^2 = I\alpha$$

Angular acceleration of pulley

$$\alpha = 4t - t^2$$

$$\Rightarrow \quad \frac{d\omega}{dt} = 4t - t^2$$

$$\Rightarrow \quad \int_0^{\omega} d\omega = \int_0^{t}(4t - t^2)\,dt$$

$$\Rightarrow \quad \omega = 2t^2 - \frac{t^3}{3}$$

here ω first $\uparrow$ then $\downarrow$ and it becomes zero when

$$2t^2 - \frac{t^3}{3} = 0$$

$$\Rightarrow \quad t = 6\text{s}$$

at $t = 6$s direction of pulley rotation is reversed

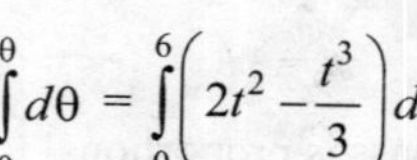

$$\frac{d\theta}{dt} = 2t^2 - \frac{t^3}{3}$$

$$\int_0^{\theta} d\theta = \int_0^{6}\left(2t^2 - \frac{t^3}{3}\right)dt$$

$$\Rightarrow \quad \theta = \left[\frac{2t^3}{3} - \frac{t^4}{12}\right]_0^6 = \frac{2}{3} \times 216 - \frac{(6)^4}{12} - 0$$

$$\Rightarrow \quad \theta = 36 \text{ rad}$$

$$\text{No of turns} = \frac{\theta}{2\pi} = \frac{36}{2\pi} = 5.73$$

Ans. (D)

Sol. 24

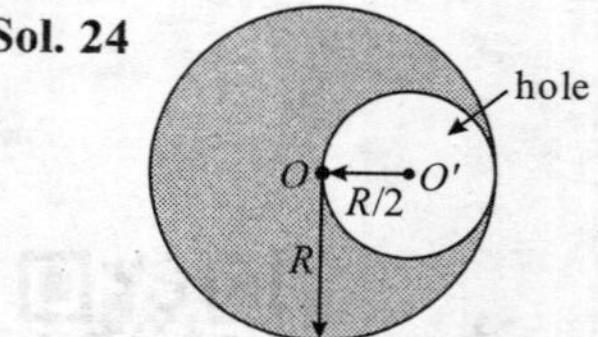

MI of whole disc is

$$I_0 = \frac{1}{2}MR^2$$

Mass of small (hole) disc is

$$m = \frac{M}{\pi R^2} \times \frac{\pi R^2}{4} = \frac{M}{4}$$

MI of small disc about axis at O is

$$I_{\text{hole}} = I_{O'} + \left(\frac{M}{4}\right)\left(\frac{R}{2}\right)^2$$

$$\Rightarrow \quad I_{\text{hole}} = \frac{1}{2}\left(\frac{M}{4}\right)\left(\frac{R}{2}\right)^2 + \left(\frac{M}{4}\right)\left(\frac{R}{2}\right)^2$$

$$\Rightarrow \qquad I_{hole} = \frac{3}{2} \times \frac{M}{4} \times \frac{R^2}{4} = \frac{3}{32} MR^2$$

MI of remaining disc is

$$I = I_0 - I_{hole}$$

$$\Rightarrow \qquad I = \frac{1}{2}MR^2 - \frac{3}{32}MR^2 = \frac{13}{32}MR^2$$ **Ans. (D)**

Sol. 25 Translational $KE_T = \frac{1}{2}mv^2$ ...(1)

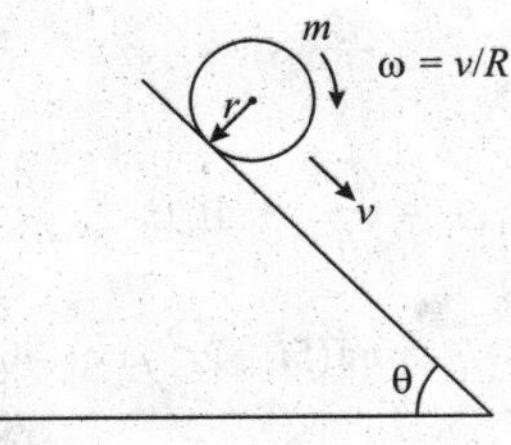

Rotational $KE_R = \frac{1}{2}I\omega^2 = \frac{1}{2}\left(\frac{2}{5}mR^2\right)\left(\frac{v}{R}\right)^2$

$$KE_R = \frac{1}{5}mv^2 \qquad \text{...(2)}$$

By (2)/(1) ⇒ $\frac{KE_R}{KE_T} = \frac{2}{5}$

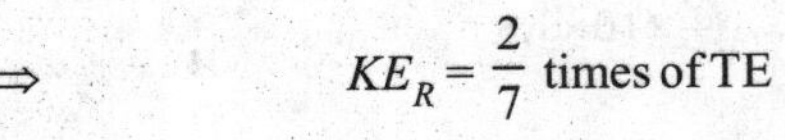

$$\Rightarrow \qquad KE_R = \frac{2}{7} \text{ times of TE}$$

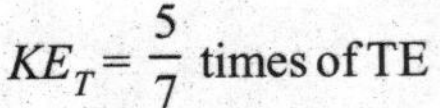

$$KE_T = \frac{5}{7} \text{ times of TE}$$ **Ans. (B)**

Sol. 26 If there is No torque ⇒ $L \to$ constant

we use $L = I\omega$

and $K = \frac{1}{2}I\omega^2 = \frac{L^2}{2I}$

⇒ As $L \to$ constant so on increasing I ⇒ KE decreases.

S-1 is false.

S-2 is true. **Ans. (B)**

Sol. 27 Angular momentum of revolving stone is

$$L = mvr = C \text{ (constant)}$$

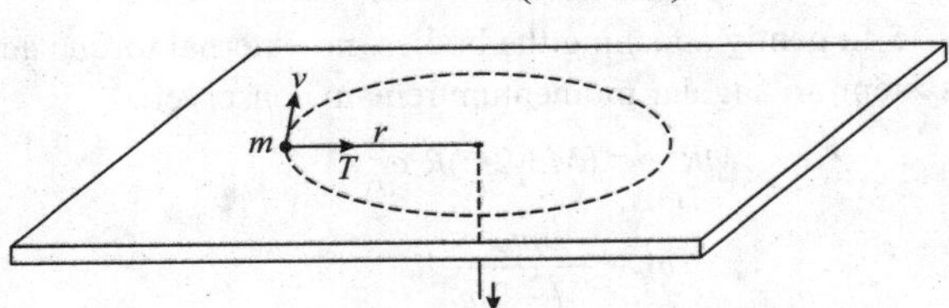

Considering stable AB (r is gradually decreased) circular motion we use

$$T = mv^2/r$$

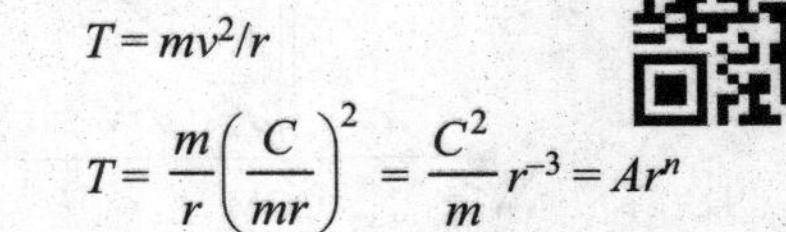

$$\Rightarrow \qquad T = \frac{m}{r}\left(\frac{C}{mr}\right)^2 = \frac{C^2}{m}r^{-3} = Ar^n$$

$$\Rightarrow \qquad n = -3$$ **Ans. (D)**

Sol. 28 Initial speed of sphere should be sufficient to take sphere to top when its $v_f = 0$.

So using work-energy theorem we have

$$\frac{1}{2}mv^2 + \frac{1}{2}\left(\frac{2}{5}mr^2\right)\left(\frac{v}{r}\right)^2 - mgh = 0$$

$$\left(\frac{1}{2} + \frac{1}{5}\right)mv^2 = mgh$$

$$\Rightarrow \qquad v = \sqrt{\frac{10}{7}gh}$$ **Ans. (D)**

Sol. 29 In case of pure rolling, the speed attained by the body at bottom of incline is

$$v_0 = \sqrt{\frac{2gh}{1 + \frac{k^2}{R_0^2}}} \qquad \text{...(1)}$$

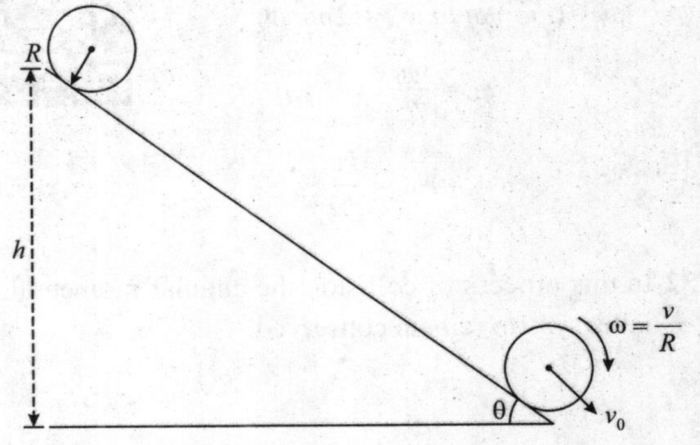

In case of smooth incline no rotational KE is gained by body so speed attained is

$$v = \sqrt{2gh} = \frac{5v_0}{4} \qquad \text{...(2)}$$

Using (2)/(1) gives $\frac{5}{4} = \sqrt{1 + \frac{k^2}{R_0^2}}$

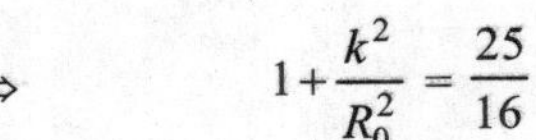

$$\Rightarrow \qquad 1 + \frac{k^2}{R_0^2} = \frac{25}{16}$$

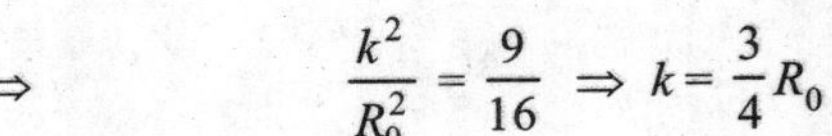

$$\Rightarrow \qquad \frac{k^2}{R_0^2} = \frac{9}{16} \Rightarrow k = \frac{3}{4}R_0$$ **Ans. (B)**

Sol. 30

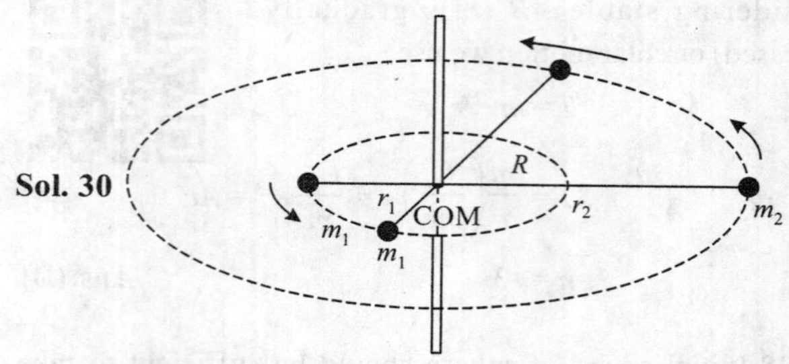

As no external force is acting on the system of these two particles

$\Rightarrow$ Their COM will remain at rest

$\Rightarrow$ During revolution the two masses will always remain opposite to each other as shown on the two sides of COM.

$\Rightarrow$ Their time period will be same for them to be on opposite sides of COM

$\Rightarrow$ $\omega_1 = \omega_2$ (independent of m_1 & m_2) **Ans. (B)**

Sol. 31 At pure rotting we use

$$v_f = r\omega_f$$

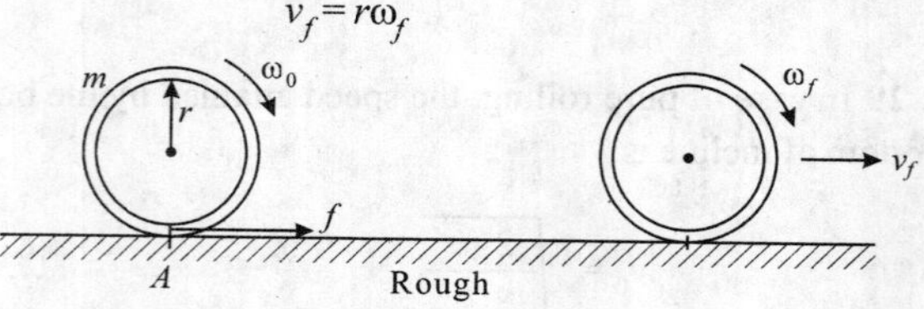

By conversation of angular momentum about point A, we use

$$(mr^2)\omega_0 = (mr^2)\omega_f + mv_f r = 2mr^2\omega_f$$

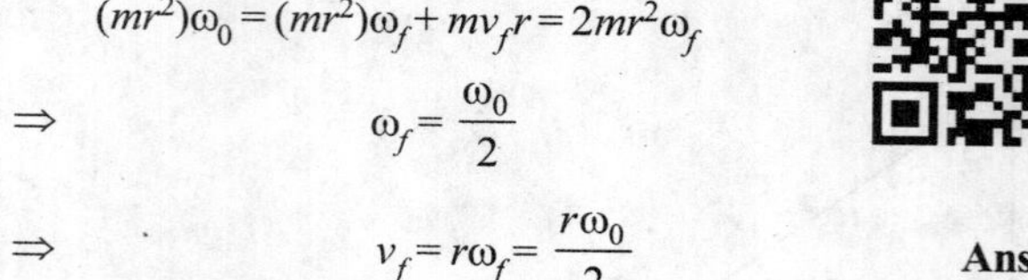

$$\Rightarrow \quad \omega_f = \frac{\omega_0}{2}$$

$$\Rightarrow \quad v_f = r\omega_f = \frac{r\omega_0}{2}$$ **Ans. (C)**

Sol. 32 In this process of collision the angular momentum of door + bullet system remain conserved.

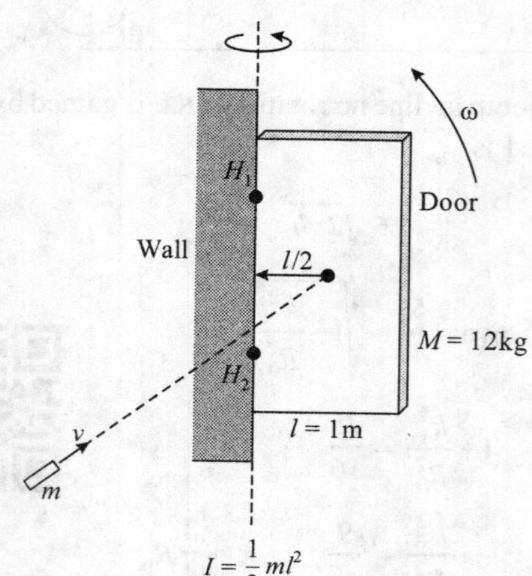

As angular momentum of door + bullet system remain conserved, we use

$$mv\left(\frac{l}{2}\right) = \frac{1}{3}Ml^2\omega$$

$$\Rightarrow \quad \omega = \frac{3mvl}{2Ml^2} = \frac{3\times0.01\times500}{2\times12\times1} = \frac{15}{24}$$

$$\Rightarrow \quad \omega = 0.625 \text{ rad/s}$$ **Ans. (B)**

Sol. 33 Angular momentum

$$\vec{L} = m(\vec{r}\times\vec{v})$$

Where $\vec{r} = 5\hat{i} - 2t^2\hat{j}$

and $\vec{v} = \frac{d\vec{r}}{dt} = -4t\,\hat{j}$

$$\Rightarrow \quad \vec{L} = m[(5\hat{i} - 2t^2\hat{j})\times(-4t\hat{j})]$$

$$\Rightarrow \quad \vec{L}_{(t=2s)} = 2[(5\hat{i} - 8\hat{j})\times(-8\hat{j})]$$

$$\vec{L}_{(t=2s)} = 2\times[-40\hat{k}] = -80\hat{k}$$ **Ans. (A)**

Sol. 34 By work-energy theorem from 0 to A, we have

$$0 + mg(1.8) = \frac{1}{2}mv^2 + \frac{1}{2}\left(\frac{2}{3}mR^2\right)\left(\frac{v}{R}\right)^2 = \frac{5}{6}mv^2$$

$$\Rightarrow \quad v = \sqrt{\frac{6}{5}\times10\times1.8}$$

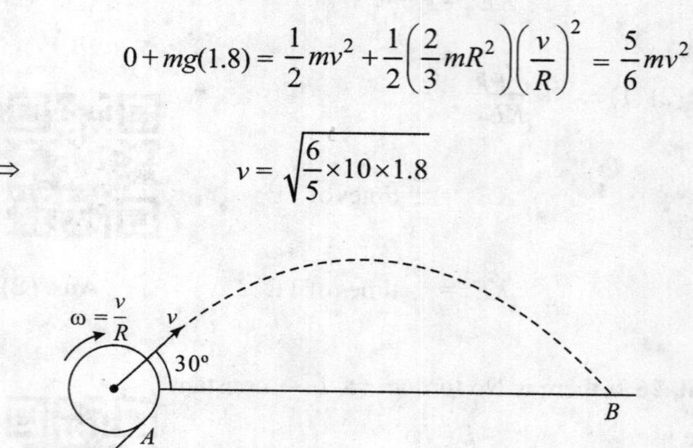

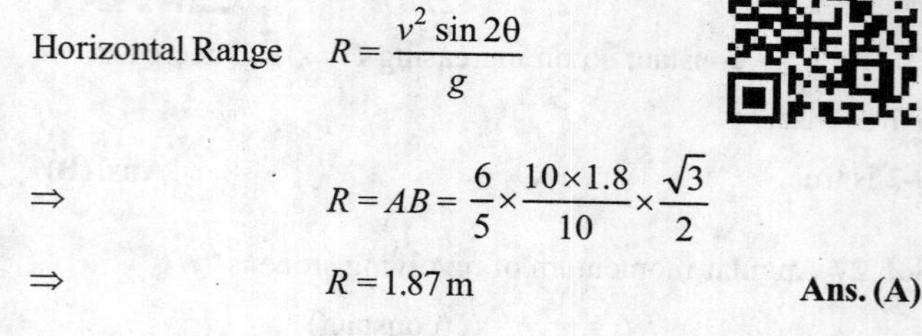

Horizontal Range $R = \frac{v^2\sin 2\theta}{g}$

$$\Rightarrow \quad R = AB = \frac{6}{5}\times\frac{10\times1.8}{10}\times\frac{\sqrt{3}}{2}$$

$$\Rightarrow \quad R = 1.87\text{ m}$$ **Ans. (A)**

Sol. 35 In gently attaching the bodies, no external torque acts on system, so angular momentum remain conserved.

$$MR^2\omega = (M+2m)R^2\omega_f$$

$$\Rightarrow \quad \omega_f = \frac{m\omega}{M+2m}$$

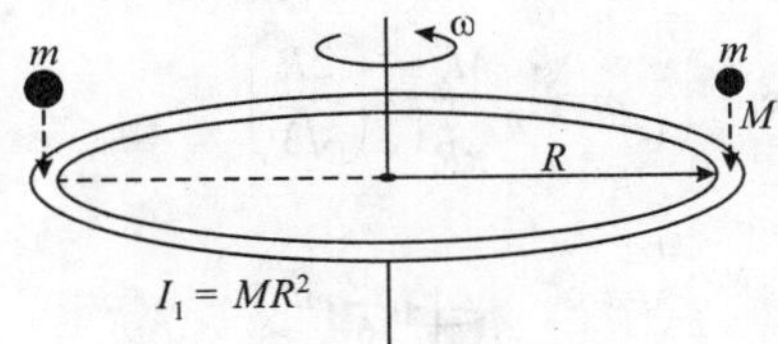

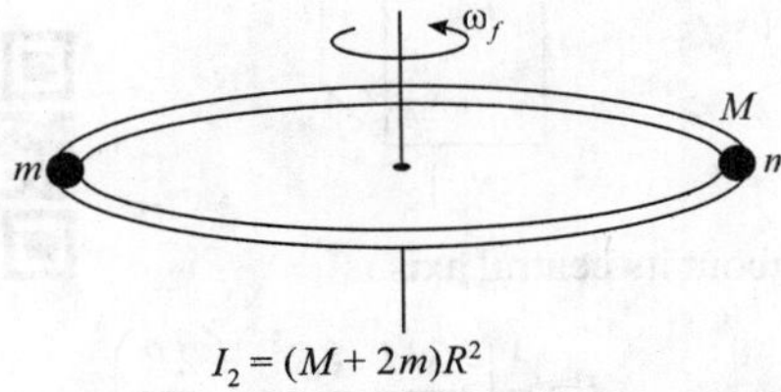

Loss in kinetic energy is given as

$$\Delta K_{\text{Loss}} = K_i - K_f$$

$$\Rightarrow \quad \Delta K_{\text{Loss}} = \frac{1}{2}I_1\omega^2 - \frac{1}{2}I_1\omega_f^2$$

$$\Rightarrow \quad \Delta K_{\text{Loss}} = \frac{1}{2}(MR^2)\omega^2 - \frac{1}{2}(M+2m)R^2\left(\frac{M}{M+2m}\right)^2\omega^2$$

$$\Rightarrow \quad \Delta K_{\text{Loss}} = \frac{1}{2}MR^2\omega^2 - \frac{1}{2}\frac{M^2R^2}{(M+2m)}\omega^2$$

$$\Rightarrow \quad \Delta K_{\text{Loss}} = \frac{1}{2}R^2\omega^2\left[M - \frac{M^2}{M+2m}\right]$$

$$\Rightarrow \quad \Delta K_{\text{Loss}} = \frac{1}{2}R^2\omega^2\left[\frac{2mM}{M+2m}\right] = \frac{mMR^2\omega^2}{(M+2m)}$$

Ans. (C)

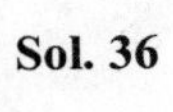

Sol. 36

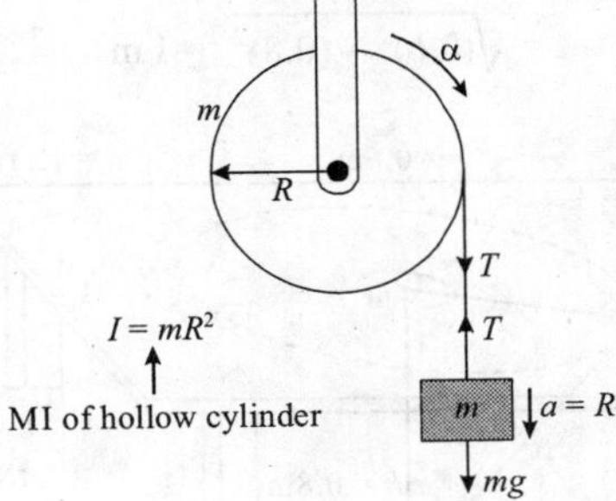

Equation of motion for falling mass

$$mg - T = ma \quad \ldots(1)$$

For cylinder $\quad TR = (mR^2)\left(\dfrac{a}{R}\right) \quad \ldots(2)$

$(1) + (2) \Rightarrow \quad mg = 2ma$

$\Rightarrow \quad a = g/2$

Ans. (B)

Sol. 37

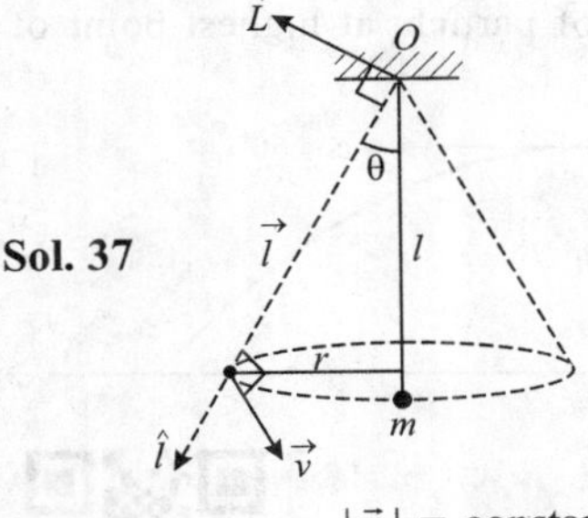

$$|\vec{v}| = \text{constant}$$

Angular momentum of bob about point O is

$$\vec{L} = m(\vec{l} \times \vec{v})$$

Direction of $\vec{L}$ is $\perp$ to both $\vec{l}$ and $\vec{v}$, as shown in figure and its magnitude is

$$L = mlv \rightarrow \text{constant}$$

Ans. (C)

Sol. 38 relative to rug we consider cylinder is having acceleration a, for which equations of motion of cylinder are

$$ma - f = Ma_1 \quad \ldots(1)$$

$$fR = \left(\frac{1}{2}MR^2\right)\left(\frac{a_1}{R}\right) \quad \ldots(2)$$

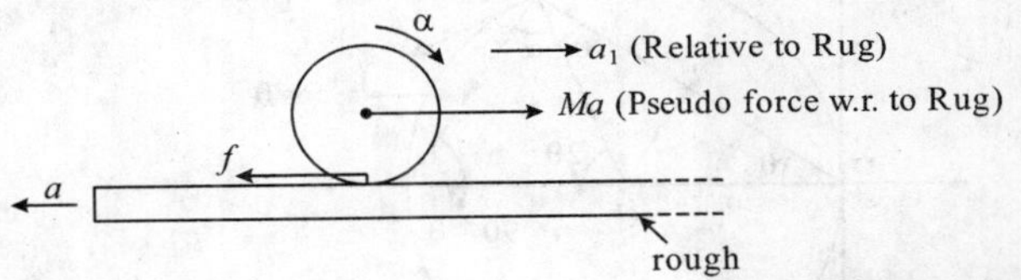

From (1) and (2), we have

$$Ma - f = 2f$$

$$\Rightarrow \quad 3f = Ma$$

$$\Rightarrow \quad f = \frac{1}{3}Ma$$

Ans. (D)

Sol. 39 For pure rolling of a body on incline plane, acceleration is given as

$$a = \frac{g\sin\theta}{\left(1 + \dfrac{k^2}{R^2}\right)}$$

for cylinder $\quad k_c = \dfrac{R}{\sqrt{2}} \Rightarrow a_c = \dfrac{g\sin\theta}{1+\dfrac{1}{2}} = \dfrac{2}{3}g\sin\theta_c$

for sphere $\quad k_s = \sqrt{\dfrac{2}{5}}R \Rightarrow a_s = \dfrac{g\sin\theta_s}{1+\dfrac{2}{5}} = \dfrac{5}{7}g\sin\theta_s$

$$a_c = a_s \Rightarrow \frac{2}{3}g\sin\theta_c = \frac{5}{7}g\sin\theta_s$$

$$\Rightarrow \quad \frac{\sin\theta_c}{\sin\theta_s} = \frac{1}{2/3 \big/ 5/7} = \frac{15}{14}$$

Ans. (D)

Sol. 40 Angular momentum of particle at highest point of trajectory about O is given as

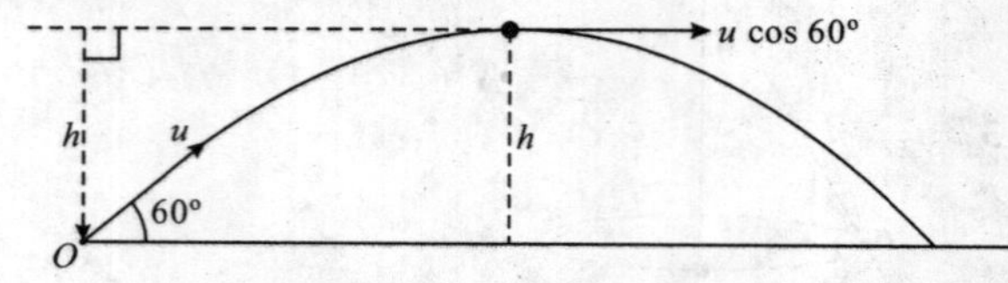

$$L_0 = m(u\cos 60°) \times h$$

$$\Rightarrow \quad L_0 = mu\cos 60° \times \frac{u^2 \sin^2 60°}{2g}$$

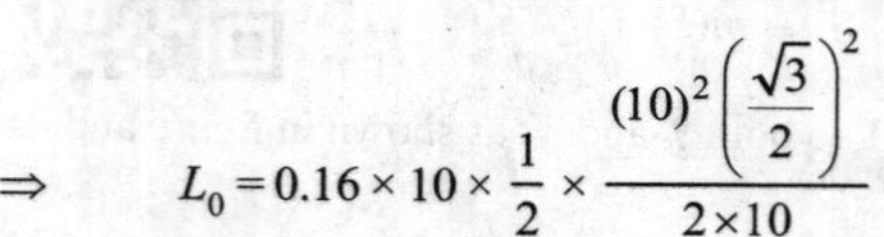

$$\Rightarrow \quad L_0 = 0.16 \times 10 \times \frac{1}{2} \times \frac{(10)^2\left(\frac{\sqrt{3}}{2}\right)^2}{2\times 10}$$

$$\Rightarrow \quad L_0 = 3 \text{ kg m}^2\text{/s}$$

Ans. (B)

Sol. 41 Angle α is given as in ΔPCA

$$\alpha = 180° - (2\theta + 90 - \theta)$$

$$\Rightarrow \quad \alpha = 90° - \theta$$

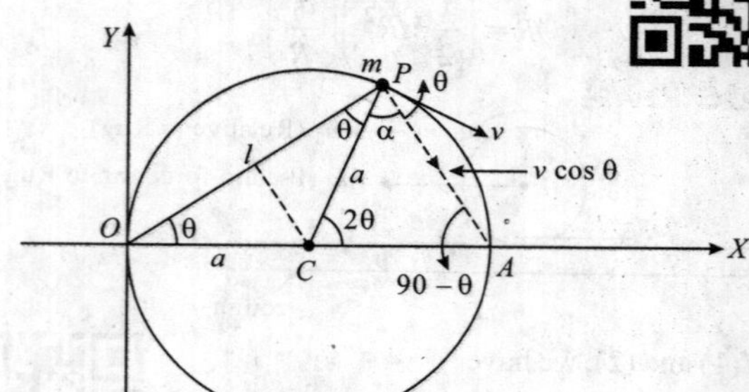

Angular momentum of mass m about O is given as

$$L_0 = m(v\cos\theta)l$$

Here $\quad l = 2a\cos\theta$

$$\Rightarrow \quad L_0 = mv\cos\theta \times 2a\cos\theta$$

$$\Rightarrow \quad L_0 = 2mva\cos^2\theta$$

$$\Rightarrow \quad L_0 = mva(1 + \cos 2\theta)$$

Ans. (A)

Sol. 42 For largest cube we use

$$2R = \sqrt{3}l$$

$$\Rightarrow \quad l = \frac{2R}{\sqrt{3}}$$

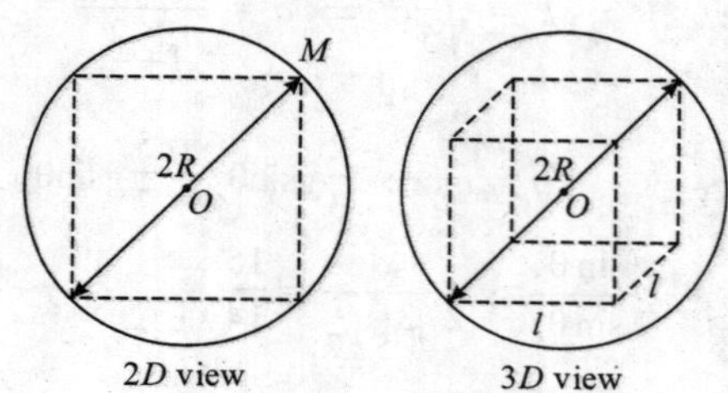

Mass of cube $\quad m = \frac{M}{\frac{4}{3}\pi R^3} \times \left(\frac{2R}{\sqrt{3}}\right)^3$

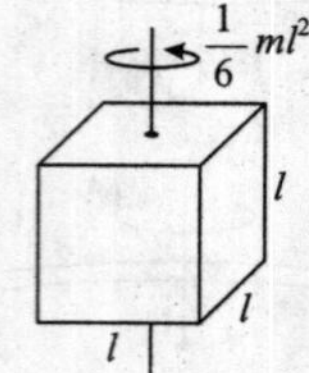

MI of cube about its central axis is

$$I = \frac{1}{6}\left(\frac{3M}{4\pi R^3}\frac{8R^3}{9\sqrt{3}}\right)\left(\frac{2R}{\sqrt{3}}\right)^2$$

$$\Rightarrow \quad I = \frac{4MR^2}{9\sqrt{3}\pi}$$

Ans. (C)

Sol. 43 Equations of motion of cylinder are

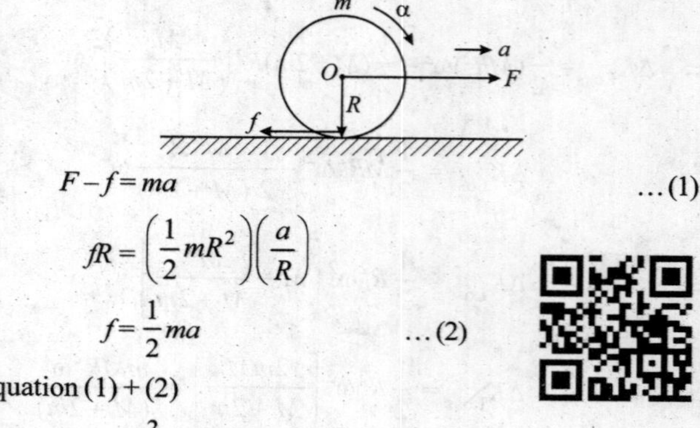

$$F - f = ma \qquad \ldots(1)$$

$$fR = \left(\frac{1}{2}mR^2\right)\left(\frac{a}{R}\right)$$

$$f = \frac{1}{2}ma \qquad \ldots(2)$$

equation (1) + (2)

$$F = \frac{3}{2}ma$$

Ans. (C)

Sol. 44

$$l = \sqrt{r^2 + h^2}$$

$$l = \sqrt{(0.6)^2 + (0.8)^2} = 1 \text{ m}$$

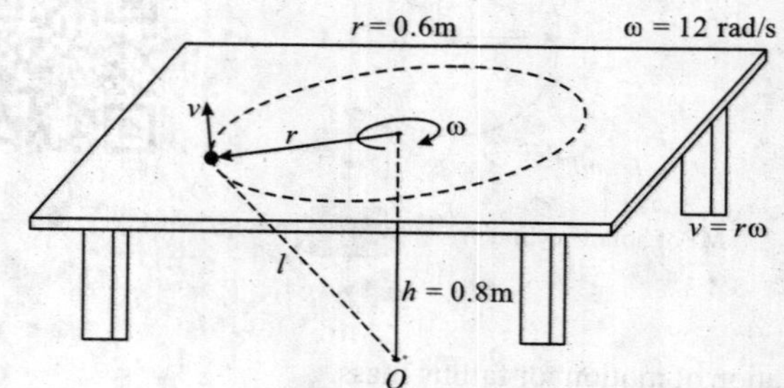

In figure angular momentum of particle about O is given as

$$L = mvl$$

$$\Rightarrow \quad L = 2 \times (0.6 \times 12) \times 1$$

$$\Rightarrow \quad L = 14.4 \text{ kg m}^2\text{/s}$$

Ans. (A)

Sol. 45 MI of a square lamina about its central AOR is given as

$$I_0 = \frac{Ma^2}{6}$$

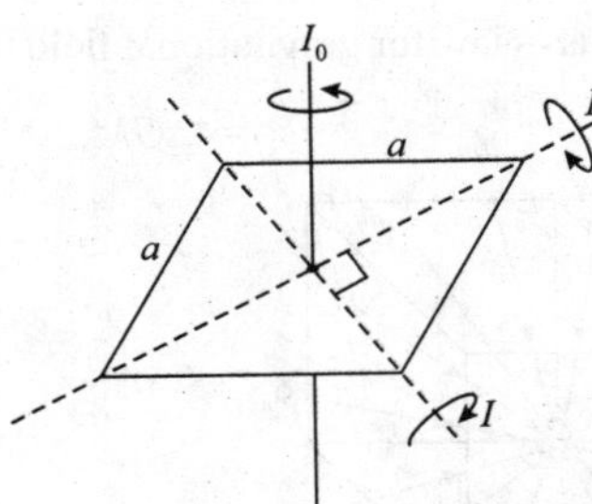

By perpendicular axes theorem we have

$$I + I = I_0$$

$$\Rightarrow \quad I = \frac{1}{2}I_0 = \frac{ma^2}{12}$$

Ans. (D)

Sol. 46 Angular momentum of particle about origin for its motion

along AB $\quad \vec{L} = mv\left(\frac{R}{\sqrt{2}}\right)(-\hat{k})$

along BC $\quad \vec{L} = mv\left(a + \frac{R}{\sqrt{2}}\right)\hat{k}$

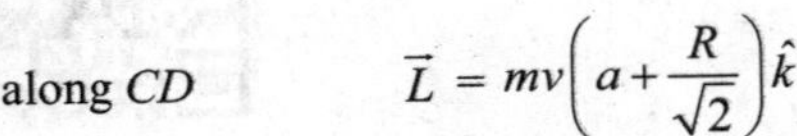

along CD $\quad \vec{L} = mv\left(a + \frac{R}{\sqrt{2}}\right)\hat{k}$

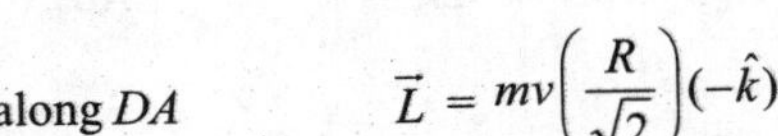

along DA $\quad \vec{L} = mv\left(\frac{R}{\sqrt{2}}\right)(-\hat{k})$

Ans. (A, C)

Sol. 47 Here we analyze friction on the bottom contact points of cones and rails

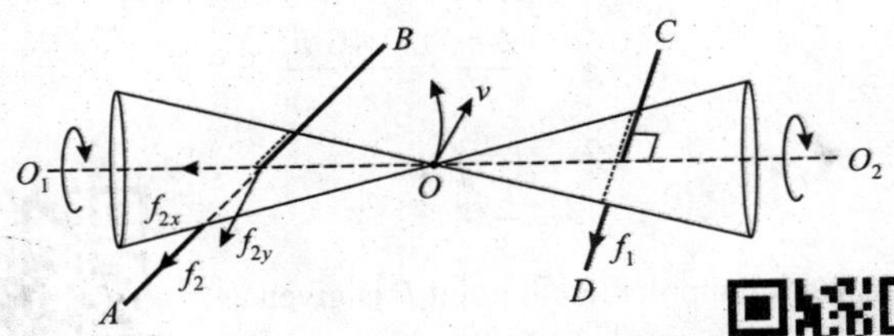

Due to a component of friction f_2 on roller at rail AB it will turn toward left. **Ans. (C)**

Sol. 48 As no torque is acting about O at the instant of impact so angular momentum of cube remain conserved about O.

$$mv\frac{a}{2} = I\omega$$

$$\Rightarrow \quad \omega = \frac{mva}{2I}$$

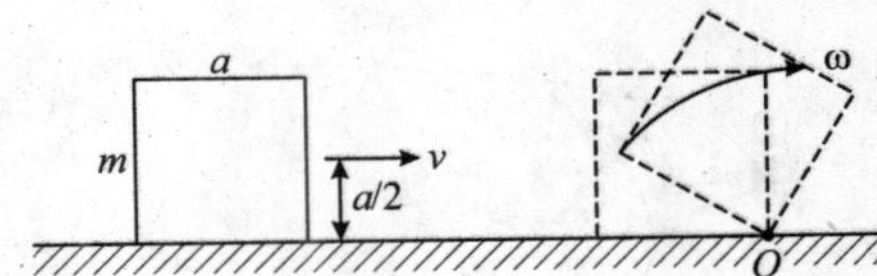

MI of cube about its corner

$$I = I_c + M\left(\frac{a}{\sqrt{2}}\right)^2 = \frac{Ma^2}{6} + \frac{Ma^2}{2}$$

$$\Rightarrow \quad I = \frac{2}{3}Ma^2$$

$$\Rightarrow \quad \omega = \frac{mva}{2\left(\frac{2}{3}Ma^2\right)} = \frac{3v}{4a}$$

$$\Rightarrow \quad \omega = \frac{3\times 2}{4\times 0.3} = 5 \text{ rad/s}$$

Ans. (B)

7.1 Gravitational Field

Sol. 1

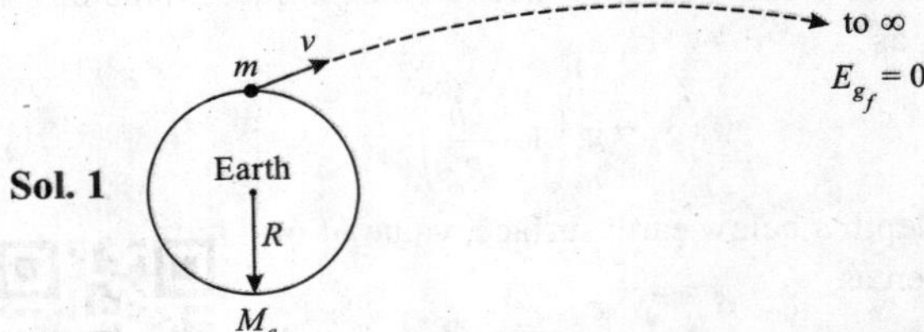

On surface of earth for the body mechanical energy is

$$E_{gi} = -\frac{GM_e m}{R} + \frac{1}{2}mv^2 = E_{gf} = 0$$

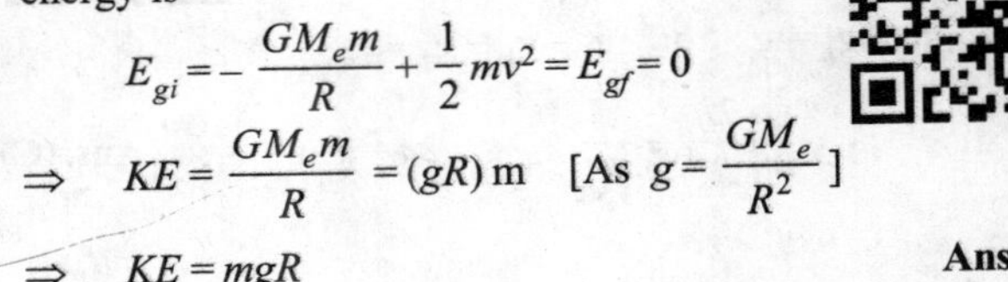

$$\Rightarrow \quad KE = \frac{GM_e m}{R} = (gR)\,\text{m} \quad \left[\text{As } g = \frac{GM_e}{R^2}\right]$$

$$\Rightarrow \quad KE = mgR$$

Ans. (C)

Sol. 2

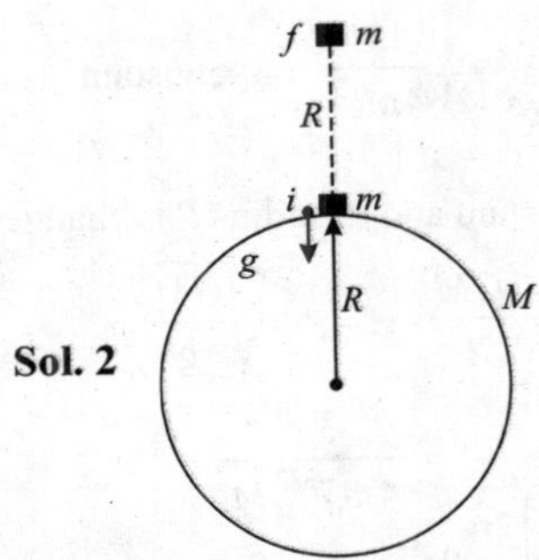

Acceleration due to gravity on

At earth surface $g = \frac{GM}{R^2} \Rightarrow \frac{GM}{R} = gR$

Gain in PE when body of mass m is raised from position i to f is

$$\Delta U = U_f - U_i$$

$$\Rightarrow \quad \Delta U = \left(-\frac{GMm}{2R}\right) - \left(-\frac{GMm}{R}\right)$$

$$\Rightarrow \quad \Delta U = \frac{GMm}{2R} = \frac{1}{2}mgR$$

Ans. (B)

Sol. 3

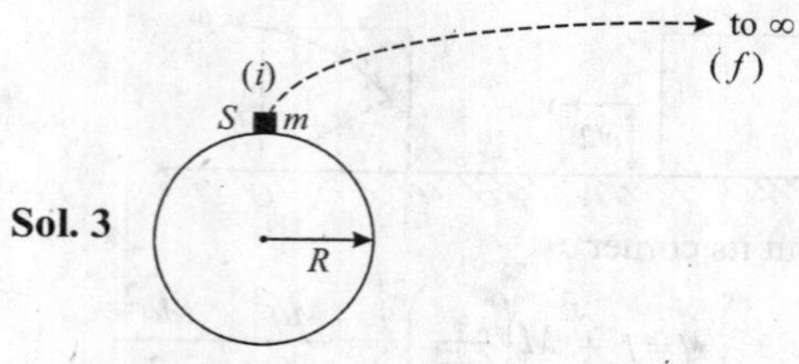

Work done in shifting mass from point S to ∞, is given as

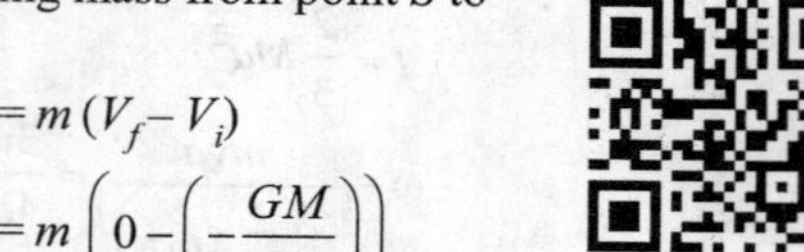

$$W = m(V_f - V_i)$$

$$\Rightarrow \quad W = m\left(0 - \left(-\frac{GM}{R}\right)\right)$$

$$\Rightarrow \quad W = \frac{GMm}{R} = \frac{6.67\times10^{-11}\times100\times10\times10^{-3}}{0.1}$$

$$\Rightarrow \quad W = 6.67\times10^{-10}\,\text{J}$$

Ans. (D)

Sol. 4 At a small height h above earth surface, value of g is given as

$$g_h = g_s\left(1 - \frac{2h}{R_e}\right) \quad \ldots(1)$$

At a depth d below earth surface, value of g is given as

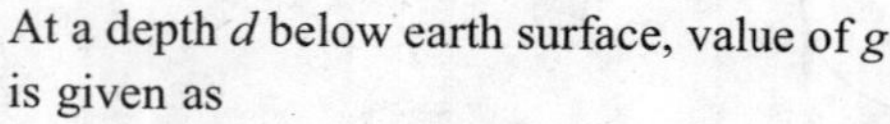

$$g_d = g_s\left(1 - \frac{d}{R_e}\right) \quad \ldots(2)$$

Given that $g_h = g_d$ or $g_s - g_h = g_s - g_d$

$$\Rightarrow \quad \frac{2h}{R_e} = \frac{d}{R_e} \rightarrow 2h = d$$

Ans. (C)

Sol. 5 For earth, its mass M and radius R are constants

$\Rightarrow$ Average density $\rho = \dfrac{M}{\frac{4}{3}\pi R^3} = \dfrac{3M}{4\pi R^3} \rightarrow$ constant

If for a planet its mass M is constant and its radius R is changed

Acceleration due to gravity $g = \dfrac{GM}{R^2} \Rightarrow R = \sqrt{\dfrac{GM}{g}}$

Average density $\rho = \dfrac{3M}{4\pi\left(\dfrac{GM}{g}\right)^{3/2}} = \dfrac{3g^{3/2}}{4\pi G^{3/2} M^{1/2}}$

$$\Rightarrow \quad \rho \propto g^{3/2}$$

If for a planet its radius R is constant and its mass M is changed

$$M = \frac{gR^2}{G}$$

Average density $\rho = \dfrac{3}{4\pi R^3} \times \dfrac{gR^2}{G} = \dfrac{3}{4\pi RG}\cdot g$

$$\Rightarrow \quad \rho \propto g$$

Ans. (C)

Sol. 6 Electronic charge is independent of g.

$$\Rightarrow \quad \frac{q_m}{q_e} = 1$$

Ans. (A)

Sol. 7 By Gauss's law for gravitational field we use

$$\phi_m = \oint \overline{g}\cdot\overline{ds} = 4\pi GM$$

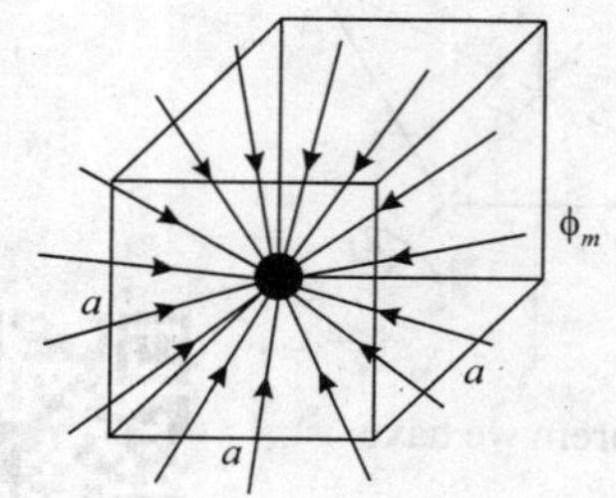

S-1 is True

By Gauss's law the gravitational field due to a point m is radially inward (radial) and for the surface enclosing the mass $\phi = 4\pi GM$.

Ans. (B)

Sol. 8 At a height h above the earth surface the value of g is given as

$$g_h = \frac{g_s}{\left(1+\dfrac{h}{R_e}\right)^2} = \frac{g_s}{9}$$

$$\Rightarrow \quad \left(1+\frac{h}{g}\right)^2 = 9$$

$$\Rightarrow \quad 1 + \frac{h}{R} = 3 \Rightarrow h = 2R$$

Ans. (C)

Sol. 9

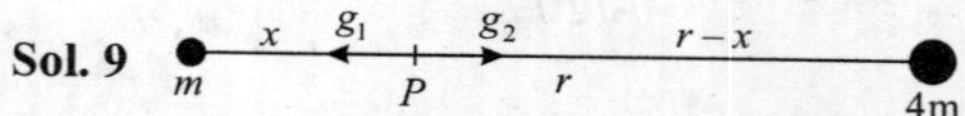

Gravitational field strength due to m and $4m$ at point P are given as

$$g_1 = \frac{Gm}{x^2} = \frac{4Gm}{(r-x)^2}$$

$$\Rightarrow \quad 2x = r - x$$

$$\Rightarrow \quad x = \frac{r}{3}$$

Gravitational potential at point P is given as

$$V_P = -\frac{Gm}{x} - \frac{G(4\text{m})}{r-x}$$

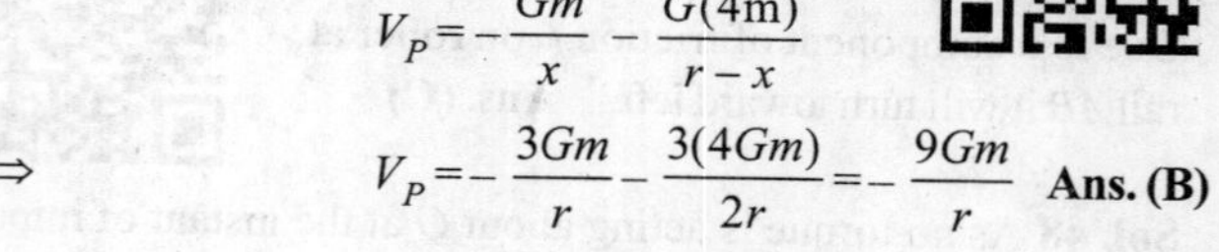

$$\Rightarrow \quad V_P = -\frac{3Gm}{r} - \frac{3(4Gm)}{2r} = -\frac{9Gm}{r}$$

Ans. (B)

Sol. 10

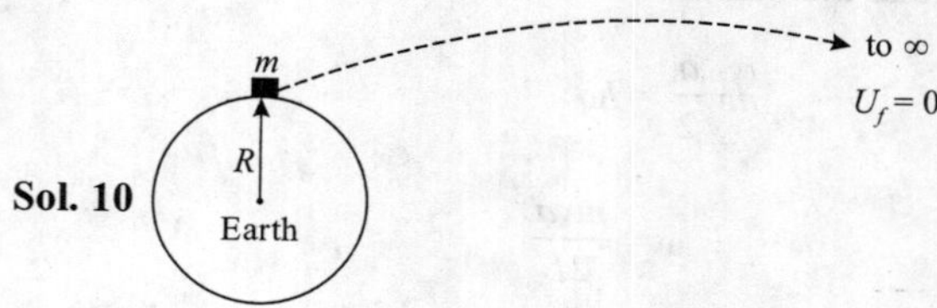

Initial gravitational PE of space ship on surface of earth is

$$U_i = -\frac{GM_e m}{R_e} = -(gR)m \quad \left[\text{As } g = \frac{GM_e}{R_e^2}\right]$$

Work done required to launch space ship to ∞ (free space) is

$$W = U_f - U_i = 0 - (-mgR) = mgR$$
$$= 1000 \times 10 \times 6400 \times 10^3$$
$$= 6.4 \times 10^{10}\text{ J}$$

Ans. (A)

Sol. 11

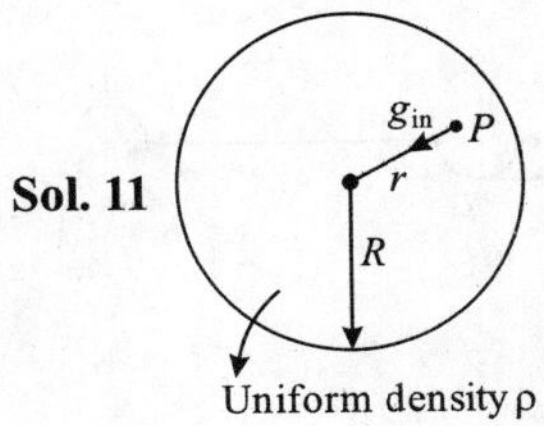

mass $M = \rho \times \frac{4}{3}\pi R^3$

For $r < R$ acceleration due to gravity inside a sphere is given as

$$g_{in} = \frac{GMr}{R^3} = \frac{G}{R^3}\left(\rho \cdot \frac{4}{3}\pi R^3\right) \cdot r$$

$$\Rightarrow \quad g_{in} = \frac{4}{3}\pi G\rho r$$

$$\Rightarrow \quad g_{in} \propto r$$

Ans. (A)

Sol. 12 Inside earth, value of g is given as

For $x < R_e$ $\quad g_{in} = \frac{GM_e x}{R_e^3}$

For $x \geq R_e$ $\quad g_{s/out} = \frac{GM_e}{x^2}$

(Where x is distance from earth centre)

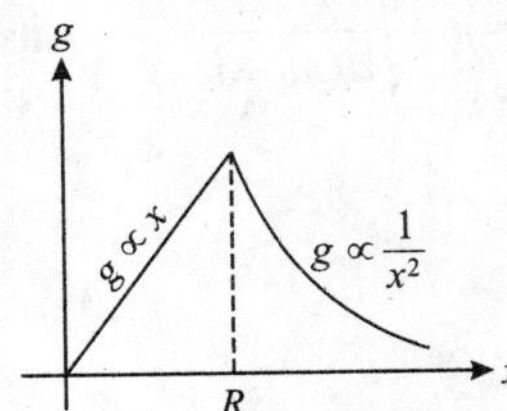

The closest/best possible option given is (B) **Ans. (B)**

Sol. 13 The mass of removed part of sphere is given as

$$m = \left(\frac{M}{\frac{4}{3}\pi R^3}\right) \times \frac{4}{3}\pi\left(\frac{R}{2}\right)^3 = \frac{M}{8}$$

Net gravitational field at point P due to remaining mass is

$$g_P = g_{full} - g_{cavity}$$

$$\Rightarrow \quad g_P = \frac{GM}{x^2} - \frac{G\left(\frac{M}{8}\right)}{\left(x + \frac{R}{2}\right)^2}$$

$$\Rightarrow \quad g_P = \frac{GM}{x^2} - \frac{GM}{8x^2}$$

$\left[\text{As } x >> \frac{R}{2} \text{ so } x + \frac{R}{2} \simeq x\right]$

$$\Rightarrow \quad g_P = \frac{7}{8}\frac{GM}{x^2}$$

Ans. (C)

Sol. 14

Change in acceleration of earth toward Sun due to change in position of moon is

$$\Delta a = a_m - (-a_m)$$

$$\Rightarrow \quad \Delta a = 2a_m$$

$$\Delta a = 2a_m = 2\left(\frac{Gm}{R^2}\right) = \frac{2 \times 6.67 \times 10^{-11} \times 7.36 \times 10^{22}}{(3.8 \times 10^8)^2}$$

$$\Rightarrow \quad \Delta a = 6.75 \times 10^{-5}\text{ m/s}^2$$

Ans. (A)

Sol. 15

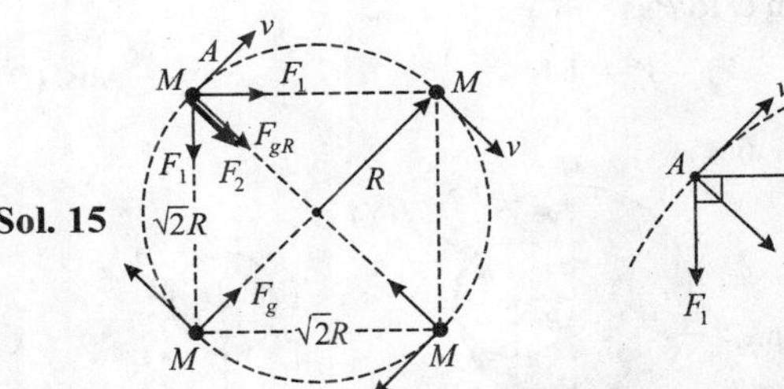

Gravitational forces acting on particle A are

$$F_1 = \frac{GM^2}{(\sqrt{2}R)^2}; F_2 = \frac{GM^2}{4R^2}$$

Net gravitational force on particle A, is given as

$$F_{gA} = F_2 + \sqrt{2}F_1$$

$$\Rightarrow \quad F_{gA} = \frac{GM^2}{4R^2} + \sqrt{2}\left(\frac{GM^2}{2R^2}\right) = \frac{Mv^2}{R}$$

$$\Rightarrow \quad \frac{GM^2}{2R^2}\left(\frac{1}{2} + \sqrt{2}\right) = \frac{Mv^2}{R}$$

$$\Rightarrow \quad v = \sqrt{\frac{GM}{4R}(2\sqrt{2} + 1)}$$

Ans. (D)

Sol. 16 Capillary height above the water level in tube is given as

$$h = \frac{2T\cos\theta}{r\rho g}$$

at earth surface $$x = \frac{2T\cos\theta}{r\rho g} \quad \ldots(1)$$

at a depth d below the surface of earth

$$y = \frac{2T\cos\theta}{r\rho\left[g\left(1-\frac{d}{R}\right)\right]} \quad \ldots(2)$$

(1)/(2) $\Rightarrow$ $\frac{x}{y} = 1 - \frac{d}{R}$ **Ans. (A)**

Sol. 17

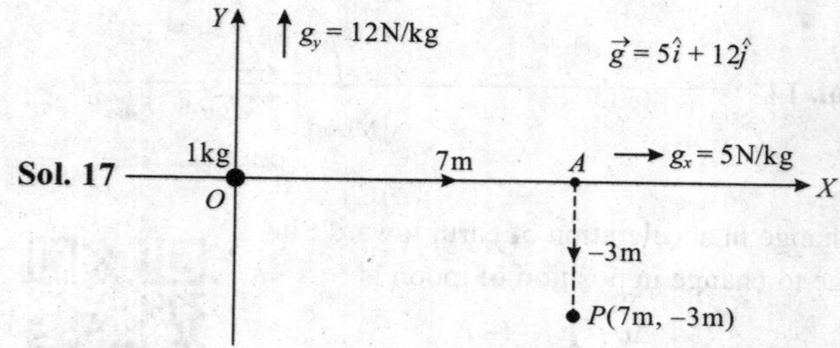

In the given situation work done in taking particle from $O \to A$ and $A \to P$ are given as

$$V_0 - V_A = 5 \times 7 = 35 \text{ J}$$

$$V_A - V_P = 12 \times (-3) = -36 \text{ J}$$

Work done or change in PE of 1 kg mass in shifting from O to P is

$$V_P - V_0 = 1 \text{ J}$$ **Ans. (D)**

Sol. 18

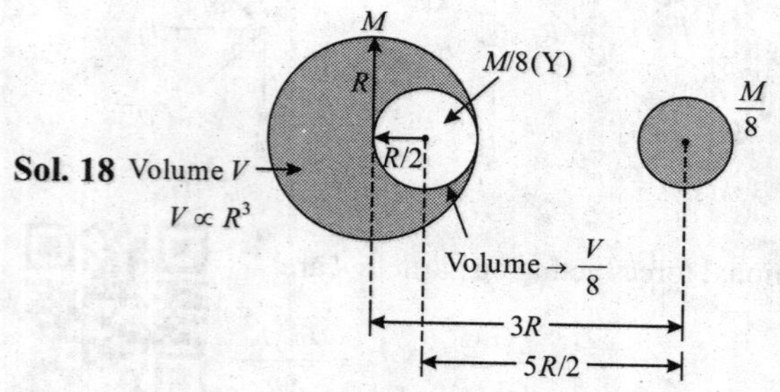

If force F_1 acts between M and $\frac{M}{8}$ than it is given as

$$F_1 = \frac{GM\left(\frac{M}{8}\right)}{(3R)^2} = \frac{GM^2}{72R^2} \quad \ldots(1)$$

If F_2 is the force between M/8 (X) and M/8 (Y) than it is given as

$$F_2 = \frac{G\left(\frac{M}{8}\right)\left(\frac{M}{8}\right)}{\left(5\frac{R}{2}\right)^2} = \frac{GM^2}{64 \times \frac{25}{4}R^2}$$

$$\Rightarrow \quad F_2 = \frac{GM^2}{400R^2} \quad \ldots(2)$$

The net force between the sphere (with cavity) and other part (x) is given as

$$F_{net} = F_1 - F_2$$

$$\Rightarrow \quad F_{net} = \frac{GM^2}{72R^2} - \frac{GM^2}{400R^2}$$

$$\Rightarrow \quad F_{net} = \frac{41GM^2}{3600R^2}$$ **Ans. (A)**

Sol. 19 (m_1 — m_1, v_1 ← d → v_2, m_2 — m_2)

By conservation of energy

$$\Rightarrow \quad E_i = E_f$$

$$\underset{PE}{0} + \underset{KE}{0} = -\frac{Gm_1m_2}{d} + \frac{1}{2}m_1v_1^2 + \frac{1}{2}m_2v_2^2 \quad \ldots(1)$$

By conservation of momentum

$$\Rightarrow \quad m_1v_1 = m_2v_1 \quad \ldots(2)$$

$$\Rightarrow \quad v_2 = \left(\frac{m_1}{m_2}\right)v_1$$

We use v_2 in equation-(1) as

$$\Rightarrow \quad \frac{Gm_1m_2}{d} = \frac{1}{2}m_1v_1^2\left[1 + \frac{m_1}{m_2}\right]$$

$$\Rightarrow \quad v_1 = \sqrt{\frac{2Gm_2^2}{d(m_1+m_2)}} = m_2\sqrt{\frac{2G}{d(m_1+m_2)}}$$

From equation-(2) $v_2 = \frac{m_1}{m_2} \cdot v_1 = m_1\sqrt{\frac{2G}{d(m_1+m_2)}}$ **Ans. (B)**

Sol. 20

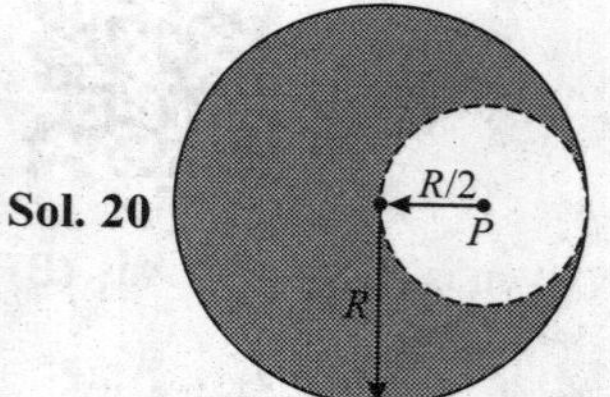

Removed mass

$$m = \frac{M}{\frac{4}{3}\pi R^3} \times \frac{4}{3}\pi\left(\frac{R}{2}\right)^3 = \frac{M}{8}$$

Gravitational potential at centre of cavity is

$$V_P = V_{\text{sphere } P} - V_{mP} \quad \ldots(1)$$

Due to a solid sphere gravitational potential at its interior point is given as

$$V_{in} = -\frac{GM}{2R^3}(3R^2 - x^2)$$

$\Rightarrow$ at $P\left(x=\frac{R}{2}\right)$ so we have

$$V_{in}=-\frac{GM}{2R^3}\left(3R^2-\frac{R^2}{4}\right)$$

$$\Rightarrow \quad V_{in}=-\frac{11}{8}\frac{GM}{R}$$

Gravitational potential due to removed mass m at centre of cavity is

$$V_{Pm}=-\frac{3}{2}\left(\frac{GM}{(R/2)}\right)=-\frac{3}{2}\frac{G(M/8)}{(R/2)}$$

$$V_{Pm}=-\frac{3}{8}\frac{GM}{R}$$

From equation-(1)

$$V_P=\left(-\frac{11}{8}\frac{GM}{R}\right)-\left(-\frac{3}{8}\frac{GM}{R}\right)$$

$$\Rightarrow \quad V_P=-\frac{GM}{R}$$ **Ans. (B)**

Sol. 21 Gravitational potential due to uniform solid spherical planet is given as

$$V_{in}=-\frac{GM}{2R^3}(3R^2-r^2) \text{ for } r<R$$

at $r=0$ $$V_c=-\frac{3}{2}\frac{GM}{R}$$

$$V_s=-\frac{GM}{R} \quad \text{for } r=R$$

$$V_{out}=-\frac{GM}{r} \quad \text{for } r>R$$ **Ans. (C)**

Sol. 22

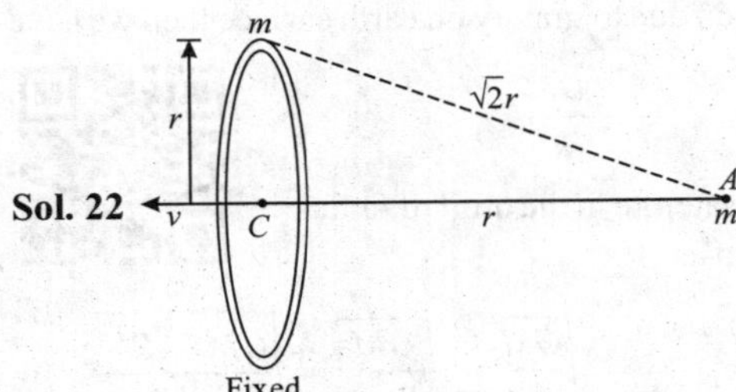

By using energy conservation, we have

$$E_{iA}=E_{fC}$$

$$-\frac{Gmm_1}{\sqrt{2}r}=-\frac{Gmm_1}{r}+\frac{1}{2}m_1v^2$$

$$\Rightarrow \quad v=\sqrt{\frac{2Gm}{r}\left(1-\frac{1}{\sqrt{2}}\right)}$$ **Ans. (C)**

7.2 Satellite Motion

Sol. 1

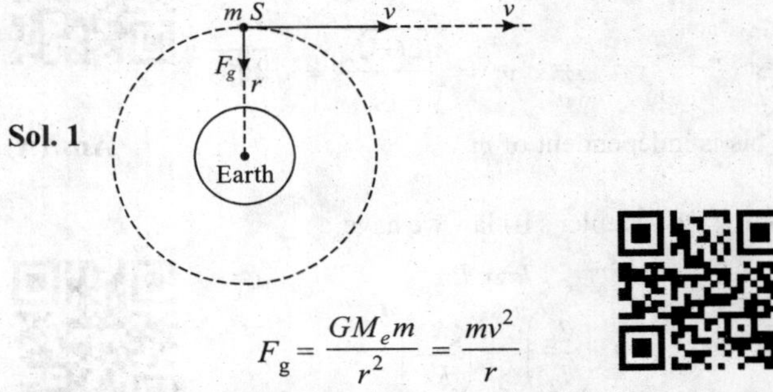

$$F_g=\frac{GM_em}{r^2}=\frac{mv^2}{r}$$

If gravitational force between earth and satellite becomes zero than there will be no centripetal force. So no circular motion will be continued and particle will move with $\vec{v}$ due to its inertia tangentially. **Ans. (B)**

Sol. 2

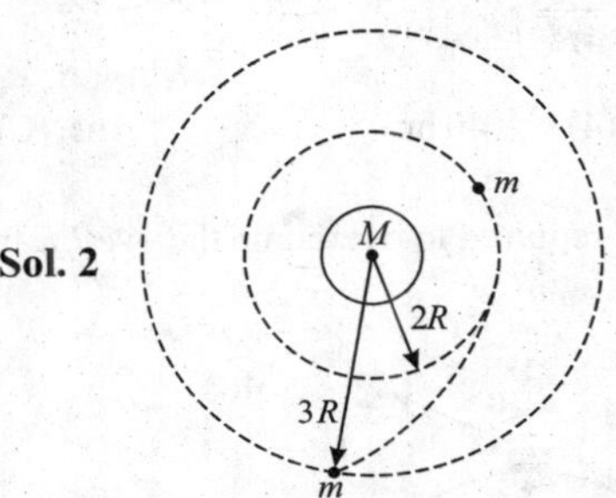

For a satellite of mass m, total energy in an orbit of radius r is given as

$$E=-\frac{GMm}{2r}$$

Initial energy of satellite ($r=2R$) $E_i=-\frac{GMm}{2(2R)}=-\frac{GMm}{4R}$

Final energy of satellite ($r=3R$) $E_f=-\frac{GMm}{2(3r)}=-\frac{GMm}{6R}$

Energy required $\Delta E=E_f-E_i=\left(-\frac{GMm}{6R}\right)-\left(-\frac{GMm}{4R}\right)$

$$\Rightarrow \quad \Delta E=\frac{GMm}{2R}\left(\frac{1}{2}-\frac{1}{3}\right)$$

$$\Rightarrow \quad \Delta E=\frac{GMm}{12R}$$ **Ans. (A)**

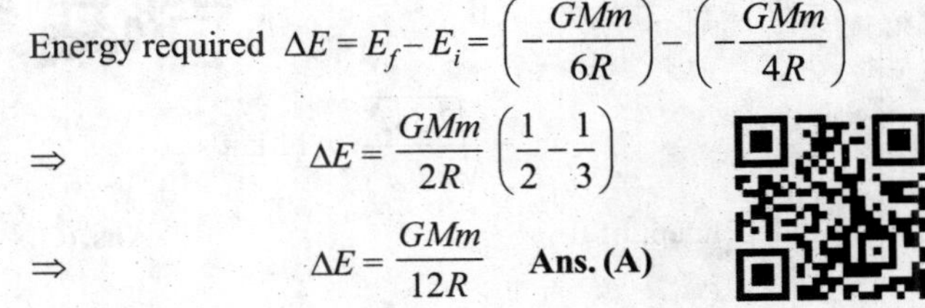

Sol. 3 v_{es} is such that its KE is numerically equal to the magnitude of gravitational PE so that $TE=0$

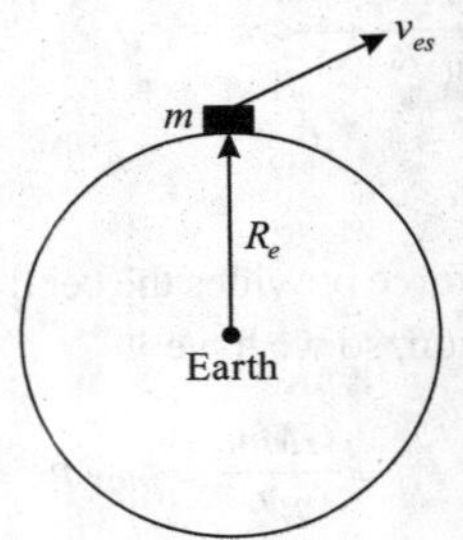

$$\frac{1}{2}mv_{es}^2 + \left(-\frac{GM_e m}{R_e}\right) = 0$$

$$\Rightarrow \quad v_{es} = \sqrt{\frac{2GM_e}{R_e}} = \sqrt{2gR_e}$$

This is independent of m **Ans. (A)**

Sol. 4 By Kepler's III law we have

$$T^2 \propto R^3$$

$$\Rightarrow \quad \left(\frac{T_1}{T_2}\right)^2 = \left(\frac{R_1}{R_2}\right)^3$$

Here $T_1 = 5$ hr

$R_2 = 4R_1$

$$\Rightarrow \quad \frac{5}{T_2} = \left(\frac{R_1}{4R_1}\right)^{3/2}$$

$$\Rightarrow \quad T_2 = 5(4)^{3/2} = 40 \text{ hr}$$ **Ans. (C)**

Sol. 5 Escape velocity is required to overcome the $-ve$ PE in body due to Earth's gravity

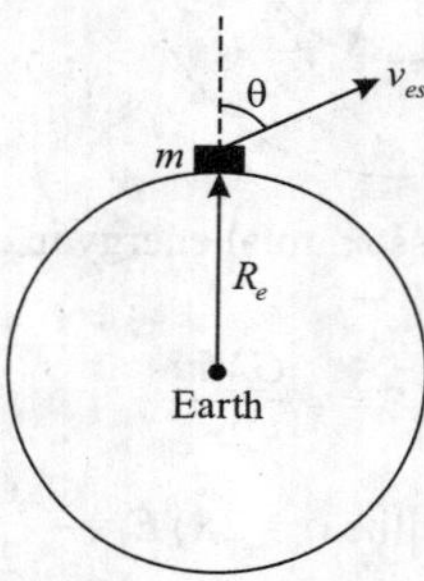

For escape velocity

$$\frac{1}{2}mv_{es}^2 + \left(-\frac{GM_e m}{R_e}\right) = 0$$

$$v_{es} = \sqrt{\frac{2GM_e}{R_e}} \simeq 11 \text{ km/s}$$

This is independent of θ **Ans. (C)**

Sol. 6

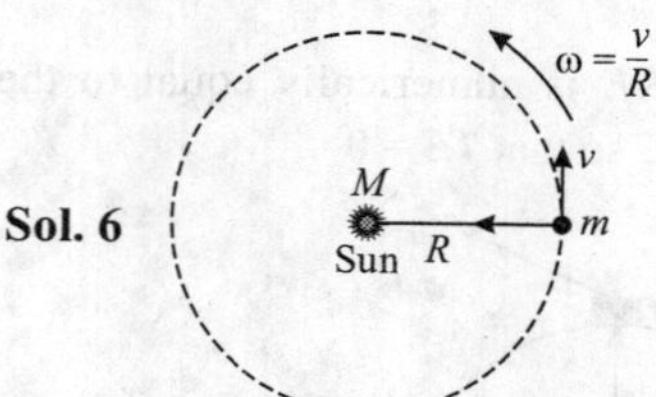

Here gravitational force provides the centripetal force to planet for its circular motion, so we have

$$F_g = \frac{GMm}{R^n} = m\omega^2 R$$

$$\Rightarrow \quad \omega = \sqrt{\frac{GM}{R^{n+1}}}$$

time period of orbital motion is

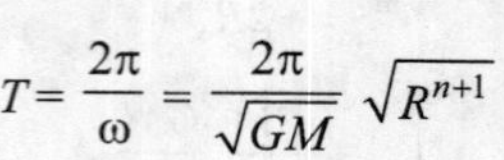

$$T = \frac{2\pi}{\omega} = \frac{2\pi}{\sqrt{GM}}\sqrt{R^{n+1}}$$

$$\Rightarrow \quad T \propto R^{\left(\frac{n+1}{2}\right)}$$ **Ans. (A)**

Sol. 7

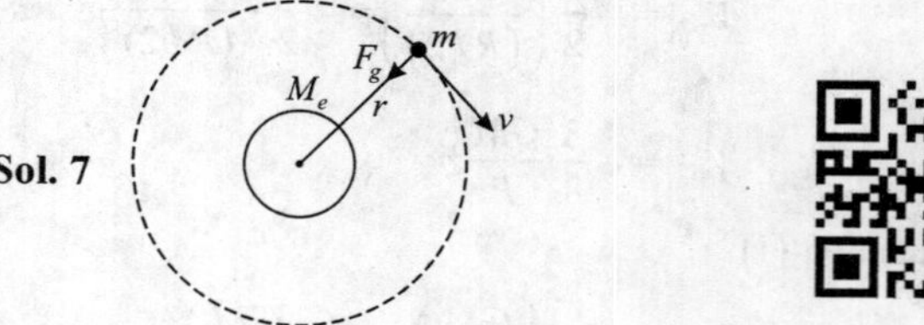

Orbital speed of a satellite in an orbit radius r is given as

$$v = \sqrt{\frac{GM_e}{r}}$$

time period of satellite is

$$T = \frac{2\pi r}{v} = \frac{2\pi}{\sqrt{GM_e}} \cdot r^{3/2}$$

T is independent of mass of satellite **Ans. (A)**

Sol. 8

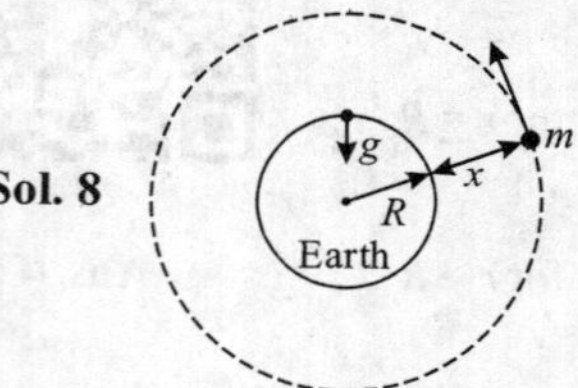

If g is acceleration due to gravity on earth surface then we have

$$g = \frac{GM}{R^2}$$

orbital speed of satellite in the orbit of radius $r = R + x$ is given as

$$v = \sqrt{\frac{GM}{r}} = \sqrt{\frac{GM}{R+x}} = \sqrt{\frac{GM}{R^2} \cdot \frac{R^2}{R+x}}$$

$$= \sqrt{\frac{gR^2}{R+x}}$$ **Ans. (D)**

Sol. 9 From a planet escape velocity is given as

$$v_e = \sqrt{\frac{2GM}{R}} \quad \text{for earth } v_{e_1} = \sqrt{\frac{2GM_e}{R_e}} = 11 \text{ km/s}$$

$$\Rightarrow \quad v_e \propto \sqrt{\frac{M}{R}}$$

For this planet $M = 10\, M_e$ and $R = \dfrac{R_e}{10}$

$$\Rightarrow \quad v_e = \sqrt{\frac{2G(10M_e)}{(R_e/10)}} = 10\sqrt{\frac{2GM_e}{R_e}}$$

$$\Rightarrow \quad v_e = 110\,\text{km/s}$$

Ans. (C)

Sol. 10

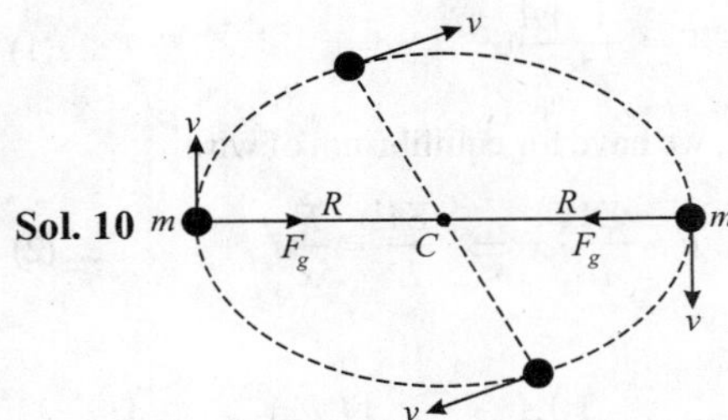

In the given double star system the gravitational force will provide the centripetal force for this circular motion, so we use

$$\frac{Gm^2}{(2R)^2} = \frac{mv^2}{R}$$

$$\Rightarrow \quad v = \sqrt{\frac{Gm}{4R}}$$

Ans. (B)

Sol. 11 For EOM elliptical orbit if time period of motion in this orbit is T then we use

$$T^2 \propto \left(\frac{a_m + a_e}{2}\right)^3 \qquad \ldots(1)$$

Semi major axis of elliptical orbit for earth if T_e be the period around sun then we use

$$T_e^2 \propto a_e^3 \qquad \ldots(2)$$

Here (1)/(2) gives

$$\frac{T^2}{T_e^2} = \left[\frac{(a_m + a_e)/2}{a_e}\right]^3$$

$$T = \left[\frac{(a_m + a_e)/2}{a_e}\right]^{3/2} T_e$$

$$T = \left[\frac{(1.5 + 2.28)/2}{1.5}\right]^{3/2} \times 365 \text{ days}$$

$$T = \left(\frac{1.89}{1.5}\right)^{3/2} \times 365 \text{ days}$$

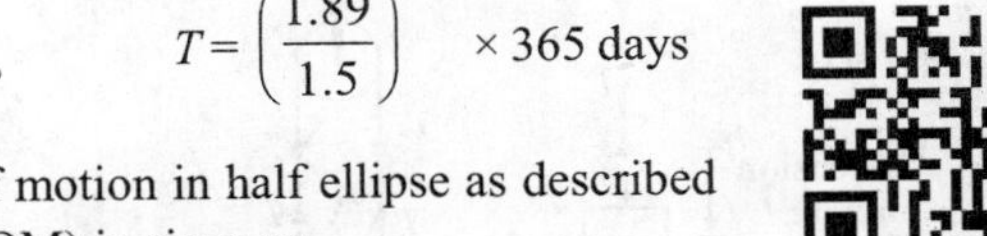

Time of motion in half ellipse as described (path EOM) is given as

$$t = \frac{T}{2} = \left[\frac{1.89}{1.5}\right]^{3/2} \times \frac{365}{2} \cong 258 \text{ days}$$

Ans. (C)

Sol. 12

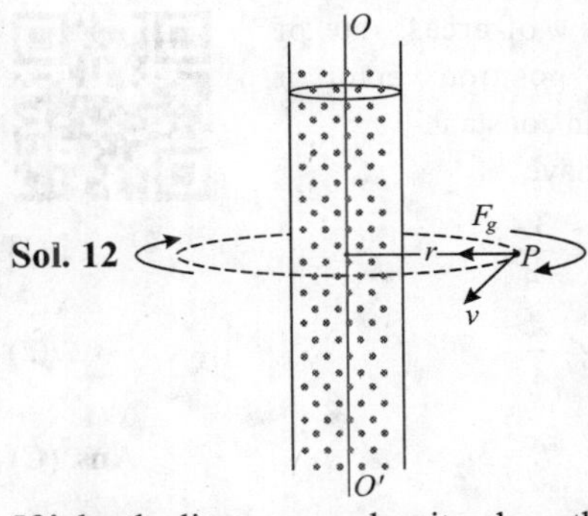

If λ be the linear mass density along the length of galaxy then gravitational field at the location of star is given as

$$g_P = \frac{2G\lambda}{r}$$

For circular motion of star, we use

$$mg_P = \frac{mv^2}{r}$$

$$\Rightarrow \quad \frac{2G\lambda}{r} = \frac{v^2}{r} \Rightarrow v = \sqrt{2G\lambda} \text{ orbital speed of star}$$

Period of revolution of star in circular orbit is

$$T = \frac{2\pi r}{v}$$

$$\Rightarrow \quad T = \frac{2\pi r}{\sqrt{2G\lambda}}$$

$$\Rightarrow \quad T \propto r$$

Ans. (A)

Sol. 13

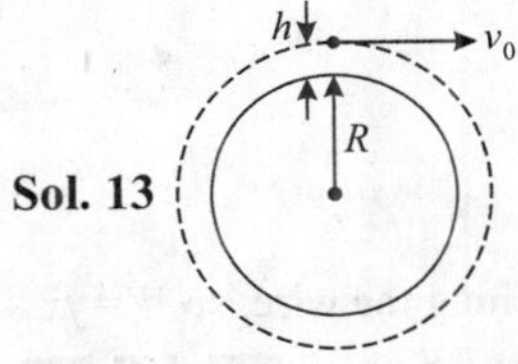

Orbital speed velocity close to earth surface is given as

$$v_0 = \sqrt{gR}$$

Escape velocity very close to earth surface is given as

$$v_e = \sqrt{2gR}$$

Additional velocity required for satellite to escape is

$$\Delta v = v_e - v_0 = \sqrt{gR}\,(\sqrt{2} - 1)$$

Ans. (D)

Sol. 14

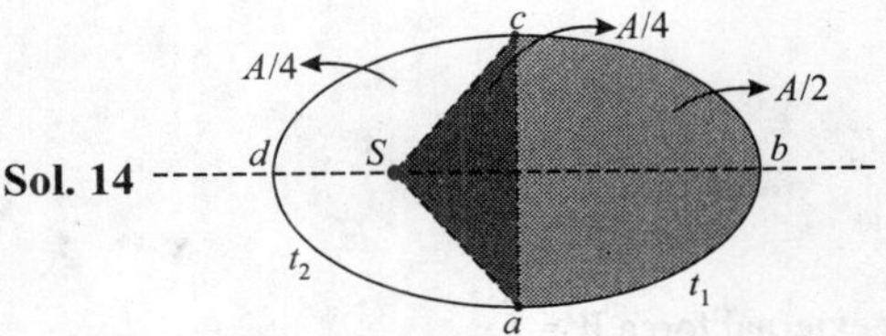

According Kepler's law of areas, rate of sweeping out area by position vector of planet w.r. to sun remain constant.

As t $\propto$ area swept, we have

$$\Rightarrow \qquad t_1 \propto \frac{3A}{4} \qquad \ldots(1)$$

$$\text{and} \qquad t_2 \propto \frac{A}{4} \qquad \ldots(2)$$

$$(1)/(2) \Rightarrow \frac{t_1}{t_2} = 3 \Rightarrow t_1 = 3t_2$$

Ans. (C)

Sol. 15

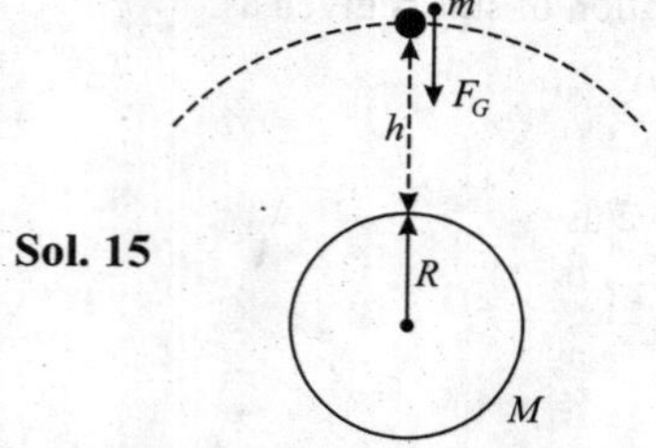

Along with satellite we consider the astronaut is also revolving around earth in orbit of radius $(R + h)$ so gravitational force on astronaut is given as

$$F_G = \frac{GMm}{(R+h)^2}$$

Here we neglect the gravitational force between astronaut and satellite.

Ans. (C)

8.1 Elasticity

Sol. 1

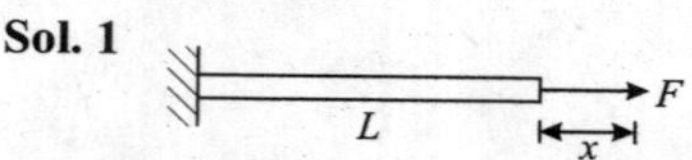

Work done by external force is stretching the wire, so $W = fx$

Half of above work is stored in elastic PE of wire, so we use

$$\text{and} \qquad U = \frac{1}{2} fx$$

$$\Rightarrow \qquad U = \frac{1}{2} \times 200 \times 1 \times 10^{-3} = 0.1 \text{ J}$$

Ans. (D)

Sol. 2

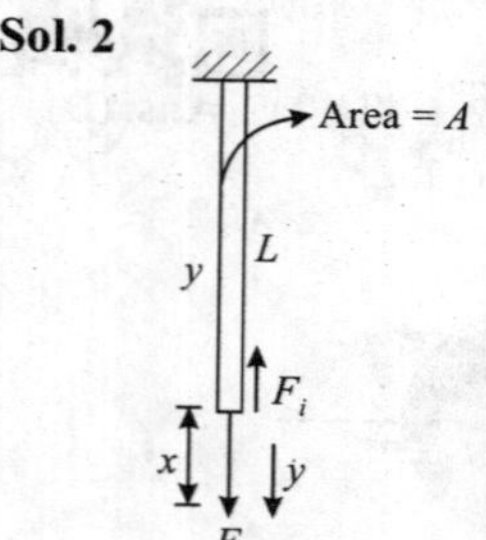

Work done by external force $W = Fx$

Due to stretching by internal force because of elasticity it develops stress in wire, using Young's modulus we have

$$Y = \frac{\text{stress}}{\text{stress}} = \left(\frac{f_i / A}{y / L}\right) \Rightarrow F_i = \frac{YA}{L} \cdot y$$

y increases from 0 to x.

$y \rightarrow$ instantaneous extension is wire

Work done by internal force

$$W_i = \int_0^x F_i day = -\frac{yA}{L} \int_0^x y\, dy$$

$$\Rightarrow \qquad W_i = \frac{1}{-2} \frac{yA}{L} x^2 \qquad \ldots(1)$$

At final extension x, we have for equilibrium of wire

$$F = \frac{YA}{L} \cdot x \Rightarrow \frac{YA}{L} = \frac{F}{x} \qquad \ldots(2)$$

from (1) and (2)

$$W_i = -\frac{1}{2} \frac{YA}{L} x^2 = -\frac{1}{2}\left(\frac{F}{x}\right) x^2 = -\frac{1}{2} Fx$$

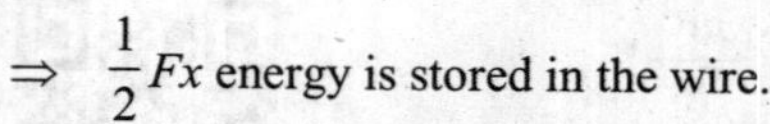

– ve sign denotes absorption of energy

$\Rightarrow \frac{1}{2} Fx$ energy is stored in the wire.

Work done in stretching by external force $= Fl$

Work done by elastic forces in stretching $= \frac{1}{2} Fl$

$$\text{Heat dissipation} = Fl - \frac{1}{2} Fl = \frac{1}{2} Fl$$

Ans. (D)

Sol. 3 If a wire is stretched by an external force then elastic PE density (J/m^3) in the wire is given as

$$u_E = \frac{1}{2} \times \text{stress} \times \text{strain}$$

By definition of Young's modulus, we use

$$y = \frac{\text{stress}}{\text{strain}} = \frac{S}{\text{strain}}$$

$$\Rightarrow \qquad \text{Strain} = \frac{S}{Y}$$

$$u_E = \frac{1}{2} \times S \times \frac{S}{Y} = \frac{S^2}{2Y}$$

Ans. (B)

Sol. 4

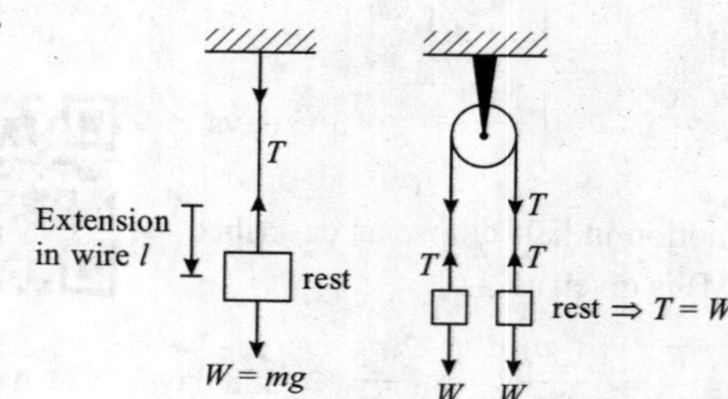

For equilibrium of load, tension in wire $T = W$

As tension in wire in the two cases is same

$\Rightarrow$ extension in these cases must be same.

Ans. (A)

Sol. 5

area $= A$

Volume of wire $\quad V = Al$

By definition of young's modulus, we have

$$Y = \frac{\text{Stress}}{\text{strain}} = \frac{(F/A)}{\Delta l/l}$$

$$\Rightarrow \quad F = \frac{YA}{l}\Delta l \times \frac{A}{A}$$

$$\Rightarrow \quad F = \frac{YA^2\Delta l}{V}$$

For same Δl and V we have

$$F \propto A^2$$

$$\Rightarrow \quad \frac{F_1}{F_2} = \left(\frac{A_1}{A_2}\right)^2$$

If $\quad A_2 = 3A \ \& \ A_1 = A$

$$\Rightarrow \quad F_2 = F_1(3)^2 = 9F_1 = 9F$$

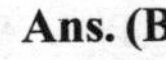

Ans. (B)

Sol. 6

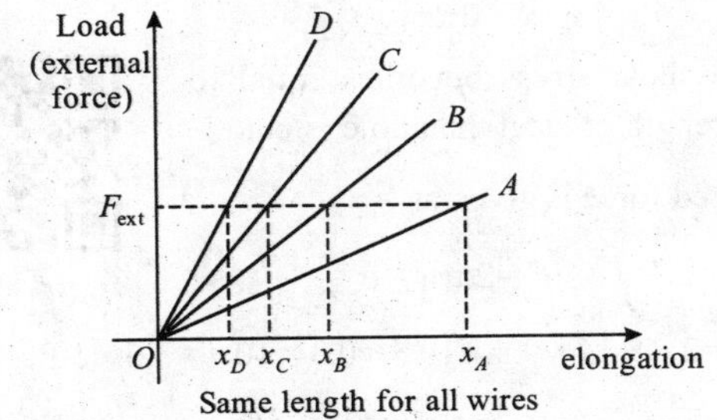

For a given value of load (external force)

$$x_A > x_B > x_C > x_D$$

As x_A is maximum

$\Rightarrow$ Strain is maximum in wire OA

$\Rightarrow$ Stress is maximum in wire OA

$$\text{stress} = \frac{F_{ext}}{A}$$

$\Rightarrow$ A is minimum for wire OA

Ans. (A)

Sol. 7 Young's modulus $Y = \dfrac{\text{Stress}}{\text{Strain}}$

$$\Rightarrow \quad \text{Strain} = \frac{\text{Stress}}{Y} = \frac{F/A}{Y} = \frac{F}{\pi r^2 Y}$$

$$\Rightarrow \quad \text{Strain} = \frac{10^5}{3.14 \times (10 \times 10^{-3})^2 \times 2 \times 10^{11}}$$

$$\Rightarrow \quad \text{Strain} = \frac{1}{628}$$

$$\% \text{ strain in wire} = \frac{1}{628} \times 100\% = 0.16\%$$

Ans. (A)

Sol. 8 Breaking force of a wire is the force at which stress in wire becomes equal to rupture strength of the wire material and it is independent of length of wire. **Ans. (C)**

Sol. 9 Stress produced in wire is given as

$$\text{Stress} = \frac{T}{A}$$

In the simple Atwood's machine shown in figure tension in wire is given as

$$T = \frac{2mm}{M+m} \cdot g = \frac{2(2m)m}{2m+m} \cdot g = \frac{4mg}{3}$$

$$\Rightarrow \quad \text{Stress} = \frac{4mg}{3A}$$

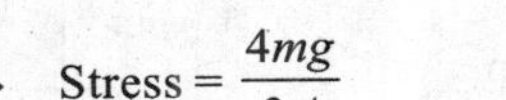

Ans. (B)

Sol. 10 Given that $\dfrac{l_{st}}{l_{br}} = a$; $\dfrac{r_{st}}{r_{br}} = b$ and $\dfrac{1/_{st}}{1/_{br}} = C$

We use $\quad Y = \dfrac{\text{Stress}}{\text{Strain}} = \dfrac{(T/\pi r^2)}{\Delta l / l}$

$$\Rightarrow \quad \Delta l = \frac{Tl}{\pi r^2 Y}$$

For steel wire $\quad \Delta l_{st} = \dfrac{3mg.l_{st}}{\pi r_{st}^2 Y_{st}}$

For brass wire $\quad \Delta l_{br} = \dfrac{2mg\, l_{br}}{\pi r_{br}^2 Y_{br}}$

$$\Rightarrow \quad \frac{\Delta l_{st}}{\Delta l_{br}} = \frac{3l_{st}}{2l_{br}} \times \frac{r_{br}^2}{r_{st}^2} \times \frac{Y_{br}}{Y_{st}}$$

$$\Rightarrow \quad \frac{\Delta l_{st}}{\Delta l_{br}} = \frac{3}{2}a \times \frac{1}{b^2} \times \frac{1}{c} = \frac{3a}{2b^2c}$$

Ans. (C)

Sol. 11 Young's modulus of wire

$$Y = \frac{\text{Stress}}{\text{Strain}} = \frac{\text{Stress}}{\Delta l/l}$$

[$l \rightarrow$ wire length & $\Delta l \rightarrow$ extension]

$$\Rightarrow \quad \frac{\Delta l}{l} = \frac{\text{Stress}}{Y} = \frac{5 \times 10^7}{2 \times 10^{11}} = 2.5 \times 10^{-4}$$

If wire is having a cross-sectional radius r than its value is

$$V = \pi r^2 l$$

$$\Rightarrow \quad \Delta V = \pi r^2 \Delta l + 2\pi r\,\Delta r l$$

$$\Rightarrow \quad \frac{\Delta V}{V} = \frac{\Delta r^2 \Delta l + 2\pi r \Delta r l}{\pi r^2 l} = \frac{0.02}{100}$$

$$\Rightarrow \quad \frac{\Delta l}{l} + \frac{2\Delta r}{r} = \frac{0.02}{100} = 2\times 10^{-4}$$

$$\Rightarrow \quad \frac{2\Delta r}{r} = (2 - 2.5)\times 10^{-4} = -0.5\times 10^{-4}$$

$$\Rightarrow \quad \frac{\Delta r}{r} = -0.25\times 10^{-4}$$

Ans. (C)

Sol. 12 As cross-sectional areas of the two wires are equal

$$\Rightarrow \quad (\text{Stress})_{Cu} = (\text{Stress})_{steel}$$

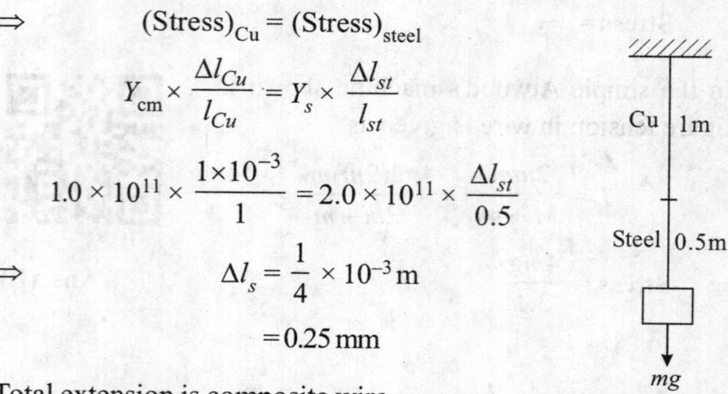

$$Y_{cm} \times \frac{\Delta l_{Cu}}{l_{Cu}} = Y_s \times \frac{\Delta l_{st}}{l_{st}}$$

$$1.0\times 10^{11} \times \frac{1\times 10^{-3}}{1} = 2.0\times 10^{11} \times \frac{\Delta l_{st}}{0.5}$$

$$\Rightarrow \quad \Delta l_s = \frac{1}{4}\times 10^{-3}\,\text{m}$$

$$= 0.25\,\text{mm}$$

Total extension is composite wire

$$\Delta l = \Delta l_{cu} + \Delta l_{st}$$

$$= 1 + 0.25$$

$$\Rightarrow \quad \Delta l = 1.25\,\text{mm}$$ **Ans. (D)**

Sol. 13

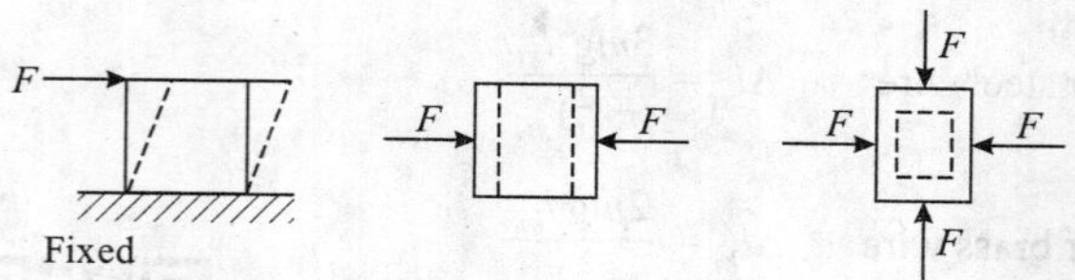

Modulus of elasticity

Shear modulus

$$\eta = \frac{\text{shear strain}}{s.\text{strain}}$$

Young's modulus

$$Y = \frac{\text{long stress}}{\text{long strain}}$$

Bulk modulus

$$B = \frac{\text{Bulk stress}}{\text{Volume strain}}$$

For equal magnitude of strains we have

Bulk stress > longitudinal stress > shear stress

$\Rightarrow \; B > Y > \eta$ **Ans. (C)**

Sol. 14 By definition of Bulk modulus

$$B = \left|\frac{\Delta P_{ex}}{\Delta V / V}\right|$$

Here $\frac{\Delta V}{V}$ is fractional compression in volume due to excess pressure ΔP_{ex}

$\Rightarrow$ For ΔP_{ex} = constant for all liquids

We have $\quad \frac{\Delta V}{V} \propto \frac{1}{B}$

$$\Rightarrow \quad \left|\frac{\Delta V}{V}\right|_{\text{Ethanol}} > \left|\frac{\Delta V}{V}\right|_{\text{Water}} > \left|\frac{\Delta V}{V}\right|_{\text{Mercury}}$$

Ans. (A)

Sol. 15

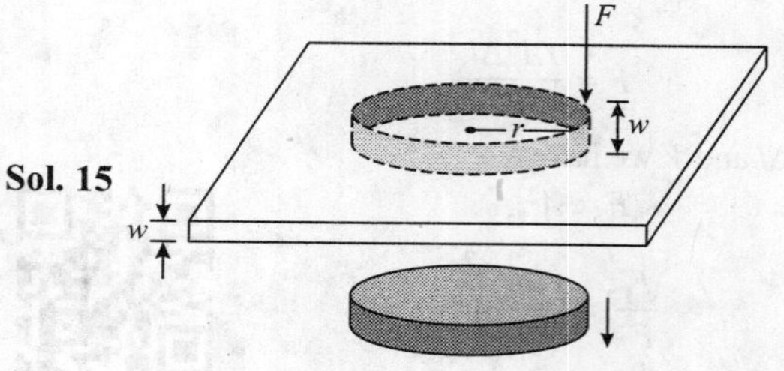

Shear stress by the applied force on the part of steel sheet (disc shaped) which is to be cut/removed is given as

Shear stress $\quad \sigma = \frac{F}{2\pi r w}$

When the shear stress becomes equal to rapture strength of steel than hole is cut

$\Rightarrow$ required force is given as

$$F = 2\pi r w \times \sigma_{max}$$

$$\Rightarrow \quad F = 2\times 3.14\times 0.5\times 10^{-2}\times 0.3\times 10^{-2}\times 3.5\times 10^{8}$$

$$\Rightarrow \quad F = 3.29\times 10^{4}\,\text{N}$$

Ans. (C)

Sol. 16

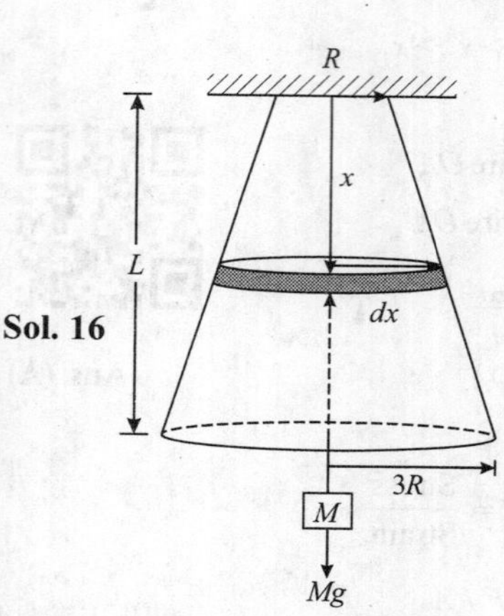

Radius of elemental disc from top end at a distance x is

$$R = \left(\frac{3R-R}{L}\right)x + R = \frac{2R}{L}x + R$$

For whole wire we can use on all such elements

$$Y = \frac{\text{Stress}}{\text{Strain}}$$

If dy is the elongation in width dx

$$\Rightarrow \quad Y = \frac{Mg/\pi r^2}{dy/dx}$$

$$\Rightarrow \quad dy = \frac{Mg\,dx}{Y\pi\left(\frac{2R}{L}x + R\right)^2}$$

Total extension in wire is

$$y = \int dy = \frac{Mg}{Y\pi}\int_0^L \frac{dx}{\left(\frac{2R}{L}x + R\right)^2}$$

$$\Rightarrow \quad y = \frac{Mg}{Y\pi}\left[\frac{L}{2R}\left(-\frac{1}{\left(\frac{2R}{L}x + R\right)}\right)\right]_0^L$$

$$\Rightarrow \quad y = \frac{Mg\,L}{2Y\pi R}\left[-\frac{1}{3R} - \left(-\frac{1}{R}\right)\right] = \frac{Mg\,L}{3\pi YR^2}$$

Total extended length of wire

$$L_f = L + y = L\left(1 + \frac{Mg}{3\pi YR^2}\right)$$ **Ans. (C)**

Sol. 17

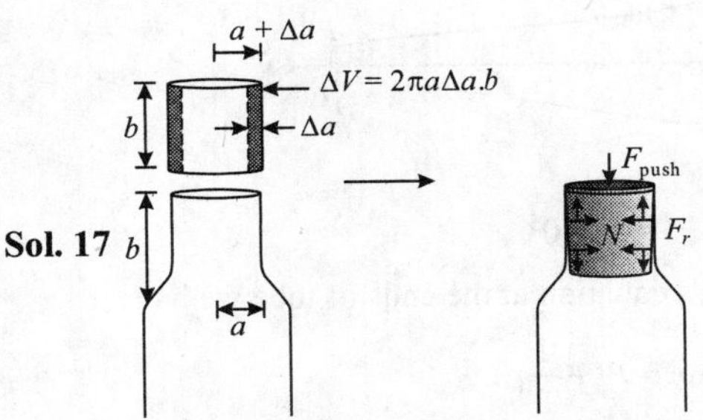

To fit the cork in the bottle opening a contact force compressive in nature is there and stress due to this, contact force on cork volume is

excess pressure $\Delta P = \frac{N}{3} = \frac{N}{2\pi ab}$

Volume compression in cork

$$\Delta V = (2\pi a\Delta a).b$$

Volume of cork

$$V = \pi a^2 b$$

Volume strain in cork

$$\Rightarrow \quad \frac{\Delta V}{V} = \frac{2\pi a\Delta a.b}{\pi a^2 b}$$

Bulk modulus of cork is given as

$$B = \frac{\Delta P_{ex}}{\left|\frac{\Delta V}{V}\right|}$$

$$\Rightarrow \quad B = \frac{N/2\pi ab}{(2\pi a\Delta ab)/\pi a^2 b} = \frac{N.a^2 b}{2\pi\Delta ab.2\pi ab}$$

$$\Rightarrow \quad N = 4\pi\Delta abB$$

to push the cork inside the bottle the external force has to overcome the friction on cork

$$\Rightarrow \quad F_{push} \geq \mu N = 4\pi\mu\Delta abB$$ **Ans. (D)**

9.1 Fluid Statics

Sol. 1 As ball sinks in liquid-1

$$\Rightarrow \quad \rho_3 > \rho_1 \quad \ldots(1)$$

and ball is not sinking in liquid-2

$$\Rightarrow \quad \rho_3 < \rho_2 \quad \ldots(2)$$

Here in jar liquid-1 is above liquid-2

$$\Rightarrow \quad \rho_1 < \rho_2 \quad \ldots(3)$$

From-(1), (2) and 3

$$\rho_1 < \rho_3 < \rho_2$$ **Ans. (D)**

Sol. 2 As $\rho_{oil} < \rho_{water}$

$\Rightarrow$ Oil will be above water in container

$$\rho_{oil} < \rho$$

$\Rightarrow$ Ball will sink in oil

$$\rho < \rho_{water}$$

$\Rightarrow$ Ball will float in water **Ans. (C)**

Sol. 3

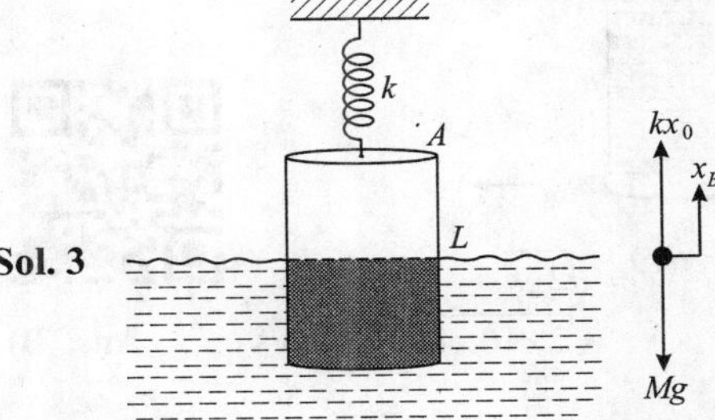

Buoyant force on cylinder due to liquid displaced by submerged part is

$$F_B = V_{\sigma g} = \left(\frac{L}{2}A\right)\sigma g$$

For equilibrium, we use

$$kx_0 + F_B = Mg$$

$$\Rightarrow \quad kx_0 = Mg - \frac{LA\sigma g}{2}$$

$$\Rightarrow \qquad x_0 = \frac{1}{k}\left(Mg - \frac{LA\sigma g}{2}\right)$$

$$\Rightarrow \qquad x_0 = \frac{Mg}{k}\left(1 - \frac{\sigma LA}{2M}\right)$$ **Ans. (B)**

Sol. 4 For equilibrium of liquids pressure at any point of a liquid is same at one horizontal level.

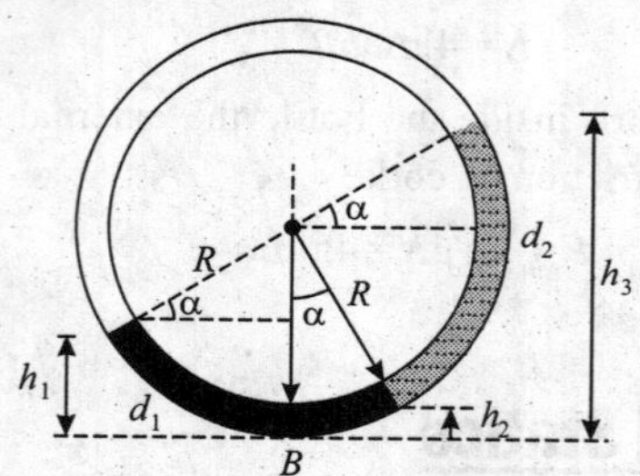

In figure if R is the radius of tube, we have

$$h_1 = R - R\sin\alpha$$
$$h_2 = R - R\cos\alpha$$
$$h_3 = R - R\sin\alpha$$

Pressure due to liquid at point B is given as

$$P_B = h_1 d_1 g$$

and $$P_B = (h_3 - h_2)d_2 g + h_2 d_1 g$$

$$\Rightarrow \qquad h_1 d_1 g = (h_3 - h_2)\, d_2 g + h_2 d_1 g$$

$$\Rightarrow \qquad (h_1 - h_2)d_1 = (h_3 - h_2)d_2$$

$$\Rightarrow \qquad \frac{d_1}{d_2} = \frac{h_3 - h_2}{h_1 - h_2} = \frac{\sin\alpha + \cos\alpha}{\cos\alpha - \sin\alpha}$$

$$\Rightarrow \qquad \frac{d_1}{d_2} = \frac{1 + \tan\alpha}{1 - \tan\alpha}$$ **Ans. (C)**

9.2 Fluid Dynamics

Sol. 1

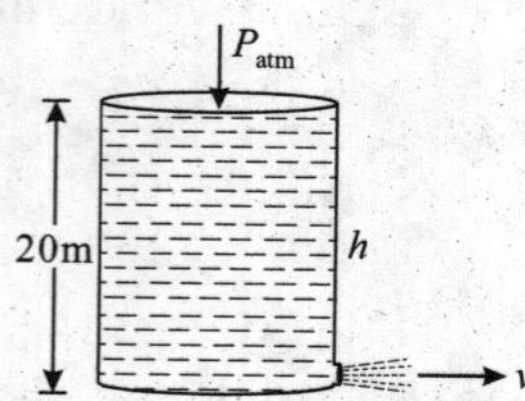

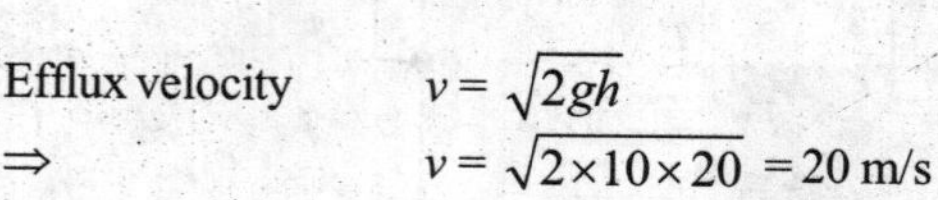

Efflux velocity $$v = \sqrt{2gh}$$

$$\Rightarrow \qquad v = \sqrt{2 \times 10 \times 20} = 20 \text{ m/s}$$ **Ans. (B)**

Sol. 2

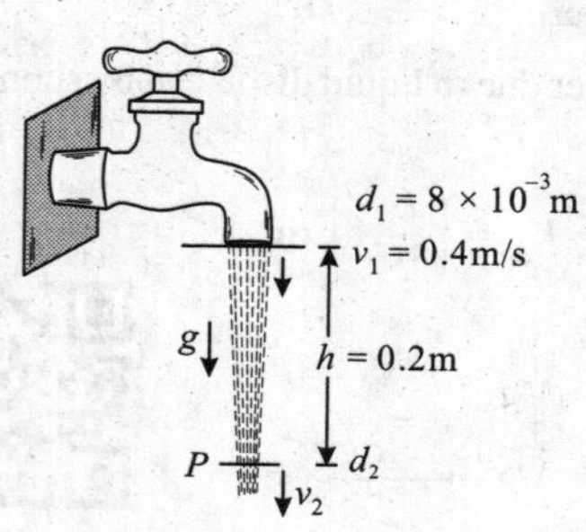

By speed equation for free fall motion of water stream we have

$$v_2^2 = v_1^2 + 2gh$$

$$\Rightarrow \qquad v_2^2 = (0.4)^2 + 2 \times 10 \times 0.2 = 4.16$$

$$\Rightarrow \qquad v_2 = \sqrt{4.16} \text{ m/s}$$

By continuity equation is stream of water, we use

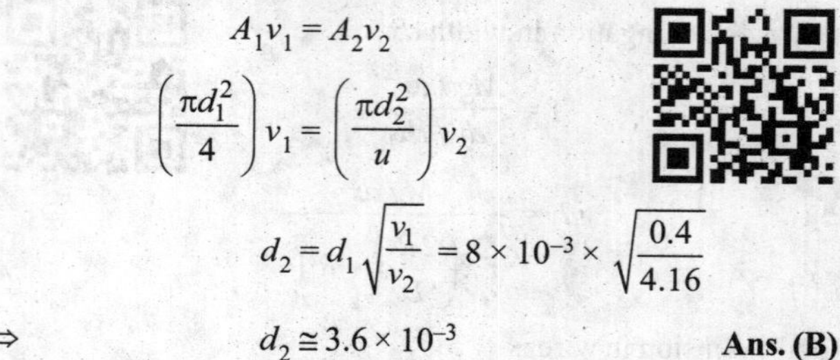

$$A_1 v_1 = A_2 v_2$$

$$\left(\frac{\pi d_1^2}{4}\right) v_1 = \left(\frac{\pi d_2^2}{u}\right) v_2$$

$$d_2 = d_1\sqrt{\frac{v_1}{v_2}} = 8 \times 10^{-3} \times \sqrt{\frac{0.4}{4.16}}$$

$$\Rightarrow \qquad d_2 \cong 3.6 \times 10^{-3}$$ **Ans. (B)**

Sol. 3 Efflux velocity of water coming out from holes

$$v_1 = \sqrt{2gh}$$

and $$v_2 = \sqrt{2g(4h)} = 2\sqrt{2gh}$$

As flows rate from holes is same, we use

$$A_1 v_1 = A_2 v_2$$

$$\Rightarrow \qquad l^2\sqrt{2gh} = \pi r^2 \times 2\sqrt{2gh}$$

$$\Rightarrow \qquad r^2 = \frac{l^2}{2\pi}$$

$$\Rightarrow \qquad r = \frac{l}{\sqrt{2\pi}}$$ **Ans. (A)**

Sol. 4

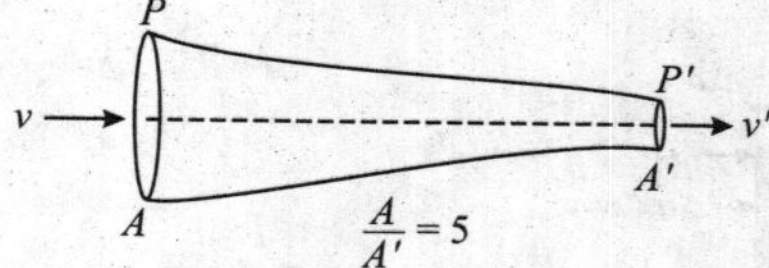

$$P - P' = 3 \times 10^5$$

Using Bernoulli's equation at the ends of tube we have

$$P + \frac{1}{2}\rho v^2 = P' + \frac{1}{2}\rho V'^2$$

$$\Rightarrow \qquad P - P' = \frac{1}{2}\rho(v'^2 - v^2) \qquad \ldots(1)$$

By continuity equation, we use

$$Av = A'v'$$

$$\Rightarrow \qquad v' = \frac{A}{A'}v = 5v$$

From (1), we use

$$3 \times 10^5 = \frac{1}{2} \times 10^3 \times 24v^2$$

$$\Rightarrow \qquad v = \sqrt{\frac{2 \times 3 \times 10^5}{10^3 \times 24}} = \sqrt{25} = 5 \text{ m/s}$$ **Ans. (A)**

Sol. 5 Efflux velocity of water from hole A is

$$v_1 = \sqrt{2gh}$$

Range of water from hole A is

$$R_A = v_1 \times \sqrt{\frac{2(H-h_1)}{g}}$$

$$R_A = 2\sqrt{h_1(H-h_1)} \qquad \ldots(1)$$

Efflux velocity of water from hole B is

$$v_2 = \sqrt{2g(H-h_2)}$$

Range of water from hole B is

$$R_B = v_2 \times \sqrt{\frac{2h_2}{g}} = 2\sqrt{h_2(H-h_2)} \qquad \ldots(2)$$

Given that $R_A = R_B$

$$\Rightarrow \quad h_1(H-h_1) = h_2(H-h_2)$$

$$\Rightarrow \quad h_1 = h_2$$

Ans. (B)

Sol. 6

Upper side

U

Cross section of an airoplane wing

L

Lower side

Wind velocity

$$v_U = 150 \text{ m/s}$$

$$v_L = 100 \text{ m/s}$$

If P_U and P_L are the air pressures at upper and lower sides of wings then we use Barnoullie's theorem, we have

$$P_U + \frac{1}{2}\rho v_U^2 = P_L + \rho v_L^2$$

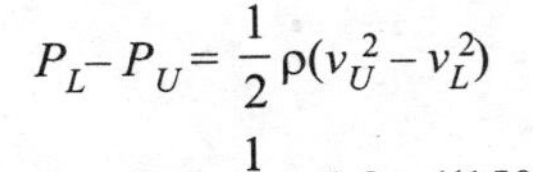

$$\Rightarrow \quad P_L - P_U = \frac{1}{2}\rho(v_U^2 - v_L^2)$$

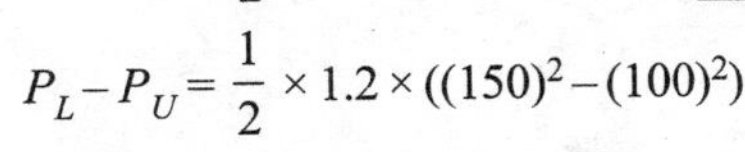

$$\Rightarrow \quad P_L - P_U = \frac{1}{2} \times 1.2 \times ((150)^2 - (100)^2)$$

$$\Rightarrow \quad P_L - P_U = 0.6 \times 10^4 \times (2.25 - 1) = 6 \times 1.25 \times 103$$

$$\Rightarrow \quad P_L - P_U = 7500 \text{ N/m}^2$$

Ans. (C)

Sol. 7

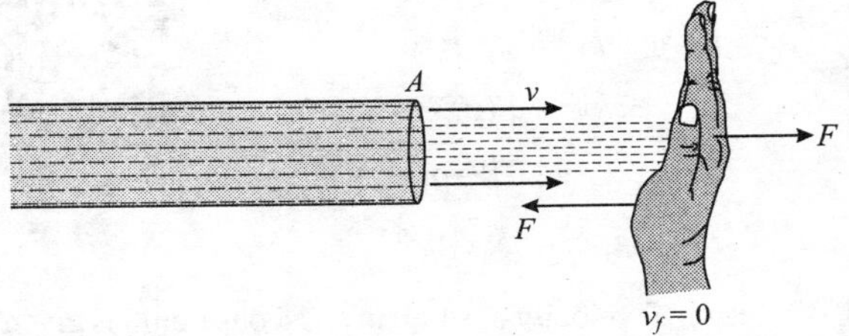

Water stops when hit the palm and it transfers momentum to the hand.

Force exerted = rate of change of momentum = momentum in hitting water/sec

$$F = \rho\,(Av) \times V = \rho A v^2$$

$$= 10^3 \times 10^{-2} \times (1.5)^2$$

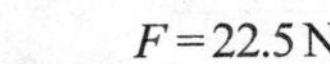

$$\Rightarrow \quad F = 22.5 \text{ N}$$

Ans (B)

$\rho \rightarrow$ density; $Av \rightarrow$ volume flow rate

Sol. 8

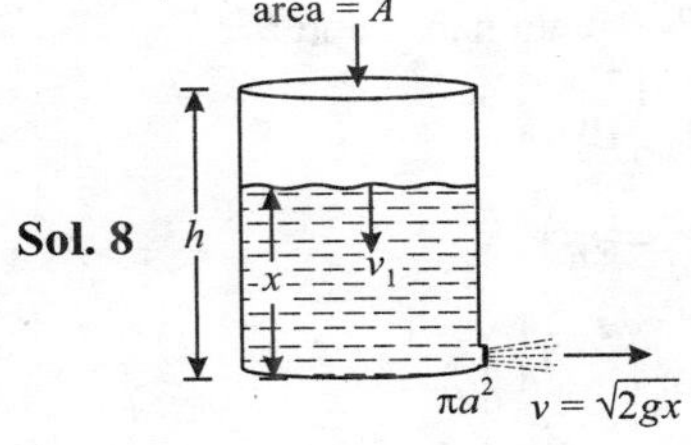

Here we can use $\quad v_1 = -\dfrac{dx}{dt}$

By equation of contains we use

$$V_1 A = \sqrt{2gx}\,.(\pi a^2)$$

$$\Rightarrow \quad -A\frac{dx}{dt} = \pi a^2\sqrt{2g}.\sqrt{x}$$

$$\Rightarrow \quad \frac{dx}{\sqrt{x}} = -\frac{\pi a^2}{A}\sqrt{2g}\,dt$$

with time x is decreasing and if in time T if the vessel is emptied than we use

$$\int_{x=h}^{x=0}\frac{dx}{\sqrt{x}} = -\frac{\pi a^2}{A}\sqrt{2g}\int_{t=0}^{t=T} dt$$

$$\Rightarrow \quad \left[2\sqrt{x}\right]_h^0 = -\frac{\pi a^2}{A}\sqrt{2g}\,[t]_0^T$$

$$\Rightarrow \quad 2\sqrt{h} = \frac{\pi a^2}{A}\sqrt{2g}\,.T$$

$$\Rightarrow \quad T = \frac{A}{\pi a^2}\sqrt{\frac{2h}{g}}$$

Ans. (B)

Sol. 9

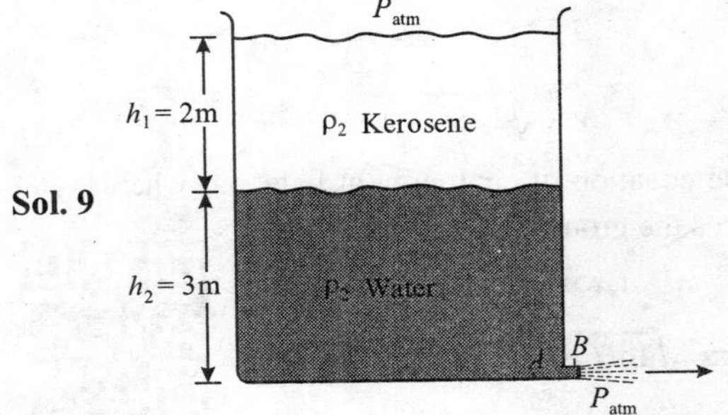

Applying Beronoulli's theorem at points A and B, we have

$$P_{atm} + h_1\rho_1 g + h_2\rho_2 g = P_{atm} + \frac{1}{2}\rho_2 v^2$$

$$\Rightarrow \quad v = \sqrt{\frac{2h_1\rho_1 g}{\rho_2} + 2h_2 g}$$

$$\Rightarrow \quad v = \sqrt{\frac{2\times2\times800\times10}{1000} + 2\times3\times10}$$

$$\Rightarrow \quad v = \sqrt{32+60} = \sqrt{92} = 9.59 \text{ m/s}$$ **Ans. (B)**

Sol. 10 We apply Beronoulli's equation at A and B

$$P_A + \frac{1}{2}\rho v_A^2 = P_B + \frac{1}{2}\rho v_B^2$$

$$\Rightarrow \quad P_B - P_A = \rho\left(v_A^2 - v_B^2\right)$$

$$\Rightarrow \quad h\rho g = \frac{1}{2}\rho v_A^2\left(-\frac{A_A^2}{A_B^2}\right)$$

$$\Rightarrow \quad v_A = \sqrt{\frac{2gh}{\left(-\frac{A_A^2}{A_B^2}\right)}} = \sqrt{\frac{2\times10\times0.05}{1-(3/5)^2}}$$

$$\Rightarrow \quad v_A = \sqrt{\frac{1}{16/25}} = \frac{5}{4} \text{ m/s}$$

By continuity equation

$$A_A v_B = A_B v_B \quad \ldots(1)$$

We have $\quad P_B - P_A = h\rho g$

From (1) $\quad v_B = \frac{A_A v_A}{A_B}$

Fluid flow rate through tube is

$$\frac{dV}{dt} = A_A v_A = 6\times10^{-6}\times1.25$$

$$\Rightarrow \quad \frac{dV}{dt} = 7.5\times10^{-6} \text{ m}^3\text{/s}$$ **Ans. (A)**

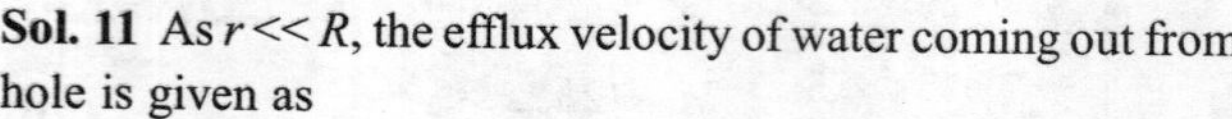

Sol. 11 As $r << R$, the efflux velocity of water coming out from hole is given as

$$u = \sqrt{2gh}$$

If v is the speed at which it hits ground

$$\Rightarrow \quad v^2 = u^2 + 2gh = 2g(H+h)$$

$$\Rightarrow \quad v = \sqrt{2g(H+h)}$$

Now we use equation of continuity at hole and where water stream strikes the ground

$$\Rightarrow \quad A_1 v_1 = A_2 v_2$$

$$\Rightarrow \quad \pi r^2\sqrt{2gH} = \pi x^2\sqrt{2g(H+h)}$$

$$\Rightarrow \quad x = r\left(\frac{H}{H+h}\right)^{1/4}$$ **Ans. (A)**

9.3 Viscosity

Sol. 1

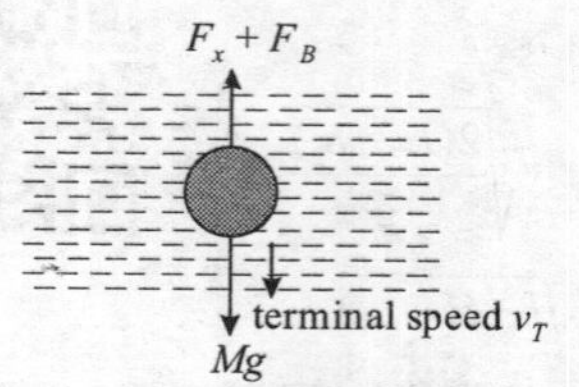

Using stoke's Rule we know before terminal speed is obtained, ball will have an acceleration which decreases because viscous force on ball is given as

$$F_v = 6\pi\eta R v$$

$$\Rightarrow \quad F_v \propto Rv$$ **Ans. (B)**

Sol. 2 In a liquid, terminal speed of sphere is given as

$$v_T = \frac{2}{9}\frac{gR^2}{\eta}(\rho_s - \rho_l)$$

For gold sphere, we have

$$v_1 = \frac{2}{9}\frac{9R^2}{\eta}(19.5-1.5) \quad \ldots(1)$$

For silver sphere, we have

$$v_2 = \frac{2}{9}\frac{gR^2}{\eta}(10.5-1.5) \quad \ldots(2)$$

Using (1)/(2) gives

$$\frac{v_1}{v_2} = \frac{18}{9} = 2$$

$$\Rightarrow \quad v_2 = \frac{v_1}{2} = \frac{0.2}{2} = 0.1 \text{ m/s}$$ **Ans. (C)**

Sol. 3

$F_B + F_{vis}$, V, ρ_1, ρ_2, V, Mg

Terminal speed is attained by ball when its acceleration $a = 0$

$$\Rightarrow \quad F_B + F_{vis} = mg$$

[F_{vis} is in opposite direction of v so need to consider-ve sign again]

$$\Rightarrow \quad V\rho_2 g + kv^2 = V\rho_1 g$$

$$\Rightarrow \quad kv^2 = V(\rho_1 - \rho_2)g$$

$$\Rightarrow \quad v = \sqrt{\frac{V(\rho_1-\rho_2)g}{k}}$$ **Ans. (A)**

Sol. 4 Terminal velocity of a ball in a viscous liquid is given as

$$v = \frac{2}{9}\frac{gR^2}{\eta}(\rho_S - \rho_L)$$

For ball falling in water

$$10 = v_w = \frac{2}{9}\frac{gR^2}{8.5\times10^{-4}} \times (7.8-1) \quad \ldots (1)$$

For ball falling in glycerine

$$v_g = \frac{2}{9}\frac{gR^2}{13.2} \times (7.8-1.2) \qquad \ldots (2)$$

From (2)/(1) we have

$$\frac{v_g}{10} = \frac{8.5\times10^{-4}}{13.2} \times \left(\frac{7.8-1.2}{7.8-1}\right)$$

$$\Rightarrow \quad v_g = 6.25 \times 10^{-4}\ \text{cm/s} \qquad \textbf{Ans. (B)}$$

Sol. 5

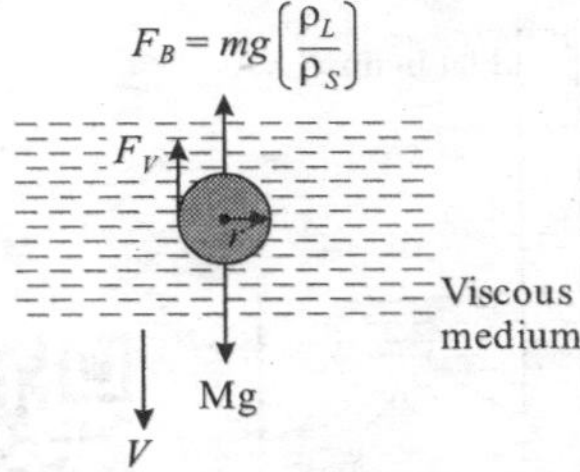

Upward viscous force on ball is given by stoke's rule as

$$F_v = 6\pi\eta r v$$

At terminal speed, all forces on sphere are balanced, so we have

$$mg = mg\left(\frac{\rho_L}{\rho_S}\right) + 6\pi\eta r v$$

$$\Rightarrow \quad \rho_3\left(\frac{4}{3}\pi r^3\right) g\left(1-\frac{\rho_L}{\rho_S}\right) = 6\pi\eta r v$$

$$\Rightarrow \quad v = \frac{2}{9}\frac{gr^2}{\eta}(\rho_S - \rho_L)$$

$$\Rightarrow \quad v \propto r^2 \qquad \textbf{Ans. (A)}$$

Sol. 6 Case-1

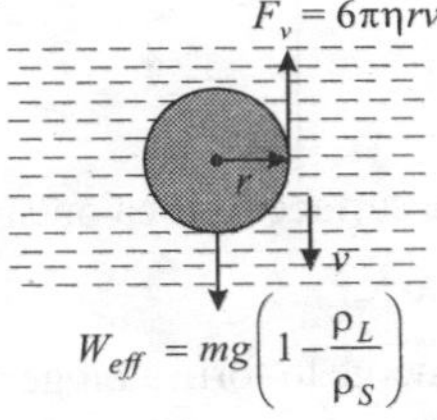

At terminal speed of ball

$$W_{eff} = 6\pi\eta r v \qquad \ldots (1)$$

When ball is pulled upward at $F_{ext} = 2W_{eff}$ then at terminal speed v', we have

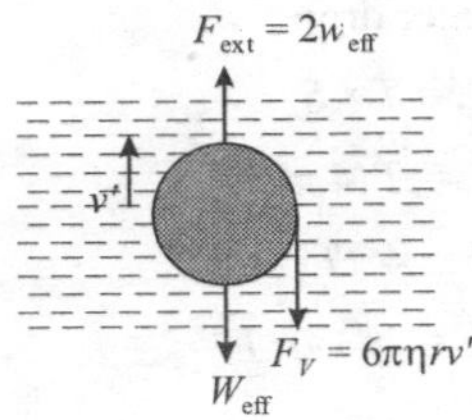

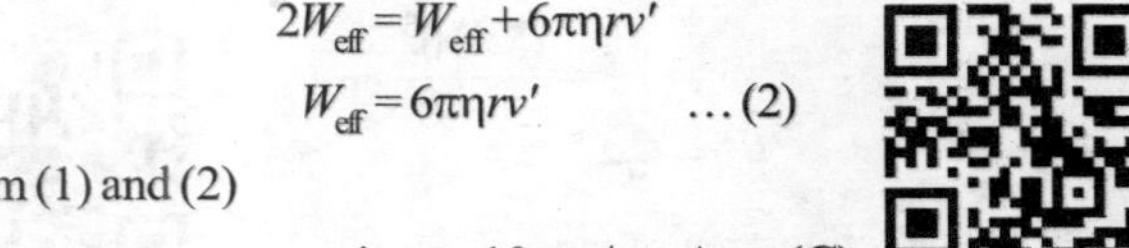

$$2W_{eff} = W_{eff} + 6\pi\eta r v'$$

$$\Rightarrow \quad W_{eff} = 6\pi\eta r v' \qquad \ldots (2)$$

From (1) and (2)

$$\Rightarrow \quad v' = v = 10\ \text{cm/s} \qquad \textbf{Ans. (C)}$$

Sol. 7

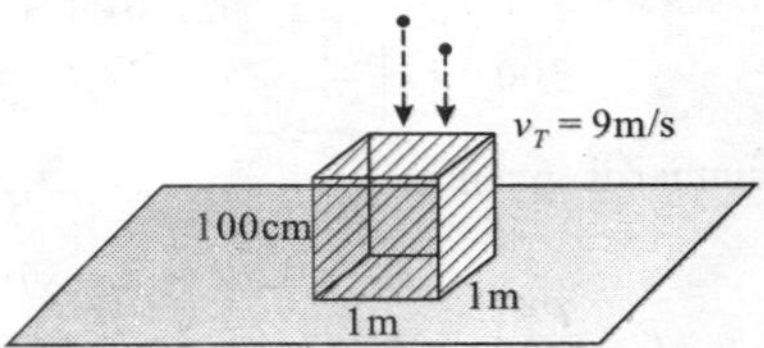

Total calculate volume of rain falling on the place per square meter in one year is

$$V = 1 \times 1 \times 100\ \text{cm} = 1\ \text{m}^3$$

KE of the rain volume which becomes zero on striking at ground is

$$\text{KE} = \frac{1}{2}(PV).\ V^2 = \frac{1}{2} \times 10^3 \times (9)^2$$

$$\Rightarrow \quad \text{KE} = \frac{81}{2} \times 1000$$

$$\Rightarrow \quad \text{KE} = 4.05 \times 10^4\ \text{J} \qquad \textbf{Ans. (B)}$$

Sol. 8

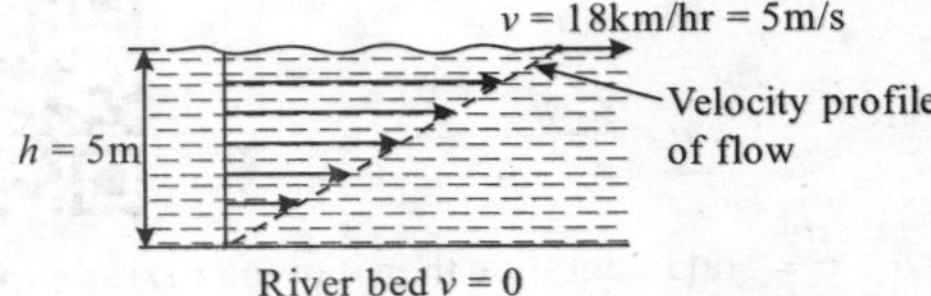

Viscous force between layers of river water is given as

$$F_v = \eta A \frac{dv}{d\pi} = \eta A\left(\frac{\Delta v}{h}\right)$$

(we assume velocity profile to be linear as shown in figure)

Shearing stress between layers of flowing water is given as

$$\text{shearing stress} = \frac{F_V}{A} = \eta\left(\frac{\Delta v}{n}\right) = \eta\left(\frac{v-0}{h}\right)$$

$$\Rightarrow \quad \sigma_s = 10^{-3} \times \frac{5}{5} = 10^{-3}\ \text{N/m}^2$$

Using 1 poise $= \frac{1}{10}$ poiseuille $= \frac{1}{10}$ N·s/m² **Ans. (C)**

Sol. 9 For a liquid flow in a pipeline, Reynolds number is given as

$$R = \frac{PvD}{\eta}$$

$v \rightarrow$ flow velocity

$P \rightarrow$ density

$D \rightarrow$ internal daintier of pipeline

The volume flow rate of water through tap is given as

$$Av = \frac{V}{t} = \frac{15\times10^3}{5\times60}\ \text{cm}^3/\text{s}$$

$$A = \pi r^2$$

Av = Cross-section area of tap

$$\Rightarrow \qquad v = \frac{15\times10^3}{300\times\pi\times\left(\frac{1}{\sqrt{\pi}}\right)^2} = 50\ \text{cm/s} = 0.5\ \text{m/s}$$

$\Rightarrow$ Reynolds number is given as

$$R = \frac{\rho v d}{\eta} = \frac{10^3\times0.5\times\frac{2}{\sqrt{3.14}}\times10^{-2}}{10^{-3}}$$

$$R = \frac{1}{\sqrt{3.14}}\times10^4 = 5643$$ **Ans. (D)**

Sol. 10

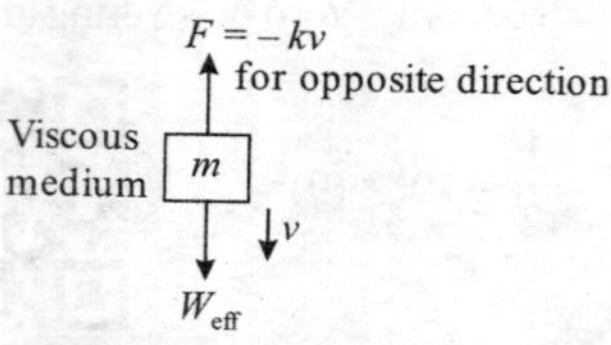

If a be the acceleration of mass, we use

$$W_{eff} - kv = ma$$

$$\Rightarrow \qquad a = \frac{W_{eff} - kv}{m}$$

[If we put $a = \frac{dv}{dt}$ and integrative then it given $v(t)$ as exponent]

Here we can see that as $v\uparrow \Rightarrow a\downarrow$ and after some (long time)

time when $v = \frac{W_{eff}}{k}$ (constant) $\Rightarrow a = 0$ **Ans. (C)**

9.4 Surface Tension

Sol. 1

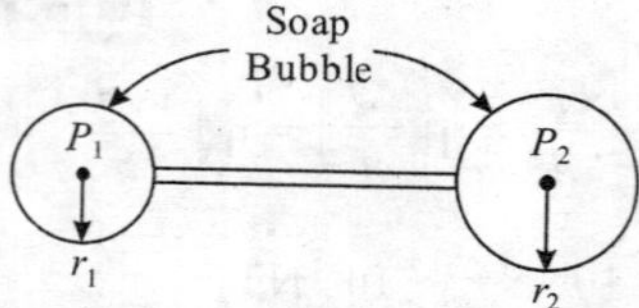

Excess pressure inside a soap bubble of radius r is given as-

$$P_{ex} = \frac{4T}{r}$$

Where $T \rightarrow$ surface tension of soap solution.

Excess pressure inside the two given soap bubble are

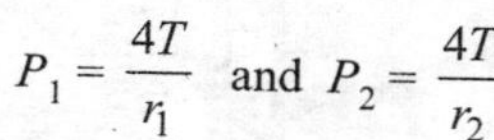

$$P_1 = \frac{4T}{r_1} \text{ and } P_2 = \frac{4T}{r_2}$$

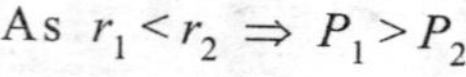

As $r_1 < r_2 \Rightarrow P_1 > P_2$

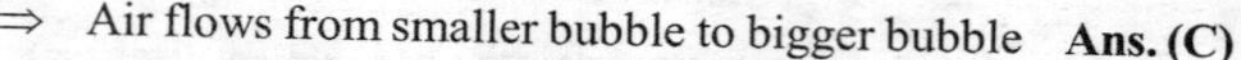

$\Rightarrow$ Air flows from smaller bubble to bigger bubble **Ans. (C)**

Sol. 2

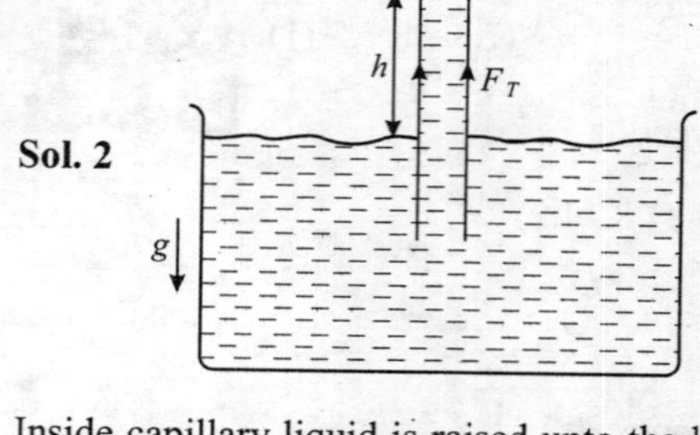

Inside capillary liquid is raised upto the level where force of surface tension balances the weight of liquid raised.

In a free falling state $g_{eff} = 0$

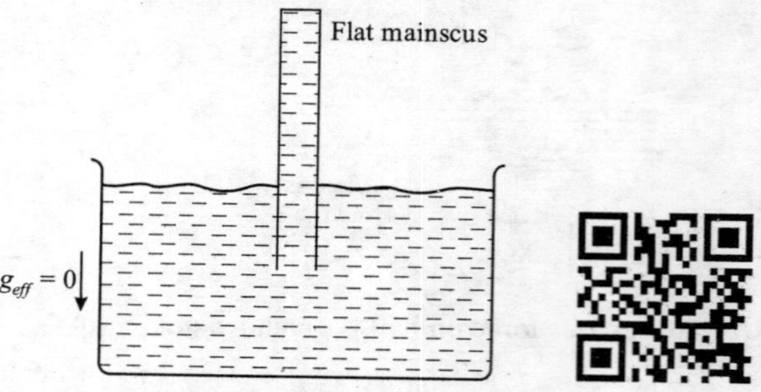

$\Rightarrow$ Effective weight of liquid raised = 0

$\Rightarrow$ F_T(upward) = 0 $\Rightarrow$ liquid will fill the complete height of capillary.

Ans. (D)

Sol. 3 As $T_{\text{soap sol.}} < T_{\text{water}}$

$\Rightarrow$ Capillary height $h = \frac{2T\cos\theta}{r\rho g}$

$$\Rightarrow \qquad h_B < h_A$$ **Ans. (C)**

Sol. 4

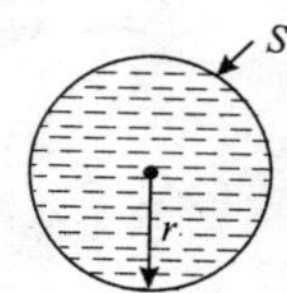

A liquid drop has only one surface of area outside

$$S = 4\pi r^2$$

When two mercury drops merge to form a bigger drop radius R then we have

$$2\times\frac{4}{3}\pi r^3 = \frac{4}{3}\pi R^3$$

$$\Rightarrow \qquad R = 2^{1/3} r$$

Surface energy of bigger drop

$$E = T\times S$$

$$\Rightarrow \qquad E = T(4\pi R^2)$$

$$\Rightarrow \qquad E = 4\pi T(2^{1/3} r)^2$$

$$\Rightarrow \qquad E = 2^{8/3}\pi r^2 T$$

Ans. (D)

Sol. 5

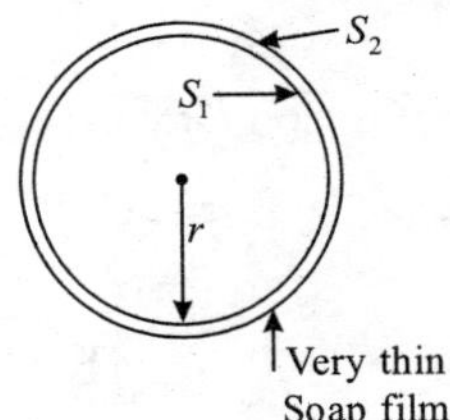

Soap bubble has the surface S_1 and S_2 which carries surface energy, given as

$$E = T \times 2(4\pi r^2) = 8\pi T r^2$$

If radius of bubble is increased from r_1 to r_2 than work done in this process is

$$W = E_f - E_i = 8\pi T(r_2^2 - r_1^2)$$

$$\Rightarrow \quad W = 8\pi \times 0.03\,[(0.05)^2 - (0.03)^2]$$

$$\Rightarrow \quad W = 0.384\,\pi\,\text{mJ} \sim 0.4\,\pi\,\text{mJ}$$ **Ans. (B)**

Sol. 6

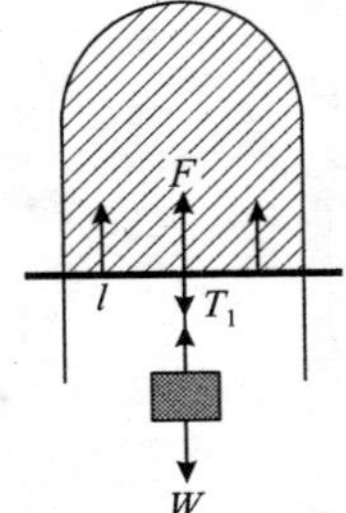

If surface tension of liquid is T than total upward force on slider due to two surfaces of the film is

$$F = 2Tl = w$$

$$\Rightarrow \quad T = \frac{w}{2l} = \frac{1.5 \times 10^{-2}}{2 \times 0.3} = 0.025\text{ N/m}$$ **Ans. (A)**

Sol. 7 If n small drops coalesce to from the big drop of radius R, we have

$$n \times \frac{4}{3}\pi r^3 = \frac{4}{3}\pi R^3 \Rightarrow n = \frac{R^3}{r^3}$$

Amount of surface energy released in process

$$\Delta E = n(4\pi r^2 T) - 4\pi R^2 T$$

$$\Delta E = 4\pi T\left[r^2 \cdot \frac{R^3}{r^2} - R^2\right] = 4\pi T R^3\left[\frac{1}{r} - \frac{1}{R}\right]$$

If v is the speed attained by big drop then we have

$$\Delta E = \frac{1}{2}mv^2$$

$$\frac{1}{2}\left(\rho \times \frac{4}{3}\pi R^3\right)v^2 = 4\pi T R^3\left[\frac{1}{r} - \frac{1}{R}\right]$$

$$\Rightarrow \quad v = \sqrt{\frac{6T}{\rho}\left[\frac{1}{r} - \frac{1}{R}\right]}$$ **Ans. (D)**

Sol. 8 Due to surface energy the outer layer (very thin) of a liquid drop if evaporates by absorption of liquid heat, whole drop can get evaporated at same temperature.

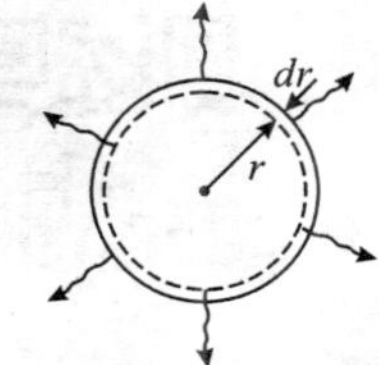

Due to evaporation of thin layer of liquid at the surface of drop the change in surface energy is

$$\Delta E = T(4\pi(r + dr)^2) - T(4\pi r^2)$$

$$\Rightarrow \quad \Delta E = T(8\pi r dr)$$

for evaporation of the thin elemental layer of liquid of width dr and out of heat to be absorbed by it is

$$dQ = dm\,L \qquad dm \rightarrow \text{mass of layer}$$

$$\Rightarrow \quad dQ = (\rho dv)L \qquad dv \rightarrow \text{volume of layer}$$

$$\Rightarrow \quad dQ = \rho L(4\pi r^2 dr) \qquad [dv = 4\pi r^2 dr]$$

The drop gets evaporated only by its surface energy if

$$\Delta E = dQ$$

$$T(8\pi r dr) = \rho L(4\pi r^2 dr)$$

$$\Rightarrow \quad r = \frac{2T}{\rho L}$$ **Ans. (C)**

Sol. 9 Capillary height in tube is given as

$$h = \frac{2T\cos\theta}{r\rho g}$$

As with temperature surface temperature describes

$\Rightarrow$ as temperature interface, h decreases

S-1 Is false

S-2 Is true as it is a fact studied in theory **Ans. (B)**

Sol. 10

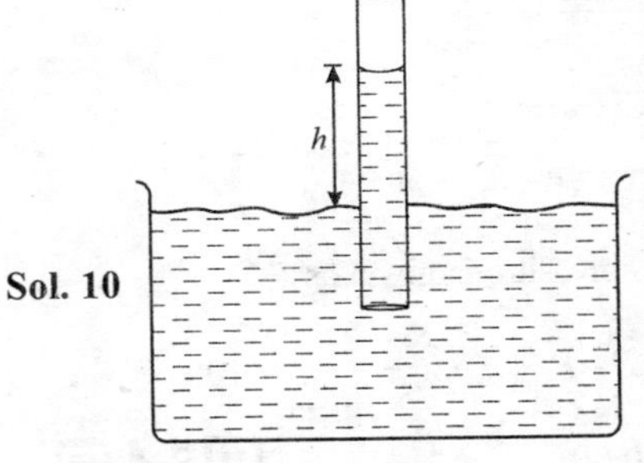

Capillary height is given as

$$h = \frac{2T\cos\theta}{r\rho g}$$

$\theta < 90°$ for glass- water interface as water wets the glass surface. When capillary is coated with wax which is not wet by water so angle of contact for wax - water surface is $\theta > 90°$

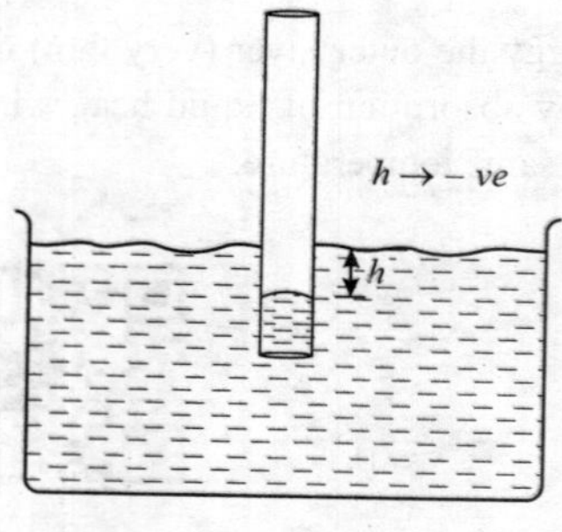

$\Rightarrow \quad \cos\theta = -ve$

$\Rightarrow \quad h = -ve$ **Ans. (C)**

Sol. 11 The excess pressure inside soap bubble is

$$P_{ex} = \frac{2T}{R}$$

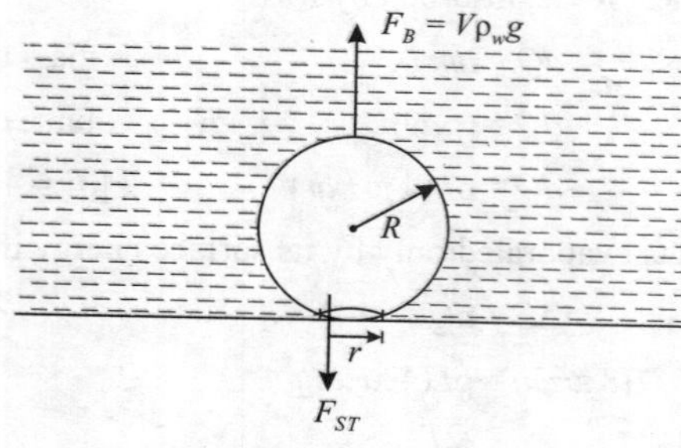

Force of surface tension at bottom on bubble is

$$F_{ST} = P_{ex} \times \pi r^2$$

At the moment spherical bubble detach from base, we use

$$F_B = F_{ST}$$

$$\Rightarrow \quad \frac{4}{3}\pi R^3 \rho_\omega g = \frac{2T}{R} \times \pi r^2$$

$$\Rightarrow \quad r = R^2\sqrt{\frac{2\rho_\omega g}{3T}}$$ **Ans. (A)**

Sol. 12

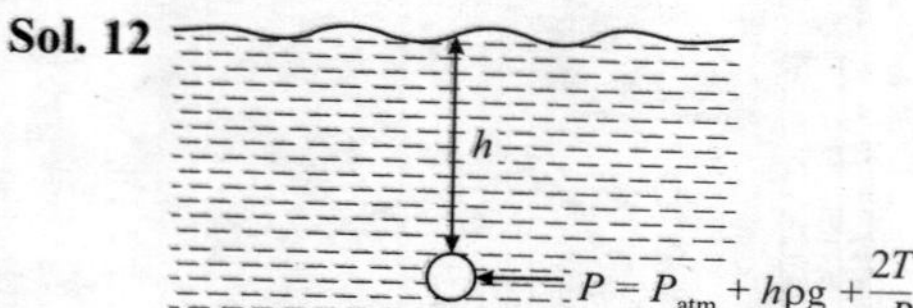

Inside the bubble excess pressure is given as

$$P_{ex} = P - P_{atm} = h\rho g + \frac{2T}{R} = 1100$$

$$\Rightarrow \quad h \times 1000 \times 9.8 + \frac{2 \times 0.06}{10^{-3}} = 1100$$

$$\Rightarrow \quad 9800h + 120 = 1100$$

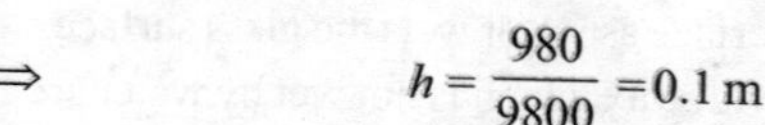
$$\Rightarrow \quad h = \frac{980}{9800} = 0.1\text{ m}$$ **Ans. (A)**

Sol. 13

P , P , $P \leftarrow$ atm pressure

P_1, R_1 + P_2, R_2 → P_f, R_0

$V_1 = \frac{4}{3}\pi R_1^3 \qquad V_1 = \frac{4}{3}\pi R_2^3 \qquad V_0 = \frac{4}{3}\pi R_0^3$

$P_1 = P + \frac{4T}{R_1} \qquad P_2 = P + \frac{4T}{R_2} \qquad P_f = P + \frac{4T}{R_0}$

If temperature is contained constant then we use

$$P_1V_1 + P_2V_2 = P_fV_0$$

$$\Rightarrow \quad \left(P + \frac{4T}{R_1}\right)\left(\frac{4}{3}\pi R_1^3\right) + \left(P + \frac{4T}{R_2}\right)\left(\frac{4}{3}\pi R_2^3\right) = \left(P + \frac{4T}{R_o}\right)\left(\frac{4}{3}\pi R_o^3\right)$$

$$\Rightarrow P\left[\frac{4}{3}\pi R_1^3 + \frac{4}{3}\pi R_2^3 - \frac{4}{3}\pi R_o^3\right] + \frac{4T}{3}(4\pi R_1^2) + \frac{4T}{3}(4\pi R_2^2) - \frac{4T}{3}(4\pi R_o^2) = 0$$

$$\Rightarrow \quad PV + \frac{4T}{3}S = 0$$

$$\Rightarrow \quad 3PV + 4TS = 0$$ **Ans. (B)**

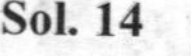

Sol. 14

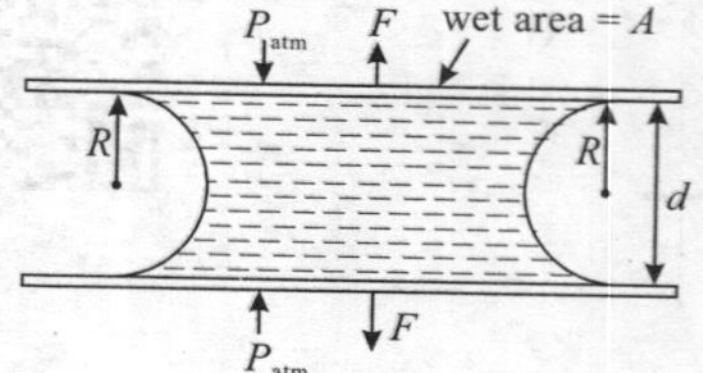

To pull apart the plates, the required force is given as

$$F = \frac{2TA}{d} = \frac{2TA}{2R} = \frac{TA}{R}$$

The pressure in water will be lower by

$$\Delta P_L = \frac{F}{A} = \frac{T}{R}$$ **Ans. (D)**

10.1 Thermal Expansion

Sol. 1

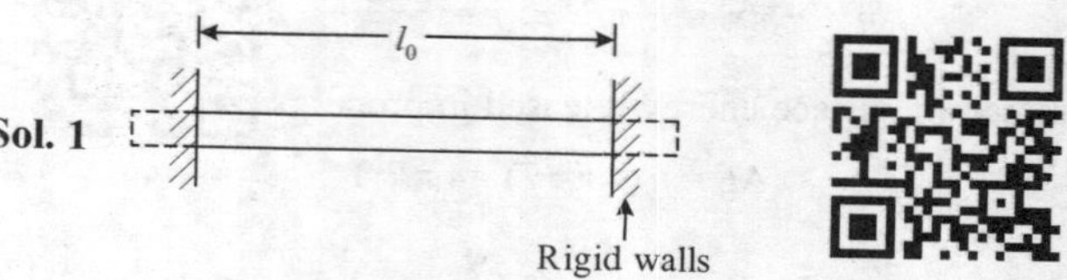

If on rising temperature by t°C rod expands by Δl then due to rigid walls, it is compressed by the same length elastically strain developed in rod due to this is

$$\text{strain} = \frac{\Delta l}{l} = \frac{\alpha l \Delta t}{l} = \alpha\Delta t = \alpha t$$

$\Rightarrow$ By definition of Young's modulus

$$Y = \frac{\text{Stress}}{\text{Strain}}$$

$\Rightarrow$ linear stress $= Y \times \text{Strain} = Y\alpha t$ **Ans. (C)**

Sol. 2 If a body of volume V is heated by ΔT then volume expansion of body is given as

$$\Delta V = \gamma V \Delta T$$

Coefficient of volume expansion $\gamma = 3\alpha$

$$\Rightarrow \quad \Delta V = 3\alpha V \Delta T = 3\alpha\left(\frac{4}{3}\pi r^3\right)\Delta T$$

$$= 3 \times 23 \times 10^{-6} \times \left(\frac{4}{3} \times 3.14 \times (10)^3\right) \times 100$$

$$= 28.88 \text{ cm}^3 \sim 28.9 \text{ cc}$$

Ans. (A)

Sol. 3 Here we consider wood is having negligible expansion coefficient compared to metal so on rising temperature by ΔT, strain due to thermal expansion which is compensated by elastic compression on cooling down is given as

$$\text{Strain} = \frac{\Delta l}{l} = \alpha \Delta T$$

$$\Rightarrow \quad \text{Stress} = \frac{F}{S} = Y \times \text{Strain} = Y\alpha\Delta T$$

force between two parts of wheel is

$$2F = 2YS\alpha\Delta T$$

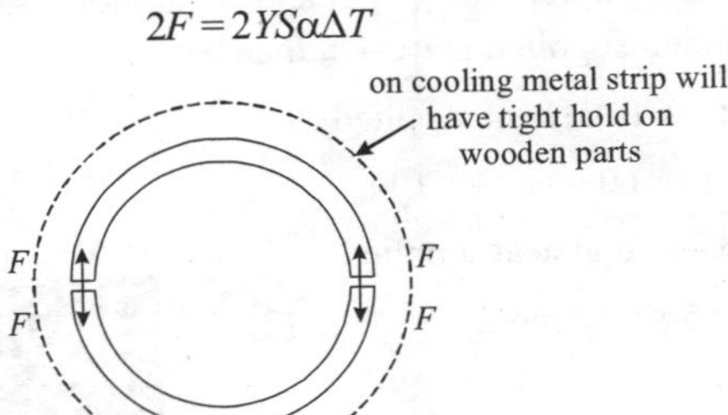

Ans. (A)

Sol. 4 For all linear scales, we use

$$\frac{\text{Reading} - LFP}{UFP - LFP} = \text{Constant}$$

For Kelvin scale & Y scale we use

$$\frac{Y - (-160)}{-50 - (-160)} = \frac{340 - 273}{373 - 273} = \frac{67}{100}$$

$$Y + 160 = \frac{67}{100} \times 110 = 73.7$$

$$\Rightarrow \quad Y = 73.7 - 160 = -86.3°Y$$

Ans. (C)

Sol. 5 Given that

$$\frac{\gamma_G}{\gamma_L} = \frac{1}{4}$$

Remain constant with temperature

V_G

V_L

$\Rightarrow$ For any rise in temperature (say ΔT) the expansion in container is equal to expansion in liquid volume.

$$\Rightarrow \quad \Delta V_G = \Delta V_L$$

$$\Rightarrow \quad \gamma_G V_G \Delta T = \gamma_L V_L \Delta T$$

$$\Rightarrow \quad \frac{V_L}{V_G} = \frac{\gamma_G}{\gamma_L} = \frac{1}{4}$$

Ans. (B)

Sol. 6 On the ends of steel wire if F is the force needed to keep its length constant then stress in wire is

$$\text{Stress} = \frac{F}{A} = Y \times \text{Strain}$$

$$\text{Strain} = \frac{\Delta l}{l} = \alpha\Delta T$$

$$\Rightarrow \quad \text{Stress} = \frac{F}{A} = Y\alpha\Delta T$$

pressure required

$$p = 2 \times 10^{11} \times 1.1 \times 10^{-5} \times 100$$

$$\Rightarrow \quad p = 2.2 \times 10^8 \text{ Pa}$$

Ans. (A)

Sol. 7. Fractional time lost/second by a pendulum clock is given as

$$\frac{\delta t}{t} = \frac{1}{2}\alpha\Delta T$$

Case-1 : When $T = 40°C$ and we consider T_g is graduation temperature of clock when it reads correct time then we have

$$\delta t = 12 \text{ s}$$

$$t = 1 \text{ day} \equiv 86400 \text{ s}$$

$$\Rightarrow \quad \frac{12}{86400} = \frac{1}{2}\alpha(40 - T_g) \quad \ldots(1)$$

Case-2 :

$$\delta t = 4\text{s}$$

$$t = 1 \text{ day}$$

$$\Rightarrow \quad \frac{4}{86400} = \frac{1}{2}\alpha(T_g - 20) \quad \ldots(2)$$

using $\frac{(1)}{(2)}$ gives

$$\frac{12}{4} = \frac{40 - T_g}{T_g - 20}$$

$$\Rightarrow \quad 3T_g - 60 = 40 - T_g$$

$$\Rightarrow \quad 4T_g = 100 \Rightarrow T_g = 25°C$$

From equation-(1)

$$\frac{12}{86400} = \frac{1}{2}\alpha(40 - 25)$$

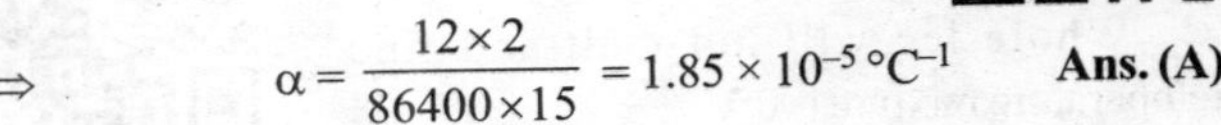

$$\Rightarrow \quad \alpha = \frac{12 \times 2}{86400 \times 15} = 1.85 \times 10^{-5} \,°C^{-1}$$

Ans. (A)

10.2 Calorimetry

Sol. 1 Specific heat → amount of heat which raises the temperature of unit mass of a substance by 1°C

Total heat required to raise the temperature of mass m by temperature t°C is

$$Q = mst \text{ (specific heat)}$$

If $t = 1$°C

$$\Rightarrow \quad Q = ms \rightarrow \text{Thermal capacity}$$

amount of heat to raise a body temperature by 1°C **Ans. (B)**

Sol. 2 By mass energy equivalence we have

$$E = mc^2$$

In case of water forming ice, it releases latent heat to surrounding

As heat is released from substance ⇒ some mass is converted to heat (energy)

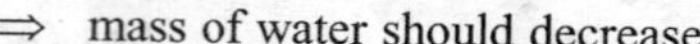

⇒ mass of water should decrease.

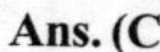

Ans. (C)

Sol. 3 Amount of heat required to change the phase of 1g water from liquid to vapour is

$$\Delta Q = mL_v = 1 \times 2256 \text{ J/g}$$

$$\Rightarrow \quad \Delta Q = 2256 \text{ J}$$

volume change due to vaporization is

$$\Delta V = 1671 - 1 = 1670 \text{ cm}^3$$

As expansion take place at constant atmospheric pressure (10^5 Pa), the work done by steam is

$$W = P\Delta V = 10^5 \times 1670 \times 10^{-6} = 167 \text{ J}$$

By first law of thermodynamics we use

$$\Delta Q = \Delta U + W$$

$$\Rightarrow \quad \Delta U = \Delta Q - W$$

$$= 2256 - 167 = 2089 \text{ J}$$

Ans. (C)

Sol. 4 Mixture = 500 gm water at 0°C + 100 gm ice at 0°C + 40 gm water (calorimeter) at 0°C

+ 10 gm steam at 100°C

heat required to melt 100 gm ice is

$$Q_{ice} = 100 \times 80 = 8000 \text{ cal}$$

Max heat which can be supplied by steam is

$$Q_{steam} = 10 \times 540 + 10 \times 1 \times 100$$

$$= 6400 \text{ cal}$$

As $\quad Q_{steam} < Q_{ice}$

⇒ Whole ice will not melt and find temperature mixture is 0°C

⇒ Amount of ice melted is given as

$$m = \frac{Q_{steam}}{L_{ice}} = \frac{6400}{80} = 80 \text{ gm}$$

⇒ Mixture= 500 gm water at 0°C + 80 gm water at 0°C + 20 gm ice at 0°C + Calorimeter (40 gm water) + 10 gm water at 0°C

In mixture finally there is 590 gm water at 0°C. **Ans. (B)**

Sol. 5 For heating 2 L water (2 kg) by 50°C (from 27°C to 77°C) amount of heat required is

$$Q = ms\Delta T = 2 \times 4200 \times 50 \text{ J}$$

Net heat supplied (rate) to water is

$$r = 1000 - 160 = 840 \text{ W}$$

(supply by coil is 1000W, loss is 160 J/s)

If in time t it happens then

$$840\,t = 2 \times 4200 \times 50$$

$$\Rightarrow \quad t = 500 \text{ s} = 8 \text{ m } 20 \text{ s}$$

Ans. (A)

Sol. 6 Let mass of water is m in gm and the uniform rate at which heat is being supplied is r cal/s, then we use

for first 10 min. → Total heat supplied

$$r \times 10 \times 60 = m \times 1 \times 100 \quad \ldots(1)$$

for next 55 min → Total heat supplied

$$r \times 55 \times 60 = m \times L_v \quad \ldots(2)$$

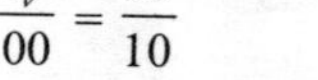

$$\frac{(2)}{(1)} \Rightarrow \frac{L_v}{100} = \frac{55}{10}$$

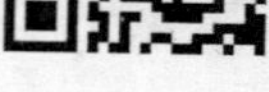

$$\Rightarrow \quad L_v = 550 \text{ cal/gm}$$

Ans. (B)

10.3 Heat Transfer

Sol. 1 By Stefan's-Boltzmann law, the heat energy radiated/sec (Thermal radiation Power) by body of surface area A is given as

$$P_{th} = \frac{dQ}{dt} = \sigma\varepsilon AT^4$$

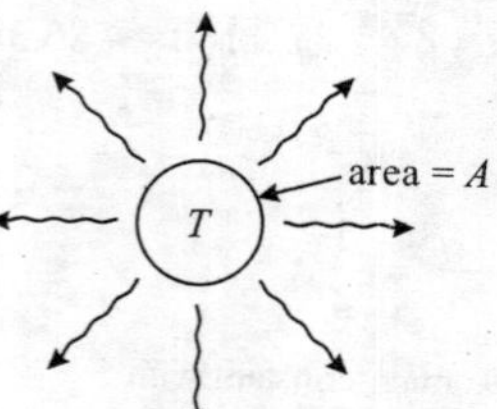

e → emissivity of body surface

$e < 1$ for general bodies

$e = 1$ for black body

For the given spheres we can use

$$P_1 = e\sigma(4\pi r_1^2)T_1^4$$

and $$P_2 = e\sigma(4\pi r_2^2)T_2^4$$

$$\Rightarrow \quad \frac{P_1}{P_2} = \frac{r_1^2 T_1^4}{r_2^2 T_2^4} = \frac{(1)^2(4000)^4}{(4)^2(2000)^4} = \frac{256}{256} = \frac{1}{1}$$

Ans. (A)

Sol. 2 (A) Spectrometer → used to analyse *EM* radiation spectrum

(B) Pyrometer → used to measure thermal radiations & radiations from a hot body

(C) Nanometer → used to measure small dimensions

(D) Photometer → used to measure light intensity **Ans. (B)**

Sol. 3 Black Body → which absorbs all the radiation incident on it and emits maximum radiation from it at a specific temperature In above options, options (A) is most suitable for choosing it close to a Black body. **Ans. (A)**

Sol. 4

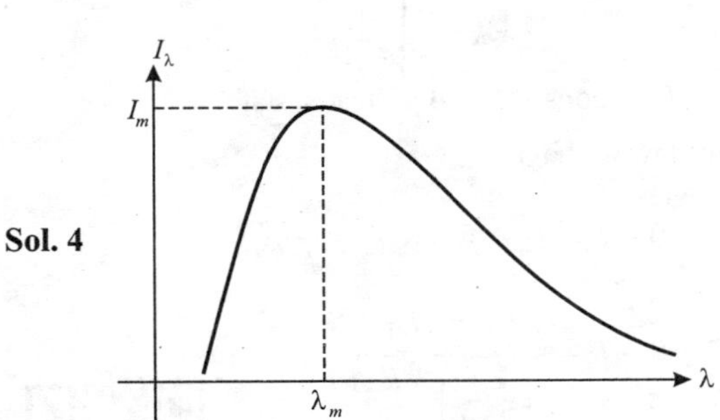

For any Black Body The *EM* radiation spectrum is given by Wien's Displacement law & Wien's fifth power law

$$\lambda_m \propto \frac{1}{T}$$

$$I_m \propto T^5$$

Ans. (D)

Sol. 5 By Newton's law of cooling the rate of cooling of a body is given as

$$\frac{\Delta\theta}{\Delta t} \propto \Delta\theta$$

($\Delta\theta$ = temperature difference of body with surrounding)

$$\Rightarrow \quad n = 1$$

Ans. (D)

Sol. 6 We consider sum as a black body and by Stefan's law, radiant power emitted by sun is given as

$$P_{\text{Rad}} = \sigma A T^4 = \sigma(4\pi R^2)T^4$$

(R → radius of Sun)

$$\Rightarrow \quad P_{\text{rad}} \propto R^2 T^4$$

If $T \to 2T$ and $R \to 2R$

Then we have $$\frac{P_f}{P_i} = \frac{(2R)^2(2T)^4}{R^2T^4}$$

$$= (2)^2(2)^4 = 64$$

$$\Rightarrow \quad P_f = 64\,P_i$$

Ans. (D)

Sol. 7

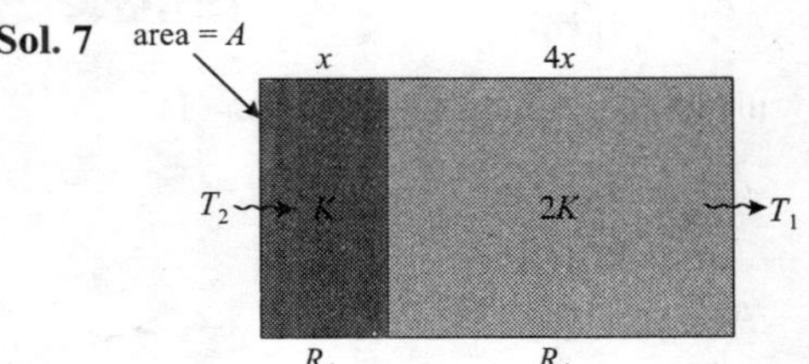

Where $$R_{th_1} = \frac{1}{k}\cdot\frac{x}{A}$$

and $$R_{th_2} = \frac{1}{2k}\cdot\frac{4x}{A}$$

Heat conduction through composite slab in steady state is given as

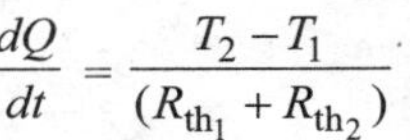

$$\frac{dQ}{dt} = \frac{T_2 - T_1}{(R_{th_1} + R_{th_2})}$$

$$\Rightarrow \quad \frac{dQ}{dt} = \frac{T_2 - T_1}{\frac{x}{kA} + \frac{2x}{kA}} = \frac{kA(T_2 - T_1)}{3x}$$

$$\Rightarrow \quad f = 1/3$$

Ans. (D)

Sol. 8

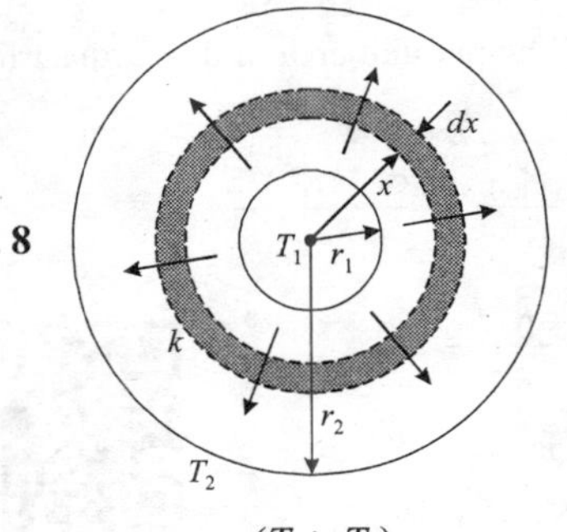

$(T_1 > T_2)$

Rate of heat flow between shells is given as

$$\frac{dQ}{dt} = \frac{T_1 - T_2}{R_{\text{th}}} \quad \ldots(1)$$

Where R_{th} is the thermal resistance for radial heat flow.

The thermal resistance of elemental shell for radial heat flow is given as

$$dR = \frac{1}{k}\cdot\frac{dx}{4\pi x^2}$$

Total thermal resistance between inner and outer shells is

$$R_{\text{th}} = \int dR = \frac{1}{4\pi k}\int_{r_1}^{r_2}\frac{dx}{x^2} = \frac{1}{4\pi k}\left[-\frac{1}{x}\right]_{r_1}^{r_2}$$

$$= \frac{1}{4\pi k}\left[\frac{1}{r_1}-\frac{1}{r_2}\right]$$

$$\Rightarrow \quad R_{\text{th}} = \frac{(r_2-r_1)}{4\pi k r_1 r_2}$$

Rate of heat flow in radial direction from equation-(1)

$$\frac{dQ}{dt} = \frac{(T_1-T_2)}{(r_2-r_1)}\times 4\pi k r_1 r_2$$

$$\Rightarrow \quad \frac{dQ}{dt} \propto \frac{r_1 r_2}{r_2-r_1}$$

Ans. (C)

Sol. 9

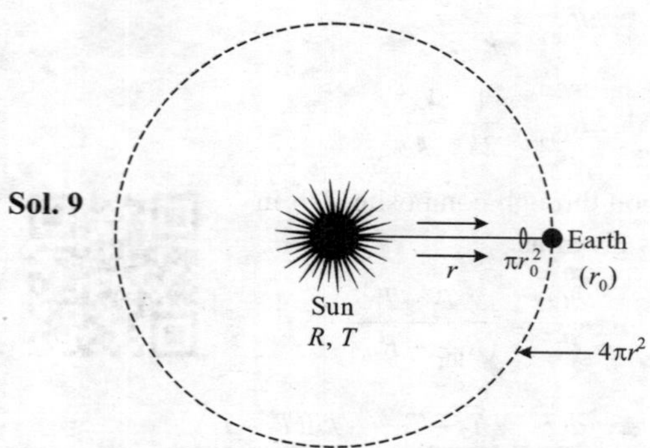

Surface area of spherical shell in which whole power of Sun will be distributed

Radiant power of Sun is

$$P_{\text{rad}} = \sigma(4\pi R^2)\,T^4$$

Radiant power of Sun falling per unit area of the earth surface (Normally) is

$$S = \frac{P_{\text{rad}}}{4\pi r^2} = \frac{\sigma(4\pi R^2)T^4}{4\pi r^2}$$

Solar constant $\quad S = \dfrac{\sigma R^2 T^4}{r^2}$

Energy incident on Earth is

$$E_e = S.(\pi r_0^2)$$

$$\Rightarrow \quad E_e = \frac{\pi\sigma R^2 r_0^2 T^4}{r^2}$$

Ans. (B)

Sol. 10

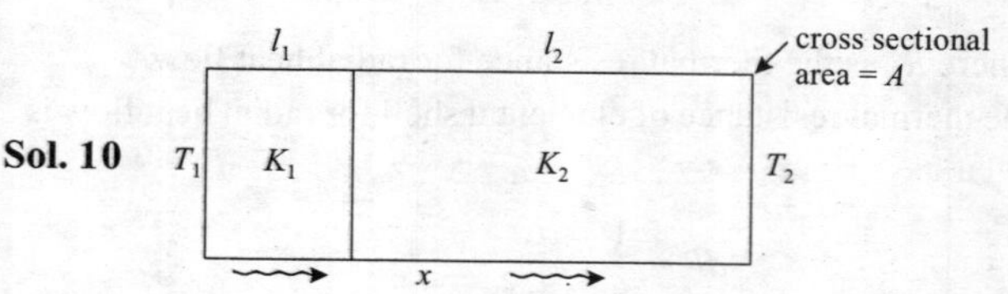

In steady state throughout the rod heat current is constant as heat absorption is zero, so we have

$$\left.\frac{dQ}{dt}\right|_1 = \left.\frac{dQ}{dt}\right|_2$$

$$\frac{T_i - x}{\left(\frac{1}{K_1}\cdot\frac{l_1}{A}\right)} = \frac{x - T_2}{\left(\frac{1}{K_2}\cdot\frac{l_2}{A}\right)}$$

$$\Rightarrow \quad x = \frac{K_1 l_2 T_1 + K_2 l_1 T_2}{K_1 l_2 + K_2 l_1}$$

Ans. (C)

Sol. 11

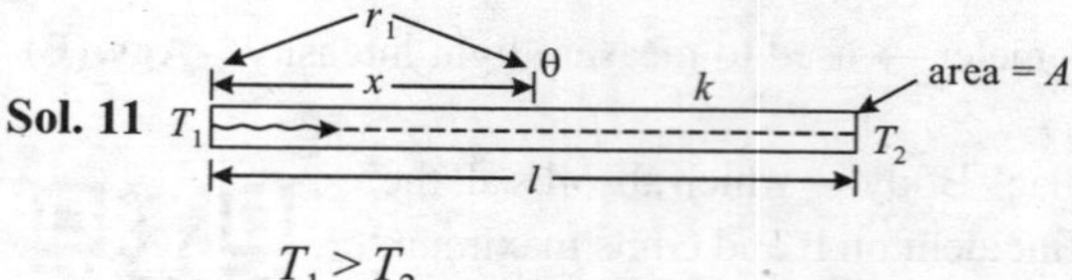

$T_1 > T_2$

Thermal current in rod is given as

$$I_{\text{th}} = \frac{dQ}{dt} = \frac{T_1 - T_2}{\left(\frac{1}{k}\cdot\frac{l}{A}\right)}$$

$\Rightarrow \quad I_{\text{th}}$ = constant under steady state

Using Ohm's law we have

$$\theta = T_1 - I_{\text{th}} r_1 \text{ where } r_1 = \frac{1}{k}\cdot\frac{x}{A}$$

$$\Rightarrow \quad \theta = T_1 - \frac{(T_1-T_2)}{\left(\frac{1}{k}\frac{l}{A}\right)}\left(\frac{1}{k}\frac{x}{A}\right)$$

$$\Rightarrow \quad \theta = T_1 - \frac{(T_1-T_2)}{l}\cdot x$$

Above equation has negative slope and positive intercept on *y*-axis.

Ans. (D)

Sol. 12 By Newton's law of cooling, the rate of colling is given as

$$\frac{d\theta}{dt} = -k(\theta-\theta_0)\ {}^\circ\text{C/s}$$

$$\Rightarrow \quad \int_{\theta_1}^{\theta}\frac{d\theta}{\theta-\theta_0} = \int_0^t -k\,dt$$

θ_1 is temperature of liquid at $t = 0$ $(\theta_1 > \theta_0)$

$$[\log_e(\theta-\theta_0)]_{\theta_1}^{\theta} = -kt$$

$$\Rightarrow \quad \log_e(\theta-\theta_0) = -kt + \log_e(\theta_1-\theta_0) \text{ (constant)}$$

$$y = mx + C \text{ [equation of a straight line]}$$

$\Rightarrow$ – ve slope straight line

Ans. (B)

Sol. 13 At such a high temperature (3000 K) we can consider the furnace like a black body so heat radiated per unit area/sec is given by Stefan's law as

$$E = \sigma T^4 \text{ J/m}^2\text{-s}$$

$\Rightarrow$ in 1 Hr. total heat/m² is given as

$$\Rightarrow \quad Q = Et = \sigma T^4.t$$

$$= 5.7 \times 10^{-8} \times (3000)^4 \times 3600$$

$$\Rightarrow \quad Q = 1.66 \times 10^{10} \text{ J/m}^2$$

$$Q \simeq 1.7 \times 10^{10} \text{ J/m}^2$$

Ans. (A)

Sol. 14 Rate of Heat conducting in steady state is given as

$$\frac{dQ}{dt} = \frac{kA(T_1 - T_2)}{l}$$

100°C | $C_u(9k)$ | (T) | Steel (k) | 0°C
$L/2$ | $L/2$

In steady state of conduction heat flow rate through the two rods will be same

$$\Rightarrow \quad \frac{(9k)A(100-T)}{L/2} = \frac{kA(T-0)}{L/2}$$

$$\Rightarrow \quad 9(100-T) = T$$

$$\Rightarrow \quad 900 = T + 9T$$

$$\Rightarrow \quad T = \frac{900}{10} = 90°\text{C}$$

Ans. (A)

Sol. 15 By Newton's law of cooling, we use rate of colling of metal is given as

$$\frac{dT}{dt} = -k(T - \theta_0)$$

$$\Rightarrow \quad \int_{\theta}^{T} \frac{dT}{T-\theta_0} = \int_{0}^{t} -kdt$$

$$\Rightarrow \quad [\ln(T-\theta_0)]_{\theta}^{T} = -kt$$

$$\ln\left(\frac{T-\theta_0}{\theta-\theta_0}\right) = -kt$$

$$\Rightarrow \quad T = \theta_0 + (\theta - \theta_0)e^{-kt}$$

at $t = 0$; $T = \theta$

at $t \to \infty$ (long time), $T = \theta_0$

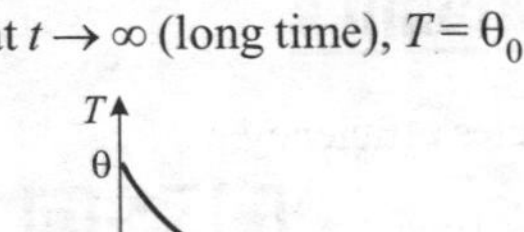

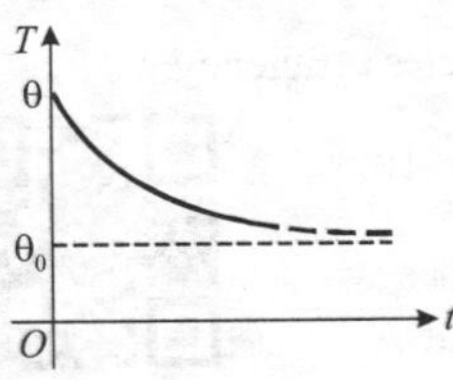

Ans. (C)

Sol. 16 By average from of Newton's law of cooling, we use

$$\frac{\Delta T}{t} = \frac{k}{(ms+\omega)}\left[\frac{T_1+T_2}{2} - T_s\right]$$

where $\Delta T = T_2 - T_1$

Initially with water, we use

$$\frac{30-25}{2} = \frac{k}{50\times 1+30}\left[\frac{30+25}{2} - T_s\right] \quad \ldots(1)$$

Then with given liquid, we use

$$\frac{30-25}{2} = \frac{k}{100s+30}\left[\frac{30+25}{2} - T_s\right] \quad \ldots(2)$$

$$\frac{(1)}{(2)} \Rightarrow \quad 50+30 = 100\,s + 30$$

$$\Rightarrow \quad s = \frac{50}{100}$$

$$= 0.5 \text{ cal/gm} = 0.5 \text{ kcal/kg}$$

Ans. (D)

Sol. 17

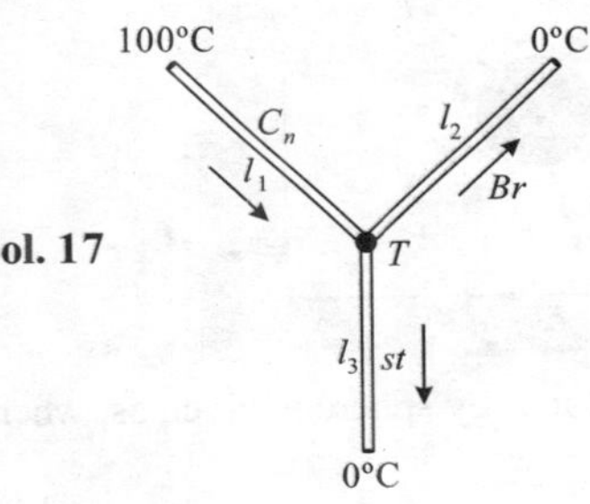

$$A = 4 \text{ cm}^2$$

$$l_1 = 46 \text{ cm}; k_1 = 0.92 \text{ CGS units}$$

$$l_2 = 13 \text{ cm}; k_2 = 0.26 \text{ CGS units}$$

$$l_3 = 12 \text{ cm}; k_3 = 0.12 \text{ CGS units}$$

Using Junction rule at temperature T, we have

$$I_{Cu} = I_{Br} + I_{st} \quad \ldots(1)$$

Thermal resistances of rods are

$$R_{Cn} = \frac{1}{k_1}\cdot\frac{l_1}{A} = \frac{1}{0.92}\times\frac{46}{4} = \frac{100}{8} \textit{CGS} \text{ Units}$$

$$R_{Br} = \frac{1}{k_2}\frac{l_2}{A} = \frac{1}{0.26}\times\frac{13}{4} = \frac{100}{8} \textit{CGS} \text{ Units}$$

$$R_{st} = \frac{1}{k_3}\frac{l_3}{A} = \frac{1}{0.12}\times\frac{12}{4} = \frac{100}{4} \textit{CGS} \text{ Units}$$

$$I_{Cu} = \frac{100-T}{R_{Cu}}; I_{Br} = \frac{T-0}{R_{Br}}; I_{st} = \frac{T-0}{R_{st}}$$

From equation (1) we have

$$\frac{100-T}{(100/8)} = \frac{T-0}{(100/8)} + \frac{T-0}{(100/4)}$$

$$\Rightarrow \quad 100-T = T + \frac{T}{2} = \frac{3T}{2}$$

$$\Rightarrow \quad 200 = 5T$$

$$\Rightarrow \quad T = 40°C$$

Heat current through *Cu*-rod is

$$\left.\frac{dQ}{dt}\right|_{Cu} = \frac{100-T}{100/8}$$

$$= \frac{100-40}{100/8} = \frac{8\times 60}{100} = 4.8 \text{ cal/s}$$

Ans. (C)

Sol. 18 Specific heat of sphere

$$s = \alpha T^3$$

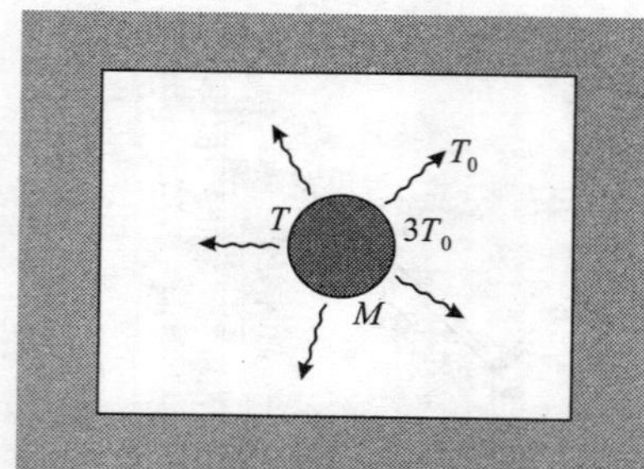

Due to radiation rate of heat loss by sphere is given as, when sphere temperature is T

$$2T_0 < T < 3T_0$$

$$\frac{dQ}{dt} = \sigma(4\pi R^2)(T^4 - T_0^4)$$

$$\Rightarrow \quad -\frac{MsdT}{dt} = 4\pi\sigma R^2(T^4 - T_0^4)$$

$$\Rightarrow \quad -\frac{M\alpha T^3 dT}{dt} = 4\pi\sigma R^2(T^4 - T_0^4)$$

$$\Rightarrow \quad \frac{T^3 dT}{T^4 - T_0^4} = -\frac{4\pi\sigma R^2}{M\alpha}dt$$

Integrating above expression, gives

$$\int_{T=3T_0}^{T=2T_0} \frac{T^3 dT}{T^4 - T_0^4} = -\frac{4\pi\sigma R^2}{M\alpha}\int_{t=0}^{t=t} dt$$

Let $\quad x = T^4 - T_0^4$

$$\Rightarrow \quad dx = 4T^3 dT$$

at $\quad T = 3T_0 \rightarrow x_1 = 80T_0^4$

and at $\quad T = 2T_0 \rightarrow x_2 = 15T_0^4$

$$\Rightarrow \quad \frac{1}{4}\int_{x_1}^{x_2} \frac{dx}{x} = -\frac{4\pi\sigma R^2}{M\alpha}\cdot t$$

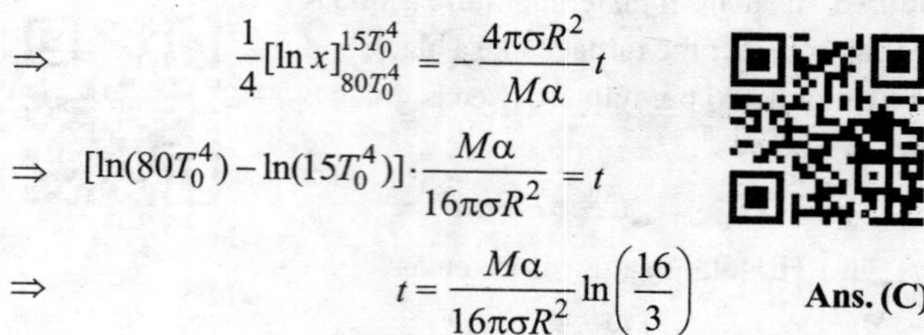

$$\Rightarrow \quad \frac{1}{4}[\ln x]_{80T_0^4}^{15T_0^4} = -\frac{4\pi\sigma R^2}{M\alpha}t$$

$$\Rightarrow \quad [\ln(80T_0^4) - \ln(15T_0^4)]\cdot\frac{M\alpha}{16\pi\sigma R^2} = t$$

$$\Rightarrow \quad t = \frac{M\alpha}{16\pi\sigma R^2}\ln\left(\frac{16}{3}\right)$$

Ans. (C)

Sol. 19 By Newton's law of cooling for a body colling down, its temperature as a function of time is given as

$$T_f = T_0 + (T_H - T_0)e^{-kt}$$

Here $T_H \rightarrow$ initial high temperature

$T_0 \rightarrow$ surrounding temperature

For case-1, we use

$$40 = 30 + 50e^{-k(5)}$$

$$\Rightarrow \quad e^{5k} = 5 \quad \Rightarrow \quad 5k = \ln(5) \qquad \dots(1)$$

For case-2, we use

$$32 = 30 + 32e^{-kt}$$

$$\Rightarrow \quad e^{kt} = 16 \quad \Rightarrow \quad kt = \ln(16) \qquad \dots(2)$$

$$\frac{(2)}{(1)} \Rightarrow \quad \frac{t}{5} = \frac{4\ln(2)}{\ln 5}$$

$$\Rightarrow \quad t = \frac{5\times 4\times 0.693}{1.609} = 8.61 \text{ min}$$

Ans. (B)

Sol. 20 Here we use average form of Newton's law of colling as

$$\frac{T_2 - T_1}{t} = k\left(\frac{T_1 + T_2}{2} - T_s\right)$$

Case-I : First 10 minimum

$$\frac{60-50}{10} = k(55 - T_s) \qquad \dots(1)$$

Case-II : Next 10 minimum

$$\frac{50-42}{10} = k(46 - T_s) \qquad \dots(2)$$

$$\frac{(1)}{(2)} \Rightarrow \quad \frac{10}{8} = \frac{55 - T_s}{46 - T_s}$$

$$\Rightarrow \quad 230\sqrt{T_s} = 220 - 4T_s$$

$$\Rightarrow \quad T_s = 230 - 220 = 10°C$$

Ans. (B)

11.1 Laws of Thermodynamics

Sol. 1 (A) False for reversible cycles efficiency

$$\eta = \frac{\text{work done}}{\text{heat input}} \times 100\%$$

for different thermodynamic processes w/o by gas in different for same heat input.

(B, C, D) True.

Ans. (A)

Sol. 2 Efficiency of a carnot engine is given as

$$\eta = \left(1 - \frac{T_2}{T_1}\right) \times 100\%$$

Where $T_2 \rightarrow$ temperature sink

$T_1 \rightarrow$ temperature of source

To achieve $\eta = 100\%$

either $T_2 = 0 \rightarrow$ Not attainable

or $T_1 = \infty$ [Impossible] **Ans. (C)**

Sol. 3 Efficiency of carnot engine is given as

$$\eta = 1 - \frac{T_{\text{Sink}}}{T_{\text{Source}}}$$

here $T_{\text{Sources}} = 627 + 273 = 900\text{ K}$

and $T_{\text{Sink}} = 27 + 273 = 300\text{ K}$

$\Rightarrow$ $\eta = 1 - \frac{300}{900} = \frac{2}{3}$

For engine efficiency relates work done and heat input as

$$\eta = \frac{\text{work done}}{\text{Heat input}}$$

$\Rightarrow$ Work done = η × heat supplied

$$= \frac{2}{3} \times 3 \times 10^6 \times 4.2$$

$$= 8.4 \times 10^6\text{ J}$$ **Ans. (B)**

Sol. 4 For an adiabatic process we use

PV^γ = constant ...(1)

We are given that $P \propto T^3$

$\Rightarrow$ $T = kP^{1/3}$

By Gas law we have

$$PV = nRT$$

$\Rightarrow$ $PV = nRkP^{1/3}$

$\Rightarrow$ $P^{1-1/3}V$ = Cost

$\Rightarrow$ $P^{2/3}\ V$ = Cost

$\Rightarrow$ $PV^{3/2}$ = Cost ...(2)

Comparing equation-(1) and (2) we have $\gamma = 3/2$ **Ans. (D)**

Sol. 5 State of a gas is indicate by thermodynamic coordinates (P, V, T) which helps in denoting gas state on indicator diagram and also we can plot process equation of ID curve. **Ans. (C)**

Sol. 6 Above statement is a consequence of "Second law of thermodynamics"

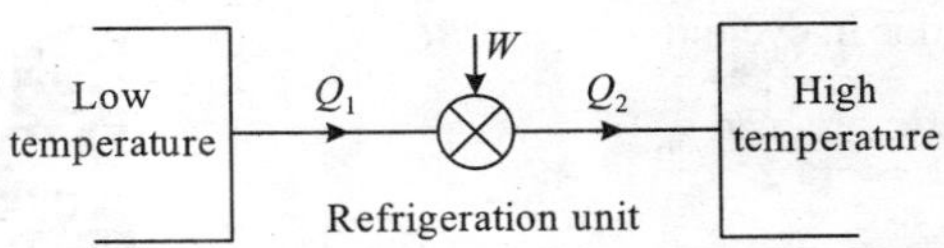

$$W + Q_1 = Q_2$$

Without external work it is impossible to transfer heat from low temperature zone to high temperature zone. **Ans. (A)**

Sol. 7. (A) As internal energy is a state function

$U = \frac{f}{2}nRT$ 'False'

This is for an isothermal process as

$$\Delta T = 0\,;\, \Delta U = 0$$

(B) 'True' Both U & S are state functions

(C) As entropy is a state function so in cyclic process or whenever a system returns to its initial state $\Delta S = 0 \rightarrow$ 'False'

(D) For adiabatic process $\Delta Q = 0 \Rightarrow \Delta W = -\Delta U \rightarrow$ 'False'

Ans. (B)

Sol. 8 As we know internal energy of a gas is a 'State function'

$$U = \frac{f}{2}nRT$$

At state A and B if internal energy of system are U_A and U_B respectively

$\Rightarrow$ $\Delta U_1 = \Delta U_2 = U_B - U_A$

As U is not a 'Path function' it does not depend on paths. **Ans. (A)**

Sol. 9 Efficiency of a heat engine is given as

$$\eta = \frac{\text{Work done}}{\text{Heat input}}$$

Heat $\rightarrow$ Area under T-S diagram

heat supplied in cycle

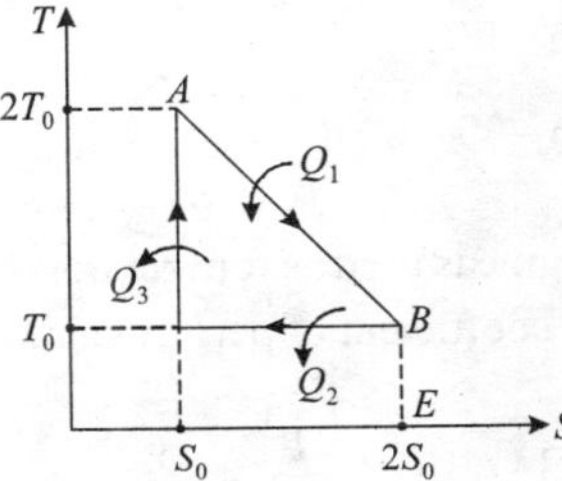

Q_1 = Area $ABEDA$

$$= T_0(2S_0 - S_0) + \frac{1}{2}T_0S_0 = \frac{3}{2}T_0S_0$$

Work done in cycle $W = \text{Area } ABC$

$$= \frac{1}{2}T_0S_0$$

$\Rightarrow$ Efficiency of cycle

$$\eta = \frac{W}{Q_1} = \frac{1/2T_0S_0}{3/2T_0S_0} = \frac{1}{3}$$ **Ans. (C)**

Sol. 10 (A) **True :** for all process (cyclic or not)

$$\Delta Q = \Delta U + \Delta W$$

or for elemental duration *FLT* is valid as

$$dQ = dU + dW$$

(B) **True :** *FLT* is defined by using energy conservation

(C) **True :** For *FLT* we use internal energy of gas/substance along with heat supplied & work done.

(D) **False :** Concept entropy is introduced in second law of thermodynamics

Sol. 11 For an adiabatic process work done is given as

$$W = \frac{nR(T_2 - T_1)}{\gamma - 1}$$

$$\Rightarrow \quad \gamma - 1 = \frac{nR(T_2 - T_1)}{W}$$

$$\Rightarrow \quad \gamma = 1 + \frac{10^3 \times 8.3 \times 7}{146 \times 10^3} = 1 + 0.4 = 1.4$$

$\gamma = 1.4$ for a diatomic gas

$$\left(f = 5 \Rightarrow \gamma = \frac{f+2}{f} = \frac{7}{5} = 1.4\right)$$ **Ans. (A)**

Sol. 12 As we know for same initial and final states of all the thermodynamic process we have

$$\overset{iaf}{\Delta U_1} = \overset{ibf}{\Delta U_2} \quad (\text{as } U \rightarrow \text{state function})$$

$$\Rightarrow \quad Q_1 - W_1 = Q_2 - W_L$$

$$\Rightarrow \quad 50 - 20 = 36 - W_2$$

$$\Rightarrow \quad W_2 = 36 - 30 = 6 \text{ cal}$$ **Ans. (A)**

Sol. 13 If same engine is used as refrigerator then relation in its efficiency (η) and coefficient of performance (k) is given as

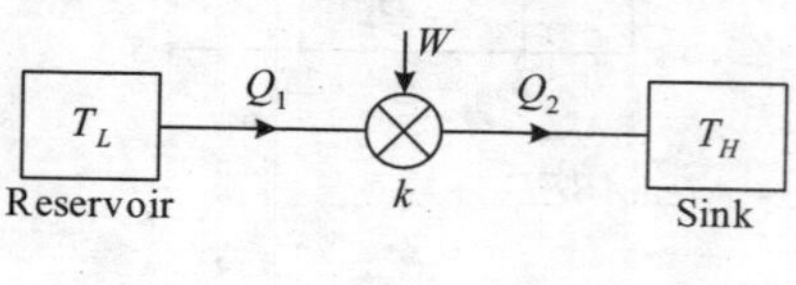

$$k = \frac{1}{\eta} - 1 = \frac{1}{1/10} - 1 = 9$$

COP of a refrigerator is given as

$$k = \frac{Q_1}{W} = \frac{\text{Heat extracted}}{\text{Work input}}$$

$$\Rightarrow \quad 9 = \frac{Q_1}{W} \quad \Rightarrow \quad Q_1 = 9 \times 10 = 90 \text{ J}$$ **Ans. (B)**

Sol. 14 Work done by gas in Isobaric Process *AB* is

$$W_{AB} = P(V_2 - V_1) = nR(T_2 - T_1)$$

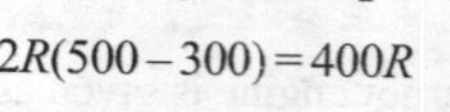

$$W_{AB} = 2R(500 - 300) = 400R$$

Work done on the gas

$$= -W_{AB} = -400R$$ **Ans. (A)**

Sol. 15 Work done by gas in Isothermal process *DA* is

$$W_{DA} = nRT \ln\left(\frac{P_1}{P_2}\right)$$

$$\Rightarrow \quad W_{DA} = 2.303\, nR\,(300)\, \log_{10}\left(\frac{1}{2}\right)$$

$$\Rightarrow \quad W_{DA} = 2.303 \times 2R \times 300 \times (-0.301) = -414R$$

Work done on the gas is

$$= -W_{DA} = 414R$$ **Ans. (D)**

Sol. 16 Total work done in complete cycle is given as

$$W_{cycle} = W_{AB} + W_{BC} + W_{CD} + W_{DA}$$

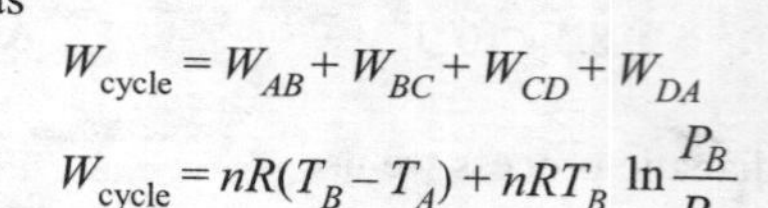

$$\Rightarrow \quad W_{cycle} = nR(T_B - T_A) + nRT_B \ln\frac{P_B}{P_C}$$

$$+ nR(T_D - T_C) + nRT_D \ln\frac{P_D}{P_A}$$

$$\Rightarrow \quad W_{cycle} = 2R(200) + 2.303 \times 2R \times 500 \log_{10}(2)$$
$$+ 2R(-200) + 2.303 \times 2R \times 300 \log_{10}(1/2)$$

$$\Rightarrow \quad W_{cycle} = 690\,R - 414\,R = 276\,R$$

Work done on the gas $= -W_{cycle} = -276\,R$ **Ans. (D)**

Sol. 17

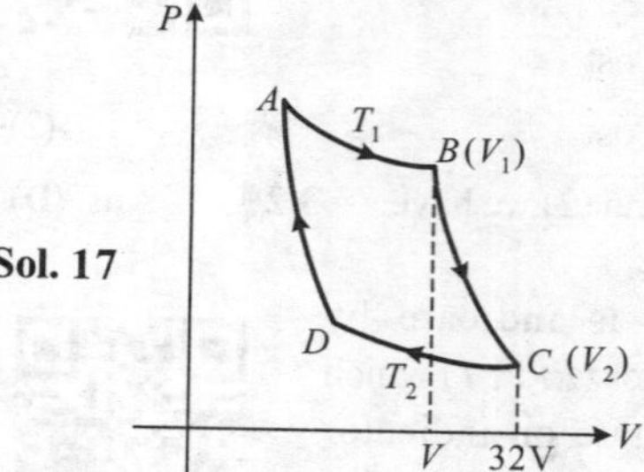

AB and *CD* $\rightarrow$ isothermal parts

BC and *DA* $\rightarrow$ adiabatic parts

$T_1 \rightarrow$ temperature of source

$T_2 \rightarrow$ temperature of sink

For adiabatic process BC, we use process equation

$$TV^{\gamma-1} = \text{constant} \quad (\text{for diatomic gases } \gamma = 7/5)$$

$$\Rightarrow \quad T_1V_1^{\gamma-1} = T_2V_2^{\gamma-1}$$

$$\Rightarrow \quad \frac{T_2}{T_1} = \left(\frac{V_1}{V_2}\right)^{\gamma-1} = \left(\frac{V_1}{32V}\right)^{7/5-1}$$

$$= \left(\frac{1}{2^5}\right)^{2/5} = \frac{1}{2^2} = \frac{1}{4}$$

Engine efficiency is given as

$$\eta = 1 - \frac{T_2}{T_1} = 1 - \frac{1}{4} = \frac{3}{4} = 0.75$$

in % $\quad \eta = \frac{3}{4} \times 100\% = 75\%$ **Ans. (C)**

Sol. 18 First law of thermodynamics increase in internal energy of gas = Amount of heat supplied

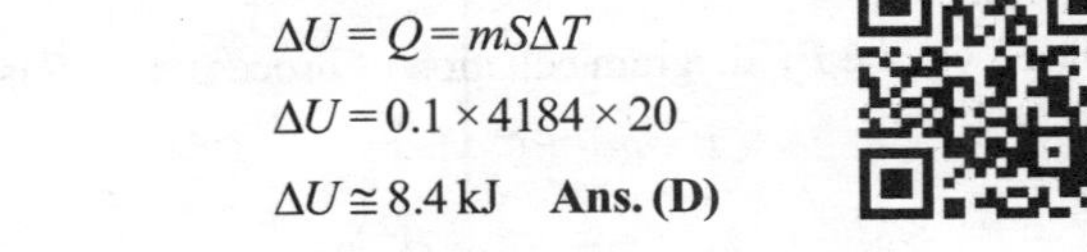

$$\Delta U = Q = mS\Delta T$$

$$\Rightarrow \quad \Delta U = 0.1 \times 4184 \times 20$$

$$\Rightarrow \quad \Delta U \cong 8.4 \text{ kJ}$$ **Ans. (D)**

Sol. 19

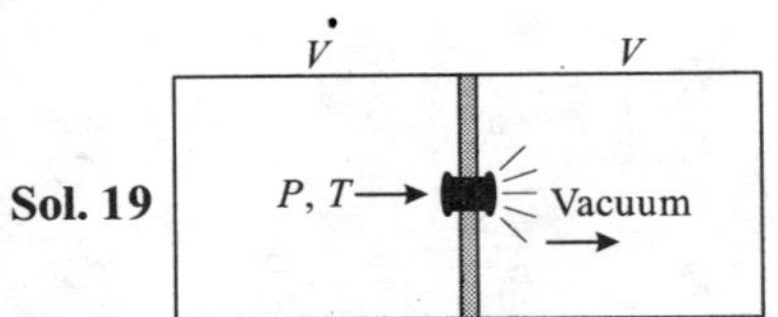

In case of 'Free expansion' (no opposition) no work is done by gas so as $\Delta Q = 0$ (insulating walls)

or $\quad U =$ constant

$\Rightarrow \quad T =$ constant

As gas temperature remain constant

we use $\quad P_1V_1 = P_2V_2$

$$PV = P_2(2V) \Rightarrow P_2 = P/2$$ **Ans. (A)**

Sol. 20 The amount of heat to be last by metal in cooling from 20 K to 4 K is

$$Q = \int dQ = -\int mSdT = -\int_{20}^{4} m\left(32\left[\frac{T}{400}\right]^3\right)dT$$

heat lost

$$\Rightarrow Q = -\frac{0.1 \times 32}{(400)^3} \cdot \left[\frac{T^4}{4}\right]_{20}^{4} = \frac{0.1 \times 32}{(400)^3 \times 4}[(20)^4 - (4)^2]$$

$$Q = 0.002 \text{ kJ}$$

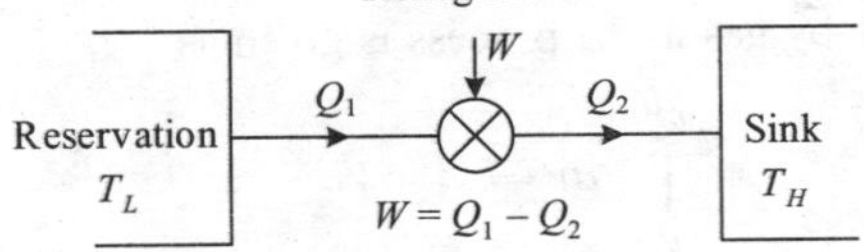

Coefficient of performance

$$K = \frac{Q_1}{W}$$

$$K = \frac{Q_1}{Q_2 - Q_1} = \frac{T_1}{T_2 - T_1}$$

At $\quad T_1 = 20\text{ K} \ \& \ T_S = 27 + 273 = 300\text{ K}$

The amount of work done in refrigeration unit is

$$\frac{Q_1}{W_1} = \frac{T_1}{T_2 - T_1} = \frac{20}{300 - 20} = \frac{20}{280}$$

$$\Rightarrow \quad W_1 = \frac{0.002\text{kJ}}{20/280} = 0.028 \text{ kJ}$$

As metal is cooled to 4 K, so at T_L = 4 K, work done by refrigeration unit is

$$\frac{Q_1}{W_2} = \frac{T_1}{T_2 - T_1} = \frac{4}{300 - 4} = \frac{4}{296}$$

$$\Rightarrow \quad W_2 = \frac{0.002\text{kJ}}{(4/296)} = 0.148 \text{ kJ}$$

As metal is cooling from 20 K to 4 K so any temperature of metal during cooling is between 20 K and 4 K so work required by refrigeration unit in between W_1 and W_2. **Ans. (C)**

Sol. 21 If $T_1 \to$ Source temperature

& $\quad T_2 \to$ Sink temperature

$\Rightarrow$ Engine efficiency $\eta = 1 - \frac{T_2}{T_1}$

Initially $\quad 1 - \frac{T_2}{T_1} = \frac{1}{6} \Rightarrow \frac{T_2}{T_1} = \frac{5}{6}$ ...(1)

Later $\quad 1 - \frac{T_2 - 62}{T_1} = \frac{1}{3} \Rightarrow \frac{T_2 - 62}{T_1} = \frac{2}{3}$ ...(2)

Solving equation-(1) and (2) we get

$$T_1 = 372 \text{ K and } T_2 = 310 \text{ K}$$ **Ans. (C)**

Sol. 22

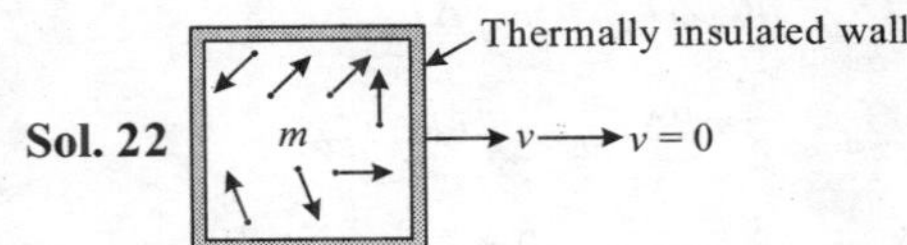

KE of gas particles due to the motion of vessel

$$K = \frac{1}{2}mv^2$$

When suddenly the vessel in brought to rest then above KE will increase the energy of random motion (thermal energy) of molecules as no energy can transmit through container walls

$$\Rightarrow \quad \frac{1}{2}mv^2 = \Delta U = n\left(\frac{R}{T-1}\right)\Delta T$$

$$\Rightarrow \quad \frac{1}{2}mv^2 = \frac{m}{M}\left(\frac{R}{\gamma-1}\right)\Delta T$$

$$\Rightarrow \quad \Delta T = \frac{Mv^2}{2R}(\gamma - 1)$$ **Ans. (B)**

Sol. 23 Efficiency of carnot engine is given as

$$\eta = 1 - \frac{T_{\text{sink}}}{T_{\text{Source}}}$$

for first engine $T_{\text{Source}} = 500\text{ K} \;\&\; \eta = 0.4$

$$\Rightarrow \quad 0.4 = 1 - \frac{T_{\text{Sink}}}{500}$$

$$\Rightarrow \quad T_{\text{Sink}} = 500 \times 0.6$$

$$\Rightarrow \quad T_{\text{Sink}} = 300\text{ K}$$

For another engine with

$$\eta = 0.6 \;\&\; T_{\text{Sink}} = 300\text{ K}$$

$$\Rightarrow \quad 0.6 = 1 - \frac{300}{T_{\text{Source}}}$$

$$\Rightarrow \quad T_{\text{Source}} = \frac{300}{0.4} = 750\text{ K}$$

Ans. (D)

Sol. 24 Cycle efficiency is given as

$$\eta = \frac{\text{Work Done}}{\text{Heat input}} \times 100\%$$

Work done by gas in cycle W = Area enclosed by $ABCD = P_0V_0$

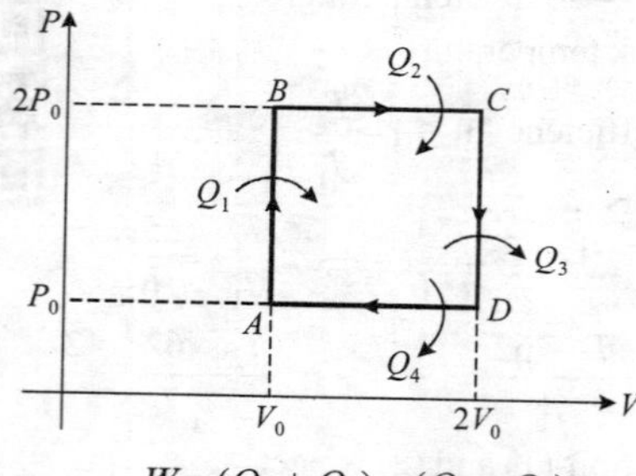

$$W = (Q_1 + Q_2) - (Q_3 - Q_4)$$

Heat input in cycle $Q_{\text{in}} = Q_1 + Q_2$

$$\Rightarrow \quad Q_{\text{in}} = nC_v\Delta T_{AB} + nC_p\Delta T_{BC}$$

$$\Rightarrow \quad Q_{\text{in}} = \frac{3}{2}nR\Delta T_{AB} + \frac{5}{2}nR\Delta T_{BC}$$

$$\Rightarrow \quad Q_{\text{in}} = \frac{3}{2}(P_0V_0) + \frac{5}{2}(2P_0V_0) = \frac{13}{2}P_0V_0$$

Cycle efficiency

$$\eta = \frac{W}{Q_{\text{in}}} \times 100\%$$

$$\Rightarrow \quad \eta = \frac{P_0V_0}{13/2P_0V_0} \times 100$$

$$\Rightarrow \quad \eta = \frac{200}{13}\% \sim 15.4\%$$

Ans. (B)

Sol. 25 Statement-2 : It is true

So carnot efficiency for source and sink at temperature 373 K and is given as

$$\eta = \left(1 - \frac{T_2}{T_1}\right) \times 100 = \left(1 - \frac{273}{373}\right) \times 100$$

$$\Rightarrow \quad \eta = (1 - 0.732) \times 100$$

$$= 26.8\% \text{ max possible}$$

Statement-1 : Is true & it is explained by Statement-2. **Ans. (D)**

Sol. 26 As in an adiabatic process there is no heat exchange

$$\Rightarrow \quad \Delta Q = 0$$

So from first law of thermodynamics, we have

$$\Delta Q = \Delta U + W$$

$$\Rightarrow \quad \Delta U = -W$$

$\Rightarrow$ Statement-1 is true

As T = constant in isothermal process $\Rightarrow$ Statement-2 is false

In adiabatic process we use $TV^{\gamma - 1}$ = constant **Ans. (B)**

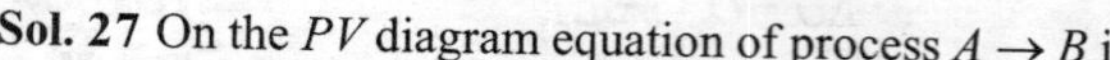

Sol. 27 On the PV diagram equation of process $A \rightarrow B$ is

$$P = mV + C \text{ where}$$

$$m = -\frac{P_0}{V_0} \text{ and } C = 3P_0$$

$$\Rightarrow \quad P = -\frac{P_0}{V_0}\cdot V + 3P_0$$

By gas law, we use

$$T = \frac{PV}{nR} = -\frac{P_0}{nRV_0}\cdot V^2 + \frac{3P_0}{nR}\cdot V \quad \ldots(1)$$

$$T \text{ is max when } \quad \frac{dT}{dV} = 0$$

$$\Rightarrow \quad -\frac{P_0}{nRV_0}(2V) + \frac{3P_0}{nR} = 0$$

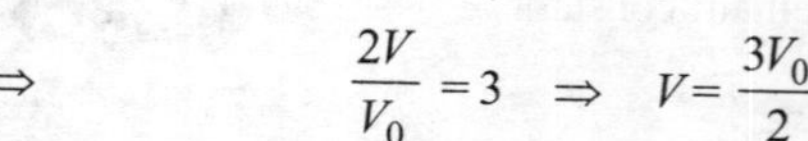

$$\Rightarrow \quad \frac{2V}{V_0} = 3 \;\Rightarrow\; V = \frac{3V_0}{2}$$

at maximum temperature

$\Rightarrow$ Maximum temperature gas in given by equation-(1) as

$$T_m = -\frac{P_0}{nRV_0}\left(\frac{3V_0}{2}\right)^2 + \frac{3P_0}{nR}\left(\frac{3V_0}{2}\right)$$

$$\Rightarrow \quad T_m = -\frac{P_0}{nRV_0} \times \frac{9V_0^2}{4} + \frac{9}{2}\frac{P_0V_0}{nR}$$

$$= \frac{P_0V_0}{nR}\left(\frac{9}{2} - \frac{9}{4}\right) = \frac{9}{4}\frac{P_0V_0}{nR}$$

Ans. (D)

Sol. 28 Gas expands from volume $V \rightarrow mV$

Work done by gas in the process is given as

$$W = \int_V^{mV} PdV = \int_V^{mV} \alpha VdV$$

$$\Rightarrow \quad W = \alpha\left[\frac{V^2}{2}\right]_V^{mV}$$

$$\Rightarrow \quad W = \frac{\alpha V^2}{2}(m^2 - 1) \quad \textbf{Ans. (D)}$$

Sol. 29 Initial state of gas for ideal monatomic gas

$$\gamma = 5/3$$

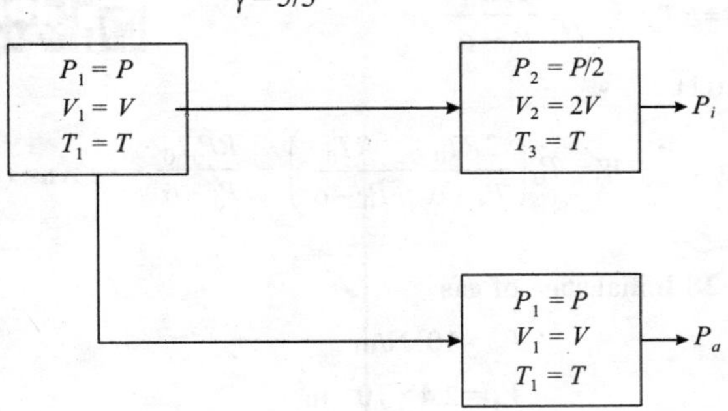

Isothermal expanded

$$T = \text{constant}$$

$$PV = \text{constant}$$

$$P.V = P_2(2V)$$

$$\Rightarrow \quad P_2 = P/2$$

Adiabatic expanded

$$\Delta Q = 0$$

$$PV^{5/3} = \text{constant}$$

$$PV^{5/3} = P'_2(2V)^{5/3}$$

$$\Rightarrow \quad P'_2 = \frac{P^{5/3}}{2}$$

Ratio $\quad \dfrac{P_a}{P_i} = \dfrac{P/2^{5/3}}{P/2} = 2^{1-5/3} = 2^{-2/3}$ **Ans. (D)**

Sol. 30 For an adiabatic process state parameters V and T are related as

$$TV^{\gamma-1} = \text{constant}$$

$$\Rightarrow \quad T_1V_1^{\gamma-1} = T_2V_2^{\gamma-1}$$

As $\quad V_2 = \dfrac{V_1}{4}$

$$\Rightarrow \quad T_1V_1^{0.5} = T_2\left(\frac{V_1}{4}\right)^{0.5}$$

$$\Rightarrow \quad T_2 = \sqrt{4}T_1 = 2T_1 = 2T$$ **Ans. (C)**

Sol. 31 Refrigerator

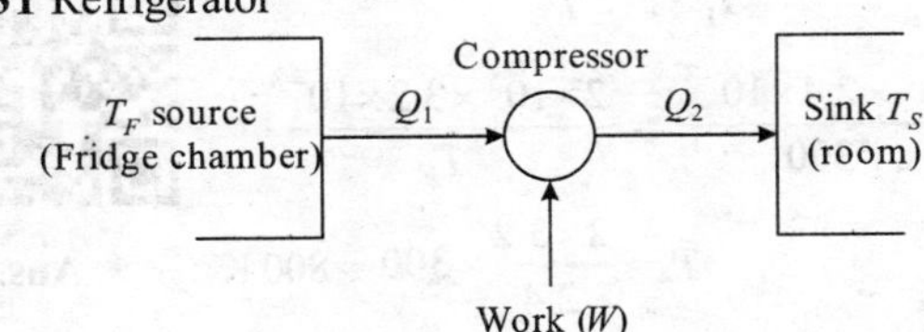

By conservation of energy

$$Q_2 = Q_1 + W$$

If door of refrigerator is kept open

$\Rightarrow$ Source and sink are same.

$\Rightarrow$ Net heat W will be given to room

$\Rightarrow$ Temperature of room increases **Ans. (D)**

Sol. 32 In the given cycle, heat extracted from the source is given as

$$Q_{out} = Q_3 + Q_4$$

$$\Rightarrow \quad Q_{out} = nC_V\Delta T_{BC} + nC_P\Delta T_{CD}$$

$$\Rightarrow \quad Q_{out} = \frac{3}{2}nR\Delta T_{BC} + \frac{5}{2}nR\Delta T_{CD}$$

$$\Rightarrow \quad Q_{out} = \frac{3}{2}\times 2P_0V_0 + \frac{5}{2}P_0V_0 = \frac{11}{2}P_0V_0$$

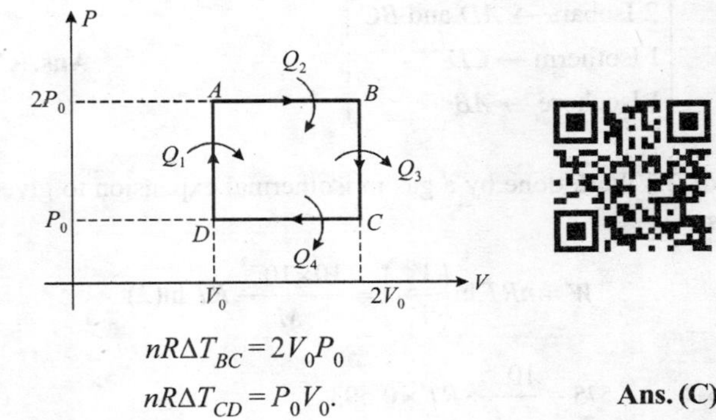

$$nR\Delta T_{BC} = 2V_0P_0$$

$$nR\Delta T_{CD} = P_0V_0.$$ **Ans. (C)**

Sol. 33

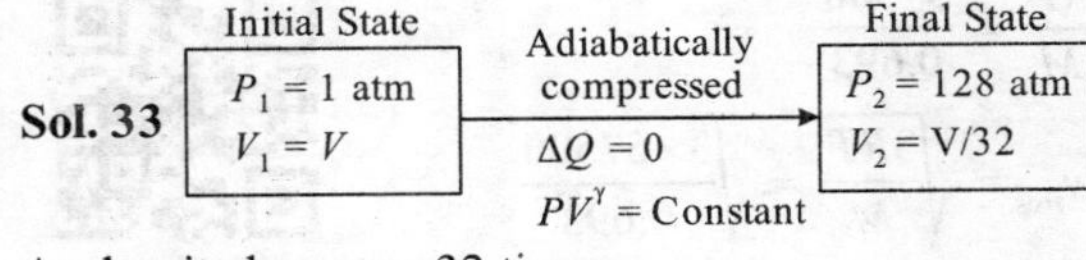

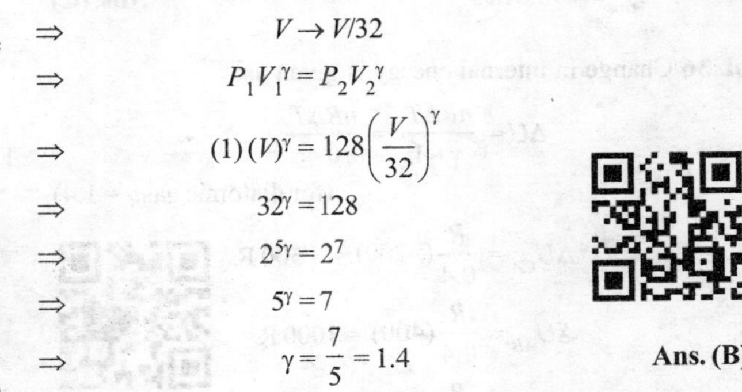

As density becomes 32 times

$$\Rightarrow \quad V \to V/32$$

$$\Rightarrow \quad P_1V_1^\gamma = P_2V_2^\gamma$$

$$\Rightarrow \quad (1)(V)^\gamma = 128\left(\frac{V}{32}\right)^\gamma$$

$$\Rightarrow \quad 32^\gamma = 128$$

$$\Rightarrow \quad 2^{5\gamma} = 2^7$$

$$\Rightarrow \quad 5\gamma = 7$$

$$\Rightarrow \quad \gamma = \frac{7}{5} = 1.4$$ **Ans. (B)**

Sol. 34 Isochores on PV-diagram

$$P = \text{constant}$$

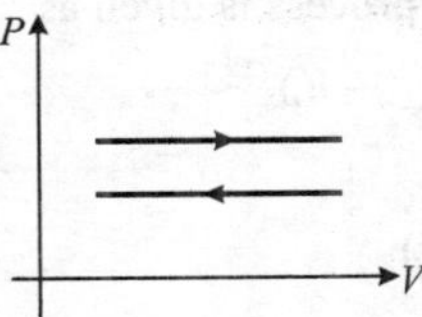

Isocharms on PV-diagram

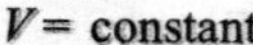

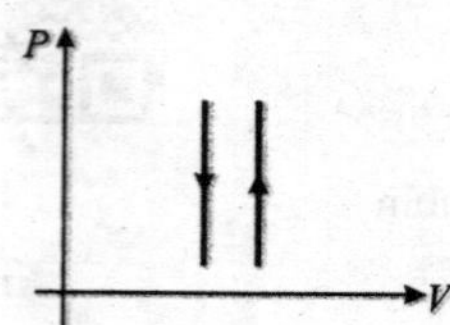

Isotherms on PV-diagram

T = constant

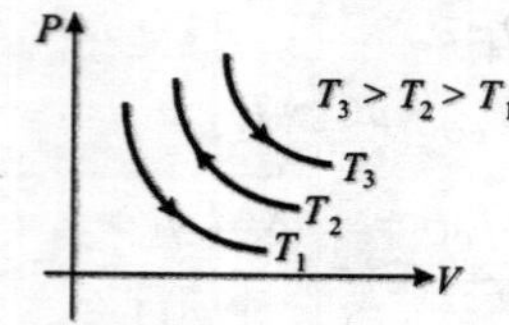

The given process has

$$\begin{bmatrix} \text{2 Isobars} \rightarrow AD \text{ and } BC \\ \text{1 Isotherm} \rightarrow CD \\ \text{1 Isochore} \rightarrow AB \end{bmatrix}$$

Ans. (C)

Sol. 35 Work done by a gas in isothermal expansion to given as

$$W = nRT\ln\left(\frac{V_2}{V_1}\right) = \frac{10\times10^{-3}}{M}RT\ln(2)$$

$$\Rightarrow \quad 575 = \frac{10^{-2}}{M}\cdot RT\times0.693$$

$$\Rightarrow \quad \frac{RT}{M} = \frac{57500}{0.693}$$

$$v_{rms} = \sqrt{\frac{3RT}{M}} = \sqrt{\frac{3\times57500}{0.693}}$$

$$\Rightarrow \quad v_{rms} = 498.6\text{ m/s}$$

Ans. (C)

Sol. 36 Change in internal energy is given as

$$\Delta U = \frac{nR\Delta T}{\gamma-1} = \frac{nR\Delta T}{0.4}$$

(for diatomic gas $\gamma = 1.4$)

$$\Rightarrow \quad \Delta U_{CA} = \frac{R}{0.4}(-200) = -500\text{ R}$$

$$\Rightarrow \quad \Delta U_{AB} = \frac{R}{0.4}(400) = 1000\text{ R}$$

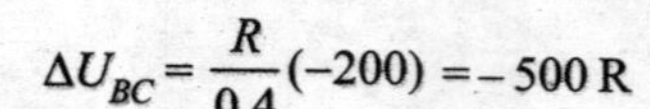

$$\Rightarrow \quad \Delta U_{BC} = \frac{R}{0.4}(-200) = -500\text{ R}$$

Ans. (D)

Sol. 37 Work done in an isobaric process is given as

$$W = P\Delta V = P(V_f - V_i)$$

as initial process is P_0

$$\Rightarrow \quad W = P_0(V_f - V_i) \qquad \ldots(1)$$

From the given equation, we have

$$PV = nRT + \alpha V$$

for $n = 1$ mole $\qquad V = \dfrac{RT}{P-\alpha}$

at $T = T_0 \rightarrow V_i = \dfrac{RT_0}{P_0-\alpha}$

at $T = 2T_0 \rightarrow V_f = \dfrac{2RT_0}{P_0-\alpha}$

from (1)

$$W = P_0\left(\frac{2RT_0}{P_0-\alpha} - \frac{RT_0}{P_0-\alpha}\right) = \frac{RP_0T_0}{P_0-\alpha}$$

Ans. (A)

Sol. 38 Initial state of gas

$$P_1 = 10^5\text{ N/m}^2$$

$$V_1 = 2.4\times10^{-3}\text{ m}^3$$

$$T_1 = 300\text{ K}$$

After expansion, gas process is

$$P_f = P_{atm} + \frac{kx}{A}$$

$$\Rightarrow \quad P_f = 10^5 + \frac{8000\times0.1}{8.0\times10^{-3}}$$

$$\Rightarrow \quad P_f = 10^5 + 10^5 = 2\times10^5\text{ N/m}^2$$

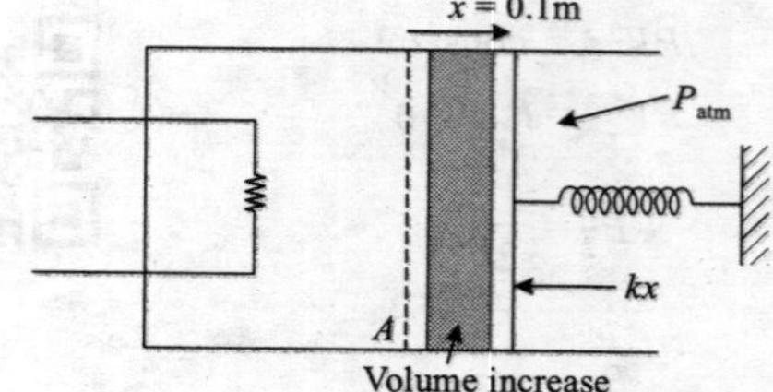

$$\Delta V = Ax$$

$$\Delta V = 8.0\times10^{-3}\times0.1$$

$$\Delta V = 0.8\times10^{-3}\text{ m}^3$$

Find state of gas

$$P_f = 2\times10^5\text{ N/m}^2$$

$$V_f = V_i + \Delta V = 2.4\times10^{-3}\text{m}^3 + 0.8\times10^{-3}\text{m}^3$$

$$= 3.2\times10^{-3}\text{ m}^2$$

$$T_f = \rho$$

As no of moles of gas are constant. So we use

$$\frac{P_1V_1}{T_1} = \frac{P_fV_f}{T_f}$$

$$\Rightarrow \quad \frac{10^5\times2.4\times10^{-3}}{300} = \frac{2\times10^5\times3.2\times10^{-3}}{T_F}$$

$$\Rightarrow \quad T_f = \frac{2\times3.2}{2.4}\times300 = 800\text{ K}$$

Ans. (B)

Sol. 39 In an adiabatic process, work done by gas is given as

$$W = -\Delta U = -\frac{nR\Delta T}{\gamma - 1}$$

given that $W = -830$ J (work done on gas) for $n = 2$ mole and $\gamma = 1.4$ for a diatomic ideal gas

$$\Rightarrow \quad W = -830 = -\frac{2 \times 8.3 \times \Delta T}{1.4 - 1}$$

$$\Rightarrow \quad \Delta T = \frac{830 \times 0.4}{2 \times 8.3} = \frac{40}{2} = 20 \text{ K}$$

$\Rightarrow$ Temperature gas increases by 20 K **Ans. (C)**

Sol. 40 By first law of thermodynamics we have

$$\Delta Q = \Delta U + \Delta W \quad \ldots (1)$$

In whole process $\Delta Q = 150$ J

and $\Delta W = P\Delta V = P(V_2 - V_1) = 100\,(1 - 2)$

$\Rightarrow \quad \Delta W = -100$ J

As gas is compressed $\Rightarrow$ work is done on the gas ($-$ *ve*)

So from equation-(1), we use

$\Rightarrow \quad 150 = \Delta U - 100$

$\Rightarrow \quad \Delta U = 250$ J

$\Rightarrow$ Internal energy increases by 250 J **Ans. (A)**

Sol. 41

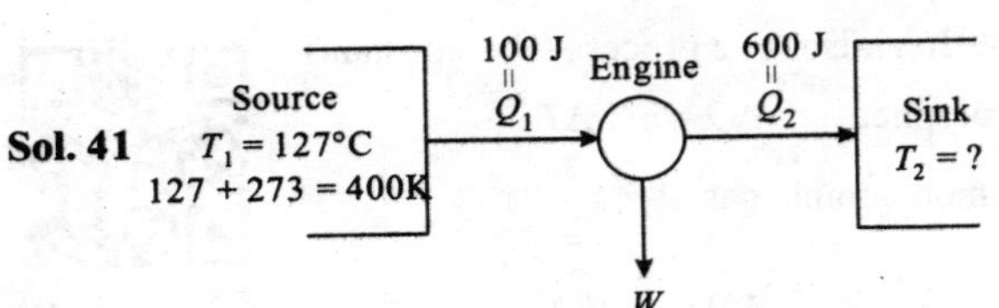

Work done per cycle by engine

$$W = Q_1 - Q_2$$
$$= 1000 - 600 = 400 \text{ J}$$

Efficiency of engine

$$\eta = \frac{W}{Q_1} \times 100 = \frac{400}{1000} \times 100 = 40\%$$

In carnot engine Q_1 and Q_2 are proportional to T_1 and T_2

$$\Rightarrow \quad \frac{Q_1}{Q_2} = \frac{T_1}{T_2}$$

$$\Rightarrow \quad \frac{1000}{600} = \frac{400}{T_2}$$

$\Rightarrow \quad T_2 = 240 \text{ K} = -33°\text{C}$ **Ans. (B)**

Sol. 42 Average time between collisions of gas molecules

$$t \propto \frac{V}{\sqrt{T}}$$

In Adiabatic process we use $TV^{\gamma-1}$ = constant

$$\Rightarrow \quad T = CV^{1-\gamma}$$

$$\Rightarrow \quad t \propto \frac{V}{\sqrt{CV^{1-\gamma}}} = C_1 V^{1 - \frac{1-\gamma}{2}} = C_1 V^{\frac{1+\gamma}{2}}$$

$$\Rightarrow \quad t \propto V^{\frac{1+\gamma}{2}} \Rightarrow q = \frac{1+\gamma}{2}$$ **Ans. (C)**

Sol. 43 Given that

$$\frac{U}{V} = kT^4$$

$\Rightarrow$ Gas pressure $P = \frac{1}{3}kT^4$

By Gas law $PV = nR_g T$

$R_g \rightarrow$ Gas constant

$$\Rightarrow \quad \frac{1}{3}kT^4 \cdot \left(\frac{4}{3}\pi R^3\right) = nR_g T$$

$$\Rightarrow \quad T^3 R^3 = \text{constant}$$

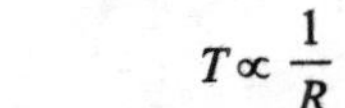

$$\Rightarrow \quad T \propto \frac{1}{R}$$ **Ans. (A)**

Sol. 44 Change in Entropy of a solid body is given as

$$\Delta S = \int \frac{dQ}{T}$$

for a solid body we use

$$dQ = CdT$$

$$\Rightarrow \quad \Delta S = \int_{T_1}^{T_2} \frac{CdT}{T} = C\ln\left(\frac{T_2}{T_1}\right)$$

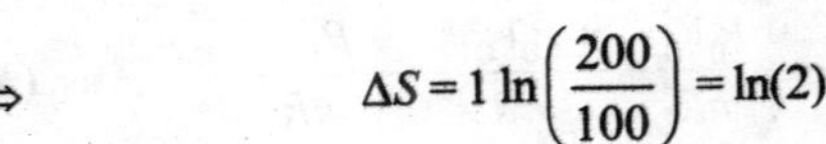

$$\Rightarrow \quad \Delta S = 1\ln\left(\frac{200}{100}\right) = \ln(2)$$

As entropy change depends only on temperature (initial & final) so in both cases ΔS remains same. **Ans. (D)**

Sol. 45 In *V-T* diagram '*ab*' and '*cd*' are straight line

$\Rightarrow$ These are isobars on *PV* diagram

Isobars on *VT* curve pass through *O* (assuming this by looking at given options)

$\Rightarrow \quad P$ = constant

from '*bc*' and '*da*' which are adiabatic

Option (B) is the correct Ans.

(B) $b \rightarrow c$ ($\rightarrow$) volume is increasing

$d \rightarrow a$ ($\rightarrow$) volume is decreasing

Corresponding to given *VT* curve.

Also slope of curve in $-ve$ and decreasing

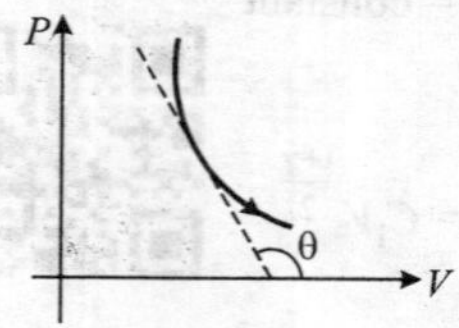

$$m = \tan\theta \rightarrow -ve$$

m is decreasing in magnitude with volume. **Ans. (B)**

Sol. 46 Equation of Straight line shown in indicator diagram is

$$P = -\frac{P_0}{V_0}\cdot V + 3P_0$$

$$\text{slope} = -\frac{P_0}{V_0}$$

$$\text{intercept} = 3P_0$$

equation $y = mx + c$

Temperature of gas during the process is

$$T = \frac{PV}{nR} = -\frac{P_0}{nRV_0}\cdot V^2 + \frac{3P_0}{nR}\cdot V$$

For maximum temperature we use

$$\frac{dT}{dV} = 0 = -\frac{2P_0}{nRV_0}\cdot V + \frac{3P_0}{nR}$$

$$\Rightarrow \quad V = \frac{3}{2}V_0$$

The maximum temperature of gas is given as

$$T_{max} = -\frac{P_0}{nRV_0}\left(\frac{3V_0}{2}\right)^2 + \frac{3P_0}{nR}\left(\frac{3V_0}{2}\right)$$

$$\Rightarrow \quad T_{max} = -\frac{9}{4}\frac{P_0V_0}{nR} + \frac{9}{2}\frac{P_0V_0}{nR} = \frac{9}{4}\frac{P_0V_0}{nR}$$ **Ans. (A)**

Sol. 47 For a polytrophic process here $n \rightarrow$ Polytropic constant

$$PV^n = \text{Constant}$$

& for this process the molar specific heat of gas is given as

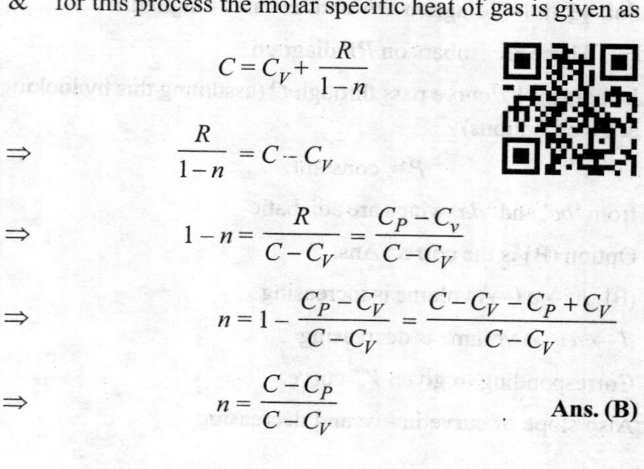

$$C = C_V + \frac{R}{1-n}$$

$$\Rightarrow \quad \frac{R}{1-n} = C - C_V$$

$$\Rightarrow \quad 1 - n = \frac{R}{C - C_V} = \frac{C_P - C_v}{C - C_V}$$

$$\Rightarrow \quad n = 1 - \frac{C_P - C_V}{C - C_V} = \frac{C - C_V - C_P + C_V}{C - C_V}$$

$$\Rightarrow \quad n = \frac{C - C_P}{C - C_V}$$ **Ans. (B)**

Sol. 48 Refrigerator

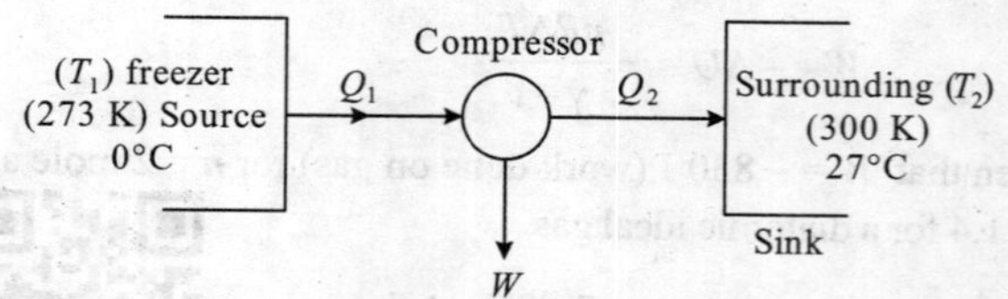

by conservation of energy

$$Q_1 + W_{ext} = Q_2$$

$$\Rightarrow \quad W_{ext} = Q_2 - Q_1$$

For a carnot freezer we use

$$\frac{Q_1}{Q_2} = \frac{T_1}{T_2} \quad \ldots(1)$$

here $Q_1 \rightarrow$ heat released by freezer in freezing ice

Here $\quad Q_1 = mL = 5 \times 336 \times 10^3 \text{ (J/kg)} \times \text{kg}$

$$= 5 \times 336 \times 10^3 \text{ J}$$

We use by equation-(1)

$$Q_2 = \left(\frac{T_2}{T_1}\right) \times Q_1 = \frac{300}{273} \times 5 \times 336 \times 10^3$$

Energy consumed by freezer in

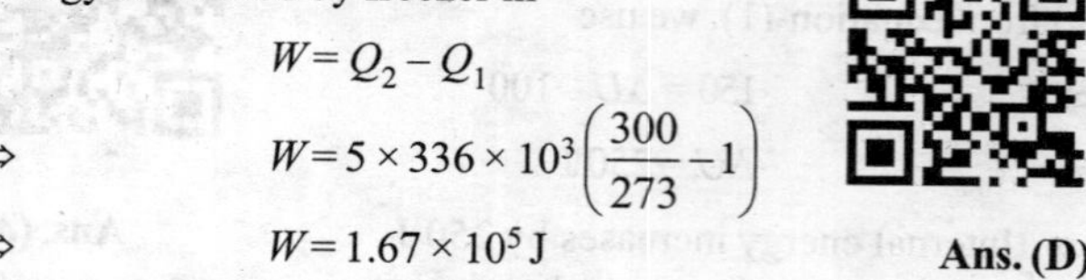

$$W = Q_2 - Q_1$$

$$\Rightarrow \quad W = 5 \times 336 \times 10^3 \left(\frac{300}{273} - 1\right)$$

$$\Rightarrow \quad W = 1.67 \times 10^5 \text{ J}$$ **Ans. (D)**

Sol. 49 In an isobaric process (P = constant)

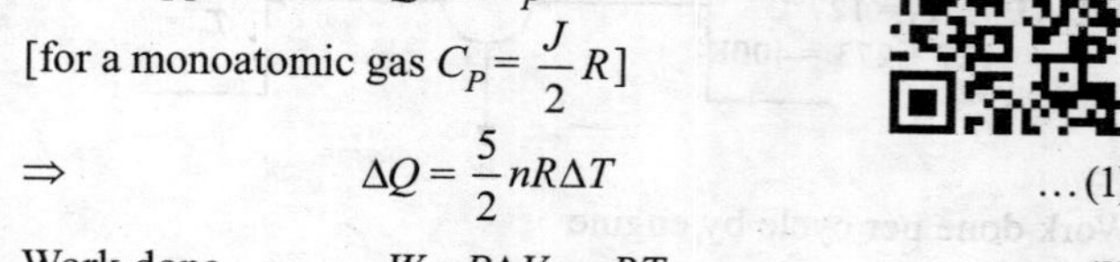

Heat supplied $\quad \Delta Q = nC_P\Delta T$

[for a monoatomic gas $C_P = \frac{J}{2}R$]

$$\Rightarrow \quad \Delta Q = \frac{5}{2}nR\Delta T \quad \ldots(1)$$

Work done $\quad W = P\Delta V = nRT \quad \ldots(2)$

$$\frac{(2)}{(1)} \Rightarrow \quad \frac{W}{\Delta Q} = \frac{nR\Delta T}{5/2nR\Delta T} = \frac{2}{5}$$ **Ans. (A)**

Sol. 50 By first law of thermodynamics

$$\Delta Q = \Delta U + \Delta W$$

If expansion of water is neglected

$$\Rightarrow \quad \Delta W = 0 \text{ (heat supplied)}$$

$$\Delta U = mS\Delta T$$

$$\Rightarrow \quad \Delta U = 0.2 \times 4184 \times 20 = 16.7 \text{ kJ}$$ **Ans. (D)**

12.1 Kinetic Theory of Gases

Sol. 1

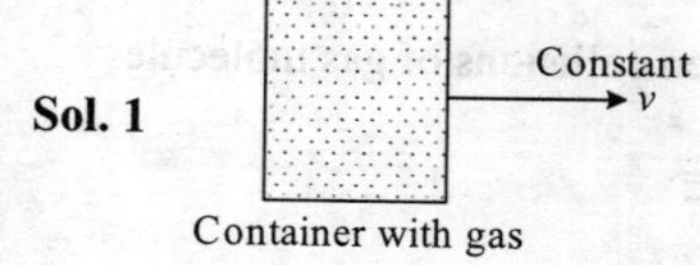

Container with gas

Temperature of gas is a measure of KE of random motion of gas molecules

$$E = \frac{f}{2}kT$$

where $f \rightarrow$ degrees of freedom

If container is moving at uniform speed in a specific direction then it does not affect the random motion of gas molecules in container. Due to v, all particles will have an ordered motion which is not affecting its T. **Ans. (C)**

Sol. 2 $T_{O_2} = 273 + 47 = 320\text{ K}$

RMS velocity of molecules is given as

$$v = \sqrt{\frac{3RT}{M}}$$

If at T_{H_2} the velocity (RMS) of H_2 molecule is equal to that of O_2 molecule at 320 K

$$\Rightarrow \quad v_{H_2} = v_{O_2}$$

$$\Rightarrow \quad \sqrt{\frac{3RT_{H_2}}{2\times10^{-3}}} = \sqrt{\frac{3RT_{O_2}}{32\times10^{-3}}}$$

$$\Rightarrow \quad T_{H_2} = \frac{2}{32}\times 320\text{K} = 20\text{ K}$$ **Ans. (D)**

Sol. 3 The equivalent value of γ for a mixture of gas is given as

$$\frac{n_1+n_2}{\gamma_{eq}-1} = \frac{n_1}{\gamma_1-1}+\frac{n_2}{\gamma_2-1}$$

$$\Rightarrow \quad \frac{1+1}{\gamma_{eq}-1} = \frac{1}{\frac{7}{5}-1}+\frac{1}{\frac{5}{3}-1}$$

$$\Rightarrow \quad \frac{2}{\gamma_{eq}-1} = \frac{5}{2}+\frac{3}{2} = 4$$

$$\Rightarrow \quad \gamma_{eq}-1 = \frac{1}{2}$$

$$\Rightarrow \quad \gamma_{eq} = \frac{3}{2} = \frac{24}{16}$$ **Ans. (C)**

Sol. 4

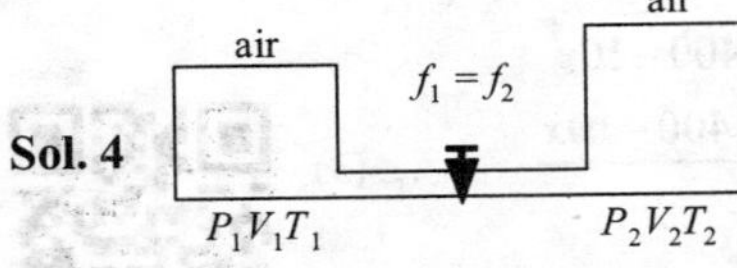

No of moles of gas (air) in the two vessels are

$$n_1 = \frac{P_1V_1}{RT_1} \text{ and } n_2 = \frac{P_2V_2}{RT_2}$$

By conservation of internal energy final equilibrium temperature of mixture is given as

$$T_f = \frac{f_1n_1T_1 + f_2n_2T_2}{f_1n_1 + f_2n_2} = \frac{n_1T_1+n_2T_2}{n_1+n_2}$$

$$\Rightarrow \quad T_f = \frac{P_1V_1+P_2V_2}{\frac{P_1V_1}{T_1}+\frac{P_2V_2}{T_2}} = \frac{T_1T_2(P_1V_1+P_2V_2)}{P_1V_1T_2+P_2V_2T_1}$$ **Ans. (C)**

Sol. 5 For equivalent γ of mixture of gases we use

$$\frac{n_1+n_2}{\gamma_{eq}-1} = \frac{n_1}{\gamma_1-1}+\frac{n_2}{\gamma_2-1}$$

$$\Rightarrow \quad \frac{1+1}{\gamma_{eq}-1} = \frac{1}{\frac{5}{3}-1}+\frac{1}{\frac{7}{5}-1}$$

$$\Rightarrow \quad \frac{2}{\gamma_{eq}-1} = \frac{3}{2}+\frac{5}{2} = 4$$

$$\Rightarrow \quad \gamma_{eq}-1 = \frac{1}{2} \Rightarrow \gamma_{eq} = \frac{3}{2}$$ **Ans. (A)**

Sol. 6 Equivalent γ for a gaseous mixture is given as

$$\frac{n_1+n_2}{\gamma_{eq}-1} = \frac{n_1}{\gamma_1-1}+\frac{n_2}{\gamma_2-1}$$

for H_e gas $\quad n_1 = \frac{m_1}{M_1} = \frac{16}{4} = 4$ mole

for O_2 gas $\quad n_2 = \frac{m_2}{M_2} = \frac{16}{32} = 0.5$ mole

$$\Rightarrow \quad \frac{4.5}{\gamma_{eq}-1} = \frac{4}{\frac{5}{3}-1}+\frac{0.5}{\frac{7}{5}-1} = 6+\frac{2.5}{2} = 7.25$$

$$\Rightarrow \quad \gamma_{eq}-1 = \frac{4.5}{7.25} \Rightarrow \gamma_{eq} = 1.62$$ **Ans. (B)**

Sol. 7 When heat flows between boxes, total internal energy of the two gases will remain constant so for this cases the final equilibrium temperature of gases is given as

$$T_{eq} = \frac{f_1n_1T_1+f_2n_2T_2}{f_1n_1+f_2n_2}$$

$$\left[\text{for } N_2 \rightarrow \begin{matrix} n_1 = 1 \\ f_1 = 5 \\ T_1 = T_0 \end{matrix} \right] \text{ and for } He \rightarrow \begin{matrix} n_2 = 1 \\ f_2 = 3 \\ T_2 = \frac{7}{3}T_0 \end{matrix}$$

$$\Rightarrow \quad T_{eq} = \frac{5\times1\times T_0 + 3\times1\times(7/3)T_0}{5\times1+3\times1}$$

$$\Rightarrow \quad T_{eq} = \frac{12T_0}{8} = \frac{3}{2}T_0$$ **Ans. (C)**

Sol. 8 C'_P and C'_V are the specific heats for an ideal gas per unit mole then we use the relation

$$C'_P - C'_V = R \quad \text{...(1)}$$

C_P and C_V per unit mass for N_2 gas can be given as

$$M = 28\text{gm}$$

$$\Rightarrow \quad C_P = \frac{C'_P}{28} \text{ and } C_V = \frac{C'_V}{28}$$

$\Rightarrow$ from equation (1), we have

$$28C_P - 28C_V = R$$

$$\Rightarrow \quad C_P - C_V = \frac{R}{28}$$

Ans. (A)

Sol. 9

P_1V_1, T_1 | P_2V_2, T_2 — Insulted container — Insulting partition

$$f_1 = f_2$$

$$n_1 = \frac{P_1V_1}{RT_1} \quad \text{and} \quad n_2 = \frac{P_2V_2}{RT_2}$$

When gases are mixed after removing partition then by internal energy conservation final equation temperature mixture is given as

$$T_f = \frac{f_1n_1T_1 + f_2n_2T_2}{f_1n_1 + f_2n_2} = \frac{n_1T_1 + n_2T_2}{n_1 + n_2}$$

$$\Rightarrow \quad T_f = \frac{T_1T_2(P_1V_1 + P_2V_2)}{P_1V_1T_2 + P_2V_2T_1}$$

Ans. (A)

Sol. 10 Energy due to thermal motion $\rightarrow$ internal energy of gas (energy of rendom motion)

For a given sample of gas its internal energy is given as

$$U = \frac{f}{2}nRT$$

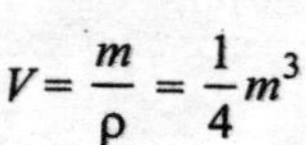

For a diatomic gas $f = 5$ and here gas volume

$$V = \frac{m}{\rho} = \frac{1}{4}m^3$$

$$\Rightarrow \quad U = \frac{5}{2}nRT = \frac{5}{2}PV = \frac{5}{2} \times 8 \times 10^4 \times \frac{1}{4}$$

$$\Rightarrow \quad U = 5 \times 10^4 \text{ J}$$

Ans. (D)

Sol. 11 For gaseous mixture, final equilibrium temperature is given as

$$T_{eq} = \frac{f_1n_1T_1 + f_2n_2T_2 + f_3n_3T_3}{f_1n_1 + f_2n_2 + f_3n_3}$$

We consider $f_1 = f_2 = f_3$

As no of moles α no of molecules

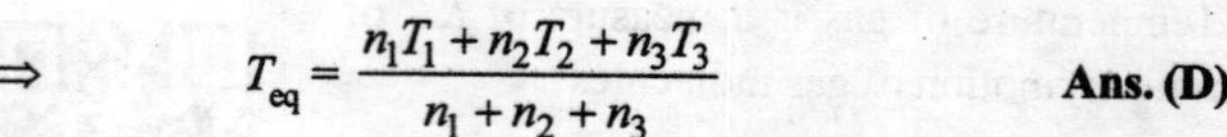

$$\Rightarrow \quad T_{eq} = \frac{n_1T_1 + n_2T_2 + n_3T_3}{n_1 + n_2 + n_3}$$

Ans. (D)

Sol. 12 As gas pressure is constant so we use by gas law

$$\frac{V_1}{T_1} = \frac{V_2}{T_2}$$

here $\quad V_2 = 2V_1$

$$\Rightarrow \quad T_2 = 2T_1 = 2 \times (273 + 27) = 60 \text{ K}$$

$$\Rightarrow \quad T_2 = 600 - 273 = 327°\text{C}$$

Ans. (A)

Sol. 13 Initial situation

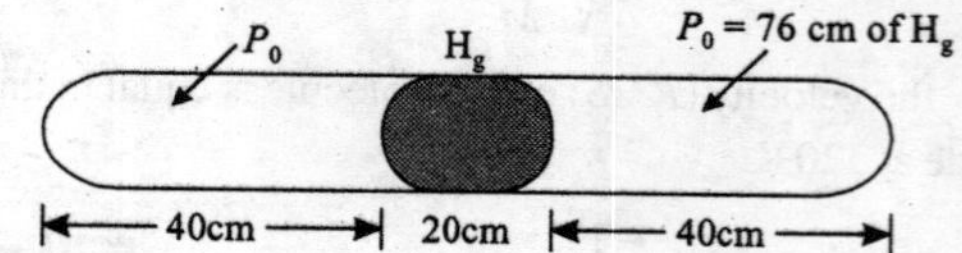

Final situation

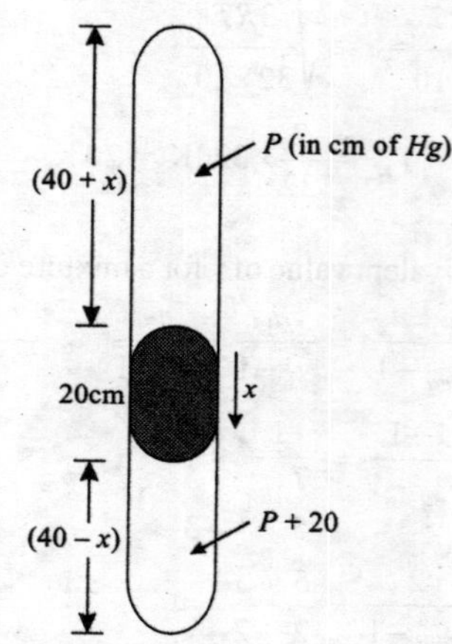

we consider constant temperature, so we have

upper section $\rightarrow P_0 \times 40 = P \times (40 + x)$ ...(1)

lower section $\rightarrow P_0 \times 40 = (P + 20) \times (40 - x)$ ...(2)

from (1) and (2)

$$40P + P_x = 40P + 800 - P_x = 20x$$

$$\Rightarrow \quad P_x = 400 - 10x$$

$$\Rightarrow \quad P = \frac{400 - 10x}{x} \quad \text{...(3)}$$

from equation (1)

$$76 \times 40 = \frac{(400 - 10x)}{x}(40 + x)$$

$$\Rightarrow \quad 3040x = 1600 - 400x + 400x - 10x^2$$

$$\Rightarrow \quad x^2 + 304x - 1600 = 0$$

$$\Rightarrow \quad x = \frac{-304 + \sqrt{(304)^2 - 6400}}{2} \simeq 5.17 \text{ cm.}$$

Ans. (B)

Sol. 14 For an isobaric process heat supplied is related to the rise in temperature as

$$Q = nC_P\Delta T$$

Slope of $Q - \Delta T$ curve $= \dfrac{Q}{\Delta T} = nC_P$

Here all gases are having same initial states $(P_1, V_1, T_1) \rightarrow$ same

$\Rightarrow$ Same have equal no of moles.

For a gas $C_P = \dfrac{f+2}{2}$

Where $f = 3$ for monoatomic gas (M)

$f = 5$ for diatomic gas (D)

$f = 6$ for polyatomic gas (P)

Maximum linear molecule

As $C_P(P) > C_P(D) > C_P(M)$ **Ans. (C)**

Sol. 15 Statement-1 : It is false because in free expansion temperature do not change as $W = 0$.

Statement-2 : True as for ideal gas we neglect *PE* as particles have no interaction but in real gas *PE* is there **Ans. (A)**

Sol. 16

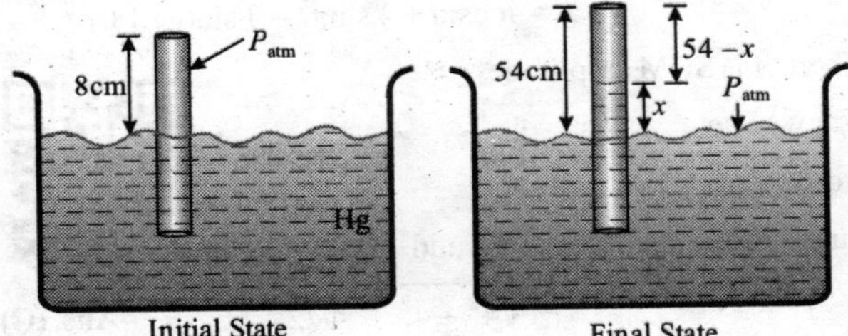

As total no of moles of air trapped in tube is constant we use

$$P_1V_1 = P_2V_2$$

$$\Rightarrow \quad 76 \times 8 = (76 - x) \times (54 - x)$$

$$\Rightarrow \quad 76 \times 8 = 76 \times 54 - 130x + x^2$$

$$\Rightarrow \quad x^2 - 130x + 76 \times 46 = 0$$

$$\Rightarrow \quad x = \frac{130 \pm \sqrt{(130)^2 - 4 \times 76 \times 46}}{2}$$

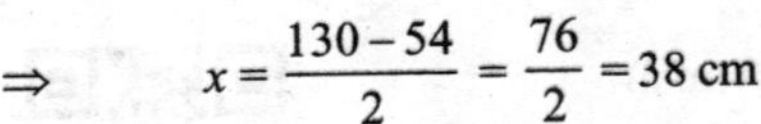

$$\Rightarrow \quad x = \frac{130 - 54}{2} = \frac{76}{2} = 38 \text{ cm}$$

Length of air column in final state

$$l = 54 - x = 54 - 38 = 16 \text{ cm}$$ **Ans. (A)**

Sol. 17 If there are N molecules in a vessel of volume V then mean distance between molecules in the vessel is given as

$$d_m = \left(\frac{V}{N}\right)^{1/3} \quad \ldots(1)$$

Using gas law, we have

$$PV = nRT$$

$$\Rightarrow \quad PV = \frac{N}{N_{AV}} \cdot RT$$

$$\Rightarrow \quad \frac{V}{N} = \frac{RT}{PN_{AV}} = \frac{8.0 \times 300}{4 \times 10^{-10} \times 6 \times 10^{23}}$$

$$= \frac{100}{10^{12}} = 10^{-11} \text{ m}^3\text{/molecule}$$

$\Rightarrow$ from equation-(1)

$$d_m = (10^{-11})^{1/2} = (10 \times 10^{-12})^{1/3}$$

$$\Rightarrow \quad d_m = 2.1 \times 10^{-4} \text{ m} = 0.21 \text{ mm.}$$ **Ans. (B)**

Sol. 18 *RMS* speed of a gas molecule is given as

$$v_{rms} = \sqrt{\frac{3RT}{M}}$$

If we consider room temperature to be at $\sim 27°\text{C} = 300 \text{ K}$.

$$\Rightarrow \quad (1930)^2 = \frac{3 \times 8.314 \times 300}{M}$$

$$\Rightarrow \quad M = \frac{3 \times 8.314 \times 300}{(1930)^2} \simeq 2 \times 10^{-3} \text{ kg}$$

Thus gas is H_2 **Ans. (A)**

Sol. 19 The (Translational) *KE* of a gas molecule at temperature T is given as

$$KE = \frac{3}{2}k_BT$$

at $T = 0°\text{C} = 273 \text{ K}$

$$\Rightarrow \quad KE = \frac{3}{2}k_B \times 273 = \frac{819}{2}k_B$$

If it rises to a height h above the earth surface

$$\Rightarrow \quad KE = Mgh = \frac{819}{2}k_B$$

[As $h << R_e$ so we consider g = constant]

$$\Rightarrow \quad h = \frac{819k_B}{2Mg}$$ **Ans. (D)**

Sol. 20 For atoms in a solid lattice we take 6 vibrational degrees of freedom $(KE + PE)$

Then molar specific heat of *Al* at constant volume is given as

$$C_v = \frac{f}{2}R = \frac{6}{2}R = 3R \text{ J/mol.K}$$

The specific heat in J/kg-K can be given as

$$s = \frac{C_v}{M} = \frac{3R}{M} = \frac{3 \times 8.314}{27 \times 10^{-3}} \text{ J/kg-K}$$

$$\Rightarrow \quad s \simeq 925 \text{ J/kg-K}$$ **Ans. (D)**

Sol. 21 The pressure exerted by gas molecules on container walls is

$$P = \frac{1}{3}\rho v_{rms}^2 \qquad \left[\text{We use } v_{rms} = \sqrt{\frac{3RT}{M}}\,\right]$$

$$\Rightarrow \quad P = \frac{\rho RT}{M} \quad \Rightarrow \quad P \propto T$$

[for a closed container $\rho \rightarrow$ constant]

$\Rightarrow$ Force on walls $\propto$ pressure by gas

Force $\propto T^{(1)}$

$$\Rightarrow \quad q = 1$$

Ans. (C)

13.1 Simple Harmonic Motion

Sol. 1

k, n parts, $k' = nk$

Each part has force constant n times of the original spring if it is divided in n equal parts.

For a force constant k, the time period of oscillations is

$$T = 2\pi\sqrt{\frac{m}{k}}$$

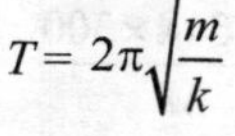

If $\quad k \rightarrow k' = nk$

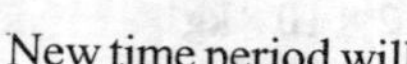

New time period will be

$$T' = 2\pi\sqrt{\frac{m}{nk}} = \frac{T}{\sqrt{n}}$$

Ans. (B)

Sol. 2 In SHM, KE and PE with position are given as

$$K_y = \frac{1}{2}m\omega^2(A^2 - y^2)$$

and

$$P_y = \frac{1}{2}m\omega^2 y^2$$

At mean position $\quad y = 0$

$$K_m = \frac{1}{2}m\omega^2 A^2 \quad \text{(max)}$$

$$P_m = 0 \quad \text{(min)}$$

At extreme position $\quad y = \pm A$

$$K_e = 0 \quad \text{(min)}$$

$$P_e = \frac{1}{2}m\omega^2 A^2 \quad \text{(max)}$$

Ans. (C)

Sol. 3 Time period of a swing (similar to simple pendulum) is given as

$$T = 2\pi\sqrt{\frac{l}{g}}$$

As boy stands up, length of pendulum decreases

$$\Rightarrow \text{ new time period } T' = 2\pi\sqrt{\frac{l'}{g}} \Rightarrow T' < T$$

Ans. (B)

Sol. 4

k, M ; k, $M+m$

Time period of SHM in first condition

$$T = 2\pi\sqrt{\frac{M}{k}} \qquad \ldots(1)$$

Time period of SHM in second condition

$$\frac{5T}{3} = T' = 2\pi\sqrt{\frac{M+m}{k}} \qquad \ldots(2)$$

$$\text{By (2)/(1)} \Rightarrow \quad \frac{5}{3} = \sqrt{\frac{M+m}{M}}$$

$$\Rightarrow \quad \frac{25}{9} = \frac{M+m}{M}$$

$$\Rightarrow \quad \frac{m}{M} = \frac{16}{9}$$

Ans. (C)

Sol. 5 SHM equation is given as

$$x = 4\cos\pi t + 4\sin\pi t = A\sin(\omega t + \theta)$$

Where A is SHM amplitude

here we use $\quad A\cos\theta = 4$

and $\quad A\sin\theta = 4$

square above equations and add

$$\Rightarrow \quad A = \sqrt{4^2 + 4^2} = 4\sqrt{2}$$

Ans. (C)

Sol. 6 Energies as a function of position x in SHM are given as

$$TE = \frac{1}{2}m\omega^2 A^2 \rightarrow \text{constant}$$

$$K_x = \frac{1}{2}m\omega^2(A^2 - x^2)$$

$$P_x = \frac{1}{2}m\omega^2 x^2$$

At mean position $\quad x = 0$

$$K_x = \frac{1}{2}m\omega^2 A^2 \text{ (max)}$$

$$P_x = 0 \text{ (min)}$$

At extreme position

$$x = \pm A$$

$$K_x = 0$$

$$P_x = \frac{1}{2}m\omega^2 A^2 \text{ (max)}$$

Ans. (A)

Sol. 7 If amplitudes of A and B are A_1 and A_2 respectively then we use $v_{\max A} = v_{\max B}$

For SHM $\quad v_{\max} = \omega A$

$$\omega_A A_1 = \omega_B A_2$$

$$\omega = \sqrt{\frac{k}{m}}$$

$$\Rightarrow \quad \frac{A_1}{A_2} = \sqrt{\frac{k_2}{k_1}}$$

Ans. (C)

Sol. 8 Time period of a simple pendulum is given as

$$T = 2\pi\sqrt{\frac{l}{g}}$$

If $l \to 1.21l \Rightarrow$ new time period will be

$$T' = 2\pi\sqrt{\frac{1.21l}{g}} = 1.1 \times 2\pi\sqrt{\frac{l}{g}}$$

$$\Rightarrow \quad T' = 1.1T$$

% increase in time period is

$$= \frac{T'-T}{T} \times 100$$

$$= \frac{(1.1-1)}{1} \times 100 = 10\%$$

Ans. (D)

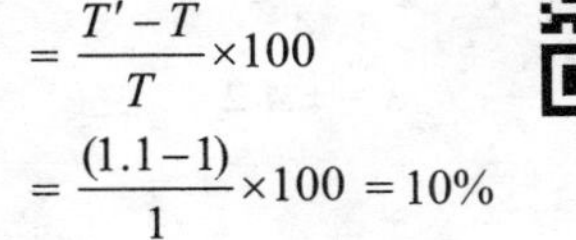

Sol. 9 Time period of a simple pendulum is

$$T = 2\pi\sqrt{\frac{l}{g}} \text{ in air}$$

$$T' = 2\pi\sqrt{\frac{l}{g_{\text{eff}}}} \text{ in water}$$

Where $g_{\text{eff}} = g\left(1 - \frac{\rho_l}{\rho_s}\right)$

$$T' = 2\pi\sqrt{\frac{l}{g\left(\frac{\rho_s - \rho_l}{\rho_s}\right)}} = T\sqrt{\frac{\rho_s}{\rho_s - \rho_l}}$$

$$\Rightarrow \quad T' = t_0\sqrt{\frac{\frac{4}{3}\times 10^3}{\left(\frac{4}{3}-1\right)\times 10^3}} = t_0\sqrt{\frac{4}{3}\times\frac{3}{1}} = 2t_0$$

Ans. (C)

Sol. 10 For first spring (force constant k_1), time period

$$t_1 = 2\pi\sqrt{\frac{m}{k_1}}$$

For second spring (force constant k_2), time period

$$t_2 = 2\pi\sqrt{\frac{m}{k_2}}$$

In series combination of springs, effective force constant k_{eq} is given by

$$\frac{1}{k_{eq}} = \frac{1}{k_1} + \frac{1}{k_2}$$

Time period of SHM using series combination is given as

$$T_{eq} = T = 2\pi\sqrt{\frac{m}{k_{eq}}} = 2\pi\sqrt{\frac{m}{k_1} + \frac{m}{k_2}}$$

Squaring gives

$$T^2 = 4\pi^2\frac{m}{k_1} + 4\pi^2\frac{m}{k_2}$$

$$\Rightarrow \quad T^2 = t_1^2 + t_2^2$$

Ans. (B)

Sol. 11 Total energy in SHM is given as

$$TE = \frac{1}{2}m\omega^2 A^2 + U_{\min}$$

Constant minimum PE does not change with position.

with position KE & PE oscillates and

$$K_x + P_x = \text{TE} \to \text{constant}$$

Ans. (C)

Sol. 12 For a forced oscillation in a damping medium if external force is $\quad F(t) = F_0\cos\omega t$

then the oscillation amplitude is given as

$$A = \frac{F_0}{\sqrt{m^2(\omega_0^2 - \omega^2)^2 + b^2\omega^2}}$$

(where $b \to$ damping coefficient)

in this question $b = 0 \Rightarrow A = \dfrac{F_0}{m(\omega_0^2 - \omega^2)}$

Ans. (B)

Sol. 13 Energy of oscillations $\propto$ (amplitude)^2

$\Rightarrow$ When amplitude is maximum, energy will also be maximum and this happens at same frequency of force

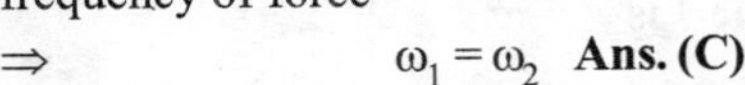

$\Rightarrow \quad \omega_1 = \omega_2$ **Ans. (C)**

Sol. 14 Acceleration of particle is given as

$$a = \frac{F}{m} = -\frac{kx}{m}$$

$$\Rightarrow \quad a = -\frac{15\times 0.2}{0.3} = -10 \text{ m/s}^2$$

Negative sign shows opposite direction.

Ans. (D)

Sol. 15 The position given is

$$y = \sin^2\omega t = \frac{1}{2}(1 - \cos 2\omega t)$$

$$\Rightarrow \quad y = \frac{1}{2} - \frac{1}{2}\cos 2\omega t$$

$$\Rightarrow \quad y = y_0 + A\cos(2\omega t + \pi)$$

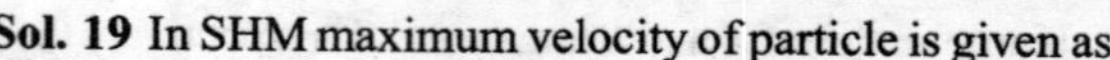

This represents a function of SHM with mean position at $y = y_0$, Amplitude A and angular frequency 2ω.

Where $A = 1/2$ and $y_0 = 1/2$

$$\Rightarrow \quad \text{Time period} = \frac{2\pi}{2\omega} = \frac{\pi}{\omega}$$ **Ans. (D)**

Sol. 16 The basic differential equation of SHM is given as

$$\frac{d^2x}{dt^2} + \omega^2 x = 0$$

where $\omega \rightarrow$ Angular frequency of SHM.

comparing both the above equation, we have

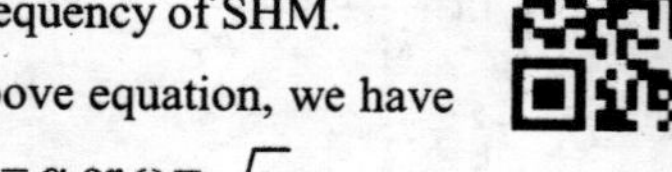

$$\omega^2 = \alpha \text{ or } \omega = \sqrt{\alpha}$$

$$\text{Time period of SHM } T = \frac{2\pi}{\omega} = \frac{2\pi}{\sqrt{\alpha}}$$ **Ans. (B)**

Sol. 17

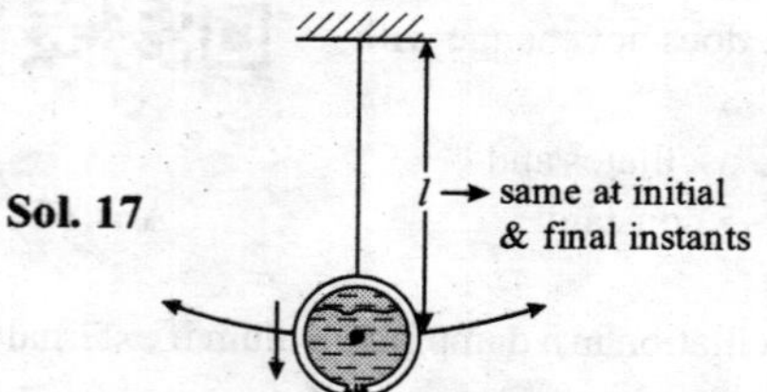

As water flows out, inside the shell water level comes down. Time period of oscillation of pendulum

$$T = 2\pi\sqrt{\frac{l}{g}}$$

As water level goes down

$\Rightarrow$ l increases as centre of mass is going down.

When shell becomes empty then again COM of shell is at its centre $\Rightarrow$ after some time l decreases.

$\Rightarrow$ T first increases then decreases to same value. **Ans. (A)**

Sol. 18 Velocity of particle-1 is

$$v_1 = \frac{dy_1}{dt} = 0.1 \times 100\pi \cos\left(100\pi t + \frac{\pi}{3}\right)$$

$$\Rightarrow \quad v_1 = 10\pi \cos\left(100\pi t + \frac{\pi}{3}\right) \quad \ldots(1)$$

Velocity of particle-2 is

$$v_2 = \frac{dy_2}{dt} = -0.1 \times 100\pi \sin(100\pi t)$$

$$\Rightarrow \quad v_2 = 10\pi \cos\left(100\pi t + \frac{\pi}{2}\right) \quad \ldots(2)$$

Phase difference between v_1 and v_2 is

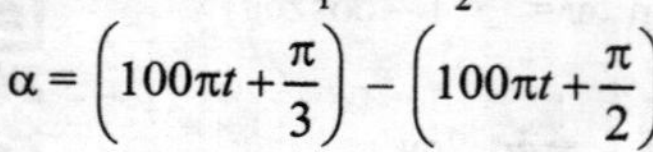

$$\alpha = \left(100\pi t + \frac{\pi}{3}\right) - \left(100\pi t + \frac{\pi}{2}\right)$$

$$\Rightarrow \quad \alpha = -\frac{\pi}{6}$$ **Ans. (A)**

Sol. 19 In SHM maximum velocity of particle is given as

$$v_{max} = A\omega = A\left(\frac{2\pi}{T}\right)$$

$$\Rightarrow \quad T = \frac{2\pi A}{v_{max}} = \frac{2 \times 3.14 \times 7 \times 10^{-3}}{4.4}$$

$$\Rightarrow \quad T = 0.01\text{s}$$ **Ans. (A)**

Sol. 20 $-x \leftarrow$ $-A$ $\quad 0 \quad$ $+A$ $\rightarrow x$

$x = A\sin\omega t$

For the particle in SHM, its KE is given as

$$K = \frac{1}{2}m\omega^2(A^2 - x^2) \quad \ldots(1)$$

$$\text{Given that at time } t \; K = \frac{3}{4}E = \frac{3}{4}\left(\frac{1}{2}m\omega^2 A^2\right)$$

$$\text{From (1) } \frac{1}{2}m\omega^2(A^2 - x^2) = \frac{3}{4}\left(\frac{1}{2}m\omega^2 A^2\right)$$

$$\Rightarrow \quad A^2 - x^2 = \frac{3}{4}A^2$$

$$\Rightarrow \quad x = \pm A/2$$

As $T = 2$s

$$\Rightarrow \quad \omega = \frac{2\pi}{2} = \pi \text{ rad/s}$$

$$\Rightarrow \quad x = A \sin\pi t$$

$$\text{at} \quad x = A/2 = A\sin\pi t$$

$$\Rightarrow \quad \sin\pi t = \frac{1}{2} \Rightarrow \pi t = \frac{\pi}{6} \Rightarrow t = \frac{1}{6}\text{s}$$ **Ans. (A)**

Sol. 21 In SHM

$$a_{max} = \omega^2 A$$

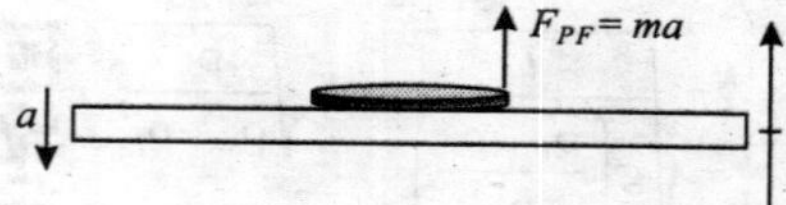

During SHM when platform goes down at acceleration a, coin experiences a pseudo force ma in upwards direction, it will leave contact when

$$ma = mg$$

$$\Rightarrow \quad \omega^2 A = g$$

$$\Rightarrow \quad A = \frac{g}{\omega^2}$$ **Ans. (B)**

Sol. 22 The SHM equation given is of the form

$$x = A\cos\omega t \quad [A = 2 \times 10^{-2}\text{ m}, \omega = \pi \text{ rad/s}]$$

Here particle starts SHM from external position as $t = 0, x = A$.

Particle speed is maximum in SHM when it crosses the mean position which happens at

$-A$ $t = T/4$ $+A$

$x = 0$ $t = 0$

$$t = \frac{T}{4} = \frac{1}{4}\left(\frac{2\pi}{\omega}\right) = \frac{1}{2}\text{s} = 0.5\text{s}$$

Ans.(A)

Sol. 23 SHM equation as

$$x = x_0\cos(\omega t - \pi/4)$$

velocity in SHM is given as

$$v = \frac{dx}{dt} = -\omega x_0\sin(\omega t - \pi/4)$$

Acceleration in SHM is given as

$$a = \frac{dv}{dt} = -\omega^2 x_0\cos(\omega t - \pi/4)$$

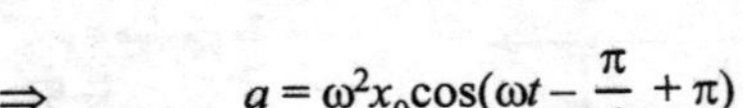

$$\Rightarrow \quad a = \omega^2 x_0\cos(\omega t - \frac{\pi}{4} + \pi)$$

$$\Rightarrow \quad a = \omega^2 x_0\cos(\omega t + \frac{3\pi}{4}) \qquad \ldots(1)$$

Comparing equation-(1) with the given acceleration we get

$$A = \omega^2 x_0$$

and $\delta = \frac{3\pi}{4}$ **Ans. (D)**

Sol. 24 The frequency of oscillation of block in this case is given as

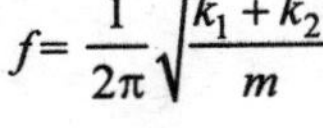

$$f = \frac{1}{2\pi}\sqrt{\frac{k_1 + k_2}{m}}$$

if $k_1 \leftarrow 4k_1$

and $k_2 \leftarrow 4k_2$

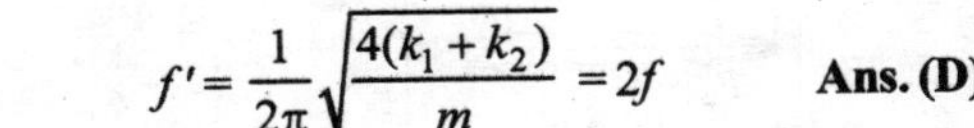

$$\Rightarrow \quad f' = \frac{1}{2\pi}\sqrt{\frac{4(k_1 + k_2)}{m}} = 2f$$

Ans. (D)

Sol. 25 Mean — Extreme

Average KE of a particle in SHM for one period (or $T/4$ period from mean to extreme position) is given as

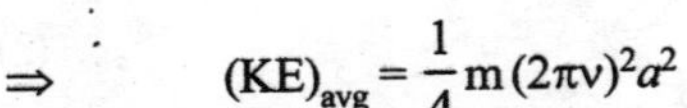

$$(\text{KE})_{\text{avg}} = \frac{1}{2}\text{TE} = \frac{1}{2}\left(\frac{1}{2}m\omega^2 A^2\right)$$

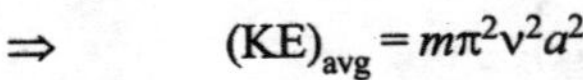

$$\Rightarrow \quad (\text{KE})_{\text{avg}} = \frac{1}{4}\text{m}(2\pi\nu)^2 a^2$$

$$\Rightarrow \quad (\text{KE})_{\text{avg}} = m\pi^2\nu^2 a^2$$

Ans. (A)

Sol. 26 In SHM $\quad a = -\omega^2 x$ and $v = \omega\sqrt{A^2 - x^2}$

(A) $-\omega^2 xT + 2\pi\omega\sqrt{A^2 - x^2}$

(B) $\frac{aT}{v} = -\frac{\omega^2 xT}{\omega\sqrt{A^2 - x^2}}$

(C) $a^2T^2 + 4\pi^2v^2 = \omega^4x^2T^2 + 4\pi^2\omega^2(A^2 - x^2)$

above options are dependent on x which varies with time.

(D) $\frac{aT}{x} = -\omega^2 T$ independent of x. **Ans. (D)**

Sol. 27

m v_2 M v_1

Mean position

$$v_1 = A_1\omega_1 = A_1\sqrt{\frac{k}{M}}$$

Due to addition of m, the new speed of blocks is given by linear momentum conservation as

$$Mv_1 = (m + M)v_2$$

$$v_2 = \frac{Mv_1}{M + m} = A_2\omega_2 \text{ [here } \omega_2 = \sqrt{\frac{k}{m + M}}\text{]}$$

$$\Rightarrow \quad A_2 = \frac{Mv_1}{(M + m)}\cdot\sqrt{\frac{m + M}{k}}$$

$$\Rightarrow \quad A_2 = \frac{M}{\sqrt{M + m}}\cdot\frac{1}{\sqrt{k}}\cdot A_1\sqrt{\frac{k}{m}}$$

$$\Rightarrow \quad A_2 = A_1\sqrt{\frac{M}{M + m}}$$

$$\Rightarrow \quad \frac{A_1}{A_2} = \sqrt{\frac{M + m}{M}}$$

Ans. (B)

Sol. 28 SHM equation of the two particles are given as

X_0 (1) (2) x

$$x_1 = A\sin\omega t$$

$$x_2 = X_0 + A\sin(\omega t + \phi)$$

separation between the particles is

$$x_2 - x_1 = X_0 + A\sin(\omega t + \phi) - A\sin\omega t$$

given that

$$(x_2 - x_1)_{\max} = X_0 + A$$

$$(A\sin(\omega t + \phi) - A\sin\omega t)_{\max} = A$$

$$\Rightarrow \quad \left[2A\cos\left(\omega t + \frac{\phi}{2}\right)\sin\frac{\phi}{2}\right]_{\max} = A$$

$$\Rightarrow \quad \left[\left(2A\sin\frac{\phi}{2}\right)\cos\left(\omega t + \frac{\phi}{2}\right)\right]_{\max} = A$$

Here $\cos\left(\omega t+\frac{\phi}{2}\right)=(+1)_{\max}$

$\Rightarrow \quad 2A\sin\frac{\phi}{2}=A$

$\Rightarrow \quad \phi=\pi/3$

Ans. (D)

Sol. 29 Under the state of equilibrium we have

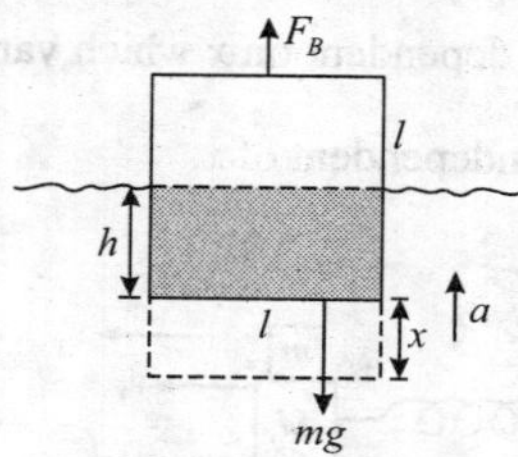

$$F_B=mg$$

$\Rightarrow \quad l^2h\rho g=l^3dg$

$\Rightarrow \quad h\rho=ld \quad \ldots(1)$

After pushing the cube by x, restoring force on it upward will be $F_B'-mg=ma$

$\Rightarrow \quad (h+x)l^2\rho g-mg=ma$

$$hl^2\rho g+xl^2\rho g-l^3dg=l^3da$$

$\Rightarrow \quad a=-\frac{\rho g}{ld}x$

–ve sign denotes opposite direction

Comparing with $\quad a=-\omega^2x$

we get $\quad \omega=\sqrt{\frac{\rho g}{ld}}$

$\Rightarrow$ Time period $\quad T=\frac{2\pi}{\omega}$

$\Rightarrow \quad T=2\pi\sqrt{\frac{ld}{\rho g}}$

Ans. (B)

Sol. 30 For a simple pendulum having damped oscillations its equation of SHM in differential form is given as

$$\frac{d^2x}{dt^2}+bv+\omega^2x=0$$

Solution to above equation is

$$x=A_0e^{-bt/2}\sin(\omega t+\phi)$$

Where $A_0e^{-bt/2}$ = Amplitude envelope.

Given that at $t=\tau$, $\quad A=\frac{A_0}{e}$

we use $\quad A=A_0e^{-bt/2}$

$\Rightarrow \quad \frac{A_0}{e}=A_0e^{-b\tau/2}$

$\Rightarrow \quad \frac{b\tau}{2}=1$

$\Rightarrow \quad \tau=\frac{2}{b}$

Ans. (A)

Sol. 31 This ring oscillates as a compound pendulum for which oscillation period is given as

$$T=2\pi\sqrt{\frac{I}{mgl}}$$

here $I=mR^2+mR^2=2mR^2$; $l=R$

$\Rightarrow \quad 1=2\pi\sqrt{\frac{2mR^2}{mgR}}=2\pi\sqrt{\frac{2R}{g}}$

squaring, we get

$\Rightarrow \quad 1=4\pi^2\times\frac{2R}{g}\Rightarrow R=\frac{1}{8}\text{m}=0.125\text{m}$ **Ans. (A)**

Sol. 32 General SHM equation

$$y(t)=A\sin\omega t$$

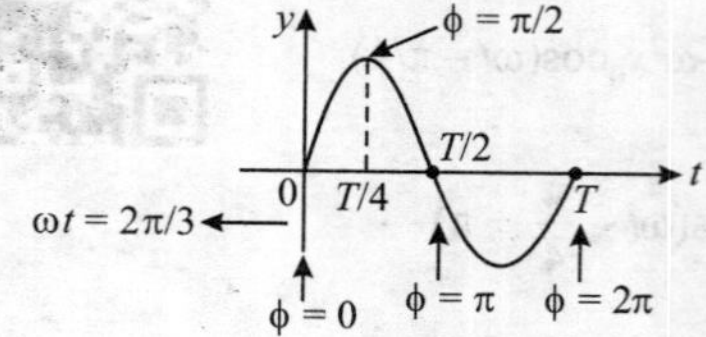

$$y=A\sin(\omega t+\phi)=A\sin\left(\omega t+\frac{2\pi}{3}\right)$$

at $\quad \omega t=-\frac{2\pi}{3}$ the function should start from $y=0$

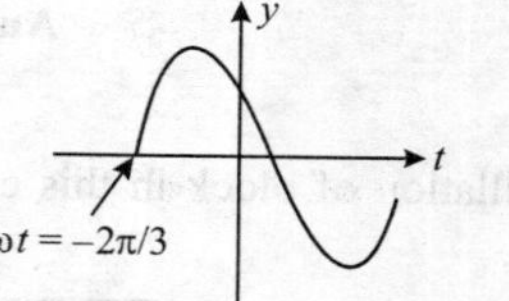

Ans. (A)

Sol. 33

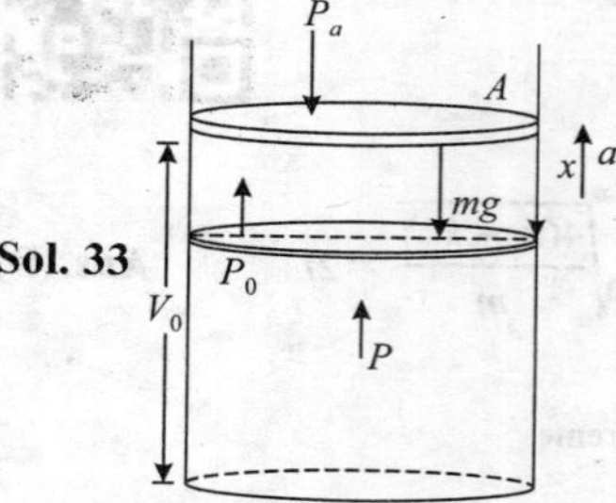

At equilibrium position, we use

$$P_0A=mg+P_aA \quad \ldots(1)$$

If after displacing piston downward gas pressure becomes P then equation of motion of piston is given as

$$PA-mg-P_aA=ma \quad \ldots(2)$$

After pushing the piston down, we use

$$P_0V_0^{\gamma}=P(V_0-Ax)^{\gamma}$$

$$\Rightarrow \qquad P_0V_0^r = PV_0^r\left(1-\frac{Ax}{V_0}\right)^{\gamma}$$

$$\Rightarrow \qquad P = P_0\left(1-\frac{Ax}{V_0}\right)^{-\gamma}$$

Using binomial expansion as $1 >> Ax/V_0$ we have

$$P = P_0\left(1+\frac{\gamma Ax}{V_0}\right)$$

From equation-(2), we have

$$\Rightarrow \quad P_0A + \frac{P_0\gamma A^2x}{V_0} - mg - P_aA = ma$$

$$\Rightarrow \qquad a = -\frac{P_0\gamma A^2}{mV_0} \qquad \ldots(3)$$

–ve sign denotes opposite direction of a compared to x.

Comparing equation-(3) with $a = -\omega^2x$

$$\Rightarrow \qquad \omega = \sqrt{\frac{P_0rA^2}{mV_0}}$$

SHM frequency of piston

$$f = \frac{\omega}{2\pi} = \frac{1}{2\pi}\sqrt{\frac{P_0\gamma A^2}{mV_0}} \qquad \textbf{Ans. (C)}$$

Sol. 34 For a damped oscillator amplitude is given

$$A = A_0e^{-bt/2m}$$

Given that at $t = 5$s we use $A = 0.9A_0$

$$\Rightarrow \qquad 0.9A_0 = A_0e^{-5b/2m}$$

$$\Rightarrow \qquad e^{-5b/2m} = 0.9$$

At $t = 15$s we use

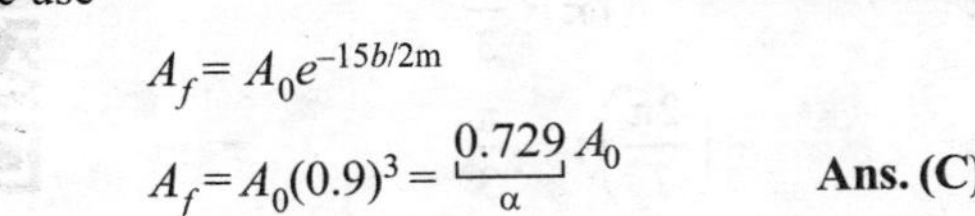

$$A_f = A_0e^{-15b/2m}$$

$$\Rightarrow \qquad A_f = A_0(0.9)^3 = \underbrace{0.729\,A_0}_{\alpha} \qquad \textbf{Ans. (C)}$$

Sol. 35

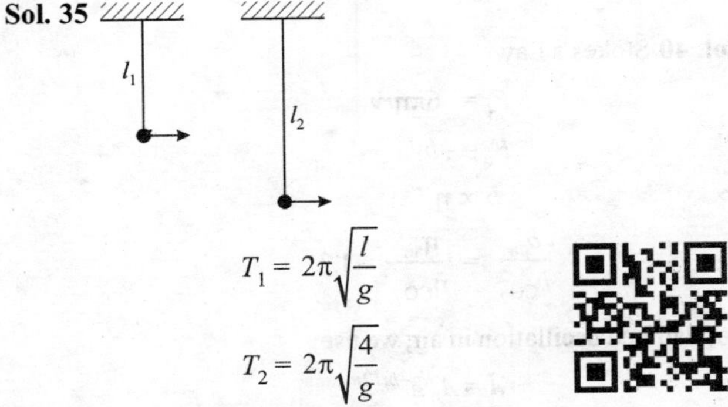

$$T_1 = 2\pi\sqrt{\frac{l}{g}}$$

$$T_2 = 2\pi\sqrt{\frac{4}{g}}$$

As $T_1 < T_2$, shorter pendulum will exceed in phase compared to longer pendulum & these will be in phase again when shorter pendulum will oscillate 1 oscillation more than longer pendulum. If by this time shorter pendulum completes N oscillations.

$$\Rightarrow \qquad N.\,2\pi\sqrt{\frac{1}{g}} = (N-1)\,2\pi\sqrt{\frac{4}{g}}$$

$$\Rightarrow \qquad N = 2N-2 \Rightarrow N = 2 \qquad \textbf{Ans. (A)}$$

Sol. 36 Angular frequency of vertical SHM of mass is

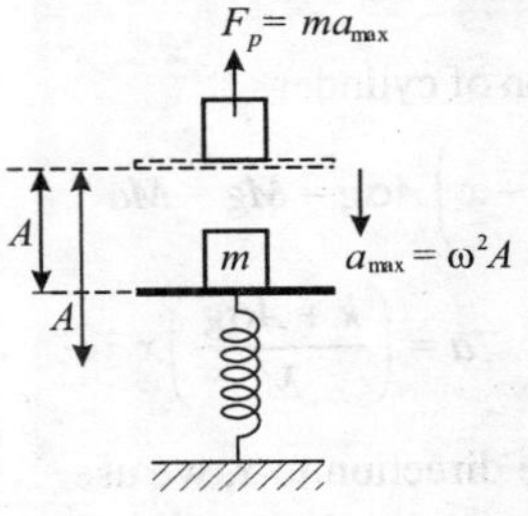

$$\omega = \sqrt{\frac{k}{m}} = \sqrt{500} = 10\sqrt{5} \text{ rad/s}$$

At upper extreme position block will experience a Pseudo force upward w.r. to pan, given as

$$F_P = ma_{max} = m\omega^2A$$

If $F_P > mg$ then block will have tendency to get detached from pan $\quad m\omega^2A > mg$

$$\Rightarrow \qquad A > \frac{g}{\omega^2}$$

$$\Rightarrow \qquad A > \frac{10}{500}$$

$$\Rightarrow \qquad A > 0.02 \text{ m} = 2 \text{ cm}$$

for $A > 2$cm somewhere at position above mean position mass can get detached from pan. **Ans. (A)**

Sol. 37 If at equilibrium spring extension is h then we have

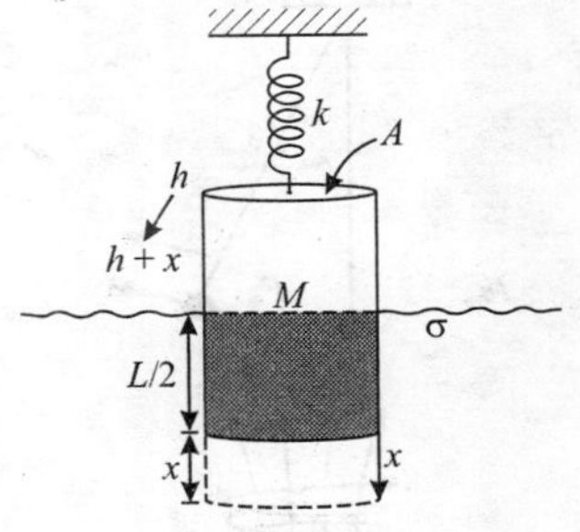

FBD of cylinder

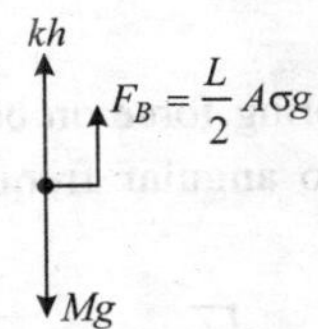

For equation of cylinder, we have

$$kh + \frac{L}{2}A\sigma g = Mg \qquad \ldots(1)$$

After pushing down the cylinder by x, its FBD is

$k(x+h)$, $F_B' = \left(\frac{L}{2}+x\right)A\sigma g$, a, Mg

Equation of motion of cylinder

$$k(x+h)+\left(\frac{L}{2}+x\right)A\sigma g - Mg = Ma$$

$$\Rightarrow \quad a = \left(\frac{k+A\sigma g}{M}\right)x$$

As a is in opposite direction to x, we use

$$a = -\left(\frac{k+A\sigma g}{M}\right)x$$

Comparing with SHM equation $a = -\omega^2 x$, we have frequency of its SHM is

$$\Rightarrow \quad \omega = \sqrt{\frac{k+A\sigma g}{M}}$$

Time period of oscillation $T = \frac{2\pi}{\omega}$

$$\Rightarrow \quad T = 2\pi\sqrt{\frac{M}{k+A\sigma g}}$$

As nothing is specified in question about damping. **Ans. (D)**

Sol. 38 Time period of oscillation for a simple pendulum

$$T = 2\pi\sqrt{\frac{l}{g}}$$

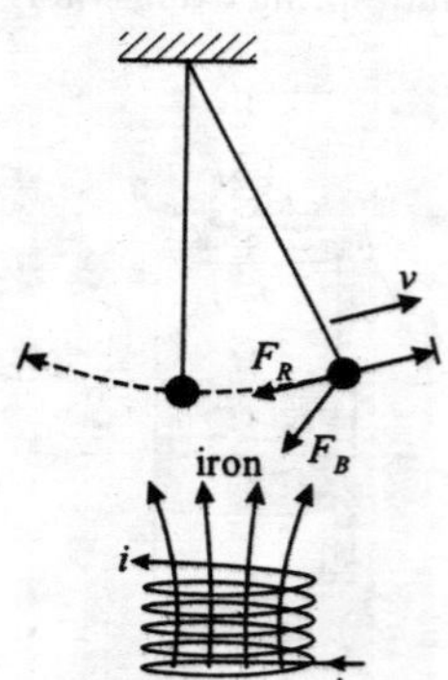

Due to coil the net restoring force on bob during oscillation increases (as shown) so angular frequency of oscillation increases $\Rightarrow$ T decreases.

$$\Rightarrow \quad T < 2\pi\sqrt{\frac{l}{g}}$$

Coil behaves as a magnet and damping is more than in air alone. **Ans. (D)**

Sol. 39

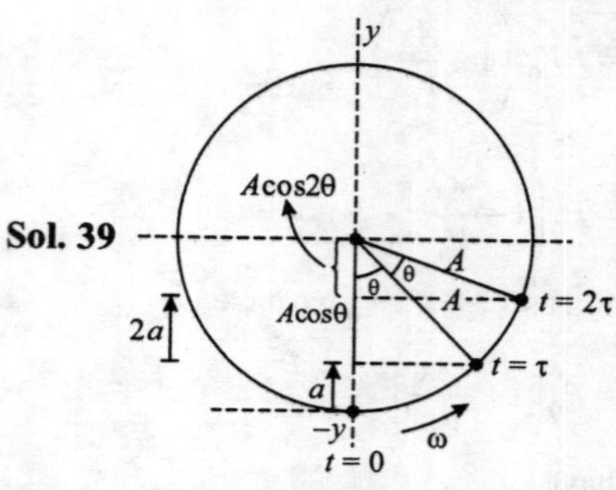

From $t = 0$ to $t = \tau$, displacement of particle in SHM is

$$a = A - A\cos(\omega\tau) \quad \ldots(1)$$

from $t = \tau$ to $t = 2\tau$, displacement of particle is $2a$

$$\Rightarrow \quad 3a = A - A\cos(2\omega\tau) \quad \ldots(2)$$

from equation (1) $\cos(\omega\tau) = \left(\frac{A-a}{A}\right)$

from equation (2) $2\cos^2(\omega\tau) - 1 = \frac{A-3a}{A}$

$$\Rightarrow \quad 2\left(\frac{A-a}{A}\right)^2 - 1 = \frac{A-3a}{A}$$

$$\Rightarrow \quad \frac{2A^2+2a^2-4aA}{A^2} = \frac{2A-3a}{A}$$

$$\Rightarrow \quad 2A^2+2a^2-4aA = 2A^2-3aA$$

$$\Rightarrow \quad 2a^2 = aA$$

$$\Rightarrow \quad A = 2a$$

From equation-(1) we have

$$\cos(\omega\tau) = \left(\frac{A-a}{A}\right) = \frac{1}{2}$$

$$\Rightarrow \quad \omega\tau = \frac{\pi}{3}$$

$$\Rightarrow \quad \left(\frac{2\pi}{T}\right)\tau = \frac{\pi}{3}$$

$$\Rightarrow \quad T = 6\tau$$

Ans. (D)

Sol. 40 Stokes's Law

$$F_v = -6\pi\eta r v$$

if $\quad F_v = -bv$

$$\Rightarrow \quad b \propto \eta$$

$$\Rightarrow \quad \frac{b_{air}}{b_{CO_2}} = \frac{\eta_{air}}{\eta_{CO_2}} = 1.3$$

For damped oscillation in air, we use

$$A = A_0 e^{-bt/2m}$$

at $t = 0, A_0 = 10$ cm

and $t = 40$s, $A = 8$ cm

$$\Rightarrow \quad 8 = 10e^{\frac{-b_{air}\times 40}{2m}} \quad \ldots(1)$$

For damped oscillations in CO_2, we use

at $t=0, A_0=10$ cm

and $t=t_1, A=5$ cm

$$\Rightarrow \quad 5=10e^{\frac{-b_{CO_2}\times t_1}{2m}} \quad \ldots(2)$$

$$\text{from equation-(1)} \quad \frac{40b_{air}}{2m}=\ln\left(\frac{5}{4}\right) \quad \ldots(3)$$

$$\text{from equation-(2)} \quad \frac{t_1 b_{CO_2}}{2m}=\ln(2) \quad \ldots(4)$$

using (4)/(3) we have

$$\frac{t_1}{40(b_{air}/b_{CO_2})}=\frac{\ln(2)}{\ln(5)-\ln(4)}$$

$$\Rightarrow \quad t_1=40\times 1.3\times\frac{0.693}{1.601-0.693}$$

$$\Rightarrow \quad t_1\approx 167\text{s}$$

Ans. (C)

Sol. 41 The time period of a simple pendulum is given as

$$T=2\pi\sqrt{\frac{l}{g}}$$

$$\Rightarrow \quad T^2=4\pi^2\left(\frac{l}{g}\right)$$

$$\Rightarrow \quad g=\frac{4\pi^2}{(T^2/l)}=\frac{4\pi^2}{(\text{slope of graph})}$$

$$\Rightarrow \quad g=\frac{4\pi^2}{4.0}=\pi^2=\left(\frac{22}{7}\right)^2=9.87\text{ m/s}^2$$

Ans. (B)

Sol. 42 As $\quad x=a_1\cos\omega t$

$$y=a_2\cos 2\omega t=a_2(2\cos^2\omega t-1)$$

$\Rightarrow$ at $t=0$, $x=a$ and $y=a_2$

$$\Rightarrow \quad y=a_2\left(\frac{2x^2}{a_1^2}-1\right)$$

$$\Rightarrow \quad x^2=\frac{a_1^2}{2a_2}y+\frac{a_1^2}{2}$$

At $y=0$, $\quad x=\pm a_1/2$

$\Rightarrow$ Trajectory is an upward open parabola. **Ans. (A)**

Sol. 43 In SHM the restoring force $\propto$ displacement from mean position $x=0$.

If $x\neq 0$ at mean position than force is a linear function of x and direction of force always toward mean position.

In option (A), (B) and (C) function depends upon x^2

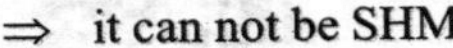

$\Rightarrow$ it can not be SHM

In option (D) it is $(-bx)$

$\Rightarrow \quad F=-bx$ (it is SHM) **Ans. (D)**

Sol. 44 $\quad A=1$ cm

$$\omega=\frac{2\pi}{T}=\frac{2\pi}{0.5}=4\pi\text{ rad/s}$$

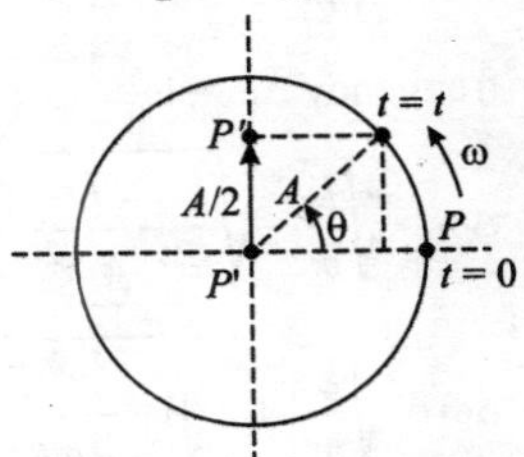

To cover distance from mean position to $A/2$.

$$\text{Phase change is} \quad \theta=\sin^{-1}\frac{A/2}{A}=\sin^{-1}\frac{1}{2}=\frac{\pi}{6}$$

time taken by SHM in going from mean position to $A/2$ is

$$t=\frac{\theta}{\omega}=\frac{\pi/6}{4\pi}=\frac{1}{24}\text{s}$$

Average velocity in moving from $x=0$ to $x=A/2$ is

$$v_{avg}=\frac{\Delta x}{\Delta t}=\frac{A/2}{1/24}$$

$$=12\text{A}=12\text{ cm/s}$$

Ans. (C)

Sol. 45

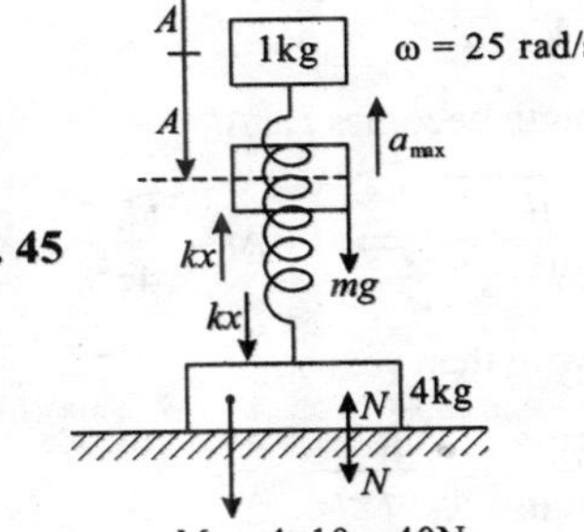

For 4 kg block, force on ground

$$N=Mg+kx|_{max} \quad \ldots(1)$$

Maximum force will be exerted on floor when 1 kg mass is at its lowest extreme so that spring compression is maximum.

Acceleration of 1 kg block at this position is

$$a_{max}=\omega^2 A=(25)^2\times 0.016=10\text{ m/s}^2$$

Equation of motion of 1 kg block is

$$kx-mg=ma_{max}$$

$$kx=mg+ma_{max}=1\times 10+1\times 10$$

$$=20\text{ N (max)}$$

From equation-(1)

$$N_{max}=Mg+kx|_{max}$$

$$=40\times 10+20=60\text{ N}$$

Ans. (C)

Sol. 46 Angular frequency of undamped oscillator

$$\omega_0 = \sqrt{\frac{k}{m}}$$

Change in angular frequency $\Delta\omega = \omega_0 - \omega$

$$\Rightarrow \quad \Delta\omega = \sqrt{\frac{k}{m}} - \sqrt{\frac{k}{m} - \frac{r^2}{4m^2}}$$

$$\Rightarrow \quad \Delta\omega = \sqrt{\frac{k}{m}}\left(1 - \sqrt{1 - \frac{r^2}{4mk}}\right)$$

$$\Rightarrow \quad \frac{\Delta\omega}{\omega_0} = \left(1 - \sqrt{1 - \frac{0.08}{4}}\right)$$

$$\Rightarrow \quad \frac{\Delta\omega}{\omega_0} = 1 - \sqrt{1 - 0.02} = 1 - (1 - 0.01) = 0.01$$

As $\quad T = \dfrac{2\pi}{\omega}$

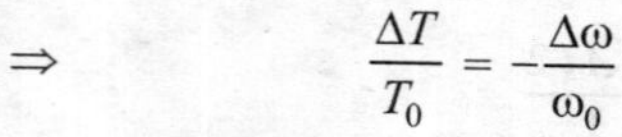

$$\Rightarrow \quad \frac{\Delta T}{T_0} = -\frac{\Delta\omega}{\omega_0}$$

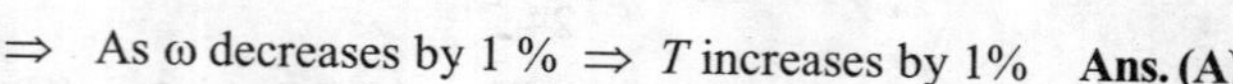

$\Rightarrow$ As ω decreases by 1 % $\Rightarrow$ T increases by 1% **Ans. (A)**

Sol. 47 If for length l of pendulum time period is T then

$$T = 2\pi\sqrt{\frac{l}{g}} \Rightarrow l = \frac{T^2 g}{4\pi^2} \qquad \ldots(1)$$

after adding a mass M, if length becomes $l + \Delta l$

then we have $\quad T_M = 2\pi\sqrt{\dfrac{l + \Delta l}{g}} \Rightarrow l + \Delta l = \dfrac{T_M^2 g}{4\pi^2} \qquad \ldots(2)$

If Y is Young's modulus of wire than we use

$$Y = \frac{\text{Stress}}{\text{Strain}} = \frac{Mg / A}{\Delta l / l}$$

$$\Rightarrow \quad \frac{\Delta l}{l} = \frac{Mg}{YA}$$

We use (2)/(1)

$$\Rightarrow \quad 1 + \frac{\Delta l}{l} = \left(\frac{T_M}{T}\right)^2$$

$$\Rightarrow \quad 1 + \frac{Mg}{YA} = \left(\frac{T_M}{T}\right)^2$$

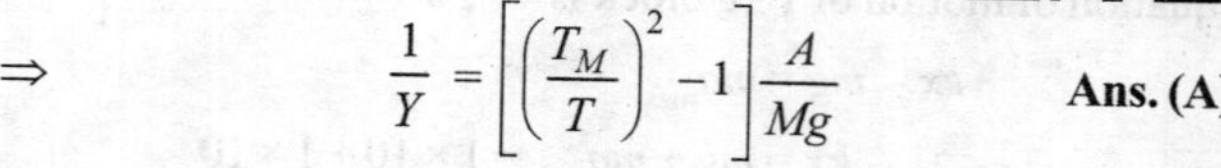

$$\Rightarrow \quad \frac{1}{Y} = \left[\left(\frac{T_M}{T}\right)^2 - 1\right]\frac{A}{Mg}$$

Ans. (A)

Sol. 48 For SHM, KE and PE as a function of displacement are given as

$$K_x = \frac{1}{2}m\omega^2(A^2 - x^2)$$

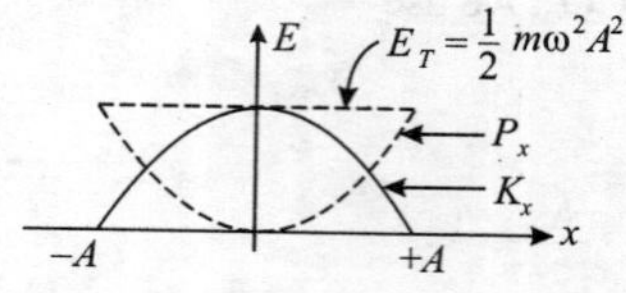

and $\quad P_x = \dfrac{1}{2}m\omega^2 x^2$ **Ans. (B)**

Sol. 49 In damped oscillations, mechanical energy as a function of time is given as

$$E = E_0 e^{-bt/m} \qquad \ldots(1)$$

at $t = 0, E_0 = 45$ J

and at $t = 15$s, $E = 15$ J

$$\Rightarrow \quad 15 = 45\, e^{-(b/m)15}$$

$$\Rightarrow \quad \frac{1}{3} = e^{-15(b/m)}$$

$$\Rightarrow \quad \ln(3) = 15(b/m)$$

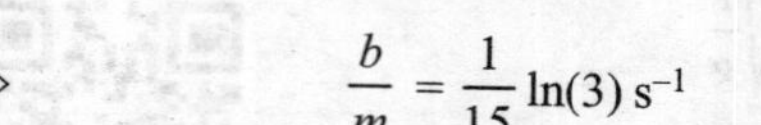

$$\Rightarrow \quad \frac{b}{m} = \frac{1}{15}\ln(3)\ \text{s}^{-1}$$

Ans. (D)

Sol. 50 As $\quad x = a\sin\omega t \quad$ at $t = 0, x = 0$

and $\quad y = a\sin 2\omega t \quad y = 0$

$\Rightarrow$ Answer could be option (A) or (C), so we check both here

(A) In one half oscillation of y, x completes its one oscillation

$\Rightarrow$ frequency of x is twice that of y.

(C) In one half oscillation of x, y completes its one oscillation

$\Rightarrow$ frequency of y is twice that of x, so this is correct answer for the given equation.

Ans. (C)

Sol. 51 Given that at $t = 0$, $x = 0$ and oscillator starts from rest $v = 0$. Checking given option for that

(A) $x = C(\sin t + \frac{1}{2}\cos t)|_{t=0} = C(0 + \frac{1}{2}) \neq 0 \quad \times$

(B) $x = C(\cot t - \frac{1}{2}\cos t)|_{t=0} \to \infty \quad \times$

(C) $x = C(\sin t + \frac{1}{2}\cos t)|_{t=0} = 0 \quad ✓$

$v = \dfrac{dx}{dt} = C(\cos t - \cos 2t)|_{t=0} = 0 \quad ✓$

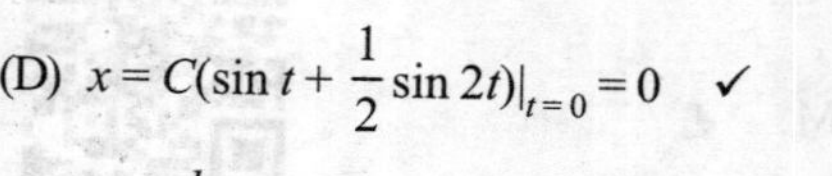

(D) $x = C(\sin t + \frac{1}{2}\sin 2t)|_{t=0} = 0 \quad ✓$

$v = \dfrac{dx}{dt} = C(\cos t + \cos 2t)|_{t=0} = 2\,C \quad \times$

Ans. (C)

Sol. 52 Speed of particle when it is at a distance $\frac{2A}{3}$ from mean position is

$$v = \omega\sqrt{A^2 - \left(\frac{2A}{3}\right)^2} = \frac{\sqrt{5}}{3}A\omega$$

After increasing the speed 3 times if new amplitude becomes A' then we use

$$3v = \omega\sqrt{(A')^2 - \left(\frac{2A}{3}\right)^2} = \sqrt{5}\,A\text{w}$$

$$\Rightarrow \quad 5A^2\omega^2 = \omega^2\left((A')^2 - \frac{4A^2}{9}\right)$$

$$\Rightarrow \quad (A')^2 = \frac{49}{9}A^2 \Rightarrow A' = \frac{7}{3}A$$ **Ans. (D)**

Sol. 53

At upper extreme position of piston washer experiences maximum upward Pseudo force w.r. to piston.

If $F_p \geq mg$ then it looses contact from piston

$$\Rightarrow \quad m\omega^2 A = mg$$

$$\Rightarrow \quad \omega = \sqrt{\frac{g}{A}}$$

$$\Rightarrow \quad f = \frac{1}{2\pi}\sqrt{\frac{10}{0.07}} = \frac{1}{2\pi}\sqrt{\frac{100}{7}} = \frac{1}{2}\sqrt{14.2}$$

$$\Rightarrow \quad f \approx \frac{3.8}{2} = 1.9\text{ Hz}$$ **Ans. (B)**

Sol. 54

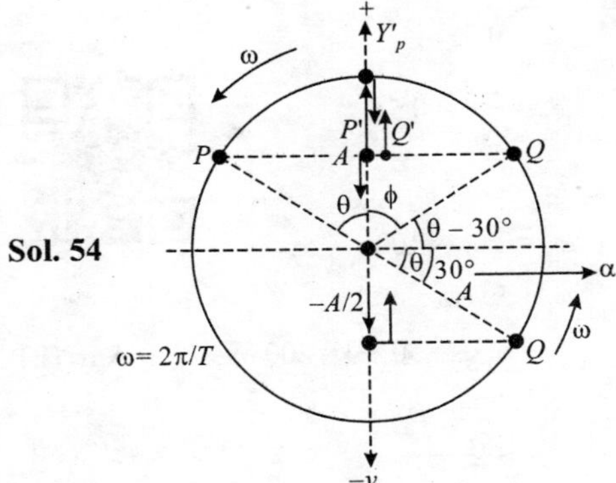

$A \sin\alpha = A/2$

$\Rightarrow \quad \sin\alpha = 1/2$

$\Rightarrow \quad \alpha = 30°$

P' and Q' are projections of P and Q in uniform circular motion along YY' which are in SHM.

In figure shown we have

$$\phi = 90° - (\theta - 30°) = 120° - \theta$$

and we have $\theta = \phi$

$$\Rightarrow \quad \theta = 120 - \theta \Rightarrow \theta = 60° = \pi/3$$

Time taken by P and Q to traverse angle $\pi/3$ is

$$t = \frac{\theta}{\omega} = \frac{\pi/3}{2\pi/T} = \frac{T}{6}$$ **Ans. (D)**

14.1 Wave Motion

Sol. 1 The given wave equation is

$$y = 10^{-4}\sin\left(600t - 2x + \frac{\pi}{3}\right) \quad \ldots(1)$$

The general wave equation is expressed as

$$y = A\sin(\omega t - kx + \alpha) \quad \ldots(2)$$

Comparing equation-(1) & (2), we have

$$\omega = 600 \text{ rad/s}$$

$$k = 2\text{ m}^{-1}$$

$$\Rightarrow \text{ Wave speed } \quad v = \frac{\omega}{k}$$

$$= \frac{600}{2} = 300 \text{ m/s}$$ **Ans. (A)**

Sol. 2 If we use sound level of I, w.r. to I_{01}

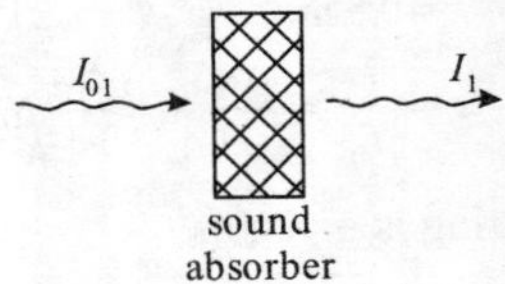

We have

$$L_{I_{01}} - L_{I_1} = 20\text{ dB}$$

$$\Rightarrow \quad 10\log_{10}\left(\frac{I_{01}}{I_0}\right) - 10\log_{10}\left(\frac{I_1}{I_0}\right) = 20$$

$$\Rightarrow \quad 10\log_{10}\left(\frac{I_{01}}{I_1}\right) = 20$$

$$\Rightarrow \quad \frac{I_{01}}{I_1} = 10^2 = 100 \Rightarrow I_1 = \frac{I_{01}}{100}$$ **Ans. (D)**

Sol. 3 The given wave equation is

$$y = 0.005\cos(\alpha x - \beta t) \quad \ldots(1)$$

General expression for a wave equation is

$$y = A\cos(kx - \omega t) \quad \ldots(2)$$

$$A\cos(kx - \omega t) = A\sin(\omega t - kx + \phi)$$

Comparing (1) and (2) we have

$$\alpha = k = \frac{2\pi}{\lambda} = \frac{2\pi}{0.08} = 25\pi$$

and $$\beta = \omega = \frac{2\pi}{T} = \frac{2\pi}{2} = \pi \quad \textbf{Ans. (A)}$$

Sol. 4 In gaseous medium speed of sound is given as

$$v = \sqrt{\frac{\gamma RT}{M}}$$

$$\Rightarrow \quad \frac{v_{O_2}}{v_{He}} = \sqrt{\frac{\gamma_{O_2}}{M_{O_2}} \times \frac{M_{He}}{\gamma_{He}}}$$

$$\Rightarrow \quad v_{He} = v_{O_2}\sqrt{\frac{\gamma_{He} M_{O_2}}{\gamma_{O_2} M_{He}}} = 460\sqrt{\frac{\frac{5}{3}\times 32}{\frac{7}{5}\times 4}}$$

$$\Rightarrow \quad v_{He} = 460\sqrt{\frac{200}{21}} \text{ m/s}$$ **Ans. (A)**

Sol. 5 Given wave equation is

$$y = 0.02 \sin\left[2\pi\left(\frac{t}{0.04} - \frac{x}{0.05}\right)\right] \quad \ldots(1)$$

General equation of a wave equation is of the form

$$y = A \sin\left[2\pi\left(\frac{t}{T_0} - \frac{x}{A}\right)\right] \quad \ldots(2)$$

Comparing (1) and (2) gives

$$T_0 = 0.04 \text{ s}$$

$$\lambda = 0.5 \text{ m}$$

$$\Rightarrow \text{ Wave speed} \quad v = \frac{\lambda}{T_0} = \frac{0.5}{0.04} = \frac{50}{4} \text{ m/s}$$

Wave speed on a string is given as

$$v = \sqrt{\frac{T}{4}}$$

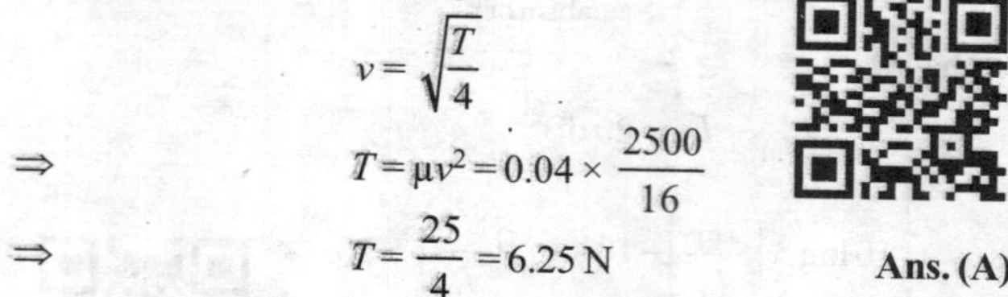

$$\Rightarrow \quad T = \mu v^2 = 0.04 \times \frac{2500}{16}$$

$$\Rightarrow \quad T = \frac{25}{4} = 6.25 \text{ N}$$ **Ans. (A)**

Sol. 6 As sound wave intensities are given as

$$I = 2\pi^2 n^2 A^2 \rho v$$

For a given medium $\rho, v \rightarrow$ constant $\Rightarrow I \propto x^2 A^2$

in S-I for first wave $n_1 = \frac{\omega}{2\pi}$; $A_1 = 2a$

For second wave $n_2 = \frac{2\omega}{2\pi}$; $A_2 = a$

$\Rightarrow I_1 = I_2$

S-I is true

As Intensity $\propto n^2 A^2$

$\Rightarrow$ S-II is false **Ans. (B)**

Sol. 7 The given expression is

$$y = e^{-(ax^2 + bt^2 + 2\sqrt{abxt})}$$

$$y = e^{-[\sqrt{ax} + \sqrt{bt}]^2}$$

It is a function of $(c_1 x + c_2 t)$ thus it represents a propagating wave. +ve sign shows that wave is travelling in $-x$ direction.

having $\omega = \sqrt{b}$ and $k = \sqrt{a}$

$$\Rightarrow \text{ Wave speed} \quad v = \frac{\omega}{k} = \sqrt{\frac{b}{a}}$$ **Ans. (D)**

Sol. 8 If a wave displacement function is given as

$$y = f(x) \text{ at } t = 0$$

For a wave travelling in +x direction at speed v, then at time $t = t$, the displacement function is given as

$$y = f(x - vt)$$

Given at $t = 0$

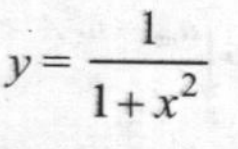

$$y = \frac{1}{1+x^2}$$

So at time t the function becomes

$$y = \frac{1}{1+(x-vt)^2} \quad \ldots(1)$$

In question at $t = 2$s displacement function is given as

$$y = \frac{1}{1+(x-1)^2} \quad \ldots(2)$$

Comparing equation-(2) with equation-(1), we get

$$vt = 1|_{t=2s}$$

$$\Rightarrow \quad v = \frac{1}{2} = 0.5 \text{ m/s}$$ **Ans. (C)**

Sol. 9 Standard wave equation in a medium can be given as

$$y = A\cos(kx - \omega t)$$

Comparing y_1 with above standard equation we get

$$A = 0.05 \text{ m}$$

and $$k_1 = \frac{2\pi}{\lambda_1} = 0.5\pi$$

$$\Rightarrow \quad \lambda_1 = 4 \text{ m}$$

$$\omega_1 = 2\pi n_1 = 100\pi$$

$$\Rightarrow \quad n_1 = 50 \text{ Hz}$$

Wave velocity $v = n_1\lambda_1 = 50 \times 4 = 200$ m/s **Ans. (B)**

Sol. 10

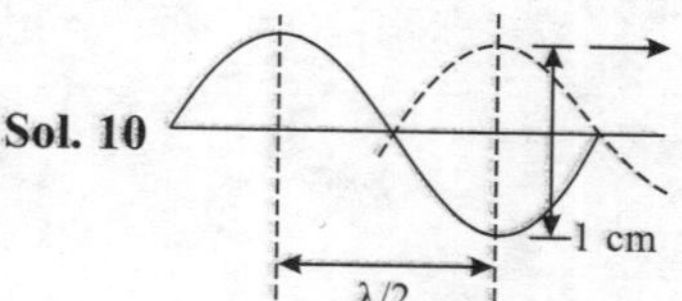

Distance between a crest and neighbouring trough is

$$\frac{\lambda}{2} = 0.4 \text{ cm}$$

$$\Rightarrow \quad \lambda = 0.8 \text{ cm}$$

It is given that $2A = 1$ cm $\Rightarrow$ $A = 0.5$ cm

As distance between two neighbouring crests is λ

$$\Rightarrow \quad t = \frac{\lambda}{v} = 0.4 \text{ s}$$

$$\Rightarrow \quad v = \frac{\lambda}{0.4} = \frac{0.8}{0.4} = 2 \text{ cm/s}$$

$\Rightarrow$ Maximum speed of vibrating particles

$$v_{max} = A\omega = A\left(\frac{2\pi v}{\lambda}\right) = \frac{0.5 \times 2\pi \times 2}{0.8}$$

$$\Rightarrow \quad v_{max} = \frac{5\pi}{2} \text{ cm/s}$$

Ans. (B)

Sol. 11

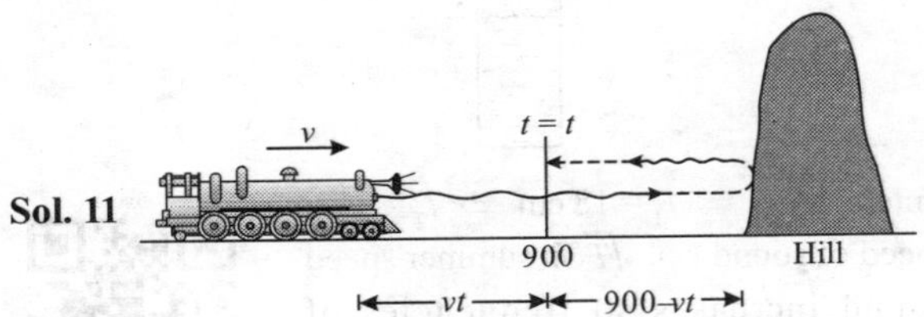

In time t when reflected sound is heard by the driver then distance travelled by sound is

$$900 + (900 - vt) = v_s . t$$

at $\quad t = 5$s

$$\Rightarrow \quad 900 + 900 - 5v = 330 \times 5 = 1650$$

$$\Rightarrow \quad 5v = 1800 - 1650 = 150$$

$$\Rightarrow \quad v = \frac{150}{5} = 30 \text{ m/s}$$

Ans. (D)

Sol. 12 Given equation of SHW is

$$y = \frac{10}{\pi}\sin\left(\frac{2\pi}{T}t - \frac{2\pi}{\lambda}x\right)$$

Comparing with $\quad y = A\sin(\omega t - kx)$

Amplitude $A = \frac{10}{\pi}$; $\omega = \frac{2\pi}{T}$; $k = \frac{2\pi}{\lambda}$

As wave velocity $\quad = 2 \times$ maximum particle velocity

$$\frac{\omega}{k} = 2 \times A\omega$$

$$\Rightarrow \quad \frac{\lambda}{2\pi} = 2 \times \frac{10}{\pi}$$

$$\Rightarrow \quad \lambda = 40 \text{ cm}$$

Ans. (A)

Sol. 13

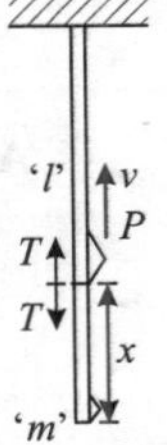

Tension at point P in string is

$$T = \left(\frac{m}{l}x\right)g$$

Wave speed in string at point P is

$$v = \sqrt{\frac{T}{\mu}} = \sqrt{\frac{\left(\frac{m}{l} \times g\right)}{\frac{m}{l}}} = \sqrt{xg}$$

$$\Rightarrow \quad \frac{dx}{dt} = \sqrt{xg}$$

$$\Rightarrow \quad \int_0^l \frac{dx}{\sqrt{x}} = \int_0^t \sqrt{g}\,dt$$

$$\Rightarrow \quad \left[2\sqrt{x}\right]_0^l = \sqrt{g}t$$

$$\Rightarrow \quad t = \frac{2\sqrt{l}}{\sqrt{g}} = 2\sqrt{\frac{20}{10}} = 2\sqrt{2} \text{ s}$$

Ans. (C)

14.2 Stationary Waves and Beats

Sol. 1 Fundamental frequencies of A and B are

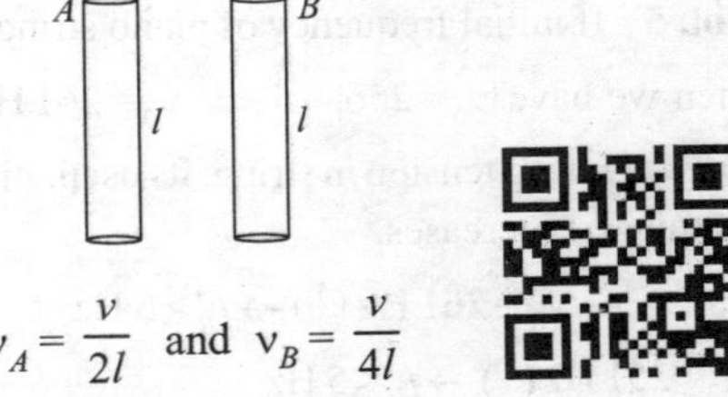

$$\nu_A = \frac{v}{2l} \quad \text{and} \quad \nu_B = \frac{v}{4l}$$

Here we ignore end correction

$$\Rightarrow \quad \frac{\nu_A}{\nu_B} = \frac{2}{1}$$

Ans. (C)

Sol. 2 If the frequency of unknown fork is ν_0 then we use Initially

$$|\nu_0 - 288| = 4$$

$$\Rightarrow \quad \nu_0 = 292 \text{ cps or } 284 \text{ cps}$$

On loading ν_0 with some wax its frequency decreases & later it produces 2 beats/s with 288 cps fork.

After loading with wax $\nu_0 \rightarrow \nu_0' = 292\downarrow$ or $284\downarrow$

for 292 → $f_B = 290 \Rightarrow$ 2 beats/sec

for 284 → $f_B > 4$ beats/s

⇒ 2 beats/s is not possible with 284 Hz. **Ans. (B)**

Sol. 3 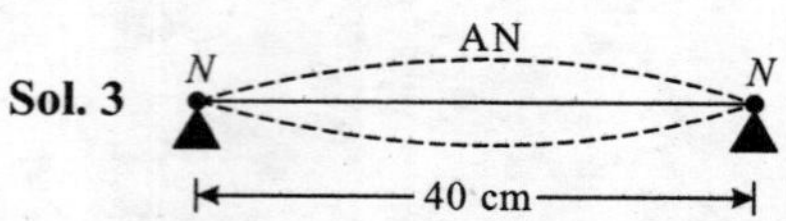

Maximum wavelength of stationary wave in a clamped string is for fundamental frequency given as

$$\nu_0 = \frac{v}{2l}$$

⇒ wavelength $\lambda = 2l = 2 \times 40 = 80$ cm **Ans. (B)**

Sol. 4 General equation of a stationary wave can be

$$y = 2A \sin kx \sin(\omega t + \alpha)$$

→ at $x = 0$; $R = 2A \sin kx = 0$

⇒ Node

or $y = 2A \cos kx \sin(\omega t + \alpha)$

→ at $x = 0$; $R = 2A \cos kx = 2A$

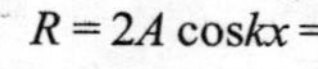

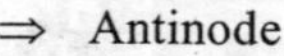

⇒ Antinode

As one wave is $y_1 = a \sin(\omega t - kx)$

with option (A) → $y_R = a \sin(\omega t - kx) + a \sin(\omega t + kx)$

$= 2A \sin\omega t \cos kx$

with option (B) → $y_R = a \sin(\omega t - kx) + a \sin(\omega t + kx)$

$= -2A \cos\omega t \sin kx$ **Ans. (B)**

Sol. 5 If initial frequency of piano string is ν_0.

then we have $|\nu_0 - 256| = 5 \Rightarrow \nu_0 = 261$ Hz or 251 Hz

On increasing tension in string, its oscillation frequency increases.

⇒ $\nu_0 \to \nu_0' = 261$ Hz (↑) → $f_B' > 5$ Hz

or 251 Hz (↑) → $f_B' < 5$ Hz

Giving that $f_B' = 2$ Hz

final beat frequency ⇒ $\nu_0 = 251$ Hz **Ans. (C)**

Sol. 6 Initially we have $\nu_1 = 200$ Hz and $\nu_2 = ?$

$$f_B = |200 - \nu_2| = 4 \text{ Hz}$$

⇒ $\nu_2 = 196$ Hz or 204Hz

On loading some tape on fork-2, its frequency decreases

$$\nu_2 \to \nu_2'$$

we use $\nu_2' = 196$ ↓ or 204 ↓

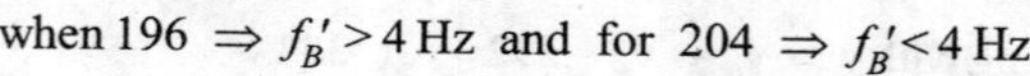

when 196 ⇒ $f_B' > 4$ Hz and for 204 ⇒ $f_B' < 4$ Hz

later it is given that

$$f_B' = |200 - \nu_2'| = 6 \text{ Hz}$$

⇒ $\nu_2 = 196$ Hz **Ans. (C)**

Sol. 7 For a clamped string oscillations all the horizontal frequencies of fundamental frequency are available for resonance so for two successive resonant frequency, we use

$$n_2 - n_1 = n_0 \ (n_0 = \text{fundamental frequency})$$

⇒ $n_0 = 420 - 315 = 105$ Hz **Ans. (A)**

Sol. 8 For resonance column experiment we know that second resonance occurs at 3 times the length of first resonance.

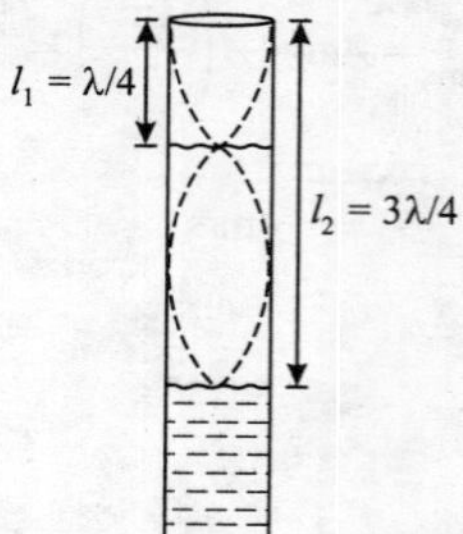

In winter $l_1 = 18$ cm ⇒ $l_2 = 54$ cm

As speed of sound $v \propto \sqrt{T}$ in summer speed of sound increases so frequencies of oscillating column are given as (frequency of tuning fork)

$$\nu_1 = \frac{v}{4l_1} = \frac{3v}{4l_2} \to \text{constant}$$

In summer as v increases ⇒ for same experiment l_2 also increases. **Ans. (B)**

Sol. 9 Considering two waves at a time beat frequency can be given as

$$\left.\begin{array}{l}\nu_1 = \nu - 1 \\ \nu_2 = \nu\end{array}\right] \to f_B = 1\text{Hz}$$ and

time of maxima $t = 0, 1, 2, 3, \ldots\ldots$ s

and $$\left.\begin{array}{l}\nu_2 = \nu \\ \nu_2 = \nu + 1\end{array}\right] \to f_B' = 1\text{Hz}$$

⇒ $t_m = 0, 1, 2, 3, \ldots\ldots$ s

and $$\left.\begin{array}{l}\nu_2 = \nu - 1 \\ \nu_3 = \nu + 1\end{array}\right] \to f_B'' = 2\text{Hz}$$

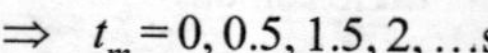

⇒ $t_m = 0, 0.5, 1.5, 2, \ldots$ s

So 0.5, 1.5 .... Very low intensity maxima

and 0, 1, 2, ... Higher maximas are produced with high intensity.

⇒ Time difference = 1s

⇒ $$f_{Bf} = \frac{1}{T} = 1 \text{ Hz}$$ **Ans. (B)**

Sol. 10 Superposition of the two waves is giving resulting displacement as $y = y_1 + y_2$

$\Rightarrow \quad y = A\sin(\omega t - kx) + A\sin(\omega t + kx)$

$\Rightarrow \quad y = 2A\sin\omega t\cos kx$

$\Rightarrow \quad y = R\sin\omega t$

Where $R = 2A\cos kx$ is amplitude of different medium particles.

For nodes $R = 2A\cos kx = 0$

$\Rightarrow \quad \cos kx = 0$

$\Rightarrow \quad kx = (2N+1)\frac{\pi}{2}\ ; N = 0, 1, 2, \ldots\ldots$

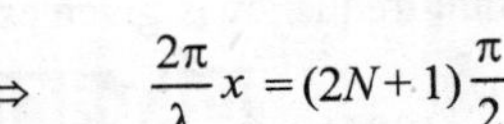

$\Rightarrow \quad \frac{2\pi}{\lambda}x = (2N+1)\frac{\pi}{2}$

$\Rightarrow \quad x = (2N+1)\frac{\lambda}{4}$ (position of Nodes) **Ans. (A)**

Sol. 11 Fundamental oscillations of an open pipe $\Rightarrow$ Antinodes at open ends and 1 node at middle

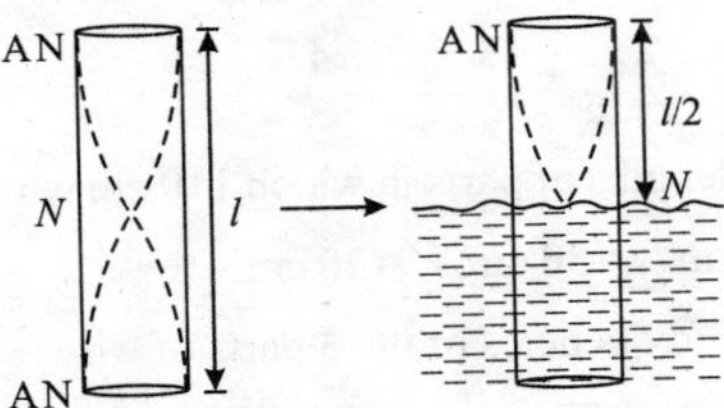

For closed pipe $\rightarrow$ Antinode at open end and node at closed end.

By looking at figures, the wavelength of sound is same in the two cases $\Rightarrow$ frequency is also same

To verify: $f_{\text{open}} = \frac{v}{2l} = f$

$f_{\text{closed}} = \frac{v}{4l'} = \frac{v}{4(l/2)}$

$= \frac{v}{2l} = f$ **Ans. (B)**

Sol. 12 Destructive interference is produced for coherent waves (same frequency) with phase difference of $(2N+1)\pi$.

In y_1 & y_2 frequency in same & phase difference is π so there SHW will produce Destructive interference.

Stationary waves are produced by superposition of two coherent waves travelling in opposite direction, it happens in y_3 & y_4. **Ans. (D)**

Sol. 13 A general equation of stationary wave can be given in two ways

$y = A_0\sin kx\sin(\omega t + \phi)$ for a node at $x = 0$

$y = A_0\cos kx\sin(\omega t + \phi)$ for an Antinode at $x = 0$

As one wave is

$y_1 = a\cos(kx - \omega t)$

if $\quad y_2 = -a\cos(kx + \omega t) = a\cos(kx + \omega t + \pi)$

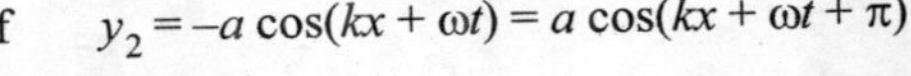

by superposition

$y = y_1 + y_2 = a[\cos(kx - \omega t) - \cos(kx + \omega t)]$

$= 2a\sin kx\cos\omega t$

at $\quad x = 0$ there will be a Node **Ans. (B)**

Sol. 14

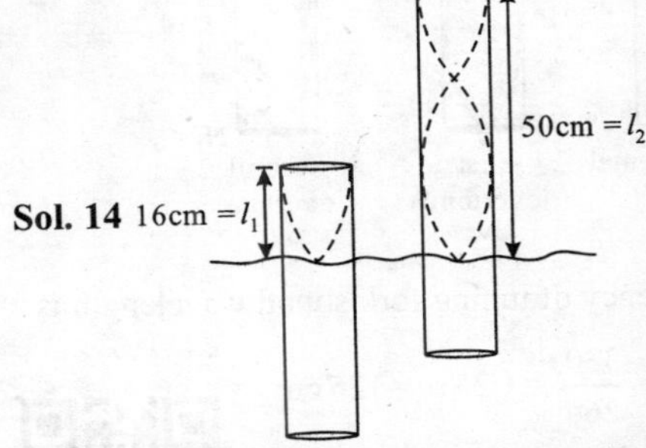

As l_2 is approx 3 times l_1 (but not exact) so we need to account end correction (say 'e'). If v is the velocity of sound than we use

$$500 = \frac{v}{4(l_1 + e)} \qquad \ldots(1)$$

and $$500 = \frac{3v}{4(l_1 + e)} \qquad \ldots(2)$$

From (1) and (2)

$\Rightarrow \quad \frac{v}{4(0.16 + e)} = \frac{3v}{4(0.5 + e)}$

$\Rightarrow \quad 0.5 + e = 0.48 + 3e$

$\Rightarrow \quad 2e = 0.02$

$\Rightarrow \quad e = 0.01$ cm

From equation-(1)

$$500 = \frac{v}{4(0.16 + 0.01)} = \frac{v}{4 \times 0.17}$$

$\Rightarrow \quad v = 500 \times 4 \times 0.17 = 20 \times 17 = 340$ m/s

When tube is pulled out of water, it behaves like an open tube

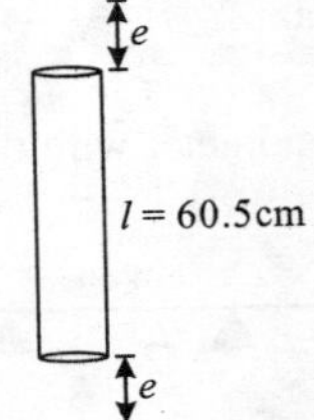

fundamental frequency of the open tube is

$$\nu_0 = \frac{v}{2(l + 2e)} = \frac{340}{2(0.605 + 0.02)}$$

$\Rightarrow \quad \nu_0 = \frac{340}{2 \times 0.625} = \frac{340}{1.25} = 272$ Hz

An open pipe has all restoring frequency which are integral multiple of its fundamental frequency. So lowest two frequencies are ν_0 and $2\nu_0 \Rightarrow 272$ Hz & 544 Hz **Ans. (D)**

Sol. 15 For a closed pipe, it resonates with a given frequency if its length is odd multiple of $\lambda/4$.

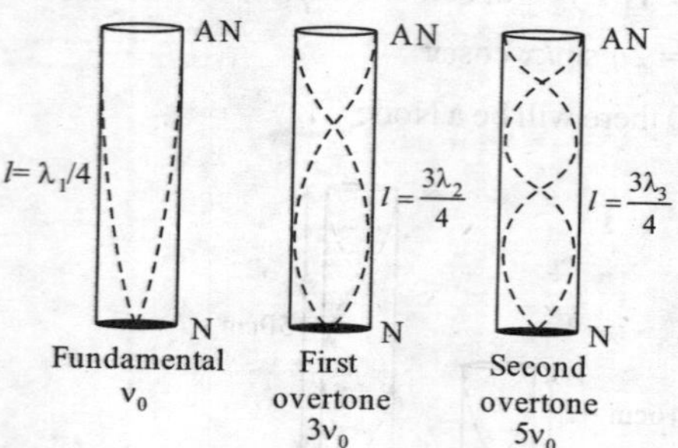

For the given frequency of tuning fork sound wavelength is

$$\lambda = \frac{v}{\nu} = \frac{330}{264} = 1.25\text{ m} = 125\text{ cm}$$

The possible length for closed pipe to resonate with above tuning fork are

$$l = \lambda/4, 3\lambda/4, 5\lambda/4, \ldots\ldots$$

$$\Rightarrow \quad l = 31.25\text{ cm}, 93.75\text{ cm}, \ldots$$ **Ans. (B)**

Sol. 16 For a stretched string if elastic deformation is there with tension T in it than we have

$$Y = \frac{\text{Stress}}{\text{Strain}} = \frac{T/A}{\text{Strain}}$$

$\Rightarrow$ String tension $T = YA \times$ Strain

Fundamental frequency of a clamped wire is given as

$$\nu_0 = \frac{1}{2l}\sqrt{\frac{T}{\mu}} = \frac{1}{2l}\sqrt{\frac{YA(\text{Strain})}{\rho A}}$$

$$\Rightarrow \quad \nu_0 = \frac{1}{2l}\sqrt{\frac{Y(\text{Strain})}{\rho}}$$

$$\Rightarrow \quad \nu_0 = \frac{1}{2\times 1.5}\sqrt{\frac{2.2\times 10^{11}\times 0.01}{7.7\times 10^3}}$$

$$\Rightarrow \quad \nu_0 = 178.2\text{ Hz}$$ **Ans. (B)**

Sol. 17 In a damped sonometer wire if l is the length between bridges then

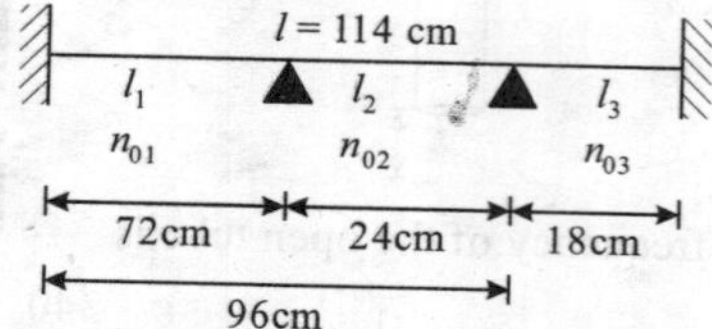

Its fundamental frequency is given as

$$\nu_0 = \frac{v}{2l} = \frac{1}{2l}\sqrt{\frac{T}{\mu}}$$

As $n \propto \frac{1}{l} \Rightarrow \frac{1}{l_1} : \frac{1}{l_2} : \frac{1}{l_3} = 1:3:4$

$$\Rightarrow \quad l_1 : l_2 : l_3 = 12:4:3$$

$$\Rightarrow \quad l_1 = \frac{12}{19}\times 114 = 72\text{ cm}$$

$$l_2 = \frac{4}{19}\times 114 = 24\text{ cm}$$

$$l_3 = \frac{3}{19}\times 114 = 18\text{ cm}$$ **Ans. (D)**

Sol. 18 For a closed pipe, fundamental frequency is given as

$$n_0 = \frac{v}{4L} = \frac{340}{4\times 0.85} = \frac{85}{0.85} = 100\text{ Hz}$$

For a closed pipe only odd harmonic frequency resonate

$\Rightarrow$ below 1250 Hz the resonating frequency are

100 Hz, 300 Hz, 500 Hz, 700 Hz, 900 Hz, & 1100 Hz

1 2 3 4 5 6 **Ans. (C)**

Sol. 19 The lengths of parts in which 110 cm wire is divided is

$$l_1 = 60\text{ cm};\ l_2 = 30\text{ cm};\ l_3 = 20\text{ cm}$$

Fundamental frequencies of the 3 parts of wire are

$$\nu_{1p} = \frac{1}{2l_1}\sqrt{\frac{T}{\mu}} = \frac{1}{2\times 0.6}\times\sqrt{\frac{400}{0.01}} = \frac{1}{2\times 0.6}\times\frac{20}{0.1}$$

$$= \frac{1000}{6}\text{ Hz}$$

$$\nu_{2p} = \frac{1}{2l_2}\sqrt{\frac{T}{\mu}} = \frac{1}{2\times 0.3}\times\sqrt{\frac{400}{0.01}} = \frac{1000}{3}\text{ Hz}$$

$$\nu_{3p} = \frac{1}{2l_3}\sqrt{\frac{T}{\mu}} = \frac{1}{2\times 0.2}\times\sqrt{\frac{400}{0.01}} = \frac{1000}{2}\text{ Hz}$$

As there wires can oscillate at any multiple of their fundamental frequency.

$\Rightarrow$ The lowest common frequency here is

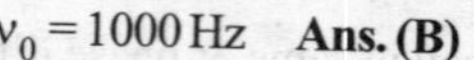

$$\nu_0 = 1000\text{ Hz}$$ **Ans. (B)**

Sol. 20 Fundamental frequency of open & closed pipes are shown below

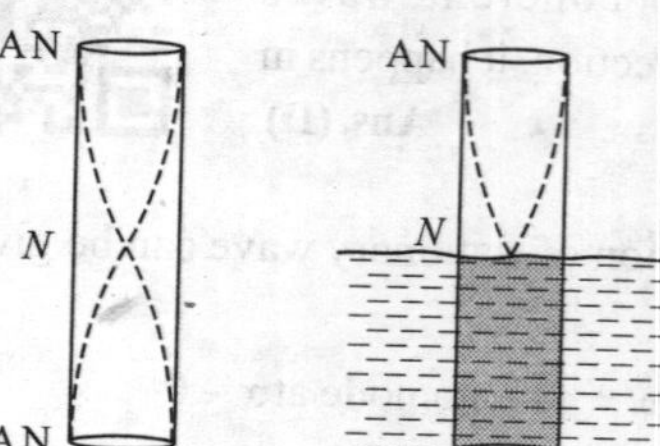

As wavelength in the above two cases is same for fundamental frequencies.

$\Rightarrow$ Their fundamental frequency must be same. **Ans. (D)**

14.3 Doppler's Effect

Sol. 1

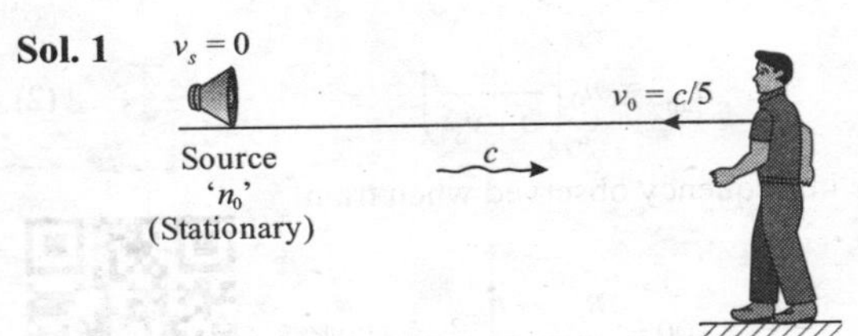

Apparent frequency is

$$\nu_{ap} = \nu_0\left(\frac{c - v_0}{c - v_s}\right) = \nu_0\left(\frac{c-(-c/5)}{c}\right)$$

$$\Rightarrow \quad \nu_{ap} = \nu_0\left(\frac{6}{5}\right)$$

$$\% \text{ increase in frequency} = \frac{\nu_{ap} - \nu_0}{\nu_0} \times 100$$

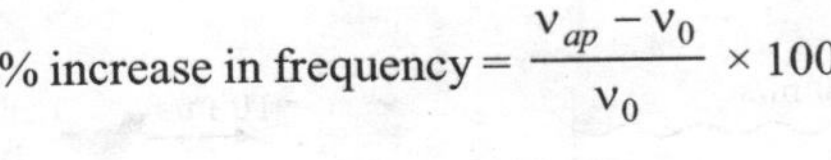

$$= \frac{1}{5} \times 100$$

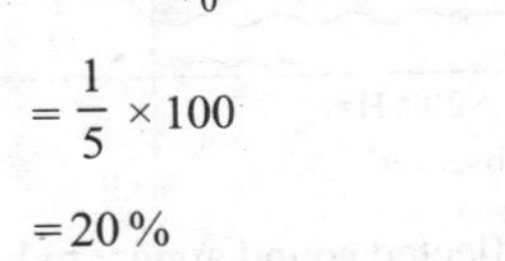

$$= 20\,\%$$ **Ans. (D)**

Sol. 2

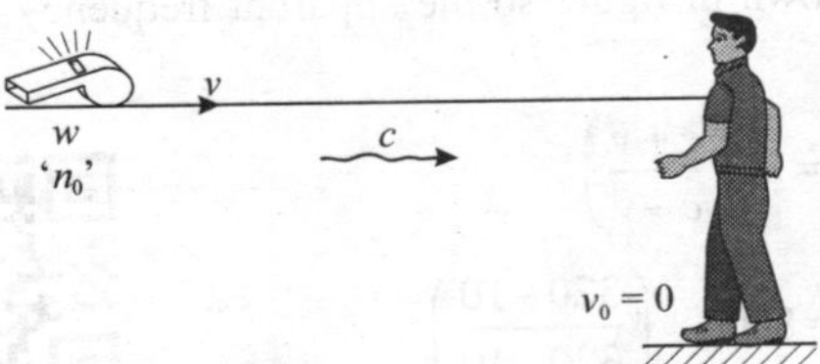

Apparent frequency heard by observer is

$$n_{ap} = n_0\left(\frac{c - v_0}{c - v_s}\right) = n_0\left(\frac{c}{c - v_s}\right)$$

As $n_{ap} = 10000$ Hz and $n_0 = 9500$ Hz

$$\Rightarrow \quad 10000 = 9500\left(\frac{300}{300 - v_s}\right)$$

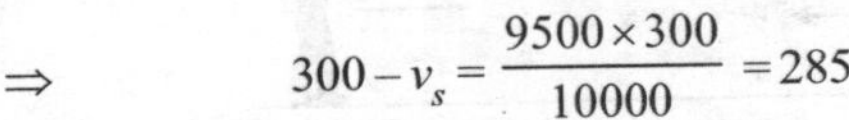

$$\Rightarrow \quad 300 - v_s = \frac{9500 \times 300}{10000} = 285$$

$$\Rightarrow \quad v_s = 300 - 285 = 15 \text{ m/s}$$ **Ans. (C)**

Sol. 3

S n_0 $u = 0$ (rest) $v_s = 0$; a; s; c; $v_M = \sqrt{2as}$

Apparent frequency is $n_{app} = n_0\left(\frac{c - v_M}{c}\right)$

$$\Rightarrow \quad \frac{94}{100} n_0 = n_0\left(\frac{c - \sqrt{2as}}{c}\right)$$

$$\Rightarrow \quad \frac{94 \times 330}{100} = 330 - \sqrt{2 \times 2 \times s}$$

$$\Rightarrow \quad s = 98 \text{ m}$$ **Ans. (D)**

Sol. 4 **S-1: Echolocation :** A phenomenon by which bats detect the objects in their surrounding.

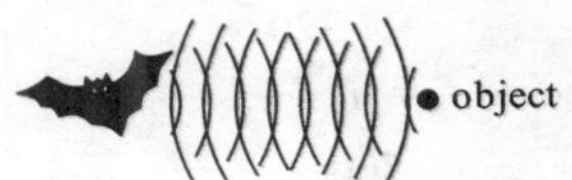

Waves reflected from object through which bats estimate the location of object.

S-1 is true. By Definition of Doppler's effects.

In general **S-2** is True.

As **S-2** is not linked with **S-1** directly. **Ans. (C)**

Sol. 5 **Case-I:**

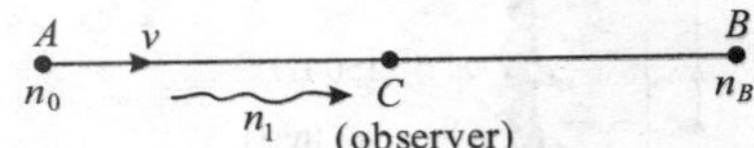

Apparent frequency of A heard by C is

$$n_1 = n_0\left(\frac{c}{c - v}\right)$$

$$\Rightarrow \quad n_1 = 500 \times \frac{340}{336} = 506 \text{ Hz}$$

$$f_B = |n_1 - n_B| = 6$$

$$n_B = 500 \text{ Hz or } 512 \text{ Hz}$$

Case-2:

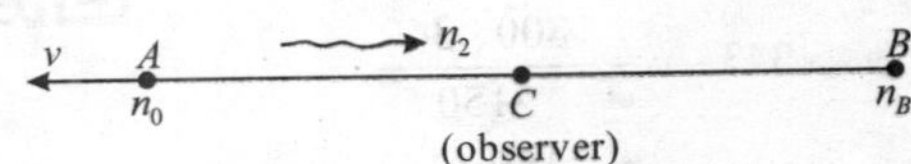

Apparent frequency of A heard by C is

$$n_2 = n_0\left(\frac{c}{c + v}\right)$$

$$\Rightarrow \quad n_2 = 500 \times \frac{340}{344} = 494 \text{ Hz}$$

$$f_B' = |n_2 - n_B| = 18$$

$$\Rightarrow \quad n_B = 512 \text{ Hz}$$ **Ans. (C)**

Sol. 6

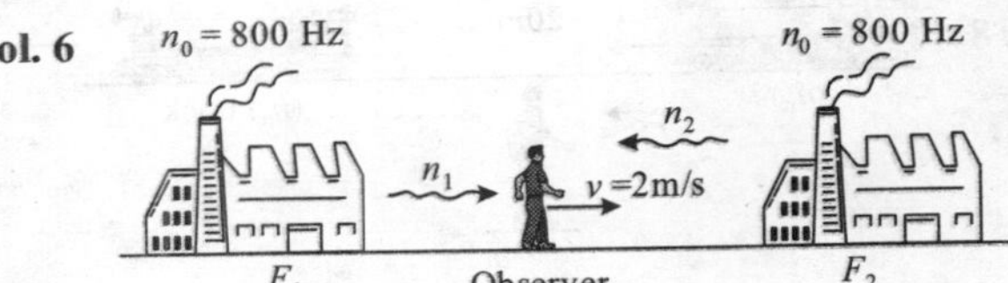

Apparent frequency of sound heard by observer are

from factory-1 it is $n_1 = n_0\left(\frac{c-v}{c}\right) = 800 \times \left(\frac{320-2}{320}\right)$

$$\Rightarrow \qquad n_1 = \frac{800 \times 318}{320}$$

from factory-2 it is $n_2 = n_0\left(\frac{c+v}{c}\right) = 800 \times \left(\frac{320+2}{320}\right)$

$$\Rightarrow \qquad n_2 = \frac{800 \times 322}{320}$$

Beat frequency heard $f_B = n_2 - n_1$

$$= \frac{800}{320}(322-318)$$

$$\Rightarrow \qquad f_B = \frac{800 \times 4}{320} = 10\,\text{Hz}$$

Ans. (D)

Sol. 7

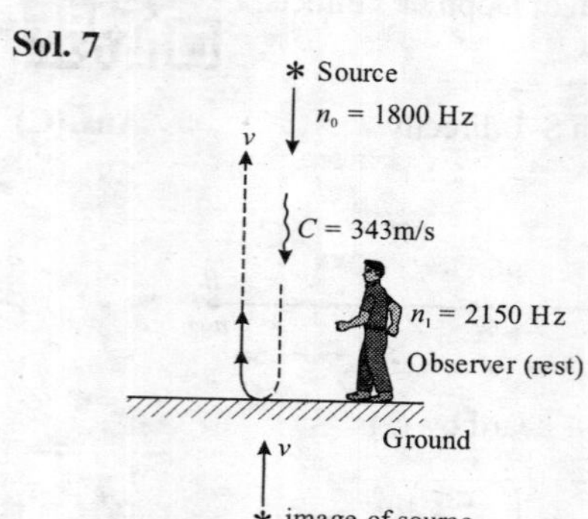

By Doppler's effect apparent frequency of sound received by observer is

$$n_1 = n_0\left(\frac{c}{c-v_s}\right)$$

$$2150 = 1800\left(\frac{343}{343-v}\right)$$

$$\Rightarrow \qquad 343 - v = \frac{1800 \times 340}{2150}$$

$$\Rightarrow \qquad v = -\frac{180 \times 343}{215} + 343 \simeq 56\,\text{m/s}$$

Reflected waves appear to be coming from the image of source in the ground so the apparent frequency received by source is reflected waves is given as

$$n_{ap} = n_0\left(\frac{c+v}{c-v}\right) = 1800 \times \left(\frac{343+56}{343-56}\right)$$

$$\Rightarrow \qquad n_{ap} = 1800 \times \frac{399}{287} = 2502\,\text{Hz}$$

Ans. (B)

Sol. 8

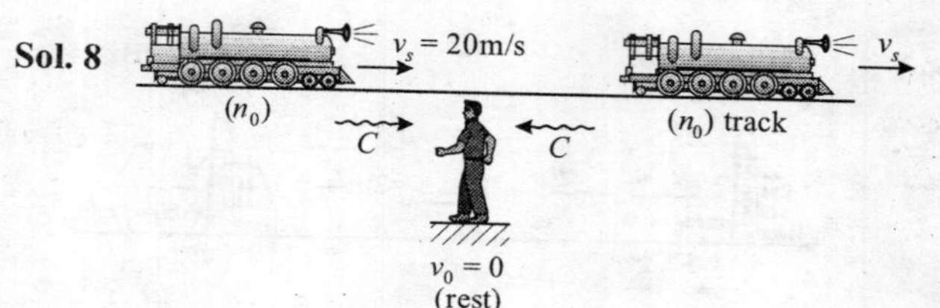

If n_{ap_2} is the frequency observed when train is approaching the person then we have

$$n_{ap_1} = n_0\left(\frac{c}{c-v_s}\right) \qquad \ldots(1)$$

If v_{app_2} is frequency observed when train reaches away from person then we have

$$n_{ap_2} = n_0\left(\frac{c}{c+v_S}\right) \qquad \ldots(2)$$

% change in frequency observed when train passes

$$\frac{\Delta n}{n_0} \times 100 = \frac{n_{ap_1} - n_{ap_2}}{n_0} \times 100\%$$

$$\%\text{ change} = \left[\frac{c}{c-v_S} - \frac{c}{c+v_S}\right] \times 100$$

$$\Rightarrow \qquad \%\text{ change} = \left[\frac{320}{300} - \frac{320}{340}\right] \times 100$$

$$\Rightarrow \qquad \%\text{ change} = 106.66 - 94.11 \simeq 12\%$$

Ans. (B)

Sol. 9

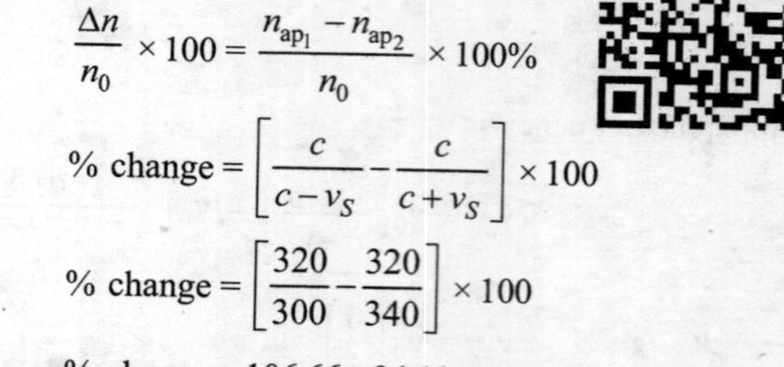

Frequency of reflected sound appear to be coming from image of bat as shown in figure so the apparent frequency heard is given as

$$f_{ap} = n_0\left(\frac{c+v}{c-v}\right)$$

$$= 8000 \times \left(\frac{320+10}{320-10}\right)$$

$$\Rightarrow \qquad f_{ap} = 8000 \times \frac{330}{310} \cong 8516\,\text{Hz}$$

Ans. (A)

Sol. 10 By Doppler's effect apparent frequency of sound heard by observer is given as

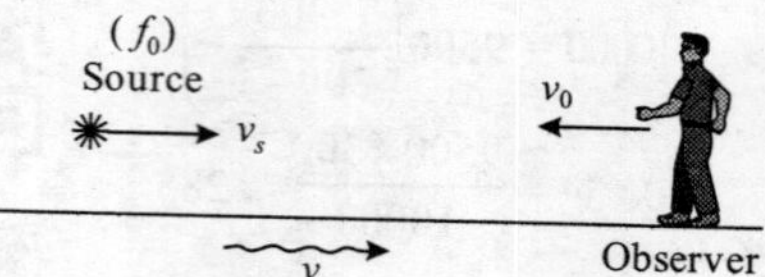

Apparent frequency $f = f_0\left(\frac{v+v_0}{v-v_s}\right)$

$$\Rightarrow \qquad f = \left(\frac{f_0}{v-v_s}\right)v_0 + \left(\frac{f_0 v}{v-v_s}\right)$$

This is of form $\quad y = mx + C$

slope of graph is $\quad m = \frac{f_0}{v-v_s}$

Ans. (C)

Sol. 11

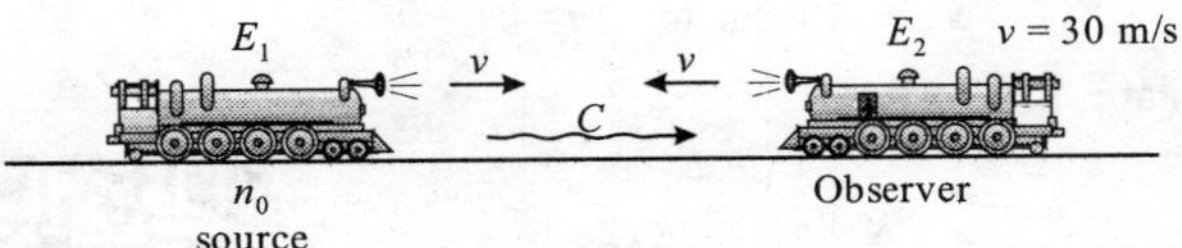

Apparent frequency heard by driver of second engine E_2 is

$$n_{ap} = n_0\left(\frac{c+v}{c-v}\right) = 540 \times \left(\frac{330+30}{330-30}\right)$$

$$\Rightarrow \quad n_{ap} = 540 \times \frac{360}{300} = 54 \times 12 = 648 \text{ Hz}$$

Ans. (D)

Sol. 12

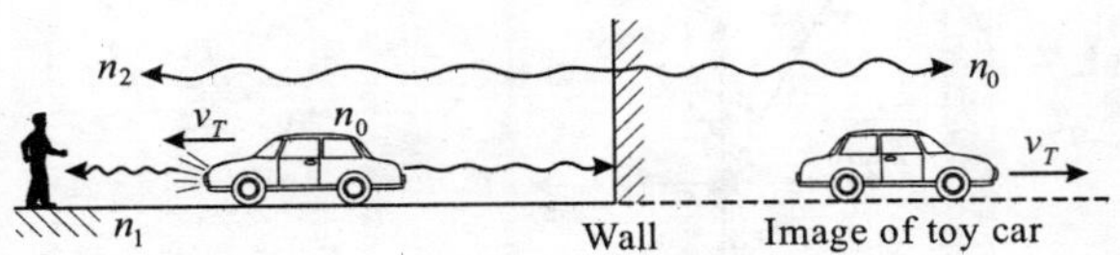

$n_1 \rightarrow$ Apparent frequency of horn from approaching toy car

$$\Rightarrow \quad n_1 = n_0\left(\frac{c}{c-v_T}\right) = n_0\left(\frac{340}{340-5}\right)$$

$$\Rightarrow \quad n_1 = \frac{340}{335}n_0$$

$n_2 \rightarrow$ Apparent frequency of horn from the receding image of toy car due to reflected wave from wall.

$$\Rightarrow \quad n_2 = n_0\left(\frac{c}{c+v_T}\right) = n_0\left(\frac{340}{340+5}\right)$$

$$\Rightarrow \quad n_2 = \frac{340}{345}n_0$$

As beat frequency heard by observer is 5 beats/s

$$\Rightarrow \quad n_1 - n_2 = 5$$

$$\Rightarrow \quad \left(\frac{340}{335} - \frac{340}{345}\right)n_0 = 5$$

$$\Rightarrow \quad n_0 = 170 \text{ Hz}$$

Ans. (D)

15.1 Electric Force and Electric Field

Sol. 1

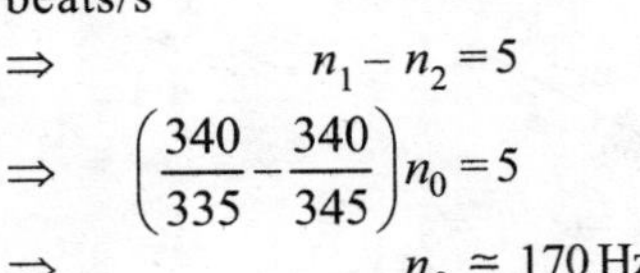

[For equation θ must be of opposite sign to Q]

For equilibrium of Q, we use

$$F_{1Q} = F_{2q}$$

$$\frac{KQ^2}{(2x)^2} = \frac{KQq}{x^2}$$

$$\Rightarrow \quad |q| = \frac{Q}{4} \quad \text{or} \quad q = -\frac{Q}{4}$$

Ans. (D)

Sol. 2 By Colomb's law

$$F_{12} = \frac{Kq_1q_2}{b^2};\ F_{13} = \frac{Kq_1q_3}{a^2}$$

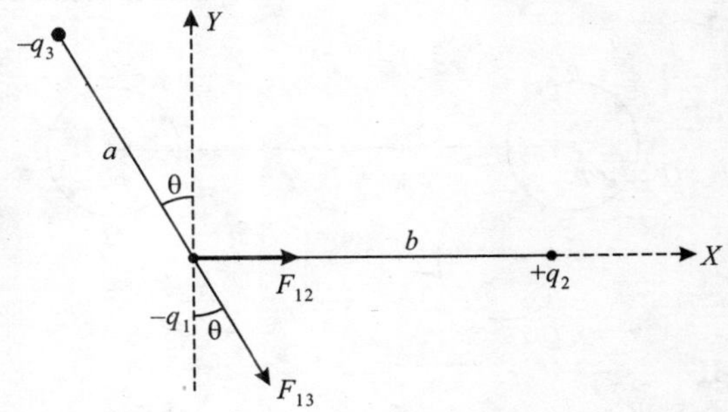

Net force on $-q_1$ along x direction is given as

$$F_x = F_{12} + F_{13}\sin\theta$$

$$\Rightarrow \quad F_x = Kq_1\left[\frac{q_2}{b^2} + \frac{q_3}{a^2}\sin\theta\right]$$

Ans. (B)

Sol. 3

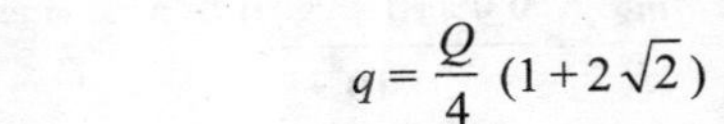

To keep net force on each of $-Q$, q has to be 'Positive'. So that for equilibrium of $-Q$ charge we have

Hare
$$F_1 = \frac{KQ^2}{a^2};\ F_2 = \frac{KQ^2}{2a^2}$$

$$F_q = F_2 + \sqrt{2}F_1$$

and
$$F_q = \frac{KqQ}{(a/\sqrt{2})^2}$$

$$\Rightarrow \quad \frac{KqQ}{a^2 2} = \frac{KQ^2}{2a^2} + \frac{\sqrt{2}KQ^2}{a^2}$$

$$\Rightarrow \quad \frac{2q}{a^2} = \frac{Q}{2a^2} = \frac{\sqrt{2}Q}{a^2}$$

$$\Rightarrow \quad q = \frac{Q}{4}(1+2\sqrt{2})$$

Ans. (B)

Sol. 4 Here to solve the case, we ignore induction effects.

$$\Rightarrow \quad r >> R$$

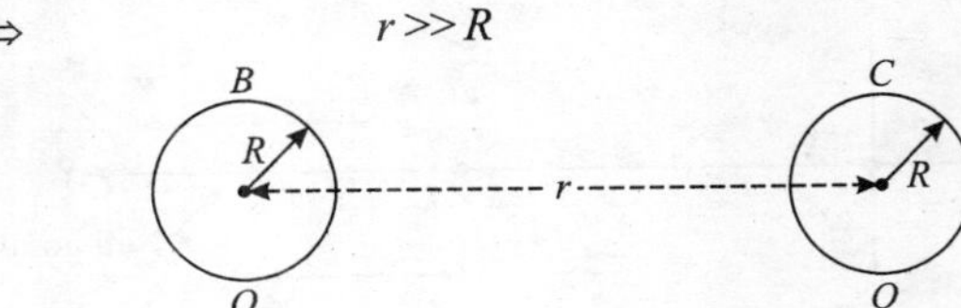

Initially the force between spheres is given as

$$F=\frac{KQ^2}{r^2}$$

In second case when the third identical sphere is located to B

Step-I

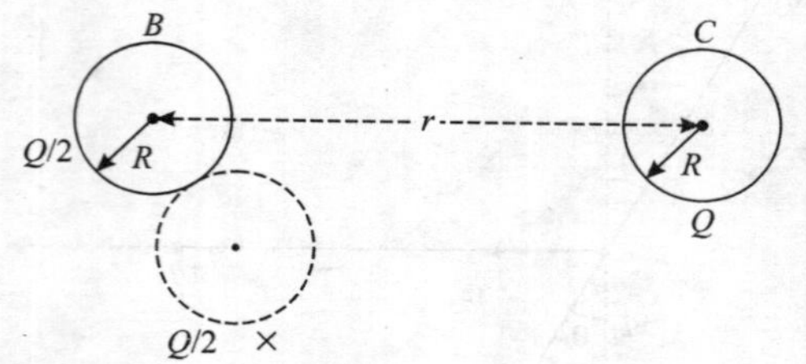

Step-II

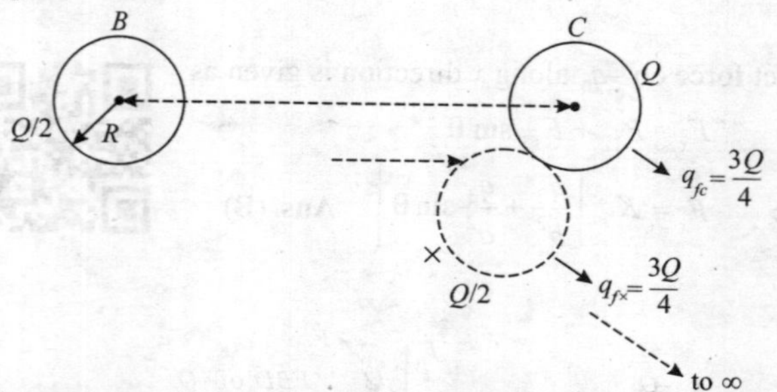

When sphere x is connected to sphere C then again their total charge will be equally distributed in than as these are identical.

$\Rightarrow$ Final charge on B and C are $Q/2$ and $3Q/4$

$\Rightarrow$ Final force between B and C is

$$F'=\frac{K(Q/2)(3Q/4)}{r^2}$$

$$=\frac{3}{8}\frac{KQ^2}{r^2}$$ **Ans. (D)**

Sol. 5 For equilibrium of drop, we have

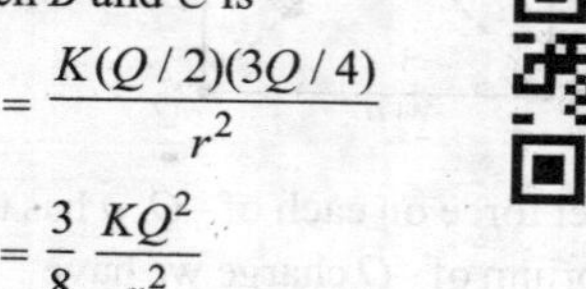

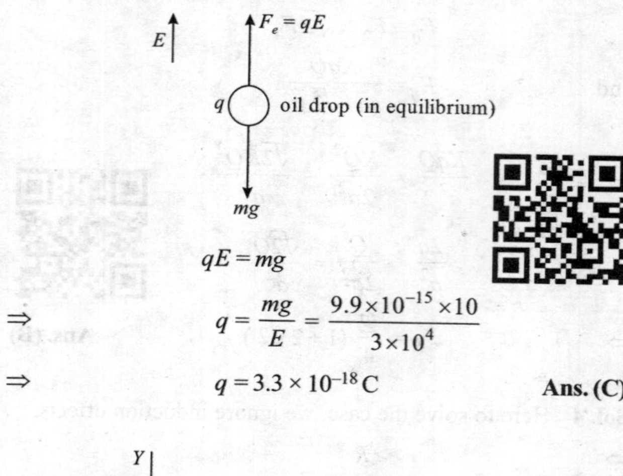

$$qE=mg$$

$\Rightarrow$ $$q=\frac{mg}{E}=\frac{9.9\times10^{-15}\times10}{3\times10^4}$$

$\Rightarrow$ $$q=3.3\times10^{-18}\,\text{C}$$ **Ans. (C)**

Sol. 6

Y, $+8q$, $x=0$, $-2q$, $x=L$, E_2, E_1, x, X, Null point, $x-L$

$E_1 \longrightarrow EF$ at x due to $8q$

$E_2 \longrightarrow EF$ at x due to $-2q$

If at x, $EF_{net}=0$

$\Rightarrow$ $$E_1=E_2$$

$$\frac{K(8q)}{x^2}=\frac{K(2q)}{(x-L)^2}$$

$\Rightarrow$ $$8(x-L)^2=2x^2$$

$\Rightarrow$ $$x=2L$$ **Ans. (A)**

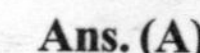

Sol. 7

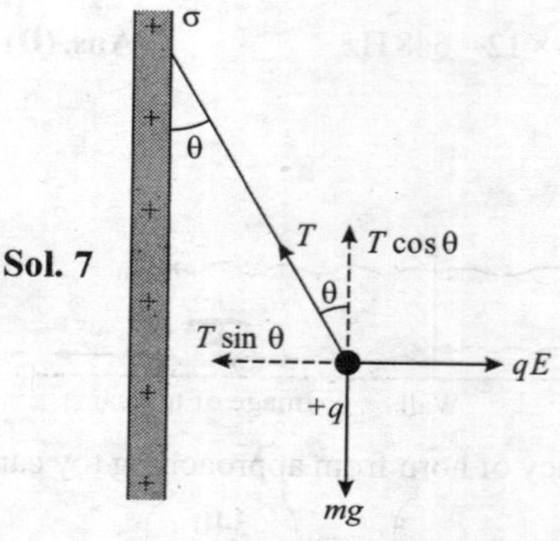

Electric field due to a large charged sheet

$$E=\frac{\sigma}{2\epsilon_0}$$

As ball is in equilibrium, we use

$$T\sin\theta=q\left(\frac{\sigma}{2\epsilon_0}\right) \quad \ldots(1)$$

$$T\cos\theta=mg \quad \ldots(2)$$

(1) ÷ (2) gives

$\Rightarrow$ $$\tan\theta=\frac{q\sigma}{2\epsilon_0 mg}$$

$\Rightarrow$ $$\sigma\propto\tan\theta$$ **Ans. (D)**

Sol. 8

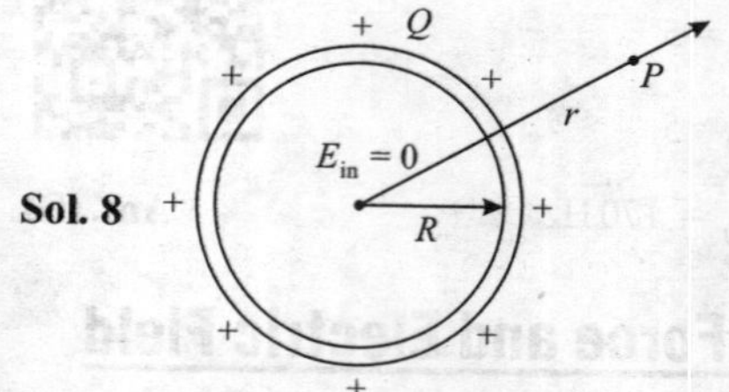

$$E=\frac{KQ}{r^2}\ \text{(For } r>R)$$

$$E\propto\frac{1}{r^2}$$

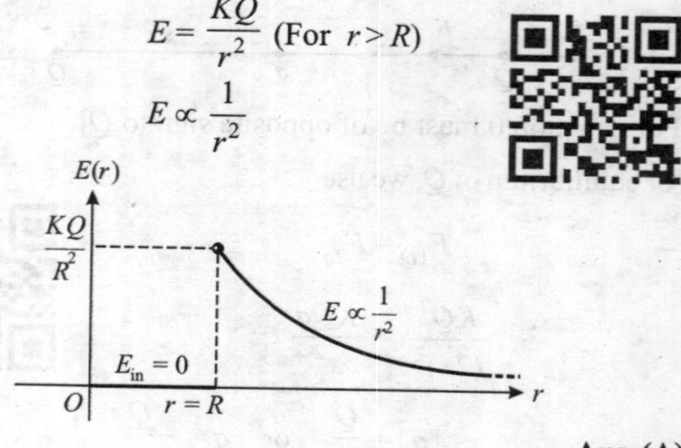

Ans. (A)

Sol. 9

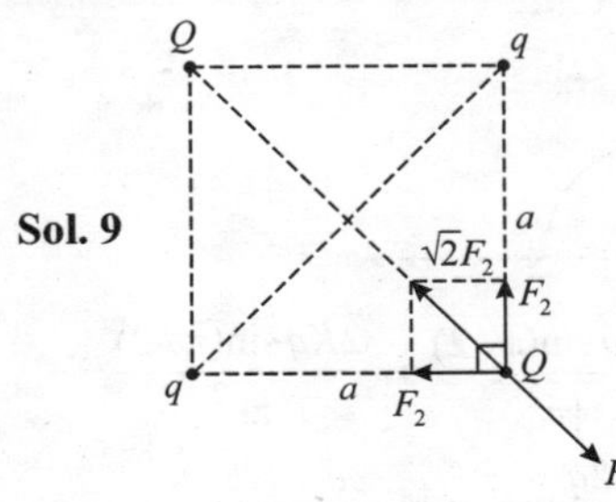

Force on Q due to other Q is $F_1 = \dfrac{KQ^2}{(\sqrt{2}a)^2}$

If not force on Q is to be zero

$\Rightarrow$ q has to be –ve so that resultant of two F_2 on Q balances F_1.

Force on Q due to each of q is $F_2 = \dfrac{KqQ}{a^2}$

As not force on Q is zero

$\Rightarrow \quad \sqrt{2}\, F_2 = F_1$

$\Rightarrow \quad \sqrt{2}\, \dfrac{KqQ}{a^2} = \dfrac{KQ^2}{2a^2}$

$\Rightarrow \quad Q = 2\sqrt{2}\, q$ in magnitude

$\Rightarrow \quad Q = -2\sqrt{2}\, q$ **Ans. (C)**

Sol. 10

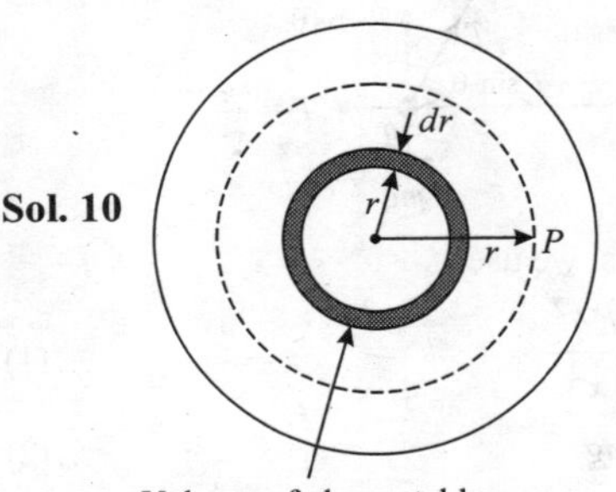

Volume of elemental layer
$dV = 4\pi r^2 dr$

The charge contained inside the thin layer of elemental shell is

$$dq = \rho(r).dV$$

$$\Rightarrow \quad dq = \frac{Q}{\pi R^4} \cdot r \cdot (4\pi r^2 dr)$$

$$\Rightarrow \quad dq = \frac{4Q}{R^4} \cdot r^3 dr$$

Total charge inside a sphere of radius r_1 is

$$q = \int dq = \int_0^{r_1} \frac{4Q}{R^4} \cdot r^3 dr$$

$$\Rightarrow \quad q = \frac{4Q}{R^4} \int_0^{r_1} r^3 dr$$

$$\Rightarrow \quad q = \frac{4Q}{R^4} \cdot \left[\frac{r^4}{4}\right]_0^{r_1} = \frac{Qr_1^4}{R^4}$$

Electric field at point 'P' due to the inside charge is given as

$$E = \frac{Kq}{r_1^2} = \frac{1}{4\pi \in_0} \cdot \frac{(Qr_1^4 / R^4)}{r_1^2}$$

$$\Rightarrow \quad E = \frac{1}{4\pi \in_0} \frac{Qr_1^2}{R^4}$$ **Ans. (A)**

Sol. 11 In Air

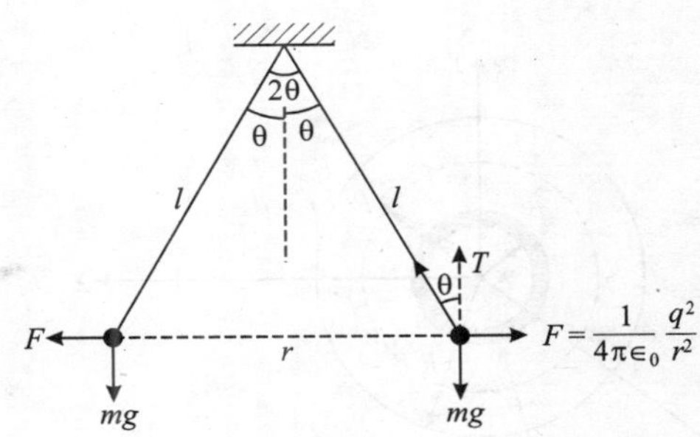

For equilibrium of bob

$$T \sin\theta = \frac{1}{4\pi \in_0} \frac{q^2}{r^2} \quad \ldots(1)$$

$$T \cos\theta = mg \quad \ldots(2)$$

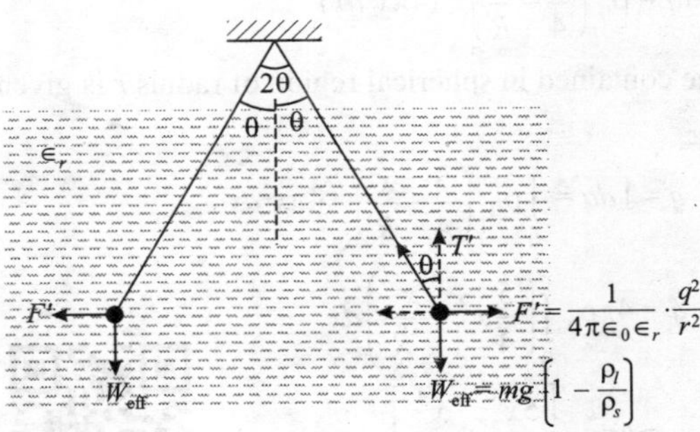

As $\quad F_B = mg \cdot \dfrac{\rho_l}{\rho_s}$

Force of Buoyancy

$$T' \sin\theta = \frac{1}{4\pi \in_0 \in_r} \cdot \frac{q^2}{r^2} \quad \ldots(3)$$

$$T' \cos\theta = mg\left(1 - \frac{\rho_l}{\rho_s}\right) \quad \ldots(4)$$

$(1) \div (2) \Rightarrow \quad \tan\theta = \dfrac{q^2}{4\pi \in_0 mgr^2}$

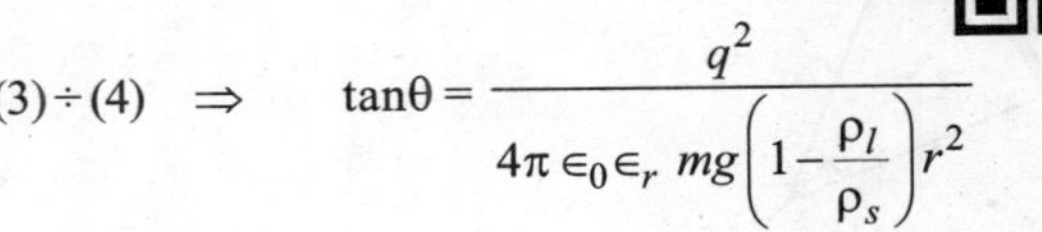

$(3) \div (4) \Rightarrow \quad \tan\theta = \dfrac{q^2}{4\pi \in_0 \in_r mg\left(1 - \dfrac{\rho_l}{\rho_s}\right) r^2}$

Here we use

$$\frac{q^2}{4\pi \epsilon_0 \, mgr^2} = \frac{q^2}{4\pi \epsilon_0 \epsilon_r \, mg\left(1-\frac{\rho_l}{\rho_s}\right)r^2}$$

$$\Rightarrow \quad \epsilon_r = \frac{1}{1-\frac{\rho_l}{\rho_s}} = \frac{1}{1-\frac{0.8}{1.6}} = 2$$ **Ans. (D)**

Sol. 12

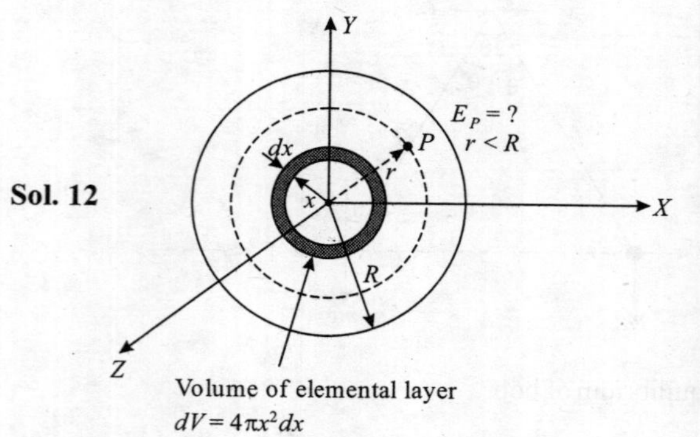

Volume of elemental layer
$dV = 4\pi x^2 dx$

Charge contained in the elemental shell is

$$dq = \rho(r) \cdot dV\big|_{r=x}$$

$$\Rightarrow \quad dq = \rho_0\left(\frac{5}{4}-\frac{x}{R}\right)\cdot(4\pi x^2 dx)$$

Total charge contained in spherical region of radius r is given as

$$q = \int dq = \int_0^r \rho_0\left(\frac{5}{4}-\frac{x}{R}\right)\cdot 4\pi x^2 dx$$

$$\Rightarrow \quad q = 4\pi\rho_0 \int_0^r\left(\frac{5}{4}x^2-\frac{x^3}{R}\right)dx$$

$$\Rightarrow \quad q = 4\pi\rho_0\left[\frac{5x^3}{12}-\frac{x^4}{4R}\right]_0^r$$

$$\Rightarrow \quad q = 4\pi\rho_0\left[\frac{5r^3}{12}-\frac{r^4}{4R}\right]_0^r$$

Electric field at the surface of inside sphere of radius r is

$$E = \frac{Kq}{r^2} = \frac{1}{4\pi \epsilon_0}\cdot\frac{4\pi\rho_0}{r^2}\left[\frac{5r^3}{12}-\frac{r^4}{4R}\right]$$

$$\Rightarrow \quad E = \frac{\rho_0 r}{4 \epsilon_0}\left[\frac{5}{3}-\frac{r}{R}\right]$$ **Ans. (C)**

Sol. 13

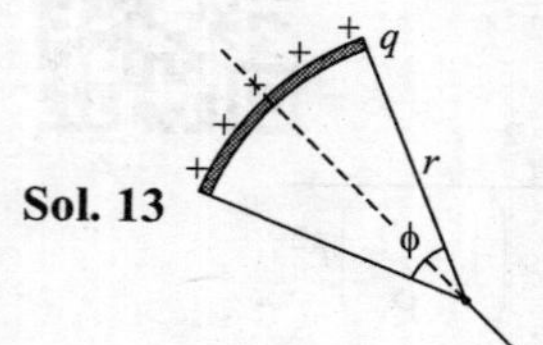

For a half ring

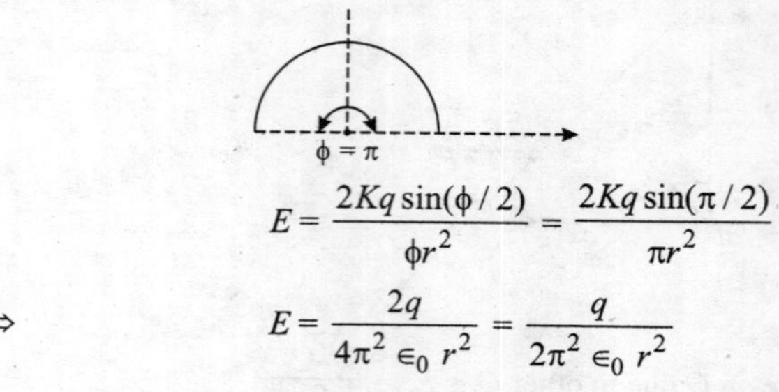

$$E = \frac{2Kq\sin(\phi/2)}{\phi r^2} = \frac{2Kq\sin(\pi/2)}{\pi r^2}$$

$$\Rightarrow \quad E = \frac{2q}{4\pi^2 \epsilon_0 r^2} = \frac{q}{2\pi^2 \epsilon_0 r^2}$$

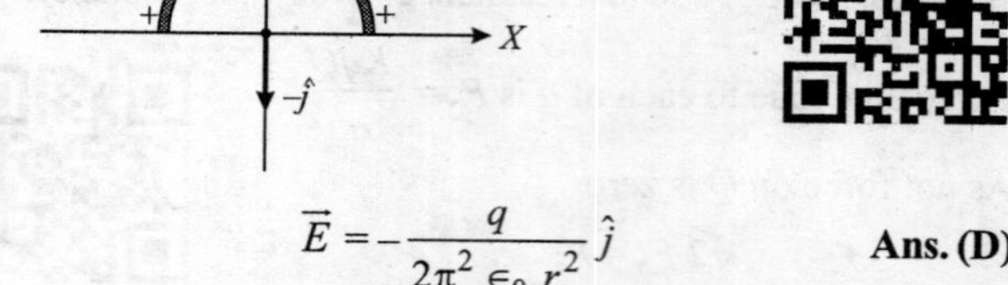

$$\Rightarrow \quad \vec{E} = -\frac{q}{2\pi^2 \epsilon_0 r^2}\hat{j}$$ **Ans. (D)**

Sol. 14

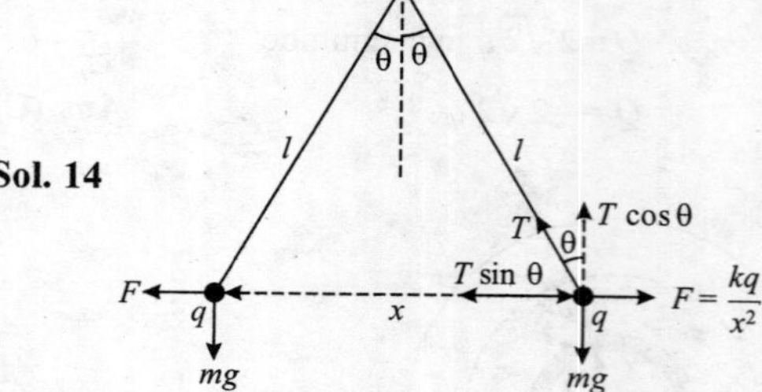

For equilibrium of spheres, we use

$$T\sin\theta = \frac{Kq^2}{x^2} \quad \ldots(1)$$

$$T\cos\theta = mg \quad \ldots(2)$$

$(1)\div(2)$

$$\Rightarrow \quad \tan\theta = \frac{Kq^2}{mgx^2} = \frac{x}{2l}$$

$\Rightarrow$ as θ is small

$$\Rightarrow \quad \tan\theta \simeq \theta = \frac{x}{2l}$$

$$\Rightarrow \quad q = \sqrt{\frac{mg}{2Kl}}\cdot x^{3/2}$$

If q starts leaking (decreasing) than x will decreases and as θ is very small, we can consider very slow variation in x. So we have rate of charge leakage (constant)

$$\frac{dq}{dt} = \sqrt{\frac{mg}{2Kl}}\left(\frac{3}{2}x^{1/2}\right)\left(\frac{dx}{dt}\right)$$

$$\Rightarrow \quad \frac{dx}{dt} = \frac{dq}{dt}\cdot\sqrt{\frac{2Kl}{mg}}\left(\frac{2}{3\sqrt{x}}\right)$$

$$\Rightarrow \quad \frac{dx}{dt} \propto \frac{1}{\sqrt{x}}$$ **Ans. (C)**

Sol. 15 In a uniformly charged sphere, electric field at a distance r from centre is given as

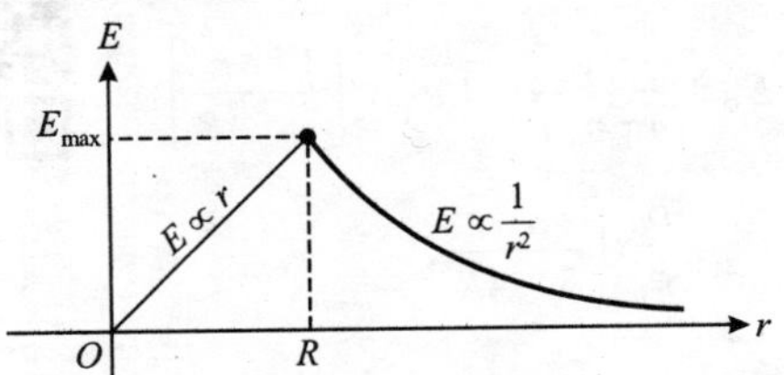

For $r > R$ $\quad E_{out} = \frac{KQ}{r^2} \longrightarrow E \propto \frac{1}{r^2} \downarrow$

For $r = R$ $\quad E_S = \frac{KQ}{R^2} \longrightarrow E_{max}$

For $r < R$ $\quad E_{in} = \frac{KQr}{R^3} \longrightarrow E \propto r \uparrow$ **Ans. (D)**

Sol. 16

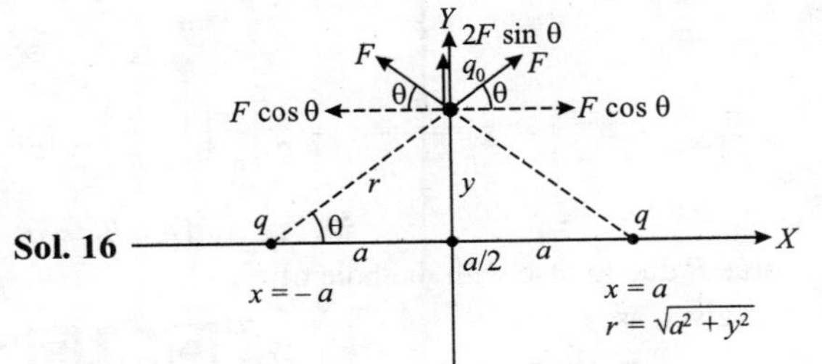

From Figure not force on q_0 due to charges on x-axis (considered fixed) is

$$F_{net} = 2F \sin\theta$$

$F \longrightarrow$ Coulombic Force

$$F = \frac{Kqq_0}{r^2} = \frac{Kqq_0}{(a^2 + y^2)}$$

$$\Rightarrow \quad F_{net} = \frac{2Kqq_0}{(a^2 + y^2)} \cdot \frac{y}{\sqrt{a^2 + y^2}}$$

As $y << a$

$$\Rightarrow \quad a^2 + y^2 \approx a^2$$

$$\Rightarrow \quad F_{net} = \frac{2Kqq_0}{(a^2 + y^2)^{3/2}} \cdot y \approx \frac{2Kqq_0 y}{a^3}$$ **Ans. (A)**

Sol. 17 In space electric force must be in downward direction so that upward electric force on $-6e$ charge balances the weight of drop.

$\Rightarrow$ At equilibrium of drop

$$qE = mg$$

Mass of liquid drop

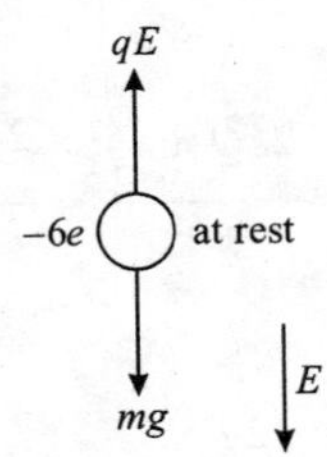

$$m = \frac{4}{3}\pi R^3 \cdot \rho$$

$$\Rightarrow \quad 6eE = \frac{4}{3}\pi R^3 \rho g$$

$$\Rightarrow \quad R = \left(\frac{9eE}{2\pi\rho g}\right)^{1/3}$$

$$\Rightarrow \quad R = \left(\frac{9 \times 1.6 \times 10^{-19} \times 25.5 \times 10^3}{6.28 \times 1.26 \times 10^3 \times 10}\right)^{1/3}$$

$$\Rightarrow \quad R = 7.74 \times 10^{-7} \text{ m}$$ **Ans. (B)**

Sol. 18 EF at a distance x from the centre of disc is

$$E_P = \frac{\rho}{2\epsilon_0}\left(1 - \frac{x}{\sqrt{x^2 + R^2}}\right)$$

At $x = 0 \rightarrow$ $\quad E_C = \frac{\rho}{2\epsilon_0}$

At $x = R \rightarrow$ $\quad E_P = \frac{\rho}{2\epsilon_0}\left(1 - \frac{R}{\sqrt{2}R}\right) = \frac{\sigma}{2\epsilon_0}\left(1 - \frac{1}{\sqrt{2}}\right)$

% reduction in electric force at P w.r.t C is

$$= \frac{E_C - E_P}{E_C} = 100\%$$

$$= \frac{\frac{\sigma}{2\epsilon_0} \cdot \frac{1}{\sqrt{2}}}{\sigma / 2\epsilon_0} \times 100\% = 70.7\%$$ **Ans. (A)**

Sol. 19

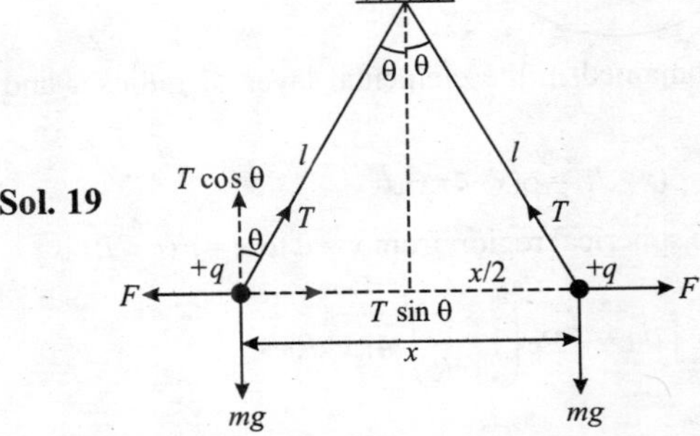

In equilibrium position, for balls, we use

$$T \sin\theta = F = \frac{Kq^2}{x^2} = \frac{1}{4\pi\epsilon_0} \cdot \frac{q^2}{x^2} \quad \ldots(1)$$

and $\quad T \cos\theta = mg \quad \ldots(2)$

$(1) \div (2)$

$$\Rightarrow \quad \tan\theta = \frac{F}{mg} = \frac{q^2}{4\pi\epsilon_0 mgx^2}$$

For small θ, we use

$$\tan\theta \simeq \sin\theta = \frac{x}{2l}$$

$$\Rightarrow \quad \frac{x}{2l} = \frac{q^2}{4\pi \in_0 mgx^2}$$

$$\Rightarrow \quad x = \left[\frac{q^2 l}{2\pi \in_0 mg}\right]^{1/3}$$

Ans. (D)

Sol. 20

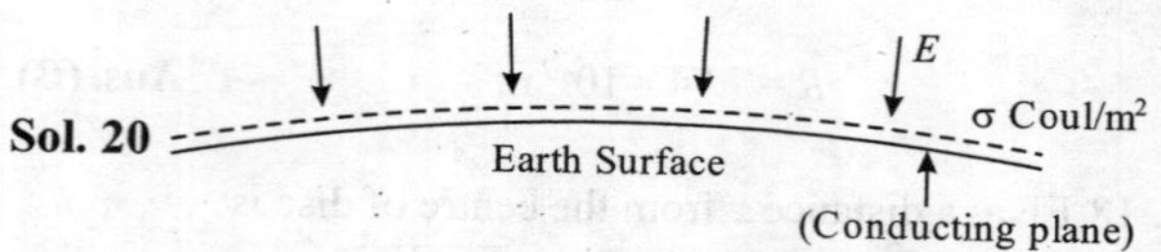

If σ C/m² (–ve) is the surface charge density on Earth surface then we use

$$E = \frac{\sigma}{\in_0}$$

$$\Rightarrow \quad \sigma = \in_0 E$$

The total surface area of earth $= 4\pi R_e^2$

⇒ Total charge on earth surface is

$$q = -\sigma \times 4\pi R_e^2 = \in_0 E \cdot 4\pi R_e^2$$

$$\Rightarrow \quad q = -8.85 \times 10^{-12} \times 150 \times 4 \times 3.14 \times (6.37 \times 10^6)^2$$

$$\Rightarrow \quad q = -676.55 \times 10^3\,\text{C} \simeq -680\,\text{KC}$$

Ans. (C)

Sol. 21

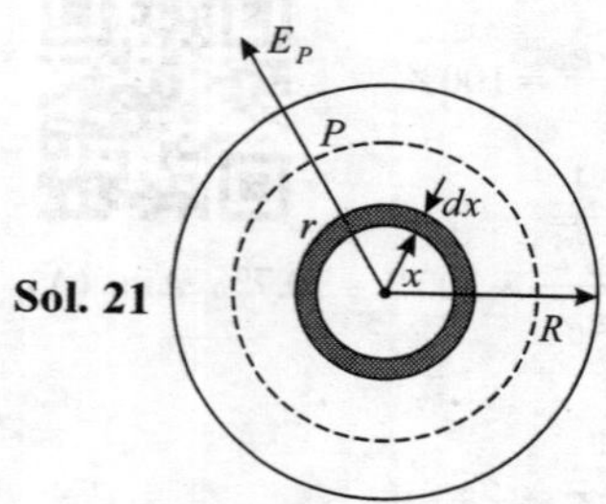

The charge contained in the elemental layer of radius x and width dx is

$$dq = \rho(x) \cdot dV = \rho(x) \cdot 4\pi x^2 dx$$

Total charge in spherical region from $x = 0$ to $x = r$ $(r < R)$ is

$$q = \int dq = \int_0^r \rho_0 \left(1 - \frac{x}{R}\right) \cdot 4\pi x^2 dx$$

$$\Rightarrow \quad q = 4\pi\rho_0 \int_0^r \left(x^2 - \frac{x^3}{R}\right) dx$$

$$\Rightarrow \quad q = 4\pi\rho_0 \left[\frac{x^3}{3} - \frac{x^4}{4R}\right]_0^r dx = 4\pi\rho_0 r^3 \left[\frac{1}{3} - \frac{r}{4R}\right]$$

Electric force strength at point P $(x = r)$ is given as

$$E_P = \frac{Kq}{r^2}$$

(For spherically symmetric distribution of charge)

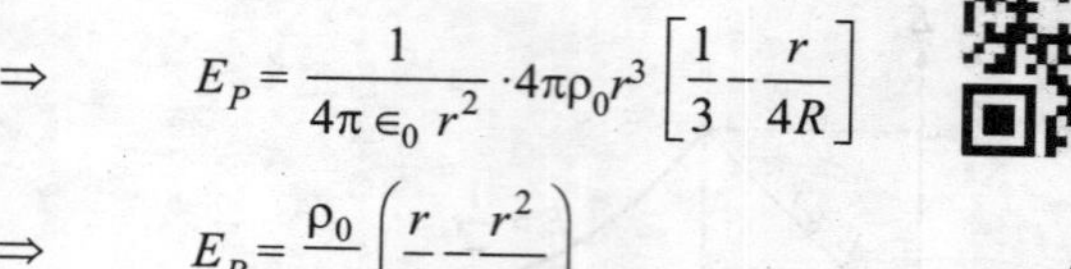

$$\Rightarrow \quad E_P = \frac{1}{4\pi \in_0 r^2} \cdot 4\pi\rho_0 r^3 \left[\frac{1}{3} - \frac{r}{4R}\right]$$

$$\Rightarrow \quad E_P = \frac{\rho_0}{\in_0}\left(\frac{r}{3} - \frac{r^2}{4R}\right)$$

Ans. (B)

Sol. 22 Due to a complete disc of radius b, electric field at point P is given as

$$E_{\text{disc}} = \frac{\sigma}{2\in_0}\left(1 - \frac{h}{\sqrt{b^2 + h^2}}\right) = \frac{\sigma}{2\in_0}\left(1 - \frac{h}{b}\right) \quad \ldots(1)$$

[As $h << b$]

Electric field at point P only due to the circular disc of radius 'a' is given as

$$E_{\text{disc}} = \frac{\sigma}{2\in_0}\left(1 - \frac{h}{\sqrt{a^2 + h^2}}\right) = \frac{\sigma}{2\in_0}\left(1 - \frac{h}{b}\right) \quad \ldots(2)$$

[As $h << a$]

Electric force P due to disc with the hole of radius 'a' is given as

$$E_{\text{given object}} = E_{\text{disc}} - E_{\text{hole}}$$

$$= \frac{\sigma}{2\in_0}\left[\left(1 - \frac{h}{b}\right) - \left(1 - \frac{h}{a}\right)\right]$$

$$= \frac{\sigma}{2\in_0}\left[\frac{h}{a} - \frac{h}{2a}\right] \quad (\text{As } b = 2a)$$

$$= \frac{\sigma h}{4\in_0 a} = Ch \quad \Rightarrow \quad C = \frac{\sigma}{4\in_0 a}$$

Ans. (A)

Sol. 23

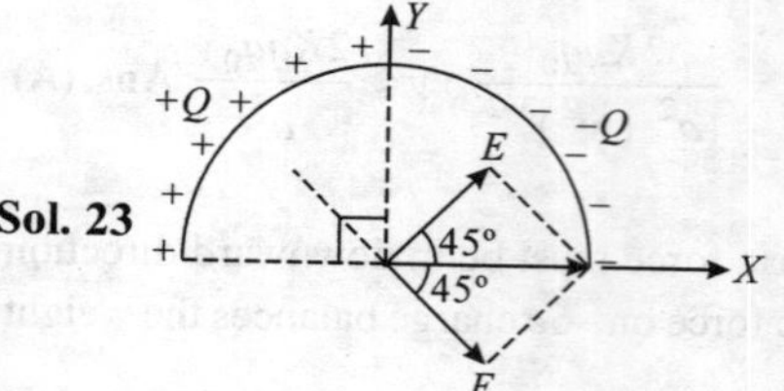

We use $\quad \pi R = L$

$$\Rightarrow \quad R = \frac{20}{\pi}\,\text{cm}$$

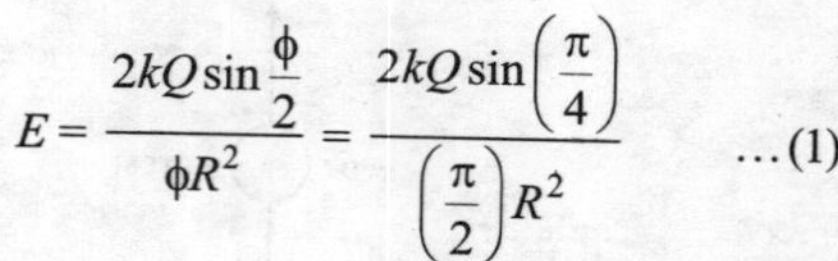

where $$E = \frac{2kQ\sin\frac{\phi}{2}}{\phi R^2} = \frac{2kQ\sin\left(\frac{\pi}{4}\right)}{\left(\frac{\pi}{2}\right)R^2} \quad \ldots(1)$$

$$E_{\text{net at } O} = \sqrt{2}\,E \quad \ldots(2)$$

From equation-(1) $E = \frac{4}{\pi R^2} \cdot \frac{1}{4\pi \in_0} \cdot Q \cdot \frac{1}{\sqrt{2}}$

$$= \frac{10 \in_0}{\pi^2 \in_0 \left(\frac{20}{\pi} \times 10^{-2}\right)^2 \sqrt{2}}$$

$$\Rightarrow \qquad E = \frac{1000}{\sqrt{2} \times 400 \times 10^{-4}} = \frac{2.5}{\sqrt{2}} \times 10^{+4} \text{ N/C}$$

From equation-(2), net electric force at O is given as

$$E_{\text{net at } O} = \sqrt{2}\, E = 2.5 \times 10^4 = 25 \times 10^3 \text{ N/C}$$

as $\qquad \vec{E}_0 = 25 \times 10^3 \hat{i}$ N/C **Ans. (D)**

Sol. 24 As net charge enclosed in cavity is $+Q - Q = 0$ so net induced charge on inner surface of shell $Q_1 = 0$.

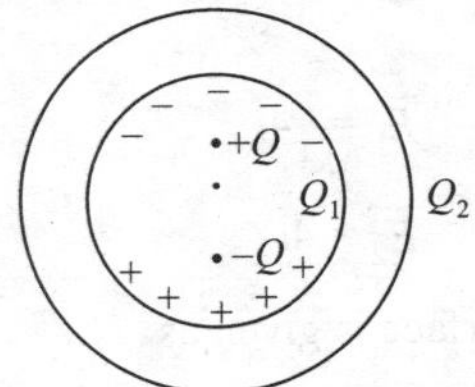

As shown we use $\sigma_1 \neq 0$ and varying with position inner surface of shell = 0

$\Rightarrow$ charge on outer surface

$$Q_2 = 0 \text{ and } \sigma_2 = 0$$ **Ans. (B)**

Sol. 25

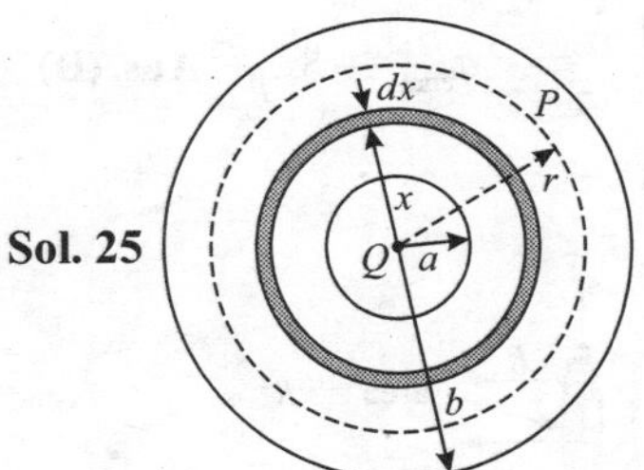

Electric field at point P is given as

$$E_P = \frac{K(Q + q_{en})}{r^2} \qquad \ldots(1)$$

Where q_{en} is the charge between charge contained within the elemental layer of radius x and width dx is

$$dq = \rho \cdot dv$$

$$dq = \left(\frac{A}{x}\right) \cdot 4\pi x^2 dx$$

Total charge in region from $x = a$ to $x = r$ is

$$q_{en} = \int dq = 4\pi A \int_{x=a}^{x=r} x\, dx$$

$$\Rightarrow \qquad q_{en} = 4\pi A \left[\frac{x^2}{2}\right]_a^r = 2\pi A r^2 - 2\pi A a^2$$

From equation-(1) $E_P = \frac{K}{r^2}(Q + 2\pi A r^2 - 2\pi A a^2) \qquad \ldots(2)$

Given that E_p in equation-(2) is a constant (independent of r) if equation-(2)

$$Q = 2\pi A a^2 \Rightarrow E = K(2\pi A) \rightarrow \text{constant}$$

$$\Rightarrow \qquad A = \frac{Q}{2\pi a^2}$$ **Ans. (A)**

15.2 Electric Flux and Gauss's Law

Sol. 1

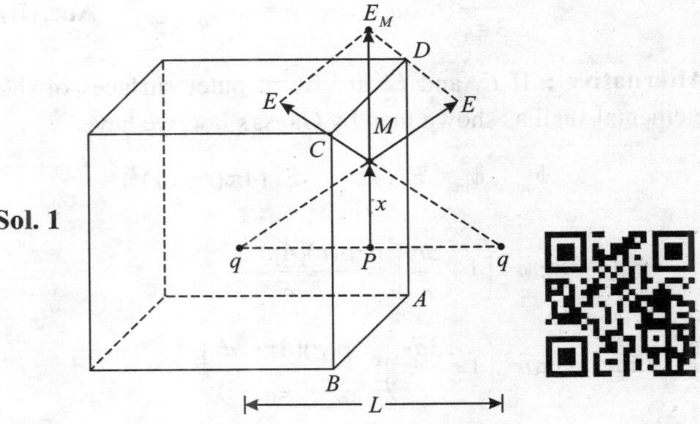

Here $P \rightarrow$ centre of square $ABCD$

$M \rightarrow$ a point in plane of square $ABCD$ at a distance x from P.

Due to the two charges, electric field resultant at any point M in plane of square $ABCD$ is parallel (tangential) to $ABCD$. So there is no electric field normal to surface $ABCD$ hence electric flux through surface $ABCD$ is zero. **Ans. (B)**

Sol. 2 Using Gauss's law, we use

$$\phi_{\text{not outward}} = \frac{q_{\text{end}}}{\in_0}$$

$$\Rightarrow \qquad \phi_2 - \phi_1 = \frac{q_{\text{end}}}{\in_0}$$

$$\Rightarrow \qquad q_{\text{end}} = \in_0(\phi_2 - \phi_1)$$ **Ans. (A)**

Sol. 3

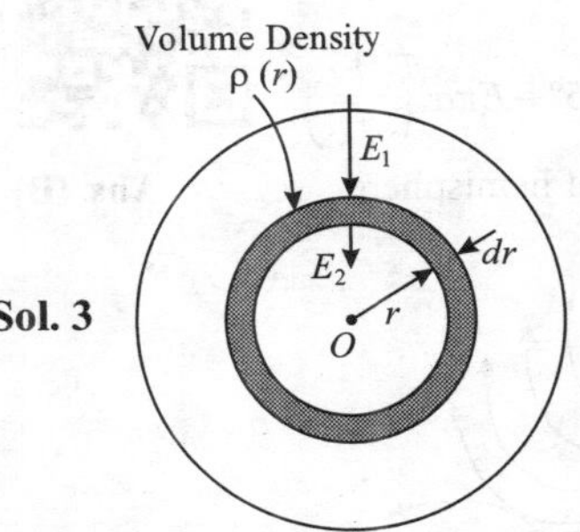

Potential at a distance r from centre is

$$\phi = ar^2 + b$$

$\Rightarrow$ EF at a distance r is given as

$$\vec{E} = -\frac{dv}{dr}\hat{r}$$

$\Rightarrow \qquad \vec{E} = -2ar\hat{r} \qquad \ldots(1)$

–ve sign implies field is in radially inward direction

$\Rightarrow$ charge on ball is –ve

From equation-(1) we can see that $E \propto r$ so this happens inside a uniformly charged ball and if its volume charge density is ρ then inside EF of this ball is given as

$$E_{in} = \frac{\rho r}{3\epsilon_0} \qquad \ldots(2)$$

from (1) and (2), we have

$$\frac{\rho r}{3\epsilon_0} = 2ar \Rightarrow \rho = 6a\epsilon_0$$ **Ans. (B)**

Alternative : If E_1 and E_2 are EF at outer surfaces of the elemental shell as shown then by Gauss's law, we have

$$\phi_{out} - \phi_{in} = E_2(4\pi r^2) - E_1(4\pi(r+dr)^2) = \frac{q_{encl}}{\epsilon_0}$$

$$8\pi ar^3 - 8\pi ar^3\left(1+\frac{dr}{r}\right)^3 = \frac{\rho(r)[4\pi r^2 dr]}{\epsilon_0}$$

$$8\pi ar^3 - 8\pi ar^3\left(1+\frac{3dr}{r}\right) = \frac{\rho(r)[4\pi r^2 dr]}{\epsilon_0}$$

$$\Rightarrow \frac{\rho(r)dr}{\epsilon_0} = -6adr$$

$$\Rightarrow \rho(r) = -6a\epsilon_0$$ **Ans. (B)**

Sol. 4

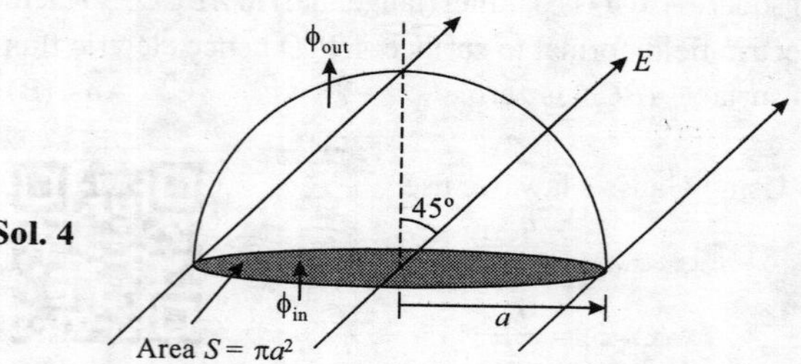

As no charge is enclosed in hemisphere

$\Rightarrow \qquad \phi_{in} = \phi_{out}$

$\Rightarrow \qquad \phi_{out} = \phi_{in} = ES\cos 45° = E\pi a^2\left(\frac{1}{\sqrt{2}}\right)$

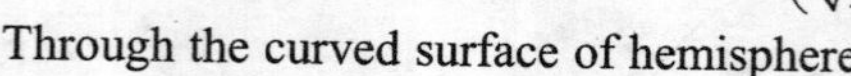

Through the curved surface of hemisphere **Ans. (B)**

Sol. 5

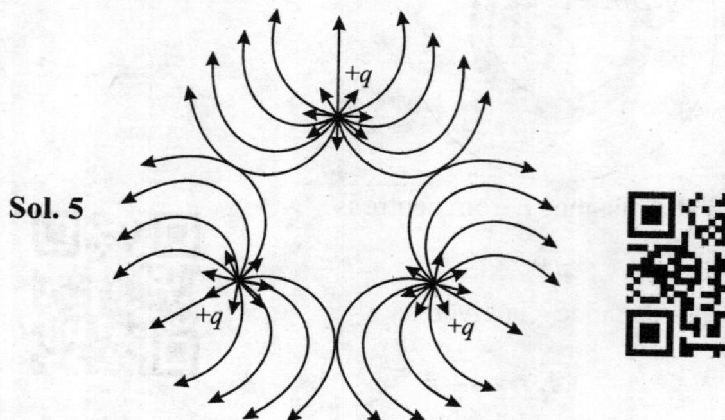

As electric lines originated from a +ve charge are repelled by other neighbouring +ve charges **Ans. (C)**

Sol. 6

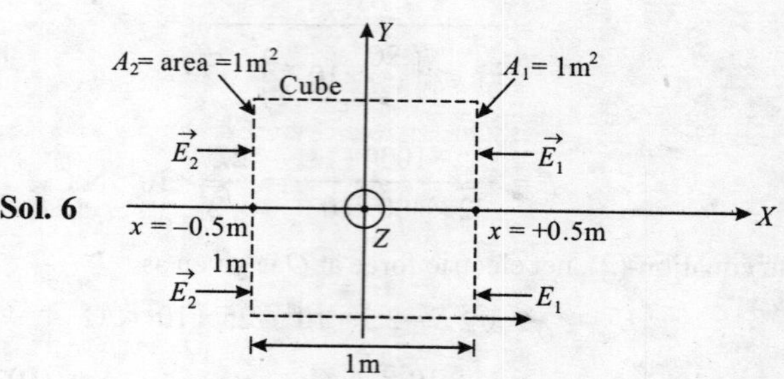

EF in the region is given as

$$\vec{E} = -\frac{dV}{dx}\hat{i}$$

at $\qquad x = 0.5\text{ m} \rightarrow \vec{E_1} = -4\hat{i}$

at $\qquad x = -0.5\text{ m} \rightarrow \vec{E_2} = 4\hat{i}$

Total flux going into the cubical surface is given as

$$\phi = \vec{E_1}\cdot\vec{A_1} + \vec{E_2}\cdot\vec{A}$$

$$\Rightarrow \qquad \phi = 4.1 + 4.1 = 8 \text{ units}$$

By Gauss's Law $\quad \phi_{out} = \frac{q_{encl}}{\epsilon_0}$

$$\Rightarrow \qquad -8 = \frac{q_{encl}}{\epsilon_0} \Rightarrow q_{encl} = -8\epsilon_0$$ **Ans. (D)**

Sol. 7

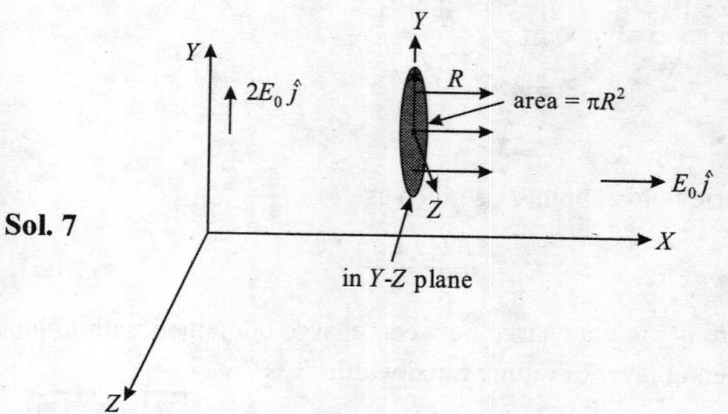

As circular area is perpendicular to X-axis (as in YZ plane) so only the electric flux due to field $E_0\hat{i}$ will pass through so we have

$$\phi = E_0 \times A = E_0 \cdot \pi r^2$$

$$= 100 \times 3.14 \times 4 \times 10^{-4}$$

$$= 12.56 \times 10^{-2}$$

$$= 0.1256 \text{ Nm}^2/\text{C}$$ **Ans. (A)**

Sol. 8

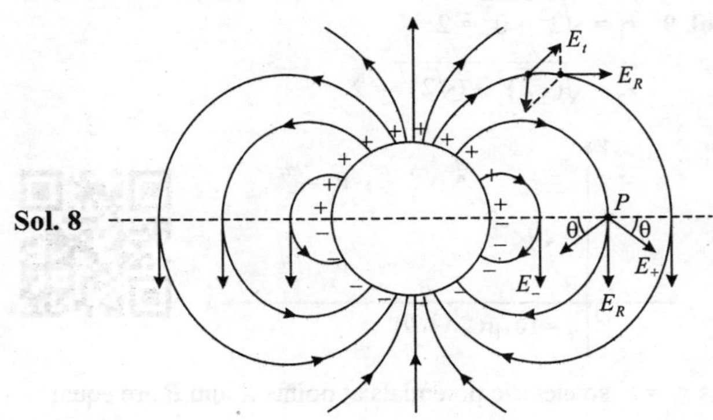

The preference of termination of electric lines is always for a –ve charge (nearly) rather at ∞. **Ans. (A)**

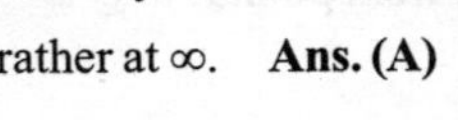

16.1 Electric Potential and Dipole

Sol. 1 Work done in moving a charge from one point to another (say A to B) is given as

$$W_{AB} = q \times (V_B - V_A) = \text{charge} \times \text{potential difference}$$

⇒ Potential difference

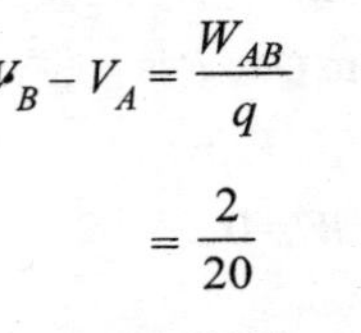

$$V_B - V_A = \frac{W_{AB}}{q}$$

$$= \frac{2}{20}$$

$$= 0.1\text{ V}$$ **Ans. (A)**

Sol. 2

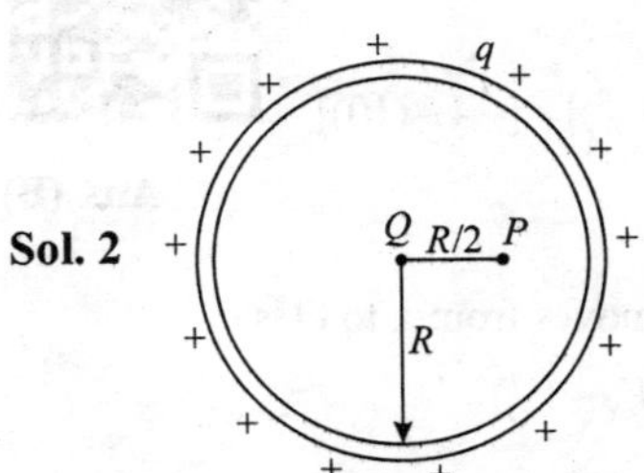

Electric potential at point P is given as

$$V_P = V_{QP} + V_{qP}$$

$$\Rightarrow \quad V_P = \frac{KQ}{\left(\frac{R}{2}\right)} + \frac{Kq}{R}$$

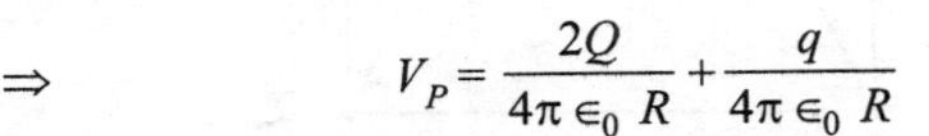

$$\Rightarrow \quad V_P = \frac{2Q}{4\pi \epsilon_0 R} + \frac{q}{4\pi \epsilon_0 R}$$ **Ans. (C)**

Sol. 3 At the point of closest approach, the KE of particle transforms into the PE of system. Thus by conservation of energy, we have

$$\Rightarrow \frac{1}{2}mv^2 + O = O + \frac{KqQ}{r} \Rightarrow r = \frac{2KqQ}{mv^2}$$

$$\Rightarrow r \propto \frac{1}{v^2}$$

If q was given a speed $2v$ then now closest approach distance will be

$$\frac{r_1}{r_2} = \left(\frac{v_2}{v_1}\right)^2 \Rightarrow r_2 = \left(\frac{v_1}{v_2}\right)^2 r_1 = \left(\frac{v_1}{2v}\right)^2 r = \frac{r}{4}$$ **Ans. (D)**

Sol. 4 Electric potential at point C_2 is

$$V_{C_2} = \left(+\frac{Kq}{\sqrt{d^2+R^2}}\right) + \left(-\frac{Kq}{R}\right)$$

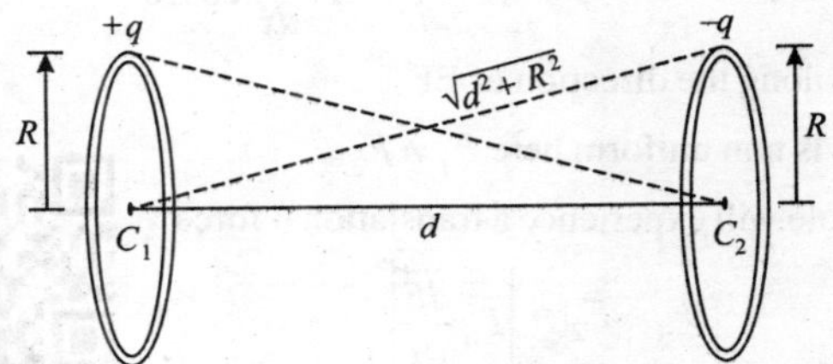

Electric potential at point C_1 is

$$V_{C_1} = V_{+q} + V_{-q}$$

$$\Rightarrow \quad V_{C_1} = \frac{Kq}{R} + \left(-\frac{Kq}{\sqrt{d^2+R^2}}\right)$$

Potential difference between centres of rings is

$$\Delta V = V_{C_1} - V_{C_2} = \frac{q}{2\pi \epsilon_0}\left(\frac{1}{R} - \frac{1}{\sqrt{d^2+R^2}}\right)$$ **Ans. (B)**

Sol. 5

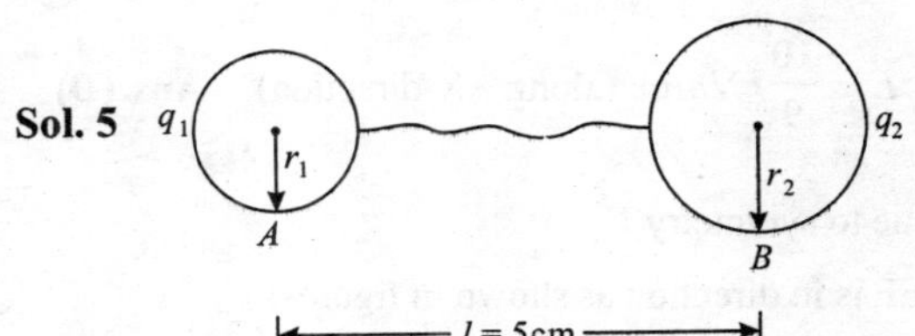

We can ignore induction effects on spheres due to charge on other sphere as separation

$$l >> r_1, r_2$$

If q_1 and q_2 are charges on A and B after connection, we have

$$V_A = V_B$$

$$\frac{Kq_1}{r_1} = \frac{Kq_2}{r_2}$$

Electric field magnitude on surfaces of A and B are

$$E_A = \frac{Kq_1}{r_1^2}$$

and $\quad E_B = \dfrac{Kq_2}{r_2}$

$\Rightarrow \quad \dfrac{E_A}{E_B} = \dfrac{r_2}{r_1} = \dfrac{2}{1}$ **Ans. (C)**

Sol. 6 Non-uniform *EF*

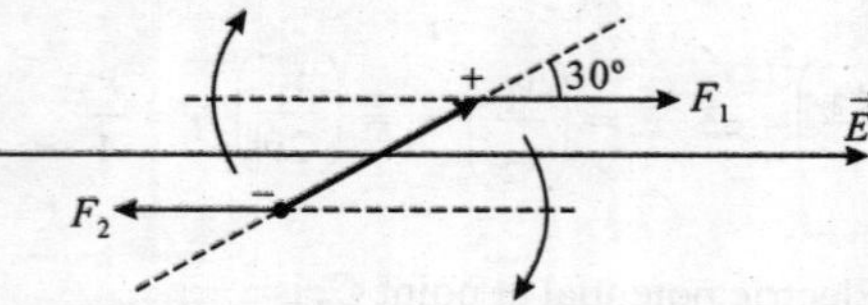

The electric force on a dipole placed in non-uniform *EF* is given as

$$F = \overline{P} \cdot \frac{\overline{dE}}{dx} = P\frac{dE}{dx}\cos 30°$$

Force along the direction of EF

As EF is non uniform here $F_1 \neq F_2$

so dipole will experience a translational force

$$|F_1 - F_2| = \left|\overline{P} \cdot \frac{\overline{dE}}{dx}\right|$$

As F_1 and F_2 are not acting along same lines of action so there will be a torque due to these forces present on dipole. **Ans. (C)**

Sol. 7 We know that EF in space is given as

$$\vec{E} = -\frac{dV}{dx}\hat{i} \quad \text{(for unidirectional EF)}$$

$$\Rightarrow \quad \vec{E} = -\left[20\left(-\frac{1}{(x^2-4)} \times 2x\right)\right]\hat{i}$$

$$\Rightarrow \quad \vec{E} = \frac{40x}{(x^3-4)}\hat{i}\Bigg|_{x=4\mu m} = \frac{40 \times 4}{(16-4)^2} = \frac{160}{144}\hat{i} \text{ V/μm}$$

$$\Rightarrow \quad \vec{E} = \frac{10}{9}\hat{i} \text{ V/μm (along + X-direction)}$$ **Ans. (D)**

Sol. 8 Due to symmetry $V_0 = 0$

At *O* net EF is in direction as shown in figure-1

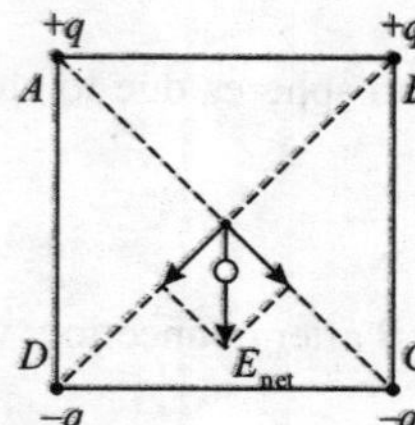

Figure-1

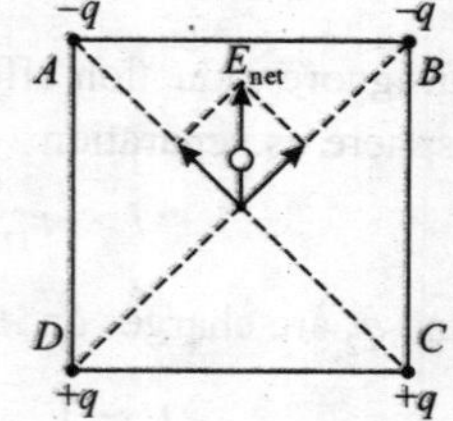

Figure-2

After interchanging charges as given in que

Still $V_0 = 0$ (remain unchanged)

As shown in figure-2 direction of $\vec{E}$ is reversed. **Ans. (D)**

Sol. 9

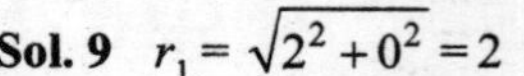

$r_1 = \sqrt{2^2 + 0^2} = 2$

$r_2 = \sqrt{(\sqrt{2})^2 + (\sqrt{2})^2} = 2$

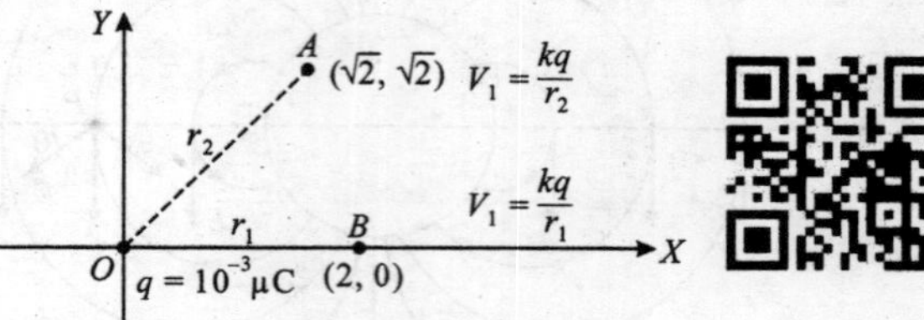

As $r_1 = r_2$ so electric potentials at points *A* and *B* are equal

$\Rightarrow \quad V_A = V_B$ **Ans. (B)**

Sol. 10 Work done in moving charge *q* from point *P* to *Q* is

$$W = q\,(V_Q - V_P)$$

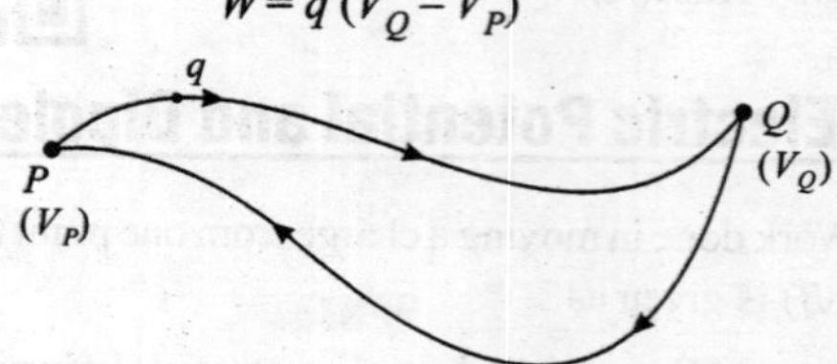

Being EF a conservative field work done does not depend on the path chosen.

Work done in moving '*q*' from *Q* to *P* is

$$W' = q\,(V_P - V_Q)$$

$$W_{closed} = W + W' = 0$$ **Ans. (D)**

Sol. 11 Work done in moving a charge *q* from point *P* to *Q* is given as

$$W = q\,(V_Q - V_P)$$

$$\Rightarrow \quad W = [100 \times (-1.6 \times 10^{-19})] \times [-4 - (10)]$$

$$\Rightarrow \quad W = 2.24 \times 10^{-16}\,\text{J}$$ **Ans. (B)**

Sol. 12 KE_{gain} of *Q* when it moves from *X* to *O* is

$$KE_{gain} = Q\,(V_X - V_O)$$

Side 1; 2a; q —a— Q X —a— q; 2a; O; $\sqrt{5}a$; $\sqrt{5}a$; −q; −q

Potential at point *X* is

$$V_X = \frac{2Kq}{a} - \frac{2Kq}{\sqrt{5}a} = \frac{2Kq}{a}\left(1 - \frac{1}{\sqrt{5}}\right)$$

Potential at point centre of square O is

$$V_O = O$$

$$\Rightarrow \quad KE_{gain} = Q(V_n - O) = QV_X$$

$$\Rightarrow \quad KE_{gain} = \frac{2KqQ}{a}\left(1-\frac{1}{\sqrt{5}}\right)$$

$$\Rightarrow \quad KE_{gain} = \frac{1}{4\pi\epsilon_0}\cdot\frac{2qQ}{a}\left(1-\frac{1}{\sqrt{5}}\right)$$ **Ans. (A)**

Sol. 13 Inside a uniformly charged sphere EF is given as

$$E_{in} = \frac{\rho r}{3\epsilon_0}$$

$\Rightarrow$ S-2 is true

Work done is moving 'q' from centre to surface of sphere is

$$W = \Delta U = q(V_S - V_C) = q\left[-\int_0^r E dr\right]$$

$$\Rightarrow \quad W = -q\int_0^r \frac{\rho r}{3\epsilon_0}\cdot dr$$

$$\Rightarrow \quad W = -\frac{q\rho}{3\epsilon_0}\frac{r^2}{2}$$

$\Rightarrow$ S-1 is false

Alternative : We can see that $\frac{q\rho}{3\epsilon_0}$ is not having dimensions of energy

$\Rightarrow$ S-1 is false **Ans. (D)**

Sol. 14 As the surface charge densities of the two shells are equal

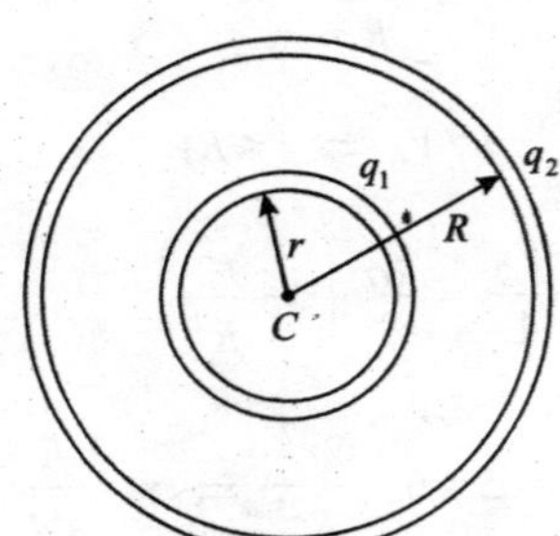

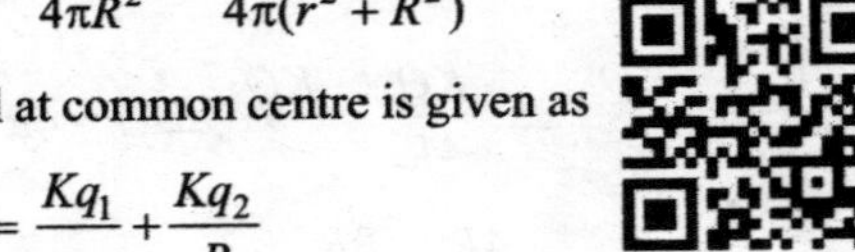

$$\Rightarrow \quad \frac{q_1}{4\pi r^2} = \frac{q_2}{4\pi R^2} = \frac{Q}{4\pi(r^2+R^2)}$$

Electric potential at common centre is given as

$$V_C = \frac{Kq_1}{r} + \frac{Kq_2}{R}$$

$$\Rightarrow \quad V_C = \frac{1}{4\pi\epsilon_0}\left[\frac{Qr^2}{r(r^2+R^2)} + \frac{QR^2}{R(r^2+R^2)}\right]$$

$$\Rightarrow \quad V_C = \frac{(r+R)Q}{4\pi\epsilon_0(r^2+R^2)}$$ **Ans. (C)**

Sol. 15

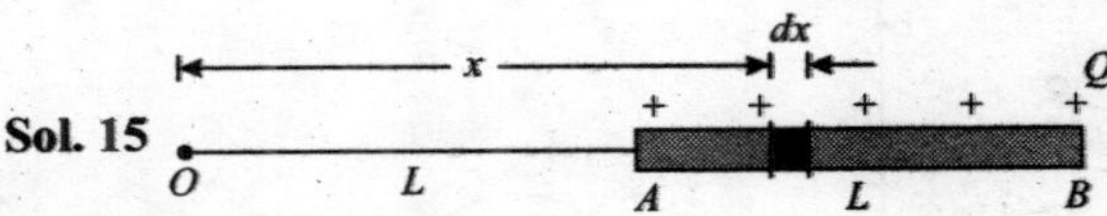

Charge on element

$$dq = \frac{Q}{L}dx$$

Potential at O due to dq is given as

$$dV = \frac{Kdq}{x} = \frac{KQ}{Lx}dx$$

Potential at O due to whole rod AB is

$$V = \int dV = \int_{x=L}^{x=2L}\frac{KQ}{Lx}dx$$

$$\Rightarrow \quad V = \frac{KQ}{L}[\ln x]_L^{2L} = \frac{KQ}{L}[\ln 2L \ln L]$$

$$\Rightarrow \quad V = \frac{KQ}{L}\ln(2) = \frac{Q}{4\pi\epsilon_0 L}\ln(2)$$ **Ans. (D)**

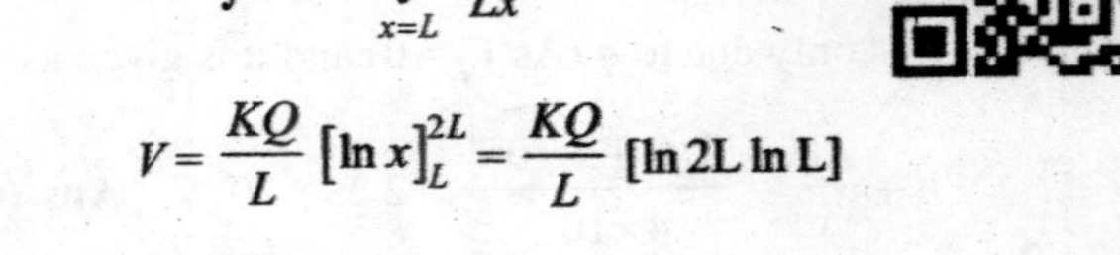

Sol. 16 As the force between dipoles placed 1 to X-axis will be zero so we consider these along X-axis as shown.

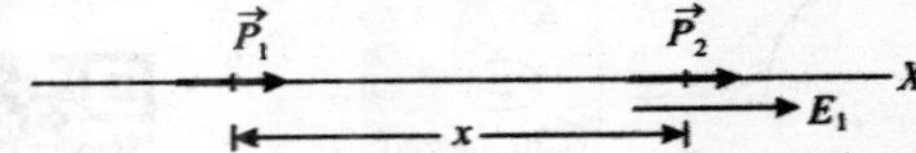

EF due to $\vec{P_1}$ at the location of $\vec{P_2}$ is given as

$$E_1 = \frac{2kP_1}{x^3}$$

In non uniform EF the force on a dipole placed along direction of EF is given as

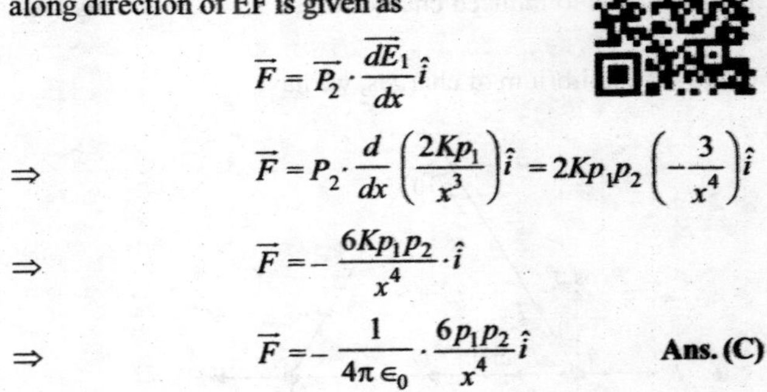

$$\vec{F} = \vec{P_2}\cdot\frac{\vec{dE_1}}{dx}\hat{i}$$

$$\Rightarrow \quad \vec{F} = P_2\cdot\frac{d}{dx}\left(\frac{2Kp_1}{x^3}\right)\hat{i} = 2Kp_1p_2\left(-\frac{3}{x^4}\right)\hat{i}$$

$$\Rightarrow \quad \vec{F} = -\frac{6Kp_1p_2}{x^4}\cdot\hat{i}$$

$$\Rightarrow \quad \vec{F} = -\frac{1}{4\pi\epsilon_0}\cdot\frac{6p_1p_2}{x^4}\hat{i}$$ **Ans. (C)**

Sol. 17 S-1 is true

Work done in moving a test charge between any two point is

$$W = q_0(V_A - V_B) = O$$

If $V_A = V_B$ (us A and B are on an equipotential surface)

S-2 is false

As at every point of equipotential surface, electric lines are ⊥ to this surface not mutually ⊥ to each other. **Ans. (C)**

Sol. 18

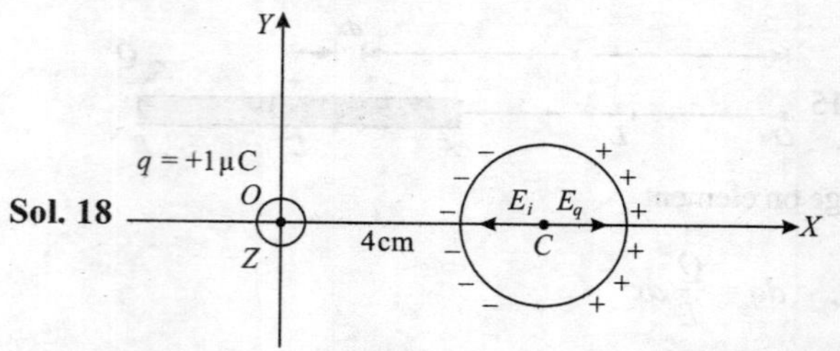

As net EF at C is zero (inside a conductor) we use

$$E_i = E_q = \frac{Kq}{x^2}$$

$$\Rightarrow \quad E_i = \frac{9\times10^9\times10^{-6}}{(4\times10^{-2})^2} = 5.625\times10^6\ \text{V/m}$$

Potential at C is only due to q (As $V_i = 0$) and it is given as

$$V = \frac{Kq}{x} = \frac{9\times10^9\times10^{-6}}{4\times10^{-2}} = 2.25\times10^5\ \text{V} \qquad \textbf{Ans. (C)}$$

Sol. 19 As in the direction of EF always potential decreases

$\Rightarrow$ we can use $\quad V_X > V_Y > V_\infty$

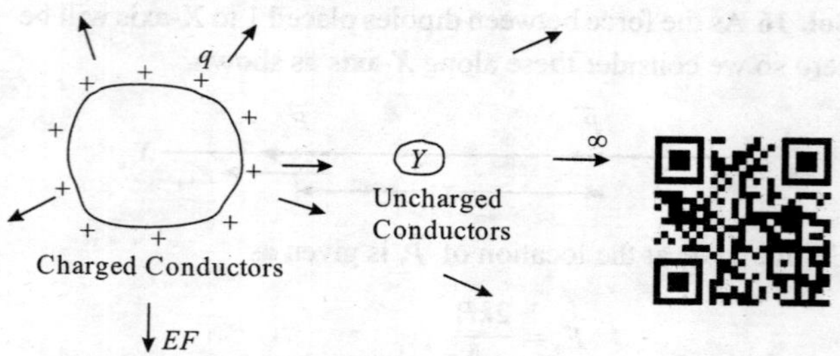

Because uncharged conductor will only affect its neighbourhood EF slightly due to induced charges on it **Ans. (A)**

Sol. 20 At equilibrium of charges, we have

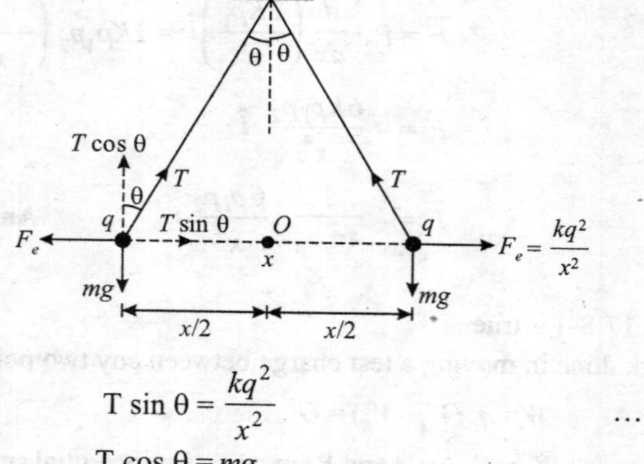

$$\text{T}\sin\theta = \frac{kq^2}{x^2} \qquad \ldots(1)$$

$$\text{T}\cos\theta = mg \qquad \ldots(2)$$

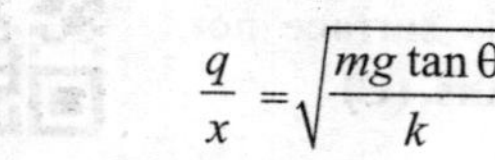

$$(1)(2) \Rightarrow \quad \tan\theta = \frac{kq^2}{mgx^2}$$

$$\Rightarrow \quad \frac{q}{x} = \sqrt{\frac{mg\tan\theta}{k}}$$

Electric potential at point O is $V_0 = \dfrac{kq}{x/2}\times 2 = \dfrac{4kq}{x}$

$$= 4k\sqrt{\frac{mg\tan\theta}{k}} = 4\sqrt{mgk\tan\theta} \qquad \textbf{Ans. (D)}$$

Sol. 21 We use

$$V_A - V_O = -\int_0^2 \vec{E}\,dx$$

here $\quad V_A < V_O$ So $V_A - V_O \rightarrow$ –ve

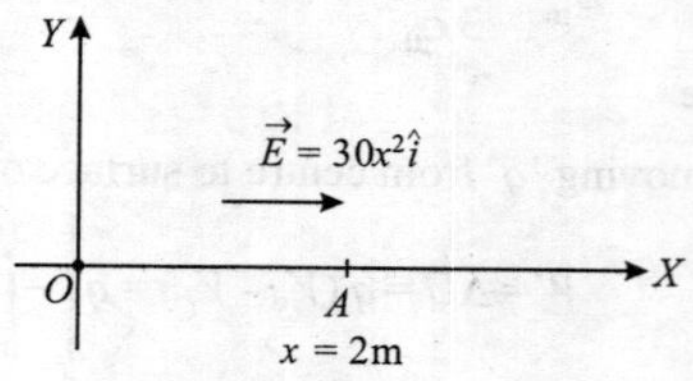

As along direction of EF potential decreases

$$\Rightarrow \quad V_A - V_0 = -\int_0^2 30x^2 dx$$

$$\Rightarrow \quad V_A - V_0 = -30\left[\frac{x^3}{3}\right]_0^2 = -10[8-0]$$

$$\Rightarrow \quad V_A - V_0 = -80\ \text{V} = -80\ \text{J/C} \qquad \textbf{Ans. (C)}$$

Sol. 22 Potential on surface of a solid uniformly charged sphere is

$$V_O = \frac{KQ}{R}$$

If at $r = R_1$, $V = \dfrac{3V_O}{2}$ $(> V_0 \Rightarrow r < R)$

$$\Rightarrow \quad \frac{5V_O}{4} = \frac{V_O}{2}\left(3 - \frac{r^2}{R^2}\right)$$

$$\Rightarrow \quad 5 = 6 - \frac{2r^2}{R^2} \Rightarrow r = \frac{R}{\sqrt{2}} = R_2$$

If at $r = R_3$, $V = \dfrac{3V_O}{4}$ $(< V_O \Rightarrow r > R)$

$$\Rightarrow \frac{V_O}{4} = \frac{KQ}{r} \Rightarrow \frac{KQ}{4R} = \frac{KQ}{r} \Rightarrow r = 4R = R_4 \qquad \textbf{Ans. (D)}$$

Here $R_4 - R_3 = 4R - \dfrac{4R}{3} = \dfrac{8R}{3} > R_2$ (As $R_2 = \dfrac{R}{\sqrt{2}}$) **Ans. (C)**

Both are correct.

Sol. 23 Along the direction of EF, potential decreases and in uniform EF, potential difference between two points is given as

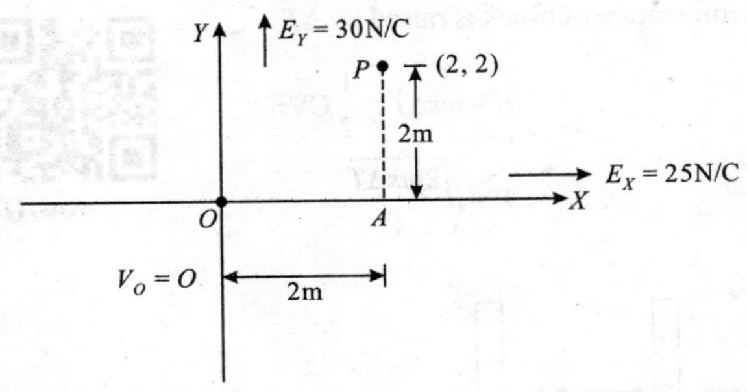

$$V_X - V_Y = Ed$$

In moving from O to P we can write

$$V_O - V_A = 25 \times 2$$

$$V_A - V_P = 30 \times 2$$

$$\Rightarrow \quad V_O - V_P = 110$$

$$\Rightarrow \quad V_P = -110\text{ V or } -110\text{ J/C}$$ **Ans. (A)**

Sol. 24 For $|Z| \leq |m$ $\quad \vec{E} = -\frac{dV}{dZ}\hat{k} = 10|Z|\hat{k}$

$-1\text{m} < Z < 1\text{m}$

and for $|Z| \geq 1\text{m}$ $\quad \vec{E} = -\frac{dV}{dZ}\hat{k} = \pm 10\hat{k}$

$Z > 1$m and $Z < -1$m constant EF

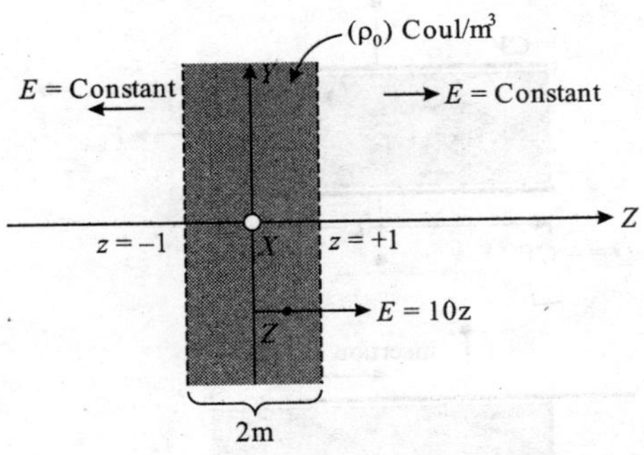

By analyzing the EF we can state that it is produced by a uniform charge distribution in a thick sheet of width 2m as shown.

Due to a thick volume charged sheet, inside at a distance Z from central plane the EF is given as

$$E_{in} = \frac{\rho_Z}{\epsilon_O} = 10z$$

$$\Rightarrow \quad \rho_0 = 10\,\epsilon_0 \quad \text{for } |z| \leq 1\text{m}$$

$$\Rightarrow \quad \rho_0 = 0 \quad \text{for } |z| \geq 1\text{m}$$ **Ans. (B)**

Sol. 25 $r_2 - r_1 = r_1 - r_0 = r_N - r_{N-1}$

$\Delta V \quad \Delta V \quad \Delta V$ Potential differences

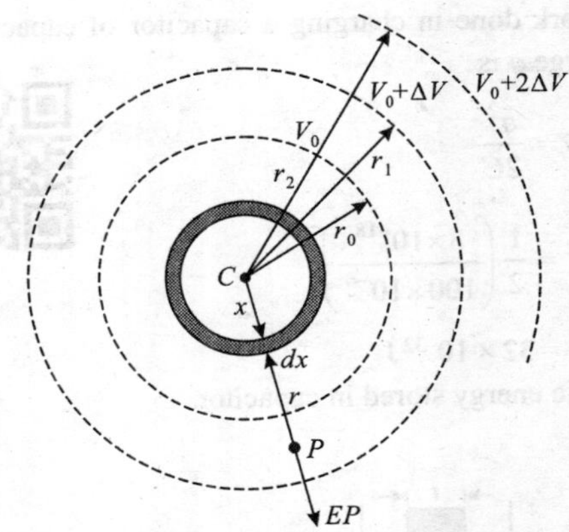

Only in uniform EF the separation between equipotential surface having same ΔV is constant.

To calculate EF at a distance r from centre of charge distribution then it is given by

$$E_P = \frac{kq}{r^2}$$

Where $q \rightarrow$ charge enclosed within sphere of rad $r = 0$ to $r = r$.

Charge in sphere of radius r is given as

$$q = \int dq = \int_0^r \rho(x) 4\pi x^2 dx$$

$\Rightarrow$ EF at point P is

$$E_P = \frac{K\int_0^r \rho(x) \cdot 4\pi x^2 dx}{r^2} = C \text{ (constant)}$$

Differentiating we get

$$\frac{d}{dr}\left[k\int_0^r \rho(x) \cdot 4\pi x^2 dx\right] = 2\text{Cr}$$

$$\frac{1}{4\pi\,\epsilon_0} \cdot [\rho(r)\, 4\pi r^2 - 0] = 2\text{ Cr}$$

$$\Rightarrow \quad \rho(r) = \frac{2C\,\epsilon_0}{r} \quad \Rightarrow \quad \rho(r) \propto \frac{1}{r}$$ **Ans. (C)**

16.2 Capacitance

Sol. 1 Capacitance of a spherical conductor is

$$C = 4\pi\epsilon_0 R$$

$$\Rightarrow \quad C = \frac{1}{9 \times 10^9} \times 1$$

$$= 1.1 \times 10^{-10}\text{F}$$ **Ans. (A)**

Sol. 2 For n identical capacitors (C) parallel combination equivalent capacitance is

$$C_{eq} = C + C + C + \ldots n \text{ times} = nC$$

Across a voltage V the energy stored is

$$U = \frac{1}{2}C_{eq}V^2 = \frac{1}{2}nCV^2$$ **Ans. (B)**

Sol. 3 Work done in charging a capacitor of capacitance C with a charge q is

$$W=\frac{q^2}{2C}$$

$$=\frac{1}{2}\left(\frac{8\times10^{-18}}{100\times10^{-6}}\right)^2$$

$$=32\times10^{-32}\text{ J}$$

Electrostatic energy stored in capacitor. **Ans. (D)**

Sol. 4

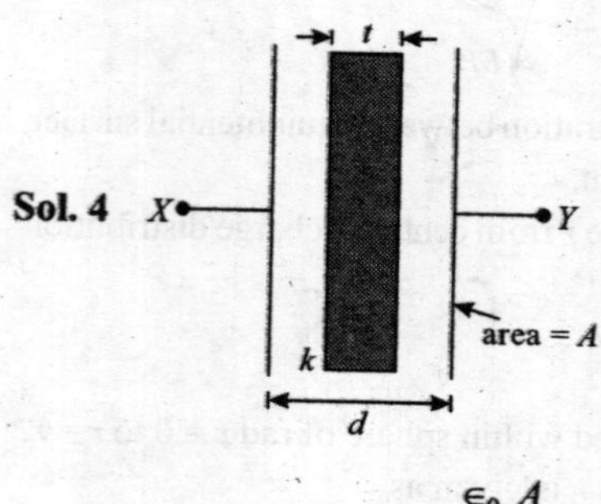

$$C_{XY}=\frac{\epsilon_0 A}{\frac{t}{k}+(d-t)}$$

If $t\to0 \Rightarrow C_{XY}=\frac{\epsilon_0 A}{d}=C$ **Ans. (B)**

Sol. 5

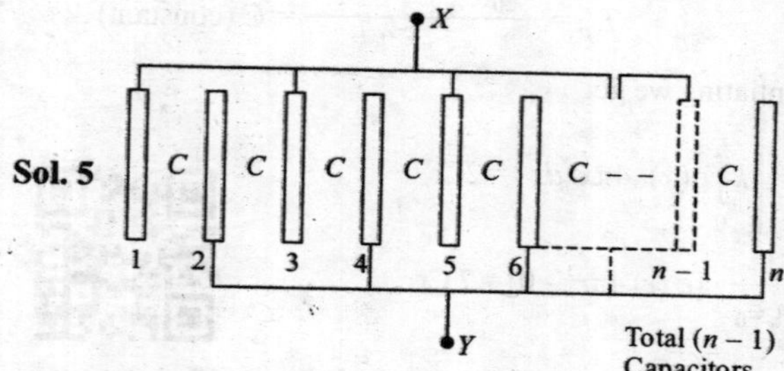

In above system of plates one plate of each capacitor is connected to Y and its other plate is connected to X. Thus all $(n-1)$ capacitors formed are in parallel combination.

$\Rightarrow \quad C_{XY}=C+C+\ldots(n-1)$ times

$=(n-1)C$ **Ans. (A)**

Sol. 6

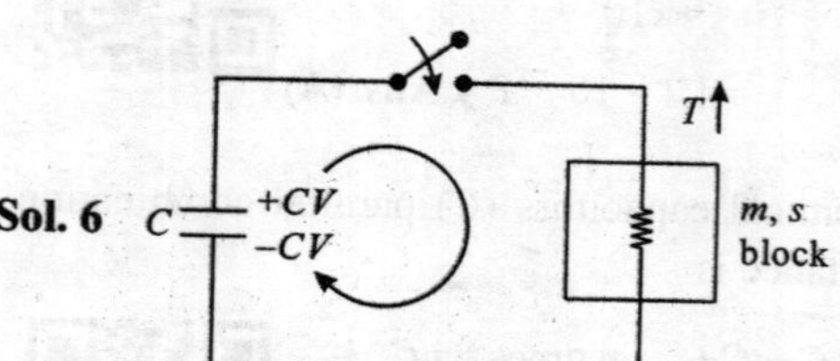

On discharging the capacitor, heat supplied to block is

$$H=U_{cap}=\frac{1}{2}CV^2$$

If temperature of block is raised by ΔT

$$\Rightarrow \quad H=ms\Delta T=\frac{1}{2}CV^2$$

$$\Rightarrow \quad V=\sqrt{\frac{2ms\Delta T}{C}}$$

Ans. (D)

Sol. 7

Work done in travelling from plate 1 to 2 on electron by the EF of plates is given as

$$W=e\times(V_2-V_1)=\Delta K=\frac{1}{2}mv^2$$

$$\Rightarrow \quad W=(-1.6\times10^{-19})\times(-20)$$

$$\Rightarrow \quad W=\frac{1}{2}\times9.1\times10^{-31}\times v^2$$

$$\Rightarrow \quad v=\sqrt{\frac{2\times1.6\times10^{-19}\times20}{9.1\times10^{-31}}}=2.65\times10^6\text{ m/s}$$ **Ans. (A)**

Sol. 8

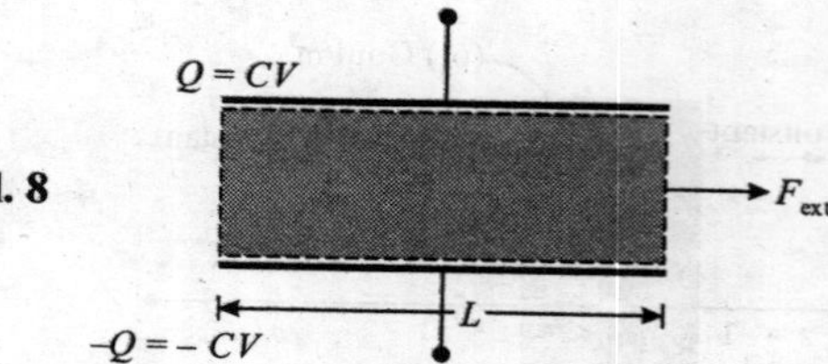

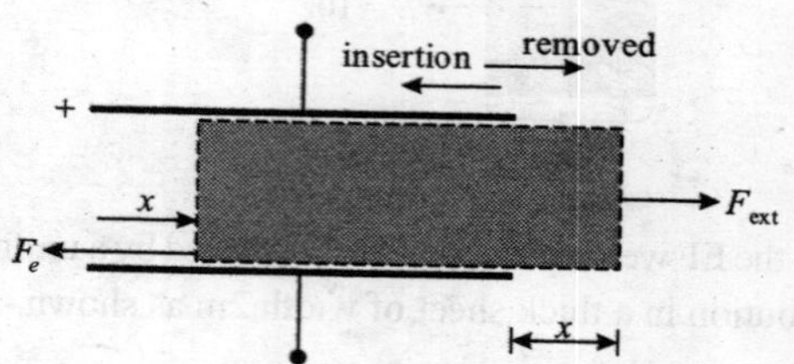

Work done in removing the dielectric slab slowly from capacitor is

$$\text{removal}\to W_1=\int_0^l F_{ext}\cdot dx$$

$$\text{insertion}\to W_2=\int_0^l F_{ext}\cdot dx$$

For slow insertion or removal of slab $F_{ext}=F_e$

Net work done is $W_1+W_2=0$ **Ans. (D)**

Sol. 9

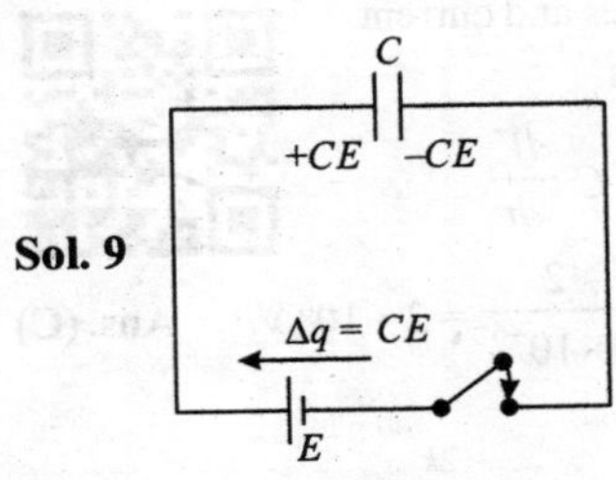

After capacitor is fully charged (when potential difference across plates is equal to that of battery EMF) charge on its plates is equal to

$$q_f = CE \text{ and } q_i = 0$$

Energy stored in capacitor is

$$U = \frac{1}{2}CE^2$$

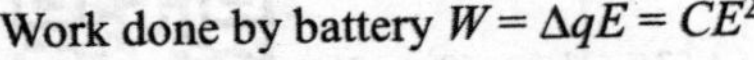

Work done by battery $W = \Delta qE = CE^2$

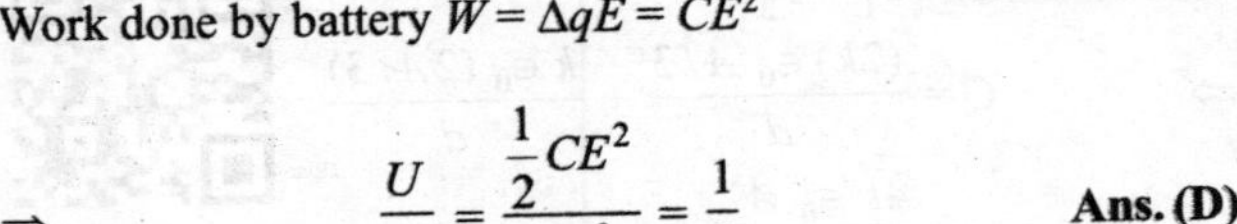

$$\Rightarrow \quad \frac{U}{W} = \frac{\frac{1}{2}CE^2}{CE^2} = \frac{1}{2}$$ **Ans. (D)**

Sol. 10

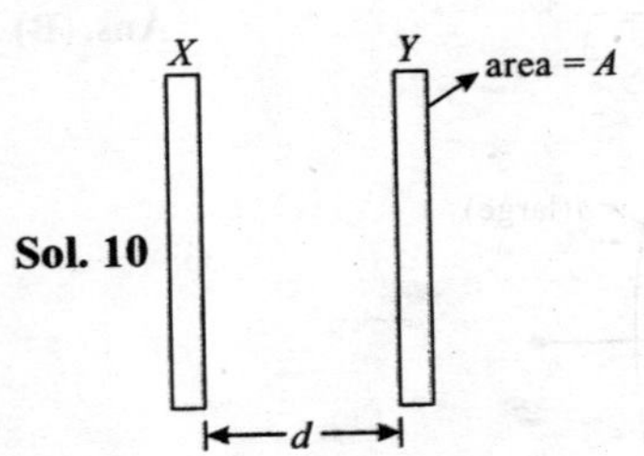

$$C = \frac{\epsilon_0 A}{d} = 9pF \Rightarrow \epsilon_0 A = 9d$$

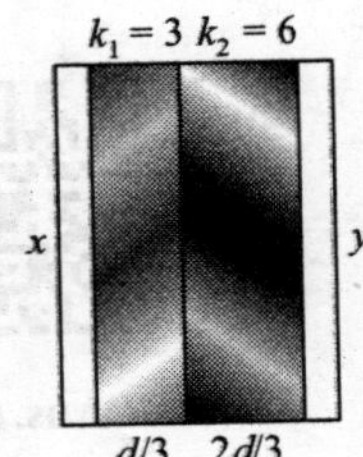

Capacitance of capacitor with multiple dielectric field slabs parallel to plates is given as

$$C' = \frac{\epsilon_0 A}{\frac{t_1}{k_1} + \frac{t_2}{k_2}}$$

$$\Rightarrow \quad C' = \frac{9d}{\frac{d/3}{3} + \frac{2d/3}{6}}$$

$$\Rightarrow \quad C' = \frac{9}{\frac{1}{9} + \frac{1}{9}} = \frac{81}{2} = 40.5 \text{ pF}$$ **Ans. (C)**

Sol. 11 (a) $V_L = \frac{2Q}{3C}$

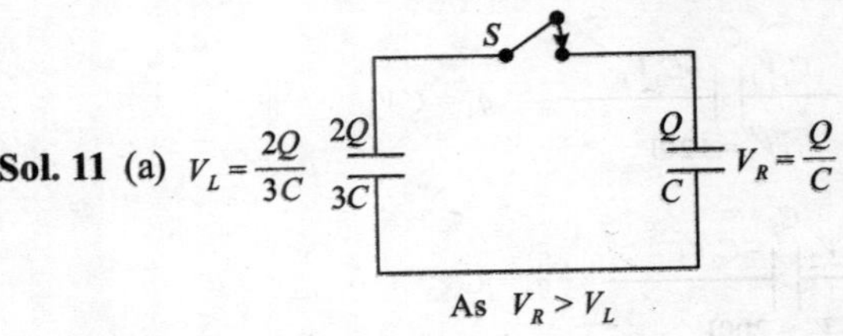

As $V_R > V_L$

then on closing S flows from R to L

(b) $V_L = \frac{Q}{C}$

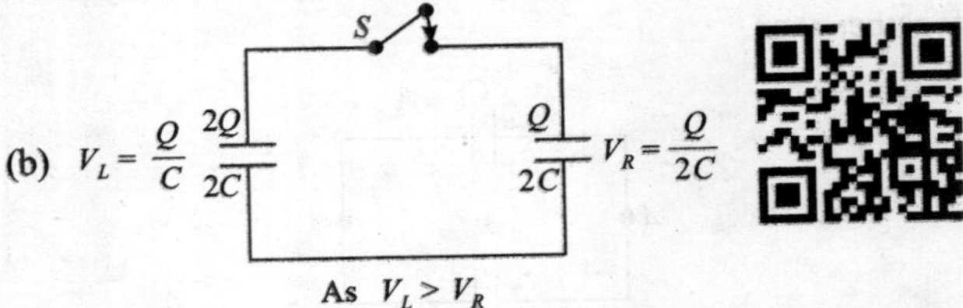

As $V_L > V_R$

then on closing S charge flows from L to R. **Ans. (C)**

Sol. 12 Case-I : n_1 capacitors, each C_1 when connected in series then its equivalent capacitance is given as

$$C_{eq_1} = \frac{C_1}{n_1}$$

⇒ Energy stored with potential difference = 4V is given as

$$U_1 = \frac{1}{2}\left(\frac{C_1}{n_1}\right)(4V)^2 \qquad \ldots(1)$$

Case-II : n_1 capacitors, each C_2 when connected in parallel then its equation capacitance is given as

$$C_{eq_2} = n_2 C_2$$

⇒ Energy stored with p.d. = V is given as

$$U_2 = \frac{1}{2}(n_2 C_2)V^2 \qquad \ldots(2)$$

Given that $U_1 = U_2$

$$\Rightarrow \quad \frac{1}{2}\left(\frac{C_1}{n_1}\right)(4V)^2 = \frac{1}{2}(n_2 C_2)V^2$$

$$\Rightarrow \quad 16\frac{C_1}{n_1} = n_2 C_2$$

$$\Rightarrow \quad C_2 = \frac{16C_1}{n_1 n_2}$$ **Ans. (D)**

Sol. 13 Statement-1 : It is true because the radius of a sphere required for making 1F cap is gives as

$$C = 4\pi\epsilon_0 R$$

$$1 = 4\pi\epsilon_0 R$$

$$\Rightarrow \quad R = \frac{1}{4\pi\epsilon_0} = 9 \times 10^9 \text{ m}$$

Statement-2 : As $6.4 \times 10^6 \text{ m} < 9 \times 10^9 \text{ m}$

⇒ It is not possible with earth

$$C_{earth} < 1\text{F}$$ **Ans. (D)**

Sol. 14 C_1: $C_1V_1 \; | \; -C_1V_1$, $V_1 = 120V$ $\quad q_1 = C_1V_1$

C_2: $C_2V_2 \; | \; -C_2V_2$, $V_2 = 200V$ $\quad q_2 = C_2V_2$

If the capacitors are joined in parallel with same polarity plates together then

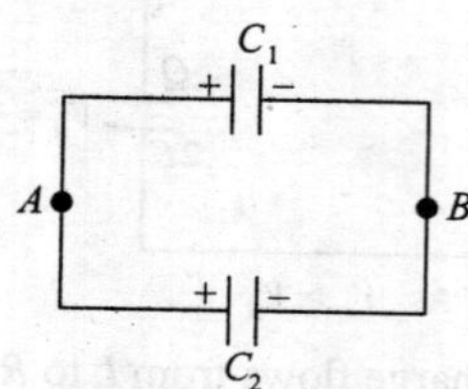

$$V_{AB} = \frac{q_1 + q_2}{C_1 + C_2} \neq 0$$

If the capacitors are joined in parallel with opposite polarity plates together then

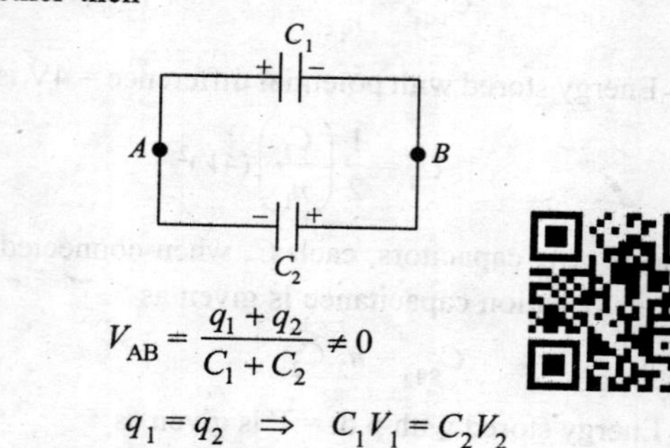

$$V_{AB} = \frac{q_1 + q_2}{C_1 + C_2} \neq 0$$

$\Rightarrow \quad q_1 = q_2 \Rightarrow C_1V_1 = C_2V_2$

$\Rightarrow \quad 120\, C_1 = 200\, C_2$

$\Rightarrow \quad 3C_1 = 5C_2$ **Ans. (B)**

Sol. 15

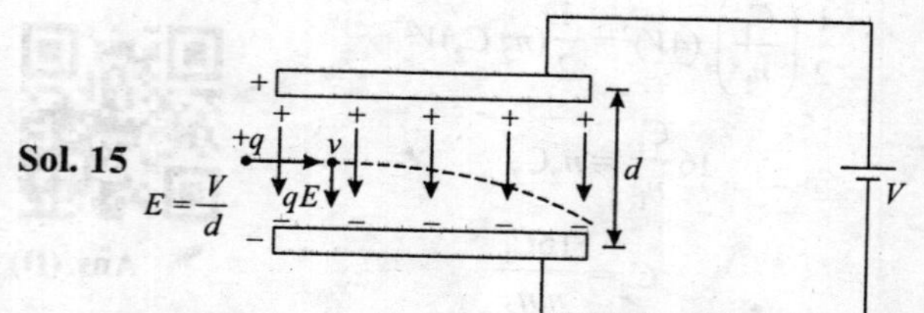

Acceleration of charged particle due to electric force is

$$a = \frac{F}{m} = \frac{qE}{m} \rightarrow \text{constant}$$

at constant acceleration, particle follows projectile motion with

$$g_{eff} = \frac{qE}{m}$$

$\Rightarrow$ path $\rightarrow$ parabolic trajectory **Ans. (C)**

Sol. 16 When a capacitor is charged to a potential difference V volt then we have

$$q = CV$$

If V starts varying then q changes and current in connecting wires is given as

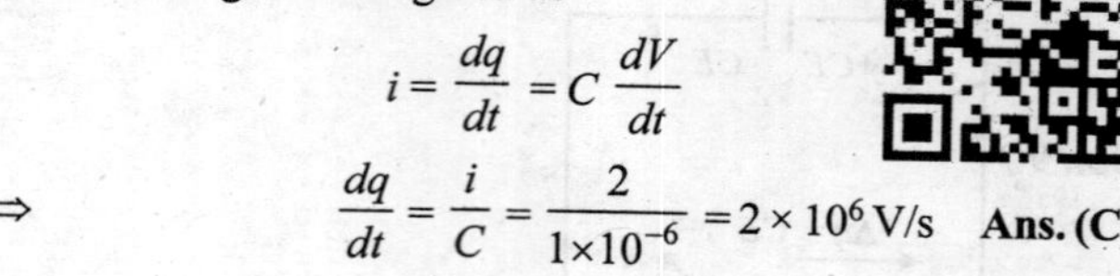

$$i = \frac{dq}{dt} = C\frac{dV}{dt}$$

$$\Rightarrow \quad \frac{dq}{dt} = \frac{i}{C} = \frac{2}{1\times10^{-6}} = 2\times10^6 \text{ V/s}$$ **Ans. (C)**

Sol. 17

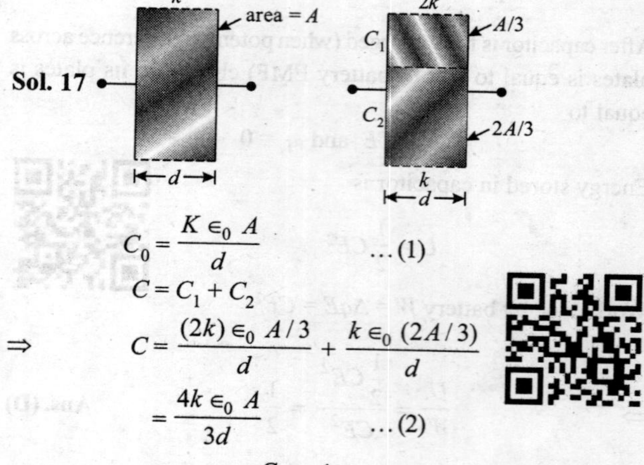

$$C_0 = \frac{K \epsilon_0 A}{d} \quad \ldots(1)$$

$$C = C_1 + C_2$$

$$\Rightarrow \quad C = \frac{(2k)\epsilon_0 A/3}{d} + \frac{k\epsilon_0 (2A/3)}{d}$$

$$= \frac{4k\epsilon_0 A}{3d} \quad \ldots(2)$$

From (1) and (2) $\Rightarrow \quad \frac{C}{C_0} = \frac{4}{3}$ **Ans. (B)**

Sol. 18

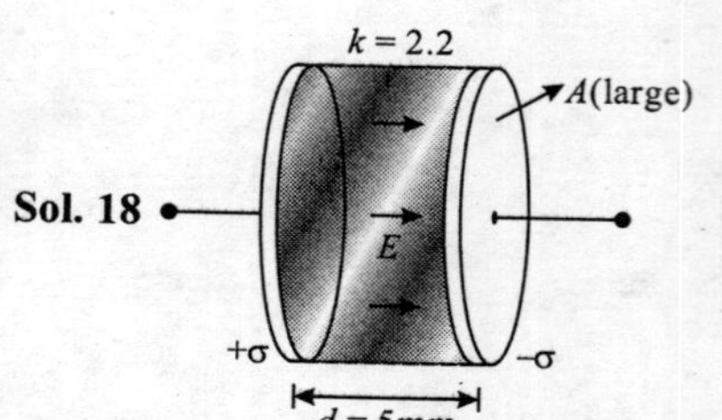

Electric field between plates of a capacitor inside dielectric is given as

$$E = \frac{\sigma}{k\epsilon_0} = 3\times10^4 \text{ V/m}$$

$\Rightarrow \quad \sigma = 3\times10^4 \times k\epsilon_0$

$\Rightarrow \quad \sigma = 3\times10^4 \times 2.2 \times 8.89\times10^{-12}$

$\Rightarrow \quad \sigma = 5.87\times10^{-7}\text{ C/m}^2$ **Ans. (A)**

Sol. 19

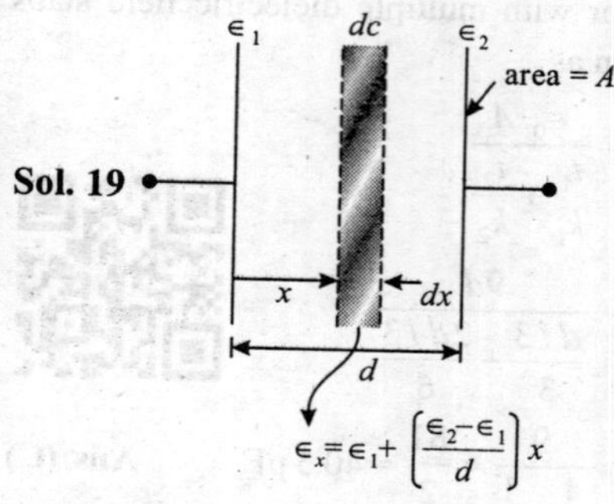

$$\epsilon_x = \epsilon_1 + \left[\frac{\epsilon_2 - \epsilon_1}{d}\right]x$$

Using $\epsilon_x = mx + C$

at $x=0, \in = \in_1$

at $x=d, \in = \in_2$

The capacitance of elemental capacitor as shown in

$$dC = \frac{\in_x \in_0 A}{dx}$$

All such dC's are in series combination so we use

$$\frac{1}{C} = \int \frac{1}{dC}$$

$$\Rightarrow \quad \frac{1}{C} = \int_0^d \frac{dx}{\in_0 A\left(\in_1 + \frac{\in_2 - \in_1}{d} \cdot x\right)}$$

$$\Rightarrow \quad \frac{1}{C} = \frac{1}{\in_0 A} \frac{d}{(\in_2 - \in_1)} \left(\ln\left[\in_1 + \frac{\in_2 - \in_1}{d} \cdot x\right]\right)_0^d$$

$$\Rightarrow \quad \frac{1}{C} = \frac{d}{\in_0 A(\in_2 - \in_1)} [\ln \in_2 - \ln \in_1]$$

$$\Rightarrow \quad \frac{1}{C} = \frac{d \ln\left(\frac{\in_2}{\in_1}\right)}{\in_0 (\in_2 - \in_1) A}$$

$$\Rightarrow \quad C = \frac{\in_0 (\in_2 - \in_1) A}{d \ln\left(\frac{\in_2}{\in_1}\right)}$$

Ans. (D)

Sol. 20 Case-I :

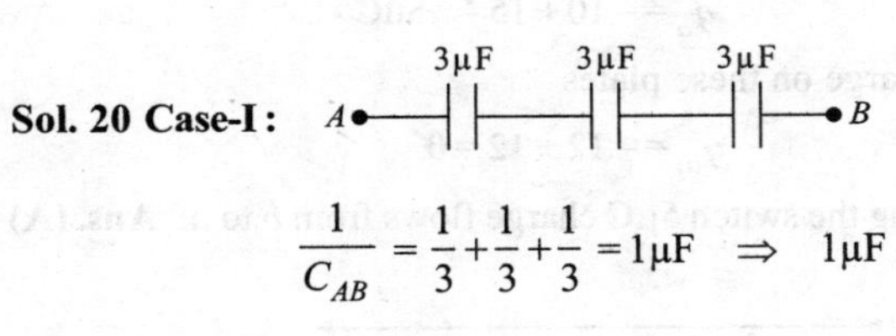

$$\frac{1}{C_{AB}} = \frac{1}{3} + \frac{1}{3} + \frac{1}{3} = 1\mu F \Rightarrow 1\mu F$$

Case-II :

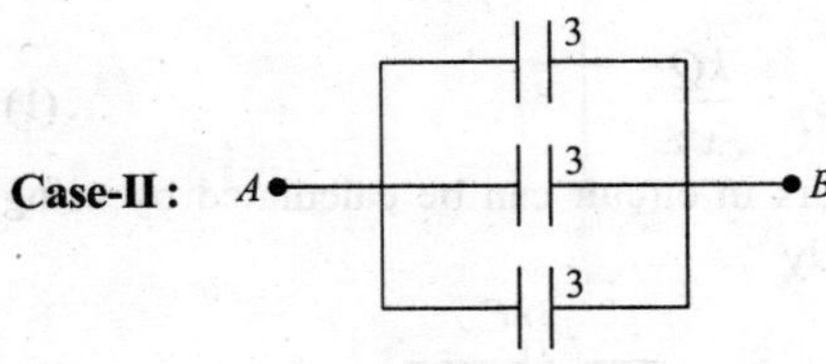

$$C_{AB} = 3 + 3 + 3 = 9\mu F$$

Case-III : A —[3μF ∥ 3μF]— 3μF — B ; (3μF ∥ 3μF = 6μF)

$$C_{AB} = \frac{6 \times 3}{6+3} = \frac{18}{9} = 2\mu F$$

Case-IV :

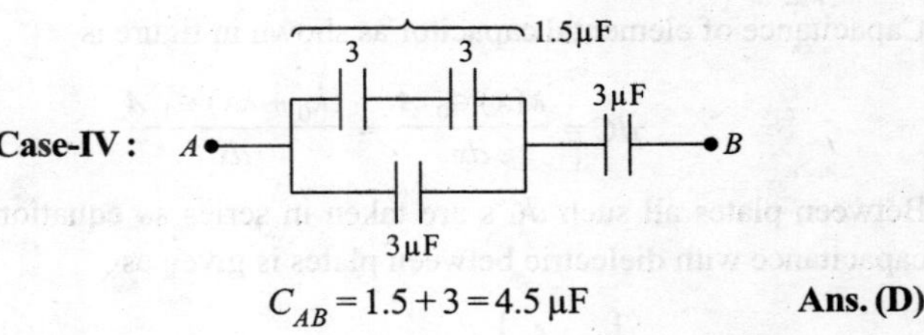

$$C_{AB} = 1.5 + 3 = 4.5\ \mu F$$

Ans. (D)

Sol. 21

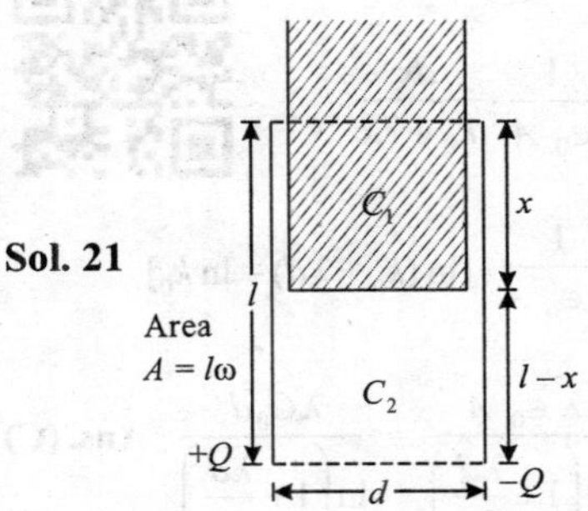

As C_1 and C_2 capacitors are in parallel with values

$$C_1 = \frac{K \in_0 (xw)}{d} \quad \text{and} \quad C_2 = \frac{\in_0 (l-x)w}{d}$$

$$C_{eq} = C_1 + C_2 = \frac{\in_0 w}{d}[l + x(k-1)]$$

Energy in capacitor with dielectric filled upto a distance x is

$$U = \frac{Q^2}{2C} = \frac{Q^2}{2\frac{\in_0 w}{d}[l + x(k-1)]}$$

$\Rightarrow$ force on dielectric is given as

$$F = -\frac{\partial U}{\partial x}$$

$$\Rightarrow \quad F = \frac{Q^2 d}{2 \in_0 w}\left[\frac{1}{[l + x(k-1)]^2} \times (k-1)\right]$$

at $x = 0$ or when dielectric is at the edge, we have

$$F_{x=0} = \frac{Q^2 d(k-1)}{2 \in_0 wl^2}$$

Ans. (C)

Sol. 22

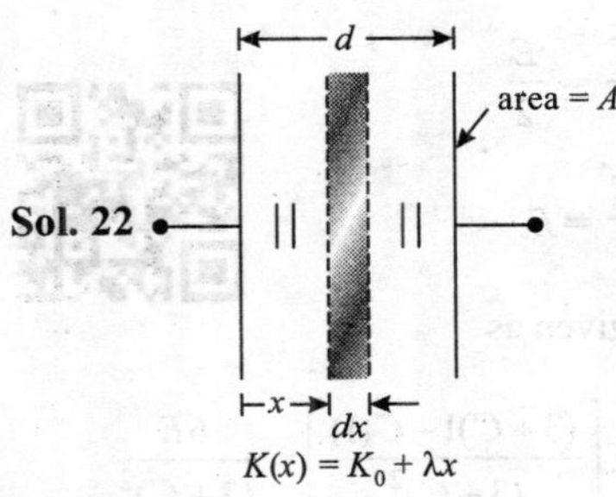

Capacitance with vacuum between plates is given as

$$C_0 = \frac{\in_0 A}{d} \qquad \ldots(1)$$

Capacitance of elemental capacitor as shown in figure is

$$dC = \frac{k(x)\in_0 A}{dx} = \frac{(k_0+\lambda x)\in_0 A}{dx}$$

Between plates all such dC's are taken in series so equation capacitance with dielectric between plates is given as

$$\frac{1}{C} = \int \frac{1}{dC}$$

$$\Rightarrow \quad \frac{1}{C} = \int_0^d \frac{1}{\in_0 A}\cdot\frac{dx}{k_0+\lambda x}$$

$$\Rightarrow \quad \frac{1}{C} = \frac{1}{\lambda \in_0 A}\cdot[\ln(k_0+\lambda d) - \ln k_0]$$

$$\Rightarrow \quad \frac{1}{C} = \frac{\lambda \in_0 A}{\ln\left(1+\frac{\lambda d}{k_0}\right)} = \frac{\lambda C_0 d}{\ln\left(1+\frac{\lambda d}{k_0}\right)}$$ **Ans. (C)**

Sol. 23 Using nodal analysis we distribute potential in given circuit as shown in figure.

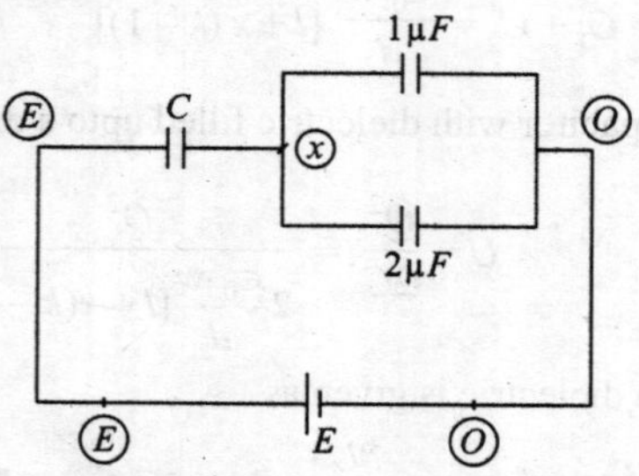

For unknown x, potential x, nodal equation is

$$1(x) + 2(x) + C(x-E) = 0$$

$$\Rightarrow \quad x = \frac{CE}{3+C}$$

charge on $2\mu F$ capacitor is

$$q_{2\mu F} = Q_2 = 2x = \frac{2CE}{3+C} \quad \text{(Not linear relation)}$$

When $C = 1\mu F \rightarrow Q_2 = \frac{2E}{4} = \frac{E}{2}$

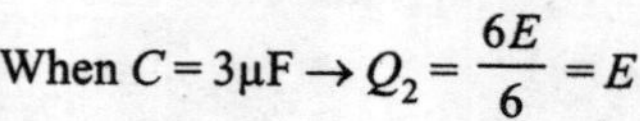

When $C = 3\mu F \rightarrow Q_2 = \frac{6E}{6} = E$

Slope of Q_2 *vs* C graph is given as

$$\frac{dQ_2}{dC} = 2E\left[\frac{(3+C)1 - C(1)}{(3+C)^2}\right] = \frac{6E}{(3+C)^2}$$

As C increase $\Rightarrow \frac{dQ_2}{dC}$ decreases **Ans. (B)**

Sol. 24

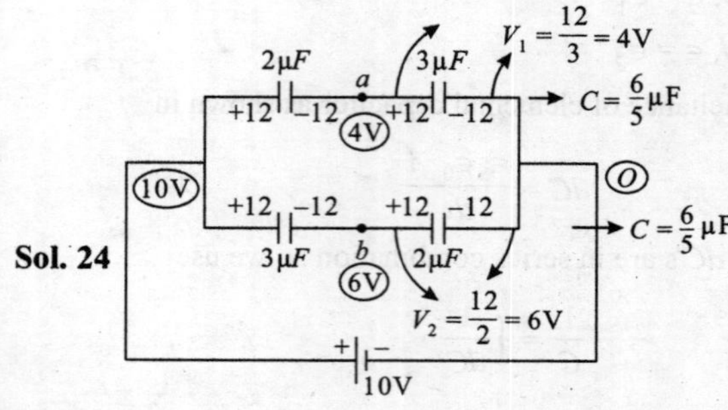

When S is open, charges on each capacitor in circuit is

$$q = CV$$

$$q = \frac{6}{5}\times 10 = 12\mu C$$

When S is closed

Charges flows from b to a

As $\quad V_B > V_A$

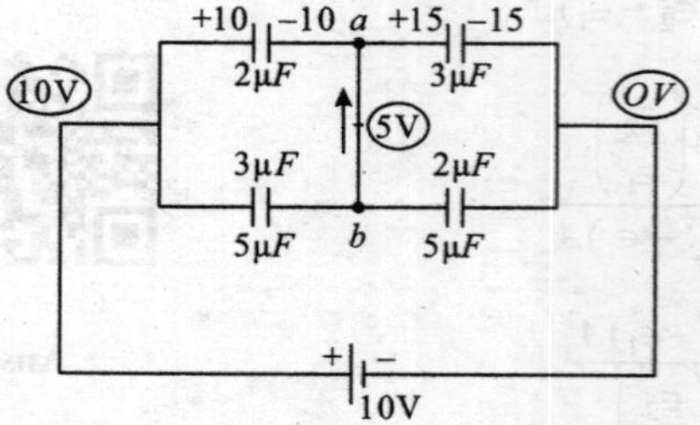

Charge connected to the two plates at point a is

$$q_a = -10 + 15 = +5\mu C$$

Initial charge on these plates

$$q_{a_i} = -12 + 12 = 0$$

On closing the switch 5μC charge flows from b to a. **Ans. (A)**

Sol. 25 $Q\bullet$ ——— x ——— P →

$$E_P = \frac{kQ}{x^2} \quad \ldots(1)$$

Charges on capacitors in circuit can be calculated by using nodal analysis quickly

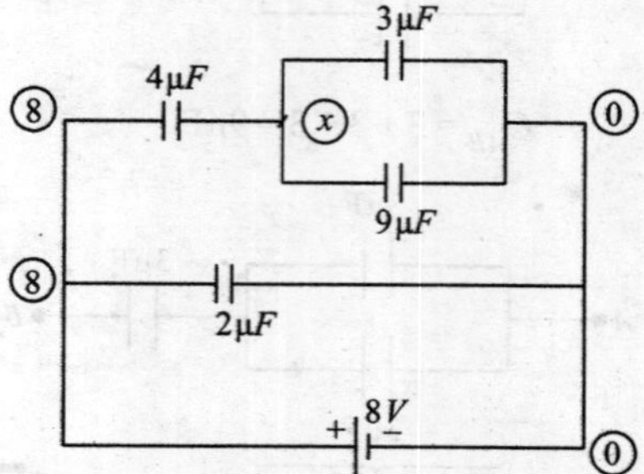

Nodal equation for potential x is given as

$$3x + 9x + 4(x-8) = 0$$

$$\Rightarrow \quad 12x + 4(x-8) = 0$$

$\Rightarrow \quad 4x+8 \Rightarrow x=2V$

$$q_{4\mu F}=4\times 6=24\mu C$$

and $\quad q_{9\mu F}=9\times 2=18\mu C$

$\Rightarrow \quad Q=24\times 18=42\mu C$

From (1) $\quad E_P=\dfrac{9\times10^9\times42\times10^{-6}}{(30)^2}$

$\Rightarrow \quad E_P=420\,N/C$ **Ans. (C)**

Sol. 26 4μF 4μF 4μF

$C_{eq}=\frac{4}{2}=2\mu F$

To get 6μF equivalent

Capacitance circuit combination is as shown in figure

Two in series and one in parallel

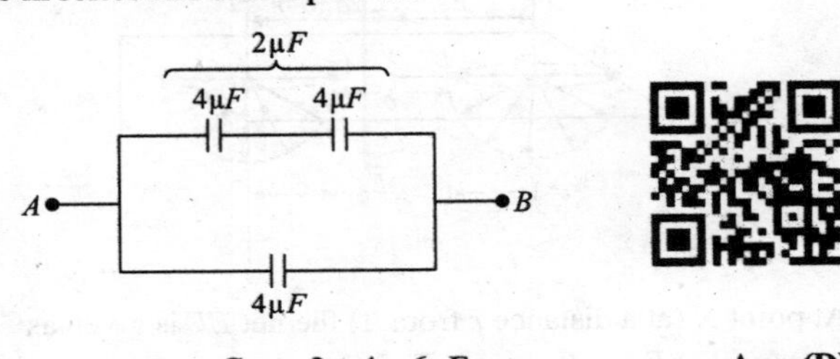

$$C_{AB}=2+4=6\mu F$$ **Ans. (D)**

Sol. 27

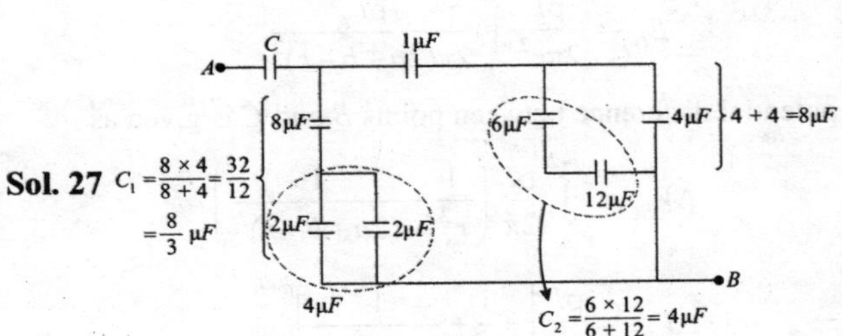

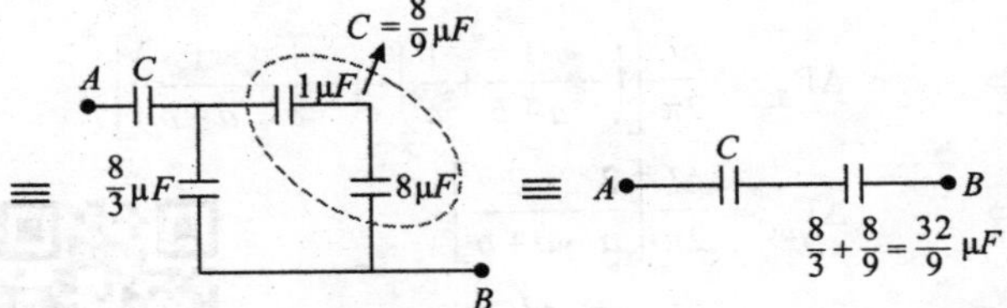

As capacitance across A and B is 1μF

$$\Rightarrow \quad \frac{1}{1}=\frac{1}{C}+\frac{1}{\frac{32}{9}}$$

$$\Rightarrow \quad \frac{1}{C}=1-\frac{9}{32}=\frac{23}{32} \quad \Rightarrow \quad C=\frac{32}{23}\mu F$$ **Ans. (A)**

17.1 Current Electricity

Sol. 1 If a resistance wire is of length l and cross sectional area A then its resistance is given as

$$R=\rho\frac{l}{A} \quad [\rho\rightarrow \text{wire resistivity}]$$

volume of wire $\quad V=RA$

$[r\rightarrow$ wire resistivity]

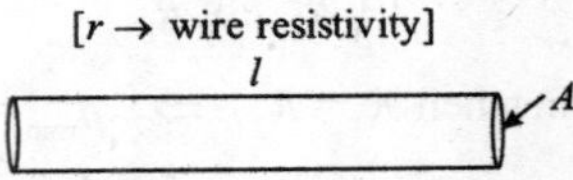

If length of wire is stretched by 100%

$$\Rightarrow \quad l_f=2l$$

As $\quad V\rightarrow$ constant $\Rightarrow \quad A_f=\dfrac{A}{2}$

$\Rightarrow$ Final resistance of wire will become

$$R_f=\rho\frac{l_f}{A_f}=\rho\left(\frac{2l}{A/2}\right)=4\rho\frac{l}{A}=4R$$

Change $=R_f-R=4R-R=3R$ **Ans. (D)**

Sol. 2 Thermistors are such resistances of which resistance changes rapidly with small change in this temperature. These are used mainly as temperature sensing devices.

Metal oxides which have high temperature coefficients of resistivity are most suitable for making thermistors. **Ans. (C)**

Sol. 3 $\dfrac{l_1}{l_2}=\dfrac{4}{3}$ and $\dfrac{r_1}{r_2}=\dfrac{2}{3} \Rightarrow \dfrac{A_1}{A_2}=\left(\dfrac{2}{3}\right)^2=\dfrac{4}{9}$

Resistances of the given wires

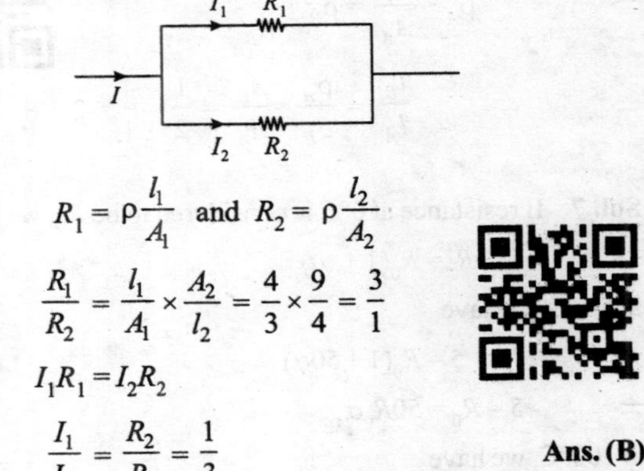

$$R_1=\rho\frac{l_1}{A_1} \text{ and } R_2=\rho\frac{l_2}{A_2}$$

$$\Rightarrow \quad \frac{R_1}{R_2}=\frac{l_1}{A_1}\times\frac{A_2}{l_2}=\frac{4}{3}\times\frac{9}{4}=\frac{3}{1}$$

$$\Rightarrow \quad I_1R_1=I_2R_2$$

$$\Rightarrow \quad \frac{I_1}{I_2}=\frac{R_2}{R_1}=\frac{1}{3}$$ **Ans. (B)**

Sol. 4 If the given resistances are R_1 and R_2

$$\Rightarrow S=R_1+R_2 \text{ and } P=\frac{R_1R_2}{R_1+R_2}$$

We use $\quad S=nP$

$$R_1+R_2=n\left(\frac{R_1R_2}{R_1+R_2}\right)$$

$$\Rightarrow \quad n=\frac{(R_1+R_2)^2}{R_1R_2}=\frac{R_1^2+R_2^2+2R_1R_2}{R_1R_2}$$

$$\Rightarrow \quad n = \frac{R_1}{R_2} + \frac{R_2}{R_1} + 2$$

$$\Rightarrow \quad n = \left(\sqrt{\frac{R_1}{R_2}} - \sqrt{\frac{R_2}{R_1}}\right)^2 + 4$$

here n is minimum when $R_1 = R_2 \Rightarrow n_{min} = 4$ **Ans. (A)**

Sol. 5 We use $R_T = R_0(1+\alpha T)$

where $R_T \rightarrow$ resistance at T°C

$R_0 \rightarrow$ resistance at 0°C

Initially at 100°C, $R_T = 100\Omega$

$$\Rightarrow \quad 100 = R_0(1+100\alpha) \quad \ldots(1)$$

Later at T°C, $R_T = 200\Omega$

$$\Rightarrow \quad 200 = R_0(1+\alpha T) \quad \ldots(2)$$

$$(2) \div (1) \Rightarrow \quad \frac{200}{100} = \frac{1+\alpha T}{1+100\alpha}$$

$$\Rightarrow \quad 2 + 200\,\alpha = 1 + \alpha T$$

$$\Rightarrow \quad T - 200 = \frac{1}{\alpha} = \frac{1000}{5} = 200$$

$$\Rightarrow T = 200 + 200 + 400°C$$ **Ans. (B)**

Sol. 6 $\rho_B = 2\rho_A$

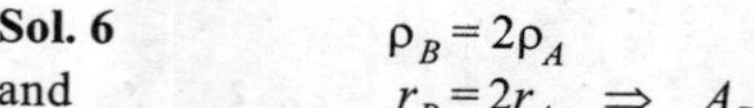

and $r_B = 2r_A \Rightarrow A_B = 4A_A$

As resistances of the two wires are equal

$$\Rightarrow \quad R_A = R_B$$

$$\Rightarrow \quad \rho_A \cdot \frac{l_A}{A_A} = \rho_B \cdot \frac{l_B}{A_B}$$

$$\Rightarrow \quad \frac{l_B}{l_A} = \frac{\rho_A}{\rho_B} \cdot \frac{A_B}{A_A} = \frac{1}{2} \times \frac{4}{1} = 2$$ **Ans. (D)**

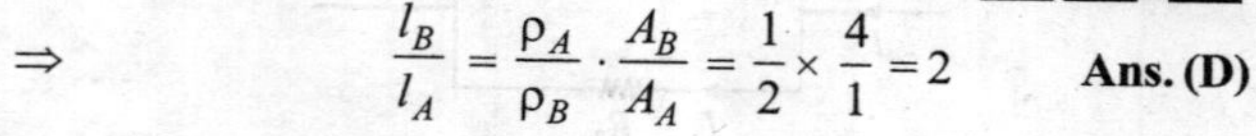

Sol. 7 If resistance at 0°C is considered to be R_0, we use at t°C

$$R_t = R_0(1+\alpha t)$$

at 50°C, we have

$$5 = R_0(1+50\alpha)$$

$$\Rightarrow \quad 5 - R_0 = 50R_0\alpha \quad \ldots(1)$$

at 100°C, we have

$$6 = R_0(1+100\alpha)$$

$$\Rightarrow \quad 6 - R_0 = 100R_0\alpha \quad \ldots(2)$$

$$\frac{(1)}{(2)} \Rightarrow \frac{5-R_0}{6-R_0} = \frac{1}{2}$$

$$\Rightarrow \quad 10 - 2R_0 = 6 - R_0$$

$$\Rightarrow \quad R_0 = 10 - 6 = 4\,\Omega$$ **Ans. (D)**

Sol. 8 Current density at a distance r from point A is given as

$$J = \frac{I}{2\pi r^2}$$

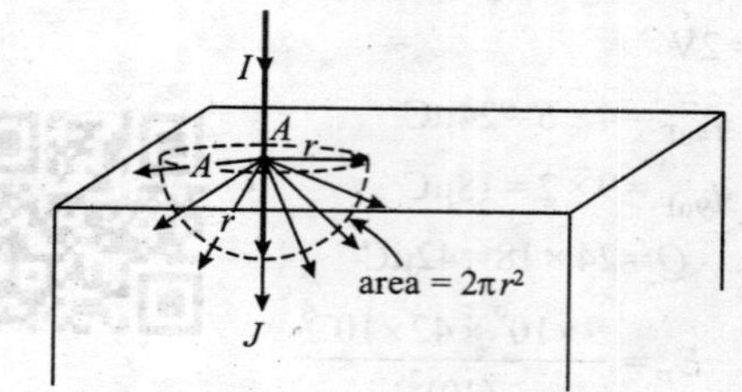

Electric field at a distance r from A is

$$E(r) = \rho J = \frac{\rho I}{2\pi r^2}$$ **Ans. (C)**

Sol. 9 Here potential difference between points B and C can be given as

$$\Delta V_{BC} = \int_B^C E_{(r)} \cdot dr$$

I, r, 2a+b−r, I, A, B, X, C, D, b, a, $\vec{E}_{(r)}$, a

At point X (at a distance r from A) the net EF is given as

$$E_{(r)} = E_{\text{due to } A} + E_{\text{dut to } D}$$

$$E_{(r)} = \frac{\rho I}{2\pi r^2} + \frac{\rho I}{2\pi(2a+b-r)^2}$$

potential difference between points B and C is given as

$$\Delta V_{BC} = \int_a^{a+b} \frac{\rho I}{2\pi}\left(\frac{1}{r^2} + \frac{1}{(2a+b-r)^2}\right) \cdot dr$$

$$\Rightarrow \quad \Delta V_{BC} = \frac{\rho I}{2\pi}\left[-\frac{1}{r} + \frac{1}{2a+b-r}\right]_a^{a+b}$$

$$\Rightarrow \quad \Delta V_{BC} = \frac{\rho I}{2\pi}\left[\left(-\frac{1}{a+b} + \frac{1}{a}\right) - \left(-\frac{1}{a} + \frac{1}{a+b}\right)\right]$$

$$\Rightarrow \quad \Delta V_{BC} = \frac{\rho I}{2\pi}\left[\frac{2}{a} - \frac{2}{a+b}\right]$$

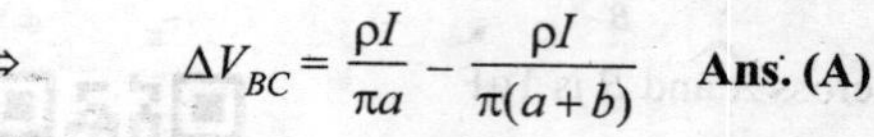

$$\Rightarrow \quad \Delta V_{BC} = \frac{\rho I}{\pi a} - \frac{\rho I}{\pi(a+b)}$$ **Ans. (A)**

Sol. 10 Using $R = R_0(1+\alpha\Delta T)$

$$\Rightarrow \quad 100 = R_0(1+\alpha(27)) \quad \ldots(1)$$

$$\Rightarrow \quad 150 = R_0(1+\alpha(227)) \quad \ldots(2)$$

$$(2) \div (1) \Rightarrow \quad \frac{150}{100} = \frac{1+\alpha(227)}{1+\alpha(27)}$$

$$\Rightarrow \quad \frac{3}{2} = (1+227\,\alpha)(1+27\,\alpha)^{-1}$$

For v small $\alpha \Rightarrow \quad \frac{3}{2} = 1 + 200\,\alpha$

$$\Rightarrow \quad \alpha = \frac{1}{400} = 2.5 \times 10^{-3}\,°C^{-1}$$

As per given values for small variations in resistance and small range of temperature variation S-1 is false.

But 27°C to 227°C is large variation as α is considered constant.

$\Rightarrow$ for given values S-1 is true if α is considered constant.

By definition S-2 is true. **Ans. (B)**

Sol. 11 For series combination at a temperature T we use

$$R_{eq} = 2R_0(1 + \alpha_S T) \qquad \ldots(1)$$

(equivalent coefficient for series combination)

at 0°C R_0 R_0
at T°C R_1 R_2

Here we have $\quad R_1 = R_0(1 + \alpha_1 T)$

and $\quad R_2 = R_0(1 + \alpha_2 T)$

Equivalent resistance of series combination as (at T°C)

$$R_{eq} = R_1 + R_2 = R_0(1 + \alpha_1 T) + R_0(1 + \alpha_2 T)$$

$$\Rightarrow \quad R_{eq} = R_0(2 + (\alpha_1 + \alpha_2)\,T)$$

$$\Rightarrow \quad R_{eq} = 2R_0\left(1 + \left(\frac{\alpha_1 + \alpha_2}{2}\right)T\right) \qquad \ldots(2)$$

Comparing (1) and (2) gives

$$\alpha_s = \frac{\alpha_1 + \alpha_2}{2}$$

$R_0 \to R_1$
$R_0 \to R_2$
at 0°C at T°C

For parallel combination

At 0°C we have $R'_{eq} = \frac{R_0}{2}$

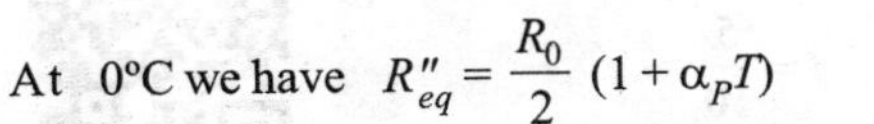

At 0°C we have $R''_{eq} = \frac{R_0}{2}(1 + \alpha_p T) \qquad \ldots(3)$

[$\alpha_p T$ = equal coefficient for parallel combination]

Equal resistance at T°C is given as

$$R''_{eq} = \frac{R_1 R_2}{R_1 + R_2} = \frac{R_0^2(1+\alpha_1 T)(1+\alpha_2 T)}{R_0(2+(\alpha_1+\alpha_2)T)}$$

[terms of consider $\alpha_1\,\alpha_2 << 1$]

$$\Rightarrow \quad R''_{eq} = \frac{R_0(1+(\alpha_1+\alpha_2)T)}{2\left(1+\left(\frac{\alpha_1+\alpha_2}{2}\right)T\right)} \text{ [term of consider } \alpha_1\,\alpha_2 << 1]$$

$$\Rightarrow \quad R''_{eq} = \frac{R_0}{2}(1 + (\alpha_1 + \alpha_2)T)\left(1 + \left(\frac{\alpha_1+\alpha_2}{2}\right)T\right)^{-1}$$

$$\Rightarrow \quad R''_{eq} = \frac{R_0}{2}(1 + (\alpha_1 + \alpha_2)T)\left(1 - \left(\frac{\alpha_1+\alpha_2}{2}\right)T\right)$$

$$\Rightarrow \quad R''_{eq} = \frac{R_0}{2}\left(1 + \left(\frac{\alpha_1+\alpha_2}{2}\right)T\right) \qquad \ldots(4)$$

[As $(\alpha_1 + \alpha_2)^2 << 1$]

Comparing (3) and (4) we have

$$\alpha_P = \frac{\alpha_1 + \alpha_2}{2}$$

Ans. (A)

Sol. 12 Tolerance of a resistance R is given as

$$\frac{dR}{R} \times 100 = 5\% \text{ for } R = 100\,\Omega$$

If we use

$$R_e = R + R + R + R = 4R$$

where $R_e = 400\,\Omega$ and $R = 100\,\Omega$

Tolerance of equivalent resistance

$$\text{Tolerance} = \frac{dR_e}{R_e} \times 100 = \frac{4dR}{4R} \times 100$$

$$= \frac{dR}{R} \times 100 = 5\%$$

Ans. (B)

Sol. 13 Resistance of a conductor is given as

$$R = \frac{\rho l}{A}$$

l $A \to$ area

When a conductor is stretched its volume remain constant

$$V = lA = \text{constant}$$

$$A = \frac{V}{l}$$

$$\Rightarrow \quad R = \left(\frac{\rho}{V}\right) l^2$$

$$\Rightarrow \quad R \propto l^2$$

Taking log on both sides

$$\ln R = \ln\left(\frac{\rho}{V}\right) + 2\ln(\rho)$$

differentiating $\quad \frac{dR}{R} = \frac{2dl}{l}$

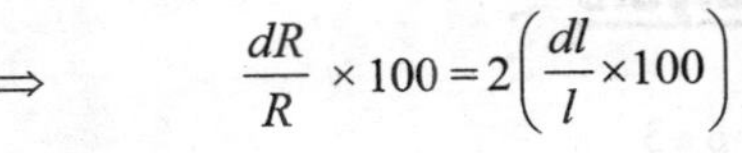

$$\Rightarrow \quad \frac{dR}{R} \times 100 = 2\left(\frac{dl}{l} \times 100\right)$$

$$= 2 \times 0.1 = 0.2\% \text{ increase}$$

Ans. (D)

Sol. 14 In final state the wire AOB behaves like two resistances $\frac{R}{2}$ in parallel combination so new resistance of shorter wire is given as

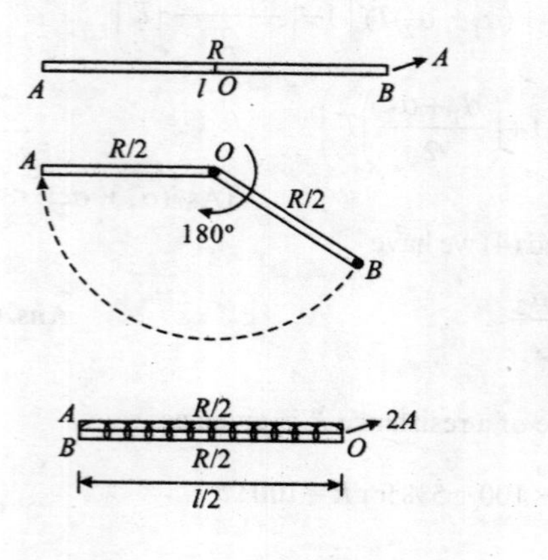

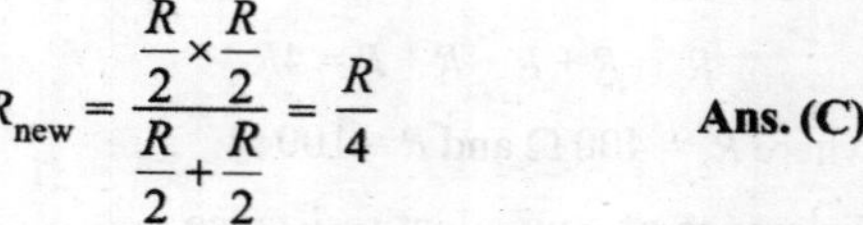

$$R_{\text{new}} = \frac{\frac{R}{2}\times\frac{R}{2}}{\frac{R}{2}+\frac{R}{2}} = \frac{R}{4}$$ **Ans. (C)**

Sol. 15 Using ohm's law for a conductor, we have

$$V = IR \quad \text{where } I = neAv_d \text{ and } R = \rho\frac{l}{A}$$

$\Rightarrow$ $$V = neAv_d \times \frac{\rho l}{A}$$

$\Rightarrow$ $$\rho = \frac{V}{nev_d l}$$

$\Rightarrow$ $$\rho = \frac{5}{8\times10^{28}\times1.6\times10^{-19}\times2.3\times10^{-4}\times0.1}$$

$\Rightarrow$ $$\rho = \frac{2}{12.8}\times10^{-4} = 1.6\times10^{-5}\,\Omega\text{-m}$$ **Ans. (D)**

Sol. 16 In a material current density is related to drift speed as

$$J = ne\,v_d$$

If $$v_d = C\sqrt{E}$$

$\Rightarrow$ $$\frac{I}{A} = ne\,C\sqrt{E}$$

As $$E \alpha V$$

$\Rightarrow$ $$I = IneC\sqrt{C_1 V}$$

$\Rightarrow$ $$I \alpha \sqrt{V} \quad \text{or} \quad I^2 \alpha V$$ **Ans. (C)**

17.2 Circuit Analysis

Sol. 1 $$R_{\text{eq}} = \frac{6\times3}{6+3} = 2\,\Omega$$

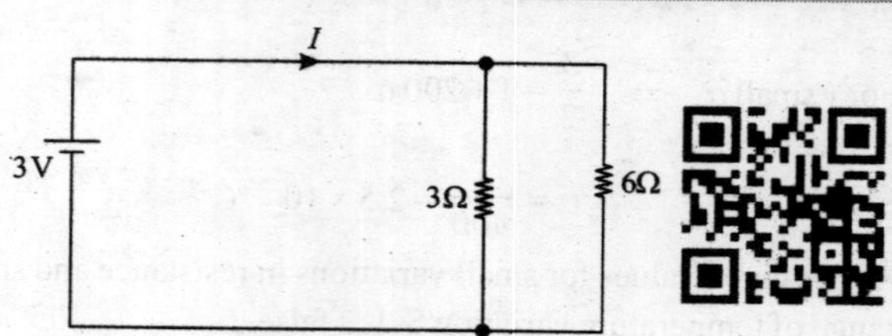

By Ohm's law, circuit current is

$$I = \frac{3}{2} = 1.5\text{ A}$$ **Ans. (B)**

Sol. 2

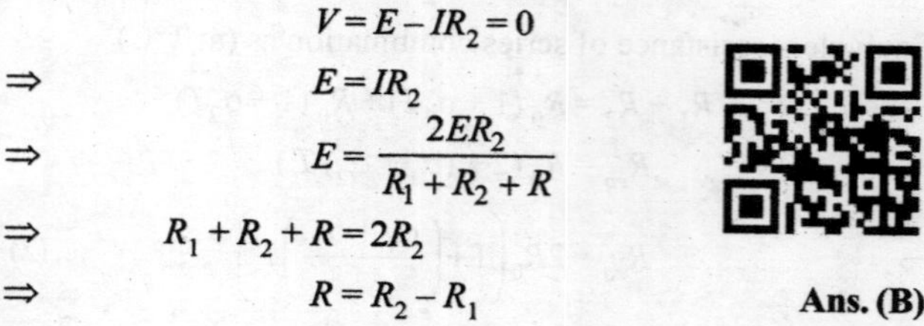

Current in circuit

$$I = \frac{2E}{R_1+R_2+R}$$

Potential difference across second source

$$V = E - IR_2 = 0$$

$\Rightarrow$ $$E = IR_2$$

$\Rightarrow$ $$E = \frac{2ER_2}{R_1+R_2+R}$$

$\Rightarrow$ $$R_1+R_2+R = 2R_2$$

$\Rightarrow$ $$R = R_2 - R_1$$ **Ans. (B)**

Sol. 3 As the circuit shown in figure is a balanced wheatstone bridge we can remove the middle resistor

$\Rightarrow$

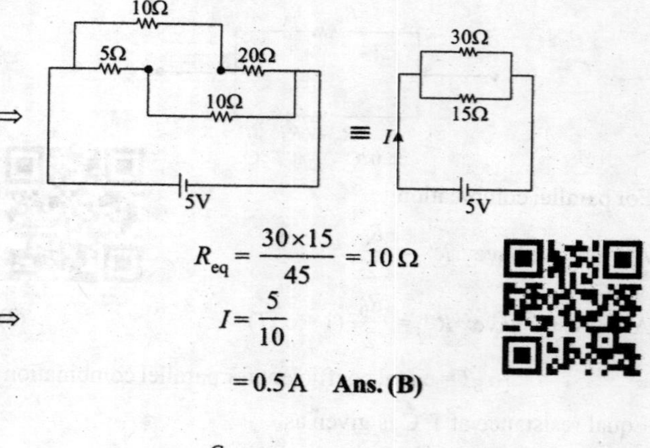

$$R_{\text{eq}} = \frac{30\times15}{45} = 10\,\Omega$$

$\Rightarrow$ $$I = \frac{5}{10}$$

$$= 0.5\text{ A}$$ **Ans. (B)**

Sol. 4

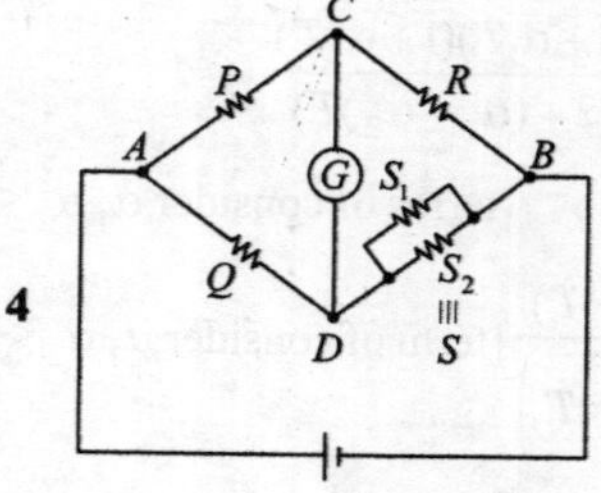

Balancing condition for the given wheatstone bridge is

$$\frac{P}{Q} = \frac{R}{S}$$

here $$S = \frac{S_1 S_2}{S_1 + S_2}$$

$$\Rightarrow \quad \frac{P}{Q} = \frac{R(S_1 + S_2)}{S_1 S_2}$$

Ans. (B)

Sol. 5 (1) Kirchhoff's first law (KCL) gives

Σi at a function = 0

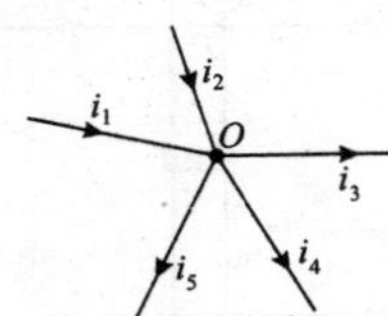

$$i_1 + i_2 = i_3 + i_4 + i_5$$

As $i \rightarrow$ charge flow/s

$\Rightarrow$ KCL is based on

"Conservation of charge".

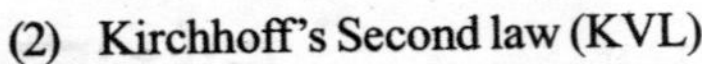

(2) Kirchhoff's Second law (KVL)

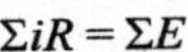

$$\Sigma iR = \Sigma E$$

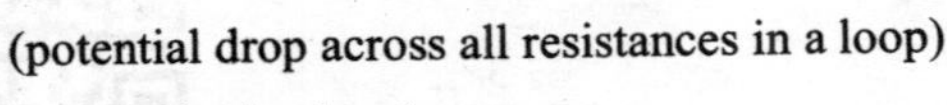

(potential drop across all resistances in a loop)

= (*EMF* in that loop)

As *EF* is conservative

$\Rightarrow$ Work done in a closed path = 0 (any loop of circuit)

$\Rightarrow$ Thus KVL is based on "Energy Conservation" **Ans. (D)**

Sol. 6

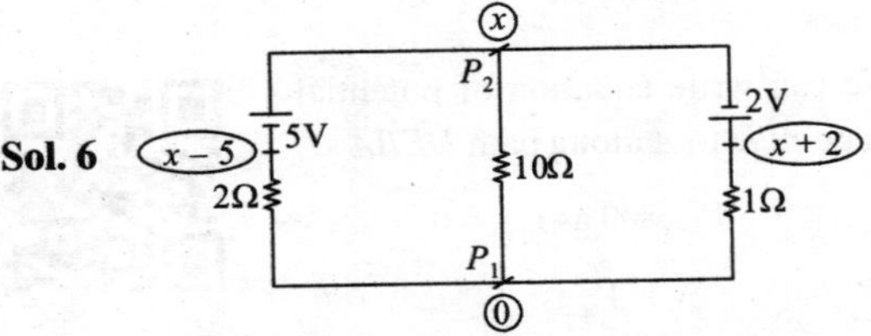

Distributing potentials in circuit and writing KCL equation for x we have

$$\frac{x-0}{10} + \frac{x+2}{1} + \frac{x-5}{2} = 0$$

$\Rightarrow x + 10x + 20 + 5x - 25 = 0$

$\Rightarrow \quad 16x = 5$

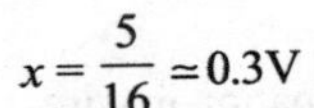

$\Rightarrow \quad x = \frac{5}{16} = 0.3\text{V}$

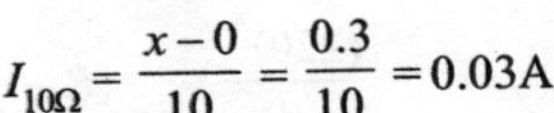

$$I_{10\Omega} = \frac{x-0}{10} = \frac{0.3}{10} = 0.03\text{A}$$

As $x > 0 \Rightarrow$ current flows from P_2 to P_1 **Ans. (C)**

Sol. 7 If E_2 is removed and potential difference across A and B is equal to $E_1 = 90\text{V}$ then on placing E_2 back in circuit no current will flow through E_2.

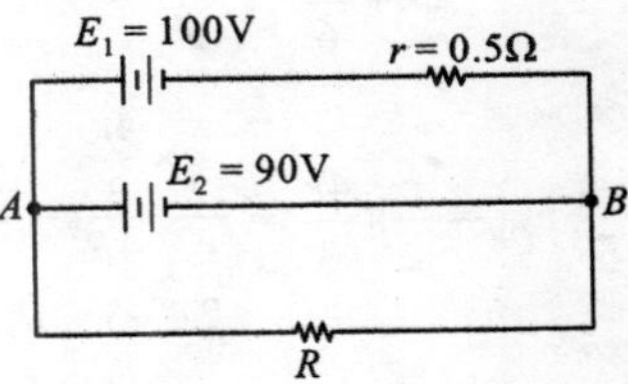

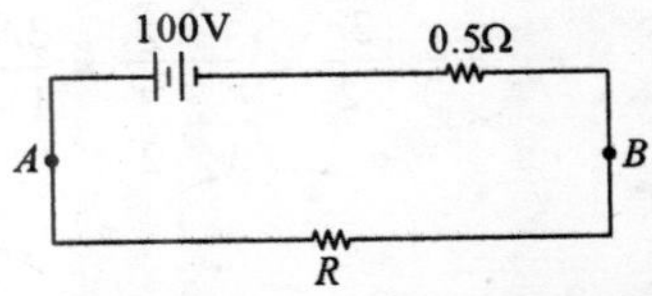

When E_2 is removed the potential difference across A and B is given as

$$V_A - V_B = \frac{100}{R + 0.5} \times R = 90$$

$\Rightarrow \quad 100R = 90R + 45$

$\Rightarrow \quad 10R = 45$

$\Rightarrow \quad R = 4.5\ \Omega$

Ans. (C)

Sol. 8

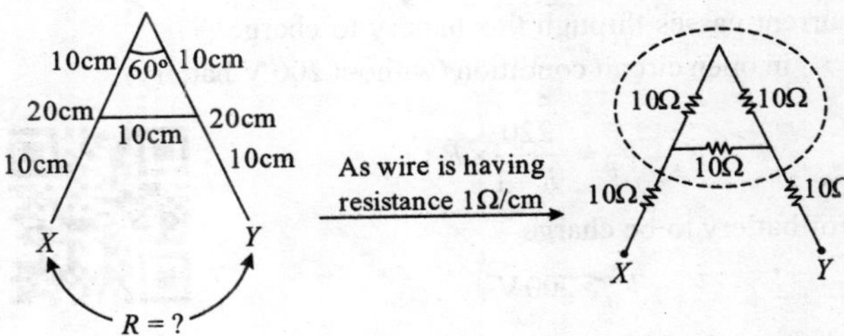

$$r_i = \frac{20 \times 10}{20 + 10} = \frac{20}{3}\Omega$$

here $$R_{xy} = 10 + \frac{20}{3} + 10$$

$$\Rightarrow \quad R_{xy} = 20 + \frac{20}{3} = \frac{80}{3}\Omega = 26.7\Omega$$

Ans. (D)

Sol. 9

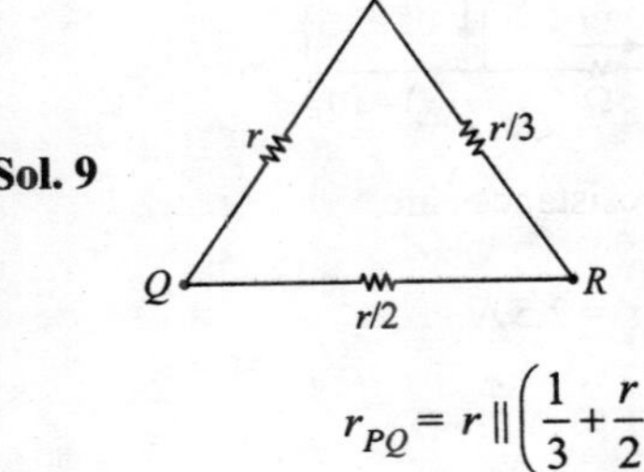

$$r_{PQ} = r \parallel \left(\frac{1}{3} + \frac{r}{2}\right)$$

$$\Rightarrow \qquad r_{PQ} = \frac{r \times \frac{5r}{6}}{r + \frac{5r}{6}} = \frac{5r}{11}$$

$$r_{QR} = \frac{r}{2} \| \frac{4r}{3} = \frac{\frac{r}{2} \times \frac{4r}{3}}{\frac{r}{2} + \frac{4R}{3}} = \frac{4r}{11}$$

and
$$r_{PR} = \frac{r}{3} \| \frac{3r}{2} = \frac{\frac{r}{3} \times \frac{3r}{2}}{\frac{r}{3} + \frac{3r}{2}} = \frac{3r}{11}$$

Highest

$$\Rightarrow \qquad r_{PQ} > r_{QR} > r_{PR}$$ **Ans. (B)**

Sol. 10

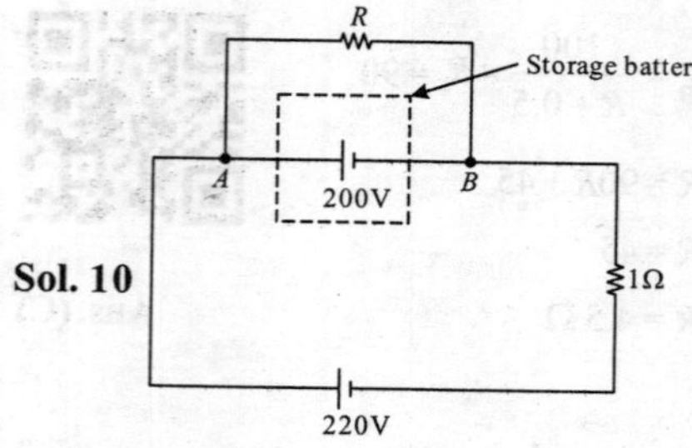

If storage battery is removed and if $V_A - V_B > 200$ V then a current passes through this battery to charge it

$\Rightarrow$ in open circuit condition (without 200 V battery)

$$V_A - V_B = \frac{220}{R+1} \times R$$

For battery to be charge

$$V_A - V_B > 200\text{ V}$$

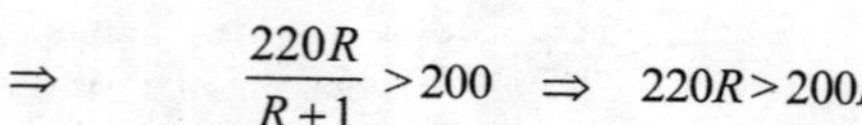

$$\Rightarrow \quad \frac{220R}{R+1} > 200 \quad \Rightarrow \quad 220R > 200R + 200$$

$$\Rightarrow \quad R > 10\,\Omega \quad \Rightarrow \quad \text{here } 11\,\Omega > 10\,\Omega$$ **Ans. (C)**

Sol. 11

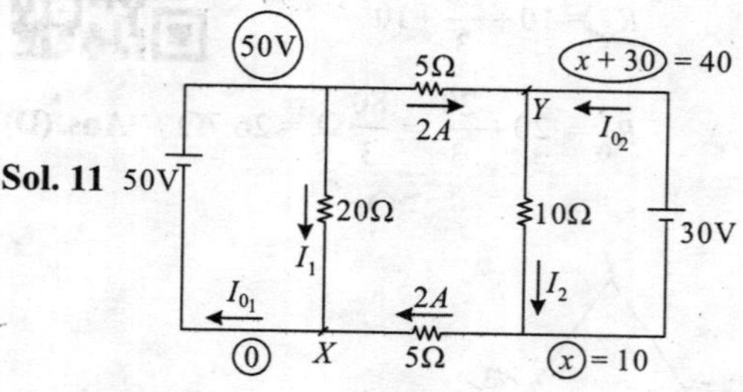

Currents is 20Ω and 10Ω resistances are

$$I_1 = \frac{50}{20} = 2.5\text{ A}$$

$$I_2 = \frac{30}{10} = 3\text{ A}$$

KCL equation for (x)

$$\frac{x + 30 - 50}{5} = 0$$

$$\Rightarrow \qquad 2x = 20\text{ V}$$

$$\Rightarrow \qquad x = 10\text{ V}$$

At junction (x) $\quad I_{0_1} = 2 + 2.5 = 4.5$ A

at junction (y) $\quad I_{0_2} = 3 - 2 = 1$ A **Ans. (C)**

Sol. 12 Modified circuit in

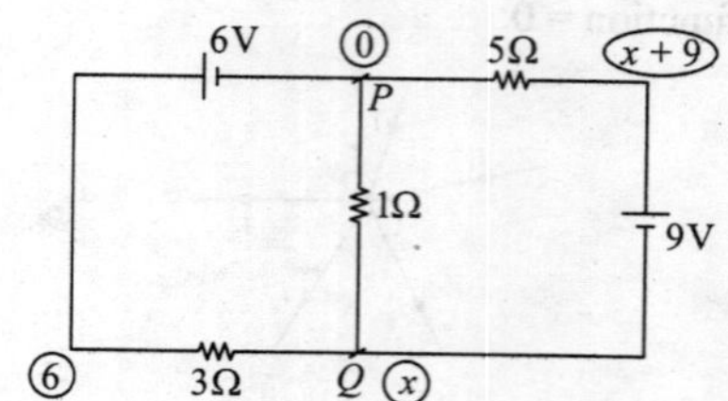

Distributing potentials in the circuit and writing KCL equation for (x), we have

$$\frac{x-6}{3} + \frac{x-0}{1} + \frac{x+9-0}{5} = 0$$

$$\Rightarrow \quad 5x - 30 + 15x + 3x + 27 = 0$$

$$\Rightarrow \qquad 23x = 3$$

$$\Rightarrow \qquad x = \frac{3}{23} V$$

(As $x > 0$ current flows from Q to P)

Current in 1Ω resistance is

$$I = \frac{x}{1} = \frac{3}{23} \simeq 0.13\text{ A}$$ **Ans. (C)**

Sol. 13 We can write equation of potential drop from point D to A along path $DEBA$

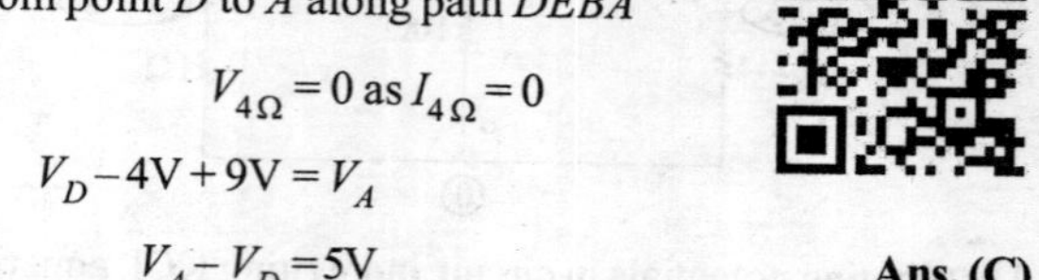

$$V_{4\Omega} = 0 \text{ as } I_{4\Omega} = 0$$

$$V_D - 4\text{V} + 9\text{V} = V_A$$

$$\Rightarrow \quad V_A - V_D = 5\text{V}$$ **Ans. (C)**

17.3 Thermal Effects of Current & RC Circuits

Sol. 1 By Faraday's first law of electrolysis

$$m = Zq = ZIt$$

$$m \propto It$$ **Ans. (B)**

Sol. 2 Initial power dissipation in wire

$$P_1 = \frac{(220)^2}{R} \qquad [R \rightarrow \text{resistance of wire}]$$

When wire cut in two equal pieces, each will have resistance

$R/2$ and these are connected in parallel

$$\Rightarrow \qquad R_{eq} = \frac{R}{4}$$

New power dissipation will be

$$P_2 = \frac{(220)^2}{R/4} = 4\left[\frac{(220)^2}{R}\right] = 4P_1$$

$$\Rightarrow \qquad P_2/P_1 = 4$$ **Ans. (B)**

Sol. 3 Here $R||2 = \frac{2R}{2+R}$ resistance is across 15V battery so power dissipation is given as

$$P = \frac{V^2}{R} = \frac{(15)^2}{2R} \times (2+R) = 150$$

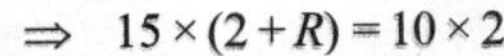

$$\Rightarrow \quad 15 \times (2+R) = 10 \times 2R$$

$$\Rightarrow \qquad 30 + 15R = 20R$$

$$\Rightarrow \qquad R = \frac{30}{5} = 6\,\Omega$$ **Ans. (B)**

Sol. 4 As minimum current that can be detected by galvanometer is

$$I_{min} = 10^{-5}\text{A}$$

If minimum temperature difference which can be measured is $\Delta\theta$ then we use

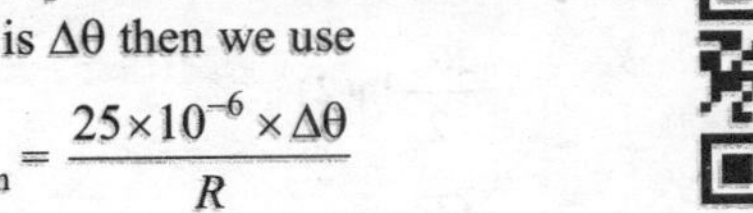

$$I_{min} = \frac{25 \times 10^{-6} \times \Delta\theta}{R}$$

$$\Rightarrow \qquad \Delta\theta = \frac{I_{min} \times R}{25 \times 10^{-6}} = \frac{10^{-5} \times 40}{25 \times 10^{-6}} = \frac{400}{25}$$

$$\Rightarrow \qquad \Delta\theta = 16\,°\text{C}$$ **Ans. (A)**

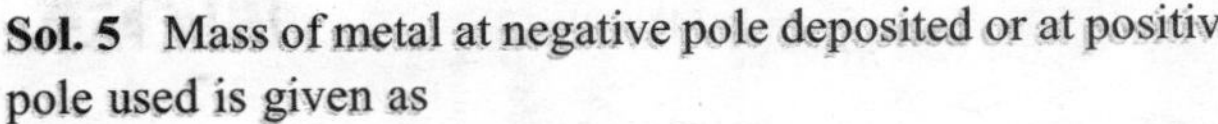

Sol. 5 Mass of metal at negative pole deposited or at positive pole used is given as

$$m = Zq$$

for Zn & Cu electrodes, we use

$$\frac{m_1}{m_2} = \frac{Z_1}{Z_2}$$

$$\Rightarrow \qquad m_2 = m_1 \times \frac{Z_2}{Z_1} = 0.13\text{g} \times \frac{31.5}{32.5}$$

$$\Rightarrow \qquad m_2 = 0.126\text{g}$$ **Ans. (C)**

Sol. 6 The resistance of bulb is

$$R = \frac{V^2}{P} = \frac{(220)^2}{1000}\Omega$$

Power consumed across 110V supply is given as

$$P' = \frac{V'^2}{R} = \frac{(110)^2}{(220)^2/1000} = \frac{1000}{4}$$

$$\Rightarrow \qquad P' = 250\text{ W}$$ **Ans. (C)**

Sol. 7 The neutral temperature is the temperature of hot junction when thermo EMF is maximum and cold junction is kept at 0°C.

Here in this case

$$E = a\theta + b\theta^2$$

E is maximum when

$$\frac{dE}{d\theta} = a + 2b\theta = 0$$

$$\Rightarrow \qquad \theta = -\frac{a}{2b} = -350°\text{C}$$

We check $\qquad \frac{d^2E}{d\theta^2} = 2b\,(+ve)$ value

$\Rightarrow$ E will never attain a maxima.

So no neutral temperature is possible is this case. **Ans. (D)**

Sol. 8 Mass of metal deposited is given as

$$m = Zq$$

charge flown $\qquad q = It = 3 \times 2 = 6\text{C}$

mass $\qquad m = 3.35 \times 10^{-7} \times 6$

$$= 20.10 \times 10^{-7}\text{ kg}$$ **Ans. (C)**

Sol. 9 The heat required to raise the temperature of 1kg water from 10°C to 40°C is

$$\Delta Q = mS_{\omega}\Delta t$$

$$\Rightarrow \qquad \Delta Q = 1 \times 4180 \times 30\text{ J} \qquad [s_{\omega} = 4180\text{ J/°C kg}]$$

It t is the time required then heat supplied by heater is

$$836t = 4180 \times 30$$

$$t = \frac{300}{2} = 150\text{ s}$$ **And.(A)**

Sol. 10 Constant current source

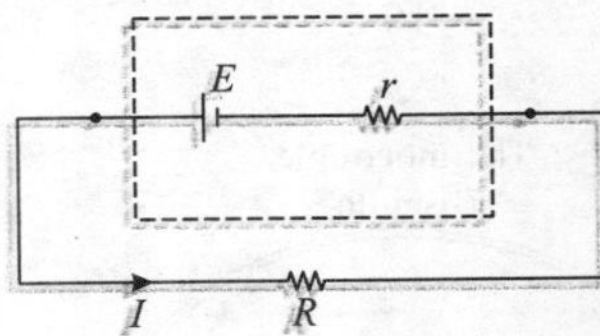

Current supplied

$$I = \frac{E}{r+R}$$

Here if $r >> R$

$$\Rightarrow \quad I = \frac{E}{r} \rightarrow \text{constant for small variations in } R$$ **Ans. (B)**

Sol. 11 If q_1 and q_2 are charges flown through copper & silver voltameter then we use

$$q = q_1 + q_2 \quad \ldots(1)$$

[As the two voltmeter are in parallel]

mass of metal deposited is given as

$$m = Zq$$

As for both, mass deposited are same

$$\Rightarrow \quad Z_1 q_1 = Z_2 q_2$$

$$\Rightarrow \quad q_1 = q_2\left(\frac{Z_2}{Z_1}\right)$$

$$\Rightarrow \quad q = q_2\left(\frac{Z_2}{Z_1} + 1\right)$$

$$\Rightarrow \quad q_2 = \frac{q}{\frac{Z_2}{Z_1} + 1}$$

Ans. (A)

Sol. 12 When a heater coil is placed across a supply of voltage V then heat produced rate is

$$H_1 = \frac{V^2}{R}$$

Each part of coil after cut has a resistance $R/2$ so now heat generation rate is

$$H_2 = \frac{V^2}{R/2} = 2\left(\frac{V^2}{R}\right) = 2H_1$$

Ans. (B)

Sol. 13 For the given temperature its hot resistance is given as

$$R_{hot} = \frac{V^2}{P}$$

$$= \frac{(200)^2}{100} = 400\,\Omega$$

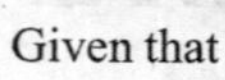

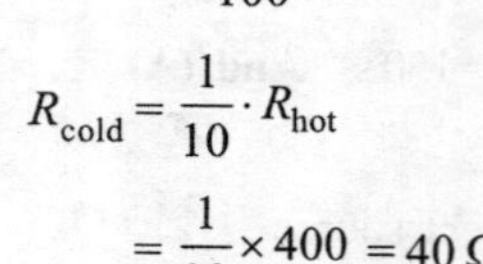

Given that $\quad R_{cold} = \frac{1}{10} \cdot R_{hot}$

$$= \frac{1}{10} \times 400 = 40\,\Omega$$

Ans. (B)

Sol. 14

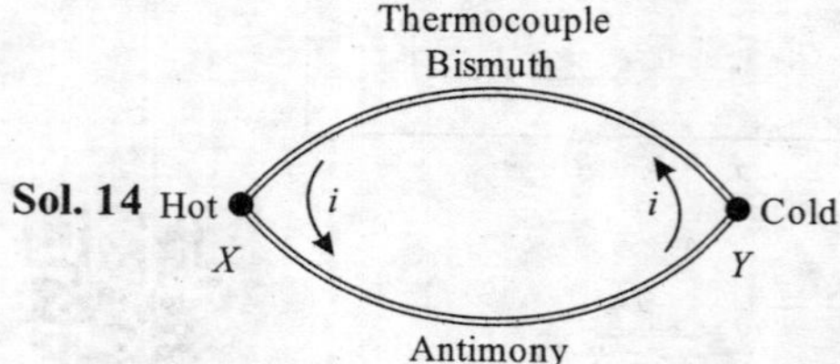

Thermoelectric series

Bismuth

↓

Antimony

Ans. (D)

Sol. 15 The resistance of bulb is

$$R = \frac{V^2}{P} = \frac{(220)^2}{100}$$

Power consumed when operated at 110V is given as

$$P_C = \frac{V_1^2}{R} = \frac{(110)^2}{(220)^2/100} = \frac{100}{4}$$

$$\Rightarrow \quad P_C = 25\text{ W}$$

Ans. (C)

Sol. 16 When a capacitor discharges through a resistor, its charge as time function is given as

$$q = Qe^{-t/RC}$$

Where Q is charge at $t = 0$

Energy in capacitor

$$U = \frac{q^2}{2C} = \left(\frac{Q}{2C}\right)^2 e^{-2t/RC} = U_0 e^{-2t/RC}$$

Given that at $t = t_1$, $U = \frac{U_0}{2}$

$$\Rightarrow \quad \frac{U_0}{2} = U_0 e^{-2t_1/RC}$$

$$\Rightarrow \quad \frac{2t_1}{RC} = \ln(2)$$

$$\Rightarrow \quad t_1 = \frac{RC}{2}\ln(2) \quad \ldots(1)$$

At $t = t_2$, $\quad q = \frac{Q}{4}$

$$\Rightarrow \quad \frac{Q}{4} = Qe^{-t_2/RC}$$

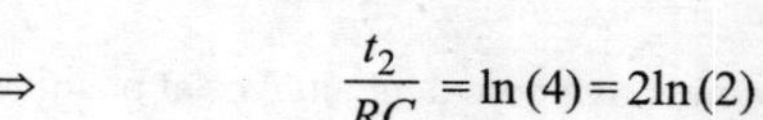

$$\Rightarrow \quad \frac{t_2}{RC} = \ln(4) = 2\ln(2)$$

$$\Rightarrow \quad t_2 = 2RC\ln(2) \quad \ldots(2)$$

$$\frac{(1)}{(2)} \Rightarrow \quad \frac{t_1}{t_2} = \frac{\frac{RC}{2}\ln(2)}{2RC\ln(2)} = \frac{1}{4}$$

Ans. (D)

Sol. 17 For discharging of capacitors in RC circuit, voltage across capacitor combination is given as

$$V = V_0 e^{-t/RC_{eq}}$$

For parallel combination $C_{eq} = 2C$ and at $t = 10$s, $V = \frac{V_0}{2}$

$$\Rightarrow \quad \frac{V_0}{2} = V_0 e^{-10/2RC} \quad \ldots(1)$$

for series combination

$C_{eq} = C/2$ and at $t = t_1$,

$$V = \frac{V_0}{2}$$

$$\Rightarrow \qquad \frac{V_0}{2} = V_0 e^{-2t_1/RC} \qquad \ldots(2)$$

Using (1) and (2) we have

$$\frac{2t_1}{RC} = \frac{10}{2RC}$$

$$\Rightarrow \qquad t_1 = \frac{10}{4} = 2.5\text{s}$$

Ans. (D)

Sol. 18

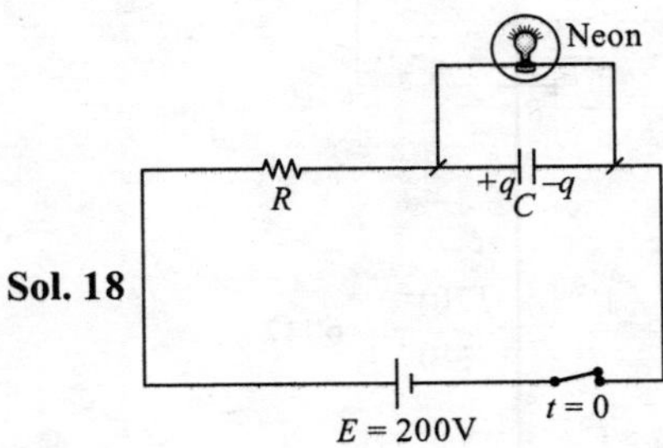

In RC circuit charge on capacitor as a function of time is given as

$$q = CE\,(1 - e^{-t/RC})$$

p.d. across capacitor as a function of time is given as

$$V = \frac{q}{C} = E(1 - e^{-t/RC})$$

at $t = 5$, $\quad V = 120\text{V}$

$$120 = 200\,(1 - e^{-5/RC})$$

$$\Rightarrow \qquad e^{-5/RC} = 1 - \frac{120}{200} = \frac{2}{5}$$

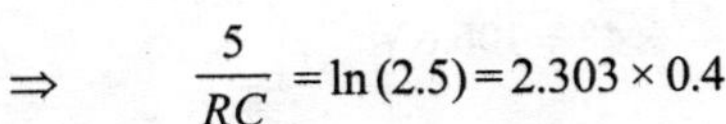

$$\Rightarrow \qquad \frac{5}{RC} = \ln(2.5) = 2.303 \times 0.4$$

$$\Rightarrow \qquad R = \frac{5}{2 \times 10^{-6} \times 2.303 \times 0.4} = 2.7 \times 10^{6}\,\Omega$$ **Ans. (A)**

Sol. 19

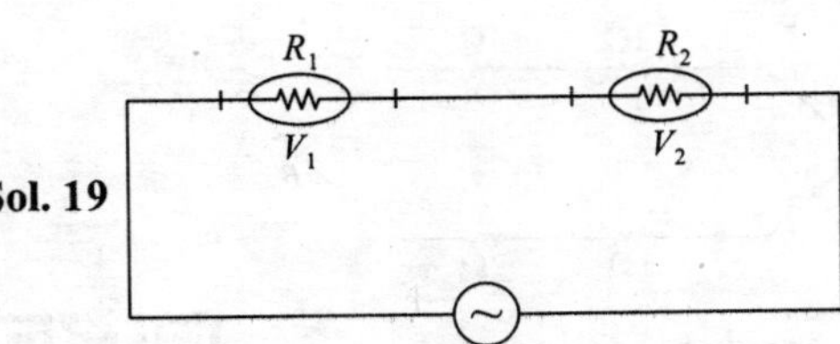

Resistances of bulbs are given as

$$R_1 = \frac{V_1^2}{P_1} = \frac{(220)^2}{25}$$

and

$$R_2 = \frac{V_2^2}{P_2} = \frac{(220)^2}{100} \Rightarrow R_1 > R_2$$

$$V_1 = \frac{440R_1}{R_1 + R_2} \quad \text{and} \quad V_2 = \frac{440R_2}{R_1 + R_2}$$

As $\quad V_1 + V_2 = 440$

$$\Rightarrow \qquad V_1 > V_2$$

$$\Rightarrow \qquad V_1 > 220\text{V} \quad \text{and} \quad V_2 < 220\text{V}$$

$\Rightarrow$ 25 W bulb will fuse **Ans. (D)**

Sol. 20 In RC discharging circuit if at $t = 0$, voltage across capacitor is V_0 then after time $t = t$, it is given as

$$V = V_0 e^{-t/RC} \qquad \text{[from graph at } t = 0,\ V_0 = 25\text{ V]}$$

where time constant $\tau = RC$

$$\Rightarrow \qquad V = V_0 e^{-t/\tau} \qquad \ldots(1)$$

at $t = 200$s from graph we can see that $V = 5$ V

from equation-(1), we use

$$5 = 25\,e^{-200/\tau}$$

$$\Rightarrow \qquad \ln 5 = \frac{200}{\tau}$$

$$\Rightarrow \qquad \tau = \frac{200}{\ln(5)} = \frac{200}{2.303\log(5)} = \frac{200}{2.303 \times 0.7}$$

[As $\log 5 = 0.698$]

$$\Rightarrow \qquad \tau \cong \frac{200}{1.6} \simeq 125\text{ s}$$ **Ans. (A)**

Sol. 21 (Fuse) it burns when its temperature exceeds the melting point of resistance material.

Heat production rate in fuse

$$H = \frac{V^2}{R}$$

When the current is switched on, R is low as it is cold (at room temperature) and with flow of current R increases and H decreases.

(due to rise in temperature)

$\Rightarrow$ Statement-1 is true.

Statement-2 : When a bulb is lit up, due to heat its resistance increases

$\Rightarrow$ Statement-2 is true & explaining Statement-1 also

Ans. (C)

Sol. 22

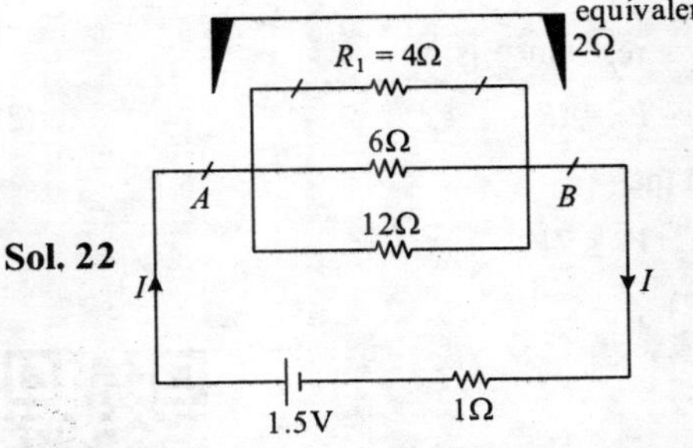

Equivalent resistance of parallel combination is

$$\frac{1}{R} = \frac{1}{4} + \frac{1}{6} + \frac{1}{12} = \frac{3+2+1}{12} = \frac{6}{12} = 0.5$$

$$\Rightarrow \qquad R = 2\,\Omega \qquad \text{(Across } A \text{ and } B\text{)}$$

Circuit current

$$I = \frac{1.5}{1+2} = \frac{1.5}{3} = \frac{1}{2} = 0.5\,\text{A}$$

Potential difference across A and B is

$$V_{AB} = IR = 0.5 \times 2 = 1\,\text{V}$$

Rate of Joule heating in 4Ω resistance is

$$P_{\text{th}} = \frac{V_{AB}^2}{R_1} = \frac{(1)^2}{4} = 0.25\,\text{W}$$ **Ans. (C)**

Sol. 23 Bulb brightess α thermal power produced in it

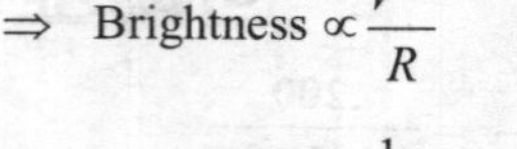

$$\Rightarrow \quad \text{Brightness} \propto \frac{V^2}{R}$$

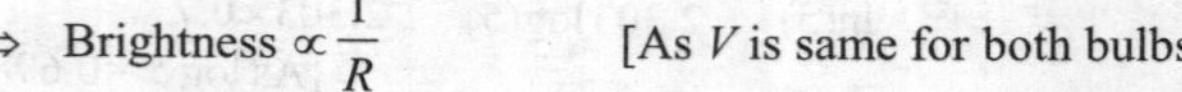

$$\Rightarrow \quad \text{Brightness} \propto \frac{1}{R}$$ [As V is same for both bulbs]

$$R_1 = 3\,\Omega \quad \text{and} \quad R_2 = 6\,\Omega$$

Bulb-1 will glow brighter **Ans. (B)**

Sol. 24

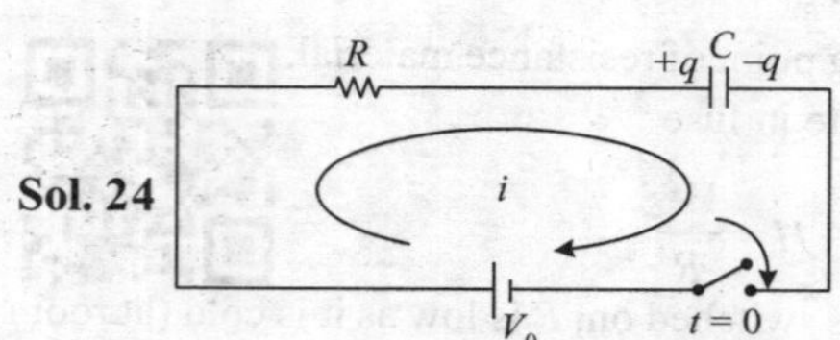

The charge on capacitor as a function of time is

$$q = CV_0\,(1 - e^{-t/RC})$$

Charge current in circuit is

$$i = \frac{dq}{dt} = \frac{V_0}{R} e^{-t/RC}$$

Voltage across capacitor at time t is

$$V_C = \frac{q}{C} = V_0(1 - e^{-t/RC}) \quad \ldots(1)$$

and voltage across resistance is

$$V_R = iR = V_0 e^{-t/RC} \quad \ldots(2)$$

At time t is given that

$$V_C = 7V_R$$

So from (1) and (2)

$$\%(1 - e^{-t/RC}) = 7\%\, e^{-t/RC}$$

$$\Rightarrow \quad 1 = 8e^{-t/RC}$$

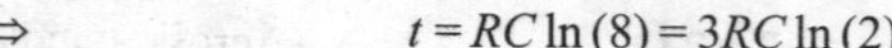

$$\Rightarrow \quad \frac{t}{RC} = \ln(8)$$

$$\Rightarrow \quad t = RC\ln(8) = 3RC\ln(2)$$ **Ans. (A)**

Sol. 25

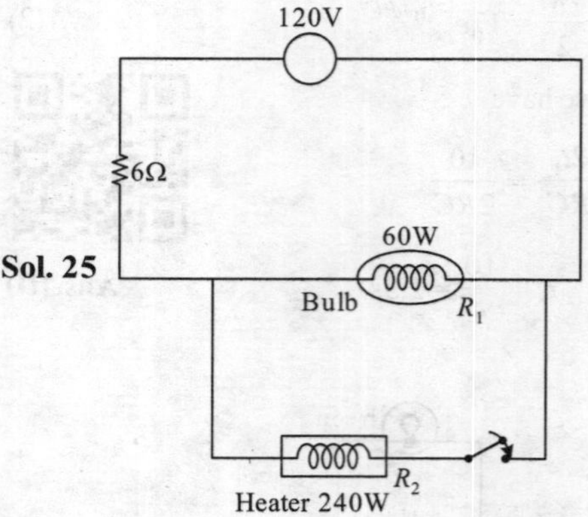

Resistance of heater

$$R_2 = \frac{V^2}{P} = \frac{(120)^2}{240} = 60\,\Omega$$

Resistance of bulb

$$R = \frac{V^2}{P} = \frac{(120)^2}{60} = 240\,\Omega$$

Initially voltage across bulb is

$$V_1 = \frac{120}{246} \times 240$$

$$\simeq 117.07\,\text{V}$$

When heater is switched on the equation equivalent of bulb and heater is

$$R_{\text{eq}} = \frac{240 \times 60}{240 + 60} = 48\,\Omega$$

Potential difference across bulb & heater combination is

$$V_2 = \frac{120}{54} \times 48 \simeq 106.6\,\text{V}$$

Change in potential difference across bulb is

$$\Delta V = V_1 - V_2 \simeq 10.04\,\text{V}$$ **Ans. (D)**

Sol. 26

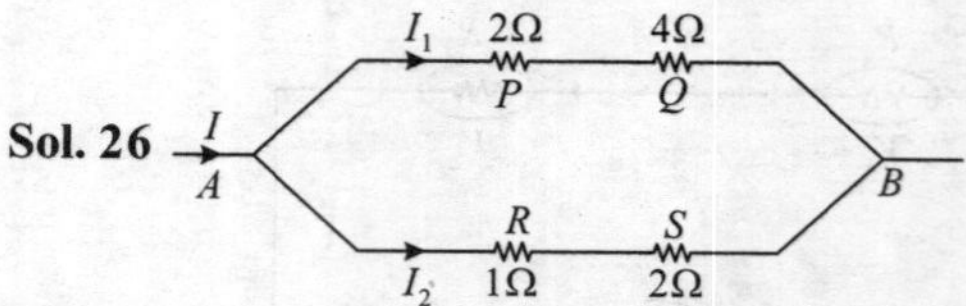

Here I_1 and I_2 are given as

$$I_1 = \frac{I}{3} \text{ and } I_2 = \frac{2I}{3}$$

Thermal power dissipated in resistances are

$$H_P = I_1^2(2) = \frac{2I^2}{9}\,;\; H_R = I_2^2\,(1) = \frac{4I^2}{9}$$

$$H_Q = I_1^2\,(4) = \frac{4I^2}{9}\,;\; H_S = I_2^2\,(2) = \frac{8I^2}{9}$$

$$\Rightarrow \quad H_S > (H_R = H_Q) > H_P$$ **Ans. (B)**

Sol. 27 Total power consumption of building at full load is

$$P = 15 \times 40 + 5 \times 100 + 5 \times 80 + 1000$$

$$\Rightarrow \quad P = 600 + 500 + 400 + 1000 = 1400\text{W}$$

The current drawn from mains supply at full load is

$$I = \frac{P}{V} = \frac{2500}{220} = \frac{125}{11} = 11.36\text{ A}$$

Maximum current supplied at full load

As fuse rating must be kept such that maximum current at full load can sustain. **Ans. (C)**

Sol. 28

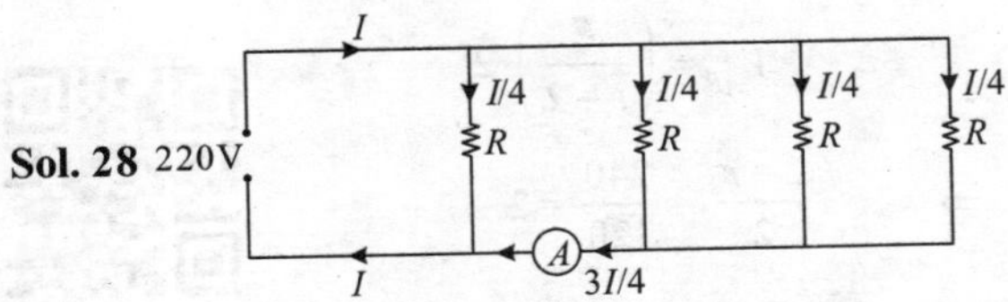

As each bulb is of 100W consumption

$$\Rightarrow \quad \frac{I}{4} = \frac{P}{V} = \frac{100}{220} = \frac{5}{11} = 0.45\text{ A}$$

The current through ammeter is

$$I_A = \frac{3I}{4} = 3 \times 0.45 = 1.35\text{ A}$$ **Ans. (C)**

Sol. 29 In steady state no current flows through capacitive branches of circuit

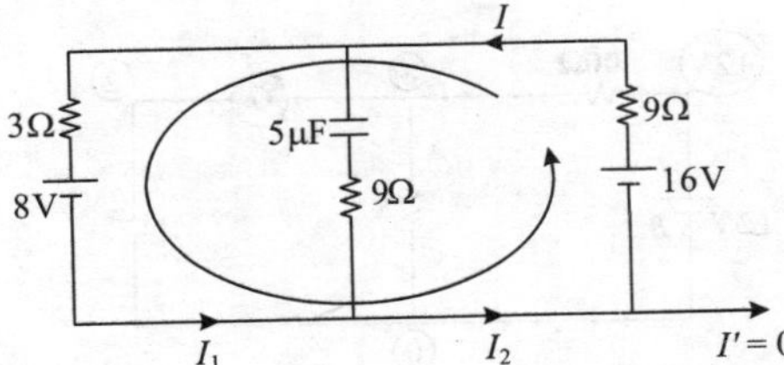

As current flows only in outer loop

$$\Rightarrow \quad I_1 = I_2 = I$$

Current in outer loop is

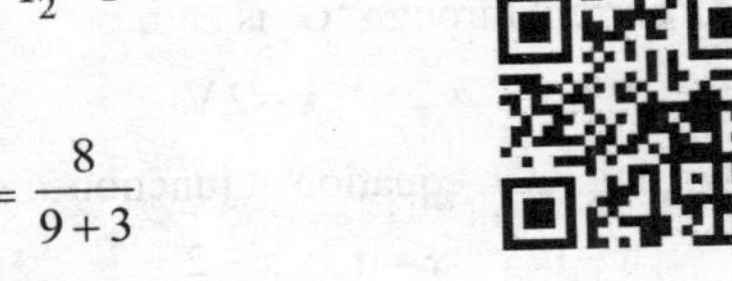

$$I = \frac{8}{9+3}$$

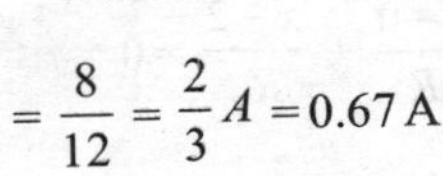

$$= \frac{8}{12} = \frac{2}{3} A = 0.67\text{ A}$$ **Ans. (B)**

Sol. 30

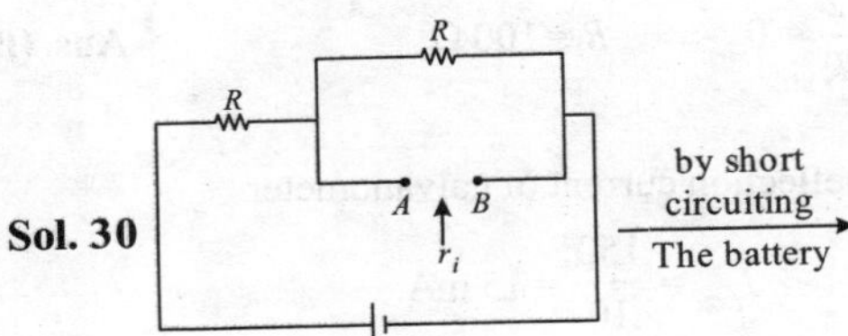

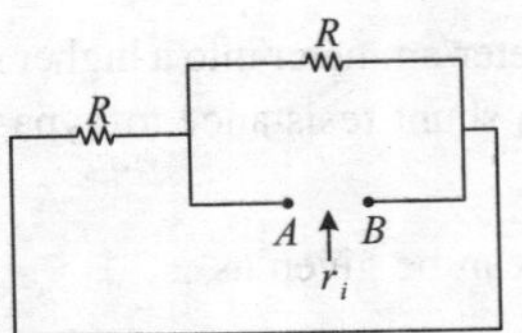

$$\Rightarrow \quad r_i = R \parallel R = R/2$$

According to maximum power transfer theorem, heat generation in r is maximum when

$$r = r_i = R/2 = fR$$

$$\Rightarrow \quad f = \frac{1}{2}$$ **Ans. (A)**

Sol. 31 At 300 K, $\quad R = 100\Omega$

and at 500 K, $\quad R = 120\Omega$

$$120 = 100\,[1 + \alpha(200)]$$

$$\Rightarrow \quad 20 = \alpha(20000) \;\Rightarrow\; \alpha = 10^{-3}\,°\text{C}^{-1}$$

When toaster is connected across $V = 200$ volt then thermal power produced is

$$P_{\text{th}} = \frac{V^2}{R} = \frac{(200)^2}{100[1 + \alpha(T - 300)]}$$

at temperature T

$$300\text{K} < T < 500\text{ K}$$

As T is raised at a constant rate (linear variation) from 300K to 500 K, so time function of temperature is given as

$$T = 300 + \frac{500 - 300}{30} \cdot t = 300 + \frac{20}{3} t$$

Total work done in these 30s of rise in temperature is

$$W = \int_0^{30} P_{\text{th}} \cdot dt = \int_0^{30} \frac{(200)^2}{100\left[1 + \alpha\left(\frac{20t}{3}\right)\right]} \cdot dt$$

$$\Rightarrow \quad W = 400 \times \frac{300}{20\alpha}\left[\ln\left(1 + \frac{200\alpha t}{3}\right)\right]_0^{30}$$

$$\Rightarrow \quad W = \frac{60}{\alpha}\left[\ln(1 + 200\alpha) - \ln(1)\right]$$

$$\Rightarrow \quad W = 60000 \ln(1.2)$$ **Ans. (None)**

None of the given option is correct.

17.4 Electrical Measuring Instruments

Sol. 1 Ammeter → its internal resistance is very low

Voltmeter → its internal resistance is very high

When we wish to convert an ammeter into a voltmeter then we connect a high resistance in series. **Ans. (C)**

Sol. 2 To convert a galvanometer/ammeter into a higher range ammeter we need to connect a shunt resistance to bypass the excess current.

The required shunt resistance can be given as

$$(I_R - I_m)R_S = I_m Rg$$

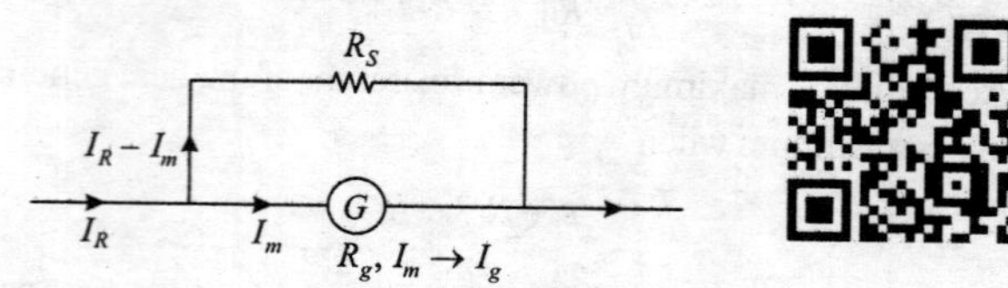

$$\Rightarrow \quad R_S = \frac{I_m R_g}{I_R - I_m} = \frac{1 \times 0.81}{10-1} = \frac{0.81}{9}$$

$$\Rightarrow \quad R_S = 0.09\,\Omega$$ **Ans. (D)**

Sol. 3 Across potentiometer wire, potential gradient is

$$\lambda = \frac{E}{L} = \frac{E}{100\text{ cm}}$$

For the given battery if unknown emf is E_{uk} and this balances at l length on wire so we use

$$E_{uk} = \lambda l = \frac{E}{100} \times 30 = \frac{30E}{100}$$ **Ans. (D)**

Sol. 4 Case-I

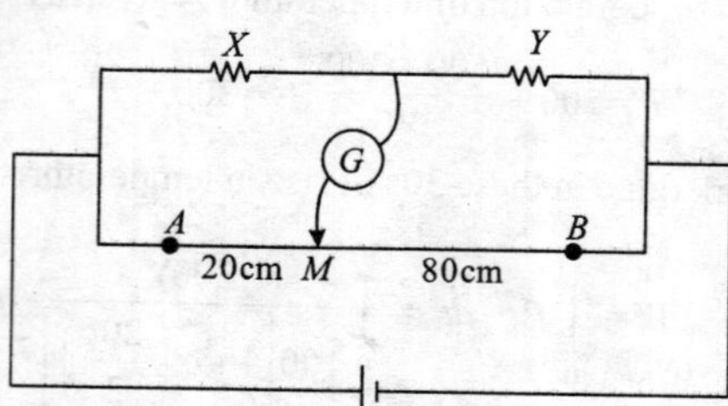

At null point we have bridge balanced

$$\Rightarrow \quad \frac{X}{20} = \frac{Y}{80} \Rightarrow y = 4x$$

At null point as bridge is balanced

$$\Rightarrow \quad \frac{4X}{l} = \frac{Y}{100-l}$$

$$\Rightarrow \quad 2l = 100$$

$$\Rightarrow \quad l = 50\text{ cm}$$ **Ans. (A)**

Sol. 5 If λ be the potential gradient on potentiometer wire then

Case-I : emf of cell is

$$E = \lambda(240) \quad \ldots(1)$$

Case-II : potential difference across cells is

$$V_{AB} = \frac{2E}{2+r} = \lambda(120) \quad \ldots(2)$$

$$V_{AB} = \left(\frac{E}{r+2}\right)\cdot 2$$

$$\frac{(1)}{(2)} \Rightarrow \frac{2+r}{2} = \frac{240}{120} = 2$$

$$\Rightarrow \quad 2 + r = 4$$

$$\Rightarrow \quad r = 2\,\Omega$$ **Ans. (D)**

Alternative : The internal resistance of a cell by potentiometer experiment is given as

$$r = \left(\frac{l_1}{l_2} - 1\right)R$$

$$\Rightarrow \quad r = \left(\frac{240}{120} - 1\right) \times 2 = 2\,\Omega$$ **Ans. (D)**

Sol. 6

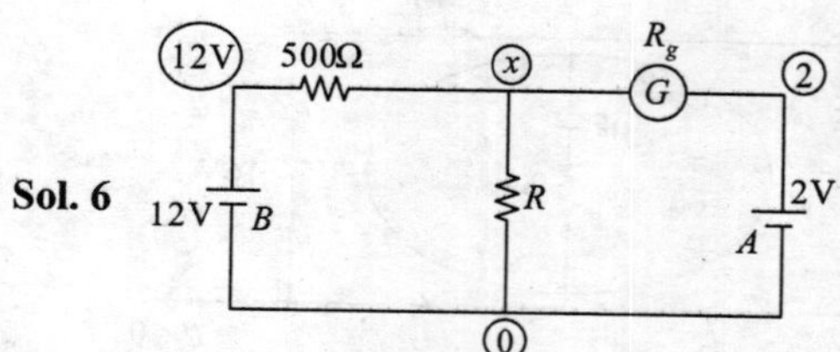

Distributing potentials at different junctions of circuit by considering zero volt reference at bottom junctions.

As current through 'G' is zero

$$\Rightarrow \quad x = 2\text{ V}$$

Writing KCL equation at junction x, we have

$$\frac{x-12}{500} + \frac{x-0}{R} + \frac{x-2}{R_g} = 0$$

$$x = 2\text{ V}$$

$$\Rightarrow \quad -\frac{10}{500} + \frac{2}{R} = 0 \Rightarrow R = 100\,\Omega$$ **Ans. (B)**

Sol. 7 Full deflection current of galvanometer

$$I_{max} = \frac{150}{10} = 15\text{ mA}$$

Full deflection voltage of galvanometer

$$V_{max} = \frac{150}{10} = 75\text{ mV}$$

at a potential difference of 75mV across galvanometer, a current of 15mA flows through it. So coil resistance is given as

$$R_C = \frac{V_{max}}{I_{max}} = \frac{75}{15} = 5\,\Omega$$

New range of galvanometer to be used as voltmeter is

$$V_R = 150 \times 1 = 150\text{ V}$$

So if R is external resistance connected in series, we use

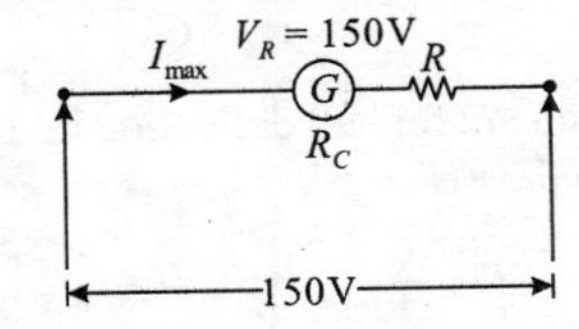

So use $\frac{150}{R+R_C} = I_{max} = 15\text{ mA}$

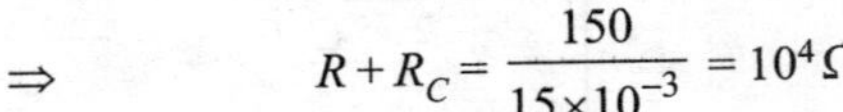

$$\Rightarrow \quad R + R_C = \frac{150}{15\times10^{-3}} = 10^4\,\Omega$$

$$\Rightarrow \quad R = 10^4\,\Omega - 5\,\Omega = 9995\,\Omega$$

Ans. (D)

Sol. 8 For bridge to be balanced we use

$$\frac{55}{20} = \frac{R}{100-20}$$

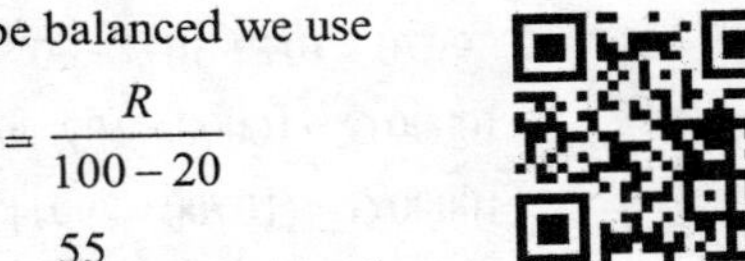

$$\Rightarrow \quad R = \frac{55}{20} \times 80 = 55 \times 4$$

$$= 220\,\Omega$$

Ans. (B)

Sol. 9

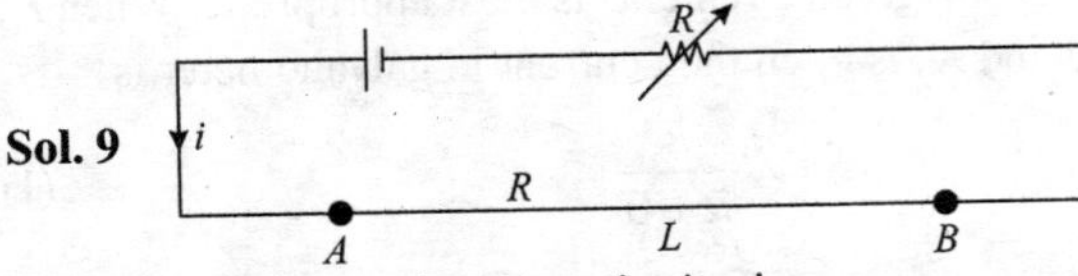

Resistance of potentiometer wire is given as

$$R = \frac{\rho L}{A}$$

Potential gradient on wire AB is given as

$$\lambda = \frac{V_{AB}}{L} = \frac{iR}{L} = \frac{i\rho}{A} = \frac{0.2\times4\times10^{-7}}{8\times10^{-1}}$$

$$\Rightarrow \quad \lambda = 0.1\text{ V/m}$$

Ans. (D)

Sol. 10 (i) $\rightarrow$ As no current flows through cell, its terminal p.d. is equal to its emf so (i) is correct.

(ii) $\rightarrow$ As potential gradient on potentiometer wire is given as

$$\lambda = \frac{V_{AB}}{L}$$

Measured emf $\quad E = \lambda\, l_{bal}$ [If λ is small then l_{bal} is large]

$\Rightarrow$ Precision will be more closer to actual value

So (ii) is correct

(iii) & (iv) are NOT correct

Ans. (C)

Sol. 11

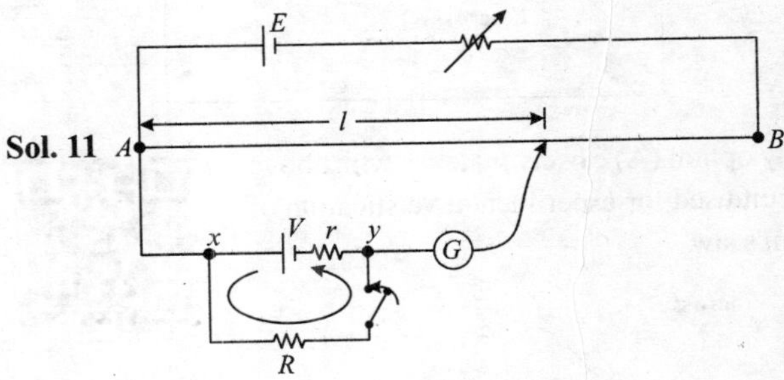

Initially when the cell of EMF V is balanced at length l then we use

$$V = \lambda l \qquad \ldots(1)$$

$$r = R$$

After connecting external resistance, we use

$$V_{xy} = \frac{V}{2R}\cdot R = \frac{V}{2}$$

If after connecting R balancing length is l' then we use

$$\frac{V}{2} = \lambda l' \qquad \ldots(2)$$

from (1) and (2) $\Rightarrow \quad l' = l/2$

Ans. (C)

Sol. 12

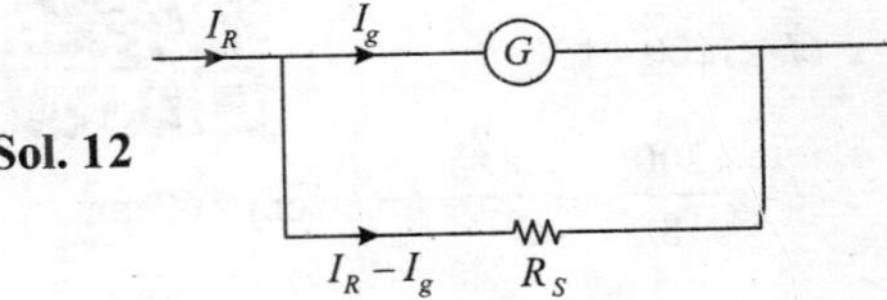

$$R_A = \frac{R_g R_S}{R_g + R_S}$$

Internal resistance of Ammeter.

If I_R increases then more current has to be bypassed through shunt resistance so R_S should be decreased or to decrease it an additional shunt is required across then ammeter.

$\Rightarrow$ Here S-1 is false & S-2 is true.

Ans. (D)

Sol. 13 To verify Ohm's law we use

$$V = IR$$

By varying R, we measure V across R and I through R & plot the graph in V and I

The graph obtained in s straight line which verifies Ohm's law.

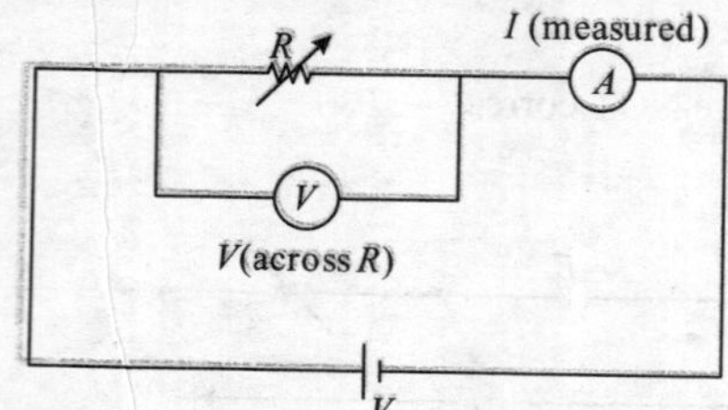

Only option (A) closely matches with above circuit used for experimental verification of Ohm's law.

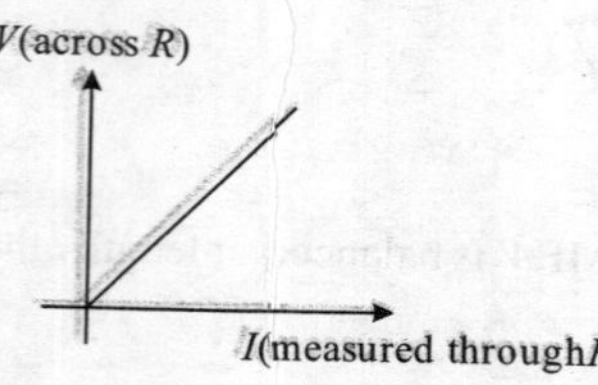

Ans. (A)

Sol. 14 Initially when balancing length is 40 cm, the balancing condition is

$$\frac{X}{40} = \frac{Y}{60} \quad \ldots(1)$$

later when $3x$ is balanced against y, if balancing length is l, then we use

$$\frac{3X}{l} = \frac{Y}{100-l} \quad \ldots(2)$$

$$\frac{(1)}{(2)} \Rightarrow \frac{l}{40\times 3} = \frac{100-l}{60}$$

$$\Rightarrow 6l = 1200 - 12l$$

$$\Rightarrow l = \frac{1200}{18} = \frac{200}{3} = 66.66\text{ cm} \sim 67\text{ cm}$$

Ans. (C)

Sol. 15

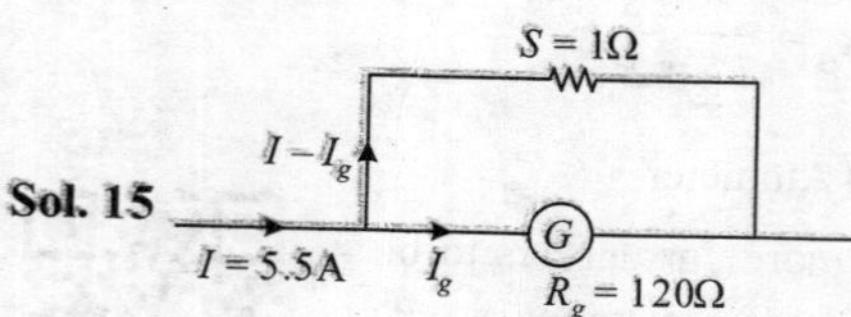

The supplied current of 5.5A will divide in inverse ratio of S and R_g and through "G" its full deflection current I_g flows so, we use

$$I_g = I \times \frac{S}{S+R_g} = \frac{5.5\times 1}{1+120}$$

$$= \frac{5.5}{1210} = \frac{55}{1210}$$

$$\Rightarrow I_g \simeq 0.045\text{ A}$$

Ans. (D)

Sol. 16 If resistance of galvanometer is G then we use

Case-1 : When $R_3 = 0$, current through galvanometer is

$$I = \frac{E}{R_1 + \frac{R_2 G}{R_2 + G}} \times \frac{R_2}{R_2 + G} \quad \ldots(1)$$

Produces deflection d

Case-2 : $R_3 = 107\ \Omega$, current through galvanometer is $[G' = G + R_3^*]$

$$I' = \frac{E}{\left(R_1 + \frac{R_2 G'}{R_2 + G'}\right)} \times \frac{R_2}{R_2 + G'} \quad \ldots(2)$$

Produces deflection $d/2$ for half deflection in galvanometer, we use

$$I' = \frac{I}{2}$$

$$\frac{E}{R_1 + \frac{R_2 G'}{R_2 + G'}} \times \frac{R_2}{R_2 + G'} = \frac{1}{2}\left(\frac{E}{R_1 + \frac{R_2 G}{R_2 + G}}\right) \times \frac{R_2}{R_2 + G}$$

$$\Rightarrow 2R_1R_2 + 2R_1G + 2R_2G = R_1R_2 + R_1G' + R_2G'$$

[here $G' = G + 107$]

$$\Rightarrow 9970 \times 30 + 2 \times 9970 \times G + 60\,G$$

$$= 9970\,G + 9970 \times 107 + 30\,G + 30 \times 107$$

$$\Rightarrow 10000\,G = 10000 \times 107 - 9970 \times 30$$

$$\Rightarrow 10000\,G = (10700 - 2991) \times 100 = 7709 \times 100$$

$$\Rightarrow G = \frac{7709 \times 100}{10000} = 77.09\ \Omega$$

Ans. (D)

Sol. 17 Among given circuits D is most appropriate. When K_1 is closed and K_2 is open then current in galvanometer is

$$I = \frac{E}{R+G} \quad \ldots(1)$$

When both K_1 and K_2 are closed current supplied by battery is

$$I' = \frac{E}{R + \frac{GS}{G+S}} \quad \ldots(2)$$

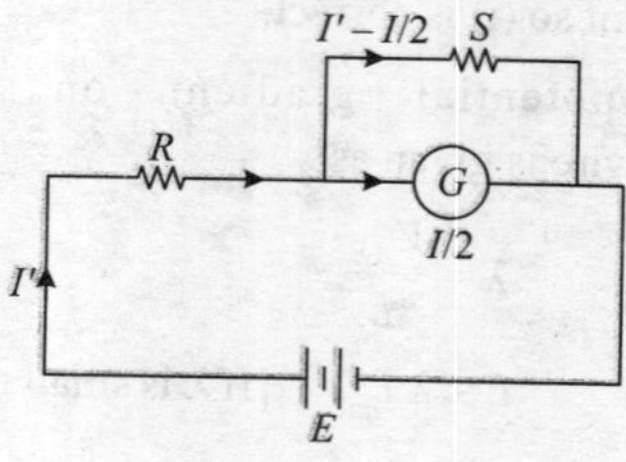

Here I' is divided in inverse ratio of S and G so we use

$$I' \times \frac{S}{S+G} = \frac{I}{2}$$

$$\frac{E.S}{RG+RS+GS} = \frac{E}{2(R+G)}$$

$$2RS+2SG = RG+RS+GS$$

$$\Rightarrow \quad G = \frac{RS}{R-S}$$ **Ans. (D)**

Sol. 18 When two batteries are connected in parallel then the terminal potential difference of this combination is given as

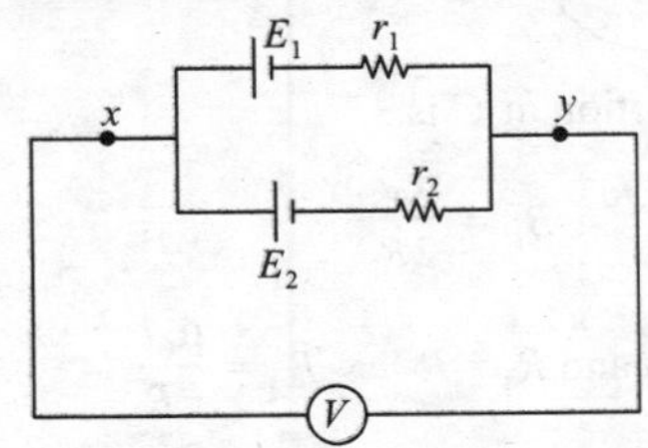

$$V_{xy} = \frac{\frac{E_1}{r_1}+\frac{E_2}{r_2}}{\frac{1}{r_1}+\frac{1}{r_2}}$$

[Already discussed in theory]

$$\Rightarrow \quad V_{xy} = \frac{\frac{10}{1}+\frac{15}{0.6}}{\frac{1}{1}+\frac{1}{0.6}} = \frac{10+25}{1+\frac{5}{3}} = \frac{35}{8/3} = \frac{105}{8}$$

$$\Rightarrow \quad V_{xy} = 13.1\text{ V}$$ **Ans. (C)**

Sol. 19

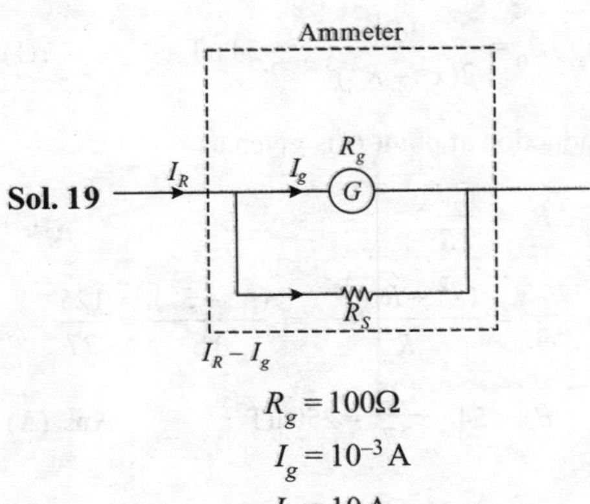

$$R_g = 100\Omega$$
$$I_g = 10^{-3}\text{ A}$$
$$I_R = 10\text{ A}$$

As R_g and R_S are in parallel we use

$$I_g R_g = (I_R - I_g)R_S$$

$$\Rightarrow \quad R_S = \frac{I_g R_g}{I_R - I_g}$$

As $I_g << I_R \Rightarrow \quad R_S = \frac{I_g R_g}{I_R} = \frac{10^{-3}\times 100}{10} = 10^{-2}\,\Omega$

Ans. (A)

Sol. 20 Step-1 :

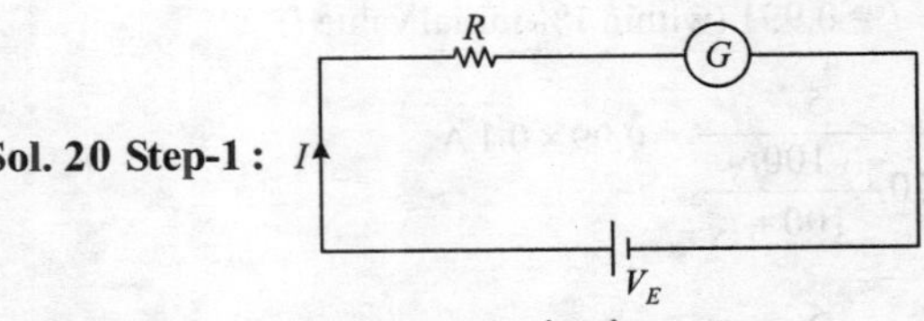

Current through galvanometer is given as

$$I = \frac{V_E}{(R+G)} \quad \ldots(1)$$

Step-2 :

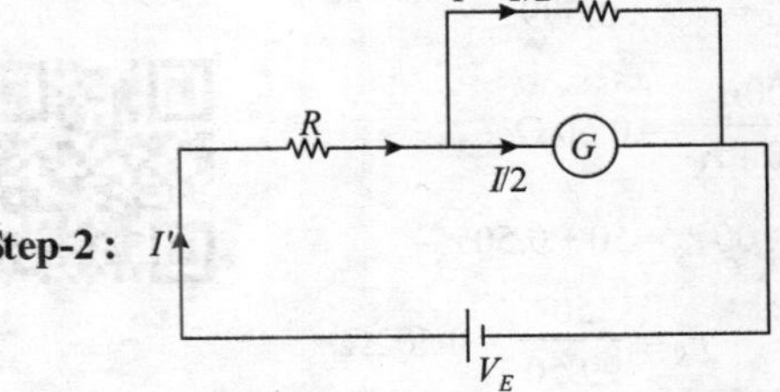

Current supplied by battery

$$I' = \frac{V_E}{R+\frac{SG}{S+G}} \quad \ldots(2)$$

Here I' is distributed in inverse ratio of S and G so we use

$$I/2 = \frac{I'S}{S+G}$$

From (1) and (2) we have

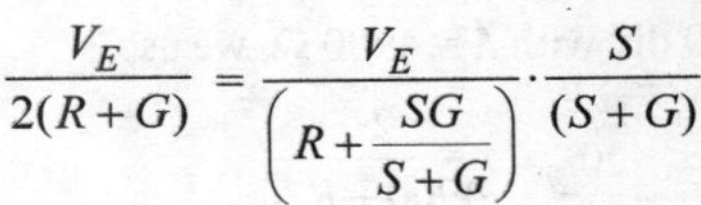

$$\frac{V_E}{2(R+G)} = \frac{V_E}{\left(R+\frac{SG}{S+G}\right)} \cdot \frac{S}{(S+G)}$$

$$\Rightarrow \quad \frac{1}{2(R+G)} = \frac{S(S+G)}{[R(S+G)SG](S+G)}$$

$$\Rightarrow \quad RS+RG+SG = 2RS+2SG$$

$$\Rightarrow \quad RG = S(R+G)$$ $\Rightarrow$ **Ans. (A)**

Sol. 21

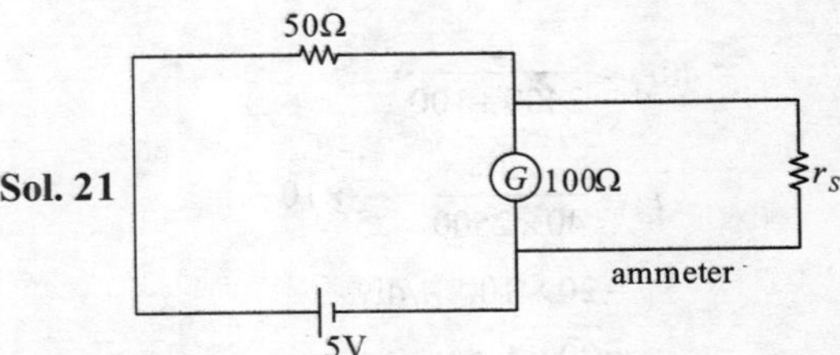

Current in circuit without the ammeter

$$I = \frac{5}{50} = 0.1\text{ A}$$

When ammeter is there is circuit, the new current will be

$$I' = \frac{5}{50+\frac{100 r_S}{100+r_S}}$$

As $I' < I \simeq I' = 0.991$ (within 1% initial value I)

$$\Rightarrow \quad \frac{5}{50+\dfrac{100r_S}{100+r_S}} = 0.99 \times 0.1\ \text{A}$$

$$\Rightarrow \quad \frac{5}{50+\dfrac{100r_S}{100+r_S}} = 0.099\ \text{A}$$

$$\Rightarrow \quad 50+\frac{100r_S}{100+r_S} = \frac{5}{0.099} = 50.50\ \Omega$$

$$\Rightarrow \quad \frac{100r_S}{100+r_S} = 0.50\ \Omega$$

$$\Rightarrow \quad 100\,r_S = 50 + 0.50\,r_S$$

$$\Rightarrow \quad r_S = \frac{50}{99.50} = 0.502\Omega$$

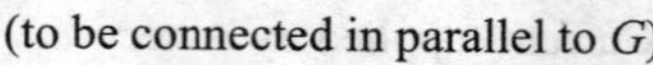

(to be connected in parallel to G)

Ans. (D)

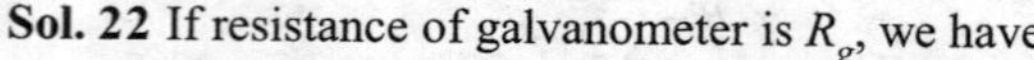

Sol. 22 If resistance of galvanometer is R_g, we have

Case-1 : At 40 div with $R = 2400\ \Omega$ if current sensitivity of "G" is i_d A/div then we use

$$40i_d = \frac{2}{2400+R_g} \quad \ldots(1)$$

Case-2 : At 20 div with $R = 4900\ \Omega$, we use

$$20i_d = \frac{2}{4900+R_g} \quad \ldots(2)$$

$$\frac{(1)}{(2)} \Rightarrow \quad 2 = \frac{4900+R_g}{2400+R_g}$$

$$\Rightarrow \quad 4800 + 2R_g = 4900 + R_g$$

$$\Rightarrow \quad R_g = 100\ \Omega$$

from equation-(1)

$$40i_d = \frac{2}{2400+100}$$

$$\Rightarrow \quad i_d = \frac{2}{40 \times 2500} = \frac{1}{5} \times 10^{-4}$$

$$= 20 \times 10^{-6}\ A/\text{div}$$

$$= 20\ \mu\text{A/div}$$

Case-3 : from 10 div if $R = R$

$$\Rightarrow \quad 10i_d = \frac{2}{R+10}$$

$$\Rightarrow \quad 10 \times 20 \times 10^{-6} = \frac{2}{R+100}$$

$$\Rightarrow \quad R + 100 = 10000$$

$$\Rightarrow \quad R = 9900\ \Omega$$

As there are total 50 div in "G"

$\Rightarrow$ Range of "G" is

$$I_{max} = 50 \times 20 \times 10^{-6}$$

$$= 10^{-3} A = 1\ \text{mA}$$

Ans. (A)

18.1 Magnetic Effects of Current

Sol. 1

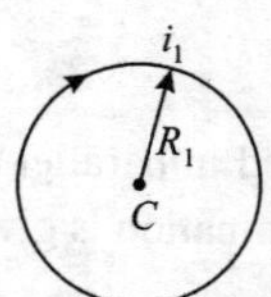

Magnetic induction at C is

$$B_C = \frac{\mu_0 i_1}{2R_1}$$

for coil A, $i_1 = i$ and $R_1 = R \Rightarrow B_A = \dfrac{\mu_0 i}{2R}$ ...(1)

for coil B, $i_2 = 2i$ and $R_2 = 2R \Rightarrow B_B = \dfrac{\mu_0(2i)}{2(2R)} = \dfrac{\mu_0 i}{2R}$ ...(2)

$$\Rightarrow \quad (1)/(2) \Rightarrow \quad \frac{B_A}{B_B} = 1$$

Ans. (A)

Sol. 2

Magnetic field induction at point O is given as

$$B_0 = \frac{\mu_0 iR^2}{2(x^2+R^2)^{3/2}} = 54\ \mu\text{T} \quad \ldots(1)$$

Magnetic field induction at point C is given as

$$B_C = \frac{\mu_0 i}{2R} \quad \ldots(2)$$

$$\Rightarrow \quad (2)/(1) \Rightarrow \quad \frac{B_C}{54} = \frac{(x^2+R^2)^{3/2}}{R^3} = \frac{(4^2+3^2)}{3^3} = \frac{125}{27}$$

$$\Rightarrow \quad B_C = 54 \times \frac{125}{27} = 250\ \mu\text{T}$$

Ans. (A)

Sol. 3

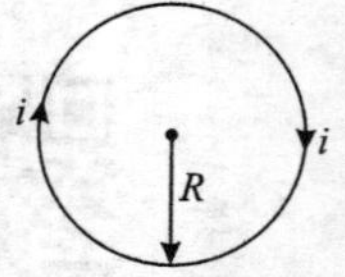

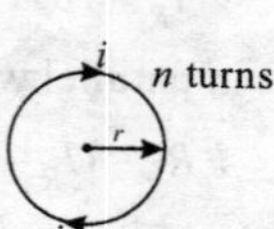

Magnetic induction at centre of one turn loop is given as

$$B = \frac{\mu_0 i}{2R} \quad \ldots(1)$$

As length of wire is constant, we use

$$2\pi R = 2\pi r \times n \Rightarrow r = R/n$$

Magnetic induction at centre of n turn loop is

$$B' = \frac{\mu_0 i}{2r} \times n = \frac{\mu_0 i n^2}{2R} = n^2 B \quad \textbf{Ans. (B)}$$

Sol. 4 Using Ampere's law on path M, we get

$$\oint_M \vec{B} \cdot \vec{dl} = \mu_0 i_{end}$$

As the conductor is hollow

$$\Rightarrow \quad i_{\text{enclosed } M} = 0$$

$$\Rightarrow \quad \oint_M \vec{B} \cdot \vec{dl} = 0$$

$$\Rightarrow \quad B_{\text{in } M} = 0 \quad \textbf{Ans. (B)}$$

Sol. 5

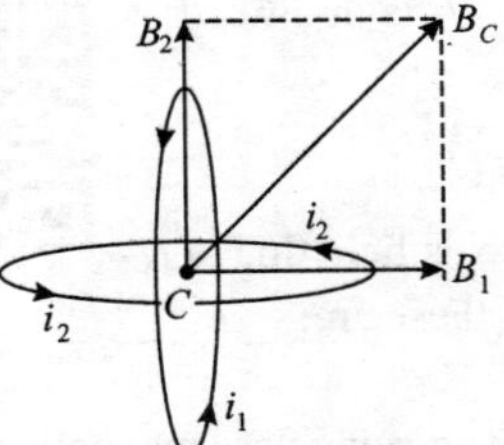

If B_1 and B_2 are magnetic induction at centre of the two coils, we use

$$B_1 = \frac{\mu_0 i_1}{2r_1} \text{ and } B_2 = \frac{\mu_0 i_2}{2r_2}$$

$$r_1 = r_2 = r = 2\pi \text{ cm}$$

Net magnetic induction at common centre of coils is given as

$$B_C = \sqrt{B_1^2 + B_2^2} = \frac{\mu_0}{2r}\sqrt{i_1^2 + i_2^2}$$

$$\Rightarrow \quad B_C = \frac{4\pi \times 10^{-7}}{2 \times 2\pi \times 10^{-2}}\sqrt{(3)^2 + (4)^2}$$

$$\Rightarrow \quad B_C = 5 \times 10^{-5} \text{ Wb/m}^2 \quad \textbf{Ans. (C)}$$

Sol. 6 For a long solenoid having turns per unit length n and current i the magnetic induction as

$$B = \mu_0 n i$$

For case-I: $n = 200$ turns/cm

$$\Rightarrow \quad 6.28 \times 10^{-2} = \mu_0 \times 200 \times 10^2 \times i \quad \ldots(1)$$

For case-II: $n = 100$ turns/cm; $i = i/3$

$$\Rightarrow \quad B = \mu_0 \times 100 \times 10^2 \times i/3 \quad \ldots(2)$$

By (2)/(1) $\Rightarrow$ $$\frac{B}{6.28 \times 10^{-2}} = \frac{1}{3 \times 2}$$

$$\Rightarrow \quad B = \frac{6.28 \times 10^{-2}}{6}$$

$$\Rightarrow \quad B = 1.05 \times 10^{-2} \text{ T} \quad \textbf{Ans. (A)}$$

Sol. 7

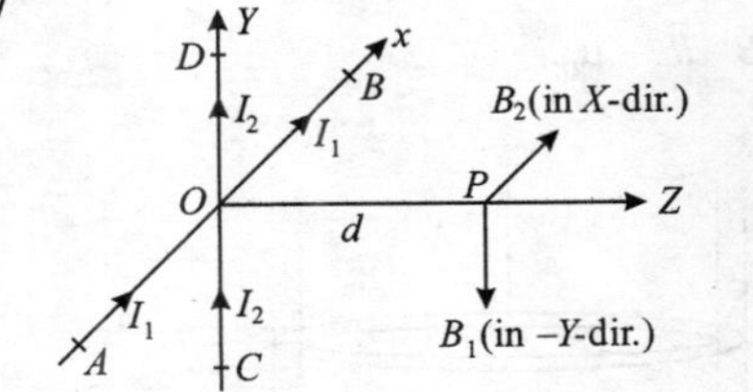

The magnetic inductions at point P due to currents I_1 and I_2 are

$$B_1 = \frac{\mu_0 I_1}{2\pi d} \text{ and } B_2 = \frac{\mu_0 I_2}{2\pi d}$$

As B_1 and B_2 are mutually perpendicular resulting magnetic induction at point P is given as

$$B_P = \sqrt{B_1^2 + B_2^2} = \frac{\mu_0}{2\pi d}\sqrt{I_1^2 + I_2^2} \quad \textbf{Ans. (B)}$$

Sol. 8 Magnetic field at interior point P of wire is given as

$$B_P = \frac{\mu_0 i x}{2\pi a^2} \quad \ldots(1)$$

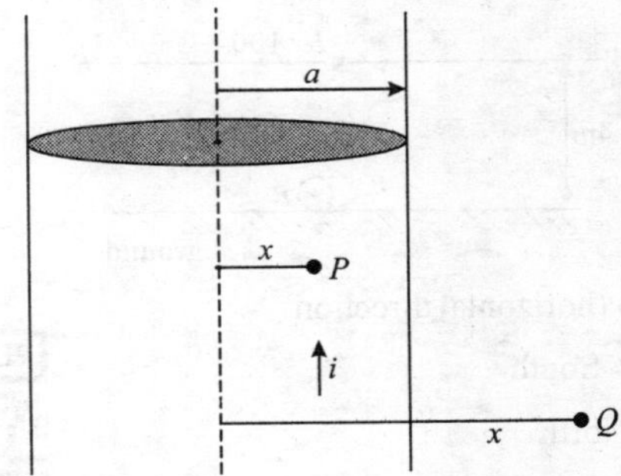

Magnetic field at outer point Q is given as

$$B_Q = \frac{\mu_0 i}{2\pi x} \quad \ldots(2)$$

at $\quad x = \frac{a}{2}$

$$B_P = \frac{\mu_0 i\left(\frac{a}{2}\right)}{2\pi a^2}$$

$$\Rightarrow \quad B_P = \frac{\mu_0 i}{4\pi a}$$

at $x = 2a$

$$B_Q = \frac{\mu_0 i}{2\pi(2a)}$$

$$\Rightarrow \quad B_Q = \frac{\mu_0 i}{4\pi a}$$

$$\Rightarrow \quad \frac{B_P}{B_Q} = 1$$

Ans. (D)

Sol. 9 If we consider a path M at interior points of pipe of radius x and use Ampere's law, then

$$\oint_M \vec{B} \cdot \vec{dl} = \mu_0 . i_{\text{end}}$$

Being a hollow pipe, here

$$i_{\text{enclosed}} = 0$$

$$\Rightarrow \quad \oint_M \vec{B} \cdot \vec{dl} = 0$$

$$\Rightarrow \quad B_{\text{in } M} = 0$$

Ans. (D)

Sol. 10

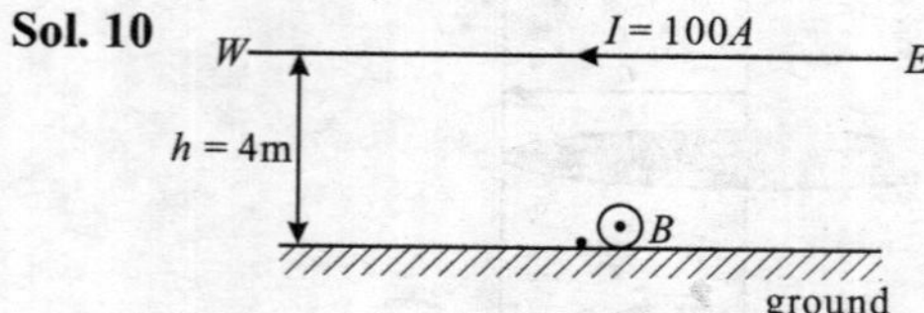

N E W S $\rightarrow$ (horizontal direction)

Outward $\rightarrow$ South

Inward $\rightarrow$ North

Magnetic induction on ground is

$$B = \frac{\mu_0 I}{2\pi h} = \frac{4\pi \times 10^{-7} \times 100}{2\pi \times 4}$$

$$\Rightarrow \quad B = 5 \times 10^{-6} \text{ T in south}$$

Ans. (C)

Sol. 11 The magnetic induction due to a circular arc carrying a current I and subtending angle θ at centre is given as

$$B = \frac{\mu_0 I \theta}{4\pi R} \quad [R \rightarrow \text{radius of arc}]$$

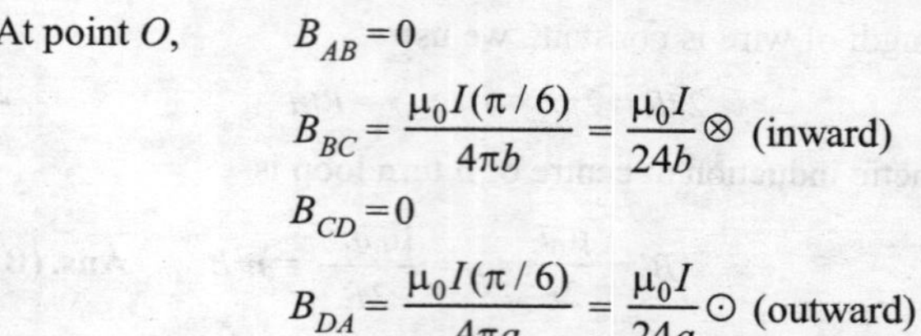

At point O, $\quad B_{AB} = 0$

$$B_{BC} = \frac{\mu_0 I(\pi/6)}{4\pi b} = \frac{\mu_0 I}{24b} \otimes \text{ (inward)}$$

$$B_{CD} = 0$$

$$B_{DA} = \frac{\mu_0 I(\pi/6)}{4\pi a} = \frac{\mu_0 I}{24a} \odot \text{ (outward)}$$

Net magnetic induction at O is given as

$$B_0 = B_{DA} - B_{BC}$$

$$\Rightarrow \quad B_0 = \frac{\mu_0 I}{24a} - \frac{\mu_0 I}{24b} = \frac{\mu_0 I}{24}\left[\frac{1}{a} - \frac{1}{b}\right]$$

$$= \frac{\mu_0 I(b-a)}{24ab}$$

Ans. (D)

Sol. 12

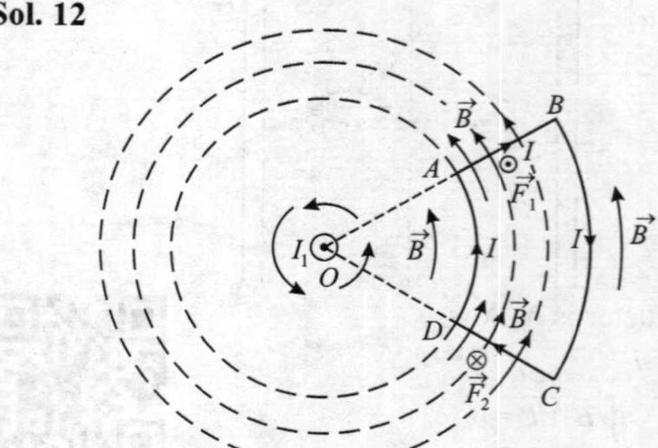

Force on wire AB due to I_1 is given in outward direction $\rightarrow \overrightarrow{F_1}$ and Force on wire CD due to I_1 is in inward direction $\rightarrow \overrightarrow{F_2}$

by symmetry we have $|\overrightarrow{F_1}| = |\overrightarrow{F_2}|$

Force on DA and BC are zero as field due to I_1 is parallel to all segments of these arc.

Ans. (D)

Sol. 13 Due to a long current carrying wire magnetic induction in its surrounding is as shown below for given situation.

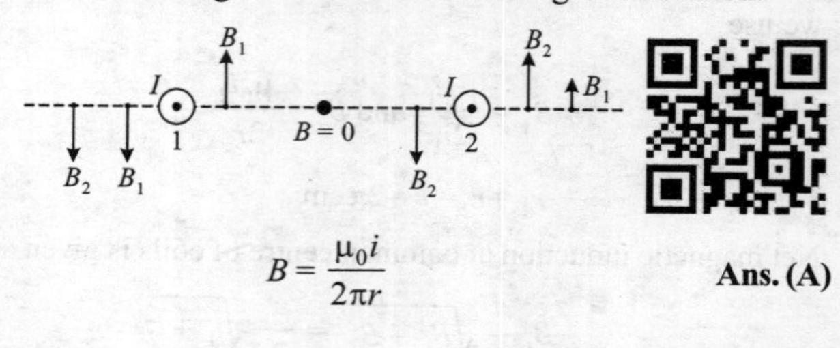

$$B = \frac{\mu_0 i}{2\pi r}$$

Ans. (A)

Sol. 14

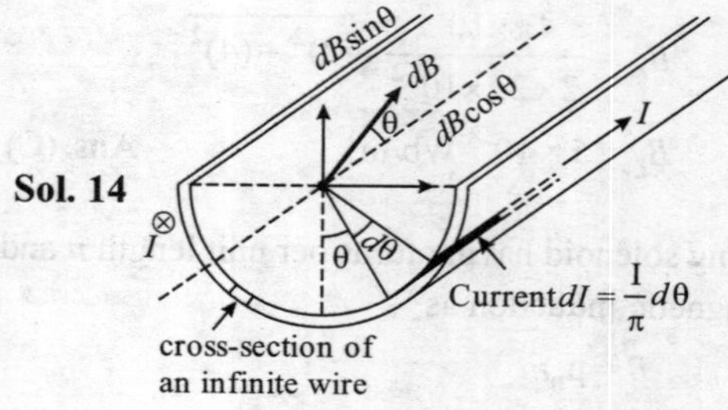

Current flowing in the elemental strip considered on surface of the half cylindrical infinite wire of width '$Rd\theta$'.

The magnetic induction due to this elemental current dI at any point on axis is given as

$$dB = \frac{\mu_0 dI}{2\pi R}$$

Net magnetic induction along axis can be given as $B = \int dB \cos\theta$

$$\Rightarrow \quad B = \int_{-\frac{\pi}{2}}^{+\frac{\pi}{2}} \frac{\mu_0\left(\frac{I}{\pi}d\theta\right)}{2\pi R}\cos\theta$$

$$\Rightarrow \quad B = \frac{\mu_0 I}{2\pi^2 R}\int_{-\frac{\pi}{2}}^{+\frac{\pi}{2}} \cos d\theta$$

$$\Rightarrow \quad B = \frac{\mu_0 I}{2\pi^2 R}[\sin\theta]_{-\pi/2}^{+\pi/2} = \frac{\mu_0 I}{2\pi^2 R}[1-(-1)]$$

$$\Rightarrow \quad B = \frac{\mu_0 I}{\pi^2 R}$$

Ans. (C)

Sol. 15

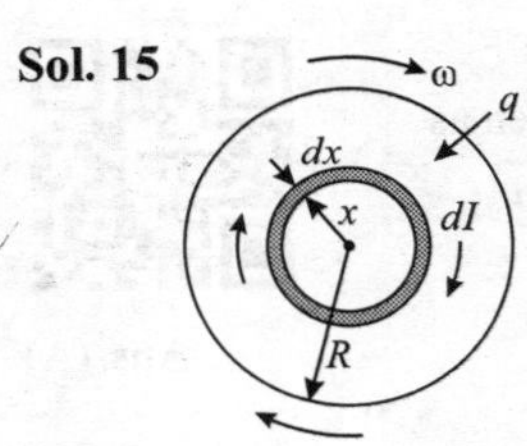

Charge on elemental ring (strip) of radius x and width dx is given as

$$dq = \frac{q}{\pi R^2}2\pi x dx = \frac{2qxdx}{R^2}$$

Current in this elemental ring is

$$dI = \frac{dq\omega}{2\pi} = \frac{qxdx\omega}{\pi R^2}$$

The magnetic induction at centre of disc due to current in the elemental ring is

$$dB = \frac{\mu_0 dI}{2x} = \frac{\mu_0}{2x}\times\frac{qx\omega dx}{\pi R^2} = \frac{\mu_0 q\omega}{2\pi R^2}dx$$

Net magnetic induction at centre of disc is given as

$$B = \int dB = \frac{\mu_0 q\omega}{2\pi R^2}\int_0^R dx$$

$$\Rightarrow \quad B = \frac{\mu_0 q\omega}{2\pi R^2}\cdot R = \frac{\mu_0 q\omega}{2\pi R}$$

$$\Rightarrow \quad B \propto \frac{1}{R}$$

Ans. (B)

Sol. 16 Magnetic induction at centre of a circular coil

$$B_1 = \frac{\mu_0 I}{2R} \quad \ldots(1)$$

MI at an axial point at a distance x from coil centre is

$$B_2 = \frac{\mu_0 IR^2}{2(R^2+x^2)^{3/2}}$$

at $x = 2\sqrt{2}R$, $\quad B_2 = \frac{\mu_0 IR^2}{2(R^2+8R^2)^{3/2}} = \frac{\mu_0 I}{54R} \quad \ldots(2)$

from (1) and (2)

$$\Rightarrow \quad \frac{B_1}{B_2} = \frac{\mu_0 I/2R}{\mu_0 I/54R} = 27$$

Ans. (B)

Sol. 17

Along the axis of a current carrying conductor magnetic induction is always zero.

$$B_M = \frac{\mu_0 i}{2\pi r}$$

and $\quad B_{\text{inside}} = \frac{\mu_0 ir}{2\pi r^2} = \frac{1}{2}\mu_0 Jr$

at P as $r = 0$ (inside) $\Rightarrow B_P = 0$

Ans. (A)

Sol. 18

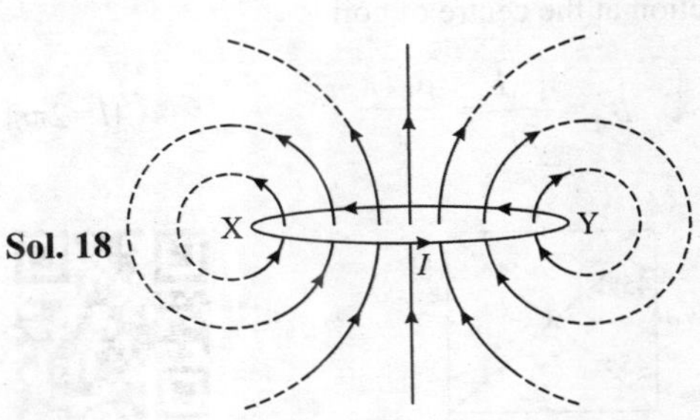

3D-view of magnetic lines configuration due to a circular loop.

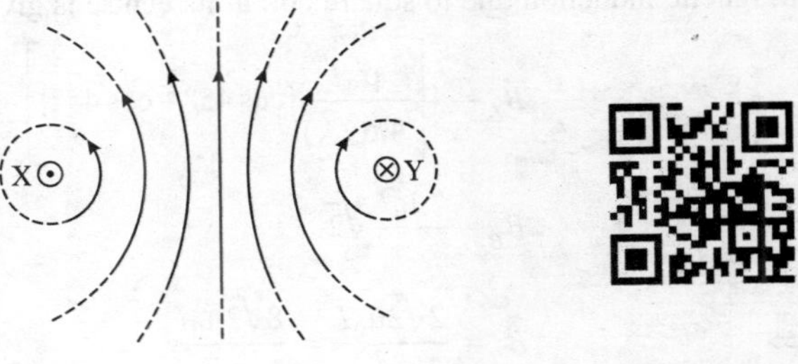

Cross-sectional view

Ans. (A)

Sol. 19 If length of wires is l then

Case I : $l = 2\pi R_1 \Rightarrow 2R_1 = l/\pi$

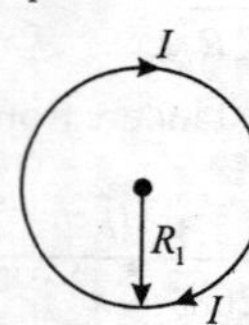

Magnetic Induction at Centre of loop is

$$B_1 = \frac{\mu_0 I}{2R_1} = \frac{\mu_0 I\pi}{l} \quad \ldots(1)$$

Case II : $l = 3\times 2\pi R_2 \Rightarrow 2R_2 = l/3\pi$

Magnetic Induction at Centre of loop is

$$B_2 = \frac{\mu_0 (I/3)}{2R_2}\times 3 = \frac{3\mu_0 I\pi}{l} \quad \ldots(2)$$

By (1)/(2) $\Rightarrow \quad \dfrac{B_1}{B_2} = \dfrac{1}{3}$ **Ans. (B)**

Sol. 20 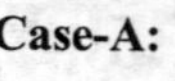

Case-A:

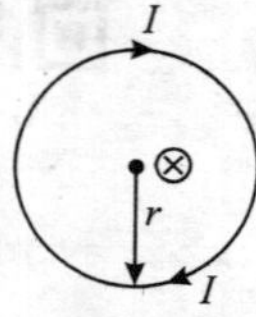

Magnetic induction at the centre of coil is

$$B_A = \frac{\mu_0 I}{2r} = \frac{\mu_0 I\pi}{l} \quad [l = 2\pi r]$$

Case-B:

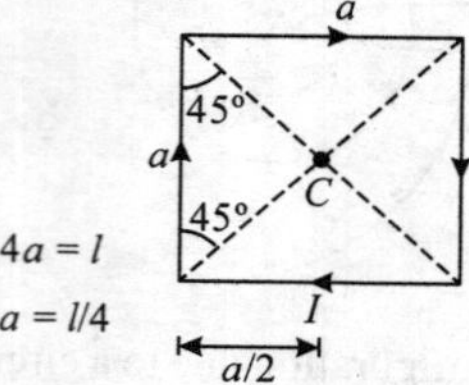

Magnetic induction due to square coil at its centre is given as

$$B_B = 4\left[\frac{\mu_0 I}{4\pi(a/2)}[\cos 45° + \cos 45°]\right]$$

$$\Rightarrow \quad B_B = \frac{2\mu_0 I}{\pi a}\sqrt{2}$$

$$\Rightarrow \quad B_B = \frac{2\sqrt{2}\mu_0 I}{\pi\left(\frac{l}{4}\right)} = \frac{8\sqrt{2}\mu_0 I}{\pi l} \quad \ldots(2)$$

By (1)/(2) $\Rightarrow \quad \dfrac{B_A}{B_B} = \dfrac{\pi^2}{8\sqrt{2}}$ **Ans. (D)**

18.2 Magnetic Force on Moving Charges

Sol. 1 If B_1 is the magnetic induction at the location of all dl on wire 2 due to wire 1, than force on dl is given as

$$F = B_1 i_2 dl$$

Here $\quad B_1 = \dfrac{\mu_0 i_1}{4\pi r}(\cos\theta + \cos\theta)$

[We use the expression of $B(r)$ due to a finite length wire]

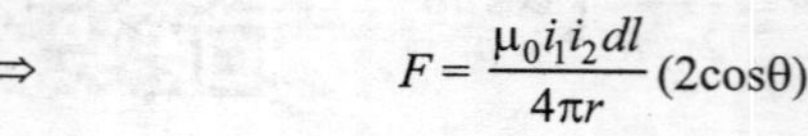

$$\Rightarrow \quad F = \frac{\mu_0 i_1 i_2 dl}{4\pi r}(2\cos\theta)$$

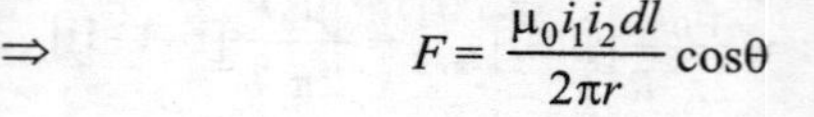

$$\Rightarrow \quad F = \frac{\mu_0 i_1 i_2 dl}{2\pi r}\cos\theta$$

Ans. (C)

Sol. 2 In uniform magnetic field the radius of circular motion is given as

$$r = mv/qB$$

$\Rightarrow$ Time period of revolution is given as

$$T = \frac{2\pi r}{v} = \frac{2\pi m}{qB}$$

$\Rightarrow$ T is independent of v. **Ans. (A)**

Sol. 3

Due to parallel currents in each turn of spring due to same direction of current flow all turns attract each other.

$\Rightarrow$ spring will get compressed. **Ans. (B)**

Sol. 4 When a charge enters in magnetic field normally then it follows a circular path of radius R given as

$$R = \frac{mv}{qB} = \frac{p}{qB} \Rightarrow R \propto \frac{1}{q}$$

As charges of e^- and p^+ are same

$\Rightarrow \quad R_e = R_p$ **Ans. (A)**

Sol. 5

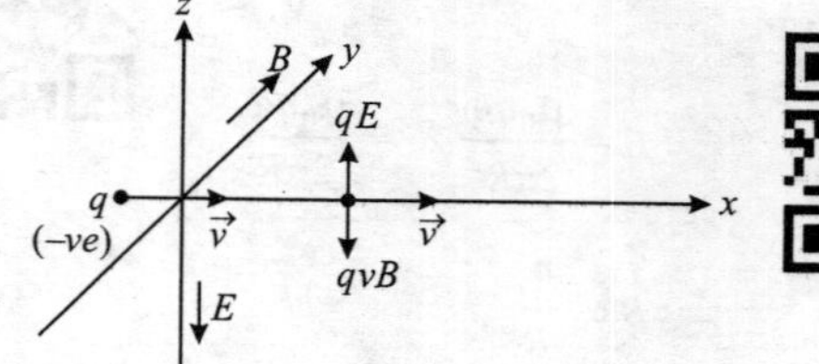

As particle continues motion in x-direction that means electric and magnetic forces on it are balanced.

$$\Rightarrow \quad qE = qvB$$

$$\Rightarrow \quad B = \frac{E}{v} = \frac{10^4}{10} = 10^3 \text{ Wb/m}^2 \qquad \textbf{Ans. (A)}$$

Sol. 6 Work done in turning a magnetic needle by angle $\theta_1 = 60°$ to $\theta_2 = 60°$ is given as

$$W = MB(\cos\theta_1 - \cos\theta_2)$$

$$W = MB(1 - 1/2) = \frac{1}{2}MB \qquad \ldots(1)$$

Torque needed to hold the needle at $\theta_2 = 60°$ to the direction of magnetic field is

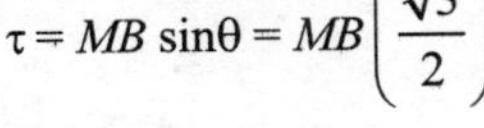

$$\tau = MB\sin\theta = MB\left(\frac{\sqrt{3}}{2}\right)$$

$$\Rightarrow \quad \tau = \sqrt{3}W \qquad \textbf{Ans. (A)}$$

Sol. 7

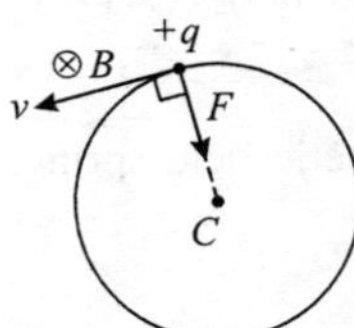

Magnetic force on a moving charge

$$\vec{F} = q(\vec{v} \times \vec{B})$$

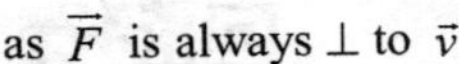

as $\vec{F}$ is always ⊥ to $\vec{v}$

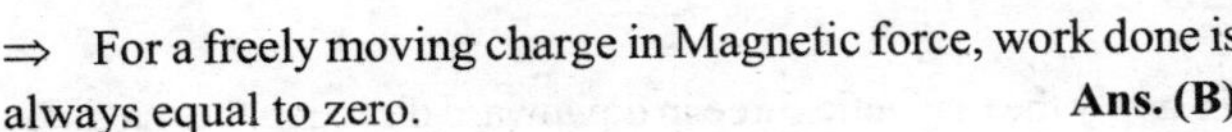

⇒ For a freely moving charge in Magnetic force, work done is always equal to zero. **Ans. (B)**

Sol. 8 **Case-I :**

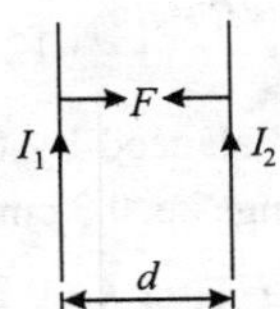

attractive force per unit length between wires is given as

$$F = \frac{\mu_0 I_1 I_2}{4\pi d} \qquad \ldots(1)$$

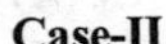

Case-II :

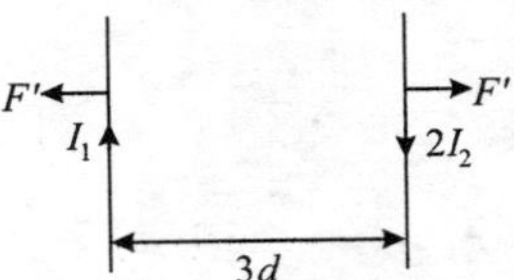

Repulsive force per unit length between wires is given as

$$F' = -\frac{\mu_0 I_1 (2I_2)}{4\pi(3d)} \qquad \ldots(2)$$

By (2)/(1) ⇒ $\frac{F'}{F} = -\frac{2}{3} \Rightarrow F' = -\frac{2}{3}F$ **Ans. (C)**

Sol. 9 For perpendicular motion of a charge particle in magnetic field, we use

$$qvB = \frac{mv^2}{r}$$

$$\Rightarrow \quad r = \frac{mv}{qB}$$

Time period of one revolution

$$T = \frac{2\pi r}{v} = \frac{2\pi}{v} \times \frac{mv}{qB} = \frac{2\pi m}{qB} \qquad \textbf{Ans. (D)}$$

Sol. 10

$B_1 \rightarrow$ magnetic induction due to wire 1 at the location of wire 2.

Force per unit length between the wires is given as

$$F = B_1 il = \left(\frac{\mu_0 i}{2\pi d}\right) il$$

$$\Rightarrow \quad \frac{F}{l} = \frac{\mu_0 i^2}{2\pi d} \qquad \textbf{Ans. (A)}$$

Sol. 11

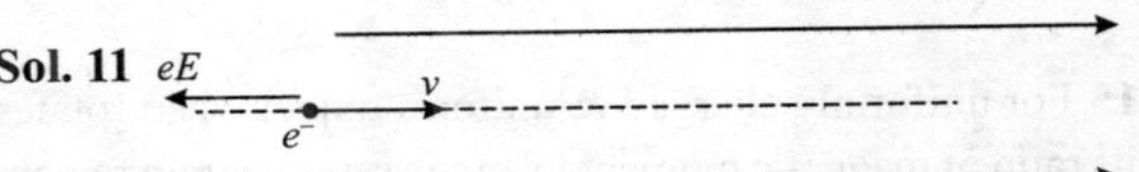

Acceleration of electron

$$a = -\frac{eE}{m}$$

As $\vec{v}$ is in same direction as $\vec{B}$ so no magnetic force will act on electron but electric force due to $\vec{E}$ in direction opposite to $\vec{v}$ so $|\vec{v}|$ will start decreasing. **Ans. (B)**

Sol. 12

Released from rest

Charge on releasing will start moving due to electric force and it moves along the direction of $\vec{E}$ and $\vec{B}$. At every point the velocity $\vec{v}$ of particle is parallel to magnetic induction $\vec{B}$.

⇒ $F_{magnetic} = 0 \Rightarrow$ path is a straight line **Ans. (B)**

Sol. 13 Whenever a charge moves perpendicular to the direction of magnetic field its path is a circular motion.

$\Rightarrow$ direction of its $\vec{v}$ continuously change and as magnitude force is $\perp$ to motion so no work is done on particle.

$\Rightarrow$ $|\vec{v}| \rightarrow$ constant

$\Rightarrow$ KE $\rightarrow$ constant **Ans. (A)**

Sol. 14

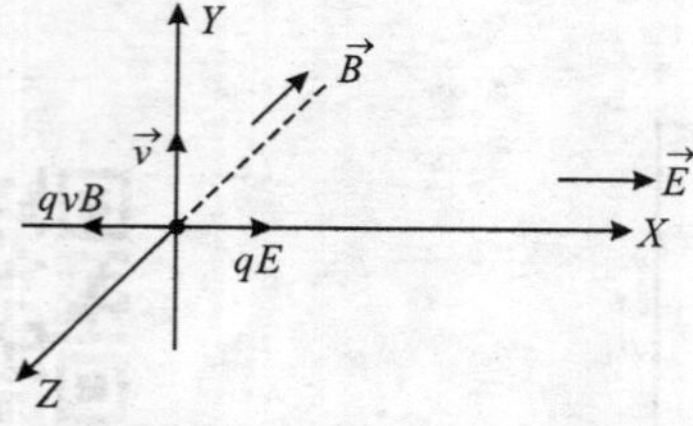

As change comes out without any change in magnitude & direction of $\vec{v}$.

$$\Rightarrow \quad qE = qvB$$

$$\Rightarrow \quad v = \frac{E}{B}$$

velocity vector will be $\vec{v} = \frac{E}{B}\hat{v}$

here we can use $\hat{v} = \frac{(\vec{E}\times\vec{B})}{EB}$

$$\Rightarrow \quad \vec{v} = \frac{E}{B}\cdot\frac{\vec{E}\times\vec{B}}{EB} = \frac{\vec{E}\times\vec{B}}{B^2}$$ **Ans. (A)**

Sol. 15 For uniformly charged & uniform object when rotates then its ratio of magnetic moment to angular momentum remain constant it is given as

$$\frac{\mu}{L} = \frac{q}{2m}$$

For disc, we use $q = \sigma \times \pi R^2$ & angular momentum $L = \left(\frac{1}{2}mr^2\right)\omega$

$$\Rightarrow \quad \mu = \frac{\sigma(\pi R^2)}{2m}\times\frac{1}{2}mR^2\omega$$

$$\Rightarrow \quad \mu = \frac{1}{4}\sigma\pi R^4\omega$$ **Ans. (D)**

Sol. 16 By Lorentz force equation, the force experienced by the charge is given as

$$\vec{F} = q\vec{E} + q(\vec{v}\times\vec{B})$$

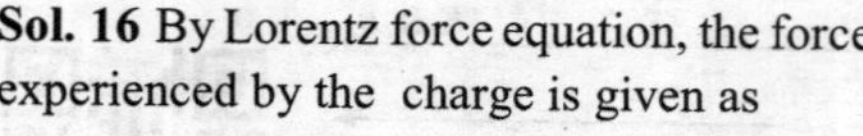

$$\Rightarrow \vec{F} = 3q\hat{i} + q\hat{j} + 2q\hat{k} + q[(3\hat{i}+4\hat{j}+\hat{k})\times(\hat{i}+\hat{j}-3\hat{k})]$$

$$\Rightarrow \vec{F} = 3q\hat{i} + q\hat{j} + 2q\hat{k} + q[(3\hat{k}-9(-\hat{j})+4(-\hat{k})-12\hat{i}+\hat{j}-\hat{i}]$$

$$\Rightarrow \vec{F} = 3q\hat{i} + q\hat{j} + 2q\hat{k} + q[-13\hat{i}+10\hat{j}-\hat{k}]$$

$$\Rightarrow \vec{F} = -10q\hat{i} + 11q\hat{j} + q\hat{k} \Rightarrow F_y = 11q$$ **Ans. (B)**

Sol. 17 In magnetic field the radius of circular motion for a charge particle is given as

$$r = \frac{mv}{qB} = \frac{\sqrt{2mk}}{qB}$$

For proton, we use $m = m_p$ & $q = +e \Rightarrow r_p = \frac{\sqrt{2m_pk}}{eB}$

For deutron, we use $m = 2m_p$ & $q = +e$

$$\Rightarrow \quad r_d = \frac{\sqrt{2(2m_p)k}}{eB} = \sqrt{2}r_p$$

For α-particle, we use $m = 4m_p$ & $q = +2e$

$$\Rightarrow \quad r_\alpha = \frac{\sqrt{2(4m_p)k}}{2eB} = r_p$$

$\Rightarrow r_\alpha = r_p < r_d$ **Ans. (C)**

Sol. 18 Initially for equilibrium of wire, we use

$$kx_1 = mg \Rightarrow k\times(0.005) = 0.01\times 10 \quad \ldots(1)$$

where k = force constant of spring

When wire is subjected to the magnetic field springs further stretch by 0.3 cm.

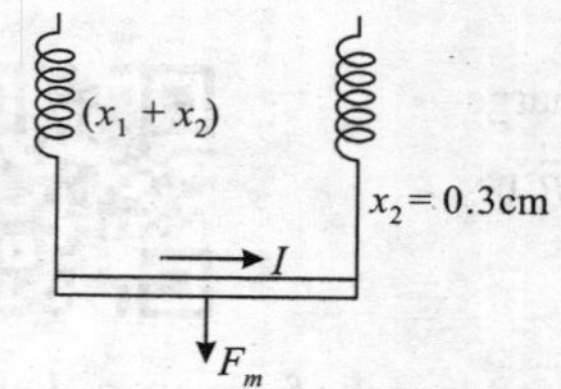

To apply the magnetic force in downward direction the magnetic field must be applied out of the page.

$$F_m = BIl = B\times\left(\frac{24}{12}\right)\times(0.05)$$

The magnetic force is balanced by the spring force due to additional stretch in springs i.e. 0.3 cm.

$$\Rightarrow \quad kx_2 = F_m \Rightarrow k\times 0.003 = B\times 2\times 0.05 \quad \ldots(2)$$

By (2)/(1) $\Rightarrow \frac{B\times 0.1}{0.1} = \frac{0.003}{0.005} = \frac{3}{5} = 0.6$

$\Rightarrow$ $B = 0.6$ T out of the page **Ans. (A)**

Sol. 19

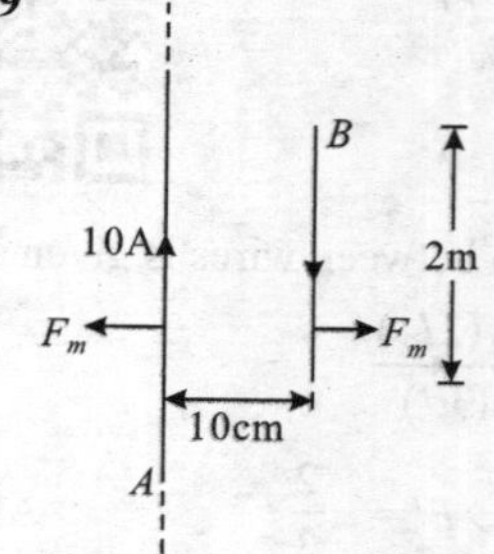

Repulsive force between two opposite and parallel currents is

$$F_m = \frac{\mu_0 I_1 I_2 l}{2\pi d}$$

$$\Rightarrow \quad F_m = \frac{4\pi\times10^{-7}\times10\times2\times2}{2\pi\times0.1}$$

$$\Rightarrow \quad F_m = 8\times10^{-5}\,\text{N}$$ **Ans. (A)**

Sol. 20 under the influence of crossed magnetic field & electric field the charge particle if pass undeflected.

$$\Rightarrow \quad \vec{F_e} = -\vec{F_m}$$

$$\Rightarrow \quad |\vec{F_e}| = |\vec{F_m}|$$

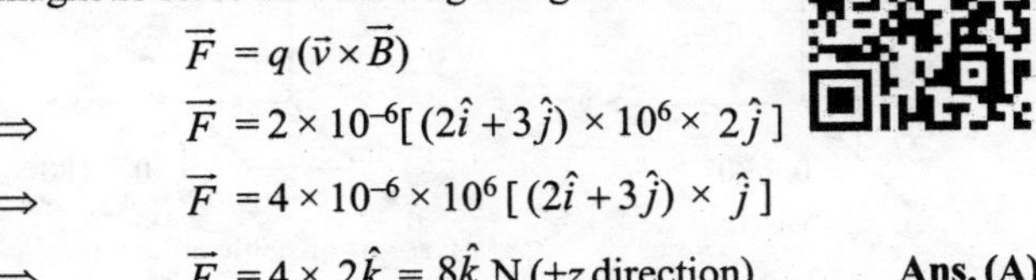

$$qE = qvB$$

$$\Rightarrow \quad v = \frac{E}{B} = \frac{7.7\times10^3}{0.14} = 55\times10^3\ \text{m/s}$$

$$\Rightarrow \quad v = 55\ \text{km/s}$$ **Ans. (C)**

Sol. 21 By Lorentz force equation, the magnetic force on a moving charge is

$$\vec{F} = q(\vec{v}\times\vec{B})$$

$$\Rightarrow \quad \vec{F} = 2\times10^{-6}[(2\hat{i}+3\hat{j})\times10^6\times2\hat{j}]$$

$$\Rightarrow \quad \vec{F} = 4\times10^{-6}\times10^6[(2\hat{i}+3\hat{j})\times\hat{j}]$$

$$\Rightarrow \quad \vec{F} = 4\times2\hat{k} = 8\hat{k}\ \text{N}\ (+z\ \text{direction})$$ **Ans. (A)**

Sol. 22 In a magnetic field radius of charge particle's circular motion is given as

$$R = \frac{mv}{qB} = \frac{\sqrt{2mk}}{qB}$$

if the particle is accelerated by a potential difference V

$$\Rightarrow \quad K = qV$$

$$\Rightarrow \quad R = \frac{\sqrt{2mqV}}{qB}$$

for proton $q = e,\ m = m_p \Rightarrow R_p = \frac{1}{B}\frac{\sqrt{2m_p eV}}{q}$

for deutron $q = e,\ m = 2m_p \Rightarrow R_D = \frac{1}{B}\frac{\sqrt{2(2m_p)eV}}{q} = R$

$$\Rightarrow \quad \frac{R_p}{R_D} = \frac{1}{\sqrt{2}} \Rightarrow R_p = \frac{R}{\sqrt{2}}$$ **Ans. (B)**

Sol. 23 S-1: In perpendicular motion to a uniform/Non uniform magnetic field as

$$\vec{F}_{\text{magnetic}} = q(\vec{v}\times\vec{B})$$

$\Rightarrow$ $\vec{F}_{\text{magnetic}}$ is $\perp$ to $\vec{v}$ so magnetic force never do work on a moving charge

$\Rightarrow$ KE $\rightarrow$ constant

$\Rightarrow$ S-1 it true

$\vec{F}_{\text{magnetic}}$ is $\perp$ to $\vec{v}$

$\Rightarrow$ **S-2 : it is true and explaining S-1** **Ans. (D)**

Sol. 24

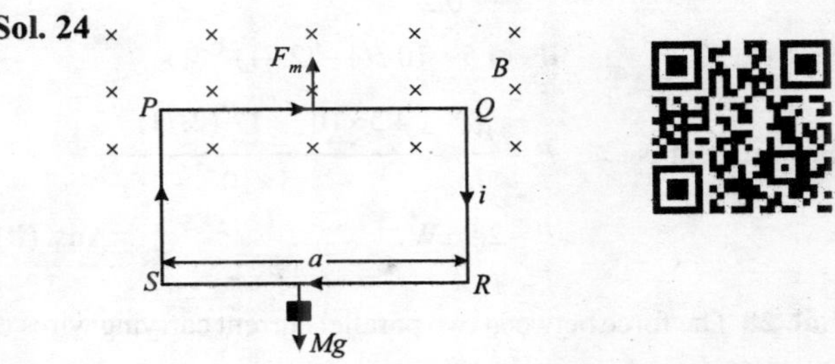

Magnetic force on loop is due to wire PQ, given as

$$F_m = Bia$$

Given that $Bia > mg \Rightarrow$ net force is in upward direction so weight rises up. As net work done by magnetic field is zero and here work is done against gravity. **Ans. (C)**

Sol. 25 As charge is not getting deflected $\Rightarrow$ no net force is acting on it.

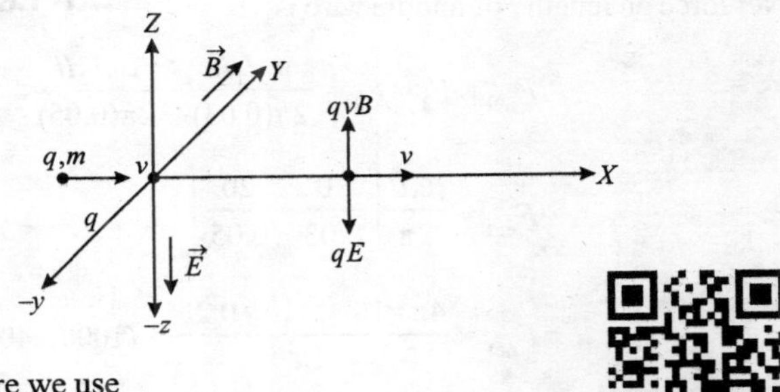

Here we use

$$qE = qvB$$

$$B = \frac{E}{v} = \frac{10^4}{10} = 10^3\ \text{Wb/m}^2$$ **Ans. (C)**

Sol. 26 Given that $E_y \propto J_x B_z$

$$\Rightarrow \quad E_y = kJ_xB_z$$

$$\Rightarrow \quad k = \frac{E_y}{J_xB_z}$$

$$\Rightarrow \quad U(k) = \frac{U(E_y/B_z)}{U(J_x)} = \frac{\text{m/s}}{\text{A/m}^2} = \frac{\text{m}^3}{\text{As}}$$ **Ans. (B)**

Sol. 27 Work done in displacing the wire by an elemental displacement dx is

$$dW = BIl dx = 3.0\times10^{-4}\times e^{-0.2x}\times10\times3\times dx$$

Total work done in displacing the wire from $x = 0$ to $x = 2$m is

$$W = \int dW = \int_0^{2.0} 9\times10^{-3}\cdot e^{-0.2x}dx$$

$$\Rightarrow \quad W = 9\times10^{-3}\left[\frac{e^{-0.2x}}{-0.2}\right]_0^2$$

$$\Rightarrow \quad W = \frac{9\times10^{-3}}{0.2}(1-e^{-0.4})$$

$$\Rightarrow \quad W = 4.5\times10^{-2}(1-(2.71)^{-0.4})\text{ J}$$

Power spent is
$$P = \frac{W}{t} = \frac{4.5\times10^{-2}\left[1-(2.71)^{-0.4}\right]}{5\times10^{-3}}$$

$$\Rightarrow \quad P = 2.96\text{ W}$$ **Ans. (B)**

Sol. 28 The force between two parallel current carrying wires is given as

$$F = \frac{\mu_0 I_1 I_2 l}{2\pi d}$$

As $F_1 > F_2$

Net force on length l of middle wire is

$$F_{\text{net}} = F_1 - F_2 = \frac{\mu_0 I_1 Il}{2\pi(0.03)} - \frac{\mu_0 I_2 Il}{2\pi(0.05)}$$

$$\Rightarrow \quad F_{\text{net}} = \frac{\mu_0 Il}{2\pi}\left[\frac{30}{0.03} - \frac{20}{0.05}\right]$$

$$\Rightarrow \quad F_{\text{net}} = \frac{4\pi\times10^{-7}\times10\times0.25}{2\pi}\times(1000-400)$$

F_{net} is acting toward right

$$\Rightarrow \quad F_{\text{net}} = 2\times10^{-7}\times10\times0.25\times600$$

$$\Rightarrow \quad F_{\text{net}} = 3\times10^{-4}\text{ N}$$ **Ans. (A)**

Sol. 29

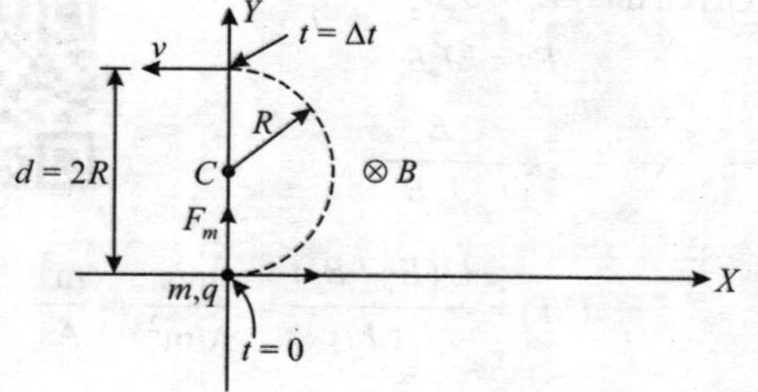

In magnetic field, radius of circular motion of charge is given as

$$R = \frac{mv}{qB} = \frac{d}{2} \quad \ldots(1)$$

Time required to complete half circle is given as

$$\Delta t = \frac{T}{2} = \frac{1}{2}\left(\frac{2\pi m}{qB}\right) = \frac{\pi m}{qB} \quad \left[\text{As } T = \frac{2\pi m}{qB}\right]$$

from equation-(1) $\Delta t = \pi\left(\frac{d}{2v}\right) = \frac{\pi d}{2v}$.

also from equation-(1) $B = \dfrac{2mv}{qd}$ **Ans. (C)**

Sol. 30 For stable equilibrium $U \rightarrow$ minimum as $U = -\vec{M}\cdot\vec{B}$
so for $\theta = 0°$ it will be in stable equilibrium
and for unstable equilibrium $U \rightarrow$ max $\Rightarrow$ at $\theta = 180°$
it will be in unstable equilibrium.

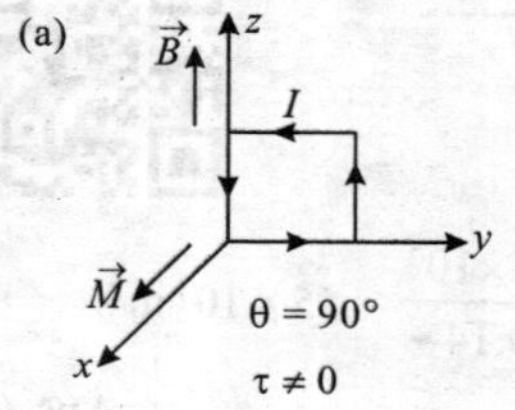

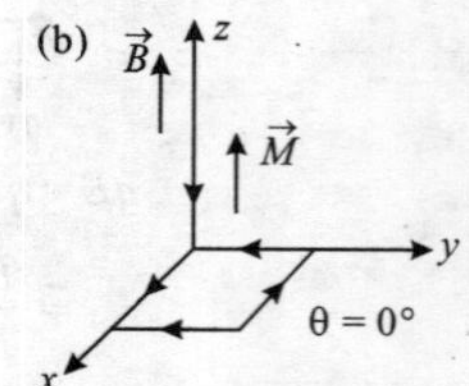

Case of stable eqlibrium

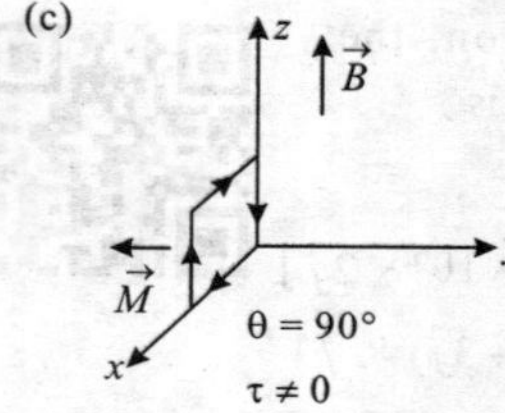

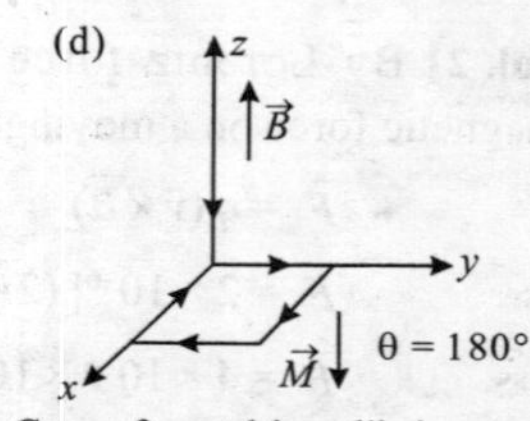

Case of unstable eqlibrium

(b) and (d) are cases of stable and unstable equilibrium respectively. **Ans. (C)**

Sol. 31

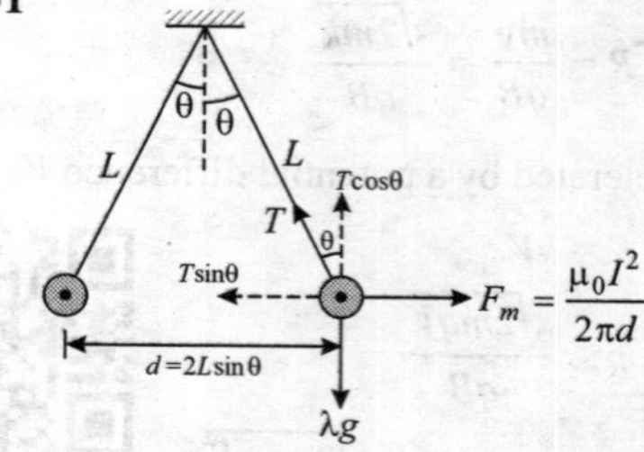

For equilibrium of wires, we have

$$T\sin\theta = \frac{\mu_0 I^2}{2\pi(2L\sin\theta)} \quad \ldots(1)$$

$$T\cos\theta = \lambda g \quad \ldots(2)$$

$$\text{By (1)/(2)} \Rightarrow \quad \frac{\sin^2\theta}{\cos\theta} = \frac{\mu_0 I^2}{4\pi L\lambda g}$$

$$\Rightarrow \quad I = 2\sin\theta\sqrt{\frac{\pi\lambda g L}{\mu_0\cos\theta}}$$ **Ans. (B)**

Sol. 32 For solenoid having closely spaced turns these behave like closed loop coils and in uniform magnetic field produced by a solenoid the net force on coils (of other solenoid) is equal to zero.

$\Rightarrow \quad \vec{F_1} = \vec{F_2} = 0$ **Ans. (A)**

Sol. 33 $F_m = BIl = 2BIR\sin\theta$ (magnetic force on wire)

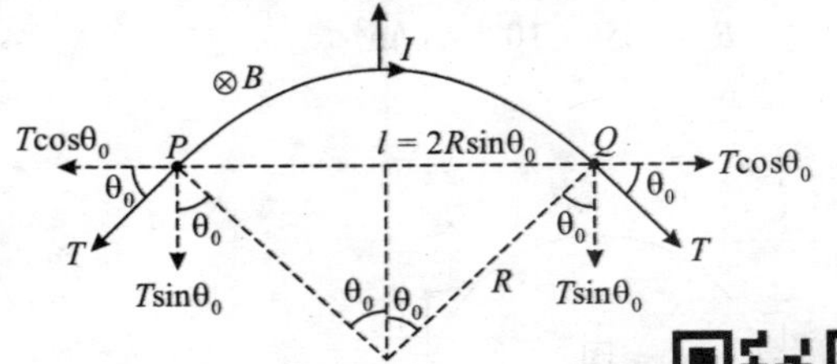

As wire is in equilibrium, we use

$$2T\sin\theta_0 = 2BIR\sin\theta_0$$

$\Rightarrow \quad T = BIR$ **Ans. (C)**

Sol. 34 Force between two parallel current carrying wires is given as

$$F = \frac{\mu_0 I_1 I_2 l}{2\pi d}$$

$\Rightarrow \quad F \propto I_1 I_2$

$\Rightarrow$ If I_1 and I_2 are in same direction (same sign) $\Rightarrow I_1 I_2 \to +\text{ve}$ then wires attract each other $\Rightarrow F \to -\text{ve}$. And

if I_1 and I_2 are opposite (opposite signs) $\Rightarrow I_1 I_2 \to -\text{ve}$ then wires repel each other $\Rightarrow F \to +\text{ve}$. **Ans. (A)**

Sol. 35

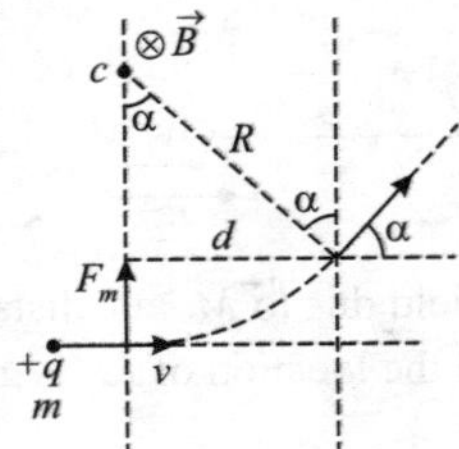

Kinetic energy of proton $K = qV = \frac{1}{2}mv^2$

The radius of proton motion inside the Magnetic Field is

$$R = \frac{mv}{qB} = \frac{\sqrt{2mk}}{qB}$$

from figure $\quad \sin\alpha = \frac{d}{R} = \frac{qBd}{\sqrt{2mK}} = \frac{qBd}{\sqrt{2mqV}}$

$\Rightarrow \quad \sin\alpha = Bd\sqrt{\frac{q}{2mV}}$ **Ans. (D)**

19.1 Classical and Terrestrial Magnetism

Sol. 1

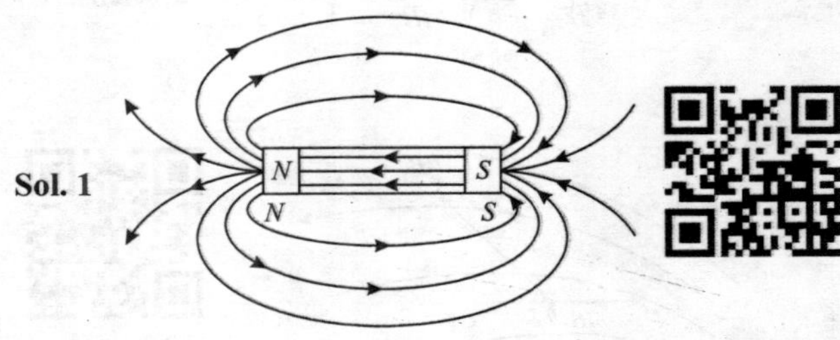

Configuration of magnetic lines in surrounding of a bar magnet. Inside a bar magnet magnetic lines travel from S to N pole.

Ans. (D)

Sol. 2 The oscillation period of a bar magnet in magnetic field is

$$T = 2\pi\sqrt{\frac{I}{MB}}$$

$$I = \frac{ml^2}{12} \quad \text{and} \quad M = m_s.l$$

If magnet is broken in two equal parts of length $l/2$ then its moment of inertia & magnetic moment will become

$$I' = \frac{(m/2)(l/2)^2}{12} = \frac{I}{8}$$

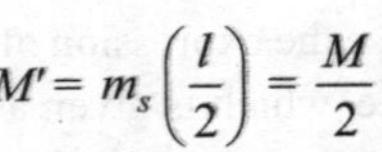

& $\quad M' = m_s\left(\frac{l}{2}\right) = \frac{M}{2}$

New time period of oscillation will be

$\Rightarrow \quad T' = 2\pi\sqrt{\frac{I'}{M'B}} = 2\pi\sqrt{\frac{I/8}{M/2B}} = \frac{T}{2}$

$\Rightarrow \quad \frac{T'}{T} = \frac{1}{2}$ **Ans. (B)**

Sol. 3 In a vibration magnetometer time period of oscillations of a magnet is

$$T = 2\pi\sqrt{\frac{I}{MB}}$$

Here $\quad I = \frac{ml^2}{12}$ (m = mass)

& $\quad M = m_s l$ (m = pole strength)

If magnet is cut in 3 parts each of length $l/3$ then we use new moment of inertia and magnetic moment of combination is

$$I' = 3\times\frac{(m/3)(l/3)^2}{12} = \frac{I}{9}$$

and $\quad M' = m_s\frac{l}{3}\times 3 = M$

New time period will be

$$T' = 2\pi\sqrt{\frac{I'}{M'B}} = 2\pi\sqrt{\frac{I/9}{MB}} = \frac{T}{3} = \frac{2}{3}\,\text{s}$$ **Ans. (B)**

Sol. 4

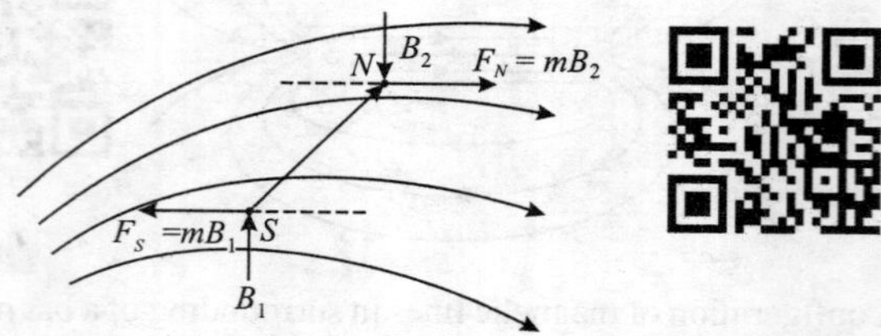

As in non uniform magnetic field $B_1 \neq B_2$

$\Rightarrow$ There will be a net force acting on the needle and as direction F_N and F_S are not along same line.

$\Rightarrow$ There will be a net torque acting as well. **Ans. (C)**

Sol. 5

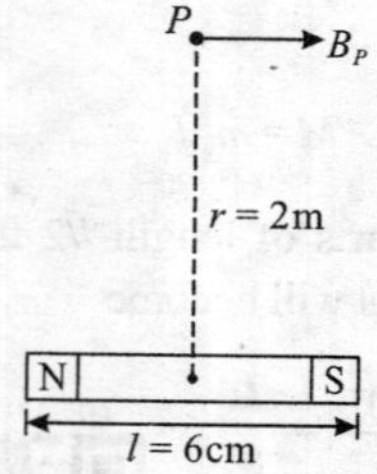

As $r >> l$, here we can use the expression of magnetic induction due to a magnetic dipole, which is given as

For equatorial points $B_P = \dfrac{kM}{r^3} = \dfrac{\mu_0}{4\pi}\dfrac{M}{r^3}$

$$\Rightarrow \quad B_P = 10^{-7} \times \frac{4}{(2)^3} = 0.5 \times 10^{-7}\,\text{T}$$

$$\Rightarrow \quad B_P = 5 \times 10^{-8}\,\text{T}$$ **Ans. (C)**

Sol. 6

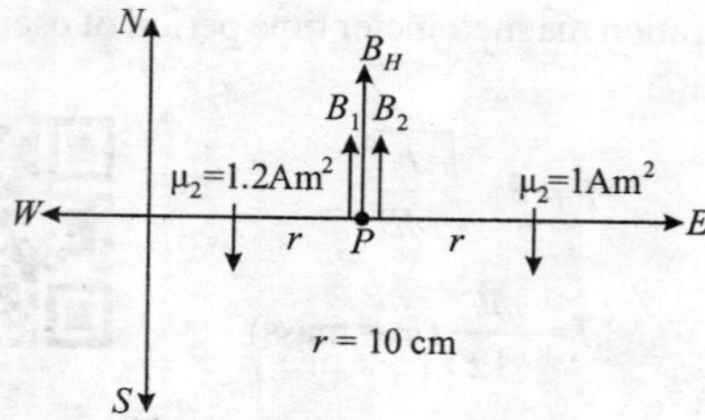

Magnetic moment of the two dipole are $\mu_1 = 1.20\ \text{Am}^2$ & $\mu_2 = 1.00\ \text{Am}^2$ and due to these dipoles, magnetic induction at mid point P are given as

$$B_1 = \frac{k\mu_1}{r^3} = \frac{\mu_0}{4\pi}\frac{\mu_1}{r^3} = \frac{10^{-7} \times 1.20}{(0.1)^3}$$

$$\Rightarrow \quad B_1 = 1.2 \times 10^{-4}\ \text{Wb/m}^2$$

and $\quad B_2 = \dfrac{k\mu_2}{r^3} = \dfrac{\mu_0}{4\pi}\dfrac{\mu_2}{r^3} = \dfrac{10^{-7} \times 1.00}{(0.1)^3}$

$$\Rightarrow \quad B_2 = 1 \times 10^{-4}\ \text{Wb/m}^2$$

$\Rightarrow$ Net magnetic induction at P is

$$B_P = B_H + B_1 + B_2$$

$$\Rightarrow \quad B_P = 3.6 \times 10^{-5} + 1.2 \times 10^{-4} + 1 \times 10^{-4}$$

$$\Rightarrow \quad B_P = 2.56 \times 10^{-4}\ \text{Wb/m}^2$$ **Ans. (B)**

Sol. 7

Magnetic induction at equatorial point P due to Earth's magnetic dipole is given as

$$B_P = \frac{kM}{R_e^3}$$

$$\Rightarrow \quad B_P = \frac{10^{-7} \times 8 \times 10^{22}}{(6.4 \times 10^6)^3}\,T$$

$$\Rightarrow \quad B_P = 0.302 \times 10^{-4}\,\text{T} = 0.302\ \text{G}$$

$$1\,\text{G} = 10^{-4}\,\text{T}$$ **Ans. (D)**

Sol. 8

[B_1 is the axial point Magnetic field due to M_1 at a distance x] Magnetic induction due to M_1 at the location of M_2 is given as

$$B_1 = \frac{2kM_1}{x^3}$$

In non-uniform Magnetic field, force on dipole M_2 is given as

$$\vec{F} = -\vec{M}_2\frac{dB_1}{dx}\hat{i}$$

In magnitude $\quad |\vec{F}| = |\vec{M}_2 \times 2kM_1\dfrac{d}{dx}(x^{-3})|$

$$\Rightarrow \quad |\vec{F}| = \frac{6kM_1M_2}{x^4} \Rightarrow F \propto x^{-4}$$ **Ans. (D)**

Sol. 9

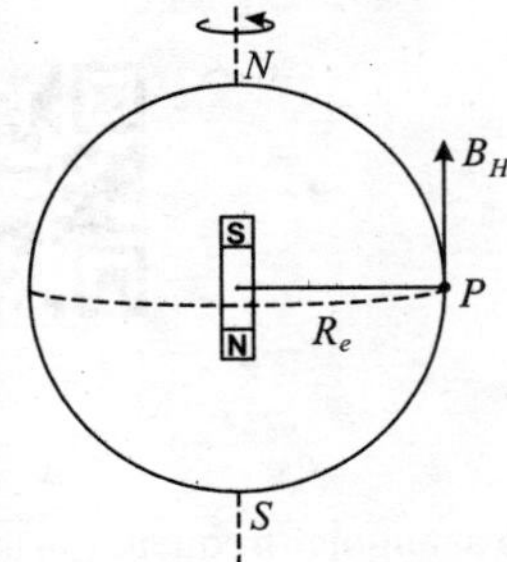

Neglecting declination

For a magnetic dipole at equatorial point, the magnetic induction is given as

$$B_H = \frac{kM}{R_e^3} = 4 \times 10^{-5}$$

$$\Rightarrow \quad M = \frac{4\times10^{-5}\times(6.4\times10^{6})^3}{10^{-7}}$$

$$\Rightarrow \quad M = 1.048 \times 10^{23}\ \text{Am}^2$$

Ans. (A)

Sol. 10

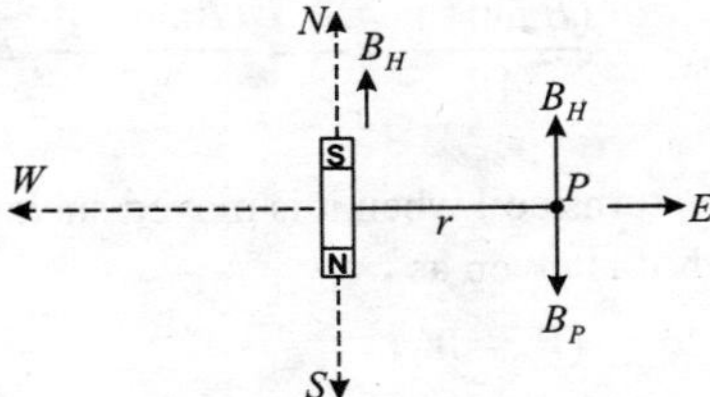

Considering the magnet as a magnetic dipole, magnetic induction at equatorial point P is given as

$$B_P = \frac{KM}{r^3}$$

As at P $\quad B_{net} = 0$ (null point) Þ $B_P = B_H$

$$\Rightarrow \quad \frac{10^{-7}\times M}{(0.3)^3} = 3.6\times10^{-5}$$

$$\Rightarrow \quad M = \frac{3.6\times10^{-5}\times27\times10^{-3}}{10^{-7}} = 9.72$$

Ans. (C)

Sol. 11

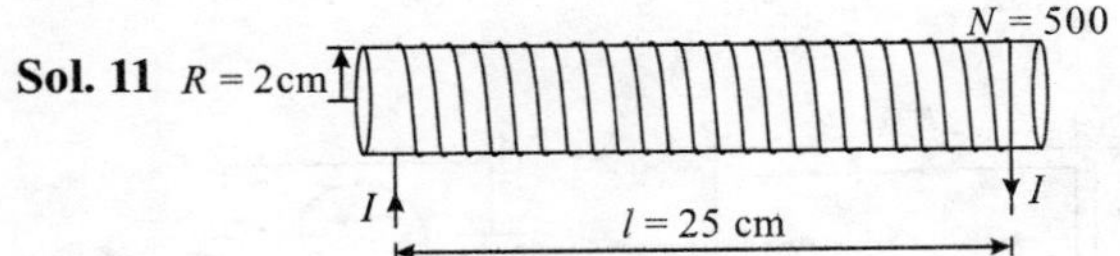

Magnetic moment of solenoid

$$\mu = I(\pi R^2)\times N$$

Volume of solenoid $V = l(\pi R^2)$

$$\text{Magnetization} \quad |\overrightarrow{M}| = \frac{\mu}{V} = \frac{I\pi R^2 N}{l\pi R^2}$$

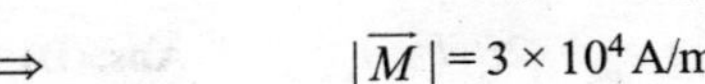

$$= \frac{IN}{l} = \frac{15\times500}{0.25}$$

$$\Rightarrow \quad |\overrightarrow{M}| = 3\times10^4\ \text{A/m}$$

Ans. (C)

Sol. 12 Stable equilibrium of a dipole in magnetic field exist when angle θ between its dipole moment and net magnetic induction is zero.

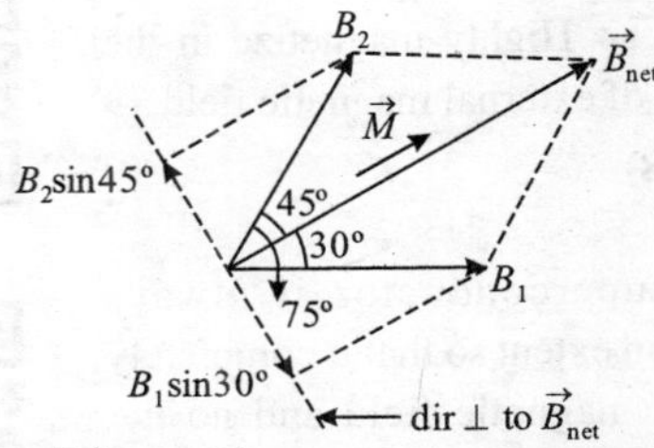

here θ between $\overrightarrow{M}$ and $\overrightarrow{B}_{net}$ should be zero. The components of B_1 and B_2 along the direction normal to $\overrightarrow{B}_{net}$ must be equal.

$$\Rightarrow \quad B_1\sin30° = B_2\sin45°$$

$$15\times\frac{1}{2} = B_2\times\frac{1}{\sqrt{2}}$$

$$\Rightarrow \quad B_2 = \frac{15}{\sqrt{2}} = 10.6\ \text{mT}$$

Ans. (B)

19.2 Magnetic Properties of Materials

Sol. 1 Curie temperature is the temperature above which a ferromagnetic material changes to paramagnetic material. **Ans. (A)**

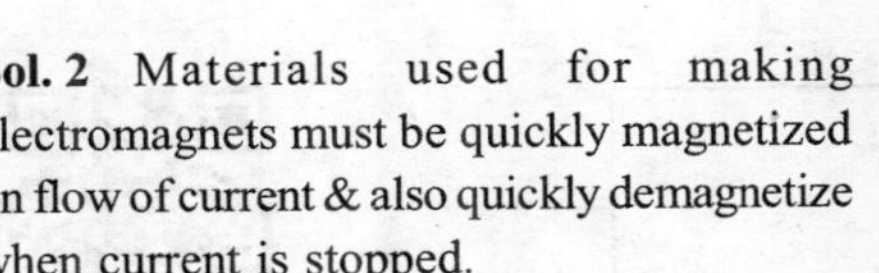

Sol. 2 Materials used for making electromagnets must be quickly magnetized on flow of current & also quickly demagnetize when current is stopped.

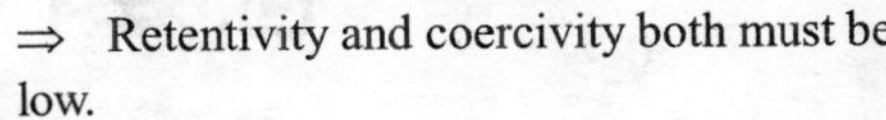

⇒ Retentivity and coercivity both must be low.

Ans. (B)

Sol. 3 Paramagnetic and Diamagnetic materials are weakly magnetized along & opposite to external field.

⇒ N_2 is attracted by external magnet & N_3 is repelled by external magnet weakly Ferromagnetic material strongly magnetized along the direction of external magnetic field.

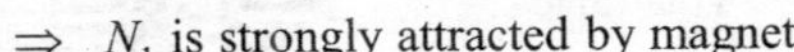

⇒ N_1 is strongly attracted by magnet.

Ans. (B)

Sol. 4 For any material always

$$\epsilon_r > 1$$

For a diamagnetic material we use

$$\mu_r < 1$$

Ans. (B)

Sol. 5 For demagnetization of magnet we use

$$H_c = \frac{B}{\mu_0} = nI = \frac{N}{l}I$$

$$I = \frac{H_c\times l}{N} = \frac{3\times10^3\times0.1}{100} = 3\ \text{A}$$

Ans. (C)

Sol. 6 Diamagnetic → repel external magnetic field → Bar B.
Paramagnetic → magnetize in same direction of external Magnetic field → Bar C.
Ferromagnetic → Highly magnetize in the same direction of external magnetic field → Bar A. **Ans. (B)**

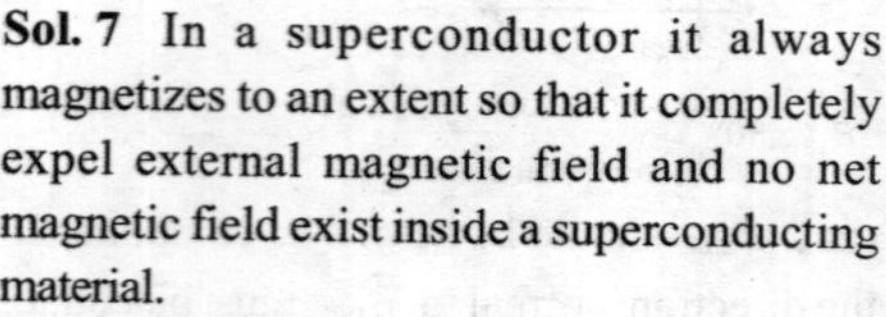

Sol. 7 In a superconductor it always magnetizes to an extent so that it completely expel external magnetic field and no net magnetic field exist inside a superconducting material.

$$\Rightarrow \quad B_{inside} = 0$$

$$\text{or} \quad B_{sup} = 0$$

Ans. (B)

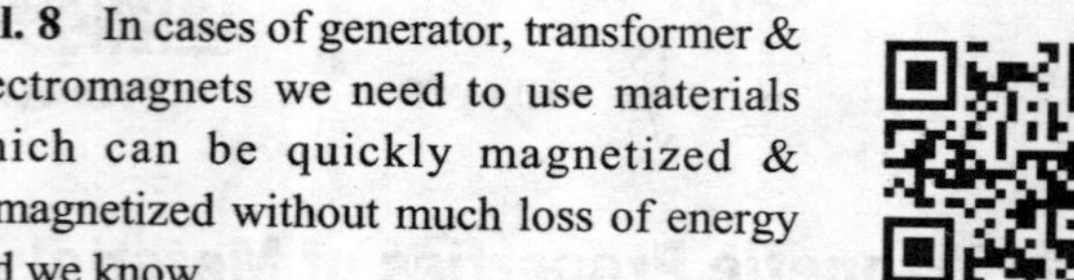

Sol. 8 In cases of generator, transformer & electromagnets we need to use materials which can be quickly magnetized & demagnetized without much loss of energy and we know.

Loss of energy/cycle ∝ area of B-H curve. **Ans. (D)**

20.1 Electromagnetic Induction

Sol. 1

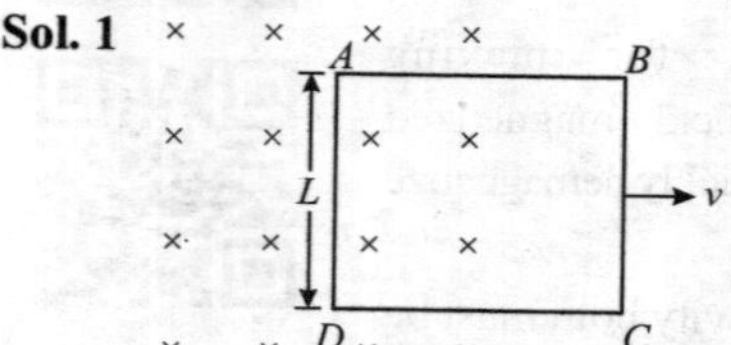

During motion, only wire segment AD will cut magnetic flux and motional emf is induced in it, which is given as

$$e_{AD} = BvL$$

$$v_A - v_D = BvL$$

Ans. (D)

Sol. 2

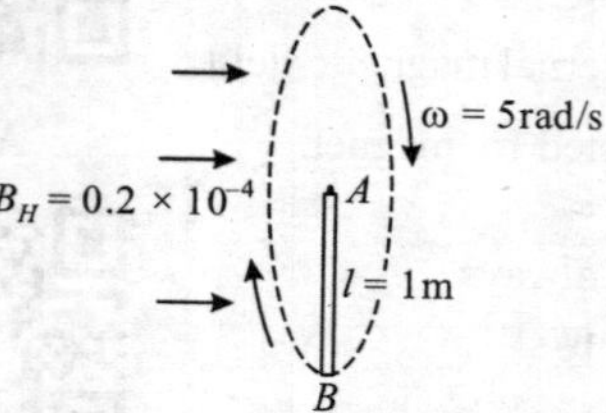

EMF induced across a rotating conductor in uniform and normal magnetic field is given as

$$e = \frac{1}{2} B\omega l^2$$

$$\Rightarrow \quad e = \frac{1}{2} \times 0.2 \times 10^{-4} \times 5 \times (1)^2$$

$$\Rightarrow \quad e = 0.5 \times 10^{-4}\, V = 50\, \mu V$$

Ans. (B)

Sol. 3

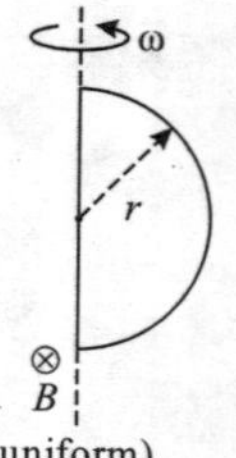

EMF induced in a rotating loop at angular frequency ω is given as

$$e = NBA \sin\omega t = \frac{B\pi\omega r^2}{2} \sin \omega t$$

induced current in loop is $i = e/R$

rate of heat generated (thermal power) in loop is

$$P_{th} = i^2 R = \frac{(B\pi\omega r^2)^2}{4R} \sin^2 \omega t$$

$$\Rightarrow \text{mean power } \langle P_{th} \rangle = \frac{(B\pi\omega r^2)^2}{4R} \langle \sin^2 \omega t \rangle$$

$$\Rightarrow \quad \langle P_{th} \rangle = \frac{(B\pi\omega r^2)^2}{4R} \times \frac{1}{2} = \frac{(B\pi\omega r^2)^2}{8R}$$

Ans. (B)

Sol. 4 For a given n turns coil when it is moved such that the flux changes through it is given as

$$\Delta\phi = n(W_2 - W_1)$$

⇒ emf induced in coil is

$$e = -\frac{\Delta\phi}{\Delta t} = \frac{n(W_2 - W_1)}{t}$$

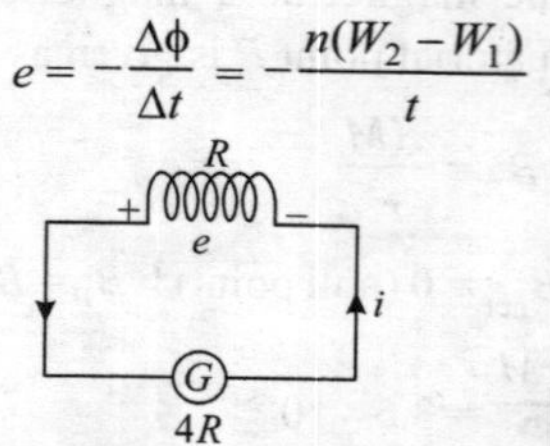

effective resistance of circuit = $5R$

⇒ Current induced in coil will be

$$i = \frac{e}{5R} = -\frac{n(W_2 - W_1)}{5Rt}$$

Ans. (B)

Sol. 5

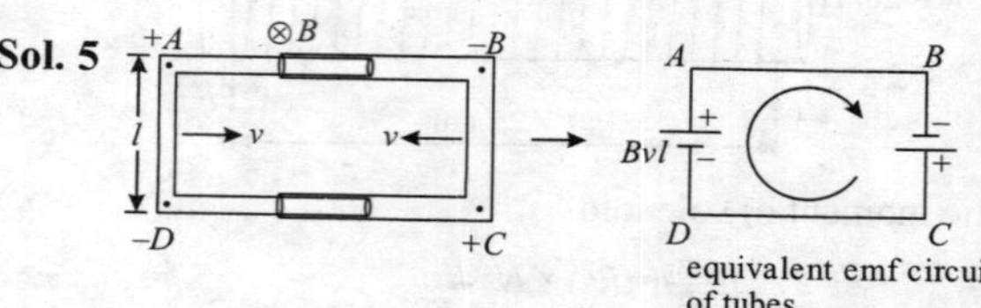

As sections AD and BC are moving normal to their lengths so emf is induced only in these sections so motional emf induced is

$$e_{AD} = Bvl \text{ and } e_{BC} = Bvl$$

Total loop emf in circuit

$$e_T = e_{AD} + e_{BC} = 2Bvl$$

Ans. (D)

Sol. 6 Motional emf across the conductor PQ is

$$e_{PQ} = Blv$$

$\Rightarrow$ equivalent circuit will be (with emf)

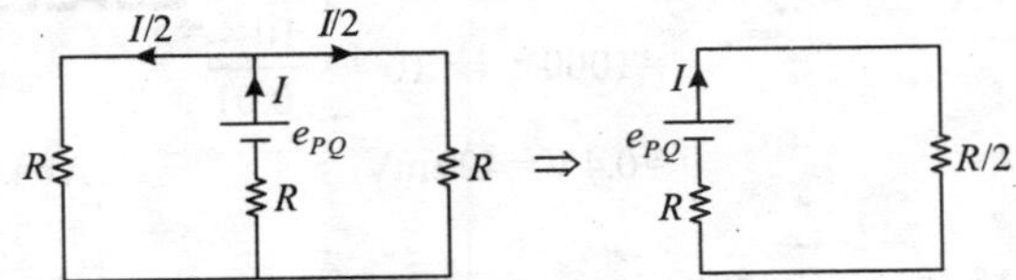

From figure, current supplied by battery is

$$I = \frac{e_{PQ}}{R + \frac{R}{2}} = \frac{Blv}{\frac{3R}{2}} = \frac{2Blv}{3R}$$

Currents through side resistances is

$$I_1 = I_2 = \frac{I}{2} = \frac{Blv}{3R}$$ **Ans. (C)**

Sol. 7 For a straight wire moving perpendicular to the magnetic field, the motional emf is given as

$$e = Bvl$$

$\Rightarrow \quad e = 0.3 \times 10^{-4} \times 5 \times 20$

$\Rightarrow \quad e = 3 \times 10^{-3}\ \text{V} = 3\ \text{mV}$ **Ans. (B)**

Sol. 8 Here $B_H = 5 \times 10^{-5}$ T (As 1T = 1 N/A-m)

$l = 2\text{m}$ [vertical]

$v = 1.5$ m/s

As vertical aerial cuts horizontal component of earth's field normally so motional emf induced in it is given as

$$e = Blv = 5 \times 10^{-5} \times 2 \times 1.5$$

$\Rightarrow \quad e = 1.5 \times 10^{-4} = 0.15\ \text{mV}$ **Ans. (B)**

Sol. 9

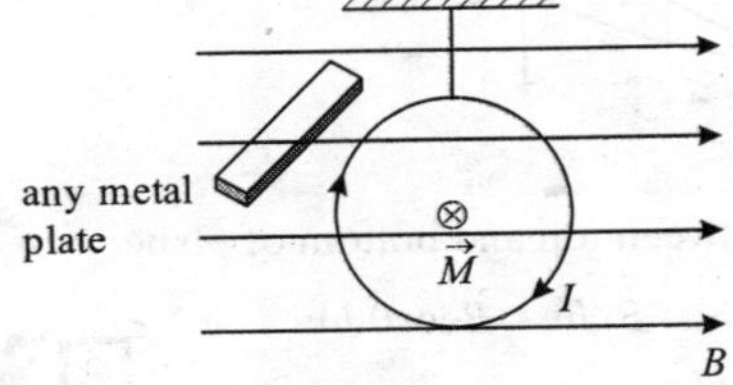

Torque on coil $\quad \vec{\tau} = \vec{M} \times \vec{B}$

$\tau = MB \sin\theta$

$\tau = MB$

at $\theta = 0°$, coil is in state of stable equilibrium about which it oscillates.

When an aluminium plate (any metal plate) is kept near the coil then due to oscillation of coil $\vec{B}_C$ due to coil will be time varying and eddy currents are induced in plate and that induction opposes its cause which is oscillation of coil so these are damped out. **Ans. (A)**

Sol. 10 When $|\Delta\phi|$ flux is changed through a coil of resistance R, then charge flown through the coil is given as

$$\Delta q_f = \frac{|\Delta\phi|}{R}$$

$\Rightarrow \quad |\Delta\phi| = \Delta q_f \times R = $ area under i-t curve $\times R$

$\Rightarrow \quad |\Delta\phi| = \frac{1}{2} \times 4 \times 0.1 \times 10 = 2$ Wb **Ans. (C)**

Sol. 11

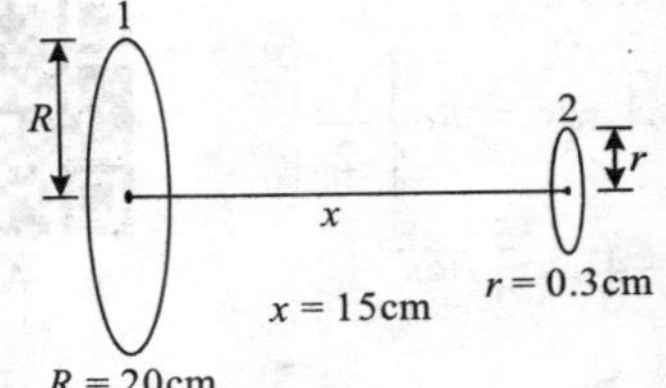

If i_2 current flows in smaller loop then flux linked with bigger loop can be given as

$$\phi_1 = Mi_2 \quad \ldots(1)$$

where $M \rightarrow$ coefficient of mutual inductance between loops 1 and 2.

To calculate M, we supply a current i, through bigger loop & calculate flux linked with smaller loop as

$$\phi_2 = Mi_1 \quad \ldots(2)$$

Magnetic induction at location of loop 2 due to loop 1 is

$$B = \frac{\mu_0 i_1 R^2}{2(R^2 + x^2)^{3/2}}$$

flux through loop -2 is $\phi_2 = B.\pi r^2 = \dfrac{\mu_0 \pi r^2 R^2}{2(R^2 + x^2)^{3/2}} i_1 \quad \ldots(3)$

Comparing equation-(2) and (3) gives

$$M = \frac{\mu_0 \pi r^2 R^2}{2(R^2 + x^2)^{3/2}}$$

Using above value of M in equation-(1), we get

$$\phi_1 = \frac{\mu_0 \pi r^2 R^2}{2(R^2 + x^2)^{3/2}} i_2$$

$$\Rightarrow \quad \phi_1 = \frac{4\pi \times 10^{-7} \times \pi \times (0.3 \times 10^{-2})^2 \times (0.2)^2 \times 2}{2 \times ((0.2)^2 + (0.15)^2)^{3/2}}$$

$$\Rightarrow \quad \phi_1 = \frac{4\pi \times 10 \times 10^{-7} \times 9 \times 10^{-6} \times 4 \times 10^{-2}}{(0.25)^3}$$

$\Rightarrow \quad \phi_1 = 9.216 \times 10^{-11}$ Wb **Ans. (A)**

Sol. 12 Motional *EMF* induced in the element of rod as shown is

$$de = B(x\omega)dx$$

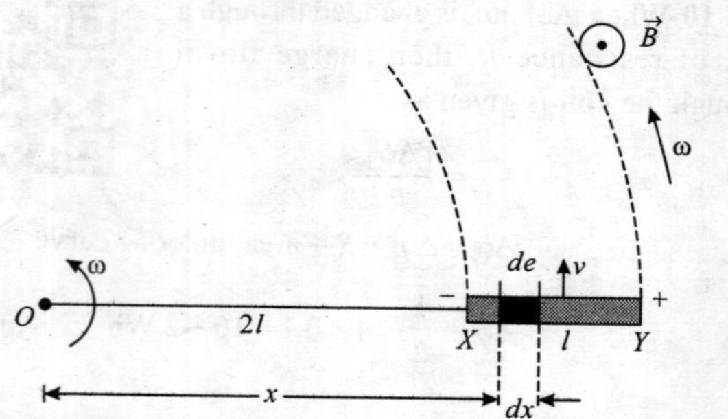

Total *EMF* induced in rod is

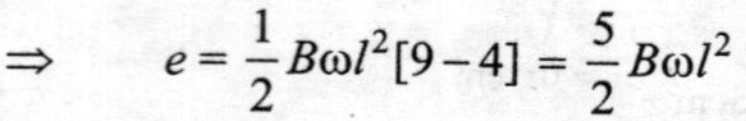

$$e = \int de = B\omega \int_{2l}^{3l} x dx = B\omega \left[\frac{x^2}{2}\right]_{2l}^{3l}$$

$$\Rightarrow \quad e = \frac{1}{2} B\omega l^2 [9 - 4] = \frac{5}{2} B\omega l^2$$

Ans. (D)

Sol. 13

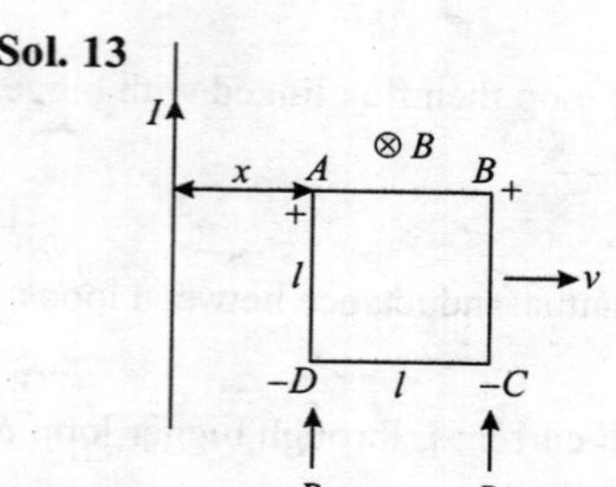

The motional emf will be induced in wire segments *BC* and *AD* which are given as

$$e_{AD} = B_1 v l = \frac{\mu_0 I}{2\pi x} vl \quad \dots(1)$$

and

$$e_{BC} = B_2 v l = \frac{\mu_0 I}{2\pi(l + x)} vl \quad \dots(2)$$

Total emf induced in loop *ABCD* is given as ($e_{AD} > e_{BC}$)

$$e_T = e_{AD} - e_{BC}$$

from (1) and (2)

$$e_T = \frac{\mu_0 I v l}{2\pi}\left[\frac{1}{x} - \frac{1}{x + l}\right]$$

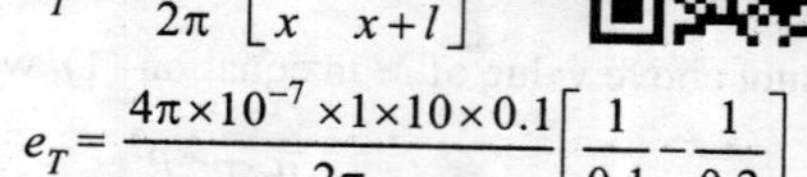

$$\Rightarrow \quad e_T = \frac{4\pi \times 10^{-7} \times 1 \times 10 \times 0.1}{2\pi}\left[\frac{1}{0.1} - \frac{1}{0.2}\right]$$

$$\Rightarrow \quad e_T = 2 \times 10^{-7} \times \frac{1}{0.2} = 10^{-6}\,\text{V}$$

$$\Rightarrow \quad e_T = 1\,\mu\text{V}$$

Ans. (B)

Sol. 14 emf induced in the coil is

$$e = \left|\frac{d\phi_L}{dt}\right|$$

[ϕ_2 - flux linked with all turns of coil]

Here $\phi_L = N \times \phi = N(BA)$

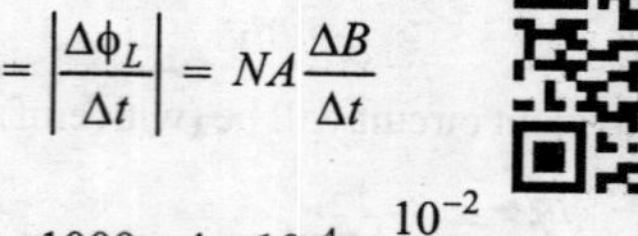

Average emf induced $e = \left|\frac{\Delta\phi_L}{\Delta t}\right| = NA\frac{\Delta B}{\Delta t}$

$$\Rightarrow \quad e = 1000 \times 4 \times 10^{-4} \times \frac{10^{-2}}{0.01}$$

$$\Rightarrow \quad e = 0.4\,\text{V} = 400\,\text{mV}$$

Ans. (A)

Sol. 15 In a cylindrical region TVMF, the induced EF at a distance *r* from axis of field is given as

for $r < R \rightarrow \quad E_i = \frac{1}{2} r \frac{dB}{dt} \Rightarrow E \propto r$

for $r < R \rightarrow \quad E_0 = \frac{1}{2}\frac{R^2}{r}\frac{dB}{dt} \Rightarrow E \propto \frac{1}{r}$

Ans. (A)

Sol. 16 Magnetic field components at Delhi

As Delhi is in Northern hemisphere, we use

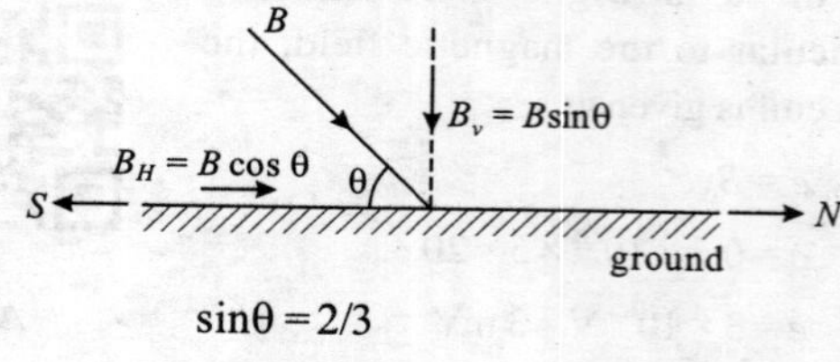

$$\sin\theta = 2/3$$

$$\cos\theta = \sqrt{1 - \sin^2\theta} = \frac{\sqrt{5}}{3}$$

Flight of plane

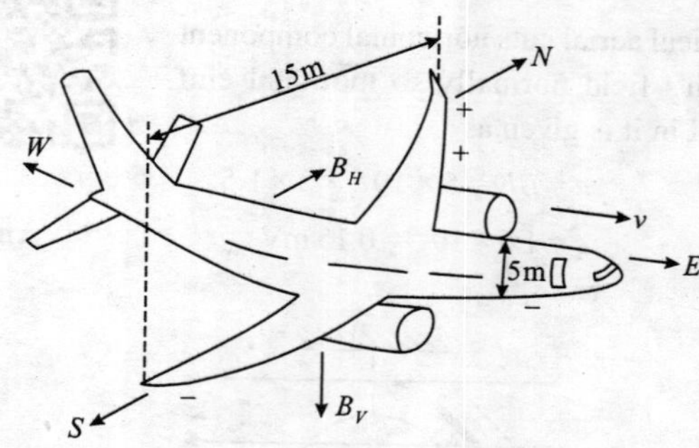

Motional EMF between top and bottom of plane

$$e_{TB} = v_B = Blv = B_H hv = B\cos\theta\, hv$$

$$\Rightarrow \quad v_B = 5 \times 10^{-5}\,T \times \frac{\sqrt{5}}{3} \times 5 \times 240$$

$$\Rightarrow \quad v_B = 44.7 \times 10^{-3}\,\text{V}$$

Motional EMF between the tips of wings is

$$e_{\text{Tips}} = v_w = Blv = B_v wv = B\sin\theta wv$$

$$\Rightarrow \quad v_w = 5 \times 10^{-5} \times \frac{2}{3} \times 15 \times 240$$

$$\Rightarrow \quad v_w = 120 \times 10^{-3}\,\text{V}$$

Ans. (D)

Sol. 17

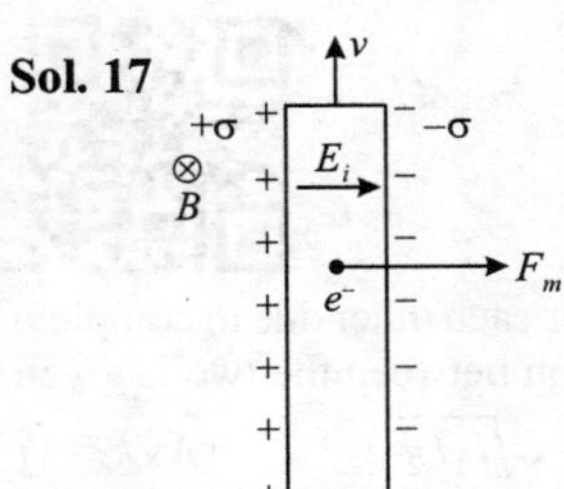

Due to motion of sheet, free electrons in sheet experience force toward right, given as

$$F_m = evB$$

Due to magnetic forces the free e^-'s drift and develops internal EF due to induced charges so that net force on free electron should be zero.

$$F_e = eE_i \quad e^- \quad F_m$$

Where $E_i = \sigma/\epsilon_0$ (due to induced charges on surface of sheet)

we use $\quad eE_i = evB$

$$\Rightarrow \quad \frac{\sigma}{\epsilon_0} = vB$$

$$\Rightarrow \quad \sigma = \epsilon_0 vB$$

$\Rightarrow$ On left and right surfaces of sheet induced charges density will be $+\epsilon_0 vB$ and $-\epsilon_0 vB$. **Ans. (B)**

Sol. 18 Magnetic flux through the loop is

$$\phi = B\pi r^2 = \pi r^2 B_0 e^{-t/\tau}$$

loop emf induced in the loop is $e = \left|\frac{d\phi}{dt}\right| = \frac{\pi r^2 B_0}{\tau} e^{-t/\tau}$

induced current in the loop is $i = \frac{e}{R} = \frac{\pi r^2 B_0}{\tau R} e^{-t/\tau}$

Total heat generated in loop is

$$H = \int_0^\infty i^2 R\,dt = \frac{\pi^2 r^4 B_0^2}{\tau^2 R} \int_0^\infty e^{-2t/\tau} dt$$

$$\Rightarrow \quad H = \frac{\pi^2 r^4 B_0^2}{\tau^2 R} \left[\frac{e^{-2t/\tau}}{-2/\tau}\right]_0^\infty$$

$$\Rightarrow \quad H = \frac{\pi^2 r^4 B_0^2}{2\tau R} \left[e^{-2t/\tau}\right]_\infty^0$$

$$\Rightarrow \quad H = \frac{\pi^2 r^4 B_0^2}{2\tau R}[1-0] = \frac{\pi^2 r^4 B_0^2}{2\tau R}$$ **Ans. (B)**

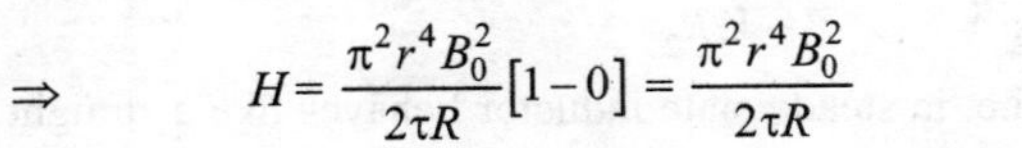

20.2 Self and Mutual Induction

Sol. 1 As in given circuit all three inductors are connected in parallel so we use

$$\frac{1}{L_{eq}} = \frac{1}{L_1} + \frac{1}{L_2} + \frac{1}{L_3}$$

$$= \frac{1}{3} + \frac{1}{3} + \frac{1}{3} = 1$$

$$\Rightarrow \quad L_{eq} = 1\text{ H}$$ **Ans. (D)**

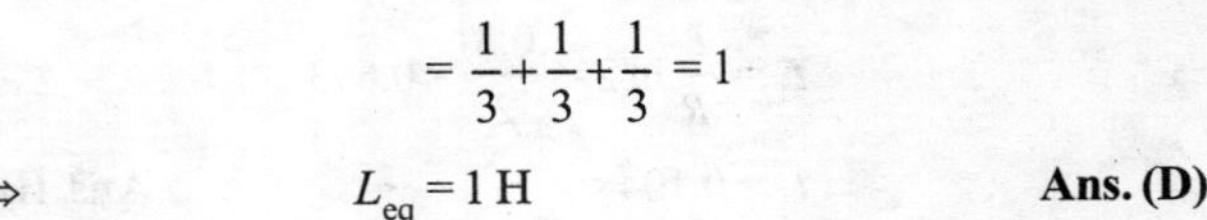

Sol. 2 If in a coil of self inductance 'L' current changes by di in time dt then magnitude of emf induced in coil is given as

$$e = L\frac{di}{dt}$$

$$\Rightarrow \quad e = L\frac{\Delta i}{\Delta t}$$

$$\Rightarrow \quad 8 = L \times \frac{4A}{0.05\text{s}}$$

$$\Rightarrow \quad L = \frac{8 \times 0.05}{4}$$

$$\Rightarrow \quad L = 0.1\text{ H}$$ **Ans. (D)**

Sol. 3 If two coils with self induction coefficients L_1 and L_2 are placed to each other than their mutual induction is given as

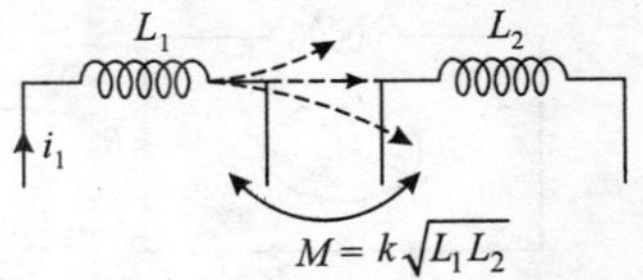

Where $k \rightarrow$ Coupling factor [depends upon the fraction of magnetic flux of first coil which in linked with second coil]

Here k indirectly depends upon separation & orientation of the two coil.

for full flux linkage we use $k = 1$

for No flux linkage we use $k = 0$

Either due to large separation or kept at 90° angle to each other. **Ans. (B)**

Sol. 4

R L i i V t = 0

In series L-R circuit the current grows according to relation

$$i = \frac{V}{R}(1 - e^{\frac{-Rt}{L}})$$

$V/R \rightarrow$ steady state current

if at $t = t_1$, $i = V/2R$

$$\Rightarrow \quad \frac{V}{2R} = \frac{V}{R}(1 - e^{\frac{-Rt_1}{L}})$$

$$\Rightarrow \quad e^{-Rt_1/L} = \frac{1}{2}$$

$$\Rightarrow \quad \frac{Rt_1}{L} = \ln(2)$$

$$\Rightarrow \quad t_1 = \frac{L}{R}\ln 2 = \frac{0.3}{2} \times 0.693$$

$$\Rightarrow \quad t_1 = 0.104\text{ s}$$ **Ans. (B)**

Sol. 5 emf induced in a coil due to time varying magnetic flux is given as

$$e = -\frac{d\phi}{dt}$$

$$\Rightarrow \quad e = -\frac{d}{dt}(10t^2 - 50t + 250)$$

$$\Rightarrow \quad e = -[20t - 50]$$

at $t = 3\text{s}$, $\quad e = -[20 \times 3 - 50] = -10\text{ V}$ **Ans. (B)**

Sol. 6 When circuit is in steady state, current through inductor is $\quad I_0 = E/R$

Now battery is disconnected & terminals A & B are short circuited.

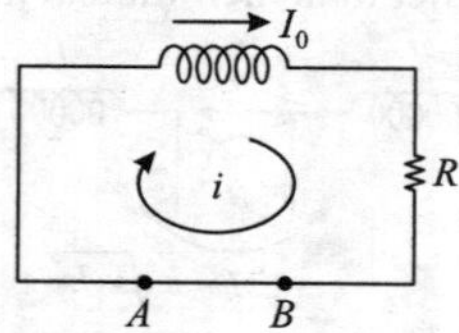

During decay current in circuit is given as

$$i = I_0 e^{-Rt/L} = \frac{E}{R} e^{-Rt/L}$$

$$\Rightarrow \quad i = \frac{100}{100} e^{\frac{-100\times10^{-3}}{100\times10^{-3}}} = e^{-1}$$

$$\Rightarrow \quad i = \frac{1}{e}\text{ A}$$ **Ans. (A)**

Sol. 7

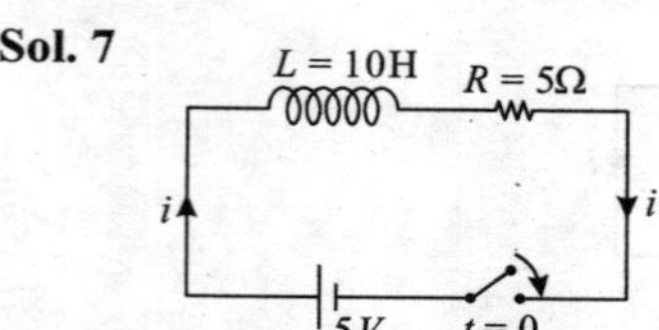

For R-L circuit current as a function of time is given as

$$i = \frac{V}{R}\left(1 - e^{\frac{-Rt}{L}}\right)$$

$$\Rightarrow \quad i = \frac{5}{5}\left(1 - e^{\frac{-5\times2}{10}}\right)$$

$$\Rightarrow \quad i = 1 - e^{-1}$$ **Ans. (D)**

Sol. 8

N_1 $\quad L_1 \quad A = 10\text{cm}^2$

$l = 20$ cm $\quad N_2 \quad L_2$

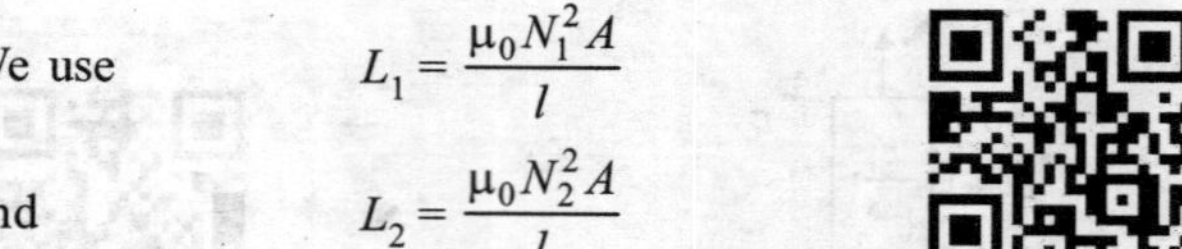

We use $\quad L_1 = \dfrac{\mu_0 N_1^2 A}{l}$

and $\quad L_2 = \dfrac{\mu_0 N_2^2 A}{l}$

As the two solenoids are wound over each other due to complete linkage of flux, the mutual induction between the two is given as $\quad M = k\sqrt{L_1 L_2} = \sqrt{L_1 L_2}$ $\quad$ [As $k = 1$]

$$\Rightarrow \quad M = \frac{\mu_0 A}{l} N_1 N_2$$

$$\Rightarrow \quad M = \frac{4\pi\times10^{-7}\times10\times10^{-4}}{0.2} \times 300 \times 400$$

$$\Rightarrow \quad M = 2.4\pi \times 10^{-4}\text{ H}$$ **Ans. (D)**

Sol. 9

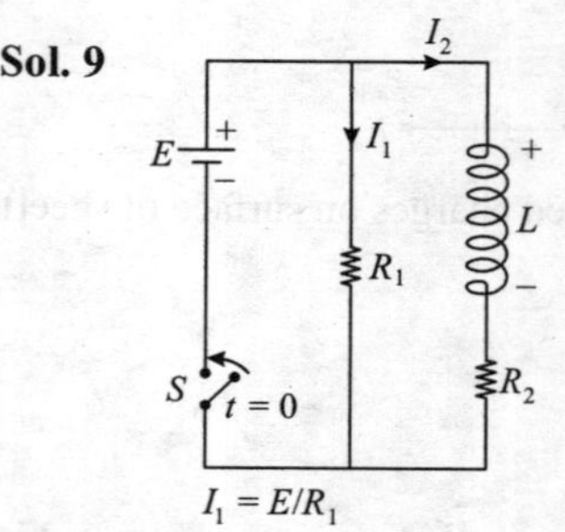

Current I_2 is given as

$$I_2 = \frac{E}{R_2}\left(1 - e^{\frac{-R_2 t}{L}}\right)$$

Potential drop across L is given as

$$e_L = L\frac{dI_2}{dt} = \frac{LE}{R_2}\left(e^{\frac{-R_2 t}{L}} \times \frac{R_2}{L}\right) = E\,e^{-R_2 t/L}$$

$$\Rightarrow \quad e_L = 12\,e^{\frac{-2t}{0.4}} = 12\,e^{-5t}\text{ V}$$ **Ans. (B)**

Sol. 10 At $t = 0$, inductor behaves like an open circuit so we use

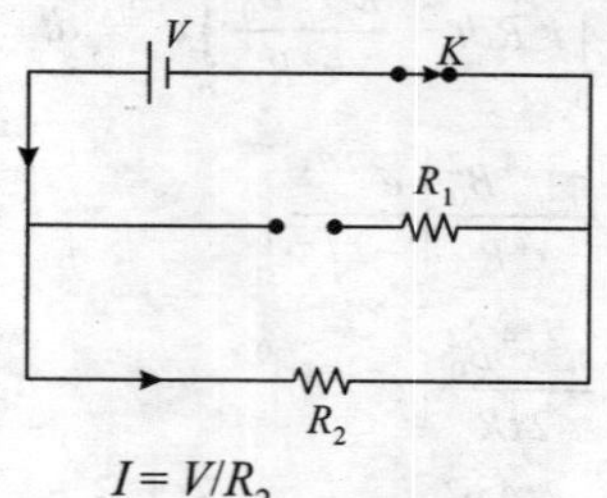

$\Rightarrow$ at $t = 0$, $\quad I = V/R_2$

At $t = \infty$, i.e. in steady state inductor behaves like a straight wire so we use

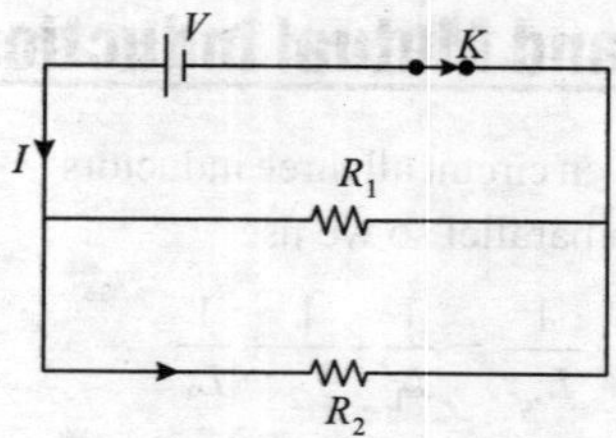

$$R_{eq} = \frac{R_1 R_2}{R_1 + R_2}$$

$$\Rightarrow \quad I = V/R_{eq} = \frac{V(R_1 + R_2)}{R_1 R_2} \quad \textbf{Ans. (C)}$$

Sol. 11 Ideally magnetic induction inside a solenoid everywhere remain constant

$$B = \mu_0 nI = \mu_0 \left(\frac{N}{L}\right) I$$

Magnetic flux linked with solenoid is

$$\phi = NBA = N\left(\frac{\mu_0 NI}{L}\right)\pi r^2 \qquad [\because A = \pi r^2]$$

$$\Rightarrow \quad \phi = \left(\frac{\mu_0 \pi N^2 r^2}{L}\right) I$$

Here self inductance of the solenoid is

$$L_{sol} = \left(\frac{\mu_0 \pi N^2 r^2}{L}\right) I$$

As magnetic induction on the sides of solenoid is less than $\mu_0 nI$

$$\Rightarrow \quad \phi = L_{sol} I$$

Here $\quad L_{sol} < \dfrac{\mu_0 \pi N^2 r^2}{L}$

$\Rightarrow$ **S-1** is true

S-2 is its explanation **Ans. (B)**

Sol. 12

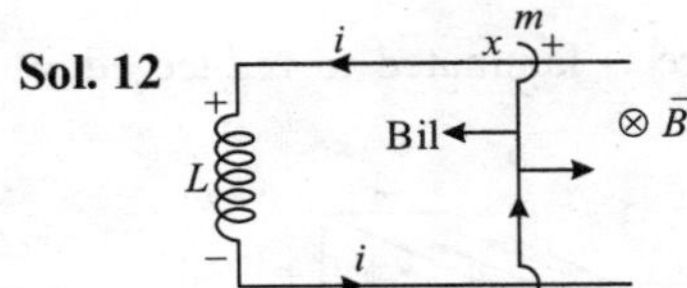

Motional emf induced in connector xy is

$$e_{xy} = Bvl$$

For the inductor as it is in parallel to connector xy, we use

$$Bvl = L\frac{di}{dt} \qquad \ldots(1)$$

If a be the acceleration (–ve) of connector we use

$$a = -\frac{Bil}{m} \qquad \ldots(2)$$

From equation-(1) $\int di = \dfrac{Bl}{L}\int vdt$

$$\Rightarrow \quad i = \frac{Bl}{L}\cdot x$$

[Where $x = \int vdt$ is the displacement of connector]

From equation-(2) $\quad a = -\dfrac{Bl}{m}\left[\dfrac{Bl}{L}\cdot x\right]$

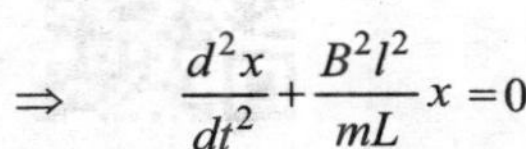

$$\Rightarrow \quad \frac{d^2x}{dt^2} + \frac{B^2l^2}{mL}x = 0$$

This is the differential equation of SHM so connector is executing SHM. **Ans. (D)**

Sol. 13 As S_2 is kept open so the circuit is simple RC transient and charge on capacitor is given at (time function)

$$q = CV(1 - e^{-t/RC})$$

$$q = CV(1 - e^{-t/\tau})$$

At $t = \tau \rightarrow \quad q = CV(1 - e^{-1})$

At $t = 2\tau \rightarrow \quad q = CV(1 - e^{-2})$ **Ans. (C)**

Sol. 14 for two closely spaced coils, emf induced in one coil due to current variation in other coil is given as

$$V(t) = -M\frac{dI(t)}{dt}$$

[M = mutual inductance between coils]

$$\Rightarrow \quad V(t) = -M \times \text{slope of } I(t) \text{ curve}$$

$$\text{slope} = -\frac{V(t)}{M}$$

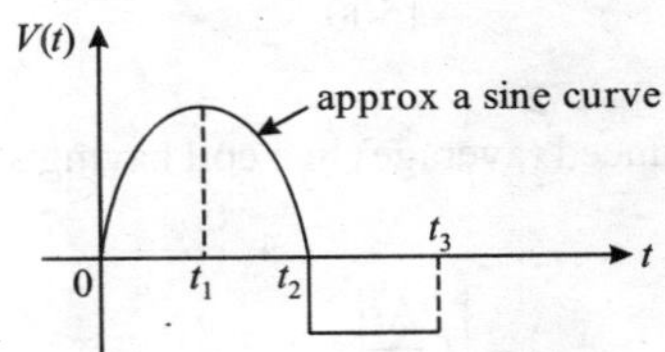

from $\quad$ 0 to $t_1 \rightarrow$ Slope of $I(t)$ curve is increasing (+ve)

t_1 to $t_2 \rightarrow$ Slope of $I(t)$ curve is decreasing (+ve)

t_2 to $t_3 \rightarrow$ Slope of $I(t)$ curve is constant (+ve) as $V(t)$ is –ve

$\Rightarrow$

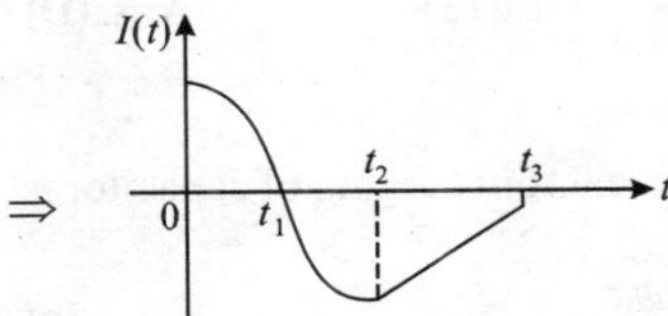

$\Rightarrow$ None of the given options is correct. **Ans. (None)**

Sol. 15 After point C is connected to B then circuit will be

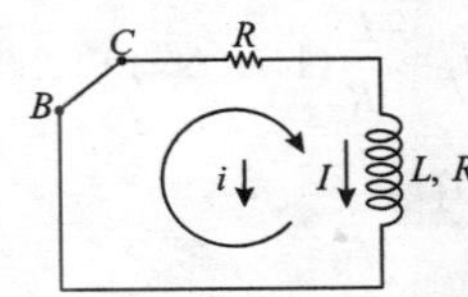

in the given loop we can write

$$V_R + V_L = 0$$

$$\Rightarrow \quad \frac{V_R}{V_L} = -1 \quad \textbf{Ans. (C)}$$

Sol. 16 frequency of LC oscillation is given as

$$f = \frac{1}{2\pi\sqrt{LC}}$$

for $L_1 (> L_2)$ we use $f_1 < f_2$ or $T_1 > T_2$

In case of L_1 maximum charge on capacitor Q_{max} will decrease more slowly. **Ans. (A)**

Sol. 17 When K_1 is closed the steady current in circuit is given as-

$$I_0 = \frac{V}{R} = \frac{15}{150} = 0.1 \text{ A}$$

When at $t = 0$, K_1 is opened and K_2 is closed then inductor current I_0 will start decaying through R and its time function as

$$i = I_0 e^{-Rt/L} = 0.1 \times e^{-150\times 10^{-3}/0.03}$$

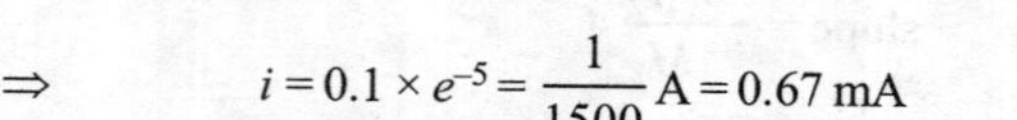

$$\Rightarrow \quad i = 0.1 \times e^{-5} = \frac{1}{1500} \text{ A} = 0.67 \text{ mA} \quad \textbf{Ans. (D)}$$

Sol. 18 Emf induced (average) in a coil having self inductance L is given as

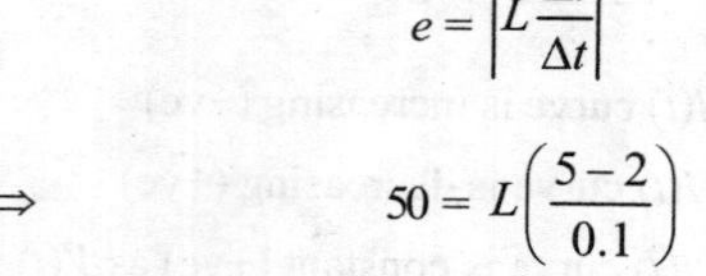

$$e = \left| L\frac{\Delta i}{\Delta t} \right|$$

$$\Rightarrow \quad 50 = L\left(\frac{5-2}{0.1}\right)$$

$$\Rightarrow \quad L = \frac{50}{30} = \frac{5}{3} = 1.67 \text{ H} \quad \textbf{Ans. (D)}$$

Sol. 19 In series RC circuit current for charging of capacitor is

$$i_a = \frac{E}{R} e^{-t/RC} \quad \ldots (a)$$

[RC - Transient circuit]

for series LR circuit growth of current is

$$i_b = \frac{E}{R}(1 - e^{-Rt/L}) \quad \ldots (b)$$

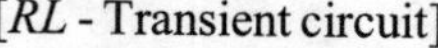

[RL - Transient circuit] **Ans. (C)**

21.1 Alternating Current

Sol. 1 By transformer equation, we have

$$\frac{e_1}{e_2} = \frac{N_1}{N_2} \quad \ldots (1)$$

and for an ideal transformer we use its power equation for primary and secondary coil is

$$e_1 i_1 = e_2 i_2 \quad \ldots (2)$$

From (1) and (2) we have

$$\frac{i_2}{i_1} = \frac{N_1}{N_2}$$

$$\Rightarrow \quad i_2 = \frac{N_1}{N_2} i_1 = \frac{140}{280} \times 4$$

$$\Rightarrow \quad i_2 = 2 \text{ A} \quad \textbf{Ans. (B)}$$

Sol. 2

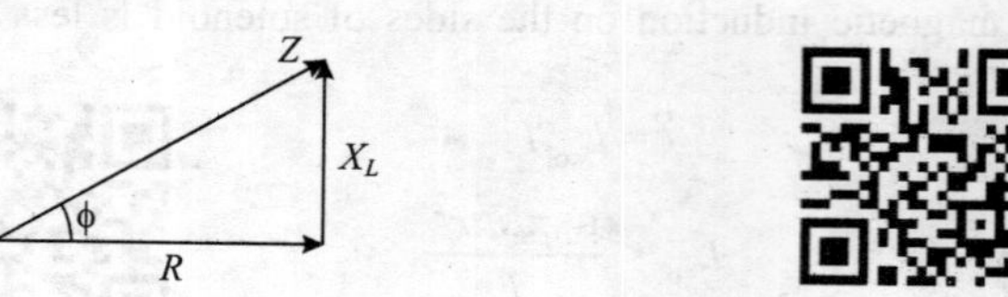

$$X_L = \omega L \lfloor \pi/2$$

$$R = R \lfloor 0^\circ$$

Impedance triangle

$$\text{Power factor} \quad \cos\phi = \frac{R}{Z} = \frac{R}{\sqrt{R^2 + \omega^2 L^2}} \quad \textbf{Ans. (B)}$$

Sol. 3 The transformer core is laminated to reduce eddy current losses.

Non laminated core :

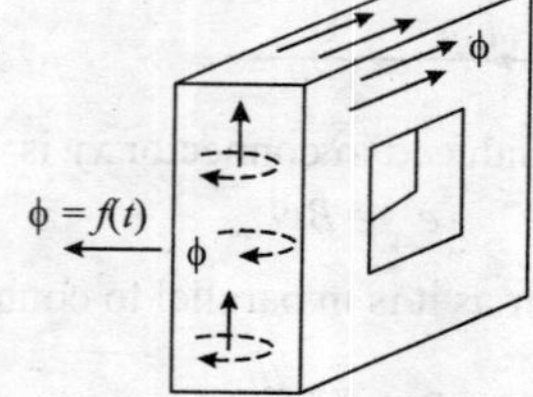

Time varying magnetic flux causes eddy currents to induced over all the cross-section

Laminated core :

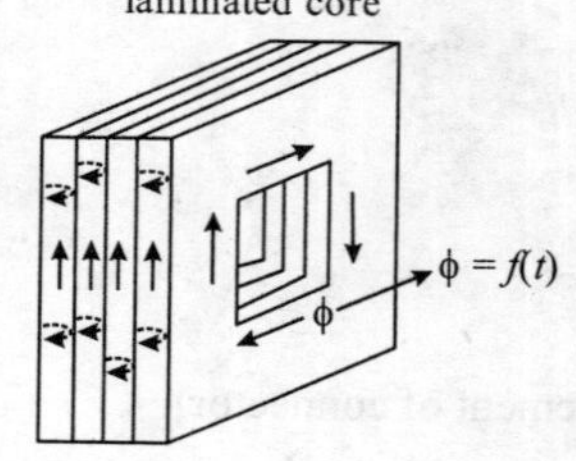

Due to laminated core eddy currents are induced within laminated strips only so losses due these miniature current are reduced. **Ans. (A)**

Sol. 4

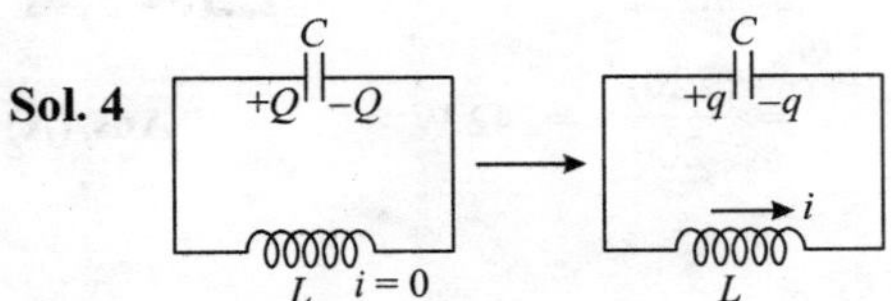

By conservation of energy

$$\frac{Q^2}{2C} = \frac{q^2}{2C} + \frac{1}{2}Li^2$$

When capacitor & inductor have equal amounts of energy stored we use

$$\frac{q^2}{2C} = \frac{1}{2}Li^2$$

$$\frac{Q^2}{2C} = 2\left(\frac{q^2}{2C}\right)$$

$$\Rightarrow \quad q^2 = \frac{Q^2}{2}$$

$$\Rightarrow \quad q = \frac{Q}{\sqrt{2}}$$

Ans. (C)

Sol. 5

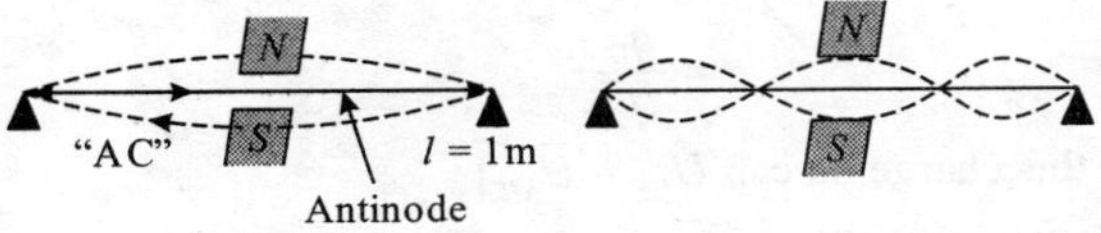

$$T = 10 \times 9.8\,\text{N}$$

$$\mu = 9.8 \times 10^{-3}\,\text{kg/m}$$

Here the fundamental frequency of oscillation of wire is given as

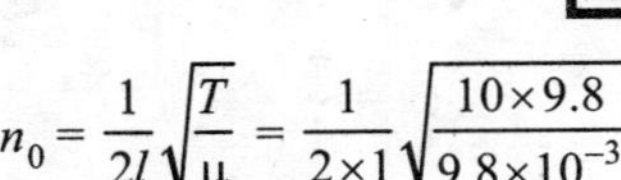

$$n_0 = \frac{1}{2l}\sqrt{\frac{T}{\mu}} = \frac{1}{2\times 1}\sqrt{\frac{10\times 9.8}{9.8\times 10^{-3}}}$$

$$\Rightarrow \quad n_0 = \frac{1}{2} \times 100 = 50\,\text{Hz}$$

So when $n = n_0$ or $3n_0$ or $5n_0$ ... the wire will oscillate in resonance.

50 Hz, 150 Hz, 250 Hz.... **Ans. (A)**

Sol. 6 For a given LCR circuit, its resonant frequency is given as

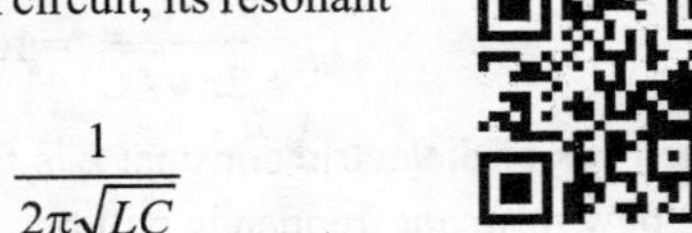

$$f_R = \frac{1}{2\pi\sqrt{LC}}$$

If $C \to 2C$ then to keep f_R same we must use $L \to L/2$

So that product $LC \to$ constant. **Ans. (C)**

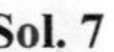

Sol. 7

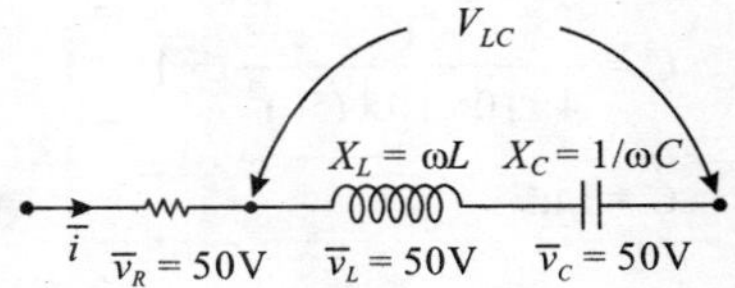

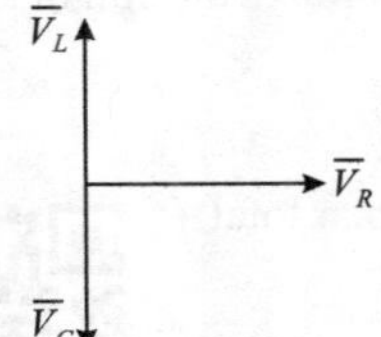

As $\overline{V}_C$ is 90° lagging w.r.t. to current $\overline{i}$ and $\overline{V}_L$ is 90° ahead w.r. to current $\overline{i}$. So we have $\overline{V}_L$ and $\overline{V}_C$ at phase difference of 180°.

Here $\quad \overline{V}_{LC} = \overline{V}_L + \overline{V}_C = 0$

As $\quad |\overline{V}_L| = |\overline{V}_C|$ **Ans. (D)**

Sol. 8 A *DC* ammeter measures the average value of current passing through it.

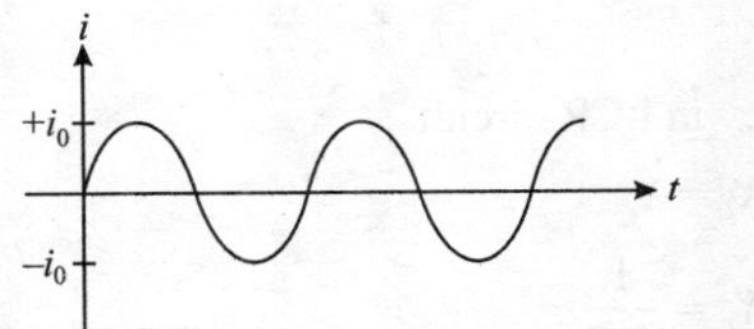

Thus average of a symmetric *AC* is zero. **Ans. (C)**

Sol. 9 Due to an inductor $L \to$ current legs behind emf by $\pi/2$ in phase.

Due to a capacitor $C \to$ current leads emf by $\pi/2$ in phase.

If a resistance R is there in AC circuit then the phase difference between current and emf is between 0 and $\pi/2$.

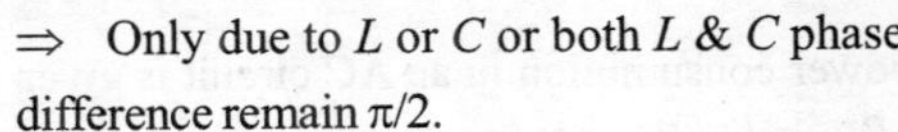

$\Rightarrow$ Only due to L or C or both L & C phase difference remain $\pi/2$. **Ans. (B)**

Sol. 10 For a given AC circuit power factor is given as

$$\cos\phi = R/Z$$

$$\Rightarrow \quad \cos\phi = \frac{12}{15} = \frac{4}{5} = 0.8$$

Ans. (A)

Sol. 11 Power is maximum at resonant frequency given as

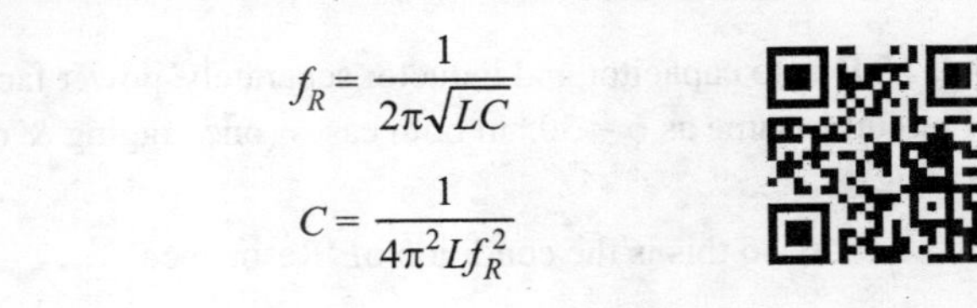

$$f_R = \frac{1}{2\pi\sqrt{LC}}$$

$$\Rightarrow \quad C = \frac{1}{4\pi^2 L f_R^2}$$

$$\Rightarrow \qquad C = \frac{1}{4\times10\times10\times(50)^2} = 10^{-6}\,\text{F}$$

$$\Rightarrow \qquad C = 1\,\mu\text{F}$$ **Ans. (C)**

Sol. 12 The magnetic flux passing through the coil of area A in magnetic field is given as

$$\phi = \vec{B}\cdot\vec{A}$$

When coil in at an angle $\theta = \omega t$ then total linked flux with coil is

$$\phi_L = N(BA\cos\omega t)$$

emf induced in coil is

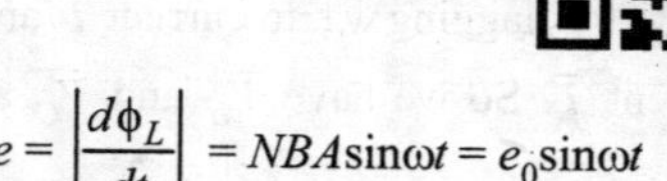

$$e = \left|\frac{d\phi_L}{dt}\right| = NBA\sin\omega t = e_0\sin\omega t$$

(AC induced emf in generator)

Maximum emf $\quad e_0 = NBA\omega$ **Ans. (D)**

Sol. 13

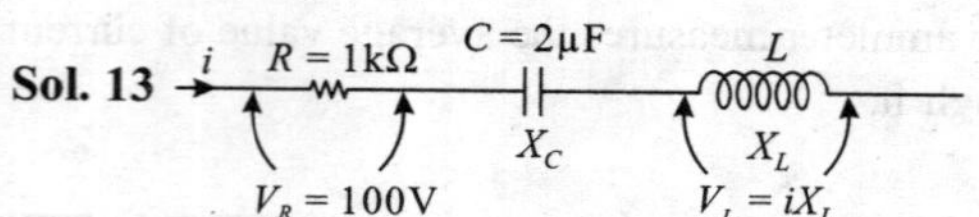

At resonant frequency in LCR circuit

$$X_L = X_C$$

$$X_L = \frac{1}{\omega C}$$

Circuit current $\quad i = \frac{V_R}{R} = \frac{100}{1000} = 0.1\,\text{A}$

Voltage across inductor is given as

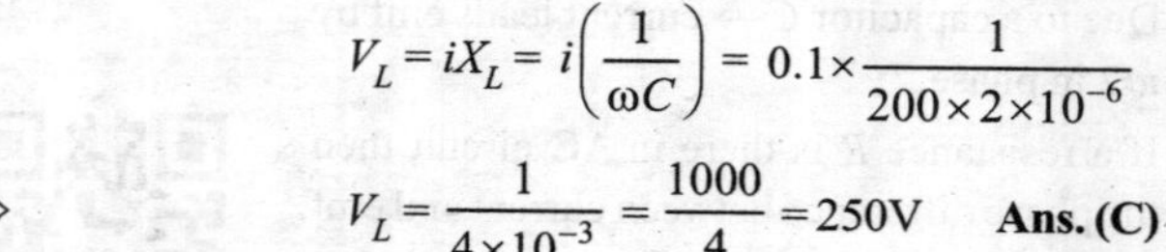

$$V_L = iX_L = i\left(\frac{1}{\omega C}\right) = 0.1\times\frac{1}{200\times2\times10^{-6}}$$

$$\Rightarrow \qquad V_L = \frac{1}{4\times10^{-3}} = \frac{1000}{4} = 250\text{V}$$ **Ans. (C)**

Sol. 14 Average power consumption in an AC circuit is given as $\quad P_{avg} = E_{rms}I_{rms}\cos\phi \qquad \ldots(1)$

Here ϕ is the phase difference between emf and current in circuit

Here $\quad E = E_0\sin\omega t$

and $\quad I = I_0\sin(\omega t - \pi/2)$

$\Rightarrow \quad \phi = \pi/2$

$\Rightarrow$ From equation-(1)

$$P_{avg} = 0$$ **Ans. (B)**

Sol. 15 Due to capacitor and inductor separately, power factor of circuit is same as $\phi = 30°$ in both cases (one lagging & one leading)

$\Rightarrow X_L = X_C$ so this is the condition of 'Resonance'.

In LCR circuit at resonance, power dissipation is given as

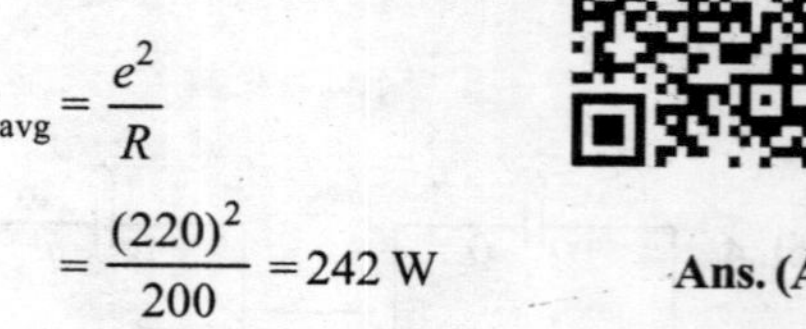

$$P_{avg} = \frac{e^2}{R}$$

$$= \frac{(220)^2}{200} = 242\,\text{W}$$ **Ans. (A)**

Sol. 16

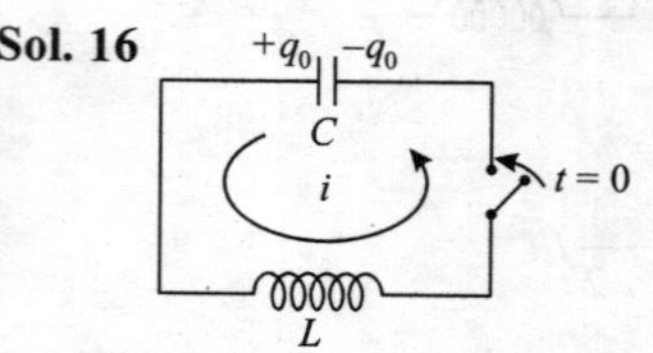

The frequency of LC oscillations is $\omega = \frac{1}{\sqrt{LC}}$

So the charge on capacitor as a function of time can be given as

$$q = q_0\sin(\omega t + \alpha)$$

at $t = 0$, $q = q_0$

$$\Rightarrow \qquad \alpha = \pi/2$$

$$\Rightarrow \qquad q = q_0\cos(\omega t) \qquad \ldots(1)$$

If after t, when charge on capacitor is q such that

$$\frac{q_0^2}{2C} = \frac{q^2}{2C} + \frac{1}{2}Li^2 \qquad \left[\text{with } \frac{q^2}{2C} = \frac{1}{2}Li^2\right]$$

$$\Rightarrow \qquad \frac{q_0^2}{2C} = 2\times\frac{q^2}{2C}$$

$$\Rightarrow \qquad q = \frac{q_0}{\sqrt{2}}$$

[At this charge on cap $U_{EF} = U_{MF}$]

from equestion-(1) we have

$$q = q_0\cos\omega t$$

$$\Rightarrow \qquad \frac{q_0}{\sqrt{2}} = q_0\cos(\omega t)$$

$$\Rightarrow \qquad \omega t = \frac{\pi}{4}$$

$$\Rightarrow \qquad \frac{1}{\sqrt{LC}}t = \frac{\pi}{4}$$

$$\Rightarrow \qquad t = \frac{\pi}{4}\sqrt{LC}$$ **Ans. (D)**

Sol. 17 For a given circuit having an inductor L and a capacitor C, the resonant frequency is given as

$$f_R = \frac{1}{2\pi\sqrt{LC}} = 10000\,\text{Hz} \qquad \ldots(1)$$

When gas of dielectric constant k is filled then $C \to kC$

$\Rightarrow$ new resonant frequency will be

$$f_R' = \frac{1}{2\pi\sqrt{kLC}} = 9950\,\text{Hz} \qquad \ldots(2)$$

By (1)/(2) $\Rightarrow \sqrt{k}=\dfrac{10000}{9950}$

$\Rightarrow \quad k=\left(\dfrac{1000}{995}\right)^2 \simeq 1.01$ **Ans. (C)**

Sol. 18 We can see in figure that $V_L = V_C$ this happens at resonance only

$\Rightarrow \quad V_R = e = 220\text{ V}$

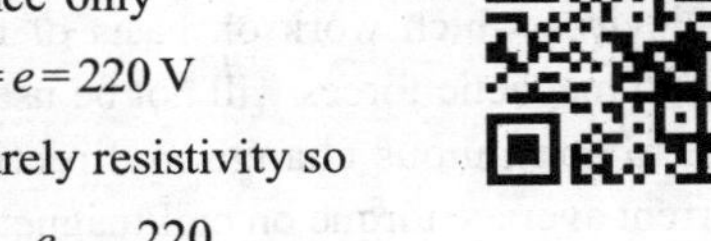

and circuit current is purely resistivity so

$$i=\frac{e}{R}=\frac{220}{100}=2.2\text{ A}$$ **Ans. (D)**

Sol. 19 In series LCR circuit at resonance circuit current is maximum so voltage across R is also maximum & it happens at resonant frequency, given as

$$\omega_R=\frac{1}{\sqrt{LC}}=\frac{1}{\sqrt{24\times 2\times 10^{-6}}}$$

$$\Rightarrow \quad \omega_R=\frac{1000}{\sqrt{48}}=\frac{1000}{6.9}=144.5\text{ Hz}$$

Closest option is (B) **Ans. (B)**

Sol. 20

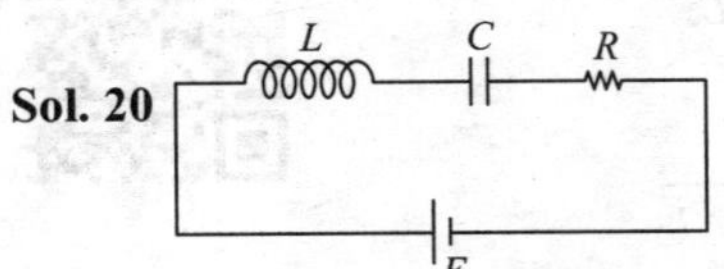

Initially when a DC voltage is applied then in steady state after a long time charge on capacitor is given as

$$q = CE$$

$$\Rightarrow \quad E=\frac{q}{C}=\frac{10^{-9}}{10^{-11}}=100\text{ V}$$

Now DC source is replaced by an AC source of peak value 100 volt.

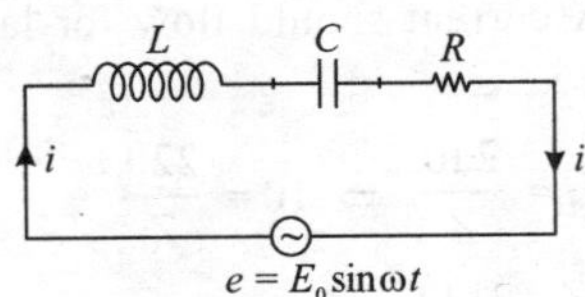

At resonance $\omega=\dfrac{1}{\sqrt{LC}}$ and circuit current will be

$$i = e/R$$

Peak current as $\quad i_0=\dfrac{E_0}{R}=\dfrac{100}{100}=1\text{A}$

Peak voltage across capacitor at resonance is given as

$$V_C=i_0X_C=1\cdot\left(\frac{1}{\omega C}\right)$$

Peak charge on capacitor is

$$q=CV_C=1\cdot\left(\frac{1}{\omega C}\right)=\sqrt{LC}$$

$$\Rightarrow \quad q=\sqrt{10^{-5}\times 10^{-11}}$$

$$\Rightarrow \quad q=10^{-8}\text{ C}$$ **Ans. (D)**

Sol. 21 For a series RLC circuit quality factor is given as

$$Q=\frac{\omega_0}{\Delta\omega}$$

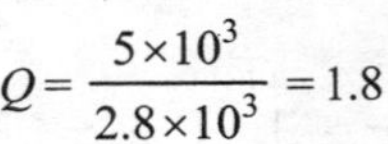

Here resonant frequency $\omega_0 \rightarrow$ maximum power in circuit

from plot $\quad \omega_0 = 5\text{ kHz}$

and bandwidth $\Delta\omega \rightarrow$ difference of half power frequencies

$$\Delta\omega=\omega_2-\omega_1$$

From plot we use $\quad \omega_1 \cong 3.6\text{ kHz}$ and $\omega_2 \cong 6.4\text{ kHz}$

$\Rightarrow$ Bandwidth $\quad \Delta\omega \cong 6.4-3.6=2.8\text{ kHz}$

So quality factor of circuit is given as

$$Q=\frac{5\times 10^3}{2.8\times 10^3}=1.8$$

Closest option here is (B) **Ans. (B)**

Sol. 22

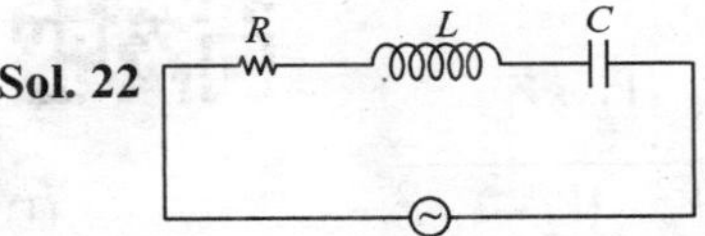

(A) At resonance $X_L = X_C$ so circuit impedance is purely resistive so $\phi = 0°$ and circuit current is in same phase with applied voltage. "It is correct".

(B) At resonant frequency $\omega=\dfrac{1}{\sqrt{LC}}$ we have $\omega L=\dfrac{1}{\sqrt{LC}}$ "It is correct".

(C) At resonance circuit current is $i = e/R$

if R is reduced $\Rightarrow$ i increases.

So voltage across capacitor $V_C = iX_C$ increases with i.

"It is correct".

(D) At resonance circuit impedance is $Z=\sqrt{R^2+(X_L-X_C)^2}$

As $X_L = X_C \Rightarrow Z$ is minimum.

"It is Not correct". **Ans. (D)**

Sol. 23 Case-I :

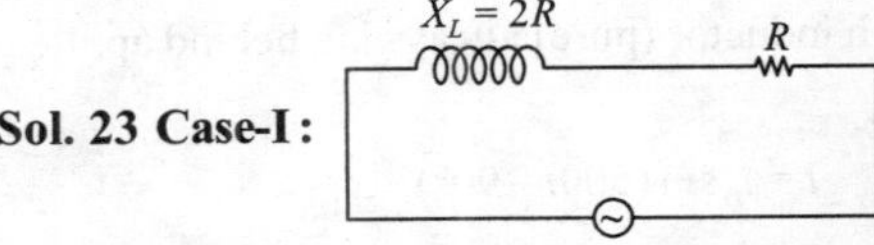

Circuit impedance $\quad Z_1=\sqrt{R^2+X_L^2}=\sqrt{5}R$

Power factor $\quad \cos\phi_1=\dfrac{R}{Z_1}=\dfrac{1}{\sqrt{5}}$

Case - II :

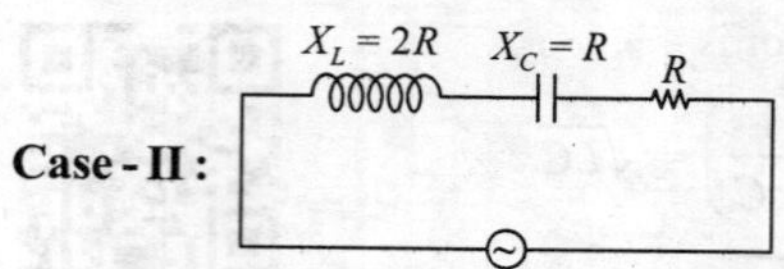

Circuit impedance $Z_2 = \sqrt{R^2 + (X_L - X_C)^2} = \sqrt{2}R$

New power factor, $\cos\phi_2 = \frac{R}{Z_2} = \frac{1}{\sqrt{2}}$

Ratio of new power factor to old power factor is

$$\frac{\cos\phi_2}{\cos\phi_1} = \frac{1/\sqrt{2}}{1/\sqrt{5}} = \sqrt{\frac{5}{2}}$$ **Ans. (D)**

Sol. 24

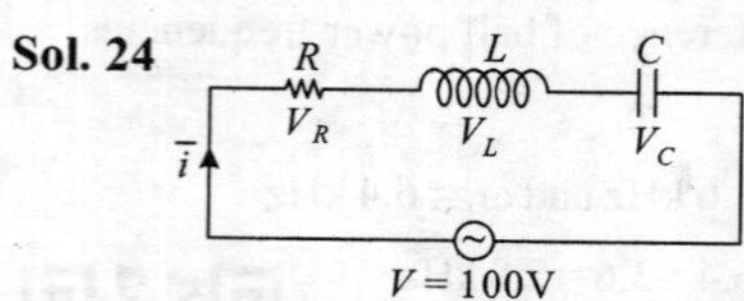

Phasor diagram of voltages is shown below

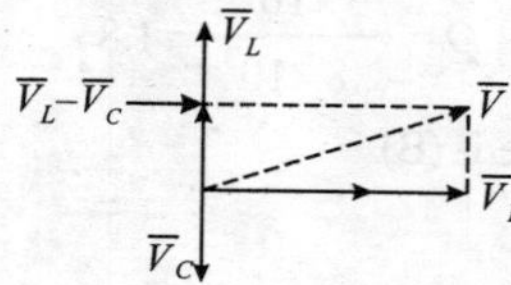

In phasor form $\bar{V} = \bar{V}_R + \bar{V}_L + \bar{V}_C$

in magnitude $V = \sqrt{V_R^2 + (V_L - V_C)^2}$ ...(1)

if $V_L : V_C : V_R = 1 : 2 : 3$

Then we can use in magnitudes $V_L = k, V_C = 2k, V_R = 3k$

From equation-(1) we have

$$100 = \sqrt{(3k)^2 + (k)^2} = \sqrt{10}k$$

$\Rightarrow$ $k = 10\sqrt{10}$

Here we have $V_R = 3k = 30\sqrt{10} \cong 94.5$

Closest option here is option (C) **Ans. (C)**

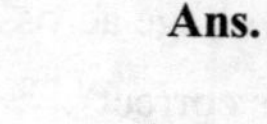

Sol. 25

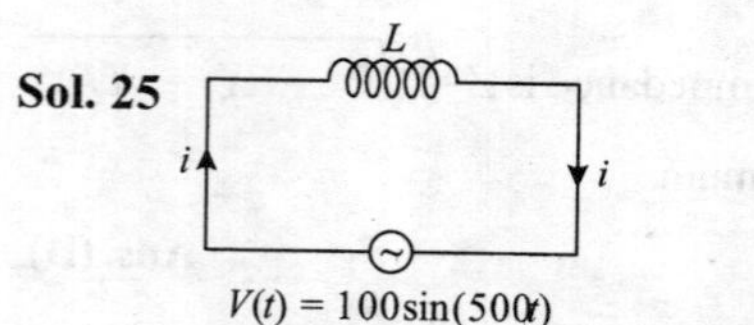

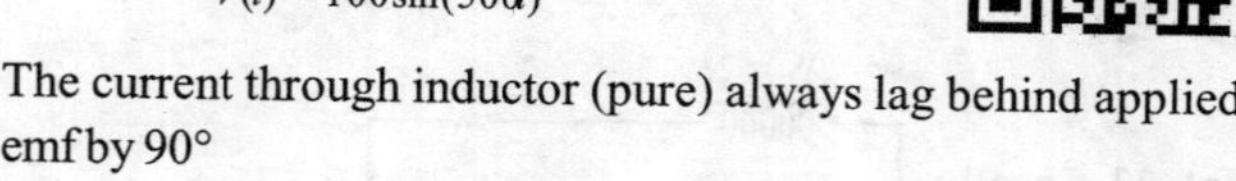

The current through inductor (pure) always lag behind applied emf by 90°

$\Rightarrow$ $i = i_0 \sin(500t - 90°)$

Here $i_0 = \frac{e_0}{Z} = \frac{e_0}{X_L} = \frac{e_0}{\omega L} = \frac{100}{500 \times 0.02}$

$\Rightarrow$ $i_0 = \frac{100}{10} = 10\text{ A}$

$\Rightarrow$ $i = 10\sin(500t - \pi/2)$

$\Rightarrow$ $i = -10\cos(500t)$ **Ans. (B)**

Sol. 26 As currents & voltages can be measured (RMS value) using Hot wire type meters which use the amount of power dissipation as thermal energy in the meter coil. This does not be affected by change in direction of current.

In devices which work on basis of torque due to magnetic forces will not be useful as due to continuous change in direction of current average torque on coil/magnet = 0. **Ans. (A)**

Sol. 27 Initially current is leading the applied voltage

$\Rightarrow$ $X_C > X_L$ or $\frac{1}{\omega C} > \omega L$

When C' is connected with C, $X_{CC'} = X_L$

$\Rightarrow$ $\frac{1}{\omega C_{eq}} < \frac{1}{\omega C}$ so as $C_{eq} > C \Rightarrow C'$ is connected in parallel to C, so we have

$$C_{eq} = C + C'$$

After C' is connected we use for resonance

$$\frac{1}{\omega(C + C')} = \omega L$$

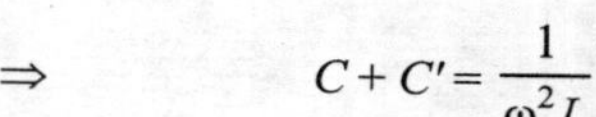

$\Rightarrow$ $C + C' = \frac{1}{\omega^2 L}$

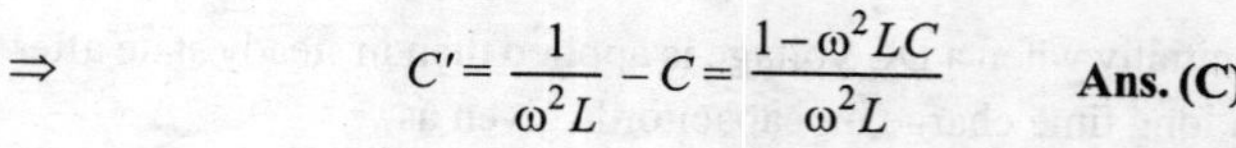

$\Rightarrow$ $C' = \frac{1}{\omega^2 L} - C = \frac{1 - \omega^2 LC}{\omega^2 L}$ **Ans. (C)**

Sol. 28 using direct current 10A current flows at 80V emf

$\Rightarrow$ Resistance of arc lamp $R = \frac{80}{10} = 8\Omega$

$\Rightarrow$ When arc lamp is connected with an inductor across AC supply then 10A current should flow for lamp to function properly.

$\Rightarrow$ $i = \frac{220}{Z} \Rightarrow 10 = \frac{220}{Z}$

$\Rightarrow$ $Z = 22\,\Omega$

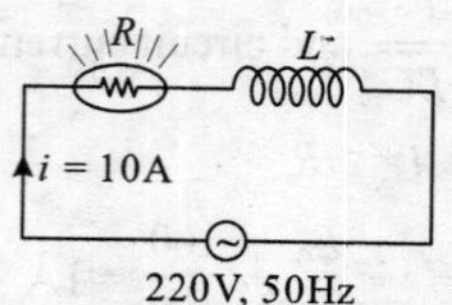

For a series LR circuit impedance is given as

$$Z = \sqrt{R^2 + \omega^2 L^2}$$

[Here $\omega = 2\pi(50) = 100\pi$ rad/s]

$$\Rightarrow \quad 22 = \sqrt{(8)^2 + (100\pi)^2 L^2}$$

$$\Rightarrow \quad 64 + (100\pi)^2 L^2 = (22)^2$$

$$\Rightarrow \quad (100\pi)^2 L^2 = 484 - 64 = 420$$

$$\Rightarrow \quad L = \frac{\sqrt{420}}{100\pi} = 0.0648\ \text{H} \simeq 0.065\ \text{H}$$ **Ans. (D)**

Sol. 29 Across a series LR circuit when AC emf is connected, circuit impedance will be

$$Z = \sqrt{R^2 + \omega^2 L^2}$$

and current in circuit is given as

$$i = i_0 \sin(\omega t - \phi)$$

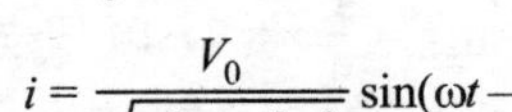

$$\Rightarrow \quad i = \frac{V_0}{\sqrt{R^2 + \omega^2 L^2}} \sin(\omega t - \phi)$$

Where $\phi = \cos^{-1}\left(\frac{R}{\sqrt{R^2 + \omega^2 L^2}}\right)$ and $i_0 = \frac{e_0}{\sqrt{R^2 + \omega^2 L^2}}$

Ans. (D)

22.1 Electromagnetic Wave

Sol. 1 For an EM wave frequency always remain same and if its wavelength changes from λ to λ' then we use

$$\frac{c}{\lambda} = \frac{v}{\lambda'} \qquad \ldots(1)$$

(Where v is wave speed in other medium)

As nothing is specified, we consider medium as non-magnetic ($\mu_r = 1$).

So wave speed in medium is

$$v = \frac{1}{\sqrt{\mu_0 \epsilon_0 \epsilon_r}} = \frac{c}{\sqrt{4.0}} = \frac{c}{2}$$

From (1) $\Rightarrow \frac{c}{\lambda} = \frac{c}{2\lambda'} \Rightarrow \lambda' = \frac{\lambda}{2}$ **Ans. (A)**

Sol. 2 Total power of source = 4×10^3 W

Energy of one photon in eV

$$E = \frac{4 \times 10^3}{10^{20}} \times \frac{1}{1.6 \times 10^{-19}}\ \text{eV}$$

$$\Rightarrow \quad E = 2.5 \times 10^2 = 250\ \text{eV}$$

Wavelength of these photons can be given as

$$\lambda = \frac{hc}{E} = \frac{12431}{250}\ \text{Å} = 49.72\ \text{Å}$$

As X-Ray wavelength range varies from 0.1Å to 100Å **Ans. (B)**

Sol. 3 Polarization direction of EMF is always along the plane of oscillation of electromagnetic force.

$\Rightarrow \quad \vec{X}$ is parallel to $\vec{E}$

direction of propagation of an EM wave is given by poynting vector which gives direction of flow of energy in the EM wave and it is given as

$$\vec{S} = \frac{1}{\mu_0}(\vec{E} \times \vec{B})$$

Where $\vec{E} \times \vec{B} \rightarrow$ direction of EM waves propagation.

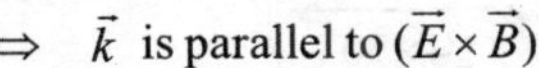

$\Rightarrow \quad \vec{k}$ is parallel to $(\vec{E} \times \vec{B})$ **Ans. (B)**

Sol. 4 The low wavelength part of EM spectrum is

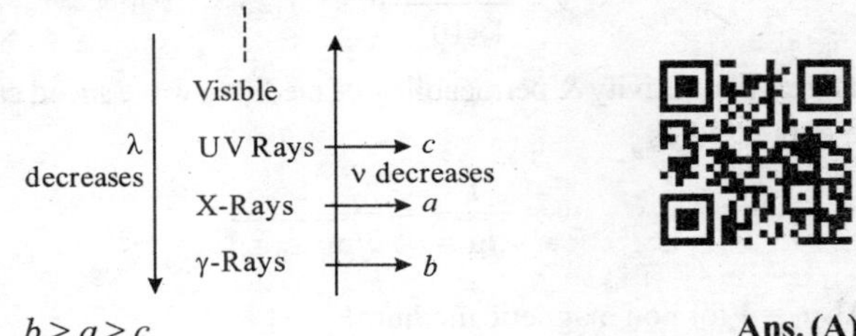

$\Rightarrow \quad b > a > c$ **Ans. (A)**

Sol. 5 Wave propagation in along $\hat{y}$ direction

$\Rightarrow \quad \vec{E} \times \vec{B}$ must be along $\hat{y}$ direction.

$\vec{E} \times \vec{B} \rightarrow$ direction of Poynting vector.

Given that magnetic field is in $+x$ direction

i.e. along $\hat{x}$

$\Rightarrow \quad \vec{E}$ must be along $\hat{z}$ direction.

Electric field function is $\vec{E} = E_0 \cos(\omega t - \frac{2\pi}{\lambda} y)\,\hat{z}$ **Ans. (C)**

Sol. 6 In EM waves propagation, peak values of electric field E_0 and magnetic field B_0 are related as

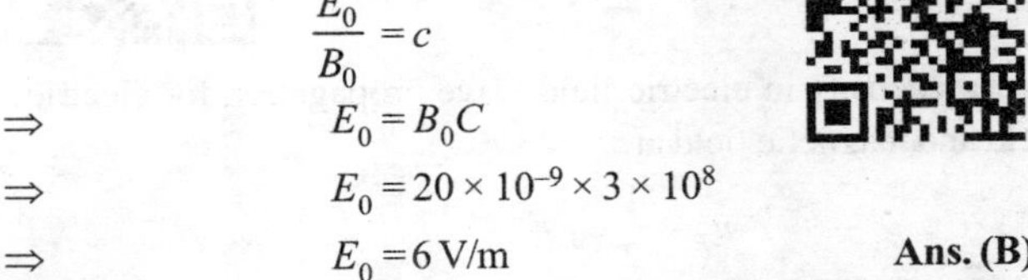

$$\frac{E_0}{B_0} = c$$

$$\Rightarrow \quad E_0 = B_0 C$$

$$\Rightarrow \quad E_0 = 20 \times 10^{-9} \times 3 \times 10^8$$

$$\Rightarrow \quad E_0 = 6\ \text{V/m}$$ **Ans. (B)**

Sol. 7 The wavelength of given radiation λ can be given as

$$E = \frac{hc}{\lambda} = 11\ \text{keV}$$

$$\Rightarrow \quad \lambda = \frac{hc}{E} = \frac{6.63 \times 10^{-34} \times 3 \times 10^8}{11000 \times 1.6 \times 10^{-19}}$$

$$\Rightarrow \quad \lambda = 11.3 \times 10^{-10}\ \text{m} = 11.3\ \text{Å}$$

As X-rays wavelength range is from 0.1Å to 100Å so this radiation is of X-Rays. **Ans. (A)**

Sol. 8 (A) False - As an EM wave can travel in a medium as well in free space as it does not require a medium for propagation.
(B) False - As EM wave consist of transverse oscillations of EF and MF so these are transverse waves.
(C) False - As EM wave are produced by time variation of EF which can be there by moving charges which accelerates.

(D) True - EM waves carry momentum as well as energy (photons) **Ans. (D)**

Sol. 9 Wave function can be expressed as $f(x - vt)$ by

$$\vec{E} = 4 \times 10^{-7}\vec{E}\left(x - \frac{50t}{4\times10^{-7}}\right)$$

The speed of EM wave in the given medium is given as

$$v = \frac{50}{4\times10^{-7}}\text{ m/s} = 1.25\times10^{8}\text{ m/s}$$

In terms permittivity & permeability of medium, wave speed can be expressed as

$$v = \frac{1}{\sqrt{\mu\in}} = \frac{1}{\sqrt{\mu_0\in_0\in_r}}$$

[As $\mu_r = 1$ for non magnetic medium]

$$\Rightarrow \quad v = \frac{c}{\sqrt{\in_r}}$$

$$\Rightarrow \quad 1.25\times10^{8} = \frac{3\times10^{8}}{\sqrt{\in_r}}$$

$$\Rightarrow \quad \sqrt{\in_r} = \frac{3}{1.25} = 2.4$$

$$\Rightarrow \quad \in_r = (2.4)^2 = 5.76$$

Ans. (B)

Sol. 10 In EM wave propagation if E is electric field and B is magnetic field then these are related as

$$\frac{E}{B} = c$$

$$\Rightarrow \quad B = \frac{E}{c}$$

Energy density in electric field wave propagation for electric field and magnetic field are

$$u_E = \frac{1}{2}\in_0 E^2$$

$$u_B = \frac{1}{2}\frac{B^2}{\mu_0} = \frac{1}{2\mu_0}\left(\frac{E}{c}\right)^2 = \frac{1}{2\mu_0}\frac{E^2}{c^2}$$

In free space we use $c = \frac{1}{\sqrt{\mu_0\in_0}}$

$$\Rightarrow \quad u_B = \frac{1}{2\mu_0}(\mu_0\in_0)E^2 = \frac{1}{2}\in_0 E^2$$

$$\Rightarrow \quad u_B = u_E$$

Ans. (C)

Sol. 11 (1) → γ-rays ~ 10^{-12} m → G
(2) → X-rays ~ 10^{-10} m → X
(3) → UV-rays ~ 10^{-7} m → U
(4) → Visible ~ 10^{-6} m → V
(5) → IR-rays ~ 10^{-4} m → I
(6) → Microwaves ~ 10^{-4} m or more → M
(7) → Radio waves ~ 10^{-3} m to several km → R
ascending order of wavelength is G, X, U, V, I, M, R **Ans. (C)**

Sol. 12 Average energy density of Electric field in EM waves is given as

$$\langle u_E\rangle = \frac{1}{4}\in_0 E^2$$

$$\Rightarrow \quad \langle u_E\rangle = \frac{1}{4}\times 8.8\times10^{-12}\times(4)^2$$

$$\Rightarrow \quad \langle u_E\rangle = 35.2\times10^{-12}\text{ J/m}^3$$

Ans. (C)

Sol. 13

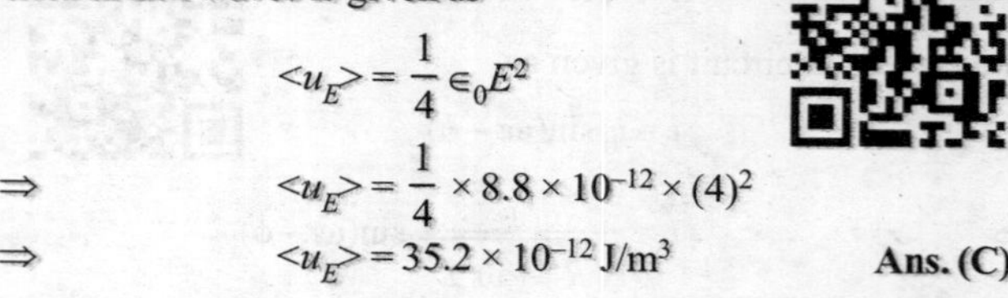

$$P_{EM} = 100\times\frac{3}{100} = 3\text{W}$$

Intensity of EM radiation at $r = 5$m from lamp is given as

$$I = \frac{P}{4\pi r^2} = \frac{3}{4\pi(5)^2} = \frac{3}{100\pi}\text{ W/m}^2$$

If E_0 is the amplitude of Electric field in wave at point M the we use

$$I = \frac{1}{2}\in_0 E^2 c$$

$$\Rightarrow \quad E_0 = \sqrt{\frac{2I}{\in_0 c}}$$

$$\Rightarrow \quad E_0 = \sqrt{\frac{2\times(3/100\pi)}{\left(\frac{1}{4\pi\times9\times10^9}\right)\times3\times10^8}} = \sqrt{7.2}\ \frac{V}{m}$$

$$\Rightarrow \quad E_0 = 2.68\text{ V/m}$$

Ans. (B)

Sol. 14 As propagation direction is $+X$ (along $\hat{i}$) so $\vec{B}$ must be along $\hat{j}$ or $\hat{k}$ or in YZ plane.

The amplitude of magnetic field is given as

$$B_0 = \frac{E_0}{c} = \frac{27}{3\times10^8} = 9\times10^{-8}\text{ T}$$

In a propagating wave general equation is written as

$$B = B_0\sin 2\pi\left(\frac{x}{\lambda} - \frac{t}{T}\right)$$

Average frequency of wave is $\omega = 2\pi\nu = 2\pi(2\times10^{14})$ Hz

Wavelength of wave is $\lambda = \frac{c}{v} = \frac{3\times10^{8}}{2\times10^{14}} = 1.5\times10^{-6}$ m

$\Rightarrow$ Most appropriate here is option (D), otherwise none is correct. **Ans. (D)**

Sol. 15 For EM wave we use always $\vec{E}\cdot\vec{B} = 0$

and direction of propagation of wave must be along $\vec{E}\times\vec{B}$

here $\vec{E}\times\vec{B}$ must be along $+\hat{k}$ (direction of propagation is z direction).

(A) $(2\hat{i}+3\hat{j}).(\hat{i}+2\hat{j}) = 2+6 = 8 \neq 0$

$\Rightarrow$ Not correct

(B) $(-2\hat{i}-3\hat{j}).(3\hat{i}-2\hat{j}) = -6+6 = 0$

$(-2\hat{i}-3\hat{j})\times(3\hat{i}-2\hat{j}) = 4\hat{k}+(-(-9\hat{k})) = 13\hat{k}$

$\Rightarrow$ Correct.

(C) $(3\hat{i}+4\hat{j}).(4\hat{i}-3\hat{j}) = 12-12 = 0$

$(3\hat{i}+4\hat{j})\times(4\hat{i}-3\hat{j}) = -9\hat{k}-16\hat{k} = -25\hat{k}$ (–z direction)

$\Rightarrow$ Not correct.

(D) $(\hat{i}+2\hat{j})(2\hat{i}-\hat{j}) = 2-2 = 0$

$(\hat{i}+2\hat{j})\times(2\hat{i}-\hat{j}) = -\hat{k}-4\hat{k} = -5\hat{k}$ (–z direction)

$\Rightarrow$ Not correct. **Ans. (B)**

Sol. 16 EM spectrum

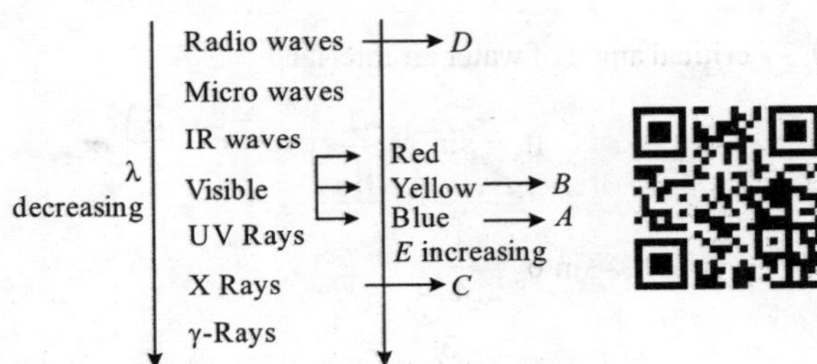

Order of increasing energy, $D \to B \to A \to C$ **Ans. (C)**

Sol. 17

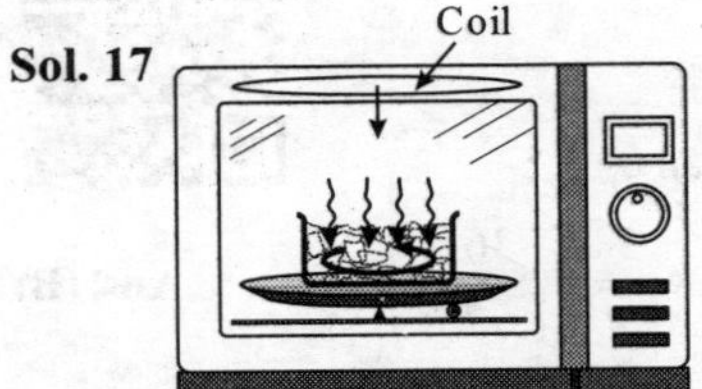

Microwave Oven

Coil of oven produces time varying magnetic field due to which microwaves are produced.

Due to vibrations in ions (water molecules in ionized state or dipoles) localized heat is produced in substance due to which cooking take place. **Ans. (C)**

Sol. 18 (A) Propagation direction $\to +Y$ and $\hat{E} = \hat{z}$ and $\hat{B} = \hat{y}$

This is not possible as $\vec{B}$ is along direction of propagation.

$\Rightarrow$ Not correct.

(B) Propagation direction $\to +Y$ and $\hat{E} = \hat{y}$ and $\hat{B} = \hat{z}$

This is not possible as $\vec{E}$ is along direction of propagation.

$\Rightarrow$ Not correct.

(C) Propagation direction $\to +X$ and $\hat{E} = \left(\frac{\hat{y}+\hat{z}}{\sqrt{2}}\right)$ and $\hat{B} = \left(\frac{\hat{y}+\hat{z}}{\sqrt{2}}\right)$

This is not possible as $\vec{E}$ and $\vec{B}$ are parallel $\Rightarrow$ Not correct.

(D) Propagation direction $\to +X$ and $\hat{E} = \left(\frac{\hat{y}-\hat{z}}{\sqrt{2}}\right)$ and

$\hat{B} = \left(\frac{\hat{y}+\hat{z}}{\sqrt{2}}\right)$

here $\vec{E}\cdot\vec{B} = 0$ and both $\vec{E}$ and $\vec{B}$ are $\perp$ to X i.e. in YZ plane and $\vec{E}\times\vec{B}$ direction is along $(\hat{y}-\hat{z})\times(\hat{y}+\hat{z}) = \hat{x}-(-\hat{x}) = 2\hat{x}$ (+x direction). Where $\vec{E}\times\vec{B}$ is direction of energy flow in EM waves. $\Rightarrow$ Correct. **Ans. (D)**

23.1 Geometrical Optics-I Reflection of Light

Sol. 1

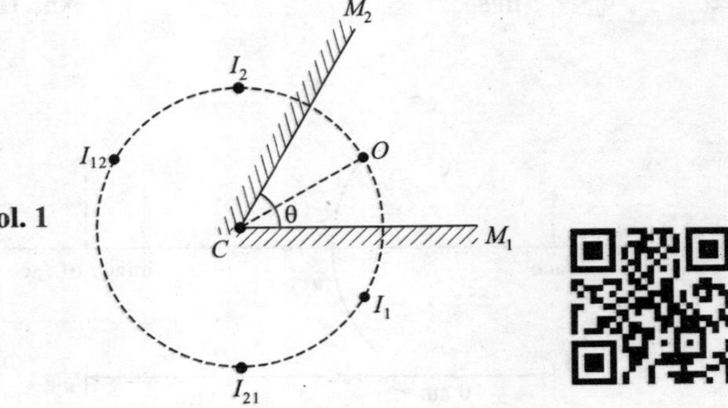

at $\theta = 60°$

$$\frac{180}{60°} = \frac{30}{\text{integer}}$$

If $\frac{180}{\theta} \in I$ then no of images produced are given as

$$N = \frac{360}{\theta} - 1$$

$$N = \frac{360}{60} - 1 = 6 - 1 = 5$$

Ans. (A)

Sol. 2 If θ is angle between mirrors that no of images obtained are

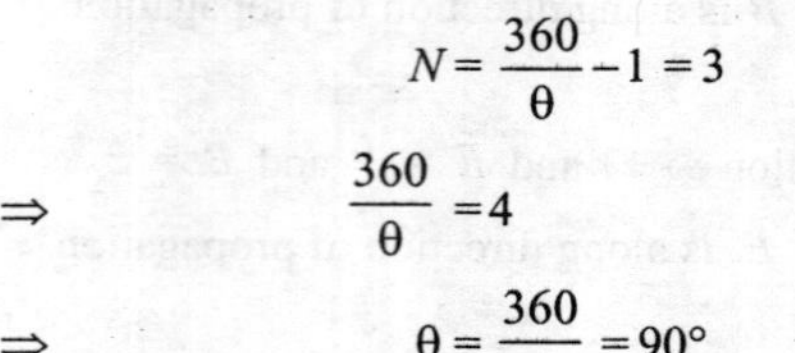

$$N = \frac{360}{\theta} - 1 = 3$$

$$\Rightarrow \quad \frac{360}{\theta} = 4$$

$$\Rightarrow \quad \theta = \frac{360}{4} = 90°$$

Ans. (B)

Sol. 3

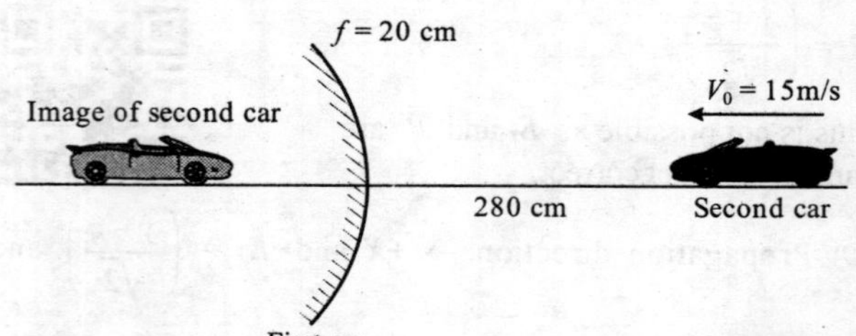

For reflection at convex mirror, we use

$$u = +280\text{ cm}$$

$$f = -20\text{ cm}$$

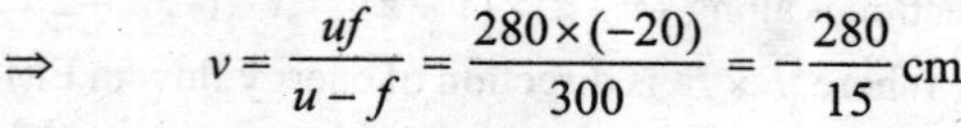

$$\Rightarrow \quad v = \frac{uf}{u-f} = \frac{280 \times (-20)}{300} = -\frac{280}{15}\text{ cm}$$

Image velocity in a mirror is given as

$$v_i = m^2 \cdot V_0 = \left|\frac{v}{u}\right|^2 \times V_0 = \left(\frac{1}{15}\right)^2 \times 15 \text{ [magnification]}$$

$$\Rightarrow \quad v_i = \frac{1}{15}\text{ m/s}$$

Ans. (D)

Sol. 4

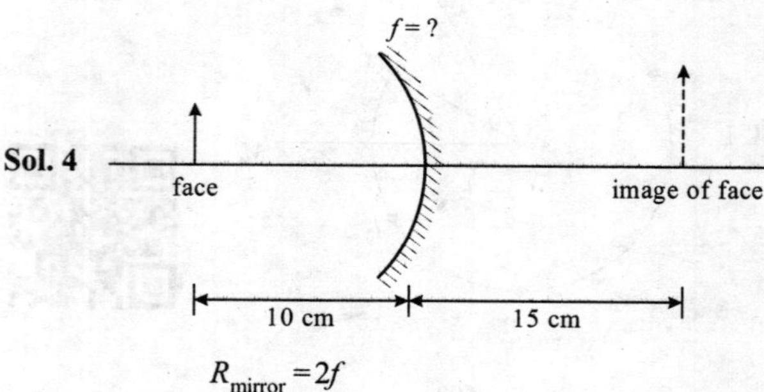

$$R_{mirror} = 2f$$

For mirror formula we use

$$u = -10\text{ cm}$$

$$V = +15\text{ cm}$$

$$\Rightarrow \quad \frac{1}{f} = \frac{1}{u} + \frac{1}{V}$$

$$\Rightarrow \quad \frac{1}{f} = -\frac{1}{10} + \frac{1}{15} = -\frac{5}{150} = -\frac{1}{30}$$

$$\Rightarrow \quad f = -30\text{ cm}$$

$$\Rightarrow \quad R = 2f = -2 \times 30 = -60\text{ cm.}$$

Ans. (C)

23.2 Geometrical Optics-II Refraction of Light

Sol. 1

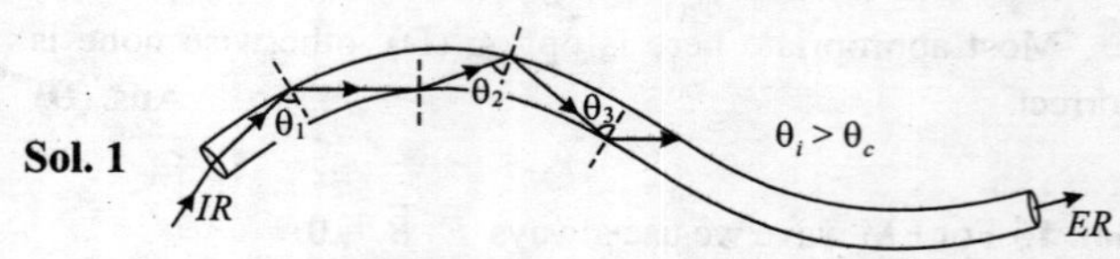

In an optical fibre at every point of inner surface light is internally reflected so light comes out only from the other end of fibre. Total internal reflection. **Ans. (A)**

Sol. 2 As light ray is internally reflected

$$\Rightarrow \quad 45° > \theta_c = \sin^{-1}\left(\frac{1}{n}\right)$$

$$\Rightarrow \quad \frac{1}{n} < \sin 45°$$

$$\Rightarrow \quad n > \sqrt{2}$$

Ans. (B)

Sol. 3

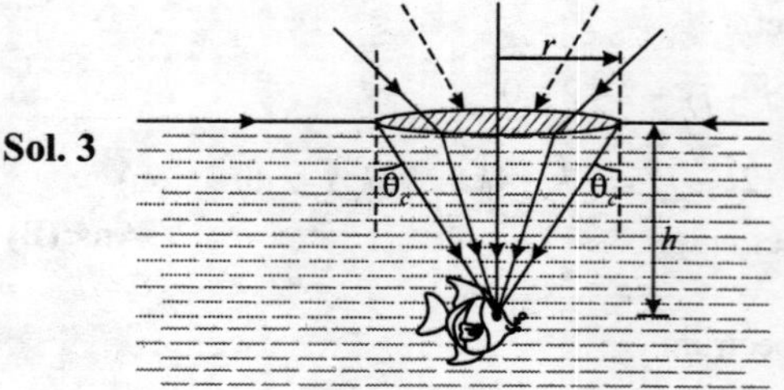

$\theta_c \rightarrow$ critical angle of water air interface

$$\theta_c = \sin^{-1}\left(\frac{1}{\mu_\omega}\right) = \sin^{-1}\left(\frac{3}{4}\right)$$

$$\Rightarrow \quad \sin\theta_c = \frac{3}{4}$$

$$\Rightarrow \quad \tan\theta_c = \frac{3}{\sqrt{7}}$$

In the figure shown, we have

$$\tan\theta_c = \frac{r}{h}$$

$$\Rightarrow \quad r = h\tan\theta_c$$

$$\Rightarrow \quad r = 12 \times \frac{3}{\sqrt{7}} = \frac{36}{\sqrt{7}}\text{ cm}$$

Ans. (B)

Sol. 4

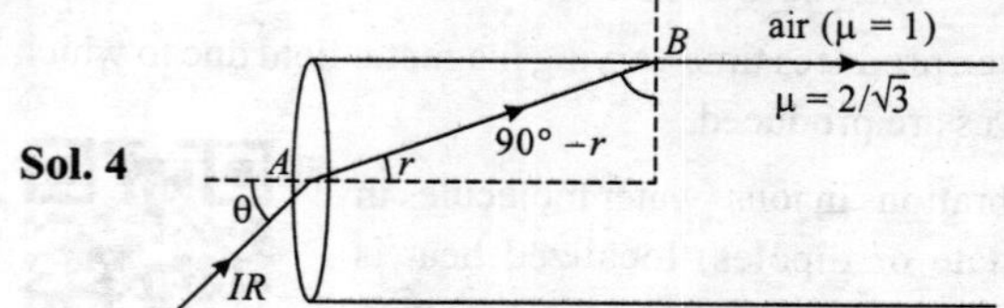

If light ray to graze along the wall of rod

$$\Rightarrow \quad 90° - r = \theta_c = \sin^{-1}\left(\frac{1}{\mu}\right) = \sin^{-1}\left(\frac{\sqrt{3}}{2}\right) = 60°$$

$$\Rightarrow \quad r = 90° - 60° = 30°$$

By Snell's law at point A we have

$$\Rightarrow \quad \sin\theta = \mu \sin r$$

$$= \frac{2}{\sqrt{3}} \times \frac{1}{2} = \frac{1}{\sqrt{3}}$$

$$\Rightarrow \quad \theta = \sin^{-1}\left(\frac{1}{\sqrt{3}}\right)$$

Ans. (B)

Sol. 5

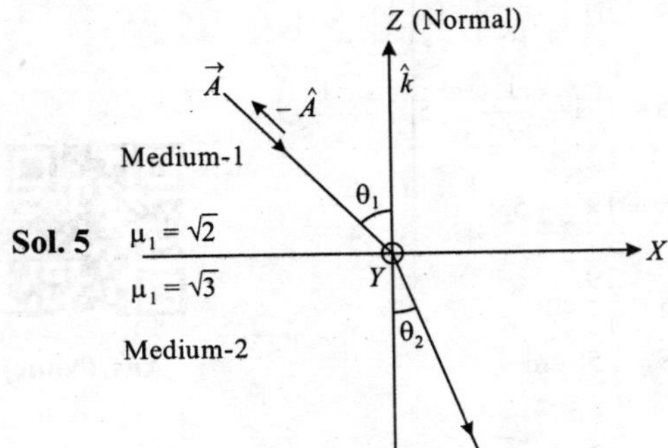

By Snell's law, we use

$$\sqrt{2}\sin\theta_1 = \sqrt{3}\sin\theta_2 \qquad \ldots(1)$$

The angle between $\hat{k}$ and $-\hat{A}$ is given as

$$\cos\theta_1 = -\hat{A}\cdot\hat{k} \qquad \ldots(2)$$

Unit vector along $\vec{A}$ is given as

$$\hat{A} = \frac{\vec{A}}{|\vec{A}|} = \frac{6\sqrt{3}\hat{i} + 8\sqrt{3}\hat{j} - 10\hat{k}}{\sqrt{(6\sqrt{3})^2 + (8\sqrt{3})^2 + (10)^2}}$$

$$\Rightarrow \quad \hat{A} = \frac{1}{20}(6\sqrt{3}i + 8\sqrt{3}\hat{j} - 10\hat{k})$$

$$\Rightarrow \quad \hat{A} = \frac{3\sqrt{3}}{10}\hat{i} + \frac{4\sqrt{3}}{10}\hat{j} - \frac{1}{2}\hat{k}$$

From equation (2), we have

$$\cos\theta_1 = -\left(\frac{3\sqrt{3}}{10}\hat{i} + \frac{4\sqrt{3}}{10}\hat{j} - \frac{1}{2}\hat{k}\right)\cdot\hat{k} = \frac{1}{2}$$

$$\Rightarrow \quad \theta_1 = 60°$$

Now from equation-(1), we have

$$\sqrt{2} \times \frac{\sqrt{3}}{2} = \sqrt{3}\sin\theta_2$$

$$\Rightarrow \quad \sin\theta_2 = \frac{1}{\sqrt{2}} \Rightarrow \theta_2 = 45°$$

Ans. (D)

Sol. 6

Object shift along normal is given as

$$S_1 = h_1\left(1 - \frac{1}{\mu_1}\right)$$

$$S_2 = h_2\left(1 - \frac{1}{\mu_2}\right)$$

Total shift of object as seen normally is given as

$$S = h_1\left(1 - \frac{1}{\mu_2}\right) + h_2\left(1 - \frac{1}{\mu_2}\right)$$

Ans. (C)

Sol. 7

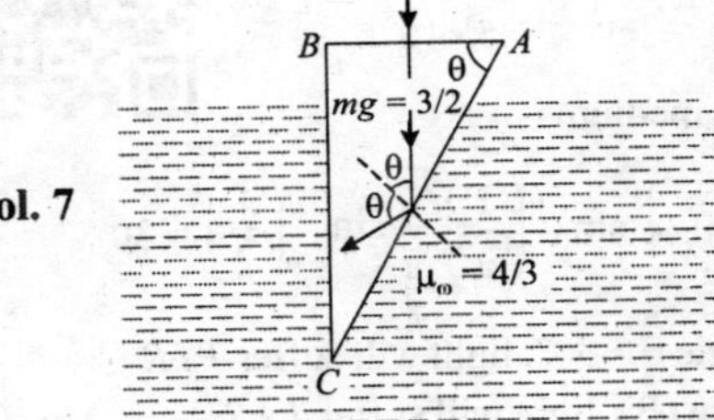

Light will be totally reflected at face AC to reach face BC if

$$\theta > \theta_c$$

[$\theta_c \rightarrow$ critical angle glass-water interface]

$$\Rightarrow \quad \sin\theta > \sin\theta_c$$

$$\Rightarrow \quad \sin\theta > \frac{1}{{}_\omega\mu_g} = \frac{\mu_\omega}{\mu g} = \frac{4/3}{3/2}$$

$$\Rightarrow \quad \sin\theta > \frac{8}{9}$$

Ans. (C)

Sol. 8

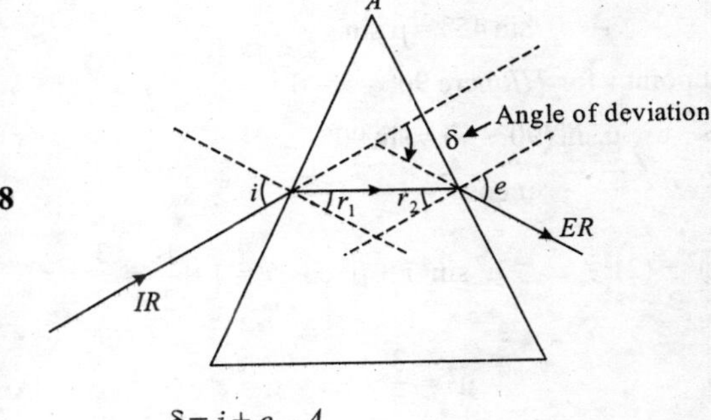

$$\delta = i + e - A$$

When $i = e \rightarrow \delta$ is minimum

$\Rightarrow$ $r_1 = r_2 = A/2$

and light passes through prism symmetrically

$$\sin i = \mu \sin r_1$$

$$\sin e = \mu \sin r_2 = \mu \sin (A - r_1)$$

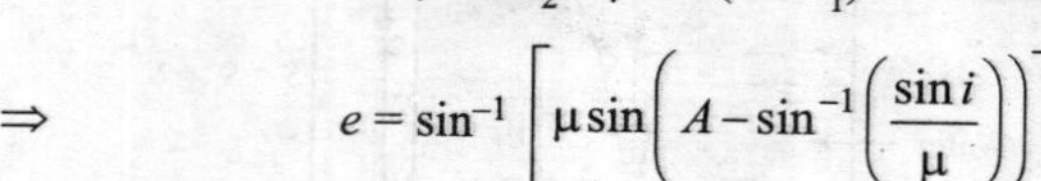

$$\Rightarrow \quad e = \sin^{-1}\left[\mu \sin\left(A - \sin^{-1}\left(\frac{\sin i}{\mu}\right)\right)\right]$$

$$\Rightarrow \quad \delta = i + \sin^{-1}\left[\mu \sin^{-1}\left(A \sin^{-1}\left[\frac{\sin i}{\mu}\right]\right)\right] - A$$

This is a non linear relation. **Ans. (C)**

Sol. 9 As light travels 30 cm in 0.2 ns, the speed of light in medium is

$$v = \frac{3\times10^{-2}}{0.2\times10^{-9}} = 1.5\times10^{8}\ \text{m/s}$$

Refractive index of medium is

$$\mu = \frac{c}{v} = \frac{3\times10^{8}}{1.5\times10^{8}} = 2$$

Critical angle for the medium is

$$\theta_c = \sin^{-1}\left(\frac{1}{\mu}\right) = \sin^{-1}\left(\frac{1}{2}\right) = 30°$$

For all incidence angle $\theta > 30°$, light will suffer TIR

In A & B only for case (B), light will suffer TIR **Ans. (B)**

Sol. 10

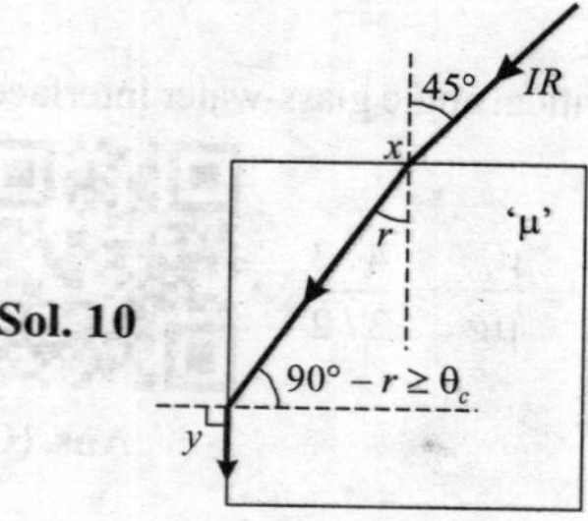

We use Snell's law at x, we have

$$\sin 45° = \mu \sin r \quad \ldots(1)$$

At point y for TIR here $90° - r = \theta_c$

$\Rightarrow$ $\mu \sin(90° - r) = \sin 90°$

$\Rightarrow$ $\mu \cos r = 1 \quad \ldots(2)$

$(1)^2 + (2)^2 \Rightarrow \mu^2 \sin^2 r + \mu^2 \cos^2 r = 1 + \frac{1}{2} = \frac{3}{2}$

$\Rightarrow$ $\mu^2 = \frac{3}{2} \Rightarrow \mu = \sqrt{\frac{3}{2}}$ **Ans. (D)**

Sol. 11

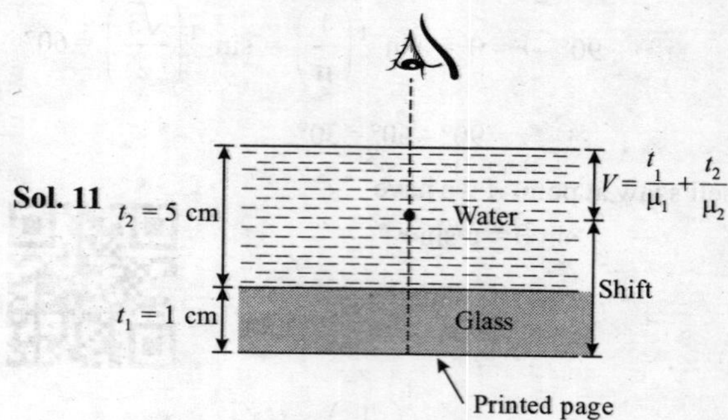

Apparent shift of printed page due to glass and water is given as

$$S = t_1\left(1 - \frac{1}{\mu_1}\right) + t_2\left(1 - \frac{1}{\mu_2}\right)$$

$$\Rightarrow \quad S = 1\left(1 - \frac{1}{3/2}\right) + 5\left(1 - \frac{1}{4/3}\right)$$

$$\Rightarrow \quad S = 1\times\frac{1}{3} + 5\times\frac{1}{4} = \frac{1}{3} + \frac{5}{4}$$

$$\Rightarrow \quad S = \frac{19}{12}\ \text{cm}$$

$$\Rightarrow \quad S \simeq 1.58\ \text{cm}$$

Ans. (None)

Sol. 12

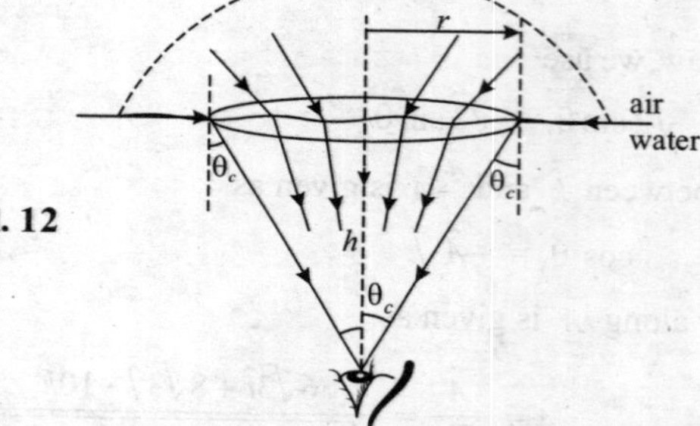

The critical angle at air-water interface is given as

$$\theta_c = \sin^{-1}\left(\frac{1}{\mu_\omega}\right) = \sin^{-1}\left(\frac{3}{4}\right)$$

$$\Rightarrow \quad \sin\theta_c = \frac{3}{4} \Rightarrow \tan\theta_c = \frac{3}{\sqrt{7}}$$

$$\tan\theta_c = \frac{r}{h}$$

$$\Rightarrow \quad r = h\tan\theta_c$$

$$\Rightarrow \quad h = h\left(\frac{3}{\sqrt{7}}\right) = \frac{15\times3}{\sqrt{3}}\ \text{cm}$$

Ans. (D)

Sol. 13

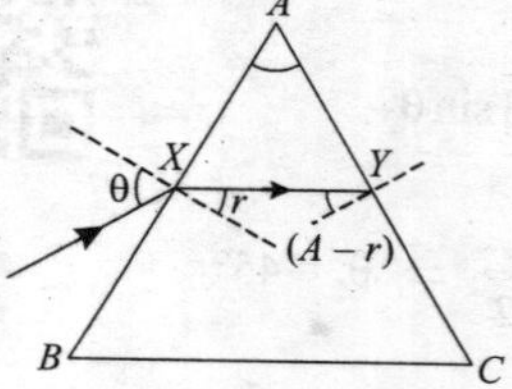

If $(A-r)>\theta_c$ then light will not get not get transmitted through force AC. So in this case we use for transmission of light

$$A-r<\theta_c \quad \ldots(1)$$

At point x, we use Snell's law

$$\sin\theta=\mu\sin r$$

$$\Rightarrow \quad r=\sin^{-1}\left(\frac{\sin\theta}{\mu}\right)$$

From equation-(1)

$$A-\sin^{-1}\left(\frac{\sin\theta}{\mu}\right)<\sin^{-1}\left(\frac{1}{\mu}\right) \quad \left[\text{As } \theta_c=\sin^{-1}\left(\frac{1}{\mu}\right)\right]$$

$$\Rightarrow \quad \sin^{-1}\left(\frac{\sin\theta}{\mu}\right)>A-\sin^{-1}\left(\frac{1}{\mu}\right)$$

$$\Rightarrow \quad \frac{\sin\theta}{\mu}>\sin\left(A-\sin^{-1}\left(\frac{1}{\mu}\right)\right)$$

$$\Rightarrow \quad \theta>\sin^{-1}\left[\mu\sin\left(A-\sin^{-1}\left(\frac{1}{\mu}\right)\right)\right]$$ **Ans. (A)**

Sol. 14 We are given with

$$\left.\begin{aligned} i&=35^\circ\\ \delta&=40^\circ\\ e&=79^\circ\end{aligned}\right] \rightarrow \delta=i+e-A$$

Prism angle is given as

$$A=i+e-\delta=35^\circ+79^\circ-40^\circ=74^\circ$$

We use RI of glass as

$$\mu=\frac{\sin\left(\frac{A+\delta_m}{2}\right)}{\sin\left(\frac{A}{2}\right)}$$

[we use $\delta_m<40^\circ$ as at 40° $i\neq e$]

$$\Rightarrow \quad \mu=\frac{\sin\left(\frac{A+\delta_m}{2}\right)}{\sin(37^\circ)} \quad [\text{As } \sin 37^\circ=3/5]$$

$$\Rightarrow \quad \mu=\frac{\sin\left(\frac{A+\delta_m}{2}\right)}{3/5}$$

$$\Rightarrow \quad \mu=\frac{5}{3}\sin(37^\circ+\theta)$$

Where $\quad \theta=\frac{\delta_m}{2}<20^\circ$

$$\Rightarrow \quad \mu=\frac{5}{3}\sin[37+(<20^\circ)]$$

$$\Rightarrow \quad \mu=\frac{5}{3}\sin[<57^\circ]$$

$$\Rightarrow \quad \mu<\frac{5}{3}\sin 57^\circ \quad \left[\text{As } \sin 60^\circ=\frac{\sqrt{3}}{2}\right]$$

$$\Rightarrow \quad \mu<\frac{5}{3}\times 1.67$$

$$\Rightarrow \quad \mu<1.45$$

Here out of given options closest possible maximum volume can be 1.5. **Ans. (A)**

Sol. 15

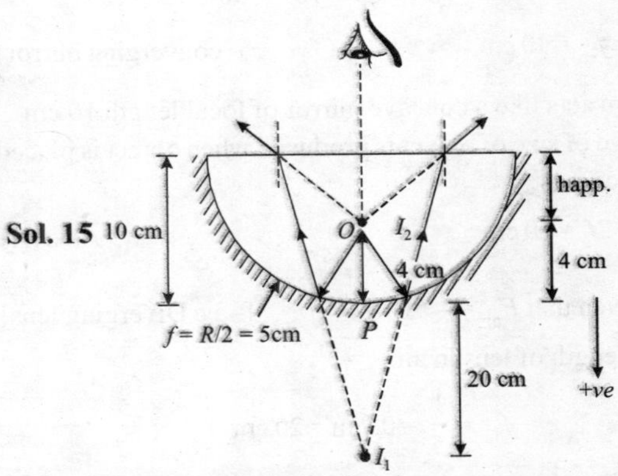

For reflection at spherical mirror we use

$$u=-4\text{ cm}$$

$$f=-5\text{ cm}$$

So from mirror formula, we have

$$\frac{1}{f}=\frac{1}{u}+\frac{1}{v}$$

$$\Rightarrow \quad \frac{1}{v}=\frac{1}{f}-\frac{1}{u}=-\frac{1}{5}+\frac{1}{4}=+\frac{1}{20}$$

$$\Rightarrow \quad v=+20\text{ cm}$$

Due to refraction from plane surface of glass to air final image is seen at

$$h_{ap}=\frac{h}{\mu}=\frac{30}{1.5}=20\text{ cm}$$ **Ans. (B)**

23.3 Geometrical Optics-III Thin Lenses

Sol. 1

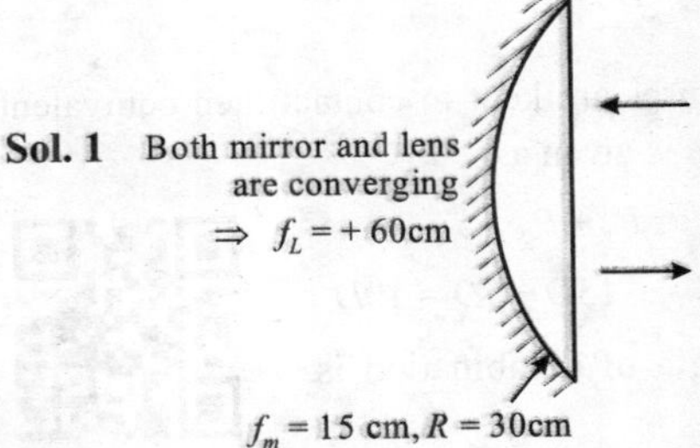

This system acts like a combination of a concave mirror and a plano convex lens

Focal length of mirror is

$$f_m=\frac{R}{2}=15\text{ cm}$$

Focal length of lens is

$$f_L=\frac{R}{\mu-1}=\frac{30}{0.5}=60\text{ cm}$$

Equivalent focal length of combination is given as

$$f_{eq} = \frac{2}{f_L} + \frac{1}{f_M} = \frac{2}{60} + \frac{1}{15} = \frac{1}{30} + \frac{1}{15} = \frac{1}{10}$$

$\Rightarrow$ $f_{eq} = 10$ cm (+ve $\Rightarrow$ converging mirror)

This system acts like a concave mirror of focal length 10 cm

A real image of size of object is produced when object is placed at a distance

$$2f_e = 20 \text{ cm}$$

Ans. (A)

Sol. 2 Given that $P_{air} = -5D$ [– *ve* Diverging lens]

$\Rightarrow$ focal length of lens in air

$$f_{air} = \frac{1}{5} = 0.2\,\text{m} = 20\,\text{cm}$$

By lens makers formula we have

$$P = (\mu - 1)\left[\frac{1}{R_1} - \frac{1}{R_2}\right]$$

$$-\frac{5}{100} = (1.5 - 1)\left[\frac{1}{R_1} - \frac{1}{R_2}\right] \quad \ldots(1)$$

If focal length of lens in liquid medium is f_L then we use

$$\frac{1}{f_L} = \left(\frac{\mu_g}{\mu_L} - 1\right)\left(\frac{1}{R_1} - \frac{1}{R_2}\right)$$

$$\Rightarrow \quad \frac{1}{f_L} = \left(\frac{1.5}{1.6} - 1\right)\left[\frac{1}{R_1} - \frac{1}{R_2}\right] \quad \ldots(2)$$

$$\frac{(1)}{(2)} \Rightarrow \quad -\frac{f_L}{20} = -\frac{0.5}{0.1} \times 1.6$$

$$\Rightarrow \quad f_L = 5 \times 20 \times 1.6 = 160\,\text{cm} = 1.6\,\text{m}$$

Power lens in liquid medium

$$P_{liq} = \frac{\mu_L}{f_L} = \frac{1.6}{1.6} = +1D$$

Ans. (A)

Sol. 3 When thin lenses are kept in contact then equivalent power of combination is given as

$$P_{eq} = P_1 + P_2$$

$$= -15D + 5D = 10D$$

equivalent focal length of combination is given as

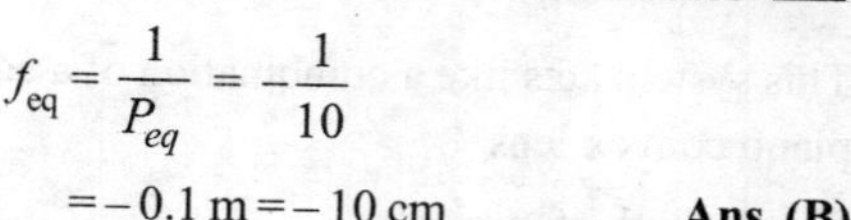

$$f_{eq} = \frac{1}{P_{eq}} = -\frac{1}{10}$$

$$= -0.1\,\text{m} = -10\,\text{cm}$$

Ans. (B)

Sol. 4 Object and image distances from a lens are related by "Lens formula", given as

$$\frac{1}{v} - \frac{1}{u} = \frac{1}{f}$$ [$u \rightarrow$ object distance from lens]

[$v \rightarrow$ image distance from lens]

$$\Rightarrow \quad v = \frac{uf}{u - f}$$

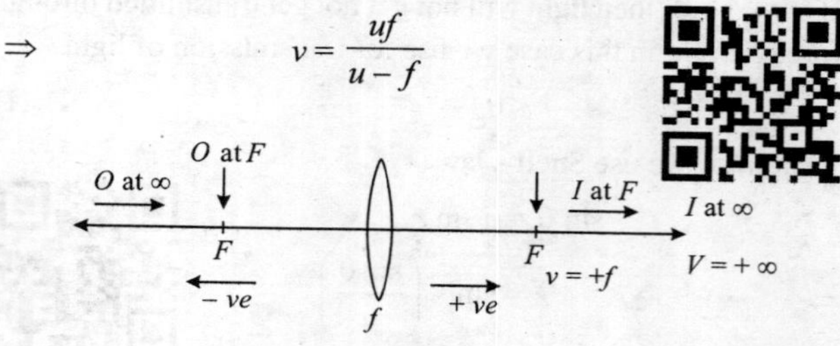

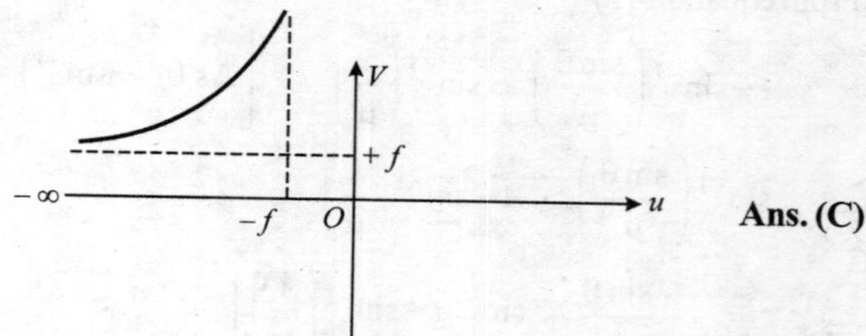

Ans. (C)

Sol. 5 For a convex lens the curve between | *u* | and | *v* | is shown as

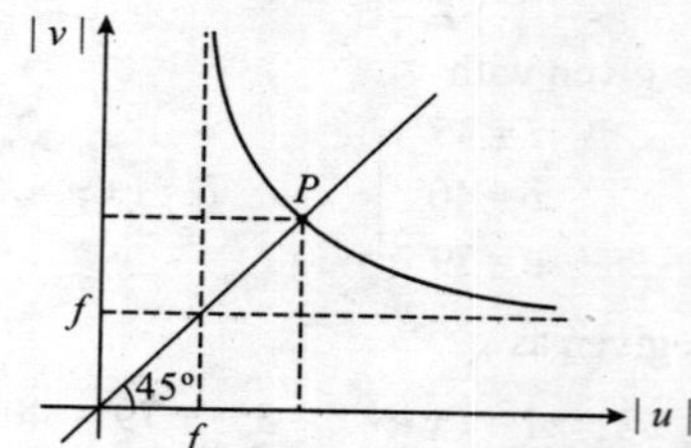

P is graph is a point where object distance and image distance are equal and in case of a convex lens for a real image

$$|u| = |v| = 2f$$

$\Rightarrow$ $P \rightarrow (2f, 2f)$

Ans. (D)

Sol. 6 **Case-I :**

Using lens formula, we have

$$u = -240\,\text{cm}$$

$$v = +12\,\text{cm}$$

$$f = ?$$

$$\frac{1}{v} - \frac{1}{u} = \frac{1}{f}$$

$$\Rightarrow \quad \frac{1}{12} + \frac{1}{240} = \frac{1}{f}$$

$$\Rightarrow \qquad f = \frac{12 \times 240}{252} = \frac{240}{21} \text{ cm}$$

Case-II :

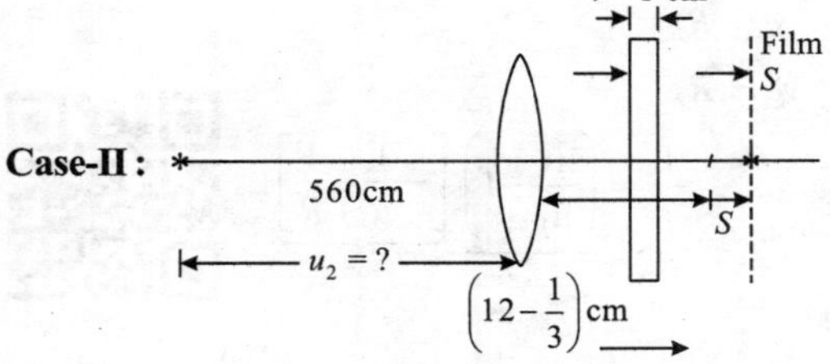

Due to glass plate image produced by lens will be shifted to right by S were

$$S = t\left(1 - \frac{1}{\mu}\right)$$

Shift
$$S = 1\left(1 - \frac{1}{3/2}\right) = 1 - \frac{2}{3} = \frac{1}{3} \text{ cm}$$

Lens has to produce the final image at a distance $\left(12 - \frac{1}{3}\right)$ cm so as to get sharp image on screen.

For case-II

$$v_2 = +\left(12 - \frac{1}{3}\right) = +\frac{35}{3} \text{ cm}$$

$$f = +\frac{240}{21} \text{ cm}$$

object distance $\quad u_2 = ?$

By lens formula

$$\frac{1}{v} - \frac{1}{u} = \frac{1}{F}$$

$$\frac{3}{35} - \frac{1}{u} = \frac{21}{240}$$

$$\Rightarrow \qquad \frac{1}{u} = \frac{3}{35} - \frac{21}{240}$$

$$\Rightarrow \qquad u = -560 \text{ cm}$$ **Ans. (A)**

Sol. 7 Refractive index of lens material is

$$\mu = \frac{c}{v} = \frac{3 \times 10^8}{2 \times 10^8} = 1.5$$

From the given information, we have (by figure)

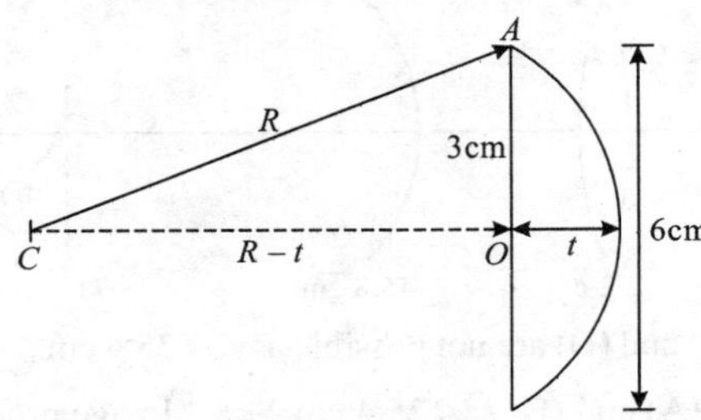

Very thin lines with thickness $t = 3$ mm

In ΔCAO, we use

$$R^2 = (3)^2 + (R - 0.3)^2$$

$$\Rightarrow \qquad R^2 = 9 + R^2 + 0.09 - 0.6R$$

$$\Rightarrow \qquad 0.6R = 9.09$$

$$\Rightarrow \qquad R = \frac{90.9}{6} \simeq 15 \text{ cm}$$

Focal length of a thin lens ($t << R$) is given by lens makes formula as

$$f = \frac{R}{\mu - 1} = \frac{15}{1.5 - 1} = 30 \text{ cm}$$ **Ans. (C)**

Sol. 8

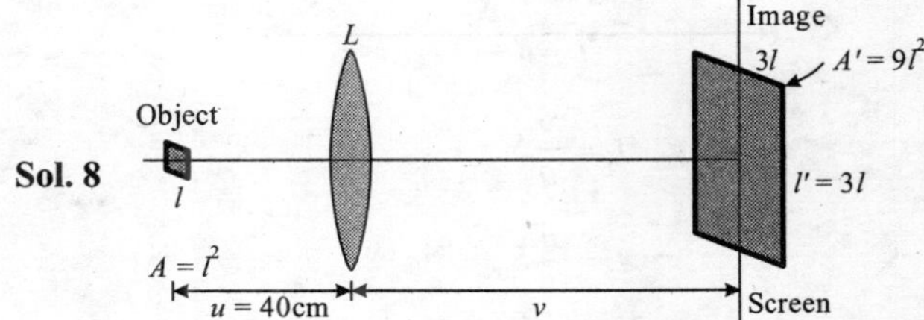

As image size in 3 times the object size

$$\Rightarrow \qquad \frac{v}{u} = 3 \Rightarrow v = 3 \times 40$$

$$\Rightarrow \qquad = 120 \text{ cm}$$

By lens formula we have

$$u = -40 \text{ cm}$$

$$v = +120 \text{ cm}$$

$$\Rightarrow \qquad \frac{1}{f} = \frac{1}{v} - \frac{1}{u} = \frac{1}{120} + \frac{1}{40} = \frac{4}{120} = \frac{1}{30}$$

$$\Rightarrow \qquad f = +30 \text{ cm}$$ **Ans. (D)**

Sol. 9 By lens makes formula

$$\frac{1}{f} = (\mu - 1)\underbrace{\left[\frac{1}{R_1} - \frac{1}{R_2}\right]}_{C}$$

$$\Rightarrow \qquad f = \frac{1}{C(\mu - 1)} = \frac{1}{C(3/2 - 1)} = \frac{2}{C}$$

When the lens is submerged in a medium of RI μ_m then we use

$$\frac{1}{f} = \left(\frac{\mu}{\mu_m} - 1\right)C$$

$$\Rightarrow \qquad f = \frac{\mu_m}{C(\mu - \mu_m)}$$

For medium having RI $\mu_1 = 4/3$, we have focal length

$$f_1 = \frac{4/3}{C\left(\frac{3}{2} - \frac{4}{3}\right)} = \frac{4/3}{C\left(\frac{1}{6}\right)} = \frac{8}{C}$$

For medium having RI $\mu_2 = 5/3$, we have focal length

$$f_2 = \frac{5/3}{C\left(\frac{3}{2}-\frac{5}{3}\right)} = \frac{5/3}{C\left(-\frac{1}{6}\right)} = -\frac{10}{C}$$

Ans. (B)

Sol. 10

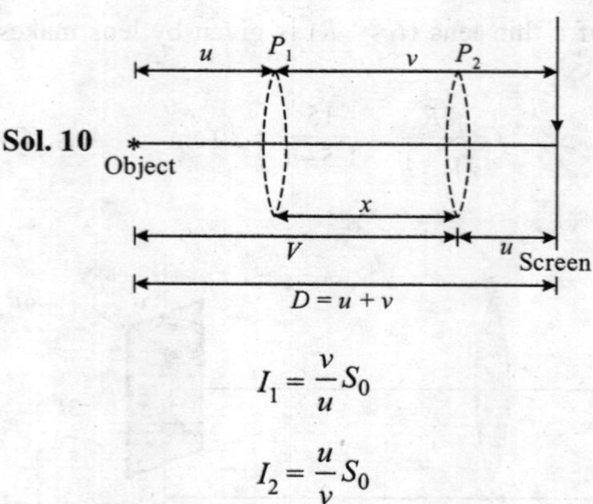

$$I_1 = \frac{v}{u}S_0$$

$$I_2 = \frac{u}{v}S_0$$

The lens displacement is given as

$$x = v - u = 10 \text{ cm} \quad \dots(1)$$

$$\frac{I_1}{I_2} = \frac{v^2}{u^2} = \frac{3}{2} \quad \dots(2)$$

from (1) and (2), we use

$$v - \sqrt{\frac{2}{3}}v = 10$$

$$\Rightarrow \quad v = \frac{\sqrt{3}(10)}{\sqrt{3}-\sqrt{2}}$$

$$\Rightarrow \quad u = \sqrt{\frac{2}{3}}(10) \Rightarrow u = \frac{\sqrt{2}(10)}{\sqrt{3}-\sqrt{2}}$$

Separation between object and screen is given as

$$D = u + v$$

$$\Rightarrow \quad D = 10\left(\frac{\sqrt{3}+\sqrt{2}}{\sqrt{3}-\sqrt{2}}\right) \text{cm}$$

$$\Rightarrow \quad D = 10\left(\frac{1.732+1.414}{1.732-1.414}\right) = 10 \times \frac{3.146}{0.318}$$

$$\Rightarrow \quad D = 98.9 \text{ cm}$$

Ans. (D)

Sol. 11 Method-1 : As we know a lens is submerged in a medium of RI greater then that of lens material then behaviour of lens is changed i.e. convex $\rightarrow$ converging

Here as $\mu_1 > \mu$, $\Rightarrow$ Concave lens converges parallel light beam.

Ans. (A)

Method-2 : Using lens makers formula

$$\frac{1}{f} = ({}_m\mu_L - 1)\left[\frac{1}{R_1} - \frac{1}{R_2}\right]$$

Here say $|R_1| = |R_2|$ (we consider an equiconcave lens) and

$${}_m\mu_L = \frac{\mu}{\mu_1}$$

$$R_1 \rightarrow -ve\,(-R)$$

$$R_2 \rightarrow +ve\,(+R)$$

$$\Rightarrow \quad \frac{1}{f} = \underbrace{\left(\frac{\mu}{\mu_1}-1\right)}_{-ve}\underbrace{\left[-\frac{1}{R}-\frac{1}{R}\right]}_{-ve}$$

As $(\mu < \mu_1)$

$\Rightarrow$ $f \rightarrow +ve$

$\Rightarrow$ Lens behave as a converging lens **Ans. (A)**

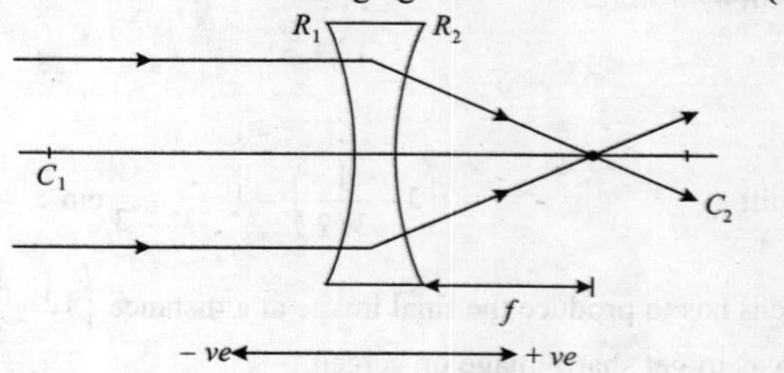

Sol. 12 The lens mirror combination behaves like a spherical mirror of which focal length f_m is given as

$$f_{plain} = \infty$$

$$f_{lens} = f$$

$$\frac{1}{f_m} = \frac{2}{f_{lens}} + \frac{1}{f_{plain}} = \frac{2}{f}$$

$$\Rightarrow \quad f_m = \frac{f}{2}$$

Using mirror formula we have

$$u = +a$$

$$V = +a/3$$

$$\Rightarrow \quad \frac{1}{f_m} = \frac{1}{u} + \frac{1}{V} = \frac{1}{a} + \frac{3}{a} = \frac{4}{a}$$

$$\Rightarrow \quad \frac{a}{4} = \frac{f}{2}$$

$$\Rightarrow \quad a = 2f$$

Ans. (D)

Sol. 13

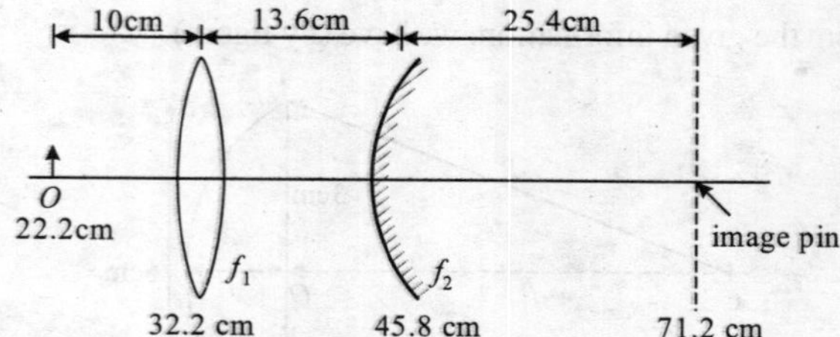

Option (C) and (D) are not possible as $f_2 \neq 25.4$ cm.

In option (A) and (B) $f_2 < 25.4$ cm $\Rightarrow$ Image produced by lens must be on right side of mirror

$\Rightarrow$ for lens $v > 13.6$ cm $\Rightarrow$ Real enlarged image produced by lens

$$\Rightarrow \qquad f_1 < 10\,\text{cm}$$

As to produce enlarged real image ($|v| > |u|$) object must be located at

$$|f_1| < u < |2f_1|$$

$\Rightarrow$ Only possible option is (A) where $f_1 = 7.8$

& here (B) is also not possible as $f_1 > 10$ cm **Ans. (A)**

Sol. 14 First refraction at convex lens L_1

$u = -60$ cm lens

$f = +30$ cm formula

$$\frac{1}{f} = \frac{1}{v} - \frac{1}{u}$$

$$\Rightarrow \quad \frac{1}{v} = \frac{1}{30} - \frac{1}{60} = \frac{1}{60}$$

$$\Rightarrow \quad v = +60\,\text{cm}$$

Second refraction at concave lens L_2 for which object is image, produced by L_1

$u = +40$ cm lens

$f = -120$ cm formula

$$\frac{1}{f} = \frac{1}{v} - \frac{1}{u}$$

$$\Rightarrow \quad \frac{1}{v} = -\frac{1}{120} + \frac{1}{40} = \frac{1}{60}$$

$$\Rightarrow \quad v = +60\,\text{cm}$$

Third refraction at L_2 again for which I_3 is the object

$u = -40$ cm

$f = -120$ cm

Using lens formula

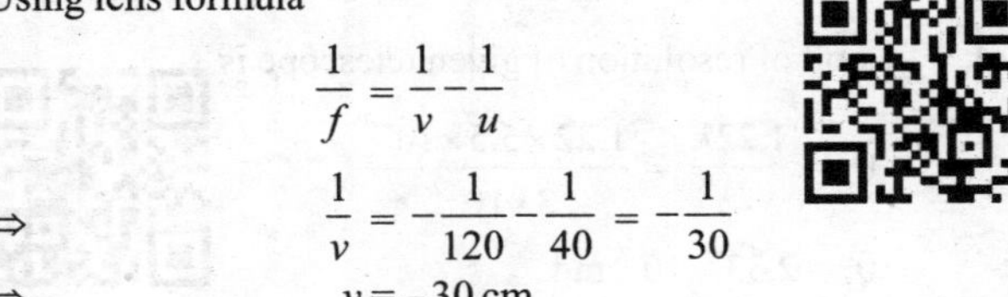

$$\frac{1}{f} = \frac{1}{v} - \frac{1}{u}$$

$$\Rightarrow \quad \frac{1}{v} = -\frac{1}{120} - \frac{1}{40} = -\frac{1}{30}$$

$$\Rightarrow \quad v = -30\,\text{cm}$$

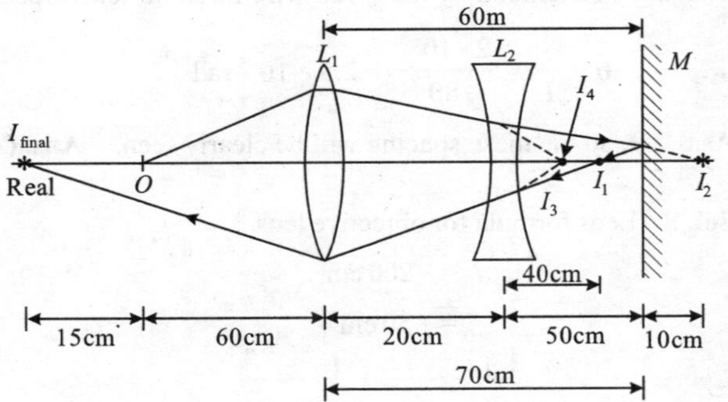

For the refraction at L_1 again for which I_4 is the object

$u = -50$ cm lens

$f = +30$ cm formula

$$\frac{1}{v} = \frac{1}{f} + \frac{1}{u} = \frac{1}{30} - \frac{1}{50} = \frac{5-3}{150} = \frac{1}{75}$$

$$\Rightarrow \quad v = 75\,\text{cm}$$

If whole combination ($L_1 + L_2 + M$) is used once then image produced I_3 is located at a distance 60 cm from the convex lens. So most appropriate answer here is option (A). **Ans. (A)**

23.4 Dispersion of Light

Sol. 1 For a prism of refracting angle A, the refractive index 'μ' and minimum deviation angle D' are related as

$$\mu = \frac{\sin\left(\frac{A+D}{2}\right)}{\sin\left(\frac{a}{2}\right)}$$

As μ increases for a given prism $\Rightarrow$ D increases

here $\mu_R = 1.520 \rightarrow D_1$

and $\mu_B = 1.525 \rightarrow D_2$

As $\mu_B > \mu_R$

$\Rightarrow$ $D_2 > D_1$ **Ans. (A)**

Sol. 2 We know that refractive index of a material, is related to light wavelength as

$$\mu = A + \frac{B}{\lambda^2}$$

So for blue light $\lambda_B < \lambda_R$

$\Rightarrow$ $\mu_B > \mu_R$

By lens makers formula, we use

$$\frac{1}{f} = (\mu - 1)\left[\frac{1}{R_1} - \frac{1}{R_2}\right]$$

As $\mu_B > \mu_R$

$\Rightarrow$ $f_B < f_R$ **Ans. (B)**

Sol. 3

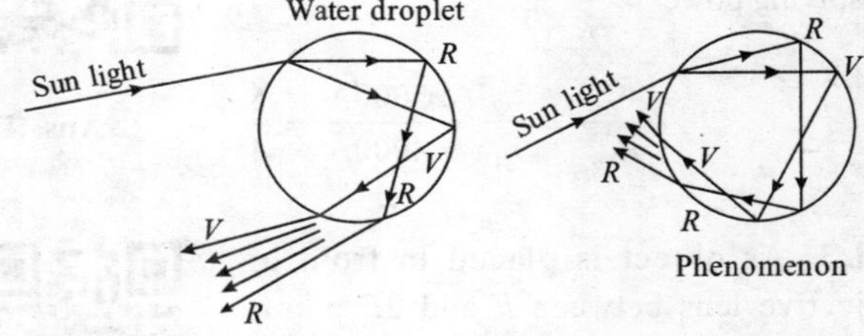

When light enters & emerges out from drop $\rightarrow$ refraction

At inner surface of drop $\rightarrow$ Internal reflection inside the drop $\rightarrow$ dispersion.

Here internal reflection is not total internal reflection but for the given options most appropriate is option (A) only. **Ans. (A)**

Sol. 4

For *TIR* at face *AC*

$$\theta_C < 45°$$

$$\Rightarrow \quad \sin\theta_C < \frac{1}{\sqrt{2}}$$

$$\Rightarrow \quad \frac{1}{\mu} < \frac{1}{\sqrt{2}} \quad \Rightarrow \mu > \sqrt{2}$$

Those colours which have $\mu > 1.414$ will suffer total internal reflection at face *AC* and will not come out.

$\Rightarrow$ Green & Blue colour light will not come out. **Ans. (D)**

23.5 Optical Instruments

Sol. 1 Resolving power of an astronomical telescope is given as

$$R_\lambda = \frac{D}{1.22\lambda}$$

$D \rightarrow$ Aperture diameter of objective lens

$\lambda \rightarrow$ Wavelength of light

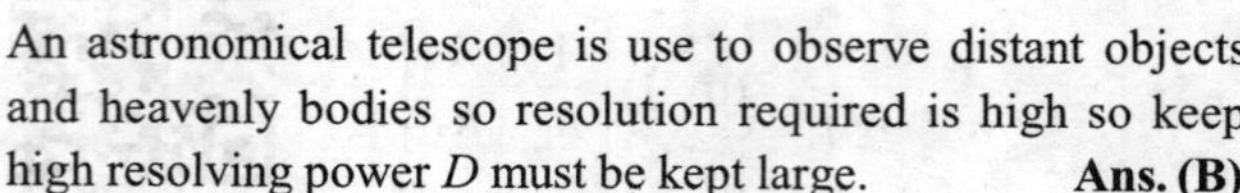

An astronomical telescope is use to observe distant objects and heavenly bodies so resolution required is high so keep high resolving power D must be kept large. **Ans. (B)**

Sol. 2 For an optical instrument we know that

$$\text{Resolving power} \propto \frac{1}{\lambda}$$

$$\Rightarrow \quad \frac{R_{\lambda_1}}{R_{\lambda_2}} = \frac{\lambda_2}{\lambda_1} = \frac{5000\text{Å}}{4000\text{Å}} = \frac{5}{4}$$ **Ans. (D)**

Sol. 3 As object is placed in front of objective lens between F and $2F$ points $\Rightarrow$ image produced is real and enlarged.

Ans. (C)

Sol. 4 Angular width of resolution

$$\theta = \frac{1.22\lambda}{D} = \frac{d}{x}$$

$$\Rightarrow \quad x = \frac{dD}{1.22\lambda} = \frac{10^{-3}\times 3\times 10^{-3}}{1.22\times 500\times 10^{-9}}$$

$$\Rightarrow \quad x = \frac{3}{1.22\times 0.5} = 4.92\text{ m} = 5\text{ m}$$ **Ans. (A)**

Sol. 5 For a travelling microscope readings are taken from meter scale on the vertical mount and vernier scale on the microscope.

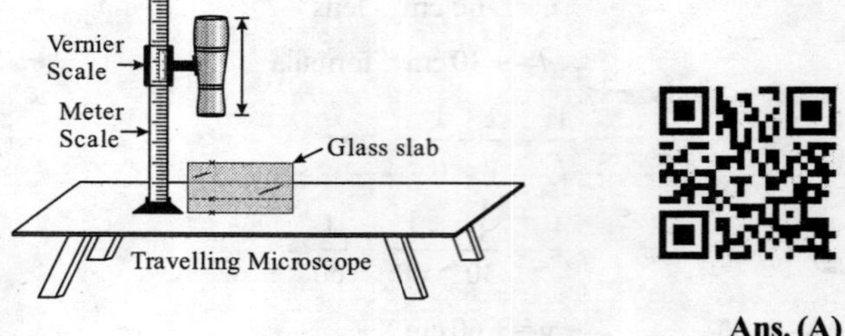

Ans. (A)

Sol. 6 For normal adjustment (to obtain final image at ∞) the image due to objective lens must be obtained at focal point of eyepiece lens as shown, lens formula for objective

$$f_e = +20\text{ mm}$$

$$u_e = -25\text{ mm}$$

$$\Rightarrow \quad \frac{1}{f_e} = \frac{1}{v_e} - \frac{1}{u_e}$$

$$\Rightarrow \quad \frac{1}{v_e} = \frac{1}{f_e} + \frac{1}{u_e} = \frac{1}{20} - \frac{1}{25} = \frac{1}{100}$$

$$\Rightarrow \quad v_e = 100\text{ mm}$$

lens separation $= f_e + v_e$

$$= 20\text{ mm} + 100\text{ mm} = 120\text{ mm}$$ **Ans. (C)**

Sol. 7 Limit of resolution of given telescope is

$$\theta_L = \frac{1.22\lambda}{D} = \frac{1.22\times 5.5\times 10^{-7}}{3\times 10^{-2}}$$

$$\Rightarrow \quad \theta_L = 2.33\times 10^{-5}\text{ rad}$$

The angle subtended by the given wire mesh on telescope is

$$\theta = \frac{x}{L} = \frac{2\times 10^{-3}}{80} = 2.5\times 10^{-5}\text{ rad}$$

As $\theta > \theta_L$ so the mesh spacing will be clearly seen. **Ans. (A)**

Sol. 8 Lens formula for objective lens

$$u_0 = -200\text{ cm}$$

$$f_0 = +50\text{ cm}$$

$$\Rightarrow \quad \frac{1}{f_0} = \frac{1}{v_0} - \frac{1}{u_0}$$

$$\Rightarrow \quad \frac{1}{50}=\frac{1}{v_0}+\frac{1}{200}$$

$$\Rightarrow \quad \frac{V}{v_0}=\frac{1}{50}-\frac{1}{200}=\frac{3}{200}$$

$$\Rightarrow \quad v_0=\frac{200}{3}\text{ cm}$$

Lens formula for eyepiece lens

$$u_e=-u_e$$

$$v_e=-D=-25\text{ cm}$$

$$\Rightarrow \quad \frac{1}{f_e}=\frac{1}{v_e}-\frac{1}{u_e}$$

$$\Rightarrow \quad \frac{1}{5}=-\frac{1}{25}+\frac{1}{u_e}$$

$$\Rightarrow \quad \frac{1}{u_e}=\frac{1}{5}+\frac{1}{25}=\frac{6}{25}$$

$$u_e=\frac{25}{6}\text{ cm}$$

Magnification produced by objective lens

$$M_0=\frac{v_0}{u_0}=\frac{+200/3}{-200}=-\frac{1}{3}$$

Magnification produced by objective lens

$$M_e=\frac{v_e}{u_e}=\frac{-25}{-25/6}=+6$$

Total magnification by telescope is

$$M_T=M_0\times M_e=-\frac{1}{3}\times 6=-2$$ **Ans. (D)**

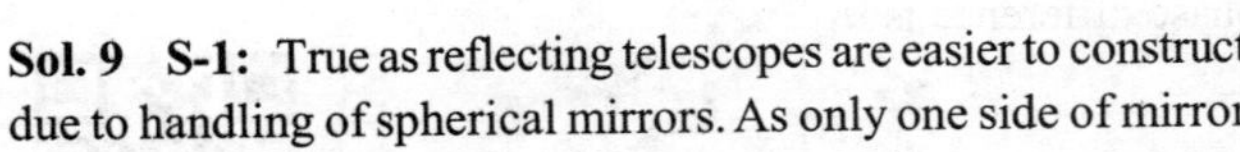

Sol. 9 S-1: True as reflecting telescopes are easier to construct due to handling of spherical mirrors. As only one side of mirror is used so on other side the mirror can be mounted where in case of lenses mounting can only be done at thin edges which is practically difficult. Thats why very large size telescopes are made by using mirrors instead of lenses

$\Rightarrow$ **S-2 :** It is true and explaining S-1. **Ans. (C)**

Sol. 10 For standard adjustment (image at D) of a telescope the magnifying power is given as

$$M=\frac{f_0}{f_e}\left(1-\frac{f_e}{D}\right)$$

$$\Rightarrow \quad M=\frac{30}{3}\left(1-\frac{3}{25}\right)$$

$$\Rightarrow \quad M=\frac{30}{3}\times\frac{22}{25}=\frac{44}{5}=8.8$$ **Ans. (D)**

Sol. 11 For normal adjustment (final image at ∞) the magnifying power of microscope is given as

$$M=\left|\frac{V_0}{u_0}\cdot\frac{D}{f_e}\right| \quad \ldots(1)$$

by using lens formula for objective lens, we have

$$\frac{1}{f_0}=\frac{1}{v_0}-\frac{1}{u_0}$$

$$\Rightarrow \quad \frac{1}{1.2}=\frac{1}{v_0}+\frac{1}{1.25}$$

$$\Rightarrow \quad \frac{1}{v_0}=\frac{1}{1.2}-\frac{1}{1.25}=\frac{1}{30}$$

$$\Rightarrow \quad v_0=30\text{ cm}$$

From-(1), we have

$$M=\frac{30}{1.25}\times\frac{25}{3}=200$$ **Ans. (A)**

Sol. 12 $D=0.25\times 2$

$$\Rightarrow \quad D=0.5\text{ cm}$$

We use for limit of resolution we have

$$\theta=\frac{1.22}{D}=\frac{d}{x}$$

$$\Rightarrow \quad d=\frac{1.22\lambda x}{D}=\frac{1.22\times 500\times 10^{-9}\times 0.25}{0.5\times 10^{-2}}$$

$$\Rightarrow \quad d=30.5\times 10^{-6}\text{ m}=30.5\ \mu\text{m}$$ **Ans. (B)**

Sol. 13 Magnifying power of telescope

$$M=\frac{\theta}{\alpha}=\frac{\text{Angle subtanded by image}}{\text{Angle subtanded by object}}$$

For normal setting we consider final image at ∞

from image $\quad \frac{\theta}{\alpha}=\frac{f_0}{f_e}$

$$\Rightarrow \quad \theta=\frac{f_0}{f_e}\cdot\alpha$$

$$\Rightarrow \quad \theta=\frac{150}{5}\times\frac{1}{20}$$

$$\Rightarrow \quad \theta=1.5\text{ rad}$$

$$\Rightarrow \quad \theta=1.5\times\frac{180^\circ}{\pi}=86^\circ$$

Closest possible option is (C). **Ans. (C)**

Sol. 14 As $\quad m=\frac{\text{Image size}}{\text{object size}}=20$

Angular magnification for normal condition

Angular size

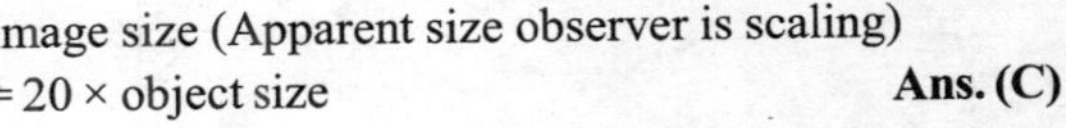

Image size (Apparent size observer is scaling)

$=20\times$ object size **Ans. (C)**

Sol. 15 Step-I : A reading of bottom surface = 'a' without slab

Step-II : A reading of bottom surface with the slab = 'b'

Step-III : A reading of top surface of slab = 'c'

$\Rightarrow$ Thickness of slab $t = a - c$ and we use

$$(a-b) = (a-c)\left[1-\frac{1}{\mu}\right]$$

$$\Rightarrow \quad 1-\left(\frac{a-b}{a-c}\right) = \frac{1}{\mu}$$

$$\Rightarrow \quad \mu = \left(\frac{a-c}{b-c}\right)$$

Thus readings a, b and c are required. **Ans. (C)**

24.1 Interference of Light

Sol. 1 Interference take place only when two or more coherent waves superpose

Coherence → The waves have exactly same frequency and constant (invarient in time) phase difference. **Ans. (D)**

Sol. 2

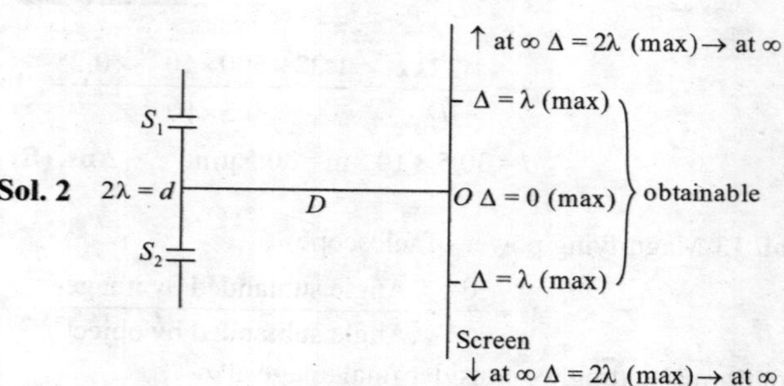

A maxima is obtained whenever path difference in waves from S_1 and S_2 is a multiple of λ, here out of 5 maxima only 3 can be obtained on screen in *YDSE*. **Ans. (C)**

Sol. 3 Case-I : If slits are considered as sources in *YDSE* for a source of light

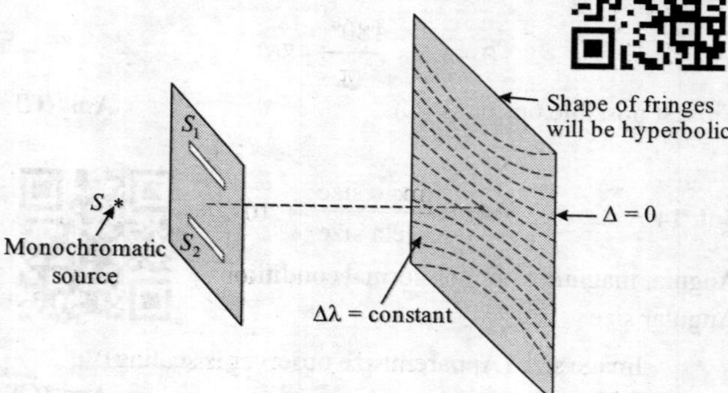

Because the locus of all points on screen which have path difference from S through S_1 and S_2 is constant is a hyperbola.

Case-II : If slits are considered as sources in *YDSE* for a line source

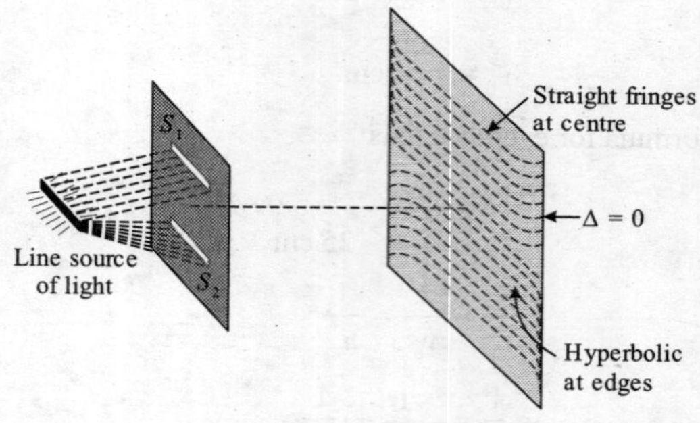

Here most appropriate is option (A). **Ans. (A)**

Sol. 4

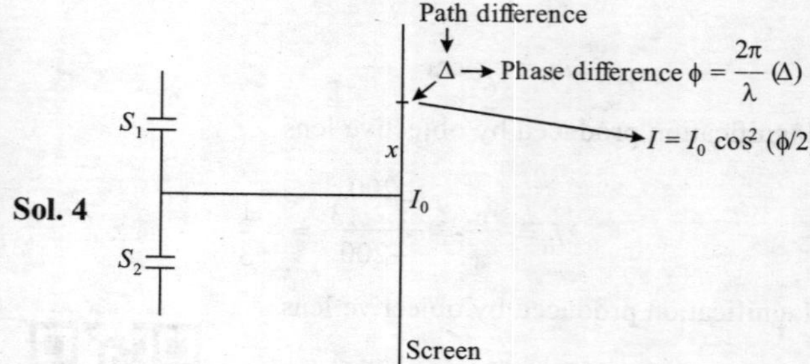

On either side of central maxima on screen the light intensity is given as

$$I = I_0 \cos^2(\phi/2) \quad \ldots(1)$$

Where $\phi \rightarrow$ phase difference between waves coming from S_1 and S_2 to that point for a point having path difference $\lambda/6$, then phase difference is

$$\phi = \frac{2\pi}{\lambda}(\Delta) = \frac{2\pi}{\lambda}\times\frac{\lambda}{6} = \frac{\pi}{3}$$

$\Rightarrow$ from equation-(1)

$$I = I_0\cos^2\left(\frac{\lambda}{6}\right) = I_0\left(\frac{\sqrt{3}}{2}\right)^2 = \frac{3I_0}{4}$$

$$\Rightarrow \quad \frac{I}{I_0} = \frac{3}{4}$$

Ans. (D)

Sol. 5 For a given wavelength of light used in *YDSE*, the distance of nth bright fringe from central maxima on screen is given as

$$x_{nB} = \frac{n\lambda D}{d}$$

[where $D \rightarrow$ distance between slit plane and screen]

[$d \rightarrow$ slit separation]

For known wavelength (λ_1) and unknown wavelength (λ_2) we use

$$\frac{3\lambda_1 D}{d} = \frac{4\lambda_2 D}{d}$$

$$\Rightarrow \quad \lambda_2 = \frac{3\lambda_1}{4} = \frac{3}{4} \times 590 \text{ nm}$$

$$\Rightarrow \quad \lambda_2 = 442.5 \text{ nm}$$

Ans. (A)

Sol. 6 Initially → beam is cylindrical

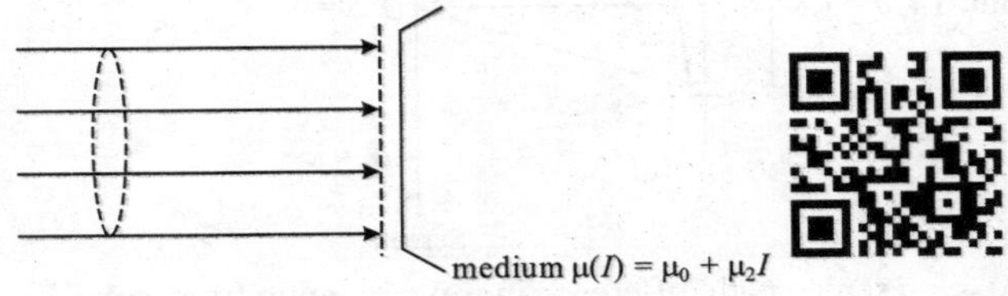

As light travel at same speed at all points of beam so wavefront will be planer. **Ans. (A)**

Sol. 7

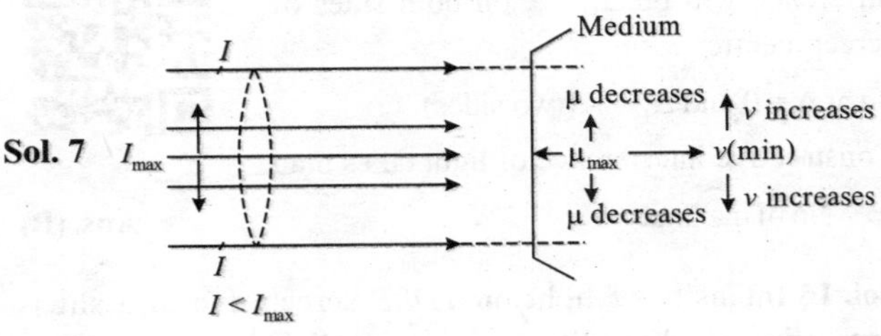

$$\mu(I) = \mu_0 + \mu_2 I \quad \ldots(1)$$

As on the two all sides of axis of beam as intensity of light decreases so from equation-(1) refractive index also decreases

$$\mu = \frac{\text{Speed of light in vaccum}}{\text{Speed in medium}} = \frac{c}{v}$$

$$\Rightarrow \quad v = \frac{c}{\mu}$$

Ans. (B)

Sol. 8

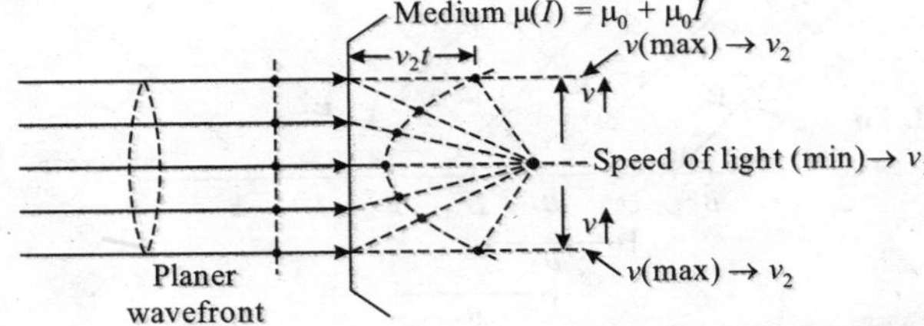

Concave wavefront after beam enters in medium

⇒ beam converges to a point. **Ans. (C)**

Sol. 9

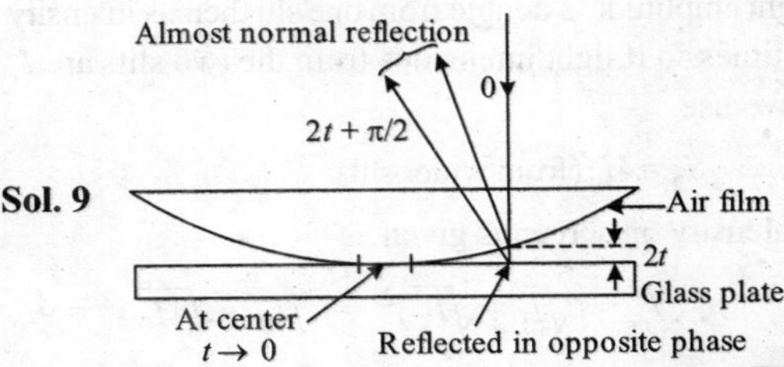

Statement-1 : It is true because a wave whenever reflected from a denser maximum suffers a phase change of π rad or a path delay of λ/2

⇒ $\Delta = \lambda/2 \to$ destructive interference ⇒ "dark"

⇒ **Statement-2 :** is true & explaining statement-1. **Ans. (D)**

Sol. 10 In first case as sources are coherent

So constructive interference take place at screen centre so the resulting intensity will be given as

$$I_1 = I_{max} = (\sqrt{I_1} + \sqrt{I_2})^2 = 4I_0 \quad \ldots(1)$$

In second case as slits are in coherent sources so no interference take place and intensity will be

$$I_2 = I_R = I_1 + I_2 = 2I_0 \quad [I_0 = kA] \quad \ldots(2)$$

Intensity due to each slit on screen

$$I_1 = I_2 = I_0$$

$$\frac{I_1}{I_2} = 2$$

Ans. (B)

Sol. 11

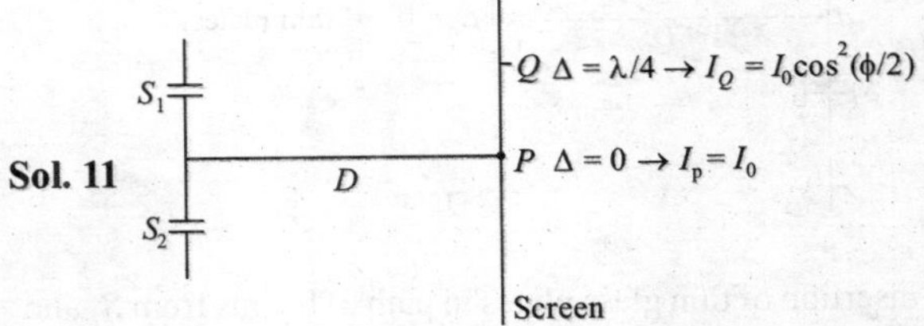

Intensity of light at a point on screen where phase difference between waves coming from S_1 and S_2 is & can be given as

$$I = I_0 \cos^2(\phi/2) \quad \ldots(1)$$

At point P as $\quad \Delta = 0 \Rightarrow \phi = 0$

So $\quad I_P = I_0$

and at point Q as

$$\Delta = \lambda/4$$

$$\Rightarrow \quad \phi = \frac{2\pi}{\lambda} \cdot \Delta = \frac{2\pi}{\lambda}\left(\frac{\lambda}{4}\right) = \frac{\pi}{2}$$

$$\Rightarrow \quad I_Q = I_0 \cos^2(\pi/4) = I_0\left(\frac{1}{\sqrt{2}}\right)^2 = \frac{I_0}{2}$$

$$\Rightarrow \quad \frac{I_P}{I_Q} = \frac{I_0}{I_0/2} = \frac{2}{1}$$

Ans. (B)

Sol. 12 If light amplitude is double from one slit then its intensity will be four times so if light intensities from the two slits are I_1 and I_2 then we use

If $I_1 = I_0 \Rightarrow I_2 = 4I_0$ (from wider slit)

Maximum intensity on screen is given as

$$I_m = (\sqrt{I_1} + \sqrt{I_2})^2 = (\sqrt{I_0} + \sqrt{4I_0})^2 = 9I_0$$

$$\Rightarrow \quad I_0 = \frac{I_m}{9}$$

For a phase difference ϕ, then resulting intensity is given as

$$I_R = I_1 + I_2 + 2\sqrt{I_1 I_2}\cos\phi \quad \ldots(1)$$

Using I_1 and I_2 in equation (1), we get

$$I_R = I_0 + 4I_0 + 2\sqrt{4I_0^2}\cos\phi$$

$$\Rightarrow \quad I_R = I_0(5 + 4\cos\phi)$$

$$\Rightarrow \quad I_R = \frac{I_m}{9}(5 + 4\cos\phi)$$

$$\Rightarrow \quad I_R = \frac{I_m}{9}(5 + 4(2\cos^2\phi/2 - 1))$$

$$\Rightarrow \quad I_R = \frac{I_m}{9}(1 + 8\cos^2\phi/2)$$

Ans. (A)

Sol. 13

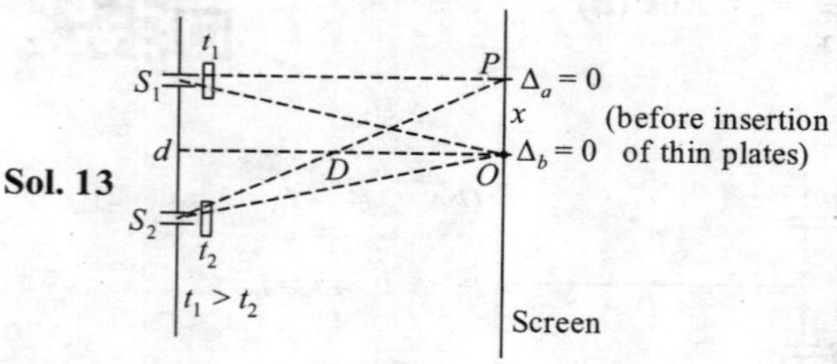

After insertion of thin glass plates in path of beams from S_1 and S_2 as shown, path difference at screen center becomes

$$\Delta_a = t_1(\mu - 1) - \mu_2(\mu - 1)$$

Say after insertion of plates at point P (above O) the physical path difference $\left(\frac{dx}{D}\right)$ will balance the optical path difference due to plates so finally effective path difference at P is zero at point P we use

$$\Delta_{ap} = \frac{dx}{D} - \Delta_a = 0$$

$$\Rightarrow \quad \frac{dx}{D} = t_1(\mu - 1) - t_2(\mu - 1)$$

$$\Rightarrow \quad x = \frac{D}{d}(\mu - 1)(t_1 - t_2) \quad \ldots(1)$$

In *YDSE* fringe width is given as

$$\beta = \frac{\lambda D}{d} \quad \Rightarrow \quad \frac{D}{d} = \frac{\beta}{\lambda}$$

$$\Rightarrow \text{ From (1)} \quad x = \frac{\beta}{\lambda}(\mu - 1)(t_1 - t_2)$$

Ans. (C)

Sol. 14 $d = 1.8\lambda$

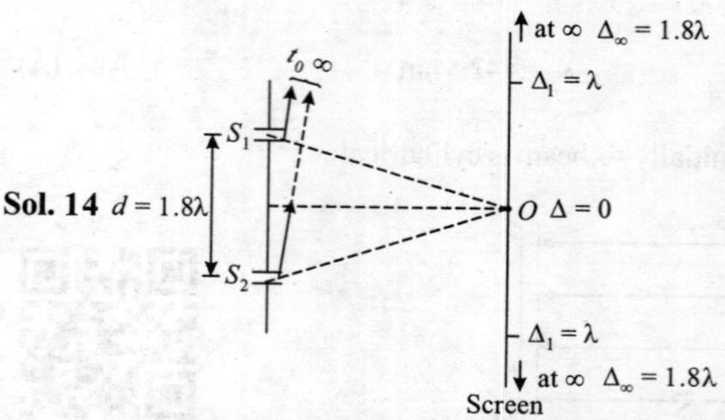

At ∞ on screen path difference in waves coming from states S_1 and S_2 is

$$\Delta_\infty = d = 1.8\lambda$$

between screen centre at ∞ somewhere path difference will be $\Delta_1 = \lambda$ on both sides of screen centre.

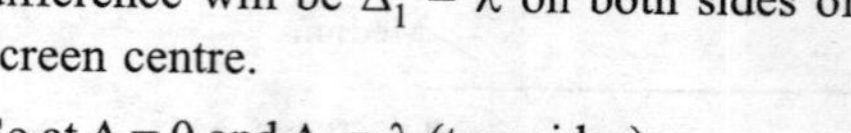

So at $\Delta = 0$ and $\Delta_1 = \lambda$ (two sides)

Constructive interference of light takes place

$\Rightarrow$ No of maxima = 3

Ans. (B)

Sol. 15 Intensity of light on *YDSE* screen due to a slit is proportional is slit width so we consider light intensities due to the two slits on screen are I_0 and 25 I_0.

The ratio of maximum to minimum intensities in interference pattern is given as

$$\frac{I_{max}}{I_{min}} = \left(\frac{\sqrt{I_1} + \sqrt{I_2}}{\sqrt{I_2} - \sqrt{I_1}}\right)^2$$

$$\Rightarrow \quad \frac{I_{max}}{I_{min}} = \left(\frac{5+1}{5-1}\right)^2 = \left(\frac{6}{4}\right)^2 = \frac{9}{4}$$

Ans. (C)

Sol. 16

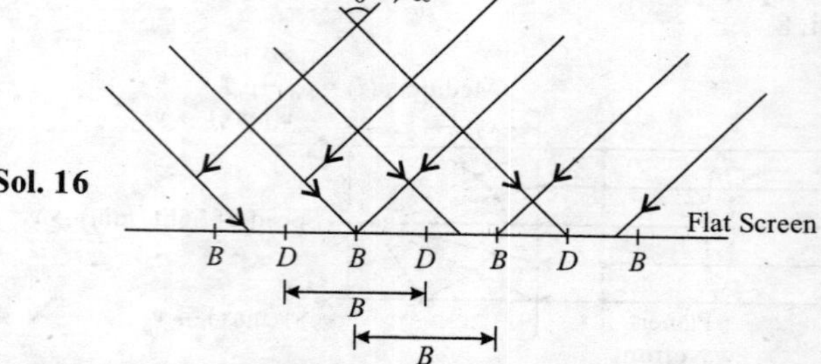

Fringe width for interference of parallel beams on a surface is given as

$$B = \frac{\lambda}{\alpha}$$

Ans. (B)

Sol. 17

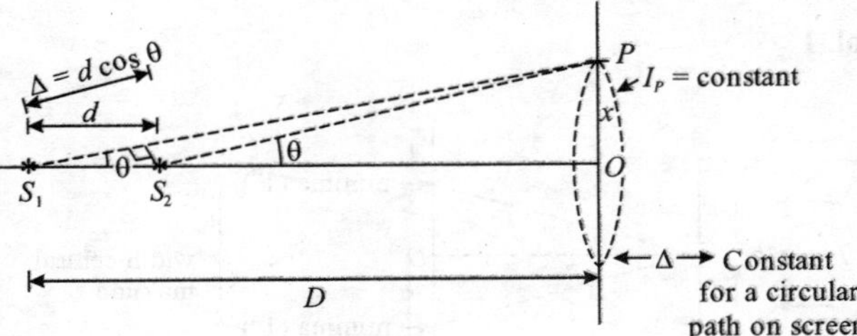

here $d << D$

On screen the locus of points where θ is a constant and at all these points path difference

$\Delta = d\cos\theta$ is a constant, will be a circle.

$\Rightarrow$ Fringes obtained are circular with centre at point O. **Ans. (D)**

Sol. 18 In *YDSE* fringe width is given as

$$\beta = \frac{\lambda D}{d}$$

$$\Rightarrow \qquad \beta \propto \lambda$$

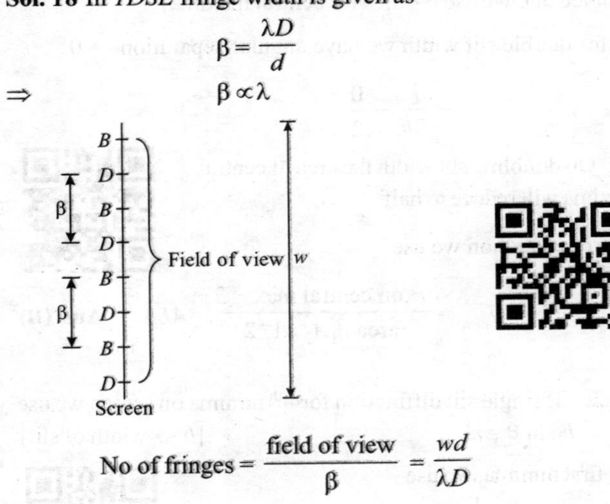

$$\text{No of fringes} = \frac{\text{field of view}}{\beta} = \frac{wd}{\lambda D}$$

$\Rightarrow$ No of fringes $\propto \frac{1}{\lambda}$

$\Rightarrow$ Statement-1 is true & statement-2 is also true and explaining statement-1. **Ans. (A)**

Sol. 19 For interference maxima of wavelength λ_1, the path difference we use bright fringe

$$\Delta = m\lambda_1 \qquad \ldots(1)$$

For interference minima (Dark fringe) of wavelength λ_2, the path difference we use

$$\Delta = (2n+1)\frac{\lambda_2}{2} \qquad \ldots(2)$$

At one point on screen if bright fringe of λ, coincides with dark fringe of λ_2 then we use

$$\Rightarrow \qquad \Delta = m\lambda_1 = (2n+1)\frac{\lambda_2}{2}$$

$$\Rightarrow \qquad \frac{m}{2n+1} = \frac{\lambda_2}{2\lambda_1} = \frac{600}{2\times 500} = \frac{3}{5}$$

For least distance from central maxima where these fringes coincide will be corresponding if

$$m = 3$$

and $\qquad 2n+1 = 5$

$$\Rightarrow \qquad \Delta = 3\lambda_1 = 3\times 500 = 1500\,\text{nm}$$ **Ans. (D)**

20.

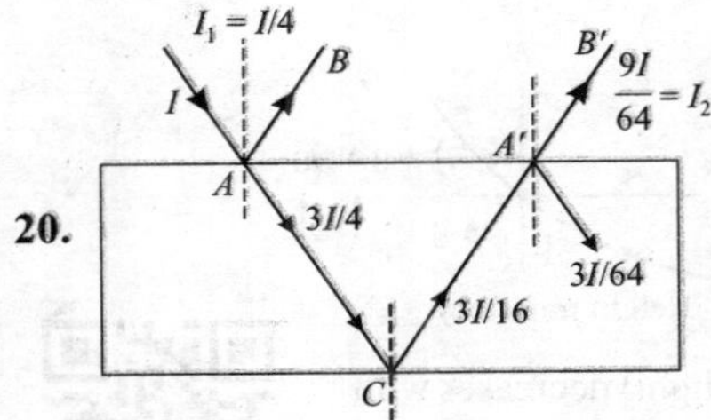

When rays AB and $A'B'$ interfere then the ratio of maximum to minimum intensity in interference pattern is given as

$$\frac{I_{max}}{I_{min}} = \left(\frac{\sqrt{I_1}+\sqrt{I_2}}{\sqrt{I_1}-\sqrt{I_2}}\right)^2 = \left(\frac{\sqrt{\frac{1}{4}}+\sqrt{\frac{9}{64}}}{\sqrt{\frac{1}{4}}-\sqrt{\frac{9}{64}}}\right)^2$$

$$\Rightarrow \qquad \frac{I_{max}}{I_{min}} = \left(\frac{\frac{1}{2}+\frac{3}{8}}{\frac{1}{2}-\frac{3}{8}}\right)^2$$

$$\Rightarrow \qquad \frac{I_{max}}{I_{min}} = \left(\frac{7}{1}\right)^2 = \frac{49}{1}$$ **Ans. (A)**

Sol. 21 For n coherent waves when, interfere constructively then resulting intensity is given as

$$I_{max} = n^2 I_0 \qquad \ldots(1)$$

for n non-coherent waves when superpose then resulting intensity at the point of superposition is given as

$$I'_{max} = nI_0 \qquad \ldots(2)$$

$$\Rightarrow \qquad \frac{I_{max}}{I_{max}} = \frac{n^2 I_0}{nI_0} = n$$ **Ans. (D)**

Sol. 22 If I_1 and I_2 are interfering intensities then maxima & minima intensities are given as

$$I_{max} = (\sqrt{I_1}+\sqrt{I_2})^2$$

and $\qquad I_{min} = (\sqrt{I_1}-\sqrt{I_2})^2$

$$\Rightarrow \qquad \frac{I_{max}}{I_{min}} = \left(\frac{4+3}{4-1}\right)^2 = \left(\frac{7}{1}\right)^2 = \frac{49}{1}$$ **Ans. (D)**

Sol. 23

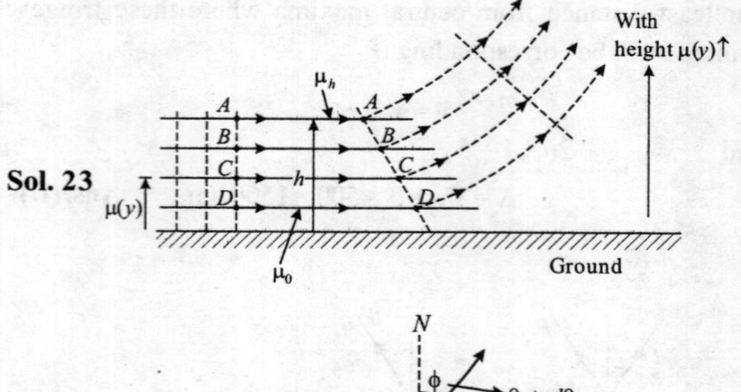

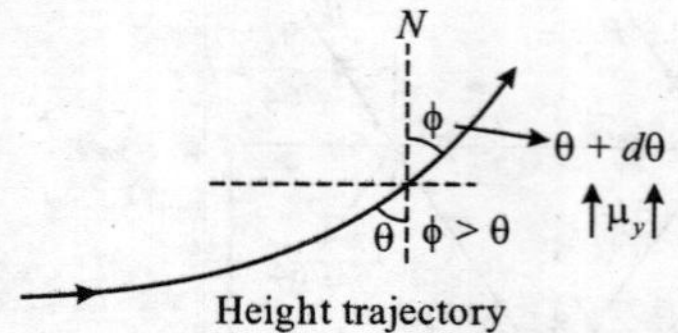

$\mu_h > \mu_0 \Rightarrow v$ (speed of light) decreases with height so the speed of light at some height is lesser then compared to ground. **Ans. (D)**

Sol. 24

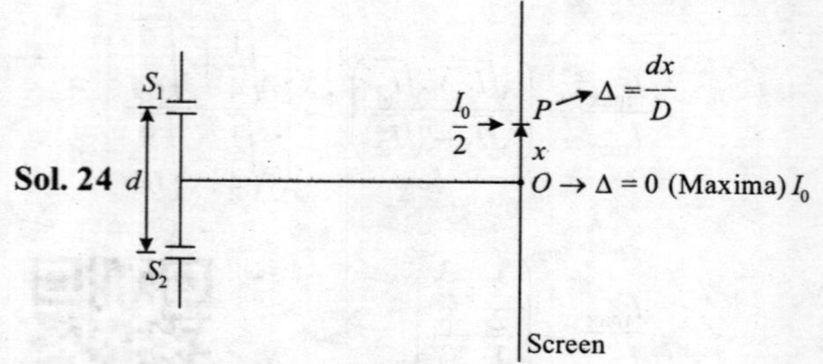

In *YDSE* fringe width is given as

$$\beta = \frac{\lambda D}{d} \qquad \ldots(1)$$

The path difference between waves reaching point P at a distance x from screen centre is

$$\Delta_P = \frac{dx}{D}$$

$\Rightarrow$ Phase difference at P

$$\phi_P = \frac{2\pi}{\lambda}\cdot\Delta_P = \frac{2\pi}{\lambda}\cdot\frac{dx}{D} \qquad \ldots(2)$$

If phase difference at point P is ϕ_P

$\Rightarrow$ Resulting light intensity at P is given as

$$I_P = I_0 \cos^2\left(\frac{\phi_P}{2}\right) = \frac{I_0}{2}$$

$$\Rightarrow \quad \cos^2\left(\frac{\phi_P}{2}\right) = \frac{1}{\sqrt{2}}$$

$$\Rightarrow \quad \frac{\phi_P}{2} = \frac{\pi}{4} \quad \text{or} \quad \phi_P = \frac{\pi}{2}$$

From equation-(2) we have

$$\phi_P = \frac{2\pi}{\lambda}\frac{dx}{D} = \frac{\pi}{2}$$

$$\Rightarrow \quad x = \frac{D\lambda}{4d} = \frac{\beta}{4}$$ **Ans. (C)**

24.2 Diffraction of Light

Sol. 1

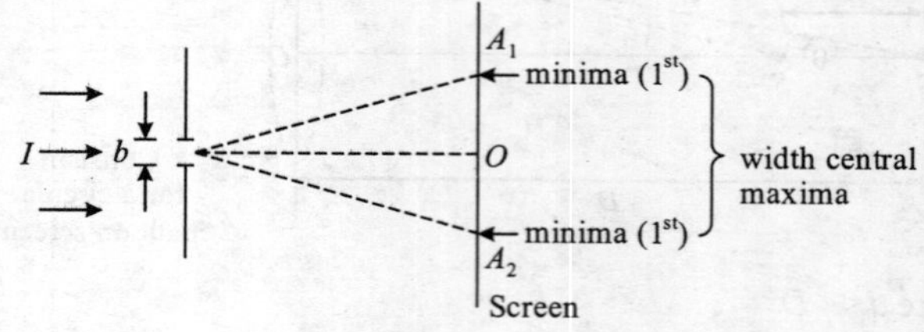

Intensity of central maxima on screen.

$$I_0 = \frac{\text{Power incident on central max}}{\text{area of screen }(A_1A_2)}$$

If slit width is doubled then power incident on screen will get doubled and we use $\theta = \frac{\lambda}{b}$ (for central maxima)

So for double slit width we have angular separation $\to \theta'$

$$= \frac{\lambda}{2b} = \frac{\theta}{2}$$

$\Rightarrow$ On doubling slit width the area of central maxima will reduce to half

So from equation we use

$$I_{new} = \frac{P \text{ on central max} \times 2}{\text{area } A_1A_2 \times 1/2} = 4I_0$$ **Ans. (B)**

Sol. 2 If single slit diffraction for n^{th} minima on screen we use

$b \sin\theta = n\lambda$ [$b \to$ width of slit]

For first minima, we use

$n = 1$

$\Rightarrow \quad b \sin\theta = \lambda$

$$\Rightarrow \quad b = \frac{\lambda}{\sin\theta} = \frac{5\times10^{-7}}{0.5} = 10\times10^{-7}\,\text{m}$$

$\Rightarrow \quad b = 10\times10^{-5}\,\text{cm}$ **Ans. (C)**

Sol. 3 **Statement-1 :** As we know wavelength of radio waves is more then that of microwaves so the diffraction possibility is more for radio waves because diffraction is more in case of wavelength of the order of obstacles in surrounding or in path of waves.

$\Rightarrow$ **Statement-1 :** is true

Statement-2 : As both are *EM* waves so for

$\lambda_R > \lambda_\mu$

$\Rightarrow \quad v_R < v_\mu$

$\Rightarrow$ **Statement-2 :** is false **Ans. (C)**

Sol. 4 The minimum separation between two lines which can be just resolved by a microscope is given as

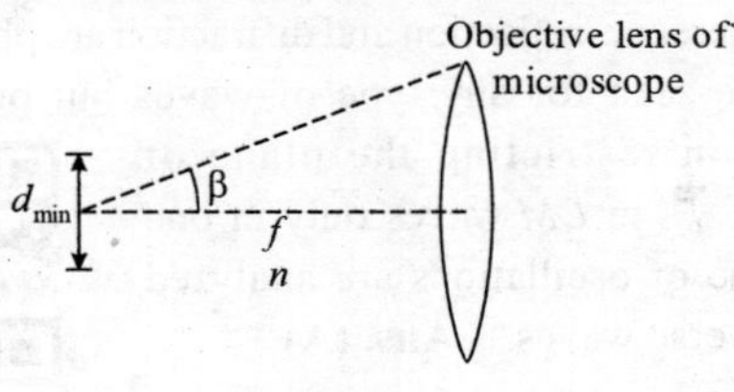

$$d_{min} = \frac{1.22\lambda}{2n\sin\beta}$$

Resolving power of microscope

$$R = \frac{1}{d_{min}} = \frac{2n\sin\beta}{1.22\lambda}$$

$$\sin 2\beta = 2\sin\beta\cos\beta$$

& for small β, we use

$$\cos\beta \simeq 1$$

$\Rightarrow$ $$R \propto n\sin 2\beta$$ **Ans. (C)**

Sol. 5

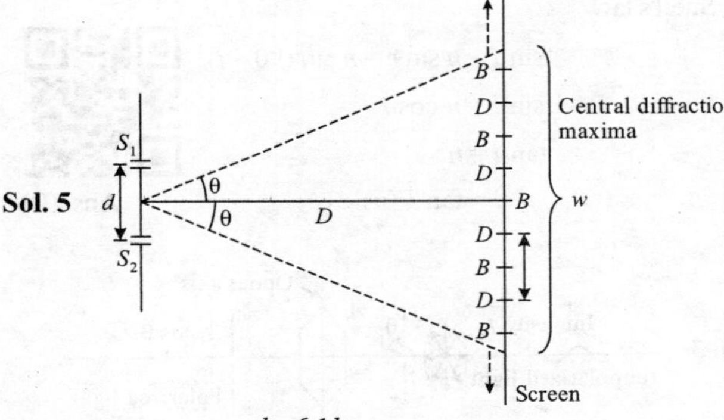

$$d = 6.1b$$

$b \rightarrow$ slit width

As interference of significant intensity of tight from the two slits will take place in the region of central diffraction maxima as shown in figure

Fringe width of *YDSE* pattern is

$$\beta = \frac{\lambda D}{d} \quad \ldots(1)$$

Angular width of central diffraction maxima is given as

$$2\theta = \frac{2\lambda}{b}$$

Width of central diffraction maxima is

$$w = 2\theta D = \frac{2\lambda D}{b} \quad \ldots(2)$$

No of bright fringes in width of central maxima is

$$N = \frac{w}{\beta} = \frac{2\lambda D}{b} \times \frac{d}{\lambda D}$$

We use $d = 1b$

$$\Rightarrow \quad N = \frac{2 \times 1.1b}{b} = 12.2$$

$\Rightarrow$ Complete 12 bright fringes are obtained in width of central maxima. **Ans. (C)**

Sol. 6 In a single slit diffraction pattern if θ is angular position of a point on screen from central maxima then we have

For a wavelength λ_1 (red light) at the position of first minimum we use

$$b\sin\theta = \lambda_1 \quad \ldots(1)$$

For one there wavelength λ_1 at the same angle θ for first maximum, we use

$$b\sin\theta = \frac{3\lambda_2}{2} \quad \ldots(2)$$

We use from (1) and (2)

$$\lambda_1 = \frac{3\lambda_2}{2}$$

$$\Rightarrow \quad \lambda_2 = \frac{2\lambda_1}{3} = \frac{2 \times 6600}{3}$$

$$= 4400 \text{ Å}$$ **Ans. (B)**

Sol. 7

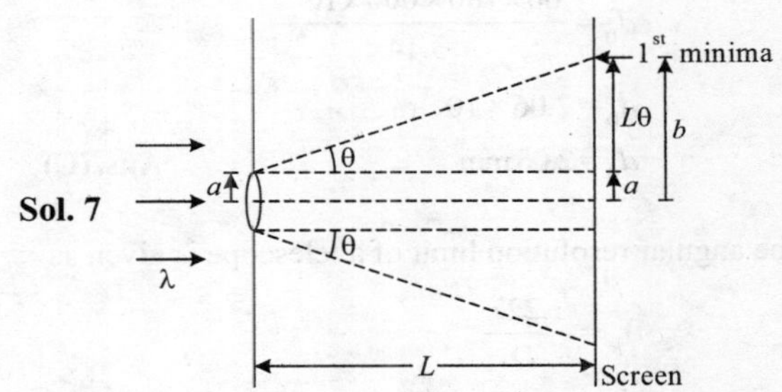

The angular position of first diffraction minima on either side of the hole is

$$a\sin\theta = \lambda \quad [n = 1]$$

$$\sin\theta = \frac{\lambda}{a}$$

For small θ we use

$$\theta = \frac{\lambda}{a} \quad [\sin\theta \simeq \theta]$$

The radius of spot can be given as

$$b = L\theta + a$$

Spread due to differaction = Geometric spread

$$\Rightarrow \quad b = \frac{L\lambda}{a} + a$$

b is minimum when

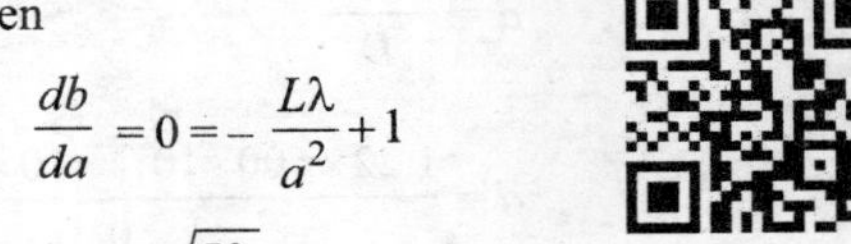

$$\frac{db}{da} = 0 = -\frac{L\lambda}{a^2} + 1$$

$$\Rightarrow \quad a = \sqrt{L\lambda}$$

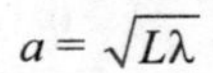

So $$b_{min} = \frac{L\lambda}{\sqrt{L\lambda}} + \sqrt{L\lambda} = 2\sqrt{L\lambda}$$ **Ans. (C)**

Sol. 8

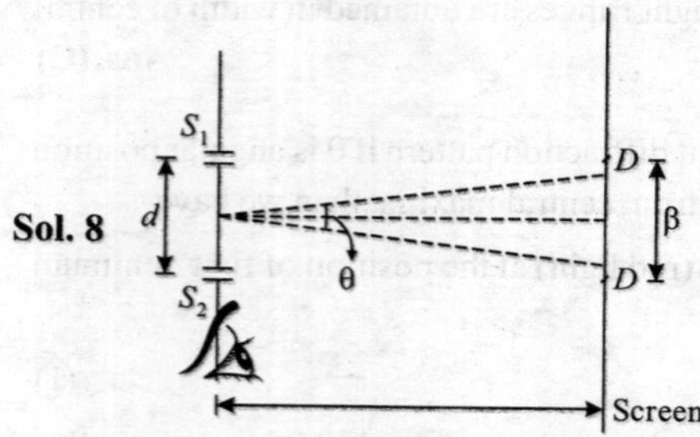

Angular fringe width in *YDSE* is given as

$$\theta = \frac{\beta}{D} = \frac{(\lambda D/d)}{D} = \frac{\lambda}{d}$$

Fringes will not be clearly seen by observer if $\theta < \theta_R$ (resolution limit of eye)

The fringes will just disappear at $d = d_0$

$\Rightarrow$ We use $\theta = \theta_R$ at $d = d_0$

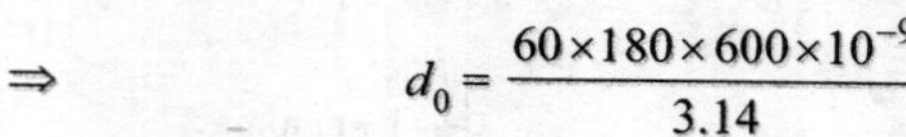

$$\frac{\lambda}{d_0} = \frac{1}{60} \times \frac{\pi}{180}$$

$$\Rightarrow \quad d_0 = \frac{60 \times 180 \times 600 \times 10^{-9}}{3.14}$$

$$\Rightarrow \quad d_0 = 2.06 \times 10^{-3}\,\text{m}$$

$$\Rightarrow \quad d_0 = 2.06\,\text{mm}$$

Ans. (C)

Sol. 9 The angular resolution limit of a telescope is given as

$$\theta_R = \frac{1.22\lambda}{D}$$

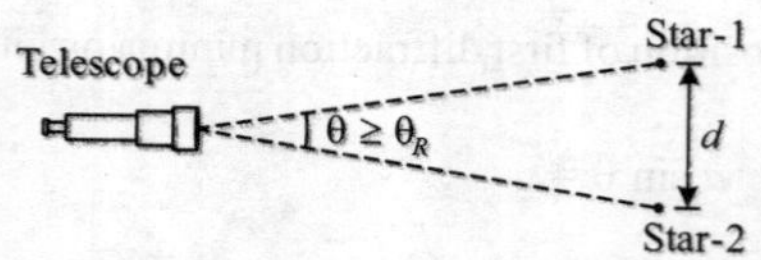

The two starts will be just resolved by the telescope when

$$L = 10 \text{ light yr}$$

$$\theta = \frac{d}{L}$$

$$\theta = \theta_R$$

$$\Rightarrow \quad \frac{d}{L} = \frac{1.22\lambda}{D}$$

$$\Rightarrow \quad d = \frac{1.22\lambda}{D}$$

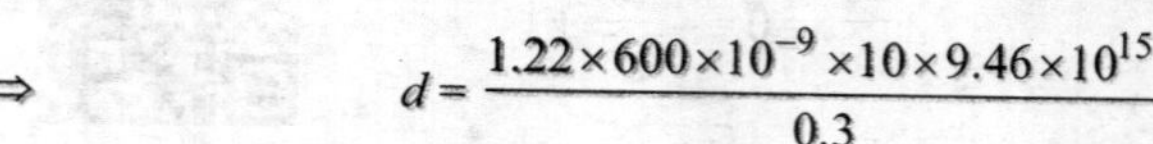

$$\Rightarrow \quad d = \frac{1.22 \times 600 \times 10^{-9} \times 10 \times 9.46 \times 10^{15}}{0.3}$$

$$\Rightarrow \quad d = 2.308 \times 10^{11}\,\text{m}$$

$$\Rightarrow \quad d = 2.308 \times 10^{8}\,\text{km}$$

Ans. (A)

24.3 Polarization of Light

Sol. 1 Interference, reflection and diffraction are phenomenon which can be seen for any type of waves but polarization is based upon restricting the plane of oscillation of $\vec{E}$ in *EM* waves only in one plane & plane of oscillations are analyzed only in transverse waves. **Ans. (A)**

Sol. 2 Using Brewster's law, we have reflected light is completely polarized when IR incident at such an angle for which reflected and refracted ray are mutually perpendicular

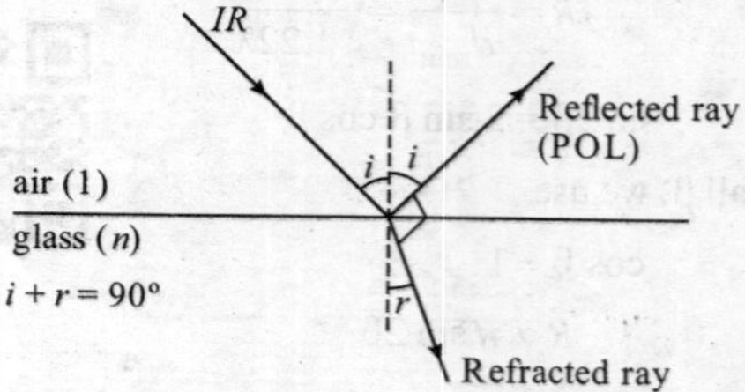

By Snell's law

$$\sin i = n \sin r = n \sin (90 - i)$$

$$\sin i = n \cos i$$

$$\Rightarrow \quad \tan i = n$$

$$\Rightarrow \quad i = \tan^{-1}(n)$$

Ans. (D)

Sol. 3

If a specific oscillation is considered before incidence on polarizer which has oscillations at an angle θ to optic axis as shown then in polarized light $A \cos\theta$ component will be transmitted so total intensity of polarized light can be given as

$$I_0 = \Sigma k A_i^2 = kA^2$$

$$I_P = k\Sigma(A_i \cos\theta_i)^2$$

$$I_P = kA_i^2\,(\Sigma\cos^2\theta_i) \text{ (average)}$$

$$I_P = kA_i^2\left(\frac{1}{2}\right) = \frac{1}{2}kA^2 = \frac{1}{2}I_0$$

Here half incident light intensity does not get transmitted.

Ans. (A)

Sol. 4 When sunlight is scattered by air particles in atmosphere

$$\text{Scattering} \propto \frac{1}{\lambda^4}$$

$\Rightarrow$ λ is least for blue/violet light so sky appears blue.

When light is seen at a specific region of atmosphere then polarized light due to scattering also enters the observer's eye so through polarizer (analyzer) light intensity varies on rotating it. **Ans. (C)**

Sol. 5

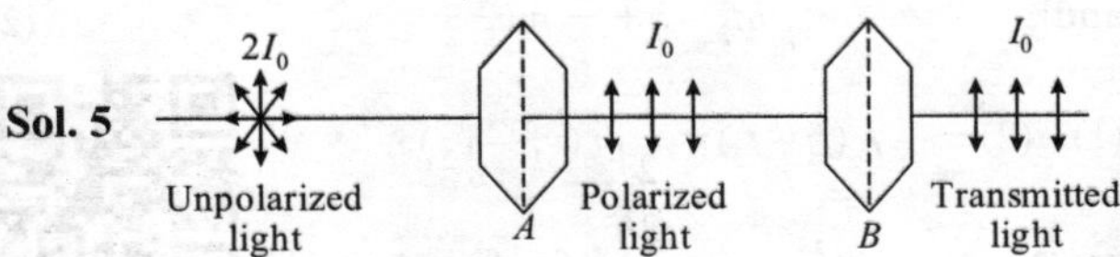

Final situation

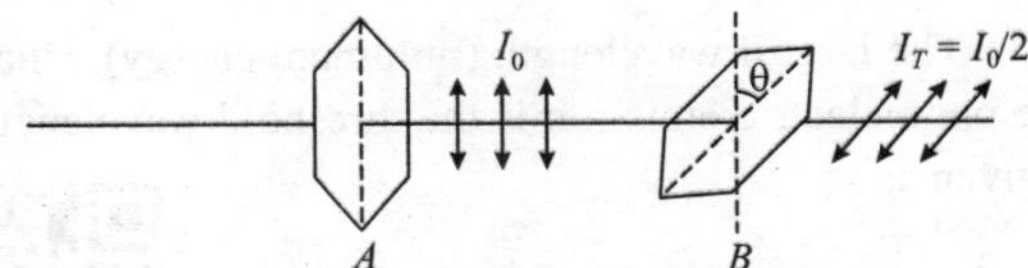

By Malus law the intensity of transmitted beam is

$$I_T = I_0 \cos^2 \theta$$

$$\Rightarrow \quad \frac{I_0}{2} = I_0 \cos^2\theta$$

$$\Rightarrow \quad \cos \theta = \frac{1}{\sqrt{2}}$$

$$\Rightarrow \quad \theta = 45°, 135°, 225°, 315°$$ **Ans. (A)**

Sol. 6

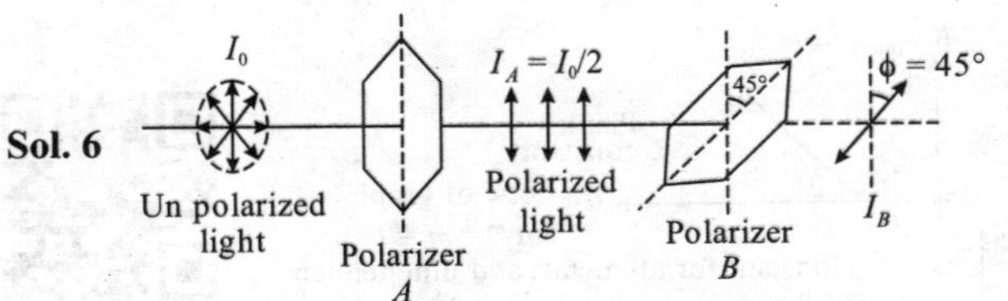

Intensity of light emerging from polarizer B is given by Malus law as

$$I_B = I_A \cos^2 \phi = \frac{I_0}{2} \cos^2(45°)$$

$$\Rightarrow \quad I_B = \frac{I_0}{2} \times \left(\frac{1}{\sqrt{2}}\right)^2 = \frac{I_0}{4}$$ **Ans. (C)**

7.

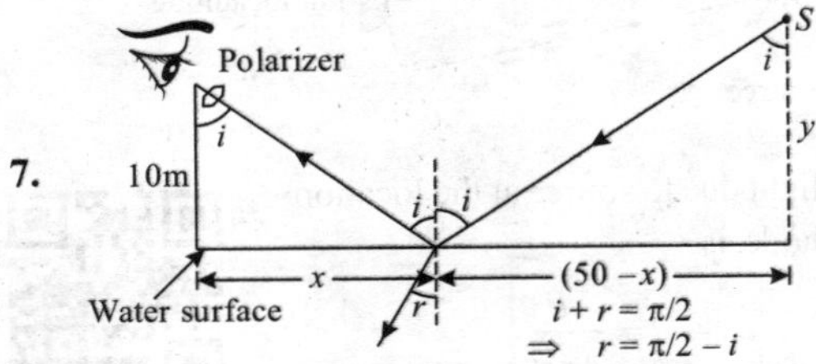

We use Snell's law at the point of reflection

$$\sin i = \mu_\omega \sin r$$

$$\Rightarrow \quad \sin i = \mu_\omega \sin\left(\frac{\pi}{2} - 1\right)$$

$$\Rightarrow \quad \tan i = \mu_\omega = \frac{4}{3}$$

In the figure shown we use

$$\tan i = \frac{x}{10} = \frac{50 - x}{y} = \frac{4}{3} \qquad \ldots(1)$$

$$\Rightarrow \quad y = \frac{10(50 - x)}{x}$$

and $$x = \frac{40}{3} m = 13.33 \text{ m}$$

$$\Rightarrow \quad y = \frac{10\left(50 - \frac{40}{3}\right)}{\frac{40}{3}} = \frac{3}{4} \times \frac{110}{3} = 27.5 \text{ m}$$ **Ans. (B)**

Sol. 8

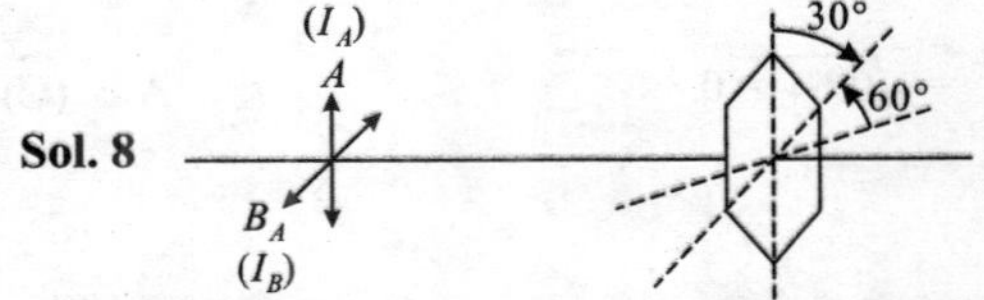

Here the polaroid axis after rotation by 30° from polarization plane of light A it is at an angle 60° from the polarization plane of light B.

By Malus law the transmitting intensities of lights A and B are

$$I_{AT} = I_A \cos^2 30°$$

and $$I_{BT} = I_B \cos^2 60°$$

Given that $$I_{AT} = I_{BT}$$

$$\Rightarrow \quad I_A \cos^2 30° = I_B \cos^2 60°$$

$$\Rightarrow \quad \frac{I_A}{I_B} = \frac{\cos^2 60°}{\cos^2 30°} = \frac{\left(\frac{1}{2}\right)^2}{\left(\frac{\sqrt{3}}{2}\right)^2} = \frac{1}{3}$$ **Ans. (D)**

Sol. 9

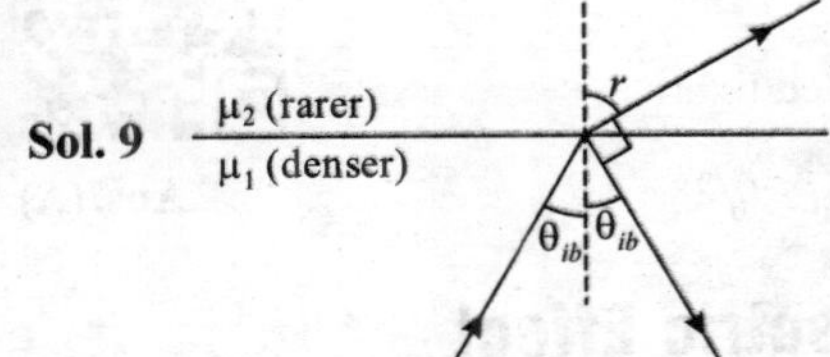

For Brewster's angle of incidence, we use

$$r = \frac{\pi}{2} - \theta_{ib}$$

By Snell's law, we have

$$\mu_1 \sin \theta_{ib} = \mu_2 \sin r = \mu_2 \sin\left(\frac{\pi}{2} - \theta_{ib}\right)$$

We use $$\sin \theta_{ic} = \frac{\mu_2}{\mu_1} \qquad \ldots(1)$$

$$\Rightarrow \quad \mu_1 \sin \theta_{ib} = \mu_2 \cos \theta_{ib}$$

We also use $$\frac{\sin \theta_{ic}}{\sin \theta_{ic}} = 1.28 \qquad \ldots(2)$$

$$\Rightarrow \quad \frac{\mu_2}{\mu_1} = \frac{\sin \theta_{ib}}{\cos \theta_{ib}} \qquad \ldots(3)$$

From (1), (2) and (3) we get

$$\sin\theta_{ic} = \frac{\sin\theta_{ib}}{\cos\theta_{ib}}$$

$$\Rightarrow \quad \cos\theta_{ib} = \frac{1}{1.28}$$

So from equation-(3), we have

$$\frac{\mu_2}{\mu_1} = \frac{\sin\theta_{ib}}{\cos\theta_{ib}} = \frac{\sqrt{1-\cos^2\theta_{ib}}}{\cos\theta_{ib}}$$

$$\Rightarrow \quad \frac{\mu_2}{\mu_1} = \sqrt{\left(\frac{1}{\cos\theta_{ib}}\right)^2 - 1} = \sqrt{(1.28)^2 - 1}$$

$$\Rightarrow \quad \frac{\mu_2}{\mu_1} = \sqrt{0.64} = 0.8$$

Ans. (C)

Sol. 10

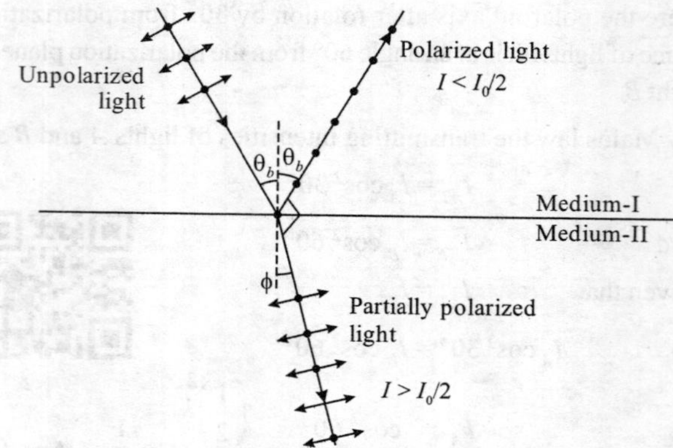

As transmitted light is partially polarized and it also contains the oscillation in the plane parallel to boundary which are there is reflected light.

So intensity of reflected light

$$I_{\text{reflected}} < I_0/2$$

Ans. (A)

25.1 Photoelectric Effect

Sol. 1 As we know work function ϕ and threshold wavelength λ_{th} are related as

$$\phi = \frac{hc}{\lambda_{\text{th}}}$$

$$\Rightarrow \quad \phi \propto \frac{1}{\lambda_{\text{th}}}$$

We use $$\frac{\phi_{Na}}{\phi_{Cu}} = \frac{\lambda_{Cu}}{\lambda_{Na}} = \frac{2.3}{4.5}$$

$$\Rightarrow \quad \frac{\lambda_{Na}}{\lambda_{Cu}} = \frac{45}{23} \simeq \frac{2}{1}$$

Ans. (C)

Sol. 2 For photoelectric effect of given light frequencies on photocathods (work function = ϕ) we use

$$hf_1 = \phi + \frac{1}{2}mv_1^2 \quad \ldots(1)$$

and $$hf_2 = \phi + \frac{1}{2}mv_2^2 \quad \ldots(2)$$

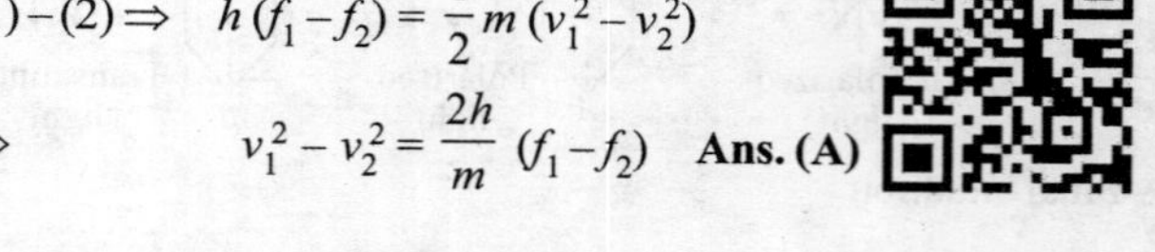

$$(1)-(2) \Rightarrow \quad h(f_1 - f_2) = \frac{1}{2}m(v_1^2 - v_2^2)$$

$$\Rightarrow \quad v_1^2 - v_2^2 = \frac{2h}{m}(f_1 - f_2)$$

Ans. (A)

Sol. 3 The largest wavelength (minimum energy) which can cause photoelectric emission is the threshold wavelength and it is given as :

$$\frac{hc}{\lambda_{\text{th}}} = \phi$$

$$\Rightarrow \quad \lambda_{\text{th}} = \frac{hc}{\phi} = \frac{6.63\times10^{-34}\times3\times10^8}{4\times1.6\times10^{-19}}$$

$$\Rightarrow \quad \lambda_{\text{th}} = \frac{12431}{4}\,\text{Å} \simeq 310.8\ \text{nm}$$

Ans. (C)

Sol. 4 In photo electric effect for a radiation frequency $\nu\,(\nu > \nu_{\text{th}})$ when falls on a metal with work function ϕ then these are related to the $KE_{(\text{max})}$ of ejected electron as

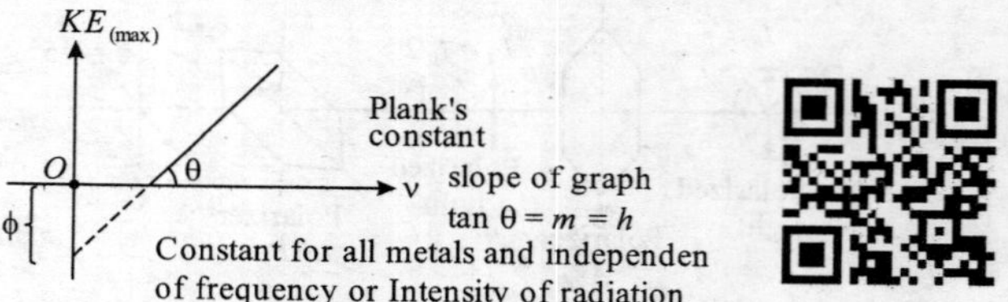

$$h\nu = \phi + KE_{\text{max}}$$

$$\Rightarrow \quad KE_{\text{max}} = h\nu - \phi$$

$$y = mx + c$$

Ans. (D)

Sol. 5

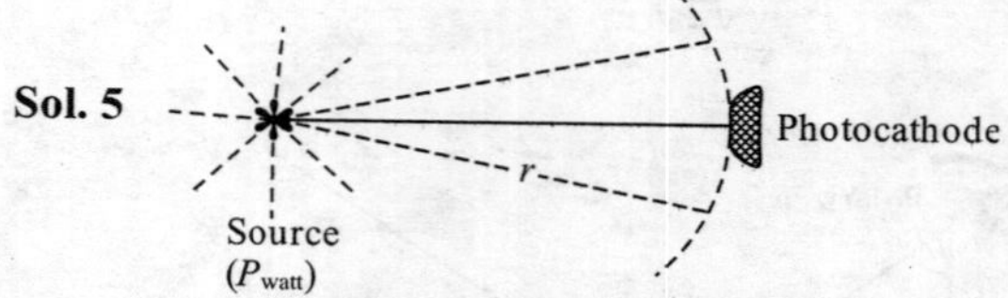

Intensity of light due to source at the location of photocathode is

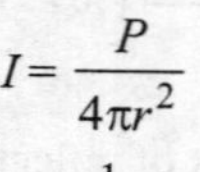

$$I = \frac{P}{4\pi r^2}$$

Here $$I \propto \frac{1}{r^2}$$

So when distance r is changed from 1 m to 0.5 m so intensity will become 4 times.

$\Rightarrow$ Number of ejected electrons will also increase by a factor of 4.

Ans. (B)

Sol. 6

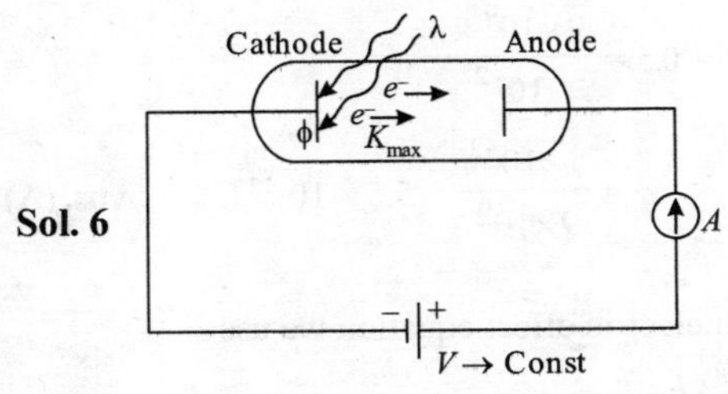

At cathode we use

$$\frac{hc}{\lambda} = \phi = K_{max}$$

As $\lambda \uparrow$ the energy $\frac{hc}{\lambda} \downarrow \Rightarrow K_{max} \downarrow$

As $K_{max} \downarrow \Rightarrow$ less electrons will reach anode $\Rightarrow$ current I decreases. **Ans. (B)**

Sol. 7 As threshold frequency gives the work function of a metal surface

$$\Rightarrow \quad \phi = h\nu_{th} = 6.2 \text{ eV}$$

Stopping potential for a metal surface gives the maximum kinetic energy for ejected photoelectrons

$$\Rightarrow \quad KE_{max} = eV_0 = 5 \text{ eV}$$

Energy of incident radiation

$$E_i = \phi = KE_{max} = 6.2 + 5 = 11.2 \text{ eV}$$

Wavelength λ of incident radiation is given as

$$\lambda = \frac{hc}{E_i} = \frac{12431}{11.2} \text{ Å} \approx 1109.9 \text{ Å}$$

As *UV* region wavelength exist from ~ 100 Å to 4000 Å

Ans. (A)

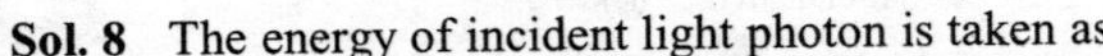

Sol. 8 The energy of incident light photon is taken as

$$E = \frac{hc}{\lambda} = \frac{12431}{4000} \text{ eV} = 3.10 \text{ eV}$$

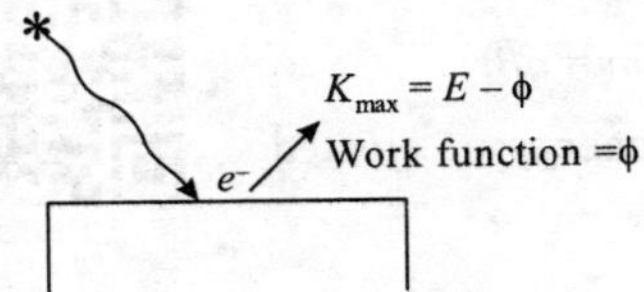

Here we use $KE_{max} = E - \phi$

$$1.68 = 3.10 - \phi$$

$$\Rightarrow \quad \phi = 3.10 - 1.68 = 1.42 \text{ eV}$$ **Ans. (D)**

Sol. 9 In Statement-1 we use

$$E_i = h\nu = \phi + KE_{max} \quad \ldots(1)$$

and stopping potential

$$V_0 = \frac{KE_{max}}{e}$$

When UV light is replaced by X-rays. Then we use $E_{i_2} > E_{i_1}$

$$\Rightarrow \quad KE_{max_2} > KE_{max_1}$$

from equation-(1) as ϕ is a constant KE_{max} increases with E_i

$$\Rightarrow \quad V_{0_2} > V_{0_1}$$

$\Rightarrow$ Statement-1 is True

In Statement-2 we have

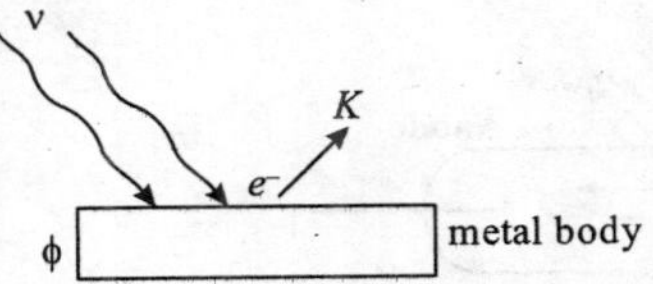

electrons in the process of ejection from metal surface looses some energy in collisions and other phenomenon so ejected KE is less than KE_{max}.

$\Rightarrow$ Statement-2 is False. **Ans. (A)**

Sol. 10 For Statement-1 we know in photoelectric effect

$$h\nu = \phi + KE_{max} \quad \ldots(1)$$

$$\Rightarrow \quad h\nu = \phi + eV_0 \quad \ldots(2)$$

Due to doubling the value of frequency ν, KE_{max} and V_0 will not get doubled.

$\Rightarrow$ Statement-1 is false and Statement-2 is true as by equation (1) and (2) it is clear that KE_{max} and V_0 are linearly dependent on frequency ν. **Ans. (B)**

Sol. 11 Photocurrent $\propto$ photon flux of incident light (Intensity of light)

and $\quad KE_{max} = h\nu - \phi$

if $\nu \leftarrow 2\nu \Rightarrow \quad KE'_{max} = 2h\nu - \phi$

$$\Rightarrow \quad KE'_{max} > 2KE_{max}$$

$\Rightarrow$ Statement-1 is False

For Statement-2

As $\quad KE_{max} = h\nu - \phi$

linear function

$\Rightarrow$ Statement-2 is True **Ans. (B)**

Sol. 12 (A) Threshold frequency $\nu_{th} = \frac{W}{h}$. So to emit electrons $\nu > \nu_{th}$

$\Rightarrow$ (A) is correct

(B) As there is no time leg in absorption of a photon and emission of electron

$\Rightarrow$ (B) is correct

(C) By photo electric effect equation max kinetic energy of ejected electrons is given as

$$KE_{max} = h\nu - W$$

$\Rightarrow$ (C) is wrong

(D) As KE_{max} depends only on incident frequency

$\Rightarrow$ (D) is correct **Ans. (C)**

Sol. 13

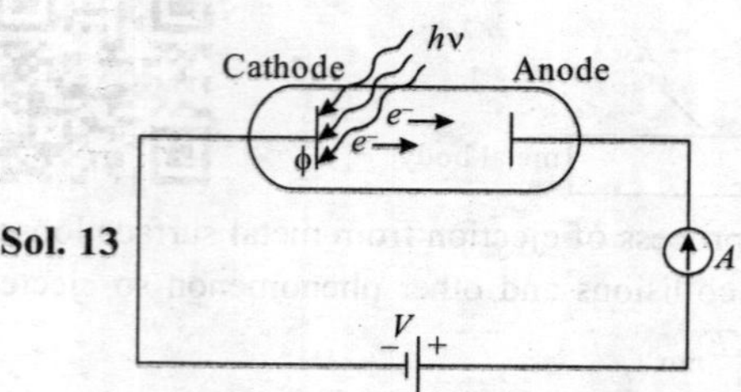

For photoelectric effect at cathode we use

$$h\nu = \frac{hc}{\lambda} = \phi + KE_{max}$$

As $\lambda \uparrow \Rightarrow \frac{hc}{\lambda} \downarrow$ and $KE_{max} \downarrow$

At lesser KE of ejected electrons the circuit current reduces. **Ans. (D)**

Sol. 14

λ = 2500Å

$KE = 0.5$ eV

$\phi = 4.47$ eV

$$r = 1\text{ cm} = 10^{-2}\text{ m}$$

Energy of incident photon is

$$E_i = \frac{hc}{\lambda}$$

$$\Rightarrow \quad E_i = \frac{12431}{2500} = 4.97\text{ eV}$$

Maximum kinetic energy of ejected e^- from ball is

$$KE_{max} = E_i - \phi = 4.97 - 4.47 = 0.5\text{ eV}$$

As positive charge gets accumulated on ball due to ejection of electrons, this positive charge will attract back the ejected electrons, these electrons will not escape from ball if ball's potential will rise to 0.5 V.

If q is the charge acquired by ball upto this time, then we use

$$V = \frac{kq}{r} = \frac{1}{4\pi\varepsilon_0} \cdot \frac{q}{r}$$

$$\Rightarrow \quad 0.5 = \frac{9\times10^9 \times q}{10^{-2}}$$

$$\Rightarrow \quad q = \frac{5\times10^{-3}}{9\times10^9} = 5.5\times10^{-13}\text{ C}$$ **Ans. (A)**

Sol. 15 By Photo electric effect equation we use

$$\frac{hc}{\lambda} = \phi + eV_0$$

$$\Rightarrow \quad V_0 = \left(\frac{hc}{e}\right)\frac{1}{\lambda} - \frac{\phi}{e}$$

Comparing with $\quad y = mx + c$

Slope of V_0 vs $\frac{1}{\lambda}$ curve is

$$\Rightarrow \quad \tan\theta = \frac{hc}{e} \rightarrow \text{constant for all metals}$$

As in graph shown slope for A and B is not same. **Ans. (D)**

Sol. 16 The radiation energy emitted in $3 \rightarrow 2$ transition is given as

$$\Delta E = E_3 - E_2 = (-1.51\text{ eV}) - (-3.4\text{ eV})$$

$$\Rightarrow \quad \Delta E = 1.89\text{ eV}$$

$n = 3$, $E_3 = -1.51$ eV; $n = 2$, $E_2 = -3.4$ eV; ΔE

$\Delta E = 1.89$ eV; $B = 3\times10^{-4}$ T; metal surface (ϕ)

In magnetic field the radius of circular motion is given as

$$r = \frac{mv}{qB}$$

$$\Rightarrow \quad p = mv = qBr$$

The maximum kinetic energy of ejected electron is given as

$$K_{max} = \frac{p^2}{2m} = \frac{q^2B^2r^2}{2m}$$

$$\Rightarrow \quad K_{max} = \frac{(1.6\times10^{-19})^2 \times (3\times10^{-4})^2 \times (10\times10^{-3})^2}{2\times9.1\times10^{-31}\times(1.6\times10^{-19})}\, eV$$

$$\Rightarrow \quad K_{max} = 0.8\text{ eV}$$

For photoelectric effect at metal surface we use

$$h\nu = \phi + KE_{max}$$

$$\Rightarrow \quad \phi = h\nu - KE_{max} = 1.89 - 0.8 = 1.09\text{ eV}$$

Ans. (B)

Sol. 17 Energy of each photon in the two radiations are

$$E_1 = \frac{hc}{\lambda_1} = \frac{12431}{4972}\text{ eV} \simeq 2.5\text{ eV}$$

and $$E_2 = \frac{hc}{\lambda_2} = \frac{12431}{6216}\text{ eV} \simeq 1.99\text{ eV} (< 2.3\text{ eV})$$

So second radiation is not capable of ejecting electrons from the metal. The power incident on 1 cm^2 of metal surface in first radiation is

$$P = IA = 1.8 \times 10^{-3} \times 10^{-4} = 1.8 \times 10^{-7}\text{ W}$$

Number of photons incident on metal/second are

$$N = \frac{P\lambda}{hc}$$

Number of electrons ejected in 2 second are

$$N_e = \frac{P\lambda}{hc} \times 2$$

$$\Rightarrow \quad N_e = \frac{1.8\times10^{-7} \times 4972\times10^{-10}}{6.63\times10^{-34} \times 3\times10^{8}} \times 2$$

$$\Rightarrow \quad N_e = 9 \times 10^{11}$$ **Ans. (B)**

Sol. 18 If ϕ be the work function of metal used, then we have

$$\frac{1}{2}mv^2 = \frac{hc}{\lambda} - \phi$$

$$\Rightarrow \quad v = \sqrt{\frac{2hc}{\lambda m} - \frac{2\phi}{m}} \quad \ldots(1)$$

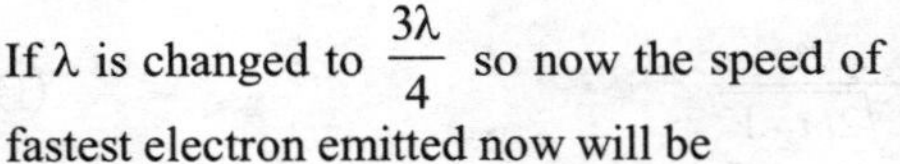

If λ is changed to $\frac{3\lambda}{4}$ so now the speed of fastest electron emitted now will be

$$v' = \sqrt{\frac{2hc}{\lambda m}\left(\frac{4}{3}\right) - \frac{2\phi}{m}} \quad \ldots(2)$$

From equation-(1) $$\sqrt{\frac{4}{3}}\, v = \sqrt{\frac{2hc}{\lambda m}\left(\frac{4}{3}\right) - \frac{2\phi}{m}\left(\frac{4}{3}\right)} \quad \ldots(3)$$

from equation-(2) and (3) comparing, we get

$$v' > \sqrt{\frac{4}{3}}\, v$$ **Ans. (A)**

Sol. 19 Using photo electric effect equation we have

$$\frac{hc}{\lambda_1} = \phi + \text{eV} \quad \ldots(1)$$

$$\frac{hc}{\lambda_2} = \phi + 3\,\text{eV} \quad \ldots(2)$$

(1) × 3 – (2) gives

$$\Rightarrow \quad \frac{3hc}{\lambda_1} - \frac{hc}{\lambda_2} = 2\phi \quad \Rightarrow \quad \phi = \frac{3hc}{2\lambda_1} - \frac{hc}{2\lambda_2}$$

When wavelength λ_3 is used

$$\frac{hc}{\lambda_3} = \phi + eV_0$$

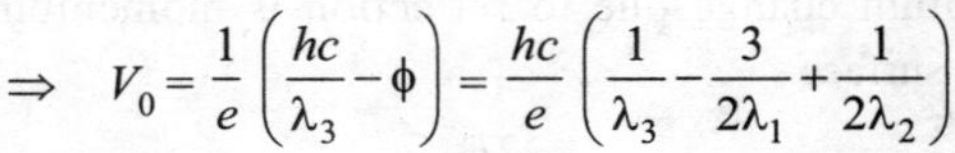

$$\Rightarrow \quad V_0 = \frac{1}{e}\left(\frac{hc}{\lambda_3} - \phi\right) = \frac{hc}{e}\left(\frac{1}{\lambda_3} - \frac{3}{2\lambda_1} + \frac{1}{2\lambda_2}\right)$$ **Ans. (D)**

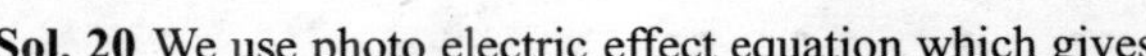

Sol. 20 We use photo electric effect equation which gives

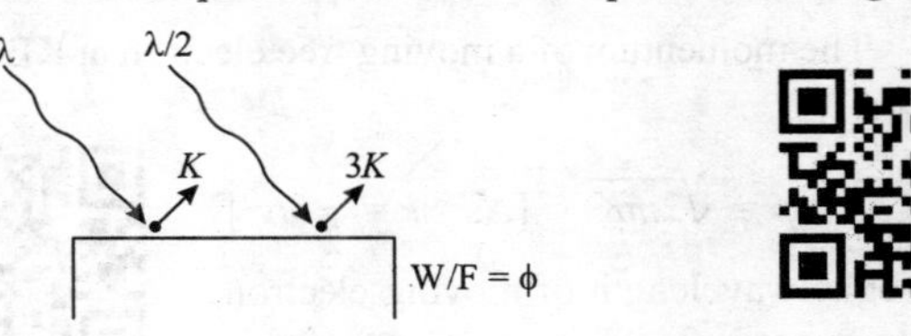

$$\frac{hc}{\lambda} = \phi + k \quad \ldots(1)$$

$$\frac{hc}{(\lambda/2)} = \phi + 3k \quad \ldots(2)$$

Using (1) × 3 – (2) $\Rightarrow \frac{hc}{\lambda} = 2\phi \Rightarrow \phi = \frac{hc}{2\lambda}$ **Ans. (A)**

25.2 Matter Waves and X-Rays

Sol. 1

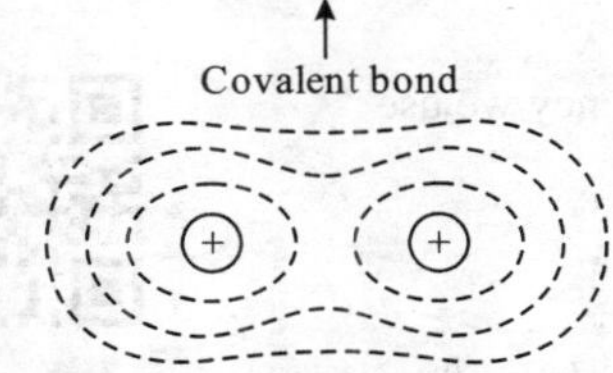

Overlapping region of electron cloud due to Van der waals force between electrons and Nu.

This is a region between two atoms where probability density of existence of electrons now exist. **Ans. (A)**

Sol. 2

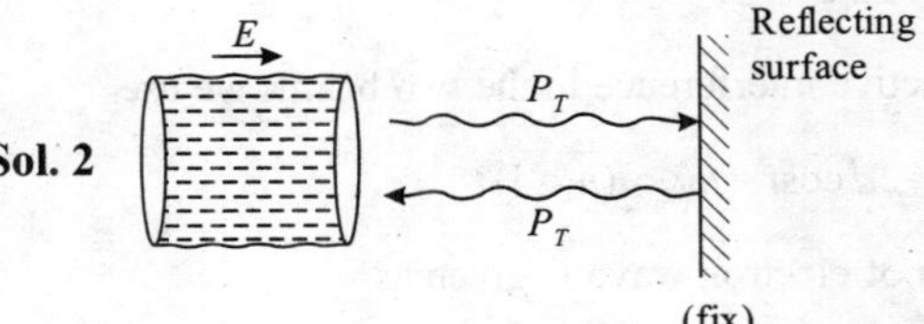

If radiation wavelength is λ, then no of photons in the radiation are $N = \frac{E}{hc/\lambda} = \frac{E\lambda}{hc}$

Each photon in radiation has momentum

$$p = \frac{h}{\lambda}$$

$\Rightarrow$ Total momentum in radiation beam is

$$p_T = \text{N} \times \frac{R}{\lambda} = \frac{E\lambda}{kc} \times \frac{h}{\lambda} = \frac{E}{c}$$

Total momentum change due to reflection is momentum transferred to surface

$$\Delta p_T = p_T - (-p_T) = 2p_T = \frac{2E}{c}$$ **Ans. (B)**

Sol. 3 The momentum of a moving free electron at KE 'K' is given as

$$p = \sqrt{2mK} \quad [\text{As } k = \frac{1}{2}mv^2]$$

De-Broglie wavelength of moving electron can be given as

$$\lambda = \frac{h}{p} = \frac{h}{\sqrt{2mK}} \quad \ldots(1)$$

If K is doubled to $2K$ then new De-Broglie wavelength is given as

$$\lambda' = \frac{h}{\sqrt{2m(2K)}} = \frac{\lambda}{\sqrt{2}}$$ **Ans. (C)**

Sol. 4 As a photon having wavelength λ has momentum associated with it is given by concept of matter wave

$$p = \frac{h}{\lambda} \quad \ldots(1)$$

If ν be the photon frequency we use

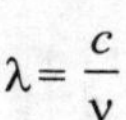

$$\lambda = \frac{c}{\nu}$$

from equation-(1) $p = \frac{h}{c/\nu} = \frac{h\nu}{c}$ **Ans. (D)**

Sol. 5 Path difference in the electron beams which are diffracted from points O and O' are

$$\Delta = 2d\cos i$$

For constructive interference in the two beams we use

$$\Delta = 2d\cos i = n\lambda \quad (n \in \text{I})$$

Wavelength of electron wave is given as

$$\lambda = \frac{h}{mv} = \frac{h}{\sqrt{2mK}} = \frac{h}{\sqrt{2meV}} \quad [\text{As } K = eV]$$

Here we have

$$2d\cos i = \frac{nh}{\sqrt{2meV}}$$

$$\Rightarrow \quad V = \frac{n^2h^2}{8med^2\cos^2 i}$$

For least value of V, we take $n = 1$

$$\Rightarrow \quad V = \frac{h^2}{8med^2\cos^2 i}$$

$$\Rightarrow \quad V = \frac{(6.6\times10^{-34})^2}{8\times9.1\times10^{-31}\times1.6\times10^{-16}\times(10^{-10})^2\times\left(\sqrt{3}/2\right)^2}$$

$\Rightarrow \quad V \simeq 50\text{ V}$ **Ans. (B)**

Sol. 6 Path difference in waves AOA' and $BO'B'$ after reflection from atomic layers is given as

$$\Delta = 2d\cos i$$

For constructive interference at angle i we use

$$\Delta = 2d\cos i = n\lambda_{dB} \quad [n \in I]$$ **Ans. (B)**

Sol. 7 **Statement-1 :** It is true as in Davisson-Germer experiment interference of electrons considering their de-Broglie wavelength was experimentally verified.

Statement-2 : It is true and explaining S-1 also. **Ans. (D)**

Sol. 8 The de-Broglie wavelength for a particle with charge q and mass m which is accelerated at potential difference V is given as

$$\lambda = \frac{h}{\rho} = \frac{h}{\sqrt{2mK}} = \frac{h}{\sqrt{2mqV}} \quad [K = qV]$$

For e^- we use $m = m_e, q = e, V = V$

$$\Rightarrow \quad \lambda_e = \frac{h}{\sqrt{2m_eeV}} \quad \ldots(1)$$

for a proton we use $m = m_p, q = e, V = 4V$

$$\Rightarrow \quad \lambda_p = \frac{h}{\sqrt{2m_pe(4V)}} = \frac{h}{2\sqrt{2m_peV}} \quad \ldots(2)$$

So we have from (1) and (2)

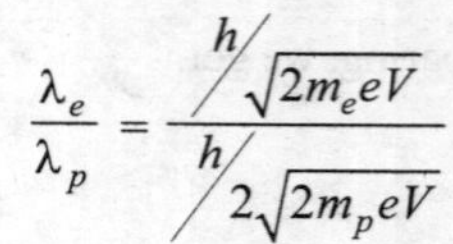

$$\frac{\lambda_e}{\lambda_p} = \frac{h/\sqrt{2m_eeV}}{h/2\sqrt{2m_peV}}$$

$$\Rightarrow \quad \frac{\lambda_e}{\lambda_p} = 2\sqrt{\frac{m_p}{m_e}}$$ **Ans. (D)**

Sol. 9 **(1)** Davisson and Germer experiment $\rightarrow$ related to diffraction of electron as a wave. $\rightarrow$(i)

(2) Millikan's oil drop experiment $\rightarrow$ used in determining e/m of an electron. $\rightarrow$(ii)

(3) Rutherfored experiment → gold foil α-scattering experiment discovered Nu. → (iv)

(4) Franck-Hertz experiment → energy level quantization. → (iii)

Ans. (B)

Sol. 10

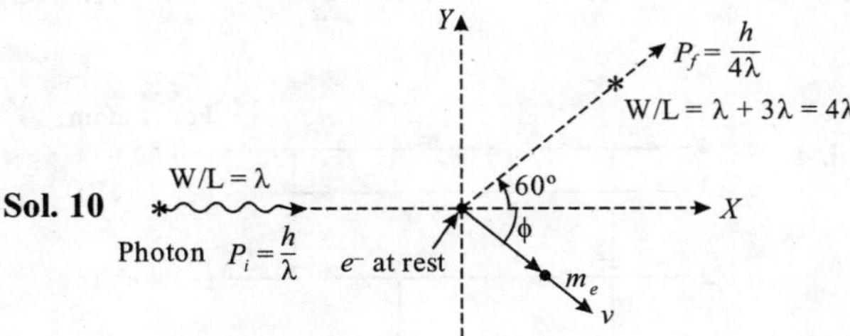

By conservation of linear momentum in above scattering, we use

X-dir → $\frac{h}{\lambda} = \frac{h}{4\lambda}\cos 60^\circ + m_e v\cos\phi$ ...(1)

Y-dir → $\frac{h}{4\lambda}\sin 60^\circ = m_e v\sin\phi$ ...(2)

From (1) and (2) we have

$$m_e v\cos\phi = \frac{h}{\lambda} - \frac{h}{8\lambda} = \frac{7h}{8\lambda} \quad ...(1)$$

$$m_e v\sin\phi = \frac{h}{4\lambda}\left(\frac{\sqrt{3}}{2}\right) \quad ...(2)$$

(2)(1) ⇒ $\tan\phi = \frac{\sqrt{3}}{7}$

⇒ $\tan\phi = \frac{\sqrt{3}}{7} \simeq 0.25$ **Ans. (C)**

Sol. 11 For a dust particle if we consider its mass

$$m \sim 1\,\mu g = 10^{-6} \times 10^{-3}\text{ kg}$$
$$= 10^{-9}\text{ kg}$$

If we consider it to be moving at 1 cm/s ~ 0.01 m/s

Then its de-Broglie wavelength is given as

$$\lambda = \frac{h}{\rho} = \frac{h}{mv} = \frac{6.63\times10^{-34}}{10^{-9}\times10^{-2}} \simeq 6.63 \times 10^{23}\text{ m}$$

In such cases where mass of a moving particle is significant than its de-Broglie wavelength is so low that experimentally it cannot be determined. **Ans. (D)**

Sol. 12 For list-1

(A) Frank-Hertz Experiment → (q) → (ii)

it has given the discrete spectral lines for H or any atom.

It was the first practical experiment which analyzed quantum behaviour of radiation emitted from an atom.

(B) Photo electric effect → (q) → (i)

Photon energy is absorbed by electron to eject from a metal surface.

(C) Davisson Germer Experiment → (r) → (iii)

Scattering and interference of electrons in a specific direction by considering de-Broglie wavelength of moving electrons.

Ans. (C)

Sol. 13 For circular motion in magnetic field we use

$$qvB = \frac{mv^2}{r} \quad ...(1)$$

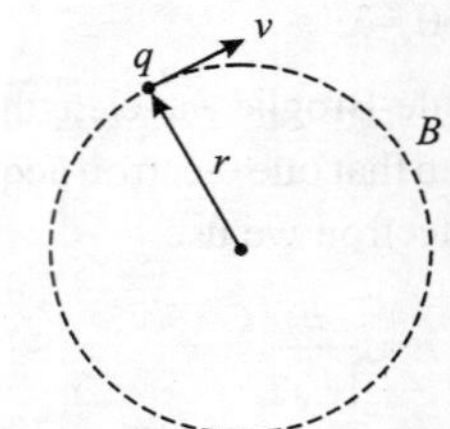

By Bohr model using quantization of angular momentum, we have

$$mvr = \frac{nh}{2\pi} \quad ...(2)$$

⇒ $r = \frac{nh}{2\pi mv}$

⇒ $mv^2 = \frac{qBnh}{2\pi m}$

from (1) and (2) we use

$$mv = qBr$$

⇒ $mv = qB\left(\frac{nh}{2\pi mv}\right)$

TE of charge particle is

$$E = \frac{1}{2}mv^2 = \frac{qBnh}{4\pi m}$$ **Ans. (C)**

Sol. 14 de-Broglie wavelength of an electron in n^{th} level is given as

$$\lambda = \frac{h}{\rho_n} = \frac{h}{mv_n} \quad ...(1)$$

As we know $v_n = \frac{2\pi kZe^2}{nh}$

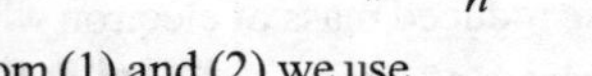

⇒ $v_n \to \frac{1}{n}$ ...(2)

From (1) and (2) we use

$$\lambda \propto n$$

⇒ For $n = 4$ we use

$$\lambda_{n=4} = 4\lambda_{n=1} \text{ (for ground state)}$$ **Ans. (B)**

Sol. 15 KE of an electron accelerated by a voltage V is

$$K = eV$$

de-Broglie wavelength of this e^- is given as

$$\lambda = \frac{h}{P} = \frac{h}{\sqrt{2mK}}$$

$$\Rightarrow \quad \lambda = \frac{6.6\times10^{-34}}{\sqrt{2\times9.1\times10^{-31}\times1.6\times10^{-19}\times50}}$$

$$\cong 1.7\times10^{-10}\,\text{m} = 1.7\,\text{Å}$$

Ans. (C)

Sol. 16 After passing through slit the first minima angular position can be given as

$$d\sin\theta = \lambda \qquad \ldots(1)$$

Where λ we consider de-Broglie wavelength of incident electron out of which it is given that one electron acquires momentum p_y in y-div so for this electron we use

$$\lambda = \frac{h}{|P_y|} \qquad \ldots(2)$$

From equation-(1) and (2) we use for all these electrons which gain momentum p_y in y-direction (one electron is given in question)

$$d\sin\theta = \frac{h}{|P_y|}$$

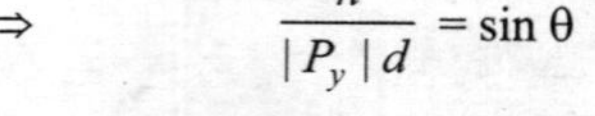

$$\Rightarrow \quad \frac{h}{|P_y|\,d} = \sin\theta$$

Here for majority of other electrons s we use $\sin\theta < 1$

$$\Rightarrow \quad \frac{h}{|P_y|\,d} < 1$$

$$\Rightarrow \quad |P_y|\,d > h$$

Ans. (A)

26.1 Atomic Structure

Sol. 1 Ionization energy (to remove on e^-) from n^{th} state of a hydrogenic atom is given as

$$IP_n = \frac{13.6Z^2}{n^2}$$

here from Li^{+2} ($Z = 3$) and $n = 2$ we use

$$IP_2 = \frac{13.6\times3^2}{2^2} = \frac{13.6\times9}{4}$$

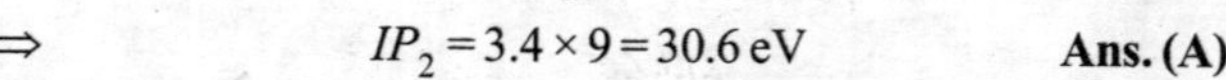

$$\Rightarrow \quad IP_2 = 3.4\times9 = 30.6\,\text{eV}$$

Ans. (A)

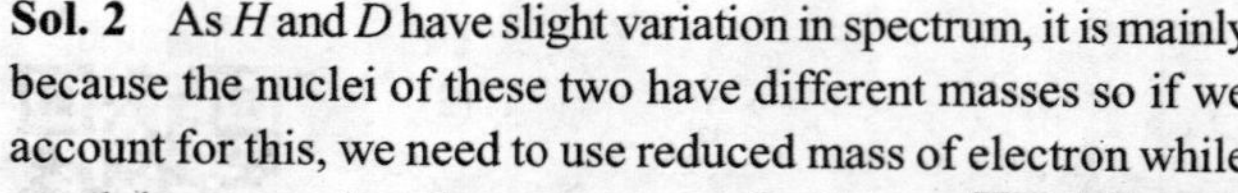

Sol. 2 As H and D have slight variation in spectrum, it is mainly because the nuclei of these two have different masses so if we account for this, we need to use reduced mass of electron while revolving around nucleus at centre of orbit. Here reduced mass of electron are different so energies of different energy levels will be slightly different. **Ans. (C)**

Sol. 3 Ionization of H-atom from $n = 1$ to ∞ requires 13.6 eV So from n^{th} state of H-atom ionization requires the energy

$$IP_n = \frac{13.6Z^2}{n^2}\,\text{eV}$$

$$\Rightarrow \quad IP_2 = \frac{13.6\times1^2}{2^2} = \frac{13.6}{4} = 3.4\,\text{eV}$$

Ans. (C)

Sol. 4

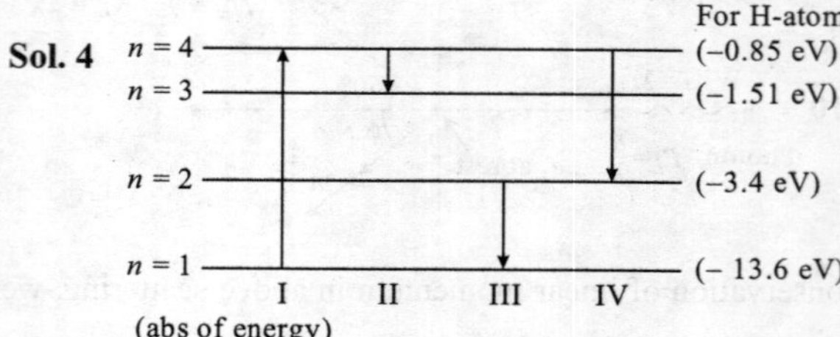

$$E_{II} = (-0.95\,\text{eV}) - (-1.51\,\text{eV}) = 0.66\,\text{eV}$$

$$E_{III} = (-3.4\,\text{eV}) - (-13.6\,\text{eV}) = 10.2\,\text{eV}$$

$$E_{IV} = (-0.85\,\text{eV}) - (-3.4\,\text{eV}) = 2.55\,\text{eV}$$

Ans. (A)

Sol. 5 Options (A) and (D) are absorbing photons

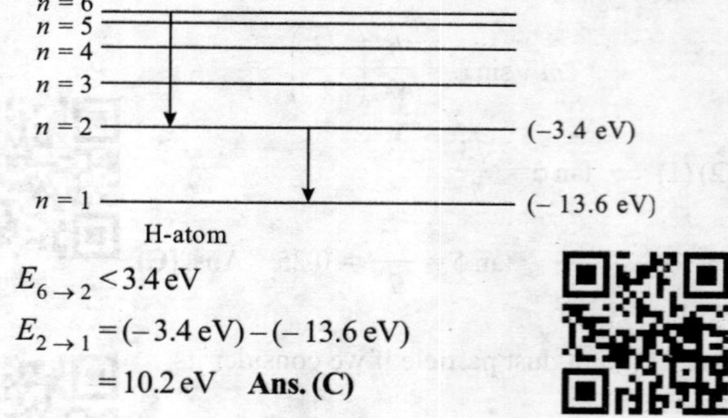

$$E_{6\to2} < 3.4\,\text{eV}$$

$$E_{2\to1} = (-3.4\,\text{eV}) - (-13.6\,\text{eV})$$

$$= 10.2\,\text{eV}$$

Ans. (C)

Sol. 6 In Bohr model for n^{th} orbit we can use for circular motion of electron

$$\frac{mv^2}{r} = \frac{k}{r}$$

$$\Rightarrow \quad mv^2 = k$$

$$v = \sqrt{\frac{k}{m}} \quad \text{(independent of } n\text{)}$$

kE of electron is $\quad T_n = \frac{1}{2}mv_n^2 = \frac{1}{2}k \quad$ (independent of n)

By Bohr's quantization postulate we have

$$mvr = \frac{nh}{2\pi}$$

$$\Rightarrow \quad r_n = \frac{nh}{2\pi mv}$$

$$\Rightarrow \quad r_n \propto n$$

Ans. (B)

Sol. 7 As $\lambda_{IR} > \lambda_{UV}$

$\Rightarrow \quad \Delta E_{IR} < \Delta E_{UV}$

For *H*-atom

n = 5
n = 4
n = 3
ΔE_{UV}
n = 2
n = 1

In *H*-atom IR radiation will be corresponding to a transition which emits energy less than $4 \rightarrow 3$ transition

(A) $E_{4\rightarrow 2} > E_{4\rightarrow 3}$

(B) $E_{5\rightarrow 4} < E_{4\rightarrow 3}$

(C) $E_{2\rightarrow 1} > E_{4\rightarrow 3}$

(D) $E_{3\rightarrow 2} > E_{4\rightarrow 3}$ **Ans. (B)**

Sol. 8 Energy involved in transition from n_1 to n_2 Bohr orbit is given as

$$\Delta E = 13.6\, Z^2 \left(\frac{1}{n_1^2} - \frac{1}{n_2^2}\right) \text{eV}$$

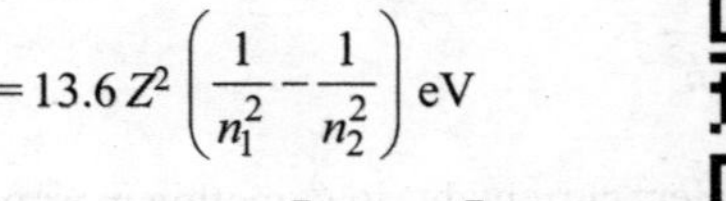

$$\Rightarrow \quad \Delta E = 13.6 \times (3)^2 \times \left[\frac{1}{1^2} - \frac{1}{3^2}\right] \text{eV}$$

$$\Rightarrow \quad \Delta E = 13.6 \times 8 \times \frac{8}{9} = 108.8 \text{ eV}$$ **Ans. (A)**

Sol. 9

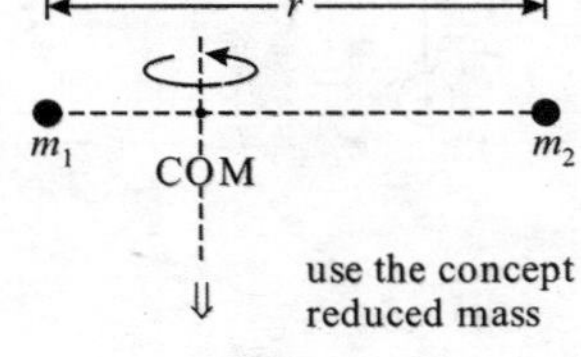

use the concept of reduced mass

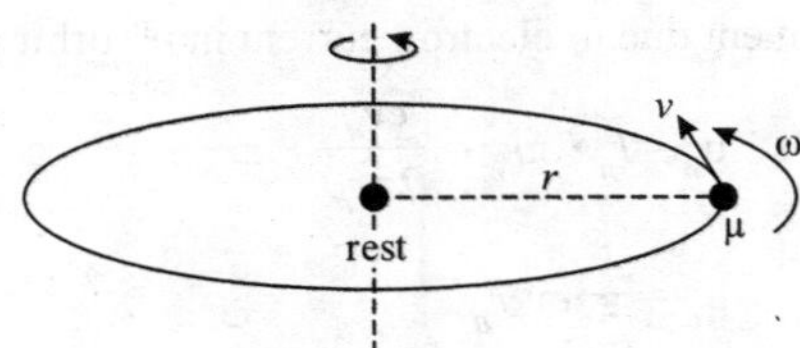

Rotational KE of system is given as

$$E = \frac{1}{2} I\omega^2 = \frac{1}{2}(\mu r^2)\left(\frac{v}{r}\right)^2 = \frac{1}{2}\mu v^2 \quad \ldots(1)$$

Where $\left(\mu = \frac{m_1 m_2}{m_1 + m_2}\right)$

Using Bohr's quantization rule, we have

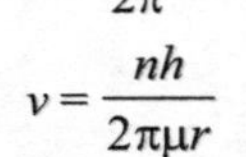

$$\mu v r = \frac{nh}{2\pi}$$

$$\Rightarrow \quad v = \frac{nh}{2\pi\mu r} \quad \ldots(2)$$

From equation (1) and (2) we have

$$E_{RE} = \frac{1}{2}\mu\left(\frac{nh}{2\pi\mu r}\right)^2$$

$$\Rightarrow \quad E_{RE} = \frac{1}{2}\mu\left(\frac{n^2h^2}{4\pi^2\mu^2 r^2}\right)$$

$$\Rightarrow \quad E_{RE} = \frac{n^2h^2}{8\pi^2\left(\frac{m_1 m_2}{m_1+m_2}\right)r^2} = \frac{(m_1+m_2)n^2h^2}{8\pi^2 m_1 m_2 r^2}$$

Most appropriate among given options is option (A). **Ans. (A)**

Sol. 10 If an atom (*H*-atom) the electron is excited to n^{th} state than no of spectral lines in emission spectrum are

$$N = {}^nC_2 = \frac{n(n-1)}{2}$$

$$\Rightarrow \quad N = \frac{4\times 3}{2} = 6$$ **Ans. (A)**

Sol. 11 By Rydberg's formula we use

$$\frac{1}{\lambda} = RZ^2\left[\frac{1}{n_1^2} - \frac{1}{n_2^2}\right]$$

[We use $n_1 = n$ and $n_2 = n + 1$]

$$\Rightarrow \quad \frac{1}{\lambda} = RZ^2\left[\frac{1}{n^2} - \frac{1}{(n+1)^2}\right]$$

$$\Rightarrow \quad \frac{1}{\lambda} = RZ^2\left[\frac{(n+1)^2 - n^2}{n^2(n+1)^2}\right]$$

$$\Rightarrow \quad \frac{1}{\lambda} = R\left[\frac{2n+1}{n^2(n+1)^2}\right]$$

$$\Rightarrow \quad \lambda = \frac{n^2(n+1)^2}{(2n+1)R}$$

For $n >> 1$

$$\Rightarrow \quad \lambda = \frac{n^4}{2nR} = \frac{n^3}{2R}$$ **Ans. (B)**

Sol. 12

n = 3 (–2 eV)
n = 2 (–6 eV)
n = 1 (–8 eV)

For the three energy levels there will be 3 emission lines in spectrum corresponding to energies

$$\Delta E_{32} = (-2) - (-6) = 4 \text{ eV}$$

$$\Delta E_{31} = (-2) - (-8) = 6 \text{ eV}$$

$$\Delta E_{21} = (-6) - (-8) = 2 \text{ eV}$$

Wavelength emitted corresponding to the energies are

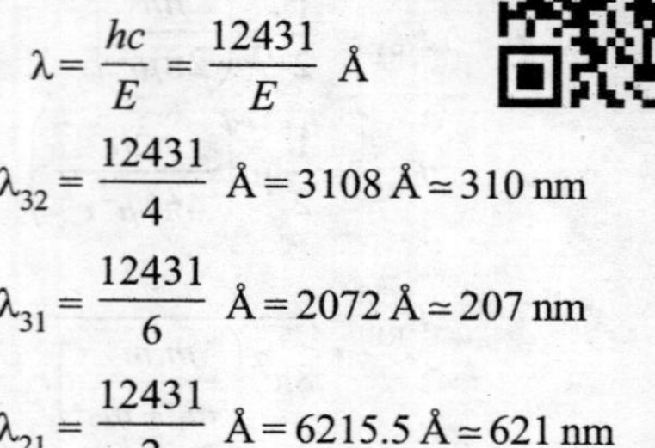

$$\lambda = \frac{hc}{E} = \frac{12431}{E}\ \text{Å}$$

$$\lambda_{32} = \frac{12431}{4}\ \text{Å} = 3108\ \text{Å} \simeq 310\ \text{nm}$$

$$\lambda_{31} = \frac{12431}{6}\ \text{Å} = 2072\ \text{Å} \simeq 207\ \text{nm}$$

$$\lambda_{21} = \frac{12431}{2}\ \text{Å} = 6215.5\ \text{Å} \simeq 621\ \text{nm}$$

$\Rightarrow$ 465 nm is not present in the spectrum **Ans. (B)**

Sol. 13 For Li^{+2} $Z = 3$ and by Rydberg's formula these wavelengths are given as :

$$\underset{n_2}{2} \longrightarrow \underset{n_1}{1} \quad \frac{1}{\lambda_{21}} = R(3)^2\left[\frac{1}{1^2} - \frac{1}{2^2}\right] = 9R \times \frac{3}{4}$$

$$\Rightarrow \quad \lambda_{21} = \frac{4}{27R}$$

$$\underset{n_2}{3} \longrightarrow \underset{n_1}{1} \quad \frac{1}{\lambda_{31}} = R(3)^2\left[\frac{1}{1^2} - \frac{1}{3^2}\right] = 9R \times \frac{8}{9}$$

$$\Rightarrow \quad \lambda_{31} = \frac{9}{72R}$$

$$\underset{n_2}{3} \longrightarrow \underset{n_1}{2} \quad \frac{1}{\lambda_{32}} = R(3)^2\left[\frac{1}{2^2} - \frac{1}{3^2}\right] = 9R \times \frac{5}{36}$$

$$\Rightarrow \quad \lambda_{32} = \frac{36}{45R}$$

$$\Rightarrow \quad \frac{\lambda_{32}}{\lambda_{31}} = \frac{36/45R}{9/42R} = \frac{32}{5} = 6.4$$

$$\frac{\lambda_{21}}{\lambda_{31}} = \frac{4/27R}{9/72R} = \frac{32}{27} = 1.2$$

Ans. (C)

Sol. 14 Speed of electron in n^{th} orbit is given as

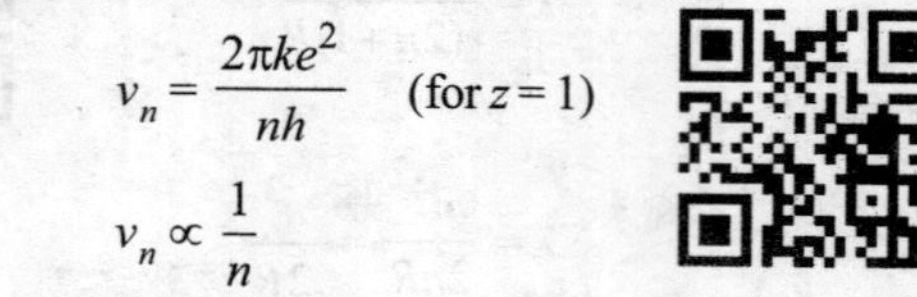

$$v_n = \frac{2\pi ke^2}{nh} \quad (\text{for } z = 1)$$

$$\Rightarrow \quad v_n \propto \frac{1}{n}$$

Graph-*B* shows the correct case **Ans. (A)**

Sol. 15 As α particles are positively charged so these must be repelled away from the nucleus so here option (C) is not possible.

Ans. (C)

Sol. 16 IP of Li^{+2} which is a hydrogenic atom can be given by Bohr model as energy required to remove third electron from Li^{+2}

$$\Rightarrow \quad \text{IP} = 13.6\,Z^2 = 13.6\,(3)^2 = 13.6 \times 9 = 122.4\ \text{eV}$$

Total energy required to remove all 3 electrons from Li atom is

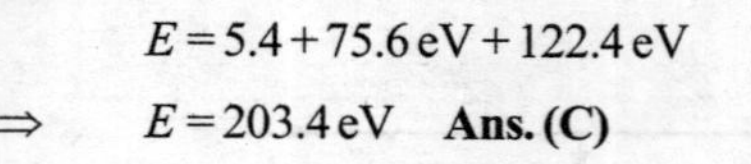

$$E = 5.4 + 75.6\ \text{eV} + 122.4\ \text{eV}$$

$$\Rightarrow \quad E = 203.4\ \text{eV} \quad \textbf{Ans. (C)}$$

Sol. 17 If ν be the frequency of radiation emitted, we use

$$\Delta E = (IP)\,Z^2\left[\frac{1}{n_1^2} - \frac{1}{n_2^2}\right]$$

(For a transition $n_2 \rightarrow n_1$)

$$\Rightarrow \quad \Delta E = h\nu = (IP)\,Z^2\left[\frac{1}{(n-1)^2} - \frac{1}{n^2}\right]$$

$$\Rightarrow \quad \nu = \frac{(IP)Z^2}{h}\left[\frac{2n-1}{n^2(n-1)^2}\right]$$

Here $2n >> 1$ and $n >> 1$

$$\Rightarrow \quad \nu = \frac{(IP)(Z)^2}{h}\left(\frac{2n}{n^4}\right) = \frac{2IP(Z^2)}{h}\left(\frac{1}{n^3}\right)$$

$$\Rightarrow \quad \nu \propto \frac{1}{n^3}$$

Ans. (D)

Sol. 18 Equivalent current due to e^- motion in n^{th} orbit is given as

$$I_n = \frac{e\omega_n}{2\pi} = \frac{ev_n}{2\pi r_n}$$

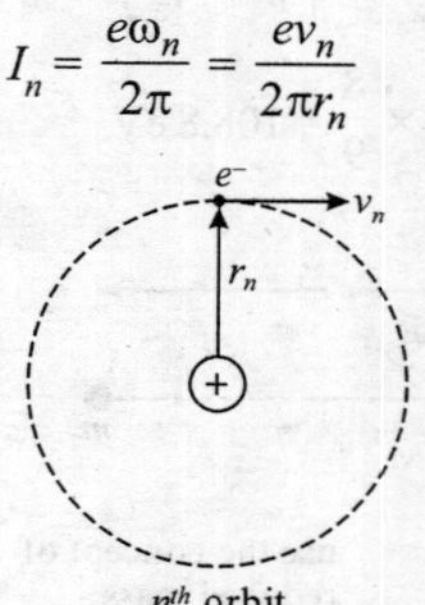

So magnetic moment due to electron current in n^{th} orbit is

$$\mu_n = I_n \times \pi r_n^2 = \frac{ev_n}{2\pi r_n} \times \pi r_n^2$$

$$\mu_n = \frac{1}{2} ev_n r_n \qquad \ldots(1)$$

For n^{th} orbit (for $Z = 1$)

$$v_n = \frac{2\pi Ke^2}{nh}$$

and $$r_n = \frac{n^2h^2}{4\pi^2 Ke^2 m}$$

From equation-(1) we use

$$\mu_n = \frac{1}{2}e\left(\frac{2\pi Ke^2}{nh}\right) \times \left(\frac{n^2h^2}{4\pi^2 Ka^2 m}\right)$$

$$\Rightarrow \quad \mu_n = \frac{enh}{4\pi m}$$

Out of given options most appropriate is option (C).
But here for n^{th} excited state $n \leftarrow n+1$. **Ans. (C)**

Sol. 19

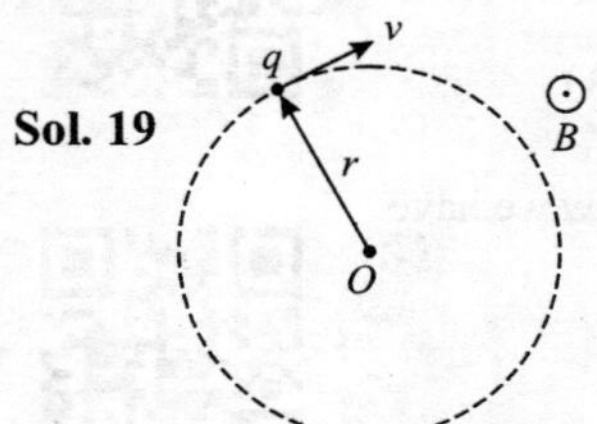

We use $2\pi r = n\lambda = n\left(\frac{h}{mv}\right)$

$$\Rightarrow \quad 2\pi r = \frac{nh}{mv} \qquad \ldots(1)$$

For circular motion in magnetic field, we have

$$qvB = \frac{mv^2}{r}$$

$$\Rightarrow \quad mv = qBr \qquad \ldots(2)$$

From (1) and (2) we use

$$2\pi r = \frac{nh}{qBr}$$

$$\Rightarrow \quad 2\pi qBr^2 = nh$$

$$\Rightarrow \quad r = \sqrt{n}$$ **Ans. (C)**

Sol. 20

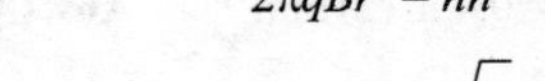

We know the excitation energies of H-atom are :

$$\Delta E_{1\to 2} = 10.2\,\text{eV}$$
$$\Delta E_{1\to 3} = 12.09\,\text{eV}$$
$$\Delta E_{1\to 4} = 12.75\,\text{eV}$$

By the collisions with incident electron, the H-atom can get excited max to $n = 3$ level

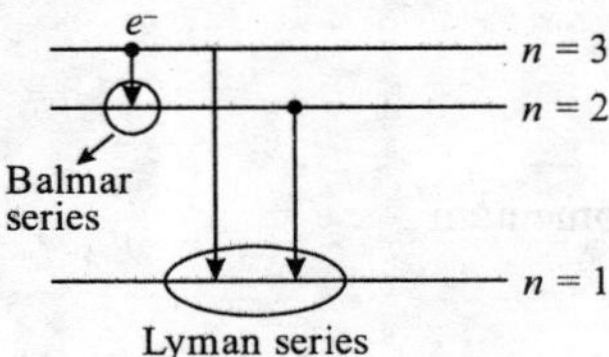

Ans. (A)

Sol. 21 For a revolving electron in speed v_n and radius r_n for n^{th} orbit, we use :

$$F = \frac{mv_n^2}{r_n}$$

$$\Rightarrow \quad \frac{e^2}{4\pi E_0}\left(\frac{1}{r_n^2}+\frac{\beta}{r_n^3}\right) = \frac{mv_n^2}{r_n} \qquad \ldots(1)$$

By using Bohr's quantization postulate we use

$$\Rightarrow \quad mv_n r_n = \frac{nh}{2\pi} \qquad \ldots(2)$$

$$\Rightarrow \quad v_n = \frac{nh}{2\pi m r_n}$$

From equation (1) we have

$$\frac{e^2}{4\pi\varepsilon_0}\left[\frac{1}{r_n}+\frac{\beta}{r_n^2}\right] = m\left[\frac{nh}{2\pi m r_n}\right]^2$$

We multiply r_n^2 in LHS and RHS gives :

$$\frac{e^2}{4\pi\varepsilon_0}[r_n+\beta] = \frac{n^2h^2}{4\pi^2 m}$$

$$\Rightarrow \quad r_n = n^2\frac{h^2\varepsilon_0}{e^2\pi m} - \beta$$

$$\Rightarrow \quad r_n = n^2 a_0 - \beta$$

Where $a_0 = \frac{h^2\varepsilon_0}{e^2\pi m}$ **Ans. (C)**

Sol. 22 For a given transition $n_2 \to n_1$, the wavelength emitted can be given as :

$$\frac{1}{\lambda} = RZ^2\left[\frac{1}{n_1^2}-\frac{1}{n_2^2}\right]$$

As $n_2 = 2$ and $n_1 = 1$ for all

$$\Rightarrow \quad \lambda \propto \frac{1}{Z^2}$$

For ${}_1H^1$ and ${}_1H^2$ we take $Z=1$

$$\Rightarrow \quad \lambda_1 \cong \lambda_2$$

and for $({}_2He^4)^+$ $Z = 2$

$$\Rightarrow \quad \lambda_3 = \frac{\lambda_1}{4}$$

and for $({}_3Li^6)^{+2}$ $Z = 3$

$$\Rightarrow \quad \lambda_4 = \frac{\lambda_1}{9}$$

$$\Rightarrow \quad \lambda_1 = \lambda_2 = 4\lambda_3 = 9\lambda_4$$ **Ans. (C)**

Sol. 23 For a given hydrogenic atom (Li^{+2}) the ionization energy for an electron in n^{th} state is given as :

$$IP_n = 13.6\frac{Z^2}{n^2}$$

Here $Z = 3$ and for first excited state we use $n = 2$

$$\Rightarrow \quad IP_{n=2} = 13.6\times\frac{(3)^2}{(2)^2}$$

$$= \frac{13.6\times 9}{4} = 30.3\,\text{eV}$$ **Ans. (B)**

Sol. 24 *KE*, *PE* and *TE* of electron in a hydrogenic atom according to Bohr model is given as :

$$TE = -\frac{KZe^2}{2r_n}\ ;\ KE = \frac{KZe^2}{2r_n}\ ;\ PE = -\frac{KZe^2}{r_n}$$

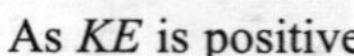

When electron makes a transition from excited state to ground state r_n decreases.

As *KE* is positive

$\Rightarrow$ $KE \uparrow$ (+ve); $PE \downarrow$ (–ve); $TE \downarrow$ (–ve) **Ans. (A)**

Sol. 25

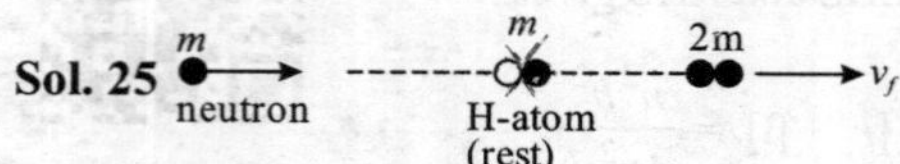

By conservation of momentum if inelastic collision occurs

$$mv = 2mv_f$$

$$\Rightarrow \quad v_f = \frac{v}{2}$$

Loss in *KE* $\quad \Delta E_2 = \frac{1}{2}mv^2 - \frac{1}{2}(2m)\left(\frac{v}{2}\right)^2 = \frac{1}{4}mv^2$

For this collision to happen ΔE_2 must be minimum 10.2 eV (Minimum energy which can be absorbed by *H*-atom in excitation from $n = 1$ to $n = 2$.)

$$\Rightarrow \quad \frac{1}{4}mv^2 = 10.2\text{ eV}$$

$$\Rightarrow \quad K_{in} = 20.4\text{ eV}$$ **Ans. (A)**

Sol. 26

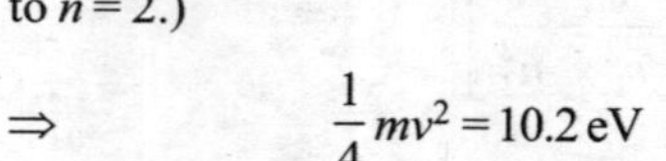

Energy required to completely remove the electron of Li^{+2} in n^{th} state is

$$\Delta E_{IP(n)} = \frac{13.6Z^2}{n^2} = \frac{13.6(3)^2}{n^2}$$

$$\Rightarrow \quad 10.2 \geq \frac{13.6\times 9}{n^2}$$

$$\Rightarrow \quad n^2 \geq \frac{13.6\times 9}{10.2}$$

$$\Rightarrow \quad n^2 \geq 12$$

$$\Rightarrow \quad n \geq 2\sqrt{3} \cong 3.5$$ **Ans. (B)**

27.1 Radioactivity

Sol. 1 Only charged particles moving in field experience magnetic force and get deflected

$\Rightarrow$ At the instant emission can contain

(i) e^- (–ve)

(ii) protons (+ve)

(iii) He^{+2} (+ve)

Will get deflected in MF **Ans. (A)**

Sol. 2 By Radioactive Decay Law we have

$$N = N_0\, 2^{-t/T}$$

at $T = 5$ years and $t = 15$ years

$$\Rightarrow \quad N = N_0\,(2)^{-15/5}$$

$$\Rightarrow \quad N = \frac{N_0}{2^3} = \frac{N_0}{8}$$ **Ans. (A)**

Sol. 3 Using Radioactive decay law, we have

$$A_c = A_{co}\, e^{-\lambda t}$$

here at $t = 0$, $A_{co} = 5000$ dis/min

at $t = 5$ min, $A_c = 1250$ dis/mim

$$\Rightarrow \quad 1250 = 5000\, e^{-\lambda(5)}$$

$$\Rightarrow \quad e^{5\lambda} = \frac{5000}{1250} = 4$$

$$\Rightarrow \quad 5\lambda = \ln(4) = 2\ln(2)$$

$$\Rightarrow \quad \lambda = \frac{2}{5}\ln(2) = 0.4\ln(2)\ \text{min}^{-1}$$ **Ans. (A)**

Sol. 4 Least wavelength $\Rightarrow$ maximum energy here γ-rays have highest energy

So it will be having least wavelength among other option

"fact based question" **Ans. (A)**

Sol. 5

X Consider at rest

m_2 ← v ; $2v$ → m_1

By conservation of linear momentum

$$m_1(2v) = m_2 v$$

$$m_2 = 2m_1$$

$\Rightarrow \quad A_2 = 2A_1 \quad A_1, A_2$ are molar atomic masses

By concept of fermi radius, the nuclear radius is given as

$$R = R_0\,(A)^{1/3}$$

$$\Rightarrow \quad R_1 = R_0\,(m_1)^{1/3}$$

and $\quad R_2 = R_0\,(2m_1)^{1/3}$

$$\Rightarrow \quad \frac{R_1}{R_2} = \frac{1}{2^{1/3}}$$ **Ans. (D)**

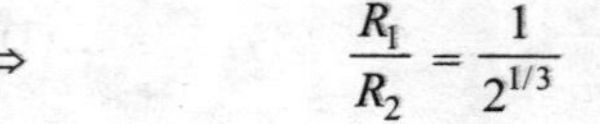

Sol. 6 We use formula of fermi radius of a Nu, given as

$$R = R_0\,(A)^{1/3}$$

For ^{27}Al we use

$$3.6 \times 10^{-15} = R_0\,(27)^{1/3} \quad \ldots(1)$$

For ^{125}Te we use

$$R = R_0\,(125)^{1/3} \quad \ldots(2)$$

(2) and (1) gives $\rightarrow \dfrac{R}{3.6\times10^{-15}} = \left(\dfrac{125}{27}\right)^{1/3} = \dfrac{5}{3}$

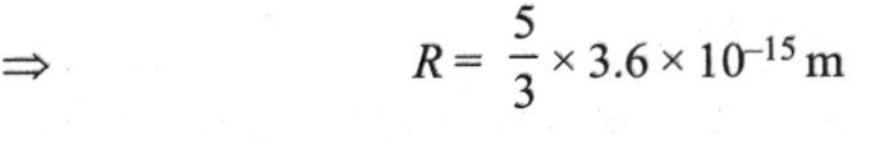

$$\Rightarrow \quad R = \frac{5}{3} \times 3.6 \times 10^{-15}\,\text{m}$$

$$= 6 \times 10^{-15}\,\text{m} = 6 \text{ fermi}$$ **Ans. (A)**

Sol. 7 Using RA decay equation we have

$$N = N_0\,(2)^{-t/T}$$

At $t = 15$ min, $N = \dfrac{N_0}{8}$ as $\dfrac{7}{8}N_0$ decay in times 15 min

$$\Rightarrow \quad \frac{N_0}{8} = N_0\,(2)^{-15/T}$$

$$\Rightarrow \quad 2^{-3} = 2^{-15/T}$$

$$\Rightarrow \quad \frac{15}{T} = 3$$

$$\Rightarrow \quad T = \frac{15}{3} = 5 \text{ min}$$ **Ans. (C)**

Sol. 8 Half life of X = Mean life of Y

If λ_X and λ_Y are decay constants of elements X and Y, we have

$$\frac{\ln Z}{\lambda_X} = \frac{1}{\lambda_Y}$$

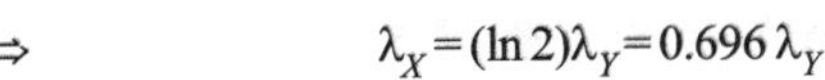

$$\Rightarrow \quad \lambda_X = (\ln 2)\lambda_Y = 0.696\,\lambda_Y$$

$$\Rightarrow \quad \lambda_X < \lambda_Y$$

$\Rightarrow$ For same N_0 we use $\lambda_X N_0 < \lambda_Y N_0$ **Ans. (B)**

Sol. 9 From *RA* decay equation we have

$$N = N_0\,(2)^{-t/T} \quad [T = 20 \text{ min}]$$

at $t = t_2$ we use $N = \dfrac{N_0}{3}$ (as $\dfrac{2}{3}N_0$ has decayed)

$$\Rightarrow \quad \frac{N_0}{3} = N_0\,(2)^{-t_2/20} \quad \Rightarrow \quad \frac{t_2}{20} = \log_2(3)$$

$$\Rightarrow \quad t_2 = 20\log_2(3) \quad \Rightarrow \quad \log_2(3) = \frac{t_2}{20}$$

at $t = t_1$ we use $N = \dfrac{2N_0}{3}$ (as $\dfrac{N_0}{3}$ has decayed)

$$\Rightarrow \quad \frac{2N_0}{3} = N_0\,(2)^{-t_1/20}$$

$$\Rightarrow \quad \frac{t_1}{20} = \log_2\left(\frac{3}{2}\right) = \log_2(3) - 1$$

$$\Rightarrow \quad \frac{t_1}{20} = \frac{t_2}{20} - 1 \quad \Rightarrow \quad t_2 - t_1 = 20 \text{ min}$$ **Ans. (A)**

Sol. 10 By RA decay equation we have $N = N_0\,(2)^{-t/T}$

For $A \rightarrow N_A = N_0\,(2)^{-80/20} = \dfrac{N_0}{2^4} = \dfrac{N_0}{16}$

Number of nuclei of A decayed in 80 min are

$$N_{AD} = N_0 - N_A = N_0 - \frac{N_0}{16} = \frac{15N_0}{16}$$

For $B \rightarrow N_B = N_0\,(2)^{-80/20} = \dfrac{N_0}{2^2} = \dfrac{N_0}{4}$

Number of nuclei of B decayed in 80 min are

$$N_{BD} = N_0 - N_B = N_0 - \frac{N_0}{4} = \frac{3N_0}{4}$$

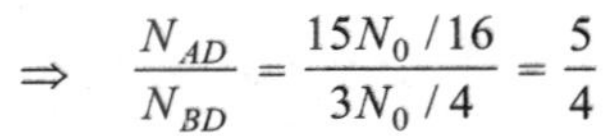

$$\Rightarrow \quad \frac{N_{AD}}{N_{BD}} = \frac{15N_0/16}{3N_0/4} = \frac{5}{4}$$ **Ans. (D)**

Sol. 11 Using radioactive decay equation we have

$$A_C = A_{C_0}\,(2)^{-t/T}$$

at

$t = 0,\ A_{C_0} = 1600$ counts/s

$t = 8\text{s},\ A_C = 100$ counts/s

$$\Rightarrow \quad 100 = 1600\,(2)^{-8/T}$$

$$\Rightarrow \quad 2^{-8/T} = 2^4 \quad \Rightarrow \quad \frac{8}{T} = 4 \quad \Rightarrow \quad T = 2\,\text{s}$$

at $t = 6\text{s}$, A_C is given as

$$A_C = 1600\,(2)^{-6/2} = \frac{1600}{2^3} = \frac{1600}{8} = 200 \text{ counts/s}$$ **Ans. (D)**

Sol. 12 Using radioactive decay equation at $t = 1$ yr we have ($T \rightarrow$ half life in yrs)

$$N_1 = N_0\,(2)^{-1/T} \quad [N_0 = 10^{20} \text{ atoms}]$$

at $t = 2$ yr $\quad N_2 = N_0\,(2)^{-2/T}$

at $t = 3$ yr $\quad N_3 = N_0\,(2)^{-3/T}$

N_0 of α-particles emitted in 3rd yr

$$\Delta N_3 = N_2 - N_3 = N_0\,((2)^{-2/T} - (2)^{-3/T}) \quad \ldots(1)$$

N_0 of α-particles emitted in 2nd yr

$$\Delta N_2 = N_1 - N_2 = N_0\,((2)^{-1/T} - (2)^{-2/T}) \quad \ldots(2)$$

N_0 of α-particles emitted in 1st yr

$$\Delta N_1 = N_0 - N_1 = N_0\,(1 - (2)^{-1/T}) \quad \ldots(3)$$

From (1) and (2) we have

$$\frac{\Delta N_3}{\Delta N_2} = \frac{N_0(2^{-2/T} - 2^{-3/T})}{N_0(2^{-1/T} - 2^{-2/T})} = 0.3$$

$\Rightarrow$ $2^{-2/T} - 2^{-3/T} = 0.32^{-1/T} - 0.32^{-2/T}$

$\Rightarrow$ $1.32^{-2/T} - 2^{-3/T} = -0.32^{-1/T} = 0$

$\Rightarrow$ $1.32^{-1/T} - 2^{-2/T} = -0.3 = 0$ [multiplied the equation with $2^{1/T}$]

Using $2^{-1/T} = x \Rightarrow x^2 - 1.3x + 0.3 = 0$

$\Rightarrow$ $x = \frac{1.3 \pm \sqrt{1.69 - 1.2}}{2} = \frac{1.3 \pm 0.7}{2} = 1$ or 0.3

Here we use $2^{-1/T} = 0.3$

From equation-(1) we have

$$\Delta N_1 = N_0(1 - 2^{-1/T}) = N_0(1 - 0.3) = 0.7\, N_0$$

$\Rightarrow$ $\Delta N_1 = 0.7 \times 10^{20} = 7 \times 10^{19}$ **Ans. (D)**

Sol. 13 (A) ✓ $A_C = \lambda N$ independent of any extra factor fission

(B) × Nuclear forces are independent of charge

(C) × Nuclei having same number of neutrons are called isotones

(D) × For photons momentum $P = \frac{h}{\lambda} \rightarrow$

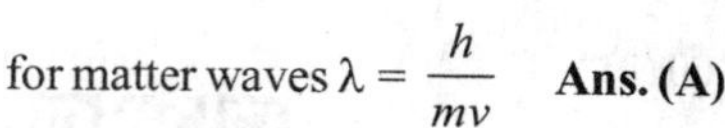

for matter waves $\lambda = \frac{h}{mv}$ **Ans. (A)**

Sol. 14 In case of simultaneous decay modes of a radioactive element equivalent decay constant is given as

$$\lambda_{eq} = \lambda_\alpha + \lambda_\beta \ [\lambda_\alpha = \frac{\ln_2}{T_\alpha} \text{ and } \lambda_\beta = \frac{\ln_2}{T_\beta}]$$

Average half life of element is

$$T = \frac{\ln_2}{\lambda_{eq}} = \frac{\ln_2}{\lambda_\alpha + \lambda_\beta}$$

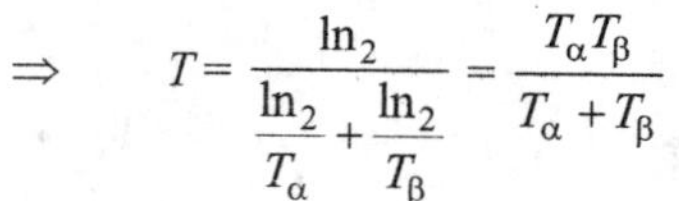

$$\Rightarrow \quad T = \frac{\ln_2}{\frac{\ln_2}{T_\alpha} + \frac{\ln_2}{T_\beta}} = \frac{T_\alpha T_\beta}{T_\alpha + T_\beta}$$ **Ans. (C)**

Sol. 15 Decay rate of a radioactive element is given as $A_C = \lambda N$. Given that half life of A = mean life of B

$$\Rightarrow \quad \frac{\ln 2}{\lambda_A} = \frac{1}{\lambda_B}$$

$\Rightarrow$ $\lambda_A = \ln(2) \cdot \lambda_B = 0.693\, \lambda_B$

$\Rightarrow$ $\lambda_B > \lambda_A$ so B will decay faster than A **Ans. (D)**

Sol. 16 If a radioactive nuclei element is produced at a constant rate r nuclei/s than the rate of accumulation of these nuclei is given as

$$\frac{dN}{dt} = r - \lambda N$$

$$\Rightarrow \quad \int_0^N \frac{dN}{r - \lambda N} = \int_0^t dt$$

$$\Rightarrow \quad -\frac{1}{\lambda}\left[\ln(r - \lambda N)\right]_0^N = t$$

$$\Rightarrow \quad \ln\left(\frac{r - \lambda N}{r}\right) = -\lambda t$$

$$\Rightarrow \quad \ln\frac{r - \lambda N}{r} = e^{-\lambda t}$$

$$\Rightarrow \quad N = \frac{r}{\lambda}(1 - e^{-\lambda t}) \qquad \ldots(1)$$

From equation-(1) $N = 50$ at time t gives

$$50 = \frac{1000}{0.5}(1 - e^{-0.5t})$$

$$\Rightarrow \quad 50 = 200(1 - e^{-0.5t})$$

$$\Rightarrow \quad \frac{1}{4} = 1 - e^{-0.5t}$$

$$\Rightarrow \quad e^{0.5t} = \frac{4}{3}$$

$$\Rightarrow \quad 0.5t = \ln\left(\frac{4}{3}\right)$$

$$\Rightarrow \quad t = 2\ln\left(\frac{4}{3}\right)\text{s}$$ **Ans. (B)**

Sol. 17 Activity at $t = 0$ (living animal) is $A_{C_0} = 16$ dpm/gm

If animal died t yrs ago then activity now is $A_C = 12$ dpm/gm using radioactive decay equation we have

$$A_C = A_{C_0}(2)^{-t/T}$$

$$\Rightarrow \quad 12 = 16(2)^{-t/T}$$

$$\Rightarrow \quad 2^{-t/5760} = \frac{4}{3}$$

$$\Rightarrow \quad \frac{t}{5760} \times \log 2 = 2\log 2 - \log 3$$

$$\frac{t}{5760} \times 0.301 = 0.602 - 0.477 = 0.125$$

$$\Rightarrow \quad t = \frac{0.125 \times 5760}{0.301} \simeq 2392 \text{ yrs}$$ **Ans. (B)**

Sol. 18 By radioactive decay equation, we have

$$A_C = A_{C_0}(2)^{-t/T} \qquad \ldots(1)$$

From freshly cut tree at $t = 0$ activity is $A_{C_0} = 20$ dpm

If a tree was cut t yrs ago its activity is $A_C = 2$ dpm

from equation-(1) $2 = 20\,(2)^{-t/5730}$

$$2^{t/5730} = 10$$

$$\Rightarrow \quad t = \frac{\log 10}{\log 2} \times 5730$$

$$\Rightarrow \quad t = \frac{5730}{0.301} = 19036.55 \text{ yrs.}$$ **Ans. (C)**

Sol. 19 Number of Na^{24} nuclei in beginning (at $t = 0$) are

$$N_0 = \frac{1\times10^{-3}\times6.023\times10^{23}}{24\times10^{-3}}$$

$$\Rightarrow \quad N_0 = \frac{6.023\times10^{23}}{24} \cong 0.25 \times 10^{23}$$

by radioactive decay equation number of Na^{24} nuclei left at $t = 7.5$ hr are

$$N = N_0\,(2)^{-t/T} = N_0\,(2)^{-7.5/15} = \frac{N_0}{\sqrt{2}}$$

Number of decays in 7.5 hr are

= Number of β emissions

$$N_\beta = N_0 - \frac{N_0}{\sqrt{2}} = N_0\left(1 - \frac{1}{\sqrt{2}}\right)$$

$$\Rightarrow \quad N_\beta = N_0\,(1 - 0.707) \simeq 0.3\,N_0$$

$$\Rightarrow \quad N_\beta = 0.3 \times 0.25 \times 10^{23} = 7.5 \times 10^{21}$$ **Ans. (B)**

27.2 Nuclear Physics

Sol. 1 Fusion will start when average thermal energy of particles in gaseous state will be equal to the PE of the fusing particles

Average thermal energy $E = \frac{3}{2}kT$

$\Rightarrow$ here $\frac{3}{2}kT \geq 7.7 \times 10^{-14}$ for fusion to start

$$\Rightarrow \quad T \geq \frac{7.7\times10^{-14}}{1.5\times1.38\times10^{-23}} \simeq 3.7 \times 10^{9}$$ **Ans. (D)**

Sol. 2 We know that in general radio active decay causes α, β and γ emissions

$\alpha \rightarrow He^{+2}$

$\beta \rightarrow e^-\,(\bar{\nu})$ or $e^+\,(\nu)$ where $\bar{\nu}$, ν are neutrinos

$\gamma \rightarrow$ EM radioactive with $\lambda < 0.1$ Å

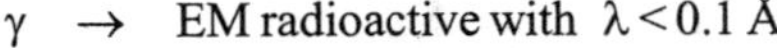

Out of given options in general protons are NOT emitted.

Ans. (A)

Sol. 3 In the decay sequence parent nucleus ($Z = 92$) is emitting

8 α particles $\Rightarrow$ this will decrease Z by $8 \times 2 = 16$ (–ve)

4 β^- particles $\Rightarrow$ this will decrease Z by $4 \times 1 = 4$ (+ve)

2 β^+ particles $\Rightarrow$ this will decrease Z by $2 \times 1 = 2$ (–ve)

Final Z of the resulting end product is

$$Z_{\text{end product}} = 92 - 16 + 4 - 2 = 92 - 14 = 78$$ **Ans. (B)**

Sol. 4 By conservation of linear momentum we use

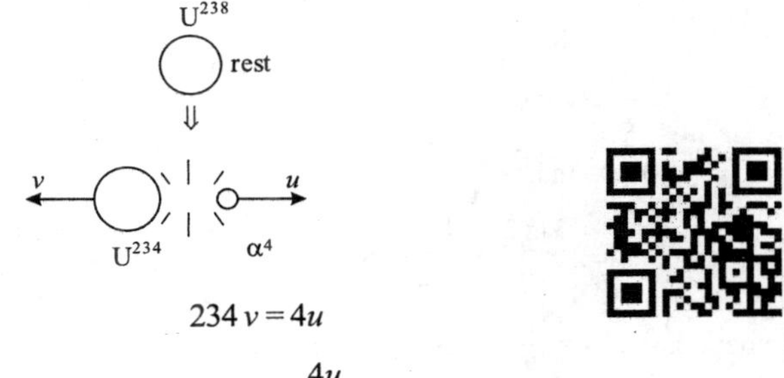

$$234\,v = 4u$$

$$\Rightarrow \quad v = \frac{4u}{234}$$ **Ans. (C)**

Sol. 5 At the point of closest approach the initial KE of α-particle gets transformed into the electrical PE of ($\alpha - U$) system, so we use

+2e
α-particle
v = 0
+ 92e
r
fixed U-nucleus
Z = 92

$$KE_i = \frac{Kq_1q_2}{r} \quad [q_1 = +92e \;\&\; q_2 = +2e]$$

$$\Rightarrow \quad r = \frac{9\times10^{9}\times92\times2\times1.6\times10^{-19}}{5\times10^{6}}$$

$$\Rightarrow \quad r = 5.3 \times 10^{-14}\,\text{m}$$

$$\Rightarrow \quad r = 5.3 \times 10^{-12}\,\text{cm}$$ **Ans. (C)**

Sol. 6 The reaction of nuclear fusion is

$${}_1H^2 + {}_1H^2 \longrightarrow {}_2H^2 + \Delta E$$

Here the Q-value of nuclear reaction (energy released) is given as

$$\Delta E = 4\,(BE_N)_{{}_2He^4} - 2 \times 2 \times (BE_N)_{{}_1H^2}$$

$$\Rightarrow \quad \Delta E = 4 \times 7 - 4 \times 1.1 = 28 - 4.4 = 23.6\,\text{MeV}$$ **Ans. (C)**

Sol. 7 $X(n, \alpha) \rightarrow {}^7_3Li$ can be written as

$${}^1_0n + {}^A_ZX \longrightarrow {}^7_3Li + {}^4_2\alpha$$

In above reaction conserving charge and mass number gives

$$1+A=7+4 \rightarrow A=11-1=10$$

$$0+Z=3+2 \rightarrow Z=5$$

Element X is ${}^{10}_{5}B$ **Ans. (B)**

Sol. 8 We use the γ-ray intensity at a penetration depth x, is gives as

$$I=I_0e^{-\mu x}$$

[$\mu \rightarrow$ absorption coefficient of lead for γ-rays]

$$I_0=I$$

and $I=\frac{I}{8}$ at $x=36$ mm

$$\Rightarrow \quad \frac{I}{8}=Ie^{-\mu(36)}$$

$$\Rightarrow \quad 36\mu=\ln 8=3\ln 2$$

$$\Rightarrow \quad \mu=\frac{3\ln 2}{36}=\frac{\ln 2}{12}\ \text{mm}^{-1}$$

In next case at $I=\frac{I}{2}$ we use

$$x=r$$

$$\Rightarrow \quad \frac{I}{2}=Ie^{-\mu r}$$

$$\Rightarrow \quad \mu r=\ln(2)$$

$$\Rightarrow \quad r=\frac{\ln(2)}{\mu}=12\ \text{mm}$$ **Ans. (D)**

Sol. 9 Fact based

emitted β-particles from a radioactive source have widely spreaded energy spectrum with speeds ranging 0.01c to 0.99c. Option (C) is most appropriate matching option. **Ans. (C)**

Sol. 10 The nuclear reaction of above given case is written as

$${}^{7}_{3}Li + {}^{1}_{1}p \longrightarrow {}^{8}_{4}Be + a$$

In every nuclear reaction the obtained product can be found in excited state which can further transit to ground state and emit gamma radiation.

$${}^{7}_{3}Li + {}^{1}_{1}p \longrightarrow {}^{8}_{4}Be^{*}$$

$${}^{8}_{4}Be^{*} \longrightarrow {}^{8}_{4}Be+\gamma$$

$$\Rightarrow \quad a=\gamma$$ **Ans. (C)**

Sol. 11 At the point of closest approach whole KE transform into electric PE

α(+2e) v $v_f=0$ r_m +Ze

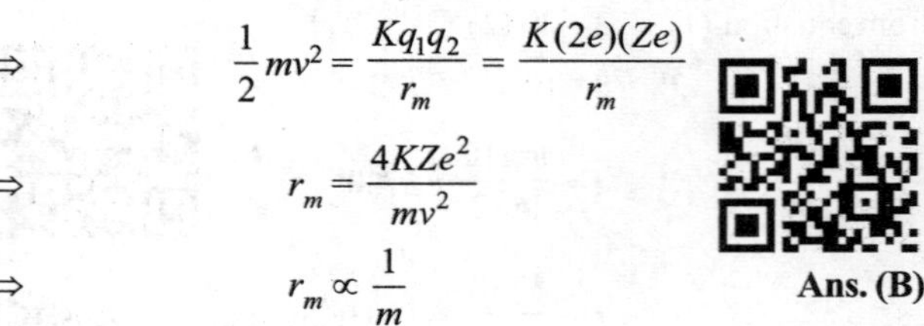

$$\Rightarrow \quad \frac{1}{2}mv^2=\frac{Kq_1q_2}{r_m}=\frac{K(2e)(Ze)}{r_m}$$

$$\Rightarrow \quad r_m=\frac{4KZe^2}{mv^2}$$

$$\Rightarrow \quad r_m \propto \frac{1}{m}$$ **Ans. (B)**

Sol. 12 In the given nuclear reaction

$$p+{}^{7}_{3}Li \longrightarrow 2\,{}^{4}_{2}He$$

As some initial energy of proton is required so by conservation of mass-energy in this equation we use

$$E_p+E_{Li}=2E_{He}$$

$$\Rightarrow \quad E_p+7\times 5.60=2\times 4\times 7.06$$

$$\Rightarrow \quad E_p=56.48-392=17.28\ \text{MeV}$$ **Ans. (B)**

Sol. 13 A gamma ray emission takes place only from on excited Nu when it transit to ground state

$${}^{A}_{Z}X^{*} \longrightarrow {}^{A}_{Z}X + \gamma\text{-photon}$$

Nucleus in excited state — Nucleus in ground state

As Z and A remain same is γ-emission so no change in proton and neutron number. **Ans. (B)**

Sol. 14 ${}^{17}_{8}O$ nucleus contains 8 protons and 9 neutrons

The mass defect in formation of nucleus ${}^{17}_{8}O$ is

$$\Delta m=8M_p+9M_n-M_O$$

energy released at the time of formation ${}^{17}_{8}O$ nucleus is

$$\Delta E=\Delta Mc^2=[8M_p+9M_n-M_O]c^2$$ **Ans. (B)**

Sol. 15 Nucleus → Neutrons, Protons

Ans. (B)

Sol. 16 In case of fission of heavy nuclei or fusion of light Nu overall $(BE)_N$ increases and energy is released

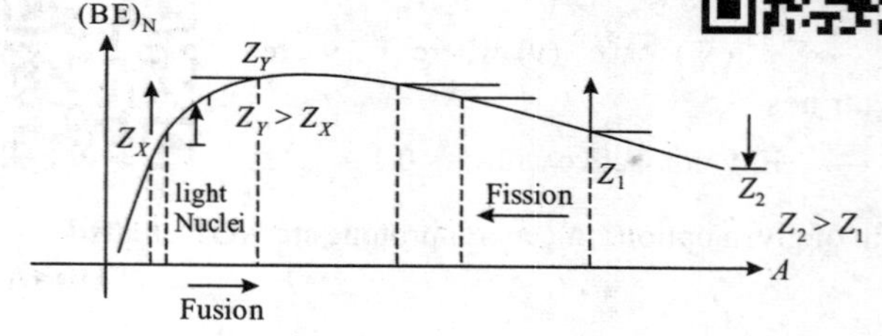

$\Rightarrow$ From above graph we can state that **S-1** is true and **S-2** is false. **Ans. (D)**

Sol. 17 In any reaction if overall BE per nucleon increases

$\Rightarrow$ Energy is released

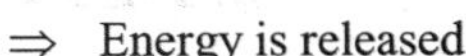

(i) $A+B \rightarrow C+E$

As $E_A, E_B < E_C \Rightarrow$ energy is released $\Rightarrow$ E is +ve

(ii) $C \rightarrow A+B+E$

As $E_C > E_A, E_B \Rightarrow$ energy is absorbed $\Rightarrow$ E is –ve

(iii) $D+E \rightarrow F+E$

As $E_F < E_D, E_E \Rightarrow$ energy is absorbed $\Rightarrow$ E is –ve

(iv) $F \rightarrow D+E+E$

As $E_D, E_E > E_F \Rightarrow$ energy is released $\Rightarrow$ E is +ve

Ans. (C)

Sol. 18 The effective nuclear reaction is

$${}^{A}_{Z}X \longrightarrow {}^{A_1}_{Z_1}Y + 3\,{}^{4}_{2}\alpha + 2F_e$$

By conservation of charge, we use

$$Z = Z_1 + 6 + 2 \Rightarrow Z_1 = Z - 8$$

By conservation mass, we use

$$A = A_1 + 12 \Rightarrow A_1 = A - 12$$

In Y ratio of neutrons to protons is $\dfrac{N_n}{N_P} = \dfrac{A_1 - Z_1}{Z_1} = \dfrac{A - Z - 4}{Z - 8}$

Ans. (C)

Sol. 19 As in the given decay process energy is evolved

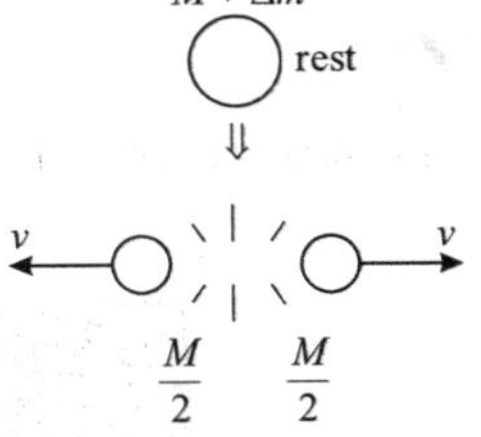

$\Rightarrow$ Final BE per nucleon must be less than initial BE per nucleon

$$\Rightarrow \qquad E_2 < E_1$$ **Ans. (C)**

Sol. 20 Energy evolved = Δmc^2

due to released energy the daughter nuclei gain KE so we use

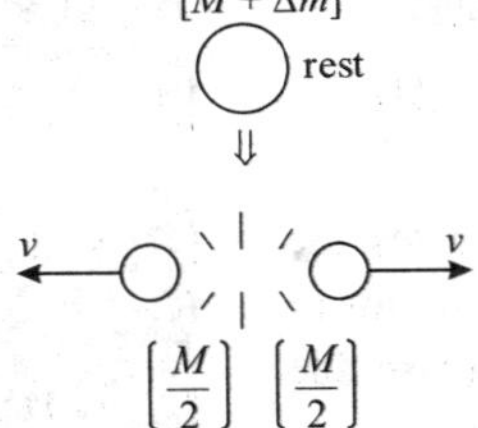

$$\Delta mc^2 = \frac{1}{2}\left(\frac{M}{2}\right)v^2 + \frac{1}{2}\left(\frac{M}{2}\right)v^2 + \frac{M}{2}v^2$$

$$\Rightarrow \qquad v = \sqrt{\frac{2\Delta m}{M}} \cdot c$$ **Ans. (C)**

Sol. 21 $0 \le E_\beta \le E_1 - E_2$

$$\underset{E_1}{(X)} \longrightarrow \underset{E_2}{(Y)} + \beta^-$$

β particles are emitted with varying energy in range from O to $E_1 - E_2$. This is because the energy different is carried by another particle called nutrino.

S-1: It is correct

S-2: By neutrino hypothesis energy and momentum conservation was considered to be valid so it explains S-1. **Ans. (C)**

Sol. 22 As $\qquad P_i = 0 \Rightarrow P_f = 0$

$$\Rightarrow \qquad P_{m_1} = P_{sm_1}$$

$P_i = 0$, $O \longrightarrow$ neutron, M

$\Downarrow$

v_2, $(\lambda')\ 5m_1$; v_1, $m_1\ (\lambda)$

We use de-Broglie wavelength of m_1 is λ

$$\Rightarrow \qquad \lambda = \frac{h}{P_{m_1}}$$

For de-Broglie wavelength of $5m_1$ we use

$$\lambda' = \frac{h}{P_{m_2}} = \frac{h}{P_{m_1}} = \lambda$$ **Ans. (D)**

Sol. 23 If charge and mass of particle X is considered a and b then we use

By conservation of mass $\rightarrow$ $235 + 1 = 141 + 92 + 3b$

$$\Rightarrow \qquad 3b = 236 - 233 = 3$$

$$\Rightarrow \qquad b = 1$$

By conservation of charge $\rightarrow$ $92 + 0 = 56 + 36 + 3a$

$$\Rightarrow \qquad 3a = 92 - 92 = 0$$

$$\Rightarrow \qquad a = 0$$

$\Rightarrow {}^{b}_{a}x \rightarrow {}^{1}_{0}x \Rightarrow {}^{1}_{0}n$ **Ans. (C)**

28.1 Semiconductor

Sol. 1 Energy band gap

in case of metals $E \sim 0$ eV [here V.B. and C.B. are overlapped]

in case of Semiconductor $E < 2 - 2.5$ eV

in case of insulators $E > 5 - 6$ eV **Ans. (C)**

Sol. 2 For conductors on increasing temperature mobility of charge carriers decrease and concentration of free charge carriers does not change.

$$\rho_c = \frac{1}{\sigma} = \frac{1}{n_e e \mu_e}$$

$\Rightarrow$ on increasing T, ρ decreases

For semiconductors on increasing temperature the concentration of charge carriers increase due to more *e-h* pair generation at high temperature

$$\rho_{sc} = \frac{1}{\sigma_{sc}} = \frac{1}{n_e e \mu_e + n_h e \mu_h}$$

$\Rightarrow$ on increasing T, ρ decreases.

Effect of temperature in a semi-conductor on n_e and n_h is high compared to μ_e and μ_h. **Ans. (C)**

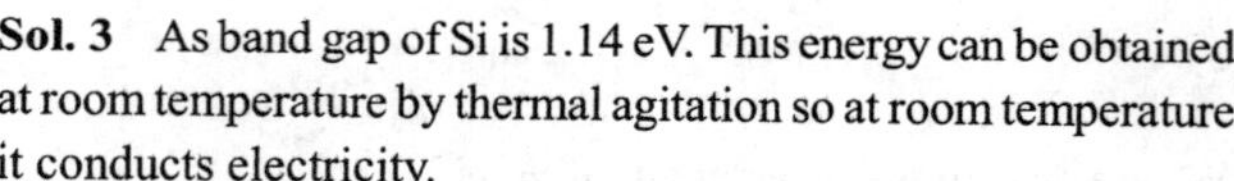

Sol. 3 As band gap of Si is 1.14 eV. This energy can be obtained at room temperature by thermal agitation so at room temperature it conducts electricity.

But at $T = 0$ K temperature no energy will be available for generation of *e-h* pairs

$\Rightarrow$ No free charge carriers will be there is Si lattice so Si behave like an insulator at 0 K temperature. **Ans. (C)**

Sol. 4 As "Copper" is a metal $\Rightarrow$ its resistance increases with rise in temperature, here as temperature is reduced, its resistance "decreases". And as "Germanium" in a semiconductor

$\Rightarrow$ its resistance decreases with rise in temperature here as temperature is reduced, its resistance "increases". **Ans. (C)**

Sol. 5 With temperature increase due to thermal agitation more e - h pairs are generated in a Semi-conductor due to which concentration of charge carriers in electricity conduction increases. **Ans. (B)**

Sol. 6

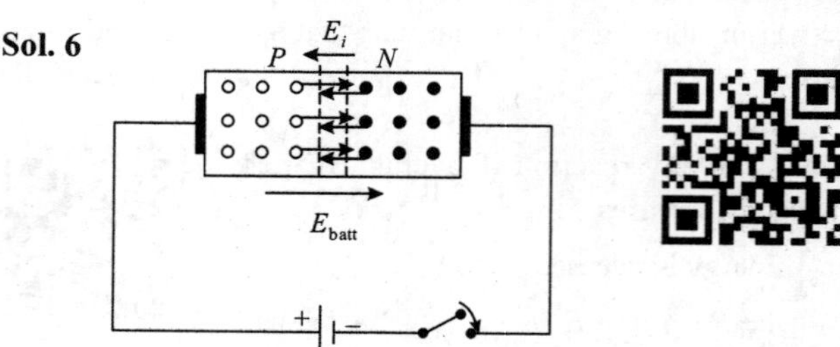

$E_i \rightarrow$ Electric field due to P and N type semi-conductor doping ions.

As external electric field due to battery overcomes the barrier field so barrier height reduces and diffusion of electrons and holes start in depletion layer so it becomes narrower. **Ans. (A)**

Sol. 7 Conductivity increases $\Rightarrow$ more e - h pair generation starts in Semi-conductor.

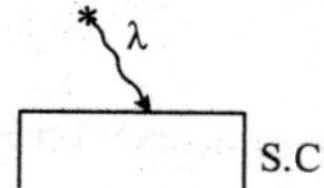

Energy band gap of Semi-conductor is given as

$$\Delta E_g = \frac{hc}{e\lambda}\text{eV}$$

$$\Delta E_g = \frac{12431}{(24800\text{Å})}\text{eV} \approx 0.5\text{ eV}$$ **Ans. (D)**

Sol. 8 The currents in the Semiconductor due to electrons and holes can be given as

$$I_e = n_e e A v_{d_e}$$

$$I_h = n_e e A v_{d_h}$$

here $A \rightarrow$ cross section area of Semi-conductor substrate.

$$\Rightarrow \quad \frac{I_e}{I_h} = \frac{n_e v_{d_e}}{n_n v_{d_h}}$$

$$\Rightarrow \quad \frac{v_{d_e}}{v_{d_h}} = \frac{I_e}{I_h} \times \frac{n_h}{n_e}$$

$$\Rightarrow \quad \frac{v_{d_e}}{v_{d_h}} = \frac{7}{4} \times \frac{5}{7} = \frac{5}{4}$$ **Ans. (C)**

Sol. 9 If conductivity increases with temperature $\Rightarrow$ the substance is a semiconductor (Si or Ge or any other)

Bonding $\rightarrow$ Covalent bonds **Ans. (B)**

Sol. 10 If density of a material increases, the energy levels in atoms become more prominent bands or E_c and E_v increase due to influence by neighbouring atoms.

On decreasing lattice constant E_c and E_v will increase and E_g decreases.

$\Rightarrow$ If lattice constant increase $\Rightarrow E_c$ and E_v will decrease $\Rightarrow E_g$ will increase $\Rightarrow$ density decrease. **Ans. (B)**

Sol. 11 The band energy gap in C, Si and Ge are

$$\Delta E_C(\text{diamond}) \approx 5.5 \text{ eV (insulator)}$$

$$\Delta E_{GE} \cong 0.7 \text{ eV}$$

$$\Delta E_{Si} \cong 1.14 \text{ eV}$$

ΔE_{Ge} and $\Delta E_{Si} < 2$ eV so these gain energy to excite electrons from valence band to conduction band at room temperature **Ans. (A)**

Sol. 12 Statement-1 : For a semiconductor as temperature rises, its conductivity increases $\Rightarrow$ Resistance decreases

$\Rightarrow$ its α is negative $\Rightarrow$ True

Statement-2 : Conductivity of a semiconductor is given as

$$\sigma = n_e e\mu_e + n_h e\mu_h$$

[n_e, $n_h \rightarrow e^-$ and hole concentration]

As temperature rises more e - h pair generation take place

$\Rightarrow$ n_e, n_h increases $\Rightarrow \sigma \uparrow$ **Ans. (D)**

Sol. 13 As Cu is a metal we use its resistivity

$$\rho = \rho_0(1 + \alpha T)$$

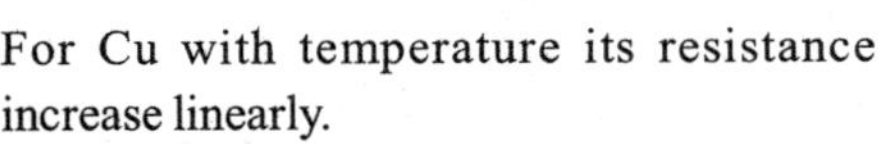

For Cu with temperature its resistance increase linearly.

For intrinsic Si the carrier concentration is given as

$$n_i = n_0 e^{-\Delta E_g / kT}$$

the conductivity of a substance $\sigma \propto n_i$

$\Rightarrow$ with increase in temperature resistivity of a Semiconductor decreases exponentially. **Ans. (A)**

28.2 PN Junction and Diodes

Sol. 1

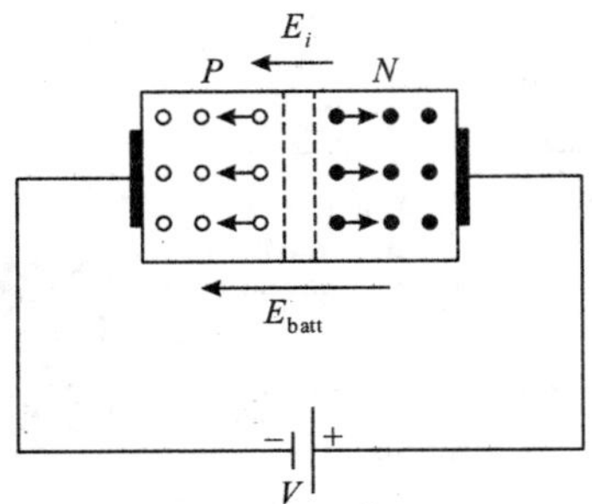

In Reverse Bias mode the electric field by battery adds up to the internal Electric field of the junction.

So barrier height increases $\Rightarrow$ Electric field in depletion layer increase in Reverse Bias condition. **Ans. (C)**

Sol. 2 As "Copper" is a metal $\Rightarrow$ its resistance increases with rise in temperature. Here as temperature is reduced $\Rightarrow$ its resistance "decreases".

And As "Germanium" is a Semiconductor $\Rightarrow$ its resistance decreases with rise in temperature.

Here as temperature is reduced $\Rightarrow$ its resistance "increases". **Ans. (C)**

Sol. 3 In above circuit for the applied battery D_2 is Forward biased and D_1 is reverse biased so the equivalent circuit for this case is

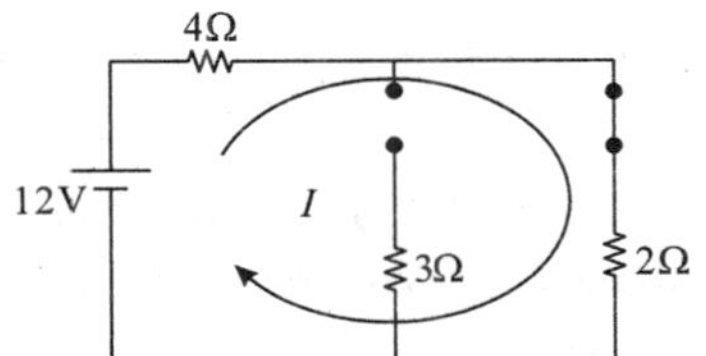

Circuit current $I = \dfrac{12}{4+2} = \dfrac{12}{6} = 2\text{A}$ **Ans. (B)**

Sol. 4 In Reverse Bias condition

P side of diode $\rightarrow$ low potential

N side of diode $\rightarrow$ high potential

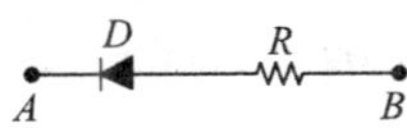

For Reverse Bias we use $V_A > V_B$ **Ans. (D)**

Sol. 5

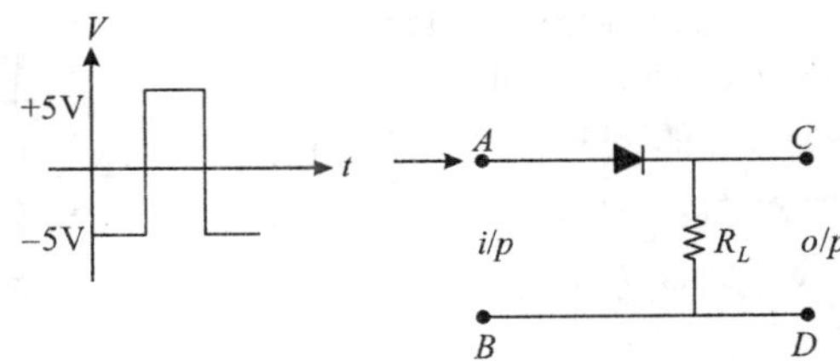

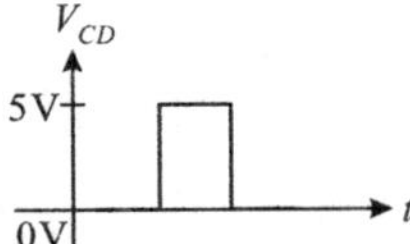

Current will pass through diode only when it is forward biased or when input voltage at A is more than 0 V so the current through R will only be there for $V_A = 0$ to 5 V. **Ans. (A)**

Sol. 6 The given circuit is using "D" as a half wave rectifier. **Ans. (B)**

Sol. 7 LED of difference band gaps emit different coloured visible radiations because the band gap is of the order of energy of visible light.

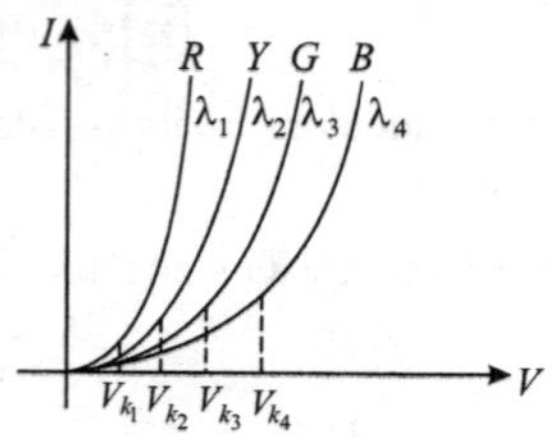

Knee point voltage increases as band gap increase $\Rightarrow$ for higher ΔE_g (for lower λ) V_K is more.

Here $\Delta E_{G_1} < \Delta E_{G_2} < \Delta E_{G_3} < \Delta E_{G_4}$

$\Rightarrow \lambda_1 > \lambda_2 > \lambda_3 > \lambda_4$ **Ans. (A)**

Sol. 8 Here in circuit we can see due to 6V battery diodes D_1 and D_2 are forward biased and D_3 is reverse biased so equivalent circuit of this case is

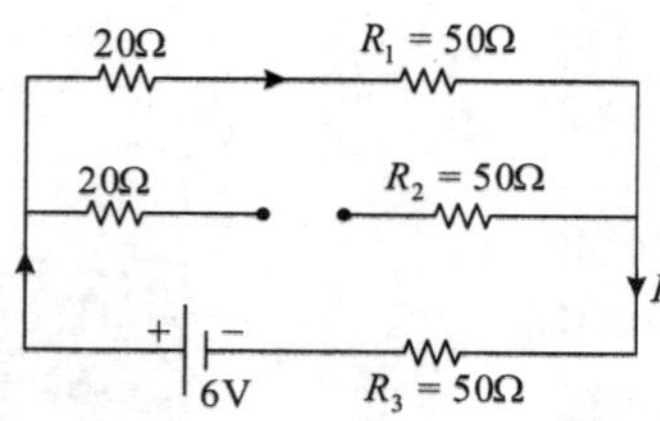

Current through R_3 (in outer loop) is given as

$$I = \frac{6}{120} = \frac{1}{20} = 50\text{ mA}$$ **Ans. (A)**

Sol. 9 In Forward Bias connection P side of diode is connected to high potential and N side is connected to low potential.

For Forward Bias $V_A > V_B$ **Ans. (A)**

Sol. 10 Equivalent circuit of given situation is shown below

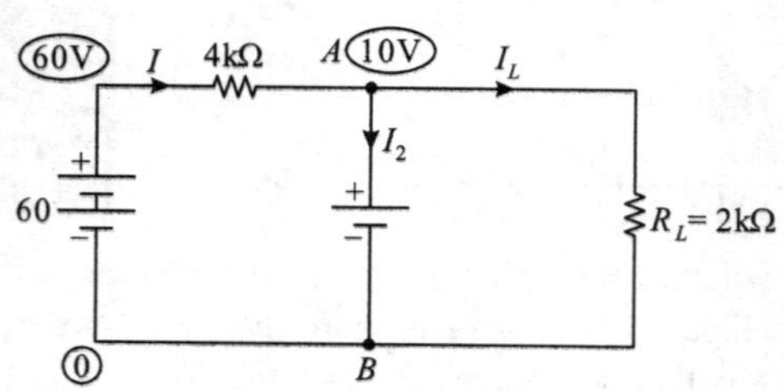

Current I in 4 kΩ resistance is

$$I = \frac{60-10}{4000} = \frac{5}{400} = 12.5\text{ mA}$$

Current in 2 kΩ resistance is

$$I_L = \frac{10-0}{2000} = 5\text{ mA}$$

and
$$I_Z = I - I_L$$
$$= 12.5 - 5 = 7.5\text{ mA}$$ **Ans. (C)**

Sol. 11 Light radiation (visible) range is form ~ 4000 Å to 7000 Å for average wavelength of about 6000 Å the corresponding energy should be

$$E\text{ (in eV)} = \frac{hc}{\lambda e} = \frac{12431}{\lambda(\text{in Å})}$$

$$= \frac{12431}{6000} \approx 2.07\text{ eV}$$ **Ans. (D)**

Sol. 12

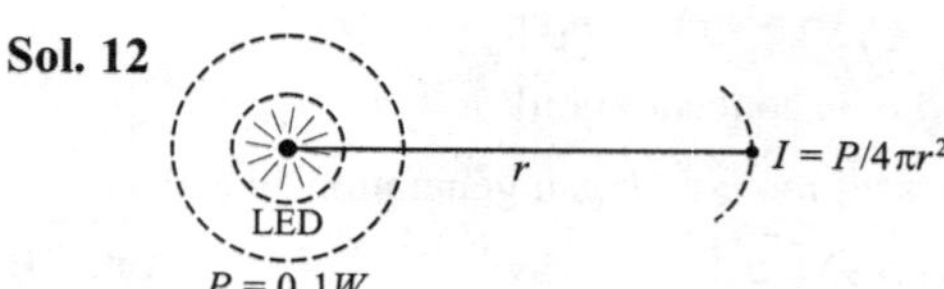

For an EM wave the energy density in light beam is given as

$$u_e = \frac{I}{c} = \frac{1}{2}\epsilon_0 E^2$$

$$\Rightarrow \quad E = \sqrt{\frac{2I}{c\epsilon_0}} = \sqrt{\frac{2P}{4\pi\epsilon_0 cr^2}}$$

$$\Rightarrow \quad E = \sqrt{\frac{2\times 0.1\times 9\times 10^9}{3\times 10^8\times (1)^2}} = \sqrt{6}$$

$$\Rightarrow \quad E = 2.45\text{ V/m}$$ **Ans. (D)**

Sol. 13

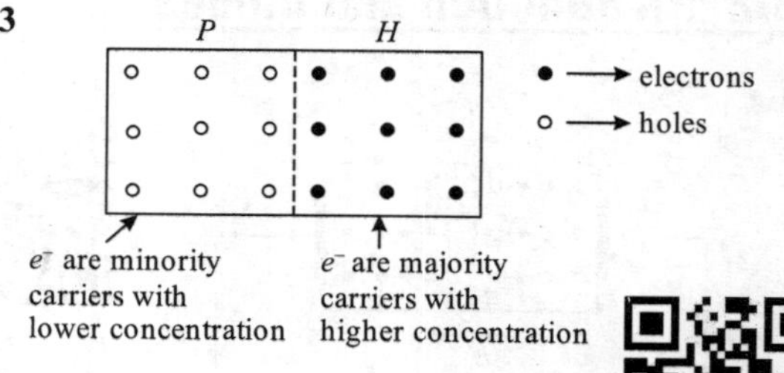

As in n-side concentration of electrons is higher compared to p-side so electron diffusion take place from n side to p side. **Ans. (D)**

Sol. 14 Situation-1 : When +ve terminal of battery is at A, circuit will be

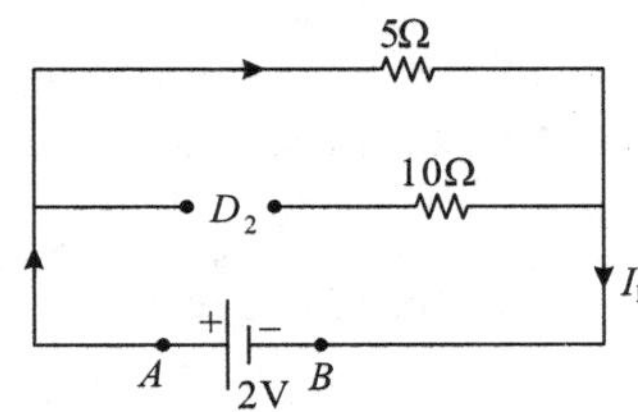

Current through battery is

$$I_1 = \frac{2}{5} = 0.4\text{ A}$$

Situation-2 : When +ve terminal of battery is at B, circuit will be

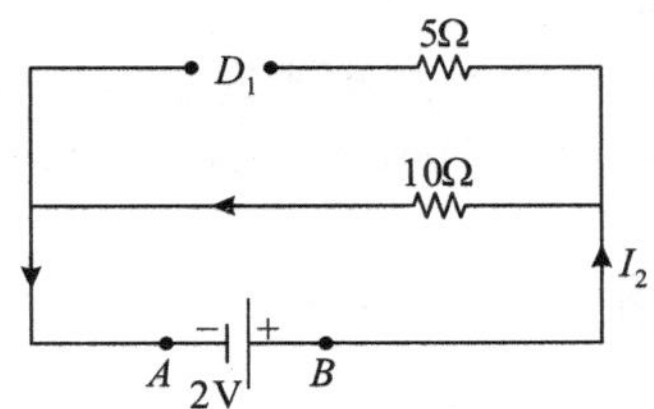

Current through battery is

$$I_2 = \frac{2}{10} = 0.2\text{ A}$$ **Ans. (A)**

Sol. 15 (i) → Normal diode

(ii) → Zener diode

(iii) → Photo cell/Solar cell (Reverse Bias)

(iv) → Light dependent resistance (Forward Bias) **Ans. (C)**

Sol. 16

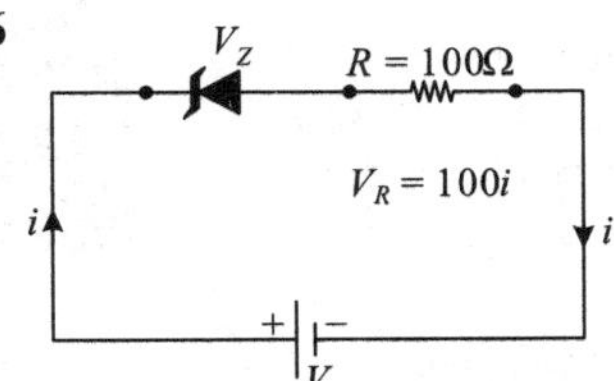

In this circuit potential drop across zener diode is

$$V_Z = V - 100\,i$$

Zener diode has a power dissipation rating of 1 W (max)

$\Rightarrow$ $V_z i = 1$

$\Rightarrow$ $(V - 100i)i = 1$

$\Rightarrow$ $Vi - 100i^2 = 1$

$\Rightarrow$ $100i^2 - Vi + 1 = 0$

For real values of i we must have

$$D \geq 0$$

$\Rightarrow$ $V^2 - 400 \geq 0$

$\Rightarrow$ $V \geq 20$ volt **Ans. (B)**

28.3 Transistors

Sol. 1 In a transistor emitter is most heavily doped as it supplies majority carriers to base or through base to collector for its functioning.

Base → lightly doped

Collector → Moderately doped

Fact based. **Ans. (A)**

Sol. 2

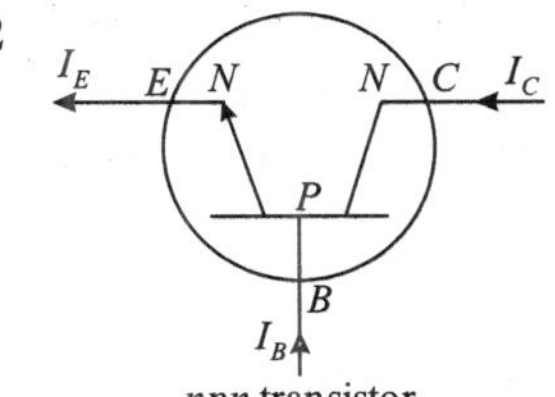

npn transistor

For normal operation of transistor BE junction is forward biased and in this condition electrons are supplied from emitter to Base and holes are supplied from Base to emitter. **Ans. (D)**

Sol. 3 In a common base amplifier input signal is applied at BE junction and output signal is taken at BC junction.

So here input current flows through emitter to collector and come out as output current.

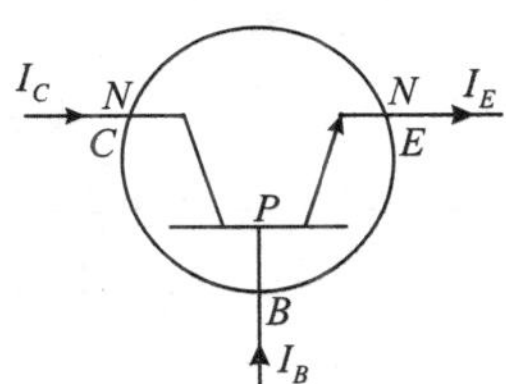

$$IC = I_E - I_B$$

Here I_C = output current and I_E = input current

All time variations pattern in I_E will also be there in I_C so the output signal is in same phase with input signal. (0°) **Ans. (D)**

Sol. 4 Base current in transistor is given as

$$I_B = I_E - I_C = 5.60 - 5.488 = 0.112\text{ mA}$$

Base current amplification factor is given as

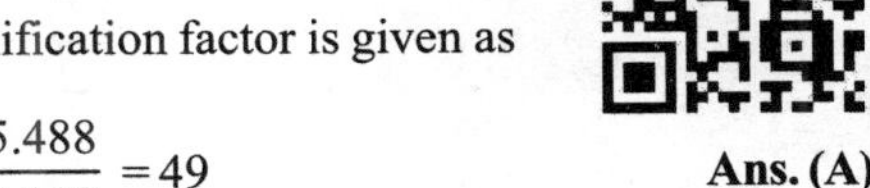

$$\beta = \frac{I_C}{I_B} = \frac{5.488}{0.112} = 49$$ **Ans. (A)**

Sol. 5 As no conduction is found between P and Q

$\Rightarrow$ P and Q are either of E and C of transistor

$\Rightarrow$ R is base

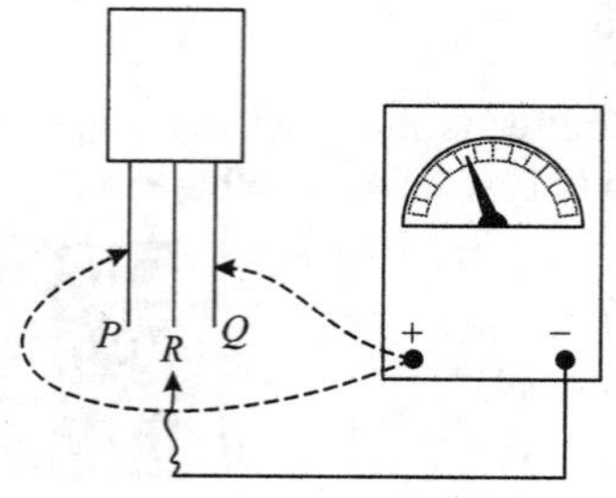

When R is kept –ve (low position) and either of P and Q +ve (high position) then some conduction is there between BE and BC junction which are in FB mode.

$\Rightarrow$ R is n side on transistor and P and Q are p sides.

$\Rightarrow$ pnp transistor. **Ans. (B)**

Sol. 6

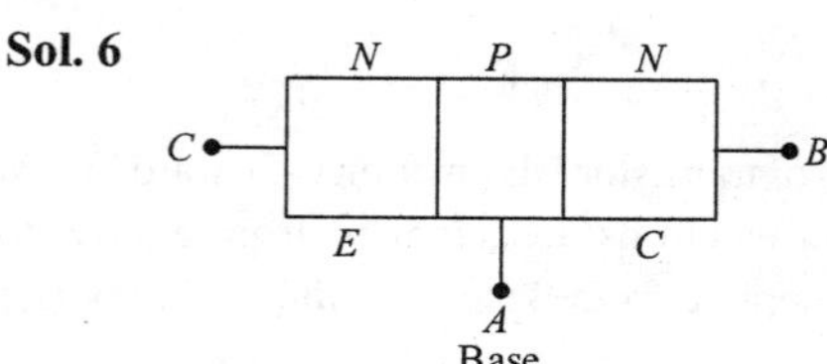

As current is supplied $\Rightarrow$ A must be P side of semiconductor as in a pn junction EF exist from N side to P side.

As conductivity of lead wires is more than moist fingers.

$\Rightarrow$ C must be emitter where doping is heavy compared to collector.

$\Rightarrow$ Large deflection (current) **Ans. (C)**

If we consider moist fingers to be equally conducting than.

Ans. (B) or (C)

Sol. 7 For a transistor currents I_E, I_C and I_B through its Emitter, Collector and Base then its current gains are defined as

$$\alpha = \frac{I_C}{I_E} \text{ and } \beta = \frac{I_C}{I_B}$$

and always we use

$$I_E = I_C + I_B$$

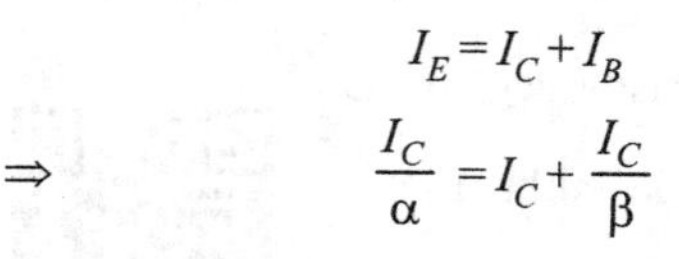

$$\Rightarrow \quad \frac{I_C}{\alpha} = I_C + \frac{I_C}{\beta}$$

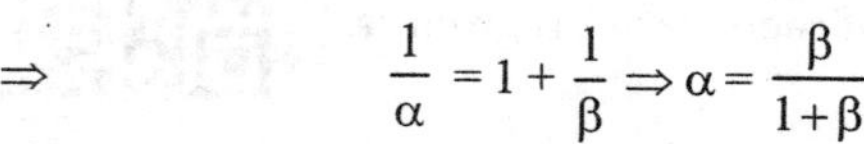

$$\Rightarrow \quad \frac{1}{\alpha} = 1 + \frac{1}{\beta} \Rightarrow \alpha = \frac{\beta}{1+\beta}$$

Ans. (B)

Sol. 8

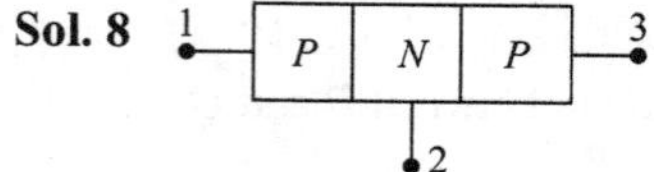

If 2 is +ve and 3 is –ve

$\Rightarrow$ Reverse Biased between 2 & 3 $\Rightarrow R_{\text{high}}$

If 2 is +ve and 1 is –ve

$\Rightarrow$ Reverse Biased between 2 & 1 $\Rightarrow R_{\text{high}}$

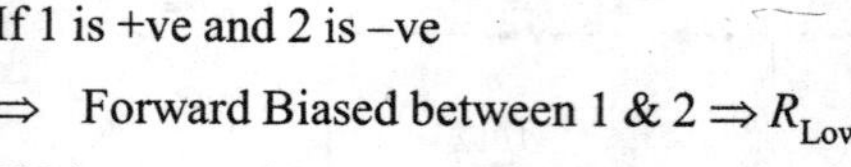

If 1 is +ve and 2 is –ve

$\Rightarrow$ Forward Biased between 1 & 2 $\Rightarrow R_{\text{Low}}$

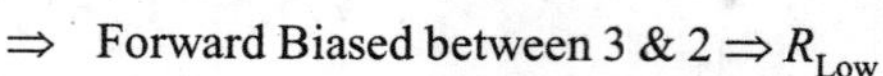

If 3 is +ve and 2 is –ve

$\Rightarrow$ Forward Biased between 3 & 2 $\Rightarrow R_{\text{Low}}$ **Ans. (B)**

Sol. 9 For a CE configuration, input resistance

$$r_i = \frac{\delta V_{BE}}{\delta I_B}$$

Generally BE junction in active region is kept forward biased so upto $V_{BE} = V_{BP} \approx 0.6$ V.

r_i should remain constant and for $V_{BE} > 0.6$V value of r_i should decreased as it happens in Forward bias p-n junction. **Ans. (C)**

28.4 Logic Gates

Sol. 1

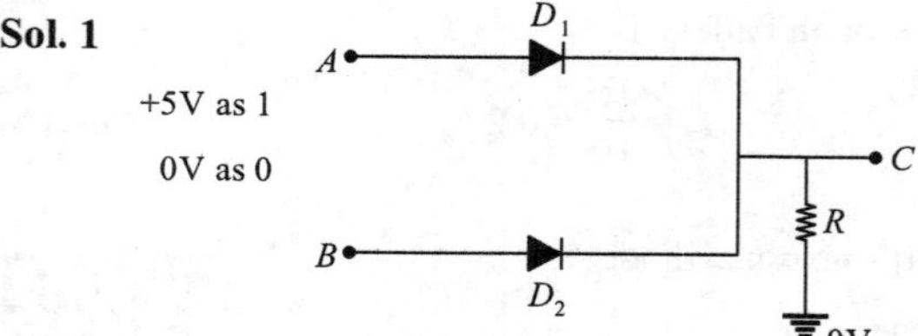

if current passes through R $\Rightarrow$ C is at high potential state (1)

Truth table of given circuit

A	B	C	
0	0	0	→ D_1, D_2 are RB
0	1	1	→ D_1 is RB & D_2 is FB
1	0	1	→ D_1 is FB & D_2 is RB
1	1	1	→ D_1, D_2 are FB

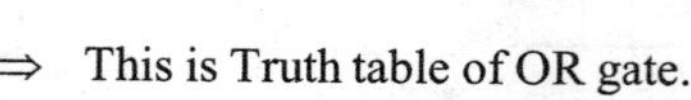

$\Rightarrow$ This is Truth table of OR gate. **Ans. (D)**

Sol. 2

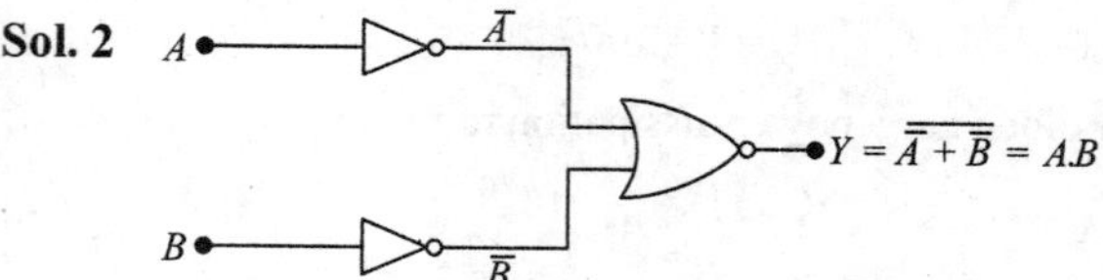

This logic circuit is equivalent to AND gate. The truth table used will be

A	B	Y
0	0	0
0	1	0
1	0	0
1	1	1

Ans. (D)

Sol. 3

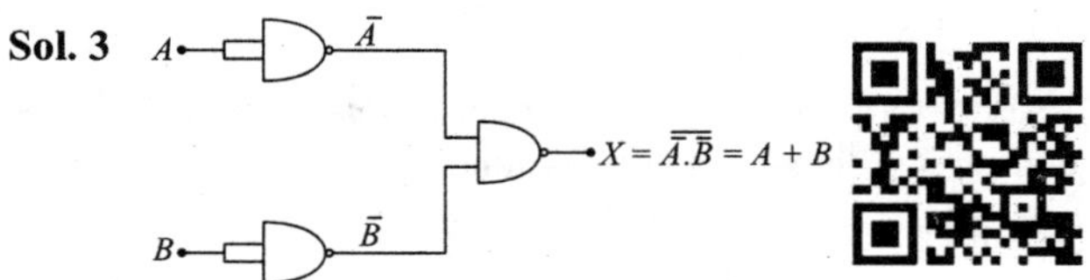

looking at output, this combination represents an OR gate.

Ans. (A)

Sol. 4

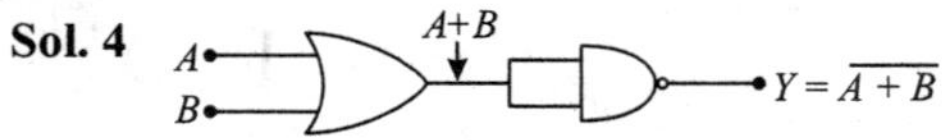

The output of this logic circuit is same as NOR Gate. **Ans. (B)**

Sol. 5

A, B, $\overline{A.B}.A$, $\overline{A.B}$, $\overline{A.B}.B$, $Y=\overline{(\overline{A.B}.A).(\overline{A.B}.B)}$

The simplified Boolean expression is

$$Y=\overline{A\cdot B}\cdot A+\overline{A\cdot B}\cdot B$$

for $A=0, B=0 \Rightarrow Y=1.0+1.0=0+0=0$

for $A=0, B=1 \Rightarrow Y=1.0+1.1=0+1=1$

for $A=1, B=0 \Rightarrow Y=1.1+1.0=1+0=1$

for $A=1, B=1 \Rightarrow Y=0.1+0.1=0+0=0$ **Ans. (A)**

Sol. 6 In the given circuit either of switches A or B is closed will make the lamp glow.

Inputs $\rightarrow$ if ON state of a switch is taken as '1' and OFF state is taken as '0'

output $\rightarrow$ lamp glow $\rightarrow$ '1'

lamp off $\rightarrow$ '0'

Truth table

A	B	Y
0	0	0
0	1	1
1	0	1
1	1	1

This is truth table of OR gate. **Ans. (B)**

Sol. 7

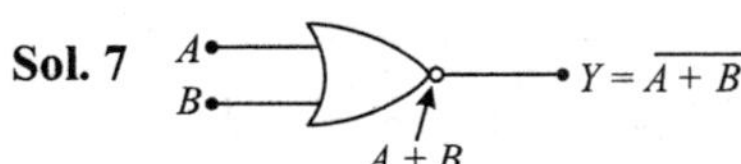

Ans. (A)

Sol. 8 Here the output of given system of gates is given as

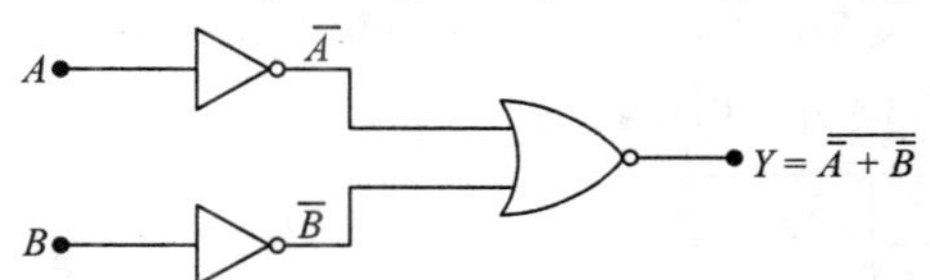

Truth table

A	B	Y
0	0	0
0	1	0
1	0	0
1	1	1

This is the truth table for AND gate. **Ans. (C)**

Sol. 9

A, B, $\overline{A+B}$, $\overline{\overline{A+B}+A}$, $\overline{\overline{A+B}+B}$, $Y=\overline{\overline{\overline{A+B}+A}+\overline{\overline{A+B}+B}}$

To make the truth table of this system we use

$A=0,0,1,1$

$B=0,1,0,1$

$$Y=\overline{\overline{\overline{A+B}+A}+\overline{\overline{A+B}+B}}$$

At $A=0, B=0 \Rightarrow$ $Y=\overline{\overline{1+0}+\overline{1+0}}=\overline{0+0}=1$

At $A=0, B=1 \Rightarrow$ $Y=\overline{\overline{0+0}+\overline{0+1}}=\overline{1+0}=0$

At $A=1, B=0 \Rightarrow$ $Y=\overline{\overline{0+1}+\overline{0+0}}=\overline{0+1}=0$

At $A=1, B=1 \Rightarrow$ $Y=\overline{\overline{0+1}+\overline{0+1}}=\overline{0+0}=1$ **Ans. (A)**

Sol. 10 (A) $C=\overline{A\cdot B+\overline{A}}$

A	B	C
0	0	0
0	1	0
1	0	1
1	1	0

(B) $C=(A+B)\cdot B$

A	B	C
0	0	1
0	1	0
1	0	1
1	1	1

(C) $C=(A\cdot B)+\overline{B}$

A	B	C
0	0	0
0	1	1
1	0	0
1	1	1

(D) $C=\overline{A.B}$

A	B	C
0	0	1
0	1	1
1	0	1
1	1	0

Ans. (A)

Sol. 11 In the given circuit if any input A or B will be at high potential +5 V (state-1) then transistor will be in ON state and C

will get connected to earth (0 V) so C will be at stable 0. Only when A & B are 0 then C will be at high position (state-1)

Truth table of this circuit will be

A	B	Y
0	0	1
0	1	0
1	0	0
1	1	0

This is Truth table of NAND gate. **Ans. (A)**

Sol. 12

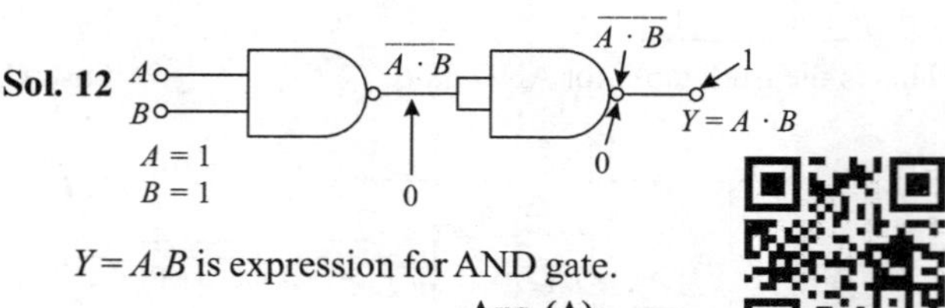

$Y = A.B$ is expression for AND gate.

Ans. (A)

Sol. 13 In given circuit V_{out} terminal is connected directly to $V_{CC} = 6\ V \Rightarrow V_{out}$ is always high at state 1.

So the output is at logic 1 irrespective of input states.

So here it is Not representing any logic gate.

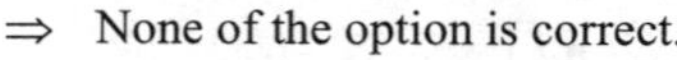

$\Rightarrow$ None of the option is correct. **Ans. (None)**

Sol. 14 For A and B both zero, output Y is zero and if either of A or B is 1, output Y is 1.

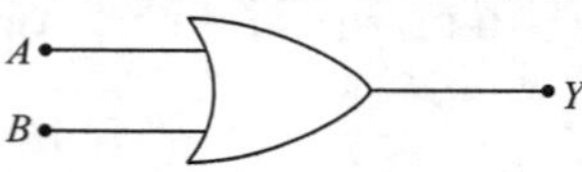

Ans. (A)

Sol. 15 Truth table for circuit

	a	b	c	Y
(A)	0	0	1	0
(B)	1	0	0	0
(C)	1	0	1	1
(D)	0	1	0	0

Boolean expression for the output of this gated circuit is

$$Y = (A + B)C$$

Ans. (C)

29.1 Communication Systems

Sol. 1 (A) True

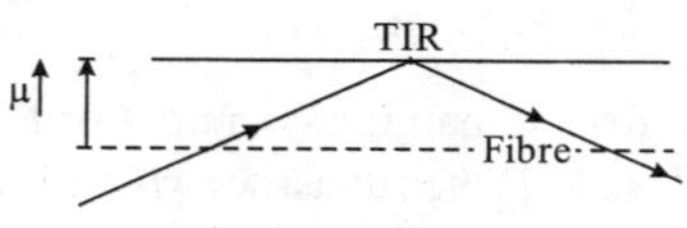

(B) Not true

As only by internal reflection light passes in optical fibre so outside interference is not possible.

(C) True

As absorption or scattering of light in OF is negligible.

(D) True

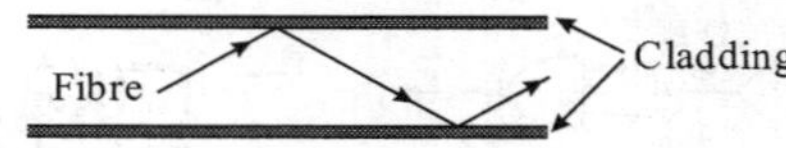

Ans. (B)

Sol. 2 **Statement-1 :** Due to energy absorption by Earth in 'Ground waves' the range of these is less so in sky wave range in relativity vary large as these are reflected from ionospheric layers.

$\Rightarrow$ True

Due to Change in state of ionization in ionosphere with temperature and other physical conditions the signals in sky waves are less stable.

$\Rightarrow$ **Statement-2 :** It is correct & explaining Statement-1 also.

Ans. (A)

Sol. 3 $h = 500$ m

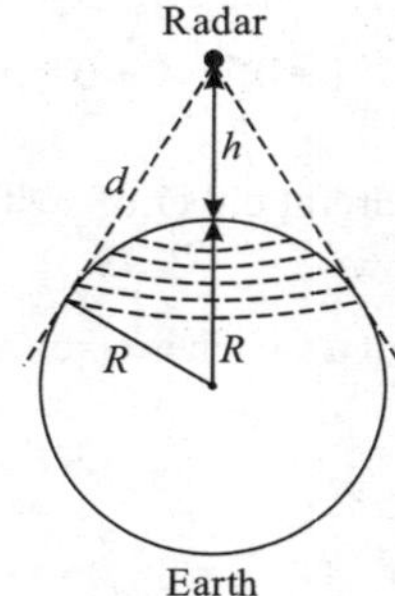

If d is the maximum distance from radar upto which objects can be detected on earth surface, we use

$$(h + R)^2 = d^2 + R^2$$

$$\Rightarrow \quad d = \sqrt{(h+R)^2 - R^2}$$

$$\Rightarrow \quad d = \sqrt{h^2 + 2hR}$$

$$\Rightarrow \quad d = \sqrt{(500)^2 + 2 \times 500 \times 6400 \times 10^3}$$

$$\Rightarrow \quad d = 500\sqrt{1 + 2 \times 6.4 \times \frac{10^6}{500}}$$

$$\Rightarrow \quad d = 80000\ \text{m}$$

Ans. (A)

Sol. 4 If a source of power P watt emits radiation of wavelength λ then number of photons emitted/s from source are

$$N = \frac{P}{hc/\lambda} = \frac{P\lambda}{hc}$$

$$\Rightarrow \quad N = \frac{10\times10^3\times500}{6.62\times10^{-34}\times3\times10^8}$$

$$\Rightarrow \quad N = \frac{5}{6.62\times3}\times10^{34-8+6} = 0.25\times10^{32}$$

$$\Rightarrow \quad N = 2.5\times10^{31}$$ **Ans. (B)**

Sol. 5 Wavelength of EM waves transmitted is

$$\lambda = \frac{c}{\nu} = \frac{3\times10^8}{830\times10^3} \simeq 361\text{ m}$$

The electric field and magnetic field in EM waves are related as

$$\frac{E}{B} = c$$

$$\Rightarrow \quad E = Bc = 4.82\times10^{-11}\times3\times10^8$$

$$\Rightarrow \quad E = 14.46\times10^{-3}$$

$$\Rightarrow \quad E = 0.01446\text{ V/m}$$ **Ans. (D)**

Sol. 6 Statement-1 : True

As in sky wave propagation we use frequency upto 30 MHz. (short waves) and long distance communication is possible due to reflection by ionospheric layers.

Statement-2 : Not correct

In ionosphere $\rightarrow$ plasma. (free ions) The frequency which are above 30 MHz can penetrate the atmosphere $\rightarrow$ No total Internal reflection occurs because with frequency Refractive Index of ionosphere changes. **Ans. (A)**

Sol. 7 (A) In sky wave signals ionization status of ionosphere changes with time due to thermal agitation change in day, night, seasons & almost every hour. (Correct)

(B) frequency which are more than 30 MHz can penetrate atmospheric layers in ionosphere. (Correct)

(C) ionosphere penetration occurs at $f > 30$ MHz (Not correct)

(D) In night ionospheric ionization is more stable due to lesser temperature variation. (Correct) **Ans. (C)**

Sol. 8 In LOS mode the maximum distance of clear communication is given as

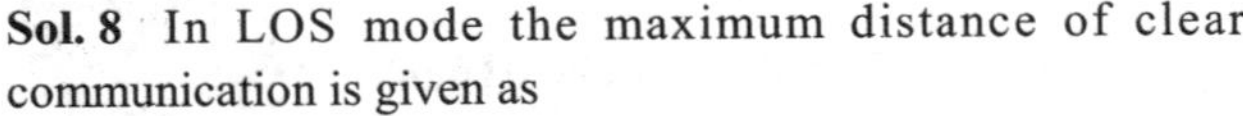

$$d_{max} = \sqrt{2Rh_T} + \sqrt{2Rh_R}$$

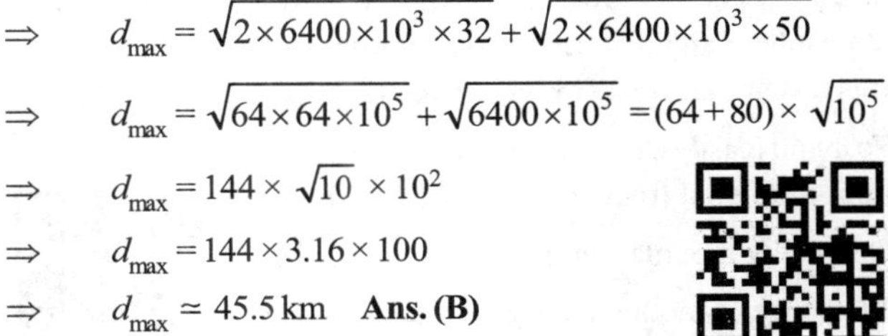

$$\Rightarrow \quad d_{max} = \sqrt{2\times6400\times10^3\times32} + \sqrt{2\times6400\times10^3\times50}$$

$$\Rightarrow \quad d_{max} = \sqrt{64\times64\times10^5} + \sqrt{6400\times10^5} = (64+80)\times\sqrt{10^5}$$

$$\Rightarrow \quad d_{max} = 144\times\sqrt{10}\times10^2$$

$$\Rightarrow \quad d_{max} = 144\times3.16\times100$$

$$\Rightarrow \quad d_{max} \simeq 45.5\text{ km}$$ **Ans. (B)**

Sol. 9 For sky wave propagation of radio waves, frequency range is

$$\Delta f_{SW} \sim 2\text{ MHz} \leftrightarrow 30\text{ MHz}$$

Among options given only option (B) is in this range.

Fact based. **Ans. (B)**

Sol. 10 for sky wave propagation radio waves, frequency range is

$$\Delta f_{SW} \sim 2\text{ MHz} \leftrightarrow 30\text{ MHz}$$

Among the given options only option (B) is in range of this.

Fact based. **Ans. (B)**

29.2 Modulation and Demodulation

Sol. 1 Modulation $\rightarrow$ using high frequency carrier frequency for long distance communication of modulation signals because of noise in direct transmission of these signals.

(A) $\rightarrow$ Speed of EM wave remain same even after modulation. Time lag between T_x and R_x is

$$t = \frac{\text{distance}}{c} \rightarrow \text{remain same (Not correct)}$$

(B) $\rightarrow$ After modulation frequency increases $\Rightarrow$ wavelength decreases $\Rightarrow$ size of antenna required reduce. (Correct)

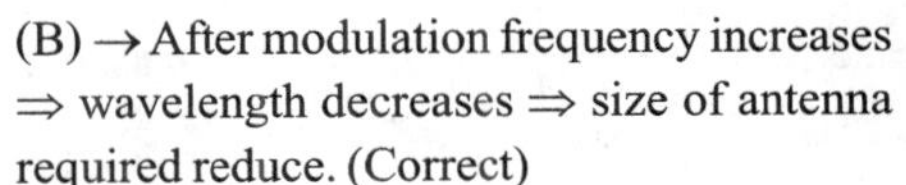

(C) $\rightarrow$ $\Delta\omega = 2\omega_m$ and fractional bandwidth $= \frac{\Delta\omega}{\omega_c} = \frac{2\omega_m}{\omega_c}\downarrow$ (Correct)

(D) $\rightarrow$ As fractional band width on spectrum decreases $\Rightarrow$ selectivity increases. (Correct) **Ans. (A)**

Sol. 2 $E = E_c\cos\omega_c t + E_m\cos\omega_m t\cos\omega_c t$

$$\Rightarrow \quad E = E_c\cos\omega_c t + \frac{E_m}{2}\cos(\omega_c - \omega_m)t + \frac{E_m}{2}\cos(\omega_c + \omega_m)t$$

where $\omega_c \rightarrow$ Carrier frequency

$(\omega_c - \omega_m) \rightarrow$ lower side band frequency

$(\omega_c + \omega_m) \rightarrow$ upper side band frequency

Ans. (B)

Sol. 3 Noise $\rightarrow$ unwanted signal which is caught from atmosphere and distort the transmitting signal.
It is low frequency (or higher wavelengths)

To avoid (easily extract) noise upto maximum limit the signal frequency is to be kept high that's why modulation is needed.

Tolerance of modulated signal against noise (Noise tolerance) is high for a high frequency wave (short wave). **Ans. (B)**

Sol. 4 During de-modulation the maximum frequency which can be detected is given as

$$f_{max} = \frac{1}{2\pi\mu RC}$$

$$\Rightarrow f_{max} = \frac{1}{2\times 3.14\times 0.6\times 100\times 10^3\times 250\times 10^{-12}}$$

$$\Rightarrow f_{max} = \frac{10^8}{6.28\times 6\times 250} = \frac{1000\times 10^5}{6.28\times 6\times 250}$$

$$\Rightarrow f_{max} \simeq 10^4\text{ Hz} \simeq 10\text{ kHZ}$$ **Ans. (B)**

Sol. 5

$A_m \sin\omega_m t \longrightarrow$ [Amplitude Modulators] $\longrightarrow y_{out} = A_m \sin\omega_m t$ $\rightarrow C_m(t)$

Modulating signal; Modulated wave

$A_c \sin\omega_c t$ Carrier wave

Where $R = A_c + A_m \sin\omega_m t$

$\Rightarrow$ Output as modulated wave is given as

$$C_m(t) = (A_c + A_m \sin\omega_m t)\sin\omega_c t$$
$$= A(1 + \sin\omega_m t)\sin\omega_c t$$

Here modulation index $\mu = \frac{A_m}{A_c} = \frac{A}{A} = 1$ **Ans. (C)**

Sol. 6 When a modulating signal of frequency ω_m is modulated on a carrier wave of frequency ω_c then the resulting modulated signal will have three frequencies

(1) Carrier frequency $\rightarrow \omega_c \rightarrow 2000$ kHz

(2) lower side band frequency $\rightarrow \omega_c \rightarrow 1995$ kHz

(2) upper side band frequency $\rightarrow \omega_c + \omega_m \rightarrow 2005$ kHz **Ans. (A)**

Sol. 7 Carrier wave is used for long distance propagation of signal using modulation.
here modulating signal $\rightarrow$ audio signal
if carrier wave is $y_c(t) = A_c \sin\omega_c t$

in AM, amplitude of carrier wave is varied in proportion to amplitude of MW (MW = audio signal modulating wave)

in FM, frequency of carrier wave is varied in proportion to amplitude of MW. **Ans. (C)**

Sol. 8 The modulated signal is

$$C_m(t) = 30\sin 300\pi t + 10\cos 200\pi t - 10\cos 400\pi t \quad \ldots(1)$$

If is of the form

$$C_m(t) = A_c \sin\omega_c t + \frac{\mu A_c}{2}\cos(\omega_c - \omega_m)t - \frac{\mu A_c}{2}\cos(\omega_c + \omega_m)t \ldots(2)$$

Comparing-(1) and (2) we get

$$A_c = 30$$
$$\Rightarrow \omega_c = 300\pi = 2\pi f_c$$
$$\Rightarrow f_c = 150\text{ Hz}$$
$$\omega_c - \omega_m = 200\pi$$
$$\omega_c + \omega_m = 400\pi$$
$$\Rightarrow \omega_m = 100\pi = 2\pi f_w$$
$$f_w = 50\text{ Hz}$$
$$\Rightarrow \frac{\mu A_c}{2} = 10$$
$$\Rightarrow \frac{\mu(30)}{2} = 10$$
$$\Rightarrow \mu = 2/3$$ **Ans. (B)**

Sol. 9 Human speech signal range ~ 200 Hz $\leftrightarrow$ 2700 Hz

$$(\Delta f_{HS}) = 2500\text{ Hz}$$

Music signal range ~ 10200 Hz $\leftrightarrow$ 15200 Hz

$$\Delta f_{MS} = 5000\text{ Hz}$$

In case both the signals are transmitted together than overall frequency range. 200 Hz $\leftrightarrow$ 15200 Hz

The frequency range for both signals will be $\Delta f_{both} = 15000$Hz

$$\frac{\Delta\omega_{both}}{\Delta\omega_{MS}} = \frac{\Delta f_{both}}{\Delta f_{MS}} = \frac{15000}{2500} = 6$$ **Ans. (C)**

30.1 Errors & Experiments

Sol. 1 Least count of main scale = 1 mm

$$\text{least count of circular scale} = \frac{\text{Pitch}}{\text{No. of CSD}} = \frac{0.5\text{ mm}}{50} = 0.01\text{mm}$$

[As 2 turns of CS gives 1mm displacement on MS]

Diameter of wire = MS + CS – *ZE*

$$= 3\text{ mm} + 35\times 0.01\text{ mm} - (-0.03\text{ mm})$$
$$= 3 + 0.35 + 0.03 = 3.38\text{ mm}$$ **Ans. (D)**

Sol. 2 Momentum of body is given as

$$p = mv = \underbrace{3.513}_{4SD} \times \underbrace{5.00}_{3SD}$$

$\Rightarrow$ $$p = 17.56500 \text{ kg m/s}$$

Rounding off to 3SD, we get

$$p = 17.6 \text{ kg m/s}$$ **Ans. (A)**

Sol. 3 Given that 29 MSD = 30 VSD

$\Rightarrow$ $$1\text{VSD} = \frac{29}{30}\text{MSD} \quad [1 \text{ MSD} = 0.5°]$$

Least count of Instrument

$$\text{LC} = 1 \text{ MSD} - 1 \text{ VSD}$$

$\Rightarrow$ $$\text{LC} = 1 \text{ MSD} - \frac{29}{30}\text{MSD}$$

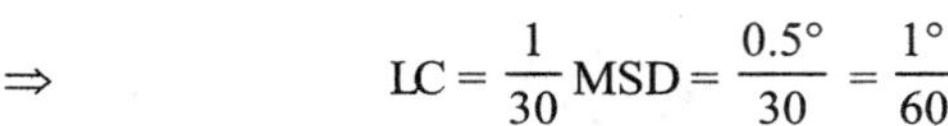

$\Rightarrow$ $$\text{LC} = \frac{1}{30}\text{MSD} = \frac{0.5°}{30} = \frac{1°}{60}$$

$\Rightarrow$ $$\text{LC} = 1'(\text{one minute})$$ **Ans. (D)**

Sol. 4

	No of SD
1st figure $\underset{12\ 345}{23.023}$	5
2nd figure $\underset{1}{0.0003}$	1
2nd figure $\underset{1\ 2}{2.1} \times 10^{-3}$	2

Ans. (A)

Sol. 5 Least count of circular scale

$$= \frac{\text{Pitch}}{\text{no. of division}}$$

$$= \frac{1 \text{mm}}{100} = 0.01 \text{ mm}$$

$$= 0.001 \text{ cm}$$

Diameter of wire = MS + CS

$$= 0 + 52 \times 0.001 = 0.052 \text{ cm}$$ 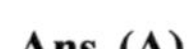 **Ans. (A)**

Sol. 6 Least count of Main Scale = 0.5°

least count of Vernier Scale $= \frac{1}{30} \times 0.5° = \frac{1°}{60}$

$$\text{Prism Angle} = 58.5\ (\text{MS}) + 9(\text{VS}) \times \frac{1}{60}$$

$$= 58.5° + 0.15° = 58.65°$$ **Ans. (C)**

Sol. 7 By Ohm's law we use $V = IR$

$\Rightarrow$ $$R = V/I$$

% (max) error in measurement of R is

$$100 \times \frac{dR}{R} = \left(\frac{dV}{V} + \frac{dI}{I}\right) \times 100$$

$\Rightarrow$ $$\frac{dR}{R} \times 100 = 3 + 3 = 6\%$$ **Ans. (A)**

Sol. 8 (A) 5.3200 cm $\rightarrow$ LC = 0.0001 cm

(B) 5.3 cm $\rightarrow$ LC = 0.1 cm

(C) 5.32 cm $\rightarrow$ LC = 0.01 cm

(D) 5.320 cm $\rightarrow$ LC = 0.001 cm **Ans. (D)**

Sol. 9 Least count = 1 MSD – 1 VSD

If we consider a and b are 1 MSD and 1 VSD lengths then we use

$$Na = (N+1)b \Rightarrow b = \frac{Na}{N+1}$$

$$LC = a - \frac{Na}{N+1} = \frac{a}{N+1}$$ **Ans. (D)**

Sol. 10 The length measured is 3.50 cm.
least count $\rightarrow$ 0.01 cm

(A) Meter scale LC = 0.1 cm

(B) Vernier Calliper LC $= \frac{1}{10}$ mm = 0.1 mm = 0.01 cm

(C) Screw Gauge LC $= \frac{1}{100}$ mm = 0.01 mm = 0.001 cm

(D) Screw Gauge LC $= \frac{1}{50}$ mm = 0.02 mm = 0.002 cm **Ans. (B)**

Sol. 11 The current is given as

$$I = (e^{1000V/T} - 1) \text{ mA} \rightarrow \text{at } I = 5 \text{ mA we have}$$

$$e^{1000V/T} = 6 \text{ mA}$$

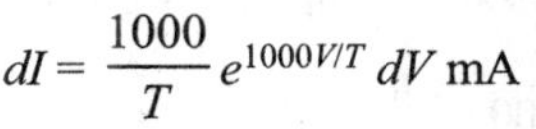

$$dI = \frac{1000}{T} e^{1000V/T}\, dV \text{ mA}$$

$\Rightarrow$ $$dI = \frac{1000}{300} \times 6 \times 0.01 \times 10^{-3}$$

$\Rightarrow$ $$dI = 2 \times 10^{-4} \text{ A} = 0.2 \text{ mA}$$ **Ans. (A)**

Sol. 12 For a simple pendulum time period is given as

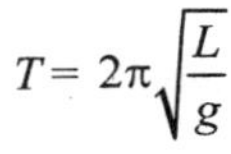

$$T = 2\pi\sqrt{\frac{L}{g}}$$

$\Rightarrow$ $$g = \frac{4\pi^2 L}{T^2}$$

Maximum relative error in measurement of g is given as

$$\frac{dg}{g}=\frac{dL}{L}+2\frac{dT}{T}$$

$$\%\frac{dg}{g}\times 100=\left(\frac{0.1}{20}+2\times\frac{1}{90}\right)\times 100$$

$$=(0.005+0.0222)\times 100=2.72\%$$ **Ans. (B)**

Sol. 13 If λ be the potential gradient on potentiometer wire than we use $V_s=\lambda l_1$

$$\Rightarrow \quad 1.1=\lambda(440) \Rightarrow \lambda=\frac{1.1}{440}=\frac{1}{400} \text{ V/cm}$$

If V_R be the potential difference across the resistance we use for balancing length $l_2=220$ cm

$$V_R=\lambda l_2$$

$$\Rightarrow \quad V_R=\frac{1}{400}\times 220=\frac{22}{40}=0.55 \text{ V}$$

As reading of voltmeter is 0.5 V so error in reading is

$$\varepsilon=0.5-0.55=-0.05 \text{ V}$$ **Ans. (D)**

Sol. 14 (1) Rotation period of earth, $T=24$ Hz $=86400$ s $\sim 10^5$ s

(2) Revolution period of earth, $T=365\times 86400\sim 10^7$ s

(3) Period of light wave ($\lambda\to 4000-8000$ Å)

$$T=\frac{\lambda}{c}=\frac{6\times10^{-7}}{3\times10^{8}}=2\times 10^{-15}\sim 10^{-15} \text{ s}$$

(4) Period of sound wave ($\nu\to 20-20000$ Hz)

$$T=\frac{1}{\nu}=\frac{1}{1000}=10^{-3} \text{ s}$$ **Ans. (A)**

Sol. 15 Using the expression of time period of simple pendulum, g is calculated as

$$g=\frac{4\pi^2 L}{T^2}$$

% relative error in measurement of g is given as

$$\frac{dg}{g}\times 100=\frac{dL}{L}\times 100+2\frac{dT}{T}\times 100$$

$$\Rightarrow \quad \frac{dg}{g}\times 100=\frac{0.01}{20}\times 100+2\times\frac{1}{90}\times 100$$

$$=(0.005+0.0222)\times 100$$

$$=0.0272\times 100=2.72\,\%$$ **Ans. (D)**

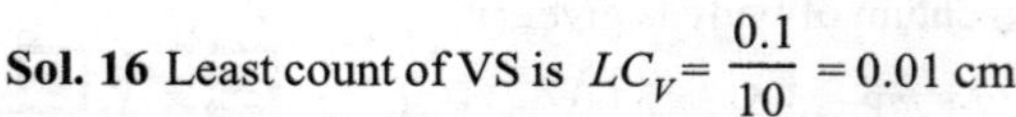

Sol. 16 Least count of VS is $LC_V=\frac{0.1}{10}=0.01$ cm

The diameter readings are

(1) $0.5+8\times 0.01-(-0.03)=0.61$ cm R_1

(2) $0.5+4\times 0.01-(-0.03)=0.57$ cm R_2

(3) $0.5+6\times 0.01-(-0.03)=0.59$ cm R_3

mean diameter of ball is

$$D=\frac{R_1+R_2+R_3}{3}=\frac{0.61+0.57+0.59}{3}$$

$$\Rightarrow \quad D=0.59 \text{ cm}$$ **Ans. (B)**

Sol. 17 Mean value of measurement

$$T_m=\frac{T_1+T_2+T_3+T_4}{4}=\frac{90+91+95+92}{4}$$

$$\Rightarrow \quad T_m=92 \text{ s}$$

Deviation values of measurements from mean value is

$$\Delta T_1=|T_1-T_m|=2\text{s}$$

$$\Delta T_2=|T_2-T_m|=1\text{s}$$

$$\Delta T_3=|T_3-T_m|=3\text{s}$$

$$\Delta T_4=|T_4-T_m|=0\text{s}$$

Mean deviation of the data set from mean value is

$$\Delta T_m=\frac{\Delta T_1+\Delta T_2+\Delta T_3+\Delta T_4}{4}$$

$$\Delta T_m=\frac{2+1+3+0}{4}=1.5 \text{ s}$$

mean time measurement

$$T_m\pm\Delta T_m=92\pm 1.5 \text{ s}$$ **Ans. (C)**

Sol. 18 Main scale least count (1 division) = 0.5 mm

Circular scale lest count $=\frac{0.5}{50}$ mm $=0.01$ mm

zero error = 5 division on the –ve side of scale

$=5\times 0.01$ mm $=0.05$ mm

Thickness of Al scale Reading = 0.5 (MS) mm + 25 (CS) × 0.01

$=0.5+0.25=0.75$ mm

As sheet thickness $=0.75-(-0.05)=0.80$ mm **Ans. (D)**

* * * * *